I0761880

STEELE SECURITY FULL SERIES

A. D. JUSTICE

BOOK 1: WICKED GAMES

Noah hasn't been the same since the day Brianna died three years ago.

When an intruder breaks into his house, he realizes a painful truth—he believed an elaborate lie.

She's alive and well.

So many questions, not enough answers.

But who's to blame for these wicked games?

WICKED GAMES.

This is a work of fiction. Names, characters, places, and incidents are a product of the author's imagination. If the location is an actual place, all details of said place are used fictitiously, and any resemblance to businesses, landmarks, living or dead people, and events is purely coincidental.

ISBN—13: 978—0692467718

ISBN—10: 0692467718

PROLOGUE

Present Day

The beads of sweat glistened in the early morning sun, running down her forehead and along her hairline before reaching her neck. Her eyes scanned the landscape around her, constantly cognizant of her surroundings. Her rhythmic breathing matched the thumping of her feet as she ran along the familiar trail. She wore her earbuds and an iPhone on her upper arm, but she rarely listened to the music. She'd discovered when others thought she was listening to music, they rarely tried to start up a conversation with her. It had become her diversionary tactic to avoid strangers, to appear to be engrossed in her own world, but still allowed her to make quick assessments of potential problems.

She ran every day, regardless of the weather, but not for the reasons most others did. She didn't want the recognition and satisfaction of completing marathons. She didn't care about fundraisers or health awareness campaigns. She was health-conscious but knew better than anyone that she needed to push herself to her limits every day. Running had become her addiction and her only way to deal with the pain inside. She pushed and punished her body with exercise to try to keep the depressive thoughts at bay. The punishment could only last for so long, though. She couldn't run day and night, but she definitely made her time count.

Boulder, Colorado, normally had mild high temperatures with lots of sunshine in early May, but today the way the dark clouds rolled in felt very ominous. She eyed the horizon while she kept her anxiety level in check internally. The approaching storm held a forewarning, and the emotions that bombarded her from every direction seemed to confirm.

Her thoughts strayed to the place she considered home. She thought, *"Damn, I miss Florida,"* as she continued to pound the pavement relentlessly. Thunderstorms were nothing new to her since she grew up in Atlanta and later moved to Miami. She actually loved storms—the rolling thunder, striking lightning, the sound of a hard rain, and the power of it all combined.

The colder Colorado spring weather had taken some acclimation, and she still wasn't crazy about it. She loved the beach, the water, and the warmth. After she'd lived in the landlocked state for three years, she'd decided that was enough to make someone crazy. Winter was absolutely depressing in every way. Miami winters were mild, to say the least, and it never snowed. However, in Boulder, there was always winter snow, and the white fluff covered everything of color. She'd recently decided to learn to snow ski in an effort to develop a new appreciation for winter weather. She knew most of her dislike stemmed from a severe case of homesickness, added to the fact that she'd never really given the city a fair chance.

She'd had an uneasy feeling for the last few days, but she couldn't pinpoint any specific incident that would account for it. She just knew to trust her instincts. They'd served her well in the past. As she continued along the trail, the hair on the back of her neck suddenly stood at full alert, and she knew someone watched her. She allowed her eyes to slowly scan the area as nonchalantly as possible. She only saw other runners and families enjoying the spring weather in the grassy areas but no obvious bad guys lurking about.

They don't usually wear a big sign to announce themselves, though, she thought sarcastically.

She'd been through too much in her twenty-seven years to dismiss the feeling as nothing. *Something* was wrong, even if she didn't know what just yet. She continued her run, intent on finishing before the rain started. She ticked off in her head each errand she needed to complete and the bills she needed to pay, but her eyes scanned the scenery as she continued on her path.

She rounded the corner of the trail and backtracked toward her townhouse. When the thoughts tried to crowd into her head, as they did now, she pushed her body harder and faster. She dug deeper, increased her pace, and controlled her breathing. She continued until the jogging trail ended then she crossed the street and continued up the sidewalk, not slowing until she reached home.

Home This isn't home. I can never really go home, she thought.

She walked the short distance from the sidewalk, up her driveway, and toward her front door. Her neighbor, Mrs. Elizabeth Stanton, called her name to get her attention, just as she did every morning after her runs. She knew the older lady was probably lonely and had very few visitors to keep her company. Mrs. Stanton's husband had died of a heart attack several years ago. She had grown children and grandchildren, but they were all busy with their lives. They didn't take much time out of their lives to visit her. In her mid-sixties, Mrs. Stanton still looked and acted like she was in her forties. She had such spunk and a zest for life.

"Hello, Kris! Out for your morning run again, I see!" Mrs. Stanton always had such a friendly tone, never prying or nosy.

"Yes, ma'am. I think it may rain soon, and you've fussed at me enough for running in the rain." No matter how long she lived here, she knew she could never get rid of her Southern drawl and slang. Her accent was evident to everyone, but so far, no one had really pushed her on why she had moved here. She genuinely liked Mrs. Stanton and often wished they'd met under better circumstances.

"Glad *someone* listens to me," she replied with the laughing tone she always used.

Kris bent over to pick up the morning paper lying in the driveway as Mrs. Stanton continued to talk to her about how she hoped the rain came soon to water her newly planted flowers and shrubs. She was naming the various newly planted flowers as Kris absently removed the rubber band from the newspaper and unrolled it. She smiled and nodded at Mrs. Stanton, trying to keep up with all the names of her landscaping, when she looked down at the headline and pictures glaring back at her.

Oh. My. God. It's him! It can't be!

Richard Hollingsworth.

Kris tried to quickly gain her composure as her heart beat so hard against her chest that she would've sworn Mrs. Stanton could hear it. She could barely hear Mrs. Stanton's jabbering over the loud swishing sound in her ears from her elevated blood pressure and pulse rate. Her eyes darted from point to point as she tried to locate the source of her anxiety. She recalled the feeling that pricked the back of her neck and thoughts that eyes watched her as she ran just mere minutes before. She knew she'd been found.

Mrs. Stanton abruptly quit talking about her flowers and gasped. "Kris! Are you all right?"

Breathe! She mentally commanded her body to comply.

"Yes, yes. I just feel a little sick all of a sudden. I think I need to eat a little and maybe lie down. I'm sorry to hurry off."

With a worried look, Mrs. Stanton offered her food, but Kris politely refused and excused herself. Mrs. Stanton promised to check on her later.

Kris entered her townhouse and closed the door as quietly as possible, leaving the front door unlocked in case she needed to get away quickly. Directly in front of the door were the stairs leading to the second level. With an open floor plan, the living room and kitchen actually looked like one big room with a bar and barstools acting as the room divider. To the right, just past the staircase, a short hallway led to the master bedroom and bath. Upstairs, there were two more bedrooms and a hall bath.

She quietly moved through each room, silently checking off in her mind that everything was where it should be. She turned toward the short hallway that led under the stairs. It was always dark under there, regardless of the time of day. She inwardly cursed the builder who designed it this way. She reached in, flicked the light switch, and slowly walked into her bedroom.

When she turned on her bedroom light, she saw a sheet of paper lying on her pillow. Her eyes quickly scanned the room to make sure she was alone. Her feet fell lightly as she searched her closet and under her bed. She didn't really know what she would've done had someone actually been hiding in there. Her nerves were on edge as she gingerly picked up the paper. There was only one word written on it: *"Brianna."* Her heart skipped a beat, and her breath caught in the back of her throat.

She finished her search of the rest of the house with a butcher knife in her hand. She realized if a man wanted to overpower her, he could do so even though she had a knife. It still made her feel better to have it ready. Satisfied she was in her house alone, she quickly locked the front door and grabbed her cell phone. She scrolled through her contacts until she found the name she needed and hit send.

On the second ring, she heard a familiar voice. "Stevens."

"What the *fuck*, Stevens?"

No introductions were needed. After she'd read the headlines splashed across the front page of the newspaper and found the note in her bedroom, she decided no pleasantries were needed either.

"We're still assessing the situation."

"Assessing the situation? That's government speak for *'we fucked up and don't know how to explain it!'* Do you have any idea what this *means?"* She knew that screaming and crying like—well, like a girl, would get her nowhere with a hardened US Marshal. So she used her anger to keep her voice low and serious. She was practically growling at the man.

Mocked by the pictures on the front page of the newspaper, she stared at the man who was *thought* to be dead by everyone except her. This man was the reason she had entered the WITSEC program and left her entire life behind three years ago. He was also a very bad man with a very good reputation and had worked hard to hide his sins. Sins she had uncovered as an investigative reporter but never shared with the media. Very few people knew she had discovered his illegal dealings, but he was one of them. Here he was, alive and well, and *home.*

Home…

~

"Look, I know how you must feel. He claims he was abducted just before getting to the airport that day. Says he's been a prisoner for the last three years and finally escaped from his captors. Could be true, could be a lie. I'm looking into his story. Just sit tight until I figure out what is going on."

She had already read the same story in the paper. He didn't tell her anything that any other person across the country couldn't readily access. With her anger at the boiling point, she kept her voice controlled but allowed the anger to flow freely. "You have no damn clue what is going on! *Think* about it, Stevens. Look at him! First of all, did his captors trim his beard and his hair for him? Don't you think it should be a little longer, if he was a *'prisoner'* for *three* years?

"Second, does he look the least bit emaciated to you? What, did his captors run out of filet mignon and caviar, so he had to survive on rib eyes instead? And then there's his appearance in general. Even Tom Hanks was dirtier in Castaway than *he* is after supposedly spending three years as a prisoner in a third world country!"

Taking a deep breath, she continued. "Third—" She could hardly get these words out. "Do you really believe he would suddenly show up, out of the blue, if he didn't already know *exactly* where I am?"

"Just stay put until you hear from me." His voice held no emotion in it—no concern, no surprise, and no intention of helping her.

"Stevens, there was a note on my bed when I got home. It has my *real name* on it."

Stevens had tried to calm her fears, but he finally admitted the situation could be dangerous, and the way it all came about was very suspicious. He didn't want her to make any rash moves that would draw attention. She knew the feelings of being watched earlier were no coincidence. She didn't believe in coincidences anyway. The note was left while she was out running. Whoever left it had been watching her, waited until she left her home, and then slipped into her house undetected.

A professional.

After hanging up with Stevens, she quickly showered and dressed. She packed a backpack with enough clothes and toiletries to last for several days. She opened a small hidden area in the wood floor and retrieved a small fireproof safe she'd hidden there three years before. It contained her alternate identification, complete with a driver's license, birth certificate, passport, credit cards, and cash. She'd prepared the stash ahead of time in the event her identity was ever compromised and she had to run with a moment's notice.

In the back of her walk-in closet, she found the small black duffel bag that contained the rest of her new identity—the hair cap, wig, adhesive, black brow pencil, and colored contacts. She pulled her long blond hair into a pile on the top of her head, pulled the head cap over her hair, tucked in any loose strands, and then put on the black wig. After making sure it was straight and looked natural, she applied the adhesive to the underside of the edges to help keep it in place.

Using the brow pencil, she applied a small amount to each eyebrow to match her new, short hair. The brown-eyed contacts covered her cobalt-blue eyes. She then applied eye makeup, using her eyeliner to reshape her eyes. She applied a dark burgundy eye shadow and thick fake eyelashes to complete her transformation. She looked in the mirror at her new image for several long minutes.

It was still midmorning yet, on a Saturday, and most of her neighbors were working in their yards. She stood to the side of the window and looked at each person. The trees behind the row of houses across the street from her townhouse were dense. She looked carefully along the line of trees, trying to spot any movement that would symbolize someone watching her. Her inner thoughts were on overload.

Is anyone out of place?

Is anyone pretending to be someone they aren't—besides me, that is?

She glanced around her townhouse and was suddenly more aware than ever that it held nothing personal that could be related to her or anyone she cared about. She'd left that all behind three long years ago. The truth was, she still saw all the pictures, faces, and smiles in her mind. She heard the laughs and voices. She felt the warmth of the hugs and kisses. Everyone she loved believed she died three years ago in a plane crash, along with Richard Hollingsworth.

Only three people in the world knew she hadn't been on that plane three years ago.

Kristina Miller, her current alias.

US Marshal Stevens.

And Richard Hollingsworth.

~

"Bosco here. She went in a while ago and hasn't left her townhouse since. No, she didn't see me. Okay."

The man, dressed in all black, gave short, clipped answers into the burner phone. He was accustomed to waiting out his targets and knew how to be invisible when he needed to be. He'd noticed she was suddenly on edge when she returned from her run, but she had been more relaxed when she first left. Something along the way spooked her. When she opened the paper, he could visibly see the panic rising in her.

He had been outside her home, watching her for a few days now, and knew she ran in the same area even though she never used the same route. She varied her routine from day to day so she could tell if someone was following her.

Smart girl. Just not smart enough, evidently. He smirked.

She hadn't seen him watching from behind the trees in the park or from his tree stand in the woods across the street from her townhouse. But from her demeanor at the end of her run, he concluded that she knew something was off. From years of watching people, gathering intelligence on them, and using that intelligence against them, he'd learned to sense when his presence had been detected.

He saw the curtains move ever so slightly in the upstairs window and knew she was looking along the tree line. Maybe if she had just looked a little higher, she would have spotted him. But for now, luck was on his side. She had no clue where he was, and he was prepared to stay there as long as needed. He'd been in worse conditions than this, even with the threat of rain. This job was a piece of cake. He straightened his legs to rest on a nearby tree branch, folded his arms behind his head, and waited.

In Miami, Richard Hollingsworth hung up the hotel phone after his call to Bosco and smiled. Soon, all the loose ends from the past would be taken care of. Three long years, he'd looked for her. That nosy, investigative reporter bitch wouldn't quit digging until she'd discovered his secret life and made him go into hiding. He'd figured out that she was onto him just in time—just before he was arrested and sent to prison for life, or worse, hung for treason.

Vengeance would soon be his.

A knock on his hotel door drew his attention. As he opened the door, he was drawn into a hug by a grizzly of a man, his best friend from years ago.

"Noah Steele, so good to see you, brother," Richard welcomed him.

CHAPTER ONE

Five Years Earlier

"Mom! I can't find my sunglasses!" Brianna yelled from her bedroom.

Diana stopped at her doorway. "They're on your head, Brianna."

Her hands flew to the top of her head. Finding them there, she smiled ruefully. "Oh. There they are."

"Relax, sweetheart. Your father has made sure you'll be very well guarded while you're away. The best soldiers will surround you in our military." Diana tried to reassure Brianna, even though, inwardly, she felt anything but happy about her daughter's choice.

"I know." She plopped down on her bed. "It's just that it'll be such a huge change. I won't be able to run to the store and get whatever I need, no takeout food. I'm leaving behind so many of the things I take for granted now."

"It'll definitely be a change of pace for you," Diana agreed as she sat beside her daughter.

Evan, Brianna's dad, walked up to the doorway, leaned against the doorframe, and watched his oldest daughter. It seemed like only yesterday when she was born. Looking back over the past few months, he was astonished at how effectively her powers of persuasion had worked on him. Somehow, she had convinced him that her true calling was in investigative reporting—in the Middle East.

Evan and Diana Tate owned a chain of luxury hotels across the United States. Their home and headquarters were in the Atlanta area, but Evan often traveled to Washington, DC to secure hotel contracts, negotiate rates, and maintain his hotel's security clearance for the VIP visits. During those visits, he made many friends who had contacts in every imaginable branch of the government.

When Brianna first approached him with her request for a special assignment to interview the elite Delta Force unit of the Army at a ghost base in the Middle East, Evan feared she'd made an immature, rash decision. Watching her pack, check items off her list, and recheck again, he saw the maturity of a determined young lady.

Still, he was her father, and he worried about his daughter's safety. "Don't make me regret this, young lady," he warned.

"Never, Daddy." Her smile beamed back at him. "This is the trip and the chance of a lifetime!"

"I can't believe you're leaving us in a week. You'll be gone for six weeks," Evan complained.

"It'll fly by, and I'll be back before you know it. I guarantee it." Brianna replied confidently, even though she hid her trepidations at leaving the comfort and security of her life.

At twenty-two, she had recently graduated with a dual bachelor's degree in communications and journalism with big plans for her future career. While in college, Brianna threw herself into her studies, taking extra classes and pushing herself so she could get out into the world and start living as soon as possible. Using this assignment as her career springboard was a gamble, but it was one she knew was right for her. The thrill of the story, getting out into the field, and putting her feet to the street was where her heart knew she belonged.

The following night, Brianna's sisters, Missy, Jessie, and Ashley, coordinated a surprise going-away party to celebrate her first big assignment and freelance job since graduating college. Missy had just turned twenty-one and was closest to Brianna in every way. Growing up not quite two years apart in age had them sharing everything from clothes to toys to boys. Missy's job was to bring Brianna to the party without giving away the surprise.

"Get ready, sis! I'm taking you out for a drink or ten. We need some quality sister time before you go jetting off to the godforsaken desert," Missy demanded as she barged into Brianna's room. "You're depriving me of six weeks of quality time, so I expect you to make it up to me tonight."

"Fine. But only because I know you won't leave me alone until I do," Brianna replied with a smile.

"You know me so well."

Once in the car, Missy and Brianna chatted casually until they reached their destination. Brianna was bouncing with excitement as they entered their favorite sports bar. Talking animatedly with Missy about her upcoming assignment, she completely missed the room full of people gathered to see her off.

"Surprise," the crowd yelled in unison.

Brianna jumped, let out a shriek, and quickly clasped her hands over her mouth. Her eyes were wide open, the shock evident on her face, and she was stunned speechless. Missy wrapped her arm around Brianna's shoulder and, leaning into her, asked, "Did I do good? Or did I do good?"

Brianna nodded before she spoke. "You definitely did well. I had no idea!"

Finally moving her feet, she made her way around the room to greet each partygoer individually. Virtually everyone she knew was there to wish her well. The party was in full swing with a packed dance floor and drinks flowing freely. By the end of the night, Brianna had lost count of how many drinks she'd fulfilled on her IOU to Missy.

When Evan approached her, his eyes conveyed his concern over her leaving. He held out his arms, and she rushed into them for a final father-daughter dance before they closed the bar. Swaying slowly in her father's arms, Brianna felt like a little girl again. She couldn't imagine not having him in her life every day, but moving on with her independence was like a siren's call. She couldn't ignore it, and she couldn't resist it.

Early one morning the following week, Evan and Diana drove Brianna to a secure military airfield. With tears in her eyes, Diana hugged her daughter tightly to her a little longer than a typical goodbye.

"I know you're in good hands, but you won't be in my hands," she said as she released Brianna and wiped her eyes.

"Don't worry, Mom." Brianna smiled reassuringly. "I'm all grown up now. I can take care of myself."

"It doesn't matter how old you are, young lady. You'll always be my baby," Diana replied. "Don't wander off alone. Stay with your escorts. Stay safe. Don't do anything stupid."

Chuckling, Brianna nodded. "You've told me that about fifty times this morning already, and the sun isn't even up yet. Not that I'll have much choice, but I'll stay close to my military escorts, and I won't wander off alone. I'll be back before you know it."

Diana dabbed her watery eyes again and drew in a ragged breath as she watched the soldiers begin to board the large military aircraft. Evan stepped forward, pulling Brianna into a bear hug, and whispered into her ear, "Come back home to us safe and in one piece. I love you, little girl."

"I love you, too, Daddy," she replied, her voice cracking. "I'd better go now."

Releasing her from his embrace, Evan and Diana watched as she boarded a C-17 military transport plane leaving out of the Atlanta area and bound for the ghost base in the Middle East. A deep feeling of dread settled in Evan's gut. He worried about his daughters enough as it was, but not knowing exactly where Brianna would be for the next six weeks made him physically ache.

As Brianna stepped aboard the plane, she immediately knew her days of pampered and comfortable living were coming to a screeching halt. A new respect for the men and women of the military grew in her mind. She decided to capitalize on that and spread it to every news outlet that would pick up her story. Ignoring the headache that threatened to make it a rough trip, she pulled out her notebook and started making notes on the topics she wanted to cover.

Since Delta Force operators are considered so clandestine that the government didn't even acknowledge their existence, her approval was granted only because the Department of Defense confidential contact was a former Delta Force operative himself and wanted the team to receive the accolades they deserved. He had already given her a list of topics that were off-limits to discuss with civilians. She knew if she asked anything classified, no one would answer her anyway. He was merely trying to save her a little trouble and frustration and help get her started on the right foot.

Settling into the uncomfortable seat for the twenty-hour flight, Brianna inserted the earplugs she'd tucked into her pocket. Knowing the planes were known to be noisy inside, she'd already researched the best methods for surviving the long flight. Many of the seats had been removed to make room for the cargo being delivered, allowing the couple dozen people onboard to spread out. Some brought blow-up mats and sleeping bags to help them pass the time after takeoff.

Brianna was too focused on her own mission and how well her article would be received once she returned home to sleep now. She considered what the public would want to know about the team. She wanted to give them due credit for their skills, the intense training they survived, and the improvised ways they kept their skills sharp. She planned to describe the less-than-desirable conditions they lived in so far from home and the lack of creature comforts most people took for granted.

But most of all, she wanted her article to remind people that, at the end of the day, these battle-hardened warriors were still just men. Courage didn't mean there was a lack of fear—it meant they carried on in spite of their fear. They had dreams and lives outside the military. They had families, wives, girlfriends, and friends they didn't see for long stretches of time.

When the plane reached cruising altitude, several people created makeshift beds on the floor of the aircraft and made themselves comfortable. Anxious to get started, Brianna briefly considered changing seats to begin talking to the service men and women on the plane with her but changed her mind when she realized the engine noise alone would prevent a lengthy conversation.

Brianna decided that a detailed diary of everything she saw, heard, felt, and experienced on her journey would help her to create the most descriptive article she could produce. With that thought, she began the arduous task of detailing every thought, decision, and conversation that led up to this assignment.

Spending most of the flight time filling the blank pages with her thoughts and feelings, Brianna began to see a story forming as her words flowed from her fingers. When she could no longer keep her eyes open or hold the pen with her cramped hand, she reclined the seat as far back as it would go and slept for the remainder of the flight.

The pilot's voice booming over the intercom and the flashing lights alerting the crew of an impending landing woke her. Gathering and stowing her things in her backpack, she couldn't stop her legs from bouncing with nervous energy as she waited to begin her exciting adventure. By the time it came to a halt and she was able to deplane, she could hardly stand the anticipation.

As she was easily recognizable in her civilian clothing, the escort team immediately picked her out of the crowd. "Miss Tate?" One of the young soldiers addressed her.

"Yes, I'm Brianna Tate." She smiled.

"Come with us, ma'am. We have strict orders to deliver you right away," he replied.

She noticed he wore the military police left armband and insignia. His name band read Roberts. "Okay, Lieutenant Roberts, lead the way."

He smiled politely as three other MPs surrounded her and led her to the waiting Humvee. Once they were securely seated inside, one of the men tied a black blindfold around her head. "Sorry, ma'am. Orders."

"It's fine. I've already been warned about the security measures." She smiled.

Brianna attempted to stay alert to the subtle noises, shifts in the vehicle, and stilted conversations inside the vehicle. She made mental notes of everything she needed to document in her diary. The vehicle slowed to a stop after several minutes of riding, and she heard three doors open and close. She had to consciously fight back the panic that tried to settle in when she heard more male voices in her near proximity, but no one spoke directly to her.

Lieutenant Roberts's voice startled her when he spoke close to her ear. "Miss Tate, I'm getting you out of the vehicle now and transferring you to another one. This is as far as I'm allowed to take you. These guys will take good care of you from here."

"Okay," she replied, knowing she had no other choice.

After changing vehicles and driving for another hour, she finally felt the vehicle come to a stop and then heard the engine cut off. An unseen person opened her door and helped her out of the vehicle.

When her blindfold was removed, the bright sun blinded her momentarily. Shielding her eyes with her hand as she absently dug her sunglasses out of her bag, she stood motionless for a moment to take in her surroundings. Her initial reaction was that the compound resembled the old TV show *MASH*, only this one had sand-colored tents instead of the standard Army green.

Large tents were scattered throughout the base. Humvees, Jeeps, and large trucks moved slowly through the streets. Troops were spread out in units of three to five. Each team handled different functions to keep the small city running smoothly.

The sun was high overhead and incredibly hot, hotter than Atlanta ever thought of being. Beads of sweat immediately sprang to the surface of her skin. She retrieved one of her notebooks from her backpack and began fanning herself to try to relieve the intense heat. One of her first questions for the men who'd agreed to an interview had already formed in her mind. How do you condition your body to stand this intense heat?

"This way, ma'am," the private carrying her luggage instructed. "Since you're our guest, you'll have your own private tent. It's right over here."

She strode toward the tent her escort pointed out with purpose, feeling both grateful and guilty for receiving special treatment. She began to mentally prepare herself for how she should approach the band of elusive soldiers. Delta Force operators were known for being the quiet professionals. They didn't boast about their missions to anyone. Handling the most extreme cases, they got in and out of a volatile area without anyone knowing they'd even been there.

As they rounded the corner of a tent, Brianna's feet halted involuntarily as her eyes drank in the sight of the men directly in front of her. One man sat in a folding chair, wearing his government-issued hat, Oakley sunglasses, no shirt, and his fatigue pants rolled up to his knees. He was working on his tan, but she couldn't tear her eyes from his chiseled chest, the muscles in his shoulders, his arms and...oh wow, his six-pack abs. She was glad she was wearing her sunglasses because she did not doubt that her eyes were as big as saucers.

His thighs were apparently just as cut as the top half of him from the form of his pants. Brianna's eyes drifted up to his face, and she instantly turned an even deeper shade of red than she already was from the heat of the scorching sun. From his megawatt smile, she knew she had been busted practically drooling over the man.

"Are you our new recruit?" There was a smile in his deep voice, teasing her, and clearly pleased that she liked what she saw.

"Um...I'm...uh...Brianna." There wasn't a coherent thought in her mind. She had no idea how she even strung those words together.

He continued smiling as he stood. Brianna couldn't hide her shock as she drew in a sharp breath. The man was huge. He had muscles bulging everywhere, and he towered over her five-foot-six-inch frame. She knew he had to be at least six-foot-four and every inch of him was rock solid.

He had short black hair, a strong, square jawline, and high cheekbones. Even though Bri couldn't see his eyes, she could feel them piercing through her. She knew she must look like an idiot just standing and staring at him, but she had literally never seen anyone like him in real life.

So much for making a good first impression, she thought to herself ruefully.

"Well, Brianna," he continued, still smiling. "Good to meet you. I'm Reaper. Meet the rest of the team." He gestured to the other men sitting in the ragged lawn chairs strewn around the outside of the tent. "This is Rebel. This here's Bull. That one is Shadow—watch out for him, and this is Judge."

Each man nodded and smiled as she said hello after Reaper introduced each of them.

Looking at the group, she smiled. "No real names. Got it."

"Maybe we can keep this one, Reap," the one called Shadow replied. "Be nice if you didn't have to hide another body today."

"The day is still young. He may have to help me hide your body before long," Brianna retorted with a playful smile.

"Oh yeah, we're keeping her all right," Rebel replied with a laugh. "Already putting Shadow in his place. I love it."

Sharing a laugh seemed to quickly break the ice between all of them, except one. Bull was the quietest man of the group and didn't smile at all. Sensing that she'd have a hard time cracking his exterior shell, she resolved to win his trust and get him to talk to her before she left this secret camp.

As she looked around at the men surrounding her, she realized that every one of them was built like a linebacker. Every inch of their bodies was covered in muscles. Every man was tall, had a thick, muscular body, and seemed to be entirely at home in these harsh surroundings.

She quickly realized these specially trained operators were able to assimilate anywhere they went because of the rigorous training they had to complete. They all also obviously took exercise and staying healthy very seriously, judging from the looks of these men.

The private cleared his throat, reminding them that he was still waiting with her belongings. Instantly feeling bad over forgetting about him, Brianna quickly finished her own introduction. "As I said, I'm Brianna Tate. I'm here on assignment to interview you and shed light on what you do for your country, why you do it, what your life out here is like, and to promote support for you to the general public.

"I'll get unpacked, and we can get started if that's okay with you."

"Sounds great," Reaper replied. After Reaper gave the private a quick nod, Brianna noticed that he turned and quickly deposited her luggage in her tent without a verbal command.

Her assignment would take the entire six weeks, and she planned to spend the majority of that time asking a lot of questions and generally getting to know each soldier. They seemed to understand her assignment and that she genuinely wanted to give them credit for the work they were doing.

Thirty minutes later, she walked back to the area where she'd left them and found everyone still there, except for Bull.

"So, who wants to go first?" she asked with a smile.

"I will," Reaper replied, removing his sunglasses and flashing his perfect smile. "Let's go over here so we can be more comfortable."

Brianna and Reaper moved to a picnic-style table in a shaded area of the camp. It was far enough away from the others that she could comfortably ask probing questions without making anyone uncomfortable. She hoped it would also ensure more in-depth answers from her participants.

"So, Reaper, huh? How'd you get that nickname?" she asked as they took a seat.

"My squadron's nicknames come from our personalities and things we're good at," he answered evasively.

"They also keep your identity secret, especially between assignments, right?" Brianna asked.

"That's right," Reaper replied.

"Am I going to have a difficult time getting to know you?" Brianna asked, trying to throw him off guard.

No such luck.

His smile slowly crawled across his face. His white teeth sparkled even in the shade, along with the mirth dancing in his blue eyes. "Most likely."

"I assume you're the leader of this squadron?"

"I am," he confirmed. "We're all officers, but I'm the ranking officer. If you tell anyone, I'll deny it and then kill you in your sleep."

"Your secret is safe with me." Brianna crossed her heart. "No need to get all scary on me."

Reaper laughed and relaxed a little. "Occupational hazard."

"I literally can't imagine. That's why I'm here. There are obviously things you can't tell me, but I'd love to tell others about you and the rest of the team to make them understand your sacrifices," Brianna replied earnestly.

Reaper carefully watched Brianna, taking in every detail of her face, posture, and body language. His training and field experience in counterterrorism, counter-surveillance, and reading micro-expressions taught him how to read and decipher a person in record time. From his assessment, she was a trusting, honest, and naïve young lady, who sincerely wanted to do a good job with her first assignment.

Plus, he'd already received a detailed background report on her before she ever boarded the plane in Atlanta. He already knew every detail of her life and anyone remotely acquainted with her. Too much was on the line for circumstances to be any different. Lives were at stake, his best friends' lives, and he wouldn't allow anyone to risk them any more than absolutely necessary.

"Okay, Brianna, fair enough. I'm sure you were briefed on what we won't discuss, but we'll help you as much as we can with your article. I'll make sure the other guys in my squadron actively participate, too. We get to read and approve it before it goes to print, though."

"Thank you so much. You have no idea how much this means to me," she gushed before smiling brightly at him.

When Brianna's eyes met his, Reaper's response was completely foreign to him. He remained calm and collected when an enemy fired a high-powered rifle at him. He could single-handedly take out multiple terrorists in a hostage situation without batting an eye or harming one hostage in the process.

But when Brianna gave him her most sincere, appreciative smile, he couldn't catch his breath. His heart sped up, skipped beats, and fluttered wildly in his chest. The warmth spread throughout his body, and his senses tingled strangely. She was definitely different from anyone he'd ever met.

"I'm looking forward to getting to know you much better over the next several weeks, Miss Tate," Reaper stated, crossing his muscular arms across his body.

Her eyes followed their movement, mesmerized by both the size and fluidity of his muscles. Darting her tongue out to wet her lips as her eyes slowly rose first to his mouth then met his gaze, she sharply inhaled when she felt his gaze physically touch her.

"I thought I was doing the interviewing here," she uttered, barely above a whisper.

"We'll just have to see about that. Won't we?"

CHAPTER TWO

The first week in the desert was the roughest week of Brianna's life. The intense heat in the triple digits during the day barely dropped below ninety degrees at night. Acclimating to the harshness was a slow process for her. She developed yet another new level of appreciation for the men and women who didn't have the luxury of time for their bodies to accept the changes.

She'd spent the majority of the week being Reaper's personal shadow. She followed him around the base, took notes of his actions, behaviors, and reactions, and she tried to build a character profile of him. She knew she wouldn't be allowed to use his nickname in her article, but she could give him a fake name and accurately describe him for her readers.

He was well-liked by everyone they encountered. Other than occasionally wearing BDUs, he was never in full uniform. After several days of watching his nonconformity to routine Army regulations, she finally garnered the nerve to ask him about it.

"Reaper, why do you not wear the standard-issue uniform?"

"My job doesn't require it. We have more lax rules than the average soldier because of the duties we're expected to perform. If I had to leave quickly to handle an issue in a large city, I have to be able to get in and out without giving away my real identity," he explains with a shrug.

"So what other regulations are you allowed to break?" she asked, intrigued.

Reaper cut his eyes to meet hers, considered what he should say, before finally answering. "Most all of them. Whatever it takes to get the job done."

She already knew Reaper was the leader of the squadron since he'd already confirmed as much. She thought she'd caught a lucky break when she overheard another soldier refer to him as Captain. Unfortunately, the private didn't follow up with his last name, and Reaper quickly shut him down from referring to him with that title again.

"I thought I was about to get lucky," Brianna blurted out.

Reaper tilted his head, humor alight in his eyes, and wore a smirk as he contemplated his reply. "I'm pretty sure that's supposed to be my line."

Her face burned with embarrassment as she gasped and buried her face in her hands. "You know what I mean," she insisted. "I thought the private was about to give away your name," she clarified, raising her eyes to meet his.

Reaper chuckled and nodded. "You may be right. But I guess it's not time for your turn yet." He grinned.

Brianna stared at him for as long as she could suppress her laugh. "Fine. You win this round. I'll have my turn, though."

"One can hope." Reaper smiled broadly.

"Yep. You're trouble. No doubt about it." Brianna shook her head but returned his smile. He was more than charming and witty, and she already knew she was getting in over her head with him.

"It's sexy when you blush. Especially when I'm the one who made you do it."

She blushed again and tucked her chin to her chest in an attempt to hide her smile. His chuckle rumbled through his chest and forced her to close her eyes as it rippled through her body. Reaper didn't have to be telepathic to know what images flashed through her mind.

"Come on. You can go with me today," Reaper offered.

"Really? Where are we going?" Brianna perked up. Her eyes widened, her lips slightly parted, and her smile engulfed her face.

She pictured going on a special operation with him. One where she was hidden behind a thick, armored car and was safe from any harm, and it provided her with a bird's-eye view of the action. Realistically, she knew that would never happen, but an aspiring journalist could dream.

"To the shooting range."

"On a first date? That's a little forward, don't you think?" Brianna joked. "I bet you take all the girls there."

"Nope. Only the ones that I'm fairly certain won't use me as the target," he deadpanned.

"Oh, so you trust me with a gun?"

"Have you ever shot one?" Reaper raised one eyebrow as his all-seeing eyes assessed her.

"Only a BB gun when I was a kid," she admitted.

"That's why I'm fairly certain you won't shoot me. I don't think you could hit me."

"Oh, you! Every time I think you're being a nice guy, you have to talk more and totally ruin it." She laughed as she playfully hit his arm.

"Come on. I'll teach you how to shoot so you can protect yourself," Reaper said. He hooked his arm around Bri's neck and pulled her with him.

The simple fact was Brianna enjoyed the time she spent with Reaper. He had an outgoing personality that made him easy to get along with, but she'd also seen the dominant, take-no-prisoners side of him. She felt sorry for anyone who had to face that part of him in a dark alley because only one would walk away in one piece. She was positive that would be Reaper.

"Wait here." Reaper released his hold on her just outside the door of the command tent. "I'll grab the keys and be right back."

When he returned with the keys, he also had a long, black cloth to use as a blindfold for Brianna.

"Really? You still don't trust me?" Her face fell, and she quickly tried to recover. From the knowing glance he gave her, she realized she didn't entirely hide the disappointment evident in her voice.

Reaper gave her a small, understanding smile. "It's not that I don't trust you, Brianna. But if you fell into the enemy's hands, they would get the location of this camp out of you. Then every life here would be in jeopardy. I have to do everything I can to help protect the integrity of this base."

"I understand," she conceded. "I wouldn't want to be responsible for putting anyone else in danger."

"That's my girl." Reaper smiled. "Hop in, and I'll blindfold you." He waggled his eyebrows suggestively at her.

"Such a sweet-talker," she mumbled as she climbed into the Humvee.

Reaper stood at her door and secured the blindfold around her eyes. "That's not too tight, is it?"

"No, it's fine."

"Okay, let's go, then."

Brianna felt the movement of the Humvee as Reaper drove them to the shooting range. She had a distinct feeling there were unnecessary turns and stops along the way. Bri had no doubt it was a tactic to throw off her sense of direction. She decided to keep it to herself that he was wasting his time. She was merely glad to spend time with him and wasn't paying too much attention to the direction they were heading.

When the vehicle finally came to a stop, Reaper killed the engine and helped Brianna to get out. Removing her blindfold, she finally got a good look at her surroundings. The rock ledges that encircled them were covered in sand but gave them some shade and natural cover. A small, makeshift shooting range had been erected with the targets clearly marked at intervals between fifteen and fifty yards.

After he removed his handgun from the holster, Reaper gave Brianna instructions on how to hold it, how to chamber a round, and how to squeeze the trigger while maintaining her aim on the target. After she'd spent several rounds, Brianna learned that she was a natural at sharpshooting.

"We may have to sign you up," Reaper praised her.

"This part is fun. I'm not sure I'd make it through the rest of basic training," Brianna chuckled.

"I'll bet you're stronger than you give yourself credit for." Reaper's ordinarily teasing tone had disappeared, replaced with sincerity.

The chemistry between Brianna and Reaper became a living, breathing being. Accidental touches that would normally be dismissed with someone else suddenly became cause for sparks to fly. While showing her how to stand and hold the gun, Reaper had to wrap his arms around her and adjust her body stance with his hands.

If I were teaching a man, I'd find a different way to show him, Reaper thought to himself. The fact that he knew he permitted himself to touch her didn't help his resolve to keep it professional. Her personality and beauty quickly got under his skin.

"So, tell me about Reaper," Brianna asked when they took a break.

"What do you want to know?" Reaper drew up to his full height, his muscles tensed, and his eyes narrowed at her.

"For starters, where are you from?"

"The vicinity of Miami." His eyes scanned the horizon as he shrugged nonchalantly.

"Do you have family there?"

"Yes. But I don't have a relationship with them anymore," he admitted. He didn't speak of his family with anyone, and he wasn't sure why he even confided that to Brianna.

"I'm sorry to hear that. It must be hard for you." She unconsciously placed her hand on his arm as she spoke.

"I've gotten used to it. What about you?" he asked, ready to be the interviewer and not the one interviewed.

"Atlanta." She tilted her head and gave him a small smile. "And yes, my family is there. I'm close to my mom, dad, and my three sisters, Missy, Jessie, and Ashley. I'm the oldest of the four. Missy is less than two years younger than me, so we've always been very close."

"What do they think about you traveling halfway around the world to come hang out with me?"

"They worry, but they're supportive. My dad actually helped me get this assignment. Your squadron isn't exactly the easiest to find." She smiled.

"No, I guess we're not. I'm glad you did, though."

"So, what else do you like to do besides shoot guns?" Brianna changed the subject abruptly.

"When I'm home, I like to go out with my friends, hang out at this club not far from my stomping grounds, and maybe dance a song or two with a hot girl."

"Do you have a girlfriend or wife waiting at home for you?" Brianna held her breath and inwardly cringed as she waited for his answer.

"No, nothing like that," he replied easily. "Even though the Army prefers that operators are married, I've somehow managed to avoid that so far."

"How old are you?"

"Twenty-nine. You?"

"Twenty-two," she replied.

"And do you have a boyfriend back home, Brianna?" Reaper stepped into her personal space as he pierced her with his gaze.

"No, no boyfriend. Not anymore anyway."

"Good." He nodded. He stood rooted to the ground, soaking in her sweet scent as it enveloped him. The urge to touch her suddenly overwhelmed his senses. He took a step back as he quickly checked his watch. "I should get you back to the base now."

He checked their surroundings carefully before he walked her back to the vehicle, secured her blindfold, and began the drive back to the base in silence. The personal conversation felt foreign to Reaper. He'd been one of the youngest operators ever to make it into the team, and it had become his life, the only way of life he knew how to live. One thing he thought he knew for sure was that he wasn't cut out for a serious relationship.

Spending an afternoon with Brianna, simply shooting at targets and talking about any and everything, was starting to make him rethink his position on the subject. He had never been able to picture having a wife and family before now. She was precisely the type of person that could make him want that very thing. The very kind of woman that could make him look forward to leaving this line of work behind just to be home with her every night.

In his mind, that very line of thinking was what would get an operator killed quicker than anything. It was true that the Army preferred married operators since they were less likely to be entrapped by a female enemy. But in Reaper's view, having his mind on his family back home and not solely on the mission at hand was even more dangerous.

When they reached the camp, Reaper removed the blindfold and called Rebel over to them.

"Your turn, man," Reaper said. "Hope you had fun today, Brianna."

She felt the sting of his sudden departure to her core. Her mouth dropped open momentarily before she caught herself. She swallowed hard and stammered out her reply. "Yeah, I did. Thanks for taking me to the shooting range, Reaper. I really appreciate it."

He heard the confused tone in her voice, gritted his teeth together, and simply nodded at her. "Anytime."

With that, he left her alone with Rebel. And he left her very confused.

She turned to face Rebel and decided to jump right into why she was there in the first place. "So, Rebel, where'd your nickname come from?"

He gave a good-natured chuckle at her question. Rebel thought about his answer for a few seconds.

"It's what I am—a rebel. I go against the grain of what most others do and say. They say I always play devil's advocate and argue the opposite view, even if I inwardly agree with them.

"The truth is, I just like to look at all the angles and make sure everyone else does, too. I'm what you'd call the most level-headed of the group. I can easily see the pros and cons of any situation and help bring balance to the team."

Brianna thought about his self-description and agreed with his assessment. Rebel was tall, had a light beard and a completely shaved head. He was obviously in great physical shape with his thick, muscular arms and chest. His broad chest tapered down to his waist, his six-pack abs showing through the tight cotton T-shirt he wore. His legs were also muscular, indicating he was thorough with his workouts. Evidence of tattoos occasionally tried to peek out from under the cuffs of his sleeves.

"How old are you?" she asked, truly interested.

"I'm thirty," he answered easily.

"Is that close to an average age for operators?"

"It's actually a little younger than the average age. It takes several years of service and training to become a full-fledged operator. Our boy Reaper is as smart as he is tough, so he was one of the youngest ever to make it. I think he had a lot to prove to himself and others, though. That helped drive him to where he is today," Rebel explained.

Brianna didn't ask, but she had a strong feeling that Reaper felt like he needed to prove himself to his family. The one he wouldn't talk about.

"Do you have a girlfriend or wife back home?" Brianna asked.

"No one to speak of," Rebel replied. "I have family—my parents and my brother."

"I have my parents and my three sisters," Brianna shared.

"Reaper mentioned he took you to the shooting range?" Rebel asked.

"Yeah, he did. Taught me how to shoot his handgun—how to chamber the bullet, hit the target, and quickly recycle. I did pretty well."

"I'm sure you did. While you're here, I can show you some hand-to-hand techniques that can save you. We try to avoid the close-quarter skirmishes, but when we have to take someone down that way, we're the best at it."

"I'd like that. You never know when I'll be walking through a dark parking garage and some freak comes up behind me," Brianna replied.

"Exactly. And I can show you how to make that bastard wish he'd never laid eyes on you."

"Sounds great. Right after we finish our interview questions," Brianna negotiated.

With a groan of disapproval, Rebel finally relented. "You should know by now that operators don't talk about themselves much. This is painful."

"If you can handle all the training you've been through, you can answer a few personal questions for me," Brianna countered.

"Let's get this over with," Rebel agreed, leading her to a more private area to share his personal information. "What do you want to know?"

"Where do you call home?"

Rebel grinned mischievously. "Wherever I hang my hat."

"Oh no, you don't. I want real answers," Brianna challenged, pointing her finger at him in a mock show of authority.

Rebel threw his head back and laughed out loud at her bravado. "Okay, okay. I'm originally from Houston, Texas."

"How long have you been in the military?"

"Since just after I turned eighteen, so twelve years."

"Do you still go home to Texas when you're on leave?" Brianna asked, genuinely interested in how he transitioned from soldier to citizen.

"Sometimes." He dropped his eyes to the ground. "I actually moved a couple of years ago and have an apartment close to Reaper."

Brianna realized there was something personal there that he didn't want to talk about, so she decided to change her line of questioning.

"Would it be easier for you to talk about the other men in your group rather than yourself? I can ask you questions about them, and you can dish all the dirt to me." Brianna's smile was playful, but she had a method to her madness. If they agreed to this, she knew she'd find out much more than if each man gave the information about himself.

"Actually, I think that's a great idea." Rebel stroked his beard with his thumb and forefinger. His eyes were cast to a faraway spot as he considered the option. "Let me talk to the other guys, make sure we're all okay with it first."

Brianna's stomach picked that moment to growl loudly. Rebel's hand slowly dropped from his face as his eyes floated to meet hers. The question in them was unmistakable, causing Brianna to blush for the hundredth time in the same day.

"Good timing," she muttered as her eyes roamed around, looking for anywhere else to land but on Rebel's amused gaze. "Guess that's my cue to go get something to eat. Let me know if they agree. If they do, you can give me the inside scoop on all of them."

"Okay." He nodded, his tone still holding amusement as he rose. "Come on. I'll walk with you to the mess hall."

CHAPTER THREE

Before Brianna had finished her meal, the four men suddenly disappeared. Without being told, she knew they'd been called out on a secret mission, and it would probably be quite a while before she saw them again. She sighed heavily with disappointment as she solemnly put her tray away and retreated to her tent. Sitting on her cot, she separated her notes into different piles to begin working on her article.

She had made several personal notes about the men she hadn't had a chance to interview thoroughly yet. Though she'd spent time around all of them as a group, she tried to focus on one at a time when she was in interview mode.

Bull was as big as a bull, though his build was somewhat different from the others. Bull's muscles weren't as cut as Reaper's, but he was taller and thicker. With those that he knew well, he was easy-going and liked to joke around. He was more reserved around outsiders, and it took longer for her to break through his wall than with the others. Once she finally did get through that tough exterior, she felt she'd have a friend for life. However, her instincts told her never to take that friendship for granted. Once his trust was betrayed, there would be no gaining it back.

Shadow often snuck up behind her, without making a sound, and scared the shit out of her. She wondered how men that big could move as stealthily as a typical house cat. He couldn't even scratch his own back because his muscles were too big for him to reach around, but he could move silently behind his unsuspecting victims. His booming laugh when she jumped out of her skin, repeatedly, was infectious, and she could never stay mad at him.

And then there was Judge. He had been Reaper's best friend in high school, and even though he wasn't part of Reaper's direct team, the remnants of their old friendship were still evident. Judge also was built like the others, but he had blond hair, blue-green eyes, and had a much more cynical personality. Where Bull was hard to get to know, Judge was hard to like. His character didn't seem to mesh with the group overall, which forced Reaper to run interference frequently.

Brianna made a quick note to ask if that was the reason why Judge wasn't on Reaper's team.

After several hours passed, she heard a small commotion outside and moved to the door to investigate. In small groups, people scurried to the Delta tent. One of the soldiers she'd met earlier passed by, smiled, and motioned for her to join them. She quickly slipped her shoes on, fell in with the others, and stepped into the large tent.

The chairs and cots had been moved to the sides, and a makeshift dance floor was prominently displayed in the middle of the tent. One man used his phone to act as a DJ, changing songs to match the mood of the partygoers. They used their footlockers as coolers, with beer bottles chilling on ice, and others began arranging tables with snacks in various locations throughout the tent.

More and more people from the base joined in the revelry and enjoyed a "night on the town" in the middle of nowhere. The impromptu party brought everyone on the base together as friends, brothers, and sisters, giving them a feeling of being at home. Two by two, couples moved to the dance floor and moved in tandem to the music.

The music was rocking, and everyone was having a great time. Brianna's eyes roamed around the tent, taking in the scene, but she still felt out of place. Her breath seized in her chest when she saw Reaper leaned against a post inside the tent, holding his chilled beer bottle. He laughed at someone's weak attempt at a popular dance move, but his gorgeous smile, tall, muscular physique, black hair, and chocolate brown eyes were all she could see.

Their playful flirting over the past couple of weeks had tortured her in her dreams. Repeatedly seeing Reaper every night made the days with him harder to bear without giving away her thoughts. Feeling his presence inside the tent overpowered her senses.

After the first song ended, the slow, sensual melody of Def Leppard's "Love Bites" immediately streamed through the speakers. Brianna was talking with one of the female soldiers, trying to keep her attention on the conversation, but her eyes involuntarily grazed over the crowd.

She silently gasped when she realized Reaper had been watching her. His lips curled into a sensuous smile, while mischief danced in his beautiful brown eyes. She felt a flutter in her chest that settled low in her abdomen, but she couldn't tear her eyes away from his. She felt a smile creep across her face, despite any attempt to keep it inside. From the fire in his eyes, he knew what he did to her insides. He turned them into molten liquid.

By the time she fully comprehended his sights were set on her, he had already pushed against the pole and walked halfway across the floor, directly toward her. She stood still as if rooted to the floor, unable to move as he cut through the densely packed dance floor with ease.

Just like a panther on the prowl, she thought.

"Want to dance?" His sensual voice soothed her nerves while his eyes saw straight through the cool façade she tried to portray.

"Sure." She hoped she at least sounded calm and collected, because inside she was anything but calm. Her heart pounded in her chest, her eyes widened when he touched her hand, and her lips parted with her sharp intake of breath.

He took her hand and led her to the dance floor, then wrapped his strong arms around her waist. She hooked her hands behind his neck as he pulled her closer to his massive body. She liked the way she fit against him, pliable under his touch, and seemed to meld with his body. She tried to think of something else—anything else—before she made a complete fool of herself.

She glanced up and realized he had been watching her intently. She felt like he could read her every thought, like a book that was laid open on full display. The heat that rose in her face was as hot as the sun, and she had the sudden urge to look away from his probing eyes.

She felt the low rumble of his chuckle vibrate in his chest more than she heard it. She looked back up and asked, innocently enough, "What?"

"I love to see you blush. It's so damn sexy."

Well, hell, so much for playing it off, she thought.

She desperately wanted to say something witty back, but she couldn't think of a single comeback.

"Hmmm...I must make you nervous. Nothing to say to that?"

"I'm not nervous. Just not giving in to your mind games!" She reasoned that comeback was only slightly better than just blurting out, *"I want you. Now!"*

"We'll see about that." His sexy smirk told her he knew exactly how much he affected her.

Shadow appeared out of nowhere, per his usual MO, and tried to cut in on their dance. Reaper narrowed his eyes, and his jaw muscles flexed before he quickly masked it. Shadow nonchalantly moved around them to dance with another girl. Brianna realized she just got her first glance at how this team was so effective. She knew they used hand signals to keep from speaking and giving away their location while out on a mission, but they also had their facial cues down to a science.

"What was that look?" she asked Reaper.

"What look?" He didn't even have the decency to look like she'd busted him in the act.

"Yeah. Exactly."

Reaper chuckled easily, and that was the end of that line of questioning.

After several more dances, beer, and ribbing between the soldiers, Brianna thanked everyone for including her and said she was heading back to her tent. Reaper threw his empty beer bottle in the garbage. "I'll walk you back to your tent," he offered.

She knew that, technically, she wasn't allowed to move around the base after dark without a military escort. But the fact that it was Reaper walking her made her as giddy as a middle school girl with her first boyfriend. She'd felt the spark between them from the moment they first met. She knew all too well that she was only on assignment for a short time. That fact was the sole reason she didn't allow herself to think of him too much.

As they walked along the sand road to her tent, she found it so easy to talk to him about anything and everything. The abrupt ending of their time together earlier that day had been forgotten. His warm, charming side was back in full force, and she was no match for it. He was the one asking all the questions now.

"Do you miss your family yet?"

"Not to sound cold, but not really. I love them, and I'll be glad to see them again, but I'm really enjoying getting to know you and the guys," she explained.

"So, tell me about this ex-boyfriend of yours."

"What ex-boyfriend?" Her eyes whipped to meet his, her feet halted in her steps, and her mind raced with possibilities. Had he looked into her background that thoroughly? Did he have someone check on her ex-boyfriend?

"You said 'no, not anymore.' So, you had one. What happened to him?"

"Oh. Well, it didn't end well, so I don't think about him anymore," Brianna stated matter-of-factly.

"Caught him with someone else, did you?"

She tilted her head to the side, narrowed her eyes, and crossed her arms over her chest as she stared Reaper down for a moment. "How did you know that?"

"Whoa, now." He chuckled, putting his arms up in mock surrender. "Of course, you were thoroughly checked out before you were allowed on base, but remember, I'm a highly trained operative. Besides, it doesn't take a rocket scientist to know from your tone that he did something pretty bad. You're not one to give up on someone so easily."

She relaxed her arms and nodded slowly. "Yes, he cheated on me. I walked in on him and his coworker in bed together. As it turns out, I may not be as sweet and harmless as you think I am."

"Oh, why's that?" Reaper's eyes danced with amusement.

"I'm pleading the Fifth to protect myself. So I can't confirm or deny that I snatched her up by the hair on her head and dragged her out of his apartment. Naked. And threw her into the hallway."

Reaper's laugh echoed through the quiet camp. "And what'd you do to him?"

"Again, I can't confirm or deny my actions. He ran out of the apartment right after I, uh, she left. I may or may not have secretly replaced his shampoo with Nair hair remover. His clothes may or may not have ended up in the garbage can…on fire. And, apparently, he subscribed to every gay, transgender, and cross-dresser dating service known to the internet."

She walked slowly and answered all of his questions about her sisters and her parents. He wanted to know everything about her life growing up, her college years, and what she liked to do for fun. Questions about college led to questions about how she got into journalism.

She explained she didn't want to be an anchorwoman because it was too stuffy and boring for her. Out in the field, with the excitement, was where she saw herself. He also correctly guessed that her parents were not thrilled with her decision to avoid the hotel management career.

It occurred to her he could garner any information he wanted from her in just the phrasing and timing of his questions. She wondered if he learned that from his advanced training or if it just came naturally to him. She knew there was no point in asking. He wouldn't answer any questions about specific training courses anyway.

Just as they reached the entrance of her tent, he grasped her elbow and stopped her in her tracks. As she turned to ask him what was wrong, he wrapped his arms around her waist. She willingly stepped into his arms as he pulled her closer. When he bent to brush his lips against hers, he pulled back for just a second to look into her eyes. She couldn't hide the same desire there that burned in his. He sensed it and covered her mouth with his with a deep, demanding kiss.

His tongue ran across her lips as he teased and tempted her to open her mouth to him. When she did, he dipped his tongue in to caress and dance with hers. Her hands locked behind his neck as she pulled her whole body up close to his. She felt his massive hand run up the back of her neck, grasp her hair in his fist, and tilt her head slightly for him to deepen the kiss even more.

He breathed heavily as he tentatively pulled back from their sensual embrace. He looked around to ensure they were still alone and unseen, then turned back to Brianna. The intensity in his eyes was palpable. It pulled her into him and made her want to succumb to desires she'd never wanted before.

"Reaper, I need to tell you something. As badly as I want this to happen, and believe me when I say I do, I don't do one-night stands."

"Noah Steele."

"What?"

"My name. It's Noah."

"Oh." She wasn't sure what to say at first. No real names were allowed because there was just too much at stake. But he told her without being asked. She didn't know what to make of that. "Noah, I don't mean to lead you on. Really."

"We won't do anything you don't want to do." His voice was low, deep, and so seductive.

"I didn't say I didn't want to..." There was that chuckle that rumbled through his chest again.

"Okay, then, no pressure. I will stop whenever you say." He brushed light kisses along her jawline, to her ear, and down her neck. She knew he must have felt her pulse increase because she could feel her heart pounding.

Barely able to speak now, she almost whispered, "Hmmm...and if I can't say when?"

"I'm here to protect you...even from yourself." He walked her backward into her tent. Then his mouth reclaimed hers with an intense desire and need. Her fingers rested on his massive shoulders, and suddenly her hands ran across his chest, down his stomach, and then around to his back. She couldn't get enough of him. Then she felt his hand splayed across her stomach, underneath her shirt. The heat from his touch seared her skin.

First, his hands traveled up her body, cupping her breast through her bra, the pad of his callused thumb rubbing her sensitive nipple. The traitorous nipple was already hard from his embrace but puckered even more at his touch. A moan escaped her mouth, and he caught it as he deepened the kiss. Then his other hand cupped her ass and pulled her even tighter to him, and she felt his erection pressed against her lower abdomen.

He deftly unhooked her front-clasp bra and ran his hands over her bare breasts, heating the desire that had pooled between her legs even more. He walked her backward, until she was against a pole, and bent his mouth to take her nipple in it. He licked and sucked on it, then drew his teeth over the sensitive skin and ran his hands over her entire midsection.

His hands made their way down her stomach to the button on her jeans. He deftly unbuttoned it with one hand and slowly slid his hand inside. She realized he was giving her ample time to stop him, but she could no more stop him than she could stop breathing. His long fingers reached the top of her lacy panties, and she was instantly glad she was at least wearing attractive ones.

His fingers lightly brushed across the top of the lace and against her stomach, as her fingers dug deeper into his shoulder muscles and the butterflies grew stronger in her stomach. He flattened his hand, and his fingers slipped under the lace, covering her mound and lightly stroking just above where she really needed his hand to be right now.

When she again didn't stop him, she felt his finger reach the mound of ultra-sensitive nerves in her clit, causing intense starbursts behind her eyelids. He rubbed in small circles, making her want him more and more. Then one of his massive fingers stroked along her sensitive folds and suddenly pushed inside her. She moaned deeply, and he pulled back to watch her face. She tried to lean into him, but he wouldn't allow her.

"I want to see you." His low, rumbling voice sounded almost pained with desire.

Even though she felt completely self-conscious and exposed, she trusted him with this intimate moment. He moved his finger slowly in and out of her, torturously slow, as her desire built higher and higher. When she didn't think she could take it anymore, his fingers stopped for a split second as he pushed his index finger and thumb together. He quickly pushed inside her again, rubbing against her most sensitive area as he increased his speed.

"Just let go. Let me watch you come apart in my arms." He was whispering in her ear now, and it was so damn sexy, she couldn't stop. She dug her fists into his shoulders, leaned her head back, and his gaze remained constant on her face. She climaxed with his fingers in her as she released a moan that relayed her complete pleasure. As she lifted her head, his mouth found hers again. But this time, the kiss wasn't urgent or demanding. It was gentle and almost sweet.

She opened her eyes to see him watching her again. "Damn, Bri. You just don't know what you do to me."

Before she could respond, a call came across his radio, ordering the team to the command center. He kissed her again,

"Duty calls."

He stopped at the opening of her tent and turned to look at her. "Don't think this was a one-night stand, Bri. It's not by a long shot." He flashed her that heart-stopping smile of his then he was gone in an instant.

"What I do to him?" she thought incredulously.

She spent the rest of the night thinking of Noah. The man had just taken her to a new high, and they hadn't even removed their clothes. Her rational mind immediately went to the fact that this could never work. A long-distance relationship rarely worked under normal circumstances, and this was far from ordinary. He was a man who was stationed half a world away from her. He lived on a little-known, top-secret base, and carried out top-secret missions. She didn't even know precisely where in the world she was.

She decided this wasn't the time for rational thinking. She wanted whatever this was between them to run its course. She didn't want rhyme or reason to take over and complicate things. She'd just enjoy his company while she could. If they weren't meant to be once she returned home, she'd at least have this time and these memories. And she'd never regret them.

CHAPTER FOUR

When the team wasn't out on an assignment, Brianna spent as much time with them as possible. She passed the days taking notes on everything they did, filled up her diary with every thought she had, and got to know the men behind the mask, so to speak. She quickly learned she genuinely enjoyed their company. One night, the guys teased Brianna about her lack of security clearance and the need to blindfold her before she could visit their base.

"Poor Brianna, she had to wear a blindfold and didn't even get to have any fun in return for it. She's just not trustworthy, I guess," Shadow joked. "You know, she could be a highly trained spy and has us all fooled into believing she's really innocent."

Shadow leaned forward with his forearms resting on his thighs. He eyed her carefully and pretended he was seriously considering it. "Yeah, look at her shifty eyes. There's no doubt that she's a double agent. We've all been fooled, gentlemen. We should just give up now."

"I'm glad you've finally figured it out. It'll make your surrender much less painful," Bri stated. "For you." She brought her arms up, flexed her biceps, and leaned her head in to kiss her right one. "These guns are deadlier than any gun you own."

The guys all burst out laughing at her gestures. Brianna was most pleased to see that Bull had also joined in on the fun. She'd had the most trouble breaking through his tough exterior. After her talk with Rebel, the guys all agreed to answer questions about each other, and she'd been able to gather much more information since then. Except from Bull. He still didn't trust her and answered her questions with only the bare minimum of words.

She still had the original black cloth that was tied around her eyes from the first time she was brought to the base. "You know," she started. "I still have that first blindfold they used when they brought me out here. I'm keeping it. It's my promise to each of you that no matter what anyone does to me, I will never give you up. I'd never willingly allow anyone to hurt a single one of you. Even though you all have nicknames and I don't have one yet." She smiled.

The mood among the men suddenly became serious, but sincere. Bull was, surprisingly, the first one to speak.

"Well, Sunny, I, for one, appreciate that."

"Sunny?"

"Yeah, Sunny, short for Sunshine, because you always have such a sunny outlook on everything."

"Couldn't you come up with something scarier? Like Skullcrusher or something cool?"

"Nope. You're Sunny. No way around it." Bull grinned. She'd never seen his "sweet" smile before. It reminded her of a little boy's smile.

"Sunny" stuck among the group, and it fit her. She claimed she didn't like it, which made everyone call her that even more.

"You'll have to accept it, Sunny." Rebel smirked. "You're our little sister now, and we'll torture you mercilessly. But know this—no one else will. You're ours to protect now. We're your brothers." He motioned around the circle of men. They all nodded in agreement, except Reaper. The look of possession in his eyes spoke of something more.

Brianna fought back the tears of emotion that threatened to overtake her. She'd finally been accepted as part of the exclusive group. Even Bull looked at her as his little sister, and she cherished the feeling. "I've always wanted a brother. Now I have several."

"You have all of us," Shadow promised. "We're proud to be your brothers. We take care of our own."

Brianna felt the shift in the bond. She had a great love for her family and was all too happy to add this wonderful group of men to the mix.

Later that night after everyone else was asleep, Noah slipped out of his barracks and into Brianna's tent. He eased onto the uncomfortable cot with her and draped his arm over her, both protectively and possessively. Her body craved his warmth and his kisses. The way he nibbled along the back of her neck sent cold chills through her entire body. He held her all night as they slept, his hand splayed across her abdomen. Before dawn, she felt his reluctance to leave her bed before anyone else woke up.

Over the following week, Reaper made it a nightly ritual to find his way to her bed. Each night, Brianna found it increasingly difficult to resist the powerful urges he created in her. If anyone in his team knew what was happening between Reaper and Brianna, they never let on. She knew damn well they were aware. It was their job to know, and it wasn't like she could even hide her feelings for him during the day when they were all together. But at least they were good-natured enough toward her not to bring it up.

With every day that passed, Brianna fell in love with Reaper just a little more. In all the nights he snuck into her bed with her, he never once tried to go further than what her grandmother had called "heavy petting." She'd laughed at that term when her grandmother first used it.

Now, the petting was making her crazy. She couldn't take her eyes off Reaper when he was around and fantasized about him when he wasn't. Right or wrong, she had decided this definitely was not a one-night stand, and she was ready to take it to the next level. She would be leaving for home the following week, and she planned to make the most of her time with him while she could.

As she got ready for bed that night, she desperately hoped he wouldn't be called out for a mission. That would ruin all her plans. She washed her face and brushed her teeth as usual, then sprayed her body with her favorite perfume. The mixture of jasmine, rose, orchid and freesia was inherently feminine and unforgettable to the senses. There hadn't been a call to use it in this godforsaken place before now. She knew the sweat from the sweltering heat during the day would have rinsed it all off her anyway. But the colder desert night air would help keep it in place, at least until he joined her.

She climbed into her bed without her pajamas this time and waited for him to join her. Within an hour of lights-out, he opened the tent door silently and slid into bed next to her. She lay on her side, and he slipped his arm around her. He suddenly jerked his head up when his hand met her cool, bare skin.

"You're sure?" he whispered.

"I've never been more certain," she replied.

She turned her body into his, looked into his eyes, and watched the chocolate brown turn to black with passion and desire. She reached up and kissed him, softly at first, then ran her fingers through his short black hair.

She ran her tongue around the outline of his lips before seductively licking in the middle to urge him to open his mouth to her. When he did, a deep rumble rolled through his chest, and the kiss suddenly turned urgent and demanding.

Her hands never left his body, as she felt the muscles in his shoulders tense, then across his chest, down his stomach to the hem of his shirt. She started to slowly pull it up over his head when he grabbed it with one hand and flung it to the floor.

He rolled her onto her back, and he moved to cover her entire body with his. Through his jogging pants, she felt his erection pressed against her lower abdomen. She raked her fingernails down his back, moved her hands to his sides, and slid her fingers under the elastic waistband. He grabbed her hands and pushed them above her head, holding them both in one hand. She realized she must have had a puzzled look on her face when he gave her the sexiest half grin she'd ever seen. He whispered, "I plan on taking my time."

Noah rose up on his forearms, cupped her face in his hands, and paused to gaze deeply into her eyes. His eyes raked over her face, taking in the slight blush from the embarrassment he knew this intense intimacy caused in her.

Her lips were still swollen from their last kiss, and her breasts heaved as they rose and fell with her increased breathing. Reaper kept his eyes on hers as he dipped his mouth to hers again, licking, teasing, and pulling away. She tried to raise her head to capture his mouth again, and he pulled farther away, still watching. When she realized what he was doing, Brianna lowered her head back to the cot.

His kissed her cheek, to her jawline, and finally moved to her earlobe. His touch sent shivers through her entire body. He licked and sucked on her ear before finally pulling on it seductively with his teeth. Then he worked his way down her neck with openmouthed kisses as he licked and bit her skin. She tried to pull her hands loose to touch him, but his grip tightened just enough to keep her hands in place, and he continued his assault on all her senses.

She inhaled deeply to breathe in his musky, masculine scent and let out a long sigh. He continued moving lower on her body. She didn't even realize the moment when he freed her hands since his mouth had found the sensitive, hardened buds of her breasts. Noah licked and bit, teased and tempted her until she grabbed his head in her hands and pulled him back to her chest. She felt the rumble of his low chuckle reverberate through her. He started again, and her back arched in response to his touch as his hand found her other breast. Slowly, painfully slow, his mouth followed his hands as he tasted every inch of her.

Her hands seemed to have a mind of their own as they moved all across his body. She was in complete awe and appreciation of every muscle in his chest, shoulders, back, and arms. He moved lower down her torso, still kissing and licking her stomach. In hushed moans, she heard him whisper, "So beautiful."

His hands moved lower still. He cupped her heated mound possessively before he found the small nub of nerves that could send her soaring. His thumb ran over it slightly and instantly made her body beg for more and more. He watched her intently as he moved in small circles while applying more pressure.

Instinctively, her hips rose slightly to meet his touch. His fingers found her soft, wet center, moving one finger along the folds, just barely touching her where she so desperately wanted to feel him.

"Noah, please, now!"

But he didn't surrender to her request. He swirled his finger around her wet heat before finally pushing all the way in. Out. In. Out. His rhythm was such sweet torture.

"Baby, you're so wet for me."

"Noah..." His name was all she could mutter before his second finger found her wet desire and plunged in. He moved his hand faster, watched her expressions, admired how responsive her beautiful body was to his touch, and how it brought her closer and closer to climax. Then he suddenly stopped.

"Uh, no! Don't stop!" she cried.

He picked her legs up, bent her knees, and put them over his shoulders. Then she felt his hot, wet tongue pressed against her clit as his two fingers danced and played in her wetness again. He increased and decreased the pressure and rhythm at a maddening pace. He again brought her closer and closer to the edge and then mercilessly took it away. When he was satisfied she could take no more, his tongue and fingers again began to work their magic.

"Bri—look at me. Look at me," he commanded.

She opened her eyes and met his piercing gaze. She ran her fingers through his hair until she could no longer hold back the intense pressure built up inside her.

"Come for me, baby." Then he felt her inner walls tighten around his fingers, felt them shudder and quiver as she tumbled over the edge.

Noah reached for his wallet, pulled out a condom wrapper and was sheathed and back on top of her before she could even move. He placed his forearms on either side of her head, their faces only a fraction of an inch apart, and he pushed his long, hard length deep inside her. He felt her body mold around and accept him. With a sharp intake of breath, she arched her back and her hips rose to take him

"God, you're so tight. You feel so good," he moaned.

Their bodies, now joined as one, found the perfect rhythm as they performed this most intimate dance. He lowered his head to catch her moan in his mouth. He sucked on her bottom lip, playfully pulled on it with his teeth, then his tongue delved into her mouth again. She held on tight to his shoulders then moved her hands down to his back. Her fingernails dug into his skin as he brought her closer and closer to the edge again. He pushed up on his hands to drive deeper into her and find her sweet spot.

"Let go, Bri. Let me feel you."

"Come with me. I'm not going over without you."

He surged harder, felt her clench around him, felt the quiver of her sensitive flesh, and watched her face change as she tumbled over the edge of passion, and then he joined her. He let his arms go limp and just lay on her beautiful, sweat-soaked body for a moment before he pulled out of her. He heard her groan of disappointment and had to chuckle.

"I know exactly how you feel, baby."

He rolled onto his side, quickly discarding the condom. As Bri turned on her side, he molded his body to fit against hers. It was not normal for him to sleep completely naked, but neither of them would dare complain.

She was so completely sated, worn out and happy, she slipped into the deepest sleep she'd had since she'd arrived on the base. At some point during the night, he got up, dressed, and silently left her tent, because he was gone when she woke up at dawn.

She showered, dressed, and walked to the mess hall for breakfast. She was devastated to learn that his team was sent out on a mission and had left about an hour before. While she sat alone with her breakfast, she was lost deep in thought as she remembered the events of the night before. She relived every moment they'd spent together up until that point in her mind.

"Where'd you go?" Judge asked.

Brianna jumped, not realizing he'd sat down beside her while she was lost in her memories of Reaper. "Oh, sorry. Just thinking about the time I've spent here."

"That's right. You'll be going home soon, won't you?" Judge nodded.

"Yes," Brianna replied solemnly. "So, you went to school with Reaper, huh?"

"Yeah. He was an overachiever even back then. It was hard for the rest of us to even try to keep up with him. Smart, handsome, athletic. I don't know of anything the guy can't do."

"Sounds like he was pretty popular." Brianna smiled as she pictured the younger version of the man she'd fallen in love with in such a short time.

"He was more than popular. Everything came so easily to him. I guess that happens when you're born with a silver spoon in your mouth, though," Judge said sarcastically.

"Silver spoon?"

"You know, the kind that rich and influential families have? That's the kind of family he comes from. He always got whatever he wanted, from whoever he wanted, whenever he wanted."

Brianna felt very uncomfortable with the contempt Judge showed toward the man who was supposed to be his friend. "That may have been true when he was a kid, but he's worked hard to get where he is today."

Judge cut his blue-green eyes to her. "The only way to get ahead is to make your own way. Working hard doesn't result in getting ahead—blazing a new path does. A real man will go after what he wants and not let anything or anyone stand in his way."

As Judge finished his rant, Brianna's thoughts strayed to how he had been such a close friend to Noah. She knew Noah's sense of loyalty ran very deep, and that was one of the most endearing qualities about him, but she couldn't stop the uneasy feeling she always had around Judge. It was one of the reasons why she stayed so close to her brothers in Noah's squadron and didn't push the interview on Judge as much.

"My time in the Army will be up soon enough," Judge continued, more to himself than to her. "I'm already making exciting plans for my future."

"That's great," she replied noncommittally. She didn't usually engage Judge in conversation more than absolutely necessary.

"I've met a few influential people in DC, and I've already started paving the road to move to a high-level position in the Department of Defense," Judge boasted.

Brianna nodded and smiled politely. "That sounds great for you, Judge. I need to go work on my article while I have some time alone. I'll see you later."

He grunted in reply as Brianna scurried past him. Relieved to retreat to the privacy of her tent, she sat on her cot and worked on her article. One ear was always tuned to the sounds that surrounded her, though, as she waited for Noah to return.

She spent the next several days in an emotional haze as she watched for them to return and waited to hear any word of their mission. Nights brought dreams of Noah and their last night together. Each day brought another round of depression when he didn't return to her yet again. Her last day on assignment finally arrived, and she wasn't ready to leave. The men didn't return before her long flight back to Atlanta.

The military convoy arrived to escort her back to the airfield. She produced the same black cloth that was previously used, they blindfolded her, and she was put in the Humvee for the long ride. She didn't mind not being able to see so much on the way in, but now she wondered if she'd passed Noah along the way out. She needed just one last look, a wave goodbye, or any sign that he was still all right.

As she left that base, the thought that she did so without seeing him, talking to him, or touching him tore her heart out of her chest. She hated that she was forced to leave him behind when she wanted nothing more than to have one more day with him.

CHAPTER FIVE

The twenty-hour flight home was even more grueling for Brianna than the flight that delivered her to the secret location. Initially, her excitement over getting the story of a lifetime was enough to keep her occupied on the uncomfortable flight. Now, the thoughts of Noah dominated her mind, and the phantom feel of his lips on her skin drove her mad.

There was no time for closure, to say her goodbyes to her new friends, and to leave no words left unspoken. As it stood, she had no way to contact Noah, no method of communication with any of them, and no way to share her information with them. Purely out of desperation, she'd considered asking Judge to pass a note on to Noah, but she couldn't shake the feeling that he just couldn't be trusted.

She finally surrendered to the emotions that welled up inside her. Brianna opened her diary, her notes, and a new notebook to start crafting her article. If every scene insisted on playing on repeat in her mind, she decided she'd make the most of it. She spent the majority of the flight time deep in thought, developed writer's cramp, and thoroughly exhausted herself mentally before she finally completed the rough draft of her article.

After she put her things away, she shifted in the uncomfortable seat as much as possible and fell asleep for the remainder of the flight. Before she knew it, the plane was wheels-down and on approach to the airfield in the Atlanta area. Mixed feelings flooded her senses. She was elated to be home and see her family again. But she was also heartbroken as she thought about Noah and the other men.

My brothers, she thought sadly as she pictured each one. She reached into her bag and fingered the black cloth that served as her blindfold. *I'll make sure this article does you proud,* she vowed.

"Bri!" Missy screeched as she rushed to wrap her arms around her sister.

Brianna smiled and dropped her bags to free her hands. She pulled Missy closer to her. "I've missed you too, sis."

"That was the longest six weeks of my life," Missy complained. "Don't ever do that again."

Brianna chuckled, knowing that Missy was usually a little on the dramatic side. "I'm home now. You don't have to worry about me leaving again for a while."

"Are you planning another trip?" Missy asked, her smile fading and the worry clouding her eyes.

"Not right away," Brianna laughed. "But if I'm going to be a real correspondent, I'll have to travel to cover the stories as they come up."

"As long as any future assignment doesn't take as long as this one did," Missy conceded.

"Glad to have you home, baby girl." Evan wrapped his arms around Brianna, nudging Missy to the side. "Safe and sound."

"I've been in good hands, Daddy," Brianna assured him. "No one would dare mess with those guys."

"They have nothing on a mother intent on protecting her children," Diana declared as she pushed Evan aside to get to her daughter. "Never do that again."

If they only knew that I've been trying to figure out a way to get myself back over there, she thought.

Jessie and Ashley stepped up and waited for their turn to welcome their older sister home. Evan picked up Brianna's bags and carried them to the car. Once they were all inside, Evan took a moment to appreciate having his family back together.

"Why don't we take our girls out to eat and then let Brianna get some rest?" Evan asked Diana.

"Sounds great to me," Diana agreed.

During their meal, Brianna filled her family in on the details of living on a ghost base, how the men worked together as a cohesive team, and how she became part of their close-knit group.

"Those hot men in uniform adopted you as their little sister?" Jessie asked, her mouth gaping open.

"They sure did." Brianna nodded, swallowing past the ball of emotion in her throat. "I have several very scary brothers now."

"I want to meet them," Missy said dreamily. "Reaper sounds exactly like my type. Think you can arrange to introduce me?"

Brianna's eyes snapped to Missy's at that comment. Her face instantly heated, her blood pressure spiked, and she was ready to tackle her sister for even suggesting it. When she saw the sparkle in Missy's eyes and the teasing grin on her face, she knew she'd just given Missy more information than she intended.

Missy's eyebrow slowly arched as she tilted her head to the side. She silently questioned Brianna, who quickly averted her gaze and refused to make direct eye contact with her again.

"They weren't allowed to give me their real names, so I definitely don't have any contact information for them. Sorry to disappoint you, Missy."

"That is very disappointing," Missy replied, her tone conveying her understanding of the situation.

Brianna finally gave in and looked at her. Missy gave her a small, reassuring smile. "But hey," Missy continued. "They're special ops guys, right? They'll find you."

That was Brianna's secret hope—that Noah would find her and they'd have the opportunity to be a couple. "I'll toast to that," Brianna replied as she raised her glass. The others joined her and lifted theirs. "To happy reunions."

Later, when Brianna crawled into her bed, her body seemed to melt into the soft sheets and plush mattress. The creature comforts of home would take some readjustment after the stark difference of the cot that had been her bed for the past six weeks. More than that, she'd grown dependent on Noah joining her, heating her body in every imaginable way, and cradling her after thoroughly loving her.

Now the bed felt cold and lonely without his thick body taking up most of the room. Tears slowly leaked from her eyes as she drifted off to sleep from sheer exhaustion. Her dreams were filled with visions of Noah—some were welcomed, and some filled her with dread.

Over the next several weeks, Brianna put the finishing touches on her article and submitted it to the *Atlanta Times Free Press* for publication. She waited on pins and needles as the editor took his time to review her writing, confirm fact checks, and make a decision on whether to run the article. By the time she finally received the call requesting a meeting to discuss it, she'd almost given up on it.

"Brianna, this is Les Vincent with the *Atlanta Times*. Can you come in this afternoon so we can discuss your article?"

"Yes, I'd love to," she replied, trying to sound outwardly confident. Inwardly, she was simultaneously screaming and feeling close to fainting.

After agreeing on a time to meet, she ran through the house in an excited frenzy. "Mom! Mom! Where are you?"

Diana stepped out of her home office, her brows drawn down in alarm and confusion. "In here, Brianna. What's wrong?"

"I just got the call from the editor. I'm going to meet with him today," Brianna blurted out.

"That's great, baby. Congratulations," Diana said as she clutched Brianna's arm. "I'm so excited for you."

"Thanks, Mom. I put a lot of work into that article, so I hope they don't change it too much."

"Don't borrow trouble, Bri. Go talk to him and see what he has to say before you start working yourself up," Diana chided her gently.

"You're right. Positive thoughts and all that jazz," Brianna replied.

~

"I'm Brianna Tate, and I have an appointment with Les Vincent." Brianna proudly introduced herself to the secretary.

"Just a moment." The older lady smiled as she checked the editor's schedule. "Here you are. If you'll have a seat, I'll let him know you're here."

After a few minutes, Brianna was led into his office. His desk was covered with stacks of paper in various heights, haphazardly strewn pens, and several bottles of water. The ultra-organized fanatic in her cringed as she took a seat across from him.

"So, you're Evan's daughter," he stated.

"Yes, I am. Do you know my dad?"

"No. I was given a directive from my boss, who was nicely asked by a golfing buddy, who knows someone who knows your dad, to read your piece," he replied dryly, his expression holding no humor.

His smile lit up his face as he continued. "And now I'm delighted that it all came down this way. To be honest, I never read unsolicited submissions from an unknown freelance writer. If I hadn't been forced to read it, I would've missed out on an excellent idea with an original focus on the sacrifices our servicemen and women make. You'll be thrilled to hear that DOD has approved your piece as-is. It looks like this story will be picked up and distributed nationally."

Brianna's blank expression and rigid posture made Les laugh. "Brianna, did you hear me?"

"Y-yes," she stammered. "I'm just speechless, literally."

His words swirled in her mind for a minute before she realized their full implication. "Did you say it's being picked up nationally?"

"Yes, I did indeed." Les smiled as he turned his chair to face her fully. "This is an amazing article, Brianna. You keep writing like this, you are going places."

As Les explained the next steps, Brianna's mind raced with possibilities. She wasn't afraid of hard work and making sacrifices to achieve her goals. She wanted to make a name for herself among the elite, the top of the top journalists. The more things seemed to fall into place, the more chaotic her life felt.

When she left for the unknown destination in a country half a world away, she faced her fears and stepped onto that plane with her own marching orders in hand. When she arrived at the base, not knowing a single person there, she quickly made friends with the men she wanted to introduce to the world. When she gave her body to Noah, she did it knowing she also gave him her heart.

Now she was stepping out into the spotlight, sharing their story with millions of people, and hoping that they found the same value in it that she did. Brianna tried to focus on Les as he talked animatedly about her future, but hopes that Noah would track her down through the trail of news coverage kept overtaking her thoughts.

"...you'll have to move to Miami," she vaguely heard Les state as he rambled on.

"Wait. What? Move to Miami?" she asked.

"Well, yeah. If you were just a freelance writer, you could live anywhere. But this is a staff position with the *Miami Herald,* so they'll want you on-site. Since both papers are owned by the same parent company, the editor in chief wants you to go there. Is that a problem?"

"No. It's not a problem at all." Brianna smiled.

Miami was where Noah called home when he wasn't off in a remote desert somewhere on assignment. She also remembered that Rebel mentioned he'd moved there not long ago to be closer to Noah. Hope that they'd be reunited grew inside her and became a new goal for her to reach.

Relaying the news to her family that night proved to be more difficult than she thought. She'd been home from her six-week stint in the desert for nearly three months, but Missy jokingly wouldn't let Brianna forget how she'd abandoned her. Brianna knew that Missy would honestly be upset that she planned to move away and start her own life.

"I have some great news," Brianna recited the lines as she'd rehearsed in the car on the way home.

"We want to hear all about it," Diana replied. "Brianna made me wait until everyone was here, so she only had to say it once." Diana laughed as she looked around the table at her family.

"I met with the editor of the *Atlanta Times* today, and he loved my article. In fact, he was so impressed with it, that he's making sure it gets picked up and distributed nationally," she began.

A round of congratulations and cheering ensued as they continued to pass the food around the table. As Brianna spooned the potatoes onto her plate, she casually added the punch line. "The editor in chief at the parent company told him to offer me a staff position...with the *Miami Herald.*"

The silence in the room was only momentary before the shouting ensued.

"No, you just got home!"

"You're not moving that far away from home all alone."

"Can I have your room?"

"Everyone calm down. This is the deal. I'm grown, I've graduated college, and I'm ready to step out and make my own life. This is a phenomenal opportunity that is unheard of for a new, unproven journalist. That one idea, that one article, has moved mountains for me.

"The staff position isn't a glamorous job or anything, but it's what I want to do. I'll still have to prove myself, take some of the stories others don't want, but this can open so many other doors. In four weeks, I'm starting my new position as a staff writer in Miami."

Evan saw the same determined young woman he'd witnessed getting on the military transport plane sitting before him now. The will and desire to excel were ingrained in her very being. Not knowing how to give up, she pursued her goals with fervor and determination.

"I'm proud of you, Brianna," Evan replied warmly. "You'll do great in Miami."

Diana dabbed her eyes with her napkin and added her agreement. "Your father's right, Brianna. I'll miss you more than I can say, but I'm very proud of you, too."

"So, I get your room?" Ashley chimed in with a teasing grin.

"No, Ashley. I expect my room to become a shrine to my memory. You'll need to pay your respects to it daily," Brianna teased.

The following four weeks seemed to move all too fast for the Tate family. As Brianna made preparations to move, every step toward her new life took her further from the safety and security of her close-knit family. When she found an apartment online that appeared to fit her needs, Missy and Brianna made a quick weekend trip to tour it in person.

"All right, we're finally away from prying eyes and eavesdropping ears. Spill it," Missy demanded as they took their seats on the plane.

"What?" Brianna asked, momentarily confused.

"You know what. It's been nearly four months since you got back from that desert, and you haven't been on a single date. Every time I've asked about what happened, you've brushed me off. Now, spill it," Missy demanded.

With a huff, Brianna nodded. "Fine. Noah and I became pretty close while I was there, but he got called off base for a mission just hours before I came back home. He didn't make it back to the base before I left, so I never had a chance to say goodbye. Or anything else, for that matter.

"He mentioned that he's from the Miami area. It sounds crazy when I say it out loud, but I really hope that he finds me through my article."

"That would be an awesome story to tell your grandkids one day, Bri," Missy assured her. "If it's meant to be, it will be."

"I know I didn't know him that long. I barely even got his real name, but I just strongly feel he's the one for me," Brianna whispered, afraid to voice her beliefs too loudly.

"So you want to be close to the place he calls home, in case he decides to look for you." Missy nodded in agreement. "I have a good feeling about this. Even though I really don't want to lose my partner in crime."

"You'll just have to come visit me often." Brianna smiled.

Sweat glistened on their brows almost immediately after stepping outside the airport into the heat and humidity of Miami. The taxi delivered them to an attractive apartment complex. Each building consisted of five floors and had meticulously landscaped flower gardens. The buildings surrounded the gated pool area and gave the aura of a secret oasis.

Brianna and Missy exchanged excited glances as they rushed into the central office. An attractive older lady sat behind the desk, busily tending to typical office duties. When she heard the door chime, she looked up and smiled at the two young ladies entering.

"Hello, how can I help you?" she asked.

"I'm Brianna Tate. I called about the apartment that's open and scheduled time to tour the grounds in person."

"Yes, Brianna." She smiled. "I'm Wanda, and I remember talking to you. I'm so glad you were able to make it. Atlanta, right?"

"That's right." Brianna nodded. "Wanda, this is my sister, Missy."

"Hello," Wanda replied. "Are you moving in, too?"

"No, I wish," Missy laughed. "I'm just here for sisterly support."

"You just let me know if you change your mind." Wanda winked. "Come right this way, ladies. I'm the best tour guide you'll ever find."

Excitement, giddiness, fear of the unknown—Brianna's feelings ran the gamut of the spectrum. The one she felt most, however, was hope. She was so very hopeful that she'd reconnect with Noah.

She took her time to walk through the empty apartment to visualize how she'd arrange her furniture. Scenes of how her life would change flashed before her eyes. In every aspect, she saw and felt Noah with her. In the kitchen cooking together, in the living room watching TV together, and in the bedroom making love every day.

"I love it. I'll take it," Brianna gushed.

CHAPTER SIX

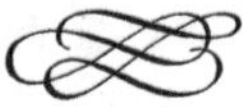

"Man, it's been a long damn day," Bull grumbled as the four men arrived back on base.

"So glad this one is over," Rebel agreed. "Being away from home gets harder the older I get."

"I've actually given this some serious thought," Reaper chimed in. "Before we were called out for this assignment, I looked into forming my own security firm. Since I haven't touched the trust fund my father set up for me, it'd be fairly easy to cover start-up costs."

"You're thinking of leaving the Army for good?" Bull asked.

"I am," Reaper confirmed. "Working for myself sounds better every day."

"Does one pretty little blonde have anything to do with that decision?" Shadow asked.

"I don't know what you're talking about, man," Reaper replied, his face stoic.

Shadow laughed heartily. "Of course not." He smiled. "I received an outside offer I've been considering too. Maybe I'll give Brianna a call when I get home. See if she wants to hook up."

Reaper rounded on Shadow, his eyes glowing with the intensity of a fire. "Don't even fucking think about it, Shadow. I don't care how big and bad you think you are, I will fuck you up."

The knowing smirk and laughter that shone in his eyes was the only answer Reaper needed to know he'd just been played. Of course, Shadow couldn't let their conversation end like that.

"To the trained ear, that would probably be an odd response for someone who's not interested in her," Shadow replied dryly.

"We're almost back to the base," Rebel chimed in. "I guess we'll see, huh?"

"Yeah, we'll see all right," Shadow laughed.

The Humvee rolled to a stop, and the four hulking men all exited at the same time. Even behind his sunglasses, Reaper knew his eyes gave him away when they searched for Brianna's tent first. His lips set in a thin line, he prepared to accept the razzing he knew his teammates would unleash on him.

"Go ahead. We'll wait here," Shadow encouraged.

He shook his head lightly, dropped his gear, and strolled over to Brianna's door. He rapped lightly on it to alert her to his presence before he swung the door open and stepped inside. He jerked his sunglasses off his face as he turned around and took in the barren furnishings.

She was gone.

He burst out of the door, almost taking it off the hinges with his force, and stomped across the way to the command tent.

"Where is Brianna Tate?" he barked out.

The private who'd carried her suitcase to her tent upon her arrival quickly stood at attention. "Her transport taking her back stateside has already left, sir."

Reaper stared the young man down for several seconds as he attempted to understand the words the private had just spoken. "I was told that transport didn't leave until twenty-three hundred hours."

"The flight plan had to be changed because of anticipated bad weather. She was taken to the airfield about two hours ago. That plane took off about an hour ago, sir," he explained.

Reaper gave him a single nod and stormed out of the tent. When he reached the other men, he snatched his gear off the ground and trudged to his own barracks. In an uncharacteristic display of aggravation, he threw his gear onto the bed and began pacing in the tight area.

Rebel approached him first, and understanding dawned as he took in Reaper's demeanor.

"I missed her. The flight left early," Reaper said through gritted teeth. "Son of a bitch!"

"I've never seen you react this way over anyone, Reap. And I've known you a long time," Rebel replied. Reaper's eyes rose to meet his. Rebel nodded. "It's time."

"Yeah. I think you're right. It is time," Reaper agreed. "Our service contracts are coming back up for renewal over the next few weeks. I'll just take the honorable discharge and my walking papers back home with me."

"Steele Security, huh?" Rebel asked.

"Count me in," Bull said from the doorway.

Reaper nodded. "Shadow, you too?" he asked.

"I've decided to take another offer, Reap. But you know anytime you need me, all it takes is a phone call," Shadow replied.

"I have no doubt about that, Shadow," Reaper replied.

"She means this much to you?" Bull asked.

Reaper inhaled deeply, filled his chest, and lifted up to his full height. He looked Bull directly in the eye when he replied. "Damn straight, she does. I'm not leaving the Army for her, but she definitely helped me make my mind up."

"We're in," Rebel said, taking a step beside Bull. "Let's do this."

They left Reaper alone in the barracks and headed to the mess hall. Reaper allowed his memories to take over his thoughts as he absently unpacked his gear. Brianna's presence had brought a different kind of peace to him, one that he hadn't known he was missing until she was gone.

Now, simply knowing that she was on her way back home, thousands of miles away from him, was a depressing thought. His nights with her had made the barren desert a tolerable place. He'd looked forward to the time he spent with her and had even stopped dreading all of her questions.

The following day, Reaper approached his commanding officer and informed him of his intent to leave the Army. After an hour of unsuccessfully attempting to persuade him to stay, his CO finally relented and agreed to start the necessary paperwork. The weeks before his discharge seemed to drag by, each day seemingly taking longer than the last.

Patience had been drilled into Reaper's mind and personality through the countless hours of training and missions he'd been on over the years. In his line of work, he had to display an enormous amount of self-control to complete his assignments successfully. But this waiting on the edge of what could be a brand-new life with Brianna was close to maddening.

The day the transport left, taking Reaper home, the mixed feelings of leaving the only life he'd known since he left home at eighteen threatened to change his mind. The thoughts of a real life with Brianna pushed him forward. Knowing he'd have his own security company, and his brothers at his side, helped give him peace about his decision.

When he briefly stopped before he boarded the plane, Reaper took a good look at the area that had been his home and silently said goodbye. It was well past time for a new life to begin.

~

"It's fucking amazing how fast this business has grown," Rebel exclaimed. "You need to hire more men, Reap. We'll have to start turning business away if you don't."

"I'm working on it. I've lined up several interviews this week with some guys who have great potential. You two get to help me," Reaper replied as he looked at Rebel and Bull. "One guy is a tech support guru—we really need someone like him. All are former military, various branches."

"Let's put them through our normal process for interviews." Bull smirked.

"Uh, Bull? We actually want these guys to like us," Rebel laughed.

"Wrong kind of interview process, then." Bull smiled.

"Have you found her yet, Reap?" Rebel asked.

"I found her the day I got back, Rebel," Reaper replied as he continued working through the stack of paperwork on his desk. "You know I'm a planning man."

"Well, if you 'plan' much longer, you may lose your chance with her." Rebel shook his head.

"Not a chance. She lives here in Miami now. She's been working nonstop to prove herself, while I've been working nonstop to make this business successful. She'll be at the Rainstorm and Bead pub with her friends this weekend to celebrate her birthday," Reaper explained. "And so will I."

"How do you know that?" Bull asked.

"It's my job to know, Bull," Reaper replied with a sly smile. "I've done my recon on my subject."

"What a good stalker-soldier," Bull replied dryly.

Reaper looked up from his task and stared at Bull. He straightened his back and slightly narrowed his eyes as he considered his friend's response.

"You like her," Reaper finally replied, his smile uncharacteristically covering his face. "She got through that thick hide of yours."

"Shut up, man," Bull dodged as he shook his head.

"Holy shit, you actually care about her," Reaper said as he stood. "I don't believe it."

"Reaper, I'd hate to kick my boss's ass, but I'll do it if you don't quit this shit," Bull threatened.

Rebel, never one to let a taboo subject go without riling Bull as much as possible, had to voice his thoughts.

"You're right, Reap." He turned toward him and continued to poke at Bull. "Shit fire. How'd she do it, Bull? You thinking of stealing Reaper's woman or what?"

Bull stood quickly, his body set in his fighting stance. "Take it back, Rebel."

"I never thought I'd see the day," Rebel goaded him. "You, Reap?"

"Never."

"Both of you shitheads better back off right now," Bull threatened through his gritted teeth and clenched jaw. "You know I'd never do that to Reaper."

"Nah, man, that part I was just giving you shit over. But you do care about Brianna. She did get to you." Rebel laughed easily.

"I meant it when I said I'd be her brother and look out for her," Bull admitted. "She's different from most."

"I agree," Reaper said and smiled at his brother. "She is different from anyone else I've met. I'm glad you like her. You know the two of you and Shadow are the only family I claim."

"So, tell us about this party." Rebel grinned.

"I'll be glad to—after the interviews. The first candidate will be here soon. His name is Brad Sullivan, and he's the tech guru I mentioned," Reaper explained.

"How many interviews do we have this week?" Bull asked, trying to hide the groan in his tone.

"Ten," Reaper replied. "Two per day."

"I don't know which is worse—spreading them out or doing them all at once to get them over with," Rebel replied.

"I spread them out, so we're not sick of asking the same questions over and over by the end of the day. That would cause us to make rash decisions. Like Bull reminded us, these aren't exactly the type of interviews we have experience conducting," Reaper explained. "We need the best men in place as soon as possible."

"Something new come up, Reap?" Bull asked.

"We may have a government contract opening up to us if the stars align just right. Judge took a position in the Department of Defense and is trying to help get the contract approved. But since he's a new employee and this is a big deal, I don't know if it'll be approved," Reaper elaborated. "He also said he'd like to be a silent partner, offered money to help fund expenses."

"You don't need his money," Rebel replied, his brow furrowed into a V between his eyes. "You have plenty of family money. Why would he do that?"

"I thought it was strange too. Judge said he didn't realize I accepted the trust fund from my parents. He thought I'd entered the military because I was penniless," Reaper replied. "I had to explain the whole story of how it was set up in my name through my parents' lawyer when I was a kid. It was automatically mine, without accepting anything from them."

There were very few secrets in the tight-knit group, and the status of Reaper's family was well known. He and his father, Steve Steele, had a long history of butting heads, bouts of not speaking, and finally coming to blows before Reaper left home for good at eighteen.

In Reaper's eyes, Steve ruled his home with his iron fist and refused to consider any opinion that differed from his own. His take-charge attitude was overbearing and cast a suffocating shadow over the household. His rules were strictly enforced and doled out without preamble.

The visiting Army recruiter made an impression on the young boy. His senior year had consisted of visiting several colleges, taking the obligatory tours, and listening to countless hours of speeches extolling the values each would bring. But each had left him feeling as if something significant were missing, like the incomplete picture presented when pieces of the jigsaw puzzle were absent.

At first, listening to the recruiter explain the benefits of a military career was no different. It simply sounded like another pitch from a sleazy used car salesman. When the recruiter began listing the sacrifices a soldier had to make, the long days and nights on patrol, and the probability of leaving the comfort of his beloved country, he knew he'd finally found someone who was real. Someone who would be honest about what he'd face in his future. Someone who would tell him how hard and dangerous life can really be.

The scary truth was exactly what he needed to hear. It was what jarred him into action, into a decision, and into the direction of a life in the military. He'd still attend college—but as a cadet with a purpose. Eventually, he'd even have a family of his own—but with a distinctly different approach than his father. Rather than seeing the world with a spoiled rich boy stigma, he would see it through the lens of an experienced man.

Just before his high school graduation, young Noah approached his father, filled with excitement about his impending plans.

"Dad, I need to talk to you," he began his carefully constructed speech. "It's very important."

Steve's arms slowly lowered the newspaper, revealing the displeasure of being interrupted on his face. "This had better be good."

"I've made a decision about my future. My plans after high school."

"Go on," Steve said as he meticulously folded the paper. His tone conveyed that he knew he wouldn't like the direction this conversation would take. "Let's hear your master plan."

"I've decided to join the Army. I talked to the recruiter for a long time and basically mapped it all out. I'll still attend college, become an officer, and make a living doing what I love to do. My mind is made up, and I've already set a date for testing and swearing in."

"You what?" Steve asked. His voice was unusually low and threatening. He leaned forward in his chair, narrowed his eyes in anger, and balled his hands into fists at his sides. He was every bit as intimidating in this position as if he stood over Noah, yelling in his face.

"I've set the date—" Noah repeated and was promptly interrupted.

"I heard you!" Steve roared. "You will not go to that testing, and you will not swear in. No son of mine will give up a prestigious future to be some grunt, sleeping in the mud or a tent with a bunch of other grunts."

Steve stood and paced back and forth across the room. Noah's eyes drifted from Steve, who was still ranting and raving, to take in the opulence of his surroundings. *It figures,* Noah thought. *All he's worried about is what his friends will think. He isn't concerned about what I want.*

That thought summed up all of Noah's life within just a few words. It was that very realization that pushed him to keep his appointment, to excel on the tests, and to complete his swearing-in ceremony. Signing on the dotted line was a formality in his mind since his heart was already committed. The day after his graduation, he took his few prized possessions and left home.

He built a long, successful career in the Army. Taking extra classes each semester, he graduated early with his degree. His tenacity in everything he tried got him noticed by both his commanding officers and the men he led. He quickly climbed through the ranks, taking every training opportunity made available to him, and expanded his capabilities. He became the youngest Delta Force member, but that still didn't bring him the personal vindication he thought it would. His father's condescending rejection of him still rang loudly in his ears.

Today, he started to feel the pride in his accomplishments that had eluded him for far too long. All of his training, skills, dedication, and hard work were beginning to pay off. Merely months prior, he started his own security firm and was already well in the black. Word of mouth had already spread quickly about his firm's abilities, making them the first choice for many high-profile clients.

Hiring several more employees would allow him to take the more complicated contracts that he'd recently received. As he worked through the scores of paperwork on his desk, his thoughts kept straying back to Brianna. The feel of her skin against his during the hot desert nights lingered in his mind even now. The sweetness of her breath, the sensual sounds she made, and the way her body felt in his hands kept him awake at night.

He would never get enough of her.

By the weekend, his plan to persuade, entice, and pursue her would be well in play.

"Reap," Rebel called to him and interrupted his thoughts. "Brad's here."

"Good. Let's get started."

Reaper moved with a new determination as he greeted Brad and ushered him into his office. After brief introductions, the trio started the interview process and professionally grilled the applicant on his skills and experience. By the end of it, all three had already made their decision and silently communicated it.

"Brad, when can you start?" Reaper asked with a smile.

"As soon as you give me the word. I'm working a temporary assignment right now, but my manager knows I'm looking for a permanent position," Brad answered.

"Next Monday, one week from today? Is that enough notice?" Reaper asked.

"That's perfect. I'm proud to be part of this agency. It's become very popular, very quickly, in the serious security circles," Brad extolled. "That's exactly the type of firm I want to be part of."

"I appreciate that, Brad. We work hard and take our responsibilities seriously here. I have no doubt you will too. Glad to have you on board," Reaper said, shaking his hand.

After Brad left, Rebel turned to the other two men and commented, "One down. Only nine more to go."

CHAPTER SEVEN

"We deserve to go on a huge bender after the week we've had," Bull declared as they stepped out of the office of Steele Security. "I'd rather run point for a month than sit through one more interview. Next person hired is an office manager, Reaper."

"You're not kidding." Reaper shook his head. "I love having this business, but interviewing has to be the worst job ever."

"Here's the Rainstorm and Bead pub. Thank God," Rebel exhaled. "Let's go have a beer or a maybe a keg."

They made a slow loop around the perimeter of the room to scan their surroundings. The trio stayed on duty even when they were off the clock. As Reaper approached the bar, he ordered three beers and let his eyes settle on Brianna.

She stood beside a tall table covered in presents, beer bottles, and a birthday cake in the middle. Several of her girlfriends surrounded her, and one placed a pointy happy birthday hat on her head. Reaper's hand froze midair as he raised his bottle to his lips. Brianna laughed heartily at the ridiculous hat but wore it with pride.

She was even more beautiful than she appeared in his dreams. Her long blond hair had lighter blond streaks as if the sun had picked specific areas to place light kisses. Her skin glowed from her Miami suntan, and her warm smile lit up her gorgeous face. If he'd had any doubts about finding her, they quickly melted away when he realized he couldn't take his eyes off her.

The thought of another man taking his place with her was enough to drive him into a blind rage. The knowledge that he'd never felt that way about anyone before convinced him to take a chance. Seeing her again solidified his feelings.

Brianna moved to the front of the table and began to open her birthday presents. He seized the perfect moment as he quickly stole up behind her, wrapped his arms around her waist, and murmured into her ear.

"Hello, Brianna. Have you missed me?"

She jumped in surprise and quickly whirled around to face him, ready to tear into the idiot who had dared to touch her. The shock of seeing him rendered her speechless for a few seconds as she openly stared at him. Then her jaw dropped open wide as the realization that he was real sank in.

"Noah!" she squealed as she automatically jumped into his arms. Her heart raced, and she couldn't contain the smile that was now permanently affixed to her face.

Of all the people she expected to see at her birthday party, Noah Steele wasn't one of them. Inwardly, she had fantasized about this moment so many times that she almost thought her daydream had taken over. But now, holding him close to her, she realized no fantasy could ever compete with the real man.

Noah effortlessly lifted her off the floor, further crushed her to him, and embraced her in the enormous bear hug that epitomized his size.

"Oh my God! I can't believe it's really you!" she whispered to him. "Are you actually here with me right now?"

"I'm definitely here, baby," he murmured.

Brianna's girlfriends were struck with the same speechless reaction as they watched the scene play out in front of them. Their eyes roamed from one man to the next, taking in the exquisite physiques and rippling muscles, all the while their mouths continued to gape open.

Reaper released Brianna, allowing her to slowly slide down his body, keeping their contact in place for as long as possible. Their eyes locked as Reaper's hand rose to cup her cheek. An uneasy throat-clearing caught her attention and reminded her they weren't alone.

Turning to their audience, Brianna ruefully explained. "Remember the guy in the Army I told you about? Reaper? This is him!"

Brianna quickly made a round of introductions, and the group rearranged tables and chairs so they could all sit together. Reaper took his seat next to Brianna, wrapped his arm possessively around her chair, and felt the puzzle pieces of his life were falling into place. The gorgeous blonde who had stolen his heart was at his side, his business was growing by leaps and bounds—almost faster than he could keep up with—and he was happier than he'd been in a very long time.

Brianna animatedly talked with her friends, regaling them with the story of how she and Reaper first met. As she finished her story, she turned toward him and drew in a ragged breath when she recognized his provocative expression.

"What's that smile for?" she asked breathily.

"It's for you," he replied smoothly.

The pub lights dimmed as the familiar sensual bass chords of "Love Bites" reverberated through the room.

"They're playing our song." The caress of Reaper's sensual tone completely captivated her, pulling her to him without conscious thought. Before she knew it, her hand was in his as he led her to the dance floor.

He wrapped his arms around her waist and pulled her body to his. She instinctively wrapped her arms around his neck. When he dipped his head to her ear, his deep voice sent cold chills cascading over her skin. "You have no idea how many times I've thought about having you in my arms again."

His hands slowly stroked up and down her ribs, his fingers flowed effortlessly over her shirt but burned straight through to her skin and left her with his unique brand. With each languid movement, her breaths became heavier and faster, her chest heaved with the exertion of restraining herself. Any rational thought about taking their relationship slowly this time quickly evaporated, exactly like the steam emanating from her overheated body.

"You're even sexier than I remember," he continued. "More than I can resist."

His lips hovered barely above the skin on her neck. He threaded his fingers through her hair, lightly grasped the silky strands, and gently tilted her head to the side. Placing wet, sensual kisses along the sensitive skin on her neck, from her ear to the dip at her collarbone, Noah continued his meticulous reacquaintance with her body.

With each word and touch, Brianna became more pliant against him. She molded her body to fit his, and they continued to sway to the music as he worked his way back up her neck. When he reached her ear, he increased her growing discomfort with his words. "By the time we step foot outside this pub, you'll be mine. If you have any objections to that, now is the time to tell me."

Before she could respond, Noah's lips found hers. A small taste quickly became an overwhelming need to consume her. Her unique flavor was the only aphrodisiac he needed. The velvety smooth brush of her tongue against his fueled his desire. She moaned softly into his mouth, so full of passion and intense need that it overflowed from her involuntarily.

"So you agree?" He smirked as he broke the kiss.

"I wholeheartedly agree," she panted as she tried to catch her breath. "As if there were ever any question about it."

"There wasn't for me," he admitted with a sexy wink. "Just had to make sure you were convinced."

"It certainly took you long enough," she challenged.

He slowly quirked one brow up, a glow of amusement lighting up his eyes. "Are you trying to say I'm slow on my game?"

She shrugged one shoulder and cut her eyes to the left as she slightly pursed her lips. "If the shoe fits and all."

"Some things are worth the extra time. Slow, deliberate movements heighten the senses. Intense, precise drives at the right time are deeply satisfying."

Keeping his voice even, his pace slow, and his eyes locked on hers, he completed his mission with a slow stroke down the front of her neck. "I'd much rather take all night, so there's no doubt about my skills.

"Honestly, you should already know that I take my recon missions very seriously," he added with a straight face.

Her reply was a groan of frustration followed by dropping her forehead to his chest. She shook her head from side to side but had to laugh at herself when she felt his chuckle rumble through him. "You'll pay for that later."

"I'll hold you to that."

Raising her eyes to his, she smirked at him. "Fell right into your trap, didn't I?"

His full-on smile had always caused the breath to seize in her chest. His straight white teeth shone against his naturally tanned skin. The crinkle around his eyes was kissable, as were his plump, sexy lips. Putting the whole man together in one package was lethal to the female population.

"Yes, you did. Now that I've caught you, I won't ever let you go, Bri." He spoke sincerely.

Hearing the words from Noah gave Brianna the courage, and the extra push, she needed to confess her own feelings. "You've had me since the moment I met you in the desert, Noah. I don't want to be let go."

The uncharacteristic display of shock on Noah's face momentarily knocked Brianna off-kilter. When he realized she'd misread his reaction, he cupped her face with his hands and poured his love into his kiss.

"Are you saying you've waited for me? All this time?" he asked, his lips brushing against hers from the closeness.

The warmth of his hands on her face seeped through her skin, warming her to the core. Nodding slowly, she silently confirmed his question. Shock turned to relief as he captured her mouth with his again. Overcoming obstacles had become a way of life for him, but this was one hurdle he'd never expected to clear.

A pure, unconditional love that was meant for only him had previously been just out of reach. He'd never felt it from his own family. He had accepted that if his parents, who were supposed to love him without stipulations, couldn't manage it, then no one could. But in the most unlikely place on earth, he'd found the very thing that had evaded him his entire life.

The slow song had ended, but neither attempted to move from the crowded dance floor. As strangers dispersed all around them, oblivious to the monumental moment that just passed between them, Noah's focus was solely on Brianna. Whether it was too soon was up for debate, but he knew he wanted Brianna and no one else. His heart was linked to hers, their fates were intertwined, and the profound connection was mutual.

"Let's get a drink," he suggested. "Sit down and talk for a while."

"Okay," she agreed.

She placed her hand in his upturned palm as they walked back to their table. When he wrapped his hand around hers, she felt cherished and protected. She'd waited for him because she couldn't picture herself with anyone else. She wasn't naïve, she didn't have a schoolgirl crush, and she didn't try to convince herself that he'd waited for her.

She just knew herself and what she wanted. She also knew no one else could ever measure up when compared to Noah.

After she'd moved to Miami, her new friends had encouraged her to go out with other guys and not spend her time waiting for Noah. They argued that she didn't know what the future held. They contended it was pointless to remain loyal when he wasn't even aware of her sacrifice.

Remaining true to herself and her feelings, despite what others said, had never felt so good.

They took their seats, and Noah ordered another round before turning his attention back to Brianna. "It seems I only have one speed with you."

"I know exactly what you mean."

"It's a good thing we're on the same page because I know how to make you disappear until you give in to my demands," he jokingly threatened before taking a drink.

"You make that sound very enticing," Brianna teased as she watched his brown eyes darken to black from desire.

"Come home with me tonight, and I'll show you," he promised as he slowly lowered his beer bottle.

"But would you still respect me in the morning?" she asked, partly joking but also part serious.

Understanding dawned in Noah's eyes, and he leaned in to give her a comforting kiss. "Nothing would make me not respect you, Brianna. If you need time to get to know me again first, I'll gladly give you whatever time you need."

"I can't wait to learn everything there is to know about the new Noah Steele," she replied earnestly.

"Let's get out of here," Noah suggested.

"Thought you'd never ask," Brianna laughed.

Rebel watched them both stand, and his knowing smirk made Brianna giggle.

"Something to say, Rebel?" she asked.

"Nothing I haven't already said to my boy, Reaper." Rebel grinned.

"Yeah, yeah, shut up, man," Noah chuckled. "We're heading out. You kids get home before curfew tonight."

"Yes, Dad," Bull deadpanned before taking a swig from his longneck bottle.

"Don't do anything we wouldn't do," Rebel added.

"Should be an interesting night in that case," Noah shot back.

As they walked hand in hand toward the door, they could still hear Bull's and Rebel's laughter carrying over the crowd. "I'm glad the guys came with you tonight. I've missed my brothers," Brianna admitted. "But where's Shadow?"

"He took another assignment," Noah replied, intentionally leaving his answer vague.

"I'm glad you didn't take another one," Brianna replied. "I'm thrilled that you're here. When did you get back home?"

"A few months ago. I've spent that entire time getting my company up and running. Business has taken off faster than I could've hoped for, and I'm so thankful," Noah explained as they walked across the parking lot.

"What company?" she asked excitedly.

"Steele Security," he replied humbly.

"I've heard of your company. You really have been busy. My editor assigned me to a piece in the lifestyle section of the paper. I don't normally report on that type of story, but he asked me to help out in a jam. Anyway, that name kept coming up when the other reporters talked about a huge event coming up soon," Brianna replied. "That's so impressive, honestly. You're already the talk of the town."

Noah's half smile and a nonchalant shrug of one shoulder conveyed exactly what he thought about the notoriety. "We're lucky to have been selected for several excellent contracts, especially for a start-up company."

"It sounds like more than luck to me," Brianna bragged on Noah. "It sounds like the secret is out about how phenomenal you are at your job."

"We'll see," Noah replied. "Enough about me. Let's talk about you."

"Why do I have the feeling you already know all there is to know about me?"

"Fair enough." Noah nodded. "I know you work at the *Miami Herald*, you take the dangerous assignments the others will hardly touch, and you're great at it."

"And?"

"And…I knew you'd be here tonight. You're the only reason I came here." He inclined his head toward the pub. "There's one thing I don't know, though."

"What?" she asked. She was still trying to catch her breath from his admission.

"Did you drive here?" he smiled.

"No, I took a taxi, so I didn't have to worry about driving."

"Good. I'll give you a ride to your apartment," he offered. As he clicked the unlock button on his key fob, the lights on his full-size SUV flashed. He opened her door, helped her into the vehicle, and stole a kiss before he moved around to his side.

"Wait. You know where I live?" Brianna asked as Noah climbed into the driver's seat. "You said apartment."

"The shocked look on your face is so cute," he laughed. "Yes, I know where you live. I'm pretty good at my job, Brianna."

He took the long route to her apartment to keep her for as long as he could. Noah then walked her to the door of her apartment. He took the keys from her hand, unlocked the door, and stepped inside first. "Wait right here."

"Why?" she asked, clearly confused.

"I need to check the apartment before I leave. Just to make sure it's safe for you," he explained.

"Noah, I walk in here alone every day." Brianna shook her head.

"That was before."

"Before what?"

Turning to look her in the eye, he replied, "Before me."

He completed his thorough search of her apartment and returned to where she waited just inside the front door.

"Satisfied that no bad men are hiding in the closets? And that there are no pictures of other men in my bedroom?" Brianna asked pointedly.

"I am now." Noah grinned mischievously.

"Yeah, you're trouble all right," Brianna retorted. "But since I'm already attached to you, I guess I'll still keep you around."

"Damn straight, you will. There's no way you'll ever get rid of me."

He wrapped his arms around her waist and pulled her to him. As he kissed her, his tongue lightly grazed the part in her lips until she opened to give him full access. He moved his hands to her face and cupped her cheeks as he tilted her head to deepen the kiss. He pushed her backward with his body until the wall was at her back.

He slid his hands down her arms until he reached her hands. He grasped them in his, pulled them above her head, and held them in place with one of his hands. The other hand trailed down her shirt, reached the hem, and moved underneath the thin material. When his fingertips found the soft skin of her stomach, she moaned softly.

He pulled away from the kiss, but his fingertips continued to draw slow figure eights on her bare skin as he gazed deeply into her eyes. "You have no idea how hard it's been to stay away from you these last several months. I had to establish my business before I could approach you, to build something for our future. But you've been on my mind every damn day and night."

"Since we're confessing our secrets, I guess I should tell you that I jumped at this job, and the opportunity to move here, because of you. I hoped you'd find me through my articles and realize that I've been in Miami waiting for you," Brianna whispered. "Because you've been on my mind every day and night, too."

The inferno that burned in Noah's eyes revealed the struggle he faced to restrain himself. He placed a soft, chaste kiss on her lips, ran his thumb across them, and let his eyes follow the trail. "If I don't leave now, I won't ever leave. Goodnight, my princess."

The bass timbre of his voice washed his whispers straight through her. She inhaled sharply, her eyes widened, her mouth parted, and the rise and fall of her chest quickened. The ache deep inside her, which spoke of her need for him, increased exponentially as she watched him back away from her toward the door. When his hand grasped the doorknob, she opened her mouth to speak, but he slowly shook his head.

"Tomorrow. Sleep well, princess." With that, Noah slipped out the door, making sure to lock it as he left.

She stood motionless and stared at the door for a full minute after he left. Brianna then finally found her voice. Exasperation and frustration filled her as the scene between them replayed in her mind.

"How the hell am I supposed to sleep now?"

CHAPTER EIGHT

Early the next morning, a knock on Brianna's door woke her. She padded to the door in her bare feet, pajama shorts, and a tank top, and peered through the peephole.

"I know you're looking at me, princess. Open the door," Noah called from the other side.

She quickly glanced in the mirror and ran her fingers through her bed hair in a hurried attempt to tame it. "Just a minute," she called.

Laughing, Noah replied, "I know what you look like when you wake up, Brianna. Let me in."

She slowly opened the door and stepped back to give him room to enter. "What are you doing here so early? The sun isn't even up yet."

"I missed you." He shrugged. "Come on." He took her hand as he led her to the bedroom. He shed his clothes down to his boxer briefs before he climbed into her bed. He lay on his side and patted the mattress beside him. "Your spot is getting cold."

She shook her head but smiled before she crawled back into the bed and took her place beside Noah. His arm draped over her from behind, and he pulled her to him, her back to his front. When they were comfortably positioned and fully relaxed, Brianna murmured to him, "I've missed this so much. I've missed you so much."

"So have I, princess. I've been awake all night thinking about how I used to sneak into your tent and crawl into your bed at night. I couldn't get this bed out of my mind, how you were all alone in it. I fought the urge to show up here for as long as I could," he whispered to her.

"Is there really any reason we should fight it anymore, Noah?" Brianna asked tentatively.

"You mean, do I think we're moving too fast?"

"Yes, that's exactly what I mean."

"For some people, it would be way too fast. But it's not for you and me. We obviously both know what we want. Fortunately, that just happens to be each other.

"If there's one thing I've learned in my line of work, it's that we don't have a promise to tomorrow. I don't want to regret not being with you every day. Just because someone, whose opinion doesn't even matter, thinks we should take things slower," Noah stated adamantly.

She turned over to face him and lovingly stroked his cheek. She reveled in the feel of his morning stubble on her skin. "I don't want to take it slowly either, Noah. If anything were to happen to one of us, I'd want you to know exactly how I feel. I'd want you to know why I waited for you to find me, to come home to me."

"Why?" Noah asked. "Tell me why, Brianna."

"Because I love you. I fell in love with you in that desert almost a year ago, and I'm still in love with you today. I'll never stop loving you," she promised.

"I am so completely in love with you, princess."

He rolled her onto her back and positioned his body above hers, with his weight resting on his forearms. As he dipped his face to hers, he covered her mouth with his and instantly brought her entire body to life at once. As he lowered his hips to meet hers, he surged upward and glided across her clit. He groaned when her fingernails dug into his flesh.

Brianna quickly pulled his shirt over his head and ran her hands over his chest and stomach. She lifted her back up off the bed as she placed open-mouth kisses on his bare skin and then trailed her tongue across his chest.

"Are you sure about this?" Noah asked, suddenly serious. "I won't be able to stop if you keep doing that."

"I'm positive, Noah. I have no doubts at all."

He stared intently into her eyes as he looked for any signs of fear or hesitation. Her eyes only spoke to him about the love she felt. It swirled in her cobalt-blue pools, lured him in, and held him as a willing prisoner.

"I want nothing more right now than to give you the things I couldn't give you in that tent. It's about to get loud in here. Hope your neighbors don't mind," he boasted.

He slid his hand down and quickly pulled her tank top over her head. As he slid his body down hers, he captured the hardened peak of her breast in his mouth. While he licked, sucked, and lightly bit it, he lavished attention on the other one with his fingers. He rolled one nipple between his thumb and middle finger then he squeezed it while he bit the other. She writhed beneath him, her fingers ran through his hair, and her moans of pleasure filled the room.

He slid farther down her body, and his mouth continued to work its magic against her skin. When he reached her boy-shorts pajamas, he hooked his fingers into the fabric at her hips and slid them off of her. He took his place between her thighs, his warm tongue circled, his lips sucked, and his teeth grazed her repeatedly until she utterly came apart.

Her screams of ecstasy and heavy breathing were only masked by her demand. "Oh my God, Noah. That was incredible. I can't wait any longer—I need to feel you now."

"Your wish is my command, princess." He smirked and shed his clothes. Within seconds, he was completely naked, sheathed, and restraining himself from pushing deep into her. "I had to let you leave before, even though I didn't want to. As of now, you are mine, and I won't let you go again," he asserted.

"You'll never have to let me go, Noah," she promised.

He leaned his head down to capture her lips again. As his tongue swirled around hers, he surged forward and drove into her as her nails once again found his bare skin. He caught her moans in his mouth as he pushed forward, arched his back, and surged into her over and over. He felt her inner muscles grip him like erotic velvet fingers. He knew she was close to tumbling over the edge.

He intentionally changed his pace, slowing and breaking their kiss. "You owe me some screams," he murmured in her ear. "I'm collecting them right now."

He hooked his arms behind her knees as he continued his initial barrage on her senses. The intense buildup of pleasure started low in her belly. Her inner muscles gripped and stroked him with each movement until the dam erupted and she screamed out his name.

"Oh my God, Noah!"

"Mmm, I love that sound. That's one."

"You're counting?"

"I'm definitely counting." He smirked before he began moving again. "The second one is coming up very soon."

An hour later, Brianna lay sprawled across the bed, breathing heavily and trying to slow her heart again after the intense physical exertion.

"The number was four, in case you lost count," he boasted.

Brianna's head rested on his chest, her arm draped across his stomach, and her leg wrapped around his. She giggled at his announcement before replying. "Yeah, I was there. I remember. Four is a great number."

"It's okay. I must be more tired than I thought," Noah teased.

"Well, I suppose you need to rest up, then," she challenged. "If that wasn't your best, I'm afraid you have more proving to do."

"You know, one of these days, that smart mouth of yours will get you into trouble," Noah laughed as he pulled her closer to him. "Good thing I'll be there to protect you."

Brianna traced the lines, bumps, and ridges of his abdominal muscles with her fingertips. His body was pure perfection after hours of intense exercise. "I know you're the best at what you do, Noah. But I've always taken pride in my independence and my ability to take care of myself. I don't really need you to protect me."

"Humor me," he replied as his fingers lovingly stroked the smooth skin on her back.

"This is going to be one of those sore spots in our relationship, isn't it?"

"Sounds like it," he replied. "You think you can handle every situation, and I want to handle every situation."

"Compromise?" she asked.

"What are you proposing?"

"If I feel like I'm getting in over my head, I'll ask you for protection," she offered.

"And if I think you're getting in over your head before you realize it?" he asked.

"Tell me. Talk to me about it. But don't try to take away my right to make decisions for myself. It's important to me," she explained.

"It's important to me for you to be safe," he explained patiently. "I understand there will usually be an element of danger in the stories you get, but you have to be smart about it. Don't walk into a situation blind. Don't think you can talk your way out of every situation. The bad guys don't work like that, baby."

"How about I keep you on speed dial, then?" she kidded.

"I'd better be on speed dial regardless. But if you're going into something dangerous, I'll be beside you," he clarified.

"Agree to disagree." She shrugged.

"Disagree all you want. As long as I'm beside you."

She shook her head as she muttered under her breath, "Stubborn man."

Noah's answering whisper made her laugh. "Stubborn woman."

Over the next several months, Noah and Brianna barely left each other's side. She joined him at Steele Security as frequently as her position allowed. She learned the business from the inside out and helped to set up the office routines efficiently. Gaining insider knowledge of how security teams were set up, how they communicated, and where their vulnerable spots were located gave her a new perspective for her own protection.

When Brianna ventured into the seedier parts of the city on a tip for a new story lead, Noah acted as her personal sentinel. He stood guard and dared anyone to make the wrong move. Pride swelled in Noah's chest every time he watched her in action.

She was a natural at making people comfortable with talking to her, giving her their innermost secrets, and willingly giving up information that could get them killed. She drew them in with her kindness, comforted them with the assurance they were doing the right thing, and encouraged them with her belief in them.

He stayed just far enough away to allow her space to talk to her subject, but close enough to intervene if necessary. She still maintained the innocence of someone who hadn't experienced the dregs of humanity—the false belief that it would always happen to someone else. Noah's line of work had proved the opposite to him. Anyone would screw others over with the right motivation.

"So, now that I know enough about Steele Security that I could be one of your agents, does that mean I can go on my assignments without you?" Brianna asked one evening.

"Nope," Noah replied casually.

"Wow. Thanks for the talk, Noah."

He leaned forward in his chair, placed his elbows on his knees, and locked his eyes on hers. With her rapt attention on him, he rephrased his original answer. "No, Brianna, that does not mean you can go without me. You know what we do, but you haven't been trained as we have. You're still way too trusting of others—people who aren't known for being model citizens."

"You don't think I could take you?"

Noah laughed heartily. "No, you can't take me. You're nowhere close to being able to take me down."

"Let's try it," she suggested.

"By all means," he said as he stood. "I'll even stand still and let you do your worst. Or best."

"Really? I can try?"

"Yes. Come at me."

Brianna stood and let her eyes roam around the large living room. She allowed time for her gaze to settle on specific areas of the room but didn't look directly at Noah. She tried to remain aloof and casual as she planned her attack. Suddenly, she burst forward, wrapped her arms around his waist, and attempted to tackle him to the ground.

Leaned forward, with her weight pushing down through her thighs, calves, and feet, she pushed with all her might. The wall of muscle wouldn't budge an inch. That is until he bent slightly at the waist, wrapped his arms around her waist, and effortlessly lifted her off the ground—and held her upside down.

He walked around the room with her in his arms, and she continued to flail, curse, and attempt to kick her way out of the predicament. To no avail. He carefully placed her on the couch before he covered her body with his, pinned her down, and prevented her from making the slightest movement.

With his face hovered just above hers, he chided her calmly. "This is why you need me with you. If any other man did this to you, I'd have to kill him, dump the body in a vat of acid, and throw it overboard into the ocean."

"You only won this round because I wasn't expecting to be picked up."

"Exactly my point. You have to be prepared for anything out there. I'm not trying to control you, Brianna. All I want is to keep you safe and sound."

"I understand."

Noah narrowed his eyes at her, knowing that she didn't actually agree with him. A knock at his door momentarily drew his attention away from the conversation. As he rose from the couch, he cut his eyes back to her. "Don't think this conversation is over yet."

"Wouldn't dream of it." She smiled sweetly.

He shook his head, ran his hand through his hair, and muttered something under his breath as he walked away.

"What was that? I couldn't hear you."

"You weren't meant to," he replied dryly.

He couldn't help but smile when he heard her laugh in response. Their relationship progressed so smoothly, so naturally that he didn't question whether they were meant for each other. It had become a given. They alternated staying at each other's places, and that hadn't been a burden at all, especially when he infinitely appreciated the company.

Before he reached the door, he checked the security camera to see who their uninvited visitor was. When he saw his old friend at the door, his strides lengthened, and he quickly swung the door open.

"Richard! So good to see you, brother," he said, giving his friend a brief, manly hug.

"You, too, man. Sorry to just drop in on you like this," Richard replied.

"You're always welcome here. Come on in," Noah said as he stepped aside to give him room to enter.

"Man, this is a nice house," Richard said, astonishment lacing his voice. "Steele Security must be doing very well."

"We are doing very well, actually. Growing more every day," Noah beamed.

"That's great. I'm proud of you. I actually have some great news for you," Richard began. "I've moved into a better position and can help influence decisions on escorts to foreign countries. I'd like to hire Steele Security. We'll have to sign a new contract for each escort, but it pays well."

"That's awesome news, Richard. Congratulations on your promotion, and thanks for your confidence in us. You know we won't let you down."

"I have no doubt about that, Reaper," Richard replied.

Brianna heard voices in the foyer, stepped out of the den, and moved toward the conversation. When she reached the doorway to the entrance, Richard turned and eyed her for a moment.

"Brianna. I didn't expect to find you here," he said, somewhat stunned.

"Hello, Judge," Brianna replied. The discomfort she'd felt around him in the desert returned to her full force, though she still couldn't identify what drove it. "How've you been?"

"I've been great, Brianna. Never better," Richard sneered. "You?"

"Same," she replied. "Never better."

"I don't think you two have ever officially been introduced—not with full names anyway," Noah said, looking between them both. "Brianna Tate, Richard Hollingsworth."

"Richard, it's nice to meet you finally," Brianna laughed.

"Likewise, Brianna," Richard replied. Turning to Noah, he continued. "Do you have time to finish the conversation about investing in your company?"

"Sure, come on into my office, Richard." Noah gestured with his arm. To Brianna, he added, "Babe, it won't take too long."

"Don't worry about me," she replied as she lifted up on her tiptoes to kiss him. "I have plenty of work to do to keep me busy."

The two men walked into the office and closed the door behind them. Taking a seat, Richard gave Noah his sly smile. "So, things are pretty hot and heavy between you and Brianna, huh? Are you already living together?"

Noah knew there would be scoffers and naysayers, so he had prepared his answers to the intrusive questions ahead of time. "We spend a lot of time together, but we each still have our own place."

"Isn't it a bit too soon for all this lovey-dovey shit? Most men I know wouldn't so willingly tie themselves down to one woman."

"We obviously don't know the same men, then," Noah replied, intentionally keeping his tone in check. "We've been together for just a few months shy of a year. But we've been alternating staying at each other's places for the majority of that time. A real man wouldn't be afraid to admit when he's in love, or care about what others think."

"Touché. I've never been in love myself, so I wouldn't know. Anyway, if you're happy, that's all that matters," Richard conceded, attempting to appease Noah. "Now, let's talk about why I came here. I'd like to invest in your company, only acting as a silent partner."

"I have a few questions about that." Noah steepled his hands. "First, why would you want to do that when you're in DC?"

"I bought a house here, and I travel back and forth on the weekends. I work in DC, but Miami is my home," Richard explained calmly.

"Second question. Wouldn't that be a conflict of interest since you have influence over the contracts?"

"Technically, I don't influence the contracts. The head of the department that executes the contracts is a good friend of mine, and he trusts my judgment," Richard shrugged. "It's best for everyone when we have escorts we can trust. Plus, you already have the highest level of security clearance there is, so that's one less hassle."

"Third question. What do you mean by 'silent partner,' exactly?" Noah asked.

"Only that I put up part of the operating money and you guarantee my contracts always come first. I'll give you plenty of notice, but I can't wait if the reigning queen of Hollywood comes to Miami and wants to hire you."

"You realize I don't need your money to operate my company, right?"

"I do. It's more like insurance that someone will always be available to cover our people. My name doesn't even have to be on any of your legal documents," Richard offered.

"I'll hold your money in escrow in the event I have to hire extra help unexpectedly. But I don't foresee a problem with being able to accommodate DOD's needs," Noah agreed.

Richard stood, extended his hand to Noah, and as they shook hands to seal the deal, he smiled widely. "Glad to be in business with you, Steele Security. This will definitely be a very lucrative business."

"Thank you for choosing Steele Security for your safety needs." Noah finished with a smile and a firm, final handshake.

CHAPTER NINE

"What was that about?" Brianna asked as Richard left without saying goodbye.

"He wants to be a silent partner in my business," Noah replied, absently rubbing his chin.

"Silent? Why?" Brianna asked.

"He said so he'll get first dibs on the escort contracts. He recommended us to his buddy in the DOD, so he wants to make sure we always have coverage for them."

"I really don't understand the loyalty you have toward Richard," Brianna blurted out.

Noah's head jerked sideways to look at her. His brows furrowed into a V, his eyes narrowed, and his mouth hung open. "He's been a friend since high school and has had my back since I first met him. Why would you say that?"

"He just gives me a really uncomfortable feeling, and you know I don't get that vibe often. I don't trust him."

"Well, I do, and I think I know him a lot better than you do."

Brianna nodded as she agreed only with his latter statement, but she wanted to drop the subject before they had their first fight over nothing more than her intuition. Her gut screamed that there was more to the story with Richard than he let on. Noah was loyal to a fault, and she feared that unyielding loyalty would end up harming him one day. If it didn't come from Richard, then it would happen with someone else whom he trusted without question. The code Reaper lived by didn't always apply in the world Noah now lived in.

"So, are you still hiring more men?" Brianna asked as she abruptly changed the subject.

"Yes, I'm building up my empire," Noah joked. "There are more requests for proposals in my inbox, and several more arrive each day. It's amazing how many people need security consultants for their homes and businesses, and how many traveling celebrities need extra security to go out in public."

"I think I may need extra security this Saturday night," Brianna admitted. "Can you spare anyone for me?"

"Where are you going Saturday night?" Noah asked as concern overtook his features. For Brianna to willingly ask for an escort, there had to be real danger involved.

"There was a tip called into the police, but they don't have the manpower to investigate. He called the paper and asked for someone there to investigate it instead. It sounds like it could be a significant story if it pans out. I have to go into northwest Miami to meet with my source," Brianna explained.

"Northwest Miami? At night?" Noah stared at her like she'd lost her mind.

"Hopefully I'll have back up."

"Today is Monday. Your meeting is being planned several days in advance. That gives anyone who wants to do you harm plenty of time to plan an attack. Why does this meeting have to wait so long to take place?"

"Because that's when my informant is off work and can talk to me," she explained.

"You're definitely not going alone. I'll call Bull and see if he's available to come with us."

"Oh, good, security in stereo," she joked. "I'll not only have the two of you in my ears, but you'll make outrageous demands and scare my source into permanent hiding."

"Bri?"

"Yeah?"

"You should run now."

She squealed with amusement as she ran through the house, toward the sweeping staircase. Just as she reached the bottom step, she suddenly flew through the air and landed on a very thick, muscular shoulder. Noah's arm wrapped around her and held her securely in place as he took the stairs two at a time. When he reached the landing at the top, he swatted her ass playfully. "Be still. You're squirming."

"Because you're carrying me over your shoulder!" she exclaimed with laughter.

"We're almost to the bedroom. It's time for you to put that sassy mouth to better use than talking," Noah replied suggestively.

"My personal Neanderthal man. What more could a girl ask for?" Brianna mocked.

"Yeah, you're way overdue for an attitude adjustment." Noah jokingly threatened her as he deposited her onto the bed.

"Well, come adjust my attitude for me, big guy," she cooed seductively.

"If you insist," Noah replied as one side of his mouth rose in his sexy, cocky grin. "I'm more than happy to oblige."

Noah and Brianna filled the rest of the week with the usual routine—completing RFPs for new contracts, researching information for her upcoming blockbuster story, alternating spending the night at his enormous house and her small apartment, and making love until exhaustion overtook them.

Saturday night, Bull arrived early for the rendezvous in one of the more dangerous neighborhoods of the northwest Miami area. Brianna used her most persuasive techniques on Noah to get him to relax about the meeting. While he loved her attempts, he refused to budge an inch when it came to ensuring her safety.

"Hey, Sunny," Bull said as he walked in. "Are you ready for your meeting tonight?"

"Hey, Bull," she replied, hugging his neck. "I am more than ready. Noah shouldn't have asked you to come along, though. He's overreacting."

"Have you ever been to that neighborhood before?" Bull asked.

"No, but it can't be any worse than the others I've been in."

"Yes, it can. You'll see, and you'll probably wish we had an army with us," Bull chuckled. "Just stick close to Reaper. He won't let anything happen to you."

"Where will you be?"

"I'll be around. Close enough to help but not where anyone will see me," Bull replied.

"This just seems like overkill to me."

"It may be, but I'm not taking any chances with my only little sister." Bull smiled.

"You know that I can't resist when you say that, Bull," she playfully admonished him. He shrugged and laughed in reply, telling her that he knew exactly what he was doing.

Bull gave her a quick kiss on the cheek and continued walking until he found Noah in his office. "Hey, Reap. You ready for tonight?"

"Yeah, I've had a couple of guys checking out things in that apartment building today. We're not walking in there blind," he replied.

"Let's see what you got."

Noah handed Bull several pictures of the area, building, and apartment layouts. He also had a full background check on the informant with the help of an old friend.

"So, we're meeting a Mr. Ammar Wasem tonight. Originally from a small village in Syria, close to the Iraqi border. Moved to the US eight years ago. Married, two young kids, and has maintained steady employment. No arrest, no blips on the radar for anything, not even speeding. Either he's legit, or he has the perfect cover for a sleeper cell member," Bull solemnly concluded.

"Either we're walking into a trap, or he really does have information about a big story for Brianna. At this point, I'm not sure which would be worse," Noah replied, clearly agitated.

Noah stepped into the doorway and called down the hall. "Brianna, can you come here for a minute, babe?"

A couple of minutes later, Brianna entered Noah's office and took a seat across the desk from him. "You rang?" She twirled her hair around her finger and gave him a playful smile.

"I did." He grinned in reply. "Tell me about this tip your source called into the police and then to your paper."

"He said there are American gunrunners in his former village, setting up a black market to sell guns to the rebels in the area. If they're successful, he said the rebels would slaughter anyone who defies them. His brother still lives there," she explained.

"Did he say who they think is behind this?" Bull asked.

"Not exactly. He alluded to the US military, but then he also said businessmen were involved. He wouldn't talk on the phone for very long since it isn't secure. He sounded terrified."

"What floor is he on?" Noah asked Bull.

"Third floor. I've already staked out my lookout spot. You'll both be well covered," Bull replied.

"You went to his apartment?" Brianna asked. "What if he saw you and got scared off?"

"I'm only seen when I want someone to see me, Sunny," Bull replied. "Since I didn't want to be seen, no one saw me."

"You know, Bull," Brianna spoke, trying to hide the smile in her voice. "I'm having a hard time deciding if I liked you better when you didn't talk to me, or now when you talk too much."

"Brianna," Bull replied, failing to hide his humor. "You'll pay for that when Reaper isn't around to protect you from me."

"If I didn't know you both better, I'd swear you were brother and sister from how you pick at each other." Noah shook his head in mock reprimand.

"She usually starts it," Bull said defensively.

"Spoken like a true big brother," Brianna retorted.

Later that evening, Noah, Brianna, and Bull left for Brianna's meeting. While the nervous energy caused Brianna's leg to jump, Noah remained calm and relaxed as his eyes assessed every aspect of their surroundings. Bull was in a separate vehicle, but he stayed back to help watch for any tails on Noah and Brianna. Even though Noah was highly skilled at identifying a tail, he'd never take chances on safety where Brianna was concerned.

Once they reached the neighborhood in northwest Miami, Brianna instinctively slid her hand over to grasp Noah's. His squeeze helped to calm her fraying nerves but didn't wholly alleviate them.

"I'm so glad you and Bull are with me tonight, Noah."

Without blatantly gawking at the surroundings, she panned the area with her eyes to take in the neighborhood. The dilapidated buildings were covered in graffiti, some with gang tags, some simply with insults hurled at anyone reading them. The bars on the windows and doors told her everything she needed to know about the crime rate of the area. The groups of people huddled at different spots along the streets slowly turned their heads and watched the sleek black SUV roll by them with blatant suspicion.

"So you don't want to go in alone?" he asked teasingly as he parked the car.

"No, I actually don't want to go in at all right now," she replied. "But if this story is real, I have to cover it, so I need to get over my irrational fears."

"Fear isn't always irrational, Bri. You have to control it—don't let it control you. But it's healthy to have fear because it keeps you on your toes, alerts you when something's not right, and can help save your life."

"Control it. Got it." She took a deep breath and looked at Noah. "Ready to go in?"

Noah checked the area around the car again and nodded. "Let's go."

Once she was out of the car, Brianna rushed to Noah's side, heeding Bull's advice to stick close. Noah wrapped his arm around her protectively and pulled her slightly in front of him. His right hand slid to the gun holster hidden at his side and quickly unsnapped it.

"Let's take the stairs," Noah said as he pushed the door open.

He quickly checked the stairwell and found it empty. They hurriedly took the stairs to the third floor. Noah covered each entry point as they passed and they worked their way to apartment 3F. Brianna stood in front of the door, took another calming breath, and knocked.

The clinking and clanking of internal locks and chains being turned and removed filled the air. The door opened a couple of inches as an eyeball filled the dark space. Noah had his back against the wall, his hand on his gun, and was ready to pounce at the first sign of trouble.

"Who are you?" the thickly accented voice of a female asked.

"I'm Brianna Tate. I'm here to talk to Ammar Wasem. He called me at the *Miami Herald*."

"Shatha, let her in," a male voice commanded from inside the apartment.

The young lady stepped back and opened the door wider to allow them to enter. When Noah stepped around to follow Brianna, Shatha's eyes grew wide as her bottom jaw dropped open. She started to protest when Brianna spoke.

"This is my bodyguard. He goes where I go. He won't interfere."

"He can wait in the kitchen," Ammar replied. "We will talk in the living room."

Shatha showed Noah to the kitchen and offered him food and drinks. He politely declined as he took a seat with a perfect line of sight to Brianna. He couldn't hear the hushed conversation from where he sat, but anyone after Brianna would have to get past him first.

When Brianna took her seat across from Ammar, she pulled her notebook and pen out of her bag to prepare for her interview. The voice-activated recorder rested on the coffee table and waited for the cue that it was time to begin.

"To recap our previous conversation, you said your brother still lives in your home village of Balikh. You believe that someone in the US military, possibly with business connections, is selling weapons to hostile rebels in the area. Is that correct?" she asked.

"That is correct. The man behind it is an American, and he is working with some evil men in Balikh. They are setting up an elaborate front to hide their sins," Ammar replied. "The blood on their hands will be great if they're not stopped in time."

"Do you have any proof of this accusation? Any names of those involved?"

"I only have the word of my brother. That is proof enough for me. He read your article on the soldiers you joined in the desert, Miss Tate. He was very impressed with how you covered it. That's why I called your paper.

"We hoped you would take this story, find out who this American is that's behind it, and stop him. It would be easier, and faster, to stop this one man than to stop many in my country. Many who are abandoning their true faith and resorting to becoming terrorists."

"I can tell you're very passionate about this subject," Brianna acknowledged. "The rebels' actions seem to be speaking for an entire ethnic group of people, don't they?"

"Yes, that's part of their plan. If a group this large is divided and fighting against each other, it makes it harder for anyone on the outside to distinguish the good guys from the bad guys. By the time you figure it out, it's too late, and the damage has already been done," he explained sadly.

"How does your brother have this information?"

"It's part of his job. He knows the inherent danger in coming forward and giving out this information. But saying nothing could result in the death of tens of thousands of people. Neither of us can live with that on our conscience."

"What is the information he has?"

"He works in customs for our country. He received a request for fast-track approval of an incoming shipment. When he looked into it further, he discovered more and more information.

"The individual pieces of the puzzle look benign, but you'll see the full picture of the cancer that's taking over Syria when you put all their pieces together. I will tell you what I can tonight, but my brother is the one who wants to speak with you," Ammar finished.

The more Ammar told Brianna about his homeland, the American, and the black-market arms dealers, the more spectacular the story sounded. Even the most unbelievable parts of the story became plausible as she felt his anguish through his words.

At the end of the interview, she thanked him for his time and hospitality. "Ammar, what you and your brother are doing is very brave. Even though you're worried about the safety of your brother and your own family, I guarantee your names won't be used or given out by me."

"Miss Tate, if you can help stop this travesty, all the worry and danger will be worth it. There's so much at stake, it's hard to pick just one or two things to focus on," Ammar replied sadly.

"I'll be back in touch soon. Please give your brother my number," she said, handing him her card. "I'm very interested in talking to him and helping to stop this from happening."

As soon as Noah and Brianna were seated back in the vehicle, Noah's phone began ringing. He transferred the call to the Bluetooth connection, and Bull's voice came across the speakers.

"Drop this story now, Brianna. Please," he pleaded.

The sincerity and concern in his voice shook Brianna. "What? Why would you say that?"

"I heard the whole conversation. If it's true, it's too dangerous for you to get mixed up in it. This operation should be a joint task force between the CIA, NSA, and the FBI—at least. You are not trained for this, Bri. You'll end up getting killed. Please don't," Bull implored her.

"Bull, you're overreacting. I'm just investigating this and getting the facts. I'm not going to apprehend them myself. I'll dig and find out who's behind it, then turn the evidence over to the authorities. I'll have the complete story out of it, then," Brianna consoled.

"Reaper, call me when you can," Bull stated flatly before disconnecting.

Brianna felt her heart drop to her feet at Bull's abrupt disconnection. She'd seen him go from burning hot to freezing cold in zero-point-two seconds with others before, but never with her. Their sibling bond had emerged in the desert and had become much stronger in the time she'd reconnected with Noah. To be shut out so heartlessly stung her to the core.

"What did he say, Brianna?" Noah cut his eyes at her.

Brianna knew deep down that it wasn't in Bull's nature to overreact to anything. She swallowed the pain rising from her chest and recounted the entire conversation for Noah. He drove wordlessly and listened intently to every word all the way back to his house.

As he pulled into his garage, Noah turned off the ignition but didn't move to exit the car. His eyes swung up to meet Brianna's. His approach with Brianna was softer than Bull's but packed no less punch.

"I can't lose you, Brianna. What we have, I've never had with anyone before. Without you, I'm only a shell of a man—completely hollow inside. Not really living, not really dying. The love I have for you could never be given to anyone else."

"You'll never lose me, Noah." She crawled over the center console to sit in his lap. She stroked his face as she spoke. "I waited for you, and I would've kept waiting if you hadn't come home when you did.

"After meeting you, spending time with you, and falling so deeply in love with you, I knew there'd never be another man in my life. We both knew that our jobs would have some danger factor to them when we started this. Don't ask me to change."

"Don't make me live through losing you," he said grimly.

Before she could answer, he wrapped his arms around her and crushed her to him. "I love you in ways I've never loved anyone. I depend on you in ways I've never depended on another. You're as much as part of me as I am, Bri."

He lifted her in his arms, slid out of the vehicle, and carried Brianna the entire way to their bedroom. He poured all the words he couldn't verbalize into their lovemaking as he spoke to her wordlessly.

You own my heart.

All of my love is yours.

Stay with me forever.

CHAPTER TEN

The courier dropped off a large envelope at Noah's house that had originally been delivered to the *Miami Herald* office. Brianna held it in her hands, felt the weight of the documents inside as they magnified and multiplied in her heart. Her source from the remote desert village found a way to get the copied documents to her so she could begin researching before meeting him in person.

She placed the unopened envelope on her desk and stared at it as if she could bore a hole in it from her gaze alone. She remembered their conversation from several weeks before, and she still felt the urgency and fear in the man's voice.

"Miss Tate," he began tentatively, his accent thick and difficult to understand over the phone. "You are a reporter, yes?"

"Yes, I'm the journalist, Brianna Tate. Who is this?" she asked, her journalistic senses tingling with a premonition that this could be exactly what she needed for a breakthrough story.

"You spoke with my brother a few weeks ago. I found your name on a story you wrote about the American military presence in the Middle East. I've stumbled upon proof that rebels are planning to buy American guns. These rebels will raid my village and kill my people. I'm asking for your help to stop this travesty."

"How did you stumble upon this proof? Who do you believe is supplying the rebels with guns? Where are you from? I'm going to need more information to go on than this," she pushed. She knew she had to verify that what this man said matched the information Ammar had given her.

"I have several documents that I found and copied. They're the shipping manifests, and I can get the separate corresponding receipt log that matches, shipment for ship-

ment. A military transport plane has been scheduled to deliver them. Someone high up must be involved, approving the shipments.

"You'll have to come here to get the receipt log in person, though. I can't risk copying and mailing it, in case the mail is intercepted," he whispered. "I would be found out instantly as I'm the only one who catalogues the shipments."

Brianna convinced him to share all of his pertinent personal information with her. Before she hung up, she had his name, exact location, and a time and place to meet. He promised to mail the copied shipping manifest documents to her. If she agreed that there was a story worth pursuing after reviewing the documents, she would then travel halfway around the world to meet with him in person.

She ripped open the cardboard envelope and quickly removed the paperwork inside to begin scouring the information. She immediately recognized the logo at the top of every manifest, and she suddenly wrapped her arms around her midsection, doubled over, and fought the intense nausea that washed over her. Her hands shook, her heart raced, and her thoughts whipped through her mind in a blur. Two words stood out like neon signs in the pitch-black night.

Steele Security.

"No, I refuse to believe Noah plays any part in this. He wouldn't do this." Brianna talked to herself as she paced back and forth.

Over the following several weeks, she spent every waking hour researching the dates and information shown on the invoices. As she pored over the documents, she found several suspicious transactions and traced offshore bank account numbers. Each new revelation brought her back to the same conclusion.

There was definitely a ringleader arranging the illegal weapon shipments. But the identity of that one person wasn't obvious. The documentation to support the armed escorts by Steele Security was all in place, all official, and all pointed to Noah Steele as the man behind the front.

The strain of all the evidence she'd found weighed heavily on Brianna's heart and mind. On the one hand, if she believed what she'd found was true, then she had to believe the worst about the man she loved more than anything in the world. She would have to face the fact that she really didn't know the man she practically lived with, gave her love to, and shared her bed with, at all. She'd have to admit to herself that she'd made an egregious mistake in trusting him with her life.

On the other hand, if she chose to ignore it, and the data were actually true, she'd be just as guilty as he was. If she let blind faith take over instead of the cold, hard facts she'd grown accustomed to, she would go against everything she ever believed in. When this story broke wide open, and it definitely would, her own reputation would be scrutinized every bit as harshly as Noah's would.

Either way, she couldn't find a solution to this situation that didn't result in losing something she didn't think she could live without. From her viewpoint, she would lose Noah, her career, or both at the same time. Her career choice provided her with access to people and documents that she wouldn't have been able to reach otherwise. She realized that what she was actually searching for was the proof that Noah was innocent.

Over those same weeks of research, she approached Noah with various questions about his line of work. After having spent so much time around a nosy, inquisitive reporter, Noah stopped questioning why she sometimes needed very specific information.

"Noah." Brianna approached him. "I have a few questions about your government contracts for security transports."

"Shoot," he replied, leaning back from his desk and giving her his full attention.

"Do you provide armed escorts for materials or weapons shipments?"

"No, we only provide armed escorts for people. Mainly officials who are traveling to highly volatile areas," he replied.

"So, your guys wouldn't be on the plane unless a person needed protection?"

"That's right," Noah confirmed.

"Why wouldn't the military just send an armed squad with them?"

"They don't always have the extra manpower to spare. Troops are stationed everywhere, and each person has a specific job to do. They can't just drop that job because one of the suits decides he needs to be in the Middle East or Africa," Noah elaborated.

"Who has the authority to set up a transport contract?" Brianna asked, trying to keep her voice calm and her breathing even as she waited.

"Well, the senior director of the Department of Defense has to sign the contract with us," Noah explained. Brianna held her breath. "But Richard is my liaison with the DOD. He has the contracts drawn up, signed, and executed."

Brianna gasped, her eyes grew wide, and her mouth gaped open. Noah's eyes narrowed at her uncharacteristic response, his head tilted to the left, and his arms slowly crossed over his body.

Richard Hollingsworth.

The man who was also known as Judge.

Richard had been coming much more frequently over the past few months. Having a house in Miami was the perfect excuse for him to show up with a contract for Noah to sign rather than sending it over the secure email system DOD used. The missing pieces of the maddening puzzle began to become clearer to Brianna. She had no proof of it, but her gut instinct told her she was on the right path.

"I just realized I forgot about a meeting. I-I'd better go," Brianna stammered.

Noah's face became unreadable. She knew he was onto her lie. Not only was her response openly obvious, Noah had been trained in all manners of reading people's expressions, so he could see straight through her ruse. She'd worked hard to keep her features schooled when she'd planned surprises for him in the past. She wanted to kick herself now because she knew she'd failed miserably during a time when she desperately needed her emotions to remain neutral.

All of her digging, researching, and questioning others had revealed more lies, more disturbing revelations, and a story that was bigger than she could handle. She couldn't break this story and expect no repercussions. Bull's dire warning when she first took this story replayed in her mind, telling her she wasn't trained for this and she'd end up hurt.

What scared her most was what would happen to Noah and his business. She knew she had been acting differently toward him since her investigation trail implicated Noah. Intense levels of worry and stress over what she should do and what she should believe had changed her, made her doubt everything she thought she knew, and kept her awake at night.

A week later, she tried to approach the subject again by asking Noah different questions. This time, she focused more on Richard specifically, rather than the business aspect of it.

"How long have you known Richard?" she asked.

"Not sure exactly, since before high school. Why do you ask?" Noah eyed her suspiciously.

"What was he like in school?" she asked.

"A lot like he is now. Hard for most people to get along with. He had a few close friends but kept his circle small. His family had money, and he liked to flaunt it a little too much. He also had a reputation for using girls and dumping them," Noah said as he tilted his head and cut his eyes at Brianna.

"Why did he decide to join the military?"

He crossed his arms over his chest as it expanded with his extra deep breath. "For the same reason I did. *To piss his father off.* Why are you asking so many questions about Richard all of a sudden?"

"I never interviewed him when we were in the Middle East. Just tying up some loose ends," she lied.

"I don't think so, Brianna." Noah slowly shook his head. "That was too long ago, and your article about that has long since been out of circulation. Want to try again?"

Sighing, Brianna had to admit she didn't have a reason to ask questions about Noah's friend that she could give him. Their relationship became more strained from Brianna's suspicions about Noah's involvement, and from Noah's suspicions about Brianna and Richard. She had always tried to remain unbiased in her reporting, always giving both sides of the story and not slanting the facts to weigh heavier to one side. But with this story, she reluctantly conceded she was desperately searching for any proof that Noah was completely innocent.

"It's complicated, Noah," she dodged.

"Complicated?" His voice rose as his brows furrowed. "What *exactly* is complicated between you and Richard?"

"You know how some of your work is classified and you can't tell me about it? How all of the missions you were on are still classified and you won't trust me with any information about them? But I don't push you for it because I know you have good reasons for not telling me. I need that same respect from you right now," Brianna insisted.

He leaned back in his chair and continuously assessed her every reaction. Reaper narrowed his eyes in anger as he spoke. "*Classified information* and *hidden information* are two very different things."

"Sometimes they're one and the same. Aren't they?" she replied sadly.

"It would seem so."

Brianna left Noah's office more hurt and confused than when she'd entered it. She still had no concrete proof to clear Noah's name, but she knew in her heart that he'd never be part of an illegal scheme. Especially not one that involved smuggling guns to rebels in third world countries. What kept her from involving the authorities was that they wouldn't care what her heart told her. On paper, Noah looked guilty as hell.

Richard had knowingly involved his longtime friend in his illegal scheme, but he'd set everything up so only Noah would be blamed. Richard's name wasn't actually on any of the paperwork, Brianna was positive of that. He had made sure all the official names and seals were in place.

Since he wasn't a senior director, he wasn't authorized to arrange security details for anyone. She concluded that Richard must have forged the senior director's signature on the contracts he arranged with Steele Security, allowing the DOD to pay the bills for transporting his weapons. She deduced that the man who was being escorted must be in on the operation, too. She still had to find rock-solid proof that Noah wasn't involved in any of the illegal business occurring.

But how? she asked herself.

Over the following week, Brianna and Noah avoided each other as much as possible. The unintentional silent treatment ate away at the thin sheet of trust they were both treading on. Noah spent more time in his office, while Brianna spent her time tracking down every possible bit of information she could find. One contact directed her to another, until she reached the desk of someone in the DOD who could answer her questions about government contracts.

"George Dant," he answered.

"Hi, this is Brianna Tate with the *Miami Herald*," she introduced herself for the twelfth time that morning. "I'm trying to find some information about a private contractor the DOD uses to escort officials and dignitaries to hostile countries. Can you help me?"

"Sure, that's an easy one. We don't have any such contractor. Government officials traveling to hot zones are only escorted by US military convoys. No private contractors can be used due to security clearance requirements," he explained. "No one outside the military and a few governmental agencies are eligible for the level needed."

"I wasn't aware of that stipulation," Brianna stammered. "Are there any situations where a privately contracted security firm would be used on a military transport plane? Especially one that had the security clearance from prior military service?"

"I suppose it's possible, though I can't think of any off the top of my head. Usually when we contract, we don't provide their transportation too. The contract would be for the whole package."

"This is very helpful. Thank you so much, George," she replied glumly.

"Anytime."

Hanging up, she glanced at her clock and realized that time was quickly slipping away from her. The tension in the air still hung thick, and their once-happy home had become oppressive. With her flight to meet with her informant approaching later that night, she decided she had to clear the air with Noah.

She'd tell him everything and allow him to help her set the record straight. She realized that was the path she should've taken from the outset, and she considered how she'd approach the subject with him. This was more his expertise anyway. This story was much bigger than she'd anticipated, and too much was at stake to make a mistake now.

When she entered his office, she kept her voice calm and even but awkwardly shifted from foot to foot as she stood in the doorway.

"Noah, can we please talk about what's really going on?"

Her voice was quiet, and for the first time since he met Brianna, she seemed almost afraid to ask him a question. He watched carefully as her eyes moved around the room, not settling on any one thing for too long. The sadness in her eyes was obvious, and he didn't know how to respond.

He mused, *Yes, Brianna, what exactly is going on?*

He'd definitely sensed a change in their relationship over the past few weeks. He had never considered it to be calm by any stretch of the imagination. She was a headstrong investigative reporter who pursued every aspect of her life with the same determination she displayed for a really interesting lead. He was a former Delta Force operative who was every bit as headstrong and determined, if not more.

He knew when he met her that she was very ambitious. She wouldn't get the good stories by sitting on the sidelines, or being afraid to ask the tough questions. She had never backed down from a good debate, especially with him. But for the last several weeks, there had been a different air between them.

"Now is not a good time, Bri," he stated flatly. "I'm very busy."

He couldn't bring himself to look her in the eye, and he felt like a coward for it. So he continued diligently studying the paper in front of him instead.

He didn't actually see one damn thing that was on the page. All he knew was that if this conversation played out how he thought it would, his world would come crashing down around him.

Facing down enemies with a fully automatic machine gun aimed squarely at his head was nowhere near as daunting as facing what he believed to be the case here. She'd become withdrawn, secretive, and intentionally created distance between them. She'd quietly creep into their bedroom at night, long after he'd gone to bed. She had stopped waking him to make love after she had a late night of researching and writing. All the signs were there, pointing to the one conclusion he wasn't ready to accept. She was preparing to leave him but hadn't decided how to tell him yet.

The thought of losing her shut him down mentally. Living without her touch shut him down emotionally. At least with a tangible enemy, he could form an effective plan of attack and protect what was his. With this, he had no plan of attack. He had no recourse. All he had was a vision of life without the one person who'd given him hope of having a happy family life.

She cleared her throat nervously, and she couldn't hide the disappointment and sadness in her voice. "Okay, Noah. I didn't mean to bother you at work. We just really need to talk. But I understand you're too busy for me."

"Yeah, lots to do. We can talk later, okay?"

He still wouldn't look her in the eye. He mentally berated himself for how he refused to deal with the situation. She stood before him, asking for his time and attention, but he was too troubled to give her what she needed. His inner voice was sorely irritated with him. *"Pussy—man up, and look at her!"*

She lingered in front of his desk for a few seconds longer and inhaled, as if she were about to say something else, but instead, she turned and slowly walked away. He allowed himself to look up at that moment and watch her leave. He noticed how her toned, athletic body moved. She had the muscle-toned body of the true yoga fanatic and long-distance runner he knew she was. He noticed how her long, straight blond hair glittered under the lights, even under the unforgiving fluorescents.

But one thing was definitely different in her stance. She had always held her head high and her shoulders back, as if she were ready to take on anything and anyone. Now, as she left his office, he noticed she looked at the ground, and her shoulders almost slumped as if she had the weight of the world on them.

He jumped to his feet, and his chair flew backward as he rounded his desk. Reading her had always been second nature to him, so he hadn't understood why he wasn't able to read her over the past few weeks. Seeing her with fresh eyes brought it all into perspective for him. He'd been trying to interpret her actions through his own feelings, instead of identifying her feelings, her actions, and her intentions.

The abnormal sorrow and defeat displayed in her posture snapped him out of his funk. Taking the steps two at a time, he reached the top of the landing just as she unzipped the suitcase lying on their bed. She robotically moved from the dresser to the suitcase, absently folding and placing items inside. Every few seconds, she wiped at her eyes, and his heart squeezed in his chest each time.

"Are we going somewhere?" he asked as he watched her quickly dry her eyes before turning to face him.

"I have to go to Turkey and meet with my source. I reminded you last week."

"That's today?" he asked disappointedly.

"Yes, I'm leaving tonight." Her voice cracked, and she quickly turned away from him. "I'll be back in a week."

"I hope you find what you're looking for," he offered.

His hands ached to touch her. His fingers craved the touch of her skin. His lips hungered for the taste of hers. But he wanted her to be the one to initiate it, to fortify that he was still in her heart.

"So do I. You have no idea how much," she replied solemnly. "I'm going to take a nap before I have to leave for the airport. I have a feeling this will be a painful flight." She crawled into their king-size bed, pulled the covers up to her chin, and closed her eyes.

Forlorn, Noah simply nodded and left Brianna alone in their bed. As he entered his office, his cell phone lying on his desk was ringing.

"Steele," he answered.

"Our client and her entourage are arriving today instead of tomorrow." Rebel's tone relayed his annoyance. "We need to get to the airport to pick them up, but we need to do a security sweep of the hotel first."

One of the many new pop music sensations was performing at an outdoor concert in Miami Beach over the weekend. This particular singer was notorious for being the ultimate diva, showing up unscheduled, and expecting others to immediately accommodate her schedule without regard to theirs.

Noah muttered a curse under his breath. "Fuck. What perfect timing."

"Yeah, no shit, man. I had plans tonight," Rebel complained. "But what are you going to do, right?"

"Right. Give me ten, and I'll be on my way to pick you up."

He hung up with Rebel and jogged back up the stairs to Brianna. He found her sleeping soundly, so he leaned over her and kissed her softly on the cheek.

"I love you, Brianna. Always," he whispered.

He quickly changed into his work clothes in the walk-in closet, and he left before she stirred. His sixth sense of dread wouldn't leave him, though. Like a black cloud hovering just over his head, the sense of trouble brewing continued to grow in his mind.

Something very bad was about to happen. He would bet money on it.

CHAPTER ELEVEN

Her arrival in Turkey was no easier on her than her departure from Miami had been. Brianna missed Noah more with every second ticking away on the clock. The painfully long flight left her with way too much time to herself, time to think about everything that had happened, and time to realize what was most important in her life: Noah "Reaper" Steele.

He was the man of her dreams, the one she'd waited for when she couldn't even contact him, and the one to whom she wanted to spend her life giving all her love. She mentally berated herself for not treating that love as a precious gift over the past several weeks.

As she distractedly exited the plane, her plan was simple. Find proof that would exonerate Noah and get back home as soon as possible. She decided she didn't care what the evidence pointed to, how many flashing neon arrows pointed at Noah, or if she had to sacrifice her job to protect him.

After a few clicks on her cell phone, she held her breath as the ringing began. The urge hit her suddenly and urgently. She had to talk to Noah, she had to apologize for the distance she'd created, and she had to admit to being in over her head.

He should've been on this trip with her. One of the few fights they'd had was over her blatant disregard for her safety, in Noah's words. Since she was young and wanted to keep her independence, she'd initially mistaken his input as an attempt to control her. The last thing she wanted was to feel as if she had to ask for permission. Now, as she looked at the unfamiliar, unfriendly faces in the airport, she realized she couldn't have been more wrong.

Noah was merely concerned about the woman he loved. He knew the dangers that were in the world all too well, and he wanted to protect her from harm. She groaned out loud in frustration with herself. "This is his job. This is what he does for a living. I am so stupid," she chastised herself.

Noah's voice filled her ear as his voice mail greeting urged her to leave a message. She listened to the smooth, bass timbre of his voice, and it quieted her nerves, helped her to refocus on her own mission.

"Noah, this is Brianna. I'm sure you're busy with your new client, but I just wanted to say a couple of things. I'd rather tell you than your voice mail. But just in case I miss you later, here goes.

"I love you more than anything or anyone in the world. It was stupid of me to come here without you, and I'm genuinely sorry about that. I wish you were here with me. I'm sorry I've acted so weirdly the last few weeks. I'll tell you everything that I've found while investigating this story. I know I should've told you before I left, but I literally just realized how stupid I am while standing in this airport.

"I'm going to see this through, and then I'm coming home to you. I love you, Noah."

Just as Brianna slipped her phone into her pocket, her suitcase appeared on the carousel in baggage claim. Once she secured her rental car, she realized how tired she was. The days and weeks of stress and turmoil had finally caught up with her. She was more than ready to reach her room and stretch out on the bed.

"Hi, I'm Brianna Tate," she said as she approached the front desk of the hotel. "I'm checking in."

"Welcome, Miss Tate," the young man behind the counter replied. "Welcome to Turkey. Your room is ready. Do you need help with your luggage?"

"No, thank you. I can manage," Brianna answered, taking her room key.

She was infinitely grateful that her meeting with Ammar's brother, Deron, wasn't until the following day. Besides Noah, all she could think about was taking a long, hot shower, followed by ordering room service, before she allowed the bed to swallow her whole.

Checking her phone for a call or text from Noah became a new obsession. She looked at the touchscreen repeatedly on her way up to her room, once she unpacked, before and after her shower, and countless times while she ate her meal. Before she slipped off to sleep, she whispered a small prayer.

"Please don't let me be too late to save us."

The next morning, Brianna dressed and checked the map one last time for the precise location where she'd meet Deron. Watching Noah over the past several months of working with him taught her to scout her surroundings ahead of time whenever possible. Check for the ways out, look for vulnerable areas, and identify the most likely hiding spots for unwelcome party crashers were all at the top of her to-do list.

The locale of the meeting was over an hour away from where her hotel was located. The time she spent driving alone through the desolate land made her extremely nervous. The paved road eventually changed to rock and sand. The city landscape disappeared in her rearview mirror, replaced by flat, barren views. Mountains made of solid rock stood tall in the distance where the road curved and winded in the canyons.

Nights of lying comfortably in Noah's arms as he recounted the missions he could talk about immediately sprang to mind. He always stressed the importance of having the high ground in a firefight. Being caught in the lower section of the canyon almost always meant sure death. Her rash, foolish decisions now mocked her, asking if her independence was such a great idea after all.

The hard-packed dirt road took her past a small village. Rectangular, flat-roofed homes made of uncolored brick and stone were placed side by side. Children played close to the unpaved road, so she slowed her speed in the event they bolted out in front of her. The hard stares from the villagers who stopped their daily chores and watched her as she drove past stole her breath.

She finally reached her destination, where she found an old, deserted village with very few structures left fully intact. She parked her rental car in an alcove, hidden by a sizable protruding boulder before she stealthily moved around the buildings to conduct a sweep of the area. Most of the roofs had long since caved in, leaving the walls standing as lone testaments to time's harshness.

She entered the building where she'd meet Deron and checked the view from each window. She had some measure of relief when she found nothing conspicuously alarming. She moved from room to room and located the doors in the back of the house that would be difficult to monitor. She moved broken pieces of brick and rock to use to block the doors from inside the house. With only one accessible entrance, she wouldn't have to be overly concerned about someone slipping in undetected.

When she moved to the adjacent building, she found a room that gave her the best viewpoint and multiple ways of escape. She'd already planned her route by foot to her car and had nothing but time now. As she made her seat as comfortable as possible, she wiped the sweat from her brow.

"How can people stand this heat all the time? This is awful," she said aloud. She took a swig of her water from the canteen and relished the feel of the cold liquid.

She pulled her phone from her pocket and checked for anything from Noah once again. She wasn't surprised to see "No Service" in the top left corner of her cell. She made a mental note to add "not buying a satellite phone" to her list of stupid decisions she'd made recently.

She wouldn't know if he'd called or texted until she was back in a cell service area. He'd be waiting to hear from her, wondering where she was, and if she was safe. "If I haven't already damaged our relationship, leaving him in the dark while I'm halfway around the world will surely do it," she whispered solemnly.

Hot, frustrated tears slowly rolled over her cheeks as she relived every moment with Noah that she could recall. She inhaled a deep, calming breath, and she focused on the positives. Noah was a good man, and he had a very caring side not many got to see. She was a fortunate recipient of that side of him, and she would beg his forgiveness for the distance she'd created between them if she had to.

"I'm really not usually so morbid," she cried. She wiped her tears away and retrieved her pen and paper. She wrote down her questions for Deron so she wouldn't forget the points she needed clarification on. "Anything to distract me from why this feels like the end all of a sudden."

In truth, that feeling started before she left Miami. All of the evidence she'd collected, including the foreign bank account numbers, was hidden inside the spare bedroom in Noah's house. She'd discovered the place by accident one day. The wood floor plank was loose, loudly creaking when she stepped on it. She carefully pried it up and found the perfect hiding spot for small items. Initially, she'd planned to hide one of Noah's Christmas presents in there. Before she left for the airport, she'd made a last-minute decision to drop the flash drive with her research saved on it into that little hole in the floor.

That decision seemed to solidify in her mind that things would not go well for her in Turkey. She'd learned to trust her gut instincts in extreme circumstances, and it hadn't led her astray so far. She silently prayed it was just her hypersensitivity to the subject matter that made it feel different on this trip.

An hour later, she heard a car pull up, the engine cut off, and a door open and close. Slowly stretching her upper body and craning her neck to peer out the window, she saw a man who very closely resembled Ammar looking around nervously. He appeared to be alone and checking to ensure no one had followed him.

When he stepped inside the building, Brianna grabbed her backpack and quickly moved to follow him. If he tried to remove the barricades she'd constructed, she reasoned she'd leave immediately without even looking back.

When she entered the abandoned house, she found Deron sitting at a makeshift table, which was simply a square, weathered piece of wood on top of an old barrel. It worked, as far as functionality went, so she took a seat on the other pile of flat rocks across from him.

"Brianna, I presume?" he asked. His accent was just as thick in person as it was on the phone.

She gave him a single nod in reply. "Ammar?" she asked, purposely mixing up their names.

He smiled. "Deron. Ammar is my brother you met in Miami. At his apartment."

"Deron, it's nice to meet you. I had to make sure you were the man who's supposed to be here," she explained.

"Understandable. You've traveled a long way, to a country with beliefs and customs very different from your country. I would not have allowed my wife to make such a trip," he replied.

The condescension in his voice was cleverly disguised under a thin veil of concern, but she knew it was there nonetheless. She smiled knowingly as she removed her pen and notebook to get to the reason why she was there.

"I assume you brought the papers with you?" she asked pointedly.

Deron reached under the table to retrieve the papers from his briefcase and slid them over to her. "Everything is there. You must be certain not to bring attention to those when you leave here. Mix them up and hide them in your other papers. If those are seen, my entire family will be killed."

"I'll be extra careful with them, Deron. Do you have any names of the Americans involved? Anything that would help me identify them?" she asked.

His black eyes hardened as he assessed her and looked for something to latch on to and put his trust in her. She could feel it in how his eyes implored hers. He wanted to trust her to help him but feared she'd use the information carelessly and put his family in jeopardy.

"It's the best way I can help you. I can get to the right people, but I need the right information to give them. I'd never give your name or anything that would implicate you. With these papers, I can match the shipping manifests and the money paid to the Americans behind it. But I need the names to keep from using these catalog copies, so I know where to start," she clarified.

"Take this picture with you. This is the man who keeps making trips here, meeting with the rebels, and arranging the shipments," Deron said as he slid a four-by-six snapshot to Brianna.

When she picked up the picture, she gasped loudly. Unable to catch her breath, she feared she'd hyperventilate and pass out in front of Deron. He immediately realized she knew the man in the picture, and his demeanor completely changed.

"I've made a mistake coming here. I must go," Deron snapped as he stood quickly.

"No, you didn't make a mistake," Brianna finally assured him. "I know this man, and part of me suspected him, but I wasn't one hundred percent sure until I saw this picture. It's both good news and bad news for me. I won't do anything to jeopardize your family, though. I give you my word."

"Thank you—" Deron started to speak.

The sound of cars approaching on the dirt road caught their attention. The hairs on Brianna's neck stood at full alert, her heart raced, and her chest heaved with rapid breaths.

"Who did you tell about this meeting?" he demanded. "Who knows?"

"Only my boyfriend, but he's still in Miami, and he didn't know exactly where we'd be. Who did you tell?" she asked as panic threatened to overtake her.

"I only told my brother. He would never turn me in," Deron spat out at her.

"We need to get out of here right now. That car is headed in our direction," Brianna said as she quickly stuffed the papers into her backpack. "Get out of here, Deron," she commanded.

She moved along her preplanned route. She rounded the corner to her car just as the two other cars slid to a halt inside the abandoned village. Deron had immediately jumped into his car and moved it out of sight a split second before the others arrived. She didn't see him on the road, however, so she assumed he'd found a place to hide and wait them out. More likely, he counted on her to be a diversion, to draw the men to her car, and give him the opportunity to reach his family safely.

If she started the ignition, the sound of the motor would undoubtedly draw attention to her location. Then she would have a matter of seconds to take off, but they'd quickly find her on the only road around for miles. Her natural curiosity got the best of her, so she climbed the rock wall to see whom she was up against. As she reached the top, she flattened her body against the sand and dirt ground to avoid being seen. Her eyes landed on a remarkably familiar figure. When he turned to face her as he looked around the village, she recognized the man who stood in front of her, without a doubt.

Richard Hollingsworth himself.

"Let's go. No one is here. There's another abandoned village about fifteen kilometers from here," one of the men called out.

Richard remained still for several seconds longer, and Brianna held her breath. She silently willed him to leave so she could make a clean getaway. Brianna didn't move a muscle until Richard got back in the car. When they were well down the road, headed in the opposite direction she needed to go, she hurried to her car.

Her hands shook uncontrollably as she tried to insert the key into the ignition switch. The adrenaline dump to her system wreaked havoc on the control of her motor skills. With the key finally in place, she rolled down the window and listened for any sounds before starting the engine. She put the car in drive, got back on the main road, and didn't take her foot off the gas until she reached her hotel.

She rushed inside the hotel, reached her room, and bolted the door. As she paced back and forth, she glanced at the time. It was very late in Miami, but Noah would want her to call, especially if he knew how dangerous the situation had become.

"What can he do to help me from Miami, though?" she asked herself.

She powered up her laptop and immediately checked for the next available flight home. "The sooner, the better," she muttered as she waited for the flight times to load.

She booked the first available flight back to Miami, eight hours away. She completed the online check-in to ensure her seat was reserved and began rushing around the room, haphazardly throwing her belongings into her suitcase. She carefully tucked the new evidence, including the picture, underneath the lining inside her purse. If anyone manually searched it, only a small hole would show in the lining. Her purse contained enough other papers and personal items to camouflage the new ones.

Now, all she had to do was get to the airport without being seen by Richard. Then she'd be home free, back in Noah's arms and completely protected. That was the only place she ever really wanted to be again.

As she entered the elevator, she hit the button for the lobby repeatedly. The doors seemed to close even more slowly, purposely taunting her. She quickened her pace once she reached the entry area. She'd already opted for the quick check-out, so she was able to go straight to her rental car and not look back.

As she turned the corner from the lobby toward the door to the parking garage, she smacked into Richard's chest and bounced off of him. The shock both of their faces wore was apparent, but Brianna knew hers also held a trace of guilt. Guilt that she knew the truth about him. Guilt that she'd spied on him. Guilt that she had a picture of him meeting with the radical leader of the rebel forces in her purse. Guilt that she would share all this information with Noah, and then Noah would help her take Richard down.

The irony that he would soon be judged himself hit her.

"Brianna, what are you doing here in Turkey?" Richard asked. His eyes lit with understanding while he waited for her to concoct a lie.

She chose to tell the partial truth instead. "I was sent here by my paper to follow a story lead. It didn't pan out, though. Made the trip for nothing, after all."

"That's too bad. I'll bet you thought you were so close to landing the story of a lifetime, too."

"Not really. Everyone has a different definition of what the story of a lifetime is. My definition would be my life with Noah," she replied as she lifted her chin in defiance. "I'm running late, so I'd better get going. By the way, why are you here?"

"I had a meeting with some local officials on behalf of my boss. Trying to improve relations."

"That sounds very interesting." Brianna smiled. *And that's not the responsibility of the DOD, Richard.* "Have a safe trip back home. I'm sure I'll see you again soon."

"Yes, indeed. Have a good flight." Richard smirked.

CHAPTER TWELVE

"How long will she be here?" Rebel asked.

"They're supposed to leave immediately after the concert," Noah replied.

"I'll believe it when I see it," Bull replied.

The hidden microphones and almost invisible earpieces kept the men in constant contact while they were nearby. Staying on top of the pop star diva's every movement had proven to be more of a challenge for the team than they'd thought. A change of plans at the last minute was usually the last resort for a security team, but it was the way Kristen Garrett operated from minute to minute.

"No matter when it is, it's not soon enough," Noah muttered under his breath.

"I heard that, man," Rebel agreed. "She's driving me crazy."

"After we get national recognition for this job, I say we hire more men to babysit. We can manage the men," Bull suggested.

"Hell yeah," Noah replied and kept his voice low. "I completely agree."

"Miss Garrett, it's time to leave for your show," Noah prompted her.

"Okay," she giggled. "I'm ready to go. It's a sold-out show, you know. Even if I'm late, they'll wait for me. It's not like they can start without me."

"No, they're not likely to start without you," Noah agreed. "But the later we wait, the more congested Miami traffic will be. Fans can get irate if they have to wait too long."

"You're probably right," she answered with a dismissive sigh.

"Miss Garrett is coming out. Is everything clear?" Noah asked.

"All clear," Rebel and Bull each replied back.

"We're clear to go." Noah smiled as he opened the door for her.

Once she was outside the safety of her hotel room, the hulking men surrounded her tiny frame and almost completely shielded her from the nosy onlookers. Her heels clicked and her gum popped as they walked through the hotel and out to her waiting limousine.

Bull and Rebel followed behind in a separate vehicle, occasionally chatting in Noah's ear while he wasn't able to reply. The distraction at least made the ride more entertaining than listening to Kristen's phone calls. When Noah delivered her on time to the backstage door, her tour manager and the arena security team met them to take over.

"You'll be well compensated for the extra time and attention our visit required of you. I'm impressed with your work, and I'm not impressed often. You'll be hearing from others in this industry very soon." The manager smiled as he shook hands with Noah.

"Thank you. I appreciate the referrals. Give me a call if you ever need our assistance again in the future," Noah replied.

He climbed into the truck with Bull and Rebel and then heaved a deep sigh of relief. "Thank God that's over. I don't think I could take one more minute of Miss Pop Star's gum-popping."

"No shit, man. I heard that popping in my earpiece and thought I'd go mad. I don't know how you stood it when you were sitting right beside her," Bull replied.

"Well, I did have you two chattering in my ear," Noah laughed. "Take me home. I'm ready to relax and have a beer. Brianna left me a message yesterday, but I haven't even been able to listen to it yet. I couldn't get away from Miss Garrett long enough to take a personal call."

"Guess Bri made it to Turkey all right," Rebel chimed in.

"Yeah, seems so. That's probably what the message says anyway. I'm starving, I'm tired, and I never want to hear pop music again as long as I live," Noah laughed. "That management idea is the best idea I've ever heard, Bull."

"Let's make it happen," he exclaimed.

"Her manager said he'll refer us to others in the industry. If we start getting a lot of high-profile people and contracts, this business will grow even faster. Exciting times."

Noah's thoughts immediately drifted to Brianna. In his mental picture of the future, he'd always been able to clearly see her beside him. They'd build a life together, have a family, and grow old side by side. Whatever troubles one faced, the other would be there to help.

The uncertainty of their relationship made that picture less clear to him now. His love for her hadn't changed or diminished, but something between them was off. He couldn't wait to listen to the voice mail, even if it was just her confirming she'd made it safely. He hoped that by hearing her voice and the tone of it would give him some clue of where her mind was.

After Bull and Rebel dropped him off, he showered and then checked the time on his watch as he finished toweling off. Turkey was eight hours ahead of Miami, making it just after seven in the morning there. Brianna's meeting was at nine, so Noah knew he wouldn't be able to reach her until later in the day.

She'd spend her early morning making the necessary preparations to meet with the stranger. Then she'd take her time asking questions, extracting every bit of information she could obtain, before settling down with all of her notes and penning the next Pulitzer Prize-winning article. With a full day ahead of her and a long day behind him, Noah climbed into bed and turned on the TV, fully intent on watching the news, then he would listen to Brianna's voice before he went to sleep.

When he opened his eyes, the sun streamed through his bedroom windows, the TV was still on, and he hadn't moved a muscle all night. He sat up in bed, cursed under his breath, and swung his feet over the side. He rubbed his eyes and reached for his cell phone, but it wasn't in its usual place.

Noah quickly stood, walked briskly to the bathroom, and found it on the vanity counter where he'd left it the night before. There were six missed calls from Brianna, all spaced several minutes apart. The times indicated that she was urgently trying to reach him as he slept.

"Shit, shit, shit," he repeatedly yelled as he scrolled through the times of her calls. "Please be okay." He prayed aloud as he tried calling her.

With each call, it went straight to voice mail. No ringing. No waiting for Brianna to pick up. Only her voice instructing the caller to leave a message and she'd call back as soon as she was able. He stomped through the house in frustration, threw on his clothes, and tried her cell again with no luck.

As he brought it back up to hit redial again, his phone rang in his hand. A strange, foreign number flashed on the caller identification, and he immediately felt hope that Brianna was calling from a local telephone. Maybe something had happened to her cell phone. Perhaps the battery had died, she'd lost it, or it had been destroyed. No matter, she was calling to tell him she was okay.

"Brianna?" he asked, panic lacing his voice as he answered.

"Is this Mr. Noah Steele?" the polite voice asked.

"Yes. Who is this?"

"This is US Ambassador Elliott's office in Istanbul, Turkey. I'm afraid I have some terrible news. My apologies for delivering such news over the phone, but I need to inform you that Miss Brianna Tate's plane experienced a mechanical malfunction during takeoff tonight. I'm very sorry, Mr. Steele, but there were no survivors," she explained.

"What?" Noah asked, confused. "What are you saying? I don't understand. Her flight isn't scheduled until tomorrow."

"The airline shows she changed her flight and checked in for the flight to Miami tonight. I'm very sorry, Mr. Steele. The officials are still at the scene, but the damage was far too extensive for any survivors. All three hundred thirty-seven passengers, plus the crew, are presumed dead," she replied. "You were listed as her emergency contact on her airline profile. I'm very sorry, Mr. Steele."

Noah dropped the phone and stared at it as if it had bitten him. The rapid rise and fall of his chest mirrored his fast breathing. His heart pounded in his chest, beating fiercely against his rib cage. The blood surged through his veins, swishing through his ears and drowning out any other sound.

His knees simultaneously buckled as his guttural cry echoed throughout his large home. "No!" He bent at the waist and let his forehead drop to the floor as his fists pounded it relentlessly. He chanted a mixture of painful pleas and sobs over and over. "Please, God, no. Don't take her from me. Bring her back home to me.

"Brianna," he whispered as tears continued to stream down his face. "I don't want to do this without you. I love you, baby. So fucking much."

He fell over to lie on his side and remained on the floor in shock. The ominous feeling he had before she left for this trip just made it harder for him to accept. He'd been warned, yet he let her go alone anyway. There was nothing he wouldn't give just to hear from her again.

"The voice mail," he said aloud. "Maybe there's another explanation. Please, God, let there be another explanation."

He scrambled to his phone and played the voice mail on his speaker. When her sweet voice spoke to him, the tears and heartache returned full force,

"I love you more than anything or anyone in the world. It was stupid of me to come here without you, and I'm genuinely sorry about that. I wish you were here with me. I'm sorry I've acted so weirdly the last few weeks. I'll tell you everything that I've found while investigating this story. I know I should've told you before I left, but I literally just realized how stupid I am while standing in this airport.

"I'm going to see this through, and then I'm coming home to you. I love you, Noah."

He rewound the message and played it repeatedly for an hour.

I'm coming home to you.

I'm coming home to you.

I'm coming home to you.

"Come home to me, Brianna! Come home to me now!" he shouted.

How do I let go of the one person I love more than life itself?

How do I carry on like I give a fuck about anything else?

How do I get past this pain that's worse than a white-hot knife cutting my heart out of my chest?

The questions and doubts assaulted Noah's thoughts and bombarded him with more pain than he'd ever thought a man could survive. If she were really dead, if he would never really hold her in his arms again, all he wanted to do was join her. His life, his business, and his will to live had been tied up in his love for her.

He'd become one of those weak men he pitied. The ones who shriveled up and lost their will to live when their woman left them. The ones he'd previously judged and found severely lacking in balls and testosterone. Now he fully understood what they'd experienced and what brought them to their knees.

The kind of love he had with Brianna was a once-in-a-lifetime type of love. Any other person, any other feeling, would fail woefully in comparison to Brianna. He sat up, his back against the wall and his head in his hands, and tried to will his body to give up. He tried to will his mind to let go. He just wanted to slip into oblivion and be happy again, because he couldn't imagine happiness ever returning to him in a world where Brianna wouldn't ever come home to him.

Rebel and Bull were suddenly at his side, asking questions and demanding answers he couldn't give voice to. He couldn't bring himself to say the words out loud and make them come true.

"Reaper, what's wrong with you? What happened?" Rebel asked.

"Come on, man. Help us out here. What's going on?" Bull added.

For a moment, Noah irrationally considered if he didn't say it, if he believed with everything he was that she wasn't really dead, she'd come back to him. But he'd seen too much death to think that. He was grasping at any shred of hope he could find, but there was none there.

"Brianna's plane crashed. She's dead," he finally replied. He hung his head, his chin to his chest, and the sobs racked his body again. "She's gone. She's never coming back."

The finality of his words hit Bull like a sledgehammer to the chest. He fell to his knees beside Noah, panting heavily, and fighting the tears that filled his eyes. "What?" he whispered, praying he'd somehow heard wrong.

Rebel sat down hard beside Noah, his back also against the wall as he stared blankly at the other wall. Tears slid down his face as he slowly shook his head from side to side. "No. That can't be right. They're wrong."

"I wish they were. The airline has her checked in for the flight. All three hundred plus passengers are dead. No survivors," Noah replied glumly. "I don't know what to do. What am I supposed to do?"

Neither answered his rhetorical question because they didn't have an answer. For the first time they could remember since being a team, they didn't have a plan of action. They didn't have a Plan B in case something went wrong. There was no fail-safe. Their tightrope didn't have a net to catch them, and they were all free-falling, hurtling toward the ground together.

A crash and burn was imminent and unavoidable. The casualties would be considerable. The devastation would be complete. But the worst was still yet to come.

"Reaper, I'm sorry to bring this up now. But has anyone called her family?" Rebel asked, fruitlessly wiping his tears.

"Fuck," he replied. "I don't know. I haven't even thought of that. I haven't thought of anything else."

"They need to be called, Reap. They deserve to know, too," Rebel added. "They love her, and they love you."

Noah nodded but just stared at his phone. "How do I tell them that—" His voice broke, and it took all the strength he could muster to swallow the sob that clogged his throat. "How am I supposed to tell them that their daughter is dead? That I didn't protect her? They'll hate me, and I deserve it."

"They won't hate you, and you don't deserve it. Give them more credit than that," Rebel urged. "As much as it hurts, they know Brianna is a grown woman and makes her own decisions."

Noah nodded and picked up his phone. He reluctantly dialed Evan's number as he prepared to hear her parents endure the barrage of emotions he was still battling through himself. When Evan answered the phone, Noah cringed at his jovial voice.

"Good morning, Noah," Evan answered. "Diana and I were just talking about you. We'd love to see our kids again soon. How are you?"

Evan and Diana had visited Miami for a long weekend, and Noah had insisted they stay at his house. Their time together that weekend was a mixture of work and business since the Tate family owned a chain of luxury hotels. Evan was considering an expansion and had appointments to look at properties in the South Beach area.

Evan and Diana adopted Noah as their own son that weekend. Brianna's weekly calls to her parents lengthened since they also expected an update from their new son. Noah's estrangement from his family had been difficult for him in so many ways. He missed his parents and his siblings, but the nature of their relationship couldn't be helped. When Evan and Diana welcomed him into their lives with open arms, showed him the parental love he'd missed, and loved him for who he was, he believed he could finally be part of a family.

For the first time, he also looked forward to having a family of his own. With Brianna. Now he had to tell her parents that one of their worst nightmares had come true.

"Evan, I really wish you and Diana were here. There's something I have to tell you," Noah began.

"What's wrong, son?" Evan asked, dread filling his voice.

"It's Brianna." Noah coughed, masking his sob. "Her plane...there were no survivors. I'm so sorry. I'm so sorry I wasn't there to save her."

Silence filled the line, and Noah pictured Evan trying to assimilate the bombshell that had just been dropped on him. He understood how Evan felt since he was utterly devastated by the news.

"What? I don't understand. Where? When?" Evan stammered.

"She was in Turkey, following up on a lead for a big story," Noah explained. "She was supposed to fly home tomorrow, but the embassy called and said she changed her flight to come home early. They didn't have very many details."

Evan's sobs tore through his body, filtered through the phone, and poured into Noah's broken heart. "Was it the same accident they've shown on the news?"

"I don't know, Evan," Noah replied, wiping his face again. "I haven't had the TV on at all."

"Noah, I have to go tell Diana," Evan stated solemnly. "Then I'll have the pilot ready the jet, and we can make the arrangements together. If you don't mind, I'm sure Diana would agree that we'd prefer to stay with you."

"Of course. Of course, you can stay with me," Noah replied. "As long as you want."

"We'll see you soon, son. We love you."

"Love you both," Noah responded. "I'm so sorry, Evan."

"Brianna loved you more than anything, Noah. She told me all the time how wonderful you were to her. You have nothing to be sorry for, son," Evan assured him. "That was not your fault or even in your control."

When he disconnected the call, Noah stumbled downstairs to the den, with Bull and Rebel close on his heels, to turn on the TV. He flipped the channel to the news and saw the footage replayed on a loop in the small picture window beside the anchorman's head.

"In case you're just tuning in, the top story of the day is the apparent plane explosion immediately after takeoff from an airport in Turkey. From the footage shot by onlookers with their cell phones, it's clear that no one could have survived that blast.

"Relatively small pieces of the plane have been found up to one hundred miles from the point of the explosion. No one has claimed responsibility for this act. At this time, it's unknown if there was some sort of issue with the plane itself or if this was the work of a terrorist group. We'll update you as soon as we know more."

Noah, Rebel, and Bull silently watched the scene repeatedly play on the flat screen until Rebel took the remote and turned it off. Noah didn't even notice it was no longer playing. The images were burned into his mind, and now he'd relive them every day of his life. He watched Brianna's last few minutes of life, he questioned if she had any idea of what happened, and the knowledge that he'd never see her again had killed his newfound zest for life.

"What did Evan say?" Bull asked.

Noah gave them a recap of the conversation. "He said it wasn't my fault," Noah added thoughtfully. "Evan doesn't blame me."

"They're good people, Reap. None of Bri's family will blame you. They know you love her more than anything. Hell, you hunted her down after only knowing her for six weeks. There's no doubt you're crazy about her," Bull replied.

Several hours later, Noah still sat in the same spot where he watched the raw footage of the exploding plane. He vacillated between extreme pain, complete numbness, and bitter anger as he attempted to deal with the effects of his loss. Bull and Rebel left earlier after Noah insisted he wanted to be alone.

The chimes of the doorbell evoked little more than a head turn in the general direction of the front door. After about a minute, someone pounded on the door, and then a voice called his name. He immediately recognized the voice, sprang from the couch, and sprinted toward the front door.

CHAPTER THIRTEEN

When he jerked it open, he found Evan, Diana, Missy, Jessie, and Ashley at his doorstep. All of their eyes were swollen and bloodshot red, but they were also apparently grateful to see him. The family surrounded him as arms wrapped wherever they could latch on to someone else. Sniffles, loud sobs, and muffled cries filled the entryway.

Evan was the first to release his hold on Noah, causing a chain reaction from all the women. As each person wiped their eyes, Noah took in his new family. Through better or worse, the special bond would remain between them.

"Come in," Noah spoke. "My home is your home."

"How are you holding up, son?" Diana asked as she sniffled and wiped her eyes.

"Me?" Noah asked incredulously. "How are you holding up?"

"I'm not really," she replied honestly. "But I worry about all of my kids, Noah. Now answer me."

He drew her into his arms and kissed the top of her head. "I'm not holding up either," he whispered. "I want to wake up from this horrible dream and have her here with me."

"So do I, Noah," Diana cried into his shirt. "So very much."

When everyone regrouped after putting their luggage in their temporary bedrooms, Evan raised the question that haunted everyone's mind.

"I don't know how to handle this," he started. "This isn't something I've ever really prepared for. On the one hand, I feel like I'm giving up all hope by saying this. On the other, I feel like I'm honoring my daughter by saying it. I can't win."

Evan dragged his hand over his face, scraping against the stubble that had grown throughout the day. He looked tired and drained of all emotion, but Noah knew it simmered just under the surface. The right or wrong word would set it off again. He knew because that's how he felt, too.

"There is no right or wrong thing in this situation Daddy," Missy soothed. "We've never been in this spot before, and we'll always second-guess everything we do. But I know you, and I know whatever it is, you're doing it with the best of intentions."

"Thank you, baby girl," Evan replied as his eyes misted. "I'd like to have a funeral for Brianna. From the news report, there's no chance that anyone survived. To honor her, to celebrate her life, and to give the family the closure we need, I think we should go forward with the funeral."

Diana's tears streamed over her cheeks, like small rivers with no end. She nodded her agreement, but she was unable to verbalize anything. Evan looked at his daughters, his eyes questioned them, and they each nodded their agreement.

"Noah." Evan turned to face his son. "I know the bond between a man and the love of his life. Just as I know the bond between a father and his daughter. This is your decision, too. You're every bit a part of this family as much as Brianna is."

Noah lifted his eyes to meet Evan's. The bond between the two men was now sealed in death, the death of one they both loved. "You don't know how much that means to me. How much all of you mean to me," he continued as he looked at each face.

"This is the worst thing I've ever been through. I think the funeral will be even worse, but paying our respects to Brianna will help us to start to heal. Just one day of living in limbo has been hell," he replied. He wanted to console the others, make them believe that healing was possible, but he didn't believe one word of it. Inside, he knew he'd never recover from this blow.

"We all agree, then?" Evan asked.

Everyone replied with a low, mumbled "yes," and Evan stood. "We can make the decisions of how and where tomorrow. There's no reason to rush. For the rest of today and tonight, I think we need time together to remember her, share stories, and try to help each other with the grief."

"It just doesn't feel real. None of this feels real. I'd swear I was in a dream," Missy said aloud.

"I agree," Jessie chimed in. "I expect her to text me any second now to ask about my day."

"Has anyone tried calling her cell?" Ashley asked.

"Yes," Noah replied. "I have. Repeatedly. It goes straight to voice mail."

A quick rap on the door drew Noah's attention just as it opened. Rebel and Bull walked in, their demeanor matching the somber mood inside. Their long, sad faces and red-rimmed eyes showed Brianna's brothers had struggled with the news on their own as long as they could stand.

"Bull came over to my place," Rebel started. "Neither of us knows what to do. I can't think straight for shit. All I know is we need to be here."

"She's our little sister," Bull added. "We love her, too."

"I know you do. She loves you both, too," Noah replied. "You're always welcome here. We were just discussing our next steps. Have a seat, guys."

"She does love you both," Missy replied. "She talks about all her 'Steele men' all the time."

Bull fought back the unexpected emotions that rose inside him. His sense of duty and honor were the attributes that defined him, and he'd failed her. He promised to protect her, and in his mind, he'd failed.

Rebel gave Missy a small smile as he pictured Brianna sharing her pet name for them, but it quickly disappeared when the vise squeezed his heart again. The beautiful, petite blonde who'd worked her way into their close-knit group, into their lives, and into their hearts would never come home again.

"What next steps?" Rebel asked Noah as he sat and attempted to rein his feelings back in.

Noah swallowed the heart-sized lump in his throat before answering. "Brianna's funeral. Her memorial service."

"Already?" Bull blurted out before he even realized he'd said it. "Sorry, I just hoped we'd get better news, someone made a mistake, that she's okay. It just feels too soon."

"We understand, Bull," Evan assured him. "Diana and I have talked about this since the minute Noah called. I've done everything I know to do. We called the embassy, I called in favors from friends, and they called in favors from other friends.

"Maybe I shouldn't admit this, but a friend checked her passport, her credit cards, and her cell phone. None have been used anywhere since the explosion. He's still monitoring them, but since I haven't heard from him, I know he hasn't found anything," Evan explained sadly.

"I'm sorry. I didn't mean to add more stress on you with my outburst," Bull apologized.

"No need for apologies here. We'll all go through a wide range of emotions for a long time to come," Diana replied. "Crying one minute, fighting mad the next."

For the rest of the evening and late into the night, Noah's family told their fondest stories of Brianna. Some were funny, some were touching, but all were the exact personifications of Brianna herself. Her strength, determination, and drive to excel were accented by her humor, her desire to help people, and the way she freely gave her love to her family and friends.

When exhaustion kicked in and eyes involuntarily closed, Noah insisted the group should retreat to their rooms and get a good night's sleep. He'd already decided he couldn't sleep in the bed he shared with Brianna. It was just too big, too cold, and too lonely. The nights he slept alone while she traveled for work were different. He still smelled her scent on her pillow and felt her presence beside him. Knowing she wouldn't be back, he didn't think he could handle those kinds of ghosts.

Stretched out on the couch with his arm slung over his eyes, Noah tried to relax and allow his mind to fall into a deep sleep. One where he could be with Brianna again in his dreams. After what felt like an eternity of waiting for sleep to overcome him, Noah was still wide awake. He turned on his side to try a different position, but that didn't work either.

Reluctantly, he rose and robotically walked the long path to their bedroom. His feet carried him closer and closer to the very place he'd tried to avoid. He crawled onto the bed and placed his head on the pillow. The tiny wisp of air from his movement released Brianna's perfume, and it immediately surrounded him.

Turning his face to the pillow, he inhaled deeply to savor her scent. Visions of her smiling and laughing instantly filled his mind. Her arms reached for him and sensually pulled him toward her. Her lips moved over his, and the sounds she made as he made love to her filled his ears. Love reserved only for him shone in her eyes as she mouthed, "I love you."

Noah hugged the pillow tightly to him as his heart shattered into a million jagged pieces, never to be put back together again. But that was where he felt her the most. That was where he could be with her still, even if it were only imaginary. Even if it was only for a short time. Enveloped by the scents, sights, and sounds of her in their bed, Noah finally drifted off to sleep.

With the bright morning sun lighting his bedroom, Noah stirred and stretched in the bed before extending his arm to pull Brianna to him. When his hand met the empty, cold sheets on her side, he opened his eyes and raised his head.

"Brianna?" he called out.

Then all the events of yesterday came crashing into him all at once.

He wished he could go back to sleep and continue his dream. He was with Brianna, and they were planning their wedding. All he cared about was planning their honeymoon, but she playfully scolded him on the importance of having the actual ceremony before they left for their honeymoon.

He was happy again in his dream. Brianna was happy—and alive. She was warm, loving, and full of life. Now that he was awake, the profound sadness returned, but now it wasn't muted by numbness and shock. The pain was excruciating and overwhelming. It threatened to steal his breath and laugh at him as he suffocated under the weight of it.

His sense of duty and responsibility to his friends and family pushed him to get up and shower. When he descended the stairs, he heard quiet voices coming from the kitchen. As he approached, he found Evan and Diana huddled together over a cup of coffee at the table.

Evan's arm was wrapped around Diana's shoulders as her sobs caused her body to shake violently. Noah knew he couldn't take their pain away when he could barely deal with his own grief. He stood behind them, bent over, and wrapped his arms around both of their shoulders.

After several minutes, Diana wiped her face and calmed her cries. "It just hit me hard again this morning," she explained apologetically. "My emotions are all over the place, and I can't seem to focus on any one thing."

"You don't have to apologize to me, Diana," Noah assured her. "I'm in the same place you are. No matter how strong I've been in the past, this has shown me that I'm pretty damn weak."

"You're too hard on yourself, Noah," Evan replied. "This has knocked the wind out of all of our sails."

"Evan and I have been talking about Brianna's memorial service. What do you think we should do?" Diana asked Noah.

"She loved the beach and the ocean. Anything to do with the water," Noah said.

"We could rent a boat and take it far offshore, way out where it's deep. For her memorial service, we can write down our favorite memories, seal them in a bottle, and throw the bottle overboard," Diana offered. "Do you think she would've liked that?"

"I think she would've loved it," Noah replied warmly. "It's unique, just like her."

"Have you noticed that we all refer to her in both present and past tense?" Diana stared off into the distance, her eyes unfocused, and her voice soft as she asked.

"I have noticed," Noah replied. "When I feel like she's here with me, I use the present tense. When I feel alone, I use past tense. It's not conscious, but it's definitely real."

"I agree," Diana replied.

"If we're set on the boat and bottle, I'll start making some calls. I have to do something," Evan stressed. "I feel so useless, and I just need to stay busy."

"Everyone deals with this differently, Evan. I've pretty much shut down. It hurts less to feel nothing than to feel everything," Noah confessed. "When I let my guard down, it hits me full force. I haven't found the best way to deal with it yet."

"I can't stop feeling everything," Diana replied. "I wish I could be numb. It would probably be a nice reprieve."

Evan stood, kissed his wife on the cheek, and walked toward the kitchen door. "I'll start calling around for boat charters while you shower, honey."

Diana rinsed out their coffee cups in the sink before going to wake her daughters to tell them the plans. Noah recognized the lost, wounded look in her eyes. It was the same one he saw looking back at him in his reflection.

Two hours later, everyone had showered and dressed. Rebel and Bull sat on the couch with Diana as they waited for Evan to finish his phone conversation. Missy, Jessie, and Ashley huddled together on the love seat, while

Noah sat in his recliner, lost in thought. Evan's voice brought him back to the present.

"I've charted a yacht to take us out tomorrow. We'll leave early tomorrow morning and spend the day out on the water. We're all under so much stress and grief. I think we all need the day away from everything else. Away from the news, away from the ghosts that haunt us, and out where Brianna would've loved to be," Evan stated.

"The yacht is large enough to give us enough space to say our own good-byes but small enough that we can also spend quality time together. It's extravagant, but my baby girl deserves the best." His voice broke, and the emotions he'd held at bay rushed to the surface.

"It sounds beautiful, Evan," Noah complimented him. "Brianna would love the gesture."

"Jessie, Ashley, and I are going shopping at the craft store. We want to pick out the bottles if that's okay. We may need more than one to hold all of our best memories," Missy added.

"That sounds perfect, sweetheart," Diana replied. "Thank you, girls. We know this is very hard for you, too."

The girls surrounded their mother, hugged her, and kissed her before they left together. Evan retrieved his laptop to show the others the yacht he'd secured. The gesture, in Brianna's honor, was important to him. Every aspect of it had to be of the highest caliber to serve the memory of his beloved daughter.

"Noah, what can we do for you?" Rebel asked.

Shaking his head, Noah gave his friend a sincere look of appreciation. "Nothing. You and Bull being here is enough."

"This is where we belong," Bull replied. "This is our family now, too."

Diana cooked for the group and insisted that everyone sit at the table together to eat. Noah did as she asked regardless of how hard it was for him to swallow any food. This was her contribution to help others, and it made her feel good to be able to care for them. He would allow her that small measure of comfort.

Several hours later, Missy, Jessie, and Ashley returned from their shopping trip with their arms full of bags from various stores. Missy put her bags down and rummaged through them until she found a specific item.

"I found this bottle to hold the memories," she said as she held it up. "It's elegant, and I think Brianna would like it." The tall, glass bottle had a light green tint, a wide mouth, and a thick cork stopper. The words "Love Lives" adorned the front in raised glass letters.

"It looks big enough to hold everyone's papers," Diana replied.

"I think so too," Missy replied. "All of our memories should be together, in one bottle, and sealed with our love. That's the only way it feels right to me."

"We also picked up some flowers to make arrangements, candles, and picture frames. We wanted to put different pictures and snapshots of Brianna around the yacht. I can also make a DVD with her favorite song playing in the background," Jessie explained.

With all the arrangements made, the entire clan found tasks to complete that kept them busy throughout the rest of the day. Mentally drained at the end of the day, Bull and Rebel left, and the rest retreated to the solitude of their rooms for the night. They never admitted it aloud, but the dread of what the next day held weighed heavily on their shoulders.

The next morning, everyone dressed and somberly drove to the marina. Evan checked them in, and they were escorted to the yacht. They took their seats inside the cabin as Missy passed out the strips of aged parchment paper and pens.

"Start writing down your favorite memories of Brianna. Roll up the strip of paper and put it in the bottle. Once it's full, we'll seal the cork stopper in it and toss it overboard," Missy explained tearfully.

She'd put a layer of small stones in the bottom, covered by sand, to help weigh it down. Once the memories were tossed into the ocean, the bottle would sink to the bottom and find Brianna's final resting place.

One by one, the memories filled up the glass bottle until there was no more room. Noah picked up the bottle and sealed it with the natural cork stopper. He eyed the bottle carefully as he thought about all of the memories contained inside. All of the memories would remain with him since they talked about each one as they dropped them into the bottle.

The crew took the flower arrangements and placed them strategically along the stern of the yacht. Beautiful bouquets of large white, yellow, pink, red, and orange lilies, paired with a multitude of candles, adorned the outside seating section. Noah felt the yacht progressively slowing until they came to a complete stop. The waves continued to rock the boat gently as Missy, Jessie, and Ashley lit the candles.

Noah walked to the edge of the boat, held up the bottle of memories, and prepared to give his eulogy.

"Brianna, you are the love of my life, and you will always live in my heart. Not one day will go by that I don't think of you, miss you, and wish you were at my side. After loving you, no one could possibly take your place in my life or my heart. This isn't goodbye, my love. This is until I see you again...until we can be together again. I love you, baby," Noah concluded and passed the bottle to Diana.

"My baby girl. It seems like yesterday when you were born. You grew up so fast and went out into the world. You were never afraid, though. You were the bravest person I know. My world is a little darker now without your smile and your beautiful personality to brighten it. You'll forever be loved," Diana finished and handed the bottle to Evan.

Evan held the bottle in his hand, his knuckles white from his tight grip. "Daddy's little girl. That's what you always were, Brianna. You had me wrapped around your finger from the first second I held you. I just never imagined I'd have to bear losing you first. If I could trade places with you, I'd do it in a heartbeat. I miss your voice so much, your bubbly personality, your gorgeous smile, your infectious laugh. I'll never be whole again without you. I love you. Always," Evan choked out.

Evan handed the bottle back to Noah. "Will you do the honors, Noah? I think it's fitting since Brianna gave her heart to you and wanted to spend her life with you."

Noah took the bottle and stared at it again. His private message to Brianna was like an unspoken prayer in his mind, but he knew she heard him. Rearing back, he threw the bottle into the deep, blue ocean and watched as it sank.

"I'll never say goodbye, baby," he whispered.

CHAPTER FOURTEEN

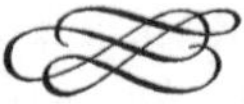

Current Day

Noah stared in amazement at his old friend Richard, whom he had thought was dead. He couldn't believe the man stood before him now, alive and well. He'd attended Richard's memorial service, had grieved his friend's passing, and visited his grave once a year to pay his respects. According to the news reports, an anti-American terrorist group with a known affiliation with the Islamic Jihadist Union had held his friend hostage all this time.

Smaller fractions of the union were located all through the Middle East and northern Africa. Noah knew Richard frequently traveled to those areas for business, but he'd never guessed that his friend was in trouble, needed his help, and waited for someone to rescue him.

Noah's guilt ate away at him. He had been living in the comfort and safety of home while his friend fought for his life every day. The shame of leaving a brother behind was overwhelming.

Noah hugged his longtime friend and patted him on the back. "Richard, I still can't believe you've been alive and held captive all this time. After Brianna's memorial service, I received word that you were also on that plane. I can't tell you how much that shook me up."

"Everything is still surreal to me. I imagine it is for everyone else too. I'm still trying to get my bearings," Richard replied.

"I have to ask this because not knowing has killed me for three years. How is it you and Brianna were both in Turkey at the same time? Did you see her?" Noah asked.

"Yes, I did see her once, and it surprised the hell out of me. She was leaving the hotel as I entered. I asked her what she was doing there, and she said she was chasing a lead that didn't pan out. She had her suitcase with her and was in a hurry to get to the airport," Richard answered.

"Then what happened?" Noah pushed. He knew he was a terrible friend, pushing for information about Brianna when Richard had just been set free, but that didn't stop him.

"My meetings with the local leaders were over, and I was ready to get home myself," Richard explained. "I realized if Brianna was headed to the airport, there had to be a flight leaving soon. I called the airline and changed my flight.

"On the way to the airport, my car was hijacked, and I was taken hostage. I'd been seen negotiating with the established leaders, and the rebels didn't appreciate my involvement. They tried to use me as leverage. If anything happened to me, the people wouldn't receive any assistance from DOD."

"How did you manage to get away?" Noah asked.

"One of the women who brought my food helped me," Richard lied. "She felt sorry for me, and for her involvement in it. We arranged for me to 'overpower' her and escape. I only hope that they believed she couldn't fight back. It's awful to even think that she paid the ultimate price just for helping me."

Richard was so sincere and so convincing that even he almost believed his story was true. Almost.

Richard felt Noah's dark, piercing eyes assessing him. He knew Noah imagined the scenario playing out in his mind as he examined every detail, looked for gaps, and pieced together the news coverage that explained his sudden return. If Noah had to die because he'd figured it all out too soon, so be it. He was just another casualty of war–or of money. *Take your pick,* Richard thought to himself.

Richard knew Noah would find a hole in his story eventually. But he planned to have already recovered precisely what he needed and be long gone again by then. Noah had always been too intelligent for his own good in Richard's mind. The two men had been Airborne Rangers and later part of the elite Delta Force together, so they were both very skilled in terrorism and counterterrorism measures.

"I'd stayed away from the news when that happened because I couldn't watch that footage of the plane exploding one more time. It was a few days later when I learned you were presumed to be on that plane too.

"I pushed hard on a lot of people to get clearance to get to the site of the explosion, but it was closed to any nonessential personnel due to the terrorist threat. I should have pushed harder. I should have looked for you," Noah insisted vehemently.

"No way," Richard shook his head. "There was no way you could've known. Even if you had somehow made it out of the States, you would've been taken as a hostage or even killed."

Noah's face became hard as he said, "We never leave a man behind. *De oppresso liber.*"

What was that quick flicker in Richard's eye? Guilt? Noah's suspicions immediately reared, and his internal radar flashed red lights. The look in Richard's eyes was gone as quickly as it came, so Noah didn't push it. Pushing the thoughts aside, he internally chided himself for doubting Richard. The man had probably endured terrible things that he couldn't discuss yet.

Richard responded, "Liberate the oppressed. And I am liberated, so let's celebrate."

Noah's thoughts kept circling back to one question. What about Bri?

"I have to ask you one more thing, Richard." Noah hesitated for a moment, not sure if he wanted the answer or not, then pushed ahead. "Was Brianna taken hostage with you? Or was she on that plane?"

Richard knew this question would come sooner or later. Letting out a deep breath, he replied, "No, Noah, she wasn't with me. I'm sorry, man."

Noah nodded, never lowering his eyes from Richard's. "At least you're home safe."

Noah and Richard easily engaged in a light banter over the next hour. Noah relayed some of the more memorable stories Richard had missed. Noah felt like a part of himself had been restored in getting his friend back, but another part of his heart felt like it had been ripped in half again.

When the news first broke of Richard, Noah had held on to some hope that Brianna would emerge alive, too. But when Richard confirmed she wasn't with him, he knew she had been on that fateful flight, and he felt like he had lost her all over again.

Noah found it challenging to keep his mind on the conversation at times, even though he was glad to be with his old friend again. His mind returned to thoughts of Brianna and how tense their relationship had become those last few weeks they were together. If only he had one more chance with her.

The conversation lagged, and Noah finally said, "I'm going to go now and let you get some rest. You probably have people coming out of the woodwork to talk to you. I'm just glad you're home, man."

Noah felt guilty for the fleeting wish that Brianna had returned instead of Richard…or even with Richard. He was glad for his friend, but something felt off about the circumstances. There were no reports of any demands for his release. The US government didn't negotiate with terrorists, so that wasn't an option either. Something didn't add up in the way that Richard suddenly appeared on the scene, in Miami, and seemingly unscathed.

You sound like a conspiracy theorist now, Reaper. He shook off his suspicious thoughts and chalked it up to the fact that the press hadn't been given a lot of information yet. More would come to light after the government officials decided what unclassified information could be released. His military career had taught him all too well how certain top-secret details would never become declassified.

Climbing into his truck, he pulled out his cell phone and punched in his friend's number. He recounted his visit with Richard to Bull. They ended the call, and Bull promised to relay the information to Rebel.

~

Richard closed the door after Noah left and smiled at his cleverness. So far, so good, he thought smugly. He believed Noah was so shocked to see him that he didn't doubt his concocted story at all. Not yet anyway.

"Now," Richard voiced aloud. "It's time to get my business back up and running."

Richard picked up the phone and dialed. "Remember me, old friend? It's time for me to come back to work. I'll need your help in getting started, and I'll definitely make it worth your while."

The voice on the other end hesitated before he answered. "Richard. Saw your picture in the paper. What can I do for you?"

"Meet me tomorrow night. We need to talk, in person," Richard demanded.

"Let me know where and what time. I'll be there," the man replied.

"One of my men will contact you tomorrow. Looking forward to it."

Richard fisted his hands as he paced in the hotel suite. Angrily, he stalked back and forth across the room, spitting out his thoughts to himself.

"That stupid little bitch. She thought she could beat me. Three years, I've had to lie low, and now I'm going to make her pay for it. Slowly and painfully."

He had a very lucrative business set up before Brianna somehow got ahold of incriminating information against him. She went deep into hiding and took that information with her. Until he got it back, his life was on the line. Technically, he had always been in danger due to the type of people with which he conducted business, but he could handle them. As long as he obtained the goods they needed, there was nothing to worry about.

But Brianna had been on a mission to tell his story, and nothing had swayed her from that. Richard had waited three years for her to show back up at Noah's door. His life and plans had been put on hold while he looked for her. If he'd reappeared before he found her, she would've annihilated him. He thought he had made sure his tracks were covered, but somehow, Brianna found out. He wouldn't make the same mistake again.

When his hired man, Bosco, called to say he'd found Brianna, Richard was elated for the first time in three years. She hadn't left the safety of her hiding place on her own, but he knew that his picture on the front page of every newspaper and internet post would jar her into action. He wagered it all on his assumption that she'd be more worried about Noah's safety than her own. For Noah, she'd let her guard down, and Richard would make sure she disappeared permanently this time.

Richard had recently received word that a dirty CIA agent wanted to make a small fortune in weapons trafficking. The agent turned out to be an old acquaintance from his military days. He planned to use his friend to build up his business again, and more importantly, keep his customers from cutting off his head. His CIA friend would have the right connections to get the specific weapons he needed for this shipment.

Richard made a few more calls to his former friends and business partners. The majority of the men he used as his security team had less than stellar backgrounds, but that type fit his plan perfectly. Someone less educated, less cunning, and with a criminal history made a great fall guy in the event something went wrong. Still, he'd be meticulous in how he set up any business meetings.

Several hours later, darkness fell in Boulder, and Bosco watched lights flicker through the windows along the row of townhouses from his spot in the tree. All of the houses, that is, except Brianna's house. He climbed down from his perch and silently moved across the yards and the street. He walked along the wall at the side of her townhouse to the back sliding glass door. He pulled on the door, and it slid open without a fight.

Bosco called Richard after he searched her townhouse. "She's gone. Yeah, I checked the house. She must have gone out the back. Clever little minx, huh? I'm on the next flight to Miami. Be there in a few hours."

Richard was extremely pleased with himself. He had secured several new contacts, talked business without anyone even knowing, and made a few new deals. His covert venture would be back in full swing soon. It was so much easier to be the bad guy when he looked and acted like the good guy. No one watched his every move when they viewed him as part of the world's elite class.

He was back in his element now, instead of hiding in some dirty third world country. *Damn, the last three years have been hell,* he thought glumly. His last shipment before going into hiding was interrupted, and the buyers were not happy. It was a good thing he had built a long relationship with them and convinced them he could help them in the future. In the meantime, he helped them develop their own supply networks and stayed alive.

His buyers helped him get back into the US because they learned of a new weapon under development, and they wanted it. Richard's DOD job and all his contacts would help him get it. He'd make enough money off this one shipment to retire to his own private island, but he knew he wouldn't stop there. He had some favors to pay back first, though.

It wouldn't be long before Brianna showed up, and he could tie up all the loose ends. He arranged for his face to be plastered across every major newspaper, but he already knew where she was hiding. He had plans for Brianna and Noah.

Noah had served his purpose. *Too bad he started thinking with his dick over that stupid little bitch,* Richard mused smugly.

~

Noah drove to his Steele Security office in downtown Miami. It was a Saturday afternoon, meaning he could've gone home instead of to work. His men were fully capable of planning and coordinating security for the foreign dignitary reception at the Miami Premiere Banquet Hall later that night. He honestly didn't want to go home yet.

The night Noah and Brianna reconnected in the Rainstorm and Bead pub replayed in his mind as he drove. He could see her across the bar, laughing and having fun with her girlfriends on her birthday. He could smell her perfume and feel her touch. The electricity between them hadn't diminished in any way.

When he'd found her, she worked for the *Miami Herald* and frequently traveled for her investigative stories. His new security business was growing by leaps and bounds and occasionally called for him to travel. Regardless of their time demands, they always made time for each other. They stayed up all night and talked for hours on end about everything and anything.

He fell in love with her in every way during their time together. Her love of life and her determination to live each day to the fullest were contagious. She loved to laugh and found humor in most anything. She didn't let daily aggravations and frustrations get her down. She always looked on the bright side and was somewhat naïve to how dangerous the world could be. He had seen the evil firsthand, but she helped balance him with the good that was still in the world.

When she caught wind of a big story that she was both excited and anxious about, she couldn't wait to dive in headfirst. As she investigated and gathered information from various sources, she talked with Noah less and less about it. Whatever it was she found, it had rocked her foundation, changed her, and altered their relationship. She became more reserved, nervous, and he was convinced she looked at him differently. He tried to talk to her about it several times, but he didn't get the answers he needed.

He knew he could push and get the answers he wanted. He was trained to interrogate suspects in numerous ways, and he was good at it, but he drew the line at using those tactics on the woman he loved. If she wasn't ready to talk about it, there was a reason, and he knew he needed to give her space.

Their last conversation continued to haunt him three years later. Brianna had approached him in his office and asked if they could talk about what was going on. He wanted to hear it, get it out in the open, and fix whatever had gone wrong between them. But losing the only woman he'd ever loved was the only thing that frightened him.

He replied that he was too busy at the moment, stating that they'd talk about it later. But his "later" never came.

"If only I'd known that would be the last time I ever saw you." Noah shook the memory from his mind.

He would forever regret how poorly he handled that conversation, the last one he had with her. He still didn't know what she'd found that had changed her so drastically over those last few weeks together. Those unanswered questions were challenging to live with after the fact. His feelings for her didn't change, still hadn't changed, but the regret of not fighting tooth and nail for her, for them, was palpable.

"They say you never know what you have until you lose it. I knew what I had, but I realized too late that I didn't do enough to keep it," he stated aloud.

Brianna was still as much a part of him today as she was on the day he found her again over four years before. It had been three years since she died, and he still thought about her every single day. Noah didn't date for a full year after Brianna's death. He just couldn't bring himself even remotely to care about another woman. He had occasional dates over the past two years, but nothing serious.

Walking into his office, he decided he had to get his mind on work and off of Brianna. The reception planned for later that night was both a blessing and a curse. On the plus side, his firm had been hired to provide additional security for the major international event. His firm worked with the local Miami police department and with various other federal organizations to coordinate coverage. His business was doing very well and had gained significant accolades from influential people in the world. The coverage from tonight would only further that, and then he would focus on opening more security firms in other major cities, employing more former military men in a position that suited their training and discipline.

The downside was he wasn't actually working the event. While he always considered himself to be on duty, his date for the evening didn't. He wasn't looking forward to spending the evening with this particular acquaintance. Alexa Bishop was part of the Miami elite club, and her wealthy family made significant contributions to political campaigns.

The woman was utterly ruthless when it came to business, but her elegant good looks and instant charm fooled many people in the boardroom. They never guessed that she was the biggest shark in the water. She knew what she wanted, and she was accustomed to getting it.

Alexa had made it clear, on more than one occasion, that what she wanted was a commitment and a ring from Noah. He had made it abundantly clear to her that scenario would never happen. He frequently encouraged her to find someone else and get married, because that life was not in the stars for him. She always sidestepped the conversation and acted as though she hadn't heard him.

He wasn't playing hard to get, and deep down, he thought Alexa knew he told her the truth. But for now, they continued to use each other and take what they needed, whether that was an occasional escort to a high-society function or for sex.

Alexa's father, William Bishop, built his business in exporting and shipping goods to other countries. Through his business dealings, he became very familiar with numerous foreign dignitaries, ambassadors, business leaders, and other officials at all levels of the US government. William would rub elbows with all the right people at the event tonight, who could grease the wheels at the shipping ports, speed up the red tape of customs, and make him even wealthier than he already was.

Noah opened his email to double-check any last-minute security changes that were required for the evening's event. He found an updated attendee list that added Richard Hollingsworth to the party.

CHAPTER FIFTEEN

The unsettling feeling of being watched wouldn't go away. So as Brianna's new identification said, "Leslie Solomon" made airline reservations for a flight leaving from Denver early that afternoon. At the beginning of her three years of WITSEC living, she had purchased an older car and parked it in a storage unit that was just over a mile from her current house.

One thing about her townhouse she was grateful for was how the backyards were arranged. Around each yard stood an eight-foot-tall wooden privacy fence with a built-in gate that led to the next yard. Another gate was positioned along the back line of fencing that led to the neighborhood directly behind the townhouses.

Her neighbor to the right of her townhouse was close to her age and had small kids. They talked at least once a week and had left their adjoining gate unlocked in case the kids' toys ended up in the wrong backyard. She knew it wasn't safe to leave through the front door, so she eased out the back sliding glass door, through the gate to her neighbor's yard, and then on to the back gate.

With her current disguise, no one watching would realize she didn't belong to that yard as she walked through the back gate. She was nothing more than a woman visiting for a neighborly chat. She continued walking through the bordering neighborhood and on to her hidden second car.

Inside the Denver airport, she checked in for her flight and walked to the line for security. She knew there were cameras all through the airport, especially at the security checkpoint, so she kept her head down as much as possible while waiting in line, without appearing suspicious. As she neared the TSA agent checking identification and boarding passes, a moment of panic hit her when she realized it had been three years since the Leslie Solomon license had been made.

Drastic changes in appearance raised too many questions in an airport. She handed her license and boarding pass to him and held her breath. He looked at the picture on the license, then at her, then back at the photo, then back at her. He finally made a few marks on her boarding pass and handed it, along with her license, back to her. He eyed her somewhat suspiciously, but when she said with her Southern twang, "Thank you so much," his look softened. He smiled and said, "Have a good flight," before turning to the next person in line.

She made it through the checkpoint without incident and walked to her gate to wait for her flight to Miami. She was sure that her Kristina Miller alias had been compromised, but she wasn't sure if Leslie Solomon had been or not. Until she knew for sure, she had to be extra careful when she arrived in Miami. The newspaper article said Richard Hollingsworth was in Miami, so she knew it wasn't him watching her. But then, she knew he wouldn't do it himself. No, she thought, he would be in Miami...with Noah.

With her thought, she let out an exaggerated and exasperated sigh. She'd have to think this through carefully. There were specific tasks she had to see to herself and plans she had to lay out carefully until this fiasco was over, one way or another. She never felt completely safe in trusting Marshal Stevens. Something about the man just didn't seem right from the beginning, and his lack of surprise over the recent turn of events solidified her resolve.

She heard the airline attendant announce over the intercom that her flight had started to board. Brianna collected her purse, stood with her boarding pass in hand, and waited for her zone to board. As she walked down the jetway, she wasn't sure if she was walking to or from hell, but she had a sneaking suspicion this would be the hardest trip to Miami she would ever make.

She settled into her seat, buckled her seat belt, and listened as the flight attendant reviewed the safety information on the TV screen in front of her. When the plane began to move, she leaned her head back against the seat, closed her eyes, and let her mind rest. She'd been running on an adrenaline-high for several hours now and was beginning to crash. She knew she was safe for at least the next four hours.

She reasoned that even if her current alias had been compromised, no one would try anything on a plane full of people. Once she landed in Miami, she would find a small hotel, pay with cash, and stay out of sight. If anyone recognized her as Brianna Tate, whatever name she used wouldn't save her anyway.

With her head resting on the back of the seat, Brianna closed her eyes as the plane lifted off. Living as someone else for the past three years had exhausted her to the bone. She figured if someone had been watching her townhouse, she had a few hours before he realized she was gone. It was still daylight, and the rain should've started by now. Nothing would appear out of place until later when the darkness inside her home would be evident. Hopefully, she would be settled into some out of the way motel in Miami before then.

She was returning to Miami as Leslie Solomon, but she wished like hell she could just be Brianna Tate and be done with this whole fiasco. She had missed her three sisters and her parents, more than she could bear at times. She had missed so much of their lives. Questions about them taunted her mind. Were any of her sisters married yet? Was she an aunt?

She thought of her mom and dad so often, she could almost see them standing before her. She worried about their health and the strain losing her had put on them. Most of all, she missed laughing with her family, regaling stories of each other during family dinners, and just spending time with them.

Her dad had been such an instrumental part of her getting her first big job after college. Her parents took a chance on real estate development at the most opportune moment. After they made their first small fortune, they decided to expand into high-rise executive offices, and they eventually established their luxury hotel chain across the Eastern US.

Neither of her parents was thrilled with her career choice since they both apparently wanted her to choose a career in business and manage their hotels. But being cooped up in an office every day was never in her plans.

Then there was Noah. She couldn't even articulate how much she still missed him every day. She dreamed of him so often that she expected to conjure him by sheer will. She never had the chance to finish that conversation with him the last day she saw him. It tore her heart out to think that would be the last time they ever talked.

As she drifted off to sleep with the gentle rocking of the plane, her unconscious mind took over and replayed the entire scene in her dreams of when she first met Noah. She woke from her nap full of regret and sadness. As the flight attendant gave instructions for landing, Brianna shifted in her seat and focused on her plans and what she needed to accomplish.

The Miami heat hit her like a brick wall when she stepped out of the airport. Three years away from the excessive heat and humidity felt like an eternity now. She hailed a taxi and gave an address that she knew was a few blocks from Noah's neighborhood. She checked her surroundings but didn't see anyone who appeared to be following her. Regardless, she refused to take any chances.

Once the taxi dropped her off, she walked for about an hour, crossed streets, doubled back, and changed her route several times. Convinced she was not being watched, she found a small, clean hotel and paid cash for her room for two nights. She also ordered the maids to stay away. She removed her pair of miniature binoculars, stowed her backpack in the closet, and started her walk through the affluent subdivision toward Noah's house.

Noah's house was actually more like an estate, set behind a stone and stucco wall that stood six feet tall, complete with a state-of-the-art security system. The wrought-iron gate across the cobblestone driveway was automatic and opened by keypad entry or a remote inside his vehicle. Once inside the house, the alarm had to be disabled within twenty seconds, or the alarm would sound and automatically notify the police.

There were several trees on his property, but she could see the circular drive where it curved at the front door. She found a hiding place and waited as she watched the area. She lifted her binoculars and carefully watched as five black SUVs pulled into the drive, punched in the key code, and drove through the gate. One man after another exited the vehicles. The entire security team was dressed in tuxedos, and all had security earpieces in place.

When Noah walked to the waiting limousine and climbed into the back, her breath seized in her chest, and her heart pounded. He was dressed to the nines in his tuxedo and looked even better than she had remembered. She remained motionless in her hiding place as the vehicles exited his property.

Once they were out of sight, she slid the binoculars into her pocket and casually strolled down the sidewalk. She approached a small café and overheard a patron seated at a sidewalk table mention the streets around the banquet hall were closed. The dining couple complained that all the visiting government officials received special attention and made it difficult for the residents to maneuver around the barricades. She immediately decided a change of plans was in order.

~

Noah and his entourage arrived at the Premiere Banquet Hall for the gala. The hall was immaculately decorated to welcome most of the foreign dignitaries and business leaders of modern civilization. Noah was dressed in his Armani tuxedo and Alexa, his date for the evening, glittered in her formfitting white ball gown on his arm. But his primary concern was always security.

He had dozens of fully capable men stationed throughout the building. Some appeared to be guests, and others were visible security personnel. He walked through the crowd with Alexa, stopped every few feet as she attempted to introduce him to new people, and mingled with the partygoers.

Brianna headed directly to the banquet hall when she figured out that was where Noah would be. She knew she could have—should have–taken that time to get into his house. He'd be preoccupied with the security detail, and the police would be preoccupied with directing traffic and avoiding international incidents. She also knew Richard would be there, but her overwhelming desire to see Noah again won out over her common sense.

She worked her way around to a back entrance, picked up a box off the delivery truck, and followed the others into the serving area. There were several complete black server outfits in various sizes hanging on a rack for the contracted servers. She grabbed a dress and shoes in her sizes and ducked into a storage room to quickly change clothes.

When she emerged fully dressed, she picked up a tray of hors d'oeuvres and exited the kitchen into the main event. She worked her way through the multitudes of people and offered small plates of elegant finger foods. Even with her disguise in place, she was still careful to keep her face turned away from anyone who potentially could recognize her.

Brianna's eyes locked on to Noah and his date. She immediately hated how they looked so happy together as they mingled with the world's elite. Alexa was flawless in this type of setting, and she knew it. She had her arm draped over Noah's arm to keep him close to her. She occasionally splayed her perfectly manicured fingers across Noah's chest as she carried on a conversation with others.

It tore Brianna's heart out to see him with someone else. He looked so happy with another woman on his arm, at his side. She never expected him to live alone for the rest of his life, but it still shredded her heart to witness it firsthand.

A familiar voice caught her attention and pulled her gaze away from Noah. Richard. She was careful to approach him from behind. She tried to eavesdrop on his conversations while keeping her back to him. She overheard him telling another guest where he was staying while in Miami and how he enjoyed the exclusivity of that luxury hotel.

Then she turned and saw Noah looking directly at her, and her heart stopped beating in her chest.

"Noah, this is Ambassador Bachar of Turkey," Alexa purred and poured on the charm. Noah had smiled, nodded, and started to introduce himself when he caught a glimpse of someone who looked vaguely familiar.

He walked a few steps away from Alexa and heard her make excuses for him "always working." He kept moving through the crowd as he tried to locate the woman he had just seen. She was dressed as one of the servers, but there was something about her he instinctively recognized.

When a large group moved directly in front of her, blocking Noah's line of sight, she turned and quickly fled to the kitchen. There were several hallways behind the kitchen used only for waitstaff and deliveries. If she could make it to the hall before Noah found her in the kitchen, she could get away. She walked as fast as she could without drawing attention to herself. She was almost to the door when she heard that familiar deep, male voice call out to her. "Hey, wait a second!"

The kitchen staff was buzzing about, keeping the food and drinks flowing, and preparing the main course meal for the hundreds of people in attendance. She glanced over her shoulder to see Noah standing in the doorway at the other end of the massive industrial-sized kitchen, with two large cooks blocking his way as they tried to exit the kitchen with the first course.

She snapped her head back around and kept walking through the door.

When she was safely in the hallway, she grabbed her stashed belongings and ran as hard as she could in heels. Once out of the building, she slowed to a casual walking pace, hopped in a taxi waiting nearby, and went straight back to her hotel room.

That was way too close, she thought.

After that near heart attack, Brianna was angry with herself for almost getting caught. *So stupid! Stupid! Stupid! Stupid!* She silently admonished herself for giving in to her curiosity and desire to see Noah again.

She opened her suitcase and pulled on her black yoga pants and a black tank top. She put a black, long-sleeve turtleneck shirt, the black spandex gloves, and a ski mask in her purse. She couldn't wear them just yet. Even at night, Miami in May was nowhere near cool enough to wear any of that type of clothing.

She sat alone in her barren motel room and waited until it was late enough that most people would be tucked away in their homes. Accustomed to planning every detail, she went over the steps she'd need to take to get into Noah's house. Watching the alarm code key through the binoculars earlier had been a stroke of luck.

Seeing Noah with another woman on his arm was excruciating. Brianna only hoped she could get in and out of his house undetected with the proof that would tie Richard to everything. Noah had obviously moved on without her, and she saw no reason to disrupt his life. She could return to Atlanta, to her family, and he'd never have to know.

The streets quieted, traffic was sparse, and most lights were off in the surrounding houses. Brianna set out on foot on her original route to Noah's house. Once she reached his street, she kept to the shadows until she reached Noah's estate. Brianna stopped behind a tree, put on the long-sleeve shirt, ski mask, and gloves, and hid her purse. She crouched down and moved along the concrete and stucco fence to the backyard.

Noah had a walk-through gate on the back of the property that would be much less conspicuous than walking up to the front gate that spanned his entire driveway. The back gate had the same keypad entry as the front one, and she crossed her fingers that she correctly read the code she'd seen used earlier.

She stayed low to keep out of the view of the cameras positioned strategically around the property. Once she reached the gate, she waited for the camera to start its movement toward the opposite direction. Then she stepped up to the keypad and entered the set of four numbers. The red light blinked. Two more tries before the alarm was tripped. She took a deep breath and held it while she entered the numbers again. She breathed a huge sigh of relief when the green light blinked, and the gate popped open.

She closed the gate behind her and stealthily approached the back door of the house. She was on the grounds, but she still needed to avoid any motion sensor lights or nosy neighbors that watched the front of the house. She pulled the tools to pick the lock out of her bra and quickly had the door open. The alarm beeped as she rushed to it. She keyed in the code to reset it before the alarm sounded.

She turned to walk away and suddenly had a second thought. On the off chance that any of his men came to the house that night, they would know someone was there if the alarm wasn't set.

A security firm owner with an elite military background who forgot to set his alarm before he left? Um, no, not happening, she thought sardonically.

She quickly reset the alarm and silently made her way to the front of the house, up the curved marble staircase to the second floor. The landing at the top of the stairs overlooked the entryway of the front door. Directly behind the landing was a long hallway with the master bedroom at the end. Brianna moved silently down the hall to one of the guest bedrooms.

CHAPTER SIXTEEN

N*o way. It couldn't have been.* Noah repeated that mantra in his head for the rest of the night. She moved like Brianna. Her hair was the wrong color, but he smelled her scent. He caught it as he followed her through the crowd and into the kitchen. He could trace that scent anywhere. It had stayed with him and tortured his mind and senses long after Brianna died.

He couldn't get into the kitchen to follow her out the back door. The kitchen manager was furious with him for delaying the first course for even a couple of minutes. He decided to wait for her to come back out to help serve, then he would look at her up close. But she never reappeared. His tolerance for this setting grew thin. His date made it clear she wasn't happy with his behavior, but damned if he cared. Alexa was the last person on his mind tonight.

He somehow managed to make it through all four courses and stood outside the building waiting for his limousine to pull up. Alexa smiled and kissed the air at everyone's cheek that passed. She said her goodbyes and had a few "let's do lunch next week" conversations. It took every bit of Noah's strength to keep from just walking home and leaving her standing on the sidewalk, alone.

Finally, he thought. The limousine arrived, and he took Alexa's elbow and guided her into the back seat. He gave the driver Alexa's address and rolled up the divider window. "So, I guess we're staying at my house again tonight," she said with a sigh of aggravation.

Alexa assumed he would spend the night with her. She had often complained they always went to her place and never his, not even once. He couldn't tell her that he couldn't share his bed with her. Not the bed he had shared with Brianna. Not the bed where her essence still slept with him every night.

She turned to him, caressed the side of his face, and moved closer to him. He knew what was on her mind. "Not tonight, Alexa," he stated with finality. "You're going to your house, and I'm going to mine tonight."

She stayed mad at him for the rest of the ride, but Noah didn't care. He just wanted to go home, alone. His ghosts were back. After he dropped Alexa off at her house, he couldn't get Brianna off his mind. She was never really far from his thoughts, but some days were worse than others. Today was one of those worse days.

After her plane exploded, Noah tried to backtrack the limited information she'd shared but came up with dead ends. He went through all her notes that were left behind, trying to find any scribbling that was remotely related to her trip to Turkey but turned up with zilch.

His current thoughts were interrupted when he felt the limousine slow down, and he realized they were pulling in his driveway. His homecoming was to a dark house. *Perfect,* he thought. *Matches my mood.*

Noah's limo dropped him off at his front door and then drove off. He walked to the front door with his head down, looking at his feet as he walked. After he unlocked the door, he moved to the keypad to turn off the house alarm and went straight to his office. He wanted to look at the list of servers again to try to narrow down which one had disappeared. After he saw his ghost, he made it a point to memorize every woman's name tag. The name of the one who gave him the slip had to be there.

His home office was on the first floor and in the back corner of the house. He wanted it away from the kitchen, entry, and bedrooms to keep the distractions to a minimum, but on the main level for a quick exit strategy. His security system cameras transmitted back to a recorder in his office, and he could watch the cameras in real-time on a flat screen TV mounted on the wall.

He sat at his desk and huffed as he went through the names on the list of servers at the banquet hall. He located the missing name, but her picture showed she was a tall, thin Hispanic woman. Definitely not the woman he saw that night. They had a security breach on his watch, and he had no idea what that even meant yet.

He picked up the remote for the TV and did a double take at what he saw on the internal security camera. Someone was in his house. On the second floor. At that very moment.

Not that he needed backup, but with the security breach at an international gathering earlier tonight, he didn't want to take any chances. He called Bull and relayed what he knew as he watched the dark figure walk down the hallway toward his bedroom. It then quickly turned right into a guest bedroom.

Bull said he would call Rebel, and they would be at his house within three minutes. Noah hung up, took off his tuxedo jacket, and started climbing the curved staircase.

His Glock .40 was drawn and held down at his leg. He wouldn't use lethal force in his house unless he had no other choice. He'd rather take the son of a bitch alive and make sure he paid for breaking in to the wrong home. He heard a creak in the wood floor and froze on the landing at the top of the stairs.

With his back against the wall, he waited to turn the corner of the wall to enter the hallway. Just as he started to turn, he heard a noise on the first floor. He had watched the cameras and was positive there was only one person in the house with him.

He went down the back stairs, Noah guessed.

He ran back down the stairs, around the corner, and into the den that was at the back of the house. Just as he reached the room, he saw a black-cloaked figure crouched down beside his leather sofa. The intruder hadn't seen him yet.

He was trained to move silently in the night, but this person was apparently less adept at it. As the intruder made a move toward the back door, Noah rammed into him. Noah heard an "oomph" when he knocked the breath out of the other guy before he fell to the ground.

Brianna didn't hear Noah come in, and she certainly didn't hear him come up behind her. *Damn, that hurts,* she thought as she struggled to right herself. Unable to take in a breath, she staggered to her feet and clumsily ran toward a row of glass patio doors. The room was full of oversized furniture—the couch, love seat, end tables, and coffee tables.

She had a straight line to the doors, but Noah had to run around his furniture. As big and quick as he was, he wasn't fast enough to get to her before she was out the door and running across the yard. It also helped that he was still wearing his tuxedo shoes and he didn't have good traction in the grass.

She made it to the wall and used a lawn ornament as a stepping stool to jump on top of the fence and scale over it. She ran until she reached her hiding spot where she gathered her purse. She took off the mask, shirt, and gloves, stuffed them into her bag, and then nonchalantly walked down the sidewalk.

"Where'd he go? Where is he?" Noah yelled, severely pissed by that point. Bull had pulled up just as the intruder jumped over the fence. Noah ran to the gate, punched in the numbers, and impatiently waited for it to open wide enough for him to get through it. He jumped into the SUV with Bull and yelled, "Go! Go!" Next, he only had to find the son of a bitch and secure him until the police got there.

Bull slowed down when he reached the intersection, and they scanned the few people milling about for anyone who fit the description. There were very few men on the street, and none of them had the right build. Noah kept looking down the road; his eyes scanned each person and mentally calculated if he or she could be the one. Then he saw her, with the short black hair, lean, muscular body, black pants, and a black tank top. There was also something black that protruded from her bag.

Noah yelled, "Her! Right there in the black! Don't let her get away!"

Bull punched the gas, and the tires screeched. She turned and looked in their direction, and Noah immediately recognized her as the woman at the banquet earlier. Bull relayed their location and situation to Rebel, who had also called in a couple extra guys. No way was anyone getting the best of him two times in one night.

When she heard screeching tires behind her, she took off in a sprint.

Oh shit, she screamed in her mind.

Brianna immediately realized she'd been made. As she turned the corner at the end of the block, she took off running in a dead heat. Her fear and adrenaline pushed her harder and harder. The sound of SUVs closing in on her drove her to a near panic attack.

She turned a sharp left and ran across a vacant lot. The SUVs had already passed the street where they could've turned, and the next street up was a one-way street in the wrong direction. She kept running until she came to a dark parking garage. She needed a break to catch her breath, so she ran inside and hid between two cars. The garage required a key card to enter and had orange and white wooden arms to prevent unauthorized entry.

The sound of wood splitting and splintering told her the arms were of very little use in this situation. The men were too determined to find her. She stayed crouched down and moved between the cars as she worked her way to the exit. She didn't know where she would go next, but she knew she was a sitting duck in this garage.

She stayed down until she didn't hear the vehicles any longer, and then she made a run for it. As quickly as she darted out from between the cars, the SUVs descended on her from every direction and boxed her in with the concrete wall behind her.

Several large men stepped out of the SUVs, guns drawn, yelling at her to put her hands up. She raised her hands above her head and watched as Noah exited the SUV directly in front of her. She tried to resist openly staring at him and only allowed her eyes to glance up at him fleetingly. She was still in her costume, with her wig, colored contact lenses, and thick eyeliner to change the shape of her eyes, but she knew she'd be found out in a split second.

As Noah stepped out of the vehicle, his eyes lasered in on the woman who dared to break in to his house. He reverted to his years of training to keep his anger under control with her. He took a step toward her and momentarily froze in his tracks. The way her body moved and the way she carried herself reminded him so much of Brianna.

She's thinner than Brianna, he thought. *Her hair is all wrong, and so is her eye color. But I see Brianna when I look at her.*

Just the thought of someone else reminding him of Brianna pissed him off. He was infuriated because a common criminal caused him even to compare her to his Brianna. He sauntered toward her and never took his eyes off hers, his anger rolling off him in waves.

Brianna knew he didn't recognize her yet, but she knew the expression on his face all too well. He smiled, but it wasn't his friendly smile at all. There was no humor in his eyes. For the first time since she met him all those years ago, she was afraid of him.

"I have a few questions to ask you. And you will answer them. You will give me all the information I want, or you will be sorry. We understand each other." He didn't ask a question. He made a statement, and it was not up for debate.

Noah glared at the lady in black who refused to look up at him. If she thought not making eye contact with him while he spoke was a sign of submission that would make him go easy on her, she was dead wrong. She didn't move a muscle. He wasn't even sure she was breathing.

Definitely scared. Definitely an amateur, Noah thought.

"You were at the banquet tonight."

Even though he didn't state it as a question, she knew he expected confirmation.

The large men with him moved toward her. She couldn't turn her head to look, but she was sure the biggest one of them stepped directly behind her. She couldn't see him, but she felt the power emanating from him. She kept her eyes trained on the floor and watched as Noah's feet approached her.

When his feet stopped, she chanced a glance up at him. He narrowed his eyes slightly at her and tilted his head to the side. From the look he shot her, he was very pissed that he hadn't received a response from her yet, but there was a hint of recognition in his eyes. She knew he'd figure it out at any second. She quickly lowered her eyes, tilted her head, and allowed the short hair from her wig to partially cover her face.

"And then you were in my house." This time, he bit the words out, anger lacing each syllable. "Now, I want to know why."

He stood so close to her that she could smell his cologne. She felt the scrutiny of his eyes as he assessed her. She knew he read her body language, read her eyes, and looked for information to use against her. She knew she probably gave him more than he needed. She didn't have a backup plan in the event she was caught, so her mind raced to come up with one at the last minute.

She quickly considered her choices.

If I speak, he will recognize my voice.

If I don't speak, I don't know what he will do with me.

If he calls the cops, then what do I do?

Is there any chance in hell I can run and get away from all these guys?

The questions flew through her mind in all of about one second, but she felt like she had been standing there, tongue-tied, for hours. She realized too late that she'd taken her eyes off the floor and had looked at the exit. That told him exactly what she thought about.

She realized her mistake, and her eyes flew back to Noah. She saw the slight nod of his head toward the giant that stood behind her and instantly knew that she was busted. Before she could move, the man behind her grabbed her upper arms, and Noah moved in on her. He then stood directly in her face.

Mmmm...he smells so good.

Stop that! Focus!

Brianna suppressed a groan. If she wasn't careful, her inner dialogue could be the death of her.

Noah grabbed her wrists in his massive hands, dug his fingers into her flesh, and squeezed as he pulled them down to put a pair of zip-tie cuffs on her.

"Oww! Damn it!" She scowled at the sudden pain in her wrists.

Noah stopped and looked at her, really looked at her, as if he were just seeing her for the first time. As if he'd just seen a ghost.

"What the hell?" He looked hard into her eyes, took a step back, as his hand flew to his face. He raked his hand across the stubble forming on his jaw and then bent to look more closely at her face.

"Bri-Brianna?"

Noah, Bull, and Rebel all looked as if they had seen a ghost. They all stood still and just gawked at her. She knew the very second they finally saw past her disguise. Noah's ordinarily unreadable face displayed his wide variety of emotion. It ranged from complete surprise and shock, to elation, and then to anger.

He was really, really angry.

Well, hell, here it comes, Brianna thought.

He paced back and forth in the garage as he tried to burn off the extra energy from his sudden adrenaline dump. His body temperature spiked from his intense fury. When he first realized she actually was Brianna, he thought his prayers had finally been answered. But when he realized that she was alive, had been at the gala, and then in his house, he knew he had been played the fool. The Brianna he loved became a figment of his imagination, replaced by the liar who'd put him through hell.

He vowed to himself to break her, just as she'd broken him.

"I understand now. Did you miss me, Bri? You crashed the party at the banquet. Then you broke in to my house." His voice trailed off, but the anger was definitely still there, and his words dripped with sarcasm.

Brianna looked from Noah to Bull. His narrowed eyes and the blatant glare in his gaze told her any trust she had previously earned from him was completely gone. And that fact really hurt.

"No, on second thought, missing me couldn't be why you're here now.

Because you let me believe you died three years ago. Clearly, you're not dead. So, no, you didn't miss me," Noah continued.

Brianna looked at Rebel and tried to get a read on him, but his face was expressionless. His face was like stone, except for the muscle that twitched ever so slightly in his jaw from clenching his teeth so hard. That wasn't a good sign either.

Noah continued. "So, baby, what exactly did you steal from my house?"

Steal from him? He thinks I broke in to take his things? Brianna's mind raced.

Brianna tried to comprehend his question, but she could only shake her head. The man behind her still held on to her shoulders so that she couldn't run. But at that moment, she knew he was probably the only thing that prevented her knees from buckling under her.

One side of Noah's mouth curved into a half grin, but she knew he found nothing funny about this situation. He took a few steps closer to her, and she instinctively tried to back up, but realized the man behind her was as hard as a concrete wall and just as immovable. Noah took another step closer so that they then stood toe-to-toe. Noah towered over her in front, and the concrete mountain of a man towered over her from behind.

In a flash, Noah raised his hand to her cheek, and she winced as though she prepared for him to hit her. His hand froze beside her face, not having made contact yet. His eyes squinted in obvious disgust and dislike of her response to him.

Like I would ever intentionally hurt her, Noah thought.

He rubbed his knuckles across her cheek and then cupped it in the palm of his hand. She leaned into it longingly as she savored the feel of his hand on her. He ran his hand around to the back of her neck and pulled her face to his. He covered her mouth with his then his tongue pushed against her lips to ask for access.

She opened her mouth to him, and he kissed her passionately. His other hand came up to meet her neckline. He softly caressed her collarbone before he moved down across the skin of her chest that showed through her tank top. The other hand moved down her back and around to her side before he gripped her hip.

Damn, you feel so good. I've missed you so much, Noah. Brianna's thoughts betrayed her.

Lost in his kiss and her thoughts, she realized too late what he'd done. He pulled her hotel key card out from under her bra strap and backed away from her. He turned to Bull and Rebel without so much as a single word to her.

"Interesting place to keep a hotel room key," Noah said as he handed the card to Bull. Brianna knew her face displayed the shock, then the anger at how easily he'd manipulated her. However, she was glad he had not felt any lower, or he would've found what else she had hidden in her bra.

"What do you want to do with her, boss? Want me to call the police?" The man behind her asked Noah. She didn't know him, and he obviously didn't know her connection to Noah, Bull, and Rebel. She wondered where Shadow was but didn't dare ask.

Noah looked at Brianna as he considered what to do with her. She didn't realize she shook her head from side to side until he spoke.

"No? Don't want the police involved?" It was a rhetorical question. He stared at her for a few seconds longer.

Brianna finally spoke. "I really don't think you want the police involved. Can we decide this somewhere other than here? I'm not sure it's safe."

Noah's anger was in full fury then as he growled. "Put her in the car. Bull, Rebel, you two ride with us."

Bull took Brianna's arm and put her in the back seat of the SUV, behind the passenger seat. He walked around to slide in behind the wheel, Rebel climbed in the front passenger seat, and Noah sat in the backseat with her, his back against the door and his body turned to face her.

"Where to, boss?" Bull asked.

"My house," Noah replied, and Bull put the SUV in gear. Brianna felt Noah's eyes on her as Bull pulled out of the garage. She didn't dare look at him yet. Traffic was light just after one o'clock in the morning, and Bull easily maneuvered into the right-hand lane of the highway. She leaned her head to her left to look around the seat and saw a traffic light a few hundred yards away. Her eyes drifted up to the rearview mirror where she saw Bull watching her intently.

The hatred in his eyes made her shrink back into her seat. She was glad she couldn't see Rebel's eyes, but she knew he wouldn't feel any different. She finally looked over her shoulder at Noah, saw the same look in his eyes, and felt the vise cinch around her heart a little tighter.

She swallowed hard and said, "Look, I know this is...complicated...but it would really be best for everyone if you just let me go."

From the front seat, she heard Rebel's sarcastic tone. "You must be joking."

Trying her hardest to keep her voice even, Brianna answered, "No, I'm not. Let me go. I will leave, and you will never see me again. I won't make any trouble. We were all friends once, weren't we?"

No response, so she continued. "I really tried not to disrupt your lives. When you realized I was really alive, how did you feel at first? Honestly?"

She had seen their faces when they realized who she was and knew they were shocked. But if they were glad to see her at all, she'd use that to try to convince them to let her go.

Noah and Bull answered in unison. "Angry."

Brianna's eyes grew wide, and her mouth gaped open. She had not expected that response at all. She felt as though all the air had been sucked out of her lungs, and the vise around her heart split it in two. She barely choked back the tears that stung the back of her eyes before she managed a response, her voice just above a whisper.

"Angry? You're angry that I'm still alive? You don't even care why?" Her eyes were darting back and forth between Noah and Bull, searching for any sliver of remorse. But she found none—only cold stares.

Softly, and with great difficulty, she choked out, "Rebel? You too?"

He had no response.

She stared out the window, pulled her feet up in the seat, and curled into her legs. As hard as she tried, she couldn't stop the tears that flowed down her face. She had expected Noah to be angry that she hadn't called or come back in the last three years. Mad that he was fooled and that she had been living somewhere else. But being mad because she was alive was just cruel. Even though their relationship had been strained before she disappeared, she never even considered that he didn't care about her welfare at all.

The past three years had been pure hell on her. Noah, her friends, and her family were always on her mind. The love she had for them was overwhelming, and each day away from them made it worse, not better. The loneliness was hard to deal with, but their safety kept her going.

Mostly to herself, she whispered, "I've lost everything." She could see Noah's face in the reflection of the glass as he watched her, studied her, and determined his next move.

"What was that? I couldn't hear you." She knew damn well he heard her. He was just being an ass.

She shook her head. "Nothing."

She didn't turn to look at him. She continued to stare out the window at nothing in particular. The tears continued to flow down her cheeks and her neck, but she didn't bother to wipe them away.

Bull pulled into the left lane to maneuver around a slow-moving car. Just as they passed it, the car sped up and pulled alongside them. Brianna shifted her eyes to look at the driver and saw him point a pistol with a silencer out of the driver's window.

She screamed, "Gun! Get down!"

She hurled her body to the left, landed with her back against Noah, and faced the gunman. She waited for the shattered glass and searing pain of the bullet. She held her breath but didn't move until Noah put his hands on her shoulders, picked her up, and sat her back in her seat. She opened her eyes and saw the glass was still intact. Bewildered, she looked at him, and he simply said, "Bulletproof glass."

The man shot two rounds at the SUV before he realized his mistake. He then turned and raced down a side street away from them. Rebel called one of the other men in the second SUV to pursue the shooter. Brianna was shaken to the core when she realized that man was probably the one who found her in Colorado.

She looked at Noah. Her voice was watery and quivered, and she was unable to stop her body from shaking. She pleaded with him. "Please, Noah. Just stop and let me out here. I'll find my way back on my own."

He looked at her as if she'd lost her mind. "A man just shot at us, and you want me to stop and let you out? You want him to come back and shoot you in the head at point-blank range?"

She shot back, "What do you care? One less thing for all of you to be angry about."

Richard and Brianna both show up alive within hours of each other? Noah knew better than to think that was a coincidence, but he hadn't yet figured out the connection.

No time like the present to find out, he thought.

Noah leaned forward, closer to her. "No, I don't think I will let you out here. Maybe I'll just take you to Richard."

Her head jerked to meet his eyes, and he saw complete terror in her eyes. That terror wasn't there before, even after the guy shot at her. That was definitely not the reaction he had expected from her. At one point, he had suspected something was going on between Richard and Brianna. He never really believed she was cheating on him with Richard, but he wasn't sure what exactly was going on.

Noah remembered Brianna brought Richard up frequently in conversation, always asking questions about him. She asked about how they met and about their business dealings. She was careful about the way she questioned him, but Noah was suspicious, nonetheless.

Brianna turned her head to appear as if she was looking straight ahead, but Noah saw her eyes darting in all directions. He could see every muscle tense in her body, and her breathing and pulse rate had increased dramatically. He knew she hit the flight-or-fight mode in an adrenaline dump, and she was definitely terrified of something.

She looked back at him, and the pain in her voice was palpable. "You would really do that to me?"

He let out a disgusted "humph" as his response.

The SUV slowed for a red light as she looked back out the side window. Lightning fast, she grabbed the door lock and the handle, jumped from the vehicle, slammed the door behind her, and ran as hard as she could.

Bull had also been watching her, but he was a split second too late on hitting the automatic door locks. Just as she slammed the door shut, Noah slid across the back seat, but he was locked in, giving her a good head start on him.

Noah chased her down the side street, as Bull honked the horn and finally got around the cars that waited at the red light. Brianna scanned the area ahead as she looked for an escape route. She saw an abandoned house with a fenced backyard. Behind it were a few more houses and what appeared to be an apartment complex.

She jumped the chain link fence and kept going until she reached the apartment complex. She hid in the shadows and stayed close to the buildings. She spotted another main road a couple of blocks down. Fear propelled her. Fear that Noah would really take her to Richard. Fear that she had misjudged him and he was really part of everything she had uncovered.

Why else would he have said that? she asked herself.

Pushing off like an Olympic runner, she headed in the direction of the cars and a crowd of people when she was suddenly engulfed from behind. Big, muscular arms circled her and pinned her arms in front. A long, muscular leg looped one of hers and made it impossible to move.

Noah's deep voice growled in her ear. "You're not going anywhere." The SUV slid into the parking lot in front of them. Bull and Rebel got out of the car and approached them as Noah released his hold on her.

She was boxed in, and there was no way out. She was close to hysterical by that time. She shook her head and held her tied hands out in front of her to keep them at bay. Through her tears, she repeated her plea. "Just let me go."

Noah didn't know what was going on, but he sure as hell intended to find out. He tried to coax her. "Bri. Just get back in the car."

"No! You're not taking me to him!"

The three men gathered around her and led her back to the SUV. She climbed in the back, Noah sat on one side, and Rebel sat on the other, sandwiching her in the middle. She pulled her feet up on the seat, wrapped her arms around her legs with her chin resting on her knees, and let the steady stream of tears continue to flow from her eyes.

Bull looked at her in the rearview mirror and saw the fear and defeat in her eyes. He was still mad that she had betrayed his trust. With his low, gruff voice, he started, "Sunny, look—"

She quickly cut him off. "Don't. Call. Me. That. That was a nickname given to me by friends, who swore always to be my brothers!"

She could feel all three sets of eyes on her, but she refused to look at any of them. She didn't want to see the hatred in their eyes, feel their icy stares, or sense their indifference toward her safety.

A few moments later, with no emotion left in her voice, she added, "Those men don't even exist anymore." Three of "those men" were in the SUV with her and had all turned their backs on her.

She leaned her head back against the headrest and closed her eyes. God, she was tired.

Once inside his house, Noah walked Brianna to the den and told her to stay there. In case she decided to run again, he activated the security alarm to lock all the doors and windows. Noah, Bull, and Rebel went into the office to watch the security tape again. The camera didn't capture whatever she did in the bedroom, and there was nothing in her hands when she came out.

They speculated that she might have planted something in there, but that didn't seem reasonable since he never used that bedroom. There was nothing in her hands when she went in. They rehashed the events of the night again, trying to make sense of it and come up with a plan.

Rebel's cell phone chirped, and he had a short conversation with the other security team. Hanging up, he looked at Noah. "Dude got away. They chased him, but he abandoned his car and took off on foot. Tags came back stolen."

Frustrated, Noah raked his hand through his hair and let out a loud sigh. "I don't know who's trying to kill her, or what she's up to. But she sure as hell didn't think of me when she brought all this shit to my front door."

Rebel leveled his gaze at Noah and said, "Brother, you know I got your back, but you may be too close to the trees to see the forest on this one."

"What do you mean?" Noah's frustration was growing.

"Man, look. I'm just looking at the facts. One, she tried to get away from you. Two, when the guy shot at her, she wasn't trying to save herself—"

"What the hell do you mean, 'she wasn't trying to save herself'?" Noah growled.

"If she were trying to save herself, she would've lain down in the seat or the floorboard or, hell, man, even just bent over. But she didn't. She used her body to shield you. We are trained to handle that kind of stress—she's not. Most any civilian—and a lot of soldiers, for that matter—would panic in that situation, Reap. I saw her face, man. She didn't know that was bulletproof glass. She was protecting you from that bullet."

Noah put his head in his hands and blew out a breath he didn't even realize he was holding.

"And three," Rebel continued. "She begged to be let out of the car, even after dude tried to shoot her. That doesn't sound like someone who's trying to bring trouble to your door."

A small voice at the door said, "He wasn't aiming at me."

All three men whirled around and looked at her, trying to take in what she said. Then Bull spat out a response. "What the hell did you just say?"

Brianna looked at each of the men, feeling partially afraid of the repercussions she would face for intruding on their male bonding time. She had only heard the last part of what Rebel was saying, but she knew he was referring to the guy who shot at them earlier.

She took a deep breath and said, "He wasn't aiming at me. He was aiming at Noah."

Rebel turned back to Noah and gave him an *I-told-you-so* look. Noah looked back at the doorway, and Brianna was gone. The three men filed out of the office and back to the den. They found her sitting on the leather couch in the darkened room. Noah turned on a lamp, sat in his recliner, and the other men each took a seat. One sat in the second recliner and one on the love seat.

Surrounded again, Brianna sighed inwardly.

Noah couldn't get used to seeing her with the short, black hair. She always had long blond hair, and he remembered how he loved to run his fingers through it.

She'd lost a lot of weight too, he realized. She was always lean and muscular, but she seemed to be thinner than he remembered. She definitely looked tired. Noah considered it had been a long day for her, but she looked utterly undone. He hesitated to ask her any questions because he was concerned she would shatter to pieces if he did. She wasn't crying any longer, but her eyes were red-rimmed, bloodshot, and swollen.

Without saying a word, he rose and walked to her, squatted in front of her, and took her wrists in his hands to remove the zip-tie cuffs. When he grabbed her wrists, she winced in pain, but she didn't say anything or make a sound. He opened his fingers, her wrists resting in the palm of his hands. He saw the lines of dark purple bruises in the shape of fingertips against her pale skin on both wrists.

"Did I do this to you?" Guilt riddled his voice because he knew the answer. His eyes searched hers for some reaction, but she just pulled her hands away and looked down. He was still outraged and hurt, but he would never physically hurt Brianna intentionally.

"It doesn't matter." There was no self-pity in her voice. She wasn't trying to make him feel bad for what he'd done. She just stated a fact, as if she deserved it.

He pulled a knife from his pocket and cut the ties from her hands. She absently rubbed the indentions they had left on her wrists, and he realized he had zipped them a little too tight. She had never complained about it. He stayed squatted in front of her and watched her, but she wouldn't look at him. He looked at Bull and then at Rebel, but they both watched her.

"Can I please use your shower?"

He didn't know how such an innocent question could hurt him so much. Brianna had had her own apartment when they first started dating, but she had practically lived there with him. She had slept in his bed. She had made love to him all night in his bed, his shower, and most everywhere else in the house. But she was asking for permission to use his shower?

"Sure. Don't even think about trying to run, though." He kept his voice even to hide all the emotions lying just underneath the surface. He stood but stayed in front of her. He offered his hand to help her up, but she didn't take it.

"Thank you." And with that, she quietly left the room as she continued to avoid looking at anyone.

Inside the bathroom, she broke down again, unable to stop the tears and body shakes. During the quiet part of the ride, she'd had time to think and sort through the events of the night. When she saw the man raise the gun and aim at Noah, her heart sank to her knees.

She knew Noah didn't love her anymore. He viewed her disappearance as betrayal, and loyalty was not an option with these guys. Noah didn't understand, and there was no way he would believe her word at that point.

Even with that, and the fact that he was angry she was even still alive, she couldn't stop her traitorous heart from loving him. And she couldn't bear the thought of him getting hurt because of her. She knew what she had to do. But first, she knew he and the others had questions that needed to be answered. She decided to tell them whatever they wanted to know.

She thought solemnly, *What could it hurt now?*

She removed the wig and the hair cap, and the pain behind her eyes let up slightly. She knew she would have one hell of a headache after crying so much. She ran her fingers through her matted hair and started the water for her shower. She made it as hot as she could stand it. She was surprised her colored contact lenses hadn't been washed away with all of her tears.

She tried to wash away the pain and dread of what she knew was still to come. She shampooed her long blond hair and applied conditioner since it would definitely need it after being under that wig for so long. Once she had rinsed off, she sat on the tile floor with her back against the built-in seat and sobbed until the water ran cold.

After she dried off, she realized she didn't bring any clothes with her to change into. They'd driven straight here, and her backpack was still in the hotel room. She wrapped the towel around her and stepped out into Noah's bedroom. She intended to ask him if he could spare a T-shirt for her to sleep in for the rest of the night, or morning, whatever it was then. She knew he had decided she would stay at his house until he figured out what he should do with her.

She walked by the bed and noticed a pair of pajamas laid out across the bed. Her heart nearly stopped when she thought that Noah's girlfriend had come over while she was in the shower. She never expected him not to date anyone after her "death," but she couldn't be in the same house with them. She couldn't sleep in the next room knowing another woman was in bed with him. Visions of them together played in her mind, and she shook her head to get rid of the images.

She felt like she was about to hyperventilate when something registered in her brain and she realized they were her old pajamas. Noah had laid out a pink cotton tank top with spaghetti straps and pink pajama pants with white polka dots for her. She quickly dressed and towel-dried her hair. She was much too tired to mess with the hair dryer right at that moment. Reluctantly, she made her way back downstairs.

She heard muffled voices in the den and knew the guys were still in there talking, so she went to the kitchen instead. Her eyes and head hurt from crying, so she left the light off and stood at the huge picture window to look at the pool water sparkle from the underwater lights.

The lights changed colors, reflecting throughout the decorative water fountains in the middle of the pool and the waterfall at the other end. Brianna always loved to watch the water at night. Water and waves had such a calming effect on her, and she desperately needed it right then.

She felt the air in the room change, energize almost, with body heat, muscles, nervous energy, and testosterone. She knew that Noah, Bull, and Rebel stood behind her in the dark.

"What do you want to know?" She didn't turn around.

"Everything," Noah said flatly as he flipped on the kitchen light. He turned to look at her and stopped dead in his tracks. Her blond hair was back, still a little damp, but no doubt, it was blond and long again.

Damn, he thought, *she's been wearing a wig this whole time.* He wondered if he'd lost his edge but quickly dismissed it as shock and stress.

He'd suspected she'd lost weight, but seeing her standing there removed all doubt. The pajamas he'd laid out for her fit her perfectly at one time. He always loved how her body filled them out. That night, they hung loosely on her, and she looked so...lost.

She stood with her back to them and stared out the window with her head slightly tilted down. Her arms were wrapped around her waist as if she tried to protect herself. Noah stood with his friends, but she was alone.

A thought hit him so hard it almost felt like a punch to the gut. Has she been alone all this time?

"Where do you want to start?" Her voice came out so soft but strained, as she worked to hold back the tears.

Noah had heard her sobs in the shower when he laid out her pajamas. Her pain sounded so raw, so real, that he almost walked into the bathroom just to hold her. The sounds were faint at first, but as Noah walked closer to the bathroom door, he distinctly heard her pain. Old feelings rose in his chest, and he put his hand on the doorknob, intent to rush in to comfort her. Then he remembered attending her funeral...her fake funeral...and he backed away from the door.

He decided that then wasn't the time to reminisce.

"Is there a boyfriend I need to be concerned about showing up here, looking for you?"

"No."

A snort and a sarcastic comment Noah couldn't withhold. "Oh, let me guess...he probably thinks you're dead, too."

Both heads snapped in his direction as Bull and Rebel looked at him. Reaper nodded and looked down momentarily. Okay, low blow.

She shook her head and paused. "There's no one. There hasn't been anyone since...since you."

Reaper, you are a dick. "Where have you been all this time?"

"Boulder, Colorado."

"Why Boulder?"

"Because that's where the US Marshals put me when I entered the Witness Protection Program."

The three men looked at each other, all puzzled. Noah's jaw dropped, and he couldn't believe what he'd just heard her say. WITSEC only happened in the movies, not in real life. Not for anyone he ever knew anyway. Bull's face showed his complete disbelief of her story, while Rebel was intrigued. Noah couldn't think of anything intelligent to say. He simply asked, "Why?"

Brianna turned to face them and stepped a few paces closer to them. Noah saw her cobalt-blue eyes and realized she'd been wearing colored contact lenses, too. *How did I miss these details about her? Because I have been so busy being angry with her for being alive,* he mentally chastised himself.

She let out a long sigh and considered how to start. "The last story I went on…in the Middle East? I got proof that some of our government officials were guilty of illegally selling weapons to terrorists. One of them tried to kill me by blowing up the plane I was supposed to be on."

Noah, Bull, and Rebel considered her story, but she could tell they were all still very skeptical. She had only given them very vague information. She supplied no names, nothing for them to run any checks on for themselves, and even she had to admit the story was pretty farfetched. Brianna kept her eyes trained on Noah. She refused to look away and give him any reason to think she was lying.

Noah finally broke the silence. "When did you last eat?"

It was Brianna's turn to look puzzled. "Um, I don't know. I guess on the plane yesterday."

Noah's face didn't soften as he asked, "A pack of peanuts? That doesn't count. When did you last eat real food?"

"Uh, I guess sometime yesterday." She glanced at the clock. It was already after two o'clock in the morning. "Well, I guess the day before yesterday, now." She shrugged nonchalantly.

"What can I fix you?"

She eyed him for a second before she resolved she wouldn't get pulled into any manipulation tactics. She said she'd answer his questions. He didn't have to play on her emotions in some cruel joke.

"Look, I don't know what your angle is. You don't have to play mind games with me. I will tell you whatever you want to know. Just be sure you want the truth before you ask the question."

"Right now, my only angle is to feed you."

"Thanks, but I'm not hungry. I don't have much of an appetite."

Noah kept his gaze leveled at her, but there was definitely a change in his eyes. They weren't quite as hard or angry anymore. He didn't trust her, but she didn't see hatred either. She knew his thoughts were about what question he'd ask next. She saw a shift briefly flicker in his eyes when he made his decision. It was then that he seemed to harden toward her again. She felt butterflies in her stomach from the anxiety of what was to come.

"I talked to Richard. I went to his hotel suite to see him."

"Oh? What did you two talk about?" She tried to sound nonchalant, but a small doubt lingered and still nagged her in the back of her mind.

He saw the same signs of terror well up in her again and wondered why Richard's name caused such a change in her demeanor. So, of course, he pushed on.

"Different things. Mostly about you." Noah shrugged.

Her big blue eyes filled with tears, but she fought them back. Noah knew she tried so hard to hold it together, but he didn't know why Richard affected her so much. And that really pissed him off.

"What does he want you to do?" Her voice cracked on her last word, and she swallowed hard.

"What do you think he wants?" Noah knew how to interrogate people and get the information he wanted. He could almost always turn their questions back on them so that they actually answered it on their own. That method gave him more information than anything he could think of alone.

"I'd say that he wants to make a deal with you. A trade."

Noah narrowed his eyes and clenched his jaw so tightly it made his whole head hurt. The muscles in his jaw twitched, and he balled his hands into tight fists. But he remained quiet and knew if he didn't push the questioning too hard, she would fill in the silence for him.

She didn't disappoint him. Her voice was soft but resolute. "I've actually been thinking about this. Especially since that guy took a shot at you tonight."

Brianna took a deep breath to calm her racing heart. She obviously didn't want to continue her current thoughts, but Noah watched her steel her nerves and proceeded anyway. Noah saw the woman he had loved standing before him. He watched her gather the courage he had never given her enough credit for possessing. He marveled at her as she drew her strength to stand tall in front of three large, intimidating men. When she nodded her head after a silent dialogue in her mind, he instantly knew she had made a decision he wasn't going to like.

Brianna took a couple of steps closer to him, wrung her hands, and still tried to fight back the tears that then rolled down her cheeks. Her watery voice quivered as she asked, "If you agree to the trade, will you be safe?"

Noah nodded, but he wasn't sure he could speak, even if his life depended on it. He had a terrible feeling in the pit of his stomach about the direction this conversation was headed. She looked down for just a second, contemplated the information, and then looked him square in the eye.

"Then I want you to agree to it. If you believe Richard, that he'll leave you alone and you'll be safe, you have to agree to it." Unshed tears glistened in her eyes, and Noah could only watch as they fell down her face.

Bull had watched the exchange. He knew what Noah was doing, but had no idea what Brianna meant. Whatever it was couldn't be good, though, so he butted into the conversation. Bull did not attempt to hide his contempt for her. His voice and his eyes were hard as he demanded an answer. "Brianna—what the hell are you talking about? What fucking trade?"

She looked at Bull and stated simply, "My life." Then she looked at Noah. He dreaded the words he knew would follow. "For Noah's."

CHAPTER SEVENTEEN

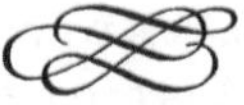

Noah kept his face unreadable, but his heart thumped against his rib cage. He knew going into it that he had a bad feeling about this conversation, but he hadn't considered this turn of events. His mind raced to put the pieces of the jigsaw puzzle together. There was no doubt that Richard was the key to everything. Her initial questions about him, followed by the terror in her eyes when Noah said he'd take her to Richard, and then this new revelation. It all so obviously pointed at Richard, but Noah didn't know what "it" was.

Rebel's deep voice reverberated through the kitchen. "Your life? Reaper, what the hell is going on? What is she talking about?"

Bull chimed in. "There's no way we would let anyone get to Reaper. What kind of bullshit are you up to, Brianna? What are you trying to do to him?" His voice was rich with hatred and close to yelling.

As he stalked toward her, Brianna absently backed up a couple of steps. She felt the pangs of guilt and pain in her heart from the knowledge she'd lost his trust. The angry look on his face scared her. She had never seen him like this before, especially toward her.

Brianna tried to keep her voice calm and not add to the anger that grew in the kitchen. "I know you don't believe me, but I'm not up to anything. I really tried to do what was best for everyone, considering.

"I can't tell you how much I've missed all of you. It has killed me to stay away for the last three years. But I had to because it was the only way to protect you. When I saw Richard came out of hiding, I knew he would come after Noah to get to me. I'm trying to help Noah."

Bull countered. "Bullshit! You're full of shit!" Turning to Noah, Bull continued. "Reaper, man, don't fall for this—" He pointed to Brianna while he considered his next expletive. Brianna's hands were steepled over her nose and mouth, her eyes closed, and her tears increased.

"Enough, Bull." Noah didn't yell, but the curt tone of his voice left no room for argument.

Before a brawl ensued in his kitchen over the bomb Brianna just dropped on them, and Bull's resulting outburst, Noah told Bull and Rebel to go home and get some rest. They all needed sleep, and they would finish the conversation later in the day. Bull and Rebel both gave Noah their secret code look before they left. Brianna didn't know what it meant, but at that point, she didn't think it really mattered.

She had made her decision, and she was at peace with it. There was just one more thing that she really wanted first. It was something that she needed, and only Noah could provide it. She waited at the base of the staircase when Noah reset the alarm system after the guys left.

He turned to her and said, "You found your pajamas. The rest of your clothes are in the guest bedroom closet. You should go on up and get some sleep."

"You-you kept all my clothes?" Surprise echoed in her voice, but Noah couldn't respond with anything more than a nod.

He had kept them all those years. They stayed in his closet until he could no longer stand the sight of them and the memories they held. He had his housekeeper move them to the other bedroom. To this day, he still couldn't bring himself to part with the only thing he had left of her.

Why would he keep them? She questioned if he kept them because he hoped she'd return one day. Maybe it was purely of sentimental value instead. She desperately wanted to ask him, but she was afraid of the answer. She bit her bottom lip and pulled it into her mouth.

He knew that look. She was nervous about something. She only did that when she was nervous.

"What is it, Brianna?"

"I…uh…was just wondering…why you didn't stay at your—" she swallowed hard "—girlfriend's house tonight."

"Girlfriend?" He had a hint of confusion in his voice.

She looked at him with a look that said she knew he was lying. "The girl you were with at the banquet."

He sighed but didn't take his eyes from hers. "She's not my girlfriend. She wants to be, but she's not."

She looked at him and cocked one eyebrow. "I overheard people at the party talking. They said you would be spending the night at Alexa's house again tonight."

He let out a long, loud huff and explained. "I have from time to time, yes. Only at her house. She's never stayed here. She's never been in our—uh, my bed."

Brianna nodded her understanding, but she still looked so sad. He still wasn't sure what to believe, and he didn't know what to feel about her. So many questions swirled through his mind.

Why would she leave me like that?

Why would she let me believe she was dead for the last three years?

Why did she break in to my house?

And if she was the bad guy here, why would she be so willing to give her life for mine?

"Why were you at the gala tonight?" he asked.

She considered lying, but he'd see straight through it, and then he wouldn't believe her at all. Even though she dreaded the backlash, she met his gaze head on and told him the truth.

"I didn't originally plan to. I didn't even know about it until I was on my way here, to your house, and I overheard someone talking about it. Then I saw you leave in your tuxedo, and all the other guys were in tuxes, so I knew your company must be in charge of the gala's security.

"It was stupid of me. I could've used the time to get in and out of your house without being caught, without turning your whole world upside down." She paused. He waited. "The truth is, Noah, I just wanted to see you. I wanted to get as close to you as I possibly could because I've missed you so much. As much as it hurt to see you with someone else, it's been worse not seeing you at all."

He still stood at the alarm pad, his hand on his hip, and he tried to look anywhere but at her. She looked like his Brianna again. Despite everything that had happened, it killed him to be so close to her but feel so far away. He had mourned her for so long and had dreamed that she would show up one day, that her death was all just a bad dream.

But he'd had to move on and get past her. He'd built up his business and was extremely good at it. The thought of her being in witness protection instead of in his protection was a complete insult to him and his abilities. She'd ultimately put her trust in someone else. Someone she didn't know and who didn't love her as he did. Another man who hadn't been forced to live without her for the last three years, who didn't have his heart ripped to shreds, and who didn't want to build a family with her.

His anger had been simmering up to that point, but it suddenly reached a boiling point.

"You know, Brianna, I'm still furious. Do you have any idea what I've been through? The plane you were on, or I thought you were on, exploded! Do you have any idea what that was like to watch the news footage over and over again? To wonder if you felt it, to question if you knew what had happened, to think you suffered and I couldn't be there to help you.

"It killed me to lose you. I died along with you every single day. The first full year, I barely even existed. We had a memorial service for you. Your friends and your family, they were so hurt. But you've been alive and well all this time, hiding in Colorado. While we all struggled to live with your death.

"Tell me something. Exactly how am I supposed to be okay with this?"

Her voice was so low, so soft, and so weak, he barely heard her from across the room. "I never wanted to hurt you. I didn't have a choice, Noah. I don't know what else to say."

"What if that isn't good enough? I deserve a better answer than that. Hell, even Bull and Rebel deserve a better answer than that. You left all of us. But what about me? Me? All I get is 'I didn't want to hurt you.' But you did!"

He knew he was ranting in half-finished thoughts, but there was just too much unfinished business to hold it in. Since he'd opened that old wound, all of his pain and suffering just poured out in the form of rage.

"It would've put your life in danger if—"

He was beyond livid and so very close to completely exploding. "What exactly did I do for a living when you met me? What do I do for a living now? Don't give me that bullshit. You didn't trust me enough to protect you. But you trusted a stranger to do it."

She knew better than to meet the hurt and anger in his tone of voice with her own. Keeping her voice as low as possible, she tried to explain. "I know, Noah, and you're a professional. The difference is you had a good idea of who your enemy was when we first met."

"And now I don't. Is that right? Is that what I'm supposed to believe?"

She crossed her arms over her body as if she were trying to hold herself together in one piece. "Noah, try to remember how it was between us. Before any of this happened. You did not doubt that I loved you then. Did you?"

"I believed you did." From his choice of words, she knew he meant that at the time he believed it, but he wasn't so sure anymore.

"Think about it for just a second, Noah. Knowing how I felt about you, why would I give up everything, everyone in my life, unless I had no other choice? You, the guys, my whole family, my whole life, Noah. Everyone who ever meant anything to me. I gave up everything and have been alone all this time. You know me better than anyone. How could I have done that if I'd had any other choice?"

Noah listened to her words and tried to consider every angle. He felt like he'd been fooled once and didn't like playing the fool. But right at that moment, he couldn't come up with any other reason than the one she gave. Not completely conceding, he shrugged. "I guess."

"Let me ask it this way. What would you have done to keep me safe back when…when you still loved me?" She bit the inside of her cheek to keep from crying again but failed miserably.

Angry that she would even question his love for her, he bit out his reply. "I would have done whatever it took, and you damn well know it."

Nodding in agreement, she replied, "Exactly, Noah. Whatever it took. Regardless of the consequences you'd face. Regardless of the pain it would've caused you. I know you would have. I'd do whatever it took to protect you, too, because I love you."

Noah seemed to accept that explanation better. At least he seemed to consider her reasoning. "I still don't understand why you trusted someone else to protect you, but I get your point about doing whatever it took."

He raked his hand through his hair and then pulled both hands over his face. When he opened his eyes again, Brianna had moved to stand directly in front of him. She was so close he could smell her shampoo and soap, and it reminded him of the many times they'd made love in the shower. And how he'd thought of that very scene every time he stepped into his shower without her over the past three years.

"There's something I want to ask you to do for me. A last request, I guess." She bit her lip again.

She looked so vulnerable and scared, and the man in him wanted to comfort her. He was still so confused, hurt, mad—no, furious—over the events of the last few hours. He tried to make sense out of anything, but he still just couldn't believe she'd hurt him like that.

"Go on." His voice had a questioning tone, and his face wore a guarded expression.

She waited so long to speak again that he didn't think she would finish her request. "You can say no. I don't want you to feel…obligated."

"What is it, Bri?"

His voice almost sounded tender for those few seconds, and she felt a glimmer of hope warm her heart. But she tamped it down because she knew better than to hope for a fairy-tale ending. He was rightfully mad, hurt, and hadn't forgiven her. She couldn't blame him.

"Can you…uh… Will you… Can I have…" Her voice trailed off again, uncertain of how to ask and even more uncertain of how he would respond.

"Just say it."

She searched his eyes for a moment before she stated her request. "For the rest of the night, can you just pretend you still love me?" Her eyes welled up with tears. As she looked down at the floor, her tears spilled over and ran down her cheeks. "I just want to spend my last night in your arms."

Brianna craned her neck up to look at him. She watched the war play out in his eyes. He debated whether he should give in, whether he even wanted to give in. It was at that moment that she knew it had been a mistake to ask.

She watched his eyes harden again, and she recognized that look all too well. His mind was set. Too much had happened, and he couldn't go back. She would spend the last night of her life as she had spent the previous three years. Alone.

She shook her head, looked down at her feet, and backed away from him. "Forget I said anything. I shouldn't have asked that of you. It was really selfish of me. I'm sorry for putting you on the spot like that."

She turned and slowly walked up the curved marble staircase to the second-floor landing. She stopped for a second as she looked down the hallway. At the end of it was the bedroom she had once shared with the man she loved more than anything. She felt the stab in her heart as she realized that she had lost him forever. All the reunion dreams she'd held on to every minute of the past three years crashed and burned before her.

She took a deep breath, walked into one of the guest bedrooms and closed the door behind her. It was symbolic to Brianna. As she closed the bedroom door, the door to her heart slammed shut. She knew Noah was her soul mate five years ago in the desert. It belonged to him, and she didn't want it back.

Noah couldn't believe what she had just asked him. Pretend to love her? He didn't know whether he should feel insulted or complimented at her request. The warring emotions in him tore him apart. On the one hand, he wanted to rush upstairs and tell her he didn't have to pretend to love her—he still loved her more than anything. On the other hand, she had betrayed him in the worst way. She let him believe she was dead. She'd never tried to contact him and still wouldn't have if he hadn't caught her.

Noah sulked. *Just what the fuck am I supposed to do now?*

~

"I need to know why you broke in to my house." Shaking her shoulder, he said again, "Brianna—I need to know why."

She opened her eyes and startled at the tall, dark figure that stood over her. It took her a second to remember where she was, but she immediately recognized the deep timbre of Noah's voice. She rubbed her eyes and looked at the clock. She'd only been asleep ten minutes. She sat up and swung her legs over the side of the bed.

Confused, she asked, "What, Noah? What did you say?"

"Tell me why you broke in to my house. I need to know."

She looked up into his eyes for a moment as she considered what she should do. She decided then was as good a time as any to give him the evidence she'd collected. She had already decided to give it to him in the morning and explain everything in detail before she went to Richard. She bent to pick up her shoe, reached inside, and brought out a flash drive. "For this," she said as she handed it to him.

He knelt down in front of her, the moonlight streaming through the window directly onto her face. "What's on it?"

"All the evidence you'll ever need is on that flash drive and in the few papers that are still in my hotel room. Keep them somewhere safe. I-I really tried to help you, Noah. I'm so sorry it wasn't enough."

He wanted to ask her what she meant. He wanted her to explain everything from start to finish. But all he could think about was that she was back in his house. After three long years of missing her, she was in a guest bedroom instead of his bed.

"It is password protected. The password is—" she put the back of her hand up to her mouth, blinked back tears, and looked away from him "—the password is Sunny, with a capital S."

Sunny, short for Sunshine.

The nickname that was given to her the night they all promised to take care of her, to be her brothers, just like they were to each other. As he looked at her then, he felt a squeezing in his chest that told him somewhere along the line, they had all let her down.

"Bri." His voice was soft and reminded her so much of how he used to sound when he said her name.

"It's only a few hours until dawn, Noah. You should get some sleep. All of this will be over soon, and you'll be able to put everything behind you. I know I have no right to ask anything of you, but this really isn't for me."

She watched his face to gauge his reaction before she continued. "Please don't tell my parents anything about my coming back. I don't want to hurt them more than I already have. I don't think they could take attending my funeral a second time."

The finality of her words was evident in the distraught look on her face. He knew she intended to see this through to the end, to her end, just as she'd said. Regardless of how hurt and mad he felt about her disappearance, he couldn't deny her genuine anguish.

She was still the same person he fell head over heels in love with so many years ago. She still put everyone ahead of herself, she still loved him unconditionally, and she willingly handed over all the documents she'd worked so hard to get. Those didn't appear to be the actions of someone who wanted to play him.

She was still his Brianna. For better or for worse, that's what he had every intention of vowing before God, friends, and family. That promise had already been made in his mind, carried out in his heart, and flowed in his veins. Their fates were already intertwined and weren't severed even in her "death."

He hooked one arm under her knees, the other under her arms, and started to lift her off the guest bed.

She pushed both hands against his chest to stop him. "Noah, no. You don't have to do this. It's okay. I get it. I've realized something since I asked you for tonight. I can't go through with this now that I know you don't love me. I thought we could pretend it all away for just one night. But I can't do it. I know it'll only hurt worse."

Brianna had no idea what he was thinking, and his eyes didn't let anything show. Her heart broke all over again with his every touch, even just being in his presence. She knew he would never really accept that she stayed away because she loved him more than anything. It broke her heart even more to know that by trading herself to Richard, she would die with Noah thinking poorly of her.

"Brianna, I can't say that I agree with what you did. I don't. At all. You should've trusted me to protect you."

With an exasperated breath, she said forcefully, "Noah, none of it was to protect me. I had to hide to protect you. Everyone who could've hurt you had to believe that I died in that explosion."

Her hand went up to his cheek, and she lovingly stroked alone his jawline. Her teary eyes held his as she continued. "I love you, Noah, more than anything, more than anyone. I've never stopped loving you. Not after I had to leave when I first met you in the desert, and I didn't stop loving you three years ago when I had to stay away from you to protect you. I've loved you with my whole heart every second that we've been apart. I hope that you can believe that—one day."

"You're not sleeping in here, Brianna." With that, he picked her up and carried her to his room. She wrapped her arms around his neck and leaned in to breathe in his scent. She silently vowed she would cherish this moment, no matter how much it broke her heart. As he set her down next to his bed, he saw the deep love that shone in her eyes, and she searched his eyes for even a sliver of reciprocation.

He shook his head, but he never took his eyes off hers as he moved in to kiss her lips lightly. His hand went up to her neck, his fingers gently stroked downward, across her collarbone to the spaghetti strap of her tank top. He pushed it off her shoulder and kissed her along the same line that his fingers had trailed. He felt her shudder under his touch. He moved to the other side and started all over. As he raised his head, he moved his hand to the back of her neck and into her hair.

He grasped a handful of hair, tilted her head, and covered her mouth with his. Their kiss suddenly became feverish and urgent. Her hands flew to his chest. She felt his muscles tense and relax under her fingers. She unbuttoned his shirt one at a time. Her fingers explored every inch of him along the way, memorized every line of his body as they went. Her fingers traced his six-pack abs to the top of his tuxedo pants and watched as they dropped to the floor. He removed his boxer briefs and stepped out of them. She reached for him and pulled him close to her.

She felt his erection on her abdomen, and her hand found his hard, thick length. She began to stroke him gently. He groaned and grabbed her hand to stop her. "Keep that up, and this won't last much longer."

He quickly pulled her tank top over her head and bent as he pulled her panties to her ankles. He kissed and licked his way back up her body. He picked her up and sat on the edge of the bed with her in his lap, while he gently stroked her face.

He couldn't stop the thoughts that whirled through his mind.

...I lost everything...

...She was protecting you...

...I tried to help you...

...My life for Noah's...

"What is it, Noah?" Brianna asked when he suddenly stopped. Her heart squeezed, and she held her breath as she expected him to say he had changed his mind. That he couldn't allow himself to go through with it. That he didn't want to spend the night with her.

He sat her on the bed beside him, rose, and walked to the window. The glow from the lights outside cast beams across his naked body and showcased his dominant form. One of his muscular arms was against the window, bent at the elbow, and his forehead rested on his forearm. Brianna felt exposed and rejected as she sat completely naked on his bed.

He changed his mind, she thought as she pulled the top sheet over her and waited for him to answer.

"You really would give up your life for mine. Wouldn't you, Bri?" The first slight hint of emotion was in his voice, just a sign that he considered she had told him the truth.

"Yes."

He noticed that she didn't hesitate in her answer. He turned to look at her for a moment and then walked back to her. The muscle in his jaw twitched, and uneasy emotions played across his face. He knelt in front of her, pulled the sheet away from her, and wrapped his arms around her waist.

"You already did, didn't you? You gave up your life here to protect me. Like you tried to protect me in the car when you thought that guy was going to shoot me." He wasn't really asking as much as he was coming to a realization. But he waited for her to answer.

She hesitated before replying, knowing the questions that would come next. "Yes."

"But why? What am I missing?"

"It's a long story, Noah. But I will tell you everything later. For right now, can you just believe me?"

"One more thing that's bothering me." She nodded, indicating for him to continue. "Why didn't you trust me? Why didn't you tell me what was going on back then? I would've helped you." His tone wasn't accusing or doubting her. She understood that he just really needed to know why.

"I did trust you, Noah. I do trust you. And I tried to tell you. But you...you got mad whenever I brought up Richard's name. Then, that last day when I tried to tell you, I wanted to tell you. But you were so busy with work. Then I had to leave on assignment before you even got home that night." Her voice trailed off.

He sighed and laid his head on her lap. "Yeah, that I remember." *I remember I was too wrapped up in myself to listen when you tried to talk to me.*

CHAPTER EIGHTEEN

She slowly ran her fingers through his hair. It was longer than before and curled slightly on the ends. She loved the silky feel of it as it moved across her hand. Her fingers made long, slow strides through it as she relished the time with him. She caressed his head as her fingers slid across his scalp. He straightened his back as he kneeled in front of her. She was face-to-face with him again after all the time apart, and her heart swelled with love. Every sensation in her came alive when he pulled her hips closer to the edge of the bed, covered her mouth with his, and then turned her head to deepen it even more.

He moved closer to her as he pushed her legs farther apart to make more room for him. He ran his fingers along the taut lines of her stomach. His fingers instinctively remembered the feel of her yoga-muscled body. He kept moving his hand down, between her legs, and his fingers found the warmth of her wetness. He felt his way along her sex. He gently stroked her and savored her soft moans of pleasure. His hand moved to her center, traced her soft wetness before he plunged his finger deep inside her. Her soft moans were enough to drive him into a frenzy.

Slowly, torturously, his hand cupped her mound and wordlessly claimed it as his own. The heel of his palm rubbed against her clit while his fingers moved in and out of her wetness. He felt her tremble as her hips instinctively rose to meet his hand. He knew her first orgasm was imminent, and he felt her velvety walls constrict around his fingers.

Her excitement and obvious need for him instantly made him unbelievably hard. The soft skin of her delicate hand wrapped around him stroked him from the base to tip and pulled his own moans from deep inside. His hips involuntarily moved in time with her hand as she continued to stroke him. His mouth covered hers again and their tongues caressed seductively.

Unable to wait any longer, he repositioned her on the bed. He gently pushed her shoulders down to lie flat on the bed as he covered her body with his. He had planned to take it slow, to make their lovemaking last, and savor every part of her. But her loving touch and submissive sounds made those plans fly right out the window. She opened her legs to invite him in, and he held the tip of his long, hard thickness at her wet center to tease her before he plunged inside her. His hips pushed in, and they both gasped from the incredible feeling of their intimate contact. He stilled his hips as his voice rumbled through his chest.

"Baby, you're so fucking tight. Am I hurting you?"

He pulled back to look at her face just as she gasped. "No, don't stop! Please." Her hands moved down to push his hips and urged him farther into her.

He moved slowly at first as he gave her body time to adjust to his size, mold around him, and fit him like a glove. As he increased his speed and thrusts, he watched her become his Brianna once again right before his eyes. She moaned and raised her hips to match his thrusts, took him to the hilt, and didn't allow him to lessen the intensity.

She screamed, unable to stop her cries. "Oh God, Noah! Don't stop!" Her voice was like an aphrodisiac to him. It pushed him to keep going when he thought he would explode.

He propped up on his forearms, framed her face with his arms, and his mouth crushed down on hers. His tongue dove in and took what was rightfully his. What should have always belonged to him. What he had missed every day for the past three years. His hunger for her was so deep, so primal, and so possessive that it thoroughly owned him. He knew he could never get enough of her.

She wrapped her legs around him and ground her heels into him when he attempted to slow his pace. She wanted him as much as he wanted her, and she showed it. "That's my girl," he murmured in her ear. "Let me hear you."

With every orgasm that rocked her body, the strong pull in her lower abdomen triggered her screams of ecstasy. His name never sounded so good, so right, as it did when it fell from her lips. Her inner walls quivered and squeezed him as he took her over the edge repeatedly. She had always been so responsive to his touch, but he felt the connection was even stronger.

"You feel too good, baby. I can't hold back any longer. Open your eyes and look at me, Bri."

She did as he commanded, and he saw the tears that were held behind her lids roll down her face. He bent his head to kiss her. "Come for me. I need to feel you come again."

He pushed up to straighten his arms and deepen his thrust. He took her over the edge of ecstasy with him, falling in tandem together. He watched her eyes and her face change as she let go, and the way his chest squeezed nearly took his breath away. Their bodies were utterly spent and thoroughly sated.

He relaxed his arms and allowed his massive body to cover hers. When he started to roll over, knowing he was crushing her, she held on and refused to let him move.

He chuckled in her ear. "Bri, I know you can't breathe."

"I'm okay. I don't want to let you go yet."

He rolled over onto his back and took her with him so that she lay entirely on top of him. She turned her head to the side and rested her cheek on his chest. He felt the warm tears as they pooled where her head lay.

"Are you okay? Did I hurt you?"

"No, you didn't hurt me." Her voice was watery and strained as she attempted to talk through the tears.

"Then why are you crying?"

She sniffled but didn't wipe her tears away. "It's just been so hard not to see you, touch you, or hear your voice. Knowing that you were so close, but so far away. I've been so alone."

His hands stroked her back lovingly as he listened to her patiently. He didn't know what to say or how he should reply.

"I'm sorry, Noah, for all of it. Everything. I know that doesn't make up for it."

The sun began to rise before they went to sleep. They made love twice more before they both passed out from exhaustion. Brianna knew she would sleep soundly for the first time in three years, safe and secure in Noah's warm embrace. He spooned her from behind, draped his arm across her body possessively, and kept her as close to him as possible.

Just before he drifted off to sleep, he heard her whisper, "I love you, Noah. I always have and I always will. I hope you remember that after tomorrow."

~

Noah felt a chill move over his body. He rolled over, his arm stretched out to pull Brianna to him, but she wasn't there. He opened his eyes and leaned up on his elbow as he strained his ears to listen for any sound. At first, he thought she might be in the bathroom.

The faint smell of coffee, bacon, waffles, and hot syrup wafted up to his bedroom, and he smiled. He loved her waffles. He had gained fifteen pounds when they first started living together. He pictured her in his kitchen, in her pajamas, dancing to the radio as she cooked breakfast.

He pulled on his shorts before he headed downstairs to the kitchen. His stomach rumbled from hunger, and everything smelled so good. It felt good to have her home. It felt right. He knew there was still a lot to talk about and pieces of the puzzle he needed to know to find closure, but he couldn't deny how glad he was to have her back.

Bull and Rebel sat at his table as they scarfed down the waffles and coffee. Noah headed straight for the cabinet to grab a coffee cup.

"Morning, boss. Sleeping in, huh?" Bull and Rebel smiled at him and then at each other. They shook their heads and resumed stuffing their palates. Noah looked at the clock and was shocked to see he'd slept past noon.

"Hey." He looked around the kitchen then back to the table. "Where's Brianna?"

They both stopped eating and looked at him. They stared at him briefly before Rebel answered. "Uh, we thought she was with you."

"She was, but she obviously made breakfast. So, where is she now?" He looked at each of the guys, who then looked at each other and back to him.

"Reap, she was down here. She cooked and talked to us for a few minutes, then said she was going back upstairs with you," Rebel answered.

"How long ago has that been?"

"About an hour ago."

Noah ran back upstairs, called her name, and looked through the bedrooms, closets, and bathrooms. She wasn't anywhere to be found. He ran back down the stairs. Rebel and Bull said they had checked the rest of the house but found no sign of her. Noah headed for the front door to check outside, and his heart dropped. He saw a white envelope taped to the door with his name on it. Tied around the oversized doorknob was the black blindfold from the desert—the symbol of her commitment to her brothers.

He strode to the door, jerked the envelope down, and tore it open.

Dear Noah,

This is the hardest letter I've ever had to write. You're probably really mad at me right now, but I hope this letter answers all of your questions and that, in time, you will see I had to do this. I know you never really intended to trade me to Richard. You're too good of a man to do that. But this the only way you'll be protected.

Richard was using you and your company to ship weapons illegally to terrorist groups in the Middle East. Your security firm was the perfect front for them to transport weapons and get them into foreign countries. He set up the contracts with you so that you'd take the blame if they ever got caught. His name is not found on any of the official documents.

This operation actually goes much further up the chain of command than just Richard. The flash drive has the documents that prove your innocence and shows that Richard is coordinating the weapons drops. There are financial records with wire transfers to his offshore bank accounts that match the dates on every contract he made with you in my backpack. When in doubt, follow the money.

On my last trip, Richard figured out I was onto him. I went into hiding after he tried to kill me. When Richard reappeared, I knew he would come after you to draw me out. The only reason he hasn't killed me yet is because he needs to destroy those documents first. But now he's sent someone to kill you and to get the evidence from me. He won't stop until you're dead.

The people involved won't let this information ever see the light of day. You'll still take the fall, and I won't let that happen to you. I found one of your wires and activated the digital recorder. Use the recording to stop him once and for all. He won't be protected once it hits the press. Then you'll be safe, and this nightmare will be over.

Thank you for giving me one last night together. I know you don't love me anymore, and I understand why. You still made last night very special for me, and I can't tell you how much that means to me. I've realized that I can't live without you again—I don't even want to try. The only thing that has kept me going the last three years is the hope we would be together again someday.

I love you, Noah. I love you more than anything. You are the best man I know, and I want you to live a long and happy life. My only hope now is that one day you'll forgive me and remember only the good times we had. That's what I'm taking with me.

Forever Yours,
Brianna

"What the fuck is she thinking?" Noah's anger reached a flashpoint. "She isn't trained for this. She'll get herself killed!" He handed the letter to Bull and paced like a caged animal, ready to pounce and maul someone.

"I don't understand why she thinks only she can save me. How many times do I have to remind her what I do for a living?" Noah growled as he paced.

"From the way this letter reads, she's convinced Richard won't allow her to live knowing what she knows. It's either you or her, and she chose to take your place," Rebel replied. "She left all the evidence with you because she knows they'll bury you both if she tries to use it. Having the additional evidence against Richard for killing Brianna will ensure your safety."

Noah propped his fists on his hips and racked his brain over her decision. He tried to see everything from her point of view to understand her reasoning, but he had the sense there was still something missing. "What did she say this morning?" Noah barked.

Rebel knew he would want a word-by-word relay of the conversation.

"She was cooking when we came in. She said good morning. We sat down and looked at the paper. I commented on how strange it was that she and Richard showed up the same day. That we were told she was dead and he was presumed dead.

"She asked what I meant by he was presumed dead. I told her about that US Marshal Stevens showing up at the office out of the blue one day. How he said he wasn't convinced Richard was on the plane. I explained that he said he didn't have any proof, he didn't really ask us many questions, and then we never heard from him again after that. I asked her if Richard's reappearance meant she was safe and if that's why they released her from WITSEC. She didn't answer me. That's when she said she was going back upstairs with you."

Noah looked at Bull. "And you?"

Bull stared at her letter he still held in his hand when he replied. "I didn't even speak to her, Reap."

"All right, she has quite a head start on us, but we need to get a plan together. Call more guys in, our best only. We have to find her. Send someone to her hotel room to clean out her stuff and see when she was last there. Bull, you still have the key?"

Bull nodded.

"Good, have the area canvassed. We have a recon mission on Richard to do. Find out where he is right now, where he'll be later, who he's with, his known contacts, recent financial transactions, his favorite foods—everything."

"You got it, boss," Rebel said as he walked away to get started.

Bull walked outside, pulled out his cell phone, hit a name, and waited. "We need your help."

CHAPTER NINETEEN

US Marshal Stevens told Rebel he didn't think Richard was on the plane. Stevens knew Richard wasn't on the plane, and he's known this whole time.

Rebel didn't realize the weight of his words and how much hidden meaning they held. He had said them so easily that he could've been talking about the weather, but Brianna connected the dots immediately. She knew she'd never fully trusted Stevens for a reason, and then she realized why.

Her mind swirled with the facts and possible scenarios that all of this meant. The questions that she should've asked from the outset, but she was too young, scared, and naïve to see it then. She couldn't think of any reason why a US Marshal would be in the Middle East.

The one reason that made sense was that he was part of the whole scheme. He was actually there with Richard in some capacity. He must work for Richard, to help prevent him from getting caught and to make his own illegal money while he was at it.

Memories of the day that changed her life flooded her mind. She'd repressed them every other time they tried to ambush her because they brought so much pain, longing for something she couldn't have and regret how she'd contributed to her circumstances. She focused on allowing them to replay so she could attempt to figure out what she had missed.

As she left the hotel in Turkey, she ran into Richard—literally smacked into him. She then sprinted to her rental car and immediately drove toward the airport. She still had to wait quite a while before her flight began boarding, but just knowing she was one step closer to going home to Noah would make her feel more secure.

She returned her rental car to the attendant and walked alone through the parking garage toward the terminal. The hairs on the back of her neck stood at attention and alerted her that something was very wrong. The uneasiness of physically feeling someone's eyes on her sent waves of panic through her. Not knowing exactly where the danger lurked added to her heightened anxiety.

Footsteps fell behind her, but she didn't dare turn around to look. She quickened her pace to reach a more populated area, but the footsteps behind her also accelerated. She placed her arms in the straps of her backpack, grabbed the straps to hold it securely against her body, and broke out in a full sprint.

When she exited the garage, she made a sharp right turn and found a covered spot where she crouched down out of sight. She waited to see who came out of the garage next. She reasoned if he stopped and looked in both directions instead of just crossing to the terminal, she'd know he really was after her.

Within a couple of seconds, a large figure took a couple of steps out of the garage and then suddenly stopped walking. He looked in both directions, took a few steps in the opposite direction from her, then suddenly did an about-face and walked a few steps in her direction. She remained crouched in her hidden spot and held her breath.

It was Richard himself, and he searched for her fervently. She'd been so foolish to think she could handle something this big on her own. She was so close to the terminal, so close to the plane that would take her home. But she knew if she stepped out into his sight, she'd never make it home again.

"Any sign of her?" Richard asked as another man approached.

"No. She's definitely fast, I'll give her that," he replied.

"Yeah. No shit. She runs all the time. One of my surveillance guys refuses to tail her anymore," Richard chuckled sarcastically. "Damn it. Find her. She can't get on that plane."

"She'll have to go through security to get on the plane," the other man replied. "She'll have to approach the airport door at some point."

Richard shook his head. "I can't go back until she's found. Deron gave her up easily enough. She has more than enough documentation to bury me, Bosco."

Before Bosco could reply, Richard's phone rang. He glanced at the screen and noticeably tensed before he answered it.

"Hollingsworth."

After an extended silence, Richard's face turned bright red with anger. With gritted teeth, he finally spoke. "Yes, crystal clear."

Richard put the phone back in his pocket and ran his fingers through his hair. Bosco watched him with a wary expression. "What was that all about?"

"That was Sayyaf. He said if I don't bring her to him in the next hour, I will regret getting on that plane," Richard replied.

"Does that mean he plans to—" Bosco's voice trailed off.

"That would be my guess," Richard huffed. "Motherfucker!" he bellowed. "I'm completely fucked if we don't find her right now. Cover the door. I'm going to look around inside for her."

The two men split up, and Brianna remained utterly still, her hands covered her mouth, and her eyes welled with tears. She watched as Bosco briskly walked away and Richard entered the airport. There weren't many places she could effectively hide in the international terminal with one man watching the doors and one watching intently inside.

If she could wait it out another hour, she hoped Sayyaf would demand Richard's presence. She'd be able to rebook her flight and get home undetected. She pulled her phone out of her pocket and tried to call Noah. With every redial, a woman's voice told her that all circuits were busy and to try her call again later. She squeezed her phone in her hand and brought it to her forehead.

"Noah, I need you so much right now," she pleaded. "I don't know what to do."

Brianna leaned her back against the wall behind her and fought back the terror that threatened to incapacitate her. She tilted her head back and looked up at the sky. The stars had just become visible in the evening sky. Her flight should be boarding by that time, and there was no way she could get through security and to her gate before the door closed. She intently watched for Richard to leave the airport terminal so she could rush inside and change her flight to the next available one.

The fates seemed to align in her favor as she watched Richard and Bosco leave the airport. Richard muttered an expletive with every long stride he took. He was obviously disgusted and angry enough to kill someone. Namely her. As the two men passed by, she heard his reply to something Bosco had said.

"Sayyaf called and ordered us to a meeting with him. Right now."

"That doesn't sound good for us," Bosco said, his tone conveying his worry.

"If he planned to kill us, he wouldn't call us to his house. He has other plans for us," Richard replied. "We probably won't like them, though."

When they were out of sight, Brianna stood and sprinted across the street toward the terminal entrance. A large jet appeared over the top of the building as it rose toward the twinkling stars. She stopped to watch it, confident it was the jet she should've been on. Her feet began to move, but her eyes remained glued to the plane as it rose higher.

In a split second, her whole world changed right before her eyes. A giant fireball consumed the plane as she watched in horror. The explosion completely obliterated the plane and sent small pieces of the fuselage in every direction for miles. The noise was deafening, and the fireball was gigantic. But the terror that resulted on the ground was complete pandemonium.

Panicked screams and heart-wrenching sobs came from every direction as onlookers realized what they had seen. Metal scraped on metal as cars crashed into others, the drivers distracted and shocked by the horrible scene. Police and airport security screamed directions in Turkish. They sounded even more terrifying yelling in a language Brianna couldn't understand.

She froze in the street with her jaw dropped open, her eyes wide from terror, and her heart pounded against her chest wall. Through the mass confusion of travelers that rushed from the building, a single voice caught her attention.

"This is US Marshal Stevens. Get Bill Jackman—it's an emergency," he yelled into his cell phone. "Bill, there's been an explosion at the airport. From what I can tell, a plane exploded upon takeoff. Appears to be an intentional attack. The authorities are evacuating the airport. I need immediate assistance and evacuation."

"You're a US Marshal?" she asked, clearly panicked. Still on the phone, he simply nodded, and she continued. "I need help. I'm a reporter from Miami. Can you help me get home? Please."

"Hang on one second, Bill," he said into the phone before he addressed Brianna. "Do you have a passport?" he asked as he eyed her carefully.

Brianna handed him her passport and nervously waited as he carefully inspected it. Her eyes continuously darted around, took in the mass confusion that surrounded them, and watched for Richard to reappear. A wave of relief washed over her when the Marshal spoke next.

"Bill, I have a young lady with a US passport here with me. She appears to be a legitimate citizen. I'm bringing her in with me," Stevens said into the phone.

After a few more clipped responses, he gave her passport back to her. "Come with me. The US Embassy personnel will pick us up, but they can't get into this area. We need to get outside the airport perimeter on foot."

"Let's run," Brianna suggested adamantly. "The sooner, the better."

"If you're sure you can keep up," he replied.

Brianna nodded in agreement, the stiff, quick jerks relaying her urgent need to move immediately. The pair bolted through the throngs of frightened people until they reached the designated area. Two large, black vehicles stopped in front of them, and three US soldiers stepped out of the first one and surrounded them.

"What's your name?" one of the soldiers demanded curtly.

"US Marshal Stevens," he replied, handing over his badge and passport.

"Brianna Tate," she replied as she gave up her passport.

"I'm Major Paul Lowe," he introduced himself. "They're good," he said to the other two soldiers. One of the men opened the back door of the second vehicle, and Major Lowe told them to get in.

As the distance between her and the airport grew, Brianna's nerves became worse. She had to remain in control while she was in the midst of danger. But when she began to feel safe and had time to contemplate on the events, she began to shake uncontrollably. Stevens noticed immediately and watched her suspiciously.

"So, what brings you to Turkey?" he asked.

"A lead for an article that was called in at my newspaper," she replied.

"You flew halfway around the world for a lead?"

"I'm a damn good investigative reporter. I did a lot of research first," she replied defensively. "Everything checked out, and it's a groundbreaking story. It just all went to hell when I got here."

"What do you mean? What went to hell?" he pressed.

She immediately knew she'd said too much and didn't want to add more to an already volatile situation. "My story. My source. Everything."

"I want to help you, Miss Tate," Stevens replied. "I really do. But I need to know what kind of trouble you're in first. You seem like a sweet girl who is a little out of her element in this part of the world. If there is even a remote possibility that your trouble is tied to that plane, you have to tell me. This could be a matter of national security, and I can't let you back into the US"

She considered his words and what it would mean for her if she couldn't get on a privately chartered flight back home. With the airport locked down and security on high alert, she knew there was no chance of arranging that outside of official government channels.

"I was supposed to be on that plane. I don't have proof that it exploded because of me, but I don't believe in coincidences. Two men are searching for me right now. And if they find me, they'll kill me because of the information I have. They're trafficking weapons and using DOD transport planes to hide them."

"You have proof of this? Any tangible evidence?"

"I have copies of the catalog pages that show the shipments of weapons have been received here on a regular basis," she offered.

A voice inside her said to still be careful and leery of everyone, so she didn't tell him about the evidence she had stashed in Noah's house. At this point, she decided no one could be fully trusted. If Stevens could get her home, she'd enlist Noah's help in how to turn the evidence over to someone who could really help.

"That would be a good start," he replied. "If you have, or can get, additional evidence, that would be even better." His statement hung in the air between them on purpose. It was to test her and see how she'd respond.

"As I said, I'm a good investigative reporter. I will keep digging until I have all the evidence I need," she replied honestly.

"Who is after you?" he asked.

"A man who works in the DOD," she replied vaguely.

"If what you're saying is true, you're in serious trouble," he warned her. "If anyone knows about this, or is involved with it, that's treason of the highest order. The penalty would certainly be death. Withholding evidence of this nature is also treason, so be sure of what you say. Are there any other Americans besides the DOD guy involved? Anyone else I need to know about?"

Brianna's thoughts immediately went to Noah and how his company was involved. She couldn't let him take the fall for what Richard had done. The evidence had to be controlled by someone who would protect Noah as she did. "No, no one else is involved in this."

"Does anyone else know about it? If you've told anyone, they could become a target themselves."

"No one knows specifics. Only the general storyline that I'm working on," she replied.

"People involved in black-market weapons trade won't care that you're a young woman. They won't care that your family and friends don't know specific details. If you go back home, these men will find them and kill them," Stevens strongly cautioned her.

"What am I supposed to do, then?" she probed. "Where am I supposed to go?"

"I can get you back to the US and into the Witness Protection Program. If you have more evidence that I can take to the State Department, I can push for arrests of anyone involved. Once we have everything we need, you'll be safe and can return home," he promised.

Sensing her hesitation, he continued. "Why do you think I'm here? I've had to help other Americans get out of here safely because of how dangerous these rebel extremists can be.

"That—" he motioned over his shoulder toward the smoke rising from the burning remnants of the jumbo jet "—is nothing compared to what they do to people they take prisoner. Don't subject your loved ones to that."

Richard was still on the loose and wanted her dead. Sayyaf was evidently a very dangerous man if even Richard was afraid of him. Bosco remained a threat, and she had no idea who else she was up against before the danger was over.

"Okay. Get me back to the US, and I'll keep digging until I have every shred of evidence. As much as I don't want to go into hiding, I don't want my family and friends to pay for my mistakes," she agreed.

Stevens contacted his friend, Palmer, at the US Embassy in Turkey and arranged for her transportation and new identification. When their plane landed, and she handed her passport to the US Customs Agent, Kristina Miller was born, and Brianna Tate ceased to exist.

After Rebel's comments, she realized that Stevens suspected she'd had proof somewhere in the US all along, so he pretended to help her in the Witness Protection Program until he knew for sure. He hounded her for all the evidence in every conversation they had. She gave him the small amount of proof that she could, but she never gave him the final link to Richard—his offshore bank account numbers.

She called him every week with questions on where the case was and when she could go home. With this information, his refusal to stop asking her for more documentation made perfect sense. He knew there had to be more because he didn't find his name associated with anything. He was somehow implicated in the evidence she gave Noah.

Department of Defense personnel.

US Marshals.

US leaders.

Foreign leaders.

Big business owners.

There were too many high-level people involved for them to leave Noah alone, to leave him out of it, even if she handed over her proof. She had brought this to Noah's door. In her mind, none of this would've ever happened if she hadn't kept digging. She couldn't let Noah pay with his life, or rot in jail for the rest of his life, for her stubbornness in getting the story.

After Rebel's offhand comment, she knew what she had to do. She finished cooking the waffles and excused herself from Bull and Rebel. They barely noticed her absence anyway since they were too busy eating breakfast. Bull hardly even looked at her, much less spoke to her. She missed her brothers, but she couldn't think of that right then. She had to hurry before Noah woke up and stopped her.

She knew the whole interrogation technique he used with his questioning. It was definitely not the same technique he would've used in the field. But he had used that on her too many times during their relationship, especially to find out any surprises she had planned for him. She couldn't keep any secrets from the man. Even though he agreed to trade her to Richard, she knew he would never go through it. Even if he hated her, he still wouldn't have done it because he was an honorable man.

So, she had to make the trade herself in a way that Richard would be caught red-handed, and his associates couldn't protect him any longer. She decided the premeditated torture and murder of a young woman, who had proof of his treasonous black-market weapons dealings, should be enough to put him away for life. The others involved would distance themselves and allow Richard to take the fall for it all.

She thought of last night and how it felt to be in Noah's arms again. Her heart hurt and tears pricked her eyes at just the idea of leaving him again. She'd watched his eyes when she asked him for her final request and knew it was too late for them. There was no going back to what they had because she had really fucked things up between them. So many regrets raged through her mind. If only she had told Noah about Richard. If only she had made him listen. If only she had stood toe-to-toe with him, fought it out, and made her case known.

If only she had one more day with Noah.

She didn't know why he changed his mind at the last second, but she almost didn't go through with it herself. The thought of him making love to her because he felt obligated in some way was just too much to bear. Once he kissed her, though, all rational thought left her. She was only glad she had that one last memory with him. But at that moment, she had to put all of her thoughts and feelings aside and focus on her plan.

Noah's security firm used state-of-the-art equipment. He had various types of surveillance gadgets and exciting toys that made the jobs more manageable. Most were at his central office in downtown Miami, but a few items always made their way home with him. Some were worn on clothes, placed in a shirt pocket, or the old-fashioned method of taping to the skin. Brianna searched his office and found a remote access digital recorder that was discreet enough to hide in plain sight.

The recorder would be found if anyone screened her for bugs, so she would wait until the last minute before turning it on. It only required a simple touch to make it start recording, but if anyone were watching, they would definitely know what she had planned. She activated the receiver for the recorder in Noah's home office, wrote him a letter to explain everything as best she could, and quietly walked out the front door. She left the blindfold tied to the front door knob because she wanted to leave them with the knowledge that she would never betray them. She had kept that with her all these years, and it seemed fitting to leave it with them then.

She ran all the way back to the hotel where her backpack still waited for her. The clerk on duty recognized her and gave her a new key card for her room. She quickly showered, dressed, and checked out. She knew Noah and a small army of men from his security team would be coming for her soon, but she planned to be well out of sight before they found her.

She took off alone down the street and to hail a taxi at the corner. She knew Richard was still in Miami, and Noah mentioned he'd gone by his hotel suite to see him. It also helped that his return was all over the news feeds. They conducted interviews at his posh hotel suite and jokingly asked how he tolerated the terrible conditions of his current residence. Hailing a cab, she gave the hotel name to the driver.

"The Villa by Barton G."

Next, all she had to do was pull off the tricky part. She needed to find out Richard's plans for the night and confront him. She wanted their meeting to be in a very public place so he wouldn't shoot her on sight. She needed to catch him in the act and make him talk to her first for her idea to work. She planned to spy on a man who was thoroughly trained and highly skilled in reconnaissance techniques. There was also no doubt Noah and his team would employ the same counter-techniques very soon.

Yeah, this will go over really well, she thought sardonically.

She stepped out of the taxi, paid the driver, and walked into the hotel lobby. Scanning the room, she didn't see Richard anywhere, but she kept her face turned from the security cameras as much as possible. She used her "Kristina Miller" identification and government-issued credit card to check in to the hotel. She knew her credit card transactions were most likely traced if what she suspected about Stevens was true. But this was the best way she knew to get close to Richard.

She pocketed her room key and exited the hotel. If she planned to fit in at the swanky establishment, she'd need more appropriate clothes. Her current clothes were nowhere near elegant enough to blend in with the other patrons. She left on foot and went in search of the high-end boutiques for a few new items—dresses, shoes, makeup, and jewelry. She also decided to buy an expensive wig that was made of real hair so it would look authentic.

She spent the afternoon shopping in several different stores to find the items she needed and buying them, regardless of the cost. After today, it wouldn't matter anyway. She was careful to watch for anyone following her as she walked from store to store. After a couple of hours shopping, there was one man who had been at more than one store with her, but he hadn't bought anything. She mistakenly turned down the wrong street and quickly found herself away from the crowds.

Brianna quickened her pace, but it was too late. A man grabbed her from behind, wrapped his hand around her mouth, and pulled her into a side alley. Her heart pounded as she struggled against his hold and tried to elbow him in the ribs. He shoved her into the back seat of an idling car, where another man was waiting for her.

She blinked rapidly and tried to catch her breath as she gave the man sitting across from her a dirty look. The man who'd grabbed her slid into the front seat of the car.

"Stevens? What the hell are you doing? Why didn't you just talk to me?" she yelled.

"Because you are not even supposed to be here. And we shouldn't be seen together in public."

"Then why not have your village idiot here—" she motioned to the other man "—talk to me instead? He's followed me for the last two hours!"

Ignoring her sarcasm, Stevens got to the point of the meeting. "Do you have the rest of the evidence for me?"

She felt completely uneasy being around him after what Rebel said earlier, so she schooled her features and lied. "No, I don't have it. I'm still working on it. I have your number."

"I need you to get it to me as soon as possible. I'll be waiting," he ordered.

Brianna jumped out of the car and hurried back to the more populated area. There were still a few things she needed to purchase before her mission was complete. The bathroom at a gourmet coffee shop served as her changing room as she transformed into a long red-haired socialite. She also made sure her eyebrows matched her new wig color.

She hailed a taxi to take her back to the hotel after her earlier mistake. She couldn't risk being seen by anyone else. She returned to the hotel, bags in hand, and walked in as though she owned the place. She didn't actually feel the confidence she outwardly displayed. She desperately wanted to be back in Noah's arms where she felt safe and secure.

CHAPTER TWENTY

Noah called an emergency meeting with a dozen of his best men in the downtown office of Steele Security. He arrived well before anyone else got there, even though every man there had immediately dropped everything and rushed in. The dry-erase board was full of information on their newest case.

"All of you have heard a lot about Brianna over the past three years," Noah explained. "We still have to find out all of the details of what happened, but she wasn't killed, and she's back. As if this weren't complicated enough, the enemy is one of our own. Richard Hollingsworth."

The rumble of expletives used to describe Richard echoed around the room. Every former military man there understood precisely what Noah meant. One of their own, a brother-in-arms, had dishonored himself and, by association, tainted their reputation.

"If Richard sees us anywhere around here, he will immediately make his move to kill Brianna. We have to assume he has a team of undercover agents, just like we do. We need eyes on Brianna and Richard—immediately. If you see Brianna, grab her no matter what. She is your first priority."

Noah concluded his mission speech and motioned for everyone to gear up. It wasn't quite like the forty-pound backpack he carried in the Army, but he was dressed for battle, nonetheless.

Bull, Rebel, and the dozen-man team joined Noah at the whiteboard as they mapped out the area around Brianna's original hotel and around Richard's hotel. The search at her hotel had turned up minimal information. She had checked out and left on foot. The clerk pointed in the general direction she walked, but her trail went cold very soon.

The computer techie of the group, Brad, had a search running on the local taxis, in the event she used a credit card in her name. The chances of finding her were essentially nil since they didn't know her alias name. Brad also worked to retrieve all the information from the flash drive Brianna gave Noah. Reviewing the data, he whistled. "Girl's done her research, Reap. This is huge."

Brad continued with his recount of the evidence Brianna had saved to the flash drive to give them more details than Brianna's letter had given. "None of these contracts are the standard ones you signed, Reaper. Your signature has been forged, and according to her notes, all the escorts you provided were illegal.

"If anyone had been caught, you would've been sent to jail for life...if anyone had let you make it that far. With the names attached to this operation, they would've buried you. She was right. This never would've hit the press. You'd be dead, and the story would've been buried along with you."

Bull lowered his head and swore under his breath. "That son of a bitch."

Noah nodded and shook his head. "With all the escorts I've approved, it could've gone wrong at any time. At best, I would've been hung for treason.

"Richard and I were friends since high school, and he purposely involved me in running guns to a band of murdering rebels," he seethed. "Then when Brianna found out, he tried to kill her. I will have Richard's head for this," Noah vowed.

Bull's phone vibrated, and he glanced down at the name on the screen. Noah looked at him expectantly, and Bull said, "I have to take this, Reap," as he stepped out of the room.

A moment later, he returned and walked to the computer where he changed the search parameters to find financial transactions for "Kristina Miller." The computer returned numerous results at several boutiques. "Got a hit," Bull called out.

They looked at the store locations on the map, and Rebel commented on how close the stores were to Richard's hotel, just as the computer returned a room charge hold for The Villa by Barton G.

"She's at the same fucking hotel. We have to find her before we're too late," Noah growled. He then passed out pictures of her to the other men, but with the charges at the wig shop, he reminded the men that she had changed her looks again.

With everyone briefed on the mission and dressed for urban warfare—meaning suits, button-downs, wireless communication earpieces, and gun holsters under their jackets and at their ankles, the security team climbed into the SUVs and drove to the hotel.

Noah decided he would check in as a guest and try to get eyes on both Brianna and Richard. Several pieces of his security equipment would help them keep watch over all the exits. If all went well, they would also have ears in Richard's suite.

Bull pulled out his cell phone again. He briefed the person on the other end on the plans for the night and ended the call. Noah turned around in his seat and stared at him as he waited for Bull to report in.

Bull said, "Don't ask, Reaper. Just trust me."

Noah stared hard at Bull. "You know I do. But if you're pulling someone else in, don't you think we need to know, so we don't shoot the wrong guy?"

Bull nodded but said, "You probably won't even know he's there, Reaper."

Still sensing the tension, Bull added, "Look, man, I've been too hard on her. Yeah, it sucks that she let us believe she was dead. But she had a damn good reason, and I didn't even give her a fucking chance." He folded his arms over his chest as he took a deep breath. "I gave my word I'd always have her back, and I let her down, man. I'm doing my damnedest to fix that."

Noah gave him a look and a nod that said he knew precisely what Bull meant.

The drive from Noah's downtown Miami firm to the South Beach hotel seemed to take forever. Noah was anxious to get there and stop her before she could do anything else stupid, or before Richard found her. He walked up to the counter and requested a suite and a meeting room. The team needed somewhere private they could set up for the night, and it would be too conspicuous for the entire team to crash his suite.

With only ten suites in the hotel, Noah was lucky to get the last one available. The concierge showed him to the meeting room, and he called the rest of the team waiting outside in the SUVs. They brought in all the gear and began to set up for surveillance. The hotel had once been a private mansion, and while definitely large and elegant for a single owner, at only three stories, it was small in comparison to other hotels.

Noah scouted the hotel as discreetly as possible. He noticed the people checking in to the suite next to Richard's had just arrived. A young man in a dark suit with a hotel name tag was carrying their bags into their room. Noah picked up a couple of bags and followed the other man into the suite. He discreetly placed a listening device on the wall shared by Richard's suite, just behind the wall sconce so it wouldn't be seen. He knew they wouldn't be able to get into Richard's room undetected, but this room gave them the closest access point that he could get.

The young man thanked Noah for his help with the bags. Noah slapped him on the back and, with a smile, said, "Anytime, kid."

Noah left the suite with no one the wiser. He called Brad to tell him what they had to work with.

Brad replied, "I will try to boost the signal to make it more sensitive. It may mean more distortion on our end, but any bit of information is better than none."

"I'm going to check Brianna's suite now. She's probably not back yet, but I have to see. It's too close to Richard's suite for me to stay here and wait, though," Noah relayed. "I'll be back in a few."

When Noah returned to the command center room, Brad informed him he had just successfully patched into the hotel's security cameras. They had eyes and ears on all floors, elevators, and the front door. Noah breathed a sigh of relief for the lucky break they'd caught. When Brianna returned to the hotel, they would know. He visualized slinging her over his shoulder and carrying her back home. One way or another, he was determined to find her and stop her.

One of the guys had food catered in for the group. To anyone else, they looked like a group of businessmen getting ready for their meeting the following morning. Their computers were all on the tables, and they were engaged in business strategy discussions, using code words only they would decipher. Brad's computer screen wasn't visible to anyone else, so he continued monitoring the cameras. When the hotel staff left the room, he switched it so everyone could see it on the projection screen.

~

Brianna entered the hotel lobby in the midst of a large group, wearing her red-haired wig, new clothes, and new makeup. When she heard a familiar voice coming from a man a few feet in front of her, she kept her face turned away from him as she listened to his incessant ramble. Richard, she sneered. He continued talking to his companion as though no one else were around.

"Make reservations for dinner at Prime 112 at eight o'clock tonight. I want my table at Mirage by eleven o'clock in the VIP room. I want a bottle of Moët chilled and ready. And make sure they have the security camera feed on the plasma this time."

His assistant was taking notes and just replied, "Got it."

Well, thank you, Richard. You just gave away your schedule much easier than I ever imagined, she thought sarcastically.

Brianna checked her watch—almost six o'clock. She had plenty of time to get ready to go to Miami's most exclusive club. She decided since Richard would have the security feed playing live in his VIP room, she shouldn't have any problems getting in. It was getting out alive that would be tricky. The loud noise in the club would make the recorder useless. She had to get him to leave the club to pull this off.

She settled in her room with the purchased clothes and accessories prepared for later tonight, along with the hidden recorder. When she finally sat on the bed, she felt exhausted to her core. She didn't get much sleep last night, or this morning, thanks to Noah. She smiled warmly at the memory. She immediately felt the sharp pain of regret and loss from losing him yet again.

She shook it off because she knew there was no other way. She ordered room service from her personal butler, compliments of the Villa suite, and retrieved her cell phone from her backpack. She knew she had time to kill since Richard would be getting ready for dinner. There were a few things she wanted to research on the internet while she waited.

She was deep in thought, taking notes, and researching the area when a light rap on her door startled her. When the butler called to her, she held the door open for him as he carried her tray of food to the small table. The smell of food reminded her how long it had been since she'd last eaten, and she suddenly realized she was starving. She sat down at the table and began to eat. Her thoughts drifted to what was to come. Her stomach seized when she realized this was most likely her last meal and she was utterly alone again.

Unable to eat any more, she decided to rest for a couple hours before she went to the nightclub. She set the alarm on her phone to wake her in time to get ready for the club. She lay down on the bed, and even though she should've been too anxious to sleep, her eyes were suddenly very heavy. Her last thoughts before she drifted off were of Noah, just like every night before.

Brianna's alarm on her phone went off just as she was in the middle of the best dream about Noah. She turned the alarm off and sat on the edge of the bed. A sudden wave of intense fear and dread washed over her because she knew what was about to happen. She kept repeating that she had to see this through to save Noah. That was the only consolation that kept her going. She prayed this would be enough to stop Richard once and for all. She rose, walked to the window that faced the ocean, and opened it. She took a few minutes to listen to the waves lapping on the beach and let the sound calm her frayed nerves.

She showered and dressed to go to the exclusive South Beach nightclub, Mirage, where Richard would be. She carefully applied her makeup and made sure everything was completely perfect. She tried on the red wig but decided against it. She knew she wouldn't walk away from Richard alive. Her last request to herself was to be Brianna for the night. She dried her long hair and styled it with the flat iron, adding curls to the ends to help accentuate her looks.

She had picked out a trendy tight-fitting dress to help her look like she belonged there. It was glittering blue and stopped above midthigh. The top tied around her neck, leaving her arms and back exposed. In the back, the tight material began again below her waist, teasing at giving a view of her ass. She moved her hand along the front hem of the dress, felt the small recording device, and breathed a sigh of relief that it was securely in place. She reasoned that it was in the best place to avoid suspicion. She could simply pull on the hem in an act of modesty to make sure the dressed covered her, and no one would know what she was really doing.

She put on her open-toe silver high heels, then her earrings, followed up with her necklace. She picked up her small matching clutch to put her license, credit card, and cash inside. She gave herself a once-over in the mirror and decided she looked very nice.

Too bad all this fuss isn't for a date night with Noah, she thought solemnly.

She stepped out of her room and asked the concierge to arrange for a limo to take her to the Mirage. She walked to the front of the hotel to wait for the limo to arrive. Within a minute, a long, black limo came, and the driver opened the door to let her slide in. He was barely out of his teens and was probably working his way through college. She caught him smiling at her while blatantly watching her ass. When he realized she saw him, his smile quickly faded, and his face turned a deep red. She laughed to herself and leaned back against the leather seat as he pulled the limo away from the hotel.

~

Steele Security sat in the plush meeting room, watching the security feed change over to different camera views on the overhead projector. When Brianna suddenly appeared in the hotel lobby, Noah yelled for Brad to switch to that camera view only. Noah watched as she walked toward the front door, then he ran out of the room after her. She wasn't there by the time he reached the lobby, so he continued outside. She wasn't outside either. He looked both ways and saw a limo about a block away.

As he ran back inside, Brad was walking to him. "There's a delay on the feed, boss. I'm sorry, I didn't know they were working on a delay on the cameras until you ran out of the room."

"Damn it!"

They walked over to the front desk and asked the clerk about the types of transportation they offered. She confirmed his belief that the limo had just left with one guest and would be back within twenty minutes. Noah asked to be next on the list for the limo and told the guys to get the SUVs ready. He would talk to the driver and find out where he dropped Brianna off.

If this guy refuses to talk to me, I'll break both his legs, he vowed.

"Twenty minutes, my ass! Where the hell is this guy? It's been forty-five minutes!" Noah bellowed. He paced back and forth along the sidewalk as he grew more and more anxious. He still had his wits about him to watch for Richard, and his team still had eyes and ears on him from the SUVs.

"Boss, he's coming down."

Noah heard Bull in his earpiece and moved out of sight. He watched as Richard left and told one of the teams to follow him and the other team to stay put for the time being. He was still waiting for the limo driver to verify where he took Brianna. As he moved back into the lobby, he saw the limo pull up to the front.

By the time the driver parked the limo, Noah had opened his door and all but dragged him out of the car. "The lady you picked up from here, where is she?"

The driver, obviously young and scared, was speechless. A huge, muscled man had just yanked him out of the car. He stammered, trying to form a coherent string of words. "I…uh…she's…um…"

"Where?"

"Mirage…nightclub…"

The black SUV slid up beside the limo, Noah jumped in, and Bull sped off to the nightclub. No one said a word as they flew through traffic, dodging cars, and running red lights. Noah fisted his hands and released them, repeatedly.

"Brad, anything on the digital recorder yet?"

"No. Nothing yet."

CHAPTER TWENTY-ONE

Brianna enjoyed the smooth ride of the limousine and asked the driver to take his time. She wanted to take in the sights and sounds one last time before going to the club. She had him drive the entire length of Ocean Drive to South Pointe Park. He waited while she walked with her toes in the sand and her shoes in her hand. She stood and listened as the waves crashed, breathed in the salty air, and enjoyed the ocean breeze for several long minutes.

She reluctantly walked back to the limo, climbed in the back, and closed her eyes as he drove her to Washington Avenue. In the back seat of the limo, the memories that she wanted to take with her took over. Her thoughts were always of Noah. She could see him, feel him, and hear him close to her. She felt as the car slowed to a stop, and she opened her eyes.

A long line of people that wrapped all the way around the block waited outside Mirage. Young ladies in various states of dress openly flirted with the bouncer. Their attempts to get in ahead of the hordes of others waiting in line were blatantly obvious, but the bouncer didn't seem to mind their advances. Small groups of guys and girls talked and laughed with each other, without a care in the world, other than having a good time.

Brianna stepped out of the limo and looked directly at the security camera, smiled, and waved. She knew it was a clear challenge that Richard wouldn't be able to resist. She showed up there willingly and waited for him to take the bait. She strolled up to the bouncer, smiled, and waited. She noticed an earpiece in his ear and knew he would soon be given orders. He looked down at his clipboard list, then back up to her, before he opened the red velvet rope and let her in. Several people called out to him to also let them in as she walked into the exclusive club.

The multilevel club was packed with bodies writhing to the music on the enormous dance floor. Strangers chatted and looked for company for the night, others waited at the bar to get another glass of their poison of choice. The DJ was set up in the middle to give everyone a good view of the show. A light show danced with the beat and changed colors on the ceiling and walls. Brianna walked through the crowd on her way to find Richard and politely refused several requests to dance and more.

She reached the VIP room and took a deep breath. It was a smaller room for more intimate gatherings but still large enough for a good-sized party. The room included its own bar and plush leather couches. Richard stood as she walked in. His eyes raked over her, and he had the type of smile that reminded her of a sleazy, snake oil salesman. She swallowed the bile that tried to rise in the back of her throat and stopped in front of him.

"Brianna. I'm so shocked to see you. I thought you were dead." He didn't even try to sound genuine.

"Well, it seems we're both back from the dead, Richard."

"To what do I owe the pleasure?"

"I'm here to ask you to leave Noah alone. Call off your dogs."

"You know what I want, Brianna. When I get what I want, you get what you want." His smile didn't reach his eyes. There was no warmth or compassion there. His eyes were stone-cold, and she knew he was lying, but she played along anyway.

Brianna looked around at the others in the room. There were several young women scattered throughout the room. They clearly enjoyed the free drinks Richard supplied. There were also several hired henchmen who waited for a reason to pounce on someone. "This really isn't the place to talk about it. Is there somewhere else we can go?"

Like the cat that had caught the mouse, he replied. "Of course, of course." He motioned for one of his men to come over.

They walked out the back door of the club and got into the back seat of Richard's car. As the man drove in silence, she watched the buildings go by in a blur. The people out having a good time were oblivious to her predicament. She took mental notes of the direction they were headed—away from crowds, hotels, clubs, and restaurants. They were headed to a more deserted area where they would have plenty of privacy.

Playing the victim, she looked at the man who drove them, then to Richard. "Where are we going?"

"Oh, just a little place I have acquired. It's a good place to talk. Very private."

They continued to hold eye contact until she finally turned her head and looked out the window. They pulled up to a windowless building made of large concrete blocks. The door was solid steel with an industrial dead bolt lock. The driver got out and opened the door for Brianna, while Richard exited from the other side. The driver unlocked and opened the building door for them and then locked it back when they were all inside.

Richard flipped on the light to reveal a large room with a single chair in the middle of it, and a long, thin table sat against the wall to the right. There was a doorway on the back wall that led to another darkened room. The second room was somewhat smaller than the one she was in, but she couldn't see what was in it.

She turned to Richard and asked, "What is this place?"

Richard didn't answer. The driver walked to the table, picked up a wand to sweep her for bugs, and walked back to her. The wand made no noise as he ran it over her front and back. "She's clean."

Then he walked back and laid the wand back on the table. The sound of a door opening came from the darkened room, and Brianna jerked her head around. Three more men strolled in and stood silently as they waited for orders.

Brianna reached down, tugged on the hem of her dress in modesty, and pulled it down. She purposely glanced around the room with a nervous gaze. She secretly activated the hidden recording device and then flattened the wrinkles in her dress.

Richard watched her but didn't seem to know what she was doing. The corners of his mouth curved up slightly as if he were amused at her attempt to cover herself in that dress.

"Oh, don't worry. These guys aren't here for that."

"Why are they here?"

With an ominous chuckle, Richard nodded toward the men, and they stalked toward Brianna.

~

Noah's second team of men had waited for Richard to leave the hotel and tailed his car to Mirage. They watched as the driver let Richard out at the front door, and he strolled straight up to the entrance. The bouncer immediately opened the red velvet rope and let him walk in ahead of the line of waiting partiers.

The driver pulled away from the curb and made a turn at the end of the block. Roman, the man in charge of the secondary team, put his team into play.

"Blake, follow the car around to the back of the building. Put a GPS tracker on it in case they leave again," Roman said as he handed the tracker off. "Watch the back and report back if you see anything at all."

Blake took it and walked around to the back of the building as he followed the path Richard's car took. He watched from the shadows as it pulled into a parking lot behind the building, and the driver jogged back around to the front. Blake moved silently through the parking lot and secured the location device to the underside of the car.

Blake conveyed his status back to the group. "The GPS is ready. There's a parking lot behind the building, and there's a back door. There's no doorknob, so it's an exit only. I'll stay back here. We'll need eyes on it in case they come out of it."

Roman found a place to park where he could watch the front door. Alex opened the GPS tracking software and confirmed the steady dot on the screen.

"Do we have any intel on this guy? Does he have a team of guys? Or another car?" Alex asked from the backseat.

"We know he has men, but we don't have any other specific info on them. We didn't have time to find out who they are or how many," Roman replied.

"So, we're flying blind," Alex stated.

"Pretty much," Roman chuckled.

"Good. I hate when people spoil the ending," Alex joked, and they both laughed.

After several minutes of waiting, Alex got out of the car and began his perimeter walk. All of the men were on edge and with good reason. They all respected and admired Noah tremendously. If he was worried about this operation, they knew they all had a reason to be worried as well. No one wanted to be the one who let him down and allowed Brianna out of his sight.

Alex walked down the street in the opposite direction from Blake. He scanned the faces in the waiting cars as he watched for Brianna. He turned the corner of the block and continued his stroll toward the back of the building. He checked every possible entry and exit point along his walk. As he reached the back alley of the club, he saw headlights illuminate a gravel parking lot.

Screeching tires, a loud crash, and hysterical screams suddenly filled the night air. Alex urgently called to his team through his communicator as he ran back to the front of the building, in the direction of the screams. "Roman. Blake. Talk to me. What's going on?"

"Almost there," Blake replied.

"Drunk driver in a small car just pulled out in front of an eighteen-wheeler barreling down the road. The car now looks like a crushed aluminum can. Driver and passenger are injured," Roman responded. "I'm calling an ambulance."

An hour after he lost sight of her at the hotel, Noah finally arrived at the nightclub. He found Roman and Alex on the sidewalk in front of the building and Blake walked toward them from the corner.

"We have a situation, Reaper." Blake hated being the one to deliver the bad news to his boss.

Noah's hard stare bored into him, and he clenched his teeth when he spoke. "What?"

He knew his men were professionals and whatever happened was probably beyond their control. But he wasn't very logical where Brianna was involved. Especially when he knew exactly what she intended to do, and he knew Richard would have no problem complying.

Roman spoke up. "We were in place, staking out the front door while we waited for Brianna to show up. Blake put a GPS tracker on the car parked in the back lot.

"There was a wreck between an eighteen-wheeler and a drunk driver in a small car. The people in the car were hurt badly, and we helped the fire department extricate them from the car. Just as we finished, we saw a limo turning at the end of the block. She may already be inside the club."

Noah rudely pushed through a group of people who were in his direct line to the bouncer. With Bull and Rebel close on his heels, no one dared to challenge him.

"Joe, I need to get in. One of my targets may be inside, and I need eyes on the prize at all times for this one," Noah said to the bouncer.

"Anything for my Steele men." Joe smiled and opened the rope to let Noah, Bull, and Rebel pass.

"Blake, go to the back door and keep your eyes on it. Do not let them leave with her," Roman instructed. "I'll keep watch in the front."

Inside the club, Noah, Bull, and Rebel split up to look for Brianna. Noah didn't really care where Richard was. His only focus was to find Brianna. The entire place was packed with wall-to-wall people.

There were multiple rooms with various seating arrangements. There were high-backed booths, soft cushioned chairs, actual beds, and some people were even sitting on the floor. He slowly walked through the crowd, and his eyes scanned everyone as he made his way through.

Rebel and Bull systematically made their way through the lower level of the club until the three men had covered every square inch. They walked up to the second-floor mezzanine and continued their search. They kept on and performed the search again on their way back to the front of the club.

"Damn, where can she be?" Noah asked aloud.

He tried to keep his mind in professional mode and not let his personal feelings enter the equation. Emotions only made it worse and prevented him from thinking logically. The three men stood just inside the front door of the club and watched people enter and leave for several minutes before they walked back outside. As they moved away from the crowds of people, Blake came running around the side of the building.

"West! They're headed west! Let's move!"

Both teams scattered to the SUVs. Their tires squealed as they drove in the direction Blake had last seen the car.

Alex looked at the GPS tracking software and said, "This isn't moving!"

Blake shot his reply back. "They had a second car!" He gave everyone a description of it as they pulled out of their parking area. Traffic was heavy with people going out to the late-night parties. By the time they pushed their way through the blaring horns of angry drivers, they had lost sight of the car.

Noah punched the dash of the SUV. "Fuuuuuccccckkkkkk!"

They split up and proceeded to canvass the area, one block at a time.

"This is fucking useless. We don't even know if they went back to the damn mainland or somewhere else on the island." Noah racked his brain to figure out what to do next, where to look, but nothing came to him. Bull kept watching as he drove block by block, intent to do anything to stay busy.

Noah raked his hand over his face, and his hand stopped just over his mouth. He propped his elbow on the door, and he stared out the passenger window. "*Bri, where the hell are you?*" he asked her silently.

Just then, Brad yelled out, "Reaper, she's activated the bug!"

"Pinpoint her location. Now!"

CHAPTER TWENTY-TWO

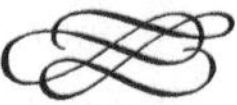

Richard's men surrounded Brianna and forcefully shoved her toward the chair. The chair was made of thick wood and was very sturdy. It was painted black and had padded armrests. The legs were reinforced with two-by-fours running between each one, on each side, front and back. Once she was sitting, she understood why it was constructed that way. They used duct tape to secure her arms to the armrests, and her feet were duct-taped to the legs.

Without saying a word or asking a single question, one man backhanded her across the face. Her body shifted violently to the left. She saw stars and felt a sudden burst of intense pain in her cheek, before the metallic taste of blood filled her mouth. Her eye immediately started to swell. Still dazed, she turned her face back to the front when another blow rocked the other side.

Blood ran down her cheek and out of her mouth as Richard walked up to face her. "You've caused me a lot of fucking trouble. I want those damn documents back, or you'll hurt a lot more than this."

"What documents?" Say it. Say it, she willed him.

"Don't play coy with me. You know damn well what documents."

She heard a loud "Thwack!" in her ear as something slammed into the side of her head. She knew she'd been hit, but she didn't know with what. A fist? A baseball bat?

Oh God, it hurts! She wanted to scream, but more than that, she didn't want to give him the satisfaction.

Her vision blurred as she struggled to hold her head up. Then she felt blows to her ribs that knocked the breath out of her. She coughed, and her chest convulsed angrily when she tried to suck in oxygen. It hurt to breathe, and it hurt not to breathe.

"You stupid fucking bitch. Give us back the weapons invoices," he growled.

She felt another blow to her head, but she was already so disoriented, she didn't feel as much pain as she had before. Or maybe her brain didn't register it. Whatever the case, she knew she wouldn't get out alive.

At some point, she passed out from the beating. She awoke to one of the men slapping her in the face. "Wake up. Come on. Wake up!"

She tried to open her eyes, but they were both almost swollen shut. Her vision was blurry, and she couldn't make out any faces, only dark figures as they moved around her. She could feel the darkness enveloping her, and confusion overtook her. She lost several seconds of time as their words faded in and out.

"Tell us now, or you die, Brianna." The male voice came from the dark figure directly in front of her. She heard the slide of the gun as he readied the bullet in the chamber. She saw the mysterious figure pull his arm up and straighten it in front of him. She couldn't see it, but she knew he held the gun in his hand.

She heard heels clicking across the floor, and a female voice taunted her. "Give me the damn gun if you can't do it, Richard. I sure as hell can."

Just as she thought it was over, she heard another voice in the room with them. It was a very familiar voice. But in the fog and haze of her battered body and brain, she couldn't quite place it.

"Put the gun down. I already told you, man. This isn't happening."

"Oh, it's happening all right. I'm putting a fucking bullet in her head and feeding her to the damn sharks."

That was Richard. I know that voice, she thought.

"I'm not asking. I'm telling you. Put the damn gun down. This is your last chance."

Who is that?

"Last chance? What? You think you can fucking stop me?"

"Yep."

Brianna saw Richard's dark figure turn from her and face the other mysterious figure that had just stopped in front of her. Richard's arm was down at his side, but she could feel the tension in the room.

"And how the hell do you plan to do that? There's five of us and one of you."

He released a menacing chuckle. "I don't need anyone else with me to take out five men."

She saw the shadow of Richard's arm lift upward, and instinctively, she knew he would soon kill her. The loud pops of gunfire filled the room, and people scurried and shuffled all around her. She heard shouting that seemed to come from everywhere and echoed off the walls. She had lost sight of Richard's dark form. There were so many by that time that she couldn't distinguish one from another. Her eyes became too heavy to keep open, and she was exhausted.

She was still taped to the chair and couldn't shield herself. She heard someone scream and realized it was her. She suddenly felt a white-hot, searing pain in her shoulder. Just before she passed out, she heard a calm voice that soothed her. "Hold on, Sunny. Help is coming."

~

Noah paced back and forth in the surgical waiting room at Jackson Memorial Hospital. He hadn't seen Brianna since the paramedics left with her in the back of the ambulance. She wasn't awake when they loaded her on the stretcher, and they were frantically working on her in the back of the ambulance as it pulled away. He didn't make many friends at the hospital when he arrived at the emergency room and couldn't find her.

A nurse finally informed him Brianna had been taken straight into surgery upon arrival. He was more than aggravated that he had to fill out registration paperwork on her before the nurse would tell him where to wait for word of her condition. After more than two hours of jumping every time any of the medical personnel walked by, a doctor came into the waiting room and called out. "Tate family?"

Noah, Bull, and Rebel rushed to the doctor. He motioned for them to sit down. "I'm Dr. Sullivan. She's out of surgery and in recovery now. She had a gunshot wound to the right shoulder. The bullet went straight through with minimal damage. We cleaned it out to help avoid infection. She will need some physical therapy to restore full range of motion."

Noah let out a sigh of relief. "Okay. We can deal with physical therapy."

Dr. Sullivan nodded, but the expression on his face showed grave concern. "I'm afraid that's not all. She was badly beaten. She has a significant concussion with large hematomas on both sides of her head, and there is some slight swelling around the brain. That is the most serious injury right now. We will continue to monitor her brain activity and swelling closely. I've asked Dr. Conley, a neurosurgeon, to oversee that part of her care. He's one of our best."

Noah's face drained of all color.

Dr. Sullivan continued. "She also has numerous cracked ribs, along with contusions on both sides of her ribs. Contusions were also found on her arms and legs. This lady has sustained significant trauma to essentially her entire body."

Noah couldn't think of a single intelligent medical question to ask. "When can I see her?"

"She'll be in PACU for at least an hour, more likely two, while we monitor her vital signs and her brain activity. If her vitals remain stable, she'll be moved to the neuro-ICU until we're sure all danger of swelling has passed. Once she's in ICU, you can go in during visiting times, as long as you're family." His eyebrows rose as he silently questioned their relationship to her.

Noah responded. "Yes, I'm her husband." *Maybe not right now, but I plan to be.*

Bull spoke up, pointing to Rebel and himself. "We're her brothers."

Dr. Sullivan nodded and said, "We will inform you of any change in her condition." He advised them to move to the neuro-ICU waiting room to wait for the updates.

The clock seemed to stand still as Noah waited to see Brianna. He paced in the waiting room, and when he couldn't bear the confines of those walls any longer, he paced back and forth along the hallway outside the neuro-ICU door. When the ICU door opened, he tried to look in, just to see her for a second. He saw the nurses station in the middle of a round room and the sliding glass doors all around the perimeter of the room.

She could be in any one of those rooms. Alone. Scared. Thinking I'm not here because I don't love her, Noah thought.

The ICU door opened again, and Dr. Sullivan walked out with another doctor.

"This is Dr. Conley." The two men shook hands as Noah waited for the news. Bull and Rebel walked up to stand behind Noah.

Dr. Conley spoke. "We've monitored her for the last couple of hours, and she is stable for now. She will stay in neuro-ICU until she wakes up. I'm afraid we won't know if there was any permanent brain damage until then. Her vitals have been stable, and we have sedated her to help her body rest and heal.

"You can see her for a few minutes, but I should warn you, she is badly bruised, swollen, and there are a lot of tubes. Right now, she's breathing on her own, but she has been intubated as a precaution. If the swelling in her neck or throat suddenly worsens as the contusions become more apparent, the ventilator may have to do the work for her."

"Thank you, Doctor. I really want to see her. She needs to know she's not here alone," Noah replied.

"I can let you see her for five minutes." Dr. Conley shook Noah's hand and walked off.

Noah stared at the ICU door for a moment. The usually calm former military man was scared of what he would find on the other side. He mentally chided himself for being such a pussy and walked inside in spite of his fears.

A nurse met him just inside the door. "You'll have to wash and sanitize your hands before going in the patient rooms."

"Which room is Brianna Tate in?" Noah asked as he turned on the water.

"She's in room eighteen," she answered.

As he walked up to her door, his breath caught in the back of his throat. She looked so small in that big hospital bed. Her hair had been pushed away from her face and was spread out on the pillow under her head.

Her face was savagely battered. Both of her eyes were blackened and swollen, her right cheek had a line of dried blood from the split skin, and her left cheek was a mixture of black and purple bruising. As he moved closer to her, he saw the swollen contusions on the sides of her head and arms. He realized the blood-red bands across her wrists were where she had been bound.

The blood pressure cuff was wrapped around her upper arm. There were tubes attached to her hand, and one went down her throat. She had wires connected to her chest, and the heart monitor above her bed beeped in time with the rhythm dancing across the screen. A nasal cannula delivered oxygen, and there was a slight hiss as the oxygen flowed through the tube.

He felt someone behind him and turned to see Bull and Rebel standing at the door. Bull's face masked the profound need for revenge that warred inside him. Rebel couldn't speak as he stepped into the room. Noah turned back to Brianna and gently touched her hand. He was afraid anywhere he touched her would cause her more pain.

He spoke gently to her. "I'm here, Brianna. I'll be here when you wake up."

Bull and Rebel left Noah alone with her for the last few minutes he had with her on this visit. They walked out to the hall to wait for him.

"We didn't fucking get there soon enough," Bull growled.

"I know, man. But it could have been worse. They could've killed her." Rebel's voice didn't hold the conviction his words tried to convey.

"They almost did. They still might have. She's not out of the woods yet." Bull fisted his hands. "You saw what they fucking did to her. You heard what Dr. Conley said. If she dies, Richard fucking dies. Painfully." Rebel nodded in agreement.

Noah walked out into the hall, and both men looked at him as they waited for any information. He was obviously upset, but he held it together for her. "Rebel. Go to my house and grab enough clothes to last a few days. I'm staying here with her until she wakes up."

"You got it. Call me if you think of anything else you need," Rebel said as he walked away.

Noah had to go to the police station to make an official statement. Over the years, he had built a good relationship with many of the guys on the police force. Tonight, he was glad those contacts gave him time at the hospital first.

"Bull, stay here and watch over Brianna while I'm at the police station. I can't take a chance that someone will come in and finish what they started," Noah said solemnly. "I'll be back as soon as possible."

"I'm not going anywhere, Reap."

Bull stood at his post guarding the ICU door. He checked the picture on the hospital identification card against the person who wore it to make sure no one got past him. If anyone objected, they didn't dare complain to the intimidating sentinel standing guard.

Noah anguished over whether or not to call Brianna's family in Atlanta. On the one hand, their daughter was in the hospital fighting for her life. On the other hand, this was the same daughter they thought was already dead.

Should he deny them the last chance they may have to see her? Or let them move on, having already somewhat accepted her death?

If the situation were reversed, he concluded that someone had damn well better tell him, or someone's head would roll. Having the chance to say goodbye was somehow better than the limbo they'd all felt from not seeing her one last time.

Plus, once she had fully healed, he had plans for their future, and her family would be part of it. It wouldn't be a good idea to start out with this kind of secret. He sighed deeply and punched the numbers on his cell phone.

"Hello?"

"Hello, Evan. This is Noah Steele. This will be an unbelievable shock. I'm not really sure how to even begin."

"What's going on, Noah?"

"It's Brianna, Evan. She's alive, and she's in the hospital here at Jackson Memorial. You and your family need to get down here as soon as possible. She's hurt pretty badly, sir."

"Wh-what did you say?" Evan sounded as if the breath had been knocked out of him.

Noah knew the feeling. He relayed as much of the story as fast as he could, without wasting any time.

"We'll be there within a couple of hours, Noah. I'm having the jet fueled as we speak. Now, I have to tell Diana and the girls."

Noah thought back to the note she'd left him. He left out that part of the story when he talked to her father. He had been turning her words over and over in his head, reading between the lines at what she didn't say. Or more accurately, what he didn't say.

She told me she loved me, showed me she loved me. She answered my questions. She made love to me all night. She waited for me. She sacrificed herself for me.

And I never once told her I loved her. Or even that I missed her.

Noah made a silent vow never to let a day go by without telling her how much he loved and needed her.

Brianna's family arrived at Jackson Memorial soon after sunrise. Every single one of them was in tears and frantic to see her. Noah warned them of her appearance much the same way as the doctor had told him. He knew that no description would really prepare them for what they were about to see. Even putting the shock of her being alive aside, the sight of her battered body with all the tubes, bells, and whistles attached to her would evoke nightmares.

Brianna's parents and her three sisters all took turns visiting her during the time they allowed. Her visits were limited to fifteen minutes at a time to keep the stimulation stress to a minimum.

Her condition was still serious, and she hadn't opened her eyes. They couldn't be sure whether she'd suffer permanent brain damage or if she'd ever wake up again at all. It killed Noah that he hadn't seen her since she first came out of surgery two days ago. He simply reminded himself that her family hadn't seen or talked to her in three years.

At the midmorning visit, Missy told Noah to take her turn. She'd already been in once that morning, and she knew he'd been patiently waiting for his turn. He hugged Missy and went straight to Brianna's room. He sat next to her bed and put his hand underneath hers to avoid hurting her.

Her bruises were slightly better than when he had first seen her. Instead of the angry black and purple bruises, they looked more purple than black, with a hint of green showing. Her eyes weren't quite as swollen, though they were still black. The contusions on the sides of her head were healing, but their presence remained obvious.

"Hey, Brianna, it's me, Noah. You probably can't hear me, but there's something I need to say. There's something I need you to know."

He stopped talking for a moment and hoped to get any type of reaction from her. He needed some indication she was waking up.

"I haven't really been living the last three years. I've only existed. The only time I feel anything is when I'm with you. So you have to get better because I can't live without you. I can't love without you. I love you, Brianna. Only you."

Noah rested his forehead on the bed rail while he said a silent prayer. His head jerked up, and he stared at her. Did she just... "Baby, did you squeeze my hand just now? Squeeze it again. Come on, Bri. Squeeze it for me, baby."

It was weak, but she squeezed his hand on command. Noah called the nurse and watched as she checked all the vital signs. Noah asked her to squeeze his hand again, and the nurse watched as her hand slightly closed around his and then released it. The nurse smiled and walked off to call the doctor.

Visiting time was over, but Noah refused to leave. He assured the nursing staff he wouldn't be a problem. He explained that he had promised Brianna he would be there when she woke up, and that was a promise he intended to keep. Dr. Conley came in, reviewed her most recent EEG, checked her pupils, and then examined her surgical site and her other wounds.

Noah reached through the slats in the rail and put his hand under hers again. She squeezed his hand lightly, and he stood to talk to her.

"Bri, you're in the hospital. You're going to be okay. You need to rest. I'm right here with you, and I'm not going anywhere. I'm not leaving you, baby." Thank you, God!

Dr. Conley and the nurse stepped back into the room and began to put gloves on.

"What's going on, Dr. Conley?" Noah watched the nurse draw up a syringe and walk to Brianna's IV. "What is that?"

"It's okay. It'll just help her relax so we can remove the intubation tube. We'll monitor her for an hour or so in here. If all goes well, we'll move her to a private room." Noah stepped out of their way but refused to leave the room.

CHAPTER TWENTY-THREE

All the events that led up to her hospital stay were still fuzzy to Brianna. She was on her second day in a private room. The first day, she slept a lot. When she had tried to talk, her throat hurt and her voice was still raspy from the intubation tube. Noah was there every time she woke, giving her water to sip on, and assuring her that she was okay. He explained again that she was in the hospital and he wouldn't leave her.

She watched him sleep on the uncomfortable hospital chair-turned-partial-bed beside her. She tried to move in the bed and gasped in pain. The stitches in her shoulder pulled, and her cracked ribs objected vehemently. In a split second, Noah was up and at her side.

"Bri, are you okay? What happened?" His voice was drenched with concern.

She smiled at him. "I'm okay. I just wanted to turn over, but the rest of my body said no."

He smiled and put his hand under hers again. Brianna had a brief glimpse of a memory that was just barely out of reach. Noah watched her face and recognized her puzzled look.

"What is it, Bri?" he asked.

"When you put your hand under my hand just now, I had déjà vu. It was so familiar."

Noah chuckled. "I've done that every time I've been in to visit you. I was afraid I'd hurt you if I held yours, so I let you hold mine."

She squeezed his hand. "It doesn't hurt, honest." They were both silent, looking deep into each other's eyes, but neither was quite sure of what to say.

Brianna started. "Noah, tell me what happened that night."

His face hardened, but he didn't drop his gaze her from her eyes. "Bri, I don't really think now's the time. You're still healing and—"

She cut him off. "Noah, I need to know. Please. I'm stronger than you think."

"That you are," he conceded.

Noah recounted the details from his perspective of what happened, up until she went into that building. He told her about finding out which hotel she'd checked in to, grabbing the poor kid driving the limo she took, following her to the club, and then losing her when they took a different car.

She was shocked to hear him describe how close he was to her at the hotel and the club. Then it hit her.

"How did you find me at the hotel? I didn't use my real name." Her eyebrows furrowed, and her eyes showed her confusion.

He smiled and replied, "Um, how do I explain this?"

She cocked an eyebrow at him. "Um…one word at a time," she mocked him jokingly.

The door to her hospital room opened, and a huge, intimidating man stood in the doorframe. The man was larger than she remembered. The black-haired, blue-eyed giant stood 6'6" tall and had rock-solid muscle on every inch of his body. A beaming smile lit up his face as Brianna called his name.

"Shadow!"

Noah strolled over to the door and gave his friend a manly hug. "Good to see you, brother!"

Shadow closed the door behind him, walked to Brianna, and gave her a tentative hug. For such a big guy, he was so gentle with her. "How are you feeling, Sunny?"

His voice stirred another memory, and the full realization hit her. "It was you!"

Shadow looked at Noah and tried to play coy with her. "Me? What did I do?"

Noah tried to hide his smile.

She eyed them both suspiciously and playfully hit his arm. "You were there that night! You came in and stopped them. I owe you my life." Then tears welled up in her eyes, but they were tears of joy and gratitude.

"Well, I can't take all the credit." Shadow's voice was teasing, but she felt the warmth and love of a brother in it. "Actually, your man, Noah, was the real hero."

She looked at Noah and saw he was no longer trying to hide a smile. His body suddenly went rigid, and that familiar mask overtook any emotions on his face. Shadow looked from Brianna to Noah as he noted the shock on Brianna's face and the emotionless expression on Noah's face.

"Ah. He hasn't told you, has he? Well, you two will have plenty to talk about, then. I just wanted to see for myself that you're on the mend, Sunny."

Shadow leaned over and kissed her on the cheek. "Bull, Rebel, and I will always have your back, Sunny."

She kissed his cheek and hugged his neck as best she could with her injuries. She told him she expected to see him again soon as he walked out the door.

"What did he mean, Noah? What have you not told me?" Her eyes searched his, and he felt that familiar squeeze around his heart.

He didn't like to think about that night, much less talk about it. It had only been a few days, but it felt like it all happened years ago. He knew she wouldn't let it go. She was hell on wheels when she was onto a story.

"You asked how I found you at the hotel under your alias." She nodded. "Actually, I didn't. Bull called Shadow and told him we needed help. Shadow works for the CIA now, so he was able to find out your WITSEC alias."

"B-Bull called Shadow? For me?"

Noah nodded and continued. "Since we had a name, we could track your financial records. Your credit card showed a room charge hold, so we went there to find you. Then we tracked you to the nightclub. We lost you because of a bad wreck that happened in front of the club, and then they took a different car when they left the club with you.

"Shadow had been investigating this group for running guns for quite a while. He pretended to be a dirty CIA operative, and Richard was more than willing to use him. He kept tabs on where Richard would be that night. When you activated the recording device, we finally got a fix on you in that building."

He stopped talking for several seconds. She watched the shadows move across his face and recognized the haunted look in his eyes.

"We were still too far away from you, but we were listening." His jaw tensed, and his jaw muscles bunched as he remembered the sounds. Through clenched teeth, he continued. "We listened to them torture you."

She reached her hand up and took his, squeezing it.

"Shadow wasn't close enough right then to stop it. He walked in just as Richard leveled the gun at your head." Noah's other hand clenched the hospital bed so tightly, she thought the metal would break. "Shadow stalled them until we could get into position, then we stormed the building."

With that, he played it off like he'd finished telling the story. But she could tell there was more, and he was holding back for some reason.

"I remember hearing a lot of people suddenly in the room, or what seemed like a lot. I remember a lot of echoes and what I thought were gunshots. I couldn't really see, and my sense of time was way off."

She continued. "Noah, what are you holding back from me?"

He shook his head and sighed loudly. "You were right. It went way further up the chain than just Richard. The woman you saw me with at the banquet, Alexa Pope. She was involved, as was her father. She was in that building with you that night, and I…I had to shoot her. She's dead."

With that revelation, he turned away from her and walked to the window. She dropped her hand from where it held his, immediately feeling the empty loneliness that had been in her life without him.

He shot the woman they said was his girlfriend. She then saw the effect it had on him. He had shot someone he was involved with intimately. He had said she wasn't his girlfriend, but she was apparently something to him. Her heart broke for him and the pain he was feeling, but more for herself. She knew he would never be able to look at her without seeing Alexa.

"I...I'm sorry, Noah. I didn't know...about her or her father. You seem to care a great deal about her. I don't know what to say. Maybe it would've been better if—" Tears streamed down her face as her thoughts finished her sentence when her voice couldn't... *If it had been me instead.*

Noah whirled around and took a giant step to the side of her bed. "Don't even think that!" He stepped back, one hand on his side and the other raking down his face. "Bri, she had a gun on you. She was squeezing the trigger right in front of me. I leveled my gun at her and yelled for her to stop. She laughed —laughed!

"I pulled the trigger, barely a split second before she did. My bullet hit her, threw her backward, and knocked her aim off. If I had been even one second later, she would've killed you. I've never been so scared in my life."

Leaning over the rail, he took her hands in his. "I love you, Bri. I've never stopped loving you. I missed you every damn day you were away from me. When I thought you died, all I wanted to do was die and be with you again. Living without you has been hell on earth."

Brianna pulled him to her and kissed him through her tears. "I love you too, Noah. I love you so much, and I've died a thousand times living without you."

"I stormed into that building to save you. There was no way I could watch you die again," he murmured against her skin.

He felt her tense underneath his hands. "What about Richard? Did he get away?"

"No, he didn't get away at all. He got better than he deserved—a bullet right between the eyes," Noah replied and showed no remorse.

Later that day, as Brianna was taking a nap, a light rap on the door alerted Noah. He looked up to see Bull walking in. "Hey, brother."

"Hey, Reap," he said softly as he looked at Brianna sleeping. "I wanted to see how she's doing." He hesitated before continuing. "And I need to apologize to her."

Noah placed his hand on Bull's shoulder and nodded in understanding. They watched her sleep for a minute before she began to stir. She opened her eyes and looked from Noah to Bull, then back to Noah.

"Something wrong?" Noah heard the slight elevation of fear in her voice.

Bull answered, "No, no—well, on second thought, yes, I guess there is. Me. I've been wrong—about you and how I treated you, Brianna. I'm sorry. I should've heard you out. You deserved at least that, and I let you down. I promised I would always protect you, and I let you down."

Brianna considered his words, and Bull waited for her to order him out of her room and out of her life.

"Sunny."

Bull looked confused. "What?"

"My name is Sunny, to you." And with that, she smiled at him. Bull was suddenly at the side of the bed, bending over to hug her.

"Always," he said as he kissed her cheek. A silent understanding that his one-word answer held a promise only a brother could make.

The following day, Brianna was discharged from the hospital, and Noah took her home to his house. His protective instincts toward Brianna were in overdrive, and he was convinced that every other driver on the road was out to get her.

"The ride home was interesting." Brianna tried to keep from laughing.

Noah slowly raised one eyebrow at her remark as he turned off the vehicle. "Are you making fun of my driving?"

"No. I wouldn't dare do that," she replied. "The rest of Miami may have something to say about it, though."

"You do realize that you're defenseless right now, right? That you literally can't defend yourself, and I can do whatever I want to do to you," he threatened teasingly.

"You do realize that I know you better than anyone in the world does, right?" she countered. "And I know that you would never do anything but protect me."

Raw emotion filled his eyes as he slowly nodded. "You've got me there. No one else knows me like you do. And there's no way in hell I'd ever hurt you. However, I will hold you hostage and never let you leave my side again."

"You can't call me a hostage if I willfully and intentionally stay with you," she whispered. "Forever."

Noah leaned across the center console and gave Brianna a long, lingering kiss. "Stay right there. I'm coming around to get you."

He walked briskly around the vehicle, opened her door, and gingerly picked her up in his arms. He carried her to the door and then up the stairs to the master bedroom. He carefully placed her on the bed and arranged the pillows under her head. After he turned on the television, he handed her the remote.

"You are on complete bed rest for the next couple of weeks. Doctor's orders—and my orders. I'm going downstairs to make your lunch, and then I'll be back. Whatever you need, I'll take care of for you." Noah gave her his dazzling, heart-melting smile before he turned to leave the room.

"Noah?" she called after him.

"Yeah, babe?"

"I love you. More than anything in the world. Thank you for loving me."

"Loving you is more natural than breathing. It's life-sustaining. I don't even have to think about it. You're not just a part of me, you're the best part of me," Noah replied sincerely.

From one week to the next, he tended to Brianna's healing wounds, catered to her every need, and reminded her how much she was loved. By the end of the two weeks of restricted activities, she playfully warned him about expectations.

"You know, since you've proven you're capable of spoiling me, I'll expect it all the time now," she laughed.

"That's a promise, sweetheart." He flashed a wicked smile and waggled his eyebrows suggestively. "When you're all better, I'll spoil you in every room of this house."

"I'm holding you to that promise as soon as I'm well enough." She winked.

"That's not all you'll be holding when you're well enough."

When she was first discharged from the hospital, she still experienced frequent dizziness from her concussion. Her sore, cracked ribs also kept her from moving quickly. But after the last couple of weeks of rest and all the doting attention from Noah, the worst of her pain and symptoms had subsided.

All the flirting, overt innuendo, and sexual tension between them pushed her beyond frustrated. Two weeks of rest had her feeling much better, but she knew Noah would still be cautious, afraid he'd hurt her. She decided she had to initiate it and not give him any reason to resist. She had been without him for too long. One night of making love, after three long years of being without him, wasn't nearly enough. She planned out her tactical maneuvers for when he joined her that night.

Once he had settled into bed and was drifting off to sleep, she moved silently until she was entirely under the covers. She licked the underside of his shaft, along the vein from shaft to tip, then around his mushroom-shaped head. He was already semi-hard when she first touched him, but he was fully erect within seconds.

She felt his breathing increase with her touch and heard him moan when she took him entirely into her mouth. Her hand gently cupped his balls as her fingers stroked them lightly, moving up his shaft as her mouth moved down. His hands came around to hold her head, and his hips began to thrust in time with her hand and mouth.

He made a louder moan, then she heard his sleepy, husky voice. "Bri...ah... damn!" He threw the covers back and raised his head off the pillow to look at her.

She lifted her head and smiled at him like the Cheshire cat. Since he couldn't deny her what she wanted, she gingerly crawled on top of him and stroked him with her wet center.

"Want me to stop?" She purred in his ear, though she already knew the answer.

His alpha-male growl reverberated to her core, exciting her even more. "Hell no, I don't want you to stop!"

She raised her hips and positioned him at her entrance. He gripped her hips with his massive hands. Slowly, she took him inside her. She relished the feel of him as he stretched and filled her as only he could. She moved slowly at first, rocking her hips and finding her rhythm until she no longer felt the soreness of her injuries and just the pleasure he gave her. He sensed her need for more, so he held tighter to her hips and thrust his up to meet hers. His thumb moved between them as he massaged her clit and she screamed his name.

He sat up and wrapped his arms around her, then turned her over to lie on her back while he supported his weight on his arms. He moved very carefully so he wouldn't hurt her, but she longed to feel his body against hers. She wrapped her arms around his back and gently tugged to pull him down to her. He cupped her face in his hands and kissed her, and then he lightly flicked his tongue across her lips. She opened her mouth to invite him in, and he took full possession of it.

He continued his kisses along her jaw, down her neck, and to the taut bud of her nipple. His teeth grazed it as he licked, sucked, and kissed on one side before he started over again on the other side. Every touch heightened her arousal even more, and her moans urged him on. He worked his way down her stomach as he kissed and licked every part of her until he reached her hot, wet core. Fully settled between her legs, he moved his hands under her hips and pulled her knees over his shoulder to put her center fully in line with his tongue.

His dark head moved in to lick her from the bottom of her slit to the top of her clit, where he stopped to suck and tug on it. Her hands flew to his head as she fisted his hair to hold him in place. She felt his chuckle rumble through her from deep in his chest.

He did it again and again until Brianna came apart in his hands. "That's my girl. Let me taste you, baby. It's been too long. Come for me, scream my name." When his mouth met her core again, he didn't stop until she loudly screamed his name over and over.

He moved to cover her body with his and kissed her fiercely. The taste of her arousal was still on his tongue and lips from when he pushed her desire into a feverish state. He bent her knees, and then she lifted and spread her legs to allow him full access. With one swift thrust, he rocked inside her and murmured words of love and ecstasy.

He sat up on his knees, put his hands on the backs of her thighs, and drove hard into her. In this position, he hit the pleasure spot with every thrust and felt her inner muscles clamp down around him as she came over and over. Her extra wetness was his undoing, and with her last cry, he growled her name as his own orgasm pumped into her.

He rolled them both to the side to avoid hurting her, but he didn't let her go. They fell asleep with their bodies still entwined, and he was still inside her.

After her initial night of persuasion, Noah was much less hesitant about her physical abilities.

Noah continued to work mostly from home over the following weeks while she continued to heal. He claimed it was because he didn't want to leave her alone in the event she had any problems post-concussion. If someone were to put a gun to his head, he'd admit that he just wanted to spend as much time with her as he could.

"I will not accept no for an answer, young lady!" Evan's voice boomed at Brianna. "The arrangements have already been made, and that's that."

Noah sat back in his recliner and smiled triumphantly. The whole family was on his side, and there was no way she was getting out of it.

"Okay, Daddy, you're right," Brianna replied casually.

Evan sat up straighter. "What did you say? Don't patronize me!"

Brianna laughed. "I said okay! What more do you want?"

"An ironclad contract would do me just fine," Noah chimed in, as Brianna gingerly took a seat on Noah's lap and wrapped her arm around his neck.

"Look, I learned my lesson. I won't go snooping around in anyone else's dangerous business anymore. I'm done with the whole investigative reporting thing. I'll take the public relations position for Sterling Luxury Resorts and work for you, Daddy." She kissed Noah's cheek and added, "But I'm staying in Miami."

Evan agreed. "Fine, fine. We're building a new Sterling Luxury Resort in Miami Beach on a piece of prime real estate. You'll be able to garner us a lot of good PR."

Diana had another motive for agreeing to it. "And maybe one day I'll get some grandchildren from one of my daughters."

Brianna rolled her eyes.

After Diana and Evan left, Noah set the alarm, picked up Brianna, and carried her to his bedroom. He'd done the same every night since she was discharged from the hospital. It had been almost eight weeks since she was shot, and she was almost completely healed.

She still had occasional soreness in her shoulder and ribs, but it had become more of a dull ache. At first, Brianna did need his help to climb the stairs. She felt safe and secure in his strong embrace. She was past the point of needing to be carried then, but Noah wouldn't hear of it. *Neanderthal*, she thought and smiled, knowing she secretly loved it too.

She loved her parents, but she needed time alone with Noah. He was still as careful with her as the first night she was forced to seduce him. She smiled at the memory of that big, dangerous man giving in to her "torture tactics," as he called them. She walked into the bathroom to prepare for bed. She dug in the bathroom closet to find more cotton balls when she came across her backpack. With everything that had happened over the past several weeks, she had forgotten all about it. As she emptied the contents, she gasped and inhaled so sharply that she felt a pull in her healing ribs.

Oh. My. God.

Noah had just hung up from a phone call as she walked back into the bedroom. "Who was that?"

"That was Shadow. Seems our friend Richard has gotten a lot of his friends in trouble."

She stepped forward to Noah, touching his arm. "You?"

He smiled and answered. "No, not me—thanks to you and those documents. Shadow and his team have rounded up everyone they could identify from the trail Richard left. They will be sent away for a very long time. Shadow told his superiors Steele Security worked with him on the wire you wore. The recording of Richard admitting he intended to kill you completely cleared me of any wrongdoing."

He reached for her, pulled her close to him, and wrapped his arms around her waist. She locked her hands around his neck as he drew her into a long, glorious kiss. His tongue tenderly stroked hers, and then he pulled away slightly to suck her bottom lip into his mouth before gently scraping his teeth across it. He peppered her jaw with kisses and trailed down her neck.

He grasped the hem of her shirt and pulled it up over her head. He savored every inch of her, tasted her, and he took his time with her body.

"Noah, I really need to tell you something."

"Brianna, I really need to show you something."

She was undone by the need in his voice and the wicked, half smile he gave her. He always made her weak in the knees. He quickly shed his boxers and stepped out of them, displaying his rock-hard erection. His fingers trailed lightly over her breasts, stopping to rub her nipples with his callused fingers, before he left a trail of fire over her stomach.

He reached for her shorts, quickly unbuttoned them, and pushed them to the floor. Then he hooked his thumbs in the sides of her panties, lowered them to the floor, and knelt in front of her.

He licked and sucked on her clit, and she fell back against the wall. Her knees threatened to buckle from underneath her. His fingers found their way to her center, caressed and pleased her, and made her wetter. She ran her fingers through his hair while her other hand dug into his shoulder as he brought her closer to the edge.

She gasped when one of his thick fingers plunged deep into her, her knees bent, and her back arched, and she pulled him in deeper. She cried out when his second finger joined the first one, stretched, and filled her as he prepared her body for him.

He stood before her, and she locked her arms around his neck. He cupped her ass and pulled her up as he pushed her back against the wall. She wrapped her legs around his waist as his mouth covered hers. Their kisses became more demanding and more intense. He grunted with intense need and drove his thick, hard shaft deep inside of her.

He placed his hands on the wall, just under her hips, and continued to pound deep into her, over and over again with fierce intensity. "Look at me, baby." She opened her eyes and felt the connection to him deep inside her chest, her love for him overflowing from her eyes.

She relished every thrust and every feeling with him. Her hands roamed everywhere over his body. Her fingernails dug into his thick muscles with every orgasm that rippled through her. Her moans, screams, and utterances drove him on even more. Unable to hold back any longer when she climaxed again, he let go and allowed her body to milk him dry.

Through heavy panting and continued sweet kisses, he held her against the wall, with her legs wrapped around his waist. "I love you so much, Bri, so fucking much. God, you just don't know how much I love you and have missed you. I will tell you and show you every day. I never want to be without you again, not even for a day."

She cupped his face in her hands and kissed him. "You are my life, Noah. I will never leave you again, no matter what. Whatever the future holds, we'll face it together."

He carried her to the bed and carefully deposited her on her pillow before he climbed in beside her and held her in his arms for the night. He pulled up close to her, molded their bodies to fit each other, and softly asked, "What did you want to tell me?"

"It can wait until tomorrow." She wanted to tell him, but he already sounded half asleep, and she knew this news would probably keep him up all night. Wrapped in his arms and his warmth, she drifted off to sleep, completely sated and completely happy again.

CHAPTER TWENTY-FOUR

She stood looking in the bathroom mirror. "Okay, Brianna. This is major. You're going to walk downstairs and tell him. Just tell him."

She stared into her own eyes. "I can't do this."

"Yes, you can. Quit being a coward."

Great, now my inner dialogue is coming out!

While she still had the courage built up—and before she talked herself out of it—she walked toward Noah's office. She called out to him as she turned the corner toward his office. "Noah, we really need to talk abou—" then she realized he was completely engrossed in his work.

He didn't look up when he said, "Uh, okay. Just a sec, babe."

"Oh, I'm sorry, Noah. I shouldn't have bothered you."

She turned to leave, but before she was even through the doorway, his arms came around her waist and gently stopped her. She hadn't even heard him get up. *How does he do that?* she mused.

"You never bother me, Bri." He tenderly nuzzled her ear. He turned her around then he sat on the back of the chair that was directly in front of his large desk. "Now, what did you want to talk about?"

"Noah, it can wait, really. You were deep in thought, and I didn't mean to interrupt you. I know you're busy."

"I'm never too busy for you. Ever. I made that mistake once, but it'll never happen again." His tone was resolute. She couldn't stop the butterflies it gave her to know how sincere he was.

She wiped her palms on her shorts, suddenly aware that they were sweating, and she felt really nervous. Her eyes darted around the room as she tried to think of the best way to tell him.

He immediately noticed how she chewed on her bottom lip, a sure sign that she was nervous. He tried to remain calm because they were in a better place in their relationship. Still, it put him on full alert to see her worried demeanor.

"Um, look. I'll understand if you get mad at me when I tell you this. But I really didn't do it on purpose," she began.

The words were flying out so quickly that it was as if she had to spit them out or hold them in forever. Her tone of voice pleaded with him, and he knew she was scared—–of him, of how he would react, to whatever it was.

He stood up, took her hands in his, and kept his tone gentle. She had been through enough, and he vowed he would never be the source of her insecurity again. "Bri, you never have to be scared of me—to talk to me or to tell me anything. Whatever it is, we'll work through it together. Okay?"

She nodded and bit her lower lip again. He kept holding her hands as he stroked the tops with his thumbs to give her reassurance. She continued. "You see, the thing is, with everything that's happened... I didn't even expect to see you, much less anything else to happen... Then I got shot, and I was in the hospital."

Noah smiled reassuringly. "Bri, just tell me what's going on. Let me help with whatever it is."

"I just realized last night that I, um, haven't been on my birth control pills." She spoke each word slowly to watch his reaction.

"Since? When, exactly?" His face became the unreadable mask again, and his thumbs that had stroked her reassuringly suddenly stilled. His whole body went as rigid as stone. Brianna was afraid she'd hyperventilate before she could answer him.

Take deep breaths. Breathe! "Since that first night you caught me here in your house. My bag was still at the hotel. Noah, I'm late."

He was silent. Too silent. She was about to hit full panic mode. It wasn't that she didn't trust him. She did—with her life. He wasn't the type of man who would turn his back on her when she needed him the most, and he definitely wasn't the type of man who'd turn his back on his baby.

The issue simply was that she knew he didn't trust her yet. Their relationship had just started to get back on track. They were becoming closer and felt more comfortable with each other again, but sometimes she sensed his resentment from what she'd done. An unplanned pregnancy tended to make some men feel trapped. She didn't know how she'd survive losing him again.

Since he still hadn't spoken, she felt the need to fill in the silence. "Look, Noah. I didn't do it on purpose. I swear. I may not even be pregnant. It could just be all the stress I've been under lately. I planned to go to the store this morning to get a pregnancy test. Just to be sure, but...

"Damn it. Should I not have told you yet? I just didn't want to keep something that big from you. I don't want to keep anything from you. I didn't want you to think I went behind your back if I took the test without you. Maybe I should've made sure before I said anything?"

I'm in full panic mode, and he's just standing there! She knew she was rambling, and she couldn't stop herself. His lack of response rattled her more than if he'd been mad and yelled at her about it.

"Noah, say something—anything. Please. Are you mad?" She hesitated before asking the next question. "Do you want me to leave?" She looked down at her hands and chewed on her lip.

"Woo-hoo!" Noah yelled as he scooped her up in his arms and twirled her around. "We're having a baby!" He beamed as he kissed her, and then he sat her back down.

"Noah, wait. We don't know for sure yet," Brianna said with a nervous laugh. But she quickly saw that it was useless even to try to tell him. He grabbed his keys off his desk, pulled her hand, and headed to the car.

"Well, let's find out for sure. Right now!"

Back from the store and with the pregnancy test in hand, Brianna walked into the bathroom. Noah desperately wanted to follow, but he thought he should give her a little privacy to pee on the stick.

How long can it possibly take to piss? He paced impatiently outside the bathroom door, hesitated with his hand on the knob several times, then she finally opened the door to let him in.

"Well?" Like a kid on Christmas morning, he could hardly stand to wait.

She laughed. "Noah, I just now took it. It takes a couple of minutes for the results to show."

He stood over the stick for what seemed like hours. After a couple of seconds, he asked, "Are you sure you did it right?"

"Yeah, it's kind of hard to pee wrong, Noah." She laughed and shook her head at him. She took a couple of steps away and sat on the edge of the enormous garden tub in his master bath. And waited.

After an eternity, Noah turned to her and knelt with his perfectly chiseled body snuggled between her legs. His eyes held the passion and feelings that he usually kept buried and hidden from others.

He lifted her shirt, slowly bent his head to her stomach, and kissed it. "You're carrying my baby."

At Noah's insistence, Brianna made an emergency appointment with a doctor nearby. She drove separately so Noah could go to his downtown office after the appointment. As she glanced around at the other women in the waiting room of the obstetrician's office, she noted their various stages of pregnancy. She tried to picture how she would look as her pregnant belly expanded.

Brianna had explained her worries to the receptionist when she made the appointment. She wasn't sure how many weeks it had been, she had been under anesthesia and given other medications. She and Noah just wanted reassurance that her baby would be healthy.

The receptionist scheduled her for an ultrasound and told Brianna to bring the medical records from the hospital so the doctor could review them.

Noah was ready to tell everyone about the baby, but Brianna convinced him to wait until after the first office visit when they'd have more information. The nurse called Brianna's name, and they followed her down the hall to the exam room. Brianna changed into the paper gown and sat on the examination table.

Noah rummaged through everything in the room while Brianna and he waited for the doctor. He opened the cabinet doors, rifled through the supplies, and flipped through the magazines on the counter. Finally, the doctor strolled in the room, said hello, and then motioned for her to put her feet in the stirrups. He performed his usual physical exam and tapped on her belly. Brianna watched his face for any sign of worry. Not seeing any evidence of it didn't make her feel better, though.

"Well, what do you say we have a look at that baby?" he asked.

The nurse had gathered the materials for the ultrasound and squirted lubricating gel into a condom. She picked up the ultrasound wand, put the condom on it, and handed it to the doctor.

Noah's eyes locked on to it and grew wide. With his threatening tone, he asked, "Where are you putting that, exactly?"

The doctor chuckled. "The baby is too small at this stage to see it by regular ultrasound. We only need to insert it just past the tip. It looks worse than it really is."

Soon the black-and-white picture appeared on the screen. The doctor pointed out the baby from all the various lines and squiggles on the screen. The doctor began taking measurements of the size of the baby, the size of her uterus, and the volume of amniotic fluid. Noah moved to Brianna's side, kissed her cheek, and grabbed her hands. Together they watched in amazement at the images on the screen.

"Well, from the measurements, it looks like you're somewhere around six to eight weeks. I can only give you an estimate right now, but we'll do more measurements as you get further along."

Brianna did a quick calculation and realized conception could've occurred just before she was battered and hospitalized, or just after her release from the hospital. Just those few days could make such a huge difference.

The doctor told her to get dressed and meet him in his office so they could talk about her medical records, what to expect over the next several months, and any other questions they had. Brianna's hands were shaking as she dressed because she was so nervous.

Noah put his arms around her and pulled her close. "It'll be okay, baby." He kissed the top of her head, and they walked to the doctor's office.

The doctor was friendly, but matter-of-fact, as he spoke. "We try to give as little medication as possible to pregnant women, especially in your first trimester. I can't guarantee anything, but I don't see any medications that alarm me."

Brianna let out a sigh of relief and felt Noah squeeze her hand. She looked at him and saw his unfaltering smile. His strength seemed to move through his hand and into her. She had to believe that everything would be fine, that the baby would be healthy. Once outside the office, she began to breathe easier and felt truly happy.

"I have to go into the office for a meeting now. Will you be okay?" Noah's voice was laced with concern. She could tell he didn't want to leave her yet.

"Yes, I'll be fine. Quit worrying about me and get to work." She replied in a teasing and playful tone.

Noah kissed her goodbye, climbed into his truck, and drove off toward his downtown office. He really didn't like leaving her, especially after their first doctor visit. He wanted to take her home and spoil her for the next fifty or sixty years. He knew it was somewhat irrational to worry so much about her. He couldn't seem to shake the feeling that there could still be some repercussions after the fiasco with Richard.

Brianna walked across the parking lot to one of the Steele Security SUVs she drove until she got her car. Out of the corner of her eye, she saw a full-size SUV drive slowly behind her. She reached for the door handle when a man grabbed her from behind, covered her head with a black cloth, and pulled her into the back of the SUV.

He tied her hands and growled into her ear. "Don't fight if you want to live."

She sat motionlessly, trying to calm herself and figure out what to do next. Her voice couldn't hide her fear as she asked, "What do you want with me?"

She felt the car move and knew they were on the main road. She tried to figure out where they were headed, but her sense of direction was off under the hood she was wearing. Thoughts of Noah and their baby kept her from going into complete panic mode. She tried to keep her stress levels as low as possible, but at the moment, she didn't feel very successful.

After several stops, starts, and turns, she heard the vehicle's engine turn off. Rough hands grabbed her from the back seat, yanked her out, and pushed her forward. One hand grabbed the back of her arm and guided her in the darkness. After more turns and pushes, she was guided to what felt like a soft chair. She asked again, "What do you want?"

His angry, hushed voice responded. "I want those documents, Brianna. Give them to me, or your family will get you back in pieces."

Her hand went instinctively to her lower abdomen to protect her baby. Bile rose in the back of her throat, and she fought to push it back down.

"I-I don't have them."

His voice held disgust and disdain for her. "Then what good are you?"

Keep him talking. "I don't have them with me. I can get them."

"Can you now?" He didn't believe her.

"Yes, just...don't hurt me."

He didn't answer, and she knew he was considering his options.

"If you let me call Noah, he can get them. He can meet you somewhere, or he can leave them somewhere. You can let me go. Just take the documents and let me go."

She recognized the man's voice as US Marshal Stevens's. Over the last couple of months, Noah had told her about several high-ranking officials that had been arrested during Shadow's investigation of Richard's scheme. She hadn't heard Noah mention Stevens's name, but she had just assumed he'd been arrested too.

That was a stupid assumption to make, Bri. Now you're here with him...wherever here is, she chastised herself.

He didn't answer her, but she heard him move around the room. She heard him rummage through something, but his movements were so fast she couldn't figure out what he was doing. She heard muffled sounds as items moved, then cabinet doors opened and closed. At one point, he talked to himself. She strained her ears with every sound for clues that would tell her what he was doing.

How long until Noah realizes I'm gone? she wondered.

CHAPTER TWENTY-FIVE

Noah finished his meeting at his office in downtown Miami and was very pleased with the new contract he'd acquired. Shadow had done his best to keep Noah's name and his business name out of the negative press. His old friend had been instrumental in helping him recover from the potential backlash that scandal could've caused.

Noah's new client owned a significant computer software business and had offices located throughout the nation. The owner wanted a security detail at each location for the next twelve months as they worked to develop a new product line. This contract would put Steele Security on the map like no other before it. The best part was it was entirely legitimate.

After his meeting ended, Noah worked on planning for resources to staff that many locations in his first long-term contract. He was so engrossed in his work that he quickly lost track of time. When he finally looked up, he realized he had been at it for hours, but Brianna hadn't called him once. He grabbed his cell phone to check for missed calls, but there were none.

He tapped the screen and dialed her number. It rang several times before rolling to voice mail. He tried the house phone, but no one answered it either. Don't panic. She could be busy or taking a nap or… He turned to his computer, tapped a few keys, and checked his home security system. It hadn't been turned off or rearmed since they left the house together that morning.

"Bull. Rebel. Can you two come here for a minute?" he called down the hall.

"What's up, boss?" Rebel asked.

"Brianna isn't answering her cell or the home phone. I just checked the alarm system, and she hasn't been back since we left early this morning. I have a bad feeling," he explained.

"Reap, she's probably out shopping or something. Give her a little time and space. I guarantee she won't leave you again," Bull assured him.

Noah blew out an exasperated breath and considered what he was about to tell them. If he was wrong and she was fine somewhere, she would have his head. But he couldn't face the alternative.

"Brianna's pregnant. We just found out this morning. We haven't told anyone yet, not even her family, because we just went to the doctor today to confirm the baby's healthy. She'll be pissed at me telling you without her here, but if anything has happened to her..."

Bull and Rebel were visibly stunned.

"Congratulations, Reaper." Rebel beamed. "That's awesome news. So she's probably out buying baby stuff, then. Fifty bucks says she has her arms full and can't answer her phone."

Bull laughed with Rebel, but he knew Noah was worried. "Let's find out where she's blowing your money, Reaper. Wasn't she driving one of our SUVs today?"

Bull pulled up the GPS tracking software for their fleet of Steele Security SUVs on the computer. Every vehicle had been fitted with a tracking device so employees could be found in case of an emergency. He located the one assigned to Brianna and looked up the address where it was parked.

He turned to Noah, the worry visible on his face. "Reaper, she never left the doctor's office this morning."

The three men sprang into action. Rebel called in backup as they walked toward the parking garage. They'd start at her last known location and determine their next step from what they found at the doctor's office. The ride from the downtown office to the doctor's office took no time with Bull's driving.

As Bull had stated, the SUV still sat in the parking lot exactly where she'd met Noah that morning. He looked all around the car but found nothing to help them. He used the spare key to check for car trouble, but it started without a hitch and had a full tank of gas. Noah went inside to talk to the receptionist and learned Brianna didn't come back into the office.

Running back across the parking lot, he called Brad. "I need you to hack into the area traffic cameras, and any other security cameras at this location, and find out what happened to Bri. Now!"

Bull had his phone out and called Shadow to have him stay on alert. Shadow was back in Miami, and they all decided to meet at Noah's house, including Brad, to search for Brianna. Noah called Brianna's phone several more times, but it rolled to voice mail every time. He knew without a doubt that she was in danger.

Brad's tone of voice startled Noah from his thoughts. "Noah, I got something here!"

Noah rushed to his computer as Brad played the video again. He watched as a man in a black mask grabbed Brianna, dragged her into the back of an

SUV, and sped away with her. The camera caught the direction the vehicle traveled for another twenty seconds before it panned in the opposite direction.

"I'm working on cleaning up the image for the license plate."

"Email that image to me," Shadow commanded.

Within a few minutes, Shadow had an email back from his contact at Langley. The email was a clear picture of the SUV, the license plate, along with the owner's name, address, and all known phone numbers.

US Marshal Michael Stevens.

"He was Brianna's handler when she was in the WITSEC program," Shadow added.

"Hey, wait a minute." Rebel recalled a conversation and worked to put the pieces together in his head.

"What, Rebel? You know something? Talk to me!" Noah's agitation was evident in his tone.

"That morning she made waffles. I told her that US Marshal Stevens came by to talk to us. He told us that he didn't think Richard was on that plane and he thought Richard had been taken hostage.

"She didn't say he was assigned to her. She must have figured out that this dude was dirty. How could he not be if he knew Richard was still alive? They never reported he was taken hostage until he showed up. This one guy knew they were both alive."

"And he knows Brianna was the key to the investigation." Noah was beginning to realize what they were dealing with and how much danger Brianna was in with Stevens.

Noah dialed the cell phone number from Shadow's email. He was surprised when the man answered.

"Stevens."

"You took something of mine today, Stevens. I will tear you limb from limb with my bare hands if even one hair on her head is missing." Noah's voice was calm but low. He was serious and determined to get Brianna back and carry out his threat against Stevens.

"And you have something I want. How about a swap?"

Noah didn't like Stevens's cocky tone. He sounded so sure of himself and not at all threatened by Noah's statement.

"What do you want?"

"I want the documents Brianna collected. Every single piece of it. Save it all on a flash drive. I know you still have a copy of it."

"Let me talk to her first. I want to know she's not hurt."

"Noah?" Bri called to him.

"Bri—I'm coming to get you!"

"Not until I get what I want, you're not."

"Just say where and when, Stevens."

He gave an address where he wanted to meet in one hour. As expected, he told Noah to come alone. Brad saved a copy of the documents from his computer to a flash drive and gave it to Noah.

They geared up for battle. This time in their work fatigues, guns and knives, communication devices, stun guns, smoke grenades, and mace in various holsters and hiding places. Noah sent one team to the address listed in the email Shadow received, just in case Stevens was sending them on a wild goose chase. Shadow called his friends at Langley to initiate a search for any other local addresses that were even remotely associated with Stevens.

When I get my hands on him, he won't have to worry about going to prison. He'll be going to a morgue, Noah vowed. There was a reason why his nickname was Reaper, and he was determined to put it to good use.

~

"Come on. We're going for a ride," Stevens said as he yanked her up from the chair.

"Stevens, you don't have to do this."

"Do you know how much trouble you've caused me over the last three years?" he asked as he pushed her into the front seat of the SUV.

As he closed her door, she felt something at her feet and quickly leaned over to touch it. My purse! She quickly grabbed her cell phone out of the side pocket. As he slid into the driver's seat, she tucked it between her right thigh and the edge of her seat, as far away from Stevens as she could get it. She kept her hands at her sides and only moved her fingers as she unlocked the screen.

With her head held just right, she could barely see the touchscreen of her phone from underneath her hood. She quickly hit the speed dial button for Noah's cell and let the phone stay on. She hoped he could somehow track her cell phone signal and find her. She at least felt better knowing he was on the other end of the line.

"Where are we going, Stevens?"

"Oh, I'm going to meet your boyfriend and be done with all this shit," he replied nonchalantly.

"And what do you plan to do with me?" she asked tentatively.

"You'll see soon enough."

Is he seriously enjoying this? "How did you get involved in this? You're supposed to be one of the good guys."

"Good guys finish last, sweetheart. Haven't you heard? Hollingsworth screwed me over after I helped him. He owes me."

"But your name didn't even come up in any of those documents. You were safe."

"He screwed me over. That's why my name wasn't there. At first, I thought you were playing me when I kept asking for them, and you never gave them to me," Stevens shared.

"I wasn't playing you. I didn't know you were even involved."

"Yeah, I figured that out. Richard cut me out completely. He took all the money for himself, but you have all the offshore bank account numbers."

"So you can take all the money and just disappear," she concluded.

"Such a smart girl. Unfortunately for you, you're too smart for your own damn good."

Stevens felt very confident in his plans. He gloated about how he had beaten Richard after he'd tried to screw Stevens out of his cut. A brilliant thought had come to him when he realized that Brianna didn't know of his involvement.

While the feds are busy arresting and scheduling trials, I'll clean out the bank accounts and never be found again.

He was confident that this plan would work out perfectly for him. He only had a couple of minor details to take care of first. One of those was Brianna, and the other was Noah. They both had to die for him to be able to disappear.

He laughed to himself at the thought of how love-sick Noah would come barging in to rescue his damsel in distress, only to find out what genuine suffering meant. He had planned every detail of this scenario in his head, over and over, for the past three years.

He knew Brianna would eventually run straight back to Noah and straight back to the evidence. He didn't know where the stupid bitch had hidden the documents, but he knew she didn't have them on her. He had searched her townhouse plenty of times while she was out on her runs.

She didn't even know he was the one who'd convinced Richard's buyers there was a "new weapon" in the making. His brilliant schemes even surprised him sometimes. That thought brought a real smile to his face. Richard and that Alexa Pope bitch were both dead, her old man was arrested, and every day he heard of someone else in the circle who had been caught red-handed.

Maybe Richard cutting me out of the circle did me a favor, he mused, *since now everyone's money will be mine.* And as Brianna had pointed out, no one even suspected he was part of it.

In a few minutes, the only two people who could delay my departure from the country will be dead, he sneered. *I'll take the account numbers from Noah's cold, lifeless hands and disappear.*

He had secured Brianna to a wooden post in the old farmhouse that had once belonged to his grandmother. It had long since been condemned, and she moved in to a nursing home. He'd held on to the property in hopes that it would be worth something one day.

He laughed at his own witty self again. Tonight, this condemned house will be worth hundreds of millions of dollars. It would be valued at more than any other property in the world. The house was made of wood—old, rotten wood. It would burn to the ground with a single spark. And there was no doubt that there would be sparks.

All around the room, he had set trip wires that crossed over another. No matter which way Noah rushed in, he'd set off the small bombs Stevens had crafted. His time spent on the LAPD bomb squad paid off in the end. He'd learned how to dismantle bombs, but in doing so, he also learned how to build them.

The ones he set in the house were little more than Molotov cocktails and didn't take any real genius to rig. The trip wire would ignite the flares that sat beneath the rag hanging from the gasoline bomb. It was a short rag, so it would be a short fuse to burn. Once one went off, the whole house would catch fire, automatically igniting the others. With a fire burning that hot, everything should burn away without a trace. He knew there was no way Noah would leave Brianna in there to die alone.

Stevens left Brianna inside as he quietly moved around the side of the house. He crouched down in the darkness as he waited for Noah to arrive. He planned to kill Noah first, take the flash drive from him before dragging him inside the house. Once the flares went off in the house, they'd both burn beyond recognition. Then, he would just drive away and never be seen again. Such a perfect plan.

~

Noah jerked the phone up when he saw Brianna's name light up his screen. He hit the button, heard her conversation with Stevens, and knew exactly what she was doing. He put the call on mute and transferred it to the vehicle Bluetooth link so the team could listen through the speakers.

"Brad, track her cell phone and find her!"

Brad was already on it. He was sure what he was doing was illegal, but Shadow gave him the nod to continue. He hacked in to the cell carrier's website and identified the towers that returned the pings from Brianna's phone. A few calculations later, he had triangulated her position within a few hundred yards.

Noah listened as Brianna continued to talk and kept Stevens talking. That was a small consolation, just knowing she was still alive and didn't sound hurt. But Noah had also heard Stevens's comment and his tone of voice. Stevens wasn't leaving any loose ends, and Brianna knew too much just to let her go. He planned to kill her as soon as he got the bank numbers.

Noah sped to the location Brad indicated and saw the SUV turn into a long, gravel driveway. The house couldn't be seen from the road, so the team would be forced to go in blind. There was a row of trees on either side of the driveway, and they ran parallel with the road. He pulled over and told the guys to work their way up to the house. He was instructed to show up alone, and he would, but they would be close behind him.

The other men quickly disappeared into the night, and Noah drove on alone. He carefully took in the scenery as his SUV crawled along the gravel drive. He looked for any signs of traps. He knew what to look for since he had both set and been in enough of them in his military career. *Just like riding a bike,* he thought. *Some training never really leaves you.*

A single light shone through the window in the house at the end of the drive. He knew better than to think rescuing her would be that easy. He caught a glimpse of movement outside, on the other side of the house, and knew it wasn't any of his men. They would approach from the opposite direction, and they couldn't have beaten him here. Stevens was lying in wait for him, and he would be damn sure Stevens was disappointed.

He stopped the car in the gravel driveway. He left it far enough away from the house that it wouldn't be seen but would completely block the only exit. He turned off the dome light of the SUV and silently slipped out the door. He crouched down beside the wheel as he searched the perimeter of the house. His gun was drawn at his side as he ran toward the house. He stopped to look in Stevens's empty car before crouching beside the front of the house.

He raised his head slightly to look in the window where the light was on and saw Brianna sitting on the floor. His eyes quickly scanned the room, but it took a moment to comprehend. When his mind registered what he saw, his heart stopped in his chest.

That fucking bastard is already dead. He just doesn't know it yet.

Noah knew his men were within radio range and, as quietly as possible, whispered, "He's mine." He moved silently along the front of the house toward the direction he saw Stevens going. As he turned the corner of the back of the house, he saw a dark figure crouched by a large bush in the backyard. His eyes scanned the area around Stevens, looking for anything out of the ordinary. He caught a movement in his peripheral vision. His men were setting up for an ambush.

Noah stole up behind Stevens, as silent and deadly as the Grim Reaper himself, caught him in a headlock with his left arm and the barrel of his Glock against his right temple. "Make a move, asshole. I dare you."

Stevens went rigid and stilled his movements. Noah had hoped for more of a fight than this. He didn't like to kill anyone in cold blood if he didn't have to. But this one time he might make an exception for Stevens. He also might just enjoy it. Stevens's hand shot back, and a brief glint of moonlight reflected off his Bowie knife.

Noah was too close to avoid the nine-and-a-half-inch knife entirely. He jumped back and to the left, but the blade sliced Noah's right side and left a gaping wound. Burning pain tore through him as his left arm dropped to hold his injured side, and Stevens whirled around to face him. Charging, Stevens extended his arm and stabbed the knife toward Noah again. Noah's powerful roundhouse kick knocked the knife out of Stevens's hand. As he dove for it, Noah shot at him. The bullet hit him in the side of his chest, and this time, Stevens didn't get up.

Noah gave him a hard kick in the side, but Stevens didn't move or even groan in pain. If he were still alive, he wouldn't have been able to take that kick. Especially since Noah strategically placed it right at the bullet's entry wound. Noah walked away from Stevens while still holding his wounded side. Noah moved quickly to get Brianna out of the house before it went up in flames.

The other men watched the interaction between Reaper and Stevens, but no one interfered. They understood Reaper's innate need to handle Stevens on his own. Reaper briefed the men on what he'd seen in the house, and even though he didn't need to, he stressed to every man to be careful where they stepped inside the house. They carefully entered the dilapidated house and stepped over numerous trip wires. Blake and Roman worked on removing as much of the threat as possible while the others helped free Brianna from her bonds.

Once she was outside the house, Brianna saw Noah's blood-soaked shirt. She looked up at him with fear in her eyes. Not for her own safety, but fear of losing him. "Oh my God, Noah! You're hurt!"

He tried to relieve her fears when he gave his best smile and boasted, "It's nothing. I've had worse."

She knew better than to believe the wound was nothing. One of the guys gave her his shirt. She folded it and held it firmly against Noah's side, putting pressure on the wound to help stop the blood loss as much as possible. She wrapped her arm around his waist to help him walk to the vehicle.

A noise from behind them startled her, and when she glanced over her shoulder, she saw Stevens lunge at Noah with his large knife. With her free hand, she grabbed the gun from Noah's holster. She quickly turned to face Stevens, squeezed the trigger, and watched as the bullet hit him right between the eyes.

She felt Noah take the gun from her shaking hand as she stood staring at Stevens's dead body. Bull walked up beside her, put his arm around her shoulders, and quipped, "Our little sister doesn't miss when she aims her gun."

"My brothers trained me well." She gave Bull a weak smile and leaned into him briefly. She stepped back into Noah's embrace to assist him into the SUV. "It's time to take you to the hospital, Noah."

CHAPTER TWENTY-SIX

"I don't know about that, Noah. I'm sure going to miss him being in the CIA," Brianna teased in her Southern drawl as she curled another strand of hair.

Noah had just told her that Shadow was turning in his notice at the CIA and coming to work for Steele Security. He half jokingly said to her that Shadow saw more action in the time that Brianna was up to no good than in all his years with the company combined. The truth was Shadow knew he was going to be an uncle soon, and he wanted to be with his family. Noah was thrilled to have him join his security firm.

Brianna was preparing for their date night. She stood in the bathroom in her camisole and matching lacy panties. Noah walked to her, rubbed his hand across the little bump on her stomach, kissed her, and then knelt to kiss the baby. She loved when he did that, and it had quickly become a daily ritual.

~

She said she would be right down, Noah thought for the twentieth time. He called up the stairs from the foyer, where he'd been waiting for the last fifteen minutes. "Brianna! Don't make me come up there and get you!"

She appeared on the second-floor landing, looked down at him, and quirked her eyebrow up. "Oh, and just what do you plan to do with me?"

He flashed his wicked, half grin at her. He knew how that smile made her blood boil in the best way possible.

Finally dressed and ready to go, she walked down the stairs, and he never took his eyes off her. Her baby bump had made most of her clothes a little too tight for comfort. She'd shopped for new clothes to wear on their date night.

At Noah's insistence, she had someone from Steele Security close on her heels at all times. There were still people who wouldn't be happy with being implicated in the scandal she broke, and Noah refused to take another chance.

She'd picked an elegant aqua blue dress to wear out. The straps made a V up from the center of her chest and looped around her neck. It was gathered and belted below her breasts to draw the eye to them. The flowing material hung down over her bump and stopped at mid-thigh. She wore her long hair pulled up in an elegant ponytail, with small wisps of curls that hung down strategically around her face. Her white-gold bracelets adorned her arms, and matching earrings twinkled when she walked. Her slingback silver heels matched her silver purse that hung over her shoulder.

"Wow. Maybe we should just stay home, after all." He was only half serious, but if she agreed to it, he wouldn't argue. His eyes moved slowly up and down her body, and she could feel him undress her as she walked down the staircase toward him.

"Not a chance, Mr. Steele. You are taking me out tonight." Brianna smiled as she approached him, put her hands on his chest, and lovingly stroked the hard muscles underneath. "You look very handsome yourself, Noah."

Noah had made reservations at the most romantic spot he could think of for her. He knew her love of the water, any kind of water, and he had arranged for a four-course dinner on a private yacht. A small band would be onboard to supply the romantic music. She took his arm as he led her out to the waiting limo.

He watched her face as they drove toward the marina. Confused, she looked at him, but he just shrugged his shoulders. She knew she wouldn't get any information out of him, so she snuggled up to him and enjoyed the ride. She really didn't care where they went, as long as she was with him. Anywhere was better with him by her side.

She looked even more puzzled when they boarded a small boat and sped out into the dark ocean, but she complied. His pride swelled when he realized she didn't question him at all; she just completely trusted him. When they approached the yacht anchored just offshore, her eyes grew big. She looked at him so lovingly and with the biggest smile on her face.

He smugly gave himself a mental pat on the back. *Oh yeah, score one for Reaper!*

He helped her board the large vessel, and the crewman led them up the stairs to the top deck. The table was set with white linens, china plates, and crystal champagne flutes. There was no alcohol for her, though, but she savored every bite as the staff brought out one delicious dish after another. The band played slow, romantic songs, and just before dessert, Noah stood and asked her to dance with him.

On the dance floor, she wrapped her arms around his neck, as he wrapped his around her waist and pulled her close to him. He whispered in her ear.

"You are so beautiful." He kissed her neck and along her jaw until he reached her mouth. "I love you, Bri."

Looking up into his eyes, she said, "I love you so much, Noah. This is all such a wonderful surprise. Thank you."

He leaned down and kissed her tenderly, loving the feel of her fingers playing with the hair at the back of his neck. Noah thought about how right it felt to hold her again. He knew he was the luckiest man in the world to have a second chance at creating a life with her.

The staff brought out their dessert plates, and he led her back to the table. Under the lid, a small black velvet box sat propped open on her plate. It held a three-carat round-cut diamond solitaire, set in a white-gold band, with fourteen diamond side-stones that wrapped around the band. She gasped, and her hand flew to her mouth.

She looked up to find Noah down on one knee beside her. He picked up the box and held up the ring.

"Brianna, I can't spend one more day without you by my side. I've loved you from the moment I met you. Will you give me the greatest pleasure of going to sleep in my arms every night and waking up in them every morning, of having my children, and taking my name?"

With tears streaming down her face, and smiling from ear to ear, she jumped into his arms and yelled, "Yes! Yes! Of course, yes!"

Noah helped her back to her seat as she continued to stare at her engagement ring. "It's gorgeous, Noah. I absolutely love it. You didn't have to pick out the biggest one they had, but it's too late to take it back since it's mine now."

Noah laughed at Brianna's honesty and humor. "I'll never take that back, Brianna. That promise will last a lifetime."

"I completely melt when you whisper sweet nothings like that to me," she replied. "You spoil me so much more than you should, but that's not why I love you. Your devoted heart owns me. Your sensual touch commands me. You protect me, help me, calm me, and excite me all at once."

"I do aim to please." He winked.

"Your aim is dead on, then, because you definitely please me."

"Well, I'll make sure the neighborhood knows that when we get home."

"Share your dessert with me so we can get out of here faster." Brianna stretched her arm across the table and helped herself to his plate.

"I love when you take charge," Noah chuckled. "Now I'm taking you home, where my heart can own you, and my touch can command you. I need to try these new features out."

~

Brianna and her sister, Missy, had a girls' day out shopping. Missy was as excited about the wedding as Brianna was, and they finally had a chance to spend the day as sisters and enjoy each other's company. Missy insisted Brianna try on every wedding dress she could find until they found the perfect one. Then the perfect veil. Followed by the perfect shoes. Next was the perfect jewelry. Add to that too many bridal magazines. By the time Brianna got home, she was exhausted.

"Have fun with your sister today, baby?" Noah greeted her as she walked in.

"Yeah, I really did. I've missed her. She's so excited about the wedding." Brianna's face lit up when she saw Noah. He was barefoot, and his jeans hung low on his hips. He was shirtless and showed off his sculpted chest, arms, and abs. She'd never get tired of looking at him. He held his arms wide open, and she walked straight into them.

She had dropped all her bags, except one long garment bag. "Is that what I think it is, Brianna?" Noah asked as he took the bag from her hand.

"Yes, that's my wedding dress." She beamed, but then her smile fell.

"Hey, what's wrong, Bri?"

She let out a small chuckle and said, "I look fat. In every dress I tried on, I looked fat. It's a girl thing, I guess."

After he hung the garment bag on the coat rack, Noah knelt in front of her, lifted her shirt, and splayed his hands across her belly.

"I think this little bump is so sexy, Brianna. I love that my baby is growing inside you."

She ran her fingers through his hair as he kneeled in front of her. He looked up at her with intense desire in his eyes, and she felt her knees go weak.

As Noah rose to stand, he lightly dragged his hands up her body as he went. He pulled her shirt up over her head and tossed it aside. Then he gently stroked her cheek before his fingers lightly brushed down both sides of her neck to her collarbones. His hands flowed over her skin and left goose bumps in his wake until he reached her bra. He quickly unhooked the front clasp and let out a guttural growl as her growing breasts sprang free. He rubbed his thumbs over her sensitive nipples before leaning in to take one in his mouth.

She gasped as he sucked and pulled on her, and her back instinctively arched into him. One hand continued to rub the other breast, while his other hand left a heated path across her stomach to the button of her shorts. He swiftly unbuttoned them, pushed them down to her ankles, and she readily stepped out of them. He moved to take her other breast in his mouth. She pulled him closer to her and demanded that he take more.

His hand continued its exploration over her lacy panties to the heated pool of liquid between her legs. He could feel her wetness through them, and his already full-grown erection throbbed painfully.

"Damn, Bri, I will never get enough of you." His deep voice was husky, filled with desire for her. Before she could respond, he removed her panties, his finger explored her sensitive folds, and he found her small nub of pleasure nerves.

She dug her fingers into his shoulder and moaned in pleasure. He increased the pressure with his thumb as his fingers plunged deep inside her. With a sharp intake of breath, she cried out, "Oh, Noah!"

He felt her inner walls quiver as he increased his speed. He knew she was close to climaxing. Her normal breathing turned into rapid panting, and her hips moved in time with his fingers.

"Mmm, don't stop!" Her raspy voice pleaded with him.

"Come for me, baby. Let me feel you come."

She felt his hot breath in her ear as his deep voice whispered and urged her on. He felt her entire body tense as her head dropped back. She gripped his shoulders harder, and he felt the ripples roll through her, clench around his fingers, and drench them as she cried out his name. "Noah!"

As she raised her head and opened her eyes, she saw the smug, sexy smile on his face just before his mouth covered hers. His tongue pushed into her mouth as he slowly and tenderly caressed her tongue. She raked her fingernails over his chest, down his abdominal muscles, to the top of his jeans.

She slipped one finger under his waistband, lightly rubbed across the hypersensitive skin, and just skimmed across the top of his erection. He groaned into her mouth. She quickly unbuttoned his jeans and slid her entire hand in to grasp him.

The kiss soon became urgent and demanding, as she stroked him up and down with one hand and pushed his clothes off him with the other hand. He pulled away from the kiss, quickly lifted her, and carried her up the stairs to the bedroom. Setting her in the middle of the bed, he stopped to look at her beautiful naked body and began to lower his head to make love to her with his mouth and tongue. She grabbed his face in her hands and barely breathed out, "I can't wait, Noah. I need you inside me, now!"

"Okay, Brianna, but just this once." She felt the deep rumble of his laughter through his thick chest. He moved his body to cover hers. Using his knee to part her legs, he settled between them and framed her face with his forearms. He paused at her wet opening, stared into her eyes, and she wrapped her legs around him as she tried to push him forward while she moved her hips toward him.

He laughed again.

"My baby is so impatient." He pushed deep into her. She cried out in pleasure and arched her back. They soon moved in time, his hips surged, and hers rose to meet him. He was amazed and quite pleased with himself that with her every orgasm, she wanted more and more.

At last, she cried out, "Noah, I can't take anymore! Come with me, baby."

He thrust into her and felt her excitement as it built. Her inner walls milked him as they squeezed and quivered around him. He let go as he whispered words of love and emptied himself into her.

He rolled off her to his side, pulled her close to him, and rubbed her small baby bump. He nuzzled his face into her hair as he murmured, "I think I'll just keep you pregnant all the time. I really love how you can't get enough of me."

She felt him smile against her, and she responded, "I don't have to be pregnant not to get enough of you, Noah. That'll never happen." Then she added playfully, "I'll be glad to let you try to make me, though."

He loved her challenge. "You got a deal, and I'm holding you to that."

Brianna smiled and rolled to her side, snuggling into Noah's body as his arm wrapped around her. They drifted off to sleep, sated and happy.

She awoke in the middle of the night and walked to the bathroom. When she returned to bed, she had to admit that maybe the pregnancy hormones were adding to her libido, because she couldn't go to sleep until she had him again. He slept soundly as she planted featherlight kisses along his jaw, down his neck, and then took him in her mouth. He groaned in pleasure, and his hands went into her hair.

"Damn, woman, are you trying to kill me?" His tone was playful, but he was aroused and more than willing. He pulled her head up with a groan, and she rose to straddle him.

She held him at her core and intentionally impaled herself on him slowly. She watched him as he watched her. She rocked back and forth slowly as she enjoyed the ride and the feel of his thick length entirely inside her. She moved one hand up to her breast and pulled at her nipple.

His eyes darkened, and the look on his face was feral as his hands gripped her hips and forced her to move faster. As she increased her speed, he thrust up into her. She ran both of her hands down her torso, then one hand held tight at the base of his erection as she moved up and down, while the other hand reached around to gently stroke his balls. She felt it as he shot into her, and she climaxed with him.

Both of their chests heaved as they tried to catch their breath. They rolled onto their sides and snuggled. Noah confirmed his original plan on a pant. "Oh yeah, I'm definitely keeping you pregnant from now on."

Noah woke early the next morning, eased out of bed to let Brianna sleep, and went down to the kitchen to cook her breakfast. The smell of bacon and coffee woke her, and she smiled when she realized where he was. She picked up his T-shirt that was on the chair beside the bed, pulled it over her head, and watched as the hem fell to midthigh. In the bathroom, she ran her fingers through her hair, brushed her teeth, and then made a beeline for the kitchen.

Noah looked up as she walked in, and she recognized the hunger in his eyes and the gruffness of his voice. "You look good enough to eat. Seeing you wearing my shirt turns me on."

She stood on her tiptoes and planted a heated kiss on his lips. "I'll let you show me just how much later in the shower."

She turned toward the coffee and heard him growl. Suddenly, she was lifted in the air, seated on the counter, and Noah stepped in between her legs. She wrapped her legs around him and pulled him in close to her. The look in his eyes was one of pure love. It was so warm and inviting that she felt it reach deep inside her.

He cradled her face in his hands. He opened his mouth to say something but stopped short. She saw raw emotions in his eyes and knew he wasn't the type to easily share his innermost feelings.

Brianna put her hand on his, leaned her cheek into his palm, and patiently urged him on. "What do you want to say, Noah? It's just me—you can tell me anything."

He moved his hands to her hips but didn't take his eyes off hers. "I need you to hear me out, okay? So I can get it all out at once." Brianna nodded in agreement.

"When I first met you, in the desert, I knew it was a bad idea to get involved—the secret missions, and we lived literally a world apart. But I couldn't stay away from you, and I really tried. I fell completely in love with you out there. I found you on purpose that night in the bar. That wasn't luck or coincidence. It was luck that some guy didn't have his hands on you when I walked in, because I would've killed him."

He took a step back from her, inhaled a deep breath, and raked his hand over his jaw before he continued. Brianna didn't interrupt. She knew he wasn't finished, but her heart lurched over the distance he suddenly put between them.

"When you started asking me a lot of questions about Richard, I got jealous. It seemed like you were talking about him all the time, and I started thinking maybe you were cheating on me with him. Really thinking that you were, Bri, and I pulled away from you."

He took another step away from her and leaned against the island. "That day you came to me wanting to talk, I was so wrapped up in my own bullshit, I couldn't think straight. I said I was too busy with work, but I wasn't. I was afraid you were going to say you were leaving me. I've never run from anything in my life, Bri, but I ran from that."

She nodded that she understood what he meant and looked down at the floor. She'd never even considered that he thought she would cheat on him. She suddenly noticed he was quiet, so she looked back up at him. He was waiting for her full attention, and he was giving her time to digest what he'd said.

"Then you left for your assignment, and you didn't come back. When they called to tell me you were dead, I..." His voice trailed off, and his hands were balled into tight fists. "I didn't think I would make it. I was on suicide watch. I don't know how long Bull and Rebel stayed here with me because I didn't want to live without you."

Brianna didn't speak, but the tears steadily flowed down her cheeks as his words created the mental images. She'd often wondered what exactly had happened, but hearing it was more painful than she'd thought possible.

"They say time heals all wounds, but that's not true. Time made it worse. Time reminded me of all the things that we would never do together. I learned to live with the pain, but it never left. The day you came back, I was torn between being so damn grateful that you were alive and so fucking mad that you were alive."

He saw the hurt flash in her eyes again and immediately realized how the words sounded.

"Not mad that you were alive. That came out wrong. I was angry that you stayed away from me all that time—three long years. I mean, how could you have ever loved me if it was so easy for you to live without me, you know?

"Anyway, when you stayed with me that night, you told me and showed me how much you loved me in so many ways. When I got up the next morning, I actually felt better. I smelled the waffles, and it was like those three years were just a bad dream. You were here with me again."

He next spoke through clenched teeth as he held back the anger and myriad other emotions that swirled in his eyes. "And then I realized you were gone again. I know why you did it. But, Bri, while I was searching for you, all I could do was listen while they beat you and threatened to kill you. I ran into that building just as she was squeezing the trigger. The gun was point-blank at your head... One second later and I would've watched you die!"

He started pacing the floor but kept his eyes on hers as he kept talking. "Brianna, you willingly gave up your life to save me—twice! You are so much stronger than I ever gave you credit for being. I thought I was strong, but you seemed to be just fine without me. I need to understand how that is."

CHAPTER TWENTY-SEVEN

Brianna was still and silent as her tears continued to flow. When she heard Noah describe what he went through, the pain she put him through, it tore her heart out. She wanted to explain, to give him some consolation without making excuses. She thought the best way to do that was just to state it.

With a watery voice, she started. "I'd appreciate it if you'd hear me out now. I will tell you whatever you want to know. I want you to know that I don't mean for anything I say to sound like an excuse. I'm only trying to explain my thoughts and feelings, okay?"

Noah nodded and closed the distance between them when he moved back between her legs and rested his hands on her hips. He kissed her forehead and waited for her to gather her thoughts.

With a small smile, she explained. "I'm sure you knew, but I was head over heels in love with you when we first met. I had to leave before you returned from your mission, and it killed me to wear that blindfold. Thinking I might pass you on your way back, get just a glimpse of you, or maybe a wave before I left. And it wasn't luck that I wasn't with another guy when you walked into that bar, Noah. It was love. There was no one else for me after we made love that night in the desert."

He cocked an eyebrow in disbelief, but as agreed, didn't say anything.

"There wasn't. I had offers, a few guys asked me out, but I never went. No one else even held a candle to you. And I'm sure you know this by now, but just in case, I never cheated on you with Richard. Or anyone else, for that matter. Not even in the three years we were apart. That day I went to talk to you and you were busy, I thought you were about to leave me. I had no idea you thought I was seeing him."

He knew she was telling the truth, but he still couldn't believe his ears. *Did she remain faithful to me all that time?* He didn't have to say anything for Brianna to know what he was thinking.

"My heart still belonged to you, Noah. No one else could ever take your place. And even though you didn't know, I still thought of myself as, well, yours, and I would never betray you like that."

"I know it feels like I did betray you, and I can't blame you for feeling that way. I guess, in a way, you're right. I let you believe a lie, even if it was meant for your good. Richard was there when I went on that last assignment. I didn't even know that at first, though. I met my informant, and Richard showed up to kill us both. Then I rushed back to my hotel."

"Richard had already figured out I was investigating him, and he knew I had evidence that proved his guilt and your innocence. He tried to kill me over there. All those innocent people on the plane died in my place. Before I went to Turkey, I had a bad feeling, and I didn't take the evidence with me. I hid it here in the house before I left. I don't know why I did that. I'd never done that before, but something just told me I needed to."

A shudder ran through her body at the thought of what would've happened had she taken it with her. "Anyway, I escaped from him and rushed to the airport. I was running back to you—to tell you everything that had happened. But Richard and his hit man got to the airport before I did, and I couldn't find a way in without them seeing me. So I missed the flight. I was hiding outside the airport, crying as I watched it leave without me. Then it exploded."

She was silent for a minute, tears flowing for all the people who died on that flight, when that explosion was meant for her alone. Noah sensed her pain and lovingly rubbed her arms while he patiently waited for her to continue.

She sniffled and took a deep, calming breath. "At the time, I didn't think about how strange it was that a US Marshal walked out of the airport in the Middle East. My first thought was just that he could get me home to you. So, I gave him the condensed version of what had happened. It wasn't until later that I realized he asked me if I had the evidence on me.

"When I said it was still in the US, that's when he agreed to get me home. But he wouldn't let me come back here to you. I was so scared after everything that had happened. He spun a great story of why I had to go into WITSEC to protect you, especially since you were heavily implicated.

"The Marshal kept asking for all the evidence the whole three years, but I didn't know why until recently. He didn't believe I had given him everything, because I never found his name in it. Well, you heard the rest of that conversation when I was in the car with him. But Richard knew I still had it, too and he wanted it.

"Stevens knew Richard wasn't on the plane, even though he showed on the manifest. I didn't know that for sure until that morning when Rebel said

Richard was presumed dead, but not from the plane exploding. When Richard showed up in the paper, I knew he'd found me. And since I was already 'dead,' the only way he could get me to cooperate was through you.

"I'm sorry doesn't even begin to make up for what I did. There are no words even to explain how sorry I feel for what you went through. I wish I could take it all back. I wish I had run to you anyway and figured out something else. Those three years were pure hell for me, Noah.

"Knowing that you were only a plane ride away from me haunted me. I cried myself to sleep every single night. I wished you were there with me, I wondered whom you were with, and I knew you had to move on with your life. The only thing that kept me going was a small hope that we could be together again one day.

"I was just so alone, Noah. I thought you were leaving me. We had become so distant in those last few weeks before I left for Turkey. I wanted to talk to you and tell you everything, but you barely talked to me. You had even quit sleeping in the bed with me. You started taking night shifts and staying gone. I didn't think you wanted me to live here with you anymore. Then I was in some third world country, and everything went wrong."

She shook her head. "There's still no excuse for hurting you like that. I just want you to try to understand that I couldn't let them destroy you because of me. You would've gone to prison, or they would've killed you. It would've been entirely my fault.

"I believed they would leave you alone if everyone thought I was dead. I thought you were leaving me anyway, so I guess I didn't really think you would've taken the news that badly. I only wanted to protect you, Noah, because I love you so much."

Noah leaned in to kiss her, but she gently stopped him by putting her palms on his chest. He felt her back as it went straight as a rod and her muscles tensed.

"You asked me to marry you, to have a family with you, and there's nothing I want more. But there is something I need to know now. I need you to be honest—with yourself as much as with me."

He nodded and then asked, "What do you need to know?"

"I need to know if…" Her mouth was suddenly dry.

She didn't want to finish the question, because she was afraid of his answer. It could change everything. Her hand went to her stomach as she instinctively protected their baby that grew inside her. Tears filled her eyes as she looked at his handsome face and felt the same anxiety rise in her chest that she felt every night she had slept without him.

Noah tried his best to figure out what was on her mind that had upset her so much. He saw her hand move to her stomach as if she was shielding their baby from something hurtful. He saw the tears well up, even as she tried to fight it. He kept his voice low and soothing. "What, baby? Tell me what you need to know."

She had to know for sure before they could move forward. She knew she had to get the words out. "I need to know if you can forgive me."

Noah didn't answer, but his eyes silently questioned her.

She took a deep breath. "I know you love me and care about me. I know you want our baby. But love isn't all it takes to make a happy marriage and a happy home. If you can't forgive me, if this is always between us, we can't ever really be happy. Everything has happened so quickly with us since I came back here. Maybe you should take some time to be alone and think about it. I will understand if you do."

Noah finally answered. "You're exactly right."

She tentatively asked, "About?"

"We can't be happy without forgiveness. There hasn't been one day that I haven't loved you. Not one day that I didn't want to be with you. I've never wanted you to leave, Bri. Forgive me for ever making you feel that way."

Brianna stared at him like he had lost his mind. That sexy smile crept across his face.

"And I will forgive you if you promise to never, ever, leave me like that again." His face turned serious, as he punctuated each word. "Brianna. I. Can't. Lose. You. Again."

"I promise, Noah. I promise," she cried as she pulled him to her. He kissed her and pulled her into his strong arms.

~

"Noah?" Brianna's tone was cautious when she approached him as he was working in his home office.

He looked up from his computer screen and smiled. "Hey, baby. Come here." She walked to him, and he pulled her into his lap. He wrapped one arm behind her, and the other hand rested on her baby bump. He kissed her and asked, "What's on your mind?"

"I was just working on the wedding invitations. I know you've never wanted to talk about it before, but I just wanted to ask. Are you sure you don't want to invite your family to the wedding?"

Noah looked down at his hand as it rubbed her belly. "The only family I need is already right here with me." Brianna's hand gently lifted his chin up to look at his eyes.

Noah explained. "Every family has a black sheep, right? In my family, I guess that's me. When I chose the Army over a career in my father's business, he told me never to come back, so I didn't. You, our baby, Bull, Rebel, Shadow, and the rest of the guys—the ones who are always here for me. That's who my real family is, Bri."

Her heart broke for him as she tried to put herself in his place. She tried to picture how she would've reacted if her father had disowned her when she refused to work for him and became an investigative reporter instead. She couldn't imagine her father ever saying she could never come back, then she immediately thought of the baby growing inside her. What kind of parents could do that to their child?

"Do they even know where you are?" She pulled back and looked at him, as he answered.

"Couldn't say. But they don't live too far from here. If they really wanted to find me, my dad has the resources to do it." Noah's voice was flat, but Brianna could feel the undercurrent of hurt in him.

"I was just thinking about how excited my parents are about the baby. After all this time, I bet your family would be thrilled to see you and find out they'll be grandparents soon."

He shook his head. "I don't think so, baby."

She put her arms around his neck and held him tight as she promised, "You will always have me, Noah." She felt his arms tighten around her. "And if you ever decide to talk to them, I will be at your side."

~

Brianna's wedding planner arranged their late August wedding with little effort. Brianna chose a barefoot beach wedding at sunset. Her mother, Diana, and her sister, Missy, both helped Brianna get ready. Brianna loved spending this special time with them. She was about to marry the man of her dreams, and she had her entire family there to share the big day.

"An outdoor wedding. In late August. In Miami. Whose idea was this anyway? I can't do anything with my hair!" Missy had been in front of the mirror for twenty minutes working on the same section of uncooperative hair.

Brianna laughed and threw a hair clip at her. "It was my idea, thank you very much!"

Missy picked up the clip and pulled back the section of hair. With the snap of the clip, she said, "Perfect! Thanks, sissy!" Looking at the time, Missy touched Brianna's shoulder, and her voice hitched when she spoke. "Bri, it's time to get your dress on."

When Brianna looked up at her sister, tears sprang to her eyes when she saw tears glistening in Missy's eyes. Blinking back tears, Brianna chided Missy teasingly. "Don't cry! You're going to make me cry, and I just finished my makeup!"

Brianna stood and hugged Missy. Within a couple of seconds, their mother had wrapped her arms around them both. "I love my girls!"

Missy helped Brianna put on her wedding gown. It was sleeveless with a straight A-line fit and stopped about midthigh. The folds in the fabric lined each side of the dress, starting just above her breasts and extended to her hips in a rounded pattern. The folds gathered at her midline, just below the V-shape in the neckline, by a diamond-encrusted pearl pendant.

Diana took Brianna's hands in hers and held her arms out to the sides as she beheld her daughter. "You look absolutely elegant, Brianna." Tears spilled over Diana's eyelashes, and she dabbed them with a tissue. "I can't tell you how blessed I feel—to have you back, to see you get married, and to know I'll be a grandmother soon." She pulled Brianna in for a tight hug as she whispered, "I'm so proud of you, and I love you so much, Bri."

Brianna couldn't speak. It took every ounce of energy to fight back the tears. So she hugged her mom even tighter.

Diana spoke for her. "Momma knows, Bri." She smiled as she pulled back from her. "I know, I know—you just finished your makeup."

Just when she thought she would get out of her dressing room without crying, her father showed up at the door. "You are absolutely gorgeous, Brianna. Noah is a very lucky man." Brianna saw water shimmer in Evan's eyes, and the first tears fell before she could stop them when he finished speaking. "How can I give you away? You were my girl first."

Brianna's arms flew around his neck, and she squeezed him tightly. She managed to squeak out, "I'll always be your girl, Daddy."

"All right, enough of the waterworks! You're going to be late for your own wedding!" Missy was back in charge and shooing everyone out of the dressing room. She quickly touched up Brianna's makeup and reassured her. "You look perfect. Ready?"

"Ready."

Brianna and Missy joined Evan outside the dressing room and walked to the staging area, where the wedding coordinator, Emily, waited with Brianna's other bridesmaids—her sisters, Jessie and Ashley. They hugged Brianna just as Bull, Rebel, and Shadow walked up.

The three men pulled Brianna to the side. Bull kissed her cheek as he started. "Sunny, you are glowing. Really. We have a gift for you, and we thought you might want to wear it for the ceremony."

Shadow pulled a square velvet box from his pocket and opened it. Brianna gasped when she saw the necklace. The elegant dog tag hung on a white-gold chain by a diamond-studded lobster clasp. The front of the dog tag was polished white gold, the edges were lined with diamonds, and an infinity symbol was engraved in the middle.

Rebel removed it from the box and said, "Read the back."

"Out loud," called Missy, who had evidently eavesdropped on their conversation. Everyone laughed and gathered closer to Brianna.

Brianna turned the dog tag over, and her hand flew up to cover her heart. She read aloud. "A brother's love never ends." She looked at each man, tears brimming again, unable to speak for a moment. "I love it. I-I can't thank you enough."

She hugged each man, thanking each individually. With a kiss on the cheek, she whispered, "I love you."

Bull then took the necklace and clasped it around her neck. "It looks great on you, Sunny."

Emily said, "It's time, everyone." She motioned for the music to start and sent Jessie and Rebel down the white carpet toward the minister. When Jessie was a quarter of the way down, Ashley and Shadow followed. Bull held out the crook of his arm to Missy, she slipped her hand in, and they started their walk down the aisle.

The music changed to announce the bride as Brianna slipped her arm around Evan's. He looked at her and asked, "Ready, sweetheart?"

She took a deep breath and said, "Ready, Daddy."

They walked out, arm in arm, and Brianna witnessed the perfect sunset. The sky was different shades of pink and purple as the sun shimmered on the water and hung just over the horizon of the ocean. The slight ocean breeze made the humidity and heat at least tolerable.

As they turned the corner to face Noah, Brianna's heart leaped at the sight of him. Noah wore a sky-blue short-sleeve button-down with white cargo shorts. His dark tan against the blue shirt made him look even sexier than usual. She could feel his eyes move over her, take her in, and she saw the admiration in his face. She smiled as she walked toward him and her future.

Noah couldn't move or breathe when Brianna stepped into his line of sight. Everyone else faded away when he saw her, as if they were the only two people in the world. She was more radiant than anyone he had ever seen. And she was all his. His chest swelled with pride as she walked down the aisle, to him, to be his, forever.

Evan had a visibly hard time releasing her when the minister asked who gave her away. His voice was strong as he responded, "Her mother and I do."

But Noah saw Evan squeeze her arm tighter as he said it. As Evan's eyes met Noah's, the unspoken message was unmistakable. "*Take care of my daughter, or I'll take care of you.*" Noah nodded, hiding his smile, and took Brianna's hands.

After a few words from the minister, he said, "I understand the bride and groom have written their own vows." He nodded to Noah to start reciting his vows.

Bull handed Noah the ring as Noah spoke. "Brianna, I promise to be the best husband I can possibly be. You will have all of my love, all of my heart, and all of me for the rest of my life. I will do everything in my power to protect you, provide for you, and make you the happiest woman in the world, every single day. I love you today, tomorrow, and forever." Noah pushed the ring onto her finger as she watched breathlessly.

Tears brimmed in Brianna's eyes as she took Noah's hand and slid the ring onto his finger. "Noah, since the first day we met, you have been in my heart, on my mind, and my only love. I promise to stand by you, be your soul mate, and support and love you in every way possible. My life starts and ends with you. From this day forward, you are my everything. I will freely give you all of my love, every day, for the rest of my life."

The minister declared, "You may now kiss the bride." Noah took Brianna in his arms and kissed her deeply as the guests cheered. After what felt like forever of taking pictures, the wedding party moved to the reception area. Their friends and family watched as Noah and Brianna took the floor for their first dance as Bryan Adams's song "(Everything I Do) I Do It for You" started playing.

Noah wrapped his arms around her waist as she slipped her arms around his neck. He pulled her as close to him as possible and leaned his head down to whisper in her ear. "I love you, Mrs. Steele. I can't wait to get you away from all these people."

The low timbre of his voice and warm breath so close sent shivers down her spine. She turned her head slightly and kissed him lightly at first, then more passionately. As she pulled back, she whispered, "Let's go find a broom closet somewhere." She felt his chuckle rumble through his chest.

They managed to stay through the rest of the reception before they made their exit. The guests showered them with birdseed on their way to the limo waiting to take them on their honeymoon.

No one noticed the lurking figure watching from the shadows.

BOOKS BY A.D. JUSTICE

Steele Security Series

Wicked Games (Book 1)

Wicked Ties (Book 2)

Wicked Nights (Book 3)

Wicked Intentions (Book 4)

Wicked Shadows (Book 5)

Crossing Lines Series

Fine Line

Blurred Line

Hard Line

The Vault Series

Warning Part One

Warning Part Two

Warning Part Three

The Crazy Series

Crazy Maybe (Book 1)

Crazy Baby (Book 2)

Crazy Love (Book 3, Free Short Story)

Dominic Powers Series

Her Dom (Book 1)

Her Dom's Lesson (Book 2)

Stand—alone Novels

Saving Grace

Completely Captivated

Intent

Mistletoe Not Required

Immortal Envy

Just One Summer

ACKNOWLEDGMENTS

I want to personally thank those who specifically helped with this book.

First and foremost, I want to thank my Lord and Savior for His continuous grace and love.

My husband for believing in me and supporting my endeavors, my long nights, and the days I missed with him.

My friends who stuck by me: T.K. Leigh, Michelle Dare, and Tabitha Stokes. I love every one of you!

My editor, Lisa Hollett, for her gift of words and her sense of humor.

My readers, love, like, or hate this book, thank you for giving it a chance!

An extra special THANK YOU goes to the very special bloggers who are part of my blogger group. I appreciate your help and support so very much! You are my trusted few who get first dibs at any book I write because I know it's in good hands. MUAH!!!

BOOK 2: WICKED TIES

Colton "Bull" Lanier lived by a strict code—duty, honor, and trust no one outside his small circle of friends.

The *she* entered his life.

His new client was in trouble and kept secrets, but he couldn't ignore her plea for help.

When their attraction flared hot enough to scorch them, he gave her something very rare—*his trust*. But their worlds collided, and he was left questioning everything he'd ever believed.

Then she disappeared, and he was left to face one cold, hard fact: the truth changes everything.

PROLOGUE

"Colt! Coming to you, buddy! Get ready!"

Colt widened his feet and slightly bent his knees, getting into his stance as the batter took a swing. Just as his coach predicted, the ball flew in low toward him in his shortstop position and bounced off the ground once before he caught it and whisked it to first base.

"Out!"

"Great job, Colt!" Colt heard his father call from the stands but he didn't take his eyes off the field. The sun was in his eyes but his baseball cap helped some in shielding his face. The bright spring day was perfect weather for a game. The vividness of the tulips, pansies, and daffodils in bloom colored the landscape. The slight breeze kept the sun from being too hot, but the heat didn't matter to Colt. He played all summer in the sweltering heat and loved every second of it. But this, this was a perfect spring Saturday for baseball with his dad watching.

Colt punched his glove a couple of times and took his stance again as the next batter swung. He loved this—the smell of the dirt, the feel of swinging the bat, and the sting of catching a line-drive. He was only seven, but he knew he wanted to be a professional baseball player when he grew up. That would make his daddy so proud.

"Let's get 'em, son!" He knew his dad's voice anywhere. He could pick it out of the crowd of parents on both sides of the dugouts with his eyes closed. He loved the game, he loved the crowds, he loved everything about baseball—but none of it compared to how much he loved his father.

His father, John, worked a lot of hours and had to travel frequently, but he never failed to make time for Colt. Every day that he was home, John spent time doing something—anything—with Colt. He taught him everything he knew about baseball in their backyard. They had just started working on football, too, since Colt was close to being old enough to start playing on the local recreation league team. But Colt insisted that baseball would always be his first love.

John also made it a point to teach Colt from an early age how to treat a lady. Even at seven years old, Colt could see how much John and his mother, Beth, loved each other. They unfailingly showed one another complete respect and trust. They were affectionate with each other and with Colt—keeping their small town Alabama home as cozy as possible. Colt felt loved, safe, and secure with his parents.

After Colt's team won the game, John took the family out for the standard celebratory dinner of pizza and ice cream. Afterward, John and Beth strolled hand in hand toward their home on the oak-lined street of their small town. Colt was secure on John's broad shoulders and thoroughly enjoyed being able to touch the lowest branches of the trees as they walked and chatted.

Late that very night, Colt heard voices coming from the kitchen. Sneaking out of his bed, he crept down the hallway, crouching low against the wall to keep out of sight. Just as he reached the opening to the kitchen, he heard his parents speaking in hushed tones. He could tell they were concerned about something but he couldn't hear what they were saying. When they started moving toward him, Colt rushed back to his room and jumped in the bed. Several minutes later, John knelt at Colt's bed, ran his fingers through Colt's hair and whispered, "Just remember I love you. Always, son."

The next morning, he woke to his mother's quiet sobs. Walking softly to his parents' room, he saw his mother holding a piece of paper. He silently crept closer and closer to her until he could read the note over her shoulder. She never knew he was there and he silently made his way back to his own room.

He was only seven, but he could read the one line the note contained. And he knew he was forever changed because of those eight little words.

"You and Colt are better off without me."

CHAPTER ONE

The reception for the newlyweds, Mr. and Mrs. Noah and Brianna Steele, was in full swing. They intentionally kept the wedding small, with only immediate family and close friends invited. Some of the close friends in attendance—like Shadow, Rebel and Bull—were all also employees of Steele Security, Noah's security firm located in downtown Miami. The unbreakable bond was sealed between the "brothers" when all the men served together in the Army as Rangers, and finally in a remote area in the Middle East in the clandestine Delta Force unit.

Noah and Brianna exchanged vows at sunset on the beach, with the bride radiantly glowing in her early pregnancy and the groom smiling from ear to ear, like he was the luckiest man in the world. Noah and Brianna's relationship had been through hell and back over the past several years. But with Brianna's return to Miami, they managed to pull the pieces back together and move forward as man and wife, stronger than ever.

Engrossed in their nuptials and having eyes only for each other, neither Noah nor Brianna noticed the figure lurking in the shadows. The one person who tracked their every move, while keeping out of sight of the guests, the wedding planner, the caterer, and other workers. The one uninvited guest, who had crashed their private party, but remained unannounced, unseen, and unheard. The one who patiently waited for the right opportunity to make a move toward the happy couple.

When the wedding party moved inside an outdoor event tent, the uninvited visitor patiently waited outside. There were plenty of ways to blend into the background—to be invisible and silent—when it was absolutely necessary. This was one of those times. It was absolutely necessary to keep quiet and stay hidden. The intruder's sole focus was to wait them out, knowing that they eventually would *have* to leave the sanctity of the tent and head for their waiting limousine.

The intruder patiently waited as the wedding guests danced, laughed, and thoroughly enjoyed themselves inside the fully air-conditioned tent. For everyone except the blushing bride, the champagne flowed freely.

Bull, Rebel, and Shadow all met Brianna in the Middle East when she was on assignment as an investigative reporter. They were actually her assignment, but in a short span of time, they developed a close relationship. They became her brothers, in the same manner that Noah was their brother, and they each took that unspoken oath seriously.

Bull's commitment to Brianna and Noah was unconditional and unwavering. As Brianna and Noah's brother, he felt a keen responsibility to keeping them safe, watching their backs, and being available whenever they needed him. He loved Brianna like the little sister he never had and she had more than proven her worth in his eyes.

Brianna shared dances with her new husband, Noah, and then with Shadow and Rebel, throughout the evening. But Bull waited until the end of the evening to request his dance. He viewed his relationship with Brianna as a special one. He didn't easily trust people and she had earned his trust—actually twice in one lifetime. *No one* had ever lost his trust and then won it back again. No one until Brianna, that is.

"Can I have this dance?" Bull's smile lit up his handsome face as he leaned down and offered his arm to Brianna. She had just taken a seat next to her husband to rest her weary, swelling feet when Bull approached.

When Brianna first met the team, it was Bull who was the hardest for her to get to know. She knew right away that he regarded loyalty and trust as the ultimate test of friendship. If anyone failed that test, they would never get another chance. For those who passed the test, they would never find a more loyal friend.

"I don't know if that's a good idea, man. Her feet are-," Noah started to respond, but Brianna cut him off.

"It's okay, Noah," she patted his arm and turned to Bull, smiling warmly. "I would love to dance with my brother. I thought he'd never ask." Brianna smiled as she stood and walked to the dance floor with Bull.

Noah smiled proudly as he watched one of his best friends walk off with his glowing bride on his arm. There was no jealousy in their relationship. Noah knew very well how Bull viewed allegiance, honor, and trust in their tight-knit group. He knew when he met Brianna in the desert that he would one day marry her. There was absolutely no reason to ever question her love and faithfulness to him. She'd already proven that to him with everything they had been through.

Bull was hurt when he thought Brianna had betrayed him. His trust in her was temporarily shattered. After she revealed the truth, and Bull understood all the events of the past, he realized he had been wrong about Brianna's intentions.

When Noah thought about it, he had to admit to himself that he was relieved that Bull was able to forgive Brianna for her breaching his trust—even if it was for a good cause. It would've been hell living between the two strong-willed, hard headed people he loved had Bull not relented.

Arm in arm, Bull escorted Brianna to the dance floor and gently twirled her around to face him as they began swaying to the slow music. Bull looked around the tent, taking in all the happy faces, the toasts and cheers accompanied by glasses clinking. The bride and groom's deep-rooted love was evident to anyone who even glanced at either of them. He knew his friends would have a perfect life together. Not that there would never be problems, but their trials had only made them stronger and better prepared to face whatever the future may bring.

Bull had accepted long ago that he would never have *this*—a wife, someone who holds his heart, someone with whom to share his thoughts or someone he could trust with every facet of his life. He was happy for his friends but it just could never be in his cards. That decision was made for him—inside him—long ago. He didn't share his feelings, dreams, fears—or his love—with anyone outside of his group. He sure as hell didn't give his heart away to anyone who could hurt him.

"You look gorgeous, Sunny," Bull said, referring to her with the nickname she'd earned when she first met them while on assignment. "It was a beautiful wedding and Noah is a lucky man. I can't wait to be an uncle and help Noah teach that baby boy a few hand-to-hand techniques."

Brianna burst out laughing and put her forehead on Bull's expansive chest. His high school football coach gave him that nickname because of his enormous and formidable stature. Following through on his duties was tantamount to his sense of honor—and one of his duties was to be an uncle to the baby growing inside of her. And his honor would not be impugned.

Brianna shook her head in only slight disbelief at his statement and asked, "What if it's a girl?"

With an equally serious face and tone of voice, Bull answered. "She can learn, too."

When Brianna laughed, Bull finally conceded and laughed along with her. "Seriously, Brianna, I am looking forward to being an uncle. You and Noah will be great parents."

"Thank you, Bull. That's so sweet of you. I mean that," Brianna responded before straining on her tiptoes to kiss his cheek.

"I want you to have fun on your honeymoon, but I want you to be careful, too, Bri. Don't leave Noah's side if you can help it. I don't want anything to happen to you. *Promise me.*" His smile was gone and so was any glint of humor. He was instantly back on soldier duty and she was his charge.

Bull's sudden seriousness and frankness caught her by complete surprise.

Bull was normally a man of few words, but when he did find it necessary to issue a command, he meant what he said. For him to specifically ask her to stay close to Noah and be careful meant he knew something she didn't know. She'd learned that much about him, and she also knew better than to quiz him about it. Years of working on a "need to know" basis made him keep information to himself much more than the average person.

Still, Brianna searched his eyes for any trace of worry or any other sliver of information she could use later to pry everything out of Noah. Bull felt her penetrating stare, knew what she was looking for, and steeled himself against it. The last thing he wanted was to add undue stress on her, especially while she was pregnant, but he learned to rely on his instincts many years ago. Those instincts had kept him alive in many hazardous conditions.

Realizing she would have better luck penetrating Fort Knox than penetrating Bull's thoughts and feelings, Brianna nodded in agreement. She responded, "I promise, Bull. I don't intend to leave Noah's side the whole two weeks unless I absolutely have to."

Satisfied with her word, Bull escorted her back to Noah, who waited patiently at the bride and groom table. As they approached, Bull watched Noah's eyes take in his new wife. He was amazed with how they instantly filled with love and admiration every time Noah looked at Brianna. They also demonstrated how possessive and protective he was of Brianna.

He became even more possessive and protective of her after he learned of her pregnancy. In honor of the love that flowed between Noah and Brianna, Bull made a silent oath to do whatever it took to keep Brianna safe. He meant what he said—he was looking forward to being an uncle and he would use any means necessary to protect his family.

Noah's eyes reluctantly left Brianna and met Bull's. Brianna saw the immediate shift in Noah's demeanor—the crinkling of the outer corners of his eyes, the hard set of his jaw, and the deep breath he inhaled that drew Noah up even taller than his normal Greek-god self. She knew he saw something in Bull's countenance that set him on guard. Noah and Bull had worked together for too long and had too many full conversations without ever saying a word for Noah to have missed it. She just wished *she* knew what it was.

Noah took Bri's hand and pulled her into him for a full body embrace. Since he towered over her, Brianna couldn't see the looks he and Bull exchanged or even guess at what the looks conveyed to the other. When she pulled back, Noah lowered his head and gently brushed his lips on hers, his hands on either side of her face, then deepened it to kiss her thoroughly and completely.

It really didn't matter how many times he'd kissed her in exactly that manner, every time made her weak in the knees and gave her heart palpitations. Mr. Noah Steele was one fine specimen of a man, and she was so thankful that their lives were reunited.

"It's time to go on our honeymoon, *Mrs. Steele*. Let me take you away from here now," Noah whispered seductively to Brianna. Brianna knew full well that his words held a triple meaning. It actually was time to leave, he wanted to get her alone, and he knew something was wrong and he wanted her as far away from it as possible. She decided to go with the meaning that she liked the most.

"Take me away, Mr. Steele. *Take. Me. Away,*" she replied as she wrapped her arms around his neck, stretched on her tiptoes, and kissed him back. As his strong arms wrapped around her, she forgot about Bull's warning. She forgot about the guests who were most likely watching. She forgot about anything and everything else that the world wanted to throw at them.

It was time for her honeymoon with the man she loved.

CHAPTER TWO

The wedding reception ended with the tradition of the bride throwing the bouquet and the groom removing and shooting her garter into the crowd. The crowd whistled catcalls when Noah lifted Brianna's dress and slowly dragged the garter down her leg. She blushed bright red when he stopped midway and softly kissed her thigh. The smoldering look he gave her left no room for doubt of exactly what he had in mind.

Bull, Rebel, and Shadow each took their assigned locations to guard all sides. Each man automatically covered and protected Noah and Brianna's flank without giving it conscious thought. Bull's position put him in the optimal location to catch the lucky garter when Noah shot it into the crowd.

The surprised and disgusted look on Bull's face at catching the feminine adornment was priceless. He was such a big, macho man but he had no clue what he was expected to do with the girly garter Noah had just removed from Brianna's leg. He turned it over in his hands, smirking at the crowd of people who clapped him on the shoulder to congratulate him, though he had no idea why they thought it was such a big deal.

Brianna teased him, telling him it was the male equivalent of the bridal bouquet. It meant he would be the next male there to get married. He quickly tried to pawn it off on any other single, unsuspecting male but no one would have it. He vehemently argued with his brothers that he would never get married. He had big plans to be a career bachelor.

With the festivities and fun coming to an end, Brianna and Noah left the shelter and sanctity of the tent and took their exit as man and wife. Their friends and family tossed birdseed onto them as they left. They entered the waiting limousine with beaming smiles, obviously excited to leave for their two-week honeymoon at a secluded resort in Fiji.

The uninvited guest was still hiding in the shadows, trying unsuccessfully to catch a glimpse of the newlyweds as they walked from the massive tent to the waiting stretch limousine. A giant man strategically blocked every viewpoint of the bride and groom. None of the men moved until the happy couple was safely tucked away in the limousine and the car was then driving away.

Bull, Shadow, and Rebel exchanged glances and turned back toward the tent and beach area, each man taking a different route and moving with the confidence and prowess of a well-trained reconnaissance team. After a few minutes of nonchalantly mingling with the few remaining friends and family members, each man's eyes conveyed the path he would cover as they separated. A few members of Brianna's family were still gathering the last of the wedding gifts as the three men made their way around to the area behind the enormous tent.

Their time together in the military made them a lethal machine that could operate without any verbal communication. The way they could anticipate and read the other's thoughts was more than a little intimidating to others. They stealthily moved into position, quickly identified the culprit's location, and descended. Focusing too much on where Noah and Brianna were, and not enough on the immediate surroundings, the intruder was suddenly cornered by the three intimidating giants. And there was no way out.

One of the giants spoke first, his voice low and instinctively threatening. "This is a private party. And since I don't know you, I know you weren't invited."

When the intruder didn't answer, Bull spoke more forcefully. "Tell me what you want with the bride and groom. *Now.*"

"I have business with Noah Steele," she finally answered, tentatively.

"Not today you don't," Bull responded in an end-of-discussion tone.

"You don't understand. I have to talk to him," she argued.

"No. *You* don't understand. He's married now, so whatever you think the two of you had once upon a time is long over. You have no business with him now."

Confusion etched her face for a moment as Bull's words sunk in. "Oh, no, it's not like that at all. I, um, I," she stammered under his watchful glare.

"Yes?" he prodded, his irritation and disbelief obvious in his voice.

"I'm in trouble and I need protection. Noah Steele—he owns Steele Security, right?" she hedged, pressing on with her questions about Noah.

Bull's threatening stance toward her didn't change. He instinctively knew there was more to this lady than she revealed. Her persistence in reaching Noah, at his wedding of all places, was blatant and now she was asking questions to which she obviously already knew the answers. He decided that he would get answers from her and then he would personally escort her from the premises.

Bull narrowed his eyes, tilted his head, and thoroughly examined her from head to toe. He knew from the first glance that she was accustomed to looking and behaving in a more refined manner than her current casual appearance displayed. She wasn't someone who had lived a life in the criminal element. In other words, she didn't appear to be very street smart, but Bull never trusted anyone at face value.

She had long, black hair that was thick and naturally wavy. The natural tan glow of her skin made her mint-green eyes stand out and be noticed. Her lean, muscular frame fit her five-foot-seven height with perfect proportions.

She wore khaki mini-shorts with a stylish, flowing tank top that showed off her tanned arms and shoulders. Her fingernails and toenails were expertly manicured and she wore the exact amount of jewelry that was considered appropriate but not overdoing it. She was truly a beautiful lady and he would definitely be interested under better circumstances. Interested for a night or maybe two, that is.

When her mint-green eyes fearfully looked up into his, Bull felt electricity arcing between them. The attraction was immediate but he didn't trust that feeling. He was never one to give in to sudden impulses, so he mentally shook those thoughts away and continued with what he knew best.

"I think you know Noah *Steele* owns *Steele* Security. But what I don't know is why you came to his *wedding* to ask for protection instead of calling his *office*. The office that has manned phones, twenty-four hours a day, seven days a week," Bull retorted, his Southern drawl more evident now than earlier. He'd learned to hide his accent fairly well, but it was still ingrained in him.

The extra few seconds that it took her to respond told Bull everything he needed to know. She didn't have an answer for not calling Noah's business line and she had no business being at his wedding. He reached down and took her hand, intending to lead her away. Her reaction was completely unexpected.

"No, please don't!" she pleaded as quietly as she could while she resisted his attempts to move her. "Please—I'm really scared." Her eyes were wide open and darting around the open area, looking for hidden dangers and safe passages. She recoiled into the shadows, trying to stay hidden from sight.

Bull stopped moving but kept her hand in his. He squeezed it lightly to catch her attention. He knew that look—the wounded look, deer-caught-in-the-headlights look, the near full-blown-panic-attack look.

"You really need our help?"

"Yes," came the whispered, strained reply. He knew she was simultaneously fighting tears while internally determining whether she would fight or flee. He was leaning heavily to the flee option, if her demeanor was an accurate indication.

Taking a deep breath and letting it out with an acceptance of resignation, Bull softened his voice. "All right. You'll have to come with me and answer a few questions. We'll figure out how to best help you."

Shadow and Rebel silently witnessed the entire exchange. Bull looked at each of them and the unspoken request was conveyed. They surrounded her and walked her to Bull's waiting Steele Security SUV. Once she was safely seated inside, Bull pulled away from the curb and stole a glance at her.

She drew her sandaled feet up in the seat, bent her knees, and rested her chin on them. Her arms were bent and also resting on her knees, almost completely covering her face as her eyes darted back and forth from the windshield to the side window. Bull realized this part of her story was true—she was very scared of something or someone.

"What's your name?" Bull asked, breaking the silence and making her jump unexpectedly.

"Chaise," she answered after several long seconds. Bull noted she didn't give a last name. "What's yours?"

"Bull," he answered, thinking to himself that two could play that game.

"I can see why," she mumbled under her breath.

Bull chuckled at her bravado, the sound reverberating through his chest, and said, "Let's start over. I'm one of Noah's best friends and a long-term employee of Steele Security, Colton Lanier."

Bull held out his hand to shake hers while keeping the other one on the wheel. She looked at him for a second before relenting and taking his hand in hers. "Chaise," she paused and Bull noted that her eyes darted to the *Quickie-Mart* sign as they passed before she added, "Martin."

"Well, Chaise *Martin*, it's nice to meet you," Bull replied, emphasizing her last name and letting her know that he didn't believe her, but he decided he shouldn't push the issue any farther. He knew true fear when he saw it and she wasn't so good of an actress that she could fool him on that aspect. Her terror was real and he would allow her some anonymity for now—until he felt he had given her enough time to trust him.

She nodded once in response and let go of his hand to wrap her arms around her legs again. She let out a long breath of exasperation and Bull had the feeling she was about to start crying on him. He didn't do *feelings* too well.

"Want to tell me what's going on, Chaise?" Bull asked in a much more relaxed tone than he felt inside. He didn't want to add to her stress and make her start crying, but he needed to know what he was dealing with in this case. He had to keep himself and the other men safe, but his main concern at the moment was Brianna and Noah's safety.

She started to speak a couple of times but stopped both times before she got the first word out. She studied Bull's profile, trying to determine what she should and shouldn't say. He could tell by her rapid eye movement and her increased breathing rate that she was very uncomfortable in his presence. He just didn't know why that was.

"Um, Colton, right?"

Bull nodded. It felt strange being called by his given name. But she seemed more comfortable with it, so he would deal with the discomfort for the sake of a client.

"Colton, I'm scared, okay? Really, *really* scared," she spoke slowly and emphasized each word. "I don't know who I can trust."

"But you trust Noah?" Bull asked and noticed how her body immediately tensed even more at the mention of his name. Bull stopped at the red light and turned to look her directly in the eye. "Chaise, do you trust Noah?"

She nodded her response and bit her bottom lip in apprehension. "Yes, I do. But I know him." She turned her face away and peered out the side window for a few seconds before adding, "Or, I used to, anyway."

Bull clenched his jaws and gritted his teeth. He really didn't like the vibes he was getting from Chaise *Martin* regarding Noah and Brianna.

"Look, Chaise. It seems like something else is going on here. I told you—whatever you think you and Reaper had together, you don't. He got married today, and even if he wasn't married, he's completely in love with Brianna. I will protect them both from anyone or anything that comes against them."

"The light's green," she answered, purposely avoiding Bull's direct comments. Bull stomped on the gas in response.

"You need to start explaining some things to me, Chaise, or this is the end of the line. You can get out here and call a cab," Bull stated with finality.

Chaise obviously believed him because she jerked her head in his direction, her mouth parted in surprise, and her eyes opened wide in fear. "I told you—it's not like that. I knew Noah when we were in school. He's a little older than I am, but we were not romantically involved *at all*. I just didn't know anyone else to go to."

"About?" Bull asked, but before Chaise was able to answer, Bull continued in a stern, commanding voice. "Hang on, Chaise. And keep your head down."

Bull jerked the wheel to the right and made a sudden last-second turn. The car immediately behind him did the same and he knew without a doubt that they had a tail. He calmly picked up his cell phone and called Rebel. Chaise had no time to process his command or to even determine if she should be afraid.

"Black full-size truck, Florida tags, black-out tinted windows. Yeah. Let me know. Thanks, man."

Bull's clipped phone conversation gave Chaise no indication of his intentions or why he was talking about a black truck with tinted windows. His demeanor change was almost imperceptible. The only real difference was now his eyes darted between his rearview mirror and the road ahead instead of being trained on her.

"Colton, what's going on?"

"We're being followed. Rebel is going to shake our tail for us so we don't call unnecessary attention to ourselves," Bull answered in a tone that belied the severity of the situation. It was as if she had asked for the time and he was merely supplying her with the information.

"Shake our tail?" she asked, dumbfounded.

Bull laughed. "You know, I never really thought about how that sounded until you said it like that. Rebel's going to make the bad guys lose us in four, three, two, one."

Suddenly, another Steele Security SUV darted out from a side street immediately in front of the large, black truck that had been tailing them. The driver of the truck barely had time to slam on the brakes to keep from hitting Rebel. With nowhere else to go, thanks to oncoming traffic and Rebel's SUV blocking the rest of the road, the black truck had to come to a complete stop.

Bull drove on and watched as Rebel and Shadow exited the SUV and approached the truck with their pistols drawn. Confident the two men were capable of handling whoever was following so closely that their tail was immediately made, Bull took Chaise to one of the rarely used mainland buildings of Steele Security.

CHAPTER THREE

Securely inside one of the safest buildings in the state, Bull escorted Chaise to a 'discussion room' for a little talk. The staff didn't like to call them 'interrogation rooms' because that term immediately created a negative image. These discussion rooms were plush, with comfortable, over-stuffed leather chairs and couches, easy lighting, and a warm, inviting appeal. When they weren't sure of their guests' integrity, they found this atmosphere was much more likely to promote information sharing than the old rooms they used during their military days.

Chaise took a seat in the comfortable leather chair and Bull poured her a drink before taking the seat opposite her. He noticed a slight tremble in her hands as she took the tumbler from him. Again, he noted that she wasn't acting, but he still didn't trust her. Her words and actions had shown that she was too invested in Noah and not enough in Brianna. That didn't bode well with him. There was no way she was a current friend of Noah's but didn't know about Brianna.

"Back to our conversation earlier. You say you trust Noah, right?" Bull asked nonchalantly while keeping his all-seeing eyes fixed on Chaise's reaction.

She didn't make eye contact when she said, "Right."

"Then you can trust me. I've known Reaper for a long time. We've had each other's backs more times than I can count or even talk about."

"Why do you call him '*Reaper*'?" Chaise asked, her voice full of curiosity.

"Same reason he calls me 'Bull,'" he answered with a single shoulder shrug.

"Were you and he in the military together or something?"

"Yes."

Chaise waited for Bull to expand on his tour of duty with Noah. The noncommittal answers of his were wearing on her already frayed nerves. She knew he needed to feel like he could trust her, but she needed some confirmation that she could also trust him. After all, she was the one who had people coming after her to prevent her from sharing vitally important and damning information.

She looked at him expectantly and twirled her hand in the universal sign to keep talking. Bull considered her request for a moment before carefully continuing.

"Yes, we were in the Army together. He was my Captain and he's been my friend for a great many years now. I've worked for him since the day I left the military and he opened Steele Security," Bull explained.

"How many years has that been?" Bull could see Chaise trying to do the math in her head, counting back the years.

"Six or so," he answered. He knew exactly how long it had been, down to the exact day, but he would only give her answers in approximates.

Her head nodded in understanding, but her eyes said she was deep in thought, worlds away from the room they were in. She was thinking about the last *'six or so'* years that Noah has been out of the service.

"How long since you last saw Reaper—um, I mean Noah?" Bull asked.

Chaise looked back down at her glass for a second then turned her face away from Bull. Her hand came up and quickly whisked away a tear before she turned back to him to answer. "Um, I'm not sure, much longer than that, obviously." Her voice was shaky and she actually sounded hurt by just the thought of their length of time apart.

Bull's eyes narrowed to mere slits in suspicion. "You know his *wife* is pregnant, right?"

Chaise quickly looked Bull in the eye and her mouth was agape. "I-I thought she may be," she stammered, "but I couldn't really see them very well from where I was standing. I did notice he kept putting his hand on her stomach. There's usually only one reason a man would do that." She finished with a humorless laugh.

"My soon to be nephew," Bull said proudly, "or niece. Either way, I'll be *Uncle Bull* soon." All the color drained from Chaise's face at his statement and her eyes welled up with tears that she quickly tried to tamp down.

She didn't know what to say when Bull confirmed that Brianna was pregnant with Noah's baby. A million different feelings flooded her instantly and she knew his keen eyes didn't miss a thing. She tried to mask the hurt and regret that filled her eyes as quickly as possible at the thought of Noah's baby.

Bull continued, "And the *only* person who will protect that baby better than *me*, is Noah himself. And that's only because I don't live with them." He looked at her pointedly to make sure she caught his meaning.

Chaise swallowed hard, fighting back the tears and trying but failing to hide the pain that flashed across her face. "I'm sure you will make an excellent uncle, Colton."

Bull couldn't help but smile at this. "That I will, Chaise. That I will."

An hour, two drinks, and a couple of cartons of Chinese food later, Bull realized he had enjoyed his amiable meal and conversation with Chaise. He actively fought against his almost instant attraction to her. He kept trying to remind himself that she was a client at best and a threat at worst. But there was something about her, something that drew him in and made him want to get to know her better—as a person, not as a part of his job.

These warring emotions were so far removed from Bull that he wasn't sure how to handle them. His training told him to proceed with caution. The man in him urged him to pursue the attraction and enjoy it while it lasted. The logical part of him told him to play the middle of the road as long as possible so that he could find out her true intentions and assess the threat she posed to Noah and Brianna.

Bull was intentionally friendly and relaxed with Chaise as he continued to gauge her body language. When he was content in his ability to make Chaise feel at ease in his presence and trust him, he decided it was time for her to start sharing her story. He needed to know the whole story—why she was hiding, what scared her so much, why she needed Noah's help, and why they were followed.

It was time for her to give him a few answers.

Chaise had watched Bull all evening—from the moment she saw him standing by Noah at the wedding, when he approached her outside the tent, in the SUV on the way to the building, and inside the comfortable, cozy room. She didn't want to feel the intense attraction toward him.

But, dear lord, the man was *fine*. The natural blond highlights in his light brown hair were no doubt from the strong Miami sun, as was his tanned skin. His stark blue eyes innately penetrated and captivated anyone who dared to hold his gaze. He was intense, and though he had been friendly over dinner, he was also powerful and intimidating.

He was a little taller than Noah, which had to put him at about six-foot-five and he had the biggest arm muscles she'd ever seen. They just kept rippling and flowing down from his neck to his wrists. His expansive chest stretched his shirt tight across the middle, showcased his impressive build, and made her involuntarily salivate and gawk like an inexperienced school girl.

Bull had made it plain to her, in more ways than one, that he didn't trust her and he wanted her to leave. He questioned her motives, he questioned her integrity, and he questioned the reason why she specifically sought Noah out. But these things only made him more attractive—his loyalty, his protectiveness, and his unyielding resolve. He clearly loved Noah, Noah's new wife, and their unborn baby. Men of his caliber were nearly impossible to find. He reminded her of Noah in so many ways.

If she told him everything, would he believe her? Or would he turn her away, push her out the door, and leave her to figure it out alone?

No, that definitely isn't an option, she thought. *There is too much at stake to risk that.* She decided she would tell him what she could—what she had to tell him to ensure he gave his help. But she would give no more than the bare minimum until she absolutely had no other choice. If, or actually *when,* that time came, she would pay the piper then. In the meantime, she didn't really see any other choice.

Chaise could feel Bull's eyes burn into her as he studied her every movement. It was quite unsettling to be scrutinized so thoroughly, like she was a specimen under a microscope. She shifted slightly in her seat and immediately knew that Bull detected her uneasiness. His eyes narrowed slightly as his head ever so slightly cocked to the side as he studied her.

"Where is the restroom?" Chaise asked, hoping to convince him that her distress was from the need to use the facilities rather than from being so near to him. Or from having secrets she wasn't ready to disclose.

Bull stared her down for a couple of seconds too long for it to be a coincidence. He really didn't trust her in the least, but there was also something else in the way he looked at her. There was a hint of masked desire. It was so faint; Chaise wasn't positive that was what she had actually seen or if it was just the reflection of her desire in his eyes.

"This way," he finally said as he stood. He led her out of the discussion room and down a dimly lit hallway. "Right here," he motioned to the door on the left as he leaned against the wall on the opposite side. He apparently intended to wait for her to finish and escort her back to the main room.

Chaise smiled warmly at him as she entered the windowless bathroom and closed the door behind her. She looked around for a minute but the room only held the bare essentials. No doubt it was the "guest" bathroom. She took her time, washed her hands, and splashed water on her face. She dragged the towel down her face to dry it and stopped when she caught the reflection of her eyes in the mirror.

"You can do this," she whispered to herself, "you *have* to. No matter how hard this is."

A knock on the door startled her. "Everything all right in there?" Bull called from the other side.

She opened the door and put on her best smile again. "Fine. Just fine."

Leaning against the doorjamb when Chaise opened the door, Bull pushed up to his full, intimidating height as he crossed his bulging biceps over his equally bulging chest. Chaise's eyes couldn't help but wander to the impressive mounds, and for just a second, she forgot to be nervous around him.

Her slow perusal of his imposing upper body made her momentarily forget where she was. That is, until her eyes found his eyes, the ones that were hard-as-nails and were currently piercing her without saying a word.

"Look–" he started when the sound of the main door opening caught his attention. Before she could even react, Bull had pulled his gun from God knows where and was silently stalking toward the sound. Male voices came from the direction of the door and Bull suddenly stopped, holstered his weapon, and stepped into the open doorway from where the voices emanated.

"That's a damn good way to get shot, man," Bull said and then chuckled. He turned and saw Chaise was still rooted to the spot where he left her. He motioned for her to come to him, and somehow her feet got the message before her brain fully understood.

Chaise's heart was pounding and she felt dizzy as she moved toward the waiting Herculean giant. When she first heard the voices, she was certain they had found her, had come for her, and she was completely frozen with fear. Chaise couldn't remember a time when she had been so scared before.

It must have shown in everything about her because Bull's countenance changed from being stern to showing concern. "Are you all right?"

Chaise managed to nod but still couldn't make a sound to answer him. She didn't trust her voice just yet. As she reached Bull, the other two men came into view and she immediately recognized them from Noah's wedding. Finally breathing again, she held out her hand and introduced herself to them.

"I'm Chaise," she said, intentionally not stating her last name.

"Yes, this is Chaise *Martin*," Bull added, intentionally emphasizing her last name yet again. She cut her eyes to him and couldn't help but shoot him an apologetic look in return. He knew she was lying but he didn't know why yet. Maybe he would understand when she was finally able to tell him everything. She hoped so, anyway. He didn't seem to be the type of man she could cross and get away with it.

"This is Rebel and Shadow," Bull continued as he pointed at the other two men. "They both work for Noah, too. And, yes, we all served in the Army together, so you can trust them, too."

She smiled and shook their hands as Bull formally introduced them. She noted that although Shadow was bigger built than Bull, which in itself was really saying something, he had a friendlier natural carriage about him. Rebel wasn't quite as large as Bull but his eyes weren't as hard and suspicious as Bull's, either. He caught the emphasis Bull placed on her last name and gave her a look of understanding as he shook her hand. Even though Noah wasn't there, she was sure she was in good hands.

"What's the word, then?" Bull asked Rebel and Shadow. Chaise looked between the three of them and instantly felt invisible.

"Low-level hired hand. Amateur. He was supposed to follow her and see where she went. Didn't know shit about tailing someone," Shadow answered with a laugh.

Rebel picked up the story, "Thing is, he was hired by the *leader* of the Latino gang, *Tres Seises*. They're not someone a nice, pretty lady would normally mess with."

The three men turned and stared Chaise down. The weight of their stares was palpable on her skin and made her involuntarily take a step backward.

Their size alone was intimidating, but being under all three of their hard, probing stares was enough to make her squirm.

"Well, Chaise?" Bull spoke and turned to face her fully. Her eyes searched his for any hint of empathy but found none.

She felt the tears stinging the back of her eyes as she fought to keep her emotions under control. She had been on one hell of an emotional roller coaster and she was so ready to get off the damn ride.

"I think it's time for us to have that talk. Right now," Bull finished as he advanced on her. Wrapping his enormous, thick fingers completely around her bicep, he easily steered her back toward their "discussion room." Rebel and Shadow fell in step behind them and she suddenly felt something she'd never experienced before—complete claustrophobia.

With her eyes downcast to her feet, Chaise focused on putting one foot in front of the other. One step at a time, she allowed Bull to guide her as she tried her best to block out the unwanted feelings. Entering the room, he marched her to the chair she had vacated earlier and let go of her arm. She instantly missed the warmth of his touch on her and the security being linked to someone else provided, even if only for a moment. Even if he hadn't intended for his grip to be considered a lifeline, that's exactly how it had felt to her.

As Shadow started to close the door, Chaise startled. "No, please, leave it open!" Bull eyed her suspiciously again. "I'm just feeling a little claustrophobic. Can you just leave the door open?"

Wordless glances exchanged, Shadow replied in an easy manner. "Sure thing, sweetheart."

Bull watched Chaise's heaving chest carefully as her breaths slowed slightly, showing that she was at least telling the truth about her incident. Her respiration rate had been close to hyperventilation, but he wasn't convinced it was related to a sudden bout of claustrophobia. From his viewpoint, it only came on when he said it was time to talk.

Chaise took her seat and waited patiently as the men moved chairs around to make it easier for them to hold a conversation. She looked to each of them nervously and didn't even try to hide her feelings. They all knew she was scared and she had no reason to try to convince them otherwise. She wanted them to know she was scared out of her mind so they would help her.

CHAPTER FOUR

"Why would the *Tres Sieses* be interested in you?" Bull asked with obvious scrutiny. He didn't waste any time, she had to give him that. "That particular gang isn't known for having people *followed.* They're known for making people *disappear.*"

Her hand immediately went to her mouth as tears sprung to her eyes and spilled over onto her cheeks before she could stop them. Quickly wiping them away, she pursed her lips and looked down, trying to quickly collect her wits so she could intelligently explain what was happening. She knew from experience that hardened, ex-military men don't appreciate emotionally unstable, babbling women.

Swallowing her tears and anxiety, her eyes found Bull's and she asked with as much confidence as she could muster. "Do you mind if I just start at the beginning and explain? Then if you still have questions, you can ask them?"

Bull leaned back in his chair, crinkling his eyes as he slowly took in her posture. "By all means. Go right ahead then," he replied, but she detected at least a little disbelief in his voice.

"My nineteen-year-old intern is missing! Suddenly and mysteriously. It's not like her and I know someone took her. I've been looking for her and I've apparently gotten too close to someone who doesn't like it," Chaise blurted out hysterically before she could stop herself.

"Okay. What is your intern's name?" Bull calmly asked.

"Aura Perez."

Bull cut his eyes to his friend and nodded. Shadow quickly moved to click a few keys on the laptop while they continued talking.

"She's nineteen, right?" Bull asked and Chaise nodded to confirm. "That's pretty young—she's probably just off having fun with friends, not taking her job seriously. Maybe being an intern wasn't her thing," Bull suggested, shrugging his shoulders like it wasn't as big of a deal as Chaise was making it out to be.

"No, she's not like that. This is completely unlike her and she's been missing for several days now. I know they got her—somehow, somewhere. I have to find her before they do something terrible to her," Chaise retorted, desperate to make them understand.

"Have you had some kind of run in with this gang that would draw attention to you and Aura?" Shadow asked.

Chaise began wringing her hands and looking around the room at each of the men. "How long did you say Noah would be gone?"

Bull quickly answered. "I didn't say."

Rebel gave Bull an odd look and answered Chaise's question. "Two-week honeymoon on a tropical island. There's no way we can reach him without going there ourselves. And I'm not ruining *Reaper's* honeymoon."

Chaise nodded in understanding. "Well, I can't wait that long, anyway. It's already been way *too* long." She took a deep, calming breath in and let it out before continuing. "I work as a field human resources consultant. Companies without full time human resources professionals will hire me as a consultant to make sure their employee files are in order, ensure the policies and procedures are being followed, and that payroll policies are maintained. That sort of thing," Chaise explained.

"Anyway, Aura is a college student and she was assigned to me as my intern. I found some discrepancies between the employee paperwork and the payroll paperwork, so we started investigating them together. When we saw there were just too many *coincidences,* I told Aura to stop looking into the documentation. Something was terribly wrong and we were being pulled into the middle of it. I wanted to find out more on my own and leave her out of it. I'm afraid it was too late, though," she finished.

"What information did you find?" Rebel asked, as Bull shifted his position to lean in closer.

Before she could answer, an explosion from outside rocked the building, sending all three men scrambling for cover. Bull grabbed Chaise from the comfortable chair on his way to the floor, secured her in one spot, and then crawled to the windows to look out.

"There's a car on fire in the parking lot," Bull called to Shadow and Rebel. "It's the one Chaise and I rode in on the way over here."

"Time to move, people," Shadow commanded. "They know where we are and they want her. We need to get her to an unknown location. I'll have one of our other men meet the police here, but we need to split *now.*"

"Let's split up, divide their attention," Bull responded. "I'm taking her south. Rebel, head west. Shadow, head north. We'll rendezvous tomorrow at thirteen-hundred hours."

The sound of gunfire erupted outside, but Chaise appeared to be the only one concerned with it. Bull relieved some of her fear when he simply stated, "Bulletproof glass." He led Chaise down the hall, through a doorway, and down the stairs into the underground garage.

Once inside his truck, Bull slowly pulled forward to exit from a side entrance. When he was satisfied that the exit was clear, he pulled onto the street, weaved in and out of traffic, and circled several city blocks to ditch any possible tail, before heading toward the southbound interstate ramp.

Chaise watched Bull as he navigated his full-size truck expertly through the downtown Miami streets. His eyes constantly searched and assessed possible threats. He was definitely in his element and Chaise thought she caught brief glimpses of what he must have been like when he was in the military. With Noah.

"Did you do this kind of thing in the military?" Chaise asked, unable to hold her curiosity any longer.

Bull glanced at her over his shoulder before responding. "Not exactly the same thing. We learned to do most everything and anything. And we were good at it."

Chaise knew he wasn't being conceited. His tone was humble and the thoughtful look on his face conveyed his nostalgia without saying a word.

"You miss it, don't you?" she asked, trying to pry information out of the man who seemed intent on only giving single syllable answers.

"I do sometimes—I miss parts of it, anyway," he answered. "The best thing about the military is here with me, though—my brothers and Brianna."

Chaise smiled at his reference of his *'brothers and Brianna.'* "You love her, don't you?" The words poured out before she could stop them.

Bull's face took on a serious look as he answered. "She's *earned* her place as my sister. Just like the others *earned* their place as my brothers. I love her like a sister—nothing more."

"I didn't mean to offend you. I wasn't implying you'd betray Noah like that. You just always include her when you do talk about them, so it's pretty obvious that she holds a special place in your heart," Chaise explained humbly. Bull was protecting her and the last thing she wanted to do was offend him or appear unappreciative of his actions.

Bull shifted uncomfortably in his seat and took a moment before he responded. "Trust and honor are very important to me. Sunny—uh, that's Brianna's nickname—well, it's a long story, but I misjudged her and turned my back on her once. I won't ever do that again."

"Well, she's lucky to have someone like you in her corner. And while I'm at it, I'm lucky to have you in mine, too. Saying *'thank you'* seems grossly negligent, but I really don't know how else to say it. Thank you, Colton, sincerely, for helping me, saving me," Chaise fought back the emotions that were threatening to take over her voice.

Bull gave a single nod as his response. He wasn't accustomed to taking compliments. He was used to taking orders and seeing that his duty was performed to the best of his abilities. His commanding officers didn't say the words *'thank you'* for a job well done and they sure didn't show emotions when they told him he did a good job. He thought maybe he should lighten up on her since she looked like she was about to lose her composure.

Chaise wasn't normally such a crier, but the sudden dump of adrenaline was starting to wane and her emotions were on a crazy roller coaster. Everything that she had experienced up until that point was weighing on her as the severity of her situation started to sink in.

Chaise's coping mechanisms were being greatly tested. Aura was missing, a notorious gang was having her tailed, someone blew up the car she and Bull had been in, and then someone started shooting at the building. She was no military expert, but it was all a little too much to be considered a coincidence.

She chuckled under her breath at the absurdity of that thought. *A coincidence?*

"What's so funny over there?" Bull asked with an amused smirk.

"Well, Bull, it's pretty simple. It's either laugh or cry. And since I absolutely hate crying, I figured I had better start laughing really damn soon," she replied with a hint of witty sarcasm in her tone.

Bull let out a full belly laugh at her statement. Chaise was suddenly captivated at how his smile transformed his whole face. There was a light in his eyes that was normally masked, his white teeth shone against the stark contrast of his tan skin and his dark chin stubble, and the deep, masculine rumble of his laugh was hypnotizing. Having only seen his serious side, she was curious just how many people had been blessed with his rich, deep laugh that reverberated through her very core.

She felt herself smile a genuine smile for the first time in weeks–since the whole sordid mess started and she found herself in such a precarious predicament. Bull looked at her for a second or two longer, with this full-on smile still in place, before turning his eyes back to the road.

"Well, Chaise, I have to admit I'm glad to hear that. If I was a betting man, I would've put money on the tears," he replied with a smidgen of teasing and playfulness in his voice.

Chaise hoped she was beginning to see the real Colton Lanier, the one she knew he kept hidden from most everyone. The real part of himself that he kept reserved for only those whom he trusted. That thought left her with a sorrow she couldn't quite shake.

She had only met him a few hours before, but in that short time, he had helped her more than most people had in her entire adult life. But the part that was weighing most heavily on her was that she knew she wasn't being fair or completely honest with him.

"I guess it's a good thing you're not a betting man, then. Unless, of course, you'd actually made that bet with *me*," she playfully jabbed back at him.

His amused chuckle rippled through Chaise and his eyes lingered on hers again before turning back to the road. She noticed, with more than a little satisfaction, that his smile lingered just a bit longer that time. She hated to be the one to remove that smile from his gorgeous face, but with the interruptions they'd already encountered, she felt a dire need to finish as much of the story as she could.

"So, Colton, where are we going?" Chaise asked while turning sideways in her seat. She put her back against the door, the seatbelt strap under her arm, and pulled her knee up in the seat to get more comfortable.

Bull glanced over to answer her and was hit with a sudden and severe craving for all that was Chaise. The way she was sitting was unintentionally provocative and every cell in his body automatically gravitated toward her. Her question purred from her lips, inadvertently sounding alluring and sexy. Bull shifted in his seat and cleared his throat, taking a moment to gather his faculties before responding.

He had only met the woman and the attraction he felt toward her bordered on insane—for him. While he enjoyed the sight of a beautiful woman, and had enjoyed his share of one or two nights with them, he couldn't remember ever feeling such an intense pull to anyone else. Bull fought to keep his mind on the job and not on her as a person.

"We have a couple of choices—a safe house in Key Largo or we can go to my place for now. The house in Key Largo is rarely used so I doubt there are many supplies left for us. But it could be a good place for us to regroup," Bull stated confidently.

"We're, what, about an hour from Key Largo?" Chaise asked.

"Yeah, around there. Is there somewhere else you need to be?" Bull asked, somewhat playfully, still trying to keep the tension light.

"Well, I need to check my schedule," Chaise retorted with a laugh. Then she suddenly remembered. "Oh—um, can we go by my apartment first? I really need to get some clothes and other things together."

Bull checked the rearview and side mirrors and then changed lanes as he checked for any signs that they were being followed. When he was certain they were in the clear, he asked for her address and made his way to her South Beach condominium. Bull circled the block before he turned into the condo, where the armed guard on duty stopped him.

The guard cautiously approached the truck as Bull rolled his window down.

"Hi, Paul, it's me, Chaise. I don't have my gate opener with me. Do you mind letting us in?" she asked sweetly.

"No problem, Miss –"the guard started but Chaise promptly cut him off.

"Thank you so much, Paul! We really appreciate your help!" she quickly responded. Paul smiled and keyed in the electronic override code to let them through.

"Have a good night," Paul called as Bull slowly pulled through the gate. Bull waved in response.

Chaise was infinitely relieved that she was able to stop him before he said her last name. That would cause a whole new set of problems she wasn't ready to deal with, including confirming to Bull that she lied to him. He already knew, she had no doubt of that, but she wanted to be the one to explain it. Having someone else reveal it before the right time could be disastrous.

Bull gave her a knowing look as he rolled up his window and inched forward. She smiled apologetically, yet again, and the urge to explain everything was overwhelming.

"Colton," she stated hesitantly, drawing out his name. She was obviously unsure of how she could explain without explaining, and without making the situation even worse than it already was.

"Chaise, I understand. Martin isn't your last name. You're scared, and until you trust me, you want to stay anonymous. Just know that needs to change soon," he stated sincerely.

Chaise's thoughts immediately went to his statement implying that she didn't trust him. *That couldn't be farther from the truth,* she thought. She knew for a fact that if Noah could trust him, she could, too. The problem existed in him learning of *her* true identity. Would that destroy the delicate tendrils of trust that he was just beginning to form with her? Would he even give her a chance to explain?

Mentally chastising herself, she pushed those thoughts away to deal with at a later time. Bull looked at her, clearly expecting a response, and she realized she'd been lost in her own thoughts.

"I really appreciate that, Bull. You just don't know how much," she responded truthfully, maintaining eye contact with him as she reached to touch his arm. She wanted to tell him that she did trust him. With everything in her, she wanted to reassure him that he was good, honest and trustworthy. Unfortunately, she couldn't convey that to him without opening herself up for the questions she wasn't yet able to answer.

She directed him where to park in the parking garage underneath the oceanfront, high-rise condominium building. Bull looked around and gathered Chaise in close to his side to protect her. The unfamiliar arc of electricity shot through him immediately upon the physical contact. The look on her face told him she felt it, too. But she moved in closer to him, willingly wrapping her arm around his waist as he tucked her under his thick, muscled arm. Chaise couldn't imagine a safer place in the world to be.

CHAPTER FIVE

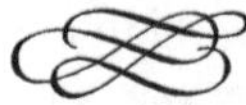

Bull stood at the massive picture window on the twenty-second floor of the luxury high-rise condominium. Chaise's *apartment* was really an eight thousand square foot, two-story luxury condo with an unbelievable view of the Atlantic Ocean from every room. A very talented interior decorator had apparently been utilized to create a natural flow from one room to the next in the open-air design. Feelings that had been stamped out and forgotten suddenly surfaced within Bull. Thoughts of ineptness and questioning if he was good enough to be there appeared from nowhere.

Bull sternly reminded himself that she was in danger and she needed the help that only he could provide. He was there for a reason and that reason was his job and *only* his job. His internal discussion proved successful as he pushed away the insecurities of his youth.

Bull slowly walked around the condo, taking in the few personal pictures that were scattered around the massive first floor, noting that Chaise wasn't in any of them. Just as he was nearing the kitchen, where a stack of mail laid piled on the counter, Chaise bounded around the corner from the back stairs and plowed into him.

She let out a shriek when she met the wall of muscle and bounced off of him. Bull grabbed her forearms, pulling her slightly toward him and steadied her footing. She let out a scared chuckle as she playfully swatted at his chest and said, "You scared the shit out of me!"

Bull laughed easily as he responded, "This place is big enough to get lost in. I'm lucky I found you at all. I must be in the wrong business."

Chaise looked around the luxury condo as she replied on a sigh. "It is great, isn't it? I'm obviously in the wrong business, too."

Bull looked at her quizzically, obviously confused by her statement.

Chase quickly amended her statement. "Oh, this place isn't *mine*. I could never afford this on my salary. It belongs to the company I'm consulting for—they use it for executives, important visitors, people like that. Since my contract with them is only for a short time, they are letting me stay here for free."

The red-alert hairs on the back of Bull's neck were now at full attention, standing on end, and making him tingle in a not so pleasant way. In his experience, if something seemed too good to be true, it usually meant that it wasn't true.

"The same company where you found discrepancies and where your intern worked when you believe she suddenly disappeared? They have access to the condo where you're living?" Bull asked slowly as his hand moved to unsnap his side holster.

All color drained from Chaise's face as she gasped and took an involuntary step back. "You don't think they'd come after me here, *do you?*"

"You haven't told me what you found, but from what I've gathered, you think there's something highly illegal going on at that company. If that's the case, I wouldn't make the mistake of underestimating them," Bull answered truthfully. "Don't forget they've already tried to come after you while you were with me."

Chaise nodded slowly, her eyes wide open, and her pupils fully dilated from fear. "I need to tell you everything, Colton. In case something happens to me, you need to know what I've found. So you can find Aura."

"Let's get out of here. You can tell me in the truck. You got everything you need?" Bull asked, pointing to the small suitcase she still held in her hand. She nodded her affirmation and he took the suitcase from her hand. Bull led the way out of the condo, stealthily moving and checking around corners to ensure a safe route for Chaise.

Bull couldn't shake the feeling of being watched. His gut instincts told him that something was awry in the condo and it wasn't safe for Chaise to stay there any longer. He pulled her in close to his back as they neared the elevator, using him body as a human shield. Once inside, he maneuvered Chaise to the front corner of the elevator. She was caged in the corner by his body. His hands were planted on the walls on either side of her face.

"We need to finish that talk real soon, Chaise." His smooth, deep voice lowered an octave as he nearly whispered his command. His face was close to hers—so close, in fact, that if she lifted herself up just enough, their lips would touch. His warm breath caressed her cheek as he leaned in closer, dropping one hand near her waist. She waited for the warmth of his touch to ignite her already pulsing body.

Instead, he reached to push the button for the lobby. Waves of disappointment rolled through her as he straightened his back and stepped away from her.

What the hell am I thinking? Chaise mentally chastised herself for such inappropriate thoughts in the most inappropriate times and places. She glanced at her watch, noted the lateness of the hour, and decided she must have been even more exhausted than she thought. She also decided she had waited way too long in between relationships.

Stress and anxiety can do funny things to the mind. That had to be reason why she was picturing Colton without his shirt on, the feel of his sinewy muscles and tan skin against hers, the silkiness of his sexy, mussed hair between her fingers. The dinging of the elevator reaching the first floor brought her out of her daydreams, or night dreams, as it was officially way too late to be considered daytime. She quickly masked the smile that was plastered on her face the instant before Bull turned to her.

"Are you ready for this?" Bull asked.

Chaise stammered for a minute, wondering if she had actually spoken the thoughts aloud before she realized he was asking if she was ready to leave the safety of the elevator. "Yes, I'm ready," she managed to respond.

"Stay close to me, Chaise."

"Okay." *No arguments from me,* she thought.

Once safely inside Bull's truck, Chaise breathed a little easier. She leaned her head on the window and closed her eyes. Her thoughts drifted to her intern, Aura, and she wondered where she could be. *Is she safe? What have they done with her?*

Bull's voice pulled her from her thoughts again. "It's late. If it's all right with you, we'll stay at my place tonight and regroup with Rebel and Shadow tomorrow to come up with a plan."

"That sounds great, Colton." Chaise's relief resounded in her tone.

Before she could start to tell him about the discrepancies and coincidences she uncovered, she fell asleep in his truck. Cocooned in the warm, leather seats, hidden from dangers by an expert ex-military man, and the rhythmic rocking and swaying of the truck gliding down the interstate lulled her into a deep sleep. She hadn't slept well since she accepted her current assignment, but her insomnia had become even worse since Aura went missing.

She opened her eyes briefly when she felt a flying sensation. She saw Bull standing outside her door, sliding his huge arms underneath her, and scooping her up from the plush seat. Chaise wrapped her arms around his neck, clung tightly to him, and laid her head on his shoulder. Within a few seconds, she was back asleep, being carried into his house as if she weighed no more than a baby.

Bull maneuvered Chaise and her bags expertly through the front door and into the spare bedroom. It had been a long day and night for both of them, but he suspected the events of the day had taken a harder toll on her than she had let on. He still had so many questions and, truthfully, was looking forward to getting a lot of answers. He was disappointed on one hand. But on the other hand, he found it strange that he was enjoying carrying her to bed, pulling back the covers, and tucking her in safely.

His training and his mental conditioning didn't allow him to rest on his laurels. There was more than some local gang going after Chaise. They didn't blow up cars and fire multiple gunshots at a building that was well outside of their known territory. No, his gut told him that it had to a bigger operation that was only using the gang as a front. Whatever the organization was, it must have a significant presence to use a well-established gang like the *Tres Sieses*. There would be no sleep for Bull that night.

Chaise startled awake, unsure if the loud noise came from her nightmares or from somewhere in the house. As her eyes somewhat focused on her surroundings, she was momentarily disoriented and unsure of where she was. She vaguely remembered Colton picking her up from his truck, so she assumed she was at his house, as planned. She eased out of bed, quietly opened the door, and crept down the hallway toward the front of the house.

There was better light in the living room, shining in the windows from the security light positioned outside, so she was able to make out the furniture in the room. The large man-cave room held an impressive array of audio-visual equipment for the large flat-screen TV, an oversized, overstuffed sectional sofa wide enough for Bull to comfortably rest on, and a matching recliner. Bull had the chair fully reclined and his eyes were closed.

Quickly glancing at the clock on the wall, she reasoned he was most likely asleep at 3:45 am. Chaise jumped when Bull's voice challenged her before his eyes even opened.

"What are you doing out of bed?"

"Bad dream," Chaise answered softly as she moved around to face him. "Mind if I lie down in here with you?"

"Is the bed not comfortable?" Bull asked with genuine concern.

"It's great. It's just that … well," her voice trailed as she started biting her fingernails.

"Just that what?" Bull prompted.

"Don't laugh. It's just that I feel safer in here with you than back there. You wouldn't know if they came through the window to get to me," she replied shyly.

Bull held back a laugh since he could tell she was seriously scared of that scenario playing out. She seemed so young to him—or maybe *sheltered* was a better word. She didn't really seem like she had experienced a lot on her own.

He surmised, from his training in reading people, that she had a controlling father who didn't want to let his little girl find her own way in the wide, wild world. She wouldn't know that he had a state of the art alarm system and no one could get on his property, much less in one of his windows, without being riddled with bullet holes first.

Bull stood and led her over to the couch where he gestured for her to lie down. When she complied, he pulled a blanket out and covered her with it. As he leaned over to cover her, their faces were once again very close.

Unable to resist the urge, Chaise rose up and kissed his cheek. When he didn't move away from her, she moved her mouth to his soft, plump lips. She softly kissed him, a chaste kiss at first, then with more fervor as her tongue lightly grazed his lips. Bull's mouth opened, giving her entrance and returning the kiss.

Bull's hands went to her face and his fingers threaded through her hair. He tilted her head to the side to deepen the kiss. His response to Chaise's kiss was unexpected, but it felt so right. Bull's logical mind kicked in and told him to slow the freight train down before it crashed.

Gently ending the kiss, Bull brushed his knuckles across her cheek and said, "Get some sleep, Chaise."

"What about you?"

"What about me?" Bull furrowed his brow and titled his head slightly.

"You need sleep, too," she replied slowly, as if he were slow and didn't understand plain English.

Bull smiled as he remembered the missions, both in the service and in the employment of Steele Security, that had kept him awake for more than thirty-six hours at a time. But she was worried about him staying up half that time. "I'll make it," he replied genially.

Chaise mumbled something about stubborn, bull-headed men and snuggled under the blanket. Bull reclaimed his comfortable recliner and watched Chaise as she drifted back to sleep. He listened to her rhythmic breathing pattern, watched the softening of her face and relaxation of her entire body, and knew the exact moment she had succumbed to sleep. A fleeting thought flashed in his mind about wanting what Noah and Brianna had but he quickly pushed it away.

Mentally reprimanding himself for the momentary lapse in discipline, Bull steeled his thoughts and relaxed in his chair. He closed his eyes and listened to the sounds around the house. He knew every creak and moan and would know immediately if anything was out of the ordinary.

Bull was more relaxed while "on duty" inside his house because Steele Security monitored his alarm system from their central location. If his system suddenly quit, as in someone cut the line or they turned his electricity off, Steele Security would call his phone and they would immediately dispatch units if he didn't answer.

CHAPTER SIX

The smell of bacon frying and coffee percolating woke Bull from the best sleep he'd had in memory. Momentarily alarmed by the unfamiliar sounds and smells, it took him a moment to remember that Chaise was in the house with him. He silently rose from his chair, noted that she was missing from the couch, and he silently crept into the kitchen. He watched her from the doorway for several minutes without her ever knowing he was there.

The thought that she was being too reckless with her safety by being unaware of her surroundings crossed his mind and he had every intention of chastising her for it. Then he realized that she'd somehow walked past him, made herself at home in his kitchen, and had their breakfast almost fully cooked before he even realized anything. He decided that the chastising should really be more of a discussion about general safety precautions.

Besides, he really enjoyed watching her cook, in his kitchen, wearing her tight spaghetti strap tank top and cotton pajama shorts. She was making herself at home, but at the same time, she was also making sure to take care of him. No one had taken care of him, other than his brothers having his back, since he'd left home.

"Something smells good," Bull finally stated, making his presence known. The sudden intrusion made her jump and she let out a startled shriek. Bull's smile grew wider, reaching his eyes and making them dance with mischief.

"Colton Lanier!" she playfully yelled while laughing, "You will stop scaring me!"

Chaise tried to sound stern but she just couldn't do it when Bull was smiling at her like that. She stood transfixed, rooted to the floor as she watched him move toward her with his confident gait. His massive muscles flexing and contracting, his keen eyes assessing but also holding an unusual glint of humor, and one side of his mouth curled up in a sexy half-grin. *The man just woke up and he still looks sexy as hell,* she thought.

"Where's the fun in that?" he asked as he stalked toward the plate of crispy bacon.

"Oh, no you don't, Mr. Lanier!"

Bull's grim look conveyed that he'd been appropriately chastised so Chaise turned back to the stove to finish cooking. Bull snatched a piece of bacon when she wasn't looking and promptly chomped on it. The crackling noise made Chaise's head spin back toward him and he immediately stopped chewing. She narrowed her eyes suspiciously at him but he feigned an innocent look. She turned her head back and then quickly snapped it back to him just as he started chewing again.

She chased him out of the kitchen with a towel wound up, ready to snap him with it. They both laughed good-naturedly, genuinely enjoying the playful banter and easy-going morning lightheartedness. Chaise dared to hope that the new repartee signaled a positive shift in their relationship.

"You're going to make me overcook the eggs!" she playfully admonished him. Bull's smile lit up his face again as he popped the rest of the bacon in his mouth and aggressively chewed it in front of her.

"Here, let me help," he said, setting the plates and forks on the table.

Chaise looked at the plates and back to Bull. "That's it? That's helping?" she asked with a straight face.

For a few seconds, Bull looked unsure of how to answer that trick question. Unable to hold back her smile, Chaise quickly turned around to hide her face from Bull's all-knowing gaze. Soon, she was unable to hold in her laughter and her shoulders started bouncing up and down as she covered her mouth with one hand.

She was suddenly hoisted in the air by two strong arms that surrounded her and heard Bull's teasing voice. "Are you making fun of me, Chaise *Martin?*"

She squealed with amusement and screamed. *"The eggs!"*

Bull lowered her body back down, skimming his front with her back. The electricity arcing off of their bodies should have short-circuited everything within a fifty-mile radius, like an miniature EMP blast. When Chaise looked over her shoulder at Bull, the sultry, sweltering look he held would have melted steel.

Bull's hands rested on her waist, still holding her tightly to him, and he knew if he merely bent his head, their lips would touch and the damn eggs could burn to ashes. He felt his head incline slowly toward her, his eyes flitting back and forth between her plump lips and her accepting eyes. The memory of last night's kiss was on both of their minds, fueling the fire raging between them.

The shrill sound of his cell phone jolted him back to reality and he quickly let go of her, putting distance between them physically and mentally, before walking off to pick up his phone. Looking quickly at the screen, he noted it was Rebel before he answered. "Yeah, man."

Chaise listened to Bull's clipped end of the conversation but was unable to ascertain anything of use from it. Putting the food on the table, she filled their glasses with juice and filled her plate. She considered waiting for Bull to join her before she started eating but petulantly decided against it. As Bull finished his phone call, Chaise was finishing her breakfast. After rinsing the breakfast dishes and putting them in the dishwasher, she wordlessly left the room to shower and dress.

Knowing what the day held—her interrogation by the Steele Security team—she was not in a hurry to finish her morning ritual. The endless questions, the uncomfortable probing, the dubious glances, and the new issue of claustrophobia made the day downright dreadful. Now, with the mixed signals and wishy-washy temperament of Bull added, the day instantly became infinitely worse.

An hour later, when she left her room, she heard multiple male voices coming from the kitchen. Slowly and quietly skirting down the hall, she tried to covertly listen to their conversation before they became aware of her presence. The chatter suddenly stopped and she knew the team had detected her presence. It was their job, after all, but she'd hoped to at least get an idea of what she would be walking into.

Rounding the corner into the kitchen, she noted Rebel and Shadow sitting at the table with Bull. Bull was fully facing her and their eyes locked. His intense desire was still there, simmering like lava just beneath the earth's surface, only masked by his cool exterior. She liked that he reacted that way to her, but sensed any movement in their current status would have to be initiated by her. Bull's sense of professionalism and duty was deep and strong—he wouldn't likely make the first move on a client.

She'd purposely dressed in a short, light green dress that made her mint green eyes sparkle. It wasn't overly provocative but it wasn't boring, either. The V-neck halter tied around her neck, leaving it open to her mid-back. The loose fitting silhouette, along with the gracefully flowing hemline, made her lean legs go on forever. She paired it with long, elegant necklaces and light brown Grecian sandals to show off her dainty, painted toes.

Bull had been leaning on his forearms on the table, but the sight of Chaise in that dress had him sitting up at full attention. Her beauty was mesmerizing and had his thoughts racing about being alone with her again. The attraction was undeniable, like a moth to the flame, just as hot and just as likely to be burned. *If this is being burned*, Bull thought, *I can definitely handle the heat.*

He watched the slight blush creep up Chaise's slender neck to her cheeks, turning them a light shade of pink. She no doubt knew the look of a man who appreciated her beauty. Knowing she was just as affected as he was, and not hiding it, made her even more attractive to Bull.

"We were just talking about you. Perfect timing, Chaise," Bull's smooth voice welcomed her.

Smiling, she responded. "Good morning, Rebel, Shadow. And just what were you guys saying about me?"

Shadow started first. "Good morning, Chaise. I conducted a search for anything on Aura Perez but I found nothing of use. There's no missing persons report on file for her. Do you know why that would be?"

Chaise stopped in mid-step, shocked and unblinking before answering, "N–no. There's no report? You're sure? Her mom said she filed it. She was worried *sick*."

Chaise took a seat at the table, confusion and unrest imprinted in her features. She looked at each man and found only his assessing stares in return. "I don't understand. What happened to her missing person report? No one's been looking for her all this time?"

Shadow's deceptively calm voice set her nerves on edge. "There wasn't a report filed, Chaise. I checked for electronic reports and paper reports. I've talked to all my contacts at the sheriff's department."

"No, that's not right! Someone told you wrong," Chase adamantly refused to believe her ears.

Shadow looked at Bull and Bull took over the conversation. "Chaise, I think it's time you start from the beginning and tell us everything."

Chaise nodded but Bull noted the apprehension and tension settle in her face. "Okay, from the beginning. I'm an HR consultant, working under contract at Viboro Distributing. Aura was my intern. She was attending the University of Miami and was assigned to help me with all the cross-referencing data."

Rebel interjected. "Who assigned her to you?"

Chaise stumbled at his question. "Um, I'm not sure what you mean. She was waiting for me at Viboro and she said she was my intern."

"So, you didn't negotiate to have an intern? The managers at Viboro didn't introduce the two of you?" Rebel pressed.

Chaise gave it some thought before answering. "No, she was waiting outside the office I was assigned to when I got there."

"Okay, go on," Bull encouraged.

"Part of my job is to make sure all the paperwork matches—cross matching dates in the personnel files and payroll files—to make sure they've maintained accurate records. I started finding discrepancies in the hire and termination dates between the personnel files and the payroll files. Two different areas maintain them but they're supposed to communicate with each other.

"At first, I didn't think anything about the discrepancies—there were only a couple in the first dataset. I find that in every large corporation. The paperwork gets lost, someone keys in a wrong date, and usually it's no big deal to correct it. But then I kept finding them and started making a comprehensive list of names, addresses, and birth dates."

Bull repositioned himself, eager to learn more and dig further into the developing mystery. "Do you still have the list?"

Chaise regarded him for a moment before answering. "Yes, I have it."

"That's great. We can easily check that list against our databases," Shadow answered.

"Shouldn't I finish telling you everything before you just jump in and take over everything?" Chaise probed irritably.

Rebel couldn't contain his amusement. "I like her," he said to Bull and Shadow. "By all means, please continue, Chaise. We're all ears."

"I noticed every name on the list was a Latino girl, between eighteen and twenty-two years old, and it all was just too suspicious for me to ignore. At first I thought it was a blatant issue of racial profiling. But when I searched for a couple of them online, I found the fliers saying they were missing persons. One after the other, Aura and I kept finding missing girls—all from Viboro Distributing, all Latino, and all very young.

"I told Aura to stop investigating it and leave it to me. I had the feeling we'd already raised too many suspicions with our questions. The next day, she didn't show up or call, so I went to her house. Her mother was absolutely distraught. She said Aura hadn't come home or called," Chaise finished.

"Did you call the police?" Rebel asked.

"No," Chaise answered tentatively. "I asked the head of security a few questions, but that didn't work out so well. Several strange things happened after that. That's why I ended up at Noah's wedding—I didn't know what else to do."

"Do you remember where Aura's mother lives?" Rebel asked.

"Yes."

"Good. Let's go talk to her mom today," Bull answered.

"All right," Chaise answered. "Can you take me to pick up my company car? I left it at the wedding reception yesterday."

"Sure," Bull answered. But Chaise didn't miss the suspicion in his eyes.

He still doesn't truly believe me, she thought solemnly.

Chaise rode with Bull, giving him directions to Aura's house, while Rebel and Shadow took a separate vehicle. When they arrived at the small house in the Hialeah Gardens area of Miami, Bull watched Chaise take a deep breath before exiting the car. They walked together to the front door while Rebel and Shadow kept watch around the perimeter of the house.

Bull knocked on the door, and when it opened, he was surprised to see an elderly Chinese man on the other side. He looked at Chaise, questioning her with his eyes, but she shook her head in confusion and had no answer for him. Bull turned back to the gentleman and gave him a warm smile.

"Hello, we are looking for Mrs. Perez. Is she home?" Bull asked.

"There's no one here by that name. I live here alone," the man answered.

"Maybe she left a forwarding address?" Bull continued his line of questioning.

"No, I think you must have the wrong address. I've lived here the last ten years," the man stated firmly, looking back and forth between Bull and Chaise.

"That can't be right—I am sure it was *this* house. I remember these red bricks on the driveway!" Chaise argued, confused and irritated about why the Chinese man insisted Mrs. Perez didn't live there.

"There are many houses in Hialeah Gardens with this kind of driveway, Miss. There's no Mrs. Perez here. Goodbye," he smarted as he stepped back in the house and closed the door in her face.

CHAPTER SEVEN

Chaise was quiet on the drive to pick up her company car from the beach area. Bull didn't have to say anything. She could tell exactly what he was thinking from the disbelieving look on his face. He made no attempt to spare her feelings with the look that he gave her. He thought she was making everything up. Glancing out the window, she saw that Rebel and Shadow were still following them.

"Why are they following us? We're just going to pick up my car, right?"

"Yes," Bull answered briskly without any further explanation.

"So, why are they following us?" Chaise pressed.

"Safety precautions," Bull answered.

Chaise knew better than to believe that excuse. Bull was keeping tabs on her because he didn't believe her and the Chinese man didn't help her case at all. "Well, I guess I should be completely safe then, right?"

"That's right," Bull snapped.

"Look, I don't know what's going on, but that's the house I went to and that's the house where I talked to Aura's mom. I'm not making this up!" Chaise could no longer hold in her frustration.

"If you say so," Bull responded with less sarcasm than before.

Chaise angrily huffed in response and was infinitely glad that they were arriving at her car. Placing her hand on the door, she readied herself to jump out and get away from the infuriating man beside her. It was just her luck that he burst that little bubble of hope before he came to a stop beside her car.

"Follow me back to my house. Shadow and Rebel will be directly behind you. You need to be on extreme alert for anything suspicious between here and my house. We will all be watching you," Bull informed her resolutely.

Chaise knew his message held the information she needed to be kept safe.

But she couldn't shake the feeling that the same message was intended to *keep* her, period. They were following her and watching out for her, but they were also watching her and doubting her. Meeting Bull's eyes, Chaise felt the familiar butterflies in her stomach—the ones she got when she felt his stare penetrating deep into her thoughts.

Can he read my mind?

"Okay, I will follow you back to your place," she agreed, placating him and avoiding any arguments. Chaise lived by the motto to choose her battles and this wasn't one she wanted to fight with Bull. She would eventually have to talk to him about going back to work the following day. She knew how that would go over, though—about as well as trying to reason with an actual bull.

Back at Bull's house after an uneventful ride, Chaise popped the trunk of her company car and started removing all the contents. Bull, Shadow, and Rebel watched with curious and dubious gazes. When she started tugging on the spare tire, Bull wordlessly stepped in and removed it for her.

"Thank you," Chaise said in all sincerity. Bull simply nodded and placed the tire on the ground.

"What are you doing?" he finally asked.

Reaching under the jack, she retrieved a small, black cartridge and handed it to Bull. Upon inspection, he realized it was a tiny flash drive.

"That's the file that I was researching when I found all the discrepancies. I highlighted the missing girls I found online but there are plenty more to be researched," she explained.

Bull handed the flash drive to Shadow who was already on his cell phone calling his confidential contacts to start the investigation. When Bull turned back to Chaise, she could still see the apparent distrust in his eyes. Releasing a sigh of resignation, she started putting the contents of the trunk back together as Shadow and Rebel walked inside, leaving Bull and Chaise alone.

Unable to stand it any longer, she turned to Bull and firmly address him. "I am not lying. I'm not making this up and I'm not crazy. I don't know what's going on but I *need* you to believe me. Even if it is for no other reason than to help me find Aura. *Please.*"

"All right," Bull responded, sensing her sincerity. "But I still have questions you haven't answered yet. Simple questions—like your last name."

"Colton, that's not as simple as you think," she quietly explained, looking down at her hands. Meeting his sharp gaze again, she continued. "What else can I do?"

"I don't know, Chaise. I guess we'll have to take it one step at a time."

As Chaise and Bull entered his house, Rebel told them that there was too much information in the flash drive for them to digest all at once. He and Shadow would take it back to Steele Security headquarters to get Brad and the other technology guys to help them pull the information together and devise a game plan.

"I strongly suggest you two lay low until we get back with you. It may take a day or two for us to get everything in order," Rebel said. Turning to Chaise, he directed, "And you need to stay off the radar completely until we get this sorted out. This is nothing to mess around with."

Chaise nodded in agreement. "I will call and take the week off next week. I'll make up something, but I don't think I can stay away from work past that."

~

The next several days seemed to drag by for Chaise. She called the general manager of Viboro and told him she had the flu and would be out a few days. She added a couple of fake coughs and made her voice sound gravelly and rough. He apparently bought her act as he told her to feel better soon.

"Well, that's done," she sighed as she hung up the phone. "That just bought me a few days off without appearing too suspicious."

Bull nodded. "Good. That gives us more time to talk. Doesn't it?"

Chaise cut her eyes to meet Bull's when he emphasized 'talk.' His vast chest expanded and contracted with his quick breaths, his nostrils slightly flared each time, and the temperature in his heated expression rolled off of him in waves. She knew without asking that *talking* was the last thing on his mind.

"Yes," she nodded while maintaining eye contact. "We have plenty of time to talk every day."

Bull blew out a forceful breath and squeezed his hands into tight fists. Chaise raised her eyebrows and flashed her best smirk at him. *So bull-headed,* she thought. *Well, two can play that game.*

Chaise enjoyed the time she had alone with Bull, getting to know him as well as he would allow it. She watched his routine and knew that he'd brought much of his military training home with him. The discipline, the organization, and the pride in keeping everything in perfect order were part of his DNA.

The unresolved sexual tension between Bull and Chaise continued to build over those several days they spent together inside the house. They had exchanged several heated glances and lingering touches during their internment. When their bodies brushed as they passed in the hallway, the heat between them was almost enough to start a fire.

"Excuse me," Bull murmured as they approached each other in the narrow hallway.

As he stepped into her personal space, Chaise turned to face him. His chest brushed across her breasts and she softly gasped at the physical contact. Her eyes met his, the longing and desire obvious in them both, and she lifted her face toward his. Bull bent his head, his lips inexplicably drawn to hers. When their lips met, her hand slid around the back of his neck while his hand slid to small of her back.

When she moaned with need, Bull pushed her into the wall and pushed his body into hers. The uncomfortable tightness behind his zipper needed relief. There was only one way he'd find that relief and that was to bury himself as deeply inside Chaise as he could get. His hand slid down her backside to the back of her thigh. He gently tugged on her leg and she willingly lifted it for him.

Just as he was about to lift her off the floor, his common sense kicked in and he slowly release her leg. After he slowed their urgent, demanding kiss, he pulled away from her to allow his erratic pulse to slow back to normal.

"What's wrong, Colton?" she whispered, confusion marking her words.

"We can't do this, Chaise," Bull answered.

"You don't want me," she asked and stated at once.

"I want you so fucking bad I can barely see straight," Bull replied through gritted teeth. "Now isn't the right time, though."

Chaise looked at the floor as she replied. "Then I guess you can just let me know when the time is right." She stepped further away from him to give him room to pass her, but kept her chin dropped to her chest. Silently, she turned and walked away from him.

Bull was almost to his breaking point when Shadow called days later and said they were on their way over with the data. His thoughts were betraying his sense of duty and his commitment to his job. His professional demeanor was waning and he was running out of excuses to keep avoiding his attraction to Chaise. She had made it painfully clear to him that she was interested. He only had to accept her invitation.

Chaise knew the distance that Bull had kept between them was intentional. She had tried to break down his walls and he had resisted her. She knew part of the reason he rejected her was because he didn't trust her. The other part of the equation was his professionalism, both on the job and in his life. When her open attempt miserably failed, she resigned herself to accept it could not be.

When Shadow and Rebel arrived at Bull's, they immediately opened the computer with the files the tech expert had dissected and had every document open and ready to discuss when Bull and Chaise joined them in the den. Shadow was busy clicking away on the secure laptop and chatting on his phone with his former CIA friends while Rebel was on the phone with Brad, the technology expert at Steele Security.

Their animated discussions centered on the information Chaise had provided. They were able to verify most of what she had already told them and linked many open cases to the girls' names on Chaise's spreadsheets. Bull raised his eyebrows at the two men and they both nodded affirmatively back at him.

"What was that all about?" Chaise asked.

"What was what all about?" Bull responded.

"Come on—I saw that. What's going on?"

"They just confirmed your story—or part of it anyway," Bull explained.

"Does that earn me any trust?" Chaise asked and Bull didn't miss the hopefulness in her tone.

"Some," he responded ambiguously. This earned him a full-watt smile from Chaise and he again felt the unfamiliar pull in his chest. He had to admit that their confirmation of her story removed some of his apprehension about her.

Relaxing his stance, Bull placed his hands on his waist and took a moment to simply observe her as she moved around his house. She moved with a fluid grace that was mesmerizing. Her long, lean body completely captivated Bull and pulled his thoughts from where he should be focused.

She walked between Shadow and Rebel, listening to their conversations and pointing out information over their shoulders as they talked about the names and the information on the lists.

"Ask them about Aura Perez," Chaise whispered to Shadow urgently.

"Yeah, can you run a check on an Aura Perez, nineteen-year-old female, University of Miami student? Thanks, man," Shadow said into his cell phone. Chaise waited on pins and needles, wringing her hands, and pacing back and forth in the three feet of space directly in front of Shadow.

When Shadow shook his head 'no' at Chaise, her pacing abruptly halted as she buried her face in her hands. Bull intently watched her every move, memorizing her body posture, her respirations, and her skin color. When she dropped her hands, he saw true fear and pain in her eyes. Chaise was sincerely worried about Aura Perez—it was no act. Seeing this, she earned another minute amount of his trust.

He waited for Shadow to finish his call before asking for an update. "What's the word, man?"

"Chaise is right—a lot of these names are tied to missing persons cases. Here's the interesting part, though. Several of these girls *used* to be listed online—pictures, fliers, everything—but now, almost all them have been taken off the Internet. I had to get a friend to hack into some servers and pull their restore files from a few weeks back to retrieve the information," Shadow explained gravely.

"What about Aura? What did they say about her? Did they find her missing persons report?" Chaise asked excitedly.

"There's no record of an Aura Perez—not at the college, not at Viboro, and not anywhere online. There's no missing persons report—not even one that's been deleted like the other girls. Either she never existed or she gave you a fake name," Shadow answered.

Bull watched Chaise's reaction to the information Shadow had obtained about Aura. She sat down hard on the sofa, confusion engraved on her face, looking around but seemingly not seeing anything in particular, then the tears started flowing uncontrollably. Before he realized it, Bull was at her side, wrapping his arm around her shoulders, and pulling her into him to console her.

"I don't *understand* what's happening," Chaise cried into Bull's chest. "She was my intern. Her mom was so distraught. Nothing makes sense!"

Bull tightened his hold on her, lightly rubbing her back as he lowered his voice to speak softly to her. "We've just started, Chaise. Don't give up hope yet."

When she wrapped her arm around his waist and hugged him tight, Bull was astonished at how *right* it felt to hold her in his arms. She fit perfectly against him, her soft but muscular body pressed to his as if she were cast from a mold that was meant only for him. The soft, sweet scent of her perfume enveloped him with her every movement.

Her soft cries into his chest propelled his protective instincts to new heights. She was his keep now and he would see things through to the end. Strange thoughts permeated his mind—thoughts of wanting her to still be around at the end of the case, to stay with him and make whatever attraction lingering between them become a living, breathing being. Whether its breath held fire or ice was yet to be determined.

Chaise's body became rigid when she realized she was wrapped around Bull and she was holding onto him so tightly. Fearing she had far overstepped her bounds, she tentatively pulled away from the safety of his comfortable embrace to look into his eyes. Both afraid and anxious to see what message they conveyed to her, she held her breath until their eyes finally met. In them, she saw desire and compassion—not the cold, unfeeling detachment she was certain she'd find. Her heart melted at the sight, and without conscious thought, her hand slowly drifted to his jaw line.

"Thank you, Colton," she whispered. "So much."

Without speaking the actual words, they both knew her appreciation was not only for how he consoled her or his oath of not giving up. They both knew the unspoken gratitude was also for the trust he was giving her—the chance that Bull rarely gave those he didn't know and never gave to those who hadn't fully earned it. He was taking an unheard of chance with Chaise and her outrageous story.

Their faces were so close. Their warm, sweet breath coated each other's faces and their lips were almost close enough to touch. Had they been alone, Chaise knew she would make the first move again, certain that Colton would not be the one to do it while he was on the job. She was thankful for the support that Shadow and Rebel were providing by researching the information she obtained. But she wished with all her might that they would suddenly disappear from the room.

Shadow and Rebel at least had the good manners of keeping their backs turned to Bull and Chaise while they reluctantly unfolded from their intimate embrace. Once they were again upright on the couch, Shadow and Rebel gathered their possessions, telling Bull and Chaise they would soon be in touch again, and Bull walked them out. Chaise took a moment to use the restroom and try to get her emotions under control.

As she entered the den, Bull was returning from outside. Their eyes collided and she was instinctively drawn to him. She couldn't have stopped her feet if she tried. It wasn't as if she had even wanted to stop. She floated across the room and directly into Bull's massive, welcoming arms. Their lips met with urgency—there was no slow, simmering kiss between them this time. It started blazing hot and continued until the fireball of desire consumed both of them.

Before she knew they had moved, Bull had backed her up against the wall and was passionately consuming her mouth. His tongue caressed hers with such finesse it felt smoother than the finest silk. Her fingers relished the feel of his hair as she feverishly massaged his head with her touch. She felt his strong hands move farther down her waist, across her hips, until he lifted her so that she could wrap her legs around his waist.

Supporting her with one leg, he used both hands to cup her face, tilting it to deepen his kiss and take more of her, which she willingly gave to him. Chaise tightened her legs around him, pulling up with her arms so that her breasts were pressed hard against him. The sensitivity of her hardened nipples increased with every brush against his shirt. The heat of his hands penetrated the thin material of her dress, searing her skin with his brand and making her wish for more at the same time.

Tearing his mouth from hers, Bull pulled his face back to look her in the eye. "Are you sure about this?"

"I've never been so sure of anything in my life, Colton," she replied decisively while maintaining his gaze. Pulling his mouth back to hers, she reclaimed it as he shifted his arms underneath her and carried her toward his bedroom.

Chaise's fingers floated down his back, appreciating the ripples and striations of his muscles, until she reached the hem of his shirt. Lifting it slowly with one hand and trailing on his hot skin with the other, she languidly removed his shirt, breaking their kiss only to fully pull it over his head and cast it away on the floor.

The short length of her dress had her most sensitive core pressed firmly against his manhood, rubbing against the rough texture of his jeans and heightening her anticipation of what was yet to come. When they reached his king-size sleigh bed, Bull stopped and stood her up at the edge of it. The yearning in his eyes and voice sent shivers down her spine when he delivered his alpha-male demand.

"My turn, Chaise—or more accurately, *your* turn," his deeply masculine whisper promised. He lifted her arms above her head. "Keep them up," he commanded and she obeyed. His hands skimmed her from her neck, moving down and around the undersides of her breasts, ever so slowly down her stomach, lightly skimming the very core of her before reaching the hem of her dress on her thighs.

When he knelt before her, she gasped audibly, incredibly aroused and eager to learn what he had planned next. Raising his face to look at her, he issued his repeat command. "Keep your arms up, Chaise."

Unable to speak, she simply nodded in agreement, until his warm hands touched her bare thighs. Her hands dropped to his head and her knees threatened to buckle simultaneously as she whimpered unexpectedly. Bull easily caught her, gently pushed her back up and said, "You can hold on to the footboard for now. But when I'm done, I want your arms back up in the air."

"Okay," Chaise complied. She was unsure of where the ability to speak suddenly appeared from or why she was instantly so willing to give in and do exactly as she was told. His take-charge personality bled over into the bedroom in an unexpected and exciting way and she didn't want to do anything to dissuade him.

Grasping the foot of the sleigh bed, Chaise held on and tightened her grip when she felt his hands on her inner thighs again. Bull took his time, lightly running his fingers across her smooth skin, leaving kisses, flicks of his tongue, and light nips of his teeth in his wake. Her approving moans of pleasure urged him on, as did her uncontrollable writhing and wiggling under his sensual attentions

She cried out and was unable to draw in a breath when she felt his warm, wet tongue lavish attention on one leg, starting inside her mid-thigh and slowly working its way up to her panty line. When he stopped and pulled away, she immediately felt the loss of his touch and the tingling sensation he created on her skin, and instantly craved more of him. Finally breathing again, her gaze began to travel downward to find him when she suddenly felt it on the other leg.

His hands followed his tongue, moving up her legs, under her dress, until he found the innermost silky edge of her panties, directly covering her now soaked core. He skimmed his fingers slowly around the edge of her panties until he finally moved around to the sides. Slipping his index finger in each side, he languidly pulled them down her legs, skimming the surface and providing sweet torture, until they were finally in a puddle at her feet. When she stepped out of them, Bull picked them up and tossed them across the room.

"You won't be needing those for a while," his deep voice rumbled.

CHAPTER EIGHT

"I can barely wait to taste you, Chaise," he murmured against her skin. "You are so fucking beautiful and sexy as hell."

Just the sound of his rich, bedroom voice was enough to melt her on the spot. Chaise moaned appreciatively, ready for anything he wanted to give her. Dropping her head back, her fingers gripped the bed frame tighter in anticipation of the wanton things he planned to do to her. Her breathing was shallow, causing her chest to heave in and out in desire.

"Chaise," Bull's voice commanded, it did not ask.

"Yes." *To whatever you want. The answer is yes!*

"Get ready to scream." Bull's fingers gripped her hips, pulling her tightly to him and to what she knew would be pure bliss. She felt his hot breath against her skin and braced herself when she felt the stubble of his jaw rub against the sensitive skin of her inner thigh. She knew heaven was less than an inch away when she felt his hot breath on her heated core. Her breaths were ragged and shallow and she felt hypnotized by him, unable to tear her eyes away from his ministrations.

"Oh, Colton," she sighed on baited breaths, waiting and desperately wanting in a manner she'd never felt before. He lifted his eyes to meet hers just as his tongue flicked out, wetting his lips in anticipation. Chaise almost let go of the bed to grab his hair in her hand to push him where she needed him. Somehow, his order to keep her hands on the bed echoed in her mind and she obeyed.

The chimes of his cell phone stilled his actions, causing Chaise to groan in exasperation. *He was so close!* Their eyes were still locked, the desire burning in his like an open white hot flame suddenly dimmed, and he sat back away from her to fish it out of his front pocket. She was still panting feverishly, still rooted to her place, her hands still gripping the footboard tightly as Bull supplied abrupt answers into the phone.

Ending his conversation, Bull stood and spoke. "The perimeter sensors have been tripped. Someone's here."

His voice held no indication of any sexual frustration or tension after what had just occurred between them was so suddenly interrupted. His demeanor was back to the normal, on-duty Bull while Chaise's head continued to spin out of control. *How can he go from red-hot to ice-cold in a matter of seconds?* Chaise thought to herself, with no small amount of annoyance and distress.

"Get ready to go. We need to leave," Bull stated matter-of-factly as he walked into the closet. He came back out with two more Glock .45 pistols and had put additional clips in his back pockets.

That sight seemed to suddenly snap Chaise into action as she dashed to his side, her eyes wide with fear and her breaths shallow, but for a completely different reason now. She followed closely behind him as he used his immense body as a human shield. His gun drawn and at the ready, he quietly moved through the house, checking the windows from the safety of the sides until he caught movement along the southern edge of his property.

"A security team is en route, but I need to get you out of here now," he turned his head to look at her. "When we get in my truck, keep your head down. Lie all the way down and don't get up until I tell you."

Chaise nodded, fear taking over and apparently rendering her voice incapable of responding at the moment. She knew someone was after her, but to hunt her down at Bull's house demonstrated an unyielding determination to get to her. *If I'm not safe here with him, I'm not safe anywhere,* she thought solemnly.

Chaise followed Bull down the hall, through the kitchen, and into his truck that was parked in the garage. Quietly opening and closing the doors, Chaise slipped in and hid in the floorboard of the backseat. The garage door was eerily quiet as it raised and Bull gunned the engine, making a quick exit from the garage until he reached the road. In his rearview mirror, Bull watched as the Steele Security teams arrived en masse to secure his home and property.

Bull had every confidence the men from Steele Security would thoroughly scrub the entire area until they either found the culprits or they deemed it clear. In the meantime, he made the decision of a safe place to take her—a place she could learn new skills to help protect herself and help him feel better. He would take her to the shooting range owned by Steele Security and teach her how to handle and shoot a pistol.

"Chaise, you can get up now," Bull had almost forgotten she was still lying in the floor in the back of his truck.

Chaise slowly rose up and looked around before sitting up fully.

"I feel like I'm being chauffeured sitting back here alone," Chaise teased.

Bull smiled at her in the rearview mirror and her stomach did somersaults. He was more than gorgeous when he smiled. He didn't smile much, but when he did, it was more than worth the wait. She couldn't help but return the smile as she asked, "Where are we going now?"

"I'm taking you somewhere safe while they clear the house. We're going to the shooting range and you're going to learn to handle a pistol," Bull stated with a glint of humor and anticipation in his eyes.

"Oh yeah, because the shooting range is the best place for me," she replied sarcastically.

"Yes, it is. You think someone will try to get to you at a Steele Security shooting range, where everyone is armed to the teeth and an expert mark? No, sweetheart, that's the safest place for you to be right now," he explained.

"If you say so," she replied while looking out the window. Chaise was seriously dreading the situation. Her secret was killing her and it just kept piling up. Should she pretend to not know how to use guns so that Bull could teach her? Or should she just go ahead and tell him that she was fairly well versed in handling guns and didn't really need instruction? Opting to reduce the backlash she was sure to get later, she decided to share some information with him.

"I'm actually pretty handy with a pistol already," she said nonchalantly.

"Really? Who taught you?" Bull was skeptical and watched her carefully in the rearview mirror.

"My dad and my brothers," she said softly. "When we were growing up, my dad always said all his kids needed to be familiar with guns so that we had a healthy respect for them. He used to take us out in the back yard once a week to practice."

"Where are your dad and brothers now?" Bull asked, clearly not happy that they weren't helping to protect her.

She leaned up between the front seats to be closer to Bull but to also try to reestablish some connection between them. She couldn't tell him everything, but she wanted to convey in some way that she was telling him everything she possibly could.

"My dad and I don't have the best relationship. We haven't for many years now. I left home and have tried to make it on my own. He is more than controlling, Colton. He is overbearing and impossible to please. I talk to my siblings occasionally but they all have their own separate lives. My mom is caught in the middle, so when I spend time with her, I try to leave everything else out."

Keeping her dress in place as best she could, Chaise worked her way between the seats and claimed the front seat beside Bull. "I know you're probably wondering why I haven't run back home to my family in all this. I just … I can't do that, Colton. If you don't want to be stuck with me, I understand—you didn't ask for this mess. I just want you to *know* … I want you to believe me when I say I mean no harm to Noah or his wife. And if my being here, with this gang and whoever else after me, puts *them* in danger, I will leave *right now* with no hard feelings."

Pulling up to a red light, Bull took a moment to read her body language, to study what she wasn't saying, and to decide what he should do next. *Do I cut her loose and protect Reaper and Brianna? Do I keep her close to keep an eye on her and protect them all?* She kept her eyes trained on him, never breaking eye contact, never flinching, and never showing that she was telling him anything but the truth.

"I don't want you go to anywhere," he finally replied. And that was the honest truth. He didn't want her to leave. He didn't know if he had it in him to pursue anything serious with her, but he couldn't deny the attraction. *For once,* he thought, *maybe I should give someone a chance.* "I believe that you don't mean them any harm. As far as danger, Reaper's job automatically puts him in danger and he's used to it—he's good at what he does. Brianna is pretty tough, too."

"She sounds great. I hope I get to meet her one day," Chaise replied absently, looking out the window. "And I hope we find Aura soon. I'm really worried about her, Colton."

After a couple of minutes, she realized he hadn't responded. Looking at him, she saw the muscle in his jaw jumping and recognized the hard set of his teeth. Aura was still a sore spot between them. Bull didn't completely believe her and she knew she wasn't lying. Before she could say anything about it, Bull pulled into the drive of a gated compound, keyed in the code, and soon they pulled into the parking area.

Bull reached across Chaise and removed a Ruger LCR .357 from his glove compartment. After grabbing a box of rounds, he and Chaise made their way through the secure building to the shooting range area. Bull wordlessly handed Chaise a pair of earplugs and the Ruger pistol. He set the rounds down on the shelf beside them and proceeded to put up a target and sent it out on the target line.

He stepped back, crossed his arms, and gestured toward the target. "Impress me."

It was definitely a challenge—and not just about her ability to shoot a pistol. She knew he was challenging everything she'd said to him. He was making her prove what she'd told him, and most likely using this test to gauge if she had told the truth about Aura. Unwilling to back down, or to risk the small advances they had already made, Chaise met his challenge head on.

She picked up the box of rounds and removed five bullets. Expertly popping the chamber open, she loaded all five bullets in and snapped the cylinder shut. She carefully put the gun down on the shelf, put her earplugs in and grabbed a pair of safety glasses. Once set, she took her shooting stance. She held the gun in her right hand, extended her arm and brought her left palm up underneath her right hand, wrapping her fingers firmly around her right hand to help steady her arm.

Letting out a calming breath, she aimed, and then slowly squeezed the trigger five times in a row. Without looking at Bull, she put the gun back on the shelf, removed her earplugs and safety glasses, and pushed the button to retrieve the target. Chaise removed it from the line and smugly handed it to Bull.

"Is a one-and-a-half inch grouping at twenty-five yards enough to impress you?" Chaise asked with a hint of sarcasm and a hefty amount of pride. She knew it was good but she waited for his confirmation. But for good measure, she also hid the intense stinging in her damn hand from firing so many of the .357 rounds in such close succession.

Bull smiled, dropped his arms, and nodded. "Impressive, indeed. Remind me not to piss you off," he replied jokingly.

After Bull finished his practice shots, Chaise helped him pick up all their belongings and they walked back toward his truck. One of the other Steele Security men stopped Bull. Bull turned to Chaise, "Can you hold onto these for me for a few minutes?"

"Sure will," she said happily, taking the few .357 rounds that were left, along with the pistol, and dropping them in her purse. Bull walked off with the other man, leaving Chaise to walk around inside the building alone for a few minutes. She saw a large picture hanging in the main hallway and approached it. Instantly recognizing it as a company all-employee picture, she searched each face looking for the men she'd recently met.

She smiled when she found Bull in the midst of the all the primarily male employees. He was younger in the picture, but he had certainly only improved with age. She kept looking through the faces until she found Shadow and then Rebel. When she found the next face, her entire body froze. She would recognize him anywhere, even if she hadn't seen him in years. He had aged, of course, since she last saw him, but there was no doubt of who it was. He was still just as handsome as she remembered. It was Noah.

Finding her breath, she turned to move away from the picture and saw Bull watching her at the end of the hallway. Not missing a step, she smiled at him as she announced, "I found you in the company picture."

Bull nodded. "Who else did you find in it?"

"All of you," she answered honestly.

"Even Reaper?" He asked, cocking his head to the side and narrowing his eyes at her as if he dared her to lie to him.

"Yes, even Noah," she answered but refused to look away from him.

"Have the gun?" Bull asked, swiftly changing topics.

"Yep," Chaise answered as she patted her purse.

Bull cocked one eyebrow up at her. "You know that's illegal, right?"

"I have a concealed carry permit. I'm legal," Chaise replied with a smile at Bull's surprised look.

Back in Bull's truck, he made a decision. "I think I need to take you away for a while until the heat dies down."

Chaise knew his comment was only related to him doing his job, but the way he said it sent shivers down her spine. The thought of going away with Bull was more than enticing. But her determination to find Aura overshadowed her desire to run away from everything with the very sexy man seated next to her.

"As much as I'd love that, Bull, I can't. I have to go to work tomorrow." She kept her voice calm, projecting a confident outer image, but inside she was dying. She had been dreading that very conversation all day.

"Chaise, in case you haven't noticed, your employer is apparently into some very bad shit. The *Tres Sieses* are after you and work is the last place you need to be. Even though the breach at my house today was a false alarm, we still have to be careful."

Bull's last statement was the termination of that conversation in his mind. He was damn good at his job but he couldn't protect her at Viboro—the very place from where she thought young girls disappeared. He was on the job for a reason and he intended to make sure she stayed safe.

"Colton, I'm going. I have to find Aura. I know you don't believe me, but she was there. I talked to her mom, and I'm going to find her! I have to go back to work and try to back trace her from there," Chaise argued.

"No."

Chaise's head whipped around to Bull, her glare burned through him and the steam that emanated from her raised the temperature in the truck ten degrees in two seconds flat.

"No?" she asked incredulously. "Are you fucking kidding me? You think you can just say 'no' and that's it?"

"Yep."

"That doesn't work on me, Colton. I left my overbearing father behind years ago. I'm the customer in this scenario and I say I'm going back to work!" Chaise shifted in her seat to turn her body toward Bull as she spoke. When she did, her already short dress hiked up her thighs even higher and Bull was reminded that, in their rush to leave his house, Chaise had left her panties behind.

He suddenly forgot what they were arguing about and he had a hard time focusing on the road. She was still sitting facing him, the flowing material of her dress moved with her every breath, shifting up and down her smooth skin. Every few seconds, it would ride up high enough just to torture and tease him with the threat of a very public display, before it moved lower again.

She was still admonishing him with everything she had, but for the life of him, he had no idea what she had said. He was simultaneously dying inside and trying to focus on not killing them both by running off the road or driving into oncoming traffic. He felt like he could breathe again when his driveway came into sight.

"Damn! Finally!" He yelled before he realized that Chaise was still raking him over the coals and he'd just interrupted her rant.

"Finally *what?"* Chaise asked irately.

Bull didn't answer her question. He simply turned into his driveway, parked his truck in the garage, and quickly jumped out. Chaise sat in the truck, stunned at his behavior, and contemplated the various scenarios that could occur should she just get her belongings and leave right away. The defiant part of her wanted to take the chance to handle everything alone.

Maybe it had been a mistake showing up at Noah's wedding and getting his company involved.

CHAPTER NINE

Chaise unbuckled her seatbelt and, with a heavy heart, resigned herself to the fact that she couldn't do it alone. Just as she started to reach for her purse, two strong arms pushed underneath her and easily lifted her out of the truck.

"What the hell-," she yelled, startled and momentarily confused.

Bull's deep-chested growl was his only reply as he swiftly moved from the truck to the door. Expertly maneuvering through the opening with her in his arms, he kicked the door shut behind him and continued straight to his bedroom. Inside, he put her down in the center of the bed and immediately covered her body with his own—clothes and all.

"Were you doing that on purpose just to make me crazy?" Bull's husky voice confronted her, desire infused in his every word as his lips hovered just above the skin on her throat.

"Doing what?" She asked him as he turned her face to the side, giving himself full access to her neck.

Her arms encircled him when he started licking and kissing her neck just below her ear. Bull's head moved downward, his teeth nipped and his tongue licked her. He sucked her soft skin into his mouth, between his teeth, in the most erotic mixture of pain and pleasure Chaise had ever felt. She grabbed his head and pulled his mouth to hers, desperate to taste him and be claimed by him.

Their mouths collided and Bull released a guttural moan of satisfaction that Chaise felt, warming every part of her body from the inside out. Bull's tongue lightly licked her lips, pushing its way through. He took his time, savored her and enjoyed the feeling of her slick, wet velvet tongue against his. Their erotic dance set Chaise on fire. She tried to take control, tried to increase the tempo, but Bull continued to keep his own pace, thwarting her attempts.

Ending their kiss, Bull raised his head to look at Chaise. Her plump, red lips were slightly swollen from their passionate kiss. Her skin was reddened and warm, her eyes were glazed over and full of heated desire. The quick rise and fall of her chest revealed her ragged breaths and her need for him to finish the sensual assault he'd started. And he had every intention of completely owning her before he was finished with her.

Using his knee to part her legs, putting him directly between her legs, he held his weight with one arm while the other hand slowly moved down her side. His touch left a trail of fire in its wake, branding her with his unique mark. When his fingers reached the outside of her leg, his skin on her skin, she thought she would come completely undone. His fingers traced circles on her skin until he reached the innermost sensitive part of her thigh.

"Oh my God, Colton. If you don't touch me now, I'm going to die!"

The carnal plea in her voice urged the primal side of him to take her right then, with no thought, rhyme or reason. *Just. Take. Her.* The protective side of him, the side that she had awakened in him, prevented him from doing just that. That voice told him to take her slowly, to build her up to heights so high she would be ruined for any other man. It urged him to make it so that she could only think of him and what he alone was capable of doing to her senses.

His deep voice lowered to a whisper against the skin on her neck. "That's how I felt in the truck. With this fucking short dress," he said as his fingers moved slowly up her thigh, "riding up on your legs."

"Colton, *please*!"

"Then it flared up, teasing me but never giving me what I wanted," he continued as if she wasn't begging. His fingers moved higher still, barely grazing the outside of her core and causing her hips to jerk toward him involuntarily. "Reminding me that your *fucking panties* were here on my floor. And I couldn't do a damn thing about it," he growled.

Chaise pulled on his short hair, pulling his face up to hers. Her eyes were like fire and her breathing was choppy and fast. "*NOW*, Colton!"

His sexy smirk didn't help matters. He was dead set on claiming her at his own pace.

"Chaise, baby, you've only *read* about the things I will do to you. By the time I'm finished with you tonight, no other man will ever be able to even come close to pleasuring you. Just relax and I'll prove it to you—one touch at a time."

The promises of pleasure from the sexy man on top of her weighed heavy on her mind and her body, like a physical being, watching and waiting to fulfill every word he'd spoken. Chaise took a deep breath, trying to calm herself before the anticipation caused an anxiety attack. As her chest rose in mid-breath, Bull's mouth caught her nipple between his teeth with light pressure. Chaise moaned loudly but made no attempt to move away, allowing him to take his fill.

"This dress is in my way," Bull's eyes flicked to hers, full of desire and wicked determination. His big hands moved slowly up her body, pushing the dress against her body, feeling every inch of her on his quest. He threw the dress over his shoulder and then took her hands in his. Pushing them above her head and holding them with one hand, their mouths met again as his other hand searched for something just out of her view.

The silky satin sensation on Chaise's wrist didn't register in her brain at first because all the nerves firing in every other part of her body. By the time she realized what he was doing, both of her wrists had been tied to the headboard. There was very little slack in the cloth. Regardless of how she moved, she couldn't reach Bull to touch him with her hands. She was both confused and excited at the possibilities. While she really hadn't known him very long, everything she saw in him told her to trust him.

"Relax, Chaise. I won't hurt you. Far from it—you'll be begging me for more," he guaranteed.

Her answering sigh was all he needed as her signal of surrender.

"That's my girl." He praised her with a deep kiss as his hands roamed over her breasts.

Finding her nipples, his fingers gently squeezed, then rolled, and squeezed again while his tongue plunged deep in her mouth. He was marking her, claiming her, and owning her every sense, her every reaction and her every desire.

Chaise's body reacted wildly, her chest arching up to push her breasts deeper into his hands. Her hands struggled against her restraints, wanting to touch him and feel him, but her manacles both prevented it and served to heighten her senses. She was pleasurably surprised at how her body responded to being tied, how her mind gave over to complete submission for him to do as he willed, and knew that she would enjoy every second of it.

When his hand left her body, she immediately missed the warmth and bliss it created. Opening her eyes, she saw a black velvet object in his hand and looked at him quizzically. He smiled assuredly and lightly stroked her cheek with it.

"Trust me, Chaise," he asked and commanded at once. Reassured by his eyes, she nodded and he slipped the mask over her eyes. "You've never been blindfolded before?"

"No," she breathed heavily.

"All you have to do is relax. I will do the rest … until you fall apart in my arms and become completely mine."

"Oh, god," Chaise gasped.

"You can call me Bull … or Colton." Chaise could feel his smirk without even being able to see his face.

"I'm going to call someone else if you don't get busy," Chaise deadpanned.

"Over *his* dead body," Bull retorted.

Before Chaise could say another word, she felt his warm, wet tongue lightly dragging down her neck and leaving chills and fire in its path. The warmth left her body for a second and then her left nipple was sucked into his mouth. The sensation of warm wetness combined with the light scraping of his teeth over her sensitive erect buds was exhilarating. The hold increased and a loud popping sound reverberated throughout the room as he released her nipple from his mouth.

Another moment of emptiness passed before his mouth found her other nipple, lavishing the same attention on it. His hand trailed down her body, between her breasts to her stomach, and circled her belly button before moving on. Bull purposely moved his hand to cup her mound, claiming it as his own without saying a word. His fingers fanned out against her skin as his mouth continued to work its own magic on her breast.

When his fingers touched the inside of her bikini line, Chaise's legs unconsciously spread to give him better access. He traced lazy patterns on her skin, exhibiting both his own self-control and his control over her body's reaction to him. His hand stayed in place as he repositioned his body lower on hers. His warm tongue tasted her skin across her abdomen, her ribs, and down to her hipbones. She could feel his warm breath blow across her core and it made her wish her hands were free so she could force his head to the center of her thighs.

"Are you wet for me, Chaise?"

If I weren't already, I would be now, Chaise thought. But the only response she could formulate was to answer in an approving moan.

"I'd better check," Bull whispered, his breath fanning out across her core, his razor stubble grating across her soft skin like an erotic form of sandpaper.

"Colton, I'm- *ooooh*," Chaise's thoughts were interrupted by the feel of Bull's finger tracing the delicate folds of her center. She felt his hand on the back of her thigh, bending her knee and pushing it toward her. Then his hand was on her other leg, bending and pushing it up and out of his way.

"Mmmm, Chaise. It does look like you're ready for me. I think I should taste you first, though," he tormented. As he spoke, his lips brushed against her—teasing, torturing, and increasing her desire with every word. She bucked her hips toward him in an attempt to rush him along. His response was his tongue laving her from bottom to top, circling her clit, and sucking it into his mouth.

Forgetting her hands were bound to the headboard, she pulled hard in her attempt to fist his hair. She moaned in both approval and frustration and felt his light chuckle between her legs.

"Relax, Chaise. Just feel it, babe," he gently chided her.

"I want to feel you, Colton," she pleaded.

"Oh, you will feel me, Chaise," he assured her.

"I mean with my hands."

"You will love this. Trust me."

Bull didn't give her a chance to reply before his finger found her innermost core and he thrust one deep into her soft channel. Her hips rose in response, her muscles contracted and pulled him deeper into her as she pulled on the satiny binds. His finger moved slowly at first, in and out, then he increased his tempo and Chaise moved in tandem with him, the wave of her orgasm building inside.

His second finger entered on the next thrust as her hips rose to meet his ministrations. Faster and harder, he kept upping his tempo until Chaise cried out his name in ecstasy and the evidence of her climax soaked his hand. Bull continued stroking her clit in circular motions as she came down from her high. Her breathing was ragged and fast, her skin was a beautiful blush color, and tiny beads of sweat covered her body.

Bull remained still for a moment, committing her every line and curve to memory.

"Colton?" her small voice penetrated the silence.

"I'm here," he whispered in her ear, sending goose bumps down her arm. He stood and shed his clothes quickly.

Chaise hummed with pleasure when his body covered hers and he seated himself between her legs. The feel of his erection on the side of her leg was breathtaking and the anticipation was stimulating. The mask kept his actions hidden so she never knew what he would do next. The release of giving over all the control she exuded in everyday life was exciting. No decisions, no consequences, no cares—just a love of life and everything he offered her.

Chaise heard the crinkling of a wrapper and Bull's ragged breaths nearby. She felt the tip of his sheathed manhood at her core, waiting for entry. His arms wrapped under and around her legs, pulling them up and readying her for his welcomed intrusion. Her hands curled into fists, holding on to the sash that held her hands captive. She felt Bull's hand move away from her leg, but she kept it held up in place. The mask over her eyes was slowly removed and she blinked, slowly opening them to see him suspended over her.

"I want to see your eyes. I want to know the exact moment that you surrender to me … the very second you realize that you belong to me," his bedroom voice whispered.

Chaise's breath seized in her chest at his words. He slowly surged his hips forward, entering her wet core, and sliding in one glorious inch at a time until he was fully inside her warm, wet channel, filling her and stretching her to accommodate his size. He moved decisively slow, feeling her muscles' every quiver and contraction around him, pulling him in deeper and holding him with a firm grip.

His eyes never left hers and she felt him reach deep inside her—physically and emotionally. And she knew what he meant. She knew immediately that he had touched her as no man had before. Even if she thought she'd been in love before, it was childish and immature compared to the barrage of emotions that flooded her at that moment. How could she explain it to anyone else when she didn't even understand? It couldn't be love—she hadn't known him long enough.

But there was a connection to him that she couldn't break and there had been from the start. Even though he didn't trust her. Even though she hadn't told him everything—he knew that—but he still protected her, he still kept his word, and he still honored his commitment. Now, he wanted her in his bed, he wanted in her head, and he wanted to own her. Even as independent and self-confident as she'd been for the last several years after getting out from under her father's thumb, she wasn't the least bit offended by his declaration.

She didn't believe it was a total domination statement. It was simply to let her know that he was staking his claim on her. That he wouldn't share her with anyone else. He meant that the intimacy was between them only and not meant for anyone else. The feeling of belonging to someone in that sense, of surrendering all to him to love and care for her, wasn't so scary. It was comforting and fulfilling. She just hoped she was right, because he owned her, he possessed her, and she willingly surrendered her all to him.

His tempo increased, moving in and out of her soft sheath with reckless abandon. His long, thick shaft filled her completely, plunging into her to the hilt until the intensity built so high, so strong, that she screamed out his name before she even realized the words were leaving her mouth.

"Colton! Oh God!"

His appreciative groan in response sent chills down her spine. "Damn, you feel so good, Chaise."

Chaise was still riding the high of her orgasm, unable to fully come down because he continued to rain down his pleasurable torture techniques on her. She knew she was done for when he leaned down and murmured in her ear.

"I'm not finished with you yet, Chaise. This is only round one."

Without giving her time to respond, Bull sat up, pulled her legs up to his shoulders, and deepened his angle. The more she screamed, the harder he drove into her, over and over until she was completely spent and limp under him. With a final thrust and resounding scream from Chaise, Bull stilled and emptied himself into her. She felt his manhood pulsing and pumping into her of its own accord. His eyes stayed glued to hers, never releasing her gaze as his hand deftly released her hands from their binds.

Repositioning her to lie in his arms, she curled up beside him with their arms and legs entwined. Content, thoroughly sated, and completed drained of all energy, she quickly fell into a deep sleep against Bull's warm body.

Bull stayed awake, listening to her breathing while he tried to keep his thoughts from racing. He had never allowed a woman he was involved with to spend the night at his place, and he'd certainly never gone to sleep with one in his arms. But something about their union felt different. Even though he knew she was still holding something back, he could only hope he wasn't wrong about her.

The next morning, Bull woke to an empty bed and felt the instant alarm run through him like an electric current. Chaise had slept with him the night before and he hadn't felt her leave the bed. Something about her was definitely throwing him off his game. Slipping on his lounging pants, he silently moved down the hall and found her in the kitchen again. She was sipping on a cup of coffee, reading the paper and was fully dressed. For work.

"How did you get the paper? It was outside and the alarm was set," Bull smarted.

"Well, good morning to you, too, Colton. Yes, I did sleep well. Actually, I slept like a rock. You know, you are *so warm* it was like having my own electric blanket! Would you like some coffee?" Chaise spoke like there was no reason for concern and like he hadn't just completely chastised her without so much as a good morning first.

They stood staring at each other for a moment until Chaise couldn't keep her eyes from roaming over his broad shoulders, firm chest, and chiseled six-pack. Her eyes trailed down the muscled V that disappeared into the waistband of his pajama pants. Her coffee cup was frozen at her lips as her eyes devoured the luscious form standing before her.

Bull's lips quirked up in one corner as he shifted his weight to one leg, placed his hand on his hip, and leveled his eyes at her. When her eyes met his, she blushed, the bright pink color filling her cheeks and neck. She smiled behind her coffee cup and quickly lowered her eyes as she took a sip.

"Oh, look at the time. I need to get going or I'll be late for work in the Miami traffic." Chaise tried to hide her ogling and announce her departure with one statement.

Out of the corner of her eye, she saw Bull's stance immediately change. Opening his legs farther apart, he crossed his muscular arms over his expansive chest and glared at her menacingly. Chaise pretended to not notice the difference in his demeanor.

"First of all, how did you disable my alarm?" Bull growled.

"I didn't—Shadow did. He brought something by for you," Chaise answered with an incline of her chin toward a large envelope on the coffee table.

"Okay. And I already said you're not going to work today. It's too dangerous," Bull commanded. "And don't forget your *missing* intern."

The suspicion in his tone felt like a literal slap to Chaise's face. She physically recoiled from the sting of his words and inflection of his voice. There it was and it may as well have been written in stone—he still didn't believe her. Not completely anyway. After everything Shadow and Rebel had recently found that corroborated her story, and after their night together, he still doubted her intentions.

Tears stung the back of her eyes and she swallowed hard to hold them back. She resolved that she would not give him the satisfaction of knowing that he hurt her as much as he did. Chaise calmly walked to the sink, poured out her coffee, put her cup in the dishwasher, and grabbed her purse off the counter. She walked directly up to Bull, who was now completely blocking the doorway and her exit route.

"Chaise, I can't let you go." Bull's tone had softened, as he was obviously aware of his mistake but he wasn't taking full ownership of it. His stance, however, was still threatening and unyielding.

"You can't stop me," Chaise retorted, emphasizing each word. "I'm not arguing with you, Colton. I am going to work and acting normal. Kindly step aside—you can't hold me against my will."

Bull drew in a deep breath, straightened his back, and pulled himself up to an intimidating height. Letting out an exasperated huff, he stepped aside to give Chaise just enough room to squeeze between him and the doorjamb. She seized the opportunity before he changed his mind and moved into the tight opening. Suddenly, both of his muscular arms came up on either side of her, boxed her in, and prevented her from moving any more than required to breathe.

"Chaise, I can't let you put yourself in danger," he said, his voice low but with a touch of tenderness to it. Her chest tightened in response, wanting to feel the intimacy he implied but the sharp sting of his prior words was still fresh.

"You can't stop me from doing anything I want to do, Colton. It's as simple as that. I'm leaving now," she stated firmly, meeting his eyes with her defiant glare.

While he was temporarily stunned, and before he could respond, she quickly ducked under his massive arm, slid her body against his, and walked quickly to the front door. She noticed that he made no attempt to stop her that time. She assumed he had done his duty—he had tried to stop her and she refused. It was by her very own decision, but part of her had foolishly hoped he would chase after her. The other part of her knew that was ridiculous since it was what she wanted to do in the first place and she had made that clear.

And this is why relationships never work. We're all damn crazy, she thought to herself as she got in her car. When she looked up, she saw Bull watching her from his front porch. His arms were crossed over his chest and his legs were spread wide in his fighting stance. But the look in his eyes stopped her. His eyes were fixed on her every move as if he was daring her to carry out her plan against his will. She couldn't explain—or escape—the feeling that she was betraying him somehow by simply doing what she'd planned to do all along. *Work.*

Remembering that she was still mad at him, she quickly put her sunglasses on, cranked her car, and pulled out of his driveway. Chaise couldn't help but wonder if she'd be welcomed back at his house at the end of her workday. She decided to cross that bridge when she came to it. She already had enough to keep her busy and stressed for the day. She'd decide what to do about Colton Lanier later.

Pulling into the parking space, she took a few deep, calming breaths before gathering her purse and walking into the building. She knew she'd been followed before going to Noah's wedding and she was sure it was because of what she'd found on the job. But she didn't want to show her hand just yet. She wanted to make them think she hadn't realized what she'd found so that she could keep digging. She wanted them to still feel smug and secure in their activities so they wouldn't change them. If they did, that would mean she'd essentially lost Aura forever. She felt responsible and wanted to find the young girl before it was too late.

She strolled into the building like she belonged there, exactly like every other morning. She smiled and said hello to the security guard at the front desk. He smiled and responded as he normally did. She breathed a sigh of relief, moved past him, and walked on to her office.

Putting her things down, she looked around her office to see if anything had been disturbed, but everything was exactly as she'd left it. If anyone had been snooping, they were experts because not one paper was out of order in her neat, organized world.

CHAPTER TEN

Deciding to face the music, Chaise drove straight back to Bull's house after work rather than going to the condo that had always given her the creeps anyway. When she first got in her car, she wasn't sure which way she should go. She hadn't heard from Bull all day and she hadn't called him, either. It stung a little that he acted so concerned about her going to work but then he never even called to see if she was safe.

As she pulled into his driveway, she had a moment of panic. She pictured him turning her away for not following his orders to not go back to work in the first place. She parked and placed her forehead on the steering wheel, conflicted and generally unsure of her next move. Her logical mind said she needed to be there with Bull but she wasn't sure she could handle the reception she'd receive.

Her car door opened and Bull's big hand gingerly wrapped around hers. She looked up at him, his cobalt blue eyes boring into hers, as he gently tugged on her to help her out of the car. He pulled her hand to his mouth and kissed each of her knuckles with his soft, plump lips. Chaise's heart both broke and melted at the sweet gesture. He was trying to be nice but there was still a huge chasm between them that she wasn't confident they would ever be able to bridge.

"I'm glad you came back here. I was beginning to wonder if you would," Bull finally spoke.

"I debated it—several times," Chaise answered truthfully.

Bull nodded in understanding. "I'm sorry for what I said, or rather, *how* I said it. I do believe that she is missing."

Bull reached in the car, turned the ignition off, and gathered Chaise's belongings. He carried them in the house with one hand and led her with his hand on the small of her back with the other hand. His words kept reverberating through her mind—both from that morning and from a few moments before. Once inside the house, Chaise decided to address the big, pink polka-dotted elephant that stood between them.

"You believe that she is missing because of the information Shadow and Rebel found. Not because of anything I've said. There's obviously a big problem between us, Colton.

"It was ridiculous of me to think last night would've changed anything—or that it meant anything to you. I *know* that, but I still wanted it to, honestly. I don't think my staying here is a good idea anymore. I won't go back to the condo, but I think I should go somewhere else," she stated sadly.

Bull admired how Chaise stood tall even though she was afraid. She faced her fears and didn't back down, although vulnerability showed in her mint-green eyes. Her long, black hair cascaded over her shoulders and her tan skin glowed with sun-kissed radiance. She was stunning at normal times, but when she was on a mission, she was absolutely spectacular.

And she was talking about leaving.

"I don't want you to leave," Bull stated plainly.

"You don't owe me anything, Colton. You've done what you said you'd do—you kept your word. This is my way of taking responsibility for my actions. I allowed … this … to happen between us and it was just way too soon. I don't regret it, but we don't really even know each other. I just don't want us to end up enemies," she said, exasperated. She was running out of steam.

All the events of the past few weeks were beginning to catch up with her and take a toll on her emotions. Discovering the missing girls, Aura's disappearance, seeking Noah after all this time, the complicated and untrusting relationship with Colton, and now going back to work where she felt eyes watching her at all times. It just all felt like too much and everything was closing in on her at once. The feeling of claustrophobia was returning with a vengeance and she wasn't even in a small space.

She was about to have a full-blown panic attack. That's what was behind that feeling of everything closing in on her. The realization of that suddenly hit her. It was the same feeling she had when she was in the Steele Security building and everything was so overwhelming. It was coming on again—just thinking about all the things she'd been through and all the things she still had to face. Alone. Again.

"Chaise? Chaise!"

She could hear his voice but it sounded muffled and distant. Her legs felt like wet spaghetti noodles—completely unable to hold her weight or move of their own accord. She felt strong arms wrap around her and gently place her on the couch. Then the strong arms wrapped around her, pulling her into a big, thick chest and shielding her from the outside world. A low, murmuring voice chanted soothing messages in her ear and plump, kissable lips placed chaste kisses on her hair, forehead, and temple.

"Just breathe. Focus on just breathing right now. You're safe here with me. I won't let anything happen to you. Breathe, baby. That's it." The reassuring voice repeated the words over and over until they sunk in and took root in Chaise's subconscious, eventually bleeding over into her conscious mind.

And then the dam broke. Everything she'd held back, bottled up, and pushed down just broke free and the tears started freely flowing. Bull felt the wetness, knew what was to come next. He pulled her securely into his lap and cradled her in his arms like a baby. Chaise welcomed it—she relished in the contact, the reassurance, and the support she felt flowing from him. She felt safe and secure in his presence and even though she would normally be embarrassed to have anyone see her cry, when her first sob broke through, she was relieved.

She felt relief that she could be herself and let the weakness show without being berated or chastised for it. She was relieved that even through her weak moments, Colton would keep his word and keep her safe. The anxiety she felt was in knowing that the troubles were not over and there were still things she needed to share with Colton. Although, maybe just not at that exact moment, since she was a blubbering mess and couldn't seem to catch her breath between sobs. His hands rubbed her back and he still muttered comforting words instead of telling her to suck it up and carry on.

The sobs subsided and she was completely wiped out. She had no fight left in her, no energy to pretend she was all right and that she didn't need help. All she could do was close her eyes, inhale the masculine musk of the man holding her close, and sink farther into his protective embrace. Within minutes, her breathing returned to normal and she fell asleep in his arms.

Bull looked down at her and marveled at how protective he'd become of her in such a short time. This type of thing never happened to him—he never allowed it. But he couldn't lie to himself and say he wasn't becoming attached to her. When he told her he didn't want her to leave, he meant it. When he said he would protect her, he meant with his life. Comforting her and calming her was new to him and he knew he'd fuck up again and cause her pain. Somehow he had to make her understand why that was and figure out how he could make it up to her when he did.

Rubbing his nose and lips along her skin, he softly called her name until she stirred again.

"How long was I asleep?" Chaise asked, a little confused and her cheeks slightly pink with embarrassment.

"Not long. I actually hated to wake you, but I need to feed you," Bull answered, keeping his voice low and calm.

Chaise made no effort to move from her spot in his arms. She looked up at him for several long seconds without speaking before she raised her hand and let her fingers stroke along his jaw. The afternoon stubble pricked her fingers and she liked the sounds it made as her nails scraped across it.

"I can't do this alone, Colton," she finally whispered her confession.

Admitting to needing someone's help was tough for Chaise. She'd been on her own for so long and had always been the resilient one.

"I know, Chaise. You don't have to," the sincerity of his tone warmed her heart. "You don't have to leave. I want you to stay here. We can take it slower; get to know each other better."

"I'd like that," Chaise replied with a smile that Bull returned. She knew full well there was no going back for her. Taking it slow or not, there was something about that man that had captured her and refused to let her go.

After cooking supper and cleaning the dishes, Bull and Chaise settled back on the couch together. The atmosphere had lightened considerably since her emotional breakdown. She was just glad they were able to spend time together—talking, laughing, and sharing.

"How was work today?" Bull asked with an unmistakable smirk.

"It was okay. I swear I felt eyes on me all day, though. Made my skin crawl to think that they were watching me," Chaise animatedly replied while gauging his reaction.

"They weren't the only ones," Bull responded.

"What do you mean?" Chaise asked while sitting up then leaning toward him in a challenging posture.

Bull smiled his full on, mega-watt smile before answering. "Brad, our techie genius, hacked into their security system and we were able to keep tabs on you all day. Why else do you think I let you leave this morning?"

Chaise was stunned beyond speech. Her bottom jaw dropped open, her eyes widened, and she sat motionless for a moment.

"*Let* me? You *let* me leave?" she asked incredulously.

Bull chuckled, "Okay, now, don't take that the wrong way. I just meant that otherwise I would've had to go with you. We would've had to do things very differently if Brad hadn't been able to get into their surveillance system."

"Damn, no wonder I felt like I was being watched all day!" Chaise swatted at his arm playfully. She laughed harder when he pretended to be hurt.

"Did you notice anything out of the ordinary?"

"No, nothing. And I looked around my office. There was nothing disturbed. Nothing out of place from where I'd left it Friday. I didn't really push my luck too much today and get into anything I'm not supposed to be in. Now that I know you're watching, I will try harder tomorrow."

Chaise noticed the change in Bull's face at that statement. He didn't like it one bit and he was biting his tongue to keep from saying anything.

"Go ahead and say it before you bite your tongue in two," Chaise deadpanned.

Bull smirked. "It's just that if they caught you, we may not be able to get to you in time to stop them from taking you somewhere. If you're dead set on doing this, we'll have to outfit you with some of our *Inspector Gadget* toys first."

"No Bond toys?" Chaise asked teasingly.

"No, you haven't graduated to *spy* yet. Baby steps," Bull joked.

~

Shadow, Rebel, and Brad came by Bull's house to bring their gadgets and show Chaise how everything worked.

"We will be able to see and hear you, but you can't hear us. The problem with that is, we won't be able to warn you if we see something happening before you do," Brad explained.

Bull recognized Chaise's worried expression as her eyes searched for reassurance from him. "Don't worry," Bull soothed her. "If it gets too dangerous, I *will* storm the building. I'll clear a path to you by any means necessary."

"You'll be close?" she asked.

"I'm never far away from you," Bull promised.

The other guys exchanged shocked glances but none of them were stupid enough to question Bull in front of her. Chaise's look of gratitude told them everything they needed to know. Whatever feelings Bull harbored for her were definitely reciprocated.

"Okay. I can do this then," Chaise replied as she stood. "Is anyone else thirsty?"

Bull, Rebel, Shadow, and Brad gave their drink requests and Chaise left the room. Rebel and Shadow took the opportunity to pounce on Bull.

"Want to tell us what the hell is going on here, man?" Shadow asked, giving Bull a pointed look, and inclining his head toward the kitchen where Chaise was.

"Uh—we are getting her ready to go in wired. Have you not been paying attention?" Bull snapped.

Rebel laughed, "You know what he's asking, man. Don't play fucking dumb with us. We know you better than that shit."

Brad was so enthralled with how the conversation was unfolding, he didn't notice at first that Bull was staring him down. Brad quickly lowered his eyes back to the electronics in front of him. Bull looked at his long-time friends and huffed out a disgusted sigh.

"Fine. Yes. Chaise. Me. Happy now?"

Rebel and Shadow both had huge, shit eating grins on their face at their friend's admission. Brad was even smiling but he didn't look up from his work to invoke the wrath of Bull for intruding on his private life. Rebel and Shadow slapped him on the back and clapped him on the shoulder. Bull, uneasy with the sudden intrusion of his privacy, told them to knock it off and walked off with them laughing heartily behind him.

Several minutes later, he reappeared with Chaise and both had their hands full of drinks for everyone. Brad took a drink of his and turned the conversation back to business.

"All right, Chaise. You're all set—just remember what we've gone over tonight. Don't get the device wet. Try to keep your hands away from it. The rustling noises make it hard to hear. And you'll need to decide your code word that tells us you're in trouble. If we hear that word, we *will* rush in, so don't use it lightly," Brad explained.

Inhaling deeply, Chaise looked at each of the four men and saw a myriad of silent reactions on their faces. Rebel cocked his head to the side, crinkled his eyes, and studied her with a somewhat concerned look. Shadow stood tall, hands on his hips, and a troubled look on his face. Brad was confident in his equipment and its ability to help keep her safe. Bull was a different matter all together. A mixture of feelings moved across his face—concern, awe, and agitation—almost simultaneously.

"I'll be fine. I have the best security team in the nation on my six. Nothing will go wrong." She tried to sound confident but it fell flat, even to her own ears.

Brad stood and placed his hand on her shoulder. "It will be fine. We will take good care of you, Chaise."

After the men had left and they were alone again, Bull turned from the door and walked directly up to Chaise.

"You don't have to do this. We can work with the local authorities. We have enough to arouse suspicion and Shadow has some significant contacts. There are other ways—better ways—to do this," Bull reasoned.

"You're right, Colton. I don't have the expertise to pull this off alone. But I'm already inside and I am in a position to snoop into anything because it's my job. It would take too much time to get someone else in there now. We may never find Aura or the other girls if I quit now."

Bull didn't respond. He knew she was right but that didn't mean he had to like it.

"I don't think I can do this without you, Colton. Don't abandon me now," Chaise asked him. Her eyes beseeched him and she held her breath waiting for his reply.

"Not a chance in hell, Chaise," came Bull's promise.

Chaise tentatively lifted her hand and stretched it out to capture Bull's hand. Once she had it, she squeezed it and gave him a small smile of appreciation.

"Well, it's late and I have a big day ahead of me tomorrow, so I guess I should get some sleep," Chaise announced but she couldn't hide the anxiety in her voice. Not only did she plan to dive headfirst into shark infested waters, so to speak, she had much more pressing problems before her.

Where should I sleep tonight?

Bull's knowing smile did nothing for her discomfort. He knew what she was thinking and there was no point in even trying to lie her way out of it. They agreed to take it slower and to get to know each other better first. But in his arms, she just felt so safe, secure, and protected that she never wanted to leave them.

"Come on. I'll take you to the guest room," Bull answered with no hint of hesitation or the disappointment that she felt to her very soul. Chaise simply nodded and followed him down the hall.

At some point during the day, Bull had moved her belongings to one of the guest bedrooms. He reminded her where the towels and other toiletries were stored and made sure she didn't need anything else before he left her alone.

After getting ready for bed, Chaise lay in the big, comfortable bed and stared at the ceiling for what felt like forever. There was absolutely nothing wrong with the bed or the bedroom. It was perfect and comfortable. It was the fact that he was so close but so far away that was driving her crazy and keeping her awake. When she was still wide-awake just after midnight, she made a decision that Bull would just have to accept.

She tiptoed through the house with only her tank top and panties on until she reached Bull's bedside. He was lying on one side, on his back, and appeared to be sleeping perfectly well without her. She knew better than to assume he was asleep after the last time she made that mistake. Not waiting, or asking for an invitation, she carefully pulled the covers back and slipped into bed beside him.

She snuggled up as close to him as she could get and instantly felt better. The tiny bubble of anxiety that had started building in her chest instantly dissipated. Just as she was thinking that it might not be a good idea to rely on him to rid her of the anxiety, he spoke and disrupted her thoughts

"Did you lose your bed?" he asked as he wrapped his arm around and pulled her closer to him. His teasing and humor tone laced his words, telling her that he didn't mind sharing his bed with her.

"Actually, I was momentarily kicked out of *my* bed but I found my way back on my own," she said in mock defense.

"Took you long enough. I was beginning to think you'd really stay in there," Bull laughingly replied.

Chaise replied with an elbow to the ribs. "You knew I didn't want to sleep in there, didn't you." It was intentionally more of a statement than a question.

"I knew," Bull replied earnestly, placing a kiss on her cheek. "And I'm glad. I wanted you in here, too."

CHAPTER ELEVEN

Chaise went to work every day that week, gathered additional information as the Steele Security team instructed, and went back to Bull's house every night. Every day she felt a little more anxious, felt more eyes watching her every move, and knew that time was not on her side. Aura had been missing too long at that point and Brad had found nothing on the other missing girls.

Bull had driven Chaise to work every day and picked her up. She had argued against it at first, feeling like her freedoms were slowly being taken from her. Bull explained that he didn't trust anyone to not tamper with her car while it was in the Viboro Distributing parking lot. If it were to break down and leave her stranded, she would be too vulnerable.

That day, she was infinitely glad that she had given in and heeded Bull's advice. The anxious feeling was at its peak and she knew she wasn't just overreacting. One of the warehouse workers had been in the office all day. He had watched every move she made, listened to her every conversation that occurred outside of her office, and leered at her without trying to disguise it. She'd had an uneasy feeling all day and practically ran out the front door to Bull's waiting SUV.

"What's wrong?" Bull asked, his facial expression and voice tone mirrored his concern.

"Can we get out of here? I'll tell you while you drive," Chaise answered, still rattled from the events of the day. "I just want to get as far away from this place as possible."

Bull pulled out into traffic, his demeanor belying his thoughts and feelings. He knew from the fret in her eyes, the furrow of her brow, and the pitch of her voice that something was inherently awry. His first order of action would be to make sure she was safe. Second, he would find and kill anyone who threatened to bring harm to her.

"Tell me what happened," Bull stated calmly. "No one said they saw or heard anything out of the ordinary from our surveillance."

"There was a guy from the warehouse who was in the office all day today. He's never worked in the office before. But all day, he was everywhere I went. He watched me, listened to my conversations, and he just gave me the creeps! I just get a really scary vibe from him," Chaise explained.

"You can show me which one he is when we get to my house. I'll get Brad to pull up the feed and we'll identify him. Could be a good lead for the case," he reassured her.

"I hope you're right. I'm ready for this to be over! I don't know how you do this all the time."

"Training, babe. I've had a lot of training to prepare me for missions. It conditioned me and taught me how to deal with intense situations. You're doing great. You've been our eyes and ears all week," he replied with a smile that relayed how impressed he was with her.

"Now you're just being nice," Chaise playfully scolded.

"No one's ever accused me of that before," Bull laughed. "I need to stop by the store first, if that's all right with you?"

"Sure, that's fine with me."

Bull and Chaise strolled through the grocery store, picking out items together as though it had always been an everyday occurrence. Chaise genuinely enjoyed his company and getting to know Colton Lanier, the man behind the Bull façade. She found that he had a heart of gold and a protective streak a mile wide.

As they walked across the vast parking lot, talking and enjoying each other's company, Bull wrapped his arm around her and pulled her close to his side. The casual movement was so natural but so intimate at the same time. Public displays of affection weren't in Bull's vocabulary but he seemed to be making a lot of concessions for Chaise.

An alarming sound caught Bull's attention just in time for him to lift Chaise off the ground, roll across the front hood of a car, and duck between the parked cars. The all black, full-size SUV narrowly missed hitting them. The SUV came to a screeching halt several yards away and four men exited the vehicle, speaking in Spanish.

"Which way did they go?" the first voice called out.

"I saw them duck between those cars over there," the second guy responded.

"Spread out and find them. Kill him. Bring her to me—unharmed," the last voice commanded.

Over your dead body, Bull thought to himself. *There's still at least one more.*

Bull kept Chaise moving through the parking lot, winding between cars and keeping low to stay out of sight. He kept the men trained in his sights, but there was still one missing. Four exited the vehicle but he only had eyes on three of them. As Bull and Chaise cornered another vehicle, he saw the fourth man.

Bull stopped dead in his tracks. All the years of training temporarily left him. He couldn't breathe. He couldn't think straight to make a decision. He couldn't make his feet move. He felt Chaise beside him, holding his arm in her tight grip, furtively whispering to him but her words held no meaning.

When the man turned around, Bull stood up in plain sight and openly gaped at the man. Within seconds, Bull was knocked to the ground as gunfire erupted around him. A large body was lying on top of him, yelling something at him that he couldn't understand. He struggled to get free but it was useless.

"Bull, dammit! Be still! What the fuck are you doing? Trying to get yourself killed?" Shadow screamed at him.

"Get the fuck off me, man!" Bull yelled back, finally finding the capacity to speak again.

"Don't do it, man. I'm warning you," Shadow growled back.

Chaise had no idea what "it," was, but Shadow's words penetrated Bull's anger. He finally nodded in agreement and relaxed his coiled muscles.

Rebel came running up at that moment. "They got away but I got the plates. May be stolen but I have a feeling it's not. Let's go find out who we're going after."

Bull stood and looked between his two brothers. His jaw was hard set, the muscles ticking and bunching in his attempts to keep his anger reined in. His face was beet red and his eyes were fierce—in a scary way.

"What the hell are you guys doing here anyway?" Bull snapped.

"You mean other than saving your ass? We're doing our fucking jobs," Shadow replied with his voice deceptively calm and low. "You nearly just got yourself and Chaise killed. What happened?"

"Nothing," Bull lied.

"Don't bullshit us, man. We saw the whole thing while we were getting into place to back you up. If you hadn't stood up, we could've had these assholes," Rebel admonished him.

"Fuck! You're right—you're right, okay? I fucked up. Let's get out of here," Bull responded when he heard sirens in the distance.

Someone surely had called the police and he wasn't ready to talk to them. He decided he'd have someone from the Steele Security office call and apprise them of the situation. He had more pressing matters to handle first.

Bull drove them back to his house, keeping both hands firmly gripped to the steering wheel. His body was rigid and his sunglasses shielded his eyes. But from what Chaise could tell, his eyes never veered in her direction. He was definitely in his own world and didn't want to be disturbed. Chaise gave him some time and space, knowing that he would have to answer for everything soon enough since Shadow and Rebel were following them.

When Bull put the truck in park, he exhaled loudly and turned to Chaise.

His face was stoic but she knew if she could see his eyes, they would be full of turmoil. Slowly reaching up to his face, she removed his sunglasses and what she saw broke her heart. It wasn't anger. It wasn't vengeance. She knew pain when she saw it—and Bull was hurting. Badly.

"Talk to me, Colton. Tell me what happened out there," Chaise asked softly.

"I could've gotten you killed because of what I did. I'm sorry, Chaise. If you want Rebel or Shadow to take over, I won't blame you," Bull answered.

"Wh-*what*? Of course I don't want either of them to take over." Chaise tried to contain the confusion, frustration, and pain his statement caused. She knew that he wasn't in the right frame of mind to realize how his words sounded. She didn't want to add to it with her insecurities. It was definitely not the time.

"Colton, whatever happened back there, I'm not leaving you. I don't trust anyone else like I do you. Besides, they would probably think something was really wrong with me if I tried to sneak into bed with them at night because I'm afraid to sleep alone." She tried to add a little brevity to the moment to get Bull to smile and realize that he wasn't alone.

Her plan worked—he gave her a small, half-smile as he rubbed his calloused fingers across her cheek.

"Over *their* dead bodies, Chaise," he countered.

"*There's* my Bull," Chaise laughed. She wasn't accustomed to using his nickname, but it seemed to fit and help remind him of his tough side.

He smirked. "I'll give you *your* Bull later tonight."

"*And* he's back, ladies and gentleman!"

Smiling, he shook his head from side to side. Bull couldn't believe how quickly and thoroughly the relationship between him and Chaise had changed, but he had to admit that he was grateful for it. She was his breath of fresh air in his stale world. After realizing how dull and lifeless his existence had become, he suddenly wanted no more of that life.

Since his father had abandoned him and his mother when he was just a young boy, he had kept personal attachments to a minimum. He had his mother, his brothers, Brianna—and that was it. He hadn't let any other woman in until Chaise. He knew without question that she was firmly seated in his heart and his life. Her support and belief in him, even though she had no idea what had just happened, solidified her place in his small band of trusted people.

Shadow and Rebel were waiting on the front porch of Bull's large, suburban home. It wasn't as big as Noah's palatial home, but it was big enough to have all the amenities he needed. His eyes cut to Shadow and Rebel as he nodded toward the door. "Let's get this over with."

Once inside the house, Shadow immediately started questioning Bull.

"What the hell happened, man? And don't tell me 'nothing'. You and I both know that's bullshit."

Bull gave them a full rundown of what had happened from his vantage point. He described the three Latino men in detail and gave a word for word recount of their conversation, including needing Chaise alive and unharmed. Then he reached the point of the story where he had to explain his actions. Or rather, he had to explain his lack of action.

"Go on," Rebel prodded, knowing that Bull was stalling.

"The fourth man with them was ... my father," Bull stated.

Stunned silence filled the room. Chaise's eyes flew from one man to the next, trying to figure out this part of the puzzle without interrupting their debriefing session.

"Shit," Shadow blurted out.

"Holy shit," Rebel echoed.

"Yeah," Bull deadpanned.

"Um, can someone explain this to me?" Chaise thought she had held her tongue long enough.

"My dad abandoned my mom and me when I was a kid. Just left one day and never came back. That was him I saw today ... in the parking lot ... with those guys who were after you." Bull looked apologetic, as if he were responsible for his dad's actions.

Then he turned his attention to Shadow and Rebel. "I have to go to my mom's. I need answers from her and I can't do this over the phone. I'm going back to Alabama."

Shadow and Rebel simply nodded their understanding.

"What about Chaise?" Rebel asked.

"What about Chaise?" Chaise repeated, irritation laced in her words. "She's right here. Maybe you can ask her."

Shadow smiled at Rebel. "I like her."

Bull was torn on what he should do with her. On one hand, he wanted to take her with him, to make sure she was protected and to get her out of the area. On the other hand, he wasn't sure what information he would obtain from his mother, and how he would react to that information, so it may be best to leave her with Shadow and Rebel.

Then he remembered her words spoken in jest while they sat in his truck.

"Chaise comes with me," Bull responded, leaving no room for argument. Chaise's responding smile conveyed she knew exactly what he was thinking when he made his decision. Bull smirked at her sarcastically and shook his head as he walked toward the kitchen.

"Beer?"

"Yeah."

"Sure."

Drinks in hand, the guys worked on their updated plan while Chaise put the remaining groceries away and started cooking supper. After a half-hour, Rebel appeared in the doorway to the kitchen.

"Damn, what smells so good in here?"

"Chicken tortilla soup, Panini sandwiches, and chips," Chaise answered as she stirred the soup.

"Bull, you go on to Alabama. I'm taking her home with me," Rebel teased.

"The hell you say," Bull challenged, positioning his body between Rebel and Chaise. Rebel grinned, knowing he'd hit a nerve with Bull.

"Let's eat," Chaise called out to no one in particular. She only wanted to quickly diffuse the tension in the room.

Brad walked in with the surveillance recording so Chaise could identify the man who'd been watching her all day. As they ate, the recording played and she watched herself move around the office as if she were watching a movie.

"That's him," she said as she pointed to the screen.

Brad stopped the video, isolated the sinister man, and uploaded his image to the facial recognition software. The software used specific facial features, such as the width between the eyes, width of the nose, and depth of the eye sockets to connect subjects to people already housed in a database. Once a match was made, the system returned a name and last known address.

"This could take a while to identify him. I'll let it keep running and contact you when it returns a hit," Brad told Bull. "We can start checking him out while you're in Alabama."

Bull nodded. "Thanks, Brad."

When the soup and sandwiches were gone and the guys had left, Bull sat on the couch with the phone in one hand and his head in the other. He had to make the dreaded call to his mother to let her know he was coming home. But he didn't want to tell her why just yet. He wanted to see her face when he told her he'd seen his father.

The couch dipped beside him when Chaise sat down and put her arm around him. She lightly stroked the back of his neck and he let her touch help ease the dread inside him.

"Do you want to talk about it before you call her, Colton?" Chaise asked supportively.

He didn't move other than to shake his head no. Her touch helped to calm him, her presence gave him strength, and he could feel her unconditional support. Without raising his head, his hand found hers and he lightly squeezed it, thankful that she was beside him. He brought her hand to his mouth and kissed her palm.

Chaise moved closer to him, aligning her body with his and wrapped her other arm around him. She kissed his cheek and then nuzzled her face against his. Inhaling the heady mixture of his masculine, musky cologne and the all-male scent that was inherently Bull, Chaise had to willfully fight the impulses he ignited in her.

Bull felt the change in the air and shifted his gaze to meet hers. He recognized the desire building in her eyes and knew his eyes mirrored hers. They'd slept together every night, but spooning had been the extent of their physical contact. With all the ambiguity in Bull's life at that moment, he wanted nothing more than to put it all behind him, take Chaise in his arms, and take her to his bed.

Bull tossed the phone onto the coffee table and pulled Chaise into his lap, straddling him so she was facing him. He crushed his mouth to hers, taking what he needed in a bruising, possessive kiss. There was no tenderness in it and he possessed no capacity for waiting. A voracious thirst had overtaken him and Chaise was the only one who could quench it.

His hands hungrily and eagerly roamed over her body. His palms covered her breasts, greedily kneading them before his thumbs found her already taut nipples. He groaned into her mouth as his tongue swept over hers. Bunching her shirt up in his fist, he quickly yanked it over her head and threw it on the floor.

Pulling the cups of her bra down, her breasts sprang free as he quickly covered one nipple with his mouth. Licking, sucking, and biting, he quickly had her worked into a frenzy. Chaise pulled his shirt over his head, leaned into him, and ran her tongue over his chest. His hands threaded through her hair and gently pulled her mouth back to his.

"Chaise," he said between kisses. "I can't wait, baby."

"Then don't," she purred.

She was instantly flying through the air and landed on her back on the soft, extra-wide couch. Bull grasped her pants and had them in a pile on the floor before she could blink. After removing a condom from his wallet, his pants soon followed and he covered her body with his. As her arms moved to wrap around him, he grabbed them and pushed them above her head. Holding both of her wrists in one of his hands, he positioned himself at her wet, waiting entrance and swiftly thrust into her.

She screamed out in pleasure at his sudden intrusion. He hooked his arm under her leg, bringing it straight up to rest on his shoulder as he straightened his body, and continued to surge into her, harder and harder with each thrust. Chaise was writhing in bliss beneath him as each plunge took him deeper and deeper inside her.

When she reached out to touch him, he captured her hands and used them as leverage to increase his drive. He felt her inner walls tighten around him, rippling and quivering as they squeezed him in the most erotic dance.

"I know you're close, baby. Give it to me—it's mine and I want it," he growled at her.

His words were all she needed to push her over the edge. Her orgasm felt like something akin to a tsunami. They rode the waves out together, until he had drained every last drop of energy from her body and she had milked him for everything he had.

When she moved her leg, he released her hands and fell forward on her body. She wrapped her arms around him, her body completely spent and sated, but her mind whirred and buzzed at what just occurred. They had agreed to take it slow, but the sexual chemistry between them was stronger than a magnet to steel.

While she tried to not read too much into it, his apparent aversion to her touching him during sex really bothered her. He didn't try to keep her at arms' length any other time. Like at that moment, as his body perfectly crushed hers into the couch, she gently stroked his back with her fingertips. But when they were at their most intimate, his walls were fully in place and she felt like she was firmly placed on the outside of them.

Bull turned his face toward her and brushed sweet kisses on her cheek and jaw. He rose up on his elbows and gently stroked her cheek with his thumb. His eyes searched hers intently but she didn't know what he was looking for yet.

"Did I hurt you?" he finally asked, concern laced his words and his expression.

"No, Colton, you didn't hurt me," Chaise whispered.

He lowered his forehead to rest on her shoulder. Chaise could feel the tension rolling off his body. The physical contact had only momentarily relieved his stress and it was coming back full force. Whatever he was dealing with, he wasn't telling Chaise.

With a deep breath, Bull stood up and pulled Chaise up with him. Wrapping his arms around her, they stood in the living room, stark naked, and just held each other for several minutes. Chaise felt the tears welling up in her eyes and fought to hold them back. She had no doubt that she was in over her head with him. There was no going back, no taking it slow, and no living in denial.

She had strong feelings for him and she was afraid of getting her heart broken. Or more accurately, of breaking her own heart when she finally told him the truth about her true identity. Every day she berated herself for not telling him sooner. Every day she knew she was a day too late in telling him the truth.

"We'll leave tomorrow on the Steele Security jet and go to my mother's. I just can't deal with calling her tonight," Bull said into her hair.

"Okay."

That was the only word Chaise could choke out without risking a total breakdown. She had to remain strong to help Bull with the turmoil in his life. He'd protected her and saved her life and it was the only way she knew to help him in return. At least, that was her rationalization.

Bull released her from his embrace and led her with his hand on the small of her back, as he always did, down the hall to his bedroom. She knew the moment he fell asleep, curled up with his front to her back, his arm protectively and possessively draped over her as he held her close. His breathing was deep and steady, his body relaxed, and she felt the tension seep from his muscles to be replaced with peacefulness.

Chaise silently cried herself to sleep.

CHAPTER TWELVE

The Steele Security jet was celebrity worthy. It had every opulent amenity anyone could possibly want, including a full-size bedroom and bathroom in the back of the jet. The front part of the Boeing Business Jet had one wall lined with soft-leather couches and small tables.

The other side was lined with cushioned leather captain chairs arranged in sets of four, positioned around a small table that was perfect for in-flight meetings. On the back wall, beside the hallway leading to the bedroom, was a large, flat screen plasma TV that was opposite a fully stocked bar. Chaise thought that Noah and Steele Security must have been doing very well to be able to afford such a luxurious asset.

Bull chose a small couch in the middle of the plane and patted the seat next to him, motioning for Chaise to sit with him. She took her seat and he immediately wrapped his arm around her, pulling her close to him. *He always does that*, she thought with a smile.

"What are you grinning about?" Bull asked.

She looked up at him, not realizing that she had an ear-to-ear smile plastered on her face until he pointed it out.

"I was actually thinking that you always do that—pull me into you when we sit down," she answered truthfully, then watched his face to gauge his reaction.

His smile remained in place. "I guess I do. Huh. How about that? Does it bother you?"

"No, it doesn't bother me at all. I like it. It's almost like I was made to fit next to you." Chaise blabbered before realizing that had just vocalized the very thought she meant to keep to herself.

Surprise registered in his eyes, but she didn't see any sign of panic.

Nothing that indicated he was ready to parachute out of the jet to get away from her and her reference to them being made for each other.

"Maybe you were made to fit with me," Bull said, partly teasing and partly serious.

Chaise desperately wanted that to be true. Bull was not the type of man who would try to feed her a line just to string her along. But she didn't think he was the type of man who wanted long-term committed relationships, either. His tone of voice and the softness in his eyes when he said that made her think that something more could come of their relationship. It made her hope that she wasn't just a temporary distraction for him that would be tossed aside as soon as the case was closed.

"What if I was, Colton? Would you keep me?" she asked with baited breath.

The flight attendant saved him from answering her question. "The pilot has indicated we are ready for departure. Please buckle your seat belts until we are at cruising altitude," she politely instructed.

Chaise moved out from Bull's arms to secure her seatbelt. Bull's first instinct was to pull her back to his side. She did fit him perfectly. Her body fit perfectly with his. He thought about how well they got along—their playful banter, their deeper conversations, and their red-hot bedroom trysts. Chaise was the first woman Bull could see himself with for the long haul. That fact alone should have him running as far in the opposite direction as fast as he possibly could go.

In less than two hours, they would reach the airport in Mobile, Alabama. While there were special circumstances, Chaise would be the first woman he'd ever introduced to his mother. The implications of that fact were enormous to Bull. It signified that he cared enough about her to take her with him instead of leaving her with Rebel or Shadow. It meant that he had to share his most private life with someone he didn't fully know. It meant that he had to let her see him when he was at his most vulnerable.

For the first time in many years, his head and his heart didn't agree. His head told him there were still too many things he didn't know about her. His logical reasoning and training told him it could never work and that she was bound to betray his trust. He still didn't know her last name, despite the intimate moments they'd shared.

Did that make them less real?

Not according to his heart.

His heart said there was more to them than their physical compatibility. When his mind said to walk away and leave her behind, his heart made sure he knew that wouldn't work. He couldn't say he was in love with her. He didn't believe in love at first sight. He believed love took a lifetime to cultivate and nurture.

But somehow she had found a way to break past his defenses and securely root herself deep inside him. When he looked at her now, he couldn't remember what he did with his free time before she came into his life.

Just a few weeks ago, in fact, he thought.

And there was his rational mind again, raging a war inside him and making him question what he thought he always wanted. He sat silently on the jet, arguing with himself over what he should do next. She was still beside him, oblivious to his entire inner monologue.

When his hand reached up to caress her cheek, he knew the instant he touched her that he wouldn't walk away. The battle had been decided and the war had been won. He walked into the situation knowing that she had secrets she was afraid to tell him. But he was a good judge of character and he could read people like a book.

At his touch, she leaned her face into the palm of his hand. She closed her eyes and hummed in pleasure at such a simple touch. He could see it on her face, he saw it in her eyes when she looked at him, and he could feel it in her every touch. He knew she felt it, too.

She was the culmination of exactly what he thought he would never want, the very thing he could never have, and now that he'd had a taste of it, he didn't think he could give it up. She trusted him, she believed in him, and she made him feel protective and possessive like no other.

Bull leaned over and placed a chaste kiss on her lips.

"Mmmm, you taste so good. I don't think one kiss is enough," he murmured against her lips.

"By all means, Colton, if you're still hungry ..." she intentionally let her voice trail off so he would fill in the rest with whatever he wanted from her.

The seatbelt light dinged off just as he was about to unfasten hers and pull her into his lap. The flight attendant appeared and asked if they wanted anything to eat or drink.

"No, thank you. Ms. Martin isn't feeling well so we're going to lie down for a while. We'd appreciate no interruptions until it's time to land," Bull responded.

Chaise tried to hide her surprise at his statement of her not feeling well. When Bull mentioned the bed, she knew exactly what he had in mind. Even so, after he helped her up, the goose bumps covered her body when he bent his head to her ear and whispered with his bedroom voice.

"Ready to join the *Mile High Club*? You'll be my first."

Her knees were suddenly weak and her panties were wet. *How can he do that to me with just his voice?* There was no way in hell she wouldn't follow him to the bedroom. She was suddenly looking forward to becoming a member of the elite group of *mile-highers* ... with Bull.

"You'll be my first, too." She couldn't stop the slight blush that crawled up her face. Bull smiled and placed his hand on his spot at the small of her back to lead her past the small galley kitchen and into the private bedroom area. He closed and locked the door behind him.

Bull wrapped his arms around her from behind. Using his chin, he moved her hair aside enough to gain access to her neck. He licked and nibbled in the erogenous zone at the base of her neck. Chaise's hand lifted and wrapped around the back of his head as he continued.

"Everything about you is so beautiful, Chaise. I can hardly take my eyes off of you. I can't keep my hands off of you. I'm falling completely under your spell," his lips whispered against her skin. His words sent shivers down her spine. She wanted to believe them. She had no reason to believe he would lie to her.

"Do you still want to slow this down?" Bull asked. Chaise knew if she said yes, he would comply. Everything in him was done with honor and integrity and he wouldn't hold it against her.

But with every fiber in her body screaming for his touch, her only response was, "No."

As she was turning to face him, Bull placed his hands on her hips to still her movement. "No, like this," he crooned in her ear.

His hand snaked down her thighs to the hem of her skirt and pulled it up. His fingers traced the lacy edge of her panties to her core. Pushing the fabric aside, his finger plunged inside her as her body reacted, saturating his hand with her sweet nectar.

"Your body already knows *this* belongs to me," his deep voice affirmed. "Doesn't it, Chaise?"

"Yessss," she hissed in response.

He languidly moved his finger inside her, collecting her wetness and spreading it on her delicate folds. His self-restraint was amazing to Chaise since all she could think of was pushing him down on the bed and finishing what he'd started.

His finger found her soaked core again as he pumped it in and out of her before suddenly adding a second. Holding her neck with this other hand, he tilted her head back to cover her mouth with his just before her orgasm took control of her senses. She moaned loudly into his mouth as his tongue caressed hers in a sensual dance.

Bull jerked her panties down her legs and, using his hands, he positioned her legs a little farther apart. Chaise looked down at him when his face suddenly appeared between her legs. His wicked grin made her knees go weak and she grabbed onto the mattress to steady herself.

"That's probably a good idea, babe," Bull warned before his tongue delved into her core. He voraciously devoured her like he was a starved man. His tongue twisted and twirled inside her, his teeth lightly scraped her sensitive nub, and just when she thought it couldn't feel any better, he added his fingers to the rousing mixture.

Despite her stronghold onto the comforter, her legs repeatedly dipped as he continued his ministrations. As he continued to lap her up, her chest heaved with deep breaths, and her moans got consistently louder. When she was able to catch her breath and look down at him, she saw his deep blue eyes watching her intently. The look of pure satisfaction was all it took to push her over the edge again.

Before she could move, Bull was once again standing behind her with his expansive chest pressed firmly against her back. He wrapped one arm around her waist and placed the other hand on her back. "Bend over for me, baby," he commanded and she willingly complied.

She heard the zipper of his jeans, the crinkling of a condom wrapper, and then the rustling of denim as he shoved his pants down his legs. He then positioned the tip of his erection at the entrance of her wet core. Chaise waited impatiently for him, slightly pushing her hips back in her attempt to feel him inside her. She felt a slight chuckle rumble through his body at her insistence.

His fingers firmly grasped her hips as he slowly pushed into her, inch by powerful inch, until he was fully buried inside her. The angle in which she was bent only deepened his penetration and intensified her pleasure. His thrusts were strong and fluid, bringing her closer and closer to ecstasy with skillful precision.

"Damn, you feel so good wrapped around me," Bull growled and immediately noticed the flush of wetness. "Mmmm, you like when I talk to you, don't you?"

"I *love* it," Chaise admitted as she gripped the comforter tighter in her fists.

"I know you do. Your body tells me, shows me," Bull claimed. "You'll be ruined for anyone but me."

Chaise knew that was already true. He knew her body's needs and desires before she even realized. He navigated her body like he owned its sole road map. And she was sure that he would completely own her heart and break it just as thoroughly … eventually.

She felt the familiar surge of pleasure and the aching feeling that built and then peaked. Waves of pleasure radiated through her core as her inner muscles squeezed and drained Bull dry as he climaxed with her.

Bull bent slightly to position his arm under her chest. Then he easily lifted her upper body to stand as he repeatedly kissed the side of her head and her cheek. He pulled her close to him as he fully wrapped his arms around her and inhaled her sweet perfume.

"That was fucking incredible, baby," he crooned as he continued to lavish her with affection. "*You* are incredible."

"You're pretty incredible yourself, Colton," she murmured, still basking in the afterglow of her multiple orgasmic experience.

Bull led her to the adjoining bathroom and she followed without asking what he had planned. After that last encounter, she decided with no small amount of pleasure that he could have his way every time and she would never regret it.

Once inside, he wet a washcloth with warm water and gently placed it between her legs. Her mint-green eyes grew wider from surprise by his tender touch and thoughtful gesture. His normally stoic eyes were suddenly hyper-expressive and they held hers captive as he silently finished. After helping her arrange her clothing, he held her face in his hands and kissed her so sweetly, so lovingly, it brought her close to tears.

"You can take a nap until it's time to land, if you'd like. We still have a little while before we land," Bull offered.

"Are you going to nap with me?"

Bull smiled appreciatively. "If that's what you want."

"I do," Chaise answered before reaching up to kiss him once more before walking away.

Chaise heard the water running and pictured Bull cleaning himself much the way he had cared for her. The sex was definitely hot, the conversations came much easier, and they got along so well. She'd tried to keep her distance, tried to keep her heart out of it, especially knowing what was still to come. But that lone act of caring for her so intimately, so thoroughly, and without expecting anything in return, had completely wrecked her plans of maintaining her space.

She knew, without a doubt, she was unequivocally his.

The bed dipped as Bull took his spot behind her. His arm reached around her and pulled her securely to him. They lay with their bodies perfectly aligned, close enough to be one, as Chaise cherished the feeling that only snuggling with him could give her.

CHAPTER THIRTEEN

Stepping off the plane in Mobile, Bull and Chaise were immediately hit with the stifling heat and humidity of southern Alabama. While Mobile Bay afforded their accustomed ocean breeze, the airport was located outside the bay area and didn't have the same attributes. Their clothes immediately clung to them as the beads of perspiration popped up and glistened in the hot sun.

The vehicle rental was much like Bull's truck in Miami minus a few of the extra amenities he had personally added. Chaise took in the sights as Bull mindlessly drove to his old home. She asked a few questions about the area and about his family but gave up after his one-syllable answers returned.

She could feel the tension radiating off of him. After everything he'd done to help her, she wanted to do something, anything, to help him in his painful situation. Chaise unbuckled her seat belt and moved across the center console and to the backseat. Bull looked at her quizzically but she proceeded with a smile.

Once she'd positioned herself, she reached her arms around the seat and began massaging Bull's shoulders and neck. His all-male groan reverberated through the truck and through her body as she felt the tense muscles begin to relax. Working out the kinks and knots she found in his muscles, she could feel his tension lighten.

After several minutes of expertly massaging, kneading, and rubbing the sore areas, Chaise knew she had successfully helped him. When she climbed back into the front seat, Bull took her hand in his, lifted it to his mouth, and kissed it. But this time, he didn't let go. He laced their fingers together and held her hand in his lap.

It felt like another turning point to Chaise. Another sign that the solid steel walls constructed around Bull may just be bending to allow her to enter.

She squeezed his hand a little as she asked about him. "Did that help any?"

Bull smiled and replied with a wink. "Yeah, if I'd known you were a secret masseuse, I would've put you to work before now."

Chaise laughed. "I'm not a secret masseuse, but anytime you need the stress worked out of you, just let me know."

The heated look Bull gave her revealed he'd intentionally twisted her meaning in his mind. She laughed and corrected her statement. "Okay, let's try that again. If you need your neck and shoulders massaged, just let me know."

Bull laughed heartily. "I think I like my interpretation better."

The rest of the ride to Sandy Bay, Alabama was in peaceful silence. Bull continued to hold on to her hand, occasionally pulling it back to his mouth to kiss it. He had a far-away look in his eyes, as if he was remembering his time spent in the area but wasn't quite ready to share his thoughts.

The truck stopped outside of a single-story, sprawling ranch-style house with lush green grass and shrubbery in the front yard. Bull sat motionless as he stared at the house. His stoic, emotionless mask was securely in place again.

"Colton, are you okay?" Chaise softly asked.

Bull nodded. "Yeah, let's get this over with."

"I can help get the bags," Chaise offered.

"We're not staying here. We'll stay at my place," Bull replied.

"Your place?" Chaise asked, confused.

"I have a small place here where I stay when I come to visit," Bull explained.

"Oh, all right."

Bull's mother, Michelle, met them at the door as they approached. She pulled Bull into her arms for an embrace as she squealed. "My baby boy's home! I didn't know you were coming! You should've called me!"

Bull hugged her back but didn't verbally respond. He pulled away and dropped his arms from around Michelle. Her face instantly changed, sensing something was wrong.

When her eyes met Chaise's, she smiled genuinely and extended her hand. "Hello, I'm Michelle Lanier, Colton's mother."

"I'm Chaise. Colton's ... friend," she said as she cut her eyes to Bull for a second.

She wasn't sure how to label what she was to him and asking him in front of his mom wasn't an option. She also noticed the tick in Colton's jaw and immediately knew he was thinking about her last name—or lack thereof. She quickly continued. "It's nice to meet you. You have a lovely home."

"Thank you, dear. Come in, come in!"

Michelle showed Chaise around her house, including Bull's old room where she'd kept things much as they were when he last lived there. His pictures from his youth and some that were more recent hung on the walls and sat out on display. It was obvious that Michelle was very proud of her son then and the man he'd become.

When they finally sat down in the den, Bull cleared his throat and started. "Mom, we need to talk."

"Do you want me to leave?" Chaise politely interrupted.

The look Bull gave her made her instantly regret asking. From the look in his eyes, it was obvious he wanted her there with him and he was disappointed that she would even ask. Chaise moved closer to him and covered his big hand with her small one. "I'll stay," she whispered.

"What's this about, Colton?" Michelle asked.

"It's about Dad."

Michelle's eyes and mouth simultaneously flew wide open in surprise. She stuttered and stammered, trying to form coherent words, but none came. She quickly averted her eyes from Bull and Chaise. Her face was bright red and her breaths suddenly increased.

"I saw him, Mom. He was with some really bad guys who shot at us, and were trying to kidnap Chaise," Bull continued without remorse. "I saw the letter he left, the one that said we were better off without him. Now, I need to know the truth about him because it's Chaise's life in danger now."

Michelle stood and walked over to the end table. She stood with her back to Colton and Chaise for several long minutes before opening the base of the table and retrieving the letter.

"I wish you'd told me you'd seen this a long time ago," she finally said as she clutched the letter to her chest.

"What difference would it have made if I had? He *abandoned* us without a second thought and you just pretended it was all fine instead of facing the truth," he spat out in anger.

"No, Colton, that's not entirely true," she sighed heavily. "I was wrong to not tell you when you were old enough to understand, but he didn't want me to say anything. He was afraid it would put you in more danger."

Michelle took a deep breath. "He didn't *abandon* us, Colton. He had to leave to *protect* us. But he's always kept watch over you and me. All these years, he's never stopped loving us."

"You're not making any sense," Colton growled.

"Your dad works undercover with the DEA, Colton. That's why he traveled so much when you were young. He was deep undercover and his cover was about to be blown. This letter you saw was our secret code, should that day ever come. His case was big and had he been discovered, it would've gotten us all killed.

"That's why we moved here. That's why you went to the military boarding school for high school. That's why I let you, and everyone else, believe he had just left without a word. It was the only way to keep us all alive."

Colton stood and started pacing the room. His hands were drawn into fists. The emotionless mask was gone and full fury had replaced it. His muscles were tightly wound, like a rattlesnake ready to strike. He looked lethal and he was only getting started.

"You really expect me to believe that all this was for *our* benefit? He could've moved with us. He could've taken on a new identity and stayed with us. He didn't have to *leave* us."

"Those were different times, Colton. He had to make it look like we were dead so we'd have a chance at a life without looking over all our shoulders all the time. We both did what we thought was best. That's all we could do," her voice rich with grief, regret, and remorse.

Chaise watched Bull intently to try to gauge his reaction. The whole conversation was a huge bombshell and she felt like she was still running to catch up to them. The silence was uncomfortable and the room felt stuffy.

"Do you still talk to him?" Bull's eyes narrowed and he crossed his arms across his huge chest.

Michelle drew in a deep breath and Chaise had a very bad feeling about what was about to occur. "Yes, Colton, I still talk to him. He's still my husband. That's why I've never remarried. It's always been him for me."

"How can you still be married if you never see him?" Bull growled.

"I do see him but not as often as I'd like at the moment. He's finishing up this current case and then he's retiring. He'll move here to be with me or we'll move somewhere together," Michelle explained with a shrug of her shoulder.

"I don't fucking believe this! He's been absent my whole life and you just take him back like what he did is nothing?" Bull's anger was reaching a scorching hot level.

"I love him, Colton. I knew what he was when we married and I knew this was a possibility. We did the best we could with what we had. He watched over you your whole life, Colton. You didn't know, but he's always watched over you and your career. He's so proud of you."

Bull paced the floor, his hands on his head and threading through his hair in frustration. There were just too many lies, too many things that were kept from him, and a lifetime of regrets caused by an absent father. The same father who had always been proud of him and would be stepping back into the family like nothing happened at all.

"Chaise and I are going to my place. I need some time to think this through." He stopped and looked her in the eye. "You shouldn't have let me find out like this. You should've told me."

"I know, son. I'm so sorry. We were only trying to protect you. I love you, Colton."

Bull nodded but Chaise had the distinct impression that he wasn't really listening to what his mom was saying. His mind was a million miles away at the moment.

In the truck after saying their goodbyes, Bull was still very quiet. He answered Chaise when she spoke, but other than that, he was very distant. Chaise reached over and put her hand over his. Without looking at her, Bull closed his hand around hers and squeezed it lightly. That was his way of thanking her for her silent support.

Bull pulled into a secluded driveway that was barely visible from the road. The shrubbery and coconut trees partially blocked the view of the drive, giving the illusion that it was an old abandoned road. Obviously, that was just how Bull wanted it to appear to keep unwanted visitors out.

At the end of the driveway sat a small house. It was immaculately kept and looked like an island oasis. The front yard was covered with lush, green grass and the backyard was the beach and ocean. Bull parked, grabbed their bags, and escorted Chaise into his home away from home.

The house was small and simple, not nearly as elaborate as his Miami home. But it was the simplicity and the back view that was the true draw. The house consisted of three bedrooms, two baths, a den, dine-in kitchen, and a large wrap-around covered porch. The back yard held the typical manly-man essentials—a grill, a fire pit, and an oversized hammock.

Chaise had always loved the beach and the ocean. She had grown up living around the water and she loved it. She was strong swimmer. The sound of the waves and the feel of the breeze was her Zen place. She looked at Bull and quipped, "I call dibs on the hammock tonight."

Her attempt at humor at least earned her a smile—the first one she'd seen since they had arrived at his mother's house. She heard, "humph," just before she was suddenly picked up and thrown over his shoulder. She squealed with laughter and he playfully swatted her ass.

"Don't even think you're sleeping *anywhere* without me, woman!"

"Oh, I do love the *'demanding Bull'* so much," Chaise teased.

"You're about to get all the 'demanding Bull' you can take," he warned with a mischievous sparkle in his eyes.

"Promises, promises," she replied sardonically. While he couldn't see the huge grin on her face, she made sure her voice conveyed her playfulness. That was all it took for Bull to want to prove her wrong. Her plan was actually working much better than she had anticipated.

Bull deposited her across the hammock and softly covered her mouth with his. He was unusually tender in his approach and Chaise felt every ounce of her body melting into the hammock. She felt the thick, rigged length of his shaft bulge against his jeans. The vibrating sensation was new, however.

"Fuck!" Bull said as he pulled his phone out of his pocket. Glancing at the screen, he saw Rebel's name just before he answered. "Yeah, man."

A few clipped words later, along with no display of emotion one way or another, Bull ended his call. Chaise looked at him expectantly as he prepared to fill her in.

"We'll have to stay here for a few days. That was Rebel. The guy you identified on the surveillance tape is not part of the *Tres Sieses*. He's actually part of a much more dangerous organization and they are apparently after you," Bull explained.

Chaise gasped audibly and the color drained from her face. "Worse than that gang? What's worse than having a gang after me?"

Bull cautiously answered her. "This is an *international* organized crime group. They are very professional and thorough, Chaise. They have their hands in several different illegal activities, including human trafficking and drugs. They don't tolerate failure, either. The guy on the video has been found shot—execution style. My guess is he was killed because he failed to get you."

The shock and terror that Chaise felt was indescribable and overwhelming. They had killed a man because he failed to kidnap her. He was supposed to kidnap her because she discovered the missing girls. The mere question of what else they could be hiding was equally as frightening as what she'd already uncovered.

"Colton, what am I supposed to do?"

His eyes revealed that his response held an intentional double entendre meaning. "Anything I tell you to do, Chaise."

"I'm serious."

"So am I," he declared. "Just stick with me, baby. I'll keep you safe."

"Come on. I know this is more serious than what you're telling me," Chaise gently chided him. "I know I haven't been a pillar of stone, but I'm not stupid."

Bull smiled gently. "I never thought you were, Chaise. Yes, it's dangerous but there's a reason why we're the best at what we do. You'll just have to trust me."

"I do trust you, Colton," she replied warmly as she stroked his cheek. Her face took a serious countenance as she continued. "I hope you know you can trust me, too."

"I'm learning that," he said sincerely as he wrapped his hand around hers. Chaise was happy to have earned that much faith from Bull in their short time together.

"So, what do we do now?"

"We'll stay here for the next few days. We'll keep off their radar and figure out our next move. Rebel and Shadow are gathering more intel on them. No one else even knows where you are."

"Let's just stay here forever, then," Chaise whispered while gazing deep into his eyes.

"That's the best plan I've heard in a long time," Bull replied. "I have all kinds of ideas for you."

"It's a good thing I have nowhere else I have to be then, isn't it? I don't even have to worry about going back to work Monday," she replied with a sultry smile.

"Come on. It's time to eat and I'll show you around," he said as he stood and helped her up from the hammock.

Bull took Chaise out to eat at an oceanfront restaurant. Tiny white lights adorned the trellis that covered the intimate patio setting, naturally creating a romantic ambiance. Large, exotic plants were placed strategically to avoid blocking the ocean view but also gave the guests a modicum of privacy.

Once the maître d' seated them, Bull emphasized his words as he leaned over the table. "You are stunning." His hooded eyes matched the bedroom quality of his voice and Chaise clenched her thighs in response. The low timbre of his voice seemed to have more control over her body than she had herself.

"You know, you said that when you tried to get me to stay home with you tonight. But, since a lady never tires of hearing how good she looks, I won't try to stop you from telling me again," Chaise flirted and teased Bull.

"I offered to feed you." Bull responded and laughed when Chaise's face heated from her blush.

The waitress appeared and saved Chaise from having to respond to his overt attempt to arouse her. Placing the menus in front of them, she recited the daily specials before taking their drink orders. Once she was gone, Chaise looked back at Bull who was still smirking.

"So, tell me something I don't know about Colton Lanier." Chaise challenged, trying to change the subject and knowing she was opening herself up to questioning as well.

"What do you want to know?" Bull leaned back in his chair and put his hands in his lap. His posture was relaxed and open. His face showed his amusement, though she wasn't sure if that was from her abrupt change in subject or her question.

"Have you ever been in love?" Chaise asked while trying to hide her hesitancy. While she wasn't naïve, she didn't know if she really wanted the answer to this question.

"Straight for the jugular, huh?" Bull asked with his panty-dropping smile. "I thought I was, once. But while I thought she was a good person, it turns out she was a lying, cheating skank behind my back. After that fiasco, I decided relationships weren't for me.

"I think, now, that it wasn't really love at all. I didn't know her like I thought I did. I ignored too many signs that were more like huge, blinking billboards. It's not a mistake I've made since."

What he didn't tell Chaise was that he had fast developed feelings for her. He wouldn't go so far as to say it was love, but he couldn't deny that he thought he *could* fall in love with her. She was the first woman who had made him feel that way—protective, possessive, and happy. For the first time in a very long time, he wanted to see how a relationship with Chaise could work.

"It sounds like you've already decided that's not something you want," Chaise replied. Bull noted that she kept her voice even and unemotional, but her eyes betrayed her and revealed her true feelings.

"For a long time, yes, it was that way. My mind isn't so set in stone now," he replied cryptically. "My turn." He immediately noticed the rigid tone of Chaise's posture and the flash of panic that crossed her face.

"Ask away," Chaise said, preparing herself for the one question she didn't want to hear.

Bull narrowed his eyes and contemplated his question. He had a visceral need to understand her connection to Reaper. He wanted to know why she reacted the way she did when Reaper's name was brought up in conversation. He wanted to ask her how she could trust him with her life and in his bed, but not with her real last name.

"Have you ever lied to me?" Bull asked.

Chaise's body relaxed and she reached her hand across the table, palm up in request for his hand. Bull complied but didn't move his gaze from hers.

"I have—but I tried to tell you I did and you said you knew. Martin isn't my last name, Colton. My last name is-," Chaise was cut off by the waitress.

"Here are your drinks. Now, are you ready to order?"

Bull squeezed Chaise's hand and answered. "Yes, I think we are."

Bull ordered their main entrees and handed the menus back to the waitress. The band started playing and Bull stood, offered his hand to Chaise, and led her to the dance floor. He wrapped his arms around her waist and she wrapped her arms around his neck. He pulled her as tightly to him as he could, just to feel her body pressed against his as they moved to the slow, melodic music.

Chaise looked up at him. "Colton, I want to tell you."

"I know you do. And for now, that's enough. It tells me you finally trust me enough. We can talk about it when we get home. Then you can explain why you had to keep it a secret."

Chaise stretched up and kissed his lips. Bull tilted his head down to meet her and deepened their kiss. The music played in the background but it was of no consequence. They were in their own world, their own time, and dancing to their own music. Their fully clothed bodies, intertwined and moving as one, was as sensual, erotic, and intimate as anything Chaise had ever experienced.

When the song finished, Bull led Chaise back to the table with his hand placed possessively on the small of her back. She liked the feeling that small gesture gave her. It announced to the world that she belonged with him. They arrived back at their table just as the wait staff arrived with their meals.

After their meals were finished, and Chaise had consumed several glasses of Moscato wine, Bull led her back to his truck. She was tipsy but not drunk, though her inhibitions were significantly lessened. The lascivious look she gave Bull left no room for misinterpretation when she purred, "I can't wait to try out that hammock, Colton."

Bull's head whipped around to look at her, shock and complete surprise at her boldness registered on his face. It was quickly replaced by wanton need and heated desire. His foot pushed the gas pedal harder as he sped back to his house.

CHAPTER FOURTEEN

Bull made himself comfortable in the hammock while Chaise took time to freshen up. He was enjoying the ocean breeze, the sway of the hammock, and the white noise from the waves breaking. A sizzle in the air caught his attention and his head snapped up from the pillow in time to see Chaise emerge from the back door.

He nearly swallowed his tongue at the outfit she had chosen in which to be more comfortable. He immediately decided she wouldn't be wearing it long enough to get comfortable. In fact, he couldn't wait to remove it from her perfectly toned body with his teeth. She was glowing with radiant beauty and the slight blush that crept up her cheeks only made her even more gorgeous.

Bull swung his legs over the side of the hammock and watched intently as she made her way to him. She was wearing a baby blue camisole that barely reached the top of her bikini line, revealing the small, triangular shaped piece of matching blue lace that covered her mound. The camisole top tied between her breasts and flowed open, revealing her toned abdomen. The four-inch black heels she wore completed her ensemble and made her legs look even longer and more toned.

She stopped directly in front of him, just barely out of his reach, as she asked, "Well, what do you think?" When she twirled around to give him a full view, his mouth dropped open when he realized her panties were actually a thong and her spectacular ass was on full display for him.

"I think if I'd known you had that here, we wouldn't have ever left the house today," Bull replied but his eyes never left her body. She saw the bulge in his pants and, as she seductively swayed toward him, she watched in amazement how the bulge continued to grow and strain against the front of his pants. Her mouth watered and she ached to be the initiator this time.

Bull stood and reached out to pull her to him but she quickly stepped back just out of his reach. He tilted his head to the side and his eyes crinkled at the corners as he attempted to figure out what she had planned. Her sly smile eased across her face as she simultaneously shook her head and her index finger at him.

"Stand still. No touching me," she warned while cocking one eyebrow at him, as if that made her directive more threatening.

"There's no fun in not touching you," he replied dryly.

"There could be," she teased. "Just try it. For me?"

Bull gave her his most seductive smile and her knees were suddenly very weak beneath her. "For you, I will try it."

Projecting confidence she didn't really possess, she sauntered up to him and deftly removed his belt and unzipped his pants. When she'd pushed them, along with his boxer briefs, down to his ankles, she dropped to her knees in front of him.

His blue eyes grew wide with surprise and then they deepened to the color of a turbulent sea. She kept her mint-green eyes trained on his and she took his thick shaft in her hand and stroked it from base to tip. Before he could reach for her, she took him in her mouth, rolling her tongue around the head of his manhood before taking him fully into her mouth.

As she worked him with her mouth and her hand, his moans of pleasure became louder. As he touched the back of her throat, she moaned loudly. The reverberation shot through him and his hands instinctively shot to her head, fisted her hair, and held her head as she continued.

"Damn, Chaise—you're killing me, baby," he growled out his pleasure. As he felt the pressure building up inside him, he dropped his head back and enjoyed the ecstasy her warm, wet mouth brought him. The pressure was about to erupt as he tried to stop her. "Baby, you have to stop now or-," but his words only spurred her on more.

Unable to contain it any longer, Bull let go of his control and allowed her to finish him, taking every last drop from him until she was sure he was completely empty. When she stopped, she looked up at him with her adoring eyes. Her heart skipped a beat from the adoring look he gave back to her.

His hands reached down and grabbed her elbows to steady her as she stood. He bowed his head and captured her mouth with his—gently and sweetly, but thoroughly kissed her. When he ended the kiss, he moved his mouth to her ear. His warm breath fanned out across her cheek as he whispered. "I seem to remember something about you wanting to try out the hammock tonight."

His chuckle rumbled through his chest when she gasped. She looked up at him from under her lashes and replied. "Oh, absolutely, Colton. We may even break that hammock tonight." His all-male growl sent shivers down her spine.

He stepped out of his pants and pulled her backward with him to the hammock. Bull sat down, and true to his thoughts, leaned forward to grasp the tiny swath of fabric between his teeth and slowly pulled them down her legs until they dropped and pooled at her feet.

Bull turned and stretched out on the hammock. "Climb aboard," he instructed with a cocky grin. Chaise kicked off her shoes, stepped out of her panties, and fished his wallet from his pants. Bull removed a condom and looked at her expectantly. Chaise took the wrapper from him and opened it with her teeth before slowly rolling it onto him. She climbed onto him and positioned herself directly above his waiting erection. As she lowered herself onto him, she relished every sensation of being stretched and filled. She moaned in delight as her wet channel grabbed him and she sank deeper onto him.

They began moving in tandem—as she came down on him, he'd thrust his hips upward into her. Every thrust brought her closer to climax. Bull's hand reached up and untied her camisole to reveal her perfect breasts and toned stomach. His hands moved down her body, taking his time with each breast and nipple. Then with his rough, calloused thumb, he applied pressure to the nub of nerve endings that made stars shoot behind her eyes.

He felt her inner walls quiver, spasm, and grab hold of him as she rocked her hips back and forth, up and down, and side to side on him. His thumb continued its assault on her nub and she began to move faster, milking him with her inner muscles with every movement.

He took her hands in his, holding them up to give her leverage to push against as she rode him. When he felt the pressure building again, he demanded, "Look at me, Chaise. I want to see your eyes when you come." The stare only intensified the feelings and soon they climaxed together.

When she leaned her head back and screamed out his name, he responded. "That's my girl. Fuck, you turn me on even more when you do that."

Chaise fell forward, splayed out on his chest, with his manhood still fully buried inside her. She loved the feeling of being connected to him and wasn't quite ready to let him go. His hand gently stroked her back as the hammock continued to gently sway. Both were unwilling to say it, but they both felt it—the shift in their relationship, the knowledge that it was more than a passing fling, and the unknown decision of what they would do about it.

Together, they fell into a deep slumber in the warm Alabama air. The gently swaying hammock rocked them to sleep and the warmth of their bodies cocooned them for the night. When the sun came up, the rays bleeding through the canopy of the trees woke Chaise. She realized that somehow she had moved from lying on top of Bull to being tucked protectively into the crook of his arm and his other was draped protectively over her. He had removed his shirt and used it to cover her.

Titling her head up, she realized that he was watching her. Chaise asked, "Did I wake you?"

"No, baby. I've been awake—just watching you sleep."

She smiled without responding.

"What is it?" he asked.

"You've started calling me 'baby.' I like it," she responded as she snuggled in tightly to him. Her top leg moved over his as she wrapped her body around him. The hammock moved slightly, rocking them as it swayed in the wind.

His arm tightened around her as he lowered his lips to her ear. "It's a good thing you do, because I wasn't going to stop."

Chaise laughed jovially as she swatted his bare chest. "Now why doesn't that surprise me?"

"It really shouldn't," he teased.

After breakfast, Bull convinced Chaise to change into her bathing suit so they could enjoy a relaxing day at the beach together. It had been way too long since Bull had taken a real vacation. Work had always been his priority and he prided himself on giving it his all.

That day, his work and his vacation were one in the same. He had to keep Chaise away from Miami to keep her safe. There was nothing else pressing that he wanted to do. In fact, continuing the conversation with his mother was the very last thing he wanted to even think about, much less actually do.

While Chaise changed, Bull gathered all the beach supplies they would need and waited patiently on the patio. His low whistle of appreciation brought a smile to Chaise's face when she stepped through the door. Her tanned body and black hair accentuated her light pink bikini. Her curves on display made Bull's mouth salivate as if he'd never tasted her before.

Or maybe it was because he already knew exactly how she tasted.

Hand in hand, they strolled across the hot sand to where the waves rolled up on the shore. Placing the bag out of reach of the water, Bull removed two masks, two snorkels, and two sets of fins. Handing one set to Chaise, he asked, "Do you know how to use these?"

"Of course," she replied casually. "I grew up around the ocean and I love the water."

"There's a manmade reef several yards off the shore. We'll swim out and have a little fun out there," Bull said with a smile.

"Let's go!" Chaise sat in the shallow water to put her fins on her feet and to fit the mask to her face. Once she was set, she floated on the shallow water until the water was deep enough for her to turn and wait for Bull.

Bull had watched her with amazement that she was bold enough to don the equipment and swim out without waiting for him. Most women, in his experience, were afraid of what the water held. She seemed to relish in the discovery of it. He waded into the water to join her and they swam off to explore.

Hours later, they were both completely exhausted from their excursions as they headed back to Bull's beachfront home. They had first explored the manmade reef just off the shore. After a light snack on the beach, they walked along the shoreline, talking and simply enjoying each other's company. Once they reached the house, Bull led Chaise to the bedroom and wrapped his arms around her for a mid-afternoon nap.

Over the next three days, they spent their time together in much the same way. After realizing how much Chaise loved the swimming, snorkeling, and the ocean in general, Bull made it a point to take her to new places each day. They explored new snorkeling spots, took long walks on the beach, and christened many new places with their lovemaking. In the evenings, he would take her to the boardwalk area to walk on the pier, shop in the beachfront stores, and eat in the local restaurants.

For brief moments, Chaise forgot that she was being pursued by a masterful criminal organization. She was in her own paradise oasis with Bull where she could happily stay. The time alone with him had given her a view into the real Colton Lanier—the man whom few seldom had the opportunity to experience.

And she knew without a shadow of a doubt that she'd fallen completely and undeniably in love with him. She never said the words, but she didn't try to hide the actions or feelings. The little things mattered to Chaise. He took such good care of her; she wanted to give what she could in return.

Every day, she rose early to cook his breakfast and make sure his black coffee was made just right. She dressed to the nines when he took her out to eat so that he would be proud to have her on his arm. When other men blatantly stared at her, she only had eyes for Bull. Lastly, she made sure that at any time he wanted her she was more than willing.

But with every time they joined, he kept her hands off of him. Before or after they made love, he seemed to love the feel of her hands on him. He acted as if he craved her touch and couldn't get enough of her. Then in midst of the their passionate encounters, he found a way to actively prohibit her from touching him.

Chaise remembered their swim on one particular day. Bull's strong arms wrapped around her and pulled her to him. Her legs instinctively wrapped around his waist as he hungrily captured her mouth with his. Her lips parted and his tongue plunged in, wrapping around hers in a slow and sensual dance.

She felt his growing erection pressing into her core and she pressed her hips downward, grinding into him. Her hand traveled down his chest and abdomen until she felt the exposed tip of his mushroom head. Pulling on the string, she loosened his shorts as his fingers pulled her swatch of bikini fabric to the side.

He broke the kiss to peer into her eyes. He placed one of his hands on her chest and lightly pushed her backward as his other hand supported her back. Chaise shot him a nervous look and he calmly assured her "Trust me, baby."

She relaxed into his hold until her back floated on the ocean water, her legs remained wrapped around his waist, and his thick shaft was poised at her core. He plunged into her wet core and then grabbed her hands in his. He pulled her toward him as his hips surged forward into her.

The low ache started deep within her as he stroked that sweet spot with every surge forward. The gentle lapping of the waves only served to enhance her ride, bringing her closer and closer to climaxing. With a last powerful thrust, the fireworks lit behind her eyes and she screamed out.

Even with the intimacy they shared, she felt something was missing between them. She had tried to broach the subject of her identity with him a couple of times, but it never seemed to be the right time. She would catch him in deep thought, but she had a good idea it had more to do with his parents than anything else. They still hadn't ventured back to his mom's house to finish their discussion. She couldn't help but feel as if she was simply Bull's escape from reality. Nothing more … nothing less.

On the fourth morning of their self-imposed beach exile, the uncertainty she felt from their relationship weighed heavily on her mind. Did she feel she had a right to demand answers? No.

Would that stop her from trying? No, most likely not; especially not considering the doubt had continuously tortured her nerves. It was the 'not knowing' part that wreaked havoc on her emotions and had started to give her a complex.

Chaise had awoken early and left Bull sound asleep in the bed. She walked down the beach to where the waves were gently lapping on the shore and waded in ankle-deep water. She was slightly bent at the waist, looking for seashells in the surf, when she heard a male voice speak to her.

She jumped and looked up into a pair of unfamiliar brown eyes. He looked to be around forty, still handsome and fit, and slightly graying at the temples. His goatee also had light speckles of gray mixed in that gave him more character than age. His smile was easy and his demeanor was laid back.

"I'm sorry. Did you say something?" Chaise asked.

The man laughed and looked slightly embarrassed. "I just asked how the fishing was this morning."

Chaise laughed in response to his attempt at humor and struck up an easy conversation with him about nothing in particular. They looked for shells and sand dollars together for several minutes. When he didn't find any, he wished her a good day and walked away down the beach.

"Who the hell was that?" she heard a familiar voice bark at her from behind.

"That was one of your neighbors, Colton. His name is Gene Castleberry," Chaise answered without looking up from her task.

"What are you doing out here alone? What if he had been one of the men sent to grab you?" Bull's menacing voice was in full effect.

"You said they didn't know where I am. So how could he be?"

"Anyone can be traced, Chaise. You could hide at the South Pole and I could find you with the right resources," Bull retorted.

"Well, I'm still here so I guess he's not one of the bad guys," Chaise replied nonchalantly.

The eerie silence forced Chaise's eyes from her search. Looking up, she recognized the storm brewing in Bull's eyes was not from concern of her safety. It was pure jealousy emanating from his eyes. She felt a twinge of satisfaction from knowing that she had somehow worked her way through his tough exterior. But that wasn't enough—she had to make him admit it before there could be any hope for them.

"Are you jealous, Colton?"

"Why would I be jealous, Chaise?"

"Oh, I don't know. Because I was talking to another man, maybe?"

"What you do with another man is not my concern. What is my concern, however, is your safety. As long as I'm responsible for your safety, you do not leave my side."

Chaise dropped the shells she held in her hand and stumbled backward in shock at his abrupt and cold answer.

"That's all I mean to you?" Her voice was soft and low, but full of unmistakable pain. She looked away from him as her hand flew to her face to whisk away the tears that were already falling.

She questioned herself. *"How could I have been so wrong?"*

She heard his exasperated sigh but she refused to look at him. She'd seen her opening to talk about what was happening between them and she took it. It wasn't his fault that he didn't give her the answer she wanted. But, damn if it didn't hurt, anyway.

CHAPTER FIFTEEN

Bull watched as Chaise walked away from him and back toward the house. He'd hurt her with words he didn't mean and didn't really feel. When he woke and she wasn't in the bed, his first thoughts were that she was cooking breakfast for him again. She'd spoiled him over the last few days and made him feel loved and cared for more than he'd felt in a very long time.

When he reached the kitchen, she was nowhere to be found. Breakfast hadn't even been started. There was nothing to even indicate she had been in there. He instantly felt a rush of adrenaline from thinking that someone had gotten to her.

He rushed outside and immediately froze in his tracks. She was in ankle deep water and she was searching for seashells with another man. They were talking and smiling. They were obviously enjoying each other's company and he didn't even warrant a second thought from her.

The man walked off before Bull was close enough to speak but the damage had been done. Chaise continued to search for shells until Bull spoke. His tone of voice shocked even him but he just kept plowing through the situation like he normally did. When the last words escaped his mouth, he only wanted to retaliate—first, for making him feel jealous, and secondly, for calling him out on it.

But he took it too far. He made her think that he didn't care about anything but the job. He basically told her she meant nothing more to him than a menial task. He called her name as she walked away from him but she ignored him, walking briskly into the house instead.

Bull gave her a few minutes to calm down and then walked into the back door.

"Chaise?" he called out as he walked into the kitchen. He heard sniffles coming from down the hall. He walked silently toward the sounds until he found her. His heart pounded in his chest when he saw her—packing her suitcase.

"Are we going somewhere?" he asked softly.

"I am," she answered. "You are free to do whatever you want with whoever you want. I'll be gone in fifteen minutes."

He walked up behind her and wrapped his arms around her. He bent his head so that his mouth was at her ear. His lips brushed against her as he spoke.

"I don't want you to go anywhere, baby," he said earnestly.

She stopped folding her clothes as she replied with a watery, strained voice. "Don't call me that. I'm just a job to you."

"No, you're not. I was worried when I couldn't find you. Then I was mad when I saw you outside with another man," he said as he tightened his grip on her a little more.

"Why would you be mad about that?" she asked.

"You were right—I was jealous. But, I didn't mean what I said. I could never share you with anyone else, Chaise."

"Tell me something, then," she started and waited for his head to nod in agreement. When he did, she continued. "Why can't I touch you when we make love?"

She felt his entire body go completely rigid. His hands stilled their gentle movements on her body. His breaths hitched in his chest. She had a fleeting thought that she shouldn't have asked, but right then was as good a time as any to find out the whole truth.

His arms slipped away from her and she felt the immediate loss of his comforting body heat. He was pulling away again. She dropped her head forward, shook it in disbelief, and started folding her clothes yet again. No matter how badly she wanted to stay, she would never stay with him under those pretenses.

"You remember I told you I thought I was in love once?" he asked. His voice didn't hold the normal self-confidence and she knew she was about to hear something she wouldn't like.

"Yes," she said softly, without turning.

"I told you she cheated on me, right?" There was so much dread in his voice that she could feel herself cringe for him. "Well, one night when we were making ...fucking ... she called me by his name. Ever since that night, I just couldn't allow anyone to touch me like that again."

"Anyone? Will that always include me?" This time, she turned and faced him. She had to know if it was something they couldn't work past. She had to know if he would always keep her—literally—at arms' length.

They stared at each other for what felt like an eternity. Chaise could see the wheels turning in Bull's brain, trying to determine how to best answer her question while being truthful at the same time. She knew he was struggling with what to say. Bull's difficulty with giving an answer unfortunately told her everything she needed to know.

Chaise couldn't hide the sadness and disappointment from her expressive eyes. Her proud shoulders dropped and her head dropped forward. She closed her eyes and fought back the tears that threatened to overtake her again. She turned her back to him while she finished packing her suitcase.

In an instant, his muscular arms whirled her around to face him. They enveloped her as he lifted her from the floor and deposited her in the center of the bed. His body covered hers as his mouth claimed hers. His kiss was fervent and needful. She let him take everything from her. Everything he needed, everything she had, everything she could give—it was all his anyway.

His hands wandered across her body, removing her clothing and his, until their naked bodies lay pressed together. Her hands were in his hair and then moved slowly down his back until her nails scraped across the perfect globes of his ass. He moaned into her mouth with anticipation and desire. His knee separated her legs, giving him perfect access to her soft, wet channel.

Bull halted his movements and peered into her eyes before he spoke. "I want to feel you, Chaise. I don't want any barriers between us. But I only want it if that's what you want, too. I've never—ever—not used a condom. I'm clean and I get tested regularly for work."

"I want that, too, Colton. I haven't been with anyone else in a long time but I still get tested yearly. I've also been taking birth control for a while. I trust you," she answered sincerely.

Bull nodded in agreement before he slowly thrust his hips forward and watched her face as he entered her. His eyes spoke volumes to her without him ever saying a single word.

He asked her not to betray his trust.

He told her he was giving her a piece of him that he'd only given away one other time.

He said he trusted her with his guard down.

Tears of joy and love slipped from her eyes and ran down her temples. She made love to every inch of his head, neck, shoulders, and his back with her fingers. She memorized the sinewy muscles, the striations they made, and how they contracted and relaxed with his every movement. She poured every last drop of her heart and soul into making love to him with her entire body.

His mouth reclaimed hers in a sweet, gentle kiss and his hips slowed to match pace. Each unhurried plunge into her brought them one step closer to bliss. One step closer to love. One step closer to becoming totally and completely lost in each other.

With his last powerful thrust, they peaked together. Bull's hands were cupped around Chaise's face as he peered lovingly into her eyes. Her fingers dug into his back, her fingernails scratching him in response to the intensity of her orgasm. His name escaped on her breath as she rode out the last wave of pleasure while feeling him still pulsing inside her.

The words were not spoken aloud. The newly formed bond was still fragile but there was no doubt they both felt it. Bull stayed fully seated inside Chaise, relishing in the feeling that was uniquely hers. His back bore the scratches from her as a badge of honor. He had allowed her inside his sacred space. He'd afforded her the privileges that others were denied. He was starting to feel whole again.

He bowed his head and kissed her lips, cheek and neck before moving off of her. She groaned her disapproval and he lightly chuckled. "I know I was crushing you, Chaise."

"No, you weren't. I love the feel of your body covering mine," she admitted.

"Come on, baby. I will cook breakfast for you today," he offered.

"If you don't mind, I'm going to shower first. I'll be quick," she promised, adding a kiss before sashaying off to the bathroom.

"Damn, I love that view," Bull called after her and gave his best catcall whistle.

Fifteen minutes later, Chaise exited the shower and towel dried her hair. When she walked into the bedroom, she realized all her clothes were in the suitcase that she had just finished packing. Rather than waste time unpacking again, she grabbed one of Bull's extra-large t-shirts from his drawer and slipped it over her head.

Bull heard her bare feet padding down the hallway. "It's about time you finished in there. I thought I would have to eat all this food myself," he teased.

Chaise turned the corner and came to a sudden halt. She blanched white as all the blood drained from her face. All the air was sucked from the room and she could not breathe when she saw that they were not alone. Her towel was slung around her shoulders, she wore nothing but Bull's t-shirt, and she stood there facing all the main operators of Steele Security.

Including Noah.

Chaise knew that Bull was at the stove intently watching her every move. She also knew that Rebel and Shadow sat at the table, though their eyes followed the others like a tennis match in progress. Another woman sat close to Noah, and from her slightly protruding stomach, she could only guess the woman was Noah's wife, Brianna.

The anxiety welled up inside her and threatened to overtake her. She hadn't told Bull yet and there she was face to face with Noah. After the advancements they had made that morning, she could see everything crumbling before her eyes.

And she had no one to blame but herself.

"*Sierra*? What the hell are you doing here? Did Dad send you to *spy* on me? So you can run back home and give him all the ammo he needs to cut me down again? And. Why. The. Fuck. Are you wearing Bull's shirt?" Noah suddenly stood, knocking the chair backward until it fell over. Brianna looked up at Noah like he'd lost his mind. She clearly felt that he had a lot of explaining to do to her—not the other way around.

"What in the fucking hell is going on, Bull?" Noah demanded as he turned to Bull.

Chaise's mouth gaped open and she grabbed the hem of Bull's shirt to hold it down in modesty. She unconsciously took a couple of steps backward out of the hostile room. She could feel daggers flying at her from both Bull and Noah. The others stared in open confusion.

"Sierra?" Bull asked in his accusatory tone, his eyes darting back and forth between her and Noah.

"Yes! *Sierra!* What the fuck have you been doing with my little sister, Bull?" Noah yelled as he advanced on Bull.

Bull's head snapped to Chaise. *"Sierra?* Your name is really *Sierra?"* He walked toward her pointing. "You fucking lied to me about *that?"*

"No, Colton, please—just give me a minute..."

"You're Sierra Steele? Noah's sister? You're his little sister?" Bull wasn't even looking at her anymore as he yelled. His hands were in his hair, pulling and raking through it.

Her anxiety attack was only being held at bay by the thought of what she would lose if she couldn't keep herself together at that very second. "Colton, please just let me explain. I can explain everything," she begged him.

Bull's face became hard. His eyes became cold. His voice was low and unemotional. "No. No explaining this away, *Sierra*. This," he motioned between them, "is finished. You should have told me."

Tears slid down her cheeks as her hand flew to her mouth in an attempt to hold in the sobs. Noah stood stock still, his face displaying his disgust and disapproval. Bull wouldn't even look at her. The only camaraderie she felt in the room came from Brianna's eyes. There was depth and understanding in them but Chaise couldn't focus on that yet.

She turned and ran down the hall to their bedroom. To *Bull's* bedroom. She quickly unpacked the clothes in which she needed to change. Once she'd dressed, she opened the door and heard shouts coming from the kitchen.

"Are you fucking kidding me? First of all, even if she wasn't my little sister, you know better than screwing a client," Noah yelled. "But the fact is, she is my sister. That's a line best friends don't cross."

"Reap, I had no idea she was your sister. You're right, I knew better than fucking a client. There's no excuse for that, but you don't know how everything went down. I'll swear an oath on my life that it'll never happen again if that makes you feel better," Bull replied.

His words speared Chaise's heart. She felt it shatter into a million pieces in her chest and knew it would never be the same again.

"You're both over-reacting," Brianna attempted to reason. "Noah, you need to sit down."

"Calm down? He didn't even know her last name. This is basic information that we collect on any client. The fact that he didn't bother honestly concerns me," Noah replied to Brianna, but with a softer tone than he used with Bull.

"Noah, babe," Brianna continued. "You weren't here. You don't know everything that happened and why. Don't jump to conclusions."

"He's right, Sunny," Bull replied. "I let him down."

Rebel and Shadow remained quiet, opting to choose their battles on another day. Chaise was completely heartbroken and drained. The anxiety attack was bubbling just under the surface, like a volcano about to erupt. She heard the resolute tone of Bull's voice. She heard the anger in Noah's voice.

There was no turning back now. She gathered her things, picked up her cell phone, and made a couple of phone calls. After she finished with her hair and makeup, she re-emerged from the bedroom with her possessions in tow. The conversation had returned to normal volumes but it was obvious that they were still talking about her when she entered the room.

Bull watched as Chaise positioned her suitcase by the door and removed something small from her purse. She walked over to stand directly in front of Bull but he wouldn't meet her gaze. She sat down on the coffee table in front of him and took a deep breath.

"You're right, Colton. I should've told you before now, and I tried to. I wanted to. My name is Sierra Chaise Steele. I haven't gone by Sierra for many, many years now." She cut her eyes at Noah as she stated the last part.

She handed Bull the business card that she had pulled from her purse. He glanced down at it long enough to verify that it did, indeed, say *Chaise Steele.*

"When I graduated college and started doing contract HR work, I changed my professional name to Chaise Steele. Too many people knew me as *Sierra-Steve-Steele's-daughter*. I told you how overbearing he was and that bled over into my professional life. I have gone by Chaise ever since then.

"As far as being Noah's sister, it's true, I am. I wanted to tell you—and I tried to tell you—but I take the full blame for that."

Turning to Noah, she explained. "Noah, he didn't know you were my brother. I gave him a fake last name so he couldn't have known. Don't blame Colton for this—blame me."

Chaise hated having the conversation in front of everyone, but there was no time and no other way to handle it. "Colton, this doesn't have to change anything between us. It doesn't change anything for me. I didn't lie about my name—it *is* Chaise. Please talk to me."

She was met with a painful, stoic silence.

"This is exactly what I thought would happen. I'm sorry I didn't tell you sooner, but I'm not sorry for anything that happened between us, Colton. I don't regret one minute of it," she said through her tears that were freely flowing down her cheeks.

She swallowed hard and stood on shaky legs to move away from Bull. She knew he would react in that way. She knew she didn't matter enough to him for him to actually hear her out. What they had between them wasn't enough for him to look past his pride. She'd known all along, deep down, that he would pull away from her as soon as she told him she was Noah's little sister. Noah had just beaten her to the punch.

An eternity passed as she made her way across the floor with all eyes burning a hole in her.

"And just where the hell do you think you're going?" Noah brazenly demanded.

"Noah Steele!" Brianna chastised him.

Chaise gave Brianna a small smile of appreciation before moving her eyes to meet Noah's. "I'm leaving."

"Like hell you are!" Noah's voiced boomed through the house. "The Cordova family is a major international drug and human trafficking organization. If they are really after you, *as you claim they are,* and if you leave here now, you may as well go turn yourself in to them. Besides, you don't even have a car here."

Chaise kept her voice calm and professional, as if she were addressing a group of executives. "Before I came in here, I made two phone calls. The first one was to Steele Security headquarters. I've paid your retainer fee. Any additional expenses I've incurred can be billed to me."

Bull still refused to look at her but she could see how hard he had clenched his jaws. She couldn't even venture a guess about what he was thinking, but at that point it really didn't seem to matter.

"The second call was for a cab. It will be here any minute now. I had no doubt everything would turn out exactly this way, so I've already made travel arrangements. I had hoped it would be different, though," she finished wistfully.

"At any rate, since I'm the customer and I've paid for the protection I've received, I am now relieving you of your duties. I no longer require your services," she stated flatly.

The room erupted in arguments—regarding her ability to make decisions, of her ability to protect herself, and of her sanity. Noah's voice boomed and cut through the fog of dissension

"If you leave now, then I have no choice but to believe this whole thing has been a ruse and you were never really in any danger. How dare you try to play me and my brothers like that?" Noah accused.

Chaise's back was to him and her hand was on the doorknob. The shock from his words hit first, then the pain, then the anger—the full-fledged, red-hot anger that that been building deep inside her. She whirled around, fire flashed in her eyes, and marched up to face Noah head-on.

"Let me fucking remind you of something, Noah. *You. Were. My. Brother. First.* You want to live by the military code of never leaving a man behind? You want to talk about honor and loyalty?"

Her entire body was shaking but there was no stopping her. The entire room watched with baited breath as she tore into Noah.

"YOU fucking left ME behind. Without a second thought. Without a backward glance. You fucking left me behind when I fucking needed you the most! You were *my* big brother! You were supposed to look out for me! But you didn't. YOU. LEFT. ME.

"So, you just fucking stay here with *'your brothers'* and pretend you're the one who has been wronged here. Keep telling yourself that and, maybe one day, even YOU will believe your own bullshit.

"Oh, and by the way, you're fired!" she yelled.

With that, Chaise stomped across the floor, yanked open the door, and hurried out to her waiting taxi. The driver put her bag in the trunk as she climbed into the backseat.

The taxi driver got in and looked at her in his rearview mirror. "Where to, Miss?"

"The airport, please."

CHAPTER SIXTEEN

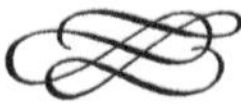

The slamming door left everyone inside the house in complete silence. Bull's eyes stayed glued to the door as if he expected Chaise to walk back in at any second. The sound of a vehicle pulling away drew Noah's attention and he raced to the window.

"Son of a bitch!" he yelled when he watched as the taxi drove away. Raking his hands over this face, Noah stood rooted to the floor, deep in thought of what their next move should be.

"Why would you think this was a ruse, Reap?" Bull finally spoke.

"What?" Noah said as he spun around. His face was contorted in confusion at Bull's question. He had already moved on to other scenarios and Bull's question pulled him back from his own world.

"You said you thought she made all this up just to get to you. Why would you think that about her?" Bull quizzed him because his own thoughts strayed to whether Chaise had used him, played him, and then walked away.

Noah sighed loudly in exasperation. "I don't—I shouldn't have said that. I've always expected my dad to send one of my siblings to guilt me into going back home. He's so manipulative—I just don't put anything past him, including using my sister," Noah explained. He turned back to the window as he continued. "I took out my anger toward my father on her. I shouldn't have done that."

"Reaper, you should know that she's really in danger. The men took shots at us and I heard them say they had orders to take her alive and kill me. If they get to her, her fate will be much worse than death," Bull continued to speak with no emotion. He could've been repeating a grocery list for all the lack of empathy his voice portrayed.

Shadow rubbed his jaw line with his hand, his thumb and middle finger meeting at his chin as he took in Bull's demeanor. Rebel sensed it, too, because he leaned forward in his seat and pierced Bull with his gaze. They knew that Bull sensed their intense gazes but he rebuffed their attempt to engage him.

Noah wasn't as easily denied. He took a couple of steps toward Bull and narrowed his eyes at him. "You sure sound concerned, Bull," Noah spat out sardonically. "So, my sister is good enough for you to fuck but not care about her wellbeing? Just another one of your whores?"

Bull was on his feet, in Noah's face, and had the front of Noah's shirt twisted in his fists in a heartbeat. He growled out, "Don't *ever* talk about her like that again."

Noah smiled at a very pissed off Bull. "Now, that's more like it."

Bull released Noah's shirt and took a step back, realization registered on his face. "You did that shit on purpose just now?"

"I did. I had to see where you really stood with her, man. That was the best way I knew how to get you to admit it," Noah replied.

"I honestly don't know where I stand with her, Reaper. I don't want anything to happen to her but I don't trust her. I can't trust her," Bull stated matter-of-factly.

"You are so full of shit, man," Rebel announced. Bull's gaze shot to Rebel and glared menacingly at him.

"What the hell is that supposed to mean?" Bull shot back.

"It means, *Bull*, that over the past several days, you haven't had any problems with trusting her. Today, you just turned your fucking back on her," Rebel replied.

"Whose side are you on, anyway?" Bull asked.

Rebel and Shadow replied simultaneously, "Chaise's."

Bull gave them both the middle finger salute.

Brianna stood and cleared her throat. "Can you boys excuse us, please? I'd like to talk to Bull alone."

Noah grinned from ear to ear, knowing Bull was about to get the ultimate tongue-lashing. "I don't know why you're smiling," Brianna said flatly. "You're next."

Noah's smile dropped and his eyes widened in surprise. "Me?"

"Oh yes, *you!* Now get out."

Brianna took Bull's hand and led him back to the couch as the other men filed out the back door to wait on the patio. She knew Noah's tactic to get Bull to admit his true feelings was brutish and would only work in the interim. Now that Bull realized what Noah was really trying to accomplish, it would be harder for Noah to get him to talk.

"I won't sugarcoat anything for you, Bull. You know as well as anyone that things between Noah and me have not been easy. We've had to work hard at rebuilding the trust between us. It wasn't easy for Noah to forgive me, Bull. He wanted to stay mad at me. His *male brain* even told him not to believe me. But, where would we be today if we hadn't worked through everything?

"The most important thing is that we both *want* this relationship. We *want* to be together because we love each other. We *forgive* each other almost daily because neither of us is perfect. It's worth all the trouble because we can't live without each other.

"You can't berate her for not telling you she's Noah's sister. She was in trouble and she needed help. Would you have helped her if you knew she was Noah's estranged sister? Sometimes, the hard road is the lesser of two evils. You can't blame her for that.

"So, you need to answer this question for yourself. *Is Chaise worth it to you?"*

Brianna stopped talking and watched Bull's reaction. He didn't verbally respond but he did nod his head once in acknowledgement.

"I'm going to leave you to think about that while I go have a little talk with my husband."

Half an hour later, Brianna, Noah, Rebel, and Shadow entered the house. Bull was standing at the front door with his bag in hand. Everyone looked at him expectantly, waiting to discover what he had decided to do.

"Let's go get her," Bull stated.

"That's what I wanted to hear," Noah replied with a brotherly slap on Bull's back. "Don't think I don't still owe you an ass-kicking for sleeping with my little sister, though."

Bull, Rebel, and Shadow laughed while Brianna gave Noah a stern look in her attempt to admonish him. He smiled and winked at her while her response was an exaggerated rolling of her eyes at him.

Boys will always be boys, she thought.

"Go on to the airport without me. There's something I need to take care of here before I leave," Bull told them.

"What's up, Bull?" Reaper asked.

"I need to go talk to my mom. My dad was one of the guys after Chaise but she says he's undercover DEA. I'll find out how to get in touch with him in case we need his help," Bull explained.

Shadow fished his vibrating phone out of his pocket and saw Brad's name on the screen. "Hey, man. Did you find her?" A few clipped sentences, a couple of 'yeahs' and 'uh-huhs' later, Shadow hung up and found all eyes on him.

"That was Brad. He found out that the cab company took Chaise to the airport. Let's get a move on in case she gets lucky and gets on an early flight," Shadow instructed.

Reaper looked at Bull and raised his eyebrows. "What do you want me to do when I find her?"

"Just try to keep her from boarding the plane until I can get there," Bull answered. Noah nodded and they all left in a race to the airport.

Several minutes later, Bull drew in a deep breath as he parked in his mother's driveway. He couldn't bring himself to turn off his truck yet. Sitting alone, he reflected upon everything he thought he knew about his life. He thought his father had abandoned his mother and him. He had accepted that his mother had lied to him, but then he'd learned it wasn't for the reasons he had originally believed.

Then, with Chaise, he was facing a similar conundrum. He knew from the beginning that she had lied about her last name and he had allowed her to keep it from him all this time. Even when she said she wanted to tell him, he was in no hurry for it. Just the fact that she admitted it and wanted to tell him was enough at that moment.

The feelings he had experienced over the past few weeks were new to him. He was just beginning to learn how to deal with them when the shit hit the fan. He was just so relieved to learn that she wasn't one of Reaper's past lovers.

In retrospect, and knowing what he knew now, her questions and interest in Reaper made sense. Bull knew that Reaper hadn't seen his family in years and Chaise must have been a pre-teen when Reaper left home. Then, to find out Reaper was married and had a baby on the way must have really hurt Chaise, thinking she would never be the aunt she wanted to be.

Finally, Bull had to examine his own actions as closely as he had examined others'. For all his blustering of being the eternal bachelor, even he had to admit he started playing house with Chaise very quickly—and it all came so very easily. He had to face the truth and admit, mostly to himself, that he didn't want to lose her. He didn't want to go back to how his life was before he met her.

Bull finally left the sanctity of his truck and walked up to the front door of his mom's house. He rang the doorbell and waited, taking time to really look around at his childhood home. He finally allowed the memories to resurface and realized that he actually had really good memories of his childhood. It wasn't the constant turmoil his mind had built up.

The door opened and Michelle looked at him, her eyes hesitant and fearful.

"Hi, Mom," Bull said softly, pulling her into his arms. "How are you?"

Michelle wrapped her arms around Bull and held tightly to him. "So much better now."

They walked inside and sat down. Bull smiled at her and squeezed her hand in his way of telling her everything was fine between them. He'd always questioned her about why she never remarried. It never occurred to him that she was still married to his dad, John, or that she couldn't imagine her life with any other man.

"I need to know how to contact Dad," Bull started, knowing that his mom would be shocked at his declaration. "I may need his help with Chaise."

"Well, you can start by turning around, son," a friendly male voice boomed from behind him.

Bull jumped up from the couch and whirled around to see his father standing in the doorway. He wore an old, ratty robe, had a towel around his neck, and his hair was still wet from his shower. He had a slight smile on his face but Bull knew his father was trying to gauge his reaction.

"I know this is awkward, son. I wanted our reunion to be under better circumstances. Your mom told me about her conversation with you and everything she said is true. I am so damn proud of you. You were always a great kid and you're a damn fine man," John said with his voice full of emotion and pride.

"I appreciate that. Maybe we can spend some time together, to get to know each other and be a family again. But, right now, I have to focus on the case. I need to know why they're after Chaise," Bull said earnestly.

"Where is Chaise?" Michelle asked.

"We had some complications. She left for the airport," Bull paraphrased.

"What?" John's mouth dropped open. "You have to go get her, son. Now!"

"Tell me what's going on," Bull demanded, the urgency in his voice matching his rising blood pressure.

"I'll change and tell you in the car on the way. We have to get to her first." The worried look on John's face ate away at Bull's confidence.

I never should have let her leave, Bull thought solemnly and with a silent prayer that she was safe.

~

At the airport, Chaise approached the ticket counter to purchase her one-way ticket back to Miami. Coming in on the private company jet had been a completely different experience than flying back in the coach section of a heavily crowded commercial airplane. They had left from Steele Security's private airstrip so she didn't have to jump through all the hoops required by the major airlines.

With her boarding pass and driver's license in hand, Chaise approached the TSA agent at the first security checkpoint. After verifying her credentials, she walked to the conveyor belt, grabbed a bin, and dropped her shoes and purse inside. Then she waited for the next agent to instruct her to step inside the full body scanner.

After she'd passed the scanning procedure, she waited at the end of the conveyor belt for her purse. And waited. And waited. Another agent walked over, took her purse out of the machine and turned to her to ask, "Ma'am, is this your purse?"

"Yes, it is. Why? What's wrong?" she asked.

"We need to scan it again. Sorry for the delay," the agent explained vaguely.

Chaise shrugged and continued to wait as the agent put it back on the conveyor belt and sent it back through the x-ray machine. The agent at the monitor stopped the belt and closely examined the screen. Within a few minutes, a plain-clothed agent, wearing a suit and tie, walked up behind the seated agent and started at the monitor.

"There's nothing in there. You're welcome to look for yourself," she told them, aggravation lacing her tone.

"We're not allowed to, ma'am," one agent stated.

"What? What are you talking about?" she asked.

Other uniformed agents started grabbing luggage off the conveyor belt and putting it on the next machine. Everyone in line eyed Chaise suspiciously as her lane was shut down and everyone was moved away from her purse.

She was mortified and thought, *What the fuck is going on?*

The plain-clothes agent approached her and apprised her of the situation. "It appears there are two live rounds of ammunition in your purse. Do those belong to you?"

Her hand met her head as she dropped it forward. "Yes, those are mine. I completely forgot about them."

"Do you shoot guns a lot?" the agent asked nonchalantly.

"Yes, I do. I have my whole life," she said defensively.

"Do you have a concealed carry permit?" he continued to politely interrogate her.

"Yes, I do, actually. It's a Florida license and it's in my purse. But I can't get to my purse to show you." The people walking by, openly gawking at her, were really starting to annoy her.

"Do you know that you can't bring live ammunition through a TSA security checkpoint?"

"Yes, I know that. I just forgot they were even in there. I went to a shooting range and just dropped the extra rounds in my purse," she explained.

"Where are you headed today, ma'am?"

"Back to Miami," Chaise answered as she watched a police officer approach them. *"Are you freaking kidding me?"*

"I just need to search your purse. I understand there are live rounds inside. Is that correct?" the officer asked.

"Yes, go right ahead," she answered with a wave of her hand. Everyone else had gawked at the contents in her person so the police may as well have their go at it now.

The officer removed the two .357 rounds and she watched as they measured, photographed, and wrote their reports. The plain-clothes agent took her driver's license and said he had to run an NCIC report to check for any warrants for her arrest.

"How long is this going to take? I have a flight to catch. This was a simple mistake. I thought you were having a fit about a bottle of lotion in my purse!"

"It shouldn't take too long," he replied as he continued to complete the paperwork. Twenty minutes later, Chaise had her purse back, minus the .357 rounds they confiscated, and the agent advised she would receive a letter in the mail that advised she couldn't bring live ammunition through the TSA checkpoint.

Yeah, I got that part, she thought sarcastically.

Four hours and one connection in Atlanta later, Chaise walked out of the Miami International Airport without a clue of where she should go. She hailed a taxi to take her to retrieve her car from Bull's house. That plan at least gave her a little extra time to figure out where she was staying for the night.

She considered staying in his house since some of her stuff was still there but quickly decided against it. His entire place was meticulously guarded and monitored by Steele Security so there was no way she could get in undetected. She decided she didn't need any additional reminders of Bull, anyway. She'd had enough heartbreak for one day.

Cranking her car, she fought back the tears and her anxiety threatened to take over her mind. The dark feeling of foreboding was like a living, breathing presence in the car with her. She had effectively compartmentalized her day so that she could function; however, she had already decided that as soon as she checked into a hotel room, she was having a complete and total mental breakdown over a bottle of Moscato wine.

Thanks to her shitty day and equally shitty mindset, Chaise decided to splurge on her hotel room and stay at Loews Miami Beach Hotel in South Beach. She requested an oceanfront suite so that she could soak in a jetted tub. She had stopped on the way in to purchase two bottles of her favorite wine.

The clerk swiped her credit card, handed her room keys to her, and had the bellman take her bag up to her suite for her. Once she was settled into her room, with the door securely locked, she filled the garden tub full of hot water, turned on the jets, and sank down into the luxurious tub.

Then, she opened all the doors of the compartments she'd created over the course of the day and let the tears flow unchecked. Her whole body convulsed with sobs. She mourned losing Bull. Even with their short union, she had foolishly let herself believe she had found a good man who would stand by her through the hard times.

Her heart had shattered when she sat in front of Bull, in front of everyone, and tried to explain herself only to have him completely ignore her. Her eyes begged, her tone of voice pleaded and her body implored. She already knew what his answer would be—she knew before she left the bedroom—so she made the call to arrange a taxi to take her away from them.

She mourned losing her brother, Noah, again. She had purposely sought him out at the beginning of the whole debacle with two intentions. She missed her brother and wanted him back, and she needed his help and protection. Then, when he accused her of engineering everything solely to manipulate him, he had hurt her more than she imagined he ever could. It was as if he had told her he didn't care that her life was in danger.

Once the water turned cold, she wrapped herself in one of the thick robes, took her chilled bottle of wine to the terrace, and decided it was well past time to get plastered. All the problems of the day would still be there the next day and she would face them when the time came. For the time being, she thought she had earned some self-pity time.

CHAPTER SEVENTEEN

Brad stayed in constant contact with Shadow as he tracked Chaise's movements via her credit card transactions. He had mused to himself that people on the run would never learn that every time they used their card, the exact location was tracked, logged, and catalogued for future use.

Bull's thoughts never strayed far from what John had shared with him about the case while they drove to the airport. He wanted to kick his own ass for how he'd treated her. What was really killing him was that he allowed her to leave when he already knew that she was in danger. That was just downright cold and heartless and he knew, without a doubt, that she would've never done that to him.

"Keep your mind on the case, son, not on your feelings. Your mind needs to be clear to be able to see the next move, to be the one calling the shots, and *then* you can get her back," John attempted to comfort and impart his wisdom at the same time.

Bull nodded. "I know. We wouldn't even be in this predicament if it weren't for me. I've royally fucked this up but I plan on making up for it. She has to be all right."

John's recount of his case had Bull on edge. The Cordova family was worse than Noah knew. Their alliance with the *Tres Sieses* gang was a new development but a familiar modus operandi for that organization.

The Cordova family had recently acquired Viboro Distributing and used it mainly as a front for their illegal activities. Chaise's contract was negotiated and signed before the Cordovas bought the company. Since they didn't want to draw attention to their acquisition, the Cordovas kept her contract in place as originally agreed. Once she started identifying the missing girls, and asking about them, she became a liability.

Bull's phone rang, pulling him from his thoughts and forcing him to focus again on their current status. "Yeah, Brad, what do you have for me?"

"She was detained at the security checkpoint for a while and they ran an NCIC on her," Brad chuckled.

"They what? Why?" Bull didn't understand how a casual traveler, who fit no dangerous profile, could suddenly warrant having a National Crime Information Center report run on her.

"She had two .357 rounds in her purse and tried to go through security with them. They frown on live ammunition on the plane," Brad was openly laughing now.

"She didn't even have a gun on her. What was she going to do? Throw the bullets at them as hard as she can?" Even Bull had to laugh at that visual.

"Yeah, well, you know how tight security is now. But, they eventually let her go and she's already en route to Miami. She had a connecting flight in Atlanta but that flight has already departed," Brad advised.

"Have them get the company jet ready, Brad. We're almost to the private airstrip now," Bull ordered.

"Already called them. They're fueling up and doing their pre-flight inspection. I'll keep you updated on her whereabouts," Brad promised.

Bull hung up with Brad and called to inform Reaper, Shadow, and Rebel of the current plan. They had gone ahead to the airport to try to stop Chaise but they had just missed her fiasco at the security checkpoint.

The group met Bull and John at the private airstrip. Reaper looked as bad as Bull knew he looked. They had both fucked up their relationship with Chaise and they both wished they could go back and do it all over again. Now, they had to confront the grim possibility that they wouldn't get to her in time to prevent the Cordova family from getting to her.

Reaper looked at Bull with haunted eyes and asked, "What did she mean that I left her when she needed me the most? What happened?"

"I don't know, Reap. She told me her father was more than over-bearing and she had to get away from him. That was the reason why she couldn't go back home when all this started. She showed up at your wedding to ask you for help but we wouldn't let her near you and Brianna," Bull explained.

Reaper drew his arms up and balled his hands into tight fists. "That man probably put her through hell when I left. We were close back then. I never thought he would take my leaving out on her but it sounds like he did. *Motherfucker!"*

Reaper looked tortured at the thoughts of Chaise enduring the wrath intended for him. Brianna wrapped her arms around him and Bull watched him instantly relax from her touch.

"Noah, she's *your* little sister—give her some credit. She's strong and she has obviously made a good life for herself away from your father. It took strength to walk away and live alone. She knows she's in danger so she'll take precautions. Let's just get to her as soon as we can. Okay?"

"Brianna, have I told you today how much I love you?" Noah wrapped his arms around her and his big hand rested protectively on her baby bump. "You always know how to make me feel better."

"She has anxiety attacks," Bull interjected. "What if she gets in a situation she can't handle and has an attack?"

Brianna looked him dead in the eye and responded. "Bull, it's not about how many times she gets knocked down. She shows how strong she is just by the mere fact that she gets back up *every time*."

"You're a lucky man, Reaper," Bull said while looking at Brianna with admiration in his eyes.

"Damn straight, I am. Sounds like you are, too, Bull," Noah's tone of voice both stated and asked at the same time.

"I was. Even if we beat the Cordovas to her, she has no reason to forgive me for how I treated her," Bull replied somberly.

"Love is reason enough to forgive, Bull," Brianna answered. The answering look on Bull's face made Brianna laugh out loud. "Oh yeah, big guy—you got it bad! May as well admit it to yourself now and accept it."

Rebel called out to them, "We're boarding now. Let's get a move on, people!"

Bull made a beeline to the private jet and took his seat. The flight time for the private jet was barely over two hours but she had a big head start on them. He tried to relax and find a comfortable position in which to sit, but his thoughts kept straying to the last time he was on the plane. He was with Chaise in the plane's bedroom and he would give anything to be there with her again.

"Bull—relax, man. We haven't even taken off yet," Shadow joked. "White knuckle flyer."

"I'm not afraid of flying, Shadow. I'm just ready to go, dickhead," Bull deadpanned. Shadow and Rebel both laughed heartily at their friend's expense.

Bull made it through the two-plus hour plane ride of ridicule from his friends. He knew them well enough to trust them with his life and not question it, so he knew it was all good-natured ribbing. He had fucked up and he knew it. He would take his lashes like a man. But, he would also wait for the day to repay the favor to both of the bastards he called brothers.

Exiting the plane in Miami, Bull immediately called Brad for an update.

"Hey, Bull, she showed up at your house, got her car and left. She stopped to buy two bottles of Moscato wine and I haven't seen a swipe of her card since then. That was just over two hours ago," Brad explained.

"Text me the address where she got the wine. Check on any past purchases that shows a pattern, a place she goes to frequently, or anything like that. Let me know what you find ASAP," Bull directed.

"You got it. Call you back in a few," Brad said before disconnecting.

"Reaper, would she go back home to your dad?" Bull asked.

"No way," Reaper answered.

Bull updated the team on what Brad had found from Chaise's credit card usage. He knew she had to find somewhere to sleep that night—unless the Cordovas had found her. But he couldn't allow himself to follow that line of thinking.

Bull's phone pinged with the incoming text from Brad with the address of where she purchased the wine. "She bought wine in South Beach. Let's check the hotels around the store and see if she's checked in."

Bull called Brad and had him double check any charges from all the hotels around that location—just in case something showed up late. The team, minus a pregnant Brianna, canvassed the area hotels in South Beach looking for Chaise. Noah refused to let Brianna tag along in case they ran into trouble. Brianna informed him that if she wasn't already so tired from all the traveling they'd done, he wouldn't have won that argument. She reluctantly went home and let the men take the night shift.

After checking several high-end hotels with no luck, Shadow approached the clerk at Loews Miami Beach Hotel with his dashing smile securely in place. The clerk batted her eyes and openly flirted with Shadow, who was using his good looks to his advantage.

After a few minutes and few suggestive comments from the clerk, Shadow had the information he needed. He swaggered back to the waiting group with a smile that split his face in two.

"Who's the man?" he asked as he approached.

"She's here?" Bull asked excitedly.

"She is here. She's in a deluxe suite with an ocean view. She specifically told them she doesn't want to be disturbed tonight," Shadow explained, then gave Bull the suite number so he could go up and disturb her anyway.

"Do you mind if I go with you?" Reaper asked. "I have some making up to do myself. Then I'll leave you two alone."

"Not at all, man. I may need the backup," Bull joked.

Outside her suite door, Bull said a silent prayer and knocked on the door. When she didn't answer a couple of minutes later, he knocked harder and called her name. Soon, Bull and Reaper were both beating on the door and yelling for her to open the door.

"I'm not leaving until you let me in, so you may as well get it over with now," Bull yelled through the door. "I have things I need to say to you and I'd rather not do it like this, Chaise. Please open the door."

"Sierra Chaise Steele—open this door right now!" Reaper yelled. Turning to Bull, he asked, "What if she's not in there?"

"Excuse me. Are you two gentlemen guests here?"

Bull and Reaper turned to find an armed security guard eying them suspiciously. "We've had complaints from customers on this floor about the noise level. They said men are in the hall beating on doors and yelling at someone."

"My sister is in this suite and we're concerned about her. We're trying to get her to open the door so we can talk to her," Reaper explained politely. "So far she's not cooperating with us. We may have been a little loud. I apologize for that. I'm just really concerned for her."

"If you're not guests here, I will have to ask you to leave the premises. She may not be in there and if she is, she obviously doesn't want to talk to you. You're disturbing the other guests," the guard said as he extended his hand toward the elevators, indicating for Bull and Reaper to leave.

Bull stood firm. "I'm not leaving without talking to her and making sure she's all right. Can you at least go in the room and check on her?"

"No, I can't without just cause. You've given me no indication that she intends to harm herself. You can leave of your own volition or I can have you arrested for trespassing. Your choice," the guard threatened.

"Let's go, Bull. We won't be able to help her if we're both in jail," Reaper sighed and turned toward the elevators.

Bull reluctantly left but felt something was very wrong. Chaise knew she was in danger and understood the severity of the situation. She wouldn't put herself in more danger by being out where she could be recognized.

"Know this," Bull said to the guard, "If anything happens to her, I'll be back to see you."

"Is that a threat?" the guard asked defensively.

"That a fucking guarantee," Bull answered before turning to follow Reaper out of the hotel.

Once they reached the sidewalk, Bull pulled out his cell phone and called Chaise's cell phone first. When it rolled to voicemail, he called her hotel room. He decided he would keep alternating between calling her cell and the hotel room until she answered.

~

Chaise sat in the warm Miami breeze, enjoying her terrace ocean view. She was still in the bathrobe, had her feet propped up, and was on her last glass of wine. Her second bottle was empty and her body had run out of tears to cry. She downed the contents of her wine glass, stumbled through the sliding glass door, and made her way back into her suite.

She heard her cell phone ringing from the bedroom area but made no attempt to rush to find it. Within seconds, her hotel room phone started ringing. Thinking it was the front desk calling, she snatched the phone up.

"Hello?" she answered with a slur.

"Chaise! Are you all right?" Bull sounded frantic but he was just so glad to have finally reached her.

"I'm fine," she lied. "I'm just a *little* drunk," she said, emphasizing *little* a tad too much. She apparently found it to be funny because she couldn't contain her laughter.

"Chaise, I really need to talk to you," Bull said tenderly. "Can I come in?"

"Oh, is that you at the door? I need to tell you to fuck off," Chaise replied in a drunken, sing-song voice.

"No! Don't answer it, Chaise!" Bull yelled, but it was too late. She had already put the phone down and walked away.

He could hear Chaise telling the person to wait. He heard her unlock the door and open it. He then heard her ask, "What do you want?" The fear in her voice was unmistakable and made his heart jump out of his chest.

When he heard a scuffle, he thought he would go ballistic.

"She's in trouble!" he yelled to the other men as he ran back into the hotel.

Bull, Reaper, John, Shadow, and Rebel were met in the lobby by the hotel security team. Despite the fact that Bull insisted she was in trouble, the security team wouldn't let them pass. Splitting up, they watched the elevators and exits but Chaise was nowhere to be found.

Reaper called the general manager, explained who he was, and finally convinced him to search her room. The manager came back down and said there was nothing out of order but Chaise was not in the room. After apologizing for the earlier troubles they encountered, the manager excused himself.

Reaper and Bull joined the other three men outside and were met with downtrodden faces.

"What? What is it?" Bull asked.

John pointed at the blinking lights in the night sky, "They took her to the roof and put her in the helicopter. The Cordovas have her now."

Bull's eyes followed the helicopter's movement as it disappeared into the night sky, flying out across the ocean. "Where are they taking her?"

"I don't know, son," John answered, knowing the question was directed at him. "I haven't infiltrated their organization to that level yet."

Bull felt ice run in his veins, much like his time on clandestine operations as a Delta Force member. The old training never really leaves. It may lie dormant for a while, watching and waiting for the right time. But when those killer instincts are needed, there's no doubt it reemerges with a vengeance.

And vengeance would be his when Bull got those men in his sights.

"I just talked to Brad. He tracked down the flight plan for that helicopter. It's headed out to a tanker a few miles offshore. We need to get her before they either put her on another helicopter or that tanker takes off somewhere else with her," Shadow informed them.

Rebel said, "Let me make a call. Be right back."

Reaper's eyes stayed glued to the black horizon as he imagined what would happen to his sister if they didn't get to her in time. He looked at Bull and saw the worry in his eyes but he also saw the man he'd known while they served in the Army together. His razor-sharp edge made him lethal, his innate distrust of everyone made him naturally suspicious of anyone's intentions, and his training made him a killing machine.

It was during his assessment of Bull that Reaper had a revelation: Bull really was in love with Chaise. This was more than a job to Bull—the Cordovas had made things personal by taking Chaise. Reaper had known Bull for many years and knew him as well as any man could. He knew, without a doubt, if anything happened to Chaise, no man in the Cordova organization would be left standing.

"Let's go. I have a friend in the Coast Guard. We have enough probable cause for them to board the boat and search for her. He's letting us ride along but we have to stay on the Coast Guard cutter while they search the tanker," Rebel explained.

"I can't go, son. If they see me, my cover will be blown and they would definitely kill her then. I'll see what I can dig up here—get the word from the lower level guys," John explained.

"I'm going—I have to be there when they find her," Bull responded.

John nodded his understanding. "Son, listen. These guys won't hesitate to kill you and throw your body overboard. Watch your back out there."

"Always," Bull answered.

The men parted ways, with the guys from Steele Security rushing toward the docks and John strolling off to meet up with his local crew. John hoped some of the guys were loose-lipped and bragging so he could get more information about Chaise's whereabouts.

CHAPTER EIGHTEEN

As far as prisons went, the oceanfront presidential suite was definitely the most luxurious. However, it was still Chaise's prison. She decided the attractive man sitting in front of her couldn't be the head of the Cordova organization.

He looked entirely too young and refined to be part of any criminal activities. His smile was warm and inviting. His eyes were a rich, chocolate brown. His hair was slightly long, black, and was wavy on the ends. It was styled back off his face and gave him a polished but roguish look that was very appealing.

"Hello, Ms. Steele. I am Rico Cordova. Regretfully, we haven't had the pleasure of meeting in person before now. I apologize for the circumstances of our meeting, but I'm afraid there was no other choice," he reassured her with his silky-smooth Latino accent.

"You could've just invited me up for drinks," Chaise cooed in response. "This suite is amazing and the company is infinitely better than in my suite."

Rico smiled at her attempt to flirt with him. "I'm afraid that wouldn't have worked, Ms. Steele. I couldn't risk you declining my offer. I'm not so sure you would've accepted my invitation. So, here we are—together at last, as they say."

"You seem to have me at quite a disadvantage. I'm still in my bathrobe. I hardly think that's the appropriate apparel for any type of meeting," Chaise quipped.

"My men have brought your clothes. You may change, if that makes you more comfortable. But, I'm afraid you'll have to stay with me for quite a while now, Ms. Steele. You have been a tad too thorough in your research at Viboro Distributing," Rico explained. His voice was even and soothing, but held the undercurrent of inherent danger and unmistakable warnings.

Chills ran down her spine, her heart palpitations increased, and she was breathing so fast she was sure she would hyperventilate. He was telling her, in his kind and inviting voice, she would never be free again. The panic attack that she had staved off earlier in the evening now threatened to rear its ugly head with full force.

Swallowing down her fear and anger, she met his gaze with hers. "I'm afraid that's not an option, Mr. Cordova. I have a previous engagement that I can't break. We can finish our conversation here and I will take my things back to my own suite," she tried to project self-confidence and courage but she was sure she had failed miserably.

Rico laughed and showed his genuine amusement. "You know, Ms. Steele, I believe we could've been good friends under different circumstances. Alas, it was not meant to be."

With a flick of his eyes, the two goons who had snatched her from her room picked her up and carried her screaming into the other room. They left her with instructions to get dressed or go naked, but one way or another, she would leave the hotel with Mr. Cordova.

When they left, Chaise quickly dressed and searched through her things for her cell phone. It was missing, of course. They hadn't reached the pinnacle of the underworld organized crime ring by making careless mistakes like that.

Within minutes, someone knocked on the door and then quickly opened it. "Ah, good. You decided to go with clothes rather than without. Less attention is drawn to us that way," Rico teased. Chaise was not amused.

The two goons escorted Chaise out of the suite and down the back stairway. It was a long way down by stairs, but Rico seemed to exert no effort. The limousine was waiting in front of the hotel and Chaise was promptly escorted into the backseat.

As they drove off, she wondered if she would ever see anyone she knew again. The thoughts of the last words she spoke to her brother rang through her head like a persistent echo. The regret of not settling the unresolved issues with Bull weighed heavily on her heart.

Chaise was fairly drunk when Bull called her earlier. She had thought about just hanging up on him but there was something in his voice that stopped her. If only she hadn't insisted on answering the knock at the door instead of talking to him. Truthfully, she was hoping it was Bull outside her door, waiting to see her. *How wrong I was,* she thought.

The limousine slowed and Chaise saw what appeared to be an abandoned warehouse ahead. The large, sliding door began to move and opened just enough to allow the car to enter before closing them inside.

The section Chaise was in looked like a simple garage. There were a couple of other cars parked inside, no doubt to hide their presence from prying eyes. An inner wall had been constructed to hide the contents of the rest of the warehouse. A simple door that connected the two sections was located in the far corner.

The door opened and several more burly, scary men walked into the garage area. Chaise was escorted into the back area. There were workmen milling about the area, putting up iron bars along one wall. They were building a small prison inside the warehouse. The entire wall was being lined with prison cells, complete with locking doors.

The stench emanating from the dark, musty warehouse was putrid. She covered her nose and mouth and tried to regulate her breathing as much as she could. Chaise fought back the bile that attempted to rise in her throat—from both the smell and from the fear that was taking hold of her senses.

She heard sniffling and whimpers coming from the dark corner. She strained her eyes to see what she was walking into and gasped audibly when she made out the shapes. A sparsely furnished, makeshift cell had been constructed in the corner. The sounds came from any one of the numerous young girls who were crammed into the small space.

As she got closer, she immediately realized they were dirty and appeared to be barely fed. The stench that permeated the air seemed to emanate from their bathroom. The bathroom, which she quickly amended, was actually only a five-gallon bucket that had been haphazardly placed in the corner of the cell. Chaise's stomach roiled at the thought of what the poor, young girls had suffered.

As she passed by their cell, she noticed that the girls barely glanced up at her. Their will to live was almost gone and their fight to get out had long since vanished. Not one even tried to ask her for help. Chaise bit back the tears that stung the back of her eyes. She knew she had to keep her wits about her to have any chance of getting out of her situation and helping anyone else.

The men escorted her out the back door of the warehouse and onto a rickety old pier. The brackish water lapped at the sides of the waiting boat. Chaise had a very bad feeling about the impending trip. On land, she felt like she had a fighting chance to escape. She could run, hide, scream for help, and in Miami, someone was always within earshot.

But out on the open ocean, she would never be found.

"Where are we going?" she asked, raising her chin in defiance and stopping in her tracks.

The bigger man didn't say anything in response. He simply picked her up and placed her on the boat. He jumped onboard after untying the hitching line and nodded to the other man. The boat's engine revved as the propellers pushed them away from land. Chaise kept a cautious eye on the direction in which they were headed and made mental notes about landmarks.

After several minutes of traveling toward the horizon, the boat slowed and Chaise saw their intended destination. A large, luxurious yacht was anchored offshore. The boat she was on idled up to the back boarding platform and two more men secured it with ropes.

Chaise was escorted into the main living quarters. Though riddled with fear, her eyes took in her surroundings and noted the opulence that the criminal underworld enjoyed while she worked hard for every dime she earned. They walked her down the narrow hallway and into the dining area.

The man sitting at the head of the table was no doubt the senior Cordova. He was older, more distinguished with his slightly graying temples and crinkle lines around his eyes, but there was no mistaking the likeness between the man and Rico. Chaise approached the table and when he saw them, he quickly stood, pulled her chair out, and motioned for her to sit with him.

He called for another plate for Chaise as he took his seat. His smile seemed so genuine—the laugh lines around his eyes were evidence of his penchant for smiling. Chaise couldn't reconcile the two men in her head—the kind, thoughtful host and the evil, underground empire ruler. He must have sensed her inner turmoil as his face took on a self-deprecating grin before he spoke.

"Ah, I see you have perhaps heard of me, no?" His Spanish accent was thicker than Rico's, but it fit him perfectly. He had thick, black hair with small speckling of gray scattered throughout. His eyes were almost black and his skin was a beautiful shade of brown. He was most definitely a handsome older man.

"You must be related to Rico Cordova. He bears a striking resemblance to you," Chaise answered with a smile. She felt like the worst hypocrite, having food and drinks with the man who had effectively kidnapped her, but she thought this was her best chance at escaping. She needed to keep her enemies as close as possible.

"You are very kind to avoid offending me by assuming he is my son," he said with a smile. "Yes, in your culture, I would be known as Ricardo Cordova, Sr. In my country, it would not be so, but that is of no matter. You may call me Ricardo," he explained while pulling her hand to his mouth.

"Thank you, Ricardo. My name is Chaise," she said politely. "I see your son learned his manners from you, as well."

Chaise's plate was placed in front of her, along with a glass of water and a glass of wine. After drinking two bottles of wine earlier, she really didn't want more but she wouldn't rudely refuse him while she was still in his good graces.

"This looks delicious," she said while picking up her fork. The waiter took her linen napkin and placed it on her lap. Chaise nodded graciously at him and took a bite of her food. "Mmmm—I love this! My compliments to the chef!"

Ricardo and Chaise finished their light meal with companionable discussions, though each intentionally avoided the subject of why she was there, for how long, or if she would ever be free again. Ricardo walked Chaise to the sitting area on the middle deck of his luxury yacht. The waiter brought their drinks out and then left them alone.

"Chaise, I know you're curious about why you're here with me," Ricardo said, his voice maintaining his friendly host tone. "There are certain parts of my business that I'm not necessarily proud of, but they are a necessity. You have stumbled into that part of my business, unfortunately.

"This saddens me because I have truly enjoyed your company. I'm afraid we must part ways now, Miss Chaise. I had to meet you first, though. It has been my pleasure," Ricardo stated.

"I don't understand what you mean. I haven't stumbled across anything," she hedged. She knew she had found something big but she didn't know all the details of it yet. She hoped to use that ignorance to her advantage. "I've only found some date discrepancies in your payroll and human resources documentation. That happens in every company. Why would you want to fire me over that?"

"Let's not insult each other's intelligence by pretending. It's been far too pleasant to taint it with that kind of ending," he said.

Two of his men appeared and pulled her up to standing. "Goodnight, Miss Chaise," he called as the men walked her back to the waiting speedboat.

~

The cutter approached the tanker with Bull and Reaper pacing nervously back and forth in anticipation. Rebel's friend with the Coast Guard had come through and they were fast on their way to boarding the other vessel. Bull's hands were locked in a permanent fist and they were ready to pound the first man he came upon.

"No one but Coast Guard personnel leaves this cutter. Is that understood? We do this by the book or we won't do it at all," Commander Harper ordered.

All the men answered affirmatively except Bull. Commander Harper gave him a pointed look, raised his eyebrows, and waited for an answer. Bull huffed and reluctantly nodded his head.

"But if she's on there, you get her off that ship before you do anything else," Bull commanded.

"You have my word," Harper replied.

The cutter slowed and a small motorboat full of men who would conduct a thorough search of the vessel was lowered into the water. Bull and Reaper watched intently as the men boarded. Bull snatched up a pair of binoculars, intent on searching for Chaise in any way that he could.

When he caught one of the men in his sights, he stopped on him and examined his face. The man appeared to be looking directly at him with a shitty smirk on his face. He was mocking them and laughing at them for wasting their time searching for her. He was helping to waste time by not volunteering any information.

"Motherfucker!" Bull yelled loudly.

"What is it, Bull?" Reaper asked.

"She's not here. The whole crew is too calm and collected. The one guy on deck is pointing over here and laughing. They're making us waste our time—they've taken her somewhere else," he explained.

"You don't know that," Commander Harper countered. "Now that we're here, we will conduct a thorough search and if anything turns up, we will haul them in."

Bull shook his head. He knew a decoy when he saw one. He knew they'd been duped and the search of a tanker would take hours. He was stranded in the ocean on a cutter with no other way to get back to shore. He was positive he would have a stroke before he was able to get back to land.

Three hours later, the search of the tanker was concluded with the exact results Bull had predicted—Chaise wasn't onboard. They'd wasted all that time on a wild goose chase and he was no closer to finding her than he was when he left shore. He stood on deck, feeling the wind whipping through his hair, as he imagined how frightened she must be.

As soon as he was back on land, he stalked off while Rebel and Reaper thanked Commander Harper for his help. He held his cell phone in his hand and was conflicted on whether he should contact his father yet.

Even that thought alone was foreign to him. Contacting his father had never been an option before. He thought about all the strange turns his life had taken over the past several weeks. How his ties to Reaper led to his ties to Chaise and ultimately led him to his ties to his father. As a man who didn't believe in coincidences, he knew there was a higher power at work, bringing them all together. He had to believe it would all work out in the end.

Putting his phone away, he decided he couldn't contact John just yet. He didn't want to chance blowing his cover and losing Chaise for good. He racked his brain, trying to decide the next move they should make. The idea struck him like lightning and he grabbed his phone up again.

"Brad, it's Bull. I need you to pull a list of every piece of property the Cordovas own in Miami. Send that to us ASAP. Thanks, man," Bull said, ending the call and turning to his brothers.

"Brad is pulling the Cordova owned properties in Miami. She's here, Reap. They haven't taken her away yet. We have to find where they're keeping her," Bull explained.

"Sounds like a good plan to start. Let's see what Brad comes up with in his research. If there are too many, we can call in more men, divide them up and save some time," Reaper said. The stress and concern was infused in his voice, though he tried to maintain his edge and remain the fearless leader.

Bull's phone pinged with the incoming text from Brad. "There are twelve warehouses and two estates. The warehouses are all relatively close but the two houses are pretty far away from each other," he relayed.

"Let's get to the office and get our gear. I'll call in Blake and Roman for additional recon help on the way there. We'll get our game plan together so that we're all on the same page," Reaper directed. "We need a coordinated front to make this work. We have no idea how many men Cordova has."

Bull agreed even though it was killing him to wait another minute. He wanted to storm in with guns blazing and take Chaise from wherever it was they had her hidden. He knew Noah was right—without a plan of attack, they would unwittingly put Chaise in more danger. He just hoped that she was being held in one of the known Cordova properties.

If not, Bull didn't know where else to look. He only knew that he damn sure wouldn't ever give up. There was no explanation for how she had invaded his thoughts, his life, and his heart in such a short time. Bull only realized that he had strong feelings for Chaise and he couldn't let her go.

He would've looked for her just because he was a good man, he was good at his job, and he had a duty to act. His heart, however, was more than involved in the case. It ruled him, it ruled his decisions, and it ruled his actions. A soft, loving woman turned the tough, stoic man inside out in a matter of days. It defied logic and reason but it was no less true.

They drove to the main Steele Security headquarters to change clothes and start gathering their gear. They dressed in all black and donned a variety of weapons in numerous locations. Laying out a map of the city, they pinpointed the location of each warehouse and the private homes.

The warehouses were located fairly close to each other, as expected, and in an old rundown section on the outskirts of Miami. Where one of the houses was located, however, was a complete surprise to everyone. The first one was in Key Biscayne, an influential island town that was connected to Miami by a bridge.

The second house was on Madden Island, which was an island off the coast of South Beach that could only be accessed by boat or helicopter. Bull and Reaper exchanged concerned looks. Any rescue attempt from that island would be very tricky with such limited access points.

"One step at a time, Bull. Let's check these warehouses first. The helicopter was a decoy, so she's probably still on the mainland," Reaper said.

Looking around at the five men, Reaper continued, "We'll split up and check every warehouse. If you find her," he stopped and pierced Bull with his gaze, "*do not engage* without all of us there unless you have no other choice. Understood?"

Four of the men responded affirmatively. Reaper cleared his throat and waited for Bull to respond. "Understood," he finally answered, but his voice lacked conviction. Reaper shook his head, knowing that it was fruitless to argue with him at that point. Bull's nickname may have been originally given to him because of his size, but it also described his personality.

Once they had parked in a covered garage, they moved on foot toward the warehouses. They were all heavily armed and experienced in covert operations. The urban warfare maneuver would be a walk in the park compared to the dangers the team had collectively faced.

The Cordovas had just created an enemy they could have never imagined, even in their worst nightmares. Bull parted from his friends to conduct his search of his two assigned warehouses for any signs of Chaise. His stride was swift and confident and his determination was set in the hardness of his eyes. After he rescued Chaise, he would unleash hell at the Cordovas' front door.

CHAPTER NINETEEN

Chaise was taken back to the warehouse and put in the small, crowded cell with the younger girls. Many of them looked emaciated and almost lifeless. Their eyes were dull and their stares were vacant. Chaise had a strong suspicion that they were drugged to keep them compliant.

As she stepped over the bodies strewn across the floor, trying to avoid stepping on anyone while she looked for an empty space, she saw a familiar face. Her breath caught in her chest and her mouth gaped open. Tears sprung to her eyes and she stumbled to reach the sleeping girl in the corner.

Chaise cried, "Aura! Aura!"

The girl slowly opened her eyes and tried to force them to focus on the shadowy figure moving toward her. She heard the name Aura being called but she thought she had been dreaming. She had been in that shithole for so long, she was beginning to forget what life outside it was like.

"What did you call me?" she asked, the shadowy figure finally coming into focus.

"Aura, it's me, Chaise," she said as she knelt beside her. Chaise had suddenly forgotten the stench and the filthy conditions of the cell. All she could focus on at the moment was the fact that Aura was in front of her. She was just so relieved that Aura was still alive.

"I'm not Aura," the girl replied weakly. "I'm Ana. Aura is my twin sister." A single tear escaped from her eye. From the looks of her, she was dehydrated and malnourished; she didn't have many tears left in her to cry.

"Ana? Twin sister?" Chaise was repeating the words but they hadn't quite sunk in yet. "If you're Ana, then where is Aura? Have you seen her?"

"No. Oh God, I hope they didn't get my sister." Ana's face contorted in pain, as if her heart were breaking in two and she wanted to sob. But no tears would flow and she made no sounds as she curled into a fetal position.

Chaise easily lifted the girl's head and shoulders off the cold, concrete floor and slid her lap under her. As Chaise laid her back down across her legs, Ana's frail hand grabbed Chaise's and held on as tightly as she could muster. Chaise stroked her dirty, matted hair as she uttered words of comfort.

"I'm sure she's fine, Ana. If she isn't here, she's probably hiding somewhere," Chaise reasoned. She was beginning to get a good idea of why Aura was so adamant to help with the research at Viboro Distributing.

Leaning forward as far as she could, Chaise whispered to Ana. "Did you work at Viboro?"

Ana simply nodded her head 'yes.' In that simple gesture, she confirmed exactly what Chaise thought was happening. They would hire young, attractive Latino women and then abduct them for their own nefarious plans. Her thoughts then strayed to Aura and how responsible she'd felt for Aura's disappearance.

The young girl was trying to save her twin sister, whom she loved and missed. The poor girl who was lying in Chaise's lap, sound asleep, had obviously been mistreated and abused at the hands of her captors. Chaise wanted to ask Ana more questions but didn't have the heart to wake her up.

Chaise leaned her head back against the metal bars and fought back the panic attack festering just under the surface. The situation as a whole was too much to handle at once. She started breaking it down into bite-size chunks so she could deal with one issue at a time.

The first issue, obviously, was that she had been kidnapped and no one knew where she was. That thought alone threatened her last thread of sanity. A fleeting memory took root in her mind and it suddenly calmed her and filled her with a sense of peace. Her thoughts created a temporary refuge from her reality.

Bull had called her hotel room phone just before they knocked on her door. He knew where she was and he knew that she'd been taken. He would find her. Bull wouldn't leave her there.

Thoughts of Bull simultaneously broke her heart and gave her strength. Regret filled her over the way they parted, the way he found out who she was, and especially that she answered the hotel room door instead of just talking to him on the phone.

In her drunken stupor, she had secretly wanted to punish him for rejecting her in front of everyone. She thought they had moved past that stage of their relationship when he relented and let her touch him while they made love. Thinking she had gotten through to him in a way that no one ever had before, she wanted to be *the one* for him—like she felt he was for her.

Suddenly, she realized the deeper meaning of his call. First of all, he was back in Miami and had searched until he found her. Second, his tone of voice was a mixture of relief and regret. That told her he still cared about her and that there may still be a chance for them to salvage their budding relationship from the mistakes they'd both made. And third, it gave her even more reason to fight, to live, and to escape the situation with as many of the girls as she could take with her.

Chaise realized she must have fallen asleep at some point. She was already completely exhausted by the time she reached her hotel room. The adrenaline dump after being "escorted" to Rico's room and then Ricardo's yacht had her running on all cylinders for several hours. When she crashed, she did so sitting on the uncomfortable concrete floor, leaned against the hard iron bars, with a scared, young girl in her lap.

Her legs were asleep and the painful pin-prickling sensation ran through them like lightning bolts. Her back and neck ached and her ass just simply hurt. From the small holes near the ceiling, she could tell it was still dark outside. The male voices approaching had awakened her and put her nerves on high alert.

Chaise turned her head to the side to get a glimpse at who was approaching. She tried to hide her surprise when she saw a familiar face. It was one of the men who had shot at her and Bull in the parking lot. It was Bull's father. He was walking with the other men who had taken her from her room, talking to them like he knew them and was one of them.

When he looked at the girls in the cell, his face registered no emotion. She knew if what Michelle had said was true, then John was trained to keep his emotions locked away deep inside where they wouldn't blow his cover. His eyes raked over the bodies in the cell until they met Chaise's eyes.

The flash of recognition and concern was so quickly masked that Chaise would've missed it had she not specifically been watching for it. She didn't know if John could get word to Bull fast enough to help her. He wouldn't blow his entire case just for her safety, but maybe he could find a way to help.

"We need one of these *putas* to make a run before daylight. We have to make a stop by Rico's house, too," the tall, thin thug told John in his thick Spanish accent. Together, they walked to the cell to choose who would go out next.

"Diego, these girls look bad. Are you feeding them, man?" John asked.

"They eat sometimes," Diego replied nonchalantly. He opened the door and walked around the cell, not bothering to avoid stepping on anyone who was in his way. He approached Chaise and Ana and kicked Ana with the toe of his boots.

"*Puta*, wake up. It's your turn," he said cruelly.

"She's not a *bitch*," Chaise spat out at him, venom lacing her voice as she spoke. "And she's in no shape to go anywhere. Leave her alone."

Diego smiled at her bravado and then he backhanded her across the cheek. Her head jerked violently to the side, clashing against the metal bars and sending her toppling over onto her side. Her cheek immediately swelled and she felt a small bead of blood roll down her face from where his ring cut her skin.

Ana fell to the concrete when Chaise was knocked over. She woke and rubbed the side of her face where it had hit the concrete. Diego kicked her again with his boot and told her to get up. Ana tried to push herself up but couldn't muster the strength to finish her movement.

Chaise jumped up, faced Diego and took a step toward him to block his access to Ana. "I said she's not going anywhere. I'll go in her place. Just tell me what I need to do."

"Well, aren't you a brave little *puta*? Maybe I should teach you some manners. You need to know who *el jefe* is around here," Diego said with a snide smile.

He started to reach for Chaise when the shorter, but stockier, man's words stopped him cold. "Diego, don't touch her again."

"Okay, Manuel," Diego replied, sounding like a whipped dog. Looking at Chaise with anger and disgust in his eyes, he said, "Follow me."

Diego led her out the door that led to the docks. John and Manuel followed close behind them. Diego, Chaise, and Manuel got into the speedboat. John untied the mooring line and threw it into the boat. Manuel looked up at John and issued his command. "Stay here and watch the girls. We'll be back sometime tomorrow."

John watched until the boat disappeared into the blackness hovering over the ocean. He had to find some way to contact Colton and let him know he'd seen Chaise. He needed a way that wouldn't call attention to him and blow his cover before he was ready to close the case. There were still questions that had to be answered and people who had to be arrested before he could walk away.

The deplorable conditions the girls were left in turned John's stomach. He could easily take the men out and turn the girls loose, but that wouldn't give him what he needed to stop the Cordova family from doing it again somewhere else. His rationalization weighed heavily on his conscience and he couldn't wait to retire from the insidious underworld life.

John had already given up too much in his life under the guise of justice and protecting others. The nagging issue that kept him up at night was the injustice he'd committed toward his own family. He was young and impetuous when he made the decision to leave for the sake of his wife and son.

Looking back, he decided if he could do it all over again, he would have never left them. As soon as the case was finished, he would retire and move back home to Alabama. If Michelle wanted, they could even move to Miami and be close to Bull. One way or another, the case had to wrap-up soon because John wasn't sure how much more he could take.

As he looked at the pitiful creatures in the cell, part of him rejoiced that he had moved up in the Cordova ranks. Another part railed against him for being such a good undercover agent that he could actually pull it off. Unable to stand it any longer, he brought the girls food and water from the kitchen. He had no doubt he would hear about it later. With any luck, Chaise's connection to the case would help bring it to a close sooner than he could alone.

John wanted to go with Diego and Manuel to keep an eye on Chaise. She was obviously very important to his son and John was once again very conflicted over his duty to his country and his duty to his son. Watching them take Chaise away was one of the hardest things he'd had to do as an agent—right behind leaving his family.

His inner turmoil boiled down to one question—*Will Colton ever forgive me?*

~

Bull moved around the darkened warehouse and instinctively knew it was empty. It wasn't the location where they were holding Chaise but he could see Viboro Distributing boxes stacked on pallets. Rows and rows of boxes reaching almost twelve feet high lined the interior of the rundown building. No reputable company would use such dilapidated buildings.

That made him want to know what was inside those boxes even more. Every bit of intelligence he could collect on the Cordovas would help solve one more piece of the puzzle. Anything that helped him locate Chaise was worth whatever he had to do. Bull crept inside, keeping low and in the shadows, until he had cased the entire inner perimeter and verified no one was there.

All the boxes were exactly the same height, width, and depth. Bull opened one of them and removed a wooden box with a hinged lid. It was marked with the *Blue Cypress Casino* logo on the top. Bull opened the lid and stared at the casino chips inside. They appeared to be genuine, high-quality clay chips that were used by the higher-end casinos.

Bull picked up one of the multi-colored chips and immediately noticed the weight was wrong. He closed his fist around it and felt it start crumbling from his grip. Underneath the colored outer shell, a white, powdery substance crumbled in his hand. He looked around again at the rows and rows of boxes that were ready to be shipped.

He walked through the warehouse, looking at the shipping labels, and noted they were being sent to casinos across the country. "Holy shit," he uttered under his breath in disbelief. He unpacked one package and counted twenty wooden boxes. Each wooden box contained one thousand chips. The amount of drugs passing through just one warehouse was staggering.

Bull took pictures with his phone, capturing the names and addresses on the shipping labels. He also snapped pictures of the contents and the compressed, white powder inside the chips. He rushed back the way he entered and on to his next destination as he continued his search for Chaise.

The next warehouse search was fruitless. It obviously hadn't been used in quite some time. Dust and dirt covered everything, with no tracks or anything else to indicate anyone had been there in months. "That explains why they have so many warehouses," he said aloud to himself. "They're alternating between them to avoid getting caught."

Bull texted the others to let them know his search was complete and there was no sign of Chaise in either of his warehouses. Within a few seconds, he received texts back from all the others relaying the same information, except Shadow. Having not received a response from Shadow, he decided that was where he needed to go next.

As he silently walked through the darkened streets, he heard voices coming from behind one of the vacant buildings. He slowed his pace and listened for any sign that they knew he was there. The number of voices increased and he was able to identify six distinct voices. They were speaking in Spanish and talking about the beautiful new Cordova girl.

"Jorge, you think she'd want you, *ese*? You're crazy, man!"

"Yeah, Marco, she is hot! She'd definitely pick me over you, homes."

"You two losers don't have to worry about it. Manuel already ordered everyone to stay away from *Senorita Chaise*. If I catch you near her, I'll cut your dick off myself," an older voice chastised the younger boys.

"We were just fucking around, man," Jorge responded, clearly offended that he had been put in his place.

The voices started trailing off so Bull moved into position to follow them. They had no clue he was close behind them, monitoring their moves and waiting for them to take him to Chaise. He listened to their boasting from the shadows and gave them all the rope they needed.

Bull sensed a change in the air, a sudden charge of energy and the distinct feeling of being watched. He skirted around the corner of the building, still hidden in the shadows, and silently unsheathed his knife. Holding it firmly in his grasp, he readied himself for the man moving along the side of the building toward him.

When the other man reached the corner, Bull's arm flew up in a split second and stopped just short of the man's neck. "Shadow, what have I told you about sneaking up on me?"

Shadow's deep chuckle rumbled through his chest, "Are you getting rusty in your old age? The Bull I knew would've known the very second I moved into his range."

"Fuck you, man. Old my ass—I made you as soon as you stepped on my block," Bull said with a smile.

Shadow's tone became serious as he replied. "Come with me. They've taken Chaise to Rico's house. I couldn't get to the boat before they left. John's at the warehouse with the other girls."

Bull's blood turned to lava in his veins at just the thought of what Rico planned to do to Chaise. "Lead the way," he responded.

Shadow and Bull jogged to the waterfront warehouse where they'd held Chaise. Bull swore under his breath when he saw the girls locked up in the cell. Looking at his father, Bull asked, "You're just going to leave them in there?"

"I have no choice until I can close this case and bust the Cordova family," John answered. "I have to figure out their trade route so I can shut them down or they will just go somewhere else and start this all over again."

"This ends *tonight*, one way or another," Bull responded. "I'm not leaving here without Chaise."

John walked over to the cell and asked one of the girls to follow him. She eyed him wearily but she did as he asked. Once he had her out of earshot of the others, John and Rebel sat down with her to decipher Cordova's plans.

"What's your name, sweetheart?" Rebel asked in a calm, reassuring tone.

"Consuela," she answered meekly.

"Consuela, my name is Rebel. I won't hurt you, I promise. I'm here to help you. Can you tell us what's going on here? Why do they have you locked up in here with these other girls?"

Her eyes darted between Rebel and John and then over to the other men who were waiting a few feet away. "They send us to their contacts in other countries to pick up the drugs for them. We bring them back here and I don't know what they do with them after that."

"So they're using you as mules. That way they won't get caught trafficking," John stated. "How do they send you?"

"In the bottom of a big, dirty ship. The men on the ship are mean, too," Consuela replied with sadness permeating her voice. "Once the ship reaches US waters, it stops. We have to bring the drugs the rest of the way in a small boat. It is very dangerous with the waves and the weather. They tell us if we don't come back, they will kill our families.

"And, sometimes, we take the small boats far out into the ocean and meet another boat that looks like a submarine with a snorkel sticking up. They throw the packages in the water for us to get," she finished explaining.

"How do you know where to go?" John asked.

"The boat has a GPS-type device that shows us where to go. The men put the information in it and then send us out. We just follow the direction it shows."

"Do you know what kind of drugs they are sending you to pick up?" Rebel asked.

"Sometimes it's meth, but usually it's heroin. I've heard the men talking about it," she answered. "They have radios and someone calls out a bunch of numbers. Every time we hear that, we know they're about to send one of us out."

John looked up at Rebel. "Now we know where they're getting the coordinates to put in the GPS. If we can get one of the radios, we can monitor it and be there to trap them."

"Diego left his radio. He forgot about it after he hit the pretty lady," Consuela said as she pointed to a radio that sat on a shelf littered with garbage.

That caught Bull and Reaper's attention. Bull walked over to where they sat, turned a chair around, and straddled it. He smiled at Consuela as he asked, "What did the pretty lady look like, sweetheart?"

"She had long black hair, pretty green eyes, and she was so nice. She saw Ana and thought she was Aura, her twin sister," she pointed to Ana. "She helped Ana when Diego was being mean. She took Ana's place for the run tonight."

"She took her place?" Rebel asked.

"Yes. But I heard Manuel say they are going to *Rico's* house first. That is not good," Consuela said.

"Why is that not good?" Bull asked.

"The girls who are taken to Rico's never come back," she whispered, as if she thought he would appear just by mentioning his name. Her eyes were wide with fear and her bottom lip trembled with the thoughts of what Rico would do with Chaise.

Bull swallowed hard to keep his thoughts and feelings under control. He didn't want to frighten the poor girl with his tirade, but he was going to kill the men who took Chaise. Every one of them would soon face him and he vowed to be the last person they would ever see.

CHAPTER TWENTY

The boat slowed in the blackness of the night and Chaise sat up straighter, trying to get her bearings on where she was. Diego was at the helm and Manuel sat beside him. They put Chaise in the back of the boat so she couldn't see the modified GPS device or hear what they were saying over the engines.

As the boat came to a stop, she thought she saw something approaching from the right. There was something sticking up out of the water but her eyes could not make out what it was. Diego pulled out a spotlight and shone it across the water just as a small, semi-submersible watercraft fully surfaced.

The pipe sticking up out of the water acted as a waterproof snorkel for the craft that allowed air in but a special valve kept the water out. The top hatch opened and a man threw several large packages out into the water. The packages were strung together with a thick cord and floated in the water between the two vessels.

Diego turned to Chaise and snidely ordered her. "Go get them, *puta*. I hope you can swim."

When Chaise didn't move, Diego pulled his gun and leveled it at her. *"Ahora." Now.*

Chaise stepped up on the side of the boat and dove into the deep, black water. She quickly swam to the packages, grabbed the cord and towed it back to the boat. Manuel reached down and took the cord from her hand and pulled the packages into the boat.

"Get back in the boat or drown out here, *puta*. Your choice," Diego taunted.

Manuel shot Diego a look that made him sit back down and look away. "You know we have orders to take her to Rico, Diego," Manuel chastised.

Looking at Chaise, Manuel commanded her. "Get back in the boat."

Chaise swam to the back of the boat and hauled her body out of the water onto the small platform. Once she was back in her seat, Diego gunned the engines and they took off across the choppy waters. Chaise noticed the winds picking up and the waves getting higher. It was the middle of hurricane season in Florida and apparently another storm was about to hit.

Diego kept the bow straight to run headlong into the waves so the boat wouldn't capsize as the wave height increased. The noise from the boat's engines, the whipping wind, and the splashing waves made it nearly impossible to hear anyone speak. Chaise could see Diego and Manuel talking but couldn't hear most of what they were saying. When she made out part of Manuel's sentence, her heart dropped to her knees. Even though she was wet and the night wind was cool against her skin, she broke out into a cold sweat from her fear.

Manuel had just told Diego that they were to kill Chaise when Rico was finished with her. She knew they were taking her to Rico but she had no idea what he planned to do with her. She only knew she wasn't going to stick around and find out. While they were busy battling the wind and waves to keep the boat straight, Chaise eased up to sit on the back of her seat.

When a high wave rolled underneath them, Chaise leaned back and intentionally fell off the side of the boat. She let the surge of the wave propel her forward as she swam as hard as she could away from the boat and her captors. She knew there were other barrier islands that were close to Madden Island. She just hoped she was going in the right direction.

The sheer terror of being out in the open ocean at night was enough to render her immobile but the threat of being caught and tortured overtook her. She swam harder and faster until her foot brushed against the sandy bottom. Breathing hard, she slugged through the breaking waves until she reached the beach. She fell flat on her stomach, exhausted from the swim and the nearly debilitating fear. Within moments, she had passed out from exhaustion.

The sound of a speedboat engine woke Chaise from her slumber. She pushed up to a sitting position and tentatively looked around to get her bearings. She was momentarily lost until she remembered she swam up on the beach to escape Diego and Manuel. The sound of the motorboat caught her attention and she scrambled behind the cover of the vegetation behind her.

As the boat passed by, she recognized the outline of Bull as he stood in the middle of the boat. He was with several other men and they were headed toward several lights that appeared to be just across the channel from her. From the look of the area, she decided she was on Lauren Key and they were going to Madden Island.

From the northwest tip of the barrier island, it was only about a hundred yards across the channel. She was exhausted, not thinking clearly, and only wanted to reach Bull. She jogged along the shoreline until she reached the island point and then swam across the channel.

In the distance, she could see the boat coasting to the shore. They had obviously cut the engines before they got too close. Chaise started to run toward them when she was suddenly grabbed from behind and yanked backward. A menacing voice growled in her ear. "You caused me a lot of trouble tonight, *puta*."

Diego twirled her around to face him. The sound of his hand hitting her cheek made a loud *thwack* and sent her flying to the ground. She grabbed her already bruised cheek and cried out in pain. He yanked her up by her hair and then dragged her behind him.

When she stumbled, her hair was painfully yanked by his tight grip. Diego turned and kicked her several times in the back and legs while telling her to get up. She struggled back to her feet as he grabbed her upper arm to push her toward a mansion that was partially hidden by the beach foliage.

When they reached the door, Diego shoved her up against it as he ground his erection into her abdomen. "You are mine now, *puta*," he hissed in her ear. Chaise fought against his hold, pushing him with all her might. He stumbled back a step or two but was instantly back against her with even more force. She was just about to scream when she heard a familiar voice.

"Diego, what the fuck do you think you're doing?" Rico asked coolly.

Diego quickly jumped away from Chaise to put distance between them but he knew he'd been caught. He looked down at the ground in shame and embarrassment. He didn't dare try to give Rico a lame excuse so he kept quiet.

Rico looked at Chaise and his face registered his surprise. His eyes grew wide at first and then narrowed as he inspected the damage to her face. "Who did this to you, *mi amor*?" Rico gently eased his hand across the angry bruise and swelling on her cheek.

His fingers brushed down her arm and stopped at the bruises in the shape of fingers that were forming on her upper arm. His eyes narrowed more but he said nothing as he continued his perusal of her body. Rico took Chaise's hand in his and gently twirled her around to find the bruises beginning on the back of her legs. He lifted her shirt just enough to see the marks on her back from Diego's kicks.

As he turned Chaise back to fully face him, his voice was calm and reassuring as he spoke to her. "Chaise, I'm very sorry for the way Diego has treated you. I promise you, *mi amor*, he will never touch you again." Before Chaise could respond, Rico drew his gun from its holster and shot Diego in the head point blank.

Rico didn't bother to look at Diego as his body fell limp onto the lanai. Chaise screamed and backed away from Rico in shock. "Shhh, *mi amor*, I said he would never touch you again and I meant it. Come inside with me." He took her hand in his and forced her inside his beachfront mansion.

"You've been very hard to keep up with, Chaise. If I didn't know better, I would think you've been intentionally avoiding me," Rico continued flirting with her as he led her to a beautifully adorned kitchen. He stopped at a large island with bar stools and motioned for her to sit.

"What do you want with me?" Chaise asked with more courage than she felt.

"You will be my consort for the foreseeable future. I've chosen you and you should feel honored," Rico explained. His tone of voice indicated she should be happy about his decision as his eyes held a glimmer of insanity mixed with pure evil.

Chaise shook involuntarily as a shudder ran down her spine. Just the thought of him touching her turned her stomach and made her long for Bull even more. She had to keep Rico talking for two reasons: to keep his hands off of her and to give Bull more time to storm the house.

She knew Bull and Noah were outside somewhere, along with several other linebacker-sized men. She could picture them drawing a map in the sand to plan their attack. Stalling sounded like her best option since Rico had already shown how fast he was with his gun.

"What does being your consort entail?" she asked, feigning interest.

He smiled warmly at her and she had the fleeting thought that he was pleased with her question, as if he believed this is what she wanted. "Anything and everything that pleases me, Chaise. Don't worry—I will make sure you are pleased as well. But first, we need to get you out of those dirty, wet clothes and into something more suitable."

Pulling her up from her seat, he led her up the stairs and into the guest bedroom. He pulled out a thigh-length, satin nightgown and matching robe before escorting her to the bathroom. After giving her a towel, he instructed her to shower and dress and then come to meet him in the den. Before he left her alone, he turned and gave her a pointed look before issuing his warning.

"Don't bother trying to run, Chaise. You can't outrun a bullet."

She stayed in the shower as long as she could to stall and give the guys time to put their plans into action. Dressing in the nightgown Rico had given her, she tiptoed into the hall. None of the upstairs lights were on but she saw the glowing light filtering into the foyer below her.

The storm was rolling in even more. The rain had started and lightning flashed across the sky. If the thunder rumbling in the distance was any indication, the storm would get much worse before it passed. The wind whipping outside blew the light rain sideways. The raindrops sounded like pebbles tapping against the windows.

Slowly walking down the stairs, she strained her ears to listen for any sounds—voices, movement, or even gunfire—but there were none. Rounding the corner, she saw Rico sitting on a large, sectional sofa with a drink in his hand. He smiled lasciviously at her as he raked his eyes over her body.

"You are so beautiful, Chaise. I think you may be my best choice yet. Come sit with me."

"Your glass is almost empty. Can I refill it for you first?" she asked, trying to buy more time for herself and for her rescue.

"That would be nice," he said as he extended his arm to hand the glass to her. When her fingers grasped it, he intentionally dragged his fingers across hers and his eyes darkened with desire. Keeping her face neutral as much as she could, she asked what he was drinking.

"Evan Williams Bourbon," he responded as he watched her. "Pour yourself a glass as well."

Chaise turned toward the bar that sat to the side of the picture window. As she approached the window, her eyes landed on Bull's as he sat crouched outside. He put his finger over his lips, telling her to be quiet, before giving her a single, slow nod. In that gesture, she knew he was telling her everything would be all right.

Chaise poured two drinks and walked back to Rico. Knowing Bull had probably already moved, she couldn't help but use her body to block Rico's view of the window. She fought to keep her nervous energy under control as she handed Rico his drink. She took a small sip of hers to keep her hands and mouth busy.

Rico's laid his hand on her knee, drew lazy circles on her skin, making each one bigger than the last. His eyes were glued to her legs and where his fingers met her skin. Chaise couldn't keep her breathing under control. Her chest heaved from the ragged breaths she drew in. Rico no doubt thought she was affected in a good way when she actually wanted to claw his eyes out and bleach her skin clean.

The shrill sound of Rico's phone filled the room. Rico looked at the display and it showed a blocked number. His eyes, full of lust, met Chaise's as he apologized. "I'm so sorry, *mi amor*. I said no interruptions tonight. This must be an urgent matter for my father."

Chaise nodded, happy for the interruption. Rico answered the phone and within a minute he suddenly shot to his feet. His face contorted in anger as he started spewing curse words in Spanish. Pacing back and forth, his tirade ended with, "Come get me then, asshole. I'm waiting."

~

Bull watched Chaise walk into the den wearing the flimsy nightgown and robe. His eyes shot to Rico and his hand instantly went to the Glock .40 on his side. Reaper stilled Bull's movements and slowly shook his head from side to side. Bull wanted to kill the man for the blatantly lustful way he looked at Chaise. When she didn't sit down, Bull took a huge risk by letting her see him, but he had to let her know he was there.

He noticed she wasn't overly surprised to see him and kept moving toward the bar as if there was nothing out of the ordinary. The team had already made all their preparations to enter the house and search for Chaise. Seeing her had confirmed their suspicions and made their Plan B go into effect.

That was exactly what Bull wanted.

When Rico put his hand on Chaise's leg and kept moving his fingers up her thigh, Reaper and Shadow had to physically restrain Bull to keep him from going through the window. After they convinced him to stick to the plan, they moved into position and Bull used the secure phone to call Rico's number.

"You took someone tonight. *She. Belongs. To. Me.* Let her go now and I will *think* about not taking everything in your life away from you," Bull told Rico in a low, menacing voice.

Rico's response was to curse at him in Spanish and pace around the room. When Rico told Bull to come and get him, Bull smiled as he replied. "I was hoping you'd say that. You just wait right there for me." Before Rico could answer, Bull disconnected and nodded to the other guys.

This was the part of the job Bull loved the most. The thrill of the covert operations, the excitement of one-upping the bad guys, and the success of a job well done were his rewards. But this time, it was much more personal. This time, his heart was involved and, even though that was foreign territory for Bull, he had to admit that he wanted Chaise for himself.

The storm that was building around them couldn't begin to match the rage that Bull had inside him. He moved into position to cover his assigned area of the house. He still had eyes on Chaise and wouldn't hesitate to take Rico out if he touched her again. Bull was sure he had effectively killed Rico's libido with his phone call.

Rico was yelling into a two-way radio but no one was able to answer him. The team had already made sure that all of Rico's men were indisposed and unable to respond. Bull watched as Rico's apprehension rose to astronomical levels and chuckled to himself. Rico had no idea what was coming to him.

Whispers from Bull's earpiece told him that all the men were in position and ready to finish what they had started. While Chaise had stalled Rico, the men from Steele Security had already infiltrated the house, disarmed the security system, and made the appropriate adjustments to the house to carry out their plans.

Bull's muscles contracted and he prepared for a fight to the death when he saw Rico snatch Chaise up by her hair and drag her toward the stairs. He angrily whispered into his communication device. "He's hurting Chaise. It's time to move *now*."

Reaper gave the word and each man stealthily moved into the house. Bull rushed in toward the same direction he saw Rico taking Chaise. Slowing only to check around corners, Bull took the steps two at a time to the top. He heard Chaise's screams and rushed to find her.

CHAPTER TWENTY-ONE

The intense pain and stinging in Chaise's scalp was sudden. Before she realized what was happening, Rico had yanked her from her seat in a fit of anger and was pulling her up the stairs by her hair. She tried to fight back but he only further twisted his hand, increasing the pressure and his grasp.

"He says you belong to *him*. We'll see who you belong to by the time I'm finished with you." The disdain dripped from his words as he spat them out at no one in particular. He was mumbling, swearing under his breath, and spouting various obscenities as he ignored Chaise's cries.

Once inside his bedroom, he tossed her on the bed while he paced back and forth across the floor. As if he suddenly remembered she was there, he stopped and gave her an evil smile. Chaise instinctively moved back as he advanced on her. He crawled across the bed, grabbed her by the ankle and roughly pulled her toward him.

Chaise screamed and kicked him repeatedly with her free leg. With all the fear and adrenalin coursing through her veins, she didn't feel any pain as she kicked him with her bare feet and punched him with her fists. Blinded by rage and fueled by fear of what he planned to do to her, she didn't even realize the moment when Rico went flying across the room.

"Chaise, baby, calm down for me," Bull tried to soothe her.

Rico roared as he scrambled back to his feet. He rushed toward Bull and tried to tackle him. Had Bull not been so close to the edge of insanity, he would've laughed at Rico's pitiful attempt to assault him. However, when Bull walked in the bedroom and saw Rico attacking Chaise, and how hard Chaise fought to keep him off of her, Bull saw red.

Simply throwing Rico across the room didn't quench his rage. Bull clenched his fists and drew his right hand back. The loud *thwack* of flesh pounding flesh echoed through the room. Chaise seemed to come to her senses as she looked at Bull in amazement.

Rico fell to the ground as his eyes rolled back in his head. Bull was tackled a second time but this time he welcomed it as he felt a soft, female body meld with his. He wrapped his arms around her and kissed the side of her head. He whispered soothing words into her ear, telling her he was there, she was safe, and he would take her away.

When he pulled back and looked at her face, his lips formed a thin line and fire burned in his eyes when he saw the angry bruises on her cheek. He attempted to keep his anger controlled so he didn't appear to be upset with Chaise, but he had to know. "Who. Hit. You?"

"Diego did this," she said, pointing to her face. "Rico shot him."

Bull gently wiped the tears from her eyes and pulled her back to him. She turned her face to the side, pressed her body against his and wrapped her arms around his waist. Just as she hugged him tight, she caught movement from the corner of her eye.

"Look out!" Chaise screamed.

Bull whirled around and pushed Chaise behind him, using his body as a shield to protect her. Rico had his gun drawn and aimed at Bull. An ugly sneer was plastered on Rico's face as he mocked Bull. "Not so tough now, are you?"

"I'm still as tough as I was when I knocked you on your ass a minute ago," Bull retorted sarcastically.

"Step aside, I want to make sure Chaise has a good view of your death," Rico ordered.

Chaise was hidden behind Bull and stood as close to him as she possibly could. She felt a bulge in the back of his waistband. Bull's arm still held Chaise safely behind him. He felt her careful movements as Chaise eased his shirt up and placed her hand on his gun. The cold steel brushed against his skin as she quickly removed it and placed the butt of it in Bull's hand.

"Whatever you want, man," Bull responded casually. He faked a step to the side, quickly raised his arm and fired two shots in rapid succession. The bullets hit Rico once in the chest and once in the head. His limp body once again hit the floor and there was no way he would get up this time.

Bull grabbed Chaise in his arms again and when he finally looked up, he saw his entire team in place. Bull smirked at them. "Thanks for the help, guys."

"You had it under control," Rebel answered with a shit-eating grin.

"Yeah, you *needed* to handle this yourself, man," Reaper replied.

The thunder boomed and the lightning strikes crackled outside the window. Bull couldn't take his eyes off of Chaise—even for the howling wind or horizontal rain beating against the windows.

"We need to get you out of here," Bull said as he pulled the cover off the bed and wrapped it around her. The flimsy material of her nightgown would look like a second skin on her if she wore it in the rain. Bull wasn't about to share *that* view with any of his brothers.

"We need to get moving before the storm gets worse or we'll be stuck on this island until it passes," Shadow said.

Bull wrapped his arm around Chaise and led her out. "I know we still have things to talk about, but I'm not letting you go."

Chaise nodded but was so overwrought with mixed emotions she couldn't respond coherently. The main emotion she felt was an overwhelming joy of getting out of the whole sordid affair alive. She snuggled in close to Bull's side and allowed him to lead her out the front door and toward the dock.

As they moved past the outer perimeter of the property, a bolt of lightning struck close to the house. The popping and sizzling of electricity hung in the air for a few seconds before the house they had just left exploded into a huge fireball. Within seconds, the entire place was engulfed in flames and smaller explosions fired in sequence.

Chaise gasped and jumped out of Bull's embrace. His hand was fast but not as fast as her eye. He nonchalantly slipped a remote detonator into his pocket and gave her a feigned innocent look.

"Did you do that?" Chaise asked, pointing at the raging inferno behind them.

"I don't understand the question," Bull answered, telling Chaise all she needed to know.

They made it back to shore despite the choppy seas and whipping wind. An uncomfortable silence settled between Chaise, Bull, and Reaper as they stood on the dock, facing each other, not knowing exactly what to say or where to start.

Chaise broke the silence. "I don't know how I can ever thank you for everything. You saved my life," her voice cracked on the last word because everything that had happened suddenly caught up with her. Tears fell from her eyes and rolled down her cheeks.

She tried to quickly wipe them away but Bull pulled her into his embrace. He wrapped his thick arms around her and nuzzled his face in her hair. The bass timbre of his whispers made her weak in the knees and temporarily helped her forget where she was.

"I've got you, Chaise. You're mine and I'm never letting you go again. I was a fucking idiot for not stopping you before. Never again, baby," Bull promised in a hushed tone.

Chaise stayed glued to Bull for what felt like an eternity. She felt rather than saw that Noah was still standing beside them. She reluctantly pulled away from Bull's embrace but smiled up at him when he took her hand in his. He honestly didn't intend to let her get far from him.

Chaise turned to Noah and searched his eyes for a few moments before speaking. "You came for me. I don't know what to say except 'thank you,' but that's not enough. I'm so very grateful and forever indebted to you."

Noah's emotions raged in his eyes and in his heart that was about to beat out of his chest. His initial estrangement was from his overbearing, controlling, and domineering father, but he'd never considered the serious impacts his absence had on his siblings. Looking at his sister, he saw the one person who had always idolized him, imitated him, and loved him with her whole heart. The searing pain he felt in his chest was like someone had stabbed him with a hot knife.

She was right—he had reneged on his duty as her brother. He had left her behind. Even though he thought it was best for her at the time, he had let her down. She was thanking him for going to find her. She was somewhat surprised that he didn't leave her behind again.

And he couldn't blame her.

Noah shook his head, took a deep breath, and stepped toward Chaise. He opened his arms and held them out to the side, inviting her to hug him. That same gesture was what he used to do when she was little and would run out of the house to meet him after school.

The tears she had managed to hold back escaped as she flew into his arms. He wrapped his arms around her and picked her up off the ground. "I'm sorry, Chaise. I'm so fucking sorry for leaving you behind," Noah's voice pleaded with her for forgiveness.

Chaise shook her head and through her tears responded. "I've missed you so much, Noah. So much. I'm just so happy to have you back. I was afraid you wouldn't want to see me."

Noah crushed her to him as his heart broke from her words. "I've missed you every day, baby sister."

Bull watched them together, brother and sister reunited after so many years apart, and a nostalgic memory from long ago resurfaced. He remembered wishing he'd had a brother or sister when he was young. Then when he joined the Army and his best friends became his brothers, he felt the missing piece of his life had been found.

As he watched them—the man he loved like a brother and the woman with whom he had fallen in love—he knew his life was complete. There wasn't one event that he could pinpoint that had given him that feeling.

It was a culmination of all the nights Chaise spent in his house and in his arms. It was the laughs they shared and the fun she brought into his life. It was the possessive and protective part of him that only she summoned. It was in the way she gave all of herself to him—even when she tried to tell him the truth and he stopped her.

Had he been honest with himself at that point, he really didn't want to know the truth. He was truly happy for the first time in a long time and he didn't feel the need to know anything about her that he didn't already know from just being with her. He didn't want anything to ruin the good thing he had with her.

Noah released Chaise from his hold as John joined them in the covered area of the docks. John nodded at Chaise as he introduced himself as Bull's father. John's voice held genuine warmth when he added, "I'm glad to see you all made it back safely." Then, he looked around and asked, "Where's Rico? Did he get away?"

"Lightning struck twice in the same place. Damnedest thing I've ever seen," Bull said with a straight face and his Southern drawl securely in place. "Whole damn place went up like kindling. He didn't make it out."

John eyed him suspiciously for a moment but Bull kept his face neutral. John cut his eyes to Chaise, but she quickly looked away and saw agents swarming around the warehouse. She pointed toward the action and asked John, "What's happening over there?"

John turned and looked toward the direction she pointed. From his profile, Chaise could tell his thoughts were already on something else. She had effectively changed the direction of the conversation and avoided any questions of what had occurred on the island. She knew the questioning would come later regardless, but she needed a momentary reprieve.

"After Colton left to find you, I talked to a few more of the girls. They had some solid information I called in to my team to investigate. We were able to gather enough hard evidence to start making arrests. The girls are being taken to the hospital and their families are being notified," John explained.

"What about Aura? Ana's twin sister? I never found her!" Chaise exclaimed.

John chuckled lightly. "Aura is fine. You really gave me a run for my money over her, Chaise."

"What do you mean?" Reaper asked.

"Aura knew something had happened to her sister at Viboro Distributing —that's why she went to work there. But she got too close to the truth and they were about to take her. So, I moved Aura and her mother to a safe house. We erased their existence from the servers. We had to work fast, because while we were busy trying to hide them, someone else was busy finding the other girls' missing persons posters."

Shadow and Rebel cleared their throats nervously, knowing that they had accessed confidential, secure servers illegally. Neither of them would ever actually admit to it since their computers were secure and untraceable. John tried to hide his knowing smile but failed miserably.

Bull shot Chaise an apologetic look, knowing she had tried to convince him that she wasn't lying about Aura but he didn't believe her. He leaned over to her ear and asked, "If I promise to never doubt you again, would that make up me for not believing you?"

"It's a start," she countered. "But I have more imaginative ways of making you pay."

"That's a deal!" Bull's smile lit up his face and Chaise was again reminded of how he made her heart flutter. He suddenly turned serious as he asked, "Did they hurt you? Do we need to go to the hospital? I won't leave you."

Chaise stroked his cheek and jaw line as her heart melted at his offer. "No, nothing like that. Diego hit me but that was about the extent of it." She moved in close to him again, comforted in the crook of his arm. Her arms wrapped around his waist and she hugged him tightly.

Daylight began to break on the horizon, reminding Chaise that she'd only had a few minutes sleep in too many hours. She felt the tiredness creeping in and overcoming her. She yawned loudly. "Since I know the girls are being taken care of, I need to get some sleep."

The full meaning of her statement didn't dawn on her until she'd said it aloud. She had nowhere to go—she had been staying with Bull for the past couple of weeks. She couldn't go back to the condo Viboro had supplied her. Her last hotel room stay didn't end well, and if she admitted it, she was afraid to be alone again. But she wouldn't admit that to anyone.

"Am I free to go now?" Chaise asked John.

John nodded. "For now. You'll have to come in and answer some questions later." John took Chaise's cell phone number and promised to contact her later. Chaise thanked him and John left them to return to help the other DEA agents.

"I will take you … home," Bull's low, bedroom voice whispered in her ear. The promise inherent in his voice and in his words made her weak in the knees but not from lack of sleep. She was suddenly very awake.

Noah's voice held concern and regret. "Get some rest, little sis. I'd like to talk to you later, if that's okay. I have a lot of making up to do, too."

"I'd like that," Chaise replied sincerely. "I've missed you, Noah." Without a second thought, Chaise's arms wrapped around Noah's neck and she kissed his cheek. "I love you, big brother."

"I love you, too," Noah replied as he squeezed her to him. Before releasing her, he pinned his gaze on his friend. "Take care of my little sister, Bull."

"You don't have to tell me twice, Reap," Bull replied.

Once Bull and Chaise arrived at Bull's house, the sun had fully risen behind the dark, black clouds. The continuous torrential downpour continued with the occasional boom of thunder and crackle of lightning. Bull pulled his truck into the garage and, gathering her into his arms, carried Chaise into the house.

She shifted in his hold just enough to wrap her arms around his neck. She nuzzled her face against his neck, inhaling his masculine scent. All of the events seemed to catch up with her all at once. She felt strong and weak at the same time. She was happy and sad, guilty and unashamed, calm and irate—and she had no way to explain any of it.

But being back in Bull's arms felt … *right*. It felt like she was home, where she belonged, where she wanted to be, and where she was welcome and safe. She could blame it on extreme circumstances, and most people probably would anyway. But, she knew that when she was away from him, he was all she thought about. When she was taken, she knew he'd come for her and she put all of her faith in him.

I love him, she thought as the realization hit her like a runaway train.

Raising her head to look at him as he carried her to the shower, she kissed his cheek.

"Bull?"

"Yeah, baby, we're home. I'll help you shower then we'll take a long nap," he replied.

"I love you."

Bull stopped in mid-stride. He drew his face back to look at Chaise, his face twisted in bewilderment and his eyes narrowed to mere slits. Chaise didn't know what response she expected to see, but that clearly wasn't it. He looked like he wanted to tell her she misunderstood his intentions, that he didn't feel the same way about her, or simply that he didn't return the sentiment.

"I just wanted to tell you. After everything that's happened, I don't want to take it for granted that I'll have time to say the things I want to say," Chaise continued.

Bull put her feet down and stood fully facing her, studying her in his way that used to make her feel like she was a freak science experiment. Now, it just felt like her heart was shattering into a million pieces, splintering inside and cutting away at her. She refused to back down—she meant what she said regardless if he felt the same.

Chaise met his gaze and lifted her chin in an act of defiance. Bull had constructed a wall around his entire life, barely letting people in, but she knew she had penetrated that wall. He was too afraid to admit it but their ties ran deeper than a casual acquaintance.

"It's okay if you can't tell me you love me," she said, choosing her words carefully.

Bull shook his head, placed his hands on his hips, and looked down. Chaise watched as he took a deep breath, his massive chest contracting and expanding with air, then he blew it out in a huff. He was wrestling with something internally but she wasn't going to let him off the hook that easily.

"Colton, look at our lives. We've both been guarded because we were hurt at a young age. You've been with *my* brother all these years. *Your* father has been investigating my employer. Our families are back together because *we're* together. We have so many common ties between us. Are you fighting it? Or do you really not feel anything for me?"

"Chaise," Bull's voice was full of need, desire, longing, and just a hint of unease. His one word statement called to her—bidding her to touch him, feel him, and to make him feel her in return.

Chaise answered his request by stepping into him, aligning their bodies and slowly raising her lips to meet his. She ran her fingers through his hair until she reached the back of his head. She placed soft, chaste kisses on his lips until his arms wrapped around her and held her. She slowly licked the part in his lips, asking for permission, until he opened his mouth and granted her entrance.

He tasted even better than she remembered. Her fingers gripped his collar and she quickly pulled his shirt up and over his head, breaking their kiss for only that split second. Shirtless Bull was a wonder to behold, but she allowed her fingers to memorize every muscle striation, every groove, and every line on him.

Deftly unbuckling his belt and pants, Chaise pushed them down to his ankles. She let her hands glide over his thighs as she reached for the band of his boxer briefs that were perfectly molded to his body. Languidly pulling them down, she let her nails lightly scrape his skin until she reached his feet.

Kneeling before him with his impressive erection in perfect alignment, she wrapped her lips around the tip. Her tongue darted out and lightly licked the waiting bead of pure desire. Bull groaned and his hips involuntarily flexed, pushing forward, but Chaise stopped him. He looked down at her as she looked up from under her lashes. Her mischievous smile spread across her face, and before he could utter a word, she quickly took him fully into her mouth.

When he hit the back of her throat, Bull thought his knees would fold underneath him. The warmth of her mouth combined with the moistness was almost his undoing. But when her tongue found the underside of his manhood, his hands automatically flew to her head and he gripped her hair in his fingers.

"Damn, Chaise," he muttered, as he leaned against the wall and watched her intently. "Ah, baby, you have to stop. I love what you're doing, but I haven't even started with you yet, and I have a lot of plans."

Bull picked Chaise up, threw her over his shoulder and marched toward the shower. She squealed in laughter and Bull playfully spanked her ass cheek. Then he added, "The other side is jealous," as he spanked that cheek.

He undressed her, taking his time as he kissed, licked, nipped, and caressed every inch of her body. The bathroom was filled with steam from the running shower by the time he guided her into the tiled shower stall. The showerhead was large and Chaise felt like she was standing in the pouring rain. She let the hot water pour over her body, washing away the tension and the events of the past few days.

While Chaise stood under the waterfall with her eyes closed, Bull soaped up a washcloth and began washing her. She opened her eyes with the initial contact of his hand, but then closed them again and let him thoroughly pamper her. When he was finished, she let out a deep, contented sigh.

"Chaise," Bull stated.

"Yes," she replied with her standard answer when it came to Bull.

"I need to hear you scream my name now."

His hot breath fanned out across her core just before his tongue found her sensitive nub. He flicked his tongue across it before lightly scraping it with his teeth. Wrapping his arm around one leg behind her knee, he carefully lifted it until he placed it across his shoulder.

"Better hold on, Chaise," he said with confidence.

Moisture flooded to her already heated center in anticipation of his intentions. Chaise grabbed onto the top of the shower door just in time as his mouth reclaimed her, owned her, and devoured her. When his tongue delved deep inside her, she cried out in pleasure.

"Not enough, Chaise. I said I need to hear you scream my name," Bull demanded.

He increased his tempo and pressure with his next attack. He wrapped one arm around her ass and held her in place. His other hand trailed up her leg, up her thigh, and into her core. When his fingers found their mark, he dipped one finger partially inside her and spread her juices to her tender folds.

The sudden intrusion of his full finger inside her sent her spiraling. Her fingers gripped the door and, had he not been holding her up, her other knee would've completely given out. He moved his finger in and out of her in a quick pace, lightly scraping her inside and hitting the spot that caused her to see stars every time.

When he added his second finger, the mixture of how he filled, stretched, and consumed her pushed her closer and closer to the edge. He continued his attentions until he heard the sound that was like music to his ears.

"Colton!"

CHAPTER TWENTY-TWO

Chaise was like putty in his hands. Her body responded to him like no other's had before. It was as if she were made especially for him—to be adored, worshipped, and thoroughly sated by only his touch. He'd fought the feelings she evoked when she told him she loved him. Part of him wanted to respond, to tell her she was the best thing that had ever happened to him, and that he loved her, too.

But another part, a deeper part, told him to back off. The part of him that shut down in emotional situations and allowed his logic and reasoning to take control told him to let her go. His mind warred over the best course of action—take a chance by telling her the truth or keep it to himself and let her go?

"Don't think you're getting off that easily," he said to Chaise with a wicked grin as he turned off the water. "Pun intended. I'm not finished with you by a long shot."

Bull grabbed a towel and dried Chaise off first and then he led her into the bedroom. He placed her on the bed and covered her body with his.

"If you weren't so tired, this would be much different," he whispered in his bedroom voice. "I'd have you bent over this bed, watching in the mirror as I make you mine all over again. But for now, you need to feel me and I need to feel you."

Bull felt her eyes searching his, looking for answers and hoping for a different one than he'd previously given her. Dipping his head, their lips met with urgency. Their tongues danced, caressed, and melded together. Bull memorized her taste, her scent, and her sounds.

He knew every part of her body and mind. Still, he didn't think he could get enough of her even if he had more than one lifetime to spend with her. She had ingrained herself in his life, his head, and his home.

One lingering doubt remained in his thoughts. *Can I give her my heart?*

As he continued to kiss her, invading all her senses and making her crazy with desire, his fingers lightly brushed across her ribs, hips, and legs until he wrapped them around the back of her knees. Pulling her legs up, he fully seated himself between them and brushed the tip of his erection across her sensitive nub. Her hips rose and her hands pulled on him, trying to demand he take her immediately.

"Chaise, do you want me?"

"Mmhmmm," she answered.

He brushed his erection harder across her moist folds, but still just barely out of reach of where she wanted him to be.

"That wasn't an answer. I asked you a question. Do you want me?"

"*Yes*, I want you, Colton," Chaise replied with a more urgent, demanding tone.

With a sudden, fluid movement, Bull fully entered her, gliding inside her to the hilt. Stretched and completely filled, Chaise cried out in response to his sudden intrusion. Bull pushed into her over and over, loving every time she screamed out his name, clawed his back, and soaked him with her essence. The feel of her hands on him again after what felt like an eternity apart was heaven.

"That's my baby," his voice rumbled low in her ear. He reached down in between their bodies, placing his thumb over her nub, and pressed in small circles as he continued to pump in and out of her. "This is mine, Chaise. Mine. And I don't share. Your body knows it belongs to me now."

His words made her blood turn to red-hot lava in her veins. His declaration of ownership of her body confused her. Questions of why he would say she was his if he didn't love her crowded her mind. She wanted to be his, but she wasn't so sure he wanted to be hers.

"I need to hear you scream my name one more time before I'm done," he said. "Are you ready?"

"Mmm, yes!"

Releasing his hold on her legs, he pushed his arms underneath her hips, raising them off the bed slightly but giving him deeper penetration. Their bodies were tightly pressed together, their eyes locked on each other's, as he pounded harder and deeper into her.

The sensations he created in her were overwhelming. The dull pull that started low in her abdomen became strong spasms, pulling her closer and closer to the edge. She felt the sweet tension building more and more, knowing that her body could only take so much before she completely exploded.

And that was exactly what he wanted.

His eyes stayed glued to hers, daring her to even try to look away from him at that moment. They were both on the edge, holding on by a bare thread that would break at any moment. He knew all too well how to make her body hum.

When she couldn't take anymore, he felt her wet, inner walls tighten around him. As she quivered around him, the ripples in her muscles caressed, stroked, and brought him to ecstasy with her. He emptied himself deep inside her as he stilled his hips. She could feel every pulse of his manhood as her body continued to milk him.

"Fuck, baby, you feel so good," his deep voice drawled.

"Wow," Chaise gasped, drawing the one syllable word out to five or six. "That just never gets old."

Bull chuckled as he placed sweet kisses on her face and his thumbs stroked her cheeks lovingly. Those intimate moments weren't all that made Chaise think Bull was hiding his feelings from her and from himself. He had been a rock for her through the whole ordeal. Even when he had fucked up and let her leave, he came after her and saved her.

As he continued lovingly lavishing attention on her, she felt him invading her heart just a little more. And a little more. She pushed away the doubts that tried to enter her mind. Her body was well spent, completely sated, and drained of all fluids, thanks to Bull. She needed sleep to be able to function in any reasonable capacity.

Bull rolled to her side, pulled the covers up, and positioned her to spoon her from behind. He draped his arm over her body, pulling her close to him as he nuzzled his face into her hair. Sleep overtook them and, for the next several hours, Chaise had only good dreams, safe in the arms of her Bull.

The next morning, Bull awoke to an empty bed where Chaise should have been. He sat up and strained his ears to listen for voices. Hearing a faint murmuring, he put his shorts on and walked to the kitchen. Chaise, Brianna, and Noah were sitting at the table drinking coffee. He immediately noted that Chaise was fully showered and dressed. Her suitcase sat on the floor beside her.

"What's going on in here?" Bull asked, intentionally keeping his voice calm, but his eyes told of the storm that raged inside. He spoke to the group but his question was undeniably directed at Chaise.

"Just having breakfast with my sister," Noah replied as he squeezed Chaise's hand. "It's been way too long."

"We were just talking about Chaise coming to stay with us for a while until she can find her own place nearby. We thought that would give Chaise and Noah some time to reconnect. What do you think about that plan, Bull?" Brianna asked, fully aware of what she was doing. She was blatantly testing him and making him test himself.

"I think that's great for Chaise and Noah. They need to reconnect," Bull replied as he stared a hole through Chaise. "Does she really need to live with you to do that?"

"Well, we're closing the case. The arrests have been made. They have

Ricardo Cordova in custody along with the rest of his crew. Rico is dead. She doesn't need constant protection any longer," Noah explained as if it should be simple to understand.

From the corner of his eye, Bull saw Brianna attempting to hide her smile. He couldn't remove his gaze from Chaise long enough to shoot Brianna a dirty look. Bull moved toward Chaise, like a tiger stalking his prey. He moved with lethal stealth and his sights were set on her.

"Can you two excuse us for a minute? I need to talk to Chaise. Make yourselves at home," Bull said as he pulled Chaise up from her chair and out of the kitchen. He didn't slow down until he reached the bedroom. He physically sat Chaise on the bed then turned to close the door.

He paced the floor in front of her, his face showing the turmoil he had tried to hide in front of their company.

"Colton, talk to me," Chaise finally said.

He suddenly stopped pacing and fully faced her. His face was red and his eyes were narrowed in anger, "Why are you leaving me again?"

"I'm not leaving you, Colton," Chaise answered calmly. "I will still see you. What exactly did you expect would happen? Did you think I would just move in with you permanently?"

"No. I don't know. I don't know what I expected. I know I'm not ready for you to leave," he answered truthfully.

"You don't love me, Colton. I think we both know that. We haven't been together long and the time we have been has been under extreme circumstances. I think it's best that I find my own place now and we can still see each other...We'll just see where it goes," Chaise said quietly.

Bull had to concede that it was way too soon for them to consider living together. What he couldn't figure out was why he felt like she was abandoning him by getting her own place. It made sense for her to live at his house when she was in trouble and he had already gotten accustomed to having her there with him. He rationalized that simply enjoying her company was not a basis for a permanent address change.

So, why couldn't he shake the feeling that their relationship would drastically change when she left?

Unable to come up with an alternative plan, Bull sighed and conceded. "Well, it'll be good for you and Reaper to spend some time together. You and Brianna can get to know each other and look at apartments together."

Chaise swallowed hard and simply nodded her head in response. She knew it would be hard, but she never imagined that it would be nearly impossible for her to willingly leave his house. A small part of her had hoped he would be more receptive to the idea and give her a reason to leave. No such luck with that.

"Well, they're waiting so we should get back in there," Chaise finally said. They walked out of the bedroom in silence. Both of them carried a heavy heart and a lingering doubt that their relationship would survive the regular day-to-day grind.

When Bull rounded the corner into his kitchen, the breath was knocked out of him. Brianna was sitting in Noah's lap. Noah had his one arm wrapped around Brianna and the other hand was on her slightly rounded stomach. They were whispering to each other, their faces nearly touching, and the smiles on their faces conveyed their deep love for the other.

Bull finally had to admit to himself that he wanted that kind of relationship, too. He wanted someone to call his own. Someone with whom to share his life, to give his love, and have a family. He knew he wanted it, but he didn't know if he could actually go through with it.

Noah had his heart ripped out when he thought Brianna was dead. His best friend didn't really live for the three years that she was gone. Bull's mother never really went on with her life after John left. Michelle waited for John, much like Noah seemed to wait for Brianna. Those couples had found their once-in-a-lifetime love and had their hearts broken for it.

Bull had been disappointed, hurt, and scarred when John left him. He'd never really gotten over that feeling of giving all his love only to have it discarded like common trash. He seemed to be the only one holding on to old hurts, though.

Noah was so happy that Brianna was still alive, there was never any other option but for them to be together. Michelle loved John so much that there was never any other choice but to wait for him to be in her life full time.

Bull was pulled from his thoughts when Noah and Brianna sensed they were not alone. When Noah looked up, he caught the look on Bull's face, saw Chaise's long, gloomy face, and instantly knew what had occurred. He whispered into Brianna's ear and smiled warmly at her. She nodded and stood up to face Bull and Chaise.

"Ready to go, my new sister?" Brianna asked cheerfully.

"I think so," Chaise answered, uncertainty prolific in her words.

"Let's go get you settled in," Noah replied, excited to have his sister back in his life. "I had your car taken to my house."

"Thank you," Chaise replied but couldn't take her eyes off of Bull.

The tension between Bull and Chaise was thick in the air, depleting the oxygen in the room and making it harder and harder for her to breathe. She felt the panic welling up inside her again, threatening to cripple her where she stood.

Chaise thought she'd managed to put it behind her when she was in the warehouse cell. She realized she had focused on the young girls and how they needed her to be strong for them. She had no choice but to push down her own fears and do whatever it took to help them. She wasn't feeling that strength inside her at that moment.

"Colton, I don't know what to say other than thank you for everything you've done for me. You took me in, protected me, helped me, and saved my life. I didn't give you any reason to help me, but you went out of your way to do it anyway. You're a good man—you have a good heart," Chaise said, fighting back tears and trying to keep her panic from consuming her.

She was really leaving the safe haven she'd found in Bull's home. Safe in his arms.

Chaise lifted up on her tiptoes and wrapped her arms around his neck. His arms wrapped around her waist but the look on his face remained pensive. Covering his mouth with hers, she kissed him like she would never see him again. She poured all of her heart, all of her love, and all of her feelings into the kiss, willing him to feel it and return it to her.

When she pulled away from him, the only sign that the kiss had affected him was the furrow in his brow. Not knowing how to take that, she picked up her suitcase and turned to follow Noah and Brianna out the front door.

Bull walked them out and watched them drive away. When they were out of sight, he walked back in his house, wandered around, and recalled all the moments he'd spent with Chaise. He walked to the bedroom and stared at the bed. He still smelled her sweet perfume scent, heard the echoes of her moans of pleasure at his hand, and felt the love she had given him. Walking back to the den, he punched a hole in the drywall.

CHAPTER TWENTY-THREE

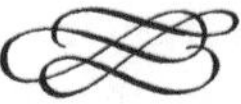

Three days. Chaise hadn't seen Bull in three days and she was going mad. She'd tried to ask Noah and Brianna about him in a round about way, but neither of them gave her any real information about him. She had a suspicion they were both acting and avoiding telling her what they knew she wanted to know. He hadn't called or come by to see her and she was miserable. All they would tell her was that Noah had sent him off on an assignment as a security escort for some corporate CEO.

Noah had to go into the downtown office of Steele Security for the day and Brianna had hotel business to attend to for her father. Chaise couldn't stand being cooped up in the house any longer. She grabbed her keys and left a note on the kitchen counter letting them know she had gone out.

Just getting out and driving around in the warm, Miami air made her feel better. She had been avoiding going back to the luxury condominium Viboro Distributing had set her up with but decided she couldn't put it off any longer. She had to pack the rest of her belongings and start looking for her own place. She already felt like a third wheel in the home of the newlyweds.

"Hi, Paul," she called to the security guard as she pulled up to the gate.

"Hello, Miss Steele! Long time, no see," he smiled warmly. "What brings you back here?"

"I have some personal belongings left in the condo, Paul. I just need to run up and finish packing. Can I drop my keys off with you when I'm finished?"

"Sure thing," he replied genially as he opened the gate for her. "Let me know if you need any help with anything at all."

"Thank you. I appreciate that," she replied as she pulled through the gate.

Chaise had been in the condo for almost an hour, packing her clothes and various other items, when the hairs on the back of her neck suddenly stood at attention. She felt the electricity in the air change and knew she wasn't alone. Turning quickly to look behind her, she shrieked as she took a few steps back.

"What are you doing here?" she demanded, fear and anger mixed in her voice.

"I'm here for you. What else?" the suave, Spanish accent answered.

"They arrested you. How did you get out?" Chaise asked.

"It's good to have many different kinds of friends, Miss Steele," he answered.

"Ricardo, you need to leave right now. The security guard knows I'm here and he will be here to check on me any minute now," she lied.

Ricardo smiled knowingly. "I don't think so, Chaise. You see, Chaise, Paul works for me. He called me the instant you showed up here."

Chaise turned and ran toward the door, leaving her packed suitcases behind. As she reached for the doorknob, two very large, very scary men grabbed her from behind. One of the men grabbed her upper arm and squeezed, tightening his grip on her and leaving finger-shaped bruises in his wake. She twisted and turned, trying to break his hold, but that only made her arm hurt worse.

"I am going to allow you to leave here for one reason only. I want the flash drive with all the information you gathered from Viboro and you're going to bring it to me," Ricardo explained.

"Why would I do that?" Chaise asked.

Ricardo pinned her with a look of pure evil in his eyes. "Because I have Aura. If you don't show up, I will kill her and feed her body to the sharks. Then, I will do the same to everyone else you know. No one will be safe."

Chaise believed him.

"You will be followed. If you tell anyone else, or if anyone follows you … Well, you know what will happen. Don't you, Chaise?"

"Yes," she replied meekly.

"Good girl," he replied sardonically, as though he were praising as dog. "Come back here when you have it."

Ricardo and his men watched her leave. She refused to turn her back to them again as she backed out of the apartment.

"You know she'll go get her brother and his team," one of the men said to Ricardo.

"I'm counting on it," Ricardo answered.

Chaise ran all the way to her car and shot Paul a dirty look as she tore out of the parking area. He had the audacity to smile and wave at her as she drove away. Taking a page from Bull's playbook, she flung her hand out of the window and gave Paul the middle finger salute.

Grabbing her cell phone from her purse, she called Aura and Ana's mother first. When Gabriela answered the phone, Chaise immediately knew Ricardo had told the truth. "Chaise! Chaise! Where is Aura? Where is my daughter?"

"Ricardo Cordova has her, Gabriela. I will get her back. I know what he wants," Chaise explained.

After several minutes of trying to console the frantic woman, Chaise disconnected and immediately called Noah.

"Noah, do you have my flash drive? The one with all the evidence against the Cordovas on it?" Chaise asked.

"No, John took it as evidence. Why?" Noah asked suspiciously.

"Are the files from it still on the computer?"

"Yes. What's going on, Chaise?"

"I need a copy of it. If I bring a flash drive, can you copy the files for me?" she asked, avoiding his question.

"Sure, come on by," Noah answered.

After an hour of Noah's brand of interrogation tactics, Chaise was finally leaving the Steele Security building with the data-packed flash drive. She was a nervous wreck just thinking about going back to that condo alone.

Chaise sat in her car, in the parking lot, for what seemed like an eternity. She played out every scenario she could dream up in her head but they all ended in disaster. She knew it had to be a trap–Ricardo wasn't stupid enough to believe he could simply take the documents and his case would be dropped.

She leaned over and put her forehead on her steering wheel. Anxiety and uncertainty flooded her senses so she just solely focused on breathing. Drawing from her memories, she imagined Bull's protective arms wrapped around her, his possessive voice telling her that she was his, and felt his masculine aura giving her strength. Lifting her head, she fished her cell phone from her purse.

"Noah? I need help," she confessed.

The deep, rumbling chuckled reverberated through her phone. "Yeah, little sis, I know. I'm waiting for you to leave so I can tail you."

"What do you know, exactly?" Chaise asked, her hackles now raised in suspicion.

"I know all kinds of things. But right now, I know you need my help and I'm not letting you go alone. They don't need to see me with you, though, so just do what you had planned to do and know that I'm with you," Noah reassured.

Chaise hesitated for a second too long, her mind asking where Bull was and why he wasn't protecting her. "It'll be fine, little sis. No one will hurt you. You can trust me," Noah urged.

"I know, Noah. It's just difficult for me. I'm going now." Chaise hung up and pulled out onto the street, heading back to the last place she really wanted to go. She had some modicum of relief in the knowledge that the head of one of the best security firms in the world was close behind her.

Chaise repeatedly searched for Noah in her rearview mirror, trying to make sure she didn't lose him at a red light. She never found him in all the Miami traffic, though, and had to concede that if he knew what he was doing, she would never find him in the crowd of cars. Ricardo said she was being followed by one of his men, too, but she didn't see them, either.

She didn't even stop to talk to Paul when she entered the security gate. His sneer was enough to turn her stomach, and though she wasn't normally a violent person, she considered using torture tactics on him that would make waterboarding seem appealing. When she was past him, she hung her arm out of her window and flipped him off again—just for good measure.

Before exiting her car in the parking garage, Chaise searched her car for a tissue to wipe her eyes. She had held back the tears as long as she could but had lost the battle. Determined to not show her weakness, she wanted to hide any remnants of her mini-breakdown before Ricardo saw her.

When she opened her glove compartment, she gasped in relief. Bull must have hidden the Ruger LCR .357 she used at the shooting range in her car because it was staring her in the face. She grabbed the low profile, concealable revolver and slipped it in the back band of her pants.

She wiped her palms on her pants and made the lonely walk to the elevators. She still hadn't seen Noah anywhere but she had to trust him to handle the situation the way he knew best. Chaise tried to keep her thoughts on Aura and the possibility of saving her.

Once she reached the condo door, she took a deep breath and tentatively opened the door. The foyer opened up into the large living area, giving her a good vantage point to see where the enemy was waiting. She quickly slipped the gun out of her waistband and slid it behind a large flower vase on the table just inside the entrance.

"Ah, Chaise. So nice of you to join us," Ricardo's smooth voice called out. His men chuckled at Ricardo's sick joke. Aura was sitting in a chair that had been moved from the dining room. Chaise realized Aura's hands and feet were taped to the chair arms and legs. She also realized that without Noah's help, neither of them would get out of the situation alive.

"You didn't leave me any choice, Ricardo," she replied sarcastically. She reached into her pocket and removed the flash drive. "Here, take this and let her go," she said, extending her palm to offer the evidence.

Ricardo laughed heartily. "I love that you are so trusting. I don't need that, Chaise. I have you—that's all I need."

"I don't understand," Chaise stalled. "What do you mean?"

Ricardo smiled at her but his eyes held no mirth. They were black, cold, and void of compassion. "I think you know exactly what I mean. You're very clever."

"Ricardo, you asked me for the data I found at Viboro Distributing. I got that for you and I came back here on my own. Now, take what you asked for and let Aura go," she replied with a stern voice.

"No. Neither of you are leaving here alive, Chaise. You will pay for what you did to Rico. Your boyfriend will pay, too," he hissed.

Ricardo seemed to have suddenly snapped. He started rambling nonsensical words, muttering to himself and pacing back and forth. Fire danced in his eyes and he flexed and contracted his fists over and over. As he passed one of his men, he grabbed the gun from the man's side and pointed it at Aura's head.

"You can watch her die, Chaise. That'll be a good punishment for you since you care about her so much," Ricardo laughed maniacally.

"She hasn't done anything to you, Ricardo. I'm the one you want. Let her go and do what you have to do to me," Chaise bargained.

Ricardo studied Chaise for a moment before he apparently had an epiphany. His face lit up and a smile tugged at the corner of his mouth. He moved the gun away from Aura's head and signaled to one of the men to cut her bonds.

"You can go now, Aura. If you stay, you will be shot," Ricardo said dryly.

Aura gave Chaise a panicked look before Chaise assured her. "It's okay, Aura. Get out of here. Now."

Aura reluctantly left and Chaise exhaled when she heard the door click and knew that Aura was safely out of Ricardo's reach. He walked toward Chaise and grabbed her by her shirt. He shoved the gun against her temple and spat his intentions out at her.

"I'm going to shoot you. Right here. *Right in the fucking head.* Then, I'm going to hang your body off the side of the balcony. *Like a fucking beacon for your boyfriend to find you.* And when he finds you, I will give him enough time to cut your dead, broken body down before I shoot *him* in the fucking head, too."

Ricardo walked her backward toward the balcony. His gun hand was shaking with excitement and anticipation of carrying out his evil plan. When Chaise's back hit the glass door, she prepared for the worst. Noah hadn't made it inside yet and it would be too late for her.

All the things she wished she'd said to Bull suddenly rushed to the forefront of her thoughts. She was scared beyond the capacity of rational thought as she faced the certainty that she was about to die. Coping with that fact was more than overwhelming, but adding unrequited love and longing for Bull to the equation was downright debilitating.

The tears rolled unchecked down her face as she watched the madness grow in Ricardo's eyes. "Can you give him a message from me first?" She didn't know where she found her voice, but there was something she had to say to Colton.

"Oh, please, let me deliver your final words to him. *Such poetic justice,*" he crooned.

"Tell him … Tell him that I love him and I wish, more than anything in the world, that I had stayed at his house. I don't care that I only knew him a few weeks. I don't need more time than that to know he's the only one for me. I only wish we had more time together," Chaise said.

"Oh, that is so sweet," Ricardo said mockingly. "But I will gladly relay your message just before I blow his fucking head off."

"Say your goodbyes to me now, Chaise," Ricardo said as he opened the large, sliding glass door behind Chaise.

"You say goodbye, asshole," the deep booming voice came out of nowhere. The distinct sound of the gun clicking, indicating it was ready to fire, immediately followed. "Put that fucking gun down and face me like a real man," Bull challenged.

Ricardo's head jerked around and found his men on the floor, unconscious, and Bull had his gun leveled on his head. He spun around, pulling Chaise with him and using her body as a shield from Bull's aim.

Bull kept advancing on Ricardo, his arm fully extended and his deadly aim still fixed on the spot between Ricardo's eyes. There was no way Bull would allow Ricardo to hurt Chaise or to walk away from the scene alive. He knew Ricardo would never stop his cat and mouse game and there was no way in hell Bull would let him threaten Chaise ever again.

"Your choice, man. You escaped from jail and the Feds have been looking for you. They're on their way now. They can either take you away in handcuffs or in a fucking body bag. My choice would be the latter," Bull threatened.

"You won't shoot me with your precious girlfriend in front of me. You might miss and hit her. We can't have that now, can we?" Ricardo asked as he leaned his face into Chaise's.

His tongue darted out and licked the side of her face as Bull watched in disgust. "She's so sweet. No wonder you want her back so badly. Maybe I should have some fun with her before I kill her. I would let you watch, but I'm not into that. I will let you live long enough to hear her screams, though."

"Over *your* dead body," Bull said menacingly, taking another step forward as he prepared for his next move.

"Chaise, baby," Bull said soothingly, effectively getting her attention as he kept his eyes and gun trained on Ricardo. "Remember what I told you I'd do to you if you hadn't been so tired that day? I need you to do that right now."

Understanding dawned on her and she knew this was her best chance at escaping without risking Bull being shot or killed. She jerked her body forward, bending at the waist with all the force she could muster.

The sudden movement caught Ricardo off guard and he was momentarily dazed when she slipped out of his grip. He was left exposed and Bull took the opportunity to end their standoff immediately. The bullets hit Ricardo in the chest before the sound of rapid gunfire registered in his brain. The blunt force of the bullets sent Ricardo flying backward, out onto the balcony, and over the railing.

Bull lowered his weapon and rushed to Chaise. He gathered her in his arms and held her tightly to him as she cried. Her whole body shook with an overdose of adrenaline and fear. She grabbed him with all her might and held onto him as if he were her only lifeline on a sinking ship.

"Well, looks like our work is done here," Noah said, appearing out of nowhere. "You did good, little sister. Although, next time, don't give up your gun so easily." He placed the .357 on the table beside Bull and Chaise before clapping Bull on the shoulder.

Rebel and Shadow were suddenly standing behind Bull, both with smiles splitting their faces in two. They seemed to be laughing with each other over some private joke.

"What's so funny, guys?" Noah asked.

"We're just being stupid, Reap. We were laughing about how it sounds when you sing, *'Chaise and Bull, sitting in a tree. F-U-C-.*"

The look on Reaper's face stopped them cold for a split second and then they both doubled over with laughter.

"Shit man, I forgot she was your sister for a minute there. Sorry, dude," Rebel said between fits of laughter.

CHAPTER TWENTY-FOUR

It was dark by the time they finished with all the police questions and paperwork. Bull led Chaise to his truck and drove her straight to his house. He didn't ask her first. He didn't give her an option of going anywhere else.

And he had no intentions of letting her leave again. Ever. He had claimed her as his own.

Bull helped her out of his truck and walked her inside, his hand in his possessive spot on her lower back. Chaise expected him to lead her to the bedroom, as he normally did after an intense situation and he couldn't express himself any other way. But he surprised her by steering her toward the couch instead.

This is new, she thought.

Bull sat down and pulled her down onto his lap. She fit perfectly in the bend of this arm and the crook of his shoulder. She inhaled his purely all-Bull, masculine and sandalwood scent. She had recently associated that scent with love and safety. It was Bull's unique aroma that she wanted to bottle and keep all to herself.

"Chaise, baby, look at me," he asked softly. She raised her head and met his gaze. The worry in his eyes melted her heart. He was concerned about her and was being as gentle as Bull knew how to be.

"What you did in the condo was so brave. I was amazed at your courage. I am so proud of you—you got Aura out of there and to safety. You willingly took her place," he continued.

All the intense feelings were building up inside her again. She was thankful that a panic attack wasn't one of those feelings. They never happened when she was in Bull's arms. She had a sudden feeling of alarm, however, when he narrowed his eyes and firmly set his jaw before he continued.

Through gritted teeth, he finished. "*Don't. Ever. Fucking. Do. That. Again.* I thought I was going to lose you, Chaise. I thought he was going to shoot you before I could get you away from him."

He crushed her to him as both of his muscled arms wrapped around her. Chaise could barely breathe under the weight of his embrace. But, she wouldn't complain about it even if she were able to speak. She thought to herself, *'This is home. This is where I belong.'* She had already decided she would wait for Bull to love her in return. It was better to be with him and be the object of his desire and affections than to keep living without him at all.

"Promise me. *Swear to me* that you'll never do that again," Bull demanded. "I watched my mom lose my dad. I watched Reaper lose Brianna. It killed them both. Even though they kept going, the spark that gave them life died when they lost their true love. I don't know if I'm as strong as they are. I don't know if I could stand losing you and I never want to find out.

"I heard what you said to Ricardo—your message to me. You have no idea how fucking hard that was to stand there and listen to you say your goodbyes. Your final words would've been confessing your love for me, Chaise. I still can't believe that. You didn't ask for anything else," he said sincerely.

"I didn't want anything else, Colton. I knew he wouldn't let me go. I knew Noah had followed me but I didn't see him anywhere, so I thought he would get there too late. I just needed you to know how I felt," she explained.

"How do you feel, Chaise?" he asked purposefully.

"I love you, Colton. I know it's too soon but I meant what I said. I don't need more time to know there's no one else for me."

"I love you, too, baby," he whispered, his mouth hovering just above hers.

His lips lightly brushed against hers as he spoke, sending cold chills down her spine and an intense tingling feeling in other more important regions. His words finally caught up with her senses.

"You love me?" she asked hopefully.

"I love you," Bull answered resolutely. "I have never said those words to anyone outside my family before you. I will never say them to another woman. You're it for me, too, Chaise. I'm yours just as much as you are mine."

"Wait a minute. Noah said you were off on an assignment. Where have you been? How did you know I was even there?" Chaise asked, narrowing her eyes at him.

Bull cleared his throat before smiling mischievously at her. "Well, I was on assignment, but *you* were my assignment," he confessed. "We knew Ricardo had escaped from federal custody and it was only a matter of time before he came after you. I was right in thinking that something was wrong with that condo. They had security cameras hidden inside so they could watch everything that happened there. Brad happened to come across the feed—while he was surfing the Internet," Bull smiled as he lied, "so we were able to keep an eye on the place.

"When we received word that Aura was missing, we knew there was no way you wouldn't help her. So, we arranged to be there with you."

Chaise leaned into him, grabbed his face in her hands, and thoroughly kissed him. Straddling him, she moved her mouth to his jaw line and then on to his neck. She worked her way up to his ear and whispered seductively to him. "Remember what you said you'd do if I wasn't so tired?"

She felt his hands tighten on her back in anticipation of what she'd say next. The very thought of him being revved up over her gave her the courage she needed.

"What if it wasn't bending me over the bed? What if it was bending me over the couch instead? There's a mirror right there," she cooed.

Chaise screamed, as she was suddenly airborne while Bull hopped over the back of the couch with her in tow. "That is one thing you'll never have to ask me twice, my love."

Within seconds, Bull had them both stripped naked and the standing mirror positioned exactly where he wanted it. He stepped into her, pressing his front to her back, as he moved her hair to the side. "I will go slower next time, but right now, I just want to feel you."

"You're taking too long, Colton. We really need to talk about your lack of focus," Chaise playfully chided him.

His hand went to the center of her back and he pushed her head down and over the couch. "Now I can see your face. You know what I want to hear, Chaise."

"Your name, screamed from the rooftop for all the neighbors to hear," she replied.

"Damn straight," he answered before he pushed into her without warning. She screamed with delight at the full sensation he created in her. "I don't think the neighbors at the end of the street heard you. I better up my game."

Before she could respond with something equally smartass, he made good on his promise. And so did she.

~

Four weeks later, the whole gang was at Noah and Brianna's house for a cookout. Brianna's tiny baby bump had grown into a more noticeable protrusion and Noah couldn't keep his hands off of her stomach.

"Noah, if you don't let me walk without you being attached to my stomach, I'm going to scream," Brianna laughed.

"You are walking close to dangerous weapons. What if you hurt my baby?" Noah replied sincerely.

"It's called a spatula, Noah, and it's not a dangerous weapon." Brianna bent at the waist from laughter.

"Hmph," was Noah's only response.

Chaise watched the two of them together and tried to reconcile the story Bull had told her about Brianna's disappearance. She couldn't imagine those two not being together for three years. They were so obviously made for each other.

Bull had said that their spark had died when they were apart and that reference just clicked as she watched her big brother with his pregnant wife. Anyone could see that Brianna was Noah's greatest strength and biggest weakness. And Noah was Brianna's as well. One didn't exist without the other.

Bull got up to get them both another drink and Noah sat down beside Chaise. "What are you thinking about, little sister?"

"About you and Brianna. Colton told me about what happened with you two. The three years apart," Chaise's voice trailed off when she saw the shadow cross his face at the memory. The spark was extinguished for that split second.

"I was gone from your life much longer than that, little sister," he said apologetically.

His voice held so much regret and remorse that Chaise's heart broke for him. She'd been so young when he left and she had only focused on how hard it had been on her. That line of thinking had continued her whole life. She'd never even considered that he might not have wanted to be separated from her.

"I have you back now. That's what matters, Noah. I'm never letting you leave me again, though. Losing you was hard enough the first time. I can't do it again," she told him.

"Ditto."

"You and Brianna are perfect together. I love her, too," Chaise said as she watched Brianna playfully teasing Bull.

"We were meant to be. I firmly believe that," Noah said. "But, it seems that you and Bull are pretty firm in your relationship, too."

"Yeah, I think we are. I love him. I can't imagine my life without him—as cliché as that sounds," Chaise laughed.

"It's not cliché if it's true. It is for me and I had to live my life without her for three years. It was the worst three years of my life," Noah said as he looked at Brianna. It was as if Brianna could feel Noah's eyes on her because she looked over at him at the same time. Brianna smiled warmly and mouthed *I love you* to him from across the deck.

"He says he loves me. He shows it, too. I've never felt more at home than I do with him. He protects me, makes me feel safe and loved," Chaise said as she watched Bull with adoring eyes.

"You love him," Noah stated.

"I do, Noah. I love him very much," Chaise admitted.

"That's all I need to know," Noah said as he stood. "Better get back to cooking. My pregnant wife needs to feed my baby."

"I heard that," Brianna called from across the deck, causing Noah to laugh in response.

Chaise laughed and as she looked over at Brianna, her eyes met Bull's. The heated look he always had for her held something more that night. She couldn't quite put her finger on it but she knew something was on his mind. She had already tried to get him to talk, but Fort Lanier was closed up tight.

Noah turned the outside speakers on and soft music filtered through the air. The sun was setting and the sparkling rays bounced off the rippling water of their expansive pool. Noah had strung small, white lights around the deck and the pool so that as the sun disappeared, the lights twinkled like stars and created a romantic atmosphere.

They talked and laughed as they ate, making up funny names for the baby, much to Noah's chagrin. At one point, he declared his baby as off limits for any conversation because they refused to keep their comments within his guidelines.

"Don't listen to them, baby. Daddy will kick their asses for you," Noah said to Brianna's stomach before cutting his eyes to the others. Laughter erupted all around and Chaise watched them, longing for her own family one day.

Bull reached over and took Chaise's hand in his. She looked at him when she felt his lips on the back of her hand. She could feel the love radiating from his intense stare. It was more than the sexual, take-charge Bull that she knew and loved. It was the man behind the mask looking at her at that moment.

It had taken them a while to get to that point. She'd had to endure several bouts of insecurity with him and their new love. But, that moment, the way he was looking at her, the way he was literally loving her with his eyes, and that he was doing it in front of others made it all worth the wait.

She knew without a doubt that they were destined to be together. There were too many links, too many ties that bound them together, for it to be any other way. While she was musing over their destined fate, Bull leaned in and kissed her lips so sweetly.

"Stop over thinking it, Chaise. I love you, baby. I'm not going anywhere. Ever," he promised.

"I believe you. Because you keep your promises," she replied. "I love you, too. More than anything."

Chaise went inside to help Brianna clean their dinner dishes while the men stayed outside to clean up around the grill. She sincerely enjoyed spending time with Brianna, getting to know her, and finding out new things about her brother. And about Colton.

Brianna told Chaise about their time in the Middle East and how she got to know Bull, Rebel, Shadow and, of course, Reaper. Chaise wasn't surprised to hear about how Bull acted when Brianna showed up after being dead for three years. She imagined Bull felt very betrayed and abandoned all over again. The fact that he forgave Brianna and still called her his sister was a miracle in itself.

"He's crazy about you, ya know?" Brianna said to Chaise. "That man loves you so much. I've never seen him like this in all the years I've known him."

"I am crazy about him, too. Maybe it seems too fast? But it just feels right. I know there's no one else for me," Chaise explained.

"It was fast for Noah and me, too. I spent time with him in the desert and things progressed rapidly, even when I thought there was no future for us. But after he was discharged, he showed up here in Miami, at a bar where I was celebrating my birthday with some friends, and we've been together ever since. Well, with the exception of the three years when I was dead, but he was still my only one then, too. When you know, you know."

A little while later, Bull and Chaise left the Steele's Miami mansion and headed home. That word had seemed so foreign to Bull at first. But now that the case was closed, and his dad was retired and back with his mother, *home* sounded better and better. The best part was that Chaise considered his house as her home. As *their* home.

When they got home, Bull let Chaise walk in the house first. She immediately thought it was strange because he always insisted on making sure the house was secure before he let her go in. But it was late and they were both tired so she didn't ask about it.

When she stepped inside, she gasped loudly and her hands flew to her face. She looked around, wide-eyed, and her jaw hung open. Her heart was pounding and her pulse was racing. She couldn't believe what she saw in front of her.

There must have been one hundred lit candles scattered throughout the house, their flames flickering and casting shadows on the walls. There were red rose petals lining a path from the garage door, through the kitchen to the den. The den held dozens of flowers in various sizes and arrangements. Soft, romantic music filled the air and set the mood.

In the center of the den sat a table with a large, white box wrapped with a huge, red velvet bow. Chaise turned to find Bull standing just behind her, watching her every move and gauging her reaction.

"When? How?" she stammered.

Bull smiled. "I would never reveal my methods, babe."

Chaise admired the different flowers, taking time to smell them and appreciate their beauty. Her eyes kept straying to the box that waited for her. Bull smiled, knowing it was killing her to wait. She eventually made her way to it and looked at him for permission.

"For me?"

"For you, baby," Bull answered sweetly.

Chaise was busy carefully untying the bow and opening the box. When she removed all the internal stuffing, she found a small, black velvet box. She held her breath as she opened it to find a sparkling, diamond ring. She turned quickly to Bull, her eyes questioning the ring's intention, but he wasn't standing beside her.

He was kneeling on one knee. His eyes wordlessly implored her to accept his promise of forever. He took her hand in his and then stole her heart all over again.

"Sierra Chaise Steele, I think I've known since I met you that you would change my life. There was something about you—even that first night—that drew me to you. Now that you've shown me what real love is, I can't live without you. Will you marry me, Chaise?"

"Yes—oh my God, yes, Colton!"

Chaise fell to her knees in front of him and wrapped her arms around his neck. Bull kissed her, slowly and sweetly at first, and the desire and urgency increased along with their tempo. Bull gently led her to lie down and he made love to her for the rest of the night. On the floor. On the couch. In the shower and eventually in their bed.

"Now that we've christened the house, maybe we should get some sleep," Chaise joked.

"I guess I can let you sleep for a little while to recharge your batteries. Then you're mine again," Bull said before sleep overtook him.

The next morning, Bull woke to hearing Chaise on the phone, telling Brianna about how he proposed. She was so excited and animated, it made him want to do it all over again, just to please her and make her feel loved.

He realized they were so much alike in that they didn't feel loved by their father when they were younger. They were both abandoned—but in different ways. His protective instincts went into overdrive when he thought about how Chaise and Noah's father must have treated her. He knew it had to be severe for her to refuse to return home when her life was in danger.

He vowed she would never have that problem again. She would always have a safe place to call home—physically and emotionally. He found he loved the responsibility of being "the man of the house," and Chaise enjoyed letting him take the reins. It made her feel safe and kept her anxiety at bay.

She didn't know that Bull had asked for Noah's permission to propose to her until Brianna explained it. The two men had a long talk about what it would mean to their families, their friendship, and their working relationship. Noah knew that no matter what, once Bull made a commitment, he would honor it to his death.

There was no doubting the love between Chaise and Bull. Noah assured Bull that he would be honored to have him as his brother in law. Noah's talk with his sister had only cemented his decision even more. They would be Aunt Chaise and Uncle Bull to Noah and Brianna's baby. They would be one big, happy family.

Bull slipped out of bed and eased up behind Chaise. He wrapped his arms around her, startling her, but she didn't miss a beat in her description of his proposal. "Tell her all the neighbors know my name is 'Oh God, Colton' now," he murmured in her ear.

Her face turned beet red and she playfully swatted him away. He laughed when she answered Brianna's question. "Oh, Colton said to tell you 'good morning,' that's all."

Chaise ended the call and took a seat in Bull's lap. "I'm so happy. Thank you for everything you did last night. It was perfect!"

"Anything for you, my love," he replied sincerely.

"Things are happening so fast. Your parents are moving down here soon," Chaise said.

"That's right. They're selling the house in Alabama and moving here to be closer to us," Bull replied with a smile.

"Brianna said her dad wants to offer me a job with his hotels. I'll be the Human Resources Manager for all of his hotels, but I'll mainly work out of the new one they're building here. It's exciting, isn't it? Starting a new life together?" Chaise asked, carefully watching his reaction.

"It's better than I ever thought it could be," Bull answered as he repositioned Chaise so that she straddled him.

Chaise leaned in and kissed him in response. "Thank you for not giving up on me when you had every reason to just walk away."

Bull shook his head from side to side. "If I had to pick one thing I would rather die than live without, it would be you. I really never thought I'd say this, but I can't wait to make you my wife."

"Well, Mr. Lanier, why don't you give me a preview of the honeymoon?" she asked seductively.

"Mmmm, I'd be glad to, future Mrs. Lanier. Your first preview will be a lesson in *Bull riding*," he wiggled his eyebrows suggestively at her. "But first, I need a date."

Chaise's eyes crinkled at the corners and her lips twisted to the side as the thought about her wedding date. Bull smiled at how cute the gestures looked on her. "I think a late April wedding. Noah and Brianna's baby will have already been born and then our whole family can be there with us."

"April it is. Now, it's time to try on your spurs," he said as he jumped up and ran down the hall with Chaise wrapped around him, laughing hysterically.

"Couldn't ask for a better start to a new life," Chaise said dreamily.

EPILOGUE

The hissing of oxygen flowing through tubes, the dinging of patient call lights, and the sterile smell of the hospital brought back memories of Brianna's hospitalization—a memory Noah would much rather forget. This visit to the hospital was under different circumstances, but no more desirable.

Chaise had received an urgent phone call from Sara Steele, their mother. Steve was in the hospital and the news was not good. He was rushed by ambulance to the emergency room during the night and was taken straight into surgery. Sara was frantic to reach all of her children. Steve was in pain but awake and asking to see them.

When Noah first heard the news, he was hesitant to agree to see him. He didn't think the hospital, post-surgery, was the best place for a family reunion after so many years apart. Sara insisted, however, and between Brianna and Chaise, Noah really didn't stand a chance.

Noah, Brianna, Bull, and Chaise all walked silently down the corridor to Steve's room in the ICU step-down unit. His condition was being carefully guarded but he wasn't in such dire straits as to need the constant monitoring of the ICU nurses.

Chaise held on to Colton's hand tightly as they walked. The impending visit weighed heavily on her mind. The anxiety level began building in her chest and she knew the only thing that kept her attack under control was the fact that Colton was with there with her. She felt him squeeze and tug on her hand lightly, asking her to look at him.

"I'm here, baby. Whatever you need, I'm here for you," he said warmly.

She nodded and squeezed his hand as she leaned into his side. "I can't imagine doing this without you here."

The beeping of the heart monitor and the ticking of the IV machine were the only sounds in the room. Sara was asleep sitting up in her chair and Steve was resting in the hospital bed with his eyes closed.

Brianna spoke up. "Maybe Bull and I should wait outside the room to give you and Chaise time to talk to your mother alone."

Noah shook his head. "No. *This* is my family now—you, our baby, Chaise, and Bull. We go in together."

Noah walked into the darkened room first and Sara sleepily opened her eyes. When she saw Noah, her eyes grew wide and she jumped up from her chair. As she rushed to him, with her arms widespread and tears in her eyes, Noah felt the regret wash over him. It had been too many years since he'd seen his mother.

He wrapped his arms around her and whispered his greeting in her ear. "Hi, Mom. How are you holding up?"

She pulled back and looked from him to Brianna, who stood proudly beside Noah. Sara's eyes dropped to Brianna's small bump and her hands flew to cover her mouth. "Noah?"

"Mom, this is my wife, Brianna. Brianna, this is my mom, Sara," he replied in hushed tones.

Sara looked at Brianna and suddenly threw her arms around her neck. Sara hugged her tightly as she cried softly. Brianna patted her on the back and whispered soothing words to her.

Sara opened her eyes and saw a large, formidable figure behind Brianna. Once her eyes adjusted, she saw his arm was wrapped around her daughter, Chaise. Turning Brianna with one hand, Sara used her other arm to grab Chaise and pull her in for a group hug.

When Sara let go of them, Chaise made her introductions. "Mom, this is Colton, my fiancé. Colton, this is Sara, my mom."

"Fiancé?" Sara asked and both Bull and Chaise nodded. "I'm so glad I didn't miss the wedding! Or my grandbaby's arrival!"

"You aren't having a family reunion without me, are you?" a weak voice called out.

All heads snapped to the direction of the voice. Steve's automatic pain medicine dispenser gave him another dose of pain medicine as Noah and Chaise moved to his bedside.

"Hi, Dad," Chaise replied. "How are you feeling?"

"Better now that the two of you are here," he answered. "I have something I need to say to you both."

Noah took a deep breath and readied himself to leave and take his family with him if Steve decided to start his usual rant. "Go ahead," Noah replied.

"I'm sorry, kids. I'm so sorry. I love you both and I want you back in my life. Not just because of this, but finding out you have Stage Three colon cancer is definitely a wake-up call for how you've lived your life. I look back and I'm not proud of the type of father I was to you two. I want a chance to make it up to you. I want to walk my baby down the aisle. I want to be a good grandfather," Steve choked up on his last words.

The room was silent. Both Chaise and Noah were stunned speechless at his admission and his request. Noah looked around at his family and they each nodded their approval.

"Apology accepted, Dad," Noah replied quietly. "Let's be a family again."

The pain medicine took effect and Steve soon slipped back into a deep sleep. Despite the prognosis, Chaise knew that her family would be whole again. Somehow everything would work out as it was intended to be.

They stood, gathered around their sick father, chatting and making introductions as Steve went in and out of sleep. Their future was ahead of them and no matter what it brought, Chaise, Colton, Brianna, and Noah would face it together.

There is strength in numbers and in family ties.

The story continues in WICKED NIGHTS.

BOOK 3: WICKED NIGHTS

First comes love. Then comes marriage. Then comes a shiny new baby carriage.

But is life ever really that simple?

An unknown danger lurked in the distance, and a family's hope began to fade into despair. Just when everything in life appeared to be perfect, will the family of Steele Security be prepared for the approaching wicked nights?

PROLOGUE

Ten Years Earlier

"Eyes on target," Reaper whispered into his comm.

The rest of the Delta Force team remained in place with their muscles tensed and ready to move when the command was issued.

"Big Eye, Reaper. Can you confirm friendlies are still in the southwest corner of the compound?" Reaper asked into the handheld radio to the reconnaissance plane that flew overhead.

"Roger that, Reaper. Thermals show five stationary warm bodies, one in motion inside the room, and one stationary outside the door."

"Copy that. Going dark. Reaper out."

He pressed the microphone button on his neck to talk to his team on the ground. "Positions."

One word was all it took for Bull, Rebel, and Shadow to move quickly into their places. They moved silently across the grounds to surround the area where the hostages were held. The houses inside the compound were all connected by doorways or covered breezeways, obviously built over time as the need to expand arose. They were constructed of a mixture of sunbaked mud and clay brick, with flat roofs and very few windows. As they covered the major entryways of the house, each man alerted their leader when he was in place and ready to take control of the situation.

When the news first broke that hostile insurgents had taken five American contractors hostage, Reaper knew his team would soon be called to intercede. The terrorists were demanding the release of one of their leaders in exchange for the five American men they currently held. For every day the government waited to make the exchange, the extremists vowed they'd behead one of the hostages. Reaper's team specialized in getting in and out of secure places, safely extracting the hostages, and effectively disabling the resistance.

When everyone was in place, Reaper gave the one-word command. "Go."

With his weapon drawn, each man crept silently through the dark in his assigned hallway until the four met in the back corner of the house. As they reached the last turn, they prepared to meet the resistance waiting for them. Rebel took his position, crouching low to the ground, ready to cover Reaper when he bolted to the opposite wall. Shadow and Bull prepared to move into similar positions immediately after the initial foe was incapacitated.

Like the well-oiled machine they'd trained to be, they executed their plan flawlessly. When the guard saw Reaper step into the hallway, his brain barely had time to register the shock before Rebel's double-tap took him out. Shadow and Bull moved into the lead positions as they continued to the door. Shouting in Arabic, followed by painful yelps, alerted the team that their enemies inside the hostage room were aware of their presence. Three men took their places on either side of the door, and then Shadow hit the door with a well-placed kick. He quickly jumped to the right side of the door, out of the way before the men inside the room opened fire.

The location of the bullet spray in the mud bricks across the hall gave the men a good indication of the enemies' locations inside the room. Rebel and Bull faced each other before one took the high position and the other took the lower one. As the guys swung around the doorframe with their weapons drawn, the guards were disarmed with minimal effort.

The team moved fully into the room, completed their full sweep, and untied the hostages. "US Army," Reaper introduced himself. "Is anyone injured?"

"Not bad. I can walk," one man answered. The others replied that they weren't injured.

Reaper pointed to the man who was obviously stronger than the others. "You stay with him—" he pointed to the slightly wounded man "—right behind me. We move at the speed of the weakest person." He finished giving the instructions on how each hostage would follow them out so that a member of the team covered each man.

"Big Eye, Reaper," he said into the radio. "Recovered. Exiting with five."

"Copy that, Reaper," came the reply. "Eyes on you."

Reaper transferred the connection from the handset to the speaker in his helmet so the recon plane could easily communicate with him. The group of men formed a line and began their withdrawal from the compound. The echo of heavy footfalls and voices became louder from the direction in which they were headed.

The voice in his helmet alerted him. "Reaper, Big Eye. Multiple hostiles are blocking your current route. Turn left at the next intersection. Proceed to the window. Extraction team being relocated."

"Copy," Reaper replied and proceeded on the updated route. Slinging his gun over his shoulder by the strap, he picked up a chair and busted a pane of the glass of the small panel window. Once the shards were cleared, he placed the chair in front of the window and motioned for Bull to go first. "Cover."

Bull nodded and deftly moved through the open window to take his place outside. "Men approaching," he said quietly into his comm.

"Big Eye, Reaper. Confirm extraction team location."

"Reaper, the team is less than half a klick from your current location."

"Copy," he replied.

He relayed the information to Bull as he helped the first hostage through the window. Rebel and Shadow remained in position with their rifles at the ready as Reaper fed the remaining men through the small opening.

"Your turn, ladies," Reaper said to Rebel and Shadow.

"Age before beauty." Shadow smirked at Rebel and jerked his head toward the exit.

"I'll be waiting on the other side of that wall to kick your ass," Rebel chuckled as he climbed out nimbly.

"You're up, big guy," Reaper said.

Shadow shouldered his weapon and followed Rebel. "Let's go, Reaper. Playtime is over," Shadow said from outside the window.

"Reaper, Big Eye. Multiple hostiles approaching your location. Take cover."

As Reaper started to turn toward the window, the first of the combatants turned the corner and spotted him. The hostile raised his rifle and took his aim at Reaper. A shot rang out and the man crumpled to the floor before he could squeeze the trigger. Reaper stepped on the chair and dove through the window, landed on his hands, and rolled in a somersault to lessen the force of his landing. Rebel simultaneously moved to cover the team, his rifle trained on the small opening.

As more men entered the hallway, Rebel squeezed the trigger of his automatic rifle. One by one, one insurgent after another fell to the floor.

"Let's go," Reaper yelled to the hostages.

They began their trek across the compound grounds toward the back wall. Armed men began pouring out of multiple doorways behind them. The men yelled curses in Arabic as they ran toward the fleeing hostages. Rebel turned and began to fire his weapon, hitting his mark repeatedly as he covered the team and hostages. One man fell from Rebel's covering fire, but he was still determined to kill the American infidels who had defiled his residence. While lying on his stomach, he raised his rifle with his bloody hands and tried to steady his shaking arms.

He fired his gun and the bullet whizzed by Rebel's head, way too close for comfort. The close proximity of the bullet to his head only fueled Rebel's anger. He turned his gun back to the wounded man and returned fire. The bullet struck the man in the head and left a gruesome, gaping wound in its wake.

A portable tactical ladder suddenly appeared over the wall, and Reaper directed the hostages to it while he and the other men provided covering fire. Several members of the extraction team climbed over the wall and moved into position in the yard, helping deter more armed opponents from approaching them. Once everyone was safely over the wall, they ran to the waiting helicopters and were safely lifted out.

Tears of joy and gratitude flowed down the faces of the rescued men. Rounds of sincere "thanks" and "thank you so much" were repeated over and over as the weight of reality set in. They were so very grateful to be going home to their families. Happy, healthy, and largely uninjured, thoughts of what could have been played through their thoughts and sent shivers down their spines.

In the courtyard of the terrorist compound, two young boys left the safety of the darkness and approached the corpse of the man who had kept shooting even after he'd been injured. The eldest of the two dropped to his knees beside the body, then dropped his pistol as his knees struck the dirt. Tears formed tracks over his cheeks through the dust that had collected on his face.

"I'm sorry, Father," he said to the lifeless man. "I failed you. I'm your first-born, and I failed to do my duty."

The younger brother placed his hand on the older one's shoulder. He was young, but he inherently understood the despair his brother felt. Family honor had been instilled in them since birth. Following orders, making their father proud, and taking a stand for their country weren't just ideals they talked about around the dinner table. The two boys had lived it every day of their young lives.

"Orphaned at barely thirteen," the older one said aloud. "It's all my fault."

CHAPTER ONE

SEPTEMBER

Current Day

The end of summer was marred by a different kind of ending. The rounds of chemotherapy and radiation therapy had begun to take their toll on the elder Steele man. The cancer that had weakened his body progressed rapidly, and the toxic treatments had a hard time keeping up with the new cell growth. The chances of improvement had begun to dwindle, and the doctors were forced to consider Steve's other options.

"Mr. Steele, it doesn't appear the treatment is working as well as we hoped we it would," Dr. Patel began. "It may be time for you and your wife to start discussing your final wishes, what lengths you're willing to go to for treatment, and at what point you want to stop treatment altogether."

Sara's soft whimpers were the only sound in the room. Steve stared at the wall straight ahead of him as he processed the bad news. Noah and Brianna sat beside Sara, both unable to string a few words together into a coherent response. Colton and Chaise sat on the other side of the bed, with Chaise holding Steve's hand while tears streamed down her face unchecked.

"Thank you, Dr. Patel. Sara and I will discuss it," Steve finally spoke.

Dr. Patel nodded and, before leaving the room, said, "Let me know if there's anything I can do to help. I'm sorry to be the bearer of such bad news. We will keep hoping for a significant change soon."

Steve and Sara both nodded at Dr. Patel in appreciation before Sara leaned over and laid her head on Steve's shoulder. Her tears dripped onto the sleeve of his hospital gown until it was soaked all the way through to his skin. She slowly started moving her head from side to side and muttering, "No. No. No."

"No!" she screamed before the sobs racked her body and her cries became long, guttural moans.

Steve maneuvered until his arm wrapped around her body, and he gently pulled her closer to him. Crawling up on the bed, Sara laid down beside Steve, wrapped her arm around him, and they simply held each other in their shared pain. Through all the ups and downs in their marriage and their family, one thing had remained constant: at the end of it all, their love was still as strong as steel.

"Dad," Chaise choked out, "we'll get a second opinion. Dr. Patel is great, but he could be wrong."

Steve shook his head. "He's the best, baby girl. He's not wrong. I had to stop my treatment a few days ago because of the severe reactions. They put me on IV rehydration for a while. If my body can't tolerate the treatment, there's nothing to keep the cancer in check.

"I plan on sticking around for a few more months anyway, so I can die a happy man. I'm going to hold my first grandbaby," he said as he looked at Noah and Brianna. Then he looked at Chaise and Bull, "And I'm going to walk my baby girl down the aisle to give her away to an honorable man who loves her. Most of all, I'll die a happy man knowing my family is whole again, and you'll all be at my side when I go.

"Sara." He paused as she raised her head from his chest. "I'm ready to get out of this hospital and go home now."

"Dad," Noah spoke then cleared his throat. "Are you sure that's really a good idea?"

"We've already talked about my options for home health care, son. I'll have around-the-clock nurses so your mom can still just spend time with me," Steve explained. "It's hard on her being at the hospital all the time."

"It's not just that, Dad. There has to be something else we can do." Noah's exasperation filled his voice.

Steve smiled at Noah. "I appreciate your concern more than you'll ever know, son. But, I'd rather spend my remaining days with my family, at home and comfortable. I'll still go for chemotherapy and radiation as long as I can, with home health care to help us out with the extra care at home."

Sara left the room to find Dr. Patel and arrange for her husband's discharge home. The weight on her heart was heavy as she walked the hospital corridor. Thinking that this could be their last trip home together threatened to knock her to her knees. She drew her strength from deep inside as her legs carried her forward until she found Dr. Patel. She approached him with a lump in her throat, inhaled deeply, and exhaled slowly.

"Dr. Patel, my husband has decided he'd like to go home. Can you arrange for his discharge and home health care as soon as possible, please?" Sara asked, rushing her words before she lost the courage to speak them.

Dr. Patel's kind eyes softened as the meaning behind her words took hold. "Yes, Mrs. Steele, I'll be glad to do it right away." Calling a nurse over, Dr. Patel gave her instructions on Steve's discharge and had her call social services to begin the paperwork for his home health care. Turning back to Sara, Dr. Patel tried to reassure her. "This is very difficult, but you'll have a lot of help and support through it. I'm very sorry I didn't have better news to deliver."

Unable to stop the tears flowing from her eyes, Sara quickly whisked each one away, only to have it replaced by another. "It's not your fault, Dr. Patel. We both know you've done everything you can do. We'll just have to keep trying and pray for a miracle. Thank you for your help."

Turning to walk back to Steve's room, Sara thought the corridor had never seemed so long before. Each step was harder for her to take than the last. Each breath became harder to breathe as she felt she might hyperventilate at any moment. The makings of a full-blown panic attack were threatening to take over and put her in a fetal position, crying and rocking in the corner.

One thought kept swirling through Sara's mind as she moved slowly down the hall.

"How can I do this?"

Hours later, the family had moved Steve from the hospital back to his home just south of Miami. The beachfront estate had every amenity a first-class businessman could hope to surround himself with. Steve Steele had made his name and fortune as the CEO of a major insurance company.

His shrewdness in running large, complex organizations had turned him into a highly sought-after commodity. Since his official retirement, he'd realized the important things he'd missed out on in life. Instead of focusing so much on making a name for himself in the marketplace, he realized he should've focused on making a better impression with his children. He'd decided the most important project he could work on was repairing his family bonds.

Then one night he landed in the hospital with unusual stomach pains and a stomach so upset he couldn't bear another second of it, and everything changed. That was the night of his emergency surgery. The night the surgeon broke the news that he had cancer and it was already advanced. He watched his plans evaporate before his eyes. No way to reconcile with his children. No time to repair what he'd so thoroughly destroyed.

Then Noah and Chaise appeared in his hospital room. At first, he thought it was a reaction to his pain medications. A hallucination conjured by his mind there to taunt him. But then he realized his visions were real as he watched Sara hug them through her tears. His children had returned—two of them anyway. There was still one son unaccounted for, but he at least felt he had a chance now.

As he lay in his own bed, Steve reflected solemnly on Dr. Patel's words. "I've worked all my life, only to retire and learn I have cancer. Terminal cancer, for all intents and purposes," he whispered to himself. "How did this happen?"

Hearing voices approach, he cut his eyes to the door and waited for Sara and the home health nurse to appear.

"Is there anything I can get you, honey?" Sara asked sweetly as she walked in.

"Just you." He smiled.

"You have me. You've always had me," she assured him as she took her spot on the bed beside him.

"I'm a lucky man," he said as he kissed her head.

"Hello, Mr. Steele. I'm Hope, and I'll be one of your nurses." The nurse extended her hand and smiled.

"Hope," Steve said thoughtfully. "I need hope, too."

She nodded, understanding his meaning. "I need to get your vitals and do your initial medical assessment. It won't take long."

"I don't seem to have any other plans right now." Steve smiled. "Let's get it done."

~

Noah paced back and forth in the great room of the house he'd grown up in. "There has to be something else we can do."

"We'll figure something out, babe. We're not giving up yet," Brianna assured him.

Sara walked into the room and all eyes snapped to her. "Hope is going over his medical information and getting his vitals. I thought I'd come check on you while they're busy."

"Mom, we're fine," Noah assured her. "You need to rest. This is taking a lot out of you."

"I'm just trying to stay busy," she admitted. "It's easier than sitting and thinking about everything."

"What can we do to help?" Brianna asked Sara. "Just say the word and we'll do it."

"We're all doing everything we can right now," Sara replied, taking Brianna's hand. "Don't feel obligated to stay here. He's not dying today. It just wasn't the news we had hoped to hear."

Noah, Brianna, Chaise, and Bull stayed with Sara as Hope worked with Steve. A couple hours later, Hope joined the family in the great room. "Mrs. Steele, I've finished with my assessment. Mr. Steele is sleeping now. That's completely normal, so don't worry. All the moving, transferring, and people poking at him just made him more tired than usual."

"Thank you, Hope. Please call us Steve and Sara," she replied with a tired smile.

"I'll be back tomorrow with more help and we'll set up our schedules. Here's my contact information," she said, handing Sara her card. "If you need anything, call me at any time."

After Sara walked Hope out, she returned to her family. "It's so good to see you all here. You're welcome to stay, but you really don't have to. He'll sleep the rest of the night, and we'll start chemotherapy and radiation again tomorrow."

"We'll go and let you get some rest then, Mom," Noah replied as he kissed her cheek. "Call if you need anything."

Chaise stood and hugged Sara. "I love you, Mom. Do you want me to stay with you?"

"No, baby," she replied. "Go home with Colton and rest. I love you all. More than you'll ever know."

After they said their goodbyes, Sara climbed into bed with Steve and snuggled up next to him. Her hot tears slid slowly out of her eyes as she drifted off to sleep.

~

The mood in the Steele Security office was still somber a week after Steve's home health care started. His treatments had resumed and, with the help of medications and hydration treatment, he began to tolerate the side effects better than before. Concern for his health and future weighed heavily on the entire extended family.

"You know," Brianna began. "Your mom reminds me so much of my neighbor in Colorado. I didn't realize how much I'd depended on her to keep me sane while I was away from you. I miss her."

"I'd like to meet her," Noah replied earnestly. "With everything that's happened in the last few months, we've barely had time to slow down. We should take a week or two and go see her. You can show me around and tell me all about your life in Boulder."

"Really?" Brianna perked up. "Do you think your parents would be okay with us leaving?"

"Yeah, I talked to Mom this morning and she said we need to stop acting like Dad is dying tomorrow," Noah chuckled. "She's right, though. Everyone has called at least once a day to ask how he is feeling. If we need to come back early, we'll have the jet so we can leave at any time."

"Let's go," Brianna agreed. "I want to surprise Mrs. Stanton, and I guess I have a lot of explaining to do to her, too."

"We're going, too," Bull chimed in.

Noah's eyebrows rose in question.

"Don't look at me like that, Reaper. Brianna is my little sister, and I missed three years with her, too. If you two are going on a stroll down memory lane, I'm strolling with you," Bull demanded as he crossed his arms over his chest.

"Using that logic, Shadow and I are going, too," Rebel spoke up.

"Hell, yeah," Shadow added. "We're not sitting this one out."

"I'm with the guys on this one, Noah," Chaise added and winked at Brianna.

"Looks like you're outnumbered, big guy." Brianna smiled. "We're taking the whole family to Colorado."

Noah glanced around the room at the family that had been at his side for nearly every major event in his life. "Fair enough. I'll have them get the jet ready to leave first thing in the morning. We'll have to brief Roman tonight and let him know he's in charge while we're away. This should be an interesting trip."

"Of course it will be. Look who's going with you," Shadow quipped.

Noah groaned and the room erupted in laughter. "I'm taking my woman home now. Meet us at the airstrip at eight tomorrow morning."

"I'll call Roman on my way home and give him the rundown, Reap," Rebel offered as he walked to the door. "See you bright and early in the morning."

"I'm right behind you, man," Shadow replied. "Have a good night, everyone."

"Let's go, Chaise. You have womanly duties to perform," Bull commanded.

"Bull. Seriously." Noah gave him a disgusted look.

"What?"

"She's my sister," Noah complained emphatically.

"Yeah, I know," Bull spoke slowly. "It's her turn to make dinner tonight, and I need her to help me pack my suitcase. What did you think I meant?"

"Nothing. I don't want to think about it," Noah amended quickly.

"Oh, wait. You thought I meant..." Bull smiled broadly. "Good idea. She definitely has those womanly duties to perform tonight."

"Get out," Noah ordered. "Get out of here right now."

"Come on, Colton," Chaise laughed. "You have some manly duties to perform for me, too."

"I can't hear you," Noah replied as his hands covered his ears. "Can't hear a word. Get out."

Chaise and Bull walked out the door laughing together and left Noah and Brianna alone. Brianna walked over to Noah, straddled his lap as she faced him, and kissed his lips. When he opened his eyes, she pulled his hands down from his ears. "They're gone now. You're safe."

"Thank God. I'll never get used to hearing that," Noah admitted.

"She's grown and he loves her, Noah. You have to accept that." Brianna smiled. "Where is your brother? Have you heard anything yet?"

"Not a word. He's deep undercover and hasn't checked in with his handler in a while now. Shadow said that's completely normal, especially if he's gathering a lot of intel and can't risk blowing his cover," Noah sighed. "I just hope that's the case, and it's not because something bad has happened to him."

"You've had a long enough day," Brianna decided. "It's time for you to take me home and perform some husbandly duties for me."

"It sounds so much better when you say it, wife." Noah's eyes darkened. "It's all my pleasure to perform my husbandly duties for you."

"Not *all* your pleasure," Brianna quipped. "I happen to get a lot of pleasure from it, too."

"Time to go," Noah replied as he shut his laptop. "Now I can't wait to get you home."

He stood, taking Brianna with him as she wrapped her legs around his waist. Her baby bump at sixteen weeks was just big enough to be noticeable but not enough to get in the way. Noah held her close to him, and she took the opportunity to kiss and lick his neck as he carried her out to the car.

"You're killing me, woman," he growled.

"Maybe I'll give you a special treat while you're driving," she purred in his ear.

"Shit, you want me to wreck," he chuckled. "Not that I'll try to stop you or anything."

"It's a good thing our SUV is nice and roomy," she replied. "I have better access to you."

"That does it. We're not going anywhere until I'm done with you. We'll just have to be like horny teenagers in the backseat."

"If you insist," she agreed.

"Damn, I love your pregnancy hormones," Noah said as he opened the back door of the SUV. After he carefully placed Brianna inside, his take-charge personality emerged again. "Strip. We're taking advantage of these new black-out windows."

Brianna slid across the seat, giving Noah room to get in. She pulled her shirt over her head, revealing her fuller breasts that spilled over the top of her lacy bra. She then adjusted her body and slid her shorts down her legs. "All yours, big guy. Show me what you got for me."

Noah climbed in, started the car to blast the air conditioner, and joined Brianna in the backseat. His eyes first went to the swell of her breasts and his fingers followed. After he pulled the lace down in the front, his mouth and hand covered them as he pulled her to lie down on the seat. The other hand slid down to her matching panties. His finger traced the edge of her panties until he reached her sensitive flesh. He moved them to one side and slid his finger across her entrance, felt the wetness, and then plunged deep inside her.

She cried out in pleasure as his finger pushed inside, then retreated as he used her juices to coat her clit and circled to start all over again. He increased his speed and pressure as her pleasure built. Her inner muscles tightened around his finger as he added a second. Her body shook and trembled when his thumb pressed against her clit, rubbing and bringing her to orgasm with finesse and ease.

"Damn, I'll never get tired of watching you come," he murmured as he moved to cover her.

Brianna's hands unzipped his pants and grasped him, pulling his cock free. She guided him to her entrance and purred up to him. "Now, Noah. I want you now."

His hips surged forward as he drove inside her. Her hips rose in automatic response to the fullness and stretching of his intrusion. "Fuck, you feel so good, baby," Noah said as he arched forward and pulled back repeatedly.

Sitting back, he put his hands on the back of her thighs and pushed forward. As he deepened his angle, her pleasure increased and she screamed his name. The sensation of her soft, inner walls clamping down around his cock was more than Noah could withstand. He let go of his control and continued to surge into her until her body had pulled every last drop from his.

"Holy shit, that was hot," Brianna panted. "We need to do this more often."

"Only if you insist." Noah smiled smugly and leaned over to kiss her softly.

"I love you, Noah," she said as she stroked his face.

"I love you, Brianna. More than life itself."

CHAPTER TWO

"Colton, are you ready, baby?" Chaise asked.

"That depends," he replied as he leaned against the doorframe. "Ready for what?"

"I know that smirk," Chaise laughed. "The answer is no. It's not happening, so don't even think about it. We don't have time for another round."

"Chaise." He grinned mischievously as he stepped toward her. "We both know I can change your mind. Don't make me prove it."

He reached his hand out and ran his finger down her arm, barely making contact but leaving chill bumps in his wake regardless. Her eyes lit with desire as his smile covered his face. "And you're mine now."

"Get out of here!" She swatted his hand away playfully.

Bull chuckled and picked up their suitcase. "Don't feel bad, baby. You can change my mind just as easily."

"I'll keep that in mind," she promised. "Let's go or we'll be late and Noah will be mad at us both."

When they reached the private airstrip, the jet was ready and waiting as Noah promised. They rushed to the stairs and entered the plane, hoping they weren't the last, just as Shadow and Rebel took their seats.

"Nice of you two to join us this morning," Shadow quipped. "What took you so long?"

Chaise blushed pink as she tilted her face downward, letting her long hair partially hide her face.

"We're right on time," Bull retorted as he and Chaise took their seats.

The flight attendant closed the cabin door and strolled through the cabin to ensure all seat belts were fastened for takeoff.

"We'll be there in about four hours," Noah announced. "The hotel rooms are taken care of, so we'll each have some privacy while we're there."

Rebel and Shadow laughed openly. Brianna also laughed before quickly coughing to cover her outburst. Taking Noah's hand in hers, she squeezed it as she beamed up at him. "Still can't get used to the fact that your sister is all grown up now, can you?"

"I realize she's grown. I just don't want to be in the same house with them while they're..." He paused, his face struck with disgust. "You know what."

"Suits me just fine, Noah. This way we can have privacy, too." Brianna grinned as she lightly stroked his arm.

"Thanks for that visual. I needed it." He leaned over to kiss her.

"I know you did," she laughed as she leaned toward him.

~

Four hours of razzing, threats, and mocking laughter later, the group of friends and family had deplaned, hauled their luggage into the waiting rental cars, and checked in to their hotel rooms. When they met in the lobby after getting settled in, Shadow started with the most important question.

"When do we eat?"

Brianna laughed. "I thought that was my line," she replied as she rubbed her pregnant belly.

"You're too slow. I'm hungry *now*," he laughingly replied.

"Let's go by my old place. I can introduce everyone to my neighbor and maybe we can talk her into going out to eat with us," Brianna offered.

"Sounds good to me. Lead the way, little sister," Bull chimed in.

On the ride to her former townhome, Brianna talked animatedly about the area, like a good hostess on a guided tour. As Noah passed by the lantern-lined pedestrian mall, Brianna smiled. "I spent a lot of time at this outdoor mall, just people-watching and not much else. A few streets over was where I used to work when I lived here."

"Where did you work?" Noah asked. "I just realized I have no idea what you did for a living while you were away."

"I worked at a pottery store, actually making the ceramic pottery on a spinning wheel." She smiled.

"Like in that movie?" he asked.

"Yes, just like that. It was so glamorous and sexy just like they portrayed it. I wasn't covered in water and sculpting compound from head to toe every single day or anything. I didn't have the mud-like clay stuck under my fingernails, in my hair, or even in my ear at all," she quipped.

"I guess I just assumed you worked for another newspaper," he mused.

"No, I couldn't. My degree and all my credentials were under my real name. I had to take a job where they didn't ask too many questions. It wasn't that bad, really. It was a small mom-and-pop store. The owners were more about making original pieces with character than turning a profit. And by character, I mean flaws, because I really sucked at it for the first six months," she explained.

When Noah pulled into the driveway, he sat motionless for a moment as he took in the townhouse where she'd lived during the three years they were apart. "So this is it, huh? This was home," he said, a spark of pain lingering in his tone.

"This was never home, Noah," she replied softly. "Home has always been with you. This was a place for shelter until I could find my way back to you."

He raised her hand and kissed the back of it, letting his lips linger on her skin as he inhaled her sweet scent. "I thank God every day that you did," he told her, his brown eyes melting to dark chocolate. "You'd better introduce me to your friend before I decide to take you back to the hotel room right now."

Giggling, she opened her car door and began to slide out. Noah still held her hand in his and stopped her with a slight tug. "I thought I'd make a clean getaway," she laughed.

"A clean getaway? Never. I'll never let you go again," he said sincerely. "I just want to make sure you're really okay with being here again."

"Noah, as long as I'm with you, I'm good anywhere we are. Bringing you and our family here chases all the old, painful ghosts away," she assured him. "It also brings new life here."

"Let's go meet Mrs. Stanton, then." He smiled.

"She was my one bright spot here. I feel bad about how I left her, too." She pursed her lips ruefully.

Exiting the vehicle, they walked hand in hand to Mrs. Stanton's front door. Brianna rang the doorbell and waited patiently. When she heard the door being unlocked, she grasped Noah's hand tightly and prepared for Mrs. Stanton's reaction to seeing her again.

When she swung the door open, Mrs. Stanton was taken aback at first by the large figure who filled her doorway. Behind him stood three more men every bit as large and intimidating. Her eyes roamed across the unfamiliar faces as she struggled to find her voice, until they landed on Brianna and recognition dawned on her.

"Kris!" she exclaimed and jumped into Brianna's arms. "I've been so worried about you. Where did you go? What happened to you?"

"Mrs. Stanton," Brianna said as she hugged her tightly. "I have a story to tell you that you'll have a hard time believing. The first thing is, my name is really Brianna Steele."

As Mrs. Stanton leaned back to look Brianna in the face, her puzzled look was impossible to hide. "Brianna?"

"Yes, ma'am. This is my husband, Noah. Noah, this is Mrs. Elizabeth Stanton."

"It's so nice to finally meet you, Mrs. Stanton," Noah said warmly.

"Call me Liz, please." She looked around at the rest of the group. "Where are my manners? Come in, all of you. I can't wait to hear this story."

The group chuckled at her honesty as they filed into her small living room. After they were all comfortably seated, Brianna introduced everyone before she began explaining everything that happened before the first time she'd arrived in Boulder. The gasps, *oohs*, and *ahhs* from Liz were the only sounds that punctuated Brianna's story. Liz's hand occasionally flew to cover her mouth as she pictured the scenes that Brianna described.

When she finished the entire story, all the way up to her current state of pregnancy, Liz's eyes were filled with tears of happiness. "Oh, Brianna." She paused. "It feels so strange to call you that, by the way. But, I'm so happy for you both. You found your way back together through all the tragedies life threw at you."

Turning to Noah, she gave him a stern look. "Don't you ever take that for granted, young man. This girl lived beside me for three long years. No matter how hard I tried to set her up with a nice man, she wouldn't have it. Now I know why—she loves you. You better take care of my girl. In all my sixty-six years, I've never met anyone like her."

"Yes, ma'am. I have every intention of loving and taking care of her for the rest of my life." Noah smiled at Liz before turning his gaze to Brianna. "She's my whole life, and soon our baby will be, too."

"He's a keeper, Brianna. I know good stock when I see it." Liz's playfulness danced in her eyes as she spoke, reminding Brianna how much she'd missed her.

"Noah is definitely a keeper." Brianna smiled. "He brought me back here because I've missed you and I owed you an explanation in person. You kept me sane while Noah and I were apart. We're here for a few days, but we'd love to take you out to eat today and spend time with you."

"I get a date with all these handsome men?" Liz asked playfully. "You there—Shadow? Are you married?"

"No, ma'am." Shadow gave her his most enticing smile. "Are you going to propose to me?"

"You're a little too young for me, son. But I'll let you take me to lunch today. Give all the people in my neighborhood something to talk about." She returned his mischievous grin.

"My kind of woman," Shadow said as he stood and offered his hand.

"I like these boys, Brianna. You have my approval," Liz said as she stood, hooked her arm in Shadow's, and walked out her front door.

The rest stood and followed them outside. When the others were safely out of earshot, Bull pulled Chaise to him and whispered in her ear. "Just so you know, even watching Grandma Liz hit on Shadow doesn't dampen my libido. I can't wait to get you back to the hotel room."

"I'm looking forward to that myself. I love the garden Jacuzzi tub in our room. Maybe we should put it to good use while we're here," Chaise challenged him.

The heated look in his eyes was the only response she needed to know that he was in full agreement. "You're playing with fire," he murmured.

"I thought I was taking the bull by the horns," she joked.

"You'll be taking Bull by something later tonight," he growled.

"Lock the door, will you, dear?" Liz called over her shoulder. Bull nodded as he pulled the door closed behind him.

As they approached the car, another car pulled into the parking spot for the neighboring townhouse. "Is that your new neighbor?" Brianna asked.

"Yes, he moved in not too long ago. He's such a nice young man—quiet, keeps to himself, doesn't have wild parties till all hours of the night." Liz shook her head. "Boring."

As her new neighbor slid out of his car, Liz called to him. "Lee, can you come over here and meet my friends?"

Lee's smile was outwardly friendly, but Noah immediately noticed how he swiftly schooled his features to hide his true annoyance. Had it simply been due to irritation with his older neighbor, Noah may have dismissed the burst of suspicion that flashed in his mind. Since he'd never been one to tamp down his instincts, he reasoned he wasn't about to start now.

When he locked eyes with Bull, Noah recognized his friend's suspicions matched his own. Quick glances at Rebel and Shadow assured him they were all on the same page. Lee was definitely hiding something. Noah silently vowed as long as Brianna and Chaise were around this guy, he'd also be there. The vibes Lee emanated were unmistakable and far too familiar to Noah, but the fact that his brothers also picked up on them solidified his resolve.

"Lee, this is Brianna. I told you about her before, but at the time her name was Kris." Liz tried to explain, but failed miserably.

Confusion flashed across Lee's face, and he opened his mouth to ask for clarification, but he shook his head slightly instead. "Brianna?" he asked to confirm when he held out his hand.

"Yes," she chuckled. "I'm Brianna, and it's a long story, so I'll spare you the details."

"And this is her husband," Liz continued, motioning to Noah.

Noah recognized the immediate change in Lee's demeanor when their eyes met. Noah narrowed his eyes slightly as he extended his hand toward Lee. The Middle Eastern accent was hidden to the untrained ear, but it was there nonetheless. The fact that Lee consciously hid his descent was very concerning. "Hey. How are ya?" Noah asked casually.

Lee's eyes swept across Noah's face as his top lip began to snarl unconsciously. He cut his eyes to Bull, then to Shadow, before finally resting on Rebel. He remained silent, not responding to Noah or accepting his hand for an uncomfortably long time. The second hand ticked away on Noah's watch as Lee stood rooted to his spot, his eyes sweeping back and forth between them.

Reluctantly grasping Noah's hand with his, he gripped it firmly and gave it a manly shake. The hatred burning in Lee's eyes was palpable, and the venom dripped from his lips when he finally replied. "I have never been better."

"Good," Noah answered. "These are friends of mine. They're just along for the ride."

Noah intentionally skimmed over the rest of the introductions. He wanted to test Lee, but he also didn't want to give him more information than they already had. He'd just decided Lee was on a strictly need-to-know basis, and he didn't need to know anything else about them.

When he released Noah's hand, Lee turned to stare down the other three men again. For someone who was roughly half his body size, Noah had to admit that Lee was brazen and bold. However, he wouldn't add intelligent to that list of characteristics just yet. His black hair, thick black eyebrows, deep brown eyes, and olive-toned skin gave him more of a Mediterranean appearance than Middle Eastern.

"It's very fortunate that I arrived home when I did," Lee replied. "Do you live around here?"

The abrupt subject change wasn't lost on Bull. "No, we don't," he replied matter-of-factly.

"Visiting Mrs. Stanton, then." Lee nodded. "Are you family?"

"I claim Brianna as my own," Liz replied. "But they're not family. She used to live in your house, Lee."

"Ah, yes. Mrs. Stanton has told me many stories about you." Lee turned to Brianna, slid his hand into hers, and lifted it toward his lips. "She's been very complimentary of you."

Noah smoothly took her hand from Lee's just before his lips touched her skin. "How nice. We need to get going. Good to meet you, Lee."

"I'm sure we'll see each other again soon," Lee replied.

"Of that, I have no doubt." Noah nodded.

As they piled into the large SUV, Noah kept his eyes on Lee. But it seemed that Lee only had eyes for Rebel.

"Rebel, you catch that?" Noah asked.

"Couldn't miss it, Reap. A flashing neon sign would've been better disguised," Rebel replied.

"Recognize him?"

"He definitely reminds me of someone from a long time ago, but I've never met *Lee* before," Rebel replied.

"You don't have to be jealous, Noah," Liz chimed in. "He was flirty with Brianna, but we can't blame him for that. I'll bet he would've been the same with Chaise if I'd had a chance to introduce them."

Liz turned to Chaise. "I'm so sorry about that. My mind must really be slipping in my old age. That was so rude of me."

Chaise chuckled easily at Liz's words. "It's fine, honestly. I'm not upset at all."

"That's right. She only wants *me* to flirt with her," Bull replied with a wink.

"Young man, I can't blame her for that. You are one handsome man," Liz replied, emphasizing her final words. "If I were thirty years younger, I'd give her a run for her money."

Laughter rumbled through the vehicle and increased at Bull's reddened face. "I'm sure you would, Liz." Chaise grinned widely. "You're still feisty now. Do you flirt with Lee?"

"I tried at first," Liz admitted. "But he's definitely an old fuddy-duddy to be so young. I've managed to get him to join me for breakfast a few times. He didn't like my store-bought honey, though. Said it wasn't as good as the kind he's used to having."

"He eats a different kind of honey?" Rebel asked.

"That's what he said. I only know of one kind—from honeybees. But whatever. Enough about him. Where are you taking me on our date, handsome?" Liz reached up and tickled Noah's ear as he drove.

"Wherever you'd like to go," Noah chuckled. "You name it, you got it."

"No wonder you ran off for this one," Liz said to Brianna. "But since he's taken and so is Bull, I guess I'll have to flirt a little harder with Rebel and Shadow."

"Oh yeah, I like her," Noah announced to the group. "It's about time that Rebel and Shadow got to be thoroughly embarrassed."

"Won't happen, man," Shadow replied. "We're the *cool ones* of the group. We're not like you and Bull—we don't get embarrassed. But we'll gladly flirt with a pretty lady." Shadow waggled his eyebrows at Liz suggestively but kept his playful grin intact.

She giggled like a schoolgirl with her first crush. "I'm sitting beside him."

When they arrived at the restaurant Liz chose, the group filed inside and appeared outwardly oblivious to the stares and gawking women who leered after the hulking men as they passed. Rebel seemed genuinely distracted and the other men knew he was deep in thought, but what caused his state wasn't clear. When Rebel finally met Noah's gaze, Noah slowly raised his eyebrows at his friend. Rebel shook his head almost imperceptibly and immediately joined the conversation.

They both knew a detailed discussion would occur later.

CHAPTER THREE

"Mrs. Steele?" Hope approached her.

"Call me Sara, please," she replied. "Yes, Hope?"

"Steve is sleeping now, but I wanted to alert you to a slight change in his condition. He seems to be more confused by everyday tasks than he was when I was last here. That's a known side effect of chemotherapy that a lot of people call 'chemo brain.' But if it gets any worse, the doctor may want to do an MRI of his head to make sure nothing else is going on," she explained.

"Are you saying it could've already spread to his brain?" Sara whispered.

"I'm saying it's something we need to watch and catch early if we can," Hope clarified. "I'm on my way out now. If you need anything, feel free to call me."

"Thank you, Hope," Sara replied absently.

Sara started her trek down the hall, and each step was more painful to take than the last. The long corridor seemed stifling as Hope's words reverberated in her mind. She just needed to see him, watch him sleep, and reassure her frantic mind that her Steve was still there. That he was still fighting to get through this and come out stronger on the other side.

Sara reached her hand out, placed her palm against the door, and pushed with light effort. The door moved in slow motion as she waited for him to come into view. As she stood in the doorway, she saw him as he currently was and not by the picture she carried in her heart. His large, strapping form had deteriorated to the point that he appeared gaunt. His skin's normally healthy glow had dimmed to a dull, flat pallor. His typically thick muscles had begun to atrophy from minimal use.

Sara's fears were becoming reality. Steve was slipping away from her. It was happening a little at a time perhaps, but steadily increasing nonetheless.

"What are you staring at, woman?" Steve smirked.

"I'm staring at my husband. You got something to say about that?" she retorted with a grin.

"You should be over here in the bed with me. Not all the way across the room."

She sighed heavily in mock contempt. "If I must. But you have to quit hogging the bed if I do."

"I've never promised you that, woman," he chuckled.

Sara crawled into their bed, laid her head on his chest, and wrapped her arms around him. She hid her worry when she felt how cold his skin was to her touch. She swallowed the tears that threatened to overtake her when the thoughts of losing him crept in. The knowledge that Steve faced his circumstances with a new attitude helped give her the strength to push it aside and simply enjoy spending time with him. She ran her fingers lightly through his thinning hair, massaging his scalp as she did.

"That feels so good," he murmured. "It's been too long since you've done that."

"You can have this every day if that's what you want," she promised.

Steve chuckled. "I won't turn it down if you're offering."

"How are you feeling today, babe?"

"Chemo is rough," he admitted. "But I'm hanging in there. Hope gave me some medicine before she left."

Within minutes, the medicine took effect and Steve drifted off to sleep. His arm was still draped around Sara. It was symbolic to her of how they'd held on to each other through so many ups and downs throughout their life together. An overwhelming feeling of anger unexpectedly hit Sara.

"Fuck you, cancer," she whispered. "You're not taking my family when we just put it back together. I've spent enough time worrying and being sad. We'll fight you every step of the way."

A sense of peace and calmness settled in her chest, bringing her hope for the first time in too many weeks. With a newfound determination, Sara allowed her muscles to relax as she closed her eyes. For the first time in a very long time, she wasn't concerned that bad dreams would cause another sleepless night. Taking a nap with her husband would become a welcome treat again.

When Steve woke from his nap, his heart filled with love when he looked down at his wife. She was curled up at his side, her arm draped across his body, and she was actually sleeping instead of staring at him. Since Dr. Patel delivered the news that the treatments weren't working as well as they'd hoped, his whole family seemed to stare at him, waiting for him to keel over in front of their eyes.

It was unnerving to Steve, to say the least. He'd always been the strong, domineering patriarch, and now he was quickly becoming a frail, pitiful shell of a man. This was one turn in his life he'd never seen coming. He mused to himself how the cancer that was killing him was the very thing that had brought his family back together. His family was his life, and he'd let them slip away from him once before.

"Never again," he muttered. "Dying to live."

Sara stirred in his arms before her eyes fluttered open. "Steve, are you okay?"

He gently stroked her cheek with his thumb. "That's the first thing you ask me every day when we wake up. Do you realize that?"

"I guess you're right," she chuckled. "I can't help it."

"Sara, I haven't done enough to deserve the love you've always given me. But I promise you, that's changing right now. For the rest of our lives, you'll never doubt how deep my love for you is," he murmured. "No more worrying about me, baby. I'm too mean to die."

"We've been together nearly forty years, Steve. You can't expect me to stop worrying about you now." Sara smiled warmly through the tears that glistened in her eyes.

"That is asking a lot, huh?" Steve winked. "I'll make a deal with you. I'll tell you if I'm feeling especially bad as long as you stop asking me how I feel every day. Unless I tell you otherwise, just assume I'm as good as I can be."

"Deal," she agreed. "But only because you asked nicely. Don't hide anything from me, though, Steve. I mean it. If you actually feel worse but don't tell me because you're trying to power through it, you could end up worse off."

"Yes, ma'am," he replied contritely. "I promise—no secrets."

"It's a deal then." Sara leaned up and placed a lingering kiss on his lips. "Sealed with a kiss."

"I'm going to shower and then we're going out for dinner," Steve decided. "I haven't taken my wife on a date in a long time."

He slowly quirked his eyebrow up at the dubious expression on her face, silently daring her to question him. Her features softened and she nodded her concession. "Where are we going?"

"Somewhere nice. Get all dressed up for me."

An hour later, Steve and Sara entered the upscale restaurant hand in hand. The music played softly in the background as the maître d' showed them to their table. Steve pulled out Sara's chair for her before taking his own. The normally welcome aroma of the various dinners quickly became a source of discomfort. As Sara looked over her menu, Steve held his breath, swallowed hard, and slowly exhaled. He inwardly vowed that he'd finish this meal with his wife or die trying.

When Sara glanced up at him, she immediately knew that the scents had intensified his nausea. Her resolve to keep her word to him was all that kept her from blurting out that they should leave. After she waited a couple of minutes, watched as he sipped on his ice water and pretended to stare at the menu longer, she was relieved when his color improved and his tense muscles relaxed.

"Have you decided what you want?" Steve asked.

"Yes. I'm ready when you are." She smiled through her worry.

Signaling for the waiter, Steve and Sara placed their orders and settled into comfortable conversation. Neither brought up the cancer, the chemotherapy drugs, the radiation treatment, or the prognosis they didn't want to face. That night was all about the couple who'd been in love for more years than not. Steve managed to consume his bland meal without incident. Even though food didn't taste the same as it had before, he felt like he was regaining some of his old strength with his body properly nourished.

"Thank you for dinner out tonight," Sara said as they walked toward the car.

"My pleasure," Steve replied. "I know you're thanking me because you're worried about me, but I appreciate that you haven't mentioned it."

"Are you going to leave me hanging here?"

Steve laughed out loud at her forwardness. "No, I know it's pure torture for you. Dinner was hard at first, but I controlled my breathing, sipped a lot of water, and chose bland foods. I actually feel better since I made myself eat."

"You know I plan to take advantage of this information." Sara grinned.

"I have no doubt of that, my love." Steve stopped walking. "In fact, I'm counting on it."

~

"Chaise, you're a dirty, dirty girl," Bull chided her softly.

"I don't know why you're blaming me. It's your fault," she retorted playfully.

"How can you say such a thing about me?" Bull feigned hurt and offense at her declaration.

"Colton Lanier, are you honestly going to stand there and deny it to my face?" Chaise's hand rested on her hip, she cocked her head to the side, and she narrowed her eyes at Bull. Her foot tapped lightly as she waited for his reply.

"I guess I need to get you out of those clothes." His voice dropped an octave as his eyes darkened with desire.

"If you think you're getting lucky while I'm standing here drenched to the bone and covered in mud, you're crazy," Chaise replied dryly. "Don't even try your moves on me, mister."

"You love my moves, though," Bull replied, emphasizing the double meaning his words held. "Let me remind you."

"Bull." She pointed at him, emphasizing the double meaning her reply held. "You are the cause of this mess. I'm trying to stay mad at you right now, so you have to let me."

The corner of his mouth lifted involuntarily as he fought to hold back his laughter. Chaise could never stay mad at him for very long. and they both knew it. Bull often used it to his advantage. "The timer on the sprinklers in Mrs. Stanton's flower beds is not my fault. It's also not my fault that you happened to be standing directly over the top of one of the sprinklers when it went off."

"Remind me again, Colton. Who was it that ran while the sprinklers soaked me?"

"Now, wait a minute—"

"Then who was it who didn't come to help me when my heels sank into the ground and I couldn't move? Then continued to stand on the sidelines when one of my heels broke off in the ground? Then laughed his ass off when I'd finally dug my heel out of the ground and slipped in the mud when I tried to run? Who was that, Colton?" she demanded.

"Reaper. And Rebel. And Shadow. Oh, and Brianna," Bull replied, his naughty grin fully in place. "Let's not forget Mrs. Stanton, the sly little lady who knew how to turn them off but didn't."

"Let's not forget Bull, my fiancé, my personal bodyguard, my big, tough soldier, who *ran from the water*," Chaise emphasized.

"I don't like wearing wet clothes," Bull explained with a single shoulder shrug.

Chaise's mouth dropped open and her eyes widened. "Are you freaking kidding me right now?"

"Not at all. I had to wear wet clothes in the Army sometimes, but I didn't have a choice," Bull started to explain.

"I'm not talking about your clothes!" Chaise yelled before stomping off to the bathroom.

Once the door was shut, Bull doubled over in laughter as the sight of Chaise angrily marching toward the bathroom replayed in his mind. One high-heeled shoe on, one off, but she still held her head high and her shoulders back. All while she tried to portray an air of authority and indignation at his insult.

When he heard the water start, he immediately stopped laughing. On the other side of that door stood a naked Chaise, whose skin begged to be lathered in soap, thoroughly washed, and meticulously worshiped. There was only one man who was up for the job. Bull unbuttoned his shirt on his way to join her. When he twisted the doorknob, he shook his head before leaning against the door.

"Chaise, unlock the door," he called.

"Nope."

"Baby, please let me in."

"Nope."

"Chaise, let me in or the hotel will have to replace the door and we'll have to go stay in the room with Noah and Brianna after they kick us out of here."

"You wouldn't dare."

"You know damn well I will," Bull replied.

He heard Chaise's huff of contempt as she unlocked the door but didn't open it for him to enter. Bull slowly turned the knob and walked into the room just as Chaise stepped into the shower. He shed his clothes and quickly followed her inside the generous shower stall. She stood under the stream of hot water with her eyes closed, soaking in the warmth and washing away the remnants of her mishap.

His eyes followed the small rivers of water that flowed over her body. His hands ached to feel the silky smoothness of her skin. His lips were drawn to the fullness of her breasts and the tautness of her nipples. His tongue longed to taste her, to lap up her essence, and bring her exquisite pleasure.

But first, he knew he had to make amends.

"I'm sorry if I hurt your feelings, baby," he said softly.

She opened her eyes and met his gaze but remained silent.

"I'm sorry I didn't help you when you were obviously having a hard time," he continued.

She still waited.

"I'm sorry I laughed at your misfortune."

Chaise picked up the shampoo and began lathering her hair but still didn't speak.

"And I'm sorry I said you looked like a frog when you were flailing around in the mud."

Bull dropped his chin to his chest, his outward display that he'd been appropriately chastised. Actually, he was attempting to hide the smile that threatened to cover his face as he envisioned the scene yet again. After a couple of seconds, the memory of the sight of Chaise sprawled out on Mrs. Stanton's front lawn, soaked to the core from the sprinklers and covered from head to toe in mud as she screamed obscenities at Bull was more than he could keep in. The repeated slips and slides from the slick mud ensured that every part of her body was thoroughly covered in dirt and flower bed mulch.

When his shoulders began to jump from his laughter, Chaise picked up the handheld showerhead, quickly turned the hot water off, and covered Bull with ice-cold water. He yelped and reached for the sprayer, but Chaise had already anticipated his moves. She ducked to the side and kept the spray of cold water centered on him.

"Chaise..." Bull's tone threatened. "When I get to you..."

"What? Think I'm scared of you?" she goaded as she continued to spray him.

Charging through the cold water, Bull wrapped his thick arms around her and pulled her to him. He smiled when she screamed because the handheld sprayer was trapped between them with the cold water still flowing strong. "You never have to be scared of me," he said softly as he adjusted the water temperature with one hand. "I'm sorry, baby. I shouldn't have laughed. I should've helped you."

Chaise shook her head and began to laugh herself. The more she laughed, the more hilarious it became. "Okay, maybe I overreacted. I'm sure it was a pretty funny sight."

"It was, but I left you when I should've helped you instead. That'll never happen again," he promised. "Now we need to finish cleaning you up, my dirty girl."

After he replaced the showerhead, Bull massaged his fingers in her hair to wash away the grime and gave her extra special attention. He gently pushed her under the spray of water, and she leaned her head back to rinse out the shampoo. After he'd repeated the process with the conditioner, he lathered her mesh travel sponge with shower gel and took his time washing every inch of her body.

"Colton?" Chaise huskily breathed his name as he gave her foot extra attention.

"Yeah, babe."

"I've waited long enough."

Bull lifted his eyes to meet hers and instantly recognized the hunger in her eyes. With a smirk, he moved deliberately slowly to increase her anticipation. "Well, if my lady is impatient, I guess I'd better do something about that."

"Colton, don't make me—*aaahhh*!"

Before she could issue her threat, the leg that had been in Bull's hand was thrown over his shoulder and his lips were wrapped around her clit. Chaise stumbled back against the shower wall while her hands searched for something hold on to. Finding nothing but the slick tile walls, she clenched her fingers on Bull's shoulders, her fingernails digging into his skin. With every flick of his tongue, graze of his teeth, and pull of his lips, Chaise saw brilliant flashes of light and stars. His wet, warm tongue voraciously lapped up her essence. He pushed his fingers inside her, filled her, and continued to increase the pressure until she screamed out his name.

"Damn, I love hearing that," Bull said as he stood.

"I'll never get tired of yelling at you for that." She smiled alluringly.

"Let's test that theory."

He turned the water off, threw Chaise over his shoulder, and sprinted toward the bed. After he deposited her in the center, he resumed feasting on her body. He pulled one taut nipple into his mouth and her back arched in response. While his tongue circled the tightened peak, he rolled the other nipple between his finger and thumb, lightly tugging on it, and silently claiming each whimper as his own. The multiple sensations his ministrations elicited in Chaise's body increased her sensitivity. Every scrape of his five-o'clock shadow pushed her closer to the edge again. Each time his teeth lightly grazed her nipple she became even more hyper-responsive.

Without forewarning, he pushed deep inside her and had to immediately still his movements when the tightness surrounding him clamped down even more. His guttural growl of appreciation echoed through the bedroom as he surged forward into her again. "I'm so fucking glad you're mine," he told her. "Always. You'll always be mine."

Chaise knew Bull well enough to read between the lines of his outward bravado. At times like this when he expressed his feelings, he showed his vulnerability. "I'll always be yours," she whispered in reply. "And you'll always be mine."

"Always," he confirmed.

CHAPTER FOUR

"They've been in and out of her townhouse for the past week. I'm positive it's them," Lee stressed into the phone. His Middle Eastern accent slipped back into the tone and inflection of his voice unconsciously when he was especially upset. "Just send me the package like I said and don't second-guess me again."

Lee hung up the phone and settled back in his chair. As he absently rubbed his chin, his mind strayed back to the moment he'd laid eyes on the four men. There was no mistaking them for anyone else. Their builds aside, the fierceness they projected, along with the carriage and confidence from their military days, was hard to hide. The way they quickly sized him up and assessed his threat level impressed Lee, but the hatred he harbored ran much deeper than any respect he could've had for them.

He pushed up from his reclining position and paced the floor, walking quickly from one end of the small room to the other. After several minutes of it, he realized he'd reverted back to his old training. He'd been twisting quickly on his heel as he prepared to turn around. "Old habits die hard," he mused to himself.

"They've visited the old lady every day this week." He abruptly changed his thoughts, going back to his original topic. "She's obviously very special to Brianna. I heard her tell Liz that they'd come back to see her soon."

His mind was on overdrive as he contemplated all the possibilities of revenge. That train of thought was dangerous, he knew, because it reduced his ability to focus on the task in front of him. But he couldn't pass up the opportunity when it presented itself so beautifully and effortlessly. It would be a sin not to take advantage of the opportunity that was so obviously a divine sign. Before he realized it, his hand had curled into a fist and he was knocking on Mrs. Stanton's door.

"Why, hello, Lee. I'm surprised to see you today," Liz greeted him.

"Hi, Mrs. Stanton." He smiled, hoping his expression didn't betray his thoughts. "How are you?"

"I'm good. Would you like to come in?" Liz stepped out of the doorway to give him room to enter. "And if I've told you once, I've told you a hundred times. Call me Liz," she laughed.

"Okay, Liz," he conceded. "It's a sign of disrespect in my family to call a lady by her first name, so it's purely out of habit."

"I can understand that." Liz nodded. "But it's also a sign of disrespect if a lady asks you to call her by her name and you don't."

"Touché," Lee laughed.

It really is unfortunate that the old lady has to die, Lee thought. *I was actually just starting to like her.*

"Would you care for some coffee or hot tea?" Liz asked.

"Hot tea would be great. Thank you."

Liz smiled and nodded. "I'll train you right eventually."

"You keep trying." He flirted playfully.

"Honey?"

"What?" Lee asked, confusion marring his attempt to be suave.

"Do you want honey in your tea?" Liz clarified.

"Yes, please," Lee replied.

After making their drinks, Liz sat at the table with Lee and they chatted amiably for a while before he brought up her recent visitors.

"Having visitors this week seems to agree with you," Lee commented.

"It was so nice having them here. I've missed Brianna so much, and I worried about her every day," she said solemnly. "I reported her as missing, and I never did understand why the police couldn't get any leads on her. Now, I understand."

"Why was that?" Lee asked.

"She was in witness protection. Whatever they were told about her was enough to keep them from looking for her. Broke my heart, though. I just thought they didn't care about her. But, she explained everything, and I can't blame her for running back to Noah. Don't think she didn't get a good tongue-lashing for not calling me as soon as she was able, though."

"I'm sure you put her in her place." Lee smiled. "Are they coming back over today?"

"No, they've all gone back home now. They promised they'd be back in a few weeks. Noah is looking into expanding his business, and he found a place here that will work out well.

"Wouldn't that be nice, Lee?" Liz exclaimed suddenly. "You know, my kids don't ever come see me. At least this way, Brianna and her family would come see me regularly."

"Why wouldn't your kids come to see you?" Lee took a sip of his tea and kept her talking.

"They're too busy with their own lives and don't have time for an old lady. My son is a doctor and his patients need him. My daughter has plenty of activities to keep her busy." Liz shrugged.

"Where do they live?"

"My son is in Texas and my daughter is in California."

"It's too bad they don't live closer to you," Lee lied. "Have you considered moving to be nearer to one of them?"

"Oh, it's crossed my mind," Liz explained as she kept her eyes trained on the table. "But I couldn't pick one over the other. Besides, it's time for them to live their lives and not worry over me. Their kids are in their early teens now and off doing their own thing. My son and daughter are enjoying just being married couples and having some time to themselves again. I'd be a third wheel to either of them."

Lee made an exaggerated show of checking the time on his watch as he quickly rose from his chair. "I'm sorry to rush out like this, Liz, but I'm late for an appointment. If you don't mind, I'd like to come by again soon. It seems we're both alone here."

"That'd be great, Lee." Liz smiled. "I have to admit, I never really thought you liked me much."

"What's not to like?" His charm oozed out of him as if it were natural. "I've had my own problems lately and I've been preoccupied. My mind is clear now."

"Glad to hear that. We don't need any muddled brains around here," Liz laughed good-naturedly.

As Lee left, his smirk covered his face. His plan would work out even better than he'd originally thought. With her only family members living multiple states away, she'd be a much easier barrier to remove. She'd become very familiar with him and could too easily identify him. That wouldn't matter after he'd exacted his revenge, but he had to eliminate any possible hindrance ahead of time.

"Say goodbye, Mrs. Elizabeth Stanton. Your time here is drawing to a close," Lee said smugly to himself as he got into his car.

Keeping up appearances would be important now. He had to appear to leave for work at the same time every day, come home after work at staggered times, and begin planting the story around the nosy neighborhood of his upcoming required business travel. Once his alibi was firmly set, the neighbors would be less likely to implicate him during the aftermath.

He could picture the neighbors' dumbfounded replies when the police finally found Liz's dead body in her townhouse.

Lee will be so upset when he gets home. He loved Mrs. Stanton.

No, officer, I don't have his cell phone number. He said he'd be back in a few days.

"By the time these idiots realize I'm not coming back, my trail will be as cold as ice," Lee said aloud.

~

"Where have you been for the last two weeks, young man?" Liz playfully chastised Lee.

"Work has been just crazy lately." He shook his head. "I finally took some time off to get a break."

"What do you do?" she probed.

"Nothing I want to talk about on my off day." He winked.

She patted his cheek in her motherly way. "One day, you'll tell me all about yourself. You think you're hiding that pain you carry around, but I see it."

He was taken aback for a few seconds. He'd never allowed anyone to get close enough to get a read on him before, but her words made him second-guess what he thought he knew. Was she really that intuitive, or had he slipped and revealed more than he realized?

"The only pain I have is that I wasn't born with a silver spoon in my mouth, independently wealthy, so I don't have to work." He attempted to play it off, avoid her directness, but the look she shot him was unmistakable. She wasn't buying it.

No matter, he thought. *It'll soon be over.*

"I hate to trouble you on your off day, but I need some help unloading bags of mulch for my flower beds. Do you mind helping me?"

"Not at all," he lied. "Lead the way."

His sole purpose was to see his plan through, and he'd planned the perfect time. At that time in September, schools in the area were starting back. Most of the parents in the neighborhood were away from home, taking their young children to school, and preoccupied with all the first day activities. In their distracted state, they wouldn't pay attention to a single man and an elderly lady.

Liz walked out the front door and toward her car. Popping the trunk open, she motioned to the bags stacked in the back, one on top of the other. "We can just put them here on the grass," she pointed. "That'll make it easier for me to put them out in the beds."

A mountain of unopened mulch bags waiting in her front yard would definitely draw attention. The whole neighborhood knew Liz loved working in her flower beds. She bragged about them to anyone within earshot who would listen. Every single day, she could be found pulling weeds, meticulously making them perfect. Lee knew there was no way he could leave it unfinished without calling attention to them both.

"Let's go ahead and spread the mulch," he suggested. "Working outside will do me good after being stuck inside behind a desk all the time."

"You're sure you don't mind?" She raised her eyebrows in disbelief.

"I don't mind at all."

For the following two hours, Lee split one of the plastic bags open, poured the mulch into the beds to Liz's exact specifications, and grabbed the next one to repeat the process. When he finally reached the last bag, the buildup of tension had him wound as tightly as a metal coil. Purposely maintaining his outward cool, he completed his task and waited for Liz to make the offer he knew was coming.

"Everything looks beautiful, Lee," she gushed. "Thank you so much for helping me."

"It's my pleasure."

"Surely you had something better to do than spend your off day with an old lady. Don't you have a nice young lady in your life?"

"No, no one like that." He shook his head.

"A wild, free-spirited girl, then?"

The twinkle in her eye almost made Lee laugh. Liz had a way of getting under his skin in a way that made him wish he still had his mother. The way she tried to mother him made a part of him long to be cared for, nurtured, and have someone he could depend on. Those feelings and sentiments had frequently been the source of fights and harsh disappointment from his father.

His father had been very traditional and had expected Lee to be the man of the family from a very early age. He'd ruled his house with an iron fist and a thick rod for the backs of children who didn't meet his expectations. When Lee remembered his father, he couldn't recall ever feeling like he'd had his father's approval. It was that feeling that drove his need for revenge. He'd been robbed of achieving his father's blessing, leaving him as only half a man.

It was this fact that helped Lee keep his eye on the goal when he was tempted to give in and just live a normal life. "No wild, free-spirited girl, either," he laughed and shook his head. "What about you? Do you have a secret man in your life?"

"There is no man who could fill the shoes my husband left behind," Liz said sadly. "I have friends. I have hobbies to keep me busy. But my heart will always belong to my husband. I'll be with him again one day."

Lee chose to take her words as a confirmation that he was doing the right thing. "My throat is getting scratchy." He rubbed his neck. "I'd better go get something to drink. Can I bring you anything?"

"Young man, you know cold drinks won't help get rid of a scratchy throat. You need some hot tea to soothe that. It's probably from all the pollen after working in the flower beds. Come inside and I'll fix our tea," Liz offered.

"Are you sure I'm not imposing?" he asked, feigning concern.

"Of course not," she insisted. "I enjoy your company. Come on in and let's talk about where you can find a free-spirited girl these days."

"Oh, I have something for you to try. Let me grab it first."

Lee jogged to his townhouse and rushed to the kitchen. He grabbed the jar from the counter and hurried back to Liz before she put that fucking awful honey of hers in his tea. "Liz, are you in here?" He cracked the door.

"In the kitchen. Come on in," she answered.

As he stepped inside, he realized that Liz was cooking a meal for them to share. "What are you making?"

"Thought we'd have some croissants and tea. I saw this recipe on a television show and it looked delicious," she replied animatedly. "You get to be my guinea pig and try them out for me."

"Only if you'll try something for me, too. It'll actually go perfectly with your croissants." He attempted to entice her.

"I'm not scared of trying something new." She placed her hand on her hip as she cocked it to one side. "You got a deal, young man."

Lee smiled smugly, pleased with how flawlessly everything was coming together. As Liz worked on creating the perfect homemade croissants, he planned his next move. Waiting weeks for her friends to return so he could kill them all at once was not an option. His pride, his honor, and earning the respect of his father forced his hand and his timetable. He suffered through the tedious conversation until the oven timer rang.

Death for whom the bell tolls, he thought.

When Liz served the hot pastries, Lee took the opportunity to open the jar. "Now it's time for you to try a real delicacy. Put some in your tea and slather it all over your croissant. You'll love it," he promised.

He dipped a small drop of honey into his tea and put another drop on his plate beside his pastry. He patiently sipped his tea while he watched Liz spoon the large blob of honey into her tea and then generously drizzled it across the top of her pastry. Lee's eyes followed the stream of honey, knowing her sweet tooth wouldn't allow her to stop when most other people would. That was exactly what he was counting on.

With every couple of bites of her pastry, she'd stop and take a drink of her tea. Lee patiently pretended to sip on his tea, raising the glass to his lips but not actually drinking it any longer. The pastries were delicious, he had to admit, and Liz had quickly scarfed hers down. When she reached for a second one, Lee sat back in his chair and watched as the intense reaction started.

The first sign was her unsteady hand as she stretched her arm across the table. When her hand dropped to pick up the croissant, she completely missed the plate. Lee lifted his eyes to hers and smirked as the bewilderment in her expression increased. She attempted to pick it up again and at last managed to succeed.

As she brought her arm back toward her body, she began to sway back and forth. Her eyes became more vacant as she started having a harder time staying upright in her chair. Her eyes swung to Lee's, fear now mixing with the confusion, knowledge that something was terribly wrong had settled in, and the uncertainty of how to convey her predicament crippled her.

"Lee?" she pleaded with one word.

He remained silent, still, and emotionless as he watched as her body succumbed to the toxins. She attempted to stand and move toward the phone, but Lee knew it was fruitless for her to even try. Her small frame crumpled to the floor as her heart rate slowed. He stood over her and watched as the life faded from her eyes.

"Goodbye, Liz," he whispered as he stepped over her, locked the door behind himself, and drove away.

CHAPTER FIVE

Noah was fully engrossed in planning a complex security detail when his cell phone on his desk rang. He absently held the phone to his ear and answered. "Steele."

"Is this Mr. Noah Steele?" the man asked.

"Speaking. Who is this?"

"I'm Special Agent Landry with the FBI in the Denver office. I need to ask you a few questions in regards to a case that landed on my desk."

Noah's curiosity was piqued enough to put the security detail to the side and focus on the phone conversation. "I'm glad to help if I can."

"Did you visit the Boulder area in late August?"

"Yes, I did. Why do you ask?" Noah replied, his senses immediately on alert.

"Did you visit with a Mrs. Elizabeth Stanton while you were in town?"

The fact that Special Agent Landry had just completely ignored Noah's question didn't go unnoticed. "Landry, right?" Noah asked, his tone of voice sharp.

"Yes," he replied, clearly not pleased that his hard-earned title had been omitted.

"Since you're calling me, I'm sure you've already been briefed on my background. There's no need for a pissing contest, because I guarantee my security clearance is higher than yours. Cut the bullshit where you try to establish your authority so we can get to the part where you tell me about the case you're working." The intent of Noah's direct and demanding tone was impossible to misunderstand.

Noah waited patiently through the few seconds of silence on the other end of the line. He could tell Special Agent Landry was fighting to keep his cool, wishing he could just hang up, but Landry knew he had called Noah called for a reason. "Mrs. Stanton was found on the floor of her home. If her son hadn't shown up exactly when he did, she would've died. Fortunately for her, he's a doctor and kept her alive until the paramedics got there to transport her to the hospital."

"Is she all right?" Noah jumped up from his desk as he asked. His first thought was to make sure Brianna was safe.

"She is now. Her heart rate dropped dangerously low and led to a heart attack. She spent a few days in CCU," Landry explained.

Noah picked up his keys and quickly moved toward the door. There was no reason for the FBI to call him to tell him about Mrs. Stanton's health scare. "Let's hear the punch line."

"The paramedic noted in his report that she had what's called widened QRS complex. The initial thought was that she'd had a bad reaction to a toxin in her system, possibly an overdose of medication. But when she regained consciousness, she was adamant that she's not on any medications."

"So, are you thinking it was an environmental accident or an intentional poisoning?" Noah climbed into his truck, intent solely on getting to Brianna, but he already knew what the agent's reply would be as he transferred the call to Bluetooth.

"Her son insisted that the medical staff figure out what had happened to his mother, so a couple of technicians went back to her townhouse with him to have a look around. There was evidence that someone else had been there with her and that they'd eaten just before her heart attack.

"The techs took the plates, food, and drinks back for testing. The results came back positive for something called grayanotoxin. It comes from *deli bal*," Landry paused.

Noah's heart also paused before racing at breakneck speed.

"Mad honey," Noah muttered disbelievingly.

"So you're familiar with it," Landry replied with a chuckle. "Why am I not surprised?"

"I spent enough time in the Middle East, Landry. Mad honey is found in a certain area of Turkey," Noah said as he pressed the gas pedal harder.

"That's right, and it's lethal in large doses. People in that area know to take it in extremely small amounts. Mrs. Stanton had a large amount in her teacup and even more left over on her plate. The second plate had a small amount that appeared to be untouched. The second cup had a miniscule amount in it, but whoever was with her didn't drink enough of it to make a difference," Landry explained.

"It was obviously someone who knew exactly what an overdose of mad honey would do. Intentional poisoning, since he was careful with how much he consumed but probably watched her use way too much." Noah envisioned the event in his head in many different scenarios, but he saw Lee in every one.

"Sounds like you have a suspect in mind," Landry probed.

"There was a weird vibe from her neighbor," Noah replied. "His name is Lee, but I didn't get his last name."

"Actually, his name is Ali Babek Turan. Mrs. Stanton positively ID'd him from a photo we showed her. He's been on an FBI Watchlist for some time, but we apparently lost him," Landry explained.

"Do you think I'm on his shit list since I was there with Mrs. Stanton?"

"I think you're on his list, but not for that reason. After I searched your name and Turan's name in a federal database, I was suddenly locked out of it completely. Spooks showed up in my director's office and took the whole case file right out of my hands. Something's obviously up, and with your impressive service history, I thought I should give you as much of a heads-up as I can."

"Thanks, Special Agent Landry. I really appreciate it. I'm sure the CIA will be waiting for me when I get home," Noah replied.

"Best of luck, Steele."

When Noah pulled into his driveway, he immediately spotted the nondescript cars on his street that hadn't been there before. Since CIA analysts needed to blend into the background wherever they went, their clothes and vehicles had to blend in as well. Most people wouldn't notice the compact car parked next to the house two doors down or the family van against the curb. But then, most people weren't trained to spot them for a living either.

The gate began to open, and he shook his head as the van moved toward him. He pressed his quick dial option for Shadow on the truck's Bluetooth.

"You're losing your touch, man. I'm already here," Shadow chuckled.

"Get your ass out of that compact car in my neighbor's driveway and get over here before the gate closes," Noah retorted. "You're too big to fit in that tiny car anyway. You'll break it."

"On my way, boss," Shadow laughed.

Noah stopped at the front door and watched Shadow climb out of the compact car with a bemused expression. Rebel and Bull pulled in the driveway just after Shadow and just before the soccer mom van that narrowly beat the closing gate.

Chaise came out of the house and walked over to stand next to Bull, her concern written on her face. She laced her fingers with his as they joined Noah. Bull gently squeezed her hand as he leaned into her. "Don't worry, baby. It'll be fine."

Two men exited the van and started walking toward the waiting crew. The front door opened and Brianna stepped outside, looking first at her family and then at the approaching men who tried a little too hard to be casual. Noah slid his arm behind her and gently pushed her until she was completely shielded by his body. "Stay there, Bri," he said over his shoulder.

"What's going on, Noah?" she whispered to his back. Her fingers gripped his shirt as she stepped closer so their bodies were touching as much as possible.

"CIA, babe. I'll tell you the rest in a minute."

"Noah Steele?" one of the men called.

"That's right," Noah replied.

"I'm Joe Brown. This is Bill Smith. We'd like to talk to you."

"Very imaginative names. What exactly can I do for the CIA? You boys here for some covert surveillance training?" Noah grinned.

Joe smiled good-naturedly as his gaze floated from one man to the next. "We've been briefed on all of you—Reaper, Bull, Rebel, and Shadow. Figured if we tried to hide too well, they'd never find our bodies."

"You'd be right about that," Shadow replied, the typical gleam of wit in his eyes.

"Mind if we talk to all of you inside?" Bill asked. "It's fortunate you're all here. Saves us a lot of time."

Noah nodded and motioned toward the door. "Come on in." As he turned, he took Brianna's hand in his and raised it to his mouth for a kiss. "You're staying with me," he said quietly.

"Just let them try to tell me to leave," Brianna replied as she opened the door.

Everyone followed Brianna into the spacious den. "Have a seat, guys," Brianna offered.

Noah sat first and pulled Brianna into his lap. She willingly took her seat, wrapped her arm around his neck, and flashed an obstinate look at Bill and Joe. Bull pulled Chaise down beside him, their thighs touching. The message was clear—this family intended to stick together no matter what was thrown at them.

Joe sat on the edge of the seat, his tense energy palpable. He clearly knew the group wouldn't be receptive to the news he had to deliver. He cleared his throat and repeated the story Special Agent Landry had already told Noah. The men remained stoic as they listened and took in every detail. The only exception was when Joe explained Liz's emergency. Noah's fingers tightened on Brianna's hip when she attempted to jump up from his lap, and a slight smile played on his lips as he shook his head.

When Joe finished, he looked at Noah. "Why does it seem like you already knew all of this?"

Noah shrugged. "Life is full of mysteries. Like why the CIA has taken over a domestic case of civilian poisoning."

Bill smiled knowingly. "It's a little more complicated than that. As Joe said, Turan was on the FBI Watchlist but he disappeared for a while. We think he's working with someone else in the US. He probably stole someone's identification and started a new life. We've checked every aspect of Mrs. Stanton's life and his cover as Lee Clover while he lived next door to her. He'd never been late for work, never missed a day, and never even had a parking ticket."

Joe chimed in. "The only trigger point we've identified is your visit to Boulder a few weeks ago. He abruptly quit his job without giving even a day's notice. He closed his checking and savings accounts. Then he poisoned Mrs. Stanton and left her for dead."

Joe and Bill paused, looked at Brianna, and then watched as Noah covered her and their baby with his free arm. Joe recognized the protective gesture and carefully weighed his next words. "Right now, the only connection we've found is Brianna's visit to the Middle East. After what happened with US Marshal Stevens, we can't discount the possibility that another member of the same international crime ring is after her."

"You think he's coming after me?" Brianna asked. Her hand flew to her stomach and joined with Noah's to shield their growing baby. "I was in Boulder every day for a week. Why not try something then?"

"There's no cause for alarm yet. We just want you to be extra vigilant about your surroundings. We're still looking at other leads and connections." Bill tried to assure her.

"But you don't know where he is or why he's here or why he tried to kill Liz. That doesn't sound like no reason to be alarmed to me," Brianna shot back. "You're in my home for a reason, aren't you? You obviously know we have every reason to be alarmed. Don't patronize me, and don't lie to me."

Noah smiled proudly at Brianna. "There's my tiger." He winked. His expression changed when he met Joe's and Bill's gazes. Noah and Reaper could be two different men at times. The man before them was definitely Reaper. "Don't disrespect my wife like that again."

"How about one of you just man up and spit it out?" Bull challenged, irritation lacing his tone.

"He has several aliases and our intel on Ali Babek Turan isn't complete, but we know that he's a merciless killer. He's never left anyone alive before, so chances are high that he thought Mrs. Stanton was dead when he walked out. Had her son not been a doctor, she probably would've been classified as another heart attack case and we would've never known about the toxin.

"Our lab guys confirmed that it came from a bee farm in Turkey from the type of rhododendron pollen in it. It was fresh, too, so he recently acquired this batch. Our computer techs are currently scouring Customs' databases for package tracking info, but I don't expect to find anything. He's been smart enough to avoid us so far, so I don't see him making that kind of mistake."

"Babek Turan doesn't make sense," Rebel interjected.

"What do you mean?" Noah asked.

"Babek is a Persian surname. Turan is a Turkish surname. It's another alias, and he's saying he identifies with both cultures," Rebel explained.

"Have you figured out why he's so familiar to you yet?" Noah asked.

Rebel shook his head from side to side, but Bill immediately picked up on the comment.

"You think he's someone you've encountered in the past?"

"No. But something about him reminds me of someone I've come across before. I've been racking my brain, going through the details of our operations, but nothing has clicked yet." Rebel stood and began pacing the room. Like a caged tiger, restless and irritated, his display of aggravation was apparent and uncharacteristic.

Joe's phone buzzed and he quickly checked the message. "Another death has just been linked to Ali Babek Turan," Joe said. "It was a sudden, unexplained death, and the circumstances too closely matched Mrs. Stanton's close call. We had it double-checked and the word just came back."

"Who was it?" Shadow asked.

"Tom Nash, a former civilian contractor for the Defense department."

Rebel's head whipped around when he heard the name. His eyes met Noah's and immediately knew what the other thought.

"What? You know something. What is it?" Joe asked.

"Tom Nash was one of the hostages we rescued from a compound in Iran, just across the border from Turkey, ten years ago," Noah answered.

"Were you detected?"

"Yeah, it ended in a firefight just as we extracted the hostages," Noah replied.

"Not that he isn't somehow part of that group, but Ali is young right now. He would've had to been just a boy ten years ago. I didn't see any kids there that night," Rebel said.

"Neither did I," Shadow confirmed. "There were a lot of grown men, but I'd remember if any kids had been part of that group. It was a close call to get some of the hostages out of there without getting shot. One thing I never wanted to face was deciding whether or not to shoot a kid."

"I don't think he's after Brianna," Rebel said and gave Brianna a reassuring smile. "I do think he's here for us, though."

"You're right. He could very well be here for all of us," Bull replied. "But killing our loved ones in the process could be an added bonus for him."

"Men, this is a matter of national security. There's more we need to brief you on, but we have to be in secure quarters." Joe retrieved four envelopes from his inside coat pocket. "By special order of the President of the United States and Commander Adkins of the United States Special Operations Command, you are all hereby served with your orders. You've been fully reinstated as Delta Force operators to assist with the capture of Ali Babek Turan, by any means necessary."

Whatever reaction Joe and Bill had expected, it was not the reaction they received. The team's faces remained expressionless, but their eyes held fire and ice. The trained killers were no doubt still lurking just beneath their civilized exteriors. Bill attempted to break the tension in the room with a moment of levity. "It's a little unnerving to have the four of you staring at us like that."

"Like what?" Bull asked.

"Like, if I look away for a second, I'd never wake up again," he replied.

"I must be losing my touch, then," Bull replied. "You shouldn't be able to tell exactly what I'm thinking."

"We need you guys. The country needs you. We could very well have an activated sleeper cell on our hands. On American soil. We have a chance to stop whatever he has planned," Bill urged.

"But the CIA doesn't have jurisdiction on American soil," Chaise interjected.

Bill and Joe both smiled. "Sure, we don't," Joe replied, intentionally cryptic.

"It's not like you have a choice, since in a way you're being drafted. But we'd much rather you join us willingly," Bill added.

"I'm in, but I have conditions," Noah spoke first.

"Let's hear them," Bill replied.

"I'm not leaving the country. We have a baby on the way, and I'm not getting stuck out on assignment somewhere and missing the birth. Or anything else that Brianna needs me here for," Noah replied.

"Deal. You stay stateside. What else?"

"If I have to leave for more than a couple of days, Brianna comes with me. I won't leave her safety in anyone's hands but these three men here with me."

"Agreed."

"Since Brianna and Chaise are in as much danger as the rest of us, they're privy to any information we get. Their safety isn't up for discussion or debate."

Joe and Bill exchanged glances, knowing that some of the information they had was classified at above top secret. Noah sensed their hesitation and chuckled humorlessly.

"Guys, you can't tell me you've never divulged a little top secret information in exchange for even better intel from a confidential informant. You're spooks. It's what you do." Noah leveled his gaze on them. "I'm not asking, gentleman. I'm telling you this is how it will be."

"You know you can agree to this, gentleman. These two civilians are under our protection and can't leave our sight," Shadow added. "It's the right thing to do."

"Fine," Joe conceded.

"What about Liz?" Brianna asked.

"She's been moved to a safe place. The neighbors don't know if she's still alive or at her son's house, and we've intentionally left it vague. With the medical laws, the hospital can't give patient status, so there's not much risk there. She's asking about you, though." Joe smiled at Brianna. "It's been hell to convince her you and the baby are safe."

Brianna chuckled. "That sounds like her."

"We have a couple of different ways we can play this to draw him out.

While we're strategizing, it's probably best if all of you move to a safe location, too," Bill suggested.

"I'll beef up security around here. Chaise can stay here with Brianna if we're away, and I'll add my best security guys to the grounds. Otherwise, I don't want to hide anywhere." Looking at his brothers, he silently confirmed their agreement.

"Your mail will be scanned and packages opened by a trained team. No delivery trucks or unknown vehicles are allowed inside the gates. Every man on your payroll has already been vetted. We're not taking any chances with this," Joe admitted.

"Good to know," Noah nodded.

Before Joe and Bill left, Joe reluctantly promised he'd have Liz contact Brianna through a clean cell phone from her safe location. "That's against every protocol on record, you know."

"I doubt you'll lose any sleep over it, Joe," Brianna deadpanned.

Later that evening, Noah and Brianna settled onto the couch together. "Is this how you felt when you were an operator all the time? A constant ball of stress in your gut?" Brianna asked as she laid her head on his chest.

"Not really stress, babe. After all the training, it becomes almost second nature. There's always a surge of adrenaline mixed with a little nervousness. That's what kept us on our toes, though," he replied. "You have nothing to be stressed about. I'll never let him get close to you."

She raised her head to look him in the eye before she spoke. "I'm not worried about me nearly as much as I'm worried about you, Noah."

"Bri, this is my job. This is what I have done for years. You don't have to worry about me. I can take care of us. I've tried to convince you of that before." He raised an eyebrow at her.

"You're never going to let me live that down, are you?"

"Nope. Not if I can use it to get what I want." He grinned slyly.

"Let me rephrase what I said to be more accurate," she said dryly. "I'm scared of losing you because I know what it's like to live without you. I don't want to do it again."

Noah's face softened as he threaded his fingers through her hair. "I feel exactly the same way. Baby, I promise we'll never know what that's like again. The security here will be thoroughly overhauled. Owning a security firm, I should've already handled that, but after you 'died,' I really just didn't care about anything. Nothing mattered except my business and protecting others, because it took my mind off what I'd lost here.

"Now I know I can't take a single thing for granted or take any chances with you and our baby. Several big enhancements will be immediately installed, so we'll both be as safe as we can possibly be," he assured her.

"You know," she purred. "All this talk of being my big, strong protector is really turning me on."

"Oh, yeah?"

"Oh, yeah," she confirmed before she lifted the hem of his shirt and pulled it over his head. "Definitely."

CHAPTER SIX

"Do you think you'll have to leave?" Chaise asked Bull on their way home.

He heard the worry in her voice, saw the concern in her eyes, and knew that her question ran deep. As much as she worried about his safety, she also worried about the anxiety that plagued her when he wasn't around. "If I have to leave you, it'll only be for the night, and you'll stay with Brianna while I'm gone. Otherwise, you will be right with me. I won't leave you for longer than that, Chaise. I promise."

She'd diagnosed herself with post-traumatic stress disorder after her ordeal with the Cordova family. She woke after having terrible nightmares at night and often had tears streaming down her face. Bull's arm would tighten around her and he'd whisper soothing words in her ear until she'd calmed down enough to fall asleep again. Her refusal to seek medical help had been the source of arguments, but Bull was often silenced when she reminded him of how he'd previously coped with stress.

"I know you think I'm weak," she half-whispered.

"No, I don't think that at all. I'm amazed at how strong you are and how well you're dealing with all the stress you've been under in the last few months."

"Colton, I depend on you way too much. It's like I can't even let you do your job without panicking over you being away. That's not who I want to be," she said solemnly.

"We depend on each other," he emphasized. "As much as I love protecting that hot body of yours, I don't want you to completely shut down if I'm away. What do you suggest we do?"

"I think taking self-defense classes may help," Chaise admitted. "Maybe my real problem is a feeling of helplessness."

"That's a great idea. You already know how to shoot and handle a gun. I can give you the names of a few places, and you can pick which class you want to go to," Bull offered.

"You're pretty slick, ya know?" She smiled playfully.

"Me? How's that?"

"The whole 'pick which class you want to go to' part. I know you did that to make me feel like I'm in control."

"You are in control. I'll even let you pick all the positions for our sexual acrobatics tonight," Bull replied.

"I think I like this 'being in control' thing."

"Yeah, don't get too used to it," Bull warned playfully.

"I'm stressing a little over planning our wedding, too," Chaise admitted.

"What's stressing you about it?"

"Several things, honestly. Not knowing what's going to happen with my dad, if he'll be able to give me away, or...if he'll even still be with us. Trying to coordinate everything around Noah and Brianna's baby. Now this guy is after us and could be part of a terrorist sleeper cell. All of this on top of the normal stress of planning a big event like this is just a lot," she explained.

"Baby, if you want a big wedding, we'll have the biggest fucking wedding ever imagined. If you'd rather run away and elope, we'll still have the loudest honeymoon anyone's ever heard. As long as you're mine forever, I'll do this however you want," Bull replied.

"You're right," Chaise decided.

"About?"

"Everything. Starting with the acrobatics tonight. Hurry up and get me home."

"Yes, ma'am." Bull saluted.

~

The next morning, Bull and Chaise met the others at Noah's house to begin the assessment, strategy, and planned reconnaissance part of their mission. Bill and Joe rejoined them and brought the files they'd collected on Turan. Each man began by reviewing every page in an attempt to identify any other ties to past missions they'd been on.

"Here you go," Joe said and handed Brianna a plain, black cell phone. "Liz will call you in a few minutes. That woman is a handful. She hasn't let her guardian have a break since we told her she can call you."

"Thanks, Joe. I appreciate this. She was my only friend for a long time, and she's very special to me," Brianna replied.

Brianna and Chaise retreated to another room in the house to wait for Liz's call. When the phone rang, Brianna immediately put it on speaker and answered excitedly. "Liz! Are you okay? Chaise is here with me, and we've been so worried about you," Brianna exclaimed.

"I'm fine now, sweet girl. I felt like I'd been run over by a semi when I first woke up in the hospital, but all the side effects are gone now," Liz assured her. "How are you and my beautiful Chaise doing? How's my baby?"

Chaise laughed at Liz's reply. "I'm fine, Liz, and I'm glad you've healed now."

"The baby's fine, too," Brianna replied. "What do you remember about the attack, Liz?"

"Not much at all," Liz said disappointedly. "This was before the poisoning, but I remember Lee coming to see me more often than he had before. Now I know why—he was studying me closer so he could pull this shit on me. I hope Shadow finds him and kicks his ass."

Chaise and Brianna both laughed at Liz's reply. "I'm sure he will, Liz. He's pretty easygoing until you rile him up, then he's lethal," Brianna said.

"Good. Just how I like my men," Liz giggled. "Do you know where I am? These damn men won't tell me anything."

"No, Liz, I'm sorry. We have no idea where they're keeping you. But, if I can arrange it, would you want to stay here with Noah and me?" Brianna asked. "Chaise will be here with us whenever the guys have to leave for the night."

"That would be heaven. This place is nice, but these guys are boring as hell. They won't even play strip poker with me," Liz huffed. She raised her voice to ensure they heard her when she continued. "It's because they know they'd lose!"

"Okay, let me see what I can do," Brianna laughed. "But, Liz, we're not playing strip poker here either."

"Fair enough. Unless everyone else leaves and Rebel or Shadow has to babysit me. Then we never had this conversation," Liz replied.

The three ladies continued talking and catching up, with Brianna asking the probing questions she'd learned as a reporter in her attempt to gather anything that could help them. After they disconnected with Liz, Brianna and Chaise rejoined the men in the den to share her suggestion. With the team on her side, she knew there was no way the CIA would stand a chance.

"We just hung up with Liz. She's doing great. Bragged on her son a lot for saving her." Brianna smiled. "We have a great idea."

All eyes swung to her, and they waited for her to continue. She met Noah's gaze and held the connection to him as she spoke.

"I'd like for Liz to come stay here with us until this is over. I think it'd be best for all of us. We'd all be in the same house to help each other. Maybe talking with us can help jar her memory of that day. She also wouldn't be there to harass the agents guarding her, even though Rebel and Shadow would have to bear the brunt of it." Brianna smiled.

"I think that's a great idea. She can flirt with me all she wants." Shadow grinned. "It's good for the ego."

"If that's what you want, I'm fine with it. We have plenty of room," Noah agreed.

"We had just decided that Reaper and I would stay here for the recon that requires more than a couple of days of travel. If that frees up two agents to help travel, it only makes sense to do it," Bull interjected.

"If you're sure you two don't mind, I can have her here tonight. She has to be in full disguise to leave the house, though. So if she goes to a doctor's appointment with you—" Joe motioned toward Brianna "—she has to be completely incognito. Turan can't know that she's still alive until we want him to know."

"We can handle that," Chaise agreed and Brianna nodded in agreement.

"Okay, it makes sense. It'll be late tonight when we move her. But if you're willing to live with her, who are we to deny you?" Bill deadpanned.

"Have you boys solved all of our other problems yet?" Brianna asked jokingly.

"Absolutely," Rebel replied. "Right down to the country's deficit."

Easy laughter rolled through the room. "We're developing a plan. One step at a time so we don't get ahead of ourselves."

Chaise's cell phone rang and she glanced at the screen. "It's Mom," she said as worry instantly infused her tone. "I'll be right back."

When Chaise left the room, Noah looked at Joe. "You have eyes on my parents right now, right?"

"Yes. He won't get to them," Joe replied confidently.

When Chaise rejoined them, her color had paled and her hands were shaking lightly, though she tried to hide it. "That was Mom. She wanted us to know they're admitting Dad back into the hospital because he's not eating enough. She said it's just a precaution and for us not to worry."

"That means she's not telling us everything," Noah replied.

"Exactly. He must be in worse shape than she's saying."

"And he must feel pretty bad to agree to go back inpatient," Noah guessed.

"We'll put extra surveillance in the hospital. We have a few agents who used to be nurses who can take a few shifts and watch over your father," Bill said and retrieved his phone from his pocket. After a clipped conversation, he had everything lined up as promised. "Everything's being put in place as we speak."

"Okay, let's get back to work and put an end to this," Rebel spoke up. "Turan needs to be stopped before anything else happens."

"Damn straight," Shadow said, and the men began their discussions again.

"Where's the file that has his work history in it?" Noah asked.

Joe and Bill exchanged glances, and Noah quickly stood, knowing immediately that they were hiding information from him. "We told you we don't have much on him." Bill avoided answering the question.

"Where is the fucking file?" Noah asked through gritted teeth. "So help me God. Withholding vital information from us is the fastest way to getting your ass kicked."

Bill retrieved a single sheet of paper from the stack and reluctantly handed it to Noah. He quickly scanned the page before advancing on Bill and Joe.

"You've got to be fucking kidding me! Why didn't you tell us this before now?"

Shadow and Bull jumped up from their seats and physically restrained Noah when he suddenly lunged for Bill. Even as strong and muscular as they both were, it took all of their strength to hold Noah back as he continued pushing, intent on plowing through them until he reached his target. With the icy tone of a killer, the fiery eyes of a madman, and the low tone of seriousness, Noah issued his warning.

"This is my family you're fucking with. I don't know you, I don't like you, and I don't trust you—especially after this. If you know anything else, you'd better speak up now because I'll cut your fucking tongue out if I find out later."

~

"Lee Clover is now dead," Ali said as he shredded his fake license. "Good riddance."

Ali had driven to Miami and arrived undetected. He had no intentions of keeping his presence here hidden, though. On the contrary, he had every plan of letting the four men and their loved ones know that he was very much alive and well, right there in their city.

"I could be right behind any one of you, and you'd never even know," he sneered.

Retrieving his multiple suitcases, he began setting up his own network in the small, furnished house he'd rented. His numerous laptops had all of the most advanced features since he'd built them himself—from the hardware parts to the operating system and the software programs. He arranged each one in the exact optimum location. The self-designed models weren't traceable like store-bought systems were—the first rule of being a genius in computer science. They also didn't have the quirks and limitations that prevented him from carrying out his commands with the speed and precision he required.

When the first one was powered up, he located several close Wi-Fi signals and ran his decryption software to retrieve their passwords. "The second rule is never use your own Internet connection, always access someone else's, then bounce the signal all over the world. By the time anyone with any intelligence locates your area, you are long gone," Ali muttered to himself. He continued to make one connection after another, projecting his unique address into different countries and making the signal zigzag in a jumbled mess that more closely resembled a mass of cooked spaghetti noodles.

He repeated the process with each machine he set up so that no two machines had the same pattern and, therefore, wouldn't have the same signature. For the average computer analyst geek employed by the government, it would take years to unravel his schematic. Ali was positive that he had plenty of time to exact his revenge and have a little fun at the team's expense along the way.

"First, let's see if you were smart enough to change your cell phone numbers." Ali shook his head. With the stroke of a few keys, he located every cell phone that had been in their possession at Liz's house. "Idiots. How can you not know to change your cell phones?"

Tapping into the cell phones' cameras remotely, he switched between each of them until he found one that was out in the open. He then activated the microphone so he had complete video and audio. He was so pleased to know they were already talking about him.

"You didn't tell us he worked as an information tech for the Army Corps of Engineers," Noah bellowed. "You knew that he's had access to all of our confidential information this whole time and didn't tell us."

"You know as well as I do that your top secret information isn't housed in the same system. It's in a stand-alone, self-contained system that couldn't be breached, even by the most notorious hacker," Bill replied.

"My family's information has been accessible to that asshole. I'm not afraid of him—let him face *me* like a man and he'll run home crying to Mommy like a little whipped pussy. But he's had access to my family's information and that's not all right with me," Noah replied loudly.

Noah pulled his phone out of his pocket and angrily punched a few keys. "Roman, I need you, Blake, and Alex over here immediately with every security upgrade we have available and some we haven't even offered yet. It's past time to lock this place down tighter than Fort Knox."

"Yes, by all means, bring in your best and see if you can barricade yourself away from me. I love the challenge," Ali replied to his computer screen.

An idea sprung to mind that was simply too good to resist. Quickly killing them when they had no clue he was there wasn't a true test of his superiority. He would torment them first, keep them on edge and constantly looking over their shoulders as they feebly attempted to outwit him. With each step and every turn, he would show them that he was better than them in all ways imaginable. Then, when it was time, he would look them in the eyes and watch the terror fill their faces as they died alone, realizing he'd beaten them.

"Yes, I know you told me to do it years ago, Roman. Just get over here and spruce it up," Noah said into the phone. "Bring extra men if you need to. And Brad. Bring Brad with you."

"Okay, they're gathering the supplies and will be here as soon as possible.

Bull, do we need to up the surveillance at your place for you and Chaise?" Noah asked as he turned.

"No, we're good. I already have the most state-of-the-art system there is. And I have a lot of big guns," Bull replied. "I also have Chaise. Any man who messes up her decorating touches should be more afraid of her than he is of me."

"Very funny, Bull." Chaise elbowed him in the ribs. "You'll pay for that later."

"See?" Bull laughed and pulled Chaise to him for a kiss.

"Rebel? Shadow? What about you two?" Noah asked.

Shadow smiled. "Nah, man, I'm good. I *hope* he comes to see me first."

"I'm good, too, Reaper. No way I'm hiding from that little sissy," Rebel replied.

Part of him was entertained at how they spoke so boldly about him when he wasn't there to defend himself. They would soon learn what he could do. But another part of him needed the rage that their insults fueled. It reminded him of why his mission was so important, why he couldn't let them have the upper hand even once, and why he had to remain patient until the time was right.

In the meantime, he would still have a little fun with them. Ali opened the cell phone's speakerphone to address his captive audience. "Yes, by all means, men. Call every security specialist you can find and have them fill your homes with their pathetic gadgets. It'll be all the more entertaining for me in the end. I'll walk through the front door of your homes as easily as if you left the light on for me and a key under the front door mat."

Ali chuckled at their confusion while they attempted to locate the source of his voice. When they followed the sounds and Noah picked up the cell phone, Ali continued with his taunts. "Aren't you the clever one? You found me in the cell phone, very impressive. Do you feel any safer yet?"

Noah's reply wasn't what Ali expected. He smiled at the blank screen of the cell phone. "Ali, I have no reason not to feel safe around a sorry little pussy like you. Picking on little old ladies doesn't take a big set of balls. How about you meet up with me somewhere? We'll see who feels safe then."

"That's a very tempting offer. Really. Alas, I will have to pass," he mocked. "However, I will accept a date with that sexy wife of yours. It may seem odd, but I've always been attracted to pregnant women. They just glow with radiant beauty.

"Or maybe your gorgeous sister? I'd bet my life that her beauty would rival the brightness of the sun if she were pregnant. Perhaps I can help her with that since your friend seems to be unable."

"What the fuck did that little piss ant just say?" Bull demanded as he jumped up from his seat beside Chaise. "I'll tear you limb from limb, you little piece of shit."

"As much as I'm enjoying our little chat, gentlemen, I'm afraid I have more work to do. But don't worry. You'll hear from me again very soon," Ali promised as he cut the connection.

He leaned back in his chair, laced his fingers behind his head, and smiled from ear to ear. This would be his favorite mission by a long shot. In fact, he was already looking forward to his next interaction with them.

He opened the image he'd saved from the live video feed of Brianna and Chaise standing side by side to stare at them longer. His smile crawled across his face before he spoke. "How about a nice game of cat and mouse, my beauties?"

CHAPTER SEVEN

OCTOBER

"Where is he?" Brianna asked, staring out the window.

Ali had systematically sent packages to Brianna over the past few weeks. One arrived at the same time every week, but a different courier delivered each one. The first package had caused a major scene outside the gate. When the agents on duty scanned it and decided it was safe to open it, a flurry of activity quickly ensued. Cars swarmed in from every direction, agents and police cornered the deliveryman to interrogate him, and Noah moved Brianna as far away from the windows as possible.

Ali had sent her an early Halloween present—a fake finger that appeared to have been cut off. He added corn syrup tinted with red food coloring to make it look more realistic. When the package was finally delivered to Brianna, she cleaned off the extra "blood" and stuck it on her middle finger. She took a picture and posted it on her social media site, knowing he was most definitely monitoring it.

The second week, he continued the theme and sent a dozen black roses to her. Not willing to be one-upped, Brianna carefully painted each one with a different color of nail polish before posting a picture of her "beautiful, multi-colored roses." After the second delivery, she'd had a talk with Bill and Joe.

"Every time a package is delivered, it draws your men from wherever they're stationed. Ali's watching every one of them and waiting to see where they're coming from. You need to take the packages to them or get a new way to scan them here. Just don't fall for his games anymore," Brianna suggested after they'd opened the second one.

"You think we don't know that?" Joe asked, somewhat amused.

"You don't act like you know that, Joe," Brianna answered honestly. "You've played into his trap both times. See what he does when you change your response to him."

"Good idea. We'll try that," Joe answered.

"Why didn't you think of that before now?" Liz asked. "And the cell phones —why didn't you know about that?

Joe and Bill exchanged glances, but they'd already learned the hard way it was best not to engage Liz directly. They'd been embarrassed one too many times by the sweet, little old lady who wasn't afraid to put them in their place or call them out on their screw-ups.

"That's exactly why we aren't taking any chances with the next package. The armored van with a portable X-ray machine in the back will be parked at the curb so any package can be viewed remotely through our secure wireless connection," Joe replied.

When the delivery van pulled up to the gate with the third package, the agents were waiting to see what Ali had sent that time. They quickly took the package, secured it in the X-ray machine, and signaled to the technician inside the house that it was ready for inspection.

"Here goes nothing," Rob, the technician, uttered to himself.

The image lit up on the screen, and Rob cringed when he recognized a couple of the more obvious items. Rob knew Reaper would be out for blood when he found out what was in it. The screening didn't reveal any explosive or dangerous contents, so Rob approved for it to be opened. When Joe brought the package inside the house, Rob quietly moved away to avoid Reaper's wrath.

"What the hell?" Reaper bellowed. "Wait until I get my hands on him."

"What is it now?" Brianna asked.

"Baby presents. *Engraved* baby presents that have his last name on them," Reaper growled. "I'm going to kill him."

Brianna put her hand on his arm, her touch instantly calming him, and she rose up on her tiptoes to place a chaste kiss on his cheek. "You know he's just trying to rile you up. Don't give him the satisfaction."

"You know I've never been rational when it comes to you," he replied. "Definitely not when another man is trying to claim my baby." His hand slid across her stomach in his protective and possessive display.

"Yeah, we all know I'm yours, Noah," she cooed.

"He's definitely toying with you. This isn't the normal MO for a terrorist group. It's possible that he's a lone wolf, banking on his seventy-two virgins waiting for him when he takes out a few infidels. But this package is much more personal, whereas the previous ones were macabre," Bill said as he inspected the contents. "Mixed signals again."

"This guy is one big screwed-up mess," Liz chimed in. "That's my official diagnosis. I'll send you my bill. But I charge extra for house calls."

Bill stared at Liz for several moments while keeping his face expressionless. In return, she gave him a toothy grin, shrugged one shoulder, and flipped her shoulder-length gray hair as she turned away from him. He shook his head and chuckled lightly to himself. It took too much energy to be aggravated with her when she so thoroughly amused him.

"What's the plan now?" Noah asked. "We've been at this for weeks now. Shadow and Rebel have been out there interviewing everyone who's had dealings with him, following up on crimes that appear to be linked to him, while we're here waiting for the next package."

His frustration level was rising with every passing minute. Brianna was his primary concern, of course, but part of him wanted to be out in the field, searching for anything that would help them put this threat to rest for good. He paced back and forth, antsy from his own inactivity, and fighting guilt over wanting to leave Brianna to help Shadow and Rebel.

Noah's new—and secure—cell phone rang and Shadow's name flashed across the screen. "Talk to me, man. What have you found?"

"Rebel and I have been comparing notes on our new friend. Seems Ali Babek Turan has had several aliases over the last few years. He worked at a major software company as an intern while he was in college. His instructors, classmates, and former employers all say he was a computer genius. He walked into the program already knowing almost as much as his instructors.

"He's been involved mostly in cybercrimes, but there are some suspicious deaths, now that we're giving them a second look. Poisoning seems to be his preferred method, although there have been a couple of deaths that were much more…intimate."

"What do you mean 'intimate'?" Reaper asked.

"You know how they say that usually when someone kills another by shooting them, the crime is colder and less personal? Emotionally detached, all that shit," Shadow began.

"Yeah. Got it. Go on," Reaper replied.

"A couple of deaths were in very close quarters with a knife. Could have been a large hunting or fighting knife, but the wounds aren't completely consistent. He's not like most killers that pick one method over another," Shadow explained.

"Are you on your way back?"

"Yeah. We'll be there in a few hours."

"Okay. You can tell me about his cybercrimes when you get here," Reaper replied.

"Roger that, Reaper. See ya soon," Shadow said before they hung up.

Brianna approached him and wrapped her arms around him from behind. "I know you're going crazy being stuck in here with us."

He turned and wrapped his arms around her. "I'd never go crazy from being with you. What's driving me crazy is not being the one out there stopping this guy."

"You will," Brianna assured him. "Was that Shadow or Rebel?"

"Shadow. They're headed back here now, but it'll be a few hours before they arrive. Shadow said they found a few things, but I said to fill me in when they get back so I don't have to repeat everything for those guys." Noah jerked his head in the direction of the CIA agents.

"Why don't we take Liz and get out of here? We need to go see your dad again," Brianna suggested. "He didn't look well last week when we were there. He's doing his best to hide it, but I can tell."

"Yeah, so can I," Noah replied grimly. "Ask Liz if she wants to go, and let's get out of here."

Brianna walked into the kitchen where Liz was trying to entice Rob into playing a game of cards with her.

"What's the matter, sonny? Scared Granny will beat you like you stole something?" Liz taunted him.

Rob's eyes darted around the room as he searched frantically for someone or something to save him from Liz. When he locked eyes with Brianna, he all but begged her to step in on his behalf. When Brianna's face lit up with her smile, he would've sworn she was an angel sent from Heaven above.

"Liz, Noah and I are going to see Steve again. Do you want to join us this time? You still haven't met his parents." Brianna continued her casual stroll into the kitchen and pretended to be oblivious to the deck of cards that Liz was flicking in Rob's face.

"I think I will," Liz replied. "I missed out last time because I thought I had Joe talked into a game of Twister, but then he got an urgent call. Damn thing lasted the whole time you were gone."

"That's too bad." Brianna feigned empathy. "Maybe you can help cheer Steve up."

"What's wrong with him? Is he on those little blue pills, too? I hear that needing those really messes with a man's mind." Liz shook her head. "Is that true, Rob?"

"Uh, I, uh… I need to go help Joe," Rob stuttered and quickly took the opportunity to leave the room.

Brianna doubled over in laughter and tears streamed down her face. "Liz, I can't tell you how much I've missed you. I love having you here with us."

"Sweet girl, I love being here with you and Noah. I think I'll stay in Miami once this is over. Don't worry. I'll get my own place. But I love being here with you and my boys," she replied.

Brianna didn't ask for clarification since she already knew that when Liz said "boys," she meant the men of Steele Security. Only Liz could get away with calling them "my boys" and not be corrected.

"So, what's going on with your father-in-law?" Liz asked.

"He has cancer," Brianna replied solemnly. "He doesn't seem to be responding to treatment as well as we hoped."

"You never told me that!" Liz exclaimed. "Let's go see him. Bring your iPad with you, Brianna. We need to FaceTime with my son while we're there."

With that, Liz rushed off to freshen up before she met Noah's parents for the first time, leaving Brianna feeling bewildered once again. From the moment they met, Liz had viewed Brianna as her own daughter. She sensed that Brianna was lonely, but she was also willingly closed off from forming close relationships. Liz continued to work on her every chance she had, and it finally paid off. Once she won Brianna over, she realized that Brianna had become the steady force in her life since her own children were seldom around.

She only hoped she had a chance to help Brianna and Noah, return the favor they'd given her when they'd so eagerly brought her into their home. Liz quickly changed clothes and rushed back downstairs to leave with Noah and Brianna. When they got in the car, Noah turned to speak to Liz.

"Don't forget to stay lying down in the backseat until we pull into my parents' garage. We don't want to risk you being seen by Ali until the CIA is ready to tell him."

"Oh yeah," Liz replied as she made herself comfortable on the spacious bench seat. "Do you know what they're waiting for?"

Over the past few weeks, Roman, Blake, Alex, and Brad had installed every imaginable security upgrade, including infrared cameras to pick up heat signatures even behind hiding places, glass-break detectors for the windows, and fog screens that billowed out smoke to disorient intruders or emit a gas that completely disabled intruders for up to twenty-four hours. Bullet-resistant doors with biometric sensors were installed throughout the house and handheld thermal imagers were brought in to conduct frequent sweeps for hidden surveillance devices.

After the upgrades had been completed, the only wild card Noah had left to contend with was Liz. Ali didn't know she'd survived, though Noah wasn't convinced that she even mattered to Ali at this point. If her death had been imperative, Ali would've employed another method and he wouldn't have left her before he was certain his plans had been carried out successfully.

"My guess is they want to use his failed attempt to taunt him, make him mad so he does something stupid. That's how a lot of men get caught. Their ego is their undoing," Noah replied.

"How about that! This tough old broad will be the criminal mastermind's undoing," Liz cheerfully boasted.

"Wouldn't that be something?" Brianna agreed. "I hope it's soon because his gifts are already on my nerves."

Before long, Noah pulled into his parents' garage and waited until the door closed securely behind him before exiting the vehicle. After the team finished the security upgrades to his house, Noah had sent them to his parents' house to update theirs as well. Constant surveillance helped ease his mind for the safety of his family, but until Ali was caught or killed, he'd always be on guard.

"Did you bring your iPad?" Liz asked Brianna.

"Got it right here." Brianna patted her oversized bag.

"Good girl. Let's see what we can do for Steve and Sara," Liz replied cryptically.

"Mom? Dad? Anyone home?" Noah called as he walked in.

"In the den," Sara called. "Come on in."

When he walked into the den, Noah had to fight to quickly rein in his shock and concern. Steve had lost even more weight since they'd last visited and his skin color had become more ashen. Noah swallowed hard, pushing down the lump of despair that had formed in his throat, and prepared to introduce Liz.

"Mom, Dad, this is Liz Stanton. We told you about her last week. She was Brianna's neighbor in Boulder, and she's staying with us for a while. Liz, this is my mom, Sara, and my dad, Steve," Noah said.

"Welcome, Liz. We're glad to finally meet you in person," Sara said when she stood to greet her.

"Nice to meet you, Liz," Steve said weakly. "Forgive me for not getting up. I'm a little under the weather today."

"It's so good to meet you both. You have a wonderful son and daughter-in-law," Liz replied. "If you don't mind my forwardness, I know a little about your medical condition, Steve. That's actually why I'm here today. I hope to be able to help you with it."

"What do you mean, Liz?" Brianna asked.

"Let's see that iPad of yours," Liz replied.

Brianna retrieved it from her bag and handed it to Liz. After a few clicks, the familiar ring of the FaceTime app filled the air.

"Hello?" a male voice answered. "Mom? Is that you?"

"You sound shocked, Daryl," Liz laughed.

"I am. I had no idea you knew how to use FaceTime."

"Of course I do. But that's not why I'm calling. Are you on your iPad, son?"

"Yes, I'm in the office today and I use it for almost everything."

"Good. I have a patient for you to consult with. Right now," Liz demanded.

Daryl recognized her tone of voice and knew this wasn't a request. This was an expectation. Since she rarely asked anything of him, he also knew that it was very important to her and he couldn't deny her—even if he was running behind on his patient appointments.

"Sure, Mom. Let's see what you've got." Daryl smiled.

"Good boy. This is Steve Steele. He has cancer. We need you to fix him," Liz replied matter-of-factly.

"No pressure there, Mom," Daryl replied sarcastically.

Steve laughed good-naturedly as Liz passed the iPad to him. "This is my son, Dr. Daryl Stanton. He thinks I pressure him."

"No pressure at all. I assume you're a doctor?"

"Yes, I'm an oncologist. Can you turn on as many lights as possible so I can get a good look at you? And tell me about your medical history." Daryl settled in behind his desk to begin making his notes and conduct his virtual assessment.

Over the next forty-five minutes, Steve and Sara answered every question, and gave detailed information about his symptoms, surgeries, and treatments. Daryl covered every aspect of Steve's medical history prior to the cancer. "If you don't mind, I'd like to contact your oncologist and talk to him. I'm not sure what my mom has told you, if anything, but I'm part of a clinical trial for a new chemotherapy drug that you may be a candidate to join. There are a few things I need to verify first, so I need to caution you against looking at this as a sure thing. We are seeing positive results from it, though. If you qualify for it, we can start it there in Miami, coordinating with your oncologist, but you'll eventually need to come to Texas for the second phase of treatment."

"I don't mind at all, Doc," Steve replied, his voice full of hope again despite his attempts not to get ahead of himself. "I'll give you all of his contact information, and you can start on it as soon as possible."

"And there's nothing preventing you from moving to Texas for the second phase of treatment? It will last for several months," Daryl clarified.

"Not if it means I have a chance to beat this. I'll move to Texas for the next several years for that remote possibility," Steve replied. "Noah, Brianna, and our grandbaby will just have to put that corporate jet to use more frequently."

"I'll have my office manager send you a few forms to sign, and we'll start gathering your medical records. We'll have to submit them to the clinical trial board to get approval to add you, but I'll do what I can to help you," Daryl promised. "But there are no guarantees of anything. I'm emphasizing that because it's human nature to grasp at anything that even hints at making us well again."

"We understand what you're saying, Dr. Stanton. We appreciate your candor, but you don't have to worry. If Steve doesn't get approved, we won't hold it against you," Sara replied.

Steve gave Daryl his doctors' names, phone numbers, and addresses, and they ended the call with Daryl's assurance he'd be in touch as soon as possible. Steve sat staring at the black iPad screen for several seconds afterward, overcome with emotion that someone who'd just met him would go to such great lengths to help him.

"Thank you so much, Liz," Steve started. "I can't tell you how much hope this gives me."

"Dad, remember he said—" Noah began.

"Not that kind of hope, son," Steve replied with a warm smile. "Hope in people again. Hope that my family will be well cared for regardless of where I am."

Looking at Liz, Steve continued. "You didn't know me at all. Never even met me before. But you walked in here with a plan specifically designed to help me, out of the goodness of your heart. Thank you for that."

"These kids love you," Liz replied and gestured toward Noah and Brianna. "If they love you, you must be good people. They mean the world to me, and they want you to get better. If getting you in touch with my son, the doctor, can help with that, then it's the very least I can do."

Misty eyes looked everywhere around the room, except where they could possibly find other misty eyes. Noah could no longer take the emotional stress and seriousness of the room.

"That's it. Group hug! We're having a pansy-ass group hug right now. Everyone. Just get this shit out of our systems and then we can move past all this heavy stuff," he bellowed. "And then we'll never speak of it again."

Laughter filled the room, sniffles ceased, and misty eyes returned to normal.

CHAPTER EIGHT

NOVEMBER

"That little bastard," Bull spit out, venom lacing his words. He shook his head in disgust as he huffed loudly. "I really want to kick his ass."

"Get in line. I called dibs on it first," Chaise replied dryly.

She flipped the sun visor down and attempted to fix her hair for the fifth time. Just as she finished, her window rolled down of its own accord for the sixth time. The air gusted into Bull's truck, whipped her hair in every direction, and she screamed in frustration. "He's really pissing me off."

"I've locked the windows, but he's evidently overriding the sensor." Bull shook his head.

All four passenger windows and the back sliding window had randomly opened and closed during their entire ride to their dinner reservation.

"Can he see us?" Chaise asked tentatively.

"I really don't know, babe," Bull replied. "But just in case, here's my one-finger salute, asshole."

The touchscreen navigation screen lit up and the automated voice filled the cab of the truck. "In five hundred feet, turn right."

Bull and Chaise looked at the screen in disbelief before they turned to look at each other. "What the hell? I didn't turn the GPS on. I know how to get to the restaurant."

"I said turn right!" The GPS voice yelled through the speakers. "Are you stupid?"

Chaise started touching all the buttons she could find to turn off the GPS, but nothing seemed to work. It continued to hurl hateful and sarcastic insults at Bull about his driving, his inability to ask for directions, and how late he would be for their dinner reservation. The more the voice spoke, the madder Bull became.

"If you can hear me, you son of a bitch, I think you're a complete pussy. Hiding behind a computer screen and taunting people doesn't make you a badass at all. Come meet me like a man and show me what you've got, face-to-face," Bull challenged.

The computer-generated voice in his GPS replied. "You will meet me again soon enough, Colton. Perhaps Chaise will be happy to be in the company of a real man then."

"Why don't you show me how you're a real man, Turan? Right now," Bull replied.

There was no response from the GPS voice, so he turned the engine off, and they walked into the restaurant.

"Hello. Welcome to The Crimson Table. How can I help you?" the hostess asked.

"We have a seven o'clock reservation for two," Bull replied.

"Wonderful. What name is it under?"

"Lanier," he replied.

She checked her computer scheduling system and verified the last name again. "I'm sorry, Mr. Lanier, but we don't seem to have a reservation for you."

Bull stared at the woman and tried to control his temper when he replied. "We've had this reservation for two weeks. We've talked to the catering chef and the restaurant manager about the menu for our rehearsal dinner. Our reservation tonight is specifically to sample our customized menu."

"One moment and I will check with them," the hostess replied.

She quickly walked away, and Bull turned to face Chaise. "You don't think he..."

"If he did," Chaise cut in, "I'll completely lose my shit. He'd better stay in hiding, that's all I'm saying."

The hostess returned and her face showed her reluctance to share what she'd learned. "I spoke to both the manager and the catering chef," she started. "They each said that you contacted them by email and canceled your reservation."

"No, I didn't. Why would I do that?" Bull countered.

"They both said they distinctly remembered the email because..." She paused. "Because it said that your fiancée had left you for a real man, and you knew when you'd been beaten."

Bull cut his eyes to Chaise. "I'm going to kill him, Chaise."

"Not if I see him first," she replied.

Chaise turned to the confused hostess and explained. "We're being cyber-stalked by a crazy man. He's obviously behind the emails the manager and chef received because neither us of sent them. We're still very much together, and we'd still like to have a rehearsal dinner for our wedding."

"I can make a new reservation, but there's no way we can do it tonight. I'm really very sorry," the hostess replied.

"I'm not making a new reservation just for him to mess with us again," Bull replied. "Let's go somewhere else, Chaise."

"You know what? You're exactly right, Colton. Let's go. I'd think that any reputable place would've called to verify an email cancelation of a rehearsal dinner menu selection," Chaise replied. "We'll take our business elsewhere."

When they reached the truck, Chaise had an even better idea. "I know what to do. I'm calling Brianna."

After several minutes on the phone with her sister-in-law, she had everything worked out. "Great news. Brianna's dad can have one of his top chefs handle our menu and the entire rehearsal dinner. We don't have to find another place. Let's just go eat somewhere easy to get in."

"I'm glad you're the brains of this team." Bull smiled at her.

"Yeah, you got real lucky there," Chaise laughed.

Her laughter stopped the second her window rolled down again. "You fucking bastard!" she yelled. She turned to Bull and gave him a sly smile. "Screw him. Roll them all down, Bull. Let's just ride with the windows down tonight."

"Another great idea," Bull said as he rolled the other windows down and opened the back sliding window.

After they settled in to enjoy the warm Miami air, all of the windows rolled up and locked in place. They both slowly turned their heads to look at each other. Chaise pulled a pen and paper out of her purse and quickly scratched out a note to Bull.

Hurry and get us home. He has too much control over the truck.

Bull nodded, his face immediately registering the seriousness of the situation. Turan controlled the truck's computer, GPS, and windows, and Bull didn't know what he may lose control of next. He changed lanes to prepare to take the next exit off the interstate. He made a split-second decision to park his truck and call a taxi to take them home. By the time Turan found the car they were in, they'd already be safely home. As the truck slowed down, he breathed a sigh of relief.

Suddenly, the truck accelerated by itself and the steering wheel locked in place. "Chaise, tighten your seat belt," Bull yelled.

Without waiting for her to react, Bull reached over, grabbed her seat belt, and hitched it up so that the safety mechanism pulled her tightly against the seat. When the tires left the pavement, the tachometer revved into the red zone as the speed continued to increase. Bull tried in vain to turn the wheel, stomp on the brakes, pull the emergency brake, and even throw the truck into park. When they hit the steep grade of the embankment, the truck's angle was inherently dangerous.

"As soon as it stops, get away from the truck," Bull commanded.

"What?" Chaise gasped, scared out of her mind.

The high speed was aggravated by the grade and angle of the truck, causing the tires on the higher side to leave the ground completely. In a split second, the top-heavy truck cab tipped over. The sound of crunching metal, breaking glass, and exploding airbags was deafening as the truck rolled over several times before coming to a stop near the bottom of the ramp.

Dazed and confused, Chaise slowly opened her eyes and was momentarily unsure where she was. Everything looked upside down and only added to her confusion. Bull's last words to her were the first coherent thought she had.

The truck. The wreck. Get away.

When she turned her head to look for Bull, her heart felt like it stopped and her already ragged breath seized in her chest. "Bull!" she yelled, forcing the air from her lungs. He was gone—she was in the truck alone. "Oh my God." The panic rose in her chest. "Bull!"

She clawed at her seat belt buckle as she tried to free herself from its tight hold. The buckle refused to release her and felt as if it continued to tighten even more as she pulled at it. Two large, warm hands covered hers and stilled her movements.

"Relax, baby," Bull's calm voice soothed. "Let me get you out."

Bull slid the knife out of the sheath strapped to his ankle. He made a couple of slices across the seat belt and helped ease her out of the seat. "Are you hurt anywhere?"

"No, I don't think so. Just terrified." Her voice quivered when she spoke, and Bull gathered her into his arms.

"I know, babe." He slowly and methodically rubbed over her back to calm her but also to check for injuries her brain hadn't yet registered in her frightened state. "Are you sure you're not hurt?"

"I'm sure. Maybe a couple of bruises and burns from the tight seat belt and the airbags, but nothing to worry about," she replied.

Within seconds, Bull's cell phone began ringing. He pulled it out of his pants pocket and saw Reaper's name on the screen. "We're okay," he said as a greeting. "My truck is totaled, but we're not injured."

"Thank God," Noah exclaimed. "I'm so glad we added the emergency alert system for our personal vehicles. We're on our way to get you."

"No, don't risk it," Bull warned. "Turan had control of my truck. Locked up the steering, took control over everything. He could've hacked in to yours, too."

"I'll call Rebel to come get you," Noah replied.

A few minutes later, Rebel arrived on the scene in his older model Jeep. He found Bull and Chaise giving detailed information about the wreck to the police. The cop was giving Bull a doubtful look as he explained how Turan had taken control of his truck, that was until the CIA and FBI agents elbowed their way in to take over the scene.

"This is Special Agent Landry with the FBI Denver office," Bill said by way of introduction. "He and his partner, Agent Daniels, will be working with us on this case in a joint CIA-FBI task force."

"You must have more information then," Rebel stated.

"There's been more chatter, both domestically and internationally. We're not taking any chances. Landry and Daniels both worked the case initially in Denver, so they're temporarily relocating to Miami," Bill explained.

"The local FBI office isn't happy about this, but we're not giving up our original case," Landry said.

Bull and Chaise retold their story from the beginning of the night, stressing they were sure Turan was also behind the mix-up at the restaurant. "He ensured you'd both be at his mercy inside the truck when he canceled your dinner reservation," Daniels agreed after Bull finished recounting their night.

"And what else does he have rigged?" Bull asked rhetorically.

"Exactly," Joe agreed. "We're towing your truck to one of our facilities to have it analyzed. Your team needs to be prepared for him to take control of anything with a computer chip that's open to a Wi-Fi signal."

"That's why I'm in my old Jeep. Everything's manual on it," Rebel replied.

"He's sending us back to the Stone Age," Chaise grumbled.

The CIA agents, FBI agents, Rebel, and Bull all snapped their heads to Chaise, then to each other. Bull stepped in front of her, pulled her face to his, and lovingly kissed her. "You're a genius, babe."

"Why? What'd I do?" Chaise asked.

~

"Are they okay?" Brianna asked when Noah hung up the phone.

"Yeah, they're fine," he replied before he rolled over to kiss her. "Rebel just dropped them off at Bull's. Chaise said she's just a little sore from the seat belt and airbags, and she's tired from a long night. She'll probably be even sorer tomorrow. It's amazing that neither of them has any major injuries."

"He could've killed them," Brianna stated. "Do you think he meant to?"

"No, I don't, because he's capable of killing them if that's what he wanted to do. I think he's still toying with us right now, but he's ramping up the stakes. The problem is, we won't know he's decided to take it to the next level until the moment it happens."

"We'll just have to catch him before he's had enough of messing with us," Brianna asserted.

"I'm all ears if you have a plan to draw him out."

"It seems like he wants to keep hiding behind his computer screen, like a bully. That's strange, though, because he didn't mind trying to kill Liz to her face. He's killed others, too, using different means. So everything has to be on his terms, according to his plans," Brianna spoke as if she were thinking aloud.

"Keep going. What are you on to?"

"When he killed people in the past, was it one-on-one, like when he tried with Liz?"

"I don't know, but I can find out. You think he's too afraid to take on more than one at a time?"

"Yes, exactly like a bully," she replied. "He'll make our lives hell while we're together and do everything he can to separate us. Once he gets us alone, he'll pounce. Of course, this is just a theory until we get more detailed information on how he murdered the others."

"We? You're getting that look in your eye again, Bri," Noah warned. "No more investigative reporting or snooping for you."

She smiled mischievously at him, but she softened her voice when she responded with feigned innocence. "Would I do that?"

"Yes, you would," he chuckled. "And don't think for one second that you're fooling me with that sweet, little girl voice."

"Wouldn't dream of it."

"Of what? Snooping or fooling me?"

"I'm not sure I understand the question," she replied.

Noah moved as quickly as lightning to cover her body with his, hovering just above her slightly protruding belly. "Brianna Leigh Steele, don't test me. I can make you disappear until this case is over, and I will do it if I have to," he spoke slowly and emphasized each word.

"It's so easy to get you riled up. Now, while you're in position, it's time for you to perform for your wife." She smiled seductively.

"For future reference, all you have to do is breathe and I'm primed to perform for my wife."

"Good to know," she replied as she raised her head from the pillow to kiss his lips. "I'm breathing."

"I feel you," he replied.

"I feel *you*," she purred.

~

Early the next morning, Brad reported to Noah's house to share what he'd found. When Noah opened the door, Brad couldn't contain his smile. In the war on the man who had made everyone's life a living hell and made the entire team feel somewhat ineffective, he finally had a solid lead.

"Come on in, Brad. You're here early," Noah said as he ushered Brad inside.

"Yeah, this is something you and the guys will want to see for yourselves," Brad replied.

Brad got his laptop set up in Noah's home office while they waited for the other men to arrive. He opened several programs, one after the other, to show a specific layout of websites. Noah took his seat just as Bull, Rebel, and Shadow filed into his office.

Brad looked around. "No CIA or FBI today?"

"No," Shadow said as he closed the door and removed a device from his pocket. He placed it on the desk and nodded at the rest of the group. "Room is secure."

"We don't trust the CIA?" Brad asked, his brow furrowed and his eyes cutting from one man to the next.

"Never trust a spy, kid." Shadow smiled.

"Weren't you in the CIA?"

"Yep."

"But you left, right?"

"You never really leave the CIA, Brad," Shadow replied flatly. "Let's hear what you've got."

"Our man Turan really is a computer genius. I've had the program back-tracking his location for the last few weeks. He built a very complex international network of signals and connections so he could stay hidden. He's good. He's very good.

"But I'm better," Brad rightfully boasted. "I've traced him back here to Miami where he's holed up, waiting to make his final move."

"You know his exact location?" Shadow asked.

"Yes, I do," Brad confirmed. "I verified it with satellite photography. He doesn't leave the house hardly at all, but he has opened the door for food delivery."

"Show us where he is," Noah said.

Brad pulled up the street-level map and also gave them satellite pictures of all sides of the house. "Are you going to go pick him up now?"

"No," Shadow interjected.

"No?" Brad asked.

"No, not yet. All we know right now is that he's being a pain in the ass to us. This can't be his only plan. And if we pick him up now, we may not find out in time. We need to let him think he's still winning, still playing us, while we continue to run our endgame on him," Shadow explained.

"You sure about this, Shadow?" Rebel asked. "This could severely backfire on us. If we don't haul him in when we have the chance, and something big happens, our asses will be on the line."

"If we haul him in too soon, and something big happens, our asses are still on the line," Bull stated.

"I'd rather catch him with both hands in the cookie jar. I don't want him sitting in jail with a smug look on his face because we missed his master plan. He's not the type to just give it up on his own," Noah surmised.

"So, we're going to have a little fun with the computer genius who's having way too much fun with us?" Rebel asked.

"What do you say, Brad?" Noah asked.

"I say, hell yeah. Let's have some fun with him, aggravate him until he fucks up," Brad replied.

"I think we may be a bad influence on him." Shadow grinned. "It's about damn time."

"It's been too long since we were an unrecognized, government-sanctioned unit," Noah stated. "This feels like we're back home again." The five men began to plan their counterattack on Ali Babek Turan. They decided it was time to turn the tables on him, use his own game against him, but with a few twists of their own.

CHAPTER NINE

"I received an interesting call from a doctor in Texas," Steve's oncologist said as he entered the room. "Dr. Daryl Stanton. Name ring a bell?"

"It sounds a little familiar." Steve smiled. "Were you two talking about me behind my back?"

"Absolutely," Dr. Patel replied jovially. "We talked about you for quite a while. I emailed him some pictures of you—fairly compromising pictures, at that."

Steve and Sara chuckled while Dr. Patel took a seat and opened the chart to read from his notes. "I believe he said he explained some of the clinical trial information to you, correct?"

"Yes. He stressed that there was no guarantee that I'd be accepted. I also understand that it doesn't mean I'll be instantly cured either," Steve answered.

"The trials have shown very promising results from the test group. Dr. Stanton called back this morning and informed me that you've been accepted into the trial." He smiled.

Steve and Sara both gawked at Dr. Patel for several seconds before either was able to speak. Sara finally forced the words out. "You're serious? He was accepted?"

Dr. Patel nodded. "Yes, this is very good news. Should I tell him you accept?"

"Yes," Steve exclaimed. "Yes, I accept!"

"You'll start phase one of it here with me, but we've set up a process so he can also monitor your status. I understand his initial assessment was done via FaceTime, so we'll continue that in the office. Once you finish the first phase, you'll have to relocate to Texas to start phase two, the more intensive phase," Dr. Patel explained.

"What am I looking at, Doc?" Steve asked, suddenly serious.

"The first phase is the administration of a single chemotherapy drug that's still under trial status with the FDA. Essentially, the preliminary results have shown that the new drug better prepares the body to accept and positively respond to the specific mixture of the two chemotherapy drugs in phase two.

"As with any chemotherapy treatment, every experience is individual. You can expect many of the standard side effects—weight loss, diminished appetite, nausea, vomiting, hair loss. But it's very likely those side effects will be more severe in phase two as the toxicity builds up in your body. The number of rounds you have to do depends on how well your cancer responds to the drugs," he concluded.

"When do we start?" Steve asked, unfazed by the daunting days ahead of him.

"I'll contact Dr. Stanton today and let him know you've agreed. We have some paperwork for you to complete, and then he'll ship the medication to me. We'll start phase one as soon as we receive the medication," Dr. Patel replied. "It should take about a week at the most, but we'll call you when it arrives. Since you've just finished a complete cycle of the current chemotherapy drug, we'll wait and start the trial drug next."

"That's great news, Dr. Patel. Thank you," Steve said as he stood to leave.

After stopping at the receptionist's area to complete more clinical trial paperwork, Steve took Sara's hand in his and they walked out together. Roman was waiting outside to drive them home. They climbed into the back of the SUV and Steve pulled Sara close to his side.

"I have an idea," he murmured in her ear.

"Oh yeah? What's that?" she whispered back.

"We need to get away together for the next week. Before the new trial drug arrives. Before our lives are centered around this cancer and my treatments again. Just the two of us—and our security detail. What do you say?"

"I say let's do it. Where do you have in mind?" Sara asked.

"Roman, do you have a girlfriend?" Steve asked.

"I'm seeing someone," he answered vaguely.

"Have you ever been to the Smoky Mountains in Tennessee?" Steve probed.

"No, can't say I have," Roman replied.

"Call your girlfriend. We're going on a trip to the mountains for the next week," Steve announced.

"Don't worry about our son. We'll take care of him," Sara added.

Roman shifted uncomfortably in his seat but didn't argue.

Steve retrieved his phone from his pocket and soon had a mountain cabin hideaway reserved for the week. He then dialed Noah's number and smiled at Sara. "Hi, son," he said when Noah answered. "Are you home? Okay, your mom and I are coming by right now. See you in a few minutes."

"You didn't give him much time to say anything in reply," Sara laughed.

"It's best not to," Steve chuckled. "Keeps him guessing."

Roman laughed and shook his head as he drove, but even he had to admit it was a good idea to get Steve and Sara away from the area while Turan was still on the loose. If that meant that he had to spend a week in the mountains, Roman decided he'd gladly take one for the team.

When they were securely inside Noah's garage, Roman opened the door and began to mentally prepare his argument for why his latest love interest should join him and the Steeles for their impromptu vacation. Before Roman joined them inside the house, he sent his girlfriend of the month, Tawnee, a quick text to persuade her to join him for a week away. After he pressed send, he slid his phone into his pocket and walked into the house to rejoin the Steele clan.

While Roman was busy on his phone, Steve and Sara found Noah inside the house and approached him together to present their idea jointly.

"Hey, Dad," Noah greeted him. "Hi, Mom. What's happened?"

Chaise heard them enter and joined her family in the foyer. She hugged her parents and stepped back. "What's going on, you two?"

Sara wrapped her arms around Steve's waist. "Your father has been accepted into the clinical trials with Dr. Stanton. Dr. Patel said the initial results have been very promising. Since your dad just finished a round of chemo, Dr. Patel said he'd wait until the new drug gets here to start the next round. So we have a week free of all treatments, and we want to take advantage of it."

Steve picked up where Sara left off. "I've rented a cabin in the Smoky Mountains, and we want to leave right away. Can you spare Roman to go with us and your pilot to fly us up there tonight?"

Noah's eyes darted between the two of them as he processed all the information that had just been thrown at him and Chaise. "First, the clinical trial is great news. I'm so relieved you got in. You definitely need a week off, and going to the mountains is a brilliant idea. Until we stop Turan, the farther away from here you are, the better.

"That is great news," Chaise exclaimed. "I'm so glad Dr. Stanton was able to get your approval so quickly."

"We are, too, sweetheart," Steve replied. "So very thankful."

"Roman, are you okay with going away for a week on such short notice?" Noah asked.

"I'm good, boss. I just need to make a quick phone call, throw some clothes in a bag, and I'll be ready to go," he replied.

"I'll call and have the plane ready to go as soon as possible," Noah replied. "I'm really glad to hear this news, Dad."

"We are, too, son," Steve replied. "Thank you both for everything you've done for us. We love you both, so much. We only wish your brother could be here, too."

"I love you, too, Daddy," Chaise replied. "I wish he were here, too. It's been so long since I've seen him."

Noah was surprised by the sudden outburst of affection from his father. He reasoned it could be just a natural side effect of the stress of the treatments, the news of the promising clinical trials, and sincere gratitude for helping them escape from it all. He hoped that was the cause behind it, but with his run of luck lately, he couldn't count on it.

"I love you both, too. But, Dad, you don't have to thank me. I'm happy to do whatever I can to help," Noah replied.

"Roman, you need a date for the week," Liz stated as she sashayed across the room toward him.

He flashed his sexy grin at Liz. "I actually just asked my girl about going with me. But, if she can't go…" He intentionally let his voice trail off, leaving Liz to infer whatever she wanted.

"You're trouble." Liz pointed her finger at him. "So, of course, I like you."

"Glad to hear that." He winked.

"Look at you, with your sexy little smile and your come-hither wink. Throw in your rugged, faded beard, that black hair, and those *drizzle-melted-milk-chocolate-all-over-my-body-and-lick-it-off* brown eyes…" Liz paused. "Dangerous combination. I'm not sure this 'girl' of yours will be safe. I should probably go and chaperone."

"I'm afraid we'd get in even more trouble if you went, Liz," Roman replied, his deep voice lowered to be more intimate. He'd watched how Liz interacted with the others, throwing them off-kilter because they didn't know how to take her. He knew how to flirt back, catch her off guard, and take control of the scene. "I'm sure my girl would be very jealous."

Liz put her hand on her side, cocked one hip higher than the other, and looked Roman square in the eye. "As well she should be."

With that, Liz turned and left the room, leaving the others in stitches as they tried to catch their breath from her comic relief.

"I have to give it to her. She knows exactly how to lighten the moment," Roman said when his fit of laughter subsided.

"I've missed her so much," Brianna said and wiped the tears from her face. "No matter how selfish it is of me, you can't take her with you this week. I need her here to help keep me sane."

"I don't know, Brianna." Roman shook his head. "I think it'd be best if she came with us. Steve may need her to call Dr. Stanton while we're away."

"I'll make sure to get his number for you before you leave," Brianna deadpanned. "You can call him from your own phone."

"You both can quit fighting over me now. My mind is made up. I'm staying here," Liz called from the other room. "I need to be here in case my boys catch Lee. They need to make sure he kisses my ass!"

Roman bit back his laugh when he met Brianna's shocked gaze. "You win."

"Obviously," she retorted, and they both laughed again.

"I have no idea how I lost control of my house," Noah said to his team, his dry sense of humor exaggerated in his tone. "One day, everything was fine. Everything ran like clockwork, with precision, down to the minute details. The next day, it just all went to shit."

"You probably just need some Pepto Bismol," Liz called. "It helps stop that problem really fast."

Snickers and coughs filled the room as Noah worked hard to resist replying. He turned back to his parents to find his mom with her hand over her mouth, covering her laughs, and his dad's broad grin lighting up his entire face. "I'll go call about the jet right now," Noah said before walking into his office.

"I'm going to my place to pack a bag and pick up Tawnee for our trip," Roman announced as he slipped his phone into his pocket. Noah stepped out of his office and lifted his eyebrow up in question at Roman.

"Is that your little tart?" Liz yelled from the den.

"That's her," Roman replied. "You want to go with me and meet her?"

"Nope. I sure don't," came Liz's clipped reply.

"Tawnee and I will take you to your house to pack your suitcase. She works for Noah, too, so she can help with security," Roman said to Steve and Sara, consciously avoiding making eye contact with Noah.

"You sly dog," Rebel laughed.

"We'll be right here. Thank you, Roman," Sara replied. "Sorry we're disrupting your life so much."

"No problem at all, ma'am. I'm looking forward to a week in the mountains," Roman assured her before he left.

Steve wrapped his arms around Sara and lightly kissed her lips. "I can't wait to have this time with you."

"I know this whole thing with Ali is added stress you don't need right now," Brianna said, her voice full of empathy. "Please remember that he's dangerous. You could be a target even if you're not right here with us."

"Brad finished the software upgrades on our fleet of vehicles so Ali can't control them any longer," Bull told them. "When he realizes that, it'll probably piss him off so much that he reacts irrationally. So far, he seems like he's a bit of a control freak."

"We'll be careful," Sara promised. "The cabin Steve reserved doesn't have Internet access and is very remote. It would be very hard for him to get to us from here."

"Just don't underestimate him," Brianna warned. "We don't know what all he's capable of or who he's in league with. There's always the possibility that he's not a lone wolf after all."

"I've lived in enough fear ever since the day I found out I had cancer," Steve replied. "We'll be safe and we won't put anyone's life in danger, but we're still going to live our lives."

Noah walked up between his parents and put his arms around their shoulders. "The jet is being fueled and prepped to go. A car will be waiting for you at a private airstrip outside of Knoxville. Let Roman do his job, Dad," Noah warned. "He and Tawnee know how to check the car and verify it's safe before you and Mom get in it. Enjoy your relaxing week in the mountains. I hope your cabin has a hot tub."

"It does, and we plan on putting it to good use." Steve elbowed him in the ribs.

"Really don't need that visual of my parents." Noah shook his head. "Could've gone all year without that."

"We'll take selfies and send them to you while we're away," Sara laughed.

"Send me some selfies of Roman in his mountain-man au naturel state," Liz yelled.

~

"Mom and Dad are safely tucked away in their mountain hideaway," Chaise told Noah. "It's been a long day for them, so they got takeout on their way to the cabin and they're staying in for the night."

"Good. They need the break from everything," Noah replied. "I wish we could get in touch with Silas."

"His handler still hasn't called back?" Chaise asked and Noah shook his head.

"Our brother is better at hiding than you are, Noah."

"It does seem like it, doesn't it?" One corner of his mouth lifted in amusement.

"Who's ready to play 'kick the Turan'?" Brad asked as he walked in.

"I am." Liz appeared out of nowhere. "What do you have in mind?"

"He just ordered pizza delivery. I think it's time to use his own tactics against him," Brad replied.

"What are we going to do? Increase his order to one hundred pizzas and breadsticks? Change his toppings to all pineapples and anchovies? Play ding-dong ditch at his front and back doors at the same time?" Liz asked excitedly.

"Actually, I thought we'd intercept the pizza delivery guy, attach a listening device on the inside flap of the pizza box, and monitor his conversations from here," Brad replied, suddenly unsure of his plan.

"Oh, well, if you want to go the *boring* route…" Liz dismissed him.

"Let's do it, Brad," Noah confirmed. "Shadow, you're up."

"On it." He smiled as he walked out.

"Bull, while he's distracted with the delivery, let's get one of our new devices on his vehicle. When he does leave, we need to know where he's going," Noah directed.

"My pleasure," he replied, retrieved the device from the office, and made his exit.

"Rebel, I had some luck in getting a few files from our missions since we've been drafted—I mean, reinstated. Why don't you take a load off and look through them, see if anything jars your memory?" Noah extended a large envelope toward Rebel.

"Sure thing, Reap," Rebel replied and took the thick package. "Anything that'll help take this shithead down."

"That's the highlight reel of our missions in the area we think he's originally from. Could be nothing in there that helps. I haven't had a chance to look through it myself, but I trust your eye anyway."

Rebel took the package into the dining room, cleared all of Brianna's decorations off the table, and started separating the documents and pictures by mission. He picked one, took a seat, and started going through every piece methodically. Many of the names and other identifying information had been redacted, but there was enough viable information left for him to fully recall the mission. When he reached the pictures, he carefully studied every face, remembered their words, dialects, and accents, and tried to make a connection to Turan.

Shadow waited outside the pizza restaurant for the deliveryman to return to his car. When he did, Shadow casually approached him, careful not to seem threatening or intimidating.

"Hey, buddy. How's it going?" Shadow asked like he was a long-lost friend.

"Good. How about yourself?"

"Can't complain." Shadow smiled warmly and glanced at his name tag. "I'm hoping you can help me out with something, Bobby."

"Sure, if I can. What do you need?"

"A buddy of mine is getting married this weekend, and a few of us have tried to get him to go out for a bachelor party tonight. He won't do it because his soon-to-be bride forbids that he have any fun at all," Shadow explained.

He leaned in close to Bobby, lowered his voice, and established eye contact to feign a friendly connection with the young man. "I have a feeling that pizza is for him, and that he's holed up inside in front of his computer again tonight."

"That sounds like the guy," Bobby confirmed. "He orders pizza several times a week. He has his whole living room set up with nothing but laptops, wires, control sticks. Guy's a serious gaming nerd."

Shadow shook his head exaggeratedly in mock contempt. "Not the games again!" he exclaimed. "Let me guess. The little Japanese creatures that don't really talk, just make strange sounds instead?"

"Every time I've seen his games, he's either playing a warfare game or a flight simulator game," Bobby replied.

"That's his life, man," Shadow replied. "Bobby, I just want to help get him out of the house so he can have some fun before his ball-and-chain makes *him* take *her* last name."

"Yeah, man, what can I do to help?" Bobby asked, fully engaged in the conspiracy.

"I need to get this microphone inside his pizza box. All I want to do is hide it where the cardboard folds. After he takes it inside, I'm going to yell at him to get the hell out of the house. He'll think I'm in the front yard. When he comes out to confront me, I'm going to sneak in the back door, lock the front door, and our friends are going to make him go out with us one last time," Shadow lied. "Can you help me out? This is my last shot at talking some sense into him before he makes the worst mistake of his life."

"Yeah, man, of course. Sounds like your friend has already surrendered his man-card. You definitely gotta help him get it back," Bobby replied as he opened the cardboard box.

"That's the damn truth, Bobby," Shadow replied. "Listen, if this works, we'll be at Club La Viva later tonight. You should stop by."

"I'm not old enough to get in yet," he replied.

"Aww, man, that's too bad," Shadow replied. "Thanks for your help, though. I really appreciate it."

Shadow gave Bobby a large tip and a manly handshake before he strolled back to his vehicle. He turned and looked at Bobby again. "Don't tell him what I'm planning now," he warned with a smile.

"Wouldn't dare," Bobby replied with a laugh. "Have fun for me, too, tonight."

"You know it." Shadow climbed into his car and waved at Bobby as he drove away. "Thanks, kid. You have no idea how much you just helped your country."

CHAPTER TEN

Turan took the pizza box from the same kid who delivered it every time and absently handed him a tip to make him go away. A slow-moving cable van on the street in front of his rented house caught his eye. He chucked the pizza box on the counter and removed the first slice as he sat back down at his homemade network. His enemies had grown smarter since they'd locked him out of controlling their cars and phones. Noah's security system was virtually impenetrable, and Turan's frustration was growing daily.

The cable van gave him a new idea. The Steele Security family most definitely had cable. "Every greedy, entitled American family has cable television to waste their time, addle their brains, and avoid doing anything remotely constructive," Ali muttered as he clicked away on his laptop.

Once he'd gained access to the cable provider's website, he quickly found Noah's and Bull's accounts. Laughing maniacally, he changed their programming options so that every channel displayed the exact same one. While he worked on his grand scheme, every possible aggravation he could add to their lives was well worth the extra time and effort.

His laptop rang and he answered the Internet call. "Yes."

"Have you accomplished today's tasks?" the older male voice asked.

"Yes, I have. You don't have to call every day to ask that," Turan retorted.

"You know that I do," the voice replied. "Your focus on your assigned tasks has been lacking of late."

"I've accomplished my goals and more," Turan argued.

"Do you have the codes?"

"You know I can't go straight to those or it'll trigger an internal alarm," he replied, exasperation lacing his voice as he'd explained this same fact too many times before. "I have to break it down one layer at a time."

"Are you still on schedule?"

"Of course," he replied indignantly.

"Until tomorrow then," the voice replied and promptly disconnected.

Turan released a litany of curse words in Farsi, flung his chair back from his desk, and jumped up to begin pacing the room to expel some of his pent-up frustration. "Fucking bastard," he yelled. "When this is over, I will make sure you get what's coming to you, too."

He grabbed a bottle of water from the refrigerator and drank half of it as he stalked back and forth, his agitation too high for him to sit still. Drawing his arm back, he hurled the bottle across the room and watched with a modicum of satisfaction as the remaining water splattered across the wall. "My talents aren't being used like they should be. I have much more potential than you give me credit for," he yelled at his computer.

"I'm tired of waiting. It's time I show more initiative. I'll never ask for forgiveness, but I won't wait for permission from anyone ever again. My rewards await me, and they're long overdue."

Turan took his seat and began typing furiously on his laptop. He talked to himself as he worked his way into the secure network his counterpart had questioned him about. "If you want to speed things up, we'll speed them up. But you won't like the consequences," he muttered.

"What is that stupid American saying?" He stopped typing, straightened his back, and stared blankly at the wall. A wicked smile covered his face when he recalled the phrase. "Oh, yes. There's more than one way to skin a cat."

His need to be in charge, to be in control of his destiny, and to exact his revenge on his own timetable began to consume him. A few keystrokes later, part one of his newly developed plan was underway.

"This should keep them busy for a while."

~

"Hear that?" Shadow asked the room.

"Sure did," Noah confirmed. "Brad, can you get a trace on where the call to Turan originated from?"

"Running it now. It's another labyrinth of networks, so it'll take a while to figure it out," Brad replied.

"The tracking device is in place on his car. He'll never find it, even if he looked right at it," Bull said. "If he leaves in that car, we'll know exactly where he goes."

"Can we remote into his computer?" Shadow asked.

"Not without him knowing. I've been combing through it, trying to find a back door, though." Brad replied. "I have to give him credit—he knows how to build electronic safeguards. He has a huge server solely dedicated to his computer network. Most medium-sized businesses don't even use a server that big."

"Why would he need one that big?" Noah asked.

"An individual wouldn't. That server has an enormous database that's housed on multiple hard drives. If one fails, the others will keep working without it," Brad explained. "He's either overcompensating for something, or he needs to access a lot of data within a split second."

A musical tone rang through the house, alerting the team that visitors had arrived at the Steele house. Noah glanced at the monitor and saw Bill, Joe, Landry, and Daniels waiting for admittance at the gate. He rolled his eyes and huffed loudly before letting them in. "Just when I thought we were getting somewhere, these clowns have to show back up."

"Remember when Chaise said he's trying to send us back into the Stone Age?" Bull asked. "Apparently our assigned agents and I had the same thought when she said that. He's a computer genius, a hardware master, a software nerd, but he also has a job to carry out and he wants revenge on us for some reason.

"Through all the harassment, he has shown us what he can do with a laptop and an Internet connection. What if his grand finale is to take away all the modern conveniences that we rely on? Phones, Internet, cars—everything we communicate with and our modes of travel. I don't mean just for the four of us, either. If he's a part of a bigger group, they could be working together to cripple multiple major cities at once." Bull leaned over, placed his hands flat on the table, and waited as his team considered his theory.

"Amazing that you've come to that conclusion," Bill stated dryly from the doorway. "Where did you get your intel?"

Bull drew up to his full height and turned to face him before he responded. "Gathering intel is my specialty. Do *you* have anything to share with *us*?"

Joe, Landry, and Daniels walked into the tension-filled room, their eyes shifting from one man to another as they read between the lines.

"Sorry to interrupt your meeting, fellows," Landry spoke first. "Daniels and I just got a judge to sign a warrant for a roving wiretap, and we have a team of guys discreetly gaining access to his computers."

"How are you doing that?" Brad asked.

"We have a few techy tricks up our sleeve that haven't been released to the public yet." Landry smiled.

"You called a friend at the NSA," Brad replied dryly.

"Well, there's that, too. Whatever it takes," Landry laughed. "We're also installing video and audio surveillance in his rental house."

"You know where he is?" Noah asked.

"Yeah…" Joe hesitated. "We know. We're watching his house."

"Oh, yeah?" Bull asked. "I guess you saw me there earlier then, huh?" The dumbfounded look the four agents gave him made Bull laugh out loud. "I'll take that as a no, then. Guess I'm not slipping as much as I thought was."

"We're not moving on him now," Noah stated. "We don't know what he's planning yet."

"We agree on that," Joe replied. "We've intercepted chatter that it's big, whatever it is. We can't wait much longer, though. If we can take him out and stop the attack in at least one area, we have to do it."

"How much time are we talking?" Noah asked.

"Impossible to say. We've located another potential person of interest, but it's more of a gut feeling than anything. If he starts making similar preparations, we'll have to move immediately," Joe answered.

"Speaking of," Brianna interjected. "We need to move immediately, Noah, if we're going to make our appointment time."

"Ready when you are, babe," Noah replied. He continued to speak and directed his statement to the others. "We'll be back later."

When they reached the doctor's office, Noah drove through the parking lot several times to check every car, every potential hiding place, and scanned surrounding businesses for anything suspicious. Satisfied that Brianna was safe, he parked and quickly escorted her inside.

"You know, people stare at me like they're trying to figure out if I'm a celebrity or something," Brianna said after they signed in for her appointment.

"Why do you say that?"

"Because you act like you're my bodyguard, walking so close and hiding me from everyone," Brianna laughed. "I need to buy a pair of huge sunglasses to complete the look."

He reached over, took her left hand, and stroked her wedding band with his thumb. He dropped his voice an octave and spoke slowly, seductively. "You belong to me. You're mine to love, protect, and cherish. To have, anytime I want to have you."

Brianna lovingly stroked the stubble growing on his face, although he'd shaved only hours before. "I'm all yours, Noah. Nothing and no one can tear us apart. And you definitely can have me *anytime* you want me."

"Brianna Steele," the nurse called from the doorway. "Are you ready?"

"I'm definitely ready," she replied, but she kept her eyes glued to Noah's.

Noah stood, extended his hand, and helped Brianna to her feet. "Keep it up, babe. We'll both get arrested for lewd conduct in public."

"We'll have to keep the 'Busted' paper for our baby book," she quipped as she stood.

Noah swatted her ass playfully. "Get back there and show me my baby, woman."

"Whatever you say, my caveman."

After Karrie, the ultrasound technician, explained the protocol, she left Brianna to change into the paper gown. Noah approached her with an unmistakable look of desire. His fingers gripped the hem of her shirt. He slowly pulled it over her head before tossing it into the empty chair. He hooked his thumbs inside the waistband of her skirt and pushed it down over her hips. His fingers skimmed across the sensitive skin of her thighs until he fully knelt in front of her.

Her skirt fell in a pile at her feet as he felt his way back up her legs to repeat the same path to remove her panties. She stepped out of them and he tossed them into the chair with her shirt. As he rose, he intentionally brushed his face against her sex. His tongue darted out and connected with her clit, instantly eliciting a needful moan deep in her chest.

"Mmm, you taste so good," he murmured against her. "Does that door lock?"

"No. Dammit," she complained, her voice thick with desire.

"That's too bad," he replied, purposely allowing his lips to brush against her as he spoke. "Maybe we won't get caught."

"You're killing me. You know I can't resist you," she purred and grasped his hair.

"I know, and I fucking love it," he replied. He quickly stood, grabbed the paper gown, and grinned wickedly. "Better get this on you before she comes back."

Fire lit her eyes, but she reluctantly agreed because she knew he was right. The tech would be back any minute. "Fine," she spat out. "But you'll pay for this later."

"Oh, I'm counting on that," he laughed. "I can hardly wait."

The rap on the door kicked Brianna into high gear to get her gown on before the door opened. Noah's laughter echoed through the room, but he did manage to call out to the nurse through the door. "Just a minute, please."

Brianna narrowed her eyes at him in mock anger. "You can let her in now."

Noah opened the door and let Karrie in while wearing a suspiciously pleased smile on his face. She stopped in their tracks, did a double take, and continued into the room. "Ready to see that baby now?"

"Yes," Brianna replied excitedly. "I can't wait. Can I just take that machine home with me?"

Karrie laughed. "You'd be surprised how many times I'm asked that question. I'm afraid not. This one is fairly high-tech so we can see finer details."

"Are we taking bets on the sex of the baby?" she asked. "We couldn't get a good view in the previous ultrasound, right?"

"That's right," Brianna replied. "I say it's a girl, but she's being stubborn like her daddy."

"I say it doesn't matter to me what sex the baby is. All I care about is that we have a healthy baby and a healthy momma," Noah added.

"Awww, you're going to be such a good daddy," Karrie cooed at him.

Brianna rolled her eyes at both of them. Not because she didn't agree—she knew Noah would be the best daddy to their children. She'd seen too many women virtually fall at his feet when he flashed his killer smile at them.

Picturing the strong, hulking man cradling a baby would definitely cause every woman's ovaries to burst into flames.

"Pregnant woman who hasn't peed in a very long time over here," Brianna reminded them.

"Well, let's press on your stomach and see that baby then," Karrie laughed.

When the lifelike image of their baby illuminated the screen, Brianna's eyes immediately filled with tears. Little hands floated up toward its face before little fingers fanned out to brush against its brow. The corners of the tiny mouth lifted slightly, teasing Mommy and Daddy, before a beautiful smile covered the baby's entire face.

Noah laced his fingers with Brianna's and leaned into her until their cheeks were pressed together. "That's you and me, Bri. That's our love," he whispered, amazement and wonder filling his voice. "Look how beautiful our love is." He gingerly wiped the tears from her face and left soft kisses in their place.

"Everything looks really good." Karrie smiled. "All of the baby measurements are tracking right on target. Do you want to know the sex today?"

"Yes," they both replied simultaneously.

Karrie moved the wand around Brianna's stomach, spreading the gel to perfectly align the view on the screen. "Congratulations, Mom and Dad. You're having a baby girl."

"A girl?" Noah asked, even though he seemed dazed.

"We're having a girl?" Brianna repeated.

Karrie printed out individual pictures while the video continued to record. She knew from experience that once the shock wore off, the parents would naturally want to examine the image more closely for themselves. She turned with a warm smile and handed them each a picture of the defining moment.

"Noah," Brianna whispered. "We're having a baby girl."

Though he held firm to his tough-guy persona, the mist that covered his eyes was unmistakable. "I think it's really hitting me that we're going to be parents. We'll be responsible for another human life, a life that we created. Her every joy and pain, her fears and dreams... They'll all be ours to the millionth degree."

"My mom always said I'd never fully understand a parent's love until I had a child of my own," Brianna sniffled. "She was so right. It's a completely different kind of love."

Karrie continued to move the wand to give them as many views of their baby girl as she possibly could. "Okay, that's all for today," she said as she cleaned the wand. "Here's your recording of the ultrasound. I'm sure you both have plenty of people who want to get their hands on that video."

"Our parents, siblings, friends," Noah chuckled. "We'll be lucky if we get to watch it again before she's born."

"Better hide it for a while." Karrie grinned. "Family and friends have ways of taking over babies. Will this be the first grandbaby?"

"Yes, on both sides. First niece, too. And between her daddy and all her uncles, she'll never be allowed to date." Brianna beamed.

Brianna stood to get dressed when Karrie left the room. Like magnets undeniably drawn together, she and Noah embraced in a moment of overwhelming emotion. His arms wrapped around her and held her securely against his body. She nestled into his body, closed her eyes, and inhaled the all-male scent that enveloped her. It was the scent that she associated with home, safety, and love, and it was unique to Noah.

"I know your job has always been dangerous," she said softly. "But please be extra careful. We need you, Noah... I can't do this without you."

His arms tightened around her. "I know exactly how you feel, Bri. One thing I know for sure is I wouldn't even make it a full day without you. And now, seeing our baby like that, it's intensified even more. I'm going to catch this asshole, I promise you."

"Let's go home, Noah. Our family will be excited to watch this video of our baby. Does Roman have the satellite phone with him?"

"Yeah, he has it. Why?"

"Let's Skype them in so your parents can watch it, too. Seeing these images of the baby may just give Steve an even stronger will to beat his cancer."

"Sounds perfect." He kissed her forehead and released her to finish dressing. "Is there anything you need from the store before we go home?"

"You already know that I want to go shopping for baby girl clothes," she laughed.

"Yeah, I know you well enough to know that," he agreed. "If you twist my arm, I'll let you talk me into buying her an outfit that says 'My Daddy Has My Heart' on it. I have a feeling I'll need that to fight Bull off."

"Bull will just mark through 'Daddy' and write 'Uncle Bull' in," she replied. "He claimed his place in our child's life as soon as he found out I was pregnant."

Before heading home, Noah drove to the shopping mall and picked out more items than Brianna did. As they walked through the department store on their way out, the display of flat-screen TVs that covered an entire wall showcased the various high-definition options. One by one, the images on every television changed to display a piece of a puzzle until the full image covered the entire wall.

The image was the 3-D still shot of Noah and Brianna's baby girl. A message appeared across the bottom of the screens that read:

Congratulations on your pink bundle of joy.
Hope you have a picture of her.
You'll need it.

CHAPTER ELEVEN

"I figured it out," Rebel exclaimed. "I know why the fucking bastard is so familiar now."

"By all means, tell us," Shadow replied.

"Remember the hostages we got out of the far northern region of Iran? He looks just like the guy who ran that compound, Hamid Madani," Rebel replied. "He shot at me as we were getting out and damn near took my head off. I returned fire and killed him."

"A family member out for revenge? A son or nephew with such a close resemblance, maybe?" Shadow suggested.

"We'll have the analysts do some digging on that name and see how it ties into Ali Babek Turan," Joe interrupted as he walked in. "Right now, we have more pressing concerns."

"What happened?" Bull asked.

"Multiple cyberattacks at once. He doesn't fit the regular mold of an extremist, and that makes me think he's going rogue," Joe replied. "Every personal cell phone on one floor of the Department of Homeland Security building in Washington, DC just started ringing at the exact same time. No two of the incoming numbers were the same."

"A couple of the employees answered their phones. It was a recording from their banks confirming $100,000 deposits into their checking accounts," Bill added.

"They all use the same bank?" Bull asked.

"No, that's the thing. It was the *same* recording from their *different* banks," Bill clarified.

"And the deposits were real?" Shadow asked.

"Yes, all of the money was transferred from the bank account of a US-owned oil refinery located in Oklahoma," Joe replied. "Since we already had the tap on his 'borrowed' Internet connection, we were able to trace it back to him pretty quickly."

"The money transfer is most likely a diversionary tactic, but he knows it can't be ignored. If I were a betting man, I'd say his real intentions are about to kick in," Bull said.

"I'd take that bet," Landry replied.

"Since you're all so ready to gamble, can I interest you in a game of poker?" Liz asked from the doorway. She waved a deck of cards at the men and flashed her sweetest smile. "I'll deal."

"That's very thoughtful of you to offer, Liz." Shadow winked at her. "Too bad we have a bad guy to catch before we can stop for playtime."

"There's always time to play, Shadow," Liz argued. "We're not promised the next breath. What if you step outside and get mowed down by a big truck? You'd die without having ever played a hand of poker with me."

"That would be tragic." Shadow nodded.

"It would be a travesty," she agreed. "There's only one solution. We should all play right now. You boys just go ahead and kick off your shoes, make yourself comfortable before we get started."

Bill and Joe exchanged glances and a shared idea seemed to pass wordlessly between them. "You thinking what I'm thinking?" Bill asked.

"I'm sure of it," Joe replied before turning his gaze. "Liz, I think it's time we play our secret card and draw him out into the light. You game?"

"For catching that little bastard?" she asked. "I'm game."

"I'll get started on the breaking news reports," Bill replied. "I'll be back in touch later today."

"I'll get our analysts up to speed. We'll need extra manpower to catch the chatter and weed out the junk," Joe added before both men walked out the door.

"Looks like that leaves us, boys." Liz smiled and began to cut the card deck.

Moments later, the driveway alert sounded, and Shadow strolled to the window to look. "Reaper's back," he called out. Concern covered his face and he quickly added, "Something's wrong. He's flying up the driveway like a bat out of hell."

Shadow, Bull, and Rebel rushed to meet Reaper and Brianna inside the garage. Reaper slammed the door as he exited the car and rushed around to help Brianna out. Even in his aggravated state, they watched as their friend visibly calmed himself before he took her hand.

"What happened, boss?" Rebel asked.

"Get me the scissors, Rebel. I'm going to cut his balls off myself," Brianna replied.

Rebel's eyes darted between Brianna and Reaper, unsure of what he should do with that statement. "Whose balls are we cutting off, little lady?"

"Turan's. He's destined to live the rest of his days as a eunuch, courtesy of yours truly," Brianna replied.

"What'd he do now?" Bull asked. His lips drew into a thin line, his nostrils flared, and his brow furrowed. He had a good idea he wouldn't like Brianna's answer at all.

"Noah and I went shopping for baby stuff after our appointment. We were walking through the store to exit, and our baby's ultrasound picture was on a giant display of TVs. He added a personal note that said congratulations, hope you have a picture of your baby, you'll need it," she replied, anger dripping from her every word. "He used the very picture we just got from the ultrasound."

Bull's hands curled into fists at his sides. "I'll tear him limb from limb."

"Get in line, brother," Reaper replied.

"He's watching you," Shadow replied. "Probably from a traffic camera around your doctor or the mall. Did you have the picture out in the open at any time?"

"When we were walking out of the office," Brianna confirmed. "I was still staring at it."

"He's not going to get to you or the baby, Sunny," Bull promised. "Maybe you should take someone else with you when you go out."

"Bull, I won't take any chances, but I won't live my life as his prisoner either. The three years I already spent in that mode were more than too much."

"We'll just have to take him out sooner rather than later," Shadow replied. "I can handle it tonight if you want."

"I found the mission that I think tied us to him," Rebel said. "It was the hostage situation in northern Iran. He looks a lot like the group leader I killed. The analysts will start looking into a real name and known associations soon."

"Good job, Rebel. That brings us one step closer to figuring out who else he's tied to, who to watch, what their endgame is. And to closing this case for good," Reaper replied. "Hold that thought, Shadow. You may actually be on to something."

"He launched another cyberattack earlier." Bull repeated the conversation they'd had with Joe and Bill to bring Reaper up to speed.

"Turan's been busy today," Reaper replied. "More so than usual. I don't like it. More reason why I think Shadow's on the right path."

"Have you heard from Mom and Dad?" Chaise asked. "Before you do anything, I just want to feel like they're safe."

"I talked to Roman on the satellite phone earlier," he confirmed. "They're fine. No landlines, no Internet, and no distractions. They're surprisingly all having a good time. Roman and Tawnee are being extra vigilant about security just in case, though."

"I'm glad to hear that. They need a break from all of this. It's too much stress on Dad in his condition," Chaise replied as she joined the conversation. "Maybe they should go on to Texas for his treatment and get away from all of this."

"That's a good idea, Chaise," Noah agreed. "We should probably talk to them about it when they get back from this trip tomorrow. I know I'd feel better if they were far away from Turan."

"Bull, it's time for us to go meet with the florist about our flowers for the wedding," Chaise said as she glanced at her watch. "We'd better hurry or we'll be late."

"Shit, I almost forgot all about that. I'm ready to go when you are." Bull leaned in and placed a kiss on her cheek. "My offer to run away and get married somewhere crazy still stands."

"Not a chance in hell, Bull," Chaise replied. "I want to see you in a tuxedo. This is the only way I can get you to wear one."

Bull shook his head because he knew Chaise would win him over, regardless of how or why he argued against it. "Let's go then, woman. Get the lead out."

"Yeah, yeah, let me grab my purse."

"Are we really moving on him tonight?" Bull asked Reaper.

"I think it's time we did something. We've listened to the CIA and the FBI. We've waited it out, kept tabs on his whereabouts, but he's still fucking with us. The flurry of activity today doesn't fit the profile of someone is who cold, calculating, and patient. It says he's becoming sloppy, desperate, and too unpredictable," Reaper replied. "If we can pull him out of there, Brad and the CIA analysts can scour through his files, pretend to be him for a little while until we find out what their plans are."

"Worth a shot. We'll be back in a few hours. Don't go without me," Bull warned.

"Wouldn't dream of it," Reaper replied when Bull and Chaise started to walk off.

Shadow rubbed his hands together in anticipation. "Let's get our mission plan laid out while Bull's picking out pansies."

"Fuck off, man," Bull called over his shoulder.

"Fuckoff? Is that a type of pansy?" Shadow retorted.

Bull flipped Shadow his signature one-finger salute over his shoulder and didn't bother to turn around for a reaction. The men laughed good-naturedly and moved their discussion inside Noah's office. Rebel grabbed the street-level map, and they began to plan their incursion on Turan's stronghold.

Liz yelled excitedly from the den. "I'm on the television. I'm a star!"

Everyone joined her to watch the breaking news alert.

The national news anchorwoman was the poster child for perfect hair, makeup, and a commanding presence. As she spoke, she owned her audience with her urgency and passion. "Ladies and gentlemen, we interrupt the regularly scheduled programming to bring you this breaking news. Government officials, speaking on the condition of anonymity, have confirmed that an elderly woman from Colorado has survived an attempt on her life. Her attacker is a member of a known terrorist group with ties to extremists in Iran. If you've seen this man" —the picture of Turan filled the screen— "please call the authorities immediately. Do not attempt to apprehend him yourself. He is considered armed and dangerous.

"I have an exclusive interview tonight with this incredibly brave lady who barely survived after he intentionally poisoned her. Tune in as she describes the close call, her thoughts on living next door to a real life sleeper-cell terrorist, and what message she'd like to send to Ali Babek Turan now. We are working to bring you more details on anyone Turan may be working with and where. Stay tuned for more."

"Can you believe that? I'm going to be interviewed on the national news tonight. Everyone will know who I am after this." Liz beamed.

"We'd better get you ready for your fifteen minutes of fame, Liz." Brianna smiled. "Come on upstairs with me while your boys finish working."

"Make me look sexy," Liz replied. "I can't go on national television looking like a slob."

"Of course not," Brianna agreed. As she passed Noah, she murmured under her breath to him, "You owe me."

"It's so worth it," he replied with a smile.

"Guess Bill and Joe are making good on their promises," Rebel said. "This kind of exposure will push Turan over the edge. Everything's been on his terms so far, but his playing field just changed."

"Maybe tonight is perfect timing, then," Reaper replied. "When the other members of his group see this, it will not end well for him. Besides blowing their covers and all the time they've invested in their mission, he just dishonored all of them."

~

When his burner phone rang, rather than the VOIP on his laptop, Turan knew without a doubt that it would be bad.

"Hello," he answered.

"Look at the news," the voice said.

"What channel?"

"It doesn't matter. It's the same on all of them."

Turan quickly pulled up the national news website and saw his reflection staring back at him. He clicked "play" on the video and watched as the news anchor described his ties to terrorism, the crimes being attributed to him, and the exclusive interview with the elderly survivor of his latest known attack.

"They have your picture," the voice spoke slowly. "They have your known aliases. They can trace you back to us. You've put our entire agenda in jeopardy with your selfish personal gains."

"I am my own man, and I don't need your permission," he stated flatly. "This news changes nothing."

"It changes everything...for you," he replied and promptly disconnected the call.

"No, it doesn't—" Turan began to argue before he realized no one was on the line.

Over the next hour, he went to every news website he could find. He read countless articles about the miraculous survival and recovery of an elderly lady who'd been poisoned by a known terrorist. He learned that he'd been on the FBI Watchlist, but he fell off their scope for a short time.

The poisoning of an American citizen on American soil by a terrorist on a government watch list was big news. It threatened the safety and security of a nation, and that nation's citizens were angry about it. They were quickly turning on him in social media posts, in replies to news articles, and in groups that encouraged local militia to take up arms and find him.

"The modern version of a lynch mob," he mused. "Let's see how well some of you work in the dark. Right after you watch Liz's interview tonight, you'll begin to understand what terror really is."

Using one of his more powerful machines, he worked his way into the local power grid controls. With a few keystrokes, he programmed a change in the electric company computers that was scheduled to go into effect at midnight.

"Soon, the lights will go out and the line crews won't be able to find anything wrong at the substation. Everything will appear to function correctly," he sneered.

A breaking news bulletin flashed across the screen of his laptop and the video automatically started playing. "Local News 3 has learned that the survivor of the terrorist attack has moved here to Miami to recuperate with friends. Stay tuned as we carry the national coverage on her interview, the harrowing details of her attack, and how she managed to survive a death sentence. Coming up next on Local News 3."

"Liz is in Miami?" Turan narrowed his eyes at the screen. "Is she really here, or are you just trying to draw me out of hiding?"

When the special news coverage started, the well-known news anchor started the program with her usual ploy to create suspense and eagerness for the latest update. Turan rolled his eyes at her penchant for drama.

"Tonight, I have the distinct honor and pleasure of interviewing someone incredible. An older lady who, for all intents and purposes, should be dead right now after being savagely poisoned by her neighbor. It turns out that her former neighbor is a wanted terrorist and is tied to several other murders. Mrs. Elizabeth Stanton may very well be the only person who has survived an attack from this brutal man.

"Mrs. Stanton joins us from a secure, remote location for her safety. This madman is still at large and is considered armed and dangerous. If you see him, do not attempt to apprehend or even approach him on your own. Call the authorities immediately and report his whereabouts. Someone out there has seen him, and you may very well be the key to ending this nightmare that our nation is currently in."

Turan laughed at her assessment of him. *A madman. Armed and dangerous. Call for help, run for cover, hide and weep.*

"And now, I'd like you to meet Mrs. Elizabeth Stanton. Welcome, Liz."

"Thank you, Julia. It's good to be here with you," Liz replied with a smile.

"Liz, let's go back to the time just before your neighbor so viciously tried to kill you. What was he like?"

"He was boring, Julia," Liz stated bluntly. "He was like a wet blanket, putting the fires out around him from pure suffocation of fun. His social skills were nonexistent and his hygiene was severely lacking. I tried to befriend him, help him out of his shell, but obviously not everyone wants to be helped."

"Are you saying he didn't know how to talk to people? He was a loner?"

"Yes, he was definitely a loner. He never had anyone visit him at his townhouse. He went to work five days a week, came home alone, and stayed inside the whole time. He's a young man; he should've been out having fun, meeting people, forming relationships. But he sat at home all alone instead."

"Talk to me about the day of the attack. What events led up to it?" Julia asked.

"He surprised me by coming over to see me all of a sudden. I'd always asked him, and sometimes he'd come in for tea—he always loved my tea—but I could tell he didn't really want to be there. But the day he tried to kill me—and failed," she stressed, "he actually did want to be there.

"He helped me unload mulch from the trunk of my car and then helped me spread it in all of my beautiful flower beds. Now I know that he was just trying to make sure there was nothing out of place in my yard. My neighbors would've known that I wouldn't leave bags of mulch on my lawn, killing the grass.

"Anyway, when I invited him in for tea and croissants, he quickly agreed to it. But first, he went to his house and brought back this awful, bitter-tasting honey that he'd been bragging on. I didn't have the heart to tell him at the time that, even though honey isn't supposed to ever go bad, his must have been the exception. It had a very bitter taste, and we all know that *real* honey is sweet."

The more she talked, the more Turan's hands curled into tight fists. Every word out of her mouth was an insult, a dishonor, and an outrage. It was clear that they weren't lying—Liz really did survive. The next words caught his attention.

"Liz, it is very serious business to have active terrorists on American soil. Here, in our country, threatening our citizens. How much of a threat do you believe Ali Babek Turan really is?"

"Julia, I can only go by what I've personally experienced. He is a bumbling, inept, thug-wannabe. Really, if he can't kill a little, old, weak lady like myself, how much of a threat can he be to a real man? Of course, it's scary to think that his friends could be better at this terrorist business than he is. Maybe he's a trainee or something. I'd feel sorry for him, you know, if he hadn't tried to kill me."

"Liz, you must have a heart of gold and the patience of a saint. If I were in your shoes, I can say I wouldn't stop until he'd been punished to the fullest extent of the law," Julia replied, her admiration of Liz clear.

"Oh, Julia, don't get me wrong. If I see him coming, he'll definitely feel the wrath of Liz Stanton. The odds of that actually happening are small, though, because that would require him to leave the safety of his four walls. He'd have to actually face another person who knows what kind of sniveling weasel he really is," Liz clarified. "He'd be too scared to face me now. I can't imagine what a disappointment he must be to his family."

"I hope you're right, Liz." Julia started her response, but Turan wasn't listening. His mind was still reeling from Liz's last statements about him. Did she know that his father never approved of him? That he never met his expectations and his father died before he could prove that he was capable of being brave? Did she know that he was always a disappointment to his father, a regret in his eyes?

CHAPTER TWELVE

"I'm really sorry, baby," Bull tried to soothe Chaise. "I know how disappointed you are."

"How is he staying a step ahead of us? I just don't get it. We have super-techy guys working this case, too."

"Nothing against Brad, but this Turan guy is a genius when it comes to programming, and apparently at hacking, too," he explained. "We know where he is, we've just been—"

"Waiting." She finished his sentence for him. "I understand not wanting to show your hand, but at some point, enough has to be enough, Colton. The man tried to kill Liz, we know he killed other people. There's enough evidence to hold him."

"Actually, we wouldn't even need that evidence with the laws on terrorism," he admitted.

"That really doesn't help right now," she replied through gritted teeth. "We know he's a terrorist. Go. Get. Him."

"We're going to his house tonight," Bull replied. "Late. We'll get him."

"Okay, as much as I want you to get him, I'm a little worried about pushing you to go to his house now. What if something happens to you?"

"Won't happen, babe. I'm too stubborn to get hurt. I'm too mean to be killed. And I'm too good at my job to be caught." He grinned at her.

"There's the cocky, confident Bull I love." She smiled back. "Please be careful tonight."

"I will, babe. I really am sorry about the flowers," he said again. "I'll kick his ass for you when I get to him if you want."

"Yes, please do. He deserves it. There's no way to get my flowers now. They'd have to be planted, grown, and harvested since he canceled my order and the ones I need were given to someone else. They were going to be perfect, too." Chaise scowled.

"We can choose another type of flower," Bull offered.

"I'll think about it. I'm just really so disappointed and disgusted right now, I can't even think straight."

"Well, it's a good thing I know what'll make you feel better, help you forget that disappointment, and have you singing from the rooftops."

"Colton, take me away," she agreed. "Shouting your name from the rooftops may be exactly what I need."

"Hell yeah." He pressed the gas pedal harder. "I'm taking you up on that—no take-backs."

"No take-backs," she agreed. "I'm all yours. I need the energy release and the whole body relaxation I get when you're finished working me over."

"You know it turns me on when you talk like that."

"I do know," she confirmed. "I'm counting on it, my lover."

"That's my girl."

When they walked inside the house, Bull leaned his back against the closed door, set the alarm system, and let his eyes rake over Chaise's body.

"You just going to stand there looking at me?" she asked coyly

"No." Bull shook his head. "I'm going to do a lot more than look at you. First, I'm going to strip every article of clothing from that gorgeous body of yours. Then I'm going to massage every inch of your body, loosen up those tight muscles, and work some of your stress out. When you're relaxed and limber, I'm going to make you mine in every known position, and maybe a few we make up on our own."

Chaise's shock was evident on her face—and in her physical reaction—as she let go of her purse at the same time her bottom jaw dropped open. Her chest rose and fell in rapid succession as her breathing became shallow. Her face flushed as desire burned through her veins like liquid fire. "You're the only one who knows how to make me forget everything else that's going on in the world."

Bull nodded slowly. "Tonight, there is nothing else, and no one else. Only you and me."

"Yes," she said breathily. "You're all I need."

He pushed off the door and walked directly to Chaise, his eyes never leaving hers as he advanced on her. "Come with me."

Bull led her into their bedroom and stopped her at the foot of the bed. As he unbuttoned her shirt, his fingers lightly brushed against her and sent chills rippling across her skin. As he pushed her skirt over her hips and down her legs, he left openmouthed kisses in his wake. He lazily traced her sensitive flesh through her silky panties with his finger. "It feels hot in here," he said as his hand reached between her legs. "Is it wet, too?"

"You can touch it and see for yourself," she offered.

"It's mine, isn't it?" he asked rhetorically. "I'll do a lot more than touch it. But I want you to tell me. So, is it wet?"

"Yes, it's very wet," she panted.

"I bet we can make it wetter," he ventured. "We haven't even started yet."

He slowly removed her panties and stood to remove her bra just as painfully slowly. His every touch branded Chaise, made her want him more, and made the wait even more excruciating. She knew if she tried to make him hurry, he would purposely make her wait even longer. His plans for her had been made known, and all she had to do was relax and let heaven come to her. Exhaling slowly, she allowed her muscles to relax and let all the stress begin to fade to black.

Bull moved her to the bed and motioned for her to lie on her stomach. When she was in place, his strong hands began massaging her neck and shoulders. Soothing scents filled the air when he removed the oil from the nightstand and poured it into his hands and rubbed them together. The friction warmed the oil enough that Chaise felt the heat seep through her skin when he began rubbing her shoulders again.

He moved down her back, running his finger along the hollow of her spine to the top of her ass. "I love this." He covered both of her cheeks with his hands and sensually squeezed. "I could feast on this all day."

While he kneaded the backs of her thighs with his strong hands, he imagined their lives together after everything settled down. He hadn't had much downtime between cases, Noah and Brianna's wedding, and planning his own wedding. The moments like this had become his refuge, his solace in the world of madness. He never imagined his life would take this turn and give him someone he couldn't imagine living without. There wasn't anything about her that he didn't love, even the things she did that drove him nuts.

"Just looking at you makes me crazy," he muttered. "You're so beautiful. And sexy. You make it impossible not to want you wherever we are. Sometimes I have to remind myself that I don't want any other man to see you naked just so I don't strip you bare when we're out somewhere."

She sighed heavily and melted even more into the bed. "If we could get away with it, would you want to have sex in a public place?"

"I think it could be fun," he replied. "But I don't think we could be quiet enough."

"You're probably right," she giggled. "It's hard to be discreet with you."

The growing bulge that strained against his zipper became painful, especially when he thought about the sounds she made and the way she looked when they made love. "This is what you do to me," he said as he slid his erection across her ass, grinding his hips against her as he moved.

She moaned appreciatively and pulled her legs up until her knees were underneath her to better accept him. When he made a second pass, his movements mimicked the act of taking her from behind. Her fingers curled into the comforter and gripped it in a vise-lock. "Colton," she begged.

The sound of his zipper and the shuffling of denim were all she needed to hear to know that he'd also reached his limit of waiting. With his clothes shed, she felt him move behind her on the bed as his legs framed hers. With one sudden thrust, he entered her soft, wet channel and dug his fingertips into her hip bones.

"Fuck, baby, you feel so good," he said. He repeatedly pulled back and pushed forward into her, drawing her moans and screams to a pinnacle. He felt her inner muscles squeeze him as if they were trying to hold him in place. "You're close," he boasted, felt the rush of warmth from her release, and then joined her in his own.

He rolled her over and she curled into him with her arm across his chest. "That was incredible. Every bit of it," she exhaled.

Bull kissed the top of her head. "You're always incredible, my love."

"Are you still going tonight?" she asked tentatively.

"Yeah, it'll be late, but I'd feel better if you wait at Reaper's while I'm gone."

"Okay. Brianna and Liz will keep me company until you get back," she agreed. "Just don't stay out past your curfew. You know I don't like to wait."

He chuckled, knowing she was joking with him. "Yes, ma'am. I'd hate to keep you waiting and get in trouble when I get home."

"You'll be in more trouble if you don't kick his ass for all the trouble he's caused us with our wedding. I want to go with you just to be the one to make him pay for it," she replied.

"If I could take you with me, just for that reason, I definitely would. You're scary when you get mad."

She playfully swatted his chest. "You'd better remember that yourself."

Bull lovingly stroked her back with his fingertips, back and forth until she was lulled into a restful sleep. He remained awake and mentally recounted the preplanned sequence of the night's events. Turan's car hadn't moved in a week, but like clockwork every night, he had food delivered to his house. Joe and Bill were being kept updated on the intercepted messages as the analysts dissected any information that was remotely close to their case. Nothing indicated that tonight would be any different than last night. No intelligence pointed to a sudden change of plans.

The plan was that the four-man team would approach the residence from different directions, each covering a specific side of the house. House blueprints, undercover pictures, and the information obtained from the wiretap were all memorized. Every step had been planned well ahead of time to avoid as many problems as possible. *Best laid plans*, was on repeat in Bull's mind.

He'd never had jittery nerves before an operation before now. Skirmishes in a foreign desert or reconnaissance work in an opulent mansion, the job had always felt like second nature to him. Get in, get what was needed, and get out. Move silently, take no prisoners, and take no shit. Stay cool, keep calm, and follow the plan—that was always how the operation went. Chaise moved in her sleep and drew his attention away from his thoughts. The change in his demeanor suddenly made sense to him.

"It's because now I have something to lose," he murmured aloud. "Something I know I never want to be without. Someone I want to make it back home to."

He let her sleep in his arms for as long as he could before he had to meet the others. He gently shook her shoulder to wake her. "Chaise, baby, we have to leave in a few minutes."

"I haven't slept that well since this whole thing started," she said sleepily. "Please be extra careful tonight. I expect you to come home to me, safe and sound and in one piece."

"Try to get rid of me," he chuckled. "Even a restraining order won't keep me from you."

Chaise and Bull got dressed and left so he could drop her off at Noah's and get to his rendezvous point well ahead of time. She held his hand with both of hers during the entire drive, gently stroked her fingers along his, and glanced nervously at him a few times.

"Here we are," Bull announced as they pulled into Noah's driveway. "Stay here with Brianna and Liz until we get back. There are security men in the yard and along the perimeter. You'll be safe."

"You need to be safe, Colton. Call or text me as soon as you can to let me know you're okay."

He smiled. He'd never had to check in with anyone before now. "I will, babe. It'll be fine—you'll see."

After a long kiss— *"until later, not goodbye"* —Chaise got out of the truck. Brianna met her at the door.

"Come on in." Brianna smiled. "We'll have a slumber party—you, Liz, and me."

"I'm not playing poker with her," Chaise stated.

"Chaise! We're playing Twister! I have everything ready," Liz yelled from the den.

"Sadly, I'm in no condition to play Twister." Brianna patted her stomach. "So, it'll be you, Liz, and the poor, unsuspecting security guy twisting," Brianna replied.

Bull waved to them both and pulled out of the drive. When he hit the road, his cell started ringing. "Hey, Reap, what's up?"

"Just making sure you remembered we have a date tonight."

"Have I ever stood you up before?" Bull asked.

"There's always a first time for everything," Reaper joked.

"Not for that," Bull replied. "Brothers don't stand each other up."

"Let's take this shithead out tonight and be done with him."

"That's what I'm talking about," Bull replied.

He pulled onto the side street that gave him the best vantage point of Turan's yard. The house was completely dark except for a small glow in the living room. The team's cell phones were turned off and their secure wireless communicators were on.

"The car hasn't moved, but either the house is empty or our boy is sound asleep. There's no movement, small glow in the front of the house, but nothing moving around on this side," Bull reported.

"Same here," Shadow replied. "That glow is from a laptop, but he's not in the living room."

"I'm below his bedroom window," Rebel whispered. "I hear snoring. Let's get this guy."

"Copy that," Reaper replied. "Everyone move into your positions. We're doing this by the book."

Bull glanced down at his watch just as he moved into his position at the back door. Two minutes until midnight. In two minutes, everything could change. This case could be closed, the bad guy could be apprehended or killed, and they could be going home to their families. Or, in two minutes, life as they knew it could all change. In the blink of an eye, everything could go wrong because they rushed into a trap set by an extremist bent on killing as many people as possible.

Bull pulled his gun close to his chest. It was locked and loaded, ready to fire. The single-word command from Reaper came across the airwaves. "Go."

Without hesitation, Bull placed a strategically swift kick to the back door and sent it flying open. He immediately stepped to the side for cover and extended his arm to aim. Quickly stepping into the room, he thoroughly searched the room before moving on to the next one. Just as he rounded the corner, he saw a door in the hallway move slightly. "Got movement," he whispered into his comm. "Door in the hallway. Going in."

"On your six," Reaper replied as Bull stepped through the door.

"Stairs, looks like a basement," Bull advised.

Light briefly illuminated the basement before it disappeared.

"He's on the move," Bull said and flew down the stairs. "There's a door down here."

Reaper was close on Bull's heels. "It's a crawl space door. He must be going for the car. Shadow, Rebel, get outside now!"

Reaper and Bull followed into the crawl space while Rebel and Shadow ran outside.

"Flashlight moving," Shadow called. "I'm on it."

"I'll cover the car and the house," Rebel replied.

Reaper and Bull emerged from the other end of the crawl space and out of the half door that Turan had exited. A bulky giant ran past them in the dark with the signature prowess of Shadow. His strides lengthened and his speed increased, then he lunged through the air and landed on a much smaller form. The scuffle only lasted a second or two before Shadow sat completely on top of him, had his arms twisted behind his back, and handcuffs locked around his wrists.

"And that's a wrap," Shadow said into his comm. "Shadow, one. Pansy-ass terrorist, zero."

The other men laughed into their comms, sharing in the revelry of the moment. As Shadow stood Turan up to walk him back into the light with the other men, the power to all the houses and businesses shut off for as far as they could see. Turan smiled from ear to ear. His face was covered in sand and dirt from his scuffle with Shadow, his clothes were dirty, and his hair was matted. But the pride on his face was evident and the fact he refrained from speaking about his accomplishment demonstrated his resolve.

This one wouldn't give up his secrets easily.

"Brianna. Chaise. Liz," Noah whispered to Bull. "Rebel, call the others and tell them it's safe to get out of their cars now. They can take custody of this asshole now."

Turan glared at Rebel as he called Joe and relayed Reaper's message. Within thirty seconds, Joe and Bill walked up. "You knew we were watching?"

Reaper looked at them like they'd just asked the dumbest question ever. "Of course, I knew. You can't tail a subject for shit," he chuckled. "Take this guy to your office and interrogate him. Call us if you need any tips on effective interrogation techniques."

"We got him," Joe replied. "Come on Ali Baba. Time to pay the piper."

"Let's get home. I don't like this at all. Something's up," Reaper said when Turan was out of earshot. "Get Brad over here to go through everything he has on these computers. We need to know what he's already done and what he's about to do."

"On it, boss," Shadow replied as Reaper put his phone to his ear.

"Brianna" The urgency in Reaper's voice was palpable. "Are you okay?"

"I'm fine, Noah. The power went out, but the generators are on and we're okay. Are you okay?"

"Yeah, babe. We got him, but it feels a little too easy. Call it a gut instinct. I'm on my way home. Keep the doors locked and keep the guns close. If anyone but me tries to get in the gate, shoot first and ask questions later," he ordered.

"Hurry home, Noah. But be careful," she replied. "I love you."

"Love you, too, babe. I'll be there within twenty minutes."

CHAPTER THIRTEEN

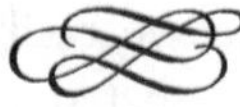

"Ladies, don't panic." Liz extended her hands out in front of her, spread her fingers, and exaggeratedly pumped them up and down. "We'll be fine. There's no reason to be scared."

"We're fine, Liz," Chaise replied calmly. "Anyway, the generators kicked on when the power went out, so the security system is still operating."

"We also have a couple of security guys outside. Plus, we're both armed." Brianna motioned between Chaise and herself.

"I won't let anything happen to either of you." Liz continued her attempts to soothe them.

"We feel so much better with you on guard," Brianna laughed.

"Are my boys all okay?" Liz asked.

"Yes, they're all fine," Chaise answered. "Colton just called and they're on the way home now."

"I'd better get the Twister mat ready for our game now," Liz replied. "Shadow and Rebel are mine tonight."

"Here, let me help you," Chaise offered. "I actually want to see this."

"Feel free to take notes, girly. You might need them later for Bull," Liz replied with a wink. "I've got the moves."

Liz and Chaise spread out the dotted mat on the floor and giggled like schoolgirls as they chatted about the mental pictures of Rebel and Shadow twisted into strange positions. They heard the squealing tires before the driveway alarm rang to alert them. Brianna rushed to the window just in time to see the tail end of Noah's truck flying into the garage. The door from the garage burst open when Noah and Bull both rushed inside, weapons drawn and aimed at the floor.

Noah stopped when his eyes met Brianna's. "You're okay?"

"We're fine, babe. Thanks for rushing home so fast, though." She smiled. "Where's Ali?"

"Joe and Bill took him in for questioning. I expect to hear from them soon," Noah replied.

Chaise walked into Bull's waiting arms. "I'm so glad you're okay," she told him.

"I'm fine, baby. We were never in any danger at all," Bull replied. "The whole thing was a piece of cake."

"Something's definitely wrong with that picture," Brianna said. "I can't believe the house wasn't booby-trapped, he didn't put up a huge fight, or really even try to wipe his hard drives."

"You know too much about this kind of thing," Chaise replied dryly to Brianna. "It scares me sometimes."

Brianna laughed. "Yeah, well, my time as a reporter, on top of my years with Noah, has taught me a few things. I've asked to officially join the team, but they won't let me."

"It was definitely too easy," Bull replied. "I'd like to know what's going on right now in that interrogation."

"Shadow and Rebel should be here soon. Let's see if Shadow can get any information from his CIA buddies," Noah suggested.

"Have you gotten used to this yet?" Chaise asked Brianna.

"Used to what? Noah putting his life in danger and waiting up to see if he'll make it home safely?" Brianna asked. "No, I'll never get used to it. He knows that. All I can do is trust that he's the best at what he does."

"Can I get a GPS tracker on you?" Chaise asked Bull. "One that sends me constant updates to let me know you're okay"

"I'll see what I can do," he chuckled.

"You and Noah could each wear one of those adventure cameras on your heads. Then Brianna and I can watch your missions together and rush in to save you if you get in trouble." Chaise grinned mischievously.

"You can use those cameras in the bedroom, too," Liz added. "Spice up your love life and all. Can I borrow it?"

"Sure, as soon as we start wearing cameras on our missions, we'll let you borrow it," Bull replied.

"Be sure to look at Shadow. A lot. From behind," Liz answered.

"Who's looking at my behind?" Shadow asked from the doorway, his sly smile covering his face.

"Bull will watch it with the adventure camera he'll wear on his head," Liz replied.

Shadow's smile faltered as his eyes bounced around the room, met the others' amused gazes, and decided it was best to not pursue the topic. "Good to know," he laughed. "Reap, Bull—need to talk to you both outside. Rebel's already out here."

"You got it," Noah replied and stepped toward Shadow.

"Be right back, babe." Bull kissed Chaise.

They met Rebel in the driveway and huddled up for the update. "Bad news, boys," Shadow started.

"What?" Noah asked, instantly on alert. "I knew it was too easy."

"Yeah, Turan has already been released," Shadow relayed. "As soon as Joe and Bill got him into the interrogation room, Bill received a call from the higher-ups. They had to release him because he has diplomatic immunity. His uncle, Bachar, is the ambassador from Turkey. Turan is also considered a diplomat since he works for his uncle."

"But he's a terrorist," Bull countered. "How can he be protected under our laws if he's a terrorist?"

"We don't have enough hard evidence to prove he is. We can't expel him back to Turkey without evidence. Legally, we're not even supposed to have the wiretap on him, and we can't use that evidence since it wasn't obtained legally."

"That's why he was smiling smugly at us," Rebel said. "He wanted us to catch him so we'd find out he's untouchable."

Reaper inhaled deeply and gave each of his brothers a hard gaze. "You all know what this means. If you want out, I understand, but this changes nothing for me. The government disavows any knowledge of my actions anyway, so I don't view this any differently. He's threatening my family and my country, and a law that protects terrorism isn't valid in my eyes."

"I'm in," Bull replied instantly.

"Me, too," Rebel answered.

"You know I have no problem with breaking silly laws like that," Shadow replied. "Landry and Daniels have been pulled from the case. Joe and Bill will still be around but, *officially*, not as much as before."

"We should expect retaliation soon," Reaper warned. "He won't be satisfied with just being let go. He'll want to cause more trouble for us."

"Exactly. He's been waiting for us to show up at his house, waiting for us to make a move on him, just so he could blatantly make his next play," Rebel replied. "He wants to rub it in our faces."

"What if we let him?" Shadow asked. "He can make his next move, get it out in the open, and we'll use his momentum against him. With every blatant attack, the news can keep carrying coverage of how he's at large. The pressure from inside is bound to reach his uncle and the rest of his cell."

"That's taking a big risk, though. Look around—we already don't have power. Have either of you heard any updates on that?" Bull asked.

"I talked to Joe," Rebel said. "They know he's behind it, and the crews are at the substation looking for the problem. Joe said Turan laughed openly, like he knew they wouldn't find anything."

"Call Brad, get him to help dig through Turan's online activities. Maybe he can identify something the crews would miss," Reaper replied.

"He's been free for almost an hour now," Shadow said. "I don't see him waiting long for the next move. We need to make some decisions—fast."

"Let's go inside and have some coffee. The emergency generators I had installed will be put to good use. It's late, or actually, early, and it doesn't look like we'll get to sleep anytime soon," Reaper said.

They walked inside and relayed the news to Brianna, Chaise, and Liz. "You should go to bed, babe. Looks like we'll be pulling an all-nighter," Noah said. "Chaise, you can pick one of the spare bedrooms and make yourself at home."

"I'm leaving the Twister mat where it is," Liz said. She pointed her finger at Shadow as she issued her demand. "Don't play without me."

"Don't worry. It wouldn't be any fun without you." Shadow winked.

Inside Reaper's home office with a full pot of coffee, the four men went over every possible scenario they could prepare for in advance. The wild card was the same as it had always been—Turan didn't fit the profile of the typical jihadist. He didn't strictly follow the cell's rules to remain invisible until the very last second, until the time his enemy had no time to react.

Contingency plans were in place for direct attacks on their households, but plans for their extended family were harder to account for. Bull's parents, John and Beth, were traveling the country and enjoying his retirement. Steve and Sara were away but due to be back in a matter of hours. Silas, Noah's brother, still hadn't been located.

"Noah," Brianna called sleepily from behind him.

"Yeah, baby?" He turned toward her, his demeanor instantly changing from trained killer to protective husband.

"Just got a call on your cell from the guys in the office. Steve and Sara's house was just broken in to and ransacked," she said grimly. "A couple of your guys are on the scene with the police. The power is still out over there, too, but they knew you'd want to know."

"Could be a trap to draw us away from here," Bull replied. "If he's been watching the house, he knows the security detail was pulled when Steve and Sara left town. I say let the men handle it until morning. We'll go over there together, pack up Steve and Sara's stuff, and send them to Texas early."

"I agree, Reap," Shadow replied. "It has to be part of his play."

The cell in Brianna's hand began to ring again. She glanced down at the screen and a concerned look covered her face. "It's the office again," she said. "Hello?"

She was silent over the next several seconds as the person on the other end relayed more information to her. "That was Brad. Good news or bad news first?"

"Bad," Noah replied.

"Turan's house just burned to the ground. We've lost all virtual connections to him and the information we were getting from the wiretap," Brianna replied.

"And the good?"

"Brad was able to retrace his keystrokes in to the power substation software just in time. He said it'll take him a couple of hours to rewrite the code, but he'll have power restored pretty soon."

"Did he say anything else about the fire?" Rebel asked.

"Obvious accelerant used—like blatantly used everywhere. It was a total loss. The crews are still on the scene making sure it's completely out before they leave," she replied.

"Reap, he couldn't have got to your parents' house and torched his house that close together. Not when they're still on the scene at Steve and Sara's house outside of Miami and the firefighters are still on the scene at his house here," Bull said.

"It'd be nice to know if we're dealing with more than one cell member in one location, or if his own cell torched his house to take him out," Reaper replied as he stood. He moved around the table to Brianna, kissed her goodnight, and took the phone from her hand. "Get some sleep, baby. I'll take phone duty for the rest of the morning."

"You know where to find me if you need any help." She smiled sleepily and stroked his cheek.

"No way am I leaving her tonight to go check out either scene," Reaper said when Brianna was out of earshot. "He's hit my parents' house and possibly torched his own place. I'm not giving him any opportunity to get to my family."

"Agreed. We should all stay here tonight and take shifts," Rebel replied. "He could've planned the fire timing with an extra-long wick or something slow-burning, just to throw us off. I think he's trying to split us up."

"You know, Brianna said the same thing a little while back. She thinks he's like a bully who's afraid to take us on as a group, so he'll try to get us alone and stab us in the back," Reaper replied. "I have to agree. He shut the power down for a reason, but I doubt he accounted for the generators keeping my security system intact."

"The sun will be up in a couple of hours. Get some sleep and I'll keep watch until daylight. I doubt he makes a move with all of us here, but I'm not willing to risk anyone's life on that," Rebel said.

"You sure? I don't mind staying up," Shadow replied.

Rebel shook his head. "No need to, man. I got this."

"We have guys outside, Rebel. Like you said, it'll be daylight in a few hours. They can handle it until then. We should all get some rest. I have a feeling it's going to take all of us to convince my parents to get out of town after they see their house in a few hours," Reaper replied.

"All right," Rebel agreed. "I just feel responsible for all of this."

"Don't. His father, or whatever relation they were, was responsible for taking those hostages. He also made the choice to fire on us," Reaper replied. "None of this is on you."

Rebel nodded slowly, not fully convinced but at least considering his friend's assessment. "All right. Let's all get some shut-eye then."

~

Turan stood outside of his rental home and stared at the charred remains in disbelief. A few firefighters still combed through the remnants of his possessions, using their picks and axes to check for smoldering fires under the larger pieces of debris. Everything he owned was in that pitiful excuse for a home. Every possession and piece of technical equipment besides the cell phone in his pocket had been inside, but now it was all burned beyond recognition by the fire and covered in water and fire retardant residue.

"I hate all of you. Bastards. You'll all pay for this," he cursed under his breath. "I'll never stop."

Turan dug his keys out of his pocket and climbed back into his car. He backed out of the driveway, put the car in drive, and aimlessly wandered around the city until the sun appeared on the horizon. The lights across the city began to flicker on, people began to stir, and he realized his grand scheme to throw Miami into a complete blackout had been thwarted. Parked in a public parking lot, desperation and defeat got the best of him. He retrieved his cell phone and dialed the number from memory. He held his breath and put the phone against his ear. Dread filled him with each ring that passed.

"I told you never to call this number," the man answered.

"I didn't have any other choice," Turan replied. "I need your help."

Silence met him, and he pictured the other man pinching the bridge of his nose in irritation and aggravation. "What do you need?"

"Money. Laptops. Somewhere to stay," Turan replied.

"You lost everything I gave you?" he asked, anger filling his tone.

"There was a fire. Everything is ruined. It was a total loss."

"You weren't there when the fire started?"

"No," Turan replied hesitantly. "I had to go out for a while. The house was burned to the ground when I got back."

"Your instructions were to remain inside and stay away from others until you were told otherwise," the man replied. "If you'd been there like you were supposed to be, maybe you could've prevented or put the fire out before you lost everything. Do you have any idea what this does to our plans?"

"I know. I've let you down, disappointed you again. I'm very sorry," Turan rambled.

"Give me a couple of hours. I'll be in touch."

With that, the line disconnected and Turan stared at his phone for several minutes. "These Americans have cost me too much. I've been too lenient, too lax in my approach. I've underestimated them for the last time," he vowed. "They've played me for a fool for far too long. I'll show them. I'll make them pay. And the only form of payment I'll accept is their blood."

Nearly four hours later, Turan sat on the beach alone and watched the waves crashing into the shore when his cell phone rang. He answered it before the second ring finished.

"Yes."

"Your apartment is waiting for you," the man spoke slowly. "Do not screw this one up. It is your last chance."

"Understood."

Turan memorized the address and thanked the man for his assistance. "Will I see you before the appointed day?"

"It is possible," the man replied. "But you really need to focus on your assigned tasks instead of worrying about that. I expect everything to be completed and ready to implement by tomorrow."

"It will be," Turan promised.

"We're counting on you," the man replied before he hung up.

Turan drove straight to the address he'd been given and climbed the stairs to his third-floor apartment. It was in even worse condition than the small rental house had been. Somehow, he'd taken yet another step down the ladder rather than up. That solemn thought seemed to accurately sum up his entire life.

New laptops, multiple display screens, and other peripherals had been placed on the desk in the bedroom. A new, preprogrammed burner cell phone lay on the bed and indicated a new text message waited.

Don't screw up again.

"If only it were that easy," Turan sighed and began to set up the new equipment.

Hours later when he had everything up and running again, he clicked on the local news website. A surveillance video on the news site's home page was on continuous replay. His name was splayed across the top of the page in a large, bold font. The video footage showed a man breaking in to the home of Steve and Sara Steele. When the frame froze, he stared into his own eyes through the security camera recording. His ties to his uncle, Ambassador Bachar, and his diplomatic immunity were being dissected and scrutinized by the public.

He turned on the television in the furnished apartment and quickly found the national news channel. He immediately knew that the commentary from the aggressive news anchor would seal his fate.

"Ali Babek Turan has been identified as the terrorist who attempted to murder his neighbor by poisoning. We've learned that he was taken in for questioning about that crime, and many others that appear to be related to him, but the authorities were forced to release him because of diplomatic immunity. We have obtained a video of Turan actively breaking in to and entering this home, and sources at the scene tell us that he vandalized it to the tune of tens of thousands of dollars.

"Knowing all of this, I'm appalled that our government officials haven't stepped up and insisted upon his deportation back to his country, at the very least, or to press

charges and have him arrested under his country's laws. It's time for the people of this great nation to stand together and demand that our rights to life, liberty, and the pursuit of happiness be taken seriously. He is a threat to all of us and does not deserve to have immunity from the consequences of his actions.

"Ambassador Bachar, it is time for you to step up and do what is right, sir. Using your political advantage to protect a murderer must stop."

Turan dropped down into the ugly, lumpy chair and stared at the video in disbelief.

CHAPTER FOURTEEN

"I am so relaxed. Nothing can take this feeling away from me," Steve boasted on the ride home from the private airstrip.

"We need to do this more often," Sara agreed. "The crisp mountain air and getting away from everything that's so stressful in our lives was just what the doctor ordered."

Roman couldn't bring himself to tell them about his conference call with Noah while they were still on the plane. Their relaxing week at the mountain lodge, hidden away from the rest of the world, was about to come to a screeching halt. The damage done to their home was substantial and would take a small army of contractors and workers to renovate it. Noah was already up and hard at work, calling construction crews in and having new plans drawn up to try to make it into a positive experience for his parents. But he knew better than to count on that.

When Roman pulled into their driveway, Steve took one look at his home and froze midsentence. Sara looked at him expectantly, waiting for him to finish his thought, before her eyes followed the path of his stare. She gasped loudly before she grabbed the door handle and jumped out of the truck.

"What the hell?" she asked aloud. "What happened here?"

"Mom, calm down," Noah spoke in low tones. "He's mad at me; he's trying to get to me however he can. If that's through you and Dad, then he'll do that. We talked about this."

"I know," she stammered. "I know we did. I guess I just didn't expect…that he'd really do it."

"On a positive note, you can remodel now." Noah smiled. "It's not a total loss. Just a really big mess."

"Did he do this?" Steve demanded, suddenly standing next to Noah. "Was this that little bastard who tried to kill Liz?"

"Yes, Dad," Noah confirmed. "It's a bit more complicated than we realized. He has diplomatic immunity, so it makes it harder for us to touch him."

"Bottom line, son. Cut to the chase," Steve ordered.

Noah looked his father square in the eye. "Okay. It'd be in your best interest to move to Texas now, do your treatments out there, and let us finish up business here. He's a slippery bastard, and he has the law on his side. His uncle is an ambassador to our country, and he's on his uncle's payroll. His house burned to the ground last night, so we lost our connection to him. It's not safe for you or Mom to be here."

Steve was shocked at Noah's candor at first, but he turned his softened gaze on Sara. "There was a time I would've been hardheaded and insisted we stay here. Guard the fort. Never be backed down by another man," Steve said softly. "But right now, all I can think about is getting you as far away from here as I can. If anything happened to you, that would be it for me."

"What if he does something worse to our home while we're away?" Sara asked as she glanced at their house.

"This building—" Steve gestured toward the house "—isn't home. It's just a structure full of furniture, clothes, and trinkets. Home is wherever you are, babe. That's all I need. I don't care about all the extra *stuff* anymore."

"You're right, Steve." Sara smiled warmly. "As long as I'm with you, I don't care about the house or anything else in it."

"We'll go to Texas, Noah," Steve replied. "If that's what you think we should do, I'm willing to follow your lead this time."

"Good. You're making the right decision," Noah replied. "I talked to Evan, Brianna's dad, this morning, and he insists that you stay at his hotel in Houston. His staff will help take care of you, and it's an ultra-swanky hotel. You'll love it, Mom."

"We can't impose on him like that," Sara replied.

"You can and you will," Brianna replied as she walked up behind her. "You're family. We'll accept nothing less."

"But we'll be there for months, what with Steve's treatment and then the clinical trials," Sara protested.

"That doesn't change anything." Brianna smiled. "Let Dad and Mom do this for you. They honestly want to help, and it's not an imposition at all."

"You're sure?" Steve asked.

"Positive," Brianna replied. "Just pick out which renovation plan you like best, and Noah and I will oversee the construction while you're away."

Steve and Sara took turns hugging Brianna and Noah. "You've both been such a big help to us. I don't know how we'll live in Texas for the next several months without you."

"We'll be there to see you after the baby's born," Noah promised. "You have to spoil her like good grandparents would."

"Her?" Steve asked.

"Her." Noah beamed. "We just found out while you were in the mountains. We're having a baby girl."

"I'm going to be a grandfather," Steve announced, as if he'd just realized it for the first time. "I'm going to get better. I'm going to kick cancer's ass. I'm going to spoil my granddaughter!"

~

"Thanksgiving wasn't the same without Mom and Dad here," Chaise commented. "It was the first one that Noah and I could've been together with them again. It's so wrong that our first Thanksgiving as one big family has been ruined by a cyberstalking, pansy-ass terrorist."

"I agree. Them not being here didn't feel right to me, either," Brianna agreed. "It wasn't the same without my parents and sisters here, either."

"I can't believe your parents went on a cruise for Thanksgiving," Chaise laughed.

"I know!" Brianna exclaimed. "They said they have to get their vacations in now because they won't leave once the baby gets here."

"Any word on Turan?" Chaise asked. "Where is he? What's he doing? Why has he been so quiet for the last couple of weeks?"

"I don't know, but it's definitely not like him. He was so smug when the guys caught him, like he knew he was untouchable. Then when that security tape was leaked to the press—" Brianna furrowed her brow, deep in thought "—everything changed."

"Joe and Bill had to be behind that," Chaise replied. "Colton said they denied it, but it's not like they'd tell the truth anyway."

"That is definitely a good possibility," Brianna agreed.

"What? What are you thinking? I know that look."

"It's not all adding up for me," Brianna began. "Something's off…something's not right."

"What do you mean?"

"The security tape—how would they have gotten it? It's on Noah's servers at the office," Brianna replied. "Noah said he didn't give it to them."

Chaise shrugged. "The CIA has their own computer guys who know how to get to whatever they want. They probably hacked in to the servers and stole it."

"You're probably right," Brianna agreed. "Still, there's something on it I want to watch again."

She opened her laptop and pulled up the video. When it reached the frame that clearly showed Turan's face, she paused it and moved it a single frame at a time. "Right there," she exclaimed. "Did you see that?"

"What? See what?" Chaise asked as she leaned toward the screen.

"Watch when the frame changes," Brianna said. Slowly moving the video frame by frame, she stopped when she reached the exact microsecond she needed. "Right here, there's a different image. It looks like this one of Turan has been placed on top of the original."

"I don't see it."

"Watch again."

"I still don't see it. I see Turan with his back to the camera. Then he turns around, like something caught his attention, and he keeps walking into the house," Chaise replied.

Brianna played it again and again, unsure of what she thought she originally watched. "Maybe I'm looking for something that's not there to be found," she sighed. "Now I'm doubting it myself."

"We all need a break. This case has been going on for way too long. The guys have been working nonstop and they're becoming crabby," Chaise laughed.

"It would be nice if Noah and I could get away one last time before the baby gets here," Brianna replied. "But I know they won't stop until they get their man. And he'd never leave them at a time like this."

Chaise sat back and thought about Brianna's comments. The bond between these men was unshakable. Knowing that any one of them would help her and protect her regardless of the situation had given Chaise a real sense of family. She wanted that same bond and closeness to carry over into the family she and Bull would have one day. "The way it's been going, Colton and I will never get married. Turan has gone out of his way to destroy my plans."

"Maybe you should just do a destination wedding and let them handle all the details. Just pick out what you want and let the consultant do all the work for you," Brianna suggested.

"That's a great idea. I think I'll steal that from you." Chaise smiled.

"Woman," Bull called. "It's time to go home."

"Whatever you say, caveman," Chaise laughed.

"You love it when I'm a caveman," Bull retorted.

"Can't deny that," she replied.

In his truck on the way home, she turned to Bull and told him about her conversation with Brianna. "What do you think about a destination wedding?"

"Sounds good to me. Can we do it tomorrow?" he asked.

"No, we cannot do it tomorrow," she chastised him playfully. "Or the next day, before you even ask."

"Damn. You're too quick." He winked. "Whatever you want, babe. As long as you're the bride and I'm the groom, I don't care if I'm in shorts and a T-shirt or a monkey suit."

"Monkey suit?"

"Yes, an actual monkey suit, complete with a tail. Not a tuxedo. I have to draw the line there."

"I'm genuinely concerned about the amount of time you're spending with Liz," Chaise quipped.

"I can't disagree with that," Bull replied thoughtfully. "I'm afraid she is starting to rub off on me. Want to play strip poker tonight?"

"No, I don't," Chaise said adamantly. "I've already planned a night of Twister."

"If you insist," Bull replied, and they both had a good laugh.

"It feels so good to laugh again. Everything has been so serious lately, thanks to Turan," Chaise said. "Any new developments with him?"

"He's apparently in hiding now. Joe said his uncle has disowned him because he publicly shamed him. It doesn't look good for an ambassador, the one person who represents the country internationally, to have a thug on his staff," Bull shrugged. "He'll have to show his face sooner or later. I'm betting on sooner."

"Do you think he'll try something else?"

"I do. I'm positive of it. He was shamed and apparently disowned, so he'll be looking for retribution."

"Is it wrong that I wish he'd just hurry up so we can get this over with?" Chaise asked.

"If you're wrong, then I'm wrong, too," Bull chuckled. "I'm ready to put this case to bed myself."

"Did you say you're ready to take Chaise to bed?"

"Yes. Yes, I did. That's exactly what I said."

"I thought that's what I heard." She grinned. "Colton, what if this case isn't finished before we get married? Will we have to postpone the wedding?"

"Not a chance," he replied. "We can still get married. I won't be able to go on a honeymoon outside the country, but that's about the only limitation I'd have."

"So I can go ahead and plan the destination wedding?"

"Yep—for as soon as possible." Bull grinned. "Before you change your mind and hightail it out of here."

"You can't get rid of me that easily, Colton Lanier. You're stuck with me."

"Stuck like crazy glue." He winked.

"I'm excited." She smiled broadly. "I feel like we're finally moving forward, and I haven't even called them yet."

"Who?"

"Our destination wedding place," Chaise said cryptically. "I want it to be a surprise."

"That means you'll have to take me there." Bull cut his eyes at her.

"That's right. That means I'll be in charge of Bull," Chaise giggled.

"I'm under no illusions about being the one in charge in this relationship," Bull laughed. "But if you want our wedding location to be a surprise, I'll go along with it. Just inside this country."

"It is." Chaise grinned mischievously. "Now I have to look at moving the date up because I'm too excited to wait. And I won't be able to keep it a secret long enough."

"Good. My plan is working then."

"Yes, you evil mastermind. Your dastardly plan of ensnaring me and forcing me to marry you in the destination wedding of my choosing has worked out perfectly. I never suspected a thing."

"I'll have to use this tactic on you again in the near future," Bull quipped. "I'll have you eating out of my hand before long."

"Yeah. Eating wedding cake out of your hand."

The following day, Chaise made several phone calls to begin the plans for her dream wedding. She had never felt so excited about planning for the wedding and couldn't wait to enlist Brianna's help. Even though she wanted to keep the location a secret, she knew she'd have to tell Brianna where it would be held and Brianna would, in turn, enlist Noah's help to get Bull there.

Noah was Colton's best man and Brianna was her matron of honor, so naturally they both had to be in attendance. Rebel and Shadow were equally as important to both Chaise and Bull, so there was no question that the whole Steele Security family had to agree to the travel. Since they'd added Liz to the group, she couldn't imagine the ceremony being complete without her there, too.

"The only people who can't be there are Mom and Dad," she said sadly. "I can't believe my parents will miss my wedding, and my daddy won't be giving me away." Steve began the new treatments the week after he moved to Texas, so there was no way he could travel so soon. Even if he were still close by, she realized he might not have the strength to walk her down the aisle after taking the strong chemotherapy drugs.

By the time she finished verifying all the details of her idea, she was convinced it was the perfect solution. "Time to get Brianna on board." She smiled. "Then Noah won't have a choice but to say yes."

An hour later, she called Brianna and gave her the details of her grand idea. "So, what do you think?"

"I think..." Brianna paused. "It's brilliant. I can't wait. This will be an epic wedding, and I'm so jealous I didn't think of it first. Now Noah and I have to get married again so I can do it, too."

Chaise burst out laughing. "Do you really mean that? You like my idea?"

"Seriously. I love it. I think Bull will, too. I absolutely cannot wait to see this wedding."

"Can you help me convince Noah that we don't have to wait until the case is over?"

"He won't take much convincing, Chaise. He loves you and he loves Bull. He wants you both to be happy," Brianna replied.

"I know he does. But I also know he's very focused on this case and may need some convincing that he's allowed to step outside of Miami for a little while."

"Leave that to me. I've got your back," Brianna laughed. "Speak of the devil. He's just getting home now."

"Oh my gosh, go work your magic on him and let me know what he says later," Chaise said hurriedly.

"Okay," Brianna laughed. "I'll talk to you later. I'm so excited!"

"What are you excited about?" Noah asked as he walked into the kitchen. "Excited because I'm home and you missed me today?"

"That's a given," Brianna cooed. "I miss you every day when you leave me. And I'm always excited when you come home."

"Who was that?" Noah asked after he made her dizzy with a thorough kiss.

"Your sister," she replied. "She's made a decision about the wedding. It's a destination wedding and she's moving the date up. We'll have to go out of town for a few days."

Noah pulled his face back to look Brianna in the eye. "With this case still open?"

"Yes, Noah. Turan has turned our lives upside down enough. We all need some normalcy, some semblance of security. This will be good for everyone, including you. We need the break, and you and I need some time alone before the baby gets here," Brianna explained.

"I love the sound of that last part." Noah flashed his sexy smile. "Where are we going?"

"If I tell you, you can't tell anyone else. Especially Bull," Brianna warned. "Chaise wants this to be a surprise for him."

Noah slowly lifted one eyebrow in amusement. "This should be good. I can't wait to hear the details. Tell me all your secrets, princess."

For the following half hour, Brianna explained every detail of the destination wedding, how they'd get Bull there without actually telling him where they were going, and about the premier package Chaise had picked out.

"I'm telling you, it's brilliant. I told her you and I have to get remarried now because I wish I'd thought of it first," Brianna laughed.

"I will marry you as often as you want and anywhere in the world you want," Noah replied before he kissed her. "You don't even have to hide the location from me."

"So, you'll do this for Chaise and Bull—without a fight?" Brianna confirmed.

"You knew you had me from the second I walked in the door," Noah replied, pinning her with his bedroom eyes.

"Of course I knew," she said as she wrapped her arms around him. "It's still good to hear it, though."

"Where you go, I go. Doesn't matter where, when, or for how long. Everything that's important to me fits right here in my arms. I can live without all the rest of it."

"You are both my strength and my weakness. I'm the luckiest woman in the world, without a doubt."

CHAPTER FIFTEEN

"You're quiet," Shadow stated. "What's going on up there?"

"It's like the calm before the storm," Rebel replied. "He's out there, waiting to pounce, and we lost him."

"Clever of him to ditch the car the way he did, huh?" Shadow replied.

"Yeah, that was great. Thought I had him with the GPS tracking, but he gave it to a homeless man who must've driven over every square inch of this city before he ran out of gas," Rebel laughed sardonically. "He was probably watching me chase that old coot from one corner to the other."

"He'll show back up. Don't worry. Roaches have ways of finding their way out of the dark and into the light."

"But what damage will he have caused first?" Rebel asked rhetorically.

"Brad has been watching for sudden spikes in broadband usage. He has to come back on the grid eventually. He's a computer geek. He's probably going through withdrawals right now."

"Could it really be that simple?" Rebel asked aloud. He jerked his cell phone out of his pocket and quickly dialed the number. "Brad, are you monitoring the deep web for Turan? He's so techy and so cocky, he's probably trolling for something illegal right now. Try high-grade weapons—ones that are really hard to get your hands on, like chemical warfare shit."

Rebel and Brad continued to talk about the difficult logistics of flushing someone out of the deep web when it was designed and used specifically for anonymity. They banked on Turan's lack of conformity to standard terrorist profiles as being his ultimate downfall. Rebel knew from experience the extent of his arsenal couldn't be limited to poisoning, stabbing, and turning the power off. He must be planning something big, something that would catch everyone completely off guard.

Rebel then had a better idea.

"Put out a hit on me," Rebel directed Brad.

"Wh-what?" Brad stammered.

"Order a hit on me. He'll bite," Rebel replied. "Give enough information about me for him to identify. Play up to him losing his father, use a similar story. Close enough to relate to him but different enough that doesn't raise any red flags."

"If you say so, Rebel. This will bring all kinds of freaks out of the woodwork, though," Brad replied.

"I'm just fishing for one freak. We'll know it when he finds it."

A week later, Rebel received a call from Brad. "Our freak-bait seems to have worked for our fishing expedition."

"What'd we catch?" Rebel asked.

"One Ali Babek Turan, who is willing and eager to relieve you of your head," Brad replied. "And he's only charging me one bitcoin to do it."

"Don't sound so excited. He doesn't get the payment until he has my head in his hands," Rebel deadpanned. "You'll get to keep all of your bitcoins."

"Good. Do you know how hard it is to generate them?"

"How do you know it's him?" Rebel asked, intentionally ignoring Brad's question.

"I have a very powerful program that can trace dark web exchanges. It's definitely him," Brad replied. "If he's known by any other name, none of our government databases has it listed."

"Good job. We're finally going to nail this prick. When is it going down?"

"He just accepted the contract, and the money is being held in escrow until he delivers on the hit. I've sent him your address and said it had to be done within a week from today. So be ready for him at any time, Rebel," Brad pleaded. "Reaper will have my head for this."

"Nah. I'll fill him in. Thanks for hiring a hit man to kill me, Brad," Rebel said as he hung up.

Rebel strode into the office with a smug smile on his face.

"What have you done?" Reaper asked.

"Who says I've done anything?" Rebel replied with a question.

"You do. Your smile gives you away every time. That's your shit-eating grin that says *'You'll never guess what shit I just pulled.'* We know you very well," Bull replied.

"Let's hear it," Reaper said.

"I got Brad to hire a hit man to kill me."

"What's the punch line?" Bull asked.

"The hit man is Turan," Rebel replied. "He's coming after me."

Reaper leaned back in his chair and narrowed his eyes at Rebel. "What if it's not him?"

"Then we'll catch whoever it is that tries to kill me." Rebel shrugged. "Either way, we'll take another bad guy off the street."

Rebel took his seat and briefed them on his entire conversation with Brad. The next seven days would be even more trying than the last couple of months had been combined. Every member of the team would have to be on their top game, adrenaline flowing, their minds set, and their bodies ready to react in a split second. When they'd stayed in that hyped-up state for extended periods of time in the past, it had always taken a big toll on their bodies and their minds.

"What if he shows up with an RPG and blows your house up?" Shadow asked, the twinkle of mischief shining in his eyes.

Rebel barked out a laugh. "Turan's not big enough to hold an RPG. The recoil alone would knock him on his ass."

"RPGs don't have recoil," Bull replied, his brow furrowed in confusion.

"Exactly," Rebel laughed.

"Okay, if we're really going to do this, we'll have a lot of backup," Reaper replied. "That's not negotiable."

"That's fine. Just don't let anyone spook him. This has been the never-ending mission, and we all need to get on with our lives," Rebel answered. "Especially me."

Reaper caught the last couple of words that Rebel muttered to himself. When their eyes met, Rebel nodded once to tell his friend that he was fine. The benefit of having his captain as one of his best friends was that they knew enough about each other to not have to verbalize everything. Rebel knew that, regardless of the situation, his brothers would have his back.

"It's a good day to catch a terrorist," Bull replied with a smile.

"Gather 'round," Reaper announced. "Let's lock this down. Everyone has to be on their best game until we catch him."

Over the following several hours, they established their plan to capture Turan in the act and use all of the evidence they'd gathered on him to help expel him from the country. They argued amongst themselves about the benefits of using him to flush out the other members of his cell, but they ultimately decided that it was best to get rid of one known terrorist than wait idly for more to show up. If his fate brought the others to their doorstep, they'd deal with it at that time.

"Let's go over tonight's assignments one last time," Reaper announced. "Rebel, you'll be inside your apartment, watching TV and relaxing. Bull, you and Roman will cover the back. If he's literally after Rebel's head, he'll try to get in as quietly as possible and come up behind him. That's the most likely point of access into Rebel's apartment, so we're counting on you.

"Shadow, take Alex and cover the east side. There are a couple of windows, one of which Rebel will be visible through.

"I'll take a couple of guys and cover the front. Blake will have one man with him on the west side. Brad will have access to satellite imagery and will be on comms with us. If anything or anyone moves, we'll know it. Let's not fuck this up."

"My head and I would appreciate it," Rebel replied. "But if he happens to slither into my place, I'll have a few surprises waiting for him myself."

"Don't do anything out of the ordinary this week, Rebel. Let's not spook him," Shadow replied. "He's most likely been watching you over the past week since the offer was posted. Checking your patterns, getting to know when you come and go, seeing if you're preparing for him. If you do anything drastically different this week, he'll know it's a setup and we'll never get this chance again."

"Copy that," Rebel replied.

"Do you even own a TV?" Bull asked.

"Yes, I have a TV, Bull," Rebel replied with a shake of his head.

"You're just not the *'relax and watch TV'* kind of guy." Bull shrugged.

"And you are?"

"Touché."

"How would you know how a hit man thinks, Shadow?" Bull asked. "You said that like you've been through this before."

"Ask me no questions, I'll tell you no lies." Shadow grinned. "That's actually a lie in itself."

"You wound me," Bull replied, mimicking a stab to the chest. "I thought we told each other everything."

"I could tell you, but then I'd have to kill you."

"You've been waiting years to use that line on me, haven't you?"

"You know me too well, Bull."

"I'll be over later and we can braid each other's hair."

"I'll be waiting with bells on," Shadow joked. "Ladies, I will see you later tonight. There are some new toys I need to prep. I've wanted to try them on a perp for a while now." Shadow waggled his eyebrows. His gaze swung to Rebel. "You've got a good head on your shoulders. You really need to keep it there."

"I agree. Hold him off at the line of scrimmage when he comes for me and we won't have to consider my taxidermy options," Rebel replied with a straight face.

"Interesting. A stuffed and mounted Rebel perched above my mantle. I could make it work with my décor," Shadow answered on his way out the door.

"You know that means he wants you to be careful tonight, right?" Reaper chuckled.

"Yeah. He's not at all ashamed to show his feminine side," Rebel retorted. "I'm headed home to act normal and pretend I'm not up to anything. Apparently I have to be more careful with that than I realized since my smile gives me away."

"Smile at Turan if you see him tonight," Bull suggested. "It'll scare the shit out of him."

"We'll cover your back, Rebel," Reaper said. "And your neck."

"Thanks, 'preciate it." He nodded. "This is going to work. Trust me."

"I don't doubt you, man," Reaper replied.

"I'm headed to the gym now. Have to keep up my ruggedly handsome good looks," he laughed and waved goodbye.

~

"This is a nice neighborhood," Turan said to himself as he walked around the block. "How different would my life be if I'd been born here in the US?"

The past couple of weeks had been increasingly difficult on him. When he first saw the video of the house vandalism, he immediately thought the men of Steele Security were behind it. *What a pitiful attempt to discredit me,* he thought smugly at the time. *Anyone with a shred of experience in videography can tell that's fake.*

But no one said it was a fake. Everyone believed that he was the one in that video. When his uncle, Ambassador Bachar, confirmed it and publicly disowned him, he knew without a doubt that his enemies weren't behind it. His own people had turned on him, offered him up as the sacrificial lamb, and left him to fend for himself.

"That was when I knew I had to move," he said aloud as he walked. "They put me up in that apartment, and they could get back inside it with no trouble. I'd be killed before I finished my own plans. I pawned all but one of the laptops and all of the peripherals, bought a junker car, and I've been living out of it ever since."

He'd gotten lucky when he replied to an ad for a dog walker. The pay wasn't great, but one dog quickly led to another, and soon he'd earned enough money to survive from day to day. They were all neighbors in the same apartment complex, making it easy to drop one off and take the next one out. He'd found being with the dogs was infinitely better than being around their humans.

"No one can be trusted, Duke," he continued speaking to the Great Dane. "That's why I'm here with you."

His eyes slowly shifted as he glanced around the complex. The second big break came when he visited a well-known hacker site in the hidden part of the Internet. The place where people only visited if they were looking for something they didn't want displayed in their search history. It was a virtual hangout that didn't track the presence of the users with cookies and ISP addresses. A place where people like him were free to post and respond to requests without the judging eyes of others watching.

The request from a comrade in similar straits caught his eye. At first, it seemed a little too good to be true and he was more than leery of it. Like any good soldier, he'd been doing his own reconnaissance work and watching his prey without anyone knowing. He'd been watching every day for almost a week and, so far, he was satisfied that he could safely take the job. He decided that accepting money for it would be an insult to his honor. One bitcoin wasn't much in the grand scheme of things, but it felt like a fitting exchange. In his mind, it was one penny for one life.

"Tomorrow, I will tell my comrade that I'll take the job," he avowed.

His target would be home anytime now if he stuck to his normal routine. "His real name has been hidden from me, Duke," he continued speaking to the dog. "But I will make him reveal it before I relieve him of his head. My knife is sharpened and ready. Sure, I could use a bullet and end this quickly, but I must look into his eyes as he dies. He must look into mine, and he must *know* I'm the one who has won."

The deep rumble of the 1969 Ford Mustang Boss 429 could be heard well before the car was seen. That was his cue that the one called Rebel was home. Loud, proud, and arrogant, his muscle car announced to the world that he'd arrived. The throaty engine turned heads all over the complex, especially from the single women who fawned over the muscle-man owner. Turan hid behind the ornamental trees in the landscaping bed and watched Rebel slide out of his car, grab his gym bag, and casually stroll to his ground-floor apartment.

Inevitably, one or two women always emerged at the precise moment Rebel arrived home and at least one needed help with something that she couldn't handle on her own.

"Can you open this jar for me? You're so strong," Turan mocked in an unusually high-pitched voice. "I'll just die if I can't eat this specific pickle right now."

Envy consumed him inside from watching the scene play out in front of his eyes. He imitated Duke's owner when she called out for Rebel's help next. "Oh, please, Mr. Muscle Head, my car won't start because I disconnected the battery cable when you weren't looking. Pay attention to me."

Duke cut his eyes up at him and quickly looked away. He laughed at his initial thought. "You're embarrassed to be seen with me? You should be embarrassed because of your owner. Look at her. She's pathetic."

Duke seemed to roll his little dog eyes, at least in Turan's mind. "Don't roll your eyes at me. I know what you're thinking. I am not jealous that she rushes outside for two seconds with him but won't even look at me."

Duke grumbled and began to walk, pulling Turan with him. They walked around the opposite end of the complex with Turan suddenly feeling superior when he realized that Rebel wasn't even aware of his presence. *He isn't as smart and cunning as he thinks he is,* Turan thought.

When Rebel finally tore himself away from his adoring fans, Turan took Duke home and purposely tried to flirt with his owner. "Hello, Greta. That color is very flattering on you."

"Thank you so much for walking him. He gets so bored inside." She dismissed him. "Same time tomorrow?"

"Sure," he replied. "I'll see you tomorrow, then."

"Good night," she called absently over her shoulder before she closed her door.

He walked to his car parked behind the apartment buildings and climbed in. He closed his eyes and let sleep overtake him. The next day, he sat outside a local café and used the free Wi-Fi to get back into the deep web. After he found his contact, he agreed to take the contract on Rebel.

Turan's suspicions were still high, even after verifying the validity of the man who hired him. He continued to walk the dogs in the complex and used the time monitoring Rebel's habits to his advantage. The day he decided to make his move, he napped in his car until darkness completely enveloped the area. There was no point in even trying to access Rebel's apartment until long after sundown with the numerous people coming and going. He laid his seat back and rested his eyes, his imagination on overdrive as he planned his exact route in his mind.

When the parking lot became quiet, Turan ensured the dome light was off before he eased out of his car. He softly closed his car door, careful to not make any loud noises that would draw attention to him. "This is one time that I actually *want* to be invisible," he muttered.

The spacious ground-floor apartments each had a back door and a small patio area. The upper-level apartments had decks, but each level was staggered so that everyone had ample access to the Florida sunshine. He moved stealthily behind the buildings until he stood on Rebel's terrace and peered into his kitchen window. Rebel walked to the pantry, retrieved a bag of popcorn, and threw it in the microwave. Then he pulled a bottle of beer out of the refrigerator and popped the top.

He moved around in the small kitchen with ease as he cleaned up after himself. Within minutes, everything had been put in its place and the counters were tidied. Rebel grabbed the popcorn and walked back toward the living room. Turan's eyes never left Rebel's form as he walked away. His smile covered his face when he felt that sense of pride return to him. Rebel didn't know he was even there.

I was staring him down and he never even knew, Turan thought.

His original plan to kill Rebel sooner rather than later morphed into a competition in Turan's mind. A competition that Rebel didn't even know he was in. Turan decided he'd test Rebel daily to see how far he could push the limits, how far his superiority would take him. He stepped closer to the back door and gripped the knob in his palm. He slowly turned it, testing it, and found it was locked, but the door opened when he pushed it. Even to his keen eyes, it appeared to be solidly closed.

A faulty lock, Rebel? So careless, he thought smugly.

He stepped into the kitchen and strained his ears to listen over the sound of the TV for any sign that Rebel was aware of his presence. After sixty long seconds of nothingness, he carefully placed one foot in front of the other until he reached the doorway to the living area. He'd looked in the front windows while walking the dogs over the past week, so he already knew that Rebel's back would be toward him.

Rebel laughed out loud at the comedian standing center stage. He held a ventriloquist's dummy dressed up as a terrorist and another doll that looked like an angry old man. The comedian and the two dummies exchanged insults, each in their own voice, and interacted as if a conversation were actually taking place. Turan became distracted by the comedian's show until Rebel's laughter jarred him out of his trance.

He slowly backed away from the entryway and made his way back to the door leading to the patio. Before he left Rebel's kitchen, he memorized everything about the room. His masculine touches around the room brought life to it, made it feel lived-in. He pictured a room full of friends and loved ones gathered around Rebel, laughing and having a good time. The same as when he got home from work, Rebel was the center of attention in his own place. Everyone clamored for his attention and time.

His eyes floated to the kitchen window he'd been watching through earlier. His reflection stared back at him, reminded him that he was an outsider, alone, and not welcome. In his own eyes, he could picture himself outside, looking in, and wishing he could change places with Rebel. His hands began to tremble and his heart began to race. Before he did something stupid like getting caught breaking in to Rebel's apartment, he quickly stepped through the door and silently closed it behind him. He retraced his steps until he reached his dilapidated car and crawled back into it.

"At least the Miami winters are mild," he sighed and cracked his windows for air. Settling into the seat for the night, he welcomed the reprieve when sleep overtook him.

CHAPTER SIXTEEN

"Say again. He's *what?*" Bull whispered into the comm. "I'm sure I heard you wrong."

"He's watching TV with Rebel," Reaper replied again. "I've said it three times now."

"Does he have a weapon? A bomb strapped to his chest?"

"Negative. He looks like he wants to laugh," Reaper replied.

"He's not shitting you, man. I can see him, too," Shadow said. "Funniest shit I've ever seen."

"He's over your right shoulder, Rebel. In the doorway to the kitchen. Laugh if you copy," Reaper instructed.

Rebel laughed louder than usual, exaggerating it to confirm his reply. His hand slipped down between the couch cushions and gripped the handle of his trusty Bowie knife. If Turan decided to make a crazy play, he'd have one hell of a fight on his hands.

"He's backing away, coming back toward you, Bull," Reaper called.

"Copy. I got eyes on him," Bull replied. "He's out now."

"Let him go if he wants to leave. We need to catch him in the act to seal his fate," Reaper replied.

"It'd be so easy, though. One shot, he'd fall," Bull replied. "And he wouldn't get back up."

"Maybe he'll try to kill me tomorrow night," Rebel replied.

"I'm following him. Seeing where he's hiding out," Shadow advised. "Stay put."

"Don't let him see you," Reaper replied.

"Do you even know who I am?" Shadow answered incredulously.

Amusement erupted over the airwaves in the form of muffled laughter and snorts. "What do you see?" Reaper asked, his mood lighter.

"He has a new ride. And it's an older, shittier car than the one he gave the homeless man," Shadow replied. "Parked behind the complex in a vacant parking lot. He just laid the seat back and is going to sleep."

"Rebel, you have three guys on duty all night—two outside and one inside. That's an order," Reaper said resolutely.

"Yes, sir," Rebel replied. His voice held respect for his CO, but the twinge of disgust wasn't completely hidden.

"I'm not taking any chances, Rebel. He could very well come back in the middle of the night with explosives and take out half the building," Reaper reminded him.

"You're right. As usual," Rebel conceded. "Go home and get your beauty rest, girls. For some reason, I think he'll want it to be much more up close and personal than an IED would be."

"Fix that lock on your back door just the same," Reaper directed. "You know how to reach me if you need me."

They silently retreated to their vehicles and met back at Reaper's house to debrief and consider changes to the lineup for the following night.

"I think our boy is more screwed up than we realized," Shadow spoke first.

"How so?" Bull asked.

"Watching TV with Rebel? Sleeping in that dilapidated car? He's an outcast who's tried to fit in everywhere, but he doesn't really belong anywhere," Shadow answered with a shake of his head.

"Feeling sorry for the guy who's planning to kill Rebel? And already tried to kill Liz?" Reaper asked. "You want to adopt him?"

"Don't go talking all crazy on me," Shadow replied. "I'm just saying, again, that he doesn't fit the profile of any murderer I know."

"You've been friends with a lot of murderers over the years, have you?" Bull asked.

"You'd be surprised," Shadow replied.

"I have to admit, when he was watching TV with Rebel, he looked…" Reaper's voice tapered off as he searched for the right word.

"Lost," Shadow interjected.

Reaper nodded in agreement.

"He's a kid, man," Shadow said with aggravation. "He should be living it up in college, partying in the fraternity house, enjoying his life. Not putting himself in a predicament where we're forced to take his life before he's even lived it."

"He's older than we were when we joined the Army," Reaper reminded him. "He's grown. Old enough to know what he's doing and be responsible for it."

"Don't get me wrong. If he makes a move for Rebel, I'll take him down in a split second. Just saying he should've made different choices for his life," Shadow clarified.

"I hear ya, man," Reaper answered. "Let's cover tomorrow night's assignments while we're here."

The three men talked about the different vantage points, the blind spots, and the vacant parking lot. "We need someone covering his car so we know what he's carrying before he even reaches Rebel's place," Reaper said. "If he happens to show up with C-4 strapped to his chest, I'd rather know as soon as possible."

"Agreed. Let's put Blake covering the parking lot. There are no windows on that side of the building anyway," Bull suggested. "One man can cover it."

After a few more changes, Bull took Chaise back to their home and Shadow left for his. Noah settled into the couch and Brianna snuggled up into his side. "Feels good to have you home again," she said and hugged him tightly. "I'm so glad you're okay."

"It was a strange night, but nothing dangerous happened," Noah replied before he kissed her. "It's good to be home with you."

"Strange how? What happened?"

"Turan went into Rebel's apartment through the back door, like we knew he would. But then he just stood behind Rebel and watched TV with him. Then he left. He didn't try anything at all. Just ...watched TV."

"He what?" Brianna sat up and looked at Noah.

"You sound like Bull now. He asked that three times," Noah laughed. "I'm not kidding. He watched TV with Rebel and then he just left."

"I heard what Shadow said about him being an outcast and how he doesn't fit in anywhere," she replied. "He's not a kid who went on a joyride in his parents' car, Noah. He tried to kill Liz. He left her for dead. He's tied to other crimes, too. You have a wonderful heart, but when it comes down to it, it'll be you or him. He will always choose to kill you. When that time comes, you can't hesitate...because our baby and I will always choose *you* over him."

"I promise, babe, I won't hesitate." Noah rubbed her belly lovingly. "There's no choice if it comes down to that. I will always choose you and our baby."

"Speaking of, we really need to start picking out a few names. Then we can narrow it down from there."

"Do you have anything in mind?"

"Noah Steele," she chastised him. "Don't think you're fooling me. I know that means you haven't even considered a name yet, and you're leaving all the work up to me."

Noah laughed, knowing he'd been busted. "Fine, fine. I've just been a little busy lately and haven't had time to look through that gigantic book of possible baby names."

"I know you have." She ran her fingers lovingly through his hair. "You always work too hard."

"Have I left you alone too much?" he asked, concern covering his face.

"I'll always take more time with you, Noah," she replied. "But, there's no reason to worry. You're home with me every night, and I fully realize I'm so very lucky for it."

"You are very lucky," Noah agreed. "And if you take me upstairs, I can be persuaded to let you get lucky several more times tonight."

"That's an irresistible offer. I think I'll take you upstairs and start *persuading* you right now."

Noah jumped up and swept Brianna up in his arms. He took the stairs two at a time and raced down the hall toward the bedroom. Brianna squealed and laughed in delight, caught up in the moment with him. When his mouth covered hers, she felt her entire body melt into his. She held his face in her hands briefly and then wrapped her arms around his neck. He tilted her head to the side and deepened the kiss, eliciting a needful whimper from her.

He kicked the door shut as they entered, and he put her down next to the bed. His hands slid down her silky nightgown, making her temperature rise with desire. He bunched the fabric up in his fingers and pulled it over her head. "You're the most beautiful woman in the world," he whispered.

"You make me believe that," she whispered back. "In the way you look at me. In the way you love me.

"I wouldn't have it any other way."

She helped him out of his work clothes, pulling his black T-shirt off and running her fingers, lips, and tongue across his expansive chest. Once she had him out of his BDUs, she gently pushed on his chest and he willingly fell back on the bed. She took her place beside him and wrapped her hand around him, surrounding him with her small fingers as she began to stroke him. Leaning over, she took him deep into her mouth and his hands tightly gripped her hair.

"Mmm, baby," he praised. "Damn, you feel so good."

She continued working him, her hand and mouth moving in tandem, until he made her stop. "Bri, babe, I want to be inside you. *Now*."

"If you insist." She grinned slyly.

She climbed over him and straddled his hips. She guided him to her core, dropped her head back when he entered her, and relished in the sensation as he stretched and filled her with his girth. She rocked her hips front to back, took him fully inside her, and dug her nails into his skin as her body adjusted to accept him. They soon found their rhythm, moving in tandem to love's intimate song and dancing to the rapid beat of their joined heart.

His fingers gripped her hips. He pushed and pulled her, lifted and lowered her, all while he continuously drove into her. She felt the pull low in her pelvis, her muscles contracting and gripping him like a velvet vise, and then her orgasm ripped through her body. She cried out his name and felt the warmth of his release immediately after hers subsided. With her body limp and satisfied, she dreamily slid back to his side, laid her head on his shoulder, and draped her arm across his chest. When her leg slid over on top of his, she was somehow touching him from head to toe.

"You okay, baby?" he asked.

"Perfect," she replied. "I may not let you out of bed tomorrow."

"Don't tease me like that," he chuckled. "You know I'd quit my job if you asked me to."

She opened her eyes and tilted her head up to fully look at him. "You love your job."

"I love you more. My job isn't my life. You are."

"Would you really quit? For me?"

"Absolutely." He stroked her arm back and forth, leaving chill bumps with his every pass. "Do you not believe me?"

"I've actually never even thought of that, Noah," she admitted. "It's so much a part of you, it would be like asking you to stop being you."

"Don't misunderstand. I enjoy having my business, doing my job, and working with the guys. Having everything means nothing without you, though. The more I see in my job, the more that fact is seared in my mind."

"If you're unhappy in your job at any time, you're not bound to it. You can do something different if you want. The only thing you can't get out of alive is this marriage." She smiled sweetly. "They'd never find your girlfriend's body."

Noah laughed at her reply. "That sounds pretty badass. It's kinda turning me on again."

"Why am I not surprised?"

"You shouldn't be," he agreed. "But you should know by now that you're the other half of my soul. I've said it in every way I know how."

"My husband. The father of my baby. The love of my life. My provider, my protector, my best friend. My lover, owner of my heart, rocker of my world. There is no part of my life that doesn't revolve around you."

Noah pulled Brianna into his arms, held her tightly to him, and they slipped off to sleep. When Noah woke the next morning, they were in the same position. Their arms and legs were still wrapped around the other. The safe, secure, and content expression on Brianna's face as she slept filled him with pride.

"What are you grinning about so early in the morning?" she asked groggily.

"You make me happy."

She managed to partially open one eye. "You make me happy, too, babe. And right now you're making me nervous. What have you done?"

"Me? Nothing," he replied. "Well, I may have rented the top floor of the hotel for Bull and Chaise's wedding present."

"Do you think they want us to stay with them for their honeymoon?" she asked dryly.

"I rented it for *them*," Noah spoke slowly. "So no one would bother them. Our rooms are at a different hotel."

"That's so sweet of you, Noah," she cooed. "I married the best man."

He leaned in and gave her a long, sweet kiss. "Time for work. I love you."

"I love you, too."

~

"On the move," Roman whispered into the comm. "Carrying a fighting knife on his belt."

"Got him," Blake replied. "Moving toward the back of the building."

"Rebel, if he goes inside, I want you to get up and move toward the kitchen. Let's see what he does. Alex, be ready to help stop him."

"Copy," Alex whispered.

"He's pulling his knife out. Looks to be between eight and nine inches long. He means business," Blake advised.

Turan tiptoed through the darkness, lurking in the shadows and scurrying across the occasional beam of light. When he'd almost reached Rebel's building, his bravado quickly grew and his guard dropped. The feeling of invincibility enveloped him and made him stand tall on his way to extinguish his enemy's light, once and for all. He stepped into the path that was illuminated by the lights in the parking lot and didn't attempt to hide.

He didn't see the arm that quickly extended out of the shadow of the building. He didn't see the light glint off of the shiny silver prongs. By the time his brain registered that something had touched him, it was much too late to react. The silver prongs dug into his skin. The arm that held the silver-pronged devil was strong and steadfast. The lightning that arced from the prongs lit up the dark night, and his screams of pain echoed off the brick walls of the numerous apartment buildings.

"Aaaah! Aaaah!" Turan screamed uncontrollably before his knees buckled and he dropped to the ground. The intense stinging that coursed through his nerves stopped for a second, only to quickly start again. Followed by his spontaneous screams and more uncontrollable body jerks.

"Take that, you little bastard," she yelled gleefully. Then she zapped him again.

"You want some more? I'll give you more." She followed with another zap. "There. Have all you want."

She moved over to his other side. "This side is jealous," she proclaimed. Then zapped him with the stun gun again.

When he screamed and convulsed, she laughed until tears rolled down her face. She danced around him as if she were chanting and performing a ritual and he was her sacrifice.

"This thing is too much damn fun," Liz exclaimed. "Watch this."

Zap. Zap-zap-zap. Zap.

She doubled over with laughter and wiped the tears from her face. "This is the best invention ever. Think I can make him pee his pants?"

She bent over and extended her arm toward his crotch, but Shadow stopped her just in time. "I think he's had enough, Liz," he chuckled. "How about you let me take that now?"

"What if he jumps up and comes after me? I have to be able to protect myself."

"If he gets up, I'll shoot him," Shadow promised. "But, for some reason, I don't think he'll be getting up on his own anytime soon."

Turan moaned and cursed her with garbled words.

"Did he just call me a white-haired she-devil?" Liz pointed at him in disbelief. "Give me that stun gun."

She reached for the stun gun, but Shadow blocked her arm. "You're quick," he said when she made a play for it with her other hand. He held it up above his head, far out of her reach.

"Shadow..." She put her hand on her hip. "I have ways of making you drop your arm, you know. That won't stop me for long."

Shadow quickly lowered his arm and drew the stun gun in close to his chest. "You're scary, Liz."

"What the hell is happening back here?" Reaper asked as he jogged up to join the others.

"Our backup got a little overzealous," Shadow reported. "Situation is under control now."

Reaper's eyes shifted to Liz and narrowed. "What are you doing here?"

"Helping you boys out. You're welcome," she replied.

Rebel walked out of his back door and tried to hide his huge smile. "Are we having a party back here? My invitation must've gotten lost in the mail."

"Lee Ali-baba Babek Turan Clover was our entertainment. Sorry you missed how he serenaded me," Liz answered. "Make Shadow give me my stun gun back, and I'll make Ali sing just for you. He sings like a girl, though."

Shadow quickly turned his back and took a few steps away from the crowd. His shoulders shook violently as he tried to regain his composure.

"He was dancing a little jig, too," Liz told Rebel. "He doesn't have the moves like I do, though." She shook her hips and danced to a song only she could hear. "He looked more like a fish out of water, flopping around on the ground."

Shadow then lost any semblance of control and horse-laughed over Liz's description of Turan being repeatedly shocked by her stun gun. "Okay, you deserve it back now. But only use it if he tries to come after you."

"Okay," Liz agreed.

Shadow turned his head to look at Reaper, who was still not sure how his team had lost control of the scene, when he heard another zap and another girly scream. He whirled around with his mouth open and looked at Liz disbelievingly.

Liz gave him a sheepish look in return. "It slipped." She shrugged. "My fingers just aren't what they used to be. What are you gonna do?"

CHAPTER SEVENTEEN

"Wait." Brianna held out her hands in the universal sign for stop. "Back up. *Liz* was there? How? Why? What?"

"Now you know exactly how I felt," Noah harrumphed. "Imagine the scene. All my professional soldiers are in place. We have every step of his path covered. He's approaching Rebel's back yard, he has a large knife on him, and we're all ready to pounce. Then Liz takes him down with a *stun gun*," Noah stressed the anticlimactic scene.

"I've already said you're welcome," Liz said as she strolled into the room. "You don't have to keep painting me as the hero."

"How did you get there?" Brianna asked. "You were supposed to be here with Chaise and me."

"Yes. Do tell Brianna how you got there," Noah urged.

"*How* isn't important. I'm just thankful that my timing was impeccable," Liz replied.

"Liz, how did you get there?" Brianna stood and arched her eyebrow at Liz.

"I may have borrowed a car," she replied.

"She stole my guy's car after she hit him with the stun gun out in the yard," Noah elaborated.

"Liz!" Brianna exclaimed.

"That'll teach him to trust strangers." She shrugged. "He didn't know me from Adam. I could've been a deranged lunatic."

"Well, clearly, we dodged that bullet," Noah replied sardonically.

"I don't know how this place even managed to run before I came here." Liz shook her head. "No worries, I'm here now."

Noah shook his head and exchanged glances with Brianna. "So, obviously you got him this time, right?" Brianna asked.

"Yes, we got him this time. Every initial in the government was represented at the scene when we called it in to Joe and Bill. They took him to a high-security federal holding center to await deportation back to Turkey," Noah replied.

"Does that mean he's also undergoing interrogation tactics to get information about the other cell members while he waits?"

"I'd say that's a 100 percent accurate assumption." Noah smiled.

"I can make him talk," Liz replied. "I can make him sing like a girl, too."

"How long will he be in holding?" Brianna asked.

"As long as they want to hold him. It could be anywhere from a couple of weeks to a couple of months. It really depends on how talkative and forthcoming he's being."

"I don't know which is worse—knowing he's still here or knowing he'll probably be freed once he gets back to his country," Brianna replied.

"Personally, I'd prefer that he stayed locked up here. At least we'd still have access to him if something else happens," Noah said.

"I'm packed. When are we leaving?" Liz abruptly changed the subject.

"First thing in the morning." Brianna smiled. "I'm so excited for Bull and Chaise. The timing worked out perfectly on the case and the last-minute cancellation they had."

"I may have had something to do with the 'last-minute cancellation' part," Noah confessed.

"What did you do?"

"I called them this morning and explained the situation with Dad. They actually didn't have an open spot, but they added one for our special circumstances." Noah shrugged nonchalantly.

"You are the best brother, the best husband, and the best man." Brianna beamed. "Why didn't you just tell them that?"

"I don't want to meddle in their business. I honestly think they should just get it done now before something else happens to delay it."

"Yeah, I think Bull would come unglued if one more thing happened," Brianna laughed.

"He still doesn't know where we're going. I love that we're all in the know and he's not," Noah laughed.

"I can't imagine Bull doing that for anyone but Chaise," Brianna said. "The Bull I met in the desert wouldn't have trusted anyone like that. It's good to see him happy."

"Are there any craps tables there?" Liz asked.

"No, Liz." Brianna shook her head. "There aren't."

"Crap."

~

"Let's go, Bull. We're going to be late," Chaise called from the den.

"On my way, babe. Keep your panties on. Or don't. That's fine, too," Bull answered as he walked down the hallway.

As he rounded the corner into the den, he came face to face with Noah, Rebel, Shadow, Brianna, Liz, and Chaise. "Whoa. What's everyone doing here?"

"It's time, Bull," Noah stated flatly.

"Time for what?"

"It's time for your ass-whooping for dating my sister," Noah replied.

"Okay. I can take it," Bull replied. "I'm not giving her up, though."

Noah smiled. "It's time for your wedding, brother. But tonight, we're having your bachelor party."

"Are you all packed, babe?" Chaise asked.

"Yep. Ready to go. Where are we going again?" Bull asked.

"Nice try." Chaise smirked. "Time to get in the car."

"Okay." Bull nodded and started toward the garage where his truck was parked.

"Not that car," Chaise said. "The one that's out front."

Bull narrowed his eyes at her and walked to the front door. His long, low whistle confirmed that she'd chosen the right transportation.

"Did you pick that out?" he asked.

"Yes, I knew you'd love it."

"I do." He kissed her. "I love you more."

"I love you, too. Let's get on the road," Chaise replied.

Bull carried their bags out to the long, black stretch Hummer limousine that seemed to take up most of the length of his driveway. The driver took the bags from him and placed them in the back with the others.

"Am I the last one to know about this?" Bull asked.

"Yep." Noah grinned and climbed inside. Rebel and Shadow laughed and climbed in behind Noah.

When Bull stuck his head inside, he was shocked by the roomy interior. The long, plush leather seats lined one entire side and wrapped around the back. Strip lights illuminated the smoke-colored mirrors on the ceiling. The minibar was lit and brimming with choices. Shadow was at the elaborate stereo system, flipping through stations and changing the settings to add more bass to the music.

"This Hummer has everything," Bull said enthusiastically. "Move over, Reaper. You're in the way."

"Make yourselves comfortable," the chauffeur spoke over the intercom. "Everything in the vehicle is stocked just for you, so feel free to help yourselves to anything you find. We'll arrive at our destination in approximately four hours. My name is Miles. Just press the button if you need anything at all."

"Four hours?" Bull mouthed.

"That's right," Chaise replied. "Now, relax and enjoy the ride."

He pulled her into his arms. "As long as I'm with you, I don't care where we go," he whispered against her skin.

"That's good, since you're about to be stuck with me for a very long time," she laughed.

"Only forever. That's not nearly enough time with you."

"You're such a sweet-talker."

"That's enough of the lovey-dovey shit," Shadow announced. "I won't be subjected to that kind of cruel and unusual punishment for the next four hours. It's bad enough that I have to endure it for the next few days."

"I think Shadow is jealous," Bull replied. "Never thought I'd see the day."

"You haven't seen the day," Shadow replied. "We're nowhere near that day."

"Is there a Mrs. Shadow in the near future? We really should meet her first, give our approval, that kind of thing," Bull continued. "Make sure she fits in our family."

"There's no future Mrs. Shadow," he replied bluntly. "There's no maybe Mrs. Shadow, or a weekend one, or any other kind of Mrs. I'm not catching your bouquet—no offense, Chaise—or your garter. I'm not next in line. For-get-it," he stressed each syllable.

Bull's wide smile covered his face and his eyes danced with laughter. "So who is she? How'd you meet her?"

Shadow stared at Bull, expressionless. "I'm not telling you anything."

"That's just mean, Shadow," Bull laughed. "I can help you out. Give you some advice when you need it."

"No."

"Chaise can help your girl, too," Bull volunteered. "She probably could use some help managing you."

"No one manages me," Shadow replied with a furrowed brow.

"That actually explains a lot." Bull smiled triumphantly.

"You shithead," Shadow laughed.

The group of friends and family enjoyed their luxurious limo ride in the best way they knew how—by relentlessly teasing, razzing, and picking on each other the entire time. The four-hour ride flew by and, before they knew it, the driver had turned into the entryway for their destination.

"Where are we anyway?" Bull asked and turned in his seat to look out the windows.

"Surprise!" Chaise exclaimed.

"I feel like a kid," Bull laughed. "Are we seriously getting married here?"

"Yes, we are. Their sign says it all. '*Walt Disney World–Where Dreams Come True*,' because this is where my dreams will come true," Chaise explained.

Bull punched the button for the chauffeur. "Miles, can you stop the car right here? Chaise and I would like to take our picture in front of the sign."

"Yes, sir," Miles replied.

Noah stepped out to take their picture in front of the sign that stretched across three lanes of traffic. As he captured the surreal moment on his phone, he flashed back to the time when his younger sister was still little. The regret over the years he missed in her life was palpable. Brianna immediately noticed the change in him when he got back in the limo.

"What is it?" she asked.

"You can smack me now. I deserve it," he admitted.

"What have you done?"

"I just realized, I mean, *really* realized, that I did the exact same thing to Chaise that I got mad at you for doing to me," he admitted. "But I was out of her life for much longer, and for much more selfish reasons."

"You're here now. You love and support her now. That's what matters," she assured him.

"You're here now. You love and support me. That's all that matters. Just wanted to be sure *you* know that."

"I do," she answered.

"We're here. Get out already," Shadow yelled as he jumped out of the limo.

"Have you ever been here before?" Noah asked.

"No. And you're wasting daylight. Check in, do your business, and let's go," Shadow demanded.

"Hang on a second," Noah replied and Shadow stopped in his tracks. "Chaise, Bull, before we check in, I should tell you that Brianna and I have a surprise for you."

"More than this?" Bull asked.

"In conjunction with this," Noah replied. "We reserved the entire top floor of the Four Seasons Resort for your wedding present. Thought you'd appreciate having some privacy for your honeymoon. We all have suites in this hotel tonight, but you'll move to the Four Seasons after the wedding."

Tears welled up in Chaise's eyes, and she threw her arms around Noah's neck. He wrapped his arms around her waist and picked her up to hug her. "Thank you so much, Noah. We appreciate it more than words can say."

"You're welcome, baby sis, and congratulations to you both. Bull's getting one hell of a wife," Noah replied.

Bull stepped up to Brianna and enveloped her in a bear hug. "Thank you, my little sister. You and Reaper are the best family a man could ask for. Soon, I'll literally be your brother."

"Bull, whether you knew it or not, you've been my brother from the second I met you in the desert. I couldn't love you more even if you and I shared the same blood," Brianna replied as she hugged him back.

"This is all very touching and beautiful," Shadow interjected. "But need I remind you people—We. Are. At. Disney. World. Move it."

"He's so bossy," Brianna teased.

"Fine. Let's check in, drop our bags off in the rooms, and meet back down in the lobby in thirty minutes," Noah decided.

"Sounds good to me," Liz replied. "I'm ready to have some fun. Can I go to the bachelor party tonight?"

"No," several voices replied in unison.

"Liz, I need you to help me tonight," Chaise explained. "With my bachelorette party."

"You got it, sweet girl." Liz patted her cheek. "It'll be a night you never forget."

They checked in and had the luggage delivered to the rooms, then met in the lobby to make plans for the rest of the day.

"What do you want to do today, Chaise?" Bull asked.

"Actually, I need Brianna and Liz to come with me today to finish up some last-minute wedding shopping. Brianna's sisters will be here later this evening, but it'll be too late by then. Why don't you guys go have fun in the parks, enjoy your bachelor party, and I'll see you back in the room tonight?"

"Will I enjoy this last-minute shopping in our room tonight?" Bull asked seductively.

Chaise laughed. "You never know what I'll find, Colton."

"Sounds good. You ladies be careful and call me every five minutes or so to let me know you're still okay," Bull joked.

"I'm taking custody of Chaise today," Brianna replied. "Don't make me hide her phone so we can spend quality sister-time together."

Once they were separated from the men, Brianna turned to Chaise. "So, wedding dress, veil, bridesmaids dresses, shoes. Pick out the cake and check on the flowers. What am I missing?"

"Matching shirts and Minnie Mouse ears for my bachelorette outing tonight," Chaise laughed. "This is all so exciting."

"I can't wait to see you in your dress," Brianna exclaimed. "You'll be the most gorgeous bride ever."

"Let's go, ladies," Liz urged. "Sounds like we have a lot to do."

"Brianna," a voice called from across the room. "Oh my gosh, look at you. You're glowing."

When she found the owner of the voice, her eyes grew big and her jaw dropped open. "Missy!"

Missy, Jessie, and Ashley rushed up to Brianna to hug her and rub her pregnant belly. "You look absolutely beautiful," Jessie gushed.

"Liz, these are my sisters." Brianna made quick introductions all around and turned back to her sisters. "What are you three doing here already? I thought you couldn't come until later tonight?"

"Change of plans. Chaise only gets married once, and we don't get to see our sister enough as it is," Missy replied. "So we came down early and we're here to help."

The ladies spent the rest of the day finalizing all the wedding plans and buying matching tank tops for their evening out. Chaise's tank top was white with "Bride" printed across the front. Brianna and her sisters' tank tops were black with "Bridesmaids."

"Time for your bachelorette party. Though it may not be as fun as it could have been." She patted her stomach. "This kind of limits what I'm able to do."

"I don't need a drunken party, Bri. That's not really my thing anyway. Spending time laughing and being silly with you ladies is plenty enough for me," Chaise replied.

"Let's go then," Missy chimed in. "Everyone have their mouse ears on?"

"I've got mine," Liz replied. "And my tank top."

The ladies burst out into laughter when they saw the tank top Liz wore. "You're our 'Chaperone' tonight?" Chaise asked.

"That's right. I'm the only one trustworthy enough to be in charge of all you girls," Liz replied. "Let's get this show on the road."

"I may have planned our night out, just a little," Jessie admitted. "First stop is dinner reservations, to feed my niece. Then, we're going to the Cirque du Soleil show. The tickets are my treat."

"That's so thoughtful of you, but you didn't have to do that," Chaise replied.

"I just thought it would be easier on Brianna. She's almost seven months pregnant now, she can't drink, and I thought being on her feet for a long time would be too hard on her," Jessie shrugged. "This way, we can all enjoy it."

Brianna hugged her. "You always think of everyone else first. Thank you, Jessie."

As they walked through the park toward the restaurant, the sight of them in matching bridal party tank tops and mouse ears turned many heads. They laughed, talked, and enjoyed their time together. Chaise's thoughts frequently turned to Bull and what he was doing for his bachelor party. When they entered the restaurant, her questions were quickly answered.

"Bull?" Chaise asked and was unable to hold back her laughter.

He shook his head from side to side, his lips drew into a thin line, and he crossed his arms over his chest. "Bastards."

Bull stood in the reservations-only restaurant wearing a bright pink tutu over his shorts, a neon green feather boa around his neck, a top hat with "Groom" written on it, and a genuine ball and chain attached to his ankle.

"Did you lose a bet?" Chaise asked.

"No," he replied curtly. "Not exactly."

"You took a dare," Brianna guessed, and Bull quickly looked away. "Oh my God! You did!"

"That's even worse than losing a bet," Liz stated. "Although I do have to admit you look very handsome in hot pink and lime green."

"Fucking bastards," he muttered under his breath.

"Would you ladies care to join us for dinner? We can ask for our tables to be put together," Noah suggested.

"I'd love that," Brianna replied.

"What else do you boys have planned for tonight?" Liz asked.

"We mysteriously had dinner reservations made for us and tickets to a show delivered to us," Rebel replied. "Know anything about that?"

"I think Jessie knows something about it," Liz replied with a laugh.

"I'm sorry." She smiled, showing she wasn't really sorry at all. "Missy, Ashley, and I just don't get to spend enough time with all of you. I didn't want to be separated for our one night of fun."

"It's all good with me," Noah replied. "We've never been conventional anyway. Why should our bachelor and bachelorette parties be?"

"Your tables are ready," the hostess said. "Follow me."

"Come on, babe." Bull smiled at Chaise. "You can sit by me."

When she wrapped her arm in Bull's, multiple cell phones emerged at once to snap pictures of them together—Chaise in her "Bride" tank top and wearing ears on her head, and Bull in his "Groom" top hat, neon green feather boa, pink tutu, and carrying his ball and chain.

"Blackmail insurance for later," Shadow said and snapped a few more pictures.

CHAPTER EIGHTEEN

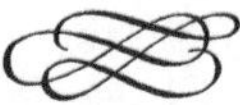

Bull walked the streets of the Venice-themed area alone, wearing his white tuxedo, silver vest, and white and silver mingled tie. The day he'd previously never believed would come was actually happening. That very morning, he realized he'd never been happier in his life. The woman he'd never dared to hope for was about to become his wife. Their life-long commitment had started well before that day, but there was a difference in the air of his wedding day.

"Colt?" a voice called to him.

His head jerked toward the voice and his eyes grew wide. "Mom? Dad?" He rushed to meet them halfway and pulled them into a warm embrace. "I thought you were traveling. What are you doing here?"

"I'd never miss my only son's wedding," his mother, Michelle, replied. "You know me better than that. Besides, it's Christmas week. What better present could you give me than a daughter-in-law?"

"I'm glad you're here, Mom."

"Looking good, son," John said. "Are you nervous?"

"Not at all," Bull replied. "I'm ready to get that ring on her finger before she comes to her senses."

"Chaise loves you, Colt," Michelle replied. "Anyone can see that."

"It's about time to take our places," John said as he looked at his watch.

"I'm ready," Bull replied.

He approached the plaza and noticed the hordes of people standing to the side, watching the small group congregate for the wedding. His parents walked down the white carpet that lined the aisle and took their seats. Brianna's parents, Evan and Diane, arrived next. Liz and Ashley approached and took their seats.

"Any second thoughts?" Noah asked from behind him.

"Not a one," Bull replied. "You have any second thoughts on being my best man?"

"Nope," Noah replied. "I'm honored to be your best man."

"I know Chaise wishes your dad were here to walk her down the aisle. I do too, truthfully."

"Yeah, we all do, including Mom and Dad. But we've got it covered," Noah replied.

Bull nodded. "Rebel okay with it?"

"You know Rebel," Noah replied and left it at that.

The music started, and that was his cue to take his place at the altar and wait for his bride's arrival. He turned to look Noah in the eye before they walked out together. "You're the best friend I could ever ask for. I promise to be the best brother-in-law you could ever ask for."

"You're already the best brother I could ask for, Bull," Noah replied sincerely.

Bull nodded once and turned to walk out of the cover of the buildings and onto the elevated plaza to declare his lifelong love in front of everyone. Family, friends, and strangers would be watching intently when he pledged himself to one woman for all of eternity. They'd listen to his vows and watch him kiss his bride. They'd all know the moment that he and Chaise became one.

And he was more than proud to let them witness this public display of affection.

He walked toward the minister to take his place. Noah, Rebel, and Shadow walked to the staging area where they'd meet the bridal party and escort them down the aisle. Noah's smile grew when he saw Brianna in her bridesmaid gown, an elegant, knee-length rendition of Belle's dress from *Beauty and the Beast*.

"You look very handsome," Brianna complimented him.

"Babe, you look gorgeous in that dress," Noah replied. "I'll be your beast later tonight."

"Ladies and gentlemen, can I get you to line up with your partner right here, please?" the wedding planner asked. "We're starting the bridesmaid procession now."

Jessie and Shadow lined up first, followed by Missy and Rebel, and finally Brianna and Noah. The ladies each held a ribbon-tied bunch of calla lilies that matched the color of their dress.

"Wait until you see your sister," Brianna whispered. "She's the most stunning bride I've ever seen."

"I'm sure she's gorgeous, but I guarantee you were still the most beautiful bride," Noah replied.

"Good reply," she giggled. "You're learning."

"I'm serious," he insisted. When they reached the end of the aisle, Noah leaned over and kissed his wife before they separated.

The bridal march started and everyone waited with bated breath to see Chaise. Especially Bull. He'd watched each of the bridesmaids approach, and he appreciated how they were all beautiful in their own way, but there was only one woman he had eyes for. He held his breath when Brianna took her place and waited for Chaise to make her grand appearance.

The clip-clop of horse's hooves hitting the pavement echoed around the plaza. Heads turned and people watched in amazement as the white pumpkin-shaped carriage stopped at the end of the aisle. A large, intimidating man stepped in front of the carriage door and assisted Chaise as she stepped out of it. Bull craned his neck, trying to see around the man to catch a glimpse of Chaise.

When she stepped into his direct line of sight, he lost his ability to breathe entirely. Her beauty stole his breath, and he couldn't tear his eyes from her. Her ball gown was strapless and formfitting at the top. The bottom was full and the sheer tulle that covered it was sprinkled with glistening sequins and glitter. Her long, dark hair was styled in an updo, revealing her long, graceful neck.

The smile on her face was solely for him.

The man who helped her out of the carriage turned to face Bull, and Chaise wrapped her arm around his. Bull's head jerked toward Noah, but his eyes didn't leave Chaise. "Reap?"

He heard Reaper chuckle. "That's Silas."

"Your brother?"

"The same."

"What are they holding?"

"My parents," Noah replied.

"What?"

When Chaise and Silas got closer, Bull realized what Noah meant. With their arms intertwined, they each held an iPad. Silas held the one that had Steve on FaceTime and Chaise held the one that had Sara. Her plan effectively brought her parents to her wedding. Her father virtually escorted her down the aisle and her mother was also able to be part of their big day.

Chaise handed her iPad off to Liz as she passed so that Sara could continue to watch the event. Everything was going perfectly with her plan. Her brother Silas stood for her father and gave her away in marriage. She'd had to convince him to give her away to a man he'd never met, never approved of, but who'd earned their brother's love and respect over the years.

When they neared the altar, Silas stopped just short of reaching Bull and thoroughly regarded him. The minister seemed to understand Silas's intent and cleared his throat. "Who gives this woman to be married to this man?"

Steve spoke up, his voice loud and sure. "Her mother, her brothers, and I do. We welcome Colton into our family."

Silas remained as motionless as a statue, staring at Bull and obviously considering his options. The few people in attendance, along with everyone who had stopped to watch the ceremony, laughed when Chaise blatantly elbowed Silas in the ribs and made him move. Even Silas, with his naturally unreadable face, smiled and lightly shook his head from side to side.

"You sure about this, baby girl?" Silas whispered, using his nickname for her. "I can still get you out of here."

"Not a chance, big brother," Chaise whispered back. "One more step."

Silas held Chaise's hand in his and took a deep breath before speaking. "You are a beautiful bride, baby girl. I'm so proud to be here with you today, standing in for Dad to help give you away. My wish for you is simple—for you to have all the love and happiness in the world."

Chaise watched with tears glistening in her eyes as Silas placed her hand in Bull's. Only because she knew him so well did she recognize the pain in his eyes. She gave him a small smile, lifted up on her toes, and kissed his cheek. "I love you, Silas."

Silas looked at Bull. "Take care of my baby sister."

"Every day of my life," Bull replied.

Silas gave a quick nod to his brother as an informal "hello" before he moved to take his seat. When he stepped away, the happy couple turned to face the minister. He was an older man with short, salt-and-pepper hair, kind eyes, and a peaceful demeanor. He smiled at Bull and Chaise and began his prepared speech.

"Dear family and friends, on behalf of Colton and Chaise, welcome to their wedding ceremony. We are here today to encourage, support, and celebrate the lifelong commitment these two will pledge before God. Their love is the reason we are here, and it is by that love that they promise to hold fast to one another, regardless of what circumstances life presents tomorrow.

"Colton and Chaise have not entered into this covenant lightly. After talking with them separately earlier today, I've learned that they're both very loyal, they both have a high degree of respect for the other, and they have the love and support of their family and friends. Those are all the ingredients for a very healthy start.

"Colton and Chaise, after forty-five years of marriage, I like to think I'm qualified to give marital advice." He paused for an impactful smile. The guests and onlookers laughed and nodded in agreement. "These five tenets, if you both abide by them, will help make a happy home. Winning an argument isn't worth losing your love. The strongest person is the one who can bend the most. No one is always right, especially you. Forgive and forget, you don't live in the past. Your spouse always comes first.

"Please face each other and hold hands," he instructed. "Colton and Chaise have each written their own vows and would now like to share them with you. Colton, you may begin."

Bull raised Chaise's hands to his mouth and kissed the back of each one.

"Chaise, you changed my life for the better the first day I met you. Every day since then, you've shown me the meaning of unconditional love. You've filled my home with the best memories with your smile. You've filled my heart with pride because I call you mine.

"I promise to make you fall in love with me every day. My heart, mind, and body are yours and yours alone. As long as I live, I promise to love, honor, protect, and cherish you. The only tears I'll ever cause you will be tears of joy, happiness, and laughter. You'll never question your place in my life, because it'll always be first."

Chaise carefully wiped the tears from her eyes and smiled lovingly at Bull. She knew how hard it must have been for him to say just those few words in front of the growing crowd that had gathered for their wedding. But, as he'd proven so many times before, he honored his commitment and came through for her.

"Chaise, you may begin your vows," the minister prompted.

"Colton, there are no words to describe how happy you make me. I've never felt more loved and protected than when I'm with you. You freely give me your strength, your love, and your trust, holding nothing back. You are my hero, my inspiration, and my love.

"I promise to be faithful and honest in our life together, always putting our love and happiness first. You will be my confidant, my best friend, and my lover through sickness and health, days of plenty and days of want, through good times and bad. I will stand beside you no matter what the day brings. With you by my side, I can face anything."

"Those are beautiful vows, Colton and Chaise. Your personalities both shine through your words," the minister said. "Now, you probably didn't know that your friends have a few words they'd like to say as well."

Bull and Chaise both froze and searched for the words to respond. Noah cleared his throat and began the litany of impromptu vows before either had a chance to react.

"Bull, as your best friend and your best man, I promise to stop threatening to kick your ass for dating my sister. If you leave our family now, I'll have to kill you."

"Bull, I promise to always take Chaise's side in an argument, because we all know you're usually wrong," Rebel added.

"Bull, I promise to use the pictures from your bachelor party as blackmail against you as often as possible," Shadow said.

The crowd erupted in laughter, cheers, and loud clapping after each man recited his vow. Bull and Chaise joined in the good-natured revelry as they laughed and accepted each vow with humility.

"If I'd known this was customary, I would've prepared vows for each of you, too. Let me see what I can do, though.

"Reaper, I promise that you'll leave this family before I willingly leave it. Rebel, I promise that Chaise really doesn't need any help to win an argument with me. And Shadow, I promise that you will suffer daily if those pictures get leaked."

After the renewed laughing, cheering, and clapping died down, the minister continued. "Despite the joking, or maybe I should say because of the joking, the love between all of you is obvious. Some of the best people I've had the privilege of calling family were no blood relation at all. But they support my wife and me, our marriage, our love, and our children. Colton and Chaise, you have that in the people here with you this evening. Never be ashamed to ask them for help when you need it.

"Colton, do you take Chaise to be your lawfully wedded wife, for all the days of your life until you die?" the minister asked.

"I do."

"Chaise, do you take Colton to be your lawfully wedded husband, for all the days of your life until you die?"

"I do."

"Colton, do you have Chaise's ring?" he asked.

Noah handled Bull the wedding band and Bull held it up.

"This small circle symbolizes never-ending love and commitment. It seals your vow that the promises you've made here today have no expiration date. Colton, place the ring on Chaise's finger, and repeat after me."

Bull slid the ring on her finger and lovingly stroked her hand with his thumb. His eyes never left hers as he repeated the words.

"This ring is a token from my heart. It symbolizes my desire for you to be mine, and for me to be yours, from this day forward, until we both shall die. Just as this ring is eternal, so is my love. With this ring, I thee wed."

"Chaise, do you have Colton's ring?"

Brianna gave Chaise Bull's wedding band. She slid the ring on his finger and repeated the same words back to Bull.

"By the power vested in me by the state of Florida, the world of Walt Disney, and the magic of Mickey, I now pronounce you husband and wife. You may now kiss the bride." The minister smiled.

"Finally!" Bull yelled. He wrapped his arms around Chaise, picked her up off the ground, and covered her mouth with his. The sound of multiple throats clearing behind him finally caught his attention and he reluctantly released her back to her spot.

"Wow—I'm not sure my legs will hold me up now," Chaise laughed.

"I'll always be here to carry you," Bull replied.

"It is my pleasure to now present Mr. and Mrs. Colton Lanier. They've asked that you join them for their reception just across the footbridge on the private terrace. Congratulations to the happy couple!"

Everyone moved to the private terrace while Bull, Chaise, and the bridal party had professional photos taken. The staff strategically placed the iPads at the reception so that Steve and Sara had an unobstructed view of the entire party. When Bull and Chaise finally joined the party, the band began playing to give them the first dance.

"I picked this song—just for you," Bull said as he pulled Chaise into his arms. They began to sway to "Amazed" by Lonestar, and he sang the lyrics to her in whispered tones. With every step, he felt her meld with him. She gripped him tightly and sighed with every verse he sang to her.

"Can I interest you in a honeymoon suite at the Four Seasons? The entire top floor happens to be reserved just for two people. We can make as much noise as we want," she whispered her proposition to him when the song ended.

"It's time to go. Everyone go home now," Bull announced loudly.

"No, you don't, young man," Bull's mom chastised him. "We still have a lot of pictures to take tonight."

Bull grinned because he knew that was the response he'd receive from at least one of the ladies.

"And you haven't cut the cake yet. And Chaise hasn't danced with Noah, your dad, or my dad yet," Brianna added. "So zip it."

"Ah, tell the truth, Sunny. You just want to dance with me," Bull replied.

"I'll dance with you," Liz answered for Brianna. "Your dance card will be full all night."

"I get the first dance with Chaise," Silas's deep voice called from behind them. "Get in line, boys."

"Silas." Chaise smiled. "You really should officially meet my husband now. Colton, Silas. Silas, Colton."

"Bull," he replied. "Only Chaise and my mom call me Colton."

Silas shook his hand. "Chaise has told me a lot about you since I arrived this morning. It seems like I've known you for years now."

"We've been trying to reach you for a while now. How'd she find you?" Noah asked.

"Mom got a message to me," Silas answered. "I've been deep undercover and couldn't risk contacting anyone until the case was over."

"So you're out now?" Chaise asked. "For good?"

"For this case, baby girl," Silas replied. "It'll be a while before I take another undercover case, though."

The band moved on to the next song and Silas smiled at Chaise. "I think they're playing our song. May I have this dance?"

"Of course," she replied. She turned to Bull and kissed his lips. "Now's a good time for you to dance with Brianna."

"Don't mind if I do." Bull smiled and took Brianna's hand. "Come on, little sister, dance with me."

The four walked onto the dance floor and started their dance. The sun had set, and the lights strung around the terrace illuminated the dance floor. The flash from several cameras cast more light on the two couples as they laughed and swayed to the music. When Noah couldn't stand it any longer, he cut in on Silas for his turn with Chaise. Silas, in turn, cut in on Bull to officially meet his sister-in-law.

"They miss you," Brianna told Silas. "They've spoken of you often. Especially since we found out about Steve's cancer."

"They're good kids" Silas replied. "It's best that I don't contact anyone when I'm undercover. Besides putting them in danger, I'm just not a nice person when I'm in character. But I'm back now, so I'll be around so much, they'll wish I was back undercover."

They danced, ate, drank, and enjoyed each other's company until the park closed for the night. Then they took their party to the reserved top floor of the swanky hotel. The floor consisted of a nine-bedroom suite, a four-bedroom suite, plus eight additional guest rooms outside the suites. Chaise walked from room to room, gawking at the amenities and the view the picturesque windows afforded.

"Noah, this is too much," she said. "You didn't have to do all this for us."

"I wanted you to have the fairy-tale wedding and the fairy-tale honeymoon you've always dreamed of. You deserve it, Chaise," he replied. "I remember you always said you'd get married at Disney when you were a little kid."

"I did," she laughed. "I never dreamed it would be like this, though."

"It is amazing."

"Thank you so much for everything you've done," she hugged him. "I love you, Noah."

"I love you, too. I only want you to be happy."

"I am. So very happy."

CHAPTER NINETEEN

Turan paced in the cell he'd been held in for what felt like several days. But in reality, it was more likely that it had been only a couple of days. There were no windows anywhere, so it was impossible for him to accurately gauge time. In fact, he was almost positive that he was deep underground in a basement somewhere. The agents who'd delivered him there wouldn't answer any of his demands to know what would happen to him. His aggravation from being at their mercy was at an all-time high, and he needed to release his pent-up energy.

However, the four walls that contained him disagreed.

One of the CIA agents opened the thick steel door to his solitary confinement and slid the barred gate across the floor until it locked into place. "Now, let's have a talk," the agent said as he sat.

"What do you want, pig?"

"You've been very busy lately. Want to tell me what you've been doing?"

Turan laughed smugly. "I don't know what you're talking about. I'm an innocent diplomatic worker. You've got the wrong man—again. Seems to be a pattern for you."

He smiled at Turan. "Your choirboy act doesn't fly with me, Turan. I can keep you here for as long as it takes for you to decide to talk. My job says I can do whatever it takes to get you to talk."

"I'm not scared of you, pig."

Turan would never admit to anything. He knew he was a genius with the computer. He could break in to secure systems others could only dream of accessing. He'd already proven it, but no one knew yet. He'd built somewhat of a safeguard into the last private network he'd accessed. If anything happened to him, the program would launch itself after seven days of inactivity.

"Have it your way." His smile didn't reach his eyes. His eyes seemed to change between warm and cold with the flip of an internal switch.

The CIA agent rolled the bars back into the wall and stared at Turan with a look that was all too familiar—he had the cold eyes of a killer. Turan was caught in his own thoughts momentarily and missed the agent's discreet movements as he slid the brass knuckles onto his fingers. The loud thwack of the metal hitting bone rang in Turan's ears before he realized his cheekbone was on fire. Turan stumbled backward, lost his balance, and landed on the floor.

Heavy, steel-toed boots repeatedly pounded his ribs, stomach, and back. He curled into a fetal position, trying to protect his head with his arms, but the bruising boots were relentless. Warm blood flowed from his busted nose, the metallic taste of blood filled his mouth, and he realized he was becoming numb. His body was shutting down.

Hands reached under his arms and around his ankles, picked him up, and placed him on something that felt harder than his bed. He was dizzy from the beating and disoriented from the blows to his head, but he knew he was being moved. *A gurney, maybe?* Cool air flowed over his injuries and made him shiver. He tried to open his eyes to see where he was and what he faced, but they were just so heavy.

"Clean him up and put him back in his cell. We'll continue when he feels better," the agent snickered.

Time passed, but Turan only drifted in and out of consciousness. It could've been hours or it could've been days, he wasn't sure. When he had brief moments of lucidity, he thought he'd felt a pinprick, but then he was quickly out again. Through the fog and haze in his mind, he realized they must have drugged him to keep him quiet. He carefully lifted one eyelid to determine where he was being held.

He was alone in his cell again. He slowly sat up on the side of the cot and waited for the dizziness to pass. When he was sure he could stand, he walked to the sheet of reflective stainless steel that served as his mirror. His wounds had been cleaned and looked better than he'd thought they would. He estimated he'd been out about three days from the appearance of his injuries.

His tray suddenly slid through the small opening at the bottom of the door, and he rushed to the window.

"Hey!" he screamed. "How long are you keeping me here? Don't I get a phone call or something?"

"No, you don't," a voice replied.

It was the only voice he'd heard since he'd arrived there besides the CIA agent who continually harassed him. The few people he'd seen refused to speak to him for any reason. The one who brought his food simply opened a small door at the bottom of the door and slid his tray inside. The two people who picked up his trays every evening didn't acknowledge his existence.

"What's happening? When will I get to go home?" he asked.

"You're not going home," the man said as he approached the steel door. He stopped to look Turan in the eye through the window as he finished, "Ever."

Turan's eyes flew open wide, his jaw dropped, and he struggled to find the words to say. "Rashad." A name was all he could manage.

"You seem surprised," Rashad replied.

"I am. I don't understand what's happening," Turan replied.

"What's happening?" Rashad mused. "You've continually screwed up, not paid attention to what's going on around you, and followed your own agenda. You've put the needs of the brotherhood last on your insignificant quest for your own revenge. That's what's happening."

"Are you working for the Americans?" Turan asked in his attempt to catch up.

Rashad released a sarcastic laugh. "No."

"They work for you?"

"I gave you a chance, Turan. You were released. You could've arranged safe passage out of the country, or even just stopped your foolishness. But I had to accept that you wouldn't stop until you'd ruined all of us."

"So what happens now?"

"Now, *I* move forward with our original plans. For *you*, now is all there is," Rashad replied. "Goodbye, Turan."

Rashad turned and walked away while Turan called his name after him, increasing in volume and intensity with each breath. Rashad left the building and placed a call on his burner phone.

"In the next two weeks," he said and hung up.

No further explanation was needed. It bothered Rashad that he'd secretly feared he wouldn't be able to say the words. If his men knew he held a soft spot for Turan, they would question his leadership skills. If they questioned his leadership skills, he'd automatically lose his position and, with it, his life. His clipped commands at least gave the illusion of control and decisiveness.

He dragged his hands over his face and through his hair. Anger filled him at being put in this predicament in the first place. "Why should I feel guilty for the problems he causes?" Rashad asked aloud. "It's not my fault. I've *told* him."

He looked back at the plain building and made peace with his decision. "Goodbye, Turan. Until we meet again."

~

"I don't want to be the one to call him," Brad insisted.

"You have to call him. You have to explain what you found," Roman replied and secretly smirked inside. He was just glad he wasn't the one who was going to interrupt Reaper on his Christmas vacation for his sister's wedding.

"Damned if I do, damned if I don't," Brad said solemnly.

"Ah, come on. Reaper's not unreasonable. Trust me, he'll want to know about this. You'll be better off telling him now than waiting until later," Roman assured him.

"Here goes nothing," Brad replied and picked up the phone.

After a few rings, Reaper picked up and Brad readied himself for the conversation.

"Steele."

"Reaper, this is Brad. Hate to bother you on your vacation, but I found something I thought you'd want to know about."

"Let's have it."

"Roman brought Turan's laptop back for me to have a look at what he's been up to. He'd hacked in to the Air Force's drone control center and set it up to launch if he hadn't logged in to the system in the previous seven days. I've found a way to disable it, but I'm frankly alarmed that he was able to do that at all," Brad explained.

"What was the drone programmed to do when it launched?"

"It was to launch a fully armed MQ-9 Reaper drone to fire on Miami. Think it's a coincidence he chose the Reaper?"

"Not at all," he replied. "I'll contact Commander Adkins and give him a heads-up. I'm sure there will be several agencies interested in hearing what you've found. Good job, Brad."

"Thank you. Sorry to bother you."

"Don't be. It's all good. I'd rather know what's going on than not know," Reaper said. "And if I don't talk to you again this week, have a Merry Christmas."

"Thanks, Reap. You, too," Brad replied before they disconnected.

~

"What was that about?" Brianna asked Noah.

"Our friend Turan is one slippery bastard," Noah replied and then relayed the conversation to the group.

"I told you he needed more shocks," Liz said to Shadow. "You should've listened to me."

"I'm not sure how that would've helped this situation, Liz," Shadow replied.

"It would've made me feel better. That's how," she replied.

Silas stared at Shadow and Liz, trying to decide which one was crazier. Liz, for the things she said, or Shadow, for continuing to try to talk sense into her. "Is your guy alerting anyone?" Silas asked Noah.

"No. I'm going to call Commander Adkins and brief him now. He can run it up the chain," Noah replied. "I'll be right back."

When Noah left the room, Silas watched his retreating back intently. When Noah closed the door, Silas stood and walked around the room until he was positioned just outside of it. He heard as Noah asked for the commander and said he'd hold. Silas feigned interest in the artwork that hung outside the bedroom in the elaborate suite.

"Silas, how long has it been since you were able to be yourself for Christmas?" Shadow asked.

"Too many years to count," he replied vaguely.

"Yeah, I'll bet it's rough when the years start blurring into one," Shadow replied. "How long were you undercover for this last case?"

"About three years," he replied, purposefully keeping his answers short. The last thing he wanted right then was to encourage a long-winded conversation.

"Do you usually jump from one case immediately into the next?" Shadow persisted.

"We have a mandatory decompression time in between," Silas answered and noted he'd let his irritation slip through his cool façade.

"I bet you've had to drastically change your appearance before, huh?"

Silas turned and completely faced Shadow. "Yeah."

Noah walked out of the bedroom, slipped his phone into his pocket, and stopped when he saw the stare-down between his brother and one of the men he considered his brother. "What's going on?"

"Nothing." Shadow smiled in triumph but didn't move his gaze from Silas. "Just talking with your brother about undercover work."

"I'm sure you two have plenty of stories to share," Noah replied.

"How's that?" Silas asked.

"I'm former CIA," Shadow replied.

Silas looked disgusted and glared at Shadow. "Is that right?"

"Get everything squared away?" Shadow asked Noah.

"Yeah, turned it over to Commander Adkins. He's scheduling a meeting with the Joint Chiefs to brief the President," Noah replied.

"Good. Let them handle it. We're out of the mix now," Shadow replied and cut his eyes to Silas.

"Couldn't agree more," Noah replied.

Silas left Noah and Shadow and walked off to his room alone. When he was out of earshot, Noah crossed his arms over his chest and quirked one eyebrow up at Shadow. "Let's have it."

"What?"

"Don't what me. You've never tried to get out of a mission before, never handed it off to someone else to finish. What's the deal?" Noah demanded.

"After all the years we've worked together, I never thought I'd have to ask you this," Shadow started. "But if it comes down to it and you have to choose, whose side would you pick? Mine—or your brother's?" Shadow asked.

"Why would I have to pick sides between you and my brother?"

"Trust me when I say I recognize the signs of a spy. Your brother isn't here only for Chaise's wedding. I don't know what his angle is, but you need to be prepared to make that choice when the time comes," Shadow replied.

Noah nodded. "Understood."

He walked to Brianna and took his seat next to her, but his mind was a million miles away. Faced with a problem he'd never even considered, he decided to do a little digging of his own. His first interrogation subject was Sara, his mother. He pulled out his phone and tapped a quick text to her. When his phone alerted him of the response, part of him didn't want to look.

Noah: Meant to ask earlier, how'd you finally get ahold of Silas?

Sara: I didn't. He called me.

Noah closed his eyes and contemplated his next move. Now that he'd confirmed the first lie, he knew he had to keep digging.

Noah: Didn't realize he called you that often.

Sara: He doesn't. This was out of the blue. Perfect timing.

Noah stared at the text for longer than he should have. The others were busy watching TV, talking, or napping, but Brianna could read him like a book. He felt her fingers in his hair before she started to play with the top of his ear. He couldn't help but smile. *Of all the body parts she has to choose from, she picks my ears to play with,* he mused.

"Something's wrong," she stated. "I know you."

He handed his cell phone to her and let her read the message. Her natural inclination to ask probing questions would kick in as soon as she read it, and she'd know exactly where his mind was. She looked up, and when her eyes met his, he knew that she completely understood what he faced.

"What are you going to do?" she asked, understanding thick in her voice.

"The only thing I can do. I'm going to confront him."

"I'll go with you, if you want. For no other reason than to support you, but I'll be by your side," she replied.

"I love you," he answered. "But I don't want you there if it turns ugly."

"Now I'm going for sure."

"Bri." He looked down at her protruding belly. "If anything happened to you or the baby, I'd go to prison."

"Fine. Just know one thing—that excuse will only work for so long. If anything happens to you, I can't be held accountable for my actions."

He chuckled at her bravado. "I'd expect nothing less from you, babe." Before he got up, he leaned in and kissed her passionately. "Wait here. I'll be back."

Shadow watched Noah rise and leave the room. He felt eyes on him and turned to see Brianna pinning him with her stare. She raised her eyebrows and inclined her head toward the door Noah had just walked through. When he didn't move fast enough, she mouthed the word *"Go!"* and made a jerking motion with her thumb stuck out. Shadow bit his lip to keep from laughing out loud and silently rose from the couch.

He stepped into the hallway outside the suite and instantly heard raised voices. He moved quietly toward the door and listened to the conversation.

"You lied to me, and I know it," Noah yelled.

"What does it matter how I got here? The point is I'm here," Silas dodged.

"No, that's not the point, and you know it."

"What are you asking me, Noah?"

"Are you working this case behind my back? Are you still undercover?"

"What makes you think that?"

"Stop answering my questions with a question. Be a man. Hell, be a *brother*. Answer me," Noah roared.

There was dead silence and Shadow readied himself to kick the door down. If he was correct in his assumption about Silas, there would be one hell of a fight but there was no way Silas would fight fair. Even with his brother. Shadow wouldn't take any chances with Noah's life.

"I think you'd better leave now," Silas replied. He was a little too calm and collected in Shadow's opinion.

"No, Silas. I think *you'd* better leave now. I'm afraid you've worn out your welcome," Noah replied.

"You really want to do that to Chaise during her honeymoon? And to Mom and Dad during Christmas, when they're already going through enough?" Silas replied.

Shadow knew Silas had used the only tactic that would get to Noah. He waited for the reply from Noah that was inevitable. Not that he blamed him, but he knew that Silas was only using their family as leverage over Noah. That was something that Noah would never do.

"Maybe you should've thought about that before you made us part of your undercover case without our knowledge. We work in dangerous conditions all the time, but we work as a team. One doesn't run off half-cocked and get us all killed. This is my family you're putting in danger. Two of them are your sister and your brother-in-law, not to mention your sister-in-law and your niece, but none of that seems to matter to you," Noah shouted. "Mom and Dad would be *ashamed* of you."

Shadow was pleasantly surprised at Noah's response. "You go, brother."

"Wait," Silas finally answered.

Shadow pictured Noah standing at the door with his hand on the knob, prepared to drop the bomb on the family and out Silas. Because they were family, Noah would give Silas one more chance to make things right. If Silas was smart and could read people at all, he'd take that chance.

"Have a seat," Silas continued. "Let's talk."

CHAPTER TWENTY

"Good morning," the nurse called as she entered the room. "How's my favorite patient today?"

"I bet you say that to all of your patients," Steve answered with a smile.

She stopped and dramatically dropped her bottom jaw. "I can't believe you'd say such a thing to me," she chastised him playfully. "And on New Year's Eve of all days." She *tsked* him and then giggled. "How are you feeling today, Steve?"

"I actually feel better today. I'm hopeful that the treatments are working. I can tell a difference in my energy level over the last few days."

"That's great. What about your diet? Are you eating well? Keeping your food down?" she probed.

"This week has been much better for that. I've eaten more and gotten to keep it down for the most part."

"The lab tech will be in this morning to draw blood. As soon as those results are ready, the doctor will be in to talk to you. Do you need anything while I'm here?" she asked.

"A sixteen-ounce T-bone steak, medium, loaded baked potato, salad with ranch dressing, and a large sweet tea," he joked.

She pretended to write it down on her hand. "Got it. You wait right here for me to bring it back to you."

This had been their daily game since Steve was admitted to the hospital a few days before Christmas. Sara and Steve still hadn't told their children that he'd had a reaction to the first dose of medication and had to be hospitalized. Dr. Stanton adjusted the amounts, and Steve had better tolerated it since that time. The lab work would tell them if the adjusted dosage was working. If not, they would have to start from square one again.

"Thank you, Heather," Steve replied. "You're the best nurse. You always make me smile. Can you work every day? Nurse Allison is the devil."

Heather tried to keep from laughing at Steve's comment. The harder she tried, the more impossible it became. "Okay, I'll give you that one. If you need anything, just hit the button. I'll be back to check on you in a bit."

"Will do." He smiled.

Steve couldn't bring himself to tell Silas, Noah, and Chaise about it during her honeymoon and their Christmas vacation. When he'd virtually walked Chaise down the aisle, he was sitting in the hospital room praying no one would notice the wall behind him. He'd sat on the side of his hospital bed wearing a suit jacket, shirt, and tie, and propped the iPad up on the tray table. He'd refused to eat anything that day in hopes that he wouldn't become ill again. He'd made it through the ceremony and partly through the reception before he'd disconnected and let exhaustion overtake him.

But on that particular day, he'd noticed a marked improvement in his energy and his appetite. He could finally joke about food without it turning his stomach. He could smell food without his skin turning a bright shade of green. At last, he dared to hope that the treatments were working and he'd soon be free of the cancer that had taken up residence in his body.

Throughout the day, Heather checked on him several times and brought his next dose of chemotherapy. His breath still hitched in his chest every time they hung the bag of IV fluids that contained his life-giving, cancer-killing toxins. Sara returned from her day of pampering that Steve insisted she do for herself.

"How's my favorite husband?" Sara asked. It had become a joke by extension that started after Heather asked about her favorite patient. The playfulness of the simple question helped make them both feel better about the situation.

"I'll ask him when he comes out of the bathroom," Steve quipped.

"Oh, look who has a sense of humor today. You must be feeling pretty good," Sara said enthusiastically.

"Sara, I really do. I'm afraid to say it out loud, but I'm actually convinced my labs will come back with positive news," he replied.

"I agree. So let it be said, so let it be done," she replied.

"You look beautiful, babe," he said as she took her seat beside his bed. "I can't wait to get out of here."

"Thank you," she replied sweetly. "I can't wait for you to get out of here either. I miss sleeping with you."

"When this is over, you won't be getting any sleep for a long time."

"Steve," she gasped. "I kind of like this side of you. Can we get some of that medicine to go?"

He laughed heartily. "If that's what it takes."

"I heard from Chaise today. They're back home, settling in to married life like they've been married for years," Sara told him. "Colton talked to me for a little while, too. I can see why Chaise loves him so much. He's really a great guy."

"It'll be nice to have everyone over for birthdays, holidays, and Tuesdays," Steve replied wistfully.

"Tuesdays?"

"Yes, Tuesday doesn't get enough attention. It's the forgotten weekday, and it needs to be celebrated. We'll have all the kids over every Tuesday," he decided.

Sara stared at him dumbfounded for several seconds. "Who is this man, and what have you done with my husband?"

"I've replaced him with the new and upgraded version. We'll have Super-Steve-Tuesdays from now on. It's part of my new leaf. So, what else did Chaise have to say?"

"She asked about you, of course. I still didn't tell her that you're in the hospital. They won't be happy when they find out," she replied.

"We'll tell them one way or another when my labs come back. We'll know more then. Is Silas still home?"

"Yes, he is. I've never known him to stay put for so long. When he comes home between cases, he's usually there no longer than two or three days before leaving out again."

"Maybe he's getting out of it and planning to stay home for good now. It's time for him to settle down anyway. He's been on so many undercover operations, he has to be risking crossing paths with the same people again," Steve replied, worry etched in his expression.

"Wouldn't that be wonderful, Steve? To have all of our kids and grandkids close to us?"

"It definitely would be."

~

"I'm never speaking to you again, so don't even start," Chaise yelled at Silas.

"I've apologized a hundred times. What more do you want me to do?"

"Well, I don't know, Silas. I've never used my sister's wedding to spy on my siblings and see what they're up to. I haven't put my family's lives in jeopardy without even telling them. And I've never hurt my brothers the way you've hurt me. So you tell me, Silas. How do you make up for something like that?"

"Baby girl, I'd never let anything happen to you."

She whirled around to face him with fire shooting out of her eyes. "That's the difference between us, Silas. I'm not thinking of only myself. My husband was there. Noah and Brianna were there, too. She's pregnant, Silas. And everyone else who I love and who has helped me through some really hard times was also there. You used all of us. How could you do that?"

His lack of response only infuriated Chaise even more.

"You're not my brother. I don't know you anymore. Is this what years of pretending to be someone else has done to you? Is the Silas I love dead and gone, only to be replaced by someone who treats his family the same way he treats criminals?"

Chaise walked away and left Silas standing alone on Noah's deck. Her words cut him to the quick, and he realized that was the first time he'd felt anything in a very long time. He turned to follow her, to try to talk to her again, but stopped when he realized he wasn't alone.

"Did Chaise ever tell you how we met?" Bull asked.

"No."

Bull nodded and his gaze drifted to just over Silas's shoulder as he remembered that day. "She was in trouble, and she was looking for Noah. She came to his wedding, lurked in the shadows, and we cornered her as soon as Noah and Brianna were safely on their way to the airport.

"She was in trouble with some very bad men who were running drugs and selling girls as sex slaves. They wanted her to join the ranks of women who had disappeared. After meeting her, I knew there was no way in hell I'd let anyone hurt her. The leader of this group had her brought to his island home. He was determined to make her his personal sex slave for a while before he disposed of her. One of his guys roughed her up pretty good on the way to deliver her to the boss. Then, the guy's father wanted to take his revenge out on me by killing Chaise.

"You're probably wondering why I'm sharing all of this with you right now. I'll be glad to tell you." Bull took a step toward Silas. "I don't give a flying fuck if you're her brother, Noah's brother, or Steve and Sara's son. If Chaise gets hurt because you're too fucking stupid to realize that even undercover cops get tailed, I'll kill you just like I did those other bastards."

Bull stared him down, willing him to make a move or say the wrong thing, but Silas looked too shocked to do either. "I never knew she was in trouble like that."

"Can't say that I'm surprised about that," Bull replied bluntly.

"How did she get dragged into that?"

"She was trying to find a missing girl."

"I need to talk to her. To apologize."

"You've done that. Now you need to leave her alone. You hurt her when you brought this to our wedding but didn't have the balls to tell us you're still working undercover. She trusted you. Saying you're sorry doesn't build that trust back," Bull stated and walked away.

Silas walked into the house and found Noah and Shadow in the office. "Can I talk to you for a minute?" Silas asked Shadow.

"Sure."

They walked back to the deck and closed the sliding glass door behind them. Silas walked to the edge of the pool and stared down into the water as he spoke. "I don't know how to be myself anymore. I think I lost myself to the job years ago. How did you make it back?"

"I never totally lost touch with the people who keep me grounded. Even if they didn't realize I was watching them, living vicariously through them. With every decision I made, I asked myself how it would look if I had to explain my actions to them one day," Shadow replied.

"Who are they? The people who keep you grounded?" Silas asked.

"Reaper, Bull, and Rebel," Shadow replied. "Brianna has been like my little sister for years, and I also watched over her when she didn't know."

"How do I turn this around?"

"Start by telling them the truth about what you know."

Silas looked up at Shadow and immediately knew he was right. He also knew that Shadow had an uncanny ability to see through him. He was as transparent as glass to this man. "You know what it means when I do that."

"I know what it means if you stay with the CIA any longer."

Silas started to deny his involvement with the agency, but the *"spare me"* expression on Shadow's face convinced him otherwise. "I'll be lost forever," he confirmed.

"It's not worth it, man. Trust me," Shadow counseled him. "It's much better to work on this side of the fence."

"What happens when I leave?"

"You never really leave the CIA, Silas."

"I've heard that saying for years, but I finally understand what it means."

"Now, don't you have some news on Turan that you need to share with us?"

"Why do I get the feeling you already know what news I have?" Silas narrowed his eyes at Shadow.

"Why do you answer my questions with a question? Why is the ocean salty when fresh water flows into it? Why do women need so many shoes? These are the questions that keep me up at night," Shadow responded.

"Fine. Let's go talk Turan," Silas agreed as he rubbed his head. "It's easier to keep up with than your line of thinking."

"Both of you boys could take lessons from me," Liz stated from behind them. "You're far too gabby to be a spy. I wouldn't even have to give either of you any sodium pentothal to get you to tell all your secrets. Take me, for example. My mind is a steel trap, an impenetrable fortress. You'd never get me to spill all my secrets."

"Liz, for the last time," Shadow spoke slowly. "I'm not falling for your bait and teaching you the tricks of the trade for you to use on some poor, unsuspecting soul."

"Shadow," Liz barked. "I need to be trained. It's a matter of national security."

"I'm positive that it's safer for national security if you're never trained in our methods. Ever," Silas replied.

Liz stood from her chair, straightened her clothes out, and looked Silas in the eye. "Young man," she started. "I can make your life hell in ways that you've never imagined. Don't test me."

With that, she walked back into the house and slammed the sliding door shut behind her. Silas and Shadow burst out in laughter and followed in her footsteps. When they reached the door, they realized that Liz had locked them outside.

"We can either bang loudly on the door and admit that Liz locked us out," Shadow said. "Or we can go over the fence, around the house, and back in the front door."

"Front door," Silas replied quickly.

"Agreed," Shadow said. "Then we never speak of this again."

"Never."

~

"So good of you boys to join us," Liz yelled as Shadow and Silas walked in the front door. "What took you so long?"

"We just took a walk," Shadow replied nonchalantly.

"Over the fence, around the house, and to the front door?" Liz asked. Snickers came from every direction around the room, but no one would make eye contact.

"I have some information to share with everyone," Silas announced and changed the subject.

"We're listening," Noah replied.

"Turan was found dead in his cell today," he announced. When it was obvious that he had the undivided attention of the room, he continued. "The medical examiner is doing an autopsy, but there were no obvious signs of injury reported. With his age, it's highly unlikely that it was from natural causes."

"Do you think someone took their questioning techniques too far?" Brianna asked.

"From what I've been told, that doesn't appear to be the reason. There were no marks on his body."

"Waterboarding doesn't leave marks, and people can die from it," she retorted.

Silas looked at her with a newfound respect for her boldness. "That's true," he said. "But waterboarding is illegal now."

"I'm sure those little technicalities stop you from using that form of questioning," Brianna replied sardonically.

"You have a point," he admitted. "He could've died from that, but I have no reason to think that. My gut tells me it's something far worse."

"Like what?" Noah asked.

"I think his cell turned on him and killed him."

"His cell turned on him?" Liz asked incredulously. "Are you one of those agents who the government did all those crazy tests on? His cell couldn't come to life and kill him."

"What? No. I meant his terrorist group, the other members of his terrorist cell," Silas replied. "Not his holding cell."

Liz gave him her evil smile to remind him of her cleverly veiled threat.

"How would they get to him in there?" Rebel asked.

"Their arm is very long. I know they have agents on their payroll, but I haven't been able to find out who they are yet."

"Why do you think it was his cell?" Rebel asked.

"Because the man I worked for in my undercover role was named Rashad. He spoke of Turan frequently, usually to curse the day he was born because Turan kept pursuing his own goals instead of the group's goal," Silas replied. "The group is geared more to causing anarchy and terror in the masses. They want to bring America to her knees."

"What did Turan want?" Noah asked.

"To bring one man to his knees."

"Me," Rebel replied.

"I believe that's correct," Silas replied. "For killing his father."

"So that was his father." Rebel nodded. "He looked a lot like his dad. They didn't have the same name, though."

"His distant uncle took him to Turkey and raised him. Hid his Iranian descent as much as he could. He taught Turan everything he knew—kid was like a sponge when it came to computers. The cell loved that because most everything in this country is managed by some kind of computer now," Silas explained. "He used 'Ali' because it means exalted. Babek and Turan are areas of Turkey and Iran that he associated his heritage with; the names meant something to him."

"Do you know who and where the other members of the cell are?" Bull asked.

"No. I'm obviously American, so there's a lot of information that Rashad wouldn't trust me with. I was supposed to come here and get close to all of you and then report back to Rashad with your weaknesses, where he could hit you hardest," Silas admitted.

"So, I hopped on a plane and showed up at Chaise's wedding, with the approval of the CIA. I've since realized that they must have known Shadow was part of this group, he'd see straight through me with his training, and that he'd set me straight. That's the story I choose to believe anyway.

"Telling you all of this means I now have to leave the CIA and this undercover life. And that actually puts all of you in even more danger. When Rashad figures out who I really am, he'll come after all of us."

CHAPTER TWENTY-ONE

"When he comes after us, he'll have one hell of a fight on his hands. We don't go down easily," Brianna said as she stood. "You have our back, we'll have yours, Silas. We're a family, and there's always room for one more."

"I'm relearning what it means to be a family, Brianna," Silas replied. "Hell, I'm relearning what it means to be *myself*."

"I don't remember you having a hard time assimilating into real life, Shadow," Rebel replied.

Silas and Shadow chuckled. "Yeah, I asked him about that," Silas admitted. "Seems he had some pretty damn good reasons to keep his head on right."

"What reasons, Shadow?" Brianna asked.

"You," Shadow replied. "And Reaper, Bull, and Rebel. You didn't know it, but I had my ways to stay close to all of you while I was undercover."

"Even while I was in Boulder?" Brianna asked.

"No, not then. But I was at your funeral," Shadow replied and cut his eyes to Reaper. "I was always there."

"Since you were able to help Shadow so much, I have every reason to believe you'll have no problem putting me in my rightful place." Silas smiled.

"Of course," Liz replied. "Especially now that I'm here. I'll be glad to put you in your place every damn day."

"I have no doubt about that, Liz," Silas laughed. "I want to be the best brother, uncle, and friend I can be."

Chaise had been silent through the entire discussion and that worried Silas. He was concerned that she wouldn't forgive him, regardless of what he did. He'd betrayed her trust and used her love to help his case. He couldn't blame her for being upset with him because he was furious with himself over it.

"Chaise?" His voice held the sadness his heart felt. He'd never considered how much his actions would hurt her.

She stood and rushed into his arms. She hugged him tightly and her tears flowed down her face. "I love you, Silas. I've missed you so much."

"I've missed you, baby girl. I didn't even realize how much until I saw you. It's been way too long. I'm so sorry. Please forgive me," he pleaded.

She nodded and squeezed him tighter. "You're forgiven."

"So what's the plan to draw Rashad out?" Rebel asked.

Silas released Chaise and looked at Rebel. "I don't think it'll take much once he realizes I'm not coming back."

"What makes you think he hasn't already followed you here?" Bull asked.

"He may have; that's a very real possibility. He obviously already knows who you guys are because of Turan, but he doesn't know about my relation to Noah and Chaise. If he had known about that when I worked for him, I'd already be dead," Silas replied.

Chaise's cell phone started ringing and she glanced at the display. "It's Mom," she announced. "Hey, Mom... Yeah, we're all here... Sure. Just a second.

"I'm putting Mom on speaker so she can give us all the news at once," Chaise told the room. "Okay, go ahead, Mom."

"Hello, everyone. Sorry to interrupt your team meeting, but I thought you'd want the latest update on Steve," Sara said.

"Yes, we do," Noah replied. "Tell us what's going on."

Sara explained that Steve had been in the hospital for the past couple of weeks and why. The group wasn't happy with them for not sharing that information earlier, but they had to agree that they understood why.

"So that brings me to what's happened now," Sara said. "Dr. Stanton just came in with the lab results and..."

She paused deliberately for dramatic effect.

"Mom!" Chaise yelled. "Tell us."

"The new treatment is working," she shrieked. "His blood work looked good, so they took him down and did an X-ray. The tumors are shrinking!"

"That's amazing," Noah replied. "Mom, that's incredible news."

"It really is," Sara sniffled. "We still have a long way to go to finish the treatment, but we'll take every piece of good news we can get."

Sara put Steve on the phone and they talked for a while longer. The good news was very welcome, especially in light of the topic they'd been discussing. When they hung up, Noah and Silas faced each other.

"I'm sorry I wasn't a better brother," Silas began. "Our family has been torn to hell, but now we're coming back together."

"Don't think you're alone in that," Noah replied. "I have my own failures as a brother to answer for. But one thing I know for sure—our family is definitely worth fighting for."

"I'm afraid we'll have quite the fight on our hands," Silas replied. "Rashad is vehement about seeing this through to the end."

"So are we," Rebel replied. "What do you need from us?"

Silas looked around the room, and each of the men signaled that he was in with a single nod of his head. "Okay. Let's take them down, then. First, we need to identify the agents and how they've been compromised."

Noah typed out a message to Brad, instructing him to track down Joe and Bill, the CIA agents, and check their bank account records. "I've had a bad feeling about them since the start of this case."

"Do you have Rashad's last name?" Rebel asked. "The one he uses now."

"Samir," Silas replied.

"On it," Shadow replied. "Looking for known accomplices and any frequently dialed numbers."

"Burner phones can't be traced, though," Liz replied.

"Sure, they can't," Shadow replied with a smile.

"Shadow, you have to teach me these tricks you know!" Liz pouted.

"I'll start checking airline records to see if Rashad is in Miami now," Bull said and walked off to the office.

"I'm going to look through that mission file again. See if anything else about Turan stands out," Rebel said.

"I'll put out some feelers with my CIA buddies," Silas replied. "See if we can cast a wide enough net to catch a bunch of terrorists."

"Sounds like we all have our marching orders," Noah said.

~

JANUARY

"I have the names and bank records for both Joe and Bill," Brad announced. "Finally. They were buried so deep, I didn't think I'd ever find them."

"Let's hear it," Noah replied.

"Joe appears to be clean, but Bill has numerous deposits in various multiples of $10,000 over a very short span. It looks like the payments were split up in differing amounts to avoid calling too much attention to them. But when you add them all up, it comes up to exactly a quarter of a million dollars," Brad explained.

"He's our guy. We need a tail on him at all times," Noah replied.

"I'll take it," Rebel volunteered. "If he leads us to Rashad, I want to be the first one there."

"Find him, tail him, and let's end this," Noah replied. "Don't engage alone if you can avoid it."

Rebel nodded. "I hope he leads us to another cell member."

"Rashad Samir is traveling as Sam Rash and he's in Miami," Bull reported. "Let's go find him and Bill."

"I'm ready," Rebel replied. "Let's go."

Rebel and Bull left to find Bill and hoped they'd also find Rashad nearby. They staked out the address listed for Bill and waited for him to arrive. When he pulled into his driveway several hours later, he walked inside without a backward glance.

"Arrogant, isn't he?" Bull asked.

"He's definitely sure that he's getting away with murder," Rebel replied. "He doesn't even check his surroundings to see if anyone's watching him."

Bull pulled out his phone and hit the speed dial. "Brad, you got that tap going?"

"It's up and running. As soon as I get a hit, you'll be the first to know," Brad replied.

Bull and Rebel continued to stake out his house, monitor his online activities, and wait for a phone call to come in. After a week and a half of driving different cars, tailing Bill everywhere he went, and monitoring his online activities, they finally got a break in the case.

"This guy really leads a boring life to be a terrorist wannabe," Bull quipped. "He has the treadmill at the gym, checking on his elderly mother at the nursing home, and a daily trip to the grocery store. He's boring me to death."

Bull's phone chimed and he looked at the text. "Huh. Brad said Bill isn't employed by the CIA anymore. He recently took a personal leave of absence for family reasons. Wonder if that's because of the mother in the nursing home or the quarter of a million dollars burning a hole in his pocket."

"I'm going to go with the latter," Rebel replied.

Thirty minutes later, Bull received another text from Brad with the phone number that Rashad was using, compliments of Shadow.

"How does he do that?" Rebel chuckled.

"It's all in those tricks he won't teach Liz about," Bull replied. "So, shall we call Rashad now?"

"Yes, let's," Rebel replied.

Bull called out the number while Rebel dialed. It rang several times before Rashad picked up. "Hello." The irritation of being interrupted was clear in his tone.

"Hello, Rashad Samir, Sam Rash, whoever you are," Rebel replied.

"Who is this?" Rashad emphasized each word.

"I'm the man who's going to put you away for life. And then I'll watch from the front row when you get the lethal injection," Rebel replied. "Ask your CIA friend Bill who I am."

"By the time you find me, it'll be much too late," Rashad replied with confidence. "But you can have Bill. I'll even help you out with that."

Rashad disconnected, and Rebel told Bull what he'd said. "What the hell does that mean?"

The explosion was so loud and violent that it blew out the glass in Bull's truck windows. Rebel jumped out of the truck and called Shadow as he ran across the front yard. "Shadow, tell me you have a list of names and numbers from Rashad's phone."

"Of course I do," Shadow chuckled. "What's all the commotion in the background?"

"Bill's house just exploded," Rebel said as he approached the raging inferno that had been Bill's home.

"Was he in it at the time?" Shadow asked.

"Yes, he went inside about thirty minutes ago," Rebel replied.

"Rashad is covering his tracks, then. He's getting ready to leave town," Shadow said. "If he hasn't already."

"He said by the time I found him, it'd be too late," Rebel said.

"He's put his plans into motion, then," Shadow replied. "I just received word that Joe has been reported missing to the agency. I don't know if he is hiding, dead, or if he's in on it and has already left town because of that. Let me make a few more calls. This just got a little harder to manage and a little more serious."

Rebel and Bull stayed until the fire department and police arrived. They explained the circumstances and as much about the case as they could provide. When they finally left the scene, they both felt defeated and like they were still several steps behind Rashad.

"Shadow thinks he may have already left the area when I talked to him," Rebel said.

"I have APBs out at all the major transit points," Bull replied. "But if he used a private charter at a private airstrip, he could bypass all of that."

"We need that info from Shadow," Rebel said. "The names and numbers of the people he's been talking to. And Joe is missing. He doesn't know if Joe is dead, hiding, or in on it."

When Bull and Rebel walked into the office, Shadow had the lists ready for them. "I've been looking into some of these names and have a few locations we need to scout out. There's a high volume of call activity to people in New York City, Atlanta, Houston, Denver, and Los Angeles. This could take some time, boys."

"I'll take LA," Silas replied. "I've done quite a bit of work out there and still have a number of undercover contacts."

"I'll take Atlanta," Noah replied. "The baby is due in a few weeks, so I'd rather not be far from home if I can help it."

"I've got NYC," Shadow replied.

"Houston," Rebel replied and ignored the glances from Bull and Noah.

"Guess I'll take Denver." Bull smiled. "Chaise can go with me if it turns out there's something to investigate there."

"Everyone set? Research these names and phone numbers. Get Brad to run background checks, searches on bank records, credit cards, and known accomplices if anyone looks suspicious," Noah instructed. "We'll have to partner with the local LEOs if we pinpoint a location."

"What does 'local LEO' mean?" Liz asked, her pen and paper ready to take notes.

"Local law enforcement office," Noah replied. "LEO so we don't have to say the whole thing every time."

"Well, aren't you clever," Liz remarked with a chuckle.

"Liz, I'm going to need your help while I'm working on this case," Noah replied.

"I'm your woman," Liz replied. "Do I get to carry a Glock?"

"No," Noah replied. "I need you to help take care of Brianna, watch out for her, make sure she's taking care of herself."

"You need me to be her bodyguard." Liz nodded. "Got it. Keep the bad guys away from her, escort her to the doctor, check the security system."

"Something like that." Noah smiled. "Can I count on you?"

"I'm on it. Don't you worry," Liz replied. She walked out of the office and began calling through the house. "Brianna? You and I are about to become even closer than we are now. Don't be embarrassed, I have all the same body parts you have."

Shadow barked out a laugh and looked at Noah. "You are a dead man. Brianna will have your head for this."

"She'll understand. I had to think of something to keep Liz busy and out of our hair," Noah laughed.

"Liz, close the door," Brianna's voice carried through the house.

"What are those? I don't have those," Liz answered.

Several minutes later, Brianna stopped in the doorway of Noah's office and glared at him. "I know what you did. You owe me, Noah Steele. When this case is over, you owe me. Don't think I won't collect either. I'm talking diamonds. *Big* diamonds."

"Anything, babe." Noah smiled. "It's worth whatever I have to pay."

~

The five men spent the following weeks combing through countless records in their attempt to pinpoint the people Rashad was in league with. When they'd narrowed their sights to a few people in each city, they started coordinating with their local contacts for stakeouts.

"Atlanta turned out to be a bust," Noah said. "The people Rashad called were employees of a news organization who ran an unfavorable story about terrorists. He was harassing everyone involved with the broadcast—the anchor, the producer, even the cameraman. None of the people on that list warrants further investigation."

"At least we can cross one city off the list. That's a relief," Silas replied. "LA isn't as fortunate. There are several indications it's a hot bed. One of my contacts out there has warned me against returning, though. Apparently I'm to be shot on sight by one of the organized crime families I infiltrated out there. They don't want a massacre in the streets, so they're doing the hard work for me. It's kind of nice to be the boss instead of the grunt."

"Houston is buzzing with activity. If you two have time on your hands, there's plenty of work to be done there," Rebel replied.

"Denver is worth looking into closer," Bull replied. "Definitely a cause for concern."

"NYC is out. The numbers he called there stemmed from a phone-sex hotline. He got the girls' private numbers and began calling them directly. Our boy is mentally unstable," Shadow replied. "I can take LA for Silas. It's been a while since I've been there. Plus, no one in LA is looking to kill me that I know of."

"Sounds good, Shadow. Sounds like Silas's contacts will have your back and get a lot of the preliminary work finished for you. The rest of us can split up and help the others cover more ground working in teams. I'll go to Houston with Rebel. Silas, you can go to Denver with Bull and Chaise," Noah replied. "Any questions or comments?"

"Yes, I have a comment," Brianna said from the doorway. Noah looked up and met her gaze. "Before you rush off to Houston, I need you to do something with me, Noah."

"Sure, babe. Whatever you need," he replied.

"I need you to take me to the hospital. My water just broke," Brianna replied.

"The baby's coming? Now?" came Noah's shocked reply.

"Right now," Brianna answered. "I've had a dull ache in my lower back all day, but I didn't think anything about it. I thought contractions would be stronger and announce their presence."

Noah's brain and ears finally caught up with each other, and he rushed to Brianna's side. "I'll grab the suitcase upstairs, and we'll go to the hospital right now."

"I've got it, Noah." Chaise smiled as she walked up with the suitcase. "I'll call Mom and Dad and Brianna's family to let them know it's time. Go ahead and take your wife to the hospital. Colton and I will be right behind you."

"Brianna, we're having a baby." Noah placed his hands on her face and lowered his mouth to hers. "You're having my baby."

"I know," she whispered. "I'm scared and excited and can't wait to meet her."

"Oh, shit," Noah hissed.

"What?" Brianna asked.

"We never picked out a name."

CHAPTER TWENTY-TWO

The contraction slammed into her like a locomotive and made her gasp for air. "I'm ready for it to go back to being a dull ache now," Brianna said through gritted teeth.

"I'm afraid there's no going back now." The nurse smiled. "The anesthesiologist will be in soon to start your epidural. You'll be able to relax and enjoy it then."

"Can you go drag him in here now?" Brianna requested.

"Let me see where he is," the nurse answered. "Don't forget to breathe through the contractions. It really does help."

"Okay. Got it," Brianna replied. "Breathe."

The nurse walked out of the room and Brianna turned to Noah. "Breathing doesn't help the pain. What a crock of shit."

Noah laughed out loud. "No, I've never found it to help my pain either. What can I do?"

"You're here with me. That's all I need." She smiled.

"It must be subsiding. You're Brianna again. In a few minutes, you'll have that evil, contorted face again," Noah chuckled.

"I'll remember that comment when the next one hits," she threatened playfully.

"Don't scare me like that," Noah retorted.

An hour later, the anesthesiologist still hadn't made an appearance, and Brianna's contractions were much stronger and closer together. Her skin was flushed, her hair was damp, and her fingers appeared to be permanently attached to Noah's hand. When the needle on the monitor redlined, her fingers clenched around his hand so she could share a small portion of her pain with him.

Bull and Chaise watched the scene play out in front of them and exchanged dubious glances. "Do you want us to leave?" Bull asked.

"Of course not. You're her aunt and uncle. Why would we want you to leave?" Noah asked.

"It looks uncomfortable," Silas answered. The muscles in his normally handsome face were drawn and contorted as if he'd felt sympathy pains.

"It is," Brianna and Noah replied in unison.

Noah hit the button to call the nurse after one especially painful contraction nearly broke his hand. The nurse promptly appeared and checked Brianna's progress. "You're very close to being fully effaced and dilated now. It won't be long before your baby arrives. Do you know what you're having?"

"A girl," she panted.

"Have you decided on her name?"

Brianna cut her eyes to Noah, and they both smiled. "No, not yet. Hopefully when we meet her," she replied.

"You'd be surprised how many people change their minds after they meet the baby for the first time," the nurse said.

A quick rap on the door caught their attention, and all heads turned to watch the anesthesiologist sheepishly enter the room with a red-faced Bull close on his heels. "I understand my presence has been requested in this room."

"Yeah, like an hour ago. Have a nice nap?" Brianna snapped.

"So, you're ready for your epidural, I presume." The doctor smiled.

The nurse anesthetist followed the doctor into the room and began assembling the items to start the epidural. "Can everyone except Dad step outside the room for a few minutes, please? We'll get her fixed up, and you can come right back in."

When everyone had left, the medical team helped Brianna sit up on the side of the bed and waited for the contraction to ease. "I'll be as easy as I can," the doctor explained. "You just have to be as still as you can possibly be. We'll have the good stuff going for you in just a minute."

The pain-numbing medicine kicked in almost immediately, and Brianna released a deeply contented sigh. The anesthesiologist checked the placement again before he left the room and wished them both the best for their delivery day.

Brianna's obstetrician then walked in and checked her progress. "Your baby is almost crowning now. I'll be back to check on you in a few minutes."

On his way out, he sent Bull, Chaise, and Silas back into the room.

"That's much better. Now I love you again, Noah," Brianna said sweetly.

"You quit loving me today?" Noah asked.

"For just a minute. When the pain was really severe. And I contemplated castrating you," Brianna joked. "Of course, I didn't really quit loving you. That could never happen."

"Let me unplug this medicine and see if you still say that." Noah pretended to search for the valve to stop the flow of medication into Brianna's epidural line.

"Don't make me have to kill you today, Noah," she retorted.

He laughed in response and leaned over the bed to kiss her. "I love you, too, babe."

"So, let's talk about a name now that I can think straight again," Brianna suggested. "Do you have anything in mind?"

"I really don't," Noah admitted. "Something unique to fit our life together."

"There's a name that's been stuck in my head," Brianna admitted.

"What is it?"

"Amelia Grace Steele," she replied.

"Why Amelia?" he asked.

"Because we've been around the world just to be together," Brianna explained.

Noah repeated it several times and played with how it rolled off his tongue. "I love it," he finally said. "I'm sold on Amelia Grace."

"I love that name," Chaise replied. "It's beautiful. I can't wait to meet my niece. Can you hurry up already?"

The family laughed and talked for the next half hour. Another knock on the door alerted them to more visitors arriving. Brianna was thrilled to see her parents and her three sisters arrive in time to be there for the delivery. "Mom, Dad! I'm so glad you made it.

"Missy, Jessie, and Ashley, get over here," she demanded as she extended her arms for a hug. They all readily complied and found a seat on her bed, surrounding her with love and support.

"We're so sorry we weren't here to give you a baby shower," Missy said solemnly. "But we're going to do one immediately after she's born. We already have it all planned out and everything's arranged."

"That's okay, Missy. We've all been very busy, and it's not easy to plan a baby shower from Atlanta," Brianna replied. "But I really do appreciate it."

"We have more good news, too," Diane quickly added.

"What? Tell me!" Brianna replied.

"We're moving to Miami!" she squealed. "The new hotel construction is well underway. We've all talked about it, and we want to be together."

"That's great news," Brianna exclaimed. "I'll be so happy to have all of my family here."

The doctor and nurse came back in the room and smiled at all of the visitors. When the doctor reached the foot of Brianna's bed, he stopped and grinned at her. "Are you ready to have a baby, young lady?"

"I am." She nodded enthusiastically. "I'm so ready to see our daughter for the first time."

Everyone left the room to give her some privacy as the doctor checked her again and confirmed that it was time. "The baby's head has completely crowned. She's ready to get out of there," he laughed.

The nurse quickly converted the bed to a delivery bed and set up everything needed for the delivery. With Noah by her side, Brianna began pushing on command. She held her breath, pushed to the doctor's count, and then lay back to rest. They repeated this process several times until the baby's head emerged.

Noah looked at Brianna with amazement when the baby's head first appeared. "Oh my God. It's our baby, Bri. That's Amelia."

"One more good push and she'll be officially delivered. You ready?" The doctor smiled.

"Yes," Brianna replied on bated breath. "I'm so ready."

Noah helped her sit up, and she pushed one last time with all of her might. She felt the immediate relief of pressure and watched as the doctor cradled the baby with one arm while he clamped the umbilical cord with his free hand.

"Would you like to cut the cord?" he asked Noah.

"Yes," Noah said and took the scissors in his hand. With one snip, he cut the cord that had connected his wife and daughter for the last nine months. "This is all so amazing."

The nurse took the baby from the doctor and cleaned her up. When she'd been weighed, measured, and monitored, the nurse placed the baby in Noah's waiting arms. The strong, alpha male, who could face bullets flying at him without so much as a blink, was completely brought to his knees by a seven-pound, twenty-inch-long baby girl.

"Amelia Grace Steele, you are so very loved," he whispered and kissed her rosy cheeks. "You look just like your mommy, my beautiful baby girl."

Noah walked to Brianna, carefully carrying his precious girl in his arms, and peered at Brianna with love brimming in his eyes. "Momma, I have someone here who would like to meet you now."

Brianna held her arms out as tears streamed down her face. "My sweet baby," she cried.

The nurse watched as Noah lovingly placed Amelia in Brianna's arms and then wrapped his muscular arms around them both. The nurse snapped pictures of them, but they were completely oblivious to anyone else in the room. She switched the camera to video mode and captured the entire moment for them.

"For as long as I have breath in my lungs, I will love and protect you both," Noah whispered. "Nothing is more important to me than my wife and my baby. You've never failed to amaze me, Brianna, and today is no exception. My life, my heart, my whole world—is right here in my arms. I love you." He kissed her softly on the temple when he finished.

The doctor and nurse finished with their tasks and left Brianna and Noah alone to spend time with their newborn. They were so completely wrapped up in everything about their daughter that they lost all track of time. They looked up when they heard a light knock on the door.

"Is everything okay in here? We're dying to meet the baby out here," Diane said.

Noah and Brianna both laughed. "Yes, Mom, everything's fine. Everyone can come in now," Brianna replied. Everyone started filing into the room, standing anywhere they could fit.

"Sorry, everyone. We got a little lost in our baby girl," Noah chuckled. "Come here and meet Miss Amelia Grace Steele."

After everyone had sufficient time with the baby, meaning Noah allowed them thirty seconds each to hold her and give her back, Missy brought in the baby shower party items. The cake was beautifully decorated with pink shoes and strollers. The gifts were wrapped in matching paper and bows. The iPads were prominently displayed so Noah's parents could participate virtually. Nothing was left undone, and Brianna felt loved beyond measure.

It was the best day of Noah and Brianna's life together. The perfect culmination of their love slept against her mother's chest, wrapped in a pink swaddling blanket.

~

FEBRUARY

"Shadow and Silas have been gone for quite a while," Liz stated. "When will they be back?"

"I'm not sure," Brianna replied. "They've been working so hard on this case for the past few weeks. Rashad hasn't left them many clues to go on."

Brianna picked Amelia up from her bassinet and sang softly to her while she changed her diaper. "I can't believe she's almost a month old now. How do does time fly so fast? It just seems like yesterday when I was still pregnant with her."

"Wait until she's grown. You'll swear that you only blinked once," Liz replied. "It's the way of things, I suppose. My mother always said the same thing, but I never understood it when I was a kid."

"I completely understand now," Brianna replied. "It's scary how life is so short. I always thought we had all the time in the world."

"Haven't we all," Liz agreed.

"Brianna," Noah called from downstairs. "Can you come here, babe?"

"On our way," Brianna replied.

When Noah saw Brianna approaching with Amelia, he had to stop and smile, just as he'd done every other time over the past several weeks. His wife and his baby together was the most beautiful sight he'd ever seen.

"Do you need something?" Brianna asked.

"Will you and Amelia be okay here if I go to Houston with Rebel?" Noah asked. "Or, would you two rather come with me? You can stay at the same hotel as my parents and visit with them while I'm working."

"We want to go with you," Brianna replied with a bright smile. "Sara and Steve have only seen her over the Internet. Besides, your parents need a break from being so focused on cancer treatments. It'll be good for them."

"I agree." Noah smiled. "Liz, you in?"

"Try to stop me from getting on that plane." She winked.

"Good. It's settled then. We all go together. Go ahead and get packed. We're leaving in a few hours."

Rebel's phone chimed, and he absently removed it from his pocket while his attention was focused on the intel he'd gathered.

"You fucking bastard," he growled loudly.

Noah, Brianna, and Liz openly gawked at Rebel's outburst because it was so unlike him. "What is it, man?" Noah asked.

Rebel held out his phone, and Noah took it from him. Rebel paced the office while Noah looked at the text.

"Motherfucker," Noah replied.

"What is it, Noah?" Brianna asked. "What's wrong?"

Noah head up the phone for Brianna to see. The screen had a picture of a beautiful nurse as she walked out of the hospital. The bright sun reflected off her short, black hair and made it almost sparkle. Her warm smile was genuine and made her instantly appealing and inviting. Brianna imagined her personality matched her smile, making her a perfect candidate to be a nurse.

"She's gorgeous. What's the big deal? Who is she?" Brianna asked.

"The message that came with this picture says, 'Don't you love my next victim?' and it's from Rashad's burner phone," Noah replied.

"He's after her now?" Brianna asked, and urgency filled her tone. "Who is she? Where is she?"

"She's in Houston," Rebel replied. His voice was like ice—cold, hard, and unfeeling. Rebel stared out the window, his hands on his hips and his back to Brianna. "And she's my wife."

EPILOGUE

Rashad watched the lovely nurse leave the hospital after her shift. She'd been working several days in a row–many more days than nurses normally worked. Three twelve-hour shifts in a row were hard enough, but with the addition of extra days and longer hours, anyone would be worn out. Rashad knew from experience when women were too tired, they weren't as aware of their surroundings as they should be. He'd used this fact to his advantage too many times to count.

If this particular pretty nurse had been watching, she would've noticed the same car following her home over the past few days. She would've seen the handsome, Middle Eastern man who followed her in the hospital halls. She would've felt his eyes on her skin. Fortunately for Rashad, she didn't notice anything out of the ordinary, and that gave him all the advantage he needed.

When he sent the picture to the man called Rebel, he simply wanted to repay an insult at first. But the more he thought about what he'd been forced to do, the more he understood Turan's obsession with revenge. The revenge he'd seek for being forced to kill his own brother wouldn't get in the way of the large-scale attack that was well underway. He decided he'd avenge his father, his brother, and his own actions all in one fatal blow.

But having a little fun by torturing Rebel along the way would definitely be an added benefit.

When he'd torched the rental house, he made sure Turan lost everything he loved and needed to carry out his specific part of the plan in the fire. All of his laptops and equipment were melted. The few articles of clothing he owned were destroyed. The roof over his head was taken away. Rashad had hoped Turan would finally give up on his quest and leave the country. But he didn't.

When their adoptive uncle publically disowned and dishonored Turan, he tried to give his brother time to get out. When he disappeared from the apartment, Rashad had hoped Turan had finally made the right decision. But then he showed up on the CIA's radar yet again after he accepted a contract as a hired killer, on the Internet of all places.

Rashad exhaled forcefully at the thought. "That was such a stupid move, Turan. How could you have been such an idiot? You knew better than anyone that nothing is safe on the web."

Killing Bill had been an added benefit for Rashad. The dirty undercover agent had become greedy and demanding. He expected Rashad to give him more money in exchange for keeping silent, looking the other way, and keeping the other agents off his trail. The fact that Bill's death happened at the exact time Rashad received the phone call was an added bonus.

Heather Reed walked by his car on the way to her car. Without so much as a glance in his direction, she continued on alone through the parking garage.

Remain oblivious to the danger all around you, Rashad thought as she crossed in front of him. *I'll see you soon.*

The story continues in WICKED INTENTIONS ... coming soon.

ABOUT THE AUTHOR

A.D. Justice is happily married to her husband of 25 years. They have two sons together and enjoy a wide variety of outdoor activities. A.D. has a full-time job by day, with a BS degree in Organizational Management and an MBA in Health Care Administration. Writing gives her the outlet she needs to live in the fantasy world that is a constant in her mind.

Thank you for reading and supporting A.D.'s books! Please take a moment to leave a review of this work. You can find her online at:

Facebook: https://www.facebook.com/adjusticeauthor
Twitter: https://twitter.com/ADJustice1
Web: www.adjusticebooks.com
Email: adjustice@outlook.com

BOOK 4: WICKED INTENTIONS

Painful secrets from Braxton "Rebel" Reed's past will be exhumed and put on full display. Desperation drives him to save the only woman he's ever loved.

Tragedy strikes in the most unexpected ways, reducing once strong walls to mere rubble.

It's been said good triumphs over evil and love conquers all. When the dust settles and the smoke clears, the last man standing wins.

PROLOGUE

June 22, 2001

Heather,

I've watched you sleep for the past few hours, and I've racked my brain trying to remember what my life was like without you in it. We've known each other as long as I can remember, and I can't recall a time when I didn't love you. There hasn't been a single day gone by I didn't know exactly how much you meant to me. You've never kept secrets from me. Your heart has always been an open book, reserved only for me to devour every word, thought, and feeling.

When we first met as kids, I was only looking for someone to play with after school. The day I knocked on your front door changed me forever. You became my partner in crime, my best friend, and the love of my life. Remember how we were inseparable? Every day, we rushed to do our chores or homework, so we'd have more time to spend together. You were, and still are, the coolest girl in the world. You could hang with me on the bicycle. You'd hold frogs and touch snakes. Every other girl would run away screaming, but never you. Nothing could make you leave my side.

As we got older, those things weren't as important to me anymore, and I saw you in a whole new light. You still had just as much spunk about you. Remember the time at the middle school dance when you punched that girl for flirting with me? I still laugh about that to this day. As if she was ever any threat to you. You said I belonged to you, even if I didn't realize it yet. You said you wouldn't put up with another girl disrespecting what we had. There are no words to describe how turned on I was when you said that. I knew I loved you then, but an awkward thirteen-year-old me didn't know how to tell you.

Then came the high school years. Yes, you remember those well, don't you? Our class schedules separated us, so I didn't see you as much during the day. The first semester of our freshman year, I thought I'd die from being apart from you for so long. Every day after school, I waited for you outside so we could go home together. Absence really did make the heart grow fonder, and I knew without a doubt it was time to tell you exactly how I felt. That day, I waited in the rain for you to come out of the school. I had my speech memorized down to the last syllable.

Then you walked out, and I watched in horror as David Richards put his arm around you and announced to the school that you were his girlfriend. You know me... there was no way I could let that stand. So I decked him. Punched his lights right out. The look on your face was priceless—you were shocked, awed, and dumbfounded all at once. You were shocked that I had finally admitted my feelings for you. Awed that I did it in such a public display. And dumbfounded that it took me so fucking long to realize what you'd always known. When I kissed you that day, you changed me again. You ruined me for any other woman. Your kiss, your taste, and your sweet scent—no one else on earth could compare to you.

So began our dating experience. We defied the odds, didn't we, babe? We showed everyone in this one-horse town that our love was real and lasting. Neither of us has ever even been on a date with anyone else. Never kissed another person in the intimate ways we kiss. Never made love to another and shared the special bond that we have together. Even after more than four years of officially dating, I can honestly say that I don't regret one minute of the time I've spent exclusively with you. Four years of football games, school dances, junior and senior proms. Weekend dates, weeknights sneaking out my bedroom window just to make out with you. Making plans and dreaming big—together.

Sometimes I look back and miss the "us" we used to be, even just a short year ago. The things we've been through have taken a hard toll on you, and I blame myself for that. You can blame me, too. I can take it, and I deserve it. More than anything, I wanted to be the one to always protect you, love you, and provide for you. Our life together was supposed to be perfect. Wonderful. Magical. Beautiful.

I failed you. I failed us. I'm sorry, baby. I'm sorry I couldn't be the man I should've been, the man you needed me to be. Because of my failures, you're all but estranged from your family, especially your dad. The stress of everything has just been too much on you, and my presence here is only adding to it.

We fight every day now over things we'd normally laugh about. We're slowly tearing each other apart, bit by bit, and I'm afraid there will be nothing left of the Heather I fell in love with before much longer. When he died, I think he took the best part of us with him. I can't keep putting you through this hell every day, baby. It's killing me to watch you slowly die right before my eyes. When you look at me, I know you blame me for not being able to protect him like I should have.

Saying all this to you in a letter is a really shitty thing to do, I know. I openly admit that I'm a coward when it comes to losing you. On one hand, I'm afraid that if I tell you I'm leaving, you'd cry and ask me to stay. And I would. For you, there's nothing I wouldn't do. On the other hand, I'm petrified that you'd tell me to go, because then I'd know that your love for me has truly died. Love that has been alive and growing since the day we met. That means I'm taking the coward's way out, so I can keep your love with me.

I'm apparently also selfish, because I can't stand to think of doing this any other way. But I'm not so selfish that I don't want you to be happy. I want you to find someone who makes you the Heather I once knew, before I brought so much pain and suffering to your life. Find someone who puts that spark in your eye, the spring in your step, and the smile on your face. Give him all of you, everything you possess, and hold nothing back so that you can be whole again. Put me in the past, where I belong, and don't look back.

Know that you have my love—all of my love, all of my heart, and all of me. Forever.

Until death do us part,
Braxton Reed

~

Braxton placed the folded letter on the empty pillow beside his wife's head and stared at her intently one last time. Over the years, he'd memorized every line, curve, and tiny freckle on her face. He knew her better than anyone else did. Better than her family members who'd done everything in their power to drive them apart. Better than her friends who'd tried to convince her to date other people before settling for him. Better than their teachers who thought they knew everything but had no idea how deeply Braxton and Heather's love ran.

Part of him wished they'd listened to at least one of the naysayers before they'd reached such a low point. Maybe if they'd broken up, dated other people, or just took a break from their all-consuming relationship, the sorrows they'd experienced wouldn't have ever happened. Maybe if they'd actually waited until they were adults, instead of pretending to be grown-ups, everything would've turned out differently.

But that wasn't the way of things. Being young and foolish, they'd made mistakes and tried to fix them. In doing so, Braxton realized they'd only made their follies worse. In his mind, the only way either of them would make it out alive was if they did something they'd never tried before. They had to split up and never look back.

In the weeks leading up to that day, Braxton had talked secretly to a recruiter about his choices and completed all the steps to enlist in the Army. By the time Heather awoke that morning, he planned to be long gone, far away from her so he couldn't hurt her again.

He paused at the door, and his hand gripped the knob as his heart shattered into a million pieces. "Eighteen, married, and divorced." He shook his head in disbelief. "How did we come to this?"

When Braxton walked out the door of the tiny, one-bedroom apartment they had briefly shared as husband and wife, he reflected on how it was the second hardest thing he'd ever done. He closed the door behind him quietly, ensured it was locked, and walked away from the woman who held his heart in her hands, who had been his best friend for as long as he could remember, and whom he'd failed in the worst way. He tried to block the visions of Heather waking and finding the letter on his pillow rather than seeing him lying there. He didn't want to think about her reaction when she read his words, regardless of what it was. The thought of her crying, brokenhearted, and feeling abandoned hurt him as much as the thought of her being relieved that he was gone.

As the bus pulled away from the station, he leaned his head on the seatback and closed his eyes. "I love you, baby. Until death do us part."

CHAPTER ONE

February, Present Day

Heather Reed stepped out of the hospital and inhaled a deep, cleansing breath before starting her trek to her car in the parking garage alone. The long, twelve-hour shift had morphed into fourteen hours, thanks to a shortage of nurses and an abundance of patients, and she was more than ready to go home. Her feet ached after the constant rushing from one room to another all day. Her lower back was stiff from all the time she spent standing in one place to complete her charting. She was more mentally drained than usual because of her heavy patient load, but taking care of others when they needed her the most was her passion. Nursing wasn't just a job she left behind when she left the floor.

When she'd found her calling in life many years ago, she'd known immediately she wouldn't be happy doing anything else. Her propensity to nurture and her desire to help others made her a natural in nursing school. Quickly rising to the top of her class, Heather insisted on taking the harder cases the other students shied away from. During her first clinical rotation in the oncology unit, she knew she'd found her niche. The work was hard and exhausting, but she knew her patients needed her more than the average.

Her mind drifted back to the first time she accompanied the oncologist to deliver the dreaded news that the treatments weren't helping and it was time to stop them. Her elderly patient was lying in the bed, watching TV like every other day. She remembered thinking how normal everything seemed, but within a matter of seconds, everything changed. The doctor sat on the edge of the bed and talked to the woman like an old friend rather than with the standard clinical distance.

By the time the doctor finished imparting the unfortunate news, the patient was at peace with the decision they'd agreed upon, while Heather was the emotional wreck. She stood at the foot of the bed and listened to the conversation, admired how well the patient accepted the bad news, and felt her heart break because she knew it wouldn't be long before the cancer ravaged the sweet lady's body. Heather's cries turned into muffled sobs, despite her desperate attempts to remain professional. When she and the doctor left the room, he stopped her in the hall and asked if she needed the sedative he'd prepared for the patient, trying to infuse humor into the situation.

No matter how many times she'd delivered the news since that day, it was always the same. She left the hospital carrying the weight of her patient's burden on her shoulders. Empathy was part of what made her such a good nurse, but it was also part of what brought all the memories flooding back. Along with the debilitating loneliness. The current patient who prompted the memories to resurface hadn't received bad news yet, but Heather couldn't shake the feeling it was coming.

She also couldn't shake the feeling she was being watched. The hairs on the back of her neck stood up at full attention. Anxiety filled her mind and a strong sense of dread filled her chest, squeezing her from the inside like a vise. Despite being tired, she quickened her steps and hurried to the safety of her car. Once she was securely locked inside, her eyes scanned the parking garage for anyone out of the ordinary. She knew just because she didn't see someone didn't mean he wasn't out there.

When she exited from the garage, she purposely turned in the opposite direction from the route she normally took home. She trusted the gut feeling that warned her she was in danger. On one hand, just the thought of it all threatened to shut off her rational mind and fill her with fear. On the other hand, her stubborn, determined side refused to be intimidated by anyone cowardly enough to watch from the shadows. Her drive took an extra hour longer than normal before she reached her house. Fortunately, the numerous stops at various stores, unexpected turns onto side streets, and a couple of double-backs revealed the car that had followed her continuously.

Armed with that knowledge, she was able to evade the person following her and reach the security of her enclosed garage. Once inside, she intentionally left the lights off and watched for approaching headlights through the bow window at the front of her house. When the car lights illuminated the street, she stepped to the side of the window, completely out of sight, and kept her eyes glued to the car as it made its way around the cul-de-sac.

The silhouette of a single occupant was visible from her viewpoint, and it had masculine characteristics. "What do you want, creeper?" she whispered to the darkness around her. "What the hell are you up to?"

The car crawled at a snail's pace back in the direction it had come from originally, before turning to continue the search on the next street over from hers. She was confident her exact location hadn't been discovered; however, she wasn't about to give up the advantage she had over him. Moving through her darkened rooms, she gathered the items she needed and showered in the hall bathroom, where the light wasn't visible from anywhere else.

She thought about driving her second vehicle instead, since he obviously knew her primary car by sight, but decided against it. If he waited in the parking garage again, he could easily spot her walking to it. "I'll park somewhere else instead," she reasoned to herself. "Leave through a different door out of the hospital, move like a ninja, undetected, right to my car. Piece of cake."

With her plan for the next day in place, she crawled into the bed and welcomed the rest that would soon follow. As tired as she was after her long day, the events of the evening had her nerves keyed up and her mind racing. She picked up her cell from the nightstand and called the first number stored in her favorites. When the call rolled to voice mail, Heather listened to the familiar voice with longing before she disconnected.

"I miss you so much," she whispered.

The next morning, Heather left for work earlier than normal, hoping to avoid giving away her exact location by beating her stalker to the punch. In her dark blue Land Rover with blackout windows, she navigated the streets with ease, taking more turns than required while constantly keeping her eyes on the traffic behind her. Rather than parking in the regular parking garage, she pulled into the lot behind the doctors' offices across the street from the hospital.

One of the benefits of working there for the past ten years was she knew every access point to gain entry. Once inside, she worked her way to the oncology floor undetected, using the secure hallways that required employee access codes to enter. But when she actually reached her unit, she knew she'd be vulnerable and completely exposed for her entire twelve-hour shift. With the substantial number of patients under her care, she didn't have time to validate every visitor who appeared on the hall.

"Becca, I need a favor." Heather approached her charge nurse and best friend in the nurses' lounge.

"Sure, hon. You're here awful early this morning. What do you need?"

"I need you to watch for anyone suspicious on the hall today. Anyone hanging around without ever actually visiting someone's room."

"You got it. But what happened? Why are you so spooked?"

"Someone followed me home from here last night. I lost him before I reached my house, but I watched him drive around my neighborhood looking for me."

"I'm alerting security right now. We need someone stationed up here until we figure out what's going on." Becca quickly moved to the desk and called security. She turned back to Heather when she hung up the phone. "Their shift changes when ours does, so they'll send someone up when the new crew gets in. We still have about forty-five minutes before shift change, though."

"Thanks, Becca. I'm going to go ahead and meet with Renee for briefing on what happened with my patients last night. The sooner I can finish the first round of pulling medications, the faster I can get out of the open hall and into my patients' rooms. With the door closed. So no one can see in."

"Don't worry, I know where to find you if I need you," Becca chuckled. "You can only hide from me for so long. If some strange guy shows up looking for you, I'll take care of him. We have plenty of shit around here that'll knock him on his ass."

"I love having you as my best friend. You are the best…and you're a little frightening when you're mad."

~

After he'd lost her the previous night, he drove for hours along every street in the enormous subdivision, determined to find her. He had to give her credit for being one of the few people he'd ever underestimated. The morning's mission was to get her work schedule so he could better track her movements. Tracing her comings and goings was becoming more cumbersome and time-consuming for him. He'd walked the halls of the hospital on more than one occasion, just to confirm she was still in the building. She'd left at different times every day she'd worked, and some days she didn't show up at all.

He was angry with himself because the night before had been the best opportunity he'd had to follow the gorgeous nurse with the short black hair back to her house. His brother, Turan, had been the computer genius, able to find anything with just a few clicks, but computers weren't his forte. Rashad had taken a more conventional preference to learning what their uncle had to teach them. He had perfected his intimidation tactics and all but eradicated any kind of feeling, but it was his proficiency with high-yield explosives that set him apart from the others. He hated to admit the moment of nostalgia that hit him when the memory of his brother snuck up on him. That moment of weakness was dangerous.

Rashad chose a spot in the parking garage and waited for Heather to show up. Cars and trucks rushed by in a mad dash to make it to work on time. When the influx of traffic slowed to a trickle and she still hadn't shown up, he muttered a curse under his breath and jerked his car door open. He moved quickly through the garage to the covered breezeway that connected to the hospital, determined not to be bested by that woman, or any woman, ever again.

Once inside, Rashad walked casually through the hospital as if he didn't have a care in the world. When others smiled or spoke to him, he replied with a feigned warmth to avoid raising any alarms or giving anyone reason to remember him. When he stepped off the elevator on her floor, he moved more carefully so his target didn't see him. Not that he was hiding from her, but when they officially met for the first time, he didn't want a flicker of recognition to light in her eyes.

With the recent shift change, the nurses were extra busy preparing for their first round to check on their patients, giving him ample opportunity to fade into the background. Patients were just waking up, call lights were going off all up and down the hall, and the breakfast trays had just arrived. While everyone scurried from one room to another, Rashad slipped into the nurses' break room to look for any information he could find on her.

One wall had a row of gray metal lockers for the nurses to store their belongings, but they all had combination locks securely fastened. There was no way he could find hers, break in to it, and leave undetected. A computer sat on a desk against the opposite wall with an uncomfortable, plastic chair. He quickly sat and tapped on a couple of keys, and the screen lit up, requesting a secure login ID.

"Damn computers," he muttered under his breath as he rose from the chair. As he walked around the table in the center of the room, the corner of a paper sticking out from under a legal pad caught his eye. He slid the paper out and smiled to himself. "Thank you for leaving me a printed copy of the floor's six-week schedule."

As he folded the paper into quarters, the break room door opened and a nurse stopped dead in her tracks when she saw him. "Can I help you, sir?"

While slipping the paper into his back pocket, he flashed his most charming smile before he replied. "I'm trying to find the break room for the family to use. You know, the one with snack machines, coffee dispenser, and bottled drinks. I'm afraid I may be lost."

"I can show you the way," she offered. "This room is only for the nurses to use."

"Ah, well, that would explain a few things," he replied, pouring on the false charm. "Lead the way."

The nurse turned and led him back to the main corridor. "Take the next hall on the right, and the vending area will be about halfway down on the left. There's a sign hanging from the ceiling just over the doorway."

"Thank you so much for your help," he replied.

"No problem," she answered. "Have a good day."

Rashad made the trek to the break room, taking the opportunity to look around nonchalantly for Heather as he walked. Not seeing her on his initial pass, he waited in the break room and bought a few snack items for appearance's sake before making the return trip. When he turned the corner back into the main hall, the first person he noticed was the security guard at the nurses' station. His first thought was he'd been made, but he released his held breath when the guard leaned over the counter and kissed the nurse.

"I'm headed home now, babe. Have a good day," the guard said. "Love you."

"Drive carefully, honey. I love you. See you tonight," the nurse cooed back.

The guard left without a backward glance, making Rashad feel more secure in his quest. As he strode down the hall, he cut his eyes to each open door, blatantly disregarding the person's privacy as he looked for Heather. When the last door came into view, his pace slowed while he considered his next move.

"I see you found the vending machines," Becca called from behind him.

"Yes, I'm afraid I found a few too many treats," he replied with his charming smile intact.

"Who are you visiting?"

He hesitated for a heartbeat, knowing he couldn't lie about a patient name. "A family friend. I'm just giving them some privacy for a few minutes."

"What's the name? I'll check to see how long it'll be before you can go in."

As luck would have it, a nurse exited from a room a few doors down just as she asked for the name. "Looks like I'm good to go in now," he inclined his head toward the open door. "Thank you for the offer, though."

She smiled and nodded her head, but he recognized the suspicion in her eyes. She wasn't moving on to continue doing her job. She was waiting him out, testing him, and calling his bluff. He had no choice but to walk into the room and at least try to stay long enough to make her believe he was actually visiting a patient. He only hoped in doing so, Heather would finally make an appearance.

Rashad walked into the room apprehensively and watched the lady lying in the bed. She appeared to be in her later sixties and was obviously once very beautiful. But the pallor of her skin expressed the severity of her condition. He took a seat in the chair beside her bed and watched her sleep for several minutes, keeping up his ruse. When she stirred and opened her eyes, she started at seeing him in her room.

"Who the hell are you?"

"I'm Greg. Would you care for a snack today?" He lied, trying to use her confusion to his advantage.

"No, I don't want anything. I'm too sick to eat."

"Okay, I'll let you get some rest and check back with you later today." He rose, snacks in hand, and left the hospital by taking the same route he'd followed in. The suspicious nurse was back at the nurses' station as he passed, but she was too busy to notice him walking out.

CHAPTER TWO

June 2001

Braxton tried to sleep with the rhythmic rocking of the bus as it continued eastward, but it was no use even to try. He could've taken the option to fly to the South Carolina base for his basic training, but he wasn't required to be there for several more days. He decided to take his time on the trip and hopefully clear his head before the intensive two-month training program began.

He would be several hours into the fifteen-hour trip before Heather woke and found his letter. She would have no way to contact him and no indication of where he was headed. He'd planned it that way intentionally so she would be forced to move on with her life. Even at eighteen, he knew when she looked at him, all she saw was a constant reminder of the worst day of their lives. After all their years spent side by side, it killed him when he saw the regret in her eyes that left no doubt in his mind she wished she'd never fallen in love with him.

He had to face the fact he had become no more than an expensive growing pain, a lesson that life had to teach them, but they were both stubborn and had to learn the hard way. For the sake of her sanity and her happiness, he had to be the one to leave. That took all the strength, drive, and courage he could muster. She'd have to be the one to file for a divorce, though. That's where he drew the line. Regardless of what the future held for him, another marriage was nowhere in the cards.

She would be his one and only love until he died.

"Where are you headed?" the older man across the aisle asked aloud.

Braxton cut his eyes toward the man to see to whom he was speaking. Most everyone on the bus was asleep since it was still dark outside. When their eyes met, the man smiled at him and waited for a reply.

"Army basic training in South Carolina. You?"

"Visiting my daughter and her family in Georgia. My son-in-law is in the Army and stationed there," the man replied. "Name's Larry, by the way."

"Braxton," he replied and accepted the offer to shake hands. "Good to meet you."

"Good to meet you, son. You're awful young to join the Army, aren't you?"

"I'm eighteen. Legal to sign my name on the dotted line and give away the next four years of my life to them."

"So you're not making it a career?"

"I haven't thought that far ahead yet," Braxton admitted. A career in the Army may not be such a bad idea. Travel the world. Associate with the best men and women, serve his country, and leave Texas behind him for as long as possible.

"What does your wife think about that?" Larry asked.

The corners of Braxton's eyes squeezed together, and his head slightly tilted in question. "What?"

Larry pointed at Braxton's left hand where his wedding ring was still prominently displayed. "You're married, right?"

"For now," he shrugged. "It didn't work out. She made a mistake marrying me."

"Marriage is hard, there's no doubt about that. My wife and I married young, too. Everyone told us not to, said we should wait until we were older. But we were headstrong, and we knew better than they did," Larry laughed in reply. His gaze drifted to another time and place as his mind's eye relived the events of the past. "After the first month of living together, we were both ready to call it quits.

"But we stuck it out. You see, we had too many people to prove wrong. More than that, we meant it when we said those vows. For better or for worse is what we've lived by all these years. Don't give up on her just yet, son. There may still be hope."

Braxton's only reply was a lopsided smile that didn't reach his eyes. There was no point in telling the man that all hope was lost and had been dead for months. Three months, to be exact. Three months since he failed Heather in a way she could never forgive him, and he could never forgive himself. In a way he knew he didn't deserve forgiveness.

"It's none of my business, and I'm just a nosy old man, I know," Larry said warmly. "But I know the look of a tormented young man. I saw it too many times in my own mirror when I wasn't much older than you are now. You'll come out of basic training a different man, Braxton. You'll be harder, more focused, and more disciplined. Use that discipline to help your marriage, son. Not hurt it."

"I will," Braxton promised. Though he didn't elaborate on how. The only way he could help his marriage was to be disciplined enough to give Heather a real chance at happiness, far away from him. "There's nothing I wouldn't do for her."

"Then you're a good man, Braxton," Larry replied. "Never forget that."

Larry settled into his seat and was asleep within minutes. His words played over and over in Braxton's mind. More times than he could count, he considered telling the bus driver to stop and let him off. He'd find a way back home on his own. He'd find a way to work things out, regardless of what had happened. But every time he started to rise from his seat, the weight of his failure held him down. With a heavy heart, Braxton closed his eyes and let sleep overtake him.

The bus shuddered to a halt, waking Braxton from the most sleep he'd had at one time in the last several months. "We'll take a thirty-minute break here, folks. Grab a bite to eat, stretch your legs, and be back on the bus at half past the hour."

Braxton's eyes surveyed the area after he exited the bus, trying to determine where they were and how much longer they had to go. The roadside diner had obviously been built first from the age of it. The truck stop next door was newer, bigger, and had a full range of facilities to cater to truck drivers. He felt someone move up beside him and knew who it was without looking.

"Want to grab a chicken sandwich and fries at four in the morning?" Larry asked with a chuckle.

"Sounds like the ultimate breakfast to me," he joked in return. "Maybe we can have apple pie for dessert. Breakfast dessert."

"That's the spirit."

The two men walked together into the diner and sat in a booth along the front windows. After the waitress took their orders, an uncomfortable silence crept into the booth, and Larry fidgeted nervously. Braxton sensed the older man wanted to resume their earlier conversation but wasn't sure how to broach it.

"It's a long, sad story." Braxton decided to save Larry the hassle. "We started out as best friends when we were kids. We finally became an official couple when we started high school. A lot of things went wrong. I'm not getting into all of the nitty-gritty details right now, though.

"In a nutshell, every day of my life that I can actually remember, I've loved her in one way or another. We were neighbors for a long time, but then her dad got one promotion after another at work. With his newfound wealth, he bought a bigger, nicer house in a ritzier neighborhood. Suddenly, I wasn't good enough for his daughter anymore.

"That didn't stop her, though. She loved me, so we stayed together despite his protests and threats and bellowing." Braxton paused and stared at a droplet of water as it slid down his glass. "As soon as we were old enough and didn't need anyone's permission, we got married. We had a go at it for a little while, tried to make it work. This is where I leave out the private details, but it all boils down to the fact that she's estranged from her entire family because of me. Especially her dad. He won't have anything to do with her as long as I'm still around.

"The stress of everything is killing her. She's torn between being with me and being with her family. I just can't stand by and watch the beautiful woman I love wither away to nothing. So, I left and made it easier for her to move on with her life."

"Did you ask her if that's what she wanted?"

The waitress returned with their orders, momentarily saving Braxton from answering what should've been an easy question. When the waitress left, Larry took a bite of his sandwich and waited for Braxton to answer.

In between bites of his food, Braxton continued recounting his story. "She's not the kind of person who would say she wanted me to leave. She can't stand hurting anyone else, so she'd take all the pain just to avoid inflicting any on someone else. Her dad or her mom called every day, pressuring her to come home, keeping her on the phone for hours at a time. She became more and more withdrawn from me. Selfishly, I hung around longer than I should have, but I just couldn't let her suffer anymore."

"Did you file for a divorce before you left?"

Braxton shook his head from side to side. "No. I won't be the one to do that."

"You really do love her, don't you?"

"It's always been her. It'll always be her."

"You know, other guys your age don't think like that."

"Those guys haven't met Heather."

Larry leaned back and studied Braxton, taking in his words and his overall demeanor. Braxton felt the appraising gaze, knew he was being sized up and measured, but he didn't care. The talk with Larry brought all the memories flooding back, tormenting him with mental pictures of the best and worst times of his life. His guts churned, the chicken sandwich and fries turned to lead in his stomach, and he had to work to swallow past the ball of emotions stuck in his throat.

"For the record, I think you're making a big mistake by leaving like this. She sounds like a great girl."

"She's the best."

"Girls like her aren't that common. Love like you just described comes once in a lifetime, if you're lucky. You won't find another one like her, Braxton."

He looked up and met Larry's gaze directly. "I know I won't. And I won't be looking for another one either. Especially not after all I've been through."

The waitress appeared with their checks. Larry picked up both at the same time and insisted on paying. "It's the least I can do for a young man who'll be serving our country. My trip ends at our next stop, so this is the last chance I'll have to do it."

"It's not necessary, but I appreciate it. Thank you."

"Take care of yourself, Braxton. I hope everything works out for you."

At the next stop, Braxton felt a deep loneliness when he said goodbye to Larry. The older man had been the first friend he'd really talked to about his predicament. He'd talked to his father often, but familial bias tainted their discussions. His friends were his age and didn't understand any of what he'd already experienced. Larry was the first person who wasn't related, wasn't too young, and didn't have any preconceived notions about their relationship. He listened, he grasped the depth of their love, and he offered advice without being condescending.

The ride from Georgia to South Carolina was both the longest and shortest of his life. He'd watched the sun rise and visualized Heather still asleep in their bed. He longed to be there with her, to hold her while she slept, to kiss her when she woke. As the bus pulled up to the station, he wondered how much longer it would be before she found his letter. Would she move out of their apartment right away, back in with her parents? Or would she wait a while to see if he came back?

"The truth is it doesn't matter what happens. Our courses are set now. In two days, I have to report to the base for basic training," he muttered to himself. He hailed a cab to take him to a hotel close to the base. After checking in and stowing his stuff, he set out on foot to take in the sights and spend the rest of his free time alone until the very last second. The two days passed by much too quickly, and it was time to check out of the hotel.

Before leaving his room, he called his mom to talk to her one last time before basic training started and all communication was cut off.

"Hello?"

"Hey, Mom." His tone was deflated, like his heart. "I'm about to leave the hotel. Just wanted to say I love you. I'll let you know when graduation is in case you and Dad can make it."

"Of course we'll be there, Brax. I love you, too, son. And I'm so worried about you."

"I'll be okay, Mom. Don't worry."

She paused for a heartbeat before replying. "Heather called this morning. She's worried to death about you, Braxton."

"Did you tell her where I am?"

"No, I didn't. You asked me not to, but you know I don't agree with how you're handling this."

"It's for the best, Mom. I have to go. Tell Dad I love him. I love you. I'll call you as soon as I can."

"Your father and I are so proud of you, Braxton. I want you to know that. We love you more than life itself."

~

August 2001

"Where did my little boy go?" Braxton's mother, Jackie, asked as she grasped her son's face in her palms.

"He left as a boy, and two months later, the Army gives us a man," his father, Bryan, beamed. "He even had a birthday while he was in basic training."

"You look so handsome in that uniform," Jackie commented through her tears. The pride and admiration she had for her son shone in her eyes and resonated in her voice.

Braxton scanned the crowd milling around the soldiers who had just graduated from basic training, searching for another familiar face he'd hoped to see. Without asking, Bryan knew exactly who his son was looking for.

"She's not here, son." Bryan placed his hand on Braxton's shoulder and squeezed to show his support. "She said..." He paused to consider his next words before he continued.

"You talked to her? What did she say?"

"She said you left her, so you know where to find her if you want to see her," Bryan replied, his face contorted with sympathy.

"She hasn't filed for a divorce?" Braxton couldn't keep the surprise from his tone. He was certain she would've filed within the first week of his absence.

"Not that we know of, Brax. She hasn't told us if she has."

"How is she?" There were a million and one questions he wanted to grill his parents with to find out every single detail about Heather. What had she been doing? Who was she talking to? Had she moved back in with her parents? Did she ask about him? Did she miss him? Did she still love him? Asking about how she was doing left the question open for interpretation, so they could share any information they thought was important.

"She's had a really rough time, son. She seemed to be doing a little better before we left to come here," Bryan replied.

"Maybe you should go talk to her, Brax. Sit down and do it face-to-face," Jackie suggested. "I think you both need that time together."

"I'm not sure I can," Braxton sighed. "I only have a couple of days to get to Arizona for AIT."

"AIT?" Jackie asked.

"Advanced Individual Training. It's training for my assigned job with the Army."

"How long will you be there?" Jackie's face fell with his reply.

"I'll be away for about six months total for AIT and jump school."

"Jump school? What is jump school?" Jackie demanded.

"Airborne School, Mom. I'm going to learn how to jump out of airplanes, control my parachute to land on specific targets, and use these skills in combat."

"I don't even want to think about that. Don't tell me anything else." Jackie shook her head from side to side, making Braxton chuckle at her discomfort.

"I'm tougher than you think, Mom."

With the graduation ceremony events completed, Braxton was able to spend what little free time he had with his parents before his more extensive training program began. While they talked, ate, and toured the grounds, his mother's words urging him to see Heather in person rang in his ears. His date to report to the training base in Arizona was nonnegotiable with the Army. But with a little extra effort, he'd already managed to get a connecting flight with an extra-long layover through the Houston airport.

The urge to see her, talk to her, be with her had been too strong for too long. He knew what he had to do the instant he was instructed to make his travel arrangements. There was no way he was flying across the country without stopping in Texas to see her again. Leaving her had been pure torture. He didn't know if seeing her again would make him feel better or worse. He only knew it had to be done.

At the end of their day together, he hugged his parents as they said goodbye, told them he loved them, and made his final preparations for leaving the base that had been his home for the previous nine weeks. The new base would be his home for the next eighteen weeks before he'd make the trek back across the country to attend the three-week jump school. He hadn't had the heart to tell his mother he'd decided to make a career of his time in the Army, and that the training he had in mind for the future would keep him away from home more and more.

Finally, the time had come to face the anguish he'd been running from for far too long. He walked out of the Houston airport with his duffle bag slung over his shoulder and hailed a taxi. They drove in complete silence to the apartment he shared with Heather. It amazed him how everything could look the same and simultaneously be completely different. The tiny little space that was barely big enough for them to turn around without bumping into each other held so many wonderful memories—and far too much pain.

He climbed the stairs, delaying the inevitable by only a couple of minutes, and stopped in front of their door. Part of him hoped she'd changed the locks, that his key wouldn't work, and he could at least say he tried as he walked away.

But he had no such luck.

His key slid into the lock without a hitch. He turned it, and the doorknob twisted with ease. He pushed the door open but stayed planted in the threshold. He felt like an intruder breaking in to someone else's house, not a husband returning home to his wife after an extended leave.

His feet moved on their own into the place he'd called home just a short eight weeks before. His legs carried him into the apartment where the sights, scents, and belongings only served to intensify the pain in his chest. He dropped his duffel bag on the floor and robotically moved through the rooms, noting what had and hadn't changed. Her clothes still hung in the tiny closet. Her makeup and toiletries still cluttered the minuscule bathroom counter.

The pictures of the two of them throughout their lives were still everywhere. According to the story the pictures told, they were more than happy together. Images of them smiling, laughing, and kissing said they couldn't get enough of each other. Their wedding picture said they belonged to each other for all time.

He walked into the kitchen and began searching for paper and a pen to write her a letter. In the event she didn't come home before he had to get back to the airport, he planned to leave her a note asking her to contact him. Telling her how monumentally he'd fucked up. Laying his feelings out on the table, without holding anything back, without regard to his vulnerability.

He wanted her back, and he could no longer deny it.

Rifling through the stack of mail and papers on the counter as he searched for a blank sheet, his eyes landed on a set of documents that made everything else fade to black around him. The black hole they created drew all of the air out of the room, leaving his chest burning as his lungs demanded oxygen. All sound instantly disappeared, replaced by the sound of his pulse beating on drums in his ears. His capacity to rationalize and reason like any other sane person dissolved, leaving only instability in its place.

Name of person filing for divorce (Petitioner): Heather Reed
Your spouse's name (Respondent): Braxton Reed
PETITION FOR DIVORCE

CHAPTER THREE

February, Present Day

In a deep sleep, Sara rolled over and snuggled against her husband, her front to his back. The contact instantly startled her awake and filled her with so much fear that she sat up and called his name out in the dark.

"Steve! Honey, what's wrong?"

She reached over to turn on the lamp beside the bed and gasped when she saw him in the light. His skin was so pale it was almost translucent, his arms were drawn up close to his chest, and his entire body appeared to be in convulsions. Had she not felt the heat radiating from his every pore, she would've thought he was having a seizure from the severity of his shivers. She placed her hand on his forehead and immediately knew she needed to call for an ambulance.

As she flew out of the bed, she grabbed the cordless phone on the nightstand and dialed 911. When the line connected to the dispatcher, she immediately began rambling information and demands.

"We're in room 1345 at Sterling Luxury Resort on Broad Street. My husband has colon cancer and is undergoing experimental chemotherapy. His fever has spiked, he's shaking uncontrollably, and he's very pale. I need an ambulance here right away to take him to the emergency room."

After she answered a few basic questions about Steve, the dispatcher assured her the ambulance was on the way. She called the front desk and alerted them to the situation before she helped Steve into a jacket, socks, and shoes. February temperatures in Houston were mild, but his high fever made

Steve feel like his body was freezing. In his condition, the chill of the evening air could cause his fever to go up even more.

Once they had him loaded onto the gurney, the paramedics wheeled him out of the luxurious hotel and into the back of the ambulance. Sara rushed to their car to meet them at the emergency room. At one point, she reached for her cell to inform Noah, Chaise, and Silas, but a quick glance at the clock stopped her. Eight minutes after three o'clock in the morning in Houston would be just after four o'clock in Miami, way too early to wake her kids until she knew more about the severity of his condition.

She racked her brain trying to remember all the side effects Dr. Stanton had warned them about, especially which ones were potentially life-threatening. Erring on the side of caution, she decided to call the answering service to at least report that Steve was en route to the hospital.

"Can I put you on hold for just a minute, Mrs. Steele? Dr. Stanton prefers to talk to his patients and their families directly," the young lady with the answering service explained.

"Of course. Thank you," Sara replied, relieved she could talk to someone—anyone—at that moment.

After a couple of minutes, the hold music abruptly quit, and a slightly groggy male voice filled the line. "This is Daryl Stanton. What's going on with Steve?"

"He was so warm and shivering so hard, he woke me up from a dead sleep. He's hot to the touch, but he's just so pale. I didn't even take his temperature before I called 911 because just seeing him in that condition rattled me so badly. I can't think straight right now, Dr. Stanton, so I can't remember when you said to get immediate help. But he scared me bad enough that I would've made him go to the hospital regardless," Sara rambled.

"You did the right thing. It's not uncommon for people to have a high fever while on chemo. It effectively destroys your immune system, so even a common cold can turn ugly very quickly. We'll do some bloodwork to rule out a systemic infection, but this could very well be a side effect of his treatment. Either way, we can make him more comfortable and get his temperature down to a safe level. I'll meet you both in the ER."

"Thank you," Sara breathed her reply, the gratitude thick in her voice.

When she was finally by Steve's side again, he was resting in a darkened exam room. The bandage on his hand made her heart rate quicken because she realized the IV had been placed in his forearm. She'd seen that happen before when he was too dehydrated for the medical personnel to hit the vein closer to his wrist. She refused to listen to the inner voice that tried to issue a dire warning concerning the sudden onset of his symptoms. She couldn't even entertain the thought of Steve succumbing to the devastating disease.

"Hi, Sara," Daryl called softly from the doorway. "I've already ordered a complete blood count, and the preliminary results should be back from the lab within in the hour. Once I get that report, I should have a better idea of what's going on. Until then, we're hydrating him, and we've started him on medication to bring his fever down. It was quite a bit higher than we like to see in chemotherapy patients, so I'm sure he was feeling pretty rough."

"It was so sudden, Dr. Stanton. He didn't say anything about feeling bad last night. But then, he still likes to think he's invincible."

"That's because I'm made of Steele," Steve mumbled his witty retort but managed to give Sara a half smile.

"Did you know you were getting sick when we went to bed last night?" Sara asked.

"I wasn't sick like this, but I did feel a little off. I didn't realize it would progress to be this bad, though. Now I know what to watch for so I can stop it before it gets too far gone."

"Absolutely," Daryl agreed. "Every symptom won't be a classic, textbook example. We'll do the best we can to manage them so you're not too miserable. I'll be back when the lab results are ready, but plan on staying for at least a day or two. You should both try to get some rest now."

Steve patted the bed beside him, so Sara crawled in and rested her cheek in the crook of his shoulder. With their arms wrapped around each other, they slept until Daryl returned with the results of his blood count. The grim expression he wore did nothing to calm Sara's fears.

"Your white blood cell count is significantly low, Steve. We're going to keep you, start you on a broad-spectrum antibiotic to help your body fight off any infection, and monitor your counts to make sure we start seeing some improvements. From the date of your last chemo round, this isn't entirely unusual, but we may need to help kick-start your bone marrow so it produces more white blood cells."

"How long will I be here this time?"

"You know the rules, Steve. We take it one day at a time," Daryl replied. "Let us finish this paperwork, and we'll get you moved to a more comfortable room."

"Sara," Steve called her name softly when Daryl had left the room. "We'll eventually have to talk about it."

"Not now, we don't. You're not giving up over this...this... It's not even a setback. It's no more than an inconvenience. If you were healthy and caught the flu, you wouldn't throw your hands up in surrender."

He knew her anger and dogged determination masked her fear of what their future may hold. He wanted to assure her he'd be fine. He wanted to soothe her frayed nerves and promise he'd kick cancer's ass. For her, he wanted to be invincible and live forever. But he couldn't promise her any of those things. Instead, he just held her close to his heart and kissed the top of her head.

When he'd been quiet for too long, she prodded him again. "Steve, promise me you're not giving up."

"I'm not giving up, babe," he whispered.

Before he drifted off to sleep again, he felt the warmth of her tears soak through his thin hospital gown.

~

"How's my favorite patient in the world today?" Heather asked as she entered Steve's room. "Even though I've missed you, it's really not necessary for you to keep pretending to be sick just to come see me."

"But I have to keep you guessing. You never know when I'll be here and when I won't," Steve joked.

"Well, to be honest, I'd much rather you show up with some food! Breakfast, lunch, snacks—it doesn't matter what it is." Heather laughed as she took a seat next to his bed.

Sara sat on the other side and watched as the two of them playfully picked on each other. With all the time they had spent in and around the oncology floor, they'd formed a special bond with Heather because of the way she cared so deeply for others. Her warm personality was genuine, but they'd also witnessed her stubborn, take-charge side. She was an advocate for her patients as much as she was their cheerleader. She'd bravely correct an intern for giving incorrect information just as she'd forcefully demand that her patient had to keep fighting until she gave them permission to give up.

Sara had also witnessed Heather handle that very painful situation with finesse and grace. A woman held on to life with every ounce of willpower she possessed while she waited for her son to arrive at her side. The lady was obviously suffering, painfully struggling to hold on until she'd heard that last goodbye from her loved one. Though her son was on his way, his trip would take too much time, and Heather realized there was no way her patient would be able to rest in peace under those circumstances.

Heather leaned in close to the lady, kept her voice low, and spoke soothingly to her.

"You carried him for nine months. Fed him, nurtured him, cared for him, loved him. Jordan knows how much you love him, sweetheart. I'll tell him how hard you fought to have him close to you just one more time. I'll tell him how much you love him. You don't have to suffer anymore. You can let go now."

Sara watched from the hallway, mesmerized by how the woman responded to Heather's words. Her labored breathing became calmer. Her clenched fists relaxed. Her face, distorted with pain, became peaceful. Then she did exactly as Heather instructed and let go. And Sara's heart broke as she watched Heather sob uncontrollably when it was all over.

The playful banter between Steve and Heather pulled Sara from her inner thoughts. Steve already seemed so much better than he was just a few hours before. As long as Heather instructed Steve to fight, Sara held on to the hope that he would be completely healed of cancer.

"I'm going to step out in the hall and call Noah. Do you need anything, Steve?"

"No, babe. I'm fine. Tell all of our kids I love them."

Sara closed the door behind her and drew in a deep breath. The daily roller coaster rides of emotions drained her mentally and physically. She knew if it affected her that much, the impact on Steve had to be so much worse. If she was considered selfish because she wanted her husband to live, and willed him to keep going regardless of how tired he was, then she'd wear the label with pride.

At the end of the hall, she pulled her cell out of her pocket and dialed Noah's number. When he picked up, she decided it was time for her to be blunt about Steve's health status. Playing down the symptoms wouldn't make them go away.

"Hey, Mom. You're calling earlier than usual. Are you and Dad all right?"

"Hi, Noah. I thought you'd want to know your dad was admitted to the hospital early this morning. He's feeling a little better now, but he had a high fever in the middle of the night. With his low white blood cell count, they're keeping him here for IV antibiotics and to monitor his counts for the next few days.

"They've, uh, had to temporarily stop his chemotherapy so his bone marrow can make more white blood cells. It's a fine line to balance the need to kill the cancer cells but not kill his immune system entirely. We'll know more in a couple of days...if he can continue in the trial, with the experimental drugs."

"There's a chance they'll drop him from the clinical trial?"

"If he can't finish the program, yes. If it's weakening his body to the point his bone marrow isn't producing blood cells, there's really no reason to continue the chemotherapy. We're not there yet, and we're not giving up hope, but I can't let you, Chaise, and Silas be blindsided by it if it does happen."

"Mom, is he worse than you're telling me?"

"He's had some ups and downs lately. Nothing in particular that any other man going through chemotherapy doesn't have. It just seems to be hitting him harder, more things at once."

"How are you, Mom? Are you eating, sleeping, taking care of yourself? I wish you'd told me sooner. We would've been there with you."

"No, son. Brianna just had a baby last month. I know you've been busy with work. You have a life and a family of your own to take care of, and that doesn't include babysitting your mother."

"It's hardly babysitting, Mom. You don't have to do this alone. Chaise and Bull could've been there with you until Brianna was able to travel. Silas could've been there. We'd work it out. How do you think that makes me feel, knowing you've been carrying this weight on your shoulders alone all this time?"

Tears escaped from Sara's eyes and rolled down her cheeks. "You're such a wonderful son—and a great man. You're all welcome to come stay here with me anytime you want to. But I understand if you can't, so I don't want you to feel obligated."

"Love is never an obligation, Mom. It's a privilege."

~

In Steve's room, Heather continued her medical assessment of Steve. The clever banter and quick comebacks demonstrated to her that his mental faculties were intact. He was alert to people, time, and place—meaning he could match faces with names, he knew what time of day and year it was, and he knew where he was. His speech was clear and concise, no audible sign of slurring his words or exaggerated forgetfulness.

The main discrepancy that concerned her was the color of his skin had significantly changed since she last saw him. That could be chalked up to a byproduct of the chemotherapy, but it was significant enough to be noted in his chart. The optimist in her hoped it was simply a side effect of the nearly lethal cocktail he'd been given to stop the progression of his disease. The realist in her told her nothing good came from kidding herself.

This was the part of her job she hated, when she had to face the fact one of her patients may no longer be responding to treatment. The time when they had to have "the talk." The one where she helped the doctor convince the patient to stop focusing on the future and start focusing on the present. The discussion that inevitably left the patient with thoughts and feelings of hopelessness, because the message they delivered essentially said to give up hope that the treatments could change the prognosis.

While Steve still joked and played along with her, she sensed a distinct change in his overall demeanor. A peaceful acceptance of what will be will be, regardless if he tried to alter the course or not, had replaced the tough as nails, hard as Steele man she'd met initially. He was no longer fixated on eradicating all the mutated cells in his body. His focus was on his family, mainly his wife, who'd been by his side every step of the way.

Steve often joked that he was made of Steele, an obvious play on his last name, but when Sara was out of earshot, he openly confessed she was actually the strong one who made him keep going. Keep trying. Keep fighting. The last time he'd said those words to Heather, her initial gut reaction was Steve was preparing to face the end of his life. He kept trying, kept fighting, kept going for Sara, but when it was clear it was no longer helping, he could accept his fate as long as she held his hand.

"Who did Sara say she was going to call?" Heather asked Steve to test his cognitive skills again and to clear the morbid thoughts from her own mind.

"Our son, Noah," Steve replied proudly.

Heather stopped writing and jerked her eyes up to meet Steve's. "Your son is Noah Steele?"

"Yep, that's my boy."

"Noah Steele from Miami?"

"Born and raised."

"Noah Steele of Steele Security?"

"That's exactly right. Wait. How did you know that? How do you know Noah?"

CHAPTER FOUR

September 2001

Heather walked into her parents' house, located in one of Houston's more upscale neighborhoods, and headed to the kitchen where she knew she'd find her mom. The house itself was gorgeous, set on just over an acre of lush green grass, professionally landscaped sweeping gardens, and a backyard pool oasis that boasted an outdoor kitchen. Inside, every room was decorated by an interior designer who stayed booked up to a year in advance. The fine dark wood trim accented both the expansive arched windows that spanned the front of the house and the wood flooring with alternating planks of light and dark shades. Everything about the inside and outside of the house exuded opulence, but it reminded Heather of a museum more than a home.

Her childhood home where she grew up next door to Braxton would almost completely fit inside the entertainment room of their current house. Their old home may have been small, but there was so much love and so many wonderful memories in it. It was pure coincidence that most of those beloved and cherished childhood memories in the other house involved Braxton in one way or another.

Kay Greer wrapped her arms around Heather and squeezed her tightly. "How's my baby? I'm so glad you're here."

"I'm fine, Mom," Heather replied, although she was actually anything but fine. Depressed. Sad. Lonely. Despondent. Those were more accurate descriptions than "fine," but that wasn't a conversation she wanted to have again that day.

"You're so thin. You've lost more weight, Heather," Kay insisted, her tone rife with genuine concern. "You're not eating, are you?"

"I said I'm fine, Mom. That means I'm fine," Heather insisted stubbornly. "Don't start. I just got here."

Emmett silently stood in the doorway through which Heather had entered, intentionally not announcing his presence so he could listen to their exchange. "Your mother's right. You've lost weight. Sit down and eat."

Heather turned her head to look at him over her shoulder. "Don't think I didn't know you were back there eavesdropping. I'm not one of your employees you can just order around. I may be your daughter, but I'm also a grown woman. I'm married. And I make my own decisions."

"Eighteen is hardly a grown woman, Heather. You're not even old enough to buy alcohol yet. But you're definitely my daughter—there's no denying you got that stubborn, defiant streak from me. Speaking of being married, did you get the papers I had my lawyer draw up?" While he meant well as a father and a businessman, Emmett had a tendency to run over everyone else's thoughts and feelings.

"Yeah, I got them all right." She made no attempt to conceal her contempt or the challenge that her arched eyebrow conveyed.

"Did you sign them?"

"Nope."

"Heather."

"Emmett," she retorted, mimicking his stance by putting her fists on her hips and staring him down.

"What did you do with the papers?" His voice was even, showing no signs of his frustration. But she knew all too well that was just part of his tactic, an act to encourage others to lower their defenses so he could pounce at the opportune moment.

"I put them on my kitchen counter," she replied.

"Good."

"With the rest of the junk mail that needs to be shredded," she added.

"That's not funny." He was beginning to lose his composure. Tiny cracks in his armored façade were beginning to show.

"It wasn't funny when I opened the packet and saw divorce papers, either," she snapped. "No warning. No heads-up. You could've said, 'Hey, Heather, my lawyer is sending some papers for you to read over. Let me know what you think.' But no, you didn't even give me that common courtesy. I thought they were from Braxton when I first opened it. Do you have any idea what that did to me? Don't you think I've been through enough already?"

"Baby, I'm sorry. I didn't even think—"

"No, that's a lie, so don't even finish that sentence. You thought about it enough to have your damn lawyer write up a very detailed, explicit legal document that divides everything between us, right down to the couch and the loveseat. You try to control everyone and everything in your life, but I will not be controlled. Do you understand me? You will not steamroll over me and my decisions for my life."

"What are you going to do, then?"

Exasperated that he would even ask that question after the outburst he just experienced, her jaw dropped open, and she blatantly glowered at him. "Whatever the hell I want to do. That's what. I don't need your permission or your approval. Or even your support. But if you want to stay in my life, let me live it myself. You're not living it through me."

"I can't talk to her," Emmett complained to Kay. "There's no reasoning with her."

"You're exactly right," Heather replied. Emmett raised his eyes to meet hers, hopeful she had seen the error of her thinking, until she continued. "So stop trying because it's really irritating when I have to keep repeating myself."

"You're still young, Heather. It'll be good for you to start over with a clean slate," Emmett pressured. "You need to trust me."

"A clean slate?" She emphasized each word as she spat out her reply. With her pointed finger in his face, she continued. "Since you're my father, I'm giving you one chance to rephrase that and then never say it again. Because if you ever even tiptoe around the words 'clean slate' to me again, as if I should just *forget*, I promise you will regret it."

"That came out wrong, Heather. Of course, I didn't mean it like that. I'm sorry. The last thing I'd ever want to do is hurt you."

"Don't you see? That's exactly what you're doing every time you want to sweep everything under the rug and pretend it never happened. It did happen —and it happened to me. Stop trying to make it seem insignificant, like a few sheets of legal paper will make it all disappear."

"I'm just trying to do what I think is best," Emmett replied softly, humbled. "I said I'm sorry, and I mean it. Forgive me. Your mother and I were just about to throw some steaks on the grill. Do you want to stay and eat with us?"

"No, I need to go. Errands to run. I just wanted to stop by for a minute to see you."

"There's no need to run off. I promise to be on my best behavior if you stay," Emmett pleaded. "I don't get to see you nearly enough."

His eyes begged her to stay. His own pain at not being able to shield his daughter from the cruel world lay just beneath the surface.

"Okay. I'll stay for a little while longer," she conceded, though she was still mad and upset with him.

"That what I want to hear. I'll go fire up the grill and burn some steaks while you ladies handle the fixings."

Heather and Kay started pulling items from the pantry and refrigerator to begin cooking the side dishes. As they worked together to accomplish the tasks, Heather instinctively knew her mother wanted to continue the conversation, but she didn't know how to approach it without alienating her daughter.

"Just come out with it already. If you keep holding it in, you'll end up in the bell tower with a high-powered rifle," Heather deadpanned.

"I didn't know your father had our lawyer draw up divorce papers, Heather. Not until you'd already received them, and it was way too late by then. I've already told him what I thought about it, but you know how he is once he gets something in his head.

"My concern is about you and your well-being. What are you going to do, Heather? Braxton has been gone for going on three months now. How long do you plan to wait for him?"

"I'm fully aware he's been gone for eleven weeks and three days. That's exactly eighty days. One thousand nine hundred twenty hours. One hundred fifteen thousand two hundred minutes, give or take, since I don't know exactly what time he left. I only know what time I found the note.

"What you and Dad don't seem to grasp is this isn't puppy love. What I feel for Braxton isn't just young love that'll fade as I get older and realize it was just infatuation. He's been my best friend for as long as I can remember. We know each other better than anyone else does. Every dirty, rotten secret we've kept from everyone else. Every good deed we did without letting anyone else know. Our imperfections and perfections only made our bond stronger. If you and Dad had faced what Braxton and I have faced, could you simply walk away from him as easily as you expect me to walk away from my husband?"

"You're right. We've underestimated how much he means to you and how being in love at your age can be just as real as being in love at my age. Your love for him really hasn't waned in the least bit, has it?"

"No, and it won't. We're both dealing with the aftermath the best way we know how. I'm partly to blame for why he left the way he did. Not that it doesn't hurt like hell, but I have to be fair about it. Sure, there are times when I get really mad at him for leaving me. I scream, cry, make stupid threats I know I'd never go through with, try to strike a bargain with God. Then I remember how I mentally checked out for a while and left him feeling responsible," Heather explained.

"You stayed away from your dad and me for a long time," Kay said sadly. "Your dad thought maybe you came back around us after Braxton left because you'd changed your mind about being married."

"I stayed away because neither of you respected my marriage, especially Dad. I didn't come back around because Braxton left. It was because I knew how badly it was hurting you."

Kay glanced out the window and saw Emmett was busy in the outdoor kitchen, fighting with the grill and marinating the steaks with his signature mixture of steak sauces and spices. "While the potatoes and rolls are cooking, let's sit down and have a little girl talk."

As they sat at the kitchen table, Kay deliberated how to share the personal information from her youth with her daughter. "I know you've loved Braxton since you were kids, but it doesn't happen like that for most people. When I was a sophomore in high school, a handsome boy my age moved in to our neighborhood and, of course, every girl in our class had a crush on him. Including me.

"When he asked me out, I was ecstatic. Out of his pick of all the girls, he chose me. We went on several dates before he asked me to officially be his girlfriend. We were perfect for each other—we were interested in similar things, we had plans to go to the same college, our families became friends. I was so in love with him I didn't feel like I could breathe without him.

"Our senior year, we debated about going to the prom. I wanted to go because it was the last one we'd ever have. He didn't want to go because our junior prom wasn't any fun at all. But because I wanted to go, and he loved me, he gave in.

"I was so excited. It was a night to dress up in a formal gown, go out to eat, dance in the arms of the love of my life, and at least pretend to be adults. Mom took me to get my hair, makeup, and nails done. My dress and shoes were a perfect fit. Dad had the camera out, ready to take more pictures than we could ever use. All the things that seemed so important at the time were working out perfectly.

"While we waited for him, Dad took several individual pictures of me. He had me doing so many poses in so many different places around the house and the yard, I didn't realize how much time had passed. When I saw the time on the clock, I knew something was wrong. Chris knew how important that night was to me, he wouldn't have intentionally made us miss our dinner reservation time.

"Mom called his house, and Chris's aunt answered, crying hysterically. Mom had to break the news to me that Chris wasn't coming. We weren't going to the prom together. We weren't going off to college together. He'd planned to make that night extra special for us, and that's why he'd tried to talk me out of going to the prom. He had planned to propose to me, but he wanted it to be in a more intimate setting. So he'd arranged to do both. We'd spend a while at the prom, then leave and have the more romantic evening he'd envisioned.

"He had a job after school and had gotten off late. So he was late picking up his tuxedo, late getting home to shower and change, late to pick up the ring he was going to use to ask me to marry him. His car had been acting up, and I remember he'd told me he needed to check it out after work...but he was late. It broke down in the middle of the road on his way to pick me up. He had his head stuck under the hood when another car came flying up behind him on the wrong side of the road. Kids who had been drinking, having fun on their way to the prom, and not paying attention to the road.

"Chris died at the scene with my ring still in his pocket. The teenage driver of the other car was charged with vehicular manslaughter, and because he had a significant blood alcohol level, he went to prison. The others in that car never recovered from what they saw, what they felt responsible for causing. And I never forgave myself for insisting we go to the prom. Because if I hadn't, then he wouldn't have been there at that exact time.

"I understand the pain you feel, like you'll never be happy again. Like you'll never have a normal life. Like you'll never experience an entire night of sleep from now on. It won't be anytime soon, but it will get better. It'll become more tolerable because you'll learn to live with the pain, but it'll never completely go away.

"Heather, what you need to take from my experience is none of us, no matter what age, has a promise for the next breath. If you love Braxton the way you say you do, and he loves you, then you need to fight for your marriage. Not sit back and wait. The longer you go without talking to him, the more damage you'll have to repair and the more risk you run that you'll never have the chance at all."

Tears soaked Heather's face as she grabbed her mother in a full embrace. Her own grief had blinded her to the pain her loved ones felt. That included Braxton, as much as she hated to admit it. He'd been her rock for so long, she took for granted that he'd save her from this nightmare, too. She'd selfishly never considered that he may need saving just as much as she did.

"I love you, Mom," was all she could manage to squeak out.

She knew Kay was right, though. She and Braxton had to talk. They had to reconnect. There was no other way to begin to heal.

Making the decision to reach out to Braxton lifted a huge weight from her heart and gave her a reason to live again. They'd still have bad days; she wasn't naïve enough to believe it would be perfect, but they loved each other. They'd figure it out together.

She ate with her parents, feeling like part of the family again for the first time in what felt like forever. Even though she enjoyed the time they spent together, she was eager to get home and write down everything she wanted to say so she wouldn't forget a single word.

It was time for her to right a few wrongs and reconnect with her husband, the love of her life, before it was too late.

CHAPTER FIVE

Present Day

Noah put his phone back in his pocket and turned to Brianna. "Dad's back in the hospital after running a high fever. Mom sounded different this time, though, and I don't have a good feeling about it."

"Different how?"

"She's usually so upbeat, with her staunch belief that he'll beat this. Maybe it's just that she's seeing him as a mortal man for the first time. It's like her denial is fading, and she's finally facing the reality that he may not make it."

"I can't say I blame her, Noah. If I were in her shoes, I wouldn't accept losing you. I'd do anything it took to keep you with me."

"You know I feel the same." He leaned over and kissed her softly. "We'll see when we get there, I guess. It feels like this flight is taking forever."

"Now that we have a little privacy, it's time for you to do a little explaining." Brianna poked him with her index finger as she spoke.

"What?" Noah's smile covered his face though he tried to appear clueless. "What are you referring to?"

"Oh, I don't know. Maybe the fact that Rebel just dropped a bomb on us when he said the lady in the picture is his wife. Did you know about her?"

"Of course I knew," Noah replied.

He bit back a laugh when she turned in her seat to face him and narrowed her eyes in threat. "Are you really not going to tell me?"

"You're putting me in a really bad position, babe. It's part of my job to know everything about every man who works for me. And they know about me. But we also have to be able to trust each other with our most intimate information. Rebel really needs to be the one to share his story when he's ready to talk about it."

"But I am your wife." Her brows drew downward as she cocked her head to the side. "So you'd keep secrets from me?"

"That nosy investigative reporter is coming out in you. I don't have any secrets from you, Bri. You know everything there is to know about me. But the facts I've learned through my top secret security clearance can't be shared. I take the promise I made to protect that information very seriously. Rebel's circumstances are very personal, and I think he deserves the right to keep it to himself if that's what he chooses."

"Fair enough. Rebel is one of my brothers, too, so he must have a good reason for keeping it secret. He'll tell me when he's ready."

"Or when you use your own counterintelligence techniques against him and start interrogating him," Noah quipped.

"Right. Whichever comes first."

Brianna chuckled as she settled back in her seat. Her eyes strayed over to where Rebel sat, and her heart broke from his pained expression. His demeanor changed the instant Rashad threatened his wife. Gone was the level-headed, easygoing man she was accustomed to seeing. This version of Rebel was the one she presumed only his enemies had the misfortune of experiencing. Rashad's threat had wounded him in a way she'd never seen before. And just as a grizzly bear becomes more dangerous when it's wounded, Rebel obviously did as well.

Judging by the intensity of Rebel's stare, Rashad had just signed his own death warrant when he issued that threat.

Rebel's gaze drifted up, and he locked eyes with Brianna. She gave him a small, understanding smile and hoped he remembered through his pain and anger she loved him like a brother. His arm stretched over to the seat beside him and he patted it, asking her to join him.

Brianna nodded, unbuckled her seat belt, and leaned over to Noah. "I'll be back in a few minutes. Rebel asked me to come sit with him. Keep an eye on Amelia." Their month-old baby was sleeping soundly in the infant car seat strapped into the seat next to hers.

"Be certain you really want to know the answer before you ask a question, princess. You may not like the answer. Once it's spoken, there's no way to unhear it," Noah cautioned.

"All I'm going to do right now is offer my shoulder or my ear, babe. He doesn't appear to be in the frame of mind to take a stroll down memory lane at the moment."

Brianna moved across the spacious aisle of the Steele Security private jet and took her seat next to Rebel. Movement caught her eye, and she looked over at her vacated seat just in time to catch Noah in the act of waking up Amelia.

"Ahem." She forcefully cleared her throat.

Noah's head jerked to meet her incredulous expression. "What? I'm lonely. You've been gone a long time."

"I literally just left your side."

"Really? It seems longer than that."

Brianna's heart swelled with more love than she thought possible when Noah's muscular arms wrapped delicately around their tiny baby, held her close to his chest, and placed soft kisses on her little cheeks. With his lips puckered to steal another kiss from Amelia's baby skin, he glanced up at Brianna and quickly flashed a smile before finishing what he'd started.

Rebel's chuckle from beside her drew her attention back to him, focusing her attention on how her friend was dealing with the latest blow. Because she knew him well, she recognized the mixture of worry and anger in his eyes even though he tried to hide it.

"Being a mom looks good on you, Sunny."

"Thank you. It feels good, too. I never knew I could love someone other than Noah this much. It's amazing."

"Being a father agrees with Reaper, too." He jerked his chin toward where his friend sat. "Don't tell him I said that, though."

Brianna laughed and leaned in toward Rebel. "Don't think he doesn't already know that."

"Don't think I can't hear both of you," Noah chimed in, causing Brianna and Rebel to both laugh out loud.

"When we get to Houston, I need you to do me a favor."

"Of course."

"Sit this one out."

"What do you mean, exactly?"

"I mean do not get involved in this case. Don't try to help find Rashad, don't put yourself in danger, and don't take any chances. That's our job, one we're extremely well-trained to handle. The risks we take are calculated, with a plan for every possible scenario that may occur and the ability to modify as needed on the fly. This case just turned very personal, and the possibility of collateral damage is very high.

"Reaper brought you and Amelia along because he wouldn't be able to concentrate if you two weren't close by where he can reach you. You're his whole world, Sunny, and I know he's yours, too. But you're my little sister, and I can't even stand the thought of losing you and Amelia on top of everything else. Promise me I have one less thing to worry about."

She heard the ominous tone of his voice and saw the undeniable deadliness lurking just underneath his calm demeanor. His request was both a forewarning and a plea, one she knew he wouldn't make lightly. He'd never asked for anything in all the time she'd known him, and she couldn't deny him this peace of mind.

"I promise I'll stay out of it. I'll only get involved if he comes after me and I have no other choice."

"Thank you, Brianna. You know you'll have a full protection detail that will never leave your side. You haven't even been released from your doctor's care yet, so don't even think you'll get away with doing anything strenuous."

"How do you know I haven't been released yet?"

He tilted his head and slowly arched one eyebrow. "It's my job to know. So don't make me have to put you in a safe house until this is over, because I'll do whatever it takes to protect my family."

"I don't doubt that for one second, Rebel. After all these years, I think I know what kind of man you are. So, I can honestly say I'm blessed to be part of your family."

"And if I know my little sister as well as I think I do, I'd say she's trying to figure out how she didn't know this very important bit of information about me."

"That has crossed my mind, yeah," she replied with a hint of jest.

"I'm sorry I haven't told you about her," he started. "I just don't think I can right now."

"There's no need to be sorry, Rebel," she replied sincerely. "One thing I've always loved about you is how you don't always go with the grain, but you always weigh the pros and cons first. So, whatever you haven't shared with me about your life, I have no doubt you have a good reason."

Rebel drew Brianna into his strong arms and kissed the top of her head. "Thank you for understanding."

"I'm always here if you need someone to talk to or if I can help in any way, Rebel. Whenever you need me," Brianna assured him as she returned his embrace. "By the way, do I get to meet her while I'm locked in the hotel room?"

Rebel couldn't help but laugh at her tenacity as he released her. "We haven't driven that reporter instinct out of you yet?"

"Never." She grinned proudly in defiance.

"I'm sure you'll get to meet her. In the bomb-proof, escape-proof, underground bunker of a safe house that we lock you both in until this case is over."

"That's not funny."

"It's a little funny."

"I love the idea. Can we make it a reality within the next couple of hours?" Noah interjected.

"We don't need your help. We weren't talking to you," Brianna retorted with a smile.

Noah shrugged, showing he didn't have a care in the world. "My wife. My jet. My team. My call."

"Uh, boss, you know you have to go to sleep at some point, right?" Rebel asked, feigning worry for his friend.

"Good point. Maybe I should stay in the underground bunker with a protection detail instead of putting the ladies in there."

"You probably should. For your safety."

While the guys continued their playful harassment, Brianna took Amelia from Noah and settled in her seat to nurse her. "Did you reach Shadow, Bull, Chaise, and Silas?"

"Chaise replied to my message a few minutes ago. Those three will meet us in Houston later today. Shadow hasn't replied yet, but he will as soon as he can. He approaches every assignment like it's a deep undercover case," Noah replied.

"Did you say Shadow is deep under the covers? I'd better help him out," Liz jumped into the conversation. "I just had a very refreshing nap in the bedroom back there, so I have plenty of energy now. Let's make a pit stop in LA first."

"Houston is nowhere near LA, Liz," Noah replied, stony-faced.

"I know that. What's your point?"

Noah stared at her disbelievingly. "Should I be concerned at all that you're our nanny and have unrestricted access to my daughter?"

"Nope. Not at all," Liz replied before turning her sights on Rebel. "It's time you and I had a talk."

"What'd I do?" Rebel asked, visibly taken aback by Liz's stern tone.

"I don't mess with married men, Rebel. So I really don't appreciate how you've carried on with me the last few months."

"What? How'd I do that?"

"Oh, you know exactly what you did. Don't play games with me. All your flirting, sneaking glances, insisting on sitting close to me so you can touch me. If I'd known you were married during all of that, I would've kicked your ass. You need to understand there'll be no more of that if we're to be friends now."

"*I* need to understand there'll be no more of that?" Rebel couldn't believe what he just heard.

"I'm glad to hear you agree." Liz nodded. As she turned to sit beside Brianna, she stopped dead in her tracks. "Brianna, I don't really know how to say this. Well, actually, yes, I do. Your boob is hanging out."

"Amelia is hungry. I can't feed her with it inside my clothes," Brianna chuckled and shook her head. "It's okay, Liz."

"In that case…" Liz began to pull her shirt up from the hem.

"What are you doing?" Noah jumped up from his seat and put his hands on hers to stop her.

"Brianna said it's okay."

"That's not what she meant," Noah insisted. "It's okay for her to feed Amelia. It's not okay for anyone else to show their boobs. Are we clear?"

"We're clear that this isn't the party plane I was promised," Liz huffed and plopped in the seat facing Brianna, who was biting her bottom lip to keep from laughing. When Liz winked at her conspiratorially, Brianna nearly lost her composure. She quickly covered it with a cough. Liz continued when Noah's suspicious gaze cut toward Brianna. "Brianna, maybe you and Amelia shouldn't try to drink at the same time. You two need to take turns. One at a time, so you don't get choked again."

Noah's conflicting feelings were written all over his contorted face. On one hand, he couldn't just leave his wife and his baby to fend for themselves. That went against every fiber of his being, the code by which he lived his life, and the vows he took when he married Brianna. On the other hand, sitting with Liz for the remainder of the flight was detrimental to his mental health, and he needed his full mental capacity to stop Rashad.

Every war has casualties, he assured himself as he took a seat across from Rebel.

Feeling her eyes boring holes into his skull, he casually turned his eyes to glance over his shoulder at Brianna. Her brows were raised to her hairline as her eyes rapidly moved between his eyes and his new seat. Noah shrugged one shoulder and pointed to Rebel. "We need to cover the plan before we get to Houston. Make sure every detail has been thought of. I have to protect you, babe."

"Uh-huh."

Noah's eyes drifted to Liz, and he immediately regretted giving in to the temptation. She lifted her hand in front of her face, pointed her index and middle fingers toward her eyes, and then turned her hand toward Noah to point one finger at him. Noah slowly nodded, not completely sure of what he may be agreeing to, and slid his eyes to Rebel. "Let's go over the plan again."

When the plane landed in Houston, Noah, Brianna, and Liz drove straight to the hospital to see Steve and Sara, while Rebel coordinated protection details at the hotel with the rest of their men. The bad feeling Noah had continued to fester, and he knew he needed to see his parents before he fully immersed himself in the role of Reaper. Stopping Rashad would take his full attention soon enough, but for the next several hours, he'd focus on enjoying having his family together.

As they walked down the hospital corridor toward his father's room, he began mentally preparing himself for what waited for him once he stepped inside it. Before he opened the door, he turned to Brianna and Liz.

"Mom said Dad has been sick. I don't know what he'll look like, so be prepared for anything. I don't want to alarm him by reacting negatively to his appearance."

"Don't worry, babe. We've got this," Brianna assured him.

When he opened the door and walked into his father's room, Noah had to consciously make his feet move. He hid his shock and concern behind his smile. The breath that had seized in his lungs was forced to exhale as he spoke. The pride on his face when introducing his daughter to his father masked the uneasiness that squeezed his heart. The love Noah felt when he placed his daughter in her grandfather's arms convinced him that his father would survive this disease. Even if it was only because of Noah's sheer will to eradicate it from his father's body.

"She's so beautiful." Steve beamed. His translucent pallor even transformed to a radiant glow. "Amelia, you're my first grandbaby. I'm going to spoil you with so much love and so many toys."

Noah turned his head away and locked eyes with Brianna. Tears filled her eyes, and she fought hard to swallow them down. "Don't think her daddy isn't already spoiling her," Brianna laughed and sat on the side of Steve's bed. "You two must be conspiring against me."

Steve smiled mischievously. "It's my job to spoil any grandkids I have. You can ask Sara. I take my job very seriously."

"He does," Sara replied. "He always has to be the best, too. So prepare for a lot of spoiling competition between these two guys."

"I say we find a way to turn this game to our advantage, Sara. We need a little spoiling action out of this, too." Brianna winked.

"I'm game if you are."

"Don't you two worry. I know exactly how to handle these men," Liz chimed in. "We'll have them peeling our grapes and feeding them to us before long."

When they finally left Steve's room, it was only because he was so completely worn-out from cooing over Amelia, gently bouncing her in his arms, and singing her to sleep. When he fell asleep with her in his arms, Brianna snapped several pictures of them with her phone.

"I'll walk you out," Sara offered.

"Come back to the hotel with us, Mom. We'll grab something to eat, you can rest for a while, and you can play with Amelia when you wake up. Brianna and Liz will be there with you if you need anything," Noah insisted.

"No, son. I'm not leaving your father yet. I'll be back at the hotel tonight. You go on ahead and get them settled. I'll be fine. I've been doing this for a while now."

With a heavy heart, Noah left his mother at the hospital beside his dad. He didn't argue the point because he knew he wouldn't be any different if it were Brianna in that hospital bed. He'd be by her side for as long as possible. Knowing that didn't make leaving his mom behind any easier, though.

CHAPTER SIX

September 2001

Braxton,

Today has been especially emotional for so many reasons, but they all seem to revolve around you in one way or another. It all started first thing today when I went to visit my parents, but not in the way I'm sure you're thinking right now. First, you probably think I went running back to them as soon as you left, but you'd be wrong. Second, you're probably also thinking they've turned me against you, but again, you'd be wrong.

Of course, my father started in on me as soon as I got there, trying to pressure me to file for a divorce. You know I've never had trouble putting him in his place, and today was no exception to that. In fact, I may have actually gotten through to him this time when I turned the tables on him. It seemed to finally sink into that thick skull of his that I meant what I said when I took those vows with you. I'm not filing for a divorce, now or ever.

Mom shared a heartbreaking story with me from when she was in school. Long story short, she lost a boyfriend who was very important to her, and the details of how and why it happened will always haunt her. After she told me about it, her words really hit home and made me think about you and me. She even encouraged me to talk to you, to make sure you know how much I still love you so we wouldn't lose any more precious time. She encouraged me to fight for my marriage and for you.

The second blow hit after I left my parents' house and rushed back to our apartment to pack a few things. Your parents have been very patient and loving to me. They've let me stay in your old room where all your childhood memories still live and

I can still feel you. The apartment has just been too lonely, and too many memories show up in my nightmares. Now, I only go by there every few days to pick up more clothes, get the mail, or check on our belongings.

On my way back to our apartment, my sole focus was to get these words on paper as fast as I could. But as soon as I stepped inside, my knees buckled and I fell to the floor. The only explanation I have for what I experienced is how I wanted you to be there with me so badly. But I swear I smelled a faint scent of you when I opened the door. That signature scent that has always been solely yours still hung in the air, as if you'd just been there a little while before.

Maybe it was simply because I didn't notice it when I stayed there every day, I'm not sure. Or maybe it was because the apartment had been closed up for a few days since I'd been gone, so the scent was so much more pronounced. Regardless of why, the tears started, and I couldn't stop them for a couple of hours after that, so I curled up on the couch and let them all out. I haven't slept at the apartment for the last several weeks because I no longer felt your presence there. But when that scent surrounded and covered me, it was almost more than I could bear.

That long, anguished cry actually felt good. It was therapeutic to finally let it all out. I've kept it bottled up inside for so long, I'm surprised I haven't exploded like a can of Coke after it's been shaken and put back on the shelf. Missing you has taken more of a toll on me than I've realized. When you left, I know you did it for me, because you thought that would be best for me. Maybe you even thought that was what I wanted.

The final blow came when I finally sat up on the couch and turned the television on for the first time in months. I've kept myself so sheltered from the world, wrapped in my cocoon of depression, I had no clue what was happening outside the four walls I've kept myself locked in. Every channel had the news on a continuous loop, and I stared in disbelief at the planes buried deep inside the buildings as they burned, the people jumping out of the broken windows, the desperation of those searching for their loved ones.

I was scared—no, I was terrified. I was confused, and no one seemed to have any answers as to why this happened. My heart was broken for all those people, their families, my country. Then I realized something important about myself. I'd numbed myself to practically everything else since that day, the day we lost him. I'd been living in a stupor, just barely surviving one day to the next, until the moment I realized that the cowardly acts of terrorism would affect you. You're in the Army now, and the terrible acts that happened earlier were an act of war against us. You'll be called upon to answer the attack.

I don't know how to live without you, Brax. I don't know how to be me without you. We've been together for so long, you've been such a huge part of my life, I've always taken for granted that you'd be there for me, to carry me when I couldn't take another step. Beside me, holding my hand. Behind me, supporting me. In front of me, protecting me. More than that, you're the other half that makes me whole.

For you to understand my insanity, I need you to take a walk down memory lane with me. I know it's hard. Believe me, I know. But we need this, Brax. We need to do this together, and I'm so sorry it's taken me this long to realize it.

Brax, I want us—our friendship, our romance, our love, our marriage—every aspect that makes this ride through life mean something, through the good times and bad. I owe you an apology that I wish I could give you in person, eye to eye, so you'd see, hear, and feel everything I'm feeling. For now, I have to hope and pray this letter will accurately convey what I need to say to you.

Here we go.

My hands were shaking so badly when I took that pregnancy test, I'm surprised I didn't pee all over myself instead of that little stick. I already knew the results before I even looked at the little window. My period had always been like clockwork until the day it just stopped showing up completely. Morning sickness had already reared its ugly head enough that I couldn't deny what was really happening. But I still needed the proof that little test provided before I'd accept it.

I remember walking out of the bathroom, hiding the test in case my parents were nearby, and rushing straight back to my bedroom. You were waiting for me, sitting on my bed and using my pencils as drumsticks, without a care in the world. You knew what the results would be, too. Unlike me, you were excited about the odds that I was really pregnant. But then, it was always hard to rile you up, unless some other guy ignorantly thought he could take your place by my side.

When I handed the pregnancy test to you without even looking at it myself, I turned around and put my head against my chest of drawers. You wrapped your arms around my waist and pulled my back flush against your front. Your hands lovingly snaked up my torso until your forearms crossed over my chest while you held me tightly. Your lips were against my ear when you whispered, "It's positive, Heather. We are pregnant."

At first, I didn't realize you'd said "we" instead of "you." I shouldn't have been surprised by it, though. You never would've made me feel like I'd have to face it alone. And I didn't, not one step of the way did I ever feel alone. When we told my parents, my dad threatened you by saying, "I'll cut your dick off and mount it over the fireplace."

You calmly replied, "Your mantle isn't big enough to hold my dick, so it sure wouldn't hold it with you mounting it."

I couldn't help but laugh out loud, and that's all it took to calm my frayed nerves so I could function again. After that, I put my dad in his place and showed them both my *place was by your side. Though the rest of conversation wasn't pleasant, you helped me make it clear we would get married and they couldn't stop us from having our own family. Of course, then we had to pretend it was our choice to wait a couple of months until we'd both turned eighteen so we could marry without their permission.*

Our wedding and reception were interesting, to say the least. My dad finally agreed to walk me down the aisle, if for no other reason than he wouldn't stand for someone else doing it instead. When the preacher asked who gave me to you, I thought he'd change his mind and drag me out of the church. But he surprised me and went through with it as planned. I've always wondered if my mom had something to do with that, whether she threatened him to make him do it.

Our reception was small but nice. Our three-tiered wedding cake was everything we could have asked for, the punch was perfect, and the candles that lit the room cast the perfect ambiance. Until Kelly leaned over to cut the cake and caught her hair on fire, that is. The flash from her hair spray igniting was both loud and bright. While the others patted her head to stop her hair from being charred, you and I were doubled over in laughter with tears streaming down our faces.

I'll never forget how you carried me over the threshold of our tiny little apartment when we finally left the reception. You refused to let me walk inside on my own two feet because you said it was your job to carry me. To you, it was symbolic of how you'd always be there to carry me, care for me, and love me. I didn't doubt your love then, Brax, and I don't doubt it now.

As my belly grew, so did our love and excitement for the future. Yes, it was hard going to school with everyone watching every pound I gained, but you made that easy for me, too. When a snarky comment was made, you either threatened to beat the guy up or to reveal an embarrassing secret about the girl if they didn't shut up. My personal bodyguard, your love and support were all I ever needed.

The day Dalton Miles Reed was born was a new experience for us both. It was the first time you were the one who'd needed consoling and protecting. You were so adorable in your panicked state—afraid something would go wrong and you'd lose me, helpless because you couldn't stop the labor pains that tore through me, and secretly dreading the gory part of the delivery. I had to keep reassuring you that I was fine, I would be fine, and you would also be fine. I think I said "fine" at least a million times that day.

Turns out, all three of us were fine excellent. After just a couple of days in the hospital, you took Dalton and me home to our little apartment. In our haste to move in together, we didn't consider the fact we'd need a separate bedroom for our son's things. So after my baby shower when we brought home the bassinet, car seat, bouncy seat, changing table, and all the baby clothes, our bedroom and living room were instantly transformed. We joked that our entire apartment had become one big nursery with no room to turn around in, but we were happy with it.

We had absolutely no clue about what colic was, how easily babies got their days and nights mixed up, or how to fix either issue. But we learned a lot about one-, two-, three-, and four-o'clock feedings, diaper changes, and what his different cries meant. The sleepless nights began to add up until we were beyond exhausted.

When I woke up that night, I immediately knew something was very wrong. I'd slept more than two hours straight for the first time in nearly three months. Dalton was in his crib beside our bed, sleeping well for the first time. I gently laid my hand on his stomach, just as I'd done so many times before when he slept, just to feel the rise and fall of his breath.

But it wasn't there.

There was no rise and fall. There was no warmth from his little baby body.

Only stillness.

My heart pounded in my chest, and my own breaths wouldn't come. I flew out of the bed and picked him up, careful to support his little head, but with an urgency I'd never experienced before. You felt me moving, and you also sensed something was terribly wrong. When you flipped the switch and the room filled with the bright overhead light, my heart splintered with unimaginable pain. The bluish hue of his skin and lips was unmistakable.

You took him from my arms and immediately started CPR while I dialed 911. Somehow, through my hysterics, I was able to tell them where we were and what had happened. Regardless of the circumstances and how badly you were hurting, you wouldn't give up, you wouldn't stop trying to revive him. All you wanted was to bring him back to us, and you did everything you could possibly do.

When the paramedics arrived and took over, Dalton still wasn't breathing. I overheard them talking when they were working on him in the back of the ambulance. They didn't know I was there when one guy asked the other if he thought Dalton would make it. He was hesitant to answer, but he finally said, "No, it doesn't look like it."

At that moment, I wanted to die. If I could've willed my heart to stop beating, I would've gladly done just that and died with him. It would've been better than living with the devastation that had just hit me like a speeding locomotive.

We didn't speak the entire ride to the hospital. I know I was lost in my prayers, begging for a miracle, trying to bargain with God to make it all a nightmare so I could wake up and gladly give up another night of sleep just to care for our baby. At the time, I didn't even realize you hadn't said a word. It wasn't because I didn't care. It wasn't that I was mad at you. I was just so very lost in mourning, afraid to hope, and afraid not to hope.

When the doctor came in to tell us our perfectly healthy eleven-week-old baby boy couldn't be revived, whatever was left of my grasp on reality completely and utterly shattered. I remember crumpling to the floor because I wished it would just swallow me whole and put me out of my misery. I remember your strong hands catching me before I hit the ground with the full force of my weight. You kneeled behind me, pulled me into your lap, and wrapped your arms around me.

Holding on to your arms was the only thing that kept me from completely checking out of my sanity. I couldn't tell you then because I couldn't even speak, but you were my lifeline. You were the only reason I continued to hold on and not give up entirely. I wish I'd told you then. I wish I'd been strong enough to explain everything I was thinking and feeling. But planning Dalton's funeral became another nail in my own coffin, and the deep depression soon overtook me.

Hindsight really hasn't been my friend because it so brilliantly highlights my failures. I have so many regrets. There are so many things I want to go back and do differently. Besides the obvious regret of not staying up all night with my eyes glued to Dalton to watch over our son as he slept, there are so many things I didn't give you enough credit for doing. I now realize so many things you did for me, to take care of me, that I took for granted. But I didn't do the same for you, and you deserved to have the same consideration you so freely gave me.

When I stood beside his little casket for hours without moving, you were beside me, holding my hand.

When they lowered his casket into the ground and my legs wouldn't hold me up, you stood behind me, supporting me.

When I had a complete mental breakdown after I realized I'd never see or kiss his little face ever again, you stood in front of me, protecting me. Shielding me. Putting me first. Even though you were dying inside, too.

I needed you, and not once did you let me down.

You needed me, and I repeatedly let you down.

At the time you needed me the most, I failed you. My lapses are truly unforgivable.

Yet, in your goodbye letter, you took all the blame. You're still protecting and supporting me, even though I retreated inside myself from the intense grief I didn't know how to deal with in my own mind.

Even though I have no right to ask this of you, I have to try. Please forgive me and give me a chance to make it up to you. I'm here for you, Braxton. I want to stand beside you and hold your hand. I want to stand behind you and support you. I want to stand in front of you and protect you. I want to take away the responsibility you feel for Dalton's death because it doesn't rest on your shoulders. I want to take away all the pain I've caused you in my ignorance, selfishness, and weakness.

I'll wait for you to come back to me for as long as it takes. My life is with you—it always has been, and it always will be. People say we're still young, we can still find love and happiness, we can still have a family one day. They're exactly right, Braxton. We can still find it all in each other—love, happiness, and a family. You're all I want, all I need, and I won't settle for anything less than what we already have together.

I'm waiting to hear from you.

I love you, Braxton. With every ounce of love I possess, I love you.

Your wife,

Heather Reed

~

Heather walked into the kitchen where Bryan and Jackie Reed sat at the table and held up a thick envelope. She was so grateful to them for taking her in and letting her stay in Braxton's old room. The apartment had become suffocating, and not from the small size. All the memories it held were impossible to escape during the best of times, but being there alone every night had become unbearable.

"I've written Braxton a long letter. I love him so much, and I can't go one more day without telling him exactly how I feel. Do you know how I can get this letter to him?"

"Yes, sweetheart, he gave me his mailing address while he's at AIT. I'll be glad to mail it for you tomorrow." Jackie wiped her eyes as she stood and took the letter from Heather. "We were just talking about all the attacks today—in New York, Washington, DC, and the plane that went down in Pennsylvania."

"It's so scary, especially since Braxton is in the service now. I'm worried about him. I can't lose him too." The tears had flowed so freely while she wrote the letter to him, she was surprised she still had tears to cry. But a mere fleeting thought of losing Braxton reduced her to tears every time.

Jackie wrapped her arms around Heather to comfort her daughter-in-law. "I know, sweetie. We have to be strong and believe he'll be okay, though. He needs all of us to believe in him and give him the strength to succeed."

~

The following week, Braxton was fully immersed in the Army's intelligence AIT program. When the attacks occurred, he'd insisted he wanted to be on the front lines of any imminent retaliation. But since he'd just started his job-specific training, he was stuck there until he finished it. Until that day, he vowed to keep his head in his training program and learn everything he could possibly learn.

"Reed!"

He heard his name being called and looked up from his training manual. "Yes, sir."

"Mail call. Come get your letter, princess. I don't deliver."

He took the thick envelope and eyed it warily. He immediately recognized the handwriting as Heather's. His heart dropped to his feet, and he wanted to stomp it into the ground so he'd never feel anything again. As packed as the envelope was, he assumed it must hold the divorce papers that were waiting for his signature.

"You'll have to get that divorce without my help, my love," he said as he put the sealed envelope away with his other private belongings. "There's no way I can sign those papers."

CHAPTER SEVEN

Present Day

Rashad Samir moved through the hospital corridor as though he belonged there, walking with purpose and a casual stride. The pretty nurse with the short black hair had continued to evade him with her cleverness and preemptive moves. At first, it only served to make him angry at her, more determined to outwit her and beat her at her own game. But after he'd had time to calm down and consider the skill it took for her to pull it off, he became impressed with her competence. Now it was a game of wills and wit to him. A way to demonstrate once and for all who would be the better opponent in the game with human chess pieces.

Dressed in clothing that closely matched the hospital's maintenance crew uniforms, Rashad blended into the background noise of the normal hustle and bustle of the hospital. Patients and their families assumed he was supposed to be there. Nurses and other hospital personnel only briefly glanced at his attire and continued what they were doing. His ball cap covered his hair, and the brim was pulled low to hide his face, completing his makeshift disguise.

As he strode past the patient rooms, he kept his ears attuned to the conversations inside for any morsel of information he could glean. He heard a man's deep laughter reverberate into the hall and immediately recognized it as belonging to the only male nurse in the oncology wing.

"Mr. Steele, you have to give Heather a break. She can't work twenty-four hours a day, seven days a week."

"No offense, Rob, but you're just not as pretty as she is."

"I can't argue with that." Rob laughed in agreement. "But I'm afraid you're still stuck with me for the next couple of days."

"I would say you could at least dress up and pretend to be her, but I'm afraid that would just make you even uglier."

The older man's voice held a blatant teasing tone. Anyone simply passing would know the two men were kidding with each other, an attempt to lighten the mood of the otherwise morose unit with their witty banter.

"You know what, Steele? Just because you've now put the idea in my head, I may just do that one day and shock the hell out of you," Rob laughed.

Rashad's curiosity got the better of him from the repeated use of the name Steele. He had to see the man's face and find out exactly who he was. He knew he was taking a huge, unnecessary risk by even stepping into the room, but he couldn't seem to stop himself. Just as he cleared the doorway, Rob the nurse turned around and looked directly at him, catching Rashad off guard.

"Hey, man. What's up?" Rob asked. He obviously knew Rashad was in the wrong room.

"I'm looking for my partner. I heard voices and thought he might be in here," Rashad lied.

"I haven't seen any maintenance guys on the floor lately except you," Rob replied. "Have you, Mr. Steele?"

Rashad shifted his gaze to the patient lying in the bed. He was obviously a sick man, judging by his color and gaunt frame. This man was older, but the similarities between him and the younger man from Miami were undeniable. Mr. Steele's hair wasn't as black or thick as the younger man's, but age and illness had a tendency of changing those characteristics. There was no denying the eyes, though. Mr. Steele's eyes had a dull sheen to them, no doubt from the cancer in his body, but they were just as piercing as his son's.

They were also just as cunning and keenly aware of his surroundings.

"No, I haven't seen any maintenance guys up here today," he confirmed, keeping his eyes locked on Rashad's. "And my door has been open the whole time."

"Okay, I'll keep looking. Thank you both."

Rashad left the room, cognizant of the fact that Mr. Steele wasn't completely buying his act. He didn't even attempt to hide the suspicion in his eyes or in the inflection of his voice. Rashad had no doubt that the elder Steele would call the younger one as quickly as he could reach for the phone. He realized he'd made the same impulsive mistake his brother, Turan, had once made.

In his quest to outwit the others and prove his superiority, he'd taken unnecessary risks that could've jeopardized his entire operation. The others he worked with, and those who worked for him, wouldn't hesitate to take his life over his foolish decisions. But they wouldn't give him as many chances to redeem himself as he'd given his brother before he finally killed Turan.

"No matter," he muttered to himself. "Maybe there's a way I can use this to my advantage, after all."

Armed with the confirmation that Heather wouldn't be at work for a few days, he knew the printed work schedule he found in the nurses' break room was accurate. While keeping his face down as he left the hospital, he carefully avoided the security cameras strategically placed around the campus and parking area. He'd done his homework, changed vehicles he used to visit the hospital, and altered his appearance to blend in, but the plan was far from over.

As he drove away, his smile covered his face when an extended plan formed in his mind. The scenes played out with expert precision as he visualized the fall of the prideful soldiers who'd invaded his childhood home. The one who'd taken his father's life would suffer first. The looks on all of their faces would be priceless when they realized how epic their failure was in the end, just before he killed them, too.

He stopped at the large merchandise store before heading back to his rented house. The magazines he was forced to buy in order to implement his plan were beyond embarrassing and insulting for a man of his caliber to have in his possession. If anyone in his group had witnessed the abomination, he would've been excommunicated and publicly disgraced when his body was returned to his homeland. But they were necessary to carry out his genius plan, and he would execute it to the fullest extent.

With the pages torn out of the numerous magazines scattered across the floor of his den, Rashad began the arduous task of cutting out individual letters. It was crass, it was obvious, and it was brilliant. Threatening notes made from the various sizes and colors of letters and words cut from magazine pages and glued to a plain white sheet of paper screamed "amateur."

"The simpleton approach will give them a false sense of security and superiority. Their foolish pride and misguided bravado will lead them directly into my trap. They won't know what hit them until the exact moment I want them to know," Rashad remarked to himself.

When the first letter was finished, he held it up in front of him to admire his handiwork. "It's really too bad Turan isn't here with me. He would appreciate this approach."

Thoughts of his brother had him picking up his laptop to perform the basic searches for information he knew how to do. With Turan's computer abilities, Rashad could've accessed even the minutest of details to help tip the scales in his favor. Without Turan, he could only find the information that was available to the general public. There were others on the team who could help, but they wouldn't. Not with this personal vendetta. Not with his personal chess game.

The names of the other soldiers were still hidden from him, locked away on a computer that was inaccessible from anywhere except onsite. In a highly secure, secret building. In a room necessitating above top secret security clearance to enter, behind an armored door that required a unique passcode and biometric identification. Protected by some of the deadliest men in the world, who would shoot first and ask no questions later if any unauthorized person attempted to enter.

When Turan had been an active member of his team, he'd installed a facial recognition program on Rashad's laptop that scoured social media sites for possible matches. With a few clicks of his mouse, he could upload a photo and the program would automatically locate anyone whose characteristics met enough distinguishing points. Not that anyone as skilled at being covert would be so foolish as to have a profile on the popular sites, but distant relations and long-lost friends could always be counted on.

That was the only way he'd been able to find Heather. The program ran day and night, scouring through millions and millions of photographs uploaded on a daily basis, looking for any connection to Rebel through her. It was as if fate herself smiled upon him, because the program finally located one potential match out of all the pictures on social media sites. The proverbial hidden needle that was lost in the haystack, the program indicated the youthful, carefree face that smiled at him from his computer screen had enough facial feature matches for an eighty-nine percent certainty the man was Rebel.

The class pictures were connected to a high school reunion in Houston, posted by someone who was very blatantly not Rebel. Heather and the unnamed young man posed together in this particular picture, smiling and very much in love. But the young man's face wasn't tagged, his name wasn't mentioned in any of the comments, and Rashad knew that for certain because he'd painstakingly checked each one. But Heather Greer's maiden name was listed, along with her married name. Rashad was able to find her fairly easily since she was a nurse and her license was on display in the state database. Unfortunately, every shred of information about her wedding—including the groom's first name—had been removed from public records everywhere. When he snapped the picture of Heather Reed and sent it as a threat, he'd played a wild card he'd only hoped would pan out.

But Noah Steele's name and information were more readily accessible because he was the owner and operator of Steele Security out of Miami. Once Rashad found the initial information on Noah, he was able to expand the search to include Noah's known family members. The demographics he found on one Mr. Steve Steele appeared to match the man he'd met earlier at the hospital. It at least gave him enough information to call the hospital and verify what he'd found.

After going through the information desk to reach the oncology unit's nurses' station, he waited patiently as the phone rang several times.

"Oncology. How can I help you?"

"I'm trying to reach a patient's room, but the phone just rings repeatedly. Is there any way you can go check on him for me? He may be sleeping, but I just need to know he's okay."

"Of course. What's the patient's name?"

"Steve Steele."

"Just a moment, let me check the census for tonight. Here he is. I'm going to put you on hold for a minute while I go check on him."

"Thank you so much. You have no idea how much I appreciate your help."

After a few minutes, she came back on the line. "He was asleep and said he didn't hear the phone ringing. He's awake now if you want to call his room again. Or I can transfer you."

"I'll just dial his room directly. You've already been so helpful. Thank you for checking on him."

"My pleasure."

With that, they disconnected, and Rashad smiled at his own cleverness. With the privacy laws, the information desk wouldn't give out patient statuses or even if the person was actually a patient there. But the caring and helpful nursing staff could always be counted on if a patient's health and well-being were in question. Going off a gut instinct and following his hunch, he got lucky in confirming his suspicions.

"Why stop at his dad, though?" Rashad laughed sardonically as he finished the cartoonish letter to threaten the elder Steele man. "Let's make it a family affair."

Going through the extended family information, he located Brianna's name. From there, it was relatively easy to find more information on her than he needed. Her time as an investigative reporter gave him plenty of ammunition to use against the entire Steele family, naming Noah's wife directly in his threats. She'd be the main topic of the next letter he created, maybe even followed by Noah's mother and then his sister.

But Heather would be the initial focus, the spark that would ignite his plan and draw Rebel out first.

~

"I'm so glad you decided to come back to the hotel with us, Sara." Brianna put her arm around her mother-in-law's shoulders. "You needed a break from the hospital, and Amelia needed to spend time with you."

"I think I need her more than she needs me. She's such a good baby."

"We've been very fortunate. She still wakes up at night to eat, but she goes right back to sleep. Of course, Noah and I sitting up longer every time just to hold her and rock her probably doesn't hurt either," Brianna laughed. "We just can't seem to get enough of her."

"You've had a long day. If you want to take a nap, I'll be glad to watch her," Sara offered.

"You've had a long day, too, Sara. In fact, you've had a long, hard few months. We talked you into leaving the hospital so you could get some rest."

"I'll have plenty of time to rest later. While you're here with my granddaughter, I want to spend time with her," Sara insisted.

"Okay. I'll go unpack all of our suitcases while Noah's on his way back to the airport to pick up Chaise, Bull, and Silas." Brianna kissed Sara's cheek and Amelia's forehead before she walked toward her bedroom.

"What about Shadow? Where's he?" Liz asked, stopping Brianna.

"He's still in LA. He'll contact Noah as soon as he can. They have specific times they're required to check in when they go off on their own, and he hasn't missed it yet."

"Well, he'll meet us here, won't he?" Liz demanded rather than asked.

Brianna hid her smile at Liz's infatuation with Shadow. "That depends on what he's found in LA. We may want him to stay there more than we want him to come here."

"There is nothing that could happen in LA that would make me want him to stay there more than I want him to come here," Liz retorted. "There are tricks of the trade he needs to teach me. He's withholding information from me."

"I don't doubt that at all, Liz."

Brianna smiled after she turned to leave the room. Liz's fascination with Shadow had more to do with his undercover spy skills than with his looks. But she also enjoyed the playful exchange of teasing and razzing the two of them engaged in. She'd lived alone for so long. After her children moved to different states and her husband died, she'd never allowed herself to hope she'd have a family again. She found a new fervor for life when they'd adopted her into the Steele family.

"Liz, let me know if you want me to help you unpack, too," Brianna offered.

"I know you think you're supermom and superwife, but you just had a baby a few weeks ago, little girl. I'll do the unpacking, and you relax in here with Sara and Amelia," Liz insisted.

"Yes, ma'am," Brianna agreed. When she took a seat, she looked at Sara and loudly whispered, "She's so bossy."

"I'm not bossy," Liz corrected. "I *am* the boss. There's a big difference."

Brianna and Sara smiled at each other as Liz continued into the master bedroom. "I hope I don't find any of those crazy sex toys in your suitcases. Blow-up dolls and such. That'd be embarrassing for Noah, because I'd blow it up and have it sitting on the couch when he walks in."

Sara and Brianna both busted out in laughter at Liz's suggestion and the way she giggled diabolically at herself.

"You don't have to worry about any of that, Liz," Brianna called out to her.

"It could be fun to get one and mess with Shadow, though," Liz replied thoughtfully, as if she were already calculating a plan.

Brianna and Sara locked gazes, each secretly hoping Liz would be successful in her endeavor, while also fearing that very thing. "Never a dull moment," Brianna quipped.

A couple of hours later, Noah, Chaise, Bull, and Silas arrived at the hotel. Chaise was the first one to join Brianna and Sara in the living area. The three-bedroom luxury suites Brianna's father, Evan Tate, had secured for them had every amenity they could possibly need. He insisted on the best for his granddaughter, plus that particular floor was inaccessible to anyone without a keycard that had been specifically programmed for it. For Noah and Brianna's suite, he'd also made sure the staff provided a crib beside the bed in the master bedroom.

There were four identical suites on the same floor that Evan had also reserved for the others in the Steele clan. If anyone who didn't belong on the floor showed their face, they'd be immediately spotted by the security team. Brianna knew the added protective measures her father had put in place for his family helped him sleep better a little better at night, even though he'd worry about them regardless.

Brianna stood to hug them as they walked into the suite, pulling Chaise into her embrace first. "Hi, Chaise. Did you go by to see your father first?"

"Yes," Chaise replied as they released each other. "He looked well rested when we got there. Noah said he was pretty worn-out by the time he agreed to let go of Amelia."

"Yes, he was. But it was his own fault," Brianna chuckled. "Where are the guys?"

"They're out in the hall having a secret decoder ring meeting." Chaise rolled her eyes. "They received a call while we were at the hospital. They wouldn't tell me what's going on, but it has to be something big about Rashad and his cell with the way they're acting all secretive about it."

"That's rude."

"They said something about it being a matter of national security. It's top secret, it's their job, blah, blah. Like we're not eyeball-deep in this case with them. Don't worry, I'll get it out of Colton later. None of his training prepared him for the torture I can inflict on him." Chaise smirked knowingly.

"It's like they don't know us at all." Brianna teasingly rolled her eyes.

"You need information out of those men? I can get it out of them," Liz added. "I'll have them singing like little girls and begging to tell me all their secrets. The trick is all in how you flick your wrist. Get a good hold and just flick it. Works every time."

"There will be no holding and flicking going on around here," Bull announced as he strode into the room. "Especially from Liz."

Noah and Silas walked in and stood behind Bull. Brianna immediately recognized the seriousness of Noah's expression and the fighting stance he innately reverted to when danger was imminent. His eyes swept around the room until they landed on hers, and for the first time since she'd seen him on a mission, there was a hint of something else in his eyes. He crossed the room, making a beeline for her, and wrapped his arms around her.

"What is it, Noah?" she murmured in his ear.

He shook his head lightly. "We've received our new orders from the top. We were also briefed on new intel about our target."

When Noah released her, she saw Sara had her arms wrapped around Silas's waist. "How's my oldest child?" she asked as she squeezed him. "I've missed you so much."

"I've missed you, too, Mom. But I'm here now, and I'm not going anywhere else," Silas replied and protectively squeezed his mother to his side.

Brianna felt Noah staring at her before she glanced up at him. "It's bad, huh?" she asked, although she already knew the answer.

"More of his team has moved into the Houston area. They haven't identified the exact target yet, but they know from the chatter that he's managed to infiltrate whatever it is they're planning to attack."

CHAPTER EIGHT

December 2001

"Surprise!" Braxton called out to his parents as he walked through the front door. "I'm home for Christmas!"

"My baby is home!" Jackie squealed and ran into his outstretched arms. "Why didn't you tell us you were coming home?"

"Because I wanted to surprise you. Besides, I wasn't sure what exact day I'd get here until the last minute."

"How long are you home, son?" Bryan asked before he pulled Braxton into a fatherly embrace.

"I get two weeks off for Christmas Exodus then I'm headed back to Arizona for more training."

"Isn't your AIT completed by now?" Bryan asked.

"I just completed the intelligence analyst training course. It was pretty grueling, but I aced it. With everything that's going on in the world right now, we need more intelligence officers. I've been offered a chance to attend counterintelligence training next. If I complete it as well as I did this one, they'll advance me up to a sergeant sooner than most."

"How'd you get picked for that?" Jackie asked suspiciously.

Braxton shrugged, giving the appearance the answer was boring and unimportant. "I guess I did pretty well during the first round of training. They said my ASVAB and test scores were high. My marksmanship is one of the best.

"Plus, I've decided to make a career out of the Army. I'm signing up for every type of advanced training I can get into. Jump school will have to wait a little longer, but I'll get there. I've been accepted to a college near the base, so I can get a degree and move up to an officer."

"Son, you're taking on way too much all at once, don't you think?" Bryan's concern for his son was written all over his face.

"Might as well do all I can while I'm young, right?"

"You won't have any spare time, Brax. You'll spend every waking moment training, going to class, or studying," Jackie warned.

"That's the point, Mom," he finally revealed. "It'll keep my mind and my hands occupied. I won't have time to think about anything else. I'm actually looking forward to it."

"You'll probably be stationed somewhere else after you finish this training, though."

"I'll just transfer and keep taking classes somewhere else. It'll be okay, Mom. Quit worrying about me so much." Braxton put his arms around her in an attempt to reassure her.

"Brax, you're my baby. I'll never stop worrying about you as long as I'm alive."

"Are you worried that I'm hungry? Because I'll let you worry about that all you want every time I come home."

Jackie released him and rolled her eyes exaggeratedly at him. "Of course, you'll let me worry about that. Come on, I'll feed you."

"Okay. I'm going to put my stuff in my room first. I'll be right there."

When he opened the door to his childhood bedroom, the past rushed over him in much the same way a tsunami crashes onto land and obliterates everything in its path. Memories of Heather filled the room—from their friendship as kids to their first time as lovers, these four walls had seen it all. The crushing weight of his past failures settled on his chest and threatened to choke the life out of him. Dumping his duffel bag on the floor by his bed, he quickly retreated back to the kitchen.

"How the fuck am I supposed to sleep in there?" he murmured to himself as he walked back down the wall.

"Brax, while your mom is cooking, I'm going next door to help Frank with his car. I'll be back in a little while."

When Bryan was out the door, Brax looked at his mom and smirked knowingly. "That wasn't obvious at all."

"What?" She feigned innocence, knowing exactly what he meant.

"Dad rushed out to help Frank with his car, but he didn't ask me to help, too? Come on. I've known him all my life," he deadpanned. "So, what is it you want to talk to me about? Let's have it."

"Okay. But just remember you asked," Jackie began. "Why haven't you answered Heather? You've kept her waiting for months now."

"Why do you think I'd answer her, Mom? If that's what she wants, she can do it without me."

"Do what without you?"

"Divorce me," Braxton bellowed. "I'm not signing those damn papers. There are other ways she can get it without my consent."

Jackie shook her head and gave him a sad smile. "Why would you think she sent you divorce papers?"

"Because I saw them myself," Braxton replied sadly. "I went back to the apartment before AIT to talk to her. They were on the kitchen counter, ready to dissolve our marriage. All they needed was our signatures."

"Oh, my baby boy." Jackie put her hands on his shoulders and shook him gently. "You didn't even open the envelope, did you?"

Braxton shook his head from side to side.

"She didn't mail divorce papers to you. Do you still have the envelope?"

"Yeah. It's in my duffel bag. I was going to leave it here with you."

"You need to go open it. I promise it's not divorce papers."

Suddenly, Braxton couldn't wait to get back to the very room he'd just left. Question after question flashed through his mind in the few steps he took toward his room.

If she didn't send the divorce papers, why did she have them?

The envelope was very thick. What else could she have sent?

Is it something I even want to read?

Dumping all of his neatly folded clothes out of his bag onto the bed, he rifled through the clothes until he found it. With his heart beating wildly against the side of his chest, he absently sat down at his old desk and slid his finger under the envelope flap. His eyes were fixed on the contents of the envelope as he gingerly removed the papers inside. After inhaling a deep breath, he held it as he unfolded the letter and began reading the words Heather had poured from her heart onto the pages in front of him.

He allowed himself to feel the emotions her words invoked. As she moved through their time together, the memories resurfaced in the form of tears flowing down his cheeks. The good and the bad times, they were all still right where he left them, and he felt them one by one all over again. Only this time, he was reliving them through her eyes, through her words, all in exactly the way she'd perceived the events as they unfolded. Thoughts and feelings they should've shared with each other, only they were blinded by youthful inexperience and their self-imposed confinement in a hellish prison.

She didn't blame him, she didn't hold him responsible, and she didn't hate him. She actually still loved him. Nothing that had happened changed or lessened her love for him, and she wanted their marriage to last. At least, she'd felt that way when she wrote the letter a few months before. His mind worried that she would've given up on him by now because he never answered.

His heart told his mind to shut the hell up because Heather would never do that.

Jumping up from his seat, he tore out of his room and ran back to the kitchen.

"Mom—"

She was waiting for him with her car keys in her opened palm. "Go, son."

After kissing her cheek and grabbing the keys from her hand, Braxton rushed out to the car and sped all the way to their apartment. He mentally berated himself for not getting more information from his mom before he left. Heather said she'd been staying in his room. For how long? When did she stop? Did she move back in to their apartment, or was she at her parents' house now?

Since it was the week before Christmas, she may not even be home. She could very well be visiting other family members. If that was the case, he didn't know what he'd do, other than wait for her, however long it took. The undeniable truth was they were made for each other. They were one of the rare couples who'd always known their union was meant to be and their hearts would never be satisfied with anyone else.

The tires skidded to a stop in the parking space, and he rushed up the flights of stairs as fast as his feet could carry him. Standing in front of the apartment door, his chest heaved forcefully from the emotion that welled up inside it. He raised his fist in the air, poised to knock on the door, but it swung open widely before his knuckles could connect.

Heather stood in the doorway. Her eyes were wide open, her mouth ajar in a silent gasp, and her muscles were tensed. She was still the most beautiful girl he'd ever seen. She was still the best friend he'd ever known, and she was still the person he loved most in the world.

She was still his wife.

Recognition that it was actually Braxton who stood before her took a few seconds to register in her shocked state. He knew the very second she realized who he was—the expression in her eyes instantly changed from slight fear to passionate love. As if to further validate their connection, they spoke at the same time.

"Heather."

"Braxton."

Desperate need for the other overtook them, their bodies collided and melded into one as their arms encircled each other. When their lips met, time and troubles melted away until there was nothing left except their love and need for each other. Lips crashed together, teeth collided, and tongues caressed with a heated fervor. Though it took all of his restraint, he slowly halted their passionate embrace.

With their foreheads touching, Braxton lovingly caressed her cheek with his thumb while keeping her held tightly against him with the other hand. "Heather." He whispered her name with such reverence, such devotion, it was as if her name had become his prayer. "I've missed you so damn much."

"Braxton, where have you been?" she implored. "I've waited so long for you to come home."

"I'm here, and I'm so sorry I've kept you waiting. I just read your letter this morning, and as soon as I finished reading it, I rushed straight over here to you."

"You only read it today? But I mailed it months ago." The confused look on her face was endearing and heartbreaking.

"Can I come in and explain?"

She smiled bashfully. "Of course you can come in. It's your home, too."

Those four words coming from her meant more than she'd ever know. He walked her backward into the apartment while not letting go of her and closed the door behind him. "Were you going somewhere?"

"Nowhere important."

"Good. Because I've been away too long, and I don't want to share you with anyone else for however long I can keep you locked away."

"What took you so long to read it?"

Knowing he put the uncertainty in her eyes cut him to the quick. *She thought I quit loving her,* he thought.

"I came by here to see you on my way to Arizona. Took the long way and rushed over here on a layover, but you weren't here. When I was looking for something to leave you a note on, I found the divorce papers on the counter. So when I received the envelope, I assumed it was the papers for me to sign."

"So if it had been those papers, you wouldn't have signed them?"

"Not a chance in hell."

"Brax, I promise I didn't want them. I've never wanted that. They were actually in with the papers I needed to shred. My dad pushed it for a while, but he knows better than to do that now."

"There are a lot of things we need to talk about, Heather. We've both been guilty of letting our misconceptions and assumptions rule us. We've been apart for way too long already."

She led him to the couch, where they sat together and talked for hours. Through their tears, they discussed the events that led up to their separation. By laying their feelings out on the table to examine, they exposed every vulnerability and made their relationship stronger.

"I never blamed you, Brax," Heather said through her tears. "My world revolved around you and Dalton, and I never doubted that your world revolved around us. The last thing I'd ever do is blame you for his death, but I understand why you'd think that. I blamed myself for not waking up to check on him earlier. Part of me just assumed you blamed me for that, too. It wasn't a conscious thought, though. In my mind, it was just a given that it was my fault."

He shook his head from side to side. "No, baby. It never occurred to me that anything was your fault. Now I have to get past the fact that I put even more pain on you when I left. At the time, I obviously wasn't thinking clearly, but I honestly thought it would be easier on you without me."

She sighed heavily and placed her palm on his cheek. "Aren't we a pair, Brax? Losing Dalton sent us both into a tailspin. One neither of us had a clue how to handle. I should've told you that your mere presence grounded me. Your love carried me through many dark nights I wasn't even sure I'd survive while we were going through it. The only thing I was sure of was you."

"Promise me something."

"Anything."

"No matter what happens in the future, this is how we talk about it. No matter what it is, no matter how hurt, mad, depressed, or confused we are. Two heads are better than one. Facts are better than assumptions."

"I promise this is how we'll talk about everything. I've been going to a therapist the last few months, and she has really helped me. I've told her everything that's happened, and she had an interesting observation."

"Yeah? What's that?"

"First, she's very impressed with our commitment to each other. I explained that we started out as best friends first and how our love and loyalty have never been in question. She doesn't think we've had a chance to develop as individuals. We went from friends to lovers to a married couple to parents, on top of being so young. She suggested we use this time apart to grow as individuals, so when we're reunited, we'll be stronger as a couple."

"How long do you plan to stay apart from me?"

She smiled at him lovingly and stroked his jaw with her fingers. "I don't plan to stay apart from you at all. But you've joined the Army now, and I don't really know how that works. Are you still in training? With everything that happened on 9/11, will you be sent away to fight? If not, where will you be stationed, and can I go with you?"

"Okay, I get your point," Braxton chuckled. "I can only take things a day at a time right now, except over the next two weeks while I have a break over the Christmas holidays. I'm finishing up my first round of individual training, but I've been selected to go for a second round with a group of handpicked soldiers. I'll be away another four months for it. After that, I have jump school in Georgia and hopefully Ranger training after that. Those two trainings will add at least another three to four months, depending on timing."

"So, almost another year of you being away, traveling and training," Heather replied.

"That was my original plan, to make the Army my career and see how far I can go with it. Heather, if you want me to take a normal Army job and settle at one base so we can be together, I'll do it. Nothing is as important to me as you are."

"No, I can't let you do that. It wouldn't be fair, Brax. Of course, I want to be with you, but I haven't seen your eyes light up when we've talked about the future for so long. But that spark was there just now when you were describing the path you want to take. I've also decided what I want to do, what I want to be."

"What do you want to be?"

"A nurse. I want to help others. Being there for them when they need help the most, being able to help them, that makes me happy. It makes me feel like my life means something. I've applied to UT for the Bachelor of Science in Nursing program."

"So four years?"

"Yeah, but I'll be able to travel to see you on the weekends, holidays, and breaks. Or you can come here. During the summer, I'll live wherever you're stationed, unless you're out of the country. We can make it work, Braxton. Don't give up on us."

"I'll never give up on us, baby. I'm all for your plan, I think it's a great idea. You'll be a wonderful nurse, and the patients will be lucky to have you. I guess that homeschooling our guidance counselor insisted on at the end of your pregnancy really paid off, didn't it?"

"Yes, I'm so glad she didn't let me get away with not finishing just because I was trying to be lazy," Heather chuckled. "I'm really excited about going back to school."

"So am I."

"You're going back to school?" Heather asked excitedly.

"I guess I left that part out. When I left for basic training, I admit I thought that was my only option at having any kind of future. But once it started, I realized it's much more than a last resort. This can be my career, a way for me to make a difference and leave my mark. With what I want to get out of it, I need a college degree, so I've decided to go for Criminal Justice."

"I'm so proud of you, Braxton."

"I love you, Heather. So damn much. It's always been you—it's only ever been you."

She moved to sit in his lap, and his arms curved lovingly around her. With one arm around his neck and the other hand resting on his chest, she felt his heart racing under her touch. "I love you, Brax. Only you—forever. And I've missed you more than you can imagine."

He watched with hooded eyes as she leaned forward and crushed her lips to his. Her hands roamed across his body. Her fingers felt each bump and ridge of his finely developed muscles. The intensity of the kiss she initiated increased markedly, conveying her need for him just as when they'd been together before their worlds crashed and burned. But in the ashes, they found the embers of a love that, once fanned, would again become white-hot and uncontainable.

He weaved his fingers through her hair, removing his lips from hers only for the split second it took to tilt her head to deepen the kiss. His tongue caressed her lips before forcing them to part. He claimed her mouth, matching and exceeding her tenacity and vigor while savoring the sweet essence that belonged only to Heather.

She broke off the kiss first but kept her lips a breath away from his. "Braxton, it's time to re-consummate our marriage."

"If that's what my wife wants, how can I deny her?"

Holding her securely in his arms, Braxton rose from the couch and carried her to their bedroom. Placed her on their bed. And showed her in every way that their marriage couldn't be bound by any type of measurement known to man. With their lips joined, he told her no amount of time would lessen his devotion. With their eyes locked, he promised his loyalty wouldn't wane with the distance between them. With their bodies joined as one, he vowed his love couldn't be measured because there was nothing that compared to its vastness.

CHAPTER NINE

Present Day

The first day off after a long stretch of twelve-hour work days didn't allow much downtime. After her intense workout first thing in the morning, she spent the rest of her day off running errands. By the time she'd had her car serviced, her hair styled, and bought groceries, she was ready to collapse on the couch and pass out in front of the television. Staying on high alert and diligently watching her surroundings every second, thanks to her would-be stalker, had only added to her fatigue.

Once she was hidden behind her garage door, she released a sigh of relief. She loaded her arms with the plastic grocery bags to avoid making a second trip and managed to unlock the door. She released a loud grunt of frustration when she finally reached the table and let the bags slide off of her arms. She inhaled a deep, calming breath, closed her eyes, and slowly released it as her chin dropped to her chest.

"I know you're in here. You're not fooling me, so don't even try to hide. You have about two seconds to show yourself." Her voice held conviction and authority as she issued her directive.

Her unannounced visitor stepped out of the darkened living room and into the kitchen directly behind her. His thick arms slid around her waist, and she willingly stepped into his embrace. "How do you always know when I'm here? I can't ever surprise you."

"I could tell you, but then I'd have to kill you," she teased.

"I've missed you so much. It's been too long since the last time I saw you."

Rebel placed a kiss just below her ear, then let his lips and tongue glide down her neck.

"Mmm," she purred and her skin prickled with yearning. "I completely agree. Even though it was technically just a few weeks ago. The last time my week off came up in the rotation."

"A few weeks is weeks too long, Heather. I'll help you put away the groceries, and then we're spending the next several hours in the bed."

"You know I love it when you get all demanding on me. Well, demanding in the bedroom, anyway."

Rebel chuckled softly against her neck. "Yeah, I know. If I tried to tell you what to do in the kitchen, I'd end up with a butcher's knife thrown at my head."

"You know me entirely too well, Brax." She turned in his arms and wrapped hers around his neck. "I'm so glad you're here. But since you're early, I have a feeling it's because someone has been following me."

One side of Rebel's lips quirked upward, and he shook his head lightly from side to side. "You already knew?"

"Of course, I knew. How long have we been married? You know, I have learned a thing or two from you over the last fourteen years."

"You've been watching me, huh?"

"I watch your every move, babe," she confirmed.

He bowed his head and captured her lips with his. A warm, welcome kiss quickly turned into a passionate, uncompromising need to consume her, reclaim her as his. Using one arm to clear the way, he easily lifted her with the other and placed her on the table directly in front of him. He gently pushed her shoulders until she lay flat on the table. His fingers gripped the sides of her yoga pants and began inching them over her hips.

"Did you forget about the groceries?" Her words reminded him, but the inflection of the desire in her voice told him her mind was on something else.

"Nope, not at all. I'm starving. I was actually hoping there would be some whipped cream in here I can use," he murmured seductively.

"If I'd known you'd be here when I got home, I would've picked some up."

"It's not a big deal. I'm still going to eat my dessert without it," he promised.

Her appreciative moan became louder as he lowered his head between her legs and his mouth covered her. His tongue darted out, laving her with its warmth. The intense pleasure caused her torso to contract and curl upward toward him, her fingers gripped his arms, and her legs fell farther apart. He curved his arms under her legs and pulled her closer to him before voraciously feasting on her again. He felt all of her muscles tense then relax with release, finishing what he'd started when his name left her lips on a guttural scream.

"Damn, baby, you have missed me," Heather praised through heavy breaths.

"I miss you that much and more every day, Heather."

"I know," she replied softly. "I miss you too. So much."

"You know how we can permanently fix this problem," he reminded her as he lifted her from the table.

"I know exactly how to fix it." She gave her standard reply. "We can move your stuff out of that crappy little apartment and into our home where you belong."

"Let me take you to our bed and see if I can convince you to move to Miami with me."

"Fine by me. As long as you know I'll be trying to convince you to stay in Houston with me."

"You are so stubborn," he chuckled as he sat her on the edge of the bed.

His fingers skimmed across her chest as he removed her shirt. The sight of her pebbled nipples through her lacy bra made him want to rush through the motions, but the limited time he had to spend with her forced him to take it slowly. He purposely brushed the pads of his thumbs across her nipples as he moved to remove her bra. When she arched her back, forcing her breasts into his palms, he paused his movements for a moment to enjoy the scene just a little longer.

When she reached for him, the sensation of her fingertips against the sensitive skin of his lower abdomen was all it took for her to completely own him. In a flash, she had removed all of his clothes, and they stood bare in front of each other. When she wrapped her hand around him, she began stroking up and down his hardened silky smoothness. He gritted his teeth, leaned his head back with his eyes closed, and savored her touch.

The moment her lips touched his hardened cock, his eyes flew open and his head jerked back upright. Then her mouth covered him, his fingers gripped her hair, and his hips bucked involuntarily when he hit the back of her throat. When she began moving her mouth and hand in tandem, he was sure he'd died and gone to heaven.

"Fuck me," he muttered under his breath.

Pausing briefly, she looked up at him through her lashes and grinned devilishly. "That's my plan, babe."

"It's time. Right now," he demanded.

Effortlessly, Rebel lifted her from her position kneeling in front of him to instantly lying supine on the bed beneath him. One swift move had him buried so deeply inside her there was no way to tell where he ended and she began. His hips surged forward, his back arched, and she writhed underneath him in sheer pleasure. Her fingers dug into his back as she lifted her hips and eagerly met each wave.

"You feel so damn good. I can't get enough of you," he murmured.

He spoke in clipped statements, driving into her with each one.

"I'd love to keep you right here."

"In this bed."

"Underneath me."

"Riding me."

"Down on all fours."

"Screaming my name."

"Over and over."

"All damn night."

His thrusts became more forceful with each one. The way her fingernails clawed at his back as she repeatedly rode the waves of ecstasy only drove him into more of a frenzy. He became intoxicated on the sweet scent of her arousal that hung in the air. With their bodies slick from sweat and breathless from exertion, they reached the summit of pleasure together.

Rebel rolled over to his side, swiveling Heather to face him as he moved. "Is this where you try to convince me to move back to Houston permanently?"

She gave him a small smile, but he detected a sense of sadness in it. "If I honestly asked you to stay here with me for good, would you?"

"Yes," he answered immediately.

"No hesitation?"

"None. I'd be here with you in a split second."

"Why now?"

"It's not something new, babe. You've always loved your independence. Maybe because you didn't have a lot of choice during all the years I was in the service. While I was on assignments all over the world, you built a life and friends here, so I understood when you didn't want to just up and leave it when we started the business in Miami. You're the one who suggested our current arrangement, but if you need more of me, all you have to do is say the word, and I'm here. I always need more of you."

"You're right, I did suggest this setup, with one of us traveling to the other so we could spend time together and still have our careers, our friends, our lives. But now I feel like we're missing out on a life we can build together," she admitted.

"So it's my turn to ask you. Why now?"

Her eyes flicked back and forth between his, telling him she was searching for the words to convey what had shaken her independent resolve.

"One of my patients recently really got to me. She was younger than me, only twenty-nine, and she had stage four breast cancer. Her biggest regret was putting so much focus on her career that she gave up the man who was her one true love. He'd wanted to get married, have kids, move to the country where they'd only have each other, no neighbors. He wanted them to build a life where their relationship was their main focus. She died without ever knowing what that life would've been like. All she knew was her job and the few friends who stayed by her side until the end.

"I feel like our time to have that kind of relationship is slipping through our fingers. And it's not even like sand where we can hold on to some part of it. It's more like trying to hold on to flowing water. Brax, I love you, I've always loved you, and I want a real life with you now. But I feel guilty because that would take you away from your friends, your brothers, and the commitments you've made to them and the business."

"You are my commitment, Heather. First and foremost, above anything else. You're my wife, and I love you more than anything and anyone else. I've been temporarily reactivated as an operator, so right now it's out of my hands because of national security. But when this case is over, I'm all yours."

"Can we start a family then?" She blurted the question out before she could stop herself, but she had an intense need to know if he was on the same page with her. She could no longer deny the two things she wanted most were to have her husband and to have a family.

"I'd love nothing more than to make a family and a full life with you, wifey."

It had always been her touch that drove him, her kiss that fueled him, and her love that invigorated him. They drifted off to sleep wrapped in each other's arms, their legs intertwined and hearts full. They'd spent long stretches of time and distance apart, but their reunions had always made up for it. This time was no different, even though it was under different circumstances.

~

The streams of light filtering in through the blinds woke Heather from a deep sleep. She reached across the bed for Rebel but found only a cold, empty space. At first, she questioned if she'd dreamed the whole thing. He'd been on her mind so strongly, and so often, she could barely make a move without thinking of him. She rolled over and grabbed his pillow, hugging it closely to her, and his scent enveloped her.

A dip in the mattress beside her startled her, and she jolted up on one elbow. "Braxton," she sighed with relief. "You're really here. It wasn't all a dream."

He smiled lovingly at her. "Well, I don't know if you're dreaming about me, but I am really here. It wasn't a dream when I ravaged your body last night. And it won't be a dream when I do it again in the shower after breakfast. Or later today in the car. Or tonight, somewhere else in the house that's to remain a surprise.

"But first, here's your coffee. Breakfast is almost ready. Get up and come eat," he demanded playfully and smacked her bare ass.

As he moved toward the door, she replied softly. "You said you'd give up everything to move here with me."

He stopped and turned his head to look at her over his shoulder, his eyes locked on to hers. She held her breath until he replied. "I did, and you know I meant it."

The look of pure, unabashed love that emanated from his eyes was solely for her. She'd never doubted him or his devotion to her, and she knew he'd never give her a reason to. "Thank you, Braxton. I'm so excited and so ready to start this new chapter of our lives together. I can't wait."

"Neither can breakfast. Come eat while it's hot."

He winked and continued back to the kitchen. She retrieved his shirt from the floor and pulled it over her head. With her steaming coffee in hand, she quickly followed him and sat at the table. She glanced around the kitchen and noticed the groceries from the night before were missing.

"You put the groceries away for me?"

"Yeah, I got back up after you fell asleep last night and put everything away so it wouldn't spoil." He set her plate full of her favorite breakfast foods down in front of her.

"This looks delicious. Thank you. I love having you home. You spoil me."

"It's my pleasure."

"Speaking of, you distracted me last night, and I didn't get a chance to interrogate you about why you're here early. It has something to do with the guy who's been following me, doesn't it?"

She watched as he took a bite of his bacon and intentionally held her gaze as he chewed, deciding what information to share and what to hold.

"Don't do that, Braxton," she warned.

"Do what?"

"Withhold information from me."

His smile crawled slowly across his handsome face. "I would never do that, babe. I was just testing your skills, making sure you're still quick on the uptake."

"You can quit stalling now, too."

He threw his head back and roared with laughter. "There's my girl. I'm afraid I've taught you a little too much over the years. By the way, Liz is with us, and she's still waiting for Shadow to teach her all of his secret spy tricks. Don't let her know that you're trained, or she'll never leave you alone."

"I can't wait to meet Liz." Heather beamed. "Actually, I can't wait to meet all of the ladies. So who's the guy following me?"

While they ate breakfast together, Rebel briefed Heather on the recent events that prompted his early return to Texas. She already knew much about the case the team had been working and why Turan had wanted to kill Rebel. During their many phone conversations, he'd kept her apprised of how the case was unfolding. When he reached the part about the picture of her being sent to him, Heather nodded in understanding.

"I knew I was being watched. All the hairs on the back of my neck were standing at attention in the parking garage. I never saw him, but I knew someone was there, so I watched my rearview mirror for a tail on my way home. Spotted him immediately. He's not very good at being covert."

"He most likely underestimated your cool ninja skills, babe."

"Yeah, he did. Then he spent a long time driving around the subdivision looking for my car. So I've been driving the Land Rover and parking in different places around the hospital when I go to work. Using different doors to enter and exit. I'm off for the next week, though. Makes it easier for you to guard my body every day."

"I will absolutely guard your body, several times a day." His heated stare expressed the true meaning behind his words. "Can you take off more time, just in case?"

"I'd have to contact Becca immediately so she can get my shifts covered," she replied, her mind drifting to her patients and how much longer she'd be away from them. "Do you have a picture of this guy I can give to security in case he shows up there?"

"Reaper has it in the file. We'll make sure it gets to them as soon as possible. But for now, it's time for you to take my shirt off. We have to take our shower so I can guard your body for the first time today. It'll take at least the next hour and all the hot water."

She slowly rose from her seat, drew his shirt over her head, and dropped it at her feet. As she stood completely naked before him, she flashed him a challenging grin. "This body? Is this the one you want to guard?"

Rebel sat back in his chair and pushed it back from the table. Arching his eyebrow in a responding challenge, he nodded slowly while his eyes raked up and down her body.

"You'll have to catch me first." She shrugged nonchalantly before taking off running at full speed toward the hall. Before she reached it, she squealed with playful laughter as she flew through the air and landed on his shoulder.

"Challenge accepted, little lady. But don't act like I didn't catch you many years ago," he chuckled as he carried her to the master bath. "You've always been mine, and I'm about to remind you why."

CHAPTER TEN

"Where did you park?" Heather asked as she and Rebel climbed into her Land Rover. "There wasn't a strange car in any of the driveways on my street."

"It's good to know I can still be invisible when I need to be." Rebel winked. "I scouted the entire neighborhood yesterday while you were out running around—at your workout, getting your hair done, buying groceries. There's a vacant house on the next street over, so I made a few calls, and it's now our command center. My rental car is parked in the garage over there."

"Were you following me yesterday?" She turned in her seat and faced him, cocking her head to the side and purposely letting her mouth fall open. Her narrowed eyes were the dead giveaway she was not pleased with the answer she already knew.

Rebel shifted uncomfortably in the driver's seat. "Babe, you know I had to follow you. I wasn't checking up on what you were doing, though. It was only to find out if anyone was tailing you."

"And?"

"No one besides me tailed you yesterday," he confirmed. "You didn't see me, though. Did you?"

She turned to sit straight forward in her seat and crossed her arms over her chest. "No," she finally admitted.

Rebel laughed, knowing that it killed her, with her fierce competitive streak, to admit that to him. "Don't be mad. I'm trained to be invisible, and I've been perfecting my technique for years and years."

"That doesn't make me feel any better," she huffed. "Maybe I should have a long talk with Liz, after all. Seems there are a few things she and I both need to learn to do."

"Don't unleash Liz on me. She's already threatened to kick my ass and accused me of leading her on."

Heather burst out laughing at the visual. "I hate that I missed seeing that in person. Liz sounds like my kind of people."

Though she'd never met Liz, Rebel had described her to a T during their nightly conversations. Since Rebel had returned from active duty, they hadn't skipped sharing the events of their day, regardless of how mundane, for even one single night. The people in Rebel's life were as important to Heather as they were to Rebel because they kept him company, they kept him sane. They kept him alive. They were like family to her, even if not all of them knew she even existed.

"They broke the mold when they made Liz. And we're all very thankful for that," he chuckled. "She's really a great woman. Regardless of how eccentric she acts sometimes, she's as good as gold. We all know she'd do anything for us, without hesitation. The way she's taken care of Brianna, Reaper, Amelia, and Reaper's parents…we couldn't ask for more."

Heather's responding silence concerned Rebel and prompted him to cut his gaze toward her. The profound sadness he saw on her face struck a chord deep inside him. He took her hand and gently squeezed it. "What's wrong, babe?"

"You'll think I'm crazy."

"I already do, so there's really no danger in telling me what's on your mind."

She smiled because she knew all he wanted was to cheer her up. "Fair enough. It's irrational, but I'm jealous of the time they get to spend with you. I'm jealous of what you experience with them, and I'm kicking myself because those memories aren't with me."

"Heather, whether you're physically with me or not, you are in every memory I have. Everywhere I go, everything I see, every emotion I feel, you are at the center of it. I understand exactly what you mean because I feel the same way when you tell me about things you do with Becca and your other friends. One reason why I share everything with you is so you'll feel like you're a part of it, too."

"I know, and I do the same with you. I told you it was irrational. It's mostly because I miss you so much. And because hindsight is twenty-twenty. There are so many things I'd do differently if we could just go back and start all over again."

"All we can do is make it the best it can be from now on."

"You're right. And we will."

He pulled into the valet parking area of the Sterling Luxury Resort and handed the keys to the attendant as he got out. When he stated the room number, Heather's head jerked in his direction and her brows furrowed, but she remained silent. Rebel led her inside, his hand possessively on her lower back, and into the elevator. He retrieved the keycard from his pocket and slid it into the reader before pressing the floor number.

When the doors closed, Heather turned to him. "You have a room here?"

"We have a room here, if we need it. It's on a secure floor that only we can access. If I need to pull you out of harm's way, you can stay here with Brianna, Chaise, and Liz. Sara will be in and out since Steve is still in the hospital."

"I didn't put two and two together when I first met Steve. He's my patient, but it was just recently that I learned he's Noah's father. I probably sounded like a lunatic when I realized it," she laughed. "This is a very elegant hotel. So, Brianna's family owns it?"

"Yes, her father built a luxury hotel empire from the ground up. He reserved this entire floor for us. There are several three-bedroom suites at our disposal."

"And the house in my neighborhood?"

"We'll use it to coordinate our activities and keep the focus away from this hotel. The more we come and go from here, the more dangerous it makes it for everyone staying here. It's too likely that someone from Rashad's cell will see us and use the hotel customers to get their point across."

The elevator doors slid open, and Rebel took Heather's hand in his as they strode to the door of one of the suites. They could hear the voices coming from inside—the laughter, the teasing, the sounds of friends and family enjoying the company they were in. Their eyes met, and they each knew what was in the other's thoughts.

"You're a member of this family, Heather." Rebel inclined his head toward the door. "When you meet Brianna, Chaise, and Liz, you'll see it doesn't matter that you didn't know them before now."

"Okay. I'm ready."

He opened the door and walked through with Heather in tow directly behind him. "Here she is, everyone. Say hello to my wife, Heather."

Before the door closed behind them, Brianna, Chaise, Liz, and Sara had surrounded Heather in a flurry of excitement. The ladies made their introductions while Rebel joined the guys at the table, reviewing the assignments and the information they'd been provided from their contact. The only one who was still missing was Shadow.

"I'm so glad you're here with him, Heather," Bull called out across the room. "You have no idea how pissy he gets when you're not around."

"I can't believe you've all kept her a secret from us all this time. What the hell is that all about?" Brianna retorted. "Every one of you knew about her and never said a word."

"I'm afraid that's partly my fault," Heather admitted.

"It's mostly mine, though," Rebel corrected as he moved back to her side. "We were already married before I joined the service. One training led to another, one mission led to the next, more dangerous mission. When I graduated college and became a Green Beret, there was just too great of a chance she'd become a target while I was out on assignment somewhere. Keeping her off the record was the best solution at the time."

"And when you left the service?" Brianna put her hand on her hip and raised her eyebrows at him.

"By then, we were already set in our routines, and we were both protective of our relationship." Rebel shrugged. "And I knew you'd give me a hard time and tell me what an idiot I've been."

"You're damn right, I would have."

The room erupted in laughter, including Brianna, and Noah wrapped his arm around his wife's shoulders. "Cut them some slack, babe."

"Braxton is covering for me," Heather replied with a sideways smirk at Rebel. "I'm a little headstrong at times, and I insisted on keeping my independence. My family and friends have always been here in Houston. He was gone on assignments a lot, especially in the early years when he was a Ranger and then a Green Beret. His deployments were shorter but more frequent, and I was in nursing school, so it's not like I could just up and move anywhere. By the time his missions slowed down enough, we were both used to it. It's just the way it has always been."

"Maybe we should've nicknamed her 'Rebel' instead of you," Bull teased.

"Rebel One and Rebel Two," Noah joked. "Heather, you haven't met my brother before now. This is Silas Steele."

"Now that we've met you, don't expect us to just let you go," Chaise asserted. "I've never believed a long-distance relationship could work, but you two have made a believer out of me."

"Don't go getting any ideas," Bull warned. "I'm not sleeping without you every night."

"So you're the one, huh?" Liz spoke up at last. "You should probably come around more, my girl. I've had to call this one down a time or two for flirting with me."

"He has told me all about you, Liz." Heather smiled broadly. "And believe me, I've already given him a piece of my mind for his antics with you."

The mischievous gleam in Liz's eyes was unmistakable. "You and I are going to get along just fine."

"As much as I'd love to continue this conversation, we need to get to work and catch this asshole as soon as possible." Rebel stopped the conversation before it got out of control.

Rebel turned and walked to the table without checking to see if the others had followed. He began reviewing the original case file and the latest intelligence Silas got from his contacts on Rashad and Turan. "Heather, come here for a minute."

When Heather reached him, he handed her a picture of Rashad. "Have you ever seen this man before?"

"Yes. At the hospital. He's been on my floor a couple of times in the past week. Is this the one who's following me?"

"That's him. His name is Rashad Samir. His brother wanted to kill me because I'm the one who killed his father in a raid on his compound ten years ago. They were just kids then. Rashad will try to take the opportunity to exact revenge on behalf of his brother."

"But based on our latest intel on Rashad, he and Turan were complete opposites in the way they work, like day and night opposites. Turan was a socially inept techie who could make a computer dance on a stripper's pole. He was dangerous as far as the havoc he could create through the internet, but he didn't offer much in the man-on-man category.

"Rashad is the polar opposite of his dead brother. He's not a tech expert in any sense of the word, but what he lacks in computer skills, he makes up for in explosives. This guy could teach one of our explosives experts a thing or two. He considers it a form of art and prides himself on finding new and exciting ways to blow shit up," Silas explained.

"Great news," Rebel deadpanned. "So we'll get to see a fireworks show up close and personal."

"It's far too likely to happen with his training and background," Silas confirmed. "We can't take any chances."

"Heather, you'll have to stay away from the hospital until this is over. With his profile, he wouldn't hesitate to take out as many patients as he can in his quest to hit us. We'll have to plan this just right. We have to let him know you're taking time off without him realizing we're feeding him the information. You've already been avoiding him, so it would raise too many red flags if you just suddenly went back to your regular routine," Rebel explained.

"So, I need to go back to work one day, let him see me accidentally on purpose so he can hear me while I tell Becca I need to take time off. Is that about it?"

Noah smiled knowingly, immediately picking up on her no-nonsense wit. "You got it. What do you need us around for?"

"For the eye candy and the company," she quipped. "I have everything else covered."

"Oh, yeah. You'll fit right in with this bunch. No doubt about it," Noah laughed.

The pride and admiration that shone on Rebel's face was reserved just for her, and she knew it without question. Guilt filled her, squeezing her heart like a heavy vise and virtually paralyzing her lungs, making it hard for her to breathe. She hid the pain of her regret behind her smile, but the ominous feeling that she'd realized what was important far too late wouldn't go away. If anything, it was multiplying with each tick of the second hand.

It felt as if she was watching a timer on a deadly bomb count down, but she was powerless to stop it.

Please don't take Braxton away from me now, she prayed silently.

"Do you need me anymore?" she asked.

"Always," Rebel replied. "But you can go get to know the ladies while we finish going over these files if you want."

"Okay," she replied softly. "You know where to find me if you need me to take over and show you boys how it's done."

Rebel chuckled and pulled her close to him, his arms wrapped around her waist, the adoration glimmering in his eyes. "You can show me how it's done all night. For now, I need to figure out how to stop the bad guy."

Amelia's cries broadcasted throughout the spacious room from the speaker of the baby monitor. In her peripheral vision, Heather saw Brianna rise from the couch and rush toward the bedroom to soothe her newborn. But the connection between Heather and Braxton held their eyes firmly locked on each other, to both comfort and share whatever strength they could muster for the other. No amount of time could lessen the loss they felt, but it did give them both time to learn to handle the pain.

"I love you," Rebel mouthed.

"I love you more," she mouthed in reply before releasing him.

He watched as she strode across the suite and sat beside Brianna to coo over Amelia. When Brianna offered to let Heather hold the baby, Rebel watched with amazement as his wife took the tiny baby in her arms, held her close to her bosom, and softly kissed her little pink baby cheeks.

Silas, Noah, and Bull began talking about the contents of Rashad's file and pulled Rebel out of his thoughts, back into the conversation. While actively participating with his team, he kept one ear attuned to Heather's conversation with the other ladies. They were dying to pry into the more intimate details of their married life, but socially acceptable decorum kept them in check. When he realized not even Liz had blurted out the questions she wanted answered, he knew Reaper must have warned them before they'd arrived at the hotel.

During a lapse in conversation at the table, Rebel looked up at Reaper. "Thanks, man."

"For what?"

"For whatever threat you issued that's keeping the ladies from bombarding Heather with questions about us."

Reaper tried to hide his smile at first, but it was pointless. "I just told them if they pushed too hard, Heather may never come around again. She's stayed away all these years, so they have to make her want to be around them."

"I always knew there was a reason why I liked you and kept you alive. You've earned your keep today."

"Good to know I'm useful for something."

"Try being useful for this case now. Where's Rashad hiding out? What's his ultimate plan? He's here for more than Heather."

"Babe?" Heather called out. "Becca just sent me a text. She said a letter was left for me at the nurse's station. It's marked personal and urgent, so I'm going to tell her to send it over here by private courier. They can have it here in a few minutes."

"There's no other name on the envelope?" He was on instant alert, knowing the courier could be followed and their location could be compromised.

"She said it only has my name, and the personal and urgent is written in capital letters under my name."

Rebel and Reaper exchanged glances, unspoken words passing between them. "Heather, have them send it to me here at the hotel." Turning to Rebel, he continued. "I'll increase security around the hotel. Extra men can be here within the hour." Reaper stepped away from the group to call in the additional contracted surveillance teams.

Within twenty minutes, the suite phone rang, making the four men turn their heads and stare at it guardedly before Reaper picked it up.

"Steele."

"Mr. Steele, a letter addressed to you has just been delivered to the front desk. Would you like me to have it delivered to your room, or would you prefer to come to the lobby to pick it up?"

"I'll come down. Who delivered it?"

"A local courier, one we've used frequently. I can give you his name and company information if you need it."

"Yes, if you can write it down for me, I'll be down in a minute to pick them both up."

After a quick trip to the lobby, Noah returned to the suite with the letter in hand. He nearly succumbed to the urge to open it in the elevator, but he knew he'd never hear the end of it from the rest of the team if he did.

Once inside the suite, he laid the letter out for everyone to read.

"What the fuck?" Rebel exclaimed.

"Dickhead is playing games. He thinks he's funny, doesn't he?" Bull replied in disgust.

Spelled out in letters cut out of magazines in different sizes, colors, and fonts was a letter addressed to Heather.

You're so good with syringes and starting IVs.
You stick them in others while you roam free.
But your turn is coming, the time is so near.
When you'll get your own stick, it's almost here.

CHAPTER ELEVEN

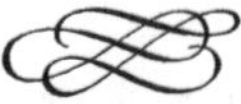

"What the hell is he up to?" Rebel asked calmly, masking the anger that welled up inside him. "It's definitely a direct threat, but what's his plan?"

"The part about her roaming free could mean he plans to snatch her," Bull reasoned. "He could be planning to drug her and take her. But the part about the stick could refer to different things. A stick in the way he started the letter, meaning he'll inject her with something. A stick of dynamite, meaning he'll blow up something. Or it could be neither one, simply meant to throw us off."

"With his background, we have to assume he's referring to bombs. Her turn is coming soon, he sent pictures of her to Rebel, and he's been following her. Left this at her nursing station, so he knew she wasn't there. But he hasn't found her house yet, or he would've left it there." Noah met Rebel's gaze dead on. "A bodyguard will be on her at all times. That's not negotiable."

Rebel nodded. "I guard her body just fine, but thanks for asking."

Noah smiled, understanding exactly how he felt. "You can't stay awake and alert for twenty-four hours a day, seven days a week until this is finished. She'll need a protection detail, even if they never touch her body."

"If they value the protruding parts of their bodies, they'll keep their hands off of her."

"Can't say I'd be any different," Noah replied.

"Hell no," Bull added. "The body would never be found if one of them touched Chaise."

"You're all pussy-whipped men," Silas sighed. "What happened to the badass Delta Operatives the three of you used to be? You know, before you traded in your man cards for women's purses."

"I'd just like to point out that I've been a badass Ranger, Green Beret, and Delta Force operative all while being married. I can carry my wife's purse better than any man, while still whipping your ass." Rebel arched a single brow at Silas in a silent mock threat.

"No need to get your girly panties all in a wad." Silas grinned.

"I'll assign the protection detail shifts to Blake, Roman, and Alex, and get Brad to start his computer magic to help find Rashad using the limited information we have so far." Bull picked up his cell phone and walked away while issuing the new orders to the other men of Steele Security.

"Rebel, I got the official word from our commander in chief while you were doing surveillance yesterday. The airwaves are full of chatter that Rashad's cell is planning something on a large scale."

"How large?"

"To rival 9/11."

"What are our orders?"

"Take no prisoners once we're sure of their plans."

"I know for a fact they won't take prisoners. While I was undercover investigating his cell's activities, the low-level guys I was allowed around couldn't wait to be promoted so they could take out as many of us as possible," Silas added. "I'm glad to hear we're ordered to take them out."

"I thought you left the CIA?" Rebel asked Silas.

"I did. Just like you left Delta Force," Silas replied.

"Delta Force doesn't even exist. I thought you spooks were smarter than that."

"And the CIA doesn't operate on American soil. So neither of us actually exists."

"Fair enough," Rebel chuckled. "Do you have any suggestions on where we should start looking for him? Or how to draw him out to us?"

"Rashad sets himself up on a pedestal, so he'd want to stay somewhere nice. His minions are more likely to be in a rat-infested motel while he stays in a suite like this one. But with what the intelligence says he's planning, he'd need somewhere with complete privacy. So I'd say he has a house here, whether it's rented, borrowed, or owned," Silas answered.

"Well, that narrows it down," Bull deadpanned.

"Exactly. Let's start narrowing it down," Noah replied. "Have Brad start searching for shipments of the most common ingredients these suicide bombers like to use. Who's moving the most paint remover and industrial-grade hydrogen peroxide? Or ammonium nitrate and diesel fuel? Cross-reference the addresses and materials. They may be splitting up deliveries of the ingredients to avoid detection."

"On it," Bull answered. "I'll have him include businesses around here, too. They may be ordering shit through an employer to hide it, too. Or stealing it."

"I'm going to take a closer look at his uncle's finances and see if anything jumps out at me now. We know there's still a connection there, but with him having immunity as an ambassador, we haven't been able to do anything about it," Rebel added.

"Let me don my disguise, and I'll go shake some local trees and see what the word on the street is." Silas stood up and turned to find Heather looking at him quizzically.

"Disguise? Shake some trees?" she asked.

"Yeah, with all of us being in Houston, the chances of being seen are just too great. I was undercover with Rashad's cell for a while, with the lowest level guys who didn't know enough to tell me anything. So, I'm going to go locate my confidential informants and find out what the word among the criminals is."

"Alone? Aren't you taking backup or anything?"

Silas smiled at her concern for his well-being. "No, I don't take backup out with me. This is what I'm trained to do, and it's best that I talk to them alone. Informants tend to clam up when people they don't know start asking them questions. Don't worry about me. I'm a big boy."

With that, Silas left the group to prepare his disguise. When he emerged again, he was unrecognizable as the handsome, fit man who'd just closed the door behind him not fifteen minutes before. He appeared heavier, his hair was shorter and light brown. His eye color had changed from the deep blue that matched Noah's to a chocolate brown. His eyebrows were bushier and matched the color of his new hair. It was the obvious changes to his face with latex prosthetic makeup that completed his transformation, making him unrecognizable as Silas Steele to everyone else.

"Who are you?" Brianna asked her brother-in-law.

"Charlie Murphy, street corner sales professional," Silas replied with a sneaky smile. "Otherwise known as a drug dealer."

"Even your teeth have changed. Are you wearing dentures?" Brianna leaned in closer to get a better look.

Silas smiled widely, giving her an opportunity to get a good look. "I sure am. These are Charlie's teeth, so I have to wear them."

"That is so cool," she replied with amazement.

"You and Shadow are keeping all the good stuff from me!" Liz stomped her foot and put her fists on her hips. "I've been asking for this for a long time now. When you get back, you're going to put some of that makeup on me and let me help with this investigation."

Silas glanced around the room, waiting for anyone to step in and act as the backup he'd just asserted he didn't need. "I'm not so sure about that, Liz. It's really too dangerous for you."

"You know what's dangerous, Silas?" Liz shifted her weight from one leg to the other and crossed her arms.

"What?" he asked tentatively.

"When you're sound asleep in your bed..." She paused for emphasis. "And I'm in the same room with you."

"One spy makeup tutorial coming up," he conceded. He made a long trip around the room for the sole purpose of looking each man in the eye as he muttered "traitor" under his breath when he passed by. Silas left the suite to begin tracking down his informants, ignoring the snickers that turned into full belly laughs when the door closed behind him.

The neighborhood Silas had to venture into was in the worst part of town, with the highest crime rate. Charlie Murphy looked as if he would not only fit right in, but it was more likely he was there to take over. His dark brown eyes were menacing and calculating as he scoured the neighborhood. He made it a point to look directly at each person he passed, leaving the distinct impression anyone who fucked with him would regret it. His confident swagger coupled with the obvious outline of the gun lying just under his untucked button-down shirt ensured others moved out of his direct path.

His appearance and demeanor perfectly fit the part of a dangerous lowlife to everyone around. Little did they know how deadly he actually was. Trained to blend in anywhere he was placed, and to also get out with the exact opposite of any identifying traits, Silas had no qualms about running into anyone in a dark alley. He knew which one of them would be walking back out on his own two feet—and which one would be wheeled away on a stretcher.

With three raps on the door in quick succession, he listened intently to the muffled sounds coming from inside the dingy, run-down apartment. Though the inhabitants attempted to be as silent as possible, hoping the person on the other side would think no one was home, they'd already made too many mistakes to pull that ruse off.

"Open up!" he commanded from the dimly lit hallway. His stern tone left no doubt he'd kick the door down if he had to tell them twice.

"Who is it?" a woman's trembling voice called back.

"That's a new low, man. Do you have any idea what kind of bad things could happen to a woman home alone in this place?"

The doorknob slowly turned, allowing the door to open only by a small crack as an eyeball peeped out.

"Pay the five dollars and install a fucking peephole. You really think that flimsy chain and your measly foot could stop me from busting in if that's what I wanted to do?" Silas asked incredulously.

The door shut softly, the ring bolt slid across the metal guide, and the chain fell against the doorjamb. Silas pushed lightly on the door, and it swung open with ease. On the other side stood Joe, the CIA agent who'd disappeared from Miami, with an overall countenance of complete deflation. His shoulders slumped, his face was crestfallen, and his eyes were lackluster.

"We don't have anything you can steal, and we can't get anything that could be of any worth to you. My wife is sick, and I've been out of work for months. What could you possibly want with us? We mind our own business and stay out of everyone else's business," Joe rambled on and on.

Silas walked in, fully aware that Joe hadn't recognized him under his disguise, and closed the door behind him. Even with Joe's down-on-his-luck demeanor, the training he received at The Farm was ingrained in his every cell. He watched Silas's movements with the precision only his years of service could provide. Once the door latched, Silas intentionally stepped out from in front of it, out of the line of fire of anyone who may show up on the other side. Joe's gaze shot up and met Silas's knowing smirk.

"Who are—?" Joe started to ask but stopped short.

"You and your *sister* need to come back with me. You're not safe here. Besides, this place is a shithole. If she's not already sick, she will be soon just from living in this dump. How do you know you haven't already contracted typhoid fever?"

Joe stared at Silas, or *Charlie,* for several long seconds. "How'd you find me?"

"Come on, Joe. You're not seriously asking me that, are you?"

"I've been very careful with every move I've made."

"Ever considered that's your problem? You're too careful, and that makes you too predictable. That'll get you killed in this job."

"I thought you quit the CIA." Recognition dawned in Joe's glare at last.

"Have you ever known anyone who actually quit? Enough with the stalling. Grab anything that could identify you, and let's go. Your sister will have a luxurious, safe place to stay, and she'll have the best company in the world."

"And where will I be?" Joe asked skeptically.

"With my brother, his team, and me. I know you took off for a reason, but now it's time to man up and make a stand."

"You don't think I tried? Too much planted evidence appeared to point at me, and I couldn't undo it."

"We know Bill was the dirty one, not you. Rashad took him out, so it's probably best that you got out of Miami. But Rashad is now in Houston, and we need to go hit up a couple of my CIs to find out the word on the street."

The color drained from Joe's face, and his eyes found his sister's worried expression. "I knew he'd end up here sooner or later. It's time to go, then. Emily, you know what we have to do."

She nodded, walked into the bedroom, and pulled the small suitcase from underneath the bed. Joe followed her, and they began filling the bag with their belongings. Silas heard Emily whisper to Joe as they packed. "Who is he? Can we trust him?"

"He's Silas Steele with the CIA. And we don't have much choice but to go with him if Rashad is here," Joe whispered back.

"Stop whispering about me. I can hear you both," Silas called. "In fact, this place is so small, I can still see you."

Emily turned her head and met Silas's knowing gaze in the mirror hanging on the bedroom wall. "I'm sorry. I'm just not cut out for all of this."

"I understand, Emily. You'll like it much better where I'm taking you."

Once in the car, Silas called Noah as an advance warning that he was bringing someone by the hotel. "Hey, little brother, I have a surprise for you."

"You know how I feel about surprises. What is it?"

"We need to make room for one more couple, one of them in the hotel and the other in the house. I'm on my way back to the hotel now to drop Emily off. Can you have Chaise come down to get her? Joe and I are going back out to get information, but it's not safe to take her with us."

"Of course. I'll let the ladies know to expect her soon. If it's the same Joe I think it is, I can't wait to hear this story, big brother."

The rest of the ride back to the hotel was quiet. Silas left Joe and Emily with their thoughts, knowing they were scared for their own safety, not quite convinced they could totally trust him, and fully aware of the havoc Rashad could rain down on their lives. In the grand scheme of things, Joe viewed Silas as the lesser of the evils he and his sister faced. Silas couldn't blame him for being concerned, but they needed Joe's help to stop whatever Rashad had planned.

When they reached the hotel, Bull and Chaise were waiting to escort Emily up to the secure floor. Noah jumped in the front seat of the car and turned to give Joe a menacing glare. "Well, well, who do we have here?"

"I believe you two have met," Silas chuckled.

"It can't be Joe Brown. The very same Joe Brown I met in Miami and who then disappeared into thin air in the middle of a national security case," Noah retorted.

"Just what I need. Two Steeles in my life. This should be fun," Joe deadpanned.

"Why'd you desert us, Joe?" Noah demanded.

"I found out Bill was dirty. I'd suspected for a while, but I couldn't get anything concrete on him. Then he started getting sloppy, blatantly prideful. I knew he'd end up getting us all killed with his arrogance. I had to get my sister away from everything. Rashad will do worse than kill her, and she's the only family I have left."

"Has he threatened her?" Noah asked.

"Yeah." Joe nodded, his eyes downcast. "He threatened to take her back to his homeland and sell her to the highest bidder. The thing is, that isn't just an idle threat. It's not his main focus, but he's done it before, and he'll do it again. Especially if it's a way of getting revenge on someone who has defied him."

Both of the back doors of the car opened simultaneously, and Rebel and Bull slid in, forcing Joe to move to the middle as they flanked him. All four men stared Joe down with their eyes lethal but their faces expressionless. Joe shook his head, resigned to being the outsider until he'd proven his allegiance to them after abandoning them before. "Let's take this bastard down," Joe finally stated resolutely.

"Let's do it. Did you girls say goodbye to your ladies?" Silas joked.

"Yeah, yeah. We're ready to go to the command center," Bull replied. "Let's get this motherfucker so I can get back to Chaise. He's being a serious cock-blocker."

"Bull. Seriously." Noah cut his deadly gaze toward his friend. "That's my sister you're talking about. How many times do I have to tell you I don't want to hear that shit?"

Bull's only reply was to flash his best friend a shit-eating grin.

"I kind of feel bad for all of you pansies since I'll still get to sleep with my wife every night. Not bad enough to give that up, though," Rebel chimed in. With a round of threats to Rebel's manhood, Silas set out for the shadier side of town to start gathering more information on Rashad's plans.

"Our informants will no doubt be thrilled to see all of us coming for them," Silas laughed.

CHAPTER TWELVE

The view of sprawling greenery of the ninth fairway was one of the most coveted in the uber-exclusive gated community, but it had nothing on the expansive Mediterranean mansion Rashad presently called home. Through his uncle's lucrative connections, he'd been able to procure one of the most luxurious houses in Houston to conduct his illegal business. The owner and his family were out of the country for business and personal travel for the next six months, ensuring Rashad's total seclusion for the duration of his mission.

Though the subdivision had plenty of houses, that specific house was situated on one of the largest lots, putting the nearest neighbor over a half acre away on either side. Inside the eight-thousand-square-foot, three-story estate, outsiders would be hard-pressed to see what he was up to regardless. The formal dining room located to the right of the expansive kitchen served as his creative space. The spacious dining table with enough seats for twelve people gave him plenty of room to spread out all his materials in a makeshift production line.

His resolve and conviction increased with each one he completed. When he had put the finishing touches on the completed product, he'd carefully move it to the sideboard buffet with the others. Alone, each ingredient was relatively harmless as long as it was handled as instructed. But mixed together, the combination became an instantly volatile and highly combustible powder.

He'd carefully planned the design himself to keep the crystallized powder secure until he was ready for it to detonate. Because it could self-detonate from the slightest friction, he insulated the outer containers with packing foam to reduce the movement of the glass cylinders. On his remote command, small devices inside each case would vibrate, creating one of the most brilliant explosions through a massive shock wave of energy.

The doorbell rang just as he placed the last one on the table. The sounds pealed throughout the house, echoing off the cathedral ceilings and carrying through the air like the most pleasant of wind chimes. Rashad glanced at his watch, and one side of his mouth quirked upward. "Right on time."

The delivery driver held the large box as Rashad signed his fake name on the delivery confirmation device. "Here you go," he said as he handed Rashad the cardboard box. "Guess I'll see you again in a day or two, huh?"

"Yeah, probably. I've ordered several things for my daughter's upcoming birthday party. It's a surprise, and we're going all out for it."

"Sounds like she'll love it. Have a good one."

"You, too," Rashad replied before closing the door. He kept up pretenses as a friendly, everyday guy next door to help to avoid blowing his cover. Not overly chatty, he gave just enough information about his fake family to keep anyone from suspecting him should anything happen to draw attention before he was ready.

He placed the box on the kitchen table and began removing the contents. One by one, he unwrapped the empty glass tubes from their protective coverings and ensured the black rubber plungers completely sealed each one before moving them to the dining room table. Once everything was in place, he began the process of filling each glass tube, carefully placing the plunger in the end, and securing it onto the custom-made trigger all over again.

His team would need an abundance of these devices to carry out their plans. Each one was small enough to carry at least ten in a standard backpack. Some would be carried in lunch coolers, others in briefcases. Obscurity was the name of the game, so the old-school suitcase-sized bombs with conspicuous wires sticking out would never work. Blending in, creating no ripples, and leaving no lasting impressions were the only surefire means of mission success.

"I wonder, Rebel, if you've considered this in all the plans you've made to find me. Has your friend Noah any idea what I'm capable of doing? I do hope you're both there to witness everything. But should you both get caught inside the grand celebration, I can live with the disappointment. However, you can't."

Rashad laughed maniacally to himself, picturing their faces as Rebel and Noah realized they were in the wrong place at the wrong time. When they realized the genius contraptions he'd built would lead to their demise and his plan would be carried out despite their pathetic attempts to stop him. It would be poetic, really, if Rashad were the type of man who believed in that kind of justice. In this case, he believed the result would be driven by divine intervention, so he would gladly accept whatever outcome lay in wait for them.

His vibrating cell phone pulled him from his inner thoughts and from the task of filling the glass vials with his concoction. He glanced at the screen before answering, instantly recognizing the name of one of the members of his team.

"Faruq, what news do you have for me, brother?" Rashad answered.

"We have teams going out tonight to locate the girl. She hasn't shown back up at the hospital, and time is running out. We need her to help complete our mission as planned."

"How do you plan to execute this idea?"

"Three teams of two men will go house to house in the neighborhood where you tracked her. We'll wait for the cover of night and look through as many windows as we can. At least we'll be able to start narrowing it down through the process of elimination so we can focus on the most likely houses."

"That's a good idea, Faruq. Tell the men to be especially careful of dogs. Any excessive barking will draw too much attention and endanger our overall mission."

"I will be sure to tell them. How are the other supplies coming along? Do you need any help with them?"

"No, they're coming along very nicely. All will be ready on schedule. I've ordered supplies in small quantities to avoid any flags of suspicious activity. I receive only enough to keep me busy for a couple of days, and then a new shipment arrives. I've timed it perfectly, though, and accounted for any delays with delivery schedules."

"It's an honor to be part of this mission with you, brother. I'll be back in touch once the men have scoured the neighborhood for the nurse."

"When they find her, have them take pictures of her and send them to me. I'll need them soon for the next step."

He disconnected and continued assembling the explosive devices. Rashad spent the rest of the day carefully measuring, cautiously constructing, and delicately moving the completed products. With each one, he pictured exactly where it would be placed and how the aftermath of the explosion would appear. That made him happy and gave him purpose, pushing him to complete what would otherwise be mundane, repetitive tasks. Each completed device was more beautiful and brilliant than the last. Each one represented a piece of the jigsaw puzzle and brought him closer to seeing the full picture in all its fiery magnificence.

~

"Why are you in disguise, Silas?" Joe finally asked. "You don't need a disguise to look creepy."

When the laughter died down, Silas explained. "I have to stay in disguise in case we run into anyone from Rashad's cell. I was undercover with them, but I never got close to him. His lower level thugs would recognize me, though. This persona is Charlie Murphy, if you need to use my name."

Once parked, the five burly men exited the vehicle and sauntered into yet another run-down, roach-infested building that should've long since been condemned. The halls were littered with garbage, dirty syringes, and empty baggies with faint white streaks as the only remnants of what was once inside. The men moved past the strung out inhabitants with red circles around their eyes so thick they almost glowed in the dimly lit space. The whites of their eyes were so bloodshot, it appeared they hadn't slept in weeks.

Silas stopped walking halfway down the hall and banged on the door with his hefty fist. He shook his head when the people inside began shuffling and whispering. He cut his eyes to Joe and said, "Paper-thin walls here too." Joe rolled his eyes in response, completely understanding his meaning.

The door creaked open, and a young teenage boy stood in the doorway. "Whatchu want?" The boy jerked his chin up defiantly as he asked, but his eyes betrayed the confidence his act projected.

"What do I want?" Silas replied casually, injecting a thick Southern accent to add to his disguise. "I want the man of the house to step out from behind that door, put his pansy-ass .22 down, and quit putting his kid in danger. He has about two seconds before I jam this door into his head and knock him the fuck out. That's what I want."

A resigned sigh fell from behind the door, and Reuben stepped out into the open. "Charlie, shit, dude. You been gone a long time, man. I thought you was dead."

Silas walked into the apartment, forcing the boy to move out of the way with his commanding presence alone. The other four men followed behind him, easily taking up all the space in the small room, especially once the door was closed. Reuben looked warily at each man, apprehension quickly overcoming his features.

"What's the word, Reuben?" Silas asked pointedly.

"Word 'bout what, man?"

"Don't play dumb with me. You know how much that pisses me off." Silas slid his Bowie knife out of the sheath and casually flipped it around in his hand.

"You talking about the dudes from the Middle East?"

Silas sheathed his knife, crossed his arms over his thick chest, and nodded.

"Yo, look here, man. I don't want none of that action. I sent their asses on down the road."

"What'd they want, Reuben?"

"They wanted military-grade shit, Charlie. Like breaking into an army base and stealing weapons and shit. You know I'm not into that, man. Yo, man, my cousin is in the military. That's like betraying my family and shit. That ain't me."

"And you know there's no way in hell you could pull that off."

"Yeah, well, I ain't no superhero, dude. I can't fly over the fences and dodge bullets and shit."

"Do you realize you end every sentence with 'and shit' or 'man'?"

"It's just the way I talk, man," Reuben replied nervously. "What else you need?"

"Have you seen them again since then?"

"I haven't. But look here, they found my boy Gustavo and wanted him to get some over-the-counter shit for them."

"Like what?"

"Paint thinner and shit, man. Those extra-large buckets of bleach like they got at the big-ass wholesale stores. Rectangular plastic or glass containers. Stuff you can walk into any store and buy right off the shelves, man. Freaked Gustavo out so bad he told them to get the fuck out of our neighborhood and don't come back."

"It freaked him out to buy legal items instead of selling them illegal ones?" Rebel clarified.

"Hell yeah, man. If some dude won't go into the store to buy his own legal shit, something is really wrong with that shit. He's up to something really bad, and he'll pin that shit on someone else while he skips town. No way is that gonna be me or my boy Gus."

"Anything else we should know?"

"Yeah, man. Me and Gus, we got ourselves real jobs now. Next month, I'm moving my family out of this shitty place. I'm making good money now, and we're moving to those better apartments off of Challenger."

"That's good to hear, Reuben. Gus, too?"

"Yeah, man. We ride to work together. Save money on gas and shit."

"I'm happy for you, Reuben. I may be back in touch soon. Don't hide behind the door with an unloaded .22 again. That's a good way to get shot."

Reuben stared at him in disbelief. "How'd you know it was unloaded?"

Silas gave Reuben a lopsided grin and moved to the door. "It's what I do, Reuben."

Back inside the car, Silas mulled over the information Reuben had shared with them. "We need to make one more stop before we go to HQ."

"Gustavo's?" Joe asked.

"No. There's an undercover agent in town working on another case, but he may have heard something that'll help us."

After a thirty-minute drive, doubling back and circling block after block, Silas finally pulled into a community park. Everyone got out of the car and instinctively scouted the area.

"Wait here. I'll be back." Silas walked off toward a small patch of trees that gave a semblance of cover.

The other men casually walked off in different directions to keep an eye out for anything suspicious while Silas conducted his clandestine spy business. Noah approached Rebel on one of his trips around the perimeter.

"Heather will be moved back to your house when we're on the way to HQ. We're coordinating the time so she'll arrive when you do."

"Shadow's back?"

"Yeah. He's at the hotel now, and he's begging us to leave ASAP because Liz has created a love nest for the two of them."

Rebel couldn't contain his laughter, especially with his imagination running wild with what ideas Liz had for Shadow. "I'm really torn, Reap. Part of me says we need to take as much time as possible to get there so Liz has plenty of time to spend with her man. But a bigger part of me really wants to spend time with my wife."

"Decisions, decisions," Noah chuckled.

"There's nothing that could make me actually want to delay seeing Heather, but I want to make Shadow squirm so badly."

"I did hear Liz yelling something about running him a nice, hot bubble bath," Noah offered and quirked one eyebrow.

"For the sake of national security and the lives of all the civilians, we must do a thorough investigation. Talk to everyone in the city if necessary."

"Thought that may help you make up your mind."

A few minutes later, Silas walked out of the woods and straight to the car. The others joined him, retaking their original seats and waiting until they were out of the park before speaking. All eyes scanned the area as they left, ever vigilant of who and what was in their peripheral vision.

"There are a few guys a little too interested in us," Noah remarked.

"Undercover Vice," Silas replied. "They haven't quite mastered the art yet, have they?"

"Not quite. For the average thug, they're good enough. For a professional, they're too obvious."

"Maybe we should start a new company and train them in the ways of the invisible?" Silas suggested.

"Not a bad idea."

"All right, let's hear it. What'd your spook friend have to say?" Rebel asked.

"I never said he was a spook." Silas cut his eyes to the rearview mirror. "But whatever's about to go down is huge. We can't screw this one up, boys. The chatter on the ground is Rashad has a large-scale attack planned and his cell is recruiting heavily."

"Large-scale, as in what? Are we talking nuclear, chemical, what?" Bull asked.

"They're still trying to figure it out. They've intercepted coded messages and signals that they're trying to decipher."

"Get them. I'm trained to analyze them," Rebel replied. "Maybe I can crack the puzzle."

"I'll see what I can do. The things he's asking for don't align with anything nuclear. I wouldn't discount the possibility of a chemical or biological attack, though."

Noah's cell started ringing, and a smile covered his face. "It's Shadow.

Wonder if Liz has him in that bubble bath yet." He smirked before answering. "Yeah, man, what's up?"

The silence in the car became deafening just before the tension notched up tenfold. The laughter immediately dissipated, each man attuned to the others' moods and mannerisms, acting and reacting as a single unit.

"I'm putting you on speaker. Say that again, Shadow."

"Another letter was delivered to the nurses' station, and we had it brought to a nearby restaurant by courier. I met him and just got back into the room to read the letter. This one is addressed to Steve.

"You've fought a good fight. You've lived a good life.
But nothing good can stay.
Now close your eyes, and say goodbye.
I'll help you pass away.

~

"Brad checked the hospital security system, and it was definitely Rashad. He was wearing a uniform that looked like maintenance, but it doesn't have the hospital logo on it. It's just close enough to blend in and not be questioned by most people. I've put one of our men on Steve's room and another undercover in the hospital."

"You know what this means, right?" Rebel asked.

"What?" Bull replied.

"First letter was to Heather. Second letter is to Steve. Brianna and Chaise are next. Maybe even Sara. He's going through our families to get to us," Rebel replied. "He's already signed his own death warrant. Now he's making it personal, and he's pissing me off."

"You mean we finally get to see Rebel get mad?" Shadow jeered. "This should be good. We'll even have front-row seats to this show."

"Should we move your dad?" Joe asked.

"We can't just yet. He's too sick as it is, and the medications for his clinical trials are there. We'll have to alert the local FBI and law enforcement so they can help with hospital security. If he's after our dad, he could take out half the hospital to get to him," Silas answered.

"Hey, Reap. Brad's program just finished running, and he's all excited about some information he uncovered. Says it's very important, and we need to get over there as soon as possible so he can translate his geek speak to regular English," Shadow interjected.

"We're on our way over there now. Get Heather and meet us at HQ. Park inside the garage, then Rebel can get her back to their house later when it's dark," Noah replied. "We'll be there within twenty minutes."

"Copy that. We're leaving now."

CHAPTER THIRTEEN

The large, two-story house on the street behind Rebel and Heather's house served as the headquarters for the team. By the time Noah and the others arrived, Roman, Alex, and Blake had finished their patrol of the neighborhood. With the miniature cameras in place to capture every possible angle around Rebel's house, they were confident any attempts made by Rashad's cell would be seen and quickly thwarted.

Brad had arranged to have furniture delivered by a team of agents who appeared to be everyday movers. The large truck sat parked by the curb for half a day while he pretended to oversee the correct placement of boxes and belongings. To anyone watching, he was simply a new neighbor waiting for the rest of his family to join him in their new home. Undercover crews arrived in nondescript construction company trucks with what appeared to be replacement sheets of drywall and a new door. A quick and simple repair job that would be quickly forgotten after a passing glance from anyone in the vicinity.

Inside those moving boxes, hidden underneath what appeared to be normal household items, was the most high-tech, military-grade equipment available. With each item Brad unpacked, he created an impressive control room in a virtually impenetrable fortress in the expansive entertainment room. The interior walls were lined with bullet-resistant panels, the wooden door was replaced with a steel door and frame, and computer monitors with a continuous display of the entire street covered the L-shaped workstation in the corner.

A large table sat in the middle of the room for the team to scour the original construction blueprints of the subdivision layout. New secure cell phones were laid out for each member of the team. The cells came complete with signal-jamming capabilities and direct chat features over constantly changing radio frequencies to prevent detection in the event of cell signal disruption. The collection of spy-worthy gear and tactical fighting equipment was enough for a small army.

Brad laughed to himself as he thought about how fitting that analogy was. Rashad may have declared his own war first, but Brad knew the Steele team would be the small army that finished it.

"What'd you find, Brad?" Noah asked as he entered the room with his entourage.

The team assembled around the table with Roman, Alex, and Blake, casually picking up their assigned gadgets and settling in for the briefing of Brad's discovery.

Brad opened his mouth to speak and immediately stopped himself when Silas stepped into his line of sight. His eyes narrowed and his brows furrowed upon taking in his appearance. "Reap, did you pick up a hitchhiking, homeless pimp on your way back?"

"Very funny, Bradford. My little brother wouldn't stop by the hotel to let me change first, so I get to be Charlie for a while longer."

"It's for your own protection. You never know when we'll run into one of Rashad's men, or if they'll see you first out somewhere. You have to stay in constant disguise," Noah retorted.

"Yeah, I know that. I have been a spy for a long time, you know. But I don't have to be *Charlie* all the time."

"Stop whining. It's not attractive when badass drug dealers whine," Noah chuckled. "Can we get back to the reason why we're here?"

"You're all here to see me," Shadow announced as he entered the room. "No small bills, please."

Heather walked to Rebel and took the seat next to him. Several of the men exchanged uncertain glances, knowing every bit of information they worked with was classified. With a determined expression, Heather reached over and laced her fingers with Rebel's in a silent declaration of her intentions.

Brad looked to Noah for direction, unsure of how to proceed in mixed company. Noah's lips quirked upward slightly on one side. "Go ahead, Brad. Heather is well aware if she hears something above top secret, we'll have to kill her."

"There are worse things than death, Reap. We could put her on Liz duty," Shadow suggested. "By the time Liz is finished with her, Heather's mind will be so jumbled, she won't know her colors from the alphabet."

"You boys think you're so funny. The truth is you're all afraid of me, and you know better than to try to kick me out of here." Heather rolled her eyes exaggeratedly, but the smile on her face belied her tone.

"I knew Liz reminded me of someone," Shadow flashed his full-on smile.

"Go ahead, Brad," Noah instructed when he quit laughing. "Before a fight breaks out in here."

"I'm still working to piece some of it together, but it's important enough you need to hear it now. I'm actually counting on your collective experience to help connect the dots. First piece is analysis of the chatter we've intercepted. Rebel, your assistance has been requested to help decipher some of these files. The messages have increased—drastically and suddenly—but they're unintelligible gibberish."

"I'll take them," Rebel replied.

"Next up, I searched for orders of anything that could be used to make bombs since that's our boy's specialty. Then I searched for any unusual items that wouldn't normally be delivered to a civilian or to a residential area. Cross-referencing the two files, I've narrowed the search area down to a few specific locations.

"A couple of them are less likely to be his hideout because of the locations and way too much public access. I wouldn't put anything past him, but I'm just not getting the feels from those areas. The one you should check out first is a gated subdivision in a high-end neighborhood. Very pricey, more than the average home, and the houses have ample room between them. This particular house has more yard than most, so it would make sense for his privacy," Brad explained.

"Was he stupid enough to have large shipments sent at once? That doesn't sound like our guy," Bull replied.

"No, these have been spaced out over a period of time. There were some shipments a few weeks ago, then they stopped, and now they've started up again. They're being shipped to that address every few days. With the access we have to government surveillance and intelligence systems, I was able to match these up in a matter of seconds. He's definitely not as tech-savvy as his brother was. Turan would've bought all this on the deep web," Brad explained. "The other addresses haven't had consistent shipments and haven't all been the same items."

"Could still be members of his cell. He could be sending parts to different people, thinking it wouldn't trip any sensors," Noah replied.

"We'll check the other addresses just to be sure. He could've been moving around, too," Shadow added.

"Reap, another letter has been delivered to the hospital. The guy watching over your dad is bringing it up. His shift just ended," Blake informed them.

Blake met him at the door and delivered the letter straight to Reaper. He was silent as he read it, but the vein popping out on his neck gave away his intense anger.

"What the hell?" Reaper demanded

"What does the little pussy have to say this time?" Bull asked.

"Our boy is quite the poet. Now he's after Brianna. Listen to this shit.

Your golden hair, your skin so fair.

Your travel abroad, your deathly fraud.
So quick your wit, so sharp your mind.
All these traits soon will make
An impressive tenth wife."

"Man, I wish he'd bring it on already. He must think his stupid little letters are getting to us, scaring us. He's really just annoying me," Bull replied.

"The problem with terrorist cells is they could go days without being seen when they're under orders to stay invisible. Stocked with enough provisions to last weeks, they could very well be inside one of the houses with the shades drawn tight and not be seen," Shadow replied.

For the following week, the men of Steele Security worked the leads they'd been given. Checking each house took time and around-the-clock monitoring. To avoid stretching their resources too thin, they each took shifts watching one house for a full forty-eight hours before moving on to the next one. They planned to keep this schedule up until someone made a move.

A call from headquarters brought all the men back to the house behind Rebel's home. Each man hoped for some kind of action that didn't involve sitting in a car, staring at an apparently empty house. The delivery of the cryptic poem had been the only physical evidence the cell was still around, and all the men were anxious to put an end to the case as soon as possible.

"Reap," Roman addressed him as soon as the men started filing into the surveillance room. "We have visitors."

All eyes swung to the monitors broadcasting the images from the surveillance cameras. Six figures moved through the darkness, exaggerated in their attempt to be stealthy in their crouched positions. Brad accessed the cameras remotely and activated the infrared night-vision setting. With their faces clearly shown, Brad captured the images and began running the facial recognition software.

"They're looking for Heather," Rebel announced as he entered the room with her in tow. "Let's help them out."

"Forcing their hand?" Silas asked.

"Something like that. I don't like feeling as if they're in control. We can let them think they are while we track them. If they're busy watching her, that car is unmanned, and we can get a tracking device on it," Rebel explained.

"Good plan. These guys are on the same step on the terrorist ladder I was when I was undercover with them. They're not his most skilled players," Silas added.

"Let's go catch some bad guys, babe." Rebel smiled at Heather. "By the way, there'd better not be cameras or bugs inside our house, Brad."

"I don't have a death wish, Rebel," Brad replied with a straight face.

"It wouldn't be me who got to you first, Brad." Rebel replied with a smirk and tugged on Heather's hand.

Following his lead, she rose and they scurried out the back door and across the lawns toward their own back door. Once inside, they strategically opened specific window coverings to limit the view of the inner details of their home. With the TV on and a shared bowl of popcorn, they snuggled closely together on the couch and waited for the terrorist recon team to work their way down the street to find them.

"When these idiots move on, you're all mine," Rebel whispered in Heather's ear. "We've been apart for far too long while I've been on this case. It's almost over, and I'll be so glad when it is."

"What do you have in mind?" she purred.

"I have every inch of your body in mind. I'm thinking about your intoxicating scent when you can't wait another second for me. I can't wait to hear the sounds you make when I put my mouth on you or my hands or my tongue. I want to feel your body underneath mine or on top of mine or both."

His mouth was close to her ear, his breath fanned out across her cheek, heating her to the core. With his arm around her and their bodies close together, it took all of her resolve to stay in place and wait them out.

"Can you hurry up and get rid of these guys?" Heather asked on a heavy breath.

"The guys walking around the neighborhood tonight? They'll be gone soon enough, and I'll have the rest of the night to remind you why you miss me so much when we're apart."

"Braxton Reed, you know exactly what you're doing to me."

"I'm just talking to you right now," he replied before placing a chaste kiss on her neck. "But soon, I'll do much more than just talk. I'll touch you. Kiss you. Lick you. Taste you. I'm a starving man, and you're the only one who can satisfy this hunger."

"Brax," she sighed.

"When I first take you upstairs, I'm going to fuck you without apology. Hard. Fast. Raw. Rough. Just when you think you can't take it a second longer, you'll beg me for more. Every time you think you can't come one more time, I'll prove you wrong. By the time I'm finished with the first round, you'll be as spent as a rag doll."

"Oh, my God." Her hooded eyes and her heaving chest left no doubt how much he affected her.

"Then I'll make love to you. I'll worship your body the way it's meant to be. Slow and steady, I'll prove beyond a shadow of a doubt your body was made to respond only to me. Every time I push inside you, I'll go deeper and your body will clench around me. Holding on to me, begging me to make you come again, until I take mercy on you and let you scream my name one last time before you pass out from exhaustion."

"Give me your gun. I'm going to shoot these guys and get it over with."

He chuckled and shook his head, knowing she was just as likely to shoot them as not. "As much as I'd like to do that myself, we have to let them lead us back to the rest of their cell."

"Brad has leads on where Rashad may be. Let the others go to those houses and find him."

"And if he's not at any of them? And if there are more members of his cell that can finish whatever he has planned?"

"I hate when you're right."

"It only happens once in a while in an argument with you. Let me have this one."

"Fine. I'll let you have it." The challenging gleam in her eye was a complete turn-on for Rebel. She lowered her voice to a seductive whisper and placed her lips against his ear. "I'll let you take me upstairs. Before you fuck me hard and rough, like you know I love it, I'll take you in my mouth and work you over until your knees buckle underneath you. By the time I'm done with you, you'll be gritting your teeth to hold on to any shred of self-control you can manage to muster."

"Fucking hell," Rebel muttered. "Look what you've done." He drew her hand to his crotch and placed it on his hardened cock.

"If you could see what you've done to me, we'd give those guys a real show when they peek through our window," she replied as she stroked him through his jeans.

He captured her mouth with his and held her face with his hands. He forced his tongue inside, taking total ownership of her without waiting for permission. When her muscles relaxed and her innate guard fell, he felt her melt into his embrace. Just when he started to lift her to straddle his lap, his cell phone began to ring.

Without asking, Heather knew who it was and why he was calling. "Your friends are severely cramping my style, Brax."

"Well, if you didn't have a madman stalking you and sending me pictures of you..." He let his teasing insinuation trail off before he answered his phone. She punched his arm as he connected. "Ow! Hello?"

"Ow, hello?" Noah laughed.

"Heather just punched me. I need hazard pay for this job, man," Rebel joked.

"Man, don't you know better than to harass a woman who has a black belt in Brazilian jiu-jitsu? She'll kick your ass and make you submit."

"Don't go dragging my sex life into this. That's not your business."

When the laughter on the other end of the line died down, Noah was finally able to brief Rebel on the latest. "They're two houses down from yours, looking in windows before quickly moving on. They're definitely looking for her. Roman and Alex are ready to tail the car, and we have GPS tracking on it. There's no way they're getting away from us tonight, but I doubt they lead us to Rashad just yet."

"We're ready and waiting. In fact, we're getting a little impatient. Can we just turn on all the outside lights and walk around in the yard? They're slow as fuck."

"Rebel, it's been several weeks since Brianna had the baby, so I know exactly how you feel. But let's not tip them off that we know they're out there, okay? We're watching the outside of your house in case they come back in the middle of the night, so you'll both be off duty. Make the most of it, then."

"Expect the favor returned as soon as you're ready, man. Just say the word."

"Taking you up on that, brother. They're moving in your direction now. Look pretty for their cameras."

With that, Noah disconnected, and Rebel hid his secure phone under his leg. When the two dark figures moved into the view of the window, Rebel and Heather both almost laughed out loud.

"It would be funny if it wasn't so damn aggravating," Heather harrumphed. "Let's just go outside, kick their asses, and be done with them already."

"You know I would if it would help stop this. We're on them, babe. Don't worry. Let them take a few pictures of us to prove to their boss they're on top of things, and we'll take them all down at the same time. You'll get to kick the whole group's ass at once."

"Promises, promises. The two stooges are gone. Take me upstairs now. You have promises you're going to make good on tonight."

"Your pleasure," he quipped. "And mine."

CHAPTER FOURTEEN

Rebel walked to the window and closed the blinds before turning his heated stare to his wife. After all the years they'd been together, nothing had ever diminished or sated his desire for her. Every touch and taste of her only made him want her more. Even if they didn't already know each other well enough to interpret every expression and every touch, there was no mistaking the desire that burned like a white-hot flame in their eyes when their gazes met.

With a determined stride, he lifted her in his arms. She locked her arms around his neck and her legs around his waist, and their mouths clashed in desperate need. He took the stairs two at a time on his way to the master bedroom. When he kicked the door closed behind him, he immediately turned and pressed her back against it. With one hand supporting her weight, he used the other to remove her shirt. His fingers deftly unhooked the front clasp of her bra, and she let it slide off her arms.

She grabbed the hem of his shirt and lifted it over his head, their lips breaking contact only for a split second. His fingers expertly kneaded her breast, slightly pinching and tugging on her sensitive nipples, while she used the door as leverage to rub against his rock-hard cock.

"Brax," she pleaded.

With a growl, his kiss became even more demanding and possessive as he all but devoured her. So consumed with the feel of his mouth on hers, she didn't realize he'd moved her to the bed until she felt her jeans being unbuttoned. When his lips left hers, she opened her eyes and watched him slide her pants down her legs. Like a predator stalking its prey, he moved with purpose when he crawled up her body. She watched with fiery desire as he dipped his head and pulled the satiny fabric of her panties with his teeth. With a slight lift of her hips, he tugged them the rest of the way off her.

When his face disappeared between her legs, she braced herself for the overwhelming sensation and intimate pleasure she knew would follow. His warm, wet tongue drove straight inside her wetness and vigorously rolled from side to side. Her fingers dug into the duvet as her body writhed against his mouth involuntarily. When he slid his hands underneath her and lifted her hips, his eyes flicked up to meet hers before he leaned in to capture her clit between his teeth. With light pressure on his bite, he narrowed his eyes teasingly at her.

"You're killing me, Brax," she moaned. "I'm dying a slow, amazing death."

"No, baby, you're not dying an amazing death yet. I'm only getting started with you. For now, my tongue gets the distinct pleasure of fucking you. Then my fingers will join in on the fun. My dick is already as hard as fucking nails, but you'll find that out firsthand soon enough."

As he spoke, he thrust his finger inside her and relished in the knowledge the intense pleasure she felt was at his hand. Literally. His finger and tongue worked in tandem before he added a second finger. The scruff of his beard rubbed against the sensitive skin of her inner thigh, making her whole body shudder from the mixture of pleasure and pain. He worked his hand and his tongue faster and harder until she fell apart under his touch.

He licked his lips as he raised his head and smirked knowingly at her. "You look so content and relaxed. You're even glowing. I'd say you need this treatment daily."

"At least daily," she agreed and rearranged their positions until he was flat on his back. "And now I'm going to remind you what you're missing when you leave me to run off to Miami."

"Babe, I don't leav— Holy shit!"

The warmth of her soft, wet mouth wrapped around the head of his cock stole his thoughts. His fingers threaded through her short black hair and held on tightly through wave after wave of her taking him deeper. The muscles throughout his body tensed, and he fought with all he had to remain in control. He wasn't anywhere near ready for their first round to be finished, but the way she pleasured him was more torture than even he could bear.

When he tried to stop her, she worked her mouth and her hand faster, leaving no doubt of her determination to finish what she'd started. Each time he hit the back of her throat, she swallowed, forcing the muscles to tighten around him and making his attempts to resist completely futile.

She recognized the signs his body innately exhibited the very second he couldn't withstand the torture by pleasure any longer. His entire body became rigid just before every muscle relaxed and the dam holding his restraint broke. After taking every drop he had to offer, she smiled up at him triumphantly. "Just a little something to think about next time you leave me."

She straddled him and lowered herself on his still hard erection until he was fully inside her. She rocked her hips back and forth as he pushed his hips upward, repeatedly driving into her. In a swift move, he switched their positions and melted her with his lustful scrutiny of her naked body. "I promised you hard and rough, didn't I?"

Before she could answer, he drove hard and fast into her, eliciting a spontaneous and unrestrained scream of passion. Between the alternating grinding and full forward thrusts, she gripped the bed tightly and reveled in the sensations only he could give her. With a matched tempo, they moved together until their bodies were slick with sweat, their breathing was labored, and their energy was spent. Their mouths connected in a kiss, tongues caressed and danced, and fingers dug into skin when they finally reached the height of their pleasure and fell over the edge together.

With one smooth motion, he rotated them both as one body to avoid crushing her under his weight. Spent from sheer exhaustion, she rested her head on his chest and his arms encircled her, holding her tightly to him, savoring the moment. Within minutes, they were both fast asleep, their bodies still entwined, their hearts beating against the other's chest. It was hours later when Rebel stirred, trying to gingerly move Heather to a more comfortable sleeping position.

"I've missed you so much, Brax," she whispered in the darkness.

"I've missed you too. For the record, I never *want* to leave you, my love. I've never wanted that, and I will never want it."

"I hate it, Brax. I hate being apart from you, and I hate that we've missed out on so much time we could've spent together all these years. I've always been supportive because it's important to you. But it kills me every time I have to watch you leave. And every time, I wonder how much longer we can stay together while we're so far apart."

Though he'd thought along the same lines himself at one point or another, hearing her say the words out loud was like a knife to his heart. The quiver in her voice when she spoke was his only clue that she was crying. "Why didn't you ever tell me you felt this strongly about it?"

"I can't make you choose between your life with me and your life without me, Brax. We agreed to this arrangement a long time ago, so it's not fair for me to expect you to give up everything you've worked for. If I'm not willing to give up my life here, I can't ask you to give up your life in Miami. Somehow, we need to make our lives into a life, though."

"You asked me if I'd give it all up for you, and I told you I would in a heartbeat. You know me well enough by now to know those aren't just idle words to placate you. I honestly mean it. It sounds like you've let this build up for a while without saying anything and you're reaching the end of your rope. I'm not going to lose you, Heather."

"I want a baby, Braxton. I want us to have a family." She held her breath after she'd spoken the words while she waited for his reply.

After several long heartbeats of silence, he finally spoke. "Are you sure? I'm strong, but I'm not strong enough to go through that again."

That. He didn't have to elaborate. She knew exactly what he meant. "Brax, Dalton died from SIDS. It wasn't anything we did or didn't do. As terrible as it was, and as much as it hurt, it wasn't our fault. Of course, I'll be a nervous wreck for the first year after having a baby just because I'll be hyperaware of everything. But after going to nursing school and to counseling, I've learned a lot about what happened to us. We didn't do anything wrong."

"I know," he conceded. "My rational mind knows that, anyway."

"Promise me you'll think about it. We're not getting any younger, you know."

"You know I will."

After a restless night, Rebel and Heather left their house to head to the hotel for a meeting with the others. Brad, Roman, Alex, and Blake were still conducting surveillance of the properties, while the rest of the team worked leads they'd managed to put together from multiple sources. Rebel had enjoyed his assignment the most—his job was to guard his wife's body from every angle, at all hours of the day and night.

"We have a tail." Heather rolled her eyes. "Will they ever give up? They're terrible at this."

Rebel laughed. "Be glad they are. We don't want to lead them to Brianna and Amelia. They've already threatened Brianna's life as it is."

"Let's turn the tables on them. Lose them, but don't lose them, and we can follow them back to where they're staying."

"We already know where they're staying, babe, from the GPS tracker tailing them the other night. But they're not the guys we need to bust just yet. Although, this is a different car, and they could very well be staying somewhere else."

"They could lead us to the ones we need to nab first. You never know."

"You're going stir-crazy," Rebel replied, suddenly understanding.

"Yes, I am. I can't stare at the same four walls for much longer. This is the last week I have off of work, and then I need to get back to it. Two weeks off is a long time in the life of an oncology nurse. I haven't even gotten to see Steve Steele."

"Okay. We'll have some fun with your inept stalkers first, and when we get to the hotel, I'll suggest we go see Steve later this evening. I know Noah and Brianna have talked to him every day, so he's still doing okay. I'm sure he'd love to see everyone in person, though. Silas will have to go in disguise again."

"We can all go in disguise. It'll be fun."

"Yeah, you're definitely getting cabin fever all right." Rebel grinned and laid his hand on her leg. With a light squeeze, he continued. "Let's see what they've got, shall we?"

"It's about time we get to do something other than hiding out inside the house. I love you, babe, but I'm used to being on the move. I've missed training at my Brazilian jiu-jitsu academy. My rolling partners will think I've dropped out," she complained.

"No, they won't. They know you're obsessed with training, sparring, rolling, and otherwise taking them to the mat to make them tap out."

"Yes, that is very true," she agreed with a nod. "Let's make *these* guys tap out now."

As the light turned yellow, Rebel gunned the engine and sped through the intersection. After making a last-second left turn, he immediately turned right and parked in a street-level parking lot. The car that tailed them got caught behind other cars at the red light. From Rebel's vantage point, he watched the two men through his binoculars. The driver banged his fist on the steering wheel, anger seared on his face, and the passenger blatantly yelled in frustration.

"I think Dude Two is trying to get Dude One to drive on the wrong side of the road," Rebel chuckled. "These two are definitely not in the upper echelon of competent terrorists. In fact, I'm not convinced they're not meant to be a distraction."

"What if they are, Brax? I didn't even think of that."

"It doesn't matter if they are, babe. We need to vet it either way. Any little bit of information we can glean is better than no information at all."

"Here they come." Heather couldn't contain the excitement in her voice when she pointed toward the gunmetal gray compact car that darted around the other vehicles immediately when the light changed.

Rebel waited patiently as they passed by without a sideways glance in his direction. Allowing a few cars in between, he pulled out of the parking lot and casually followed them. Their erratic driving pattern of speeding to the next cross street, slowing to a crawl, then speeding up again until they reached the next intersection would soon attract the attention of the local police. "They're panicking, babe. They can't find us."

Cool and calm, Rebel continued following them, hidden in plain sight within the increasingly angry pack of drivers who were unlucky enough to be trapped behind the chaos. When they finally gave up searching for Rebel, they made a quick U-turn and sped off in the opposite direction. Rebel made the same maneuver at the next light to keep distance between them and not draw their attention to the cars behind them. As he suspected, they seemed oblivious to the casual tail following them.

They followed the nondescript car to a part of town where the residents turned a blind eye and a deaf ear to anything that went on around them. Any questions created problems, and every family had enough problems of their own without inviting trouble from strangers. As long as they didn't see, didn't hear, and didn't know, they couldn't be held accountable for anyone else's actions. When the terrorists pulled into the driveway of their run-down, ramshackle house, no one even glanced in their direction.

Rebel and Heather parked one street over, a block away from their targets, and kept a vigilant watch on the house. "This isn't one of the addresses Brad found," Heather pointed out.

"No, it's not. This is new intel."

"Is this what your job is like every day?"

"Some variation of it, yeah. Some days are more exciting than doing a simple tail and sitting through a boring stakeout. Today is a good day, though, because you're with me."

"This is actually fun. I love this cloak-and-dagger shit."

"It's not so much fun when the bullets start flying, babe."

"You can teach me what to do, Brax. You know all the tricks of the trade."

He cut his eyes to her and slowly raised his eyebrows. "You want me to teach my wife, the love of my life, about participating in a live ammunition shootout?"

"Yes."

"I know that look, Heather. You're not going to let this go, are you?"

"Nope."

"All right. But you have to promise me something first."

"Okay," she replied, drawing the word out with a dubious tone. "What?"

"You absolutely will not engage in anything remotely related to a shootout until you've completed the full training for it."

"I'll make that promise, as long as you promise to actually deliver the full training program within a reasonable amount of time that'll be determined by me at a later date," she countered.

"You can't determine the length of the training when you're the trainee. I'll know when you're ready."

"And I know you, and you'll keep me as a trainee for the rest of my life. You have to guarantee I'll move past trainee status within one year." Heather crossed her arms over her chest and gave him the most obstinate expression she could muster.

"When you meet the same proficiencies we require of anyone who joins our firm, you move past trainee status. If it takes you longer than a year, that's not my fault," Rebel negotiated.

"Are these proficiencies already in writing?"

"Yes."

"Deal."

"I know I'm going to regret this."

"Let's go peek in their windows," she suggested.

"In broad daylight? Have you not watched any spy movies?"

"Come on. It'll be fun. It's boring just sitting in the car, doing nothing but staring at the front door."

"This is part of the job, babe. This is also what you're signing up for. We can't give away our position and let them move somewhere else we don't know about. Speaking of, I'll send Brad the address now." With a few clicks on his phone, he sent the information to Brad so he could start gathering information and set up full-time surveillance.

Within minutes, an older car pulled up alongside them and rolled down the passenger window. Rebel looked the two guys over carefully and smiled. "Hello, Special Agents with the FBI. Where's your Crown Vic to alert the whole neighborhood you're with the Feds?"

"We're dressed down and in a car that fits the neighborhood. What more do you want?" The agent in the passenger seat huffed and rolled his eyes.

"You need to slouch down in the seat. Your back is straight as a rod. The people around here don't sit like that, especially when they're waiting for someone to show up to do business. Mess your hair up a little more. Narrow your eyes, but not like you're squinting from the sun. More like you're daring anyone to look in your general direction. The clothes and the car do not make the undercover man, your attitude does," Rebel explained. "I don't want you boys killed on my watch."

"Appreciate the concern," the driver deadpanned.

"And don't speak so formal. That's another dead giveaway that'll get you killed."

"We're here to take over surveillance for you. I'm Stahl, and this is Baer," the driver replied.

"'Preciate it," Rebel replied pointedly as he cranked the engine. "Yell if you need anything."

On the way back to the hotel, Reaper called Rebel's cell phone. "Hey, Reap. We're on our way."

The silence caught Heather's attention, and she knew something was wrong from the expression on his face.

"I'm putting you on speaker. Can you repeat that for Heather?"

"Sure. We received another letter from Rashad today. This one is for my mother.

With Steve soon gone, my task will be done.
From you, what I want, I'll take.
From your nightmare, you'll never wake.
To a new land, you'll travel.
And before long, your son will unravel."

"That sounds like a threat to take your mom away, but also an indirect threat to you, Reap. He's going after your whole family," Rebel replied. "We'll be there in fifteen."

CHAPTER FIFTEEN

"Eyes on primary target," Shadow whispered into his comm. "Positive ID on Rashad. Shoot to kill approved?"

"Negative," Reaper replied. "Orders straight from the top. Latest intel says chatter is going wild. We've located the only known head of the cell, but he's not the top dog. We need him to find who he's taking orders from.

"Seriously?" Shadow answered, his voice thick with disappointment. "But I just got a new gun. It hasn't killed anyone yet."

Hushed chuckles reverberated through the comms. "Don't let that asshole get away with that, Reap," Rebel replied. "Primary threatened my wife first. My gun gets the pleasure."

"You win. I sure as fuck ain't getting married just to shoot someone," Shadow retorted.

"Man, if you got married, you'd be the one getting shot," Rebel countered.

Louder, uncontrollable snickers rolled through their earpieces as the men tried to contain their laughter at Shadow's expense. "I honestly can't argue with that," Shadow chuckled. "Primary on the move toward the west entrance."

"Delivery truck moving in your direction," Bull replied.

"Primary disabled the alarm system. If the delivery truck stops here, I'm gaining entry while he's distracted," Shadow whispered. "I have the alarm code if needed. Simple system, easy to bypass if I have to."

"Copy that," Reaper confirmed.

The delivery truck stopped at the curb, and the driver walked across the grass to deliver another large box of supplies. Rashad stood on the front porch with the door standing open behind him. He smiled and made idle chitchat with the driver while he signed for the package on the handheld device.

"Get the name he just used," Reaper commanded. "We're cross-checking everything."

"Copy that," Brad replied. "Rashad is signing the same name as the owner of the house. Sloppy, sloppy, sloppy. The owner has business ties back to his uncle, the ambassador."

"He doesn't know he's being sloppy. His cockiness will be his downfall," Bull responded. "It's the letters—he thinks we're distracted by them."

"And everyone he works with is spread out across the whole city. No one lives within ten miles of the others. That's for a reason," Silas advised. "Don't be fooled by his aloofness. Whatever they're planning, they have contingency plans."

"Agreed," Reaper replied. "So we take them all at once. Rebel, have you finished with those encrypted files?"

"Negative. I've partly decoded one, but they change the key frequently."

"I'm in," Shadow interjected. "Finding a comfy spot in the corner."

"I hope you took a piss before you went inside," Bull joked.

"Well. I didn't have to go, but now that you've mentioned it..."

"Delivery truck leaving," Bull noted. "Primary inside."

"He went downstairs," Shadow whispered. "There's a basement. Starting the jammer and going radio silent for a few. If there are any interior cameras, they'll be inoperable now." He retrieved a small signal jammer from his pocket and turned it on.

Shadow waited several minutes until he was sure Rashad was staying in the basement before leaving his hiding place. He moved silently through the expansive home, placing concealed cameras in various locations to provide his team with a perfect view of the interior. As small as miniature buttons, they came complete with strong adhesive on the back so they could be affixed to furniture, picture frames, or most anything else. When he'd covered all the areas he could, Shadow moved back to the door he'd entered through and crept back outside.

Shadow turned the signal jamming device off and waited for Brad to pick up the tiny spy cameras. "He forgot to turn the alarm back on," Shadow whispered when he was back in his place.

"All cameras are transmitting now," Brad notified the team. "Man, I love our new tech. Can you guys stay on active duty so we can keep everything they gave us to use?"

"You can always enlist," Bull deadpanned. "Then you can keep whatever you want."

"We need to get back into that house and see what's in the basement. I'd bet all of Brad's tech on finding more than what we need down there. I'll take first watch. If he leaves under the cover of darkness, I'm going down there," Reaper decided.

"Why don't you let me take first watch, Reap?" Shadow asked. "You need to go see your dad while he's awake. If our boy leaves, I have a few cameras left I can use in the basement."

"Ten-four. Brad, alert me immediately if Shadow enters the house again," Reaper replied.

The men left in different directions, covering their tracks and staying alert for any indication they'd been spotted. When they were each positive it was safe, they made their way back to the hotel. As soon as they walked through the door, Brianna, Chaise, and Heather were waiting impatiently for their safe return.

"Noah," Brianna sighed with relief and rushed into his arms. "It's about time."

"I was perfectly safe. Nowhere near harm, princess," he assured her.

"I think I'm getting too old for this," she laughed. "It isn't exciting anymore."

"See, Noah said there was no danger. Why couldn't I go with you?" Heather pulled her head back to look Rebel in the eye. "You said it would be dangerous."

"It would be dangerous for you to go. You'd try to storm the keep." He smiled before kissing her. "You were safer here than you would've been with me."

"Silas, come give me a hug and a big kiss," Liz asserted. "You look like you need someone to come home to."

While sputtering and coughing on the drink of water he'd swallowed just as Liz spoke, he pounded on his chest with his fist to clear his airway. "Um, well, I'd love to give you a hug, Liz." Silas wrapped his arm around her shoulders, lightly squeezed her, and kissed her on the top of the head, but his gaze swept toward Emily's amused smile.

"Where's Shadow?" Liz asked.

"He's still on the job."

"He was supposed to teach me some spy tricks this evening," Liz huffed. She looked up at Silas with wonder. "Hey, you're CIA, too. You know how to do the spy makeup tricks. I'll let you show me all your secrets." She waggled her eyebrows at him and swayed her hips a little more forcefully as she walked away. "Let's go to your room, Silas. Joe claimed he was too busy guarding all of us to teach me anything while you fellows were gone. It's time —right now."

Noah slid his hand over his mouth, trying to wipe the smile from his face, but he couldn't hide it. "You'd better get going, big brother. She doesn't like to be kept waiting. She's liable to help herself to your stuff."

"Silas," Liz called out. "What is this in here? Do you wear the thongs? I didn't know they made them for men, too. Woo, these are downright sexy."

Silas glanced around the room, catching all the snickers and stares, and was so horrified he was unable to respond.

"Oh, wait," she yelled. "It would've been sexy, but this patch of fabric is tiny. You know, I've seen commercials about these pills that enlarge your penis. You should look into those. They might help you get a girl. It didn't say how much the pills makes it grow, but even a little is better than nothing. Especially in your case."

"Liz, get out of my disguises. That's an eye patch, not a thong!" Silas yelled as he stormed into the bedroom.

"No need to be ashamed now, young man. We'll call it an eye patch if that makes you feel better."

"If anyone is going to the hospital with Bri and me, let's plan on leaving in the next fifteen minutes or so. We need to go see Dad while we can," Noah told the group.

"I'm going," Heather replied. "I need to check on my patients."

"That means I'm going, too." Rebel smiled.

"We're all going, Reap," Bull interjected. "We're family, no matter what."

Minutes later, the group reassembled in the common meeting area to go to the hospital together. When Chaise walked into Brianna's suite, she stopped short and her mouth dropped open. "Umm, how did you get into this room?"

"I can get into any room, sweetheart." The disheveled man sat casually on the couch, unconcerned with his intrusion, and held one bushy eyebrow in a defiant arc. His clothes were well-worn and varying shades of brown. So much so, he almost blended in with the couch beneath him. His short brown hair lay flat on his head, and his light five-o'clock shadow effectively hid any identifying characteristics. "What do you think you can do about it?"

"She doesn't have to do anything about it," Bull said as he stepped around Chaise, shielding her with his massive body. "That's what she has me for. You have about two seconds to start talking before you tragically fall from this luxury high-rise hotel floor."

"You can try."

Bull moved toward the man with his threatening stance and determined demeanor but was stopped by a large hand gripping his shoulder. "It's okay, Bull," Silas assured him. "Don't let him rile you."

When Bull turned and looked at Silas, he automatically stepped back and did a double take. Silas's normally black hair was sandy blond and curly. Even his eyebrows matched his lighter hair. The scruff that covered his jawline wasn't there just an hour before. His chocolate brown eyes were now a nondescript shade of green. "You have Silas's voice, but you don't look one bit like Silas."

"Well, I wouldn't *sound* like Silas if Liz hadn't stolen my voice synthesizer." Silas nodded toward the man sitting on the couch.

"Liz?" Chaise asked incredulously. "Is that you?"

"It's me, sweet pea. Silas made me up into one bad dude, didn't he?"

"So good that it's really freaking me out. How? What? I don't even know where to start with my questions," Chaise replied.

"Oh, no. Not you, too," Silas replied. "I've been tortured enough by Liz over my mad spy skills. No more trainees."

"Don't you worry, sweet girl. If you want to know anything, you just ask me. I'll get it out of Silas one way or another," Liz assured her.

Chaise laughed, knowing Liz would do just that if asked. "What's your clandestine name?"

"Chris Evans. No relation to the superhunk."

Silas shook his head and rolled his eyes at Liz. "You're supposed to pick an easily forgettable name."

"And you are?" Chaise asked Silas.

"Neil Brown."

"Boring," Liz retorted.

"How did you change your voice to a man's voice?" Chaise asked Liz.

"I could tell you, but then I'd have to kill you." Liz winked. "I've always wanted to say that. It's this little chip on my neck, hidden under a thin piece of latex that looks like skin. A little adhesive, a bit of blending, and voila—I'm a man."

"Let's go, guys," Noah announced as he, Brianna, and Amelia emerged from the bedroom. "Rebel and Heather are meeting us at the hospital, then they'll go back to their house tonight."

~

"Okay," Rebel announced.

Heather turned her attention to him as he drove and waited for him to finish his thought. After several heartbeats, she realized he had apparently already finished. "Okay? Okay, what?"

"Okay, I'm ready to have a baby. I'm ready to start a family. I'm ready to spend every day with you. As soon as this case is wrapped up and I'm off active duty again, we'll start actively trying to get pregnant. In the meantime, we'll keep practicing until we're perfect.

"I'll give my notice to Reaper as soon as possible so he can start looking to replace me. I don't want to do it just yet and distract him from the case, though. Roman is doing really well. Maybe Reap will take a chance and promote him into my position. I'll move back here, and we'll figure out the rest together."

"You're really going to quit the job you love, leave your best friends, and move back here?"

"I love you more." He shrugged. "There's never been any question about that."

"And you're sure you want to have a baby?"

"I'm sure. I watch Reaper and Bri with Amelia, and I know they're happier than they've ever been. They both wear their hearts on their sleeves, and there'll never be a day Reaper doesn't worry about them, but they'll never regret having her. You're right, we've missed enough time together living out our own lives. We put our marriage second whether we meant to or not."

"I never intentionally meant to put you or our marriage second, Brax," Heather replied in a pained whisper. Her eyes held a faraway gaze, lost in thought and retrospection.

"My best psycho-babble guess is we've lived our lives this way out of fear. Fear of a repeat. Fear that everyone was right when they told us we'd never make it. Fear that too much time together would bring all the memories flooding back to the surface and we wouldn't be able to deal with the pain. The truth is I've never been able to deal with the pain and the memories, but it's worse without you by my side.

"So before we do this—before we fully commit to it—I need you to be completely honest with me. Do I remind you of him? Of Dalton? Do you see him when you look at me?"

Heather turned in her seat to fully face him. "When I look at you, I see the one person I love most in the world. I see the boy I grew up with, the man I love, and the only one I'd ever want to be the father of my children. Of course, I think of Dalton when I look at you, but only because I would've wanted him to grow up to be just like you. The truth is, I'll see all of our children in you, and I wouldn't want to change that for anything."

"You have no idea how much I need you. You've always stood by me, loved me, believed in me, no matter what happened. You've walked through hell just to be beside me. No matter what the future holds, nothing can ever make me leave your side." Rebel squeezed her hand in his, emphasizing his sincerity.

"I feel guilty about you leaving Steele Security, your friends. I know they'll support you, too, but I also know how they've depended on you to have their backs. Will they secretly blame me for breaking up their little family?"

The concern in her eyes and her voice was sincere. The men had been through life-and-death missions together, formed bonds others couldn't comprehend, and trusted each other implicitly. The oaths they took weren't pledged lightly, and the code of honor directing their promises ran deep in their veins. Would they view her as the person who disrupted their carefully constructed world?

"My love and commitment to you have never been kept secret from them, Heather. They'll all support whatever decision we make because they're our friends and they love us. We know what's best for our life together, and that's all they want. It's not like we won't ever see them again," Rebel assured her.

"Brax, I'm so excited about this I can hardly wait. Can't we just go shoot Rashad and close the case right now?"

Rebel threw his head back in laughter. "I thought your martial arts training taught you to be patient, watch your opponent for weaknesses, and then use them against him to take him down."

"It did teach me all of that, absolutely. And Rashad's weakness is a bullet to the head. I'd like to use that weakness to take him down."

"You're a little too much like me, babe," he laughed. "It's kind of scary."

"I haven't been this excited to start a new chapter in my life in a long time. I never realized it, but looking forward to this makes it seem like the rest of my life has been put on hold, just waiting for this moment. I'm only trying to help it along."

"You have no idea how much I appreciate the gesture, but we really need to get them all at once. A bullet to Rashad's head would only give someone else a spot to move into."

Rebel parked in the hospital parking garage, and hand in hand, they walked inside. Heather's step had a new spring in it, her uncontainable delight bubbling over, while Rebel appeared invincible and proud to have the love of his life at his side. Heather's coworkers stopped their activities and watched her with questioning expressions.

"You look suspiciously happy today," Becca commented as she approached Heather. "Did you finally snap and leave all sanity behind?"

"Something like that." She beamed. "My husband is going to move in with me permanently very soon."

"You are one brave man," Becca teased. "Just going out to eat with her is scary enough. I can't imagine living with her all the time."

"Don't listen to her, babe. She has begged and begged to move in with me, but I won't let her. She's just jealous of you," Heather commented to Rebel. Turning back to Becca, she continued. "How are my patients? Have you been mean to them while I've been away?"

"Of course. That's my job, isn't it?" she joked. "You know I'm not mean to them. They love me. Steve's been asking about you, though. Since Sara has been staying here with him over the past week, he doesn't get enough first-hand information about your well-being. You should probably go see him first."

"That's exactly where I'm headed. Have you seen any strange men hanging around the last few days? Anyone you haven't seen before suddenly show up?"

"No. The big, scary guys parked outside Steve's room have been pretty effective at keeping the creepers away."

"Great, thanks. We're going to visit Steve now. I'll talk to you later."

As Heather and Rebel walked away, Heather looked up at him and whispered, "That's odd, isn't it? He sent a letter threatening Steve's life, then doesn't show up here again. Do you think he's waiting for Steve to be discharged?"

"No, I don't. I think the letters are only mean to distract us, divide up our resources, and give his cell more breathing room. He knows we have to err on the side of caution. In fact, I think he's banking on it."

Heather knocked on Steve's door and slowly pushed it open when she heard Sara call out. "How's my favorite patient in the whole world doing this evening?"

"Better now that my favorite nurse in the whole world finally showed back up," Steve replied weakly. "Are you finished being a slacker now?"

"Nowhere near finished. In fact, I'm getting a little too used to being off work. Think they'd pay me to stay away?"

By keeping up her normal, witty banter with him, she was able to hide her concern for his increasingly gray skin, gaunt appearance, and lackluster eyes. The nearly lethal cocktail of experimental chemotherapy drugs was taking a hard toll on his already compromised health. The treatment always affected people differently, but all of the more aggressive schedules eventually resulted in the same outcome.

"No way I'd let that happen," Steve smiled. "They know I'm the boss around here."

"I guess we need to get you well as soon as possible so I can kick you out of here, then," Heather teased. "Besides, it seems unfair to pick on you while you're a patient. It's just too easy."

"Don't you worry, little girl. I'm going to beat this. One way or another."

After a quick kiss to his cheek and a promise to visit him again soon, Rebel and Heather went room to room, checking in on her patients and visiting with her coworkers. Most asked when she'd return to work, but she had to keep her answers vague because of the potential threat to national security Rashad and his group posed. As long as he remained on the loose, she knew she had to limit her time around others so they didn't also become a target.

CHAPTER SIXTEEN

"This group couldn't be inconspicuous if we tried," Liz commented aloud as they walked down the hospital corridor toward Steve's room. "Look at you men. All buff, sexy, and dominant in every cell of your body. Not a single one of you blends in like I do. Face it, I was born to be a spy."

"Liz," Silas chastised her with the tone of his voice. "We're not trying to blend in. We're out in the open, in plain sight. If we didn't want to be seen, you wouldn't ever know we were there."

Turning to Noah, Silas asked, "How the hell did I become her new best friend?"

"Shadow took first watch."

"Bastard," Silas muttered under his breath.

"I heard that," Liz remarked. "You'll pay for that later."

"Sorry," he replied begrudgingly, only because he knew Liz would make good on her threat otherwise.

When they reached Steve's door, Noah turned and looked at the horde waiting behind him. "Maybe we should take turns going in and not crash in all at once?"

"You and Brianna go ahead," Chaise suggested. "Let him hold Amelia while he has some energy. By the time he gets through all of us, he'll be worn-out."

Noah kissed her cheek. "Good thinking, little sister. Bri and I will be out in a few minutes, though I have a feeling we'll have to leave Amelia with Mom."

"I'm going to roam around the halls and see if I can find my son. He may still be here making rounds," Liz announced. "I want to see how long it takes him to recognize me in this getup."

"Don't wander off too far," Noah replied. "Unless you take Silas with you."

"Ppfffttt," Liz retorted. "He'd give me away in a heartbeat. I'll be fine."

Noah, Bull, and Silas all exchanged glances as Liz sauntered away, working her best masculine walk as much as she could. She had to admit, to herself if not to Silas, her disguise was just bland enough to make her nearly invisible in the crowded hallways. No distinguishing features, nothing that was particularly interesting, and nothing that anyone would remember once they'd passed her and moved on their way. The conversations she was able to eavesdrop on amazed her and made her want it even more.

She continued her leisurely stroll, glancing around for her son the doctor when she remembered her original purpose. People everywhere shared the most personal information because they didn't realize anyone else was around. It was all far too interesting for her to ignore or resist. After a few twists and turns through the connecting hallways, she found herself in a more deserted area of the hospital. Unwavering in her quest, she continued her exploration with a relaxed casualness until a familiar face stopped her cold.

He wore a navy blue uniform that could've easily been mistaken for a maintenance crew worker. His ball cap sat low on his forehead, shielding the majority of his face, coupled with the fact that he kept his eyes on the floor as he walked. But the glimpse she got was all she needed. The similarity to Turan, the man who'd tried to kill her, was unmistakable. She had no doubt the man walking slightly ahead of her was his brother, Rashad.

The very man of the hour.

She slowed her pace, taking advantage of the advanced age her disguise suggested she was to avoid arousing his suspicion while she followed him. When he turned, opened a door, and disappeared into a room, she quickened her pace to read the plaque on the door. *Medical Gas Storage Room. Caution: Oxidizing Gas(es) Stored Within. No Smoking. No open flames.*

A chill ran down her spine, causing her whole body to shiver from the ominous undertone of the commonplace placard. A sign anyone else would pass by without a second thought suddenly became a genuine cause for panic when an explosives expert was added to the mix. Liz slipped into a janitorial closet a few doors down and on the opposite side of the hall. She left the door slightly cracked to watch for Rashad so she could try to figure out what he had planned.

When the door to the medical gases storage room opened, Rashad pushed a large metal cart loaded with oxygen tanks, the factory seal still visible on the gauges to indicate they were completely full cylinders. The tanks weren't secured in any discernible fashion and rocked unsteadily as he rolled the cart through the doorway. When he turned to lock the door behind him, one of the cylinders rolled off the bottom rack, making a loud clanging noise when it hit the floor.

Seizing her chance, Liz slipped out of the closet and strode up behind an anxious Rashad. She calmly picked up the wayward tank and handed it to him. "Seems like they'd make these carts to hold the tanks vertically so they couldn't roll off and hit your foot."

After all the years her son was in college, medical school, internship, and residency before joining his current practice, Liz knew a thing or two about hospital protocol. Like how the medical gas storage room was supposed to be locked so only personnel could access it, and the tanks were supposed to be transported in a specific vertical storage cart. Her nonchalant statement was meant to be a test of how educated Rashad was on hospital protocols.

"I should invent one and make a lot of money, huh?" Rashad replied, no hint of recognition in his eye when he briefly made eye contact. Her disguise was holding true. "It would make my job easier, anyway."

"Yeah, and at least a computer couldn't replace the work you do. All these high-tech gadgets the young people use today," *Chris Evans* tsked. "Everyone's too dependent on computers these days. Don't you agree?"

"You're right. Everything is electronic now."

Liz could tell Rashad only replied with quick, noncommittal replies to be polite while avoiding prolonging the conversation. She also knew his social skills were no match for her own.

"You look like you're fairly young, part of the Millennials who grew up with a laptop in one hand and a cell phone in the other. Think you could come to my wife's hospital room and fix our laptop for us?"

"I'm afraid I wouldn't be much help. My brother was the tech-savvy one in the family, but I never cared much for computers."

"Let me guess. You were more into the outdoorsy, physical stuff?"

"Something like that." Rashad nodded, then glanced longingly down the corridor. Away from the intruder and the conversation he wanted no part in.

"Just as well. Those techies are usually pansies. It was just a few months back when one of those wimpy boys tried to kill an old lady. You remember that? It made national news. They were somewhere in Colorado, though. Not around here. He wasn't even man enough to kill a helpless old lady. Not that I'm condoning killing old ladies, mind you. I just mean a young man should have more gumption than an old lady has."

Liz watched with masked amusement as Rashad worked his jaw, biting back his anger. He was desperate to retaliate, but he knew he couldn't without giving himself away. She opened her mouth to continue her veiled assault on Rashad's family when her cell phone began ringing. Rashad seized the opportunity to escape from his chatty captor. With a single nod goodbye to her, he quickened his stride and pushed the cart of tanks down the hall.

"Chris Evans," Liz answered.

"Liz. Where are you?" Noah asked. "We've been worried about you."

"I've just been talking to Rashad."

"You what?" Noah shouted.

"He's here in the hospital, but he's not here for us." Liz relayed her location and the entire interaction to Noah while he, Bull, and Silas made their way in her direction. When they reached her, she pointed down the hall. "He went that way, but I couldn't follow him without arousing his suspicion."

"I'll take it," Silas replied. "He'll recognize anyone else. Have Roman and Blake get the ladies out of here before Rashad sees them. Make sure Rebel and Heather are gone, too."

"They are," Bull replied. "Rebel sent me a text a few minutes ago saying they were going back to their house in case we needed them for anything."

"Liz, call your son and see if there's any way we can get Dad set up in the hotel with around-the-clock nursing care. If he can be moved, we need to do it—for his safety and everyone else's. Rashad is getting ready to make his move if he's stealing oxygen tanks," Silas directed.

"I don't understand what oxygen tanks have to do with making a move soon. But I'll call Daryl right away," Liz agreed.

"We really need Rebel to finish deciphering those encrypted files. This piece of the puzzle may shed some light on how to decode the parts he's having trouble with. I'll call him on my way back and fill him in. I'll meet you back at HQ in two hours." Silas stopped and met Noah's gaze pointedly. "Watch your six, little brother."

"Copy that. You do the same."

Noah watched his brother's back until Silas was out of his line of sight. The sinking feeling settled like a lead weight in the pit of his stomach. "Let's go," he said solemnly. "It's going to be a long night."

On their way back to Steve's room, Liz and Bull were each on their phones, making arrangements to keep their loved ones protected. Noah's phone rang, and that bad feeling he'd had suddenly turned grave.

"Let's hear it, Shadow," Noah answered.

"Reap, it's bad, man. Bad, bad. The residue indicates he's been concocting a mixture of acetone, acid, and industrial-grade hydrogen peroxide. From the amount of supplies Brad has tracked and the types of containers he ordered, his group will have very deadly and portable bombs," Shadow explained. "We need to make a move of some kind, man, or we'll look completely incompetent when everything goes down."

"Acetone, acid, and industrial-strength hydrogen peroxide? TATP. He just stole a large cart full of oxygen tanks from the hospital."

"My guess is that's where he found the high-test hydrogen peroxide, too. There aren't many other places that would need industrial-strength peroxide. The oxygen supply is self-explanatory."

"Silas is meeting us back at HQ in two hours. We're heading over there now to create our battle plan. He thinks he'll have enough intel to help Rebel piece together the last of the cipher code on those encrypted files. We can at least start contacting the cooperating agencies and arrange twenty-four-seven surveillance on all the locations we've identified," Noah replied.

"I'll be waiting for you there in twenty," Shadow replied and disconnected.

"Daryl is on his way here to make the arrangements for Steve. He'll be moved tonight, and two home health nurses will stay with them in one of the suites on our floor at all times. Your dad will be well taken care of, Noah," Liz assured him. "As much as Heather loves him, I wouldn't be surprised if she didn't insist on helping too."

"Thank you, Liz, and thank Daryl for me." He turned to the men and continued. "We need to move now. He's using TATP, so whatever he's planning will happen in the next few days, if that long."

~

"Hello, Braxton. It's been a while since I last saw you. How have you been?" Emmett asked as he stood to shake hands.

"I've been good, sir. Just very busy with work over the last few months."

The relationship between the two men was better than when Rebel and Heather first married, but not by much. Each man tolerated the other for the sake of family, but the mutual animosity simmered just under the surface. Their contention often made their standing country club dinner reservations awkward at times.

"Too busy to come home to see your wife?"

Rebel inhaled a deep breath and kept his eyes trained on Emmett's. "I can assure you the only reason I haven't been home with my wife in a while is because the case I've been on is crucial. And top secret. But I'm confident it'll wrap up soon."

"Dad," Heather interjected sternly. "I talk to my husband every single day, multiple times a day, even. Not once have I ever felt like the case came before me, nor have I ever felt the need to make him feel guilty for doing this country a great service."

"Braxton, I'm sorry—that's not what I meant, though I see how it could be easily misinterpreted. I know how important Heather is to you. I was only saying you must've been really busy if you couldn't get home to see her," Emmett clarified.

"No apology necessary," Rebel replied coolly.

"We have wonderful news," Heather stated emphatically, quickly changing the subject.

"Let's hear it," Kay encouraged her daughter.

"Braxton is leaving Steele Security after this case is wrapped up and moving back here permanently."

"Oh, Braxton, that is great news. Heather is obviously ecstatic, but I'm sure your parents are as well," Kay replied sincerely.

"I actually haven't even had a chance to tell them yet. Moving back is something I've considered for quite a while, but now I know it's time." He reached across and took Heather's hand in his before he continued. "My wife is more important to me than anything."

"I'm really so very happy for you both," Kay replied. "Have you started exploring other employment opportunities? Or will you start your own company here?"

Rebel chuckled. "We honestly haven't gotten that far in our discussions yet. This case is demanding my full attention at the moment, so I'm avoiding anything that divides my focus."

Emmett pressed his lips together into a tight line and glanced around the restaurant. He cleared his throat and looked at Rebel. "It just so happens the head of my security department is retiring soon. I need someone dependable, knowledgeable, and trustworthy to take over. In all honesty, I can't think of anyone who better fits that description than you. I won't put you on the spot for an answer right now, but think it over and let me know in a couple of days or so."

"I'll do that. Thank you, sir."

"Kay and I are leaving next week, and we'll be gone for several weeks. We're acquiring another company, and as the president and CEO, I have to be there for the final regulatory compliance review. Plus, it's just better for the overall morale of the employees who are being acquired. The whole mergers and acquisition process leaves them all feeling very vulnerable."

"If there's anything I can do to help while you're away, don't hesitate to say the word," Rebel replied. "I'm happy to do whatever you need me to."

"Just take care of my little girl, Brax. Make her happy. That's all a father can really ask of his son-in-law," Emmett replied with a genuine smile. One that confirmed he already knew Rebel wouldn't disappoint him.

Conversations during dinner flowed easier between the two men than ever before. Guards were lowered. Walls were torn down. Beginning bonds were formed, however fragile. But it was enough to allow hope to take root, along with a renewed sense of excitement for what the future would hold for their extended families.

Back in the car on the way home, Rebel glanced over at Heather, noting the natural glow on her face that only came from true happiness. "I've been waiting all damn day to get you home alone."

"Oh, yeah?" She grinned as she cut her eyes sideways toward him.

"Definitely. It's been a long fucking day, and it's going to be a long night of fucking."

"I love when you talk dirty to me," she purred.

"Yeah, I know you do. You get so wet, don't you? When I tell you everything I want to do to you. When I tell you how I'm going to take you. When I pick you up and carry you over my shoulder to the bedroom to have my way with you."

"You need to hurry up and get me home."

"We're going to start practicing to have that baby. Practice makes perfect, you know."

"You're going to make my ovaries explode from just talking about it."

Rebel reared his head back in laughter. "We can't have that. I'm going to take care of you as soon as I get you home."

The second they walked into the house, hands groped and bodies collided in desperate need of the other. Rebel explored her mouth and her neck with his mouth, licking, sucking, and nipping at her skin as he moved. He peeled her clothes off of her and dropped them on the kitchen floor right where they stood. His palms covered her breasts, his fingers kneading and caressing them. He moved one hand down across her taut stomach and covered her mound. He thrust his finger inside her and swallowed her moans of pleasure with his kiss.

Turning her around, he bent her over the table and used his foot to part her legs. With fluid perfection, he shed his clothes in a heap with hers and rubbed his thick cock against her toned ass, repeatedly pushing his hips upward in slow and enticing movements. He slid his hand around her to find her wet pussy again. With every upward thrust of his cock, he plunged his fingers deep inside her.

"Brax, I need you," she pleaded.

"You have me," he murmured.

His fingers gripped her hip bones, and he spread her legs a little farther apart. "Are you ready?" he asked.

"Yes." She drew out her reply in a mixture of a seductive hiss and a needful plea.

He wrapped his hand around his cock and guided it to her slick entrance. He rubbed the head of it against the silky wetness before surging his hips forward quickly and burying himself deeply inside her.

Her fingers curled into the table, desperate for something to hold on to as he continued to pound into her. He pulled back to the point only the tip remained inside her, then slammed his hips forward again. Her climax began to build low in her belly, the intensity of it causing her inner walls to clench around him.

"Not yet," he commanded and stepped away from her. After helping her to stand, he turned her around to face him and gently pushed her to lie back on the table. He knelt in front of her and sucked her clit into his mouth. Like a man who'd been starved, he feasted on her voraciously until she screamed his name amid other indistinguishable whimpers and sighs.

He stood, pushed both of her legs to her chest, and drove into her with reckless abandon. Close on the heels of her last orgasm, she quickly reached her climax again. He felt her body clench around him, her muscles tightened, and she held her breath to intensify the effect.

"Come for me now, baby," he demanded.

"Brax!" Her shuddering and shaking told him everything she couldn't say, and he let go of his own control and joined her in a state of complete euphoria.

CHAPTER SEVENTEEN

"You've been staring at that computer screen for hours. You're going to go blind," Heather complained.

Rebel chuckled but didn't look up. "I spent a lot of time deciphering hidden code during my time in the Army. I'm immune to blindness now."

"Are you also immune to a good, swift kick in the pants? Because that's what you'll get if you keep ignoring me."

With a smile plastered across his face, Rebel looked up from his assignment to please his wife. "Yes, my love? How can I serve you today?"

"That's better. You may continue now."

"You just wanted to see if you could make me look up, didn't you?"

"Yep. I won."

He shook his head good-naturedly. "Babe, there will never be a time you won't win when it comes to you getting my attention."

"I know," she replied as she straddled his lap, forcing him to move his laptop to the side. "I'm just so bored, Brax. I've been cooped up in this house forever."

"It's been two days, babe. Two days is not forever. And you've hardly been cooped up. We've been to the hotel to see everyone there and to HQ to meet with the guys at least a couple of times."

"HQ doesn't count. And it sure as hell feels like forever. I'm going to go to Mom's and visit with her for a while today."

"Heather, you know what's going on, what we're up against. Let's not go through this again."

"Brax, there are people out there living their lives. Carrying on with their daily activities because they have no idea something terrible is coming. I want to be one of those people. We've pretty well established he isn't actually after me. The letters and pictures were to distract you."

"No. The letters about the others were to distract us. He would kill you to hurt me because I'm the one who killed his father. Don't give him the opportunity to do that to me, Heather. There are a lot of things I can live without, but you're not one of them."

"I promise I won't take any unnecessary chances. I will go straight there and straight home. You said now that you have more concrete evidence that he's making a move soon, there are more agencies involved and more eyes on him and his crew. He's busy preparing for his grand finale fireworks show. He's not concerned with me," she argued.

"I'll take you over there. You and Kay can chill in the pool while I work on these. That'll at least give me some peace of mind and a change of scenery."

"That works for me. I'll grab both our bathing suits, in case you decide to take a break and join us. I'll be ready to go in just a few minutes."

She leaned in and planted a kiss on his lips while she rubbed her fingers through his beard. His strong arms encircled her, pulling her chest flush with his. "You are my reason for living, Heather. Your love has kept me sane through so many hard times over the years. I only want to keep you safe and with me."

"I know, babe. I am going stir-crazy, but I honestly need to discuss something important with my parents. She's home today, but I'll have to catch Daddy another time before they leave for the acquisition."

He smacked her behind playfully. "Go get ready to leave, then. One of us has work to do." She laughed along with him, loving their playful banter and the natural give-and-take they shared.

On the drive to her parents' house, Rebel was extra-vigilant about watching every car, every person crossing at the intersections, and every other thing around them when they were stopped at a red light. The serious mood inside the vehicle was so unlike Rebel's usually calm persona, Heather started to second-guess her insistence on taking the short trip. Once they pulled into the open space of her parents' three-car garage, she was finally able to relax and breathe easier.

Kay met them at the door as they walked in from the garage. She pulled Heather into her arms and kissed her cheek. "How's my girl?"

"Glad to be released from my prison cell," she joked.

"Your home is hardly a prison cell." Kay shook her head and playfully rolled her eyes.

"Shhh—don't tell Brax. That's the only reason the warden let me out for the day."

"I can hear you," Rebel replied dryly from beside her.

"Ready to swim?" she asked, smiling.

"You two go ahead. I'm making progress on this file with the information

Silas shared, and I need to try to wrap it up today if at all possible," Rebel replied.

"You can use Emmett's office, Braxton. It should have everything you need, but let me know if I can get you anything," Kay offered.

"Thanks, Kay. You ladies have fun."

Rebel left them to their mother-daughter time and made his way through the expansive home toward Emmett's study. Once seated in the plush, high-backed leather office chair, Rebel once again focused on piecing together the jagged edges of the puzzle, hoping the information he uncovered would put an end to the case once and for all. Multiple files of encrypted data had to be pieced together and interpreted without missing a key element that could change the entire meaning of the text.

After several hours of cross-referencing, double-checking, and verifying the key, he'd deciphered the hidden instructions for the extremist group. He read the message several times before the full meaning of it hit him.

Mother of Satan at Portno. Greater than eleven. Cut off fuel. Cripple the lanes. Stop the flow. Babylon falls when we slay the great harlot. Allahu Akbar!

He grabbed his secure phone and hit send. "Reaper, I discovered the hidden message." He read the message to Noah and waited for the words to sink in.

"Mother of Satan...the nickname for TATP," Noah replied. "What is Portno?"

"Port of New Orleans. The only deep-water port where foreign oil is brought into the United States."

"That could explain the 'cut off fuel' reference. And the 'greater than eleven' could mean they intend to rival the damage inflicted from the attacks on September 11. Or they want more to cause more fatalities," Noah replied. "Good work, Rebel. I knew you'd figure it out. I'll call Homeland Security and all the other agencies involved. They can send teams down there to help intercept and take them out."

"Deciphering it doesn't mean I've figured out everything he means. There's no doubt they know exactly what to do now. Does anyone have eyes on Rashad?"

"Joe has been tailing Rashad since the day Silas followed him out of the hospital. He packed up all his belongings and left the house in the gated community. He's at one of the other run-down shacks now," Noah replied. "Silas and Shadow had a talk with the director at the CIA to help clear Joe's name. I'm sure he was on the receiving end of a good tongue-lashing, and I know they'll still investigate him, but they've put him under Shadow's command for now."

"Joe had better not be hiding anything. Shadow is like a human lie detector and a revealer of secrets. He'll know every dirty little secret Joe has in no time," Rebel chuckled. "You know, if Rashad changed houses, that means he must've finished making his part of the bombs."

"That's my guess. He left in the middle of the night, and Joe said Rashad drove *very* carefully."

"Yeah, I bet he did. Those bombs are highly unstable and can go off prematurely from the slightest jarring. This could literally be going down at any time. Are we going to New Orleans?"

"We didn't do all this work to sit on the sidelines, did we?" Noah laughed. "They'll probably try to keep us out so they can take credit for it. But you know we don't do this for the fame and glory anyway."

Rebel raised his eyes to the window, watching Heather laugh and have fun with her mother in the heated pool. "No, that's not why we do it at all."

Rebel's gaze lingered on Heather, watching her every move, considering how his life would be without her, and pushing away the foreboding thoughts that the worst was yet to come. Knowing his wife like he did, he had no doubt she'd insist on going to New Orleans with him rather than staying in Houston, a safe distance away from the action. The problem was, he didn't know if he could leave her behind when the time came.

~

"You look happier than I've seen you in years." Kay smiled at her daughter with a wisp of sadness in her eyes. "Does your handsome husband have anything to do with that?"

"Maybe," she replied coyly. "I've missed him even more than I realized. It feels so good to have him home for an extended time instead of just a long weekend here and there."

"When this case is over, he'll be home every night. I'm sure working at the office and the oil fields will be a lot different than what he does now. Definitely not as exciting, but not as dangerous either. At least then he'll move back to Houston and be at home with you." Kay smiled warmly.

"That's actually what I wanted to talk to you about today. I haven't told Brax yet because I want to surprise him."

"What? You haven't told him what?" Kay leaned forward, her brow furrowed, and her eyes narrowed. "Are you pregnant?"

"No, I'm not pregnant. Don't get all excited." Heather put her hands up in front of her, palms out, indicating for her mother to calm down. "I've decided to do what I should've done a long time ago. I'm moving to Miami to be with Brax."

"But what about the job with your father? You two being here with us and his parents?"

The pleading tone of her mother's voice broke her heart, but she'd made up her mind. Her heart, her life, and her home would be with Brax.

"I can't let Brax move here and give up everything he's built in Miami. He's doing it for me, leaving his friends and the company he helped build behind. He'd never even complain about it, but part of him would always be missing."

"But your job..." Kay stammered. "You're a nurse here."

"I can be a nurse anywhere. I can transfer my nursing license, and we'll make a new life together. It'll be okay, Mom. You and Dad can come visit us anytime—we'll expect you to be there often. You'd do the same for Dad."

The tears glistened in Kay's eyes before she wiped them away. "I'm honestly shocked it took you this long to decide to move. Since the day you two met, your whole world has revolved around him. You two were meant to be together, and I guess it's way past time for you to actually live together."

Heather wrapped her arms around her mother's neck and pulled her close. "I love you, Mom. I'll miss you."

"I'll miss you, so much. When are you going to tell your dad?" Kay pulled back from their embrace. "Since he's started working on this acquisition, he stays at the office very late every day and even on weekends."

"I'll go to his office today to talk to him in person and make him give me a few minutes. I need to tell him before you go to Oklahoma for the several weeks to complete the deal."

Heather and Rebel left after having lunch with Kay on the veranda. During the ride back to their house, she approached the subject she knew would most certainly start a fight.

"Babe, I'm going to see Dad at work this afternoon. Do you want to go with me?"

"I can't go today, sweetheart. Rashad is making more moves, and we're on him. He has something big planned, no doubt. I'd rather you didn't go without me. Now isn't the time to mess around. The chatter in the intel community is deafening—even more so than usual."

"Have you deciphered the code yet?"

"Yes, but we haven't figured out all of its meaning yet. I can't help but think we missed a big part of the message. It could've been sent through a different method and the cells put the two together."

"What does it say?"

"It talks about crippling Babylon and watching the downfall of the great harlot. In both cases, they're referring to the US. One part appears to pinpoint New Orleans."

"Then he could be using Houston as his safe place and hit another city with his brainwashed sheep."

"I don't think so. Rashad is the type who would want to see it happen. He'll be a safe distance from the action, but he made the bombs here for a reason. We're not the only ones watching him. Every agency with any type of initials—and a few that don't even exist on paper—are monitoring him and his network."

"So you'll know when he makes a move. With so much attention on him and his guys, you'll stop him before it's too late. I really need to talk to Dad today, and this afternoon is the only time I'll have to do it."

"I can arrest you, ya know? Put you in shackles in a safe house, chained to the bed."

"You could, yes. But you'd have to unshackle me at some point. And when you do, your ass would be mine."

"Why now, Heather? Why can't it wait until this is over?" Rebel sighed, knowing he was about to lose this argument. As headstrong as he was, his wife was even worse when she set her sights on a goal.

"He's been really busy with this acquisition deal. He's working late and on weekends to finalize all the paperwork. In a couple of days, he'll leave for Tulsa, and he's staying there for the next several weeks as they complete the takeover. Mom's going with him, but I've already talked to her. This is really important to me, Brax. I wouldn't ask otherwise." She placed her hand on his arm, sealing their connection and stressing how important her request was.

Rebel parked in their driveway and stared at her for a long minute, warring in his mind and heart about letting her go alone. His heart wouldn't let him deny her anything she wanted, anything she asked of him. His mind knew the dangers were too real that Rashad would make good on his threats.

"Come on, Brax. Dad's offices are in one of the most heavily guarded areas and even well outside of Houston city limits. I have a hard time getting through security, and I'm the CEO's daughter."

"Fine. But you're taking one of the guys with you."

"He stays in the car. He's not coming into the office with me."

"Heather."

"Braxton."

He glared at her, intentionally giving her his meanest expression he usually reserved for criminals under interrogation. His intimidating glower caused her to break out into a fit of laughter.

"Be reasonable."

"I am, Brax. I've been vetted, and the security there knows me. I can get in and out much faster alone than if I took one of your men in with me. I could argue that I'm already unnecessarily taking a much needed set of eyes and ears out of the equation as it is. He wouldn't be allowed to keep his handy ear comms in—security would have a field day with that," she argued.

"I don't know why you picked nursing school. You'd be one hell of a politician—spinning the facts to meet your needs. Okay. Your escort waits outside. You keep your cell phone on you at all times. If there's one suspicious thing, you get out and call me first. For the record, I don't approve of this. But if I don't set it up, you'll just sneak off on your own.

"It's scary how well you know me." Heather beamed, happy she'd won that war of wills.

A couple of hours later, Roman and Heather drove together to the Port of Houston, home of the largest oil refinery in the United States. The waterways in the port were constantly busy with vessels entering and leaving with imported and exported goods. Large container ships looked more like floating cities with one large container stacked on top of the other like skyscrapers.

After clearing port security, they drove to the corporate offices where Emmett spent his days. The guard at the entrance to the parking lot eyed Roman suspiciously as he double-checked the visitor list for the day.

"I'm sorry, Ms. Reed, but I don't see you on the list for today. Is Mr. Greer expecting you?"

"No, but I need to see him. Please call and get approval," she replied.

"And your guest?"

"He'll wait in the car."

The guard looked even more suspicious and more uncomfortable with that answer. "Then I'll need to check your driver's licenses first." He nodded toward Roman. The guard walked back to his station to check Roman's identification and to contact Emmett for permission to allow Heather up to the executive wing. After several minutes, the guard finally stepped back to the vehicle window and returned their licenses.

CHAPTER EIGHTEEN

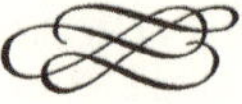

"You're cleared to go in now. Use the visitor parking spaces at the front of the building. Ms. Reed, your father said to come on up to his office. He's cleared his schedule for you." The guard smiled warmly.

"Mr. Ramsey," he addressed Roman. "I'm sorry I didn't recognize you at first. You're well-known in the sniper and sharpshooting world. It's an honor to meet you."

Roman nodded in appreciation. "Good to meet you, Bell," he replied, looking at the name tag bearing the guard's last name. "Army?"

"Yes, sir. Ranger." He directed them to the parking area and waved as they drove away.

"I recognize that look." Heather grinned slyly.

"What?"

"You think he'd make a good addition to the team. You want to recruit him."

"Don't you have a meeting to go to?" Roman asked sardonically, one side of his mouth lifting in a half grin.

Heather laughed as she opened the car door. "I won't be too long. I'm sorry to make you wait out here, but it's best I do this alone."

"No problem. I've had worse details."

She took a deep breath as she pulled the giant glass door toward her. The meeting with her dad would be hard for them both, but she'd decided on the best course of action for her life. Her priorities had changed over the years, and she'd finally realized the focus on what was most important to her had shifted.

The ride up to the twelfth floor was agonizingly slow. She had way too much time to second-guess the speech she had rehearsed to perfection.

Steeling her spine, she walked into the large executive office wing, and her father's secretary escorted her directly into his office. "You have a visitor, Mr. Greer," Betty announced.

"Come in, sweetheart. It's so good to see you. I've missed you." He rose and pulled her into his arms, hugging her close to him and kissing the side of her head. "Have a seat. Your mom said you went by to see her earlier. I've been so busy with work I haven't been home much lately."

"Yes, I know you have. That's why I came here. I know the two of you are leaving for a while to finalize this deal. This is the only way I'll get to see you before you leave."

"So, what do you have to tell me?" he asked, leveling her with his fatherly expression. "You don't just show up at my office for a chat."

"We need to talk about a couple of decisions I've made before you take off for Oklahoma. I've spent years being proud of my independence and ability to handle everything on my own. But the truth is, I've missed a lot of time with Brax over those years, and I don't want to miss one minute more.

"He's been the love of my life since the day I met him, and he will be until the day I die. We're talking about starting a family soon. Well, actually, I brought it up and told him I'm ready, and he's agreed he is, too. So, that's the good news—you'll hopefully have a grandbaby soon."

Emmett turned his chair to the side and remained uncharacteristically silent for longer than Heather felt comfortable waiting for his response.

"Say something, Daddy."

He turned his head and locked his gaze with hers. The tears shimmering in his eyes made her heart skip a beat, and the air seized in her lungs. He cleared his throat and prepared to respond.

"You've lost a lot of years and opportunities to make the best memories of your life because of me."

"Because of you?" The shock in her voice relayed her confusion.

"Yes. It's my fault—all of it. I'm the reason why Braxton left town. He joined the Army and stayed away on assignments because of me. I was so mad at him for ruining your life, all your plans for the future. You were so young when you got pregnant."

"He was the same exact age I was, Dad. We were both young and just trying to find our way."

"I know. I'm not saying I was right, sweetheart. I was slightly distraught because you were pregnant during your senior year of high school, you got married too young, and you were going to miss out on the whole college experience.

"Then Dalton died, and I was mad for all new reasons. The pain I had to watch you suffer through was almost unbearable to me. I still don't know how you were able to withstand it. I blamed him for putting you in that predicament in the first place.

"It seems he never told you about our run-in just before he left, which shouldn't surprise me because it speaks volumes about what a good man Braxton is."

He paused and inhaled deeply before forcefully releasing his breath, dreading the conversation ahead of him. "You were such a mess, sweetheart, and it killed me to see you that way. The doctor had prescribed a sedative for you, and I stood in the doorway watching you for several minutes. You were finally sleeping soundly after days of going through living hell.

"My anger reached a boiling point, and I lashed out at Braxton. When I told him it was all his fault you were going through this in the first place, he thought I was blaming him for letting Dalton die. As if he didn't do his job as a husband and father. I didn't correct him, especially when I realized it meant he was leaving. I thought that would mean a chance for you to be happy again."

"When did you ever see me unhappy with Braxton?"

He froze in place and openly gaped at her as her words sank in. The verbal slap in the face stung worse than he realized it would, though he couldn't deny he deserved it.

"I've never seen Brax make you unhappy. I've seen you get mad at him, but never to the point where you wanted to walk away."

"And I never will. You've always underestimated our bond. We started out as best friends and knew everything about each other before starting our relationship. Even now, after being apart like we have been, I couldn't imagine not having him in my life every day. Which brings me to the other reason why I'm here today, the bad news, so to speak. I've decided I'm moving to Miami to be with Braxton."

"What? Why? We already talked about him moving back here. He has a good job waiting for him right here."

"Yes, I know we did. And I appreciate you offering him a job as head of security here, but I know my husband. He'd do it for me and never hold it against me, but he wouldn't be as happy with it as he is with Steele Security. I can't do this to him or let him do it for us. I can work as a nurse in Miami as easily as I can here in Houston.

"It's time for me to be with my husband every single day I can. When we start our family, I expect you and Mom to visit us often. I'm sure his parents will too. I miss having him all the time, and I refuse to lose one more minute of being with him."

Emmett steepled his hands over his face, his forehead rested on his fingertips, and his eyes were squeezed shut. His chest rose and fell rapidly in time with his flaring nostrils. When he'd composed himself enough to speak, he cut his eyes to Heather and dropped his hands in his lap.

"All I want is for my baby girl to be happy. I want to talk to Brax again. To apologize for what I've done to you both. To tell him I'm so very proud of him, what he has accomplished, and how he's always taken care of you. I couldn't ask for a better son-in-law, and if he'd let me call him 'son,' I'd be honored."

Heather rose and flew around the large executive desk, and Emmett stood to embrace her. Father and daughter clung to each other, letting years of strife and disagreement melt away into oblivion. The healing and bonding between the two of them was long overdue, as was the release of unspoken resentments that had festered over the years.

"You have no idea how much this means to me. Thank you, Daddy," she said softly.

"I love you, Heather. And I love Brax like he's my own son. It's time I told him. Thank you for not giving up on your stubborn, hardheaded dad."

"Never. Brax loves you too. He's told me many times how he wants your approval and wants a good relationship with you. You'll just have to come to Miami to see us frequently."

Emmett pulled away, kissed her forehead, and gave her a sad smile. "You'll get sick of seeing us, we'll be there so often."

"We'll buy a house with a separate apartment so you can come as often and stay as long as you want."

Without warning or preamble, an intense rumbling emanated from all around them and shook the entire building, knocking pictures from the walls and office supplies off the desk. The windows rattled and broke into shards. Sharp pieces flew into the room, forcing them both to duck and shield their heads with their arms. Wave after wave, the noise grew louder and mixed with the sounds of people running and screaming in terror. The power blinked a few times before it completely shut off. In a matter of milliseconds, the world around Heather and Emmett ceased to make sense.

"What the hell is going on? Is this an earthquake?" Emmett bellowed and rushed to open his office door. The twelve-story building was in complete chaos. On the top floor, employees ran past his office frantically, tears streaming down their cheeks. Panic-stricken faces were contorted in pain as blood dripped down their temples, arms, and legs.

"Run, Emmett!" His chief operating officer, Russ, yelled. Emmett watched, dazed and confused, as his friend limped by. Russ rushed as quickly as his injured leg would allow, blood trickling down the side of his face and dripping from his chin.

The building was unexpectedly rocked by another blast. The force of the second explosion shook it even harder, knocking several people off-balance, and they fell to the floor. Emmett and Heather watched in horror as some were trampled underfoot by the terrified mass of people. As if in a surreal dream, Emmett stood rooted to the floor while he looked down the hall toward the direction where the blast originated. In his confounded state, his brain could barely process what his eyes saw.

What had once been a luxury office complex was now reduced to mostly rubble, devoid of any form or resemblance of what it once was. The wall at the far end of the hall that held the bank of floor-to-ceiling windows, giving a full view of the refinery operations behind the building, was completely gone. The majority of the back half of the building was missing, the floors and walls that once framed it lay in piles of wreckage and debris many stories below.

The refinery stations which had stood tall and proud had been replaced with enormous balls of orange flames. Everything outside was on fire as far as his eyes could see. The large vats that once held the refined oil were reduced to heaps of twisted metal and gnarled debris. Sirens screamed from every direction, alarms rang, and voices shouted, but their words were indecipherable.

In what remained of the office building, injured and dead bodies littered the floors below his, visible from where Emmett remained cemented in his spot. In the chaos and wreckage, nothing made sense to his logical and analytical mind. Operating with complete bedlam and turmoil surrounding him was not his strong suit.

It was like a war zone.

His mind screamed, *What the fuck is happening?*

"Dad!" Heather yelled and shook him hard. "We have to move. Now! Those blasts are timed—spaced apart intentionally. Everyone is running in one direction, and the blasts are quickly following. He's trapping everyone in one place."

"Who? Who's trapping everyone?"

"The terrorist! I'll explain it all later. We have to find another way out. Right now!"

"This way—down the back steps. They're a direct connection to the executive wing from the first floor, so there won't be many people in this stairwell."

Emmett led her to a locked door and dug his keys out of his pocket to open it. He swung the door open wide and locked the swing arm in place to keep the door propped open. "This way, everyone! Follow me!"

Emmett and Heather led the way down the stairwell, running and taking multiple steps at a time.

Twelve floors, Heather thought. *We'll never make it out in time.*

At that moment, another explosion tore through what was left of the building. More powerful than the last, the aftershock of the blast knocked their legs out from under them, split the concrete stairs in two, and separated the outer wall of the building from the stairwell. Rising to her knees, trying to steady her shaking legs, Heather peered over the edge of the broken concrete. The rebar jutted out, twisted unnaturally from the force of the blast. The platform shifted precariously underneath her, revealing more of the scenery outside and the ground below. Quickly counting back, Heather realized they'd only made it down to the eighth floor, at most.

Still at least eighty feet high, she thought. *We'd never survive a jump from this height.*

"What do we do?" a frightened woman behind Heather screamed. "Oh my God, we're all going to die! I'll never see my kids again!"

"If we die, it won't be from a lack of trying to get out," Heather yelled in response, forcing the woman to stop her hysterics long enough to make eye contact. "We can't go back up. We'll keep going down as far as we can. Then we'll jump. A broken leg is better than being buried in the rubble of this building."

"Okay," the woman sniffled. "Okay, let's go."

Emmett and Heather jumped to their feet and again led the descent down the shaky and fragile steps as fast as they could move. Heather glanced up every few seconds, watching the sway of the tons of concrete above their heads. She prayed they would reach a floor close enough to the ground so they could jump before the materials holding the now-frail building together finally gave way.

The frightened woman's cry continued to ring in her ears with every step she took. She thought about never seeing Brax again, of dying in a tomb of steel and concrete, of never fully realizing her dream of having a family with the man she loved. Those thoughts made her want to shut down, to allow the fear simply to take over so she wouldn't have to deal with the overwhelming possibility of it all for one more second.

It was the thought of letting Rashad win by using her to hurt Braxton that pushed her on. She could hear her husband's voice in her head, urging her to come to him, commanding her to never surrender, and demanding she keep going even when she didn't think she could take one more step. It was his love that gave her the strength she needed to fight off the anxiety and fear trying to incapacitate her.

With the next blast, the outer wall crumbled to the ground below. The stairwell became completely exposed to the outside elements, and the stairs began breaking beneath their feet.

"Heather, we have to jump now, or we'll be buried by the floors above us," Emmett shouted over the roar of the disintegrating building.

"Okay, let's do it, then," Heather agreed, scared out of her mind. She glanced over the edge and estimated they were somewhere around the third or fourth floor.

Thirty to forty feet to fall, she thought. *Thirty feet is the outer limit for surviving a free fall. Half the people live. But half of them die.*

"I'll lower you over the edge so you don't have as far to drop. Then I'll be right behind you," he assured her, as if he were reading her mind.

"Together," she insisted.

"No. My arms are longer, and that gives us both a better advantage." He spoke as he guided her to the edge.

She sat with her legs dangling over the side and tried to mentally prepare herself for the terrifying move she had to make. Emmett took her hands in his as he knelt behind her. She slid over the edge, and he stretched out on his stomach, lowering her as far as he could over the jagged side. Men behind him grabbed his legs, allowing him to slide the upper half of his body over the edge to get her closer to the ground.

Tears flowed from his eyes as he forced himself to turn loose of his baby girl. His daughter he'd held as soon as she was born. The little girl he'd taught to ride a bike, drive a stick shift, and enrolled in martial arts so she could always take care of herself. The little girl he'd watched grow into a beautiful, caring, independent woman.

The daughter he'd given away to another man, never truly trusting Braxton would love and care for her in the same way a father would love and care for his daughter. He'd never healed the wounds he'd inflicted on Braxton, and by extension, on her.

The daughter he'd never witnessed enjoying raising a child of her own. The joys and heartaches he could've experienced with her passed before his eyes. There were so many firsts and seconds, celebrations and disappointments, everything that makes up a life, that he'd missed out on before, and in his current predicament, knew he'd miss in the future.

So many things he'd do differently.

Her fingers slipped through his, and he watched as she landed on the ground below. She kept her knees slightly bent and rolled with the momentum of the fall, coming to a stop on her side. He watched with bated breath as she remained motionless for several seconds. Fear, horror, and grief tore through him. Fear that he'd insisted on her jumping too soon gripped him. Horror because he'd just dropped his daughter to her death rather than to safety. And grief, so much grief because the thought of life without her took away his desire to survive himself.

CHAPTER NINETEEN

A slight movement in her arm had his heart pumping in triple time. "Heather!"

She gingerly pushed up to a sitting position and looked up at him. From her blank expression and fumbling movements, she was obviously dazed from her jarring landing. But she was alive, and that was all that mattered to Emmett.

"Heather, are you okay?"

"I'm okay," she replied, her voice quivering. "Get out of there, Daddy! Jump!"

Her vacant expression faded away, and comprehension of the situation took its place. In that moment, she wished her wits hadn't returned because she was able to fully grasp the devastation laid out before her. The instability of the building petrified her, but all the frantic and pleading eyes of the people stranded in the stairwell ripped her heart out. She was shocked even part of the building was still standing. What was left would come down with the next puff of wind.

And her dad was still inside.

The shrill shriek of the panicked woman's cry abruptly filled the air and echoed off the rubble. "Tell my babies I love them. And I'm sorry I couldn't be there for them while they grow up."

Heather watched as Emmett glanced over his shoulder toward the lady, then back at the men who still held his legs. The scene played out in slow motion in Heather's mind as they each nodded before Emmett turned his gaze back to her.

When their eyes met, she knew.

"No, Daddy!" She pushed up to stand, and the pain shot through her leg.

Ignoring the intense agony, she limped closer to the building, stumbling over debris, but she kept her eyes locked on his. "No! I need you. You said you'd be right behind me."

"I love you, Heather. With all of my heart. I'm so very proud of you. I want you and Brax to have a wonderful life together. Tell your mother I love her, and I'll be waiting for her. Tell Brax I love him like the son I never had.

"Now, I have to help these people get home to their loved ones. I have to give them a fighting chance, precious."

With tears flowing unchecked down her cheeks, her vision blurred and a sob racked her body. "I love you, Daddy. Please come home with me. We need you."

Emmett took the frightened lady's hands and lowered her as far over the side as he could before he released her. One person after the other stepped up, and he dropped them to the ground below. All the while, Heather begged him to save himself, too. The slight sway of the building's remains did not bode well for the number of people still trapped, waiting for their turn to be lowered to safety.

Because they were unwilling to wait any longer or were afraid to fall from that height, many people decided to continue down the steps behind Emmett. When the first few made their move, several more fell in line behind them. The sudden movement of that many people on an already unstable structure quickly became a recipe for disaster.

Heather limped forward to shout at the people rushing down the stairs. "Go back! The stairwell is blocked. You can't go down any farther. You'll be trapped!"

The portion of the building still standing erect began to sway visibly from side to side. Slightly at first, then with more force and momentum. Heather gasped, her hand covered her mouth, and her eyes flew open wide when she realized the rocking wouldn't stop until the building had completely collapsed.

Panicked screams emanated from every floor when the final blow was dealt. A loud explosion, different from the others, filled the air just before a huge ball of fire rolled through the tattered remains of the carnage on the upper floors, consuming everything in its path.

"Dad—jump!" she pleaded.

Emmett slid over the side, gripping the concrete with his fingers and stretching his body to lessen the height of his drop.

"Just let go!" she urged. "Let go!"

"Heather!"

A voice from behind her called, and she turned to see Roman's panic-stricken face. When his expression morphed into terror before her eyes, she turned back toward the building in time to see it collapsing from the top down.

Toward her.

~

While waiting in the car, Roman heard the first blast, and his senses immediately went on high alert. The explosion could've come from a multitude of places with a variety of reasons behind it at a major oil refinery, but his gut told him this wasn't an industrial accident. Something was very wrong, and he had a very bad feeling about the outcome.

He jumped out of the car and ran in the direction of the noise. The entire area behind the office building looked like a demolition zone. Fires had erupted in multiple places at the refinery, unbridled flames shot straight up into the air and quickly jumped to the next highly flammable source. Some of the employees rushed to help the wounded, while others tried to stop the infernos that were raging out of control.

The next blast was just as powerful as the first but originated from the office building. The explosions were intentional and purposeful—that much was clear. His heart hammered in his chest as he ran toward the danger. He knew Heather and her father were still somewhere inside the building, but he didn't know where exactly. The possible locations were too numerous—in Emmett's office, searching for a safe place, attempting to get out, or worse, buried under the rubble in the blast zone.

"Brad," he barked into his cell. "I need an exact location on Heather. Then alert Rebel and get everyone down here to the port."

Brad checked the coordinates on the GPS tracker in Heather's cell and told Roman where to find her. "What happened, Roman? And what is all that noise?"

As he ran to find her, he filled Brad in on the situation, giving him all the details he could to help the team be as prepared as possible when they arrived. When he reached the area where he expected to find Heather, most of the building lay in crumbled ruins on the ground. The amount of devastation was staggering, and the task of finding her in it seemed all but impossible. Her screams registered before he could come to terms with the scene unfolding in front of him.

"Heather!"

Startled, she quickly turned her attention over her shoulder in his direction. The first set of explosions were all powerful bursts of energy, designed to cause as much structural damage as possible. The final discharge that devastated what remained of the structure had completely different elements and intentions. The ball of fire that ripped through the upper floors, which Heather and Emmett had just vacated, originated from an intense heat source designed to obliterate anything that remained after the primary blasts.

The reinforced concrete floors began to crumble, conceding to the high-temperature accelerant after all the punishment that had already been inflicted. When the top floor collapsed onto the one below, Roman knew no one else would get out alive. He ran as hard and fast as he could toward

Heather, hoping beyond hope he would make it in time to rescue her. His eyes traveled up to the many people who were still inside the stairwell when its tethers broke loose, and it tipped outward past the point of no return. With no reliable load-bearing source left, the crushing weight created a domino effect of destruction until the remains were completely unrecognizable.

Roman skidded to a halt at the edge of the debris, ignoring the cuts and bruises he'd suffered from the shards that had flown from the demolished building. His chest heaved like he'd just finished a marathon at a sprinter's pace. His heart thumped against his rib cage, ready to explode out of his chest at any moment. He bent at the waist with his hands on this thighs, gulping air. But overexertion wasn't the cause of his hypoxic state.

He had failed.

He'd failed Heather.

He'd failed Rebel.

He didn't reach her in time.

She was buried under the remnants of the razed building.

~

"They did what?" Rebel demanded, moving into his threatening stance. "How can they do that?"

"They took us off the case, with the exception of sending Blake, Alex, and Joe to New Orleans to work with our DEA liaison. Don't think I haven't argued this with everything I have," Noah replied. "I even talked directly with the president since we're taking our orders from him on this case. His advisors said it would be best to let the dual CIA-FBI Task Force take over the operations since we're coming down to the wire. Delta Force is still officially unofficial as far as the rest of the world is concerned. When Rashad is taken down, there will be so much media coverage all over it, the president is concerned we'll get caught in the cross fire of camera flashes."

"That's complete bullshit. Our team has done most of the work and found all the best leads. We should be there to take him out," Bull argued. "Fucking hypocrites."

"I agree. But we can't ignore orders to stay away from New Orleans and from any of the cell's rental houses when that order comes directly from our president," Noah replied. "You know as well as I do what'll happen to us if we disobey. I'm all for breaking the rules, but I don't want to wake up in a six-foot-by-nine-foot dark room for the rest of my life."

"Fuck them. Do you have any idea how long I worked on that damn encrypted code?" Rebel shook his head in disgust and dropped down in his chair. "If I'd known this, I would've gone with Heather to see her father at work."

"Why would she go to his office to see him instead of his house?"

"His company is buying another oil company in Oklahoma. Emmett and

Kay are leaving in a couple of days to spend the next several weeks up there, finalizing the deal and making the new employees feel more secure in their jobs. Heather said she needed to talk to him about something before he leaves, and going to his office is the only way she can get time with him."

Noah narrowed his eyes, drew his brows together, and moved quickly to rifle through the case file in the middle of the table. When he found the information, he released a haggard breath. "Is the name of that company Vessel Petroleum?"

Rebel's face fell, and his pulse quickened. He knew this couldn't be good. "Yes. Why do you ask?"

"Remember when Rashad's brother, Turan, transferred that money from an oil company to all those Homeland Security employees? It was Vessel Petroleum's account he used."

"Where'd you get that information?" Bull asked.

"A copy of the confidential case file Shadow somehow managed to get his hands on."

"You think Turan was trying to get Rashad to look into that company because of Emmett's relation to me? Why wouldn't he just tell Rashad outright?" Rebel asked.

"Maybe Rashad wouldn't listen to him. Turan pulled a lot of pranks that brought too much attention to him, whereas Rashad prefers the cover of anonymity. But Rashad didn't bother with you until after Turan disappeared, so maybe he's taken over his brother's vendetta now," Noah deduced.

"The mere fact it's the same company Emmett is preparing to take over changes everything. Portno is definitely Port of New Orleans, but what if they're planning to hit both ports at once? Taking out the Port of Houston would do just as much damage to the country's economic stability as taking out the one in New Orleans. But taking out both ports would completely cripple us.

"No imported oil coming in, no exported goods going out. On top of that, our largest oil refinery is in Houston's port. Without that production, the smaller refineries wouldn't be able to keep up with the demand, and we'd run out of fuel across the country. Can you imagine the level of chaos that would cause? Is that what they meant by 'greater than eleven'?"

"The only thing that seems certain at this point is the task force leaders have jumped the gun by taking the whole team to New Orleans. You know how I feel about coincidences," Noah replied.

"No such thing."

Shadow marched into the room, determination in his every step and masked trepidation in his expression. "Let's go. Now. We have to move."

"What's wrong?" Noah asked.

The hairs on Rebel's arms stood at attention when Shadow's eyes swung to meet his. The acid churned in his stomach, making the original sinking feeling mutate into a black hole intent on draining the life from him. He jumped to his feet, ready to move into action, and drew up to his full height. "Tell me."

"Roman just called Brad. Ringgold Refineries has just been hit, and the damage is extensive. He's calling us all in," Shadow replied stoically.

"Heather?" Rebel held his breath and waited for Shadow to answer his one-word question. The only word that held any meaning to him. The one word that could change his entire life.

"Brad used the GPS tracker on her phone to tell Roman exactly where she was about two minutes ago. Brad said there was a lot of noise in the background, and Roman said multiple bombs had been detonated. The building and refinery are presumed to be a total loss. But since Brad was able to locate her, that tells me her phone was still operable, and that's a good sign. That's all I know at this point," Shadow explained. "Can you handle going to the scene?"

"Try to stop me." Rebel quickly grabbed his gear, focusing on each task to keep his sanity in check. When he'd finished gearing up, he called over his shoulder as he rushed out the door. "I'm leaving. If you ladies are riding with me, you'd better have your asses in the truck."

With the team loaded and ready to roll, Rebel slid behind the wheel and took off like a bullet toward the port. The normal travel time from their location averaged just over thirty minutes. Rebel made the trip in less than fifteen minutes with speeds in excess of 120 miles per hour and weaving effortlessly from lane to lane through the traffic.

Nothing could've prepared him for what he saw when his truck skidded to a halt in the parking lot. He threw it into park, jumped out, and sprinted to the location Brad had given them. The devastation extended as far as he could see. Where the once regal office building had stood was now little more than a pile of rocks, twisted metal, and unidentifiable scraps.

His eyes scanned the area, frantically searching for Heather, when the sight of a man on his knees caught his attention. He was furiously moving the rocks and debris, attempting to tunnel through the carnage. The earth ceased to spin, a vacuum sealed around Rebel and squeezed the oxygen from his lungs, and his heart stopped beating in his chest.

The man hastily digging through the mounds of crumbled concrete was Roman.

"Heather!" Rebel yelled. "Hang on, baby. I'll get you out of there. Just hang on."

In the blink of an eye, Rebel was at Roman's side, moving the large pieces of concrete as if they weighed no more than a pebble. When hands on either side of him grabbed his arms and stopped his progress, he finally looked up.

"Rebel, you have to slow down. You don't want the weight to shift and cause more to fall on her," Shadow reasoned. "Methodical and calculated moves are what you need to focus on right now."

"You're right." He sat back, wiped the sweat from his brow, and tried to calm his racing heart and mind.

"This is a giant puzzle, and we have to move it one strategic piece at a time. I'm calling in the search and rescue dogs. Bull, get the professional search and rescue team out here with their equipment. They have cameras and heat-sensing equipment so we don't waste time digging in the wrong area. We're going to need all the help we can get," Noah directed.

"I'll get security in place. We don't need news helicopters and crews swarming the place, broadcasting the damage so the radicals can celebrate anything. This all has to stay under wraps for as long as possible," Shadow added.

He made a few quick phone calls and, within minutes, the entire area was cordoned off by members of the National Guard. Military and police helicopters patrolled a wide perimeter to prevent civilian aircraft from entering the airspace. Off-duty National Guard members showed up in force to assist with the search and rescue operation.

While all the plans and preparations were being made by the professionals, Rebel maintained his focus on finding his wife by moving one piece at a time. One of the dog handlers approached Rebel and spoke in a calm and reassuring manner.

"Hey, I'm Tim, and this pretty little lady is Robin. Would you mind if we help you search?"

Rebel turned to look at Tim, but he found himself face-to-face with Robin instead. Her expressive milk chocolate eyes pleaded with him to let her do her job. As if the black Labrador felt his pain, she slowly extended her snout and lovingly licked his face.

"I'd love to have some help. Thanks, Tim," he replied as he scratched behind the dog's ear. "And thank you, Robin. I really needed that."

CHAPTER TWENTY

Rashad watched all the commotion from inside the port while keeping a safe distance away from the blasts. A fiendish smile crawled across his face at the thought of seeing his mission come to fruition. The infidels had interfered with his country, his beliefs, and his family for long enough. His intentions were to prove how vulnerable the arrogant people really were, while bringing them to their knees. Part one of the current plan was well underway and coming together as expected.

He'd been warned against lingering in the port after he'd detonated the bombs, but he'd decided to take his chances. For his father, his brother, and his cause, he was obligated to see it through to the end. To him, it meant the difference in dying an honorable and worthy death, and dying a shameful and irrelevant death. A job only half completed would be dishonorable and prevent him from collecting his heavenly rewards.

The excitement that had been lacking in his life all the years he had been in the US built inside him with each explosion. With every piece of debris, shrapnel, and projectile flying from the refinery site, his elation increased from knowing he'd been instrumental in ensuring its complete destruction. Secondary explosions from the spreading fire in the fields were like a sign from Allah, praising him for his work and awarding him with a double portion for his good deeds.

The pride he felt when the first bomb detonated in the office quickly grew to a crescendo of arrogance and superiority. The final bomb in the office building culminated in the climax of his egotism. "I will be immortal now, transcending all time. Songs will be written and sung about me for the rest of time."

He'd rigged the final bomb with special care and a singular purpose in mind. The first set of bombs caused widespread devastation, but C-4 made a more impactful statement, in his opinion. The enormous, heat-generating blast was easily activated with his remote detonator and would've created an impressive explosion on its own, but the flowing oxygen from the tanks he'd procured from the hospital helped create an even more powerful force. Watching the giant ball of fire roll through several floors at the top of the building was the greatest vision he'd ever beheld. Every news outlet in the world would carry footage of his creation, memorializing his name and his innovation forever.

His cell phone began to ring just as the building made its final descent. "Yes."

"You should be well on your way to New Orleans by now. What is your current location?"

Rashad had visions of killing the man calling all the shots and giving the orders on their mission. He obeyed because he'd been ordered by his cleric to follow every command. His cleric—his teacher—was wise and was the most knowledgeable man in Islamic law he knew. For those reasons, he'd followed the rules and allowed the interloper to meddle in matters he had no business in.

Of course, he'd followed all orders with the exception of leaving the port immediately after the first explosion.

"I'm in the truck, still in the Port of Houston, making sure everything goes off without a hitch."

The silence on the other end of the line contradicted the outrage and condemnation simmering just under the surface.

"Get out of there right now," he replied through gritted teeth.

"The blasts in the second site haven't been triggered yet. Something could be wrong, and I may need to improvise. I can't do that from five hours away."

"You know as well as I do those bombs will detonate with or without you. As soon as they move the first crate, they'll all blow. Hell, even if the cargo ship slightly rocks from a wave, that's all it needs. Move your ass before you ruin this for both of us."

"As you wish," Rashad replied coolly, waiting for the day of his revenge.

"You're too damn late," he growled. "The fucking National Guard has been mobilized. They're shutting down everything and everyone in and out of the port right now. Find somewhere to park that fucking truck, get out of it, and then stay the hell out of sight." He then hung up before Rashad could respond.

"Yours is coming, my friend. Very soon, you will no longer be protected," Rashad hissed to his silent phone.

He fired up the diesel engine of the eighteen-wheeler and pulled out of his current parking spot overlooking the devastation he'd created. Several other trucks had been rerouted away from the crime scene, so he took the opportunity to fall in line with them. When they pulled into an enormous parking lot lined with one truck after the other, he smirked to himself at the brilliance of his simple hiding spot.

After he gathered his belongings that could potentially identify him from the cab of the truck, he took off on foot toward the waterway. Rashad knew from his research shutting down the port was no small feat, nor was the decision to prevent any ships from entering or leaving the area. With the enormous ships now stationary and the exits blocked by military personnel, he only had to find a seat and wait for the real fireworks to begin.

~

"Silas Steele, CIA," he introduced himself and extended his hand.

"Kevin Robbins, Port Authority Officer. Good to meet you."

"I need your help, Kevin. I'm afraid this isn't over, and something just isn't adding up for me. Can you help me out?"

"Of course. What do you need?"

"Pull up the security tapes from just before the first explosion," Silas directed. "Start with the refinery plant area first."

"You got it."

The multiple flat screens that covered the wall displayed varying images around the port. Kevin keyed in the coordinates of the refinery field and brought up every recording that captured any angle of it in the camera's range of view. Together, they reviewed each frame in the few minutes prior to the initial blast. Silas memorized where every person, vehicle, and piece of equipment was located, filing it away for easy comparison when something different jumped out at him.

An eighteen-wheeler tanker truck pulled up beside one of the large vats, and a crew of men moved toward it, gathering connectors and large hoses to begin the transfer of refined petroleum. The driver's door opened, and a pair of legs swung out into view. The driver handed the ground crewman his orders and stepped out of the big rig. Ground crew members had begun to make the connection from the vat to the truck when the blast filled the screen.

The instantly mangled truck became a deadly projectile, the damaged equipment and free-flowing gasoline became all the accelerant the fire needed to rage out of control instantaneously. Everyone in a fifty-yard vicinity of the blast was killed, and many more well past that range were severely injured.

Silas paused the recording and stared at the screen in disbelief. He noted the exact time of the blast from the recording. "Kevin, can you pull up the office building security tapes and start just a few seconds before this time?"

"Sure," he replied, clearly shaken from the graphic scene he'd just watched. When the digital recording reached the time Silas requested, Kevin put the image on the bigger screen in the middle of the wall. He had a hunch why Silas had requested that recording. "Here it is."

With his gaze carefully watching both the building and the time, Silas waited for what he knew in his gut was about to happen. At precisely the same time as the truck exploded, one end of the office building disappeared in an enormous blast of energy. Both bombs were on the same detonator, and the person holding that trigger had to be nearby. He quickly stopped the recording, unwilling to watch any further at that point because it simply hit too close to home.

"Kevin, can you trace the truck back to when it first entered the port? See if it stopped anywhere else, let anyone out, dropped anything off. Let's get a good look at the driver, possibly tie him to others who conspired in this attack. We need to take them all down."

"I'll gladly help with that. Let me know if you need an alibi."

Kevin and Silas watched the truck in rewind as it wound through the streets of the enormous industrial area. It only stopped when required. No one got in or out. Nothing was removed or put inside it. When they reached the port gates, the camera angle switched to the one on the guard's station, giving them a close-up view of the driver.

"Son of a bitch." Silas had hoped he was wrong when he saw the driver on the recording get out of the truck just before the blast. The mannerisms were the same, but he'd hoped he was wrong regardless.

"You know him?"

"Yeah. I know him. He was actually a pretty good kid. Just recently got a job here and was looking forward to being able to move to a better place soon. His name was Reuben Silva." Silas rubbed his forehead and exhaled forcefully. He'd just watched one of his confidential informants get blown up, the image forever burned into his memory.

"Hey, he said his friend Gustavo got a job here at the same time. If they're being used as pawns, his vehicle could be rigged too. Can you link into his truck's GPS and see where he is?"

"Absolutely. What's his last name?"

"Montes."

With a few clicks on his computer, he had signed in to the truck monitoring system the port maintained. "His truck is currently parked in the shipping yard cargo area. We had to use it as an overflow area for trucks because of the attack—nothing moving in or out right now."

"Get on the radio and get everyone out of that lot right now. Don't send any men into it, but contact anyone who's in there and tell them to get out. They need to leave their trucks behind. I'm on my way over to check out that truck. Jot down the license plate and description of his truck for me."

"I'll do ya one better than that. I'll print a live shot picture so you can see exactly where it is and everything surrounding it, too. Take the security Jeep parked outside." Kevin tossed the keys to Silas.

"You're a good man, Kevin."

With the picture in hand, Silas jogged out to the Jeep and squealed the tires when he pulled out of the parking lot.

"Noah," Silas yelled into his phone. "There may be another truck with a bomb in the port. I'm on my way over to check it out."

"What truck?"

Silas gave Noah a condensed version of what he'd just learned and where he was headed. "I'll be in touch soon. Or you'll hear a big bang. Either way, I'll let you know what I find."

When he reached the overflow lot, people were rushing away from the area in droves. He had no doubt the word was quickly spread regarding the possibility of another bomb. He skidded to a stop just behind the eighteen-wheeler assigned to Gustavo and cautiously approached it. He squatted low to the ground and frequently checked underneath the trailer for explosive devices. He moved along the side of the truck to the cab and slowly opened the driver's door.

He climbed up on the step and peered inside, carefully checking every possible hiding place, before moving toward the sleeping quarters. When he pulled the curtain back, Gustavo's lifeless face stared back at him.

"Shit!" Jerking his phone from his pocket, he called the Port Authority office.

"Robbins."

"Kevin—I need your help again. Can you find when this truck pulled into the overflow lot? Can you see when someone get out of it? And if so, can you get me a picture?"

"Based on where it's parked, I can check some of the trucks around it and see when they came in. That'll help narrow down a time when he pulled into that lot. Give me a sec, and I'll call you back."

While he waited for Kevin's return call, Silas walked to the back of the truck and very cautiously checked the locks before opening it. He knew with every move, he could set off another explosion, killing himself and others in the process. But if he didn't check and it hid a bomb on a timer, the results would be just as devastating. When he was confident he could safely get in the trailer, he swung the metal doors open as far as they would go, letting the failing sunlight illuminate the inside. Then he took a step back as his breath hitched in his chest.

His cell pinged and vibrated simultaneously with a text from a local number, startling him and making him jump. When he opened it, he found pictures from Kevin showing Rashad as he climbed out of the truck and left the parking lot on foot.

"Fucking hell!" he roared and hit Noah's number again. "He's here, Noah. He's still in the port. There's another truck with bombs in the trailer. I'm going in to disarm them now. There are multiple bombs connected to one timer, rigged to all go off at once. He parked it and left on foot. Gus is dead in the cab."

"You need help disarming it? I can be there in thirty seconds."

"It's a simple trigger, bro. This isn't one of his more sophisticated ones. I got this. Keep looking for Heather. Get everyone else looking for Rashad. He'll try to walk out of here after dark. I'm forwarding you a text with pictures of him getting out of the truck. Share it with everyone."

"On it. And Silas? Be careful."

"Always."

Moving slower than he'd ever moved in his life, Silas climbed into the trailer and inched toward the bomb. "These damn bomb lovers, they always make something tricky in them. They have to outsmart everyone else. Not this time, dickhead. Not this time."

After several harrowing minutes inside, he was able to breathe again when the timer stopped and the wires were disconnected from the explosives. When he climbed out of the trailer, he alerted the National Guard commander, and the explosives technicians took charge of the disposal.

It was well after dark by the time he returned to the search and rescue site. Bull was taking a break and guzzling a bottle of cold water when Silas walked up.

"Nothing on Heather yet?"

"No, not yet. There's just so much construction material to dig through. They have the dogs out there trying to lock on to a scent, but they haven't hit one so far. They're checking crevices with the heat-sensing equipment, but so far they can't get deep enough to lock on to a heat signature. Rebel has talked to Kay a few times, keeping her in the loop since they won't let anyone into the port area.

"The good news is the majority of the people who have been cleared to leave have opted to stay and help search the grounds. After you found that other truck with explosives, a growing concern there are more out there started moving through the workers. They're checking their normal work areas. If they find anything in the least bit out of the ordinary, the ordnance disposal unit will go in and check it out."

"They're allowing civilians to get involved?"

Bull shrugged. "It's a big port, and no one knows what's supposed to be in their area like the people actually doing the work. It's a matter of national security now, and every patriotic Texan wants to help. An armed National Guard member is stationed close to every major area in case anyone sees Rashad lurking in the shadows. We'd flush him out if we were out there, but Heather is our top priority, especially since *officially* we're off the case."

"She'd be our priority anyway."

Rebel, Roman, Tim, and Robin were still hard at work trying to find Heather, working in the general area Roman last saw her before the stairwell collapsed, when Silas joined them. Noah and Shadow were on the outer edge, working inward toward Rebel, so he slid his hands into a pair of gloves, joined Bull on the opposite side, and started moving the chunks of debris out of the search area.

"Good job with locating that other truck, Silas," Rebel interrupted the silence. "Listen, guys, I've been thinking a lot about the encrypted message I decoded, trying to keep my mind on something other than…just trying to stay focused while I keep digging through the rubble. The CIA analysts think 'cripple the lanes' means shutting down our interstates by cutting off our oil and gas supply. But I think their interpretation is completely wrong, and they're looking in the wrong place."

Silas glanced over at Rebel's bare hands, bleeding and raw from working nonstop over the past several hours. "What do you think it means?"

"It's pretty obvious now, isn't it? They're not just taking out our current *access* to oil and gas. They want to take out the actual *shipping* lanes—not the *driving* lanes. We'd have nothing at all coming in or out if they shut down the ports indefinitely because of a catastrophic attack. Noah and I talked about this bit earlier, before we got the call, but we didn't get to finish. The more I think about it, the more I'm convinced I'm right. Which means…"

"It means if there are more explosives, they're on the cargo ships floating in the waterway right now," Shadow replied, realization setting in. "They could have them set to explode at the same time, here and in New Orleans."

"That's why he's here," Silas muttered to himself.

"Why who's here?" Rebel asked, cutting his deadly gaze up to Silas. "Rashad is still in the port?"

"He was as of a couple of hours ago. He was caught on camera walking toward the general direction of the waterway. I thought he'd try to escape on foot after the cover of darkness, but now I think you're right."

"He may get out of the port tonight, but he will never escape from me. That I can guarantee."

CHAPTER TWENTY-ONE

Bill paced back and forth, growing angrier by the second. Rashad had always followed orders, had always performed the tasks expected of him. Until now. Until it mattered the most. Until their fucking necks were on the line and any failures would fall on Bill's shoulders.

"That little prick is pulling this shit on purpose," Bill spat out. "He's double-crossing me. Just like I knew his stupid ass would do. I should've listened to my gut on this one."

Bill shook his head and continued pacing, torn between calling Rashad again and just disappearing to let his partner take the fall alone. Everyone thought he was dead anyway. Only a couple of people knew he was still very much alive, that he wasn't the one who walked into the house minutes before it exploded that day. He'd taken advantage of an eager new recruit who was anxious to prove his exceptional disguise skills. One of two people who knew about it was Rashad himself, but that didn't bother Bill. No one would believe the word of a wanted terrorist who insisted a dead CIA agent was actually still alive—and dirty to boot.

As badly as he wanted to walk away, he also wanted what was promised to him. Rashad accepted this mission for honor, glory, and furthering their cause. The reason Bill joined them was much simpler—it had dollar signs tied to it. He was promised a life he'd like to become accustomed to rather than his life of barely scraping by. He wasn't naïve enough to think they wouldn't betray him if the opportunity presented itself.

He had the same plan himself.

But greed won over self-preservation, and he called Rashad again against his better judgment. "Status?"

"Something is wrong. The second location hasn't detonated, and it is way past time. I've been waiting for the opportunity to get onboard and check it out for myself. Have you heard from our brothers in New Orleans yet?"

"Yes, everyone is in place, and they're waiting for the final word from us. But the whole place is crawling with agents. They're methodically checking everything in the port. It's only a matter of time before they start boarding ships and checking crates. So far, they haven't interrupted our plans, but we're dangerously close to pulling the plug and walking away."

"No. We can't walk away now. There is still work to be done. The only way you get paid is when the New Orleans port is inoperable and the oil tankers are on fire. Then you can take your money and move to another country with your new name."

"You have twenty minutes to handle your part. If that means you have to sit in that tanker and blow yourself sky high, then so be it. If I don't see evidence of it in nineteen minutes and thirty seconds, you're on your own."

Bill disconnected, decided he'd take matters into his own hands, and packed a backpack with the materials he'd need to pull off his improvised changes. The original plan had called for the two separate attacks to occur simultaneously. The division in resources would cause chaos in the law enforcement agencies and FEMA response times. Whatever hiccup had caused the delay in Houston didn't mean they couldn't proceed with their plans for the port in New Orleans, though.

He reasoned the alternating attacks could wreak just as much havoc as dual, synchronized ones would. They wouldn't know where to expect the next hit. Every major government installation would be on high alert, and therefore, would hold on to their staff for defense rather than sending them to the Gulf for support. In his mind, doing something was infinitely better than doing nothing at all. And something needed to be done in order for him to be paid for his services.

Considerable extra security had been put in place at the Port of New Orleans. When Bill approached the entrance, he was stopped by soldiers in full combat gear. With a hand on his sidearm, one soldier approached the driver's side window while another circled the car with a bomb-sniffing dog. A third soldier stood off to the side, maintaining his intense glare and diligent observation.

"What brings you to the port tonight, sir?"

Bill held up his fake orders from the CIA director for inspection. "Just doing my job."

The soldier eyed his paperwork speculatively. "You're getting in a little late, aren't you?"

"Late by what standards? Do you think all of the investigation into the threats on the port is done inside here? Some of us have been out pounding the pavement to get tips and leads." Bill's displeased tone conveyed his annoyance with the soldier's questioning.

Satisfied with his response and acknowledgment of a clean car, the soldiers allowed Bill to pass through the roadblock. The truth was, Bill had long been unhappy with keeping secrets, not having the finer things in life, and envying the jet-setter mentality of the lowlife thugs he'd met with over the years. When he was approached to be the informant rather than the officer, with considerable benefits as perks, he jumped at the chance for a brand-new life. That was the precise reason why he was in the one place he shouldn't be—an area crawling with federal officers who were all bound and determined to foil a planned terrorist attack.

Once parked, he retrieved the items from his backpack and concealed his identity with the few essentials he had at his disposal. When he climbed out of his car, the tiny hairs on the back of his neck stood straight up and demanded his attention. A chill ran down his spine, and his pulse kicked up a notch. The only time he'd had that reaction in the past was when he was being watched.

Walking around his car nonchalantly, he used the time to stealthily examine his surroundings. Nothing appeared out of place to his observant eyes. No moving shadows. No lurking figures. But he was certain someone, somewhere, was watching him nonetheless. He walked toward the water, stepping into the shadow of the surrounding buildings for cover, and looked over his shoulder repeatedly for anyone tailing him.

He pulled his phone from his pocket and punched in the number for his local contact. After a couple of rings, the line connected, but he was met with silence. Bill understood the other man wasn't in a position where he could respond, prompting Bill to quietly issue his directive.

"Initiate the plan for the primary target. I'm implementing the contingency plan."

"Understood."

Bill disconnected and continued on his way to the cruise ship docks. The secondary target would destroy the few cruise ships docked in port overnight. The hint at civilian targets, and the few inevitable civilian deaths, would only serve to heighten the threat risk in other ports. Another safeguard he'd decided to employ to help ensure no additional troops were sent to his location.

He accessed the first cruise ship from the dock-level employee entrance. With all the commotion in the port, his presence onboard was barely noticed. No doubt other federal agents and port officers had made their rounds, checking anywhere and everywhere a device would be hidden to cause the most damage. The crew members onboard were busy preparing for their next voyage and had no time or interest to question him about his intentions.

"Your sacrifices will not be in vain," he mumbled to himself. "You're helping me retire to a life of luxury." He set the timer to give himself enough time to complete his tasks and get away from the last ship before the first one blew.

It was all coming together, one tactical piece at a time.

~

"He's on the move. Stay on him," Nick Tucker whispered into his comms.

"Got him," Blake replied. "He's not getting away."

"He's headed my way now," Alex replied. "On him."

"Picking up the trail now," Joe whispered.

"I'm coming up on the opposite side," Tucker replied and took off in a silent sprint.

The four-man covert team consistently rotated positions, keeping tabs on Bill's exact location as he stole through the night. With the four men watching from their hidden points when Bill entered the cruise ship, Tucker and Blake elected to take point while Joe and Alex stayed outside to cover the exits.

The organized chaos onboard the ship while the crew prepared for their next sailing was nearly as busy as the troops and agents scouring the port for weapons of destruction. The hustle and bustle helped Tucker and Blake to blend in and gave them large pallets of inventory for the perfect cover. With each bomb Bill set, Tucker and Blake immediately moved in behind him to disarm it.

"That's the last one on this ship," Tucker advised. "He's headed back out."

A couple of minutes later, Bill walked across the ramp, no longer even bothering to try to be invisible. "He's going into the next ship down," Joe alerted. "Alex and I will take this one."

"Roger that. We'll be waiting for him outside," Blake replied.

When he emerged from the second ship, Bill tossed his backpack into the water and picked up his pace in the direction of his car. Tucker chuckled lightly into his comm, making the others laugh along with him.

"Good luck with your car, buddy." Joe's tone dripped with contempt for his former partner. "See how you like being set up."

"He'll get his, Brown." Tucker's confidence was reassuring. He wasn't a man who was easily rattled—or lightly fucked with. "Soon."

In much the same manner they tailed him to the cruise docks, they coordinated tracking him to his next location. When he rounded the last building corner before returning to where his car should have been, all four men waited with smiles plastered on their faces. His cartoonish skid to a halt when he realized his car was gone elicited hushed laughs and insulting epithets from the group.

"Someone moved his cheese and left a rat trap instead. That's just rude," Alex quipped.

"Taking bets on what he does next. I say it's the typical head in the hands move," Blake hedged.

Bill ran his fingers through his hair, angrily grabbing handfuls before shaking his fists in the air. "Oh! Good call, man. He's dying to shout at the top of his lungs right now," Joe chuckled.

"He'll have that feeling again soon, but for completely different reasons." The malice in Tucker's voice was palpable.

"What are you going to do with him?" Blake asked.

Tucker glanced down at his watch. "Reaper's team is currently being advised they are back on the case, but their orders to locate and apprehend the suspects have changed."

"Changed to what?" Blake asked for clarification.

"Apprehend is no longer in their orders. It's now locate and eradicate. I think Rebel would appreciate eradicating this traitor himself, right after I help the team locate him," Tucker explained.

"Why did their orders change all of a sudden? What happened?"

"One of the tankers in Houston just blew a couple of minutes ago. They're already scrambling agents to the site. Reaper warned them this would happen, and now they're concerned it'll only get worse. My boss just now alerted me about the call to eradicate."

"He was my partner. He framed me. Maybe I should go ahead and take him out," Joe replied.

"I get that, Brown. But he helped bury Rebel's wife in Houston. That gives him first dibs in my book."

"On the move again," Blake interrupted. "Toward the oil tankers."

"He'll be looking for his new partners. We should let him help us find the rest of them."

"Good thinking, Alex. Everyone, move out. Don't lose him, no matter what." Tucker emphasized each of his last three words.

Moving effortlessly through the night, the four men followed Bill with precision and ease.

Tucker patched into the FBI command center. ""He's on the phone. Trace that call. Who's he talking to?"

"Got it. It's one of them." The FBI analyst located the exact coordinates in the port where the cell phone was located and relayed the information to the team. "Bring them in."

"Copy that," Tucker replied. "Blake, Alex—apprehend that cowardly terrorist. Joe, you're with me on Bill. Move out."

They split up, each team clear on the intentions of their mission. Bill took the long way around the port, doubling back and skirting around buildings in his attempts to lose a tail and avoid detection, adding too many precious minutes to his journey. When he finally reached his destination, a rendezvous point with the comrade he'd recently spoken to in the hull of an oil tanker, he once again found he'd reached his destination too late.

His partner in crime was gone, as were the crucial items he needed to carry out his part of the plan. Joe knew the very second the dread overcame him as understanding dawned.

"Your gut told you, didn't it? That old feeling of knowing when you're being watched. Being followed. You felt it and ignored it, thought you could get away before it was too late." Joe spoke calmly as he approached Bill from behind. Bill stood motionless, with the exception of dropping his chin to his chest. "But there's no escaping now, Bill. It would be foolish even to try. But if that's what you're thinking, go ahead and try. I won't hesitate to shoot you in the head."

"Is that any way to treat your partner?" Bill replied.

"No, it's not," Joe conceded. "But that is how traitors are treated. You betrayed me, framed me for your treachery, and left me to take the fall in your place. For that alone, you deserve to be shot."

"But that decision isn't up to us," Tucker added. Bill turned to look at him, unaware another man was in the hull of the ship with them.

"Oh? Who is it up to?" Bill asked, mock amusement in his tone and his expression.

"Rebel. The man whose wife was buried in the explosion in Houston. The man who's still digging to find her, praying she's still alive under all those tons of concrete and steel. That's who decides your fate," Tucker replied.

The shock that registered on Bill's face could not be faked. "I...I didn't know his wife was in the building."

"That doesn't matter. You knew others were in it. But the fact that *she* was sealed your fate."

"What do you owe him anyway?"

"I served under Reaper while in the Army, then worked for Steele Security for a while before taking a private security job. Now I'm DEA and I owe them my allegiance, and they have it."

"Your time here is through, Bill," Joe concluded. "Your friends have started singing like canaries, giving up the locations where you told them to put the explosives. Pity you didn't use men who were true to the cause. Hired hands have no loyalty, especially when they're facing life in prison with no possibility of parole for forty years for treason."

"Let's go. There is one person who will be glad to see you."

The five-hour ride back to Houston was mostly silent. While Tucker normally didn't approve of cold-blooded murder, what Bill had done to his friend Rebel deserved to have justice served. The orders for eradication came from the president. With no higher office in the land, it was fitting that command apply to both of the main conspirators in the plot. He had no doubt Rebel and team would find Rashad as soon as they located Heather, and delivering Bill to him was the least he could do to help his friend.

By the time they reached the Port of Houston, Rebel had been searching for Heather in the remains of the twelve-story building for more than eighteen hours. Even with the briefing of what had occurred, Tucker couldn't comprehend what his eyes saw. Before he'd seen it firsthand, he held out some hope for Heather's safe return. But the complete demolition of the building before him left the most hopeless—and helpless—feeling he'd ever experienced.

In spite of that, the first thing he did after securing his prisoner was don a pair of gloves and join the search and rescue effort. No matter how bleak the situation appeared to him, he would work nonstop as long as Rebel and his other brothers remained out there. Day and night, for as long as it took.

Reaper approached Tucker and extended his hand. "Good to see you again, Tucker. It's been a while."

"I hate that it's under these circumstances. Have you told Rebel about your change in orders yet?"

Reaper shook his head from side to side. "It wouldn't matter to him. Rashad is already dead as soon as Rebel's finished here. The fact that his death is now sanctioned means nothing."

"I brought Rashad's partner with me to give Rebel first dibs on him."

"Who is it?"

"The dirty CIA agent who faked his death, Bill Smith."

"Fucking bastard," Reaper growled. "When did DEA Special Agents start handing over dirty CIA operatives for execution?"

Tucker shrugged one shoulder and lifted one side of his mouth in a lopsided grin. "Call it an early Christmas present."

CHAPTER TWENTY-TWO

During the second day, the feeling and sensations of pain in Rebel's hands were long since gone, but he kept moving chunks of concrete, gnarled metal, and destroyed remnants of office furniture in his quest to find Heather. The twisted feelings inside him had only increased with every minute that ticked by on the clock with no real progress being made. Tim, one of the search and rescue crew members, and Robin, his loyal black Lab, had worked diligently throughout the night in solidarity with Rebel.

"Robin has bonded with you, ya know?" Tim chatted with Rebel off and on during the night, lending his moral support in every way he knew how. "Every time I try to get her to take a break, she stares at you and whines until I bring her back out here."

"She's a good girl," Rebel replied, forcing a small smile and consciously keeping his irritation under wraps. "You've trained her well. It's actually very impressive to see the search and rescue dogs in action out here."

A few other dogs and handlers had located survivors buried under the demolished building. With each round of clapping and cheering, Rebel's hope for Heather being found alive waxed and waned. His conflicting feelings of being elated there were still survivors, and envy that it wasn't his wife they'd found, created a constant war in his heart. He'd never give up until he found her, but the state he would find her in was a constant burden on his mind and his spirits.

How far underneath the debris could she be buried?

Was there enough oxygen down there to keep her alive, or would it completely run out?

Had the crumbled concrete buried and suffocated her?

When he allowed these questions to fester inside him, the desire to find

Rashad and tear him apart with his bare hands built to levels that would rival a hydrogen bomb explosion. That bled over into his interactions with everyone else. He'd tried to distance himself as much as possible because the stress of it all was tearing him apart. Tim and Robin had been a godsend in keeping him sane and level-headed for the time being, forcing him to be around at least one other person during a time he'd rather have been left alone. After she was found, he'd deal with Rashad in his own special way.

"Come on, girl. Let's get you some water," Tim called to Robin, but she ignored him. "Robin. Come."

Robin locked in place and started barking vigorously. Her excitement was almost uncontainable, causing her to jump back and forth on top of the debris. But she kept her snout pointed to a single crack between two large pieces of building material. Rebel stopped in mid-motion and stared at her for several seconds before his gaze swung to Tim. His eyes asked the question he couldn't bring himself to verbalize.

"She's got something! We need some help over here," Tim yelled.

Group members from every direction swarmed on the location Robin indicated. Reaper, Shadow, Bull, Roman, Joe, and Tucker surrounded Rebel. Everyone watched on pins and needles as a small camera on the end of a flexible tube was passed through the crack and into the darkness below. The tiny LED light illuminated the cave-like fissure, and the image was transmitted up to the screen held by the camera operator. Rebel started to move so he could see the screen, but Tim stopped him.

"Wait. There's a reason why the image isn't broadcast for everyone to see. Give him a few seconds to determine what we're dealing with down there."

In his mind, Rebel knew Tim was correct. She may still be alive, but the image of her current condition would forever be burned into his memory if he dared to look at the screen. In the event she didn't survive, Tim was only trying to save him from a lifetime of the haunting scene. Rebel nodded once, agreeing to wait for their signal it was safe to look.

Tim cupped Rebel's shoulder and squeezed. "I know I'm asking a lot of you."

"You have no idea how hard it is for me not to grab that camera from his hands and do it myself. My whole life is down there, and I don't know if she's alive or dead."

"I need you to also consider there's a possibility Robin found another victim. It's hard not to get your hopes up, but there were a lot of people in this building," Tim added.

"It's Heather," Rebel replied. "I feel her. I know it's her."

Tim nodded his head, but his dubious expression conveyed his honest thoughts. Unable to wait any longer, Rebel darted behind the camera operator and watched the live streaming images over his shoulder. What appeared to be a twisted metal cage came into view and the camera operator halted to fine-tune the resolution.

"What is that?" He talked to himself absently as he worked the equipment, moving the camera around for a different angle.

"It's the framework for the stairs. The concrete is gone, but that's the mangled steel frame the steps were built on," Rebel replied. "Zoom in right there."

When the camera zoomed in tighter, they both saw an arm move inside the cage. "There! Did you see that?" Rebel wanted to dive headfirst into the opening and bring the search and rescue mission to an end. He wanted his wife back at his side.

The camera operator adjusted the resolution again now that he had a specific target to identify. The camera panned out, giving a wider view, and Rebel's heart surged in his chest. There, buried beneath the piles of ruin and wreckage, lay the love of his life. Boulder-sized chunks of building remains surrounded her, but the thick steel frame of the stairwell had essentially cocooned her, creating a bent and contorted cage that supported the weight of the remains directly above it.

"Call the structural engineers and get them over here immediately!" The group leader instantly took control of the scene. "Everyone in the section immediately around us, carefully move to the sides. Be careful where and how you step. We don't want any shifting if we can avoid it."

Another volunteer sent a small speaker down the shaft to her and unclipped the headset from his utility belt. He extended his hand toward Rebel and passed the headset to him. "Talk to her. Let her know what we're doing and that she's not alone."

Rebel hooked it over his ear, and the volunteer gave him the go-ahead nod when he'd turned it on. For the first time in what felt like forever, he was at a loss for words of what to say to his wife. He had no idea how to reassure her. He had no way of knowing how long it would take to safely get her out of the dungeon she was buried in. He had no clue what he was supposed to say.

Her back was propped up against one side of her protective cage. The camera focused on her face, displaying the streaks of dried blood, cuts, scrapes, and bruises lying under layers of concrete dust. Her hair was matted to her head in places, wild and untamed in others. Though she kept her eyes closed, they fluttered every few seconds as she attempted to open them.

In that moment, Rebel realized he'd never seen anyone or anything more beautiful in his entire life.

"Hey, baby. I have to admit, this hiding spot was a pretty brilliant idea for our ongoing game of hide-and-seek. You've really set the bar high with this one. But as you can see, I found you. Surely by now, you know me better than to think I'd let something as trivial as a few hundred tons of steel and concrete stand in my way."

He bit back the emotions that threatened to overtake him when he saw a small smile play on her lips.

"We're using a small camera to see you and a one-way speaker to talk to you. All you have to do is nod or something to give me a sign. I'll keep talking and keep you company. You know me—I won't leave here until you're safe in my arms again. In fact, I'm never leaving you again. Not for Miami, not for the government, nothing can keep us apart again. Now that I have you in my sights, you'll be out of there as soon as possible. We have all kinds of people up here plotting and planning, brilliant minds who can figure this out in no time. I'm right here with you, Heather."

She slowly nodded to indicate she understood, her sluggish movements leaving no doubt of the trauma her body had sustained. She tried to open her eyes again but quickly shut them and winced in pain.

"Leave your eyes closed, sweetheart," Rebel coaxed her. "There's a lot of concrete dust, and it can scratch your eyes and make them hurt like hell. We'll get them rinsed good when we get you out of there. Do you remember what happened?"

She nodded, and her face fell as sadness overcame her.

"I know you're sad, and I know you're scared. But we'll get through this together, okay? You and me. Oh, and there's someone up here I can't wait for you to meet. She already loves you, and she hasn't even met you yet. She's been beside me all night, searching for you and refusing to rest until she found you. Her name is Robin, and she has the most beautiful brown eyes you'll ever see."

Heather arched one eyebrow, daring him to continue complimenting another woman to her.

Rebel laughed good-naturedly. "And she has the shiniest black hair. Come to think of it, her hair color does remind me of yours. Anyway, let me see if I can get her over here to say hello to you."

He looked up from the screen to find Tim there, smiling and waiting with Robin. Rebel knelt down beside her then Tim gave the command. "Speak to the lady, Robin."

"Rrr-ruff!" Robin barked.

Rebel ran his fingers over the screen, his heart bursting with love when Heather responded with a full smile. "Robin says hello, babe. She's a gorgeous black Lab with a heart of gold. You'll love her, and I'm pretty sure you'll want to keep her."

Engineers and construction crews approached, poised to explain the plan they'd devised for extricating her. Apprehension unlike anything he'd ever experienced before gripped him tightly, squeezing him like a vise from the inside. He put the headset on mute before he addressed them.

"I just found her after almost two days of searching. Do not do anything that could take her away from me again." The threatening timbre of his voice left no room for misunderstanding.

"We'll take good care of her. Everything will be handled one step at a time to make sure all the supports are in place." The engineer attempted to assure him, but Rebel would only rest easy when she was finally rescued.

"Okay, baby," he said softly. "We're starting the process of getting you out of there. You'll hear a lot of noise. They're bringing in heavy equipment to move the larger pieces out of the way. You'll feel vibrations, which will almost certainly shake smaller pieces onto you. Keep your head covered just in case, but I'll be here watching their every move, every second."

She mouthed *I love you* in response, and tears began to trickle down her cheeks.

"I've loved you every single day since the day we first met. You're my best friend, my lover, and my wife, and you're the best person I know. You're beautiful and sexy and caring and giving and funny and strong and independent and supportive—and so much more.

"I'm not saying goodbye, my love. You're not leaving me. Want to know how I know that? Because I can feel you. I feel you inside me, beside me, all around me. Because you're the best part of me, the part I can't live without. The day I can't feel you anymore will be the day I die. But that's not today, Heather. We still have a life to live out together. So don't you dare give up and even think about leaving me."

Her tears continued to roll down her cheeks, but the trepidation that had covered her expression was replaced with the determination he recognized. She nodded and mouthed *okay*. When the extrication work began, she did as he'd instructed and covered her head with her arms. He didn't miss the grimace of pain that flashed across her face when she raised both arms, but she didn't let it stop her.

Piece by piece, they carefully moved the largest chunks of debris at the top of the pile away from the rescue site. With every movement, the engineers reevaluated the structure of what remained and identified what to clear next. Inevitably, a portion would break loose and free-fall into the space below, tumbling through the twisted metal that imprisoned her before hitting her. Her muffled cries of pain and fright drove Rebel mad. In the tight space where she was trapped by the metal, she had nowhere to move to dodge the shards. When they'd cleared a hole barely large enough for a person to fit through on the surface, he thrust the headset back to the volunteer and jumped feet-first into the opening before anyone could stop him.

"I'm here, baby. I'm with you."

He reached his arms through the steel bars that still caged her and covered her head with his muscular arms. The metal had been driven deep into the ground around her and still supported some of the wreckage that hadn't yet been moved. Though she didn't have much room to move, she slid toward him, flush with the metal, and wrapped her arms as far around him as she could reach through the metal bars. Her fingers were battered and sobs racked her body, but she held on to him with all the strength she had left.

"You shouldn't be here." Her voice barely came across as a rough whisper with her throat and mouth coated in the dust from the devastated building.

"This is exactly where I should be—it's where you are."

Through each meticulous step of the work, Rebel stayed at her side. His strong arms protected her from falling dangers. His words soothed her frazzled nerves. His presence gave her the strength she needed to hold on. In between activities, volunteers lowered several bottles of water down to them. In the first delivery, he used the bottles meant for his rehydration to wash the grit out of her eyes and clean the dust off her face. After clearing the dust from her mouth and throat, he nursed her wounds and made sure she was well hydrated. Each time the equipment started up, he gathered her in his arms through the metal bars and used his body to shield hers.

The sun was setting again when they'd cleared enough away to safely cut the metal and get her out. A blowtorch was lowered to Rebel, and he hesitantly examined the cage that surrounded her. If the cut weakened the metal any further, the weight could shift and bury them both. But they'd been in the danger zone long enough, and the odds of something tragic happening increased. Their lives were in the hands of the structural engineers.

Rebel held his breath while he made the cuts at the precise locations in which he was instructed. When he'd cut enough away for Heather to squeeze through, he scooped her up in his arms and crushed her to him while she cried tears of joy and relief. The team above lowered harnesses down to them to pull them out to safety and freedom. He helped Heather into her harness before stepping into his own and pulling her back into his arms for safekeeping.

The thunderous roar of the crowd when they emerged from the certain death trap was humbling. Heather looked around her, blinking repeatedly from the pain and from the tears that blurred her vision, and was awed at the scene. The mass of people who'd voluntarily worked hours on end to find and free as many as possible was unbelievable.

"Brax," she choked out, unable to express anything else.

"I know, love. Believe me when I say every single one of them wanted to be here. To help in any way. And I'm so grateful for them."

Paramedics were waiting in the wings and rushed in as quickly as the workers unhooked their harnesses. At first, Heather tried to resist medical treatment.

"I'm a nurse," she rasped and waved the gurney away. "I'm okay."

"Nurses are almost as bad at being a patient as paramedics are," one of them joked but didn't move away.

"You're a wonderful nurse. You're not okay. You're injured, and you're a patient as of right now. Get on the gurney." Rebel crossed his arms over his wide chest and dared her to argue with him.

She climbed onto the gurney, careful to avoid further injury to her side and leg, and stretched out. One of the paramedics started an IV for her hydration while the other performed an initial medical assessment.

"Which hospital do you want to go to?" the one who performed the assessment asked her pointedly.

Resigned to the fact she genuinely did need medical attention, she nodded when Rebel gave the name of the hospital where she worked. The uncertainty swirling in her mind was the only reason she didn't want to leave for the hospital. She knew she needed treatment, but she wasn't ready to face the questions she couldn't bring herself to ask.

Has my dad been found?

Was he transported to the hospital?

How bad were his injuries?

When can I see him?

Is he still alive?

Loaded and ready to go, Rebel jumped into the back of the ambulance with her, staying at her side as he promised.

"Do you want us to meet you there? I don't want to intrude if the two of you need some time alone." Noah stood at the back of the ambulance, holding the edge of the door.

Heather raised her head and replied for them both. "You're our family. You don't have to ask."

Noah grinned and winked at her. "We'll be there, then. Rebel, I got a call, and we're back on for locate and eradicate. It's your call, but personally, I don't think you want to sit this one out."

Through their nonverbal conversation, Rebel read between the lines and instantly understood the difference in their assignment.

"This investigation belongs to me. There's no way in hell I'd miss it."

CHAPTER TWENTY-THREE

On the ride from the port to the hospital, Brax handed Heather his cell phone.

"Let your mom hear your voice so she knows you're okay. She's been worried sick, and they wouldn't let her in the port."

She dialed her number, and her heart ripped in two from the panic in Kay's voice when she answered.

"Brax? Is she okay?"

"I'm okay, Mom."

Completely choked with emotion, neither could speak after that simple exchange, so Rebel took the phone and finished the conversation.

"Kay, we're heading to Heather's hospital, where she knows the doctors and nurses. Meet us in the ER when you've calmed down and can safely drive. You don't have to rush, she's really okay. We'll see you soon."

Rebel leaned over and gently kissed Heather while lovingly stroking her matted hair. "It's okay, baby. You can cry all you need to. I'll be here to dry your tears and take care of you."

Kay was waiting in the emergency room when the ambulance arrived. Even though it had only been a couple of days since Heather had last seen her, she noted how the stress and worry appeared to have aged her mother by several years.

Kay rushed to her when she was wheeled in and looked her over. "Heather, are you okay? How badly are you hurt? What can I do?"

"Just my ribs and my leg hurt, Mom. I'm okay. Brax has been taking good care of me," she replied weakly.

"Thank God you were found. I don't know what I would do if..."

What Kay didn't say told Heather more than she wanted to know at the moment. Compartmentalizing the traumatic event was helping her stay sane. She wasn't prepared to know everything all at once. Whatever information Kay had about Emmett's condition couldn't be good news, and that fact nearly pushed her into a panic attack.

She was thoroughly evaluated, questioned, poked, prodded, X-rayed, treated, and medicated for the injuries she'd sustained. From the trauma and stress her body had sustained, the doctor decided to keep her for a twenty-three-hour observation and make a determination about admitting or discharging her at that time. She was moved to a large private room to give Brax enough room to stay with her.

When the doctor made his rounds the following morning, she convinced him she would convalesce much better at home than in the hospital. With assurances that Rebel, Kay, and the rest of their extended family would be there to help her, the doctor agreed to let her go home. Bull brought Heather's Land Rover to the hospital, and Rebel drove his wife home.

Later that evening, she was surrounded by her friends and family in the comfort of her own home.

"I'm fine, really. You don't have to put your lives on hold for me." Heather tried to reassure everyone she was fine, but Rebel could see through her carefully crafted façade.

After everyone left, she attempted to rest and relax, but it was fleeting. Every time she closed her eyes, she saw her father hanging from the broken steps. She saw the terrified eyes of the other victims looking to her for answers she didn't have. She saw the building collapse on her, trapping her under an enormous amount of solid concrete inside a metal cage.

She was certain she'd die in that cage. That it would become her tomb, and she'd suffer an agonizingly slow death she couldn't do anything about. She made the mistake once of turning on the television and watching the news. The list of the identified victim's names scrolled across the bottom of the screen; each one was harder to deal with than the previous. When the footage of the attack scene filled the screen, it triggered a full-on panic attack.

Over the following few days, sleep mostly escaped her because the visions turned into nightmares, and she'd wake, screaming and crying. When Kay showed up, her eyes red and nearly swollen shut from crying, Heather knew they'd found her father before her mother had spoken a word. They'd found his body several yards from where Heather had been trapped, but he hadn't been sheltered by the steel frame. He'd been buried underneath the concrete that had caved in on the stairs below him, where many other victims had been trapped despite her attempts to tell them to go back up.

As far as injuries sustained, she felt blessed to only have a broken ankle, hairline fractures in her ribs, and too many cuts, scrapes, and bruises to count.

It was the psychological injuries she wasn't confident would ever fully heal.

"Good morning, my love."

It was early morning, and they were still in the bed, facing each other. Rebel had been her lifesaver—both literally and figuratively. He'd gotten her out of that concrete tomb, and he'd been by her side through every episode of anxiety she'd endured since.

"Good morning, honey. You didn't sleep at all last night," she observed. "I can tell by your eyes."

"You don't need to be concerned about me. I'm the one who's worried about you. You didn't sleep much at all, and you were screaming and crying in your sleep."

She dropped her eyes to focus on his chest, trying to hide the fear that had a tight grip on her. "I'm sorry if I woke you. Just having bad dreams."

"Don't be sorry. When that happens, I wrap my arms around you and whisper in your ear. Your entire body relaxes against me, and you go back to sleep. I'm glad I'm here to help you."

"I'm glad you're here, too, Brax. They haven't caught Rashad yet, have they?"

She glanced up at his face and caught the flash of murderous rage before it was quickly masked again. "Not yet. Is that what's scaring you so badly? You think he'll come back after you?"

She nodded, and tears slipped from her eyes before she could stop them. "That, and I'm really not ready to attend my daddy's funeral today. How can I say goodbye?"

"You don't, sweetheart. Your love for him won't end today, and you don't have to say goodbye to it. His love for you didn't end with his death, he took it with him. You'll miss him. You'll wish he were here. But you never have to say goodbye."

"Is that how you dealt with it?"

"With losing Dalton? Yes. It took me a while, but I eventually realized that, and it helped me."

"Thank you. It does help to look at it that way."

"Back to Rashad. How much do you think about that? How often does he frighten you?"

"All the time," she admitted reluctantly.

Rebel stroked her face with his hand, wiping the tears from her eyes with the pad of his thumb. "You don't have to worry about him ever again. Very soon, he'll be no more than a memory. Memories can't come back to life and hurt you."

"Is he dead?" she whispered.

"Not yet." *But he will be.*

"You know where he is?"

"I know exactly where he is at all times."

"But you haven't taken him in yet?"

"I've been waiting until you were feeling a little better, a little more secure. When I go get him, I'll have some people come to keep you company while

I'm out. It won't take long. But no one has moved on him because his ass is mine. Now that I know he's causing you most of this fear and anxiety, I'll close up this case very soon. Today, we'll pay our respects to your father."

~

Every pew in the expansive church was full with friends, family, and employees who wanted to pay their respects to the man who was larger than life. Many who made it out of the building had asked if they could speak at his memorial, to share what he'd meant to them. Kay was so moved by the requests to honor her late husband she couldn't deny them.

One after the other approached the pulpit with their written speech in hand, but most never even referred to their notes. The graphic memories of how he'd sacrificed his own life to save theirs in the stairwell that day were forever etched onto their psyche. Notes would never do the actual event any justice.

When Heather rose and walked toward the pulpit, Rebel watched her in shocked amazement. She hadn't mentioned to him she would be one of the speakers at her father's funeral. The events had weighed on her heavily enough, and he was genuinely concerned reliving that day in front of everyone would be her breaking point. He sat on the edge of the pew, ready to spring into action and carry her out if that's what it took to save her.

He watched as she took a deep breath to calm her racing heart. She picked up a tissue and dabbed at the corners of her eyes, already fighting back the tears before she'd uttered the first word. She hid the slight tremor in her hand by gripping the sides of the podium. This was killing her, but she still faced it like a champion.

"Listening to all your stories of how my daddy saved you has been a blessing in disguise. I can't describe how very much I have dreaded this day, this service, and facing what it'll mean to my family when everything is said and done. But each of you has given me back a piece of my father to hold on to for the rest of my life, and for that, I thank you from the bottom of my heart.

"I'm not here to share the story of how he also saved my life, which he did. That's not something I can talk about just yet. But I do want to share with you a very different story about my father from that same day. You see, I went to his office to talk to him because he was rarely home while the acquisition process was underway. I love my dad very much, and I needed him to understand and support a decision I'd recently made."

Brax sat motionless and waited for her to continue, to share with him and the rest of the congregation why she went to his office on that day of all days.

"He had offered my husband a job so we could stay here in Houston and be together as a family. Brax accepted it so he could be with me. He agreed to leave behind a business he'd help build from scratch, a group of friends who are as close as family to him, and a life he was accustomed to in Miami—all for me. Because he loves me.

"That day, I told my father about two decisions I'd made and wanted to explain why they were so important to me. The first one I told him was Brax and I have decided to start a family soon. He was thrilled about that, about the prospects of being a doting grandfather and spoiling the baby even more than we could.

"The second decision was that I couldn't let Brax give up everything he'd worked so hard to build into a success just because I didn't want to give up what I was comfortable with here. It wasn't fair to my husband because I can be a nurse anywhere. So, instead of him moving here to work for my dad, I'd move to Miami and be a nurse there.

"What I thought would end up in a huge fight became the best conversation I've ever had with my father. We broke down walls that had been between us for years. We cried, we forgave, we healed, we loved. He asked me to pass on a couple of messages for him—from that conversation and then again after he saved me—because he knew he wouldn't make it out.

"Mom, he asked me to tell you he loves you and he'll be waiting for you.

"Brax, he asked me to tell you he loves you like the son he never had. In his office, he talked about some mistakes he'd made years ago, things he allowed you to believe but he never meant. He intended to ask for your forgiveness, and he said he'd be honored if you'd allow him to call you 'son.' He was proud of you and everything you've accomplished, and he was supportive of my decision to move to be with you.

"I'm sharing all of this personal information about my father with you to say this… He wasn't perfect. He made mistakes. He was stubborn and hard-headed at times. He was a hero. He saved my life. He saved many of your lives. All of these qualities and characteristics made him the man he was.

"We all have some variation of these qualities. So, in honor of my father, I simply ask this…in some way, it doesn't matter if it's big or small, be a hero to someone else who needs your help. You never know when one small thing you do makes a big difference in someone else's life."

After she took her seat next to Rebel again as the music played, he wrapped his arm around her and tucked her into his side, instinctively protecting and shielding her. He leaned over, his lips grazed her ear, and whispered to her. "I'm so proud of you for doing that. I know how hard that was for you to do. Are you sure you want to leave Houston, and move to Miami with me? Do you need time to think about it?"

She met his gaze with her tear-laden eyes. "I've thought about it for a long time now, my love. My mind was already made up before all this happened, but this has only reaffirmed to me I've made the right decision. You're everything to me, Brax, and with you is the only place I want to be."

When they left from the graveside service, Rebel noticed a familiar pair standing off to the side, patiently waiting for them to approach. He glanced over at Heather as she raised her hand to her face and wiped away the tears that continued to fall.

"Babe, I told you there was someone I wanted you to meet the night we got you out of that hole. She's here now, and I think you'd love her."

"Okay, Brax. Who is she?"

He led the way, holding her hand and giving her silent reassurances. "Heather, this is Robin. She worked with me, almost nonstop, until she locked on to your scent."

Heather leaned down in front of her and was instantly drawn into her expressive brown eyes. She fondly stroked Robin's shiny coat. "Thank you for finding me, Robin. You saved my life. You didn't even know me, but you kept working without being asked or forced to do it. I owe you everything, sweet girl."

Robin leaned into Heather, placing her head against Heather's chest. Heather lowered her head until her forehead rested on top of Robin's head, the two bonding and blocking out the rest of the world.

"Babe, this is Tim. He's Robin's handler, and he was out there helping, too. Tim and Robin were the key to my sanity out there."

Heather looked up at Tim. "I can't thank you enough, Tim. It's humbling and overwhelming when I think about how you and the others voluntarily put your own lives in danger to save complete strangers."

"We enjoy helping others. It gives us a sense of purpose, really. I have to tell you Robin has never bonded with anyone like she has the two of you. She has acted like she was in mourning for the last few days. Now that I see her with you, I know she was. She's claimed you as her family."

Rebel and Heather exchanged glances. "Are you saying you want us to take her?" Heather asked.

"If you'll love her, give her a good home, and treat her like family. She wouldn't have attached herself to you if she didn't sense you were good, honest people."

"I'd love to take her home with us, Tim. But I'd feel guilty taking your dog from you."

"She is a great dog and I love her, but she's not my only one. As sad as she's been lately, I really think she'd rather be with you."

"Then she's welcome to come home with us," Rebel replied. "I don't know how to repay you for this."

"You don't owe me anything. Give your love to Robin and we'll call it even."

The men shook hands then Heather stood and threw her arms around Tim's neck. "Thank you so much," she choked out. "Thank you."

Rebel collected Robin's things from Tim's vehicle and took his two ladies home to rest.

~

Later that evening, Rebel and Heather were alone in their home, drained from the emotional toll the day had taken on them. Heather was stretched out on the couch with her head in Rebel's lap while he lovingly massaged her head. Robin had stretched out on the love seat, content and cozy in her new home. Within minutes, Heather was sound asleep, sleeping better than she had since the whole ordeal began. Her breaths were even and her muscles were relaxed. For once, she wasn't having nightmares, reliving being buried alive, existing in fear.

Her eyes fluttered and she opened them, looking up at Rebel. Her hand followed her gaze, cupping his face in her palm and running her fingers through the stubble of his beard. "I've missed you, Brax."

"I'm right here, baby. I haven't left."

She pushed up on one hand, only wincing slightly at the pain in her side. "No, that's not what I meant."

She covered his lips with hers, teased them apart with the tip of her tongue, and then claimed ownership of his mouth. She moved cautiously, minding her injuries, and straddled his lap.

"I mean like this," she purred. "This is how I've missed you."

His fingers threaded through her short black hair before gripping a handful and holding it tightly. He tilted her head to the side, exposing the sensitive area of her neck, before he voraciously feasted on her succulent skin.

"Yes," she hissed in ecstasy. "I love how that feels."

He moved lower, removing her shirt and tossing her bra on the floor. He covered her breast with his mouth and sucked her hardened nipple between his teeth. The slight pain from the graze of his teeth mixed with the pure pleasure of his tongue was a recipe for bliss. Before she realized it, she was flat on her back, the clothes on the lower half of her body had been removed, and Rebel was working his mouth down her stomach.

He pushed her legs farther apart, flicked his tongue against her clit, and thrust his fingers deeply into her. She moaned loudly in pleasure, and her fingers gripped his head. She writhed underneath him as the warmth of his tongue started from the bottom edge of her wetness and made its way up to her clit. When he sucked it into his mouth, the sensory overload had her screaming his name.

"I want to taste you, baby. Come for me," he demanded, then eagerly dove back in, resuming his exploration of her body, relishing in the taste she left on his tongue. "Damn, you taste good. I need to be inside you now."

"Take me. Take what you want."

He grasped both of her legs, his cock poised at her entrance, and she held her breath and waited for him to surge into her. His welcome intrusion into her body caused sensations to roll through her entire being, stretching and filling her in the most erotic and pleasurable way. He leaned forward, covering her body with his, and sealed their intimate connection. He allowed his feelings to pour out into her through his eyes, through his touch, and through his heart. She accepted his love and returned her own through every kiss, every caress, and every tantalizing breath.

Their bodies slick with sweat, their hearts pounding against their chests, they made love for hours. Rediscovering one another. Reconnecting after a harrowing event. Reestablishing the connection that had carried them through so many happy and sad times throughout the years.

Their love was stronger than the blast that had rocked their world.

It was more powerful than the terrorist who had threatened their existence.

It was more consuming than the fear that had tried to tear them apart.

It was alive.

CHAPTER TWENTY-FOUR

Over the next few weeks, Rebel watched Heather become stronger and seemingly more like herself, until the sun went down and darkness covered the world like a heavy blanket shrouding the light. Her external wounds were healing, but the psychological injuries were still taking a toll on her.

He'd waited until he was certain she could manage without him continuously being at her side. Then he arranged for Brianna, Chaise, and Amelia to keep her company while he went out to finish his job. When Brianna suggested the whole family spend the day together to initiate a return to normalcy, Rebel heartily agreed.

"I'll be back as soon as I can. There are a couple of loose ends Tucker and I need to wrap up." He sealed his promise with a kiss while he lovingly stroked her cheek. "Introduce Robin to Amelia while I'm gone."

"All I want is for you to be careful and come back home to me. Say it. Promise me."

"I promise. I will be careful, and I will be back home with you before you even know I'm gone. Our house will be full of people, and they'll keep you very occupied. I have to go meet Tucker now, babe. I love you."

"I love you, Brax."

He opened the front door to leave and was greeted by a large group of their friends and family. "Look, babe. Some of our guests are already here to see you. I'll be quick."

"Oh, good! I'm glad they're here." Heather walked to the door to greet their friends, but Rebel felt her eyes boring into his back until he was out of sight.

~

Rebel drove to their rendezvous point, parked his truck, and walked in silence alongside Tucker over the last two blocks to their final destination. Rebel opened the front door, walked inside, and quickly assessed the scene. Tucker inclined his head toward Rebel and closed the door behind him on his way back out. Rebel moved around the small, dilapidated house, arranging the supplies and perfectly setting the stage.

"You're probably wondering what the fuck is happening right about now." Rebel paused when he realized Rashad was awake, and he looked down directly into Rashad's eyes. "I'll be glad to explain it to you. We don't have much time, though, so I'll have to talk while I work."

He walked to the freezer and removed the vials of TATP Rashad had already made. He carefully set them up in a row on the small end table beside where Rashad lay on the couch.

"You are about to blow yourself up with your own devices. Yeah, I know it's a little shocking since you can't move at all right now. But it'll make sense by the end of this story. Try to keep up with me.

"My wife is the best person I know. She's a nurse, as you well know since you followed her around the hospital and took pictures of her. She takes care of people who are very sick and fighting for their lives. As an oncology nurse, she's seen her fair share of tragedy over the years. But she keeps going back, she keeps trying to help, because there are always those patients who defy the odds and beat the cancer growing inside them. She's an amazing person."

Rebel rearranged the furniture in the small room as he talked, moving everything away from in front of the front window so there was nothing obstructing the view into the living room. When he was satisfied with the setup, he turned back to Rashad.

"You can't imagine the rage and fury I felt when I learned that my wife, the love of my life, the one person I can't live without, was buried alive in that explosion you created in the port. For nearly forty-eight hours straight, I did nothing but move rock, concrete, metal, and garbage, desperately looking for my wife.

"One thing you probably don't know about me is I've always been known for being very level-headed, always considering all sides of the equation before making a final decision, playing devil's advocate to get others to think differently.

"But not that night.

"That night, you changed me, Rashad. What you did to my wife flipped a switch in my brain, and the only thing that kept me focused during that forty-eight-hour journey through hell was meticulously planning every detail of how I'd kill you. And Rashad, I have a great plan.

"That plan brings us to today. You are a coward, plain and simple. You've been in hiding since the bombing, thinking you got away with it all. Thinking I didn't know exactly where you were and what you were doing every minute of every hour of every day. But I did. The only reason you've been alive the last few weeks is because my wife has needed me with her.

"Imagine my surprise when she told me she can't get past the fear of knowing you're still out here, roaming free, and could possibly hurt her again. She needs you to be dead to feel safe. I'm paraphrasing here for the sake of time. The bottom line is you'll be dead in just a couple of minutes because my wife comes first. Always.

"You may be wondering why you can't move a muscle, but you're fully aware of everything happening to you. As I mentioned, my wife is a nurse, and we've always shared every detail about our days, no matter how mundane it is. Turns out, something she mentioned a long time ago suddenly became very useful to me today.

"You can't see him because you can't turn your head, but your cohort Bill Smith is here with you. After my buddy Tucker knocked you over the head and brought you back here along with Bill, I gave each of you a shot. The medical name is long and very scientific sounding, succinylcholine, so most of the medical personnel just call it 'sux' for short. When you think about it, that's very fitting for this situation because it definitely sucks to be you right now.

"Anyway, 'sux' is a paralytic, but it allows you to remain alert and fully aware of everything happening to you and around you. I couldn't give you the full dosage because that would make your diaphragm stop working and you'd quit breathing. I don't want you to die too early. Remember I mentioned that you buried my wife in a tomb of concrete and metal? She was conscious during that whole ordeal, just like you'll both be when this house blows up with you in it.

"You're going to stay right here on this couch, and your little invention will be right here at your head. By the way, your head will be the first thing you lose when this blows, in case you haven't figured that out yet.

"Maybe you noticed I just moved some furniture around in here. That's because I need a clear line of sight to shoot these vials of TATP beside your head. When they explode, you'll be fully awake. You'll hear me leave the house. You'll hear the door latch behind me. You'll wait while the clock ticks, one excruciating second at a time. I'll take a stroll down the street to my vantage point, set the sights of my rifle on your bomb materials right here by your head, and I'll squeeze the trigger.

"When the force of my bullet connects with the temperamental nature of this compound you made, there will be nothing left of you or Bill or this house. For all intents and purposes, what little specs of DNA are left will indicate you blew up your own damn self while playing with the Mother of Satan. You'll be out of our lives forever. No ghosts. No shadows. No looking over our shoulders for psychos hell-bent on revenge.

"Speaking of psychos with a need for revenge. Yes, I shot and killed your father. But to be fair, I was rescuing hostages he'd taken from us. He shot at my friends and me first. I simply returned fire while trying to leave his house with the people who didn't belong there. Technically, he brought all that shit on himself.

"Like father, like son, I guess. I'll leave you to sort that out in the few seconds you have left alive. It's time for me to get home to my wife. Plus, that shot I gave you will start wearing off any time now. Can't have you moving around too much before the house blows to hell and back, can we?

"This is the part of the story where I'd normally tell you to bend over and kiss your ass goodbye, but you can't move. So feel free to just envision yourself doing it instead."

Rebel picked up his rifle, walked to the door, and didn't look back until he was in his spot a block away. He casually lifted his rifle to his shoulder, set his sights on the glass vials that held the volatile concoction, and squeezed the trigger with ease. The resulting explosion was so severe, it not only obliterated everything that had been in the old house, but it also knocked down the condemned houses surrounding it.

He smiled to himself. "Not a trace of evidence left."

Rebel exited through the back door and hopped into the waiting car.

"Feel better now?" Tucker asked.

"Much better. It's a beautiful morning, isn't it? Let's head back to my house now. Everyone is already there with Heather for our little get-together. We don't want to be late joining the party."

~

Rebel and Tucker pulled up to the house and found the driveway was completely full of cars.

"Shit. We're late. Everyone else beat us here."

"Will Heather ground you for it?" Tucker smirked, enjoying busting Rebel's balls.

Rebel cut his eyes sharply toward Tucker. "You know I just killed two men."

A broad, shit-eating grin crawled across Tucker's face. "Of course, I do. I helped."

"Now I know why Shadow enjoyed working with you on that case in Dallas so much. You two are so much alike."

They climbed out of the car and walked into the house, the sounds of laughter and chatter filling the air. When Rebel stepped into the living room, he immediately sought out Heather. Relief flooded him when he saw she was safe, sound, and laughing as she chatted with Liz and Becca. He walked around the room and greeted everyone individually. Becca approached him with outstretched arms and wrapped her arms around his neck.

"It's so good to see you again, Brax. I always know when you're home because Heather absolutely glows with love. Thank you so much for never giving up and saving my best friend." She wiped an errant tear from her eye when she pulled away.

"I said no crying today," Heather teasingly chastised her.

"Who's crying?" Becca challenged with a sly smile.

"Believe me, there was no way I would've left that site without my wife. Thank you for taking such good care of her in the ER. I'm surprised they didn't toss you out of there on your ear with all the demands you made." Rebel replied.

"They couldn't. I wasn't working–I was there as a visitor. Plus, they know me and they know they'd have to deal with me at some point later." Her devious smile and devilish laugh left no doubt Becca would've followed through on her veiled threat.

"If you two will excuse me, I need to speak with the boss for a minute."

After a kiss to Heather's cheek, he easily weaved through the many people celebrating Heather's recovery. When he reached Noah, he held his hand a second longer than normal when he shook hands. With a pointed look, he delivered a hidden mission update in his innocuous greeting. "It's a beautiful day for a celebration. There was a big gust of wind earlier, but it blew over in no time."

Comprehension lit in Noah's eyes. "Sometimes a nice breeze can make your whole day."

"It most certainly did that."

When Noah rejoined Brianna, Heather approached Rebel from behind and wrapped her arms around his waist. She pressed her face against his back and inhaled deeply, drawing in the scent that was uniquely his. With his hands on her arms, he lovingly caressed her while remaining cognizant of her healing wounds. He took her hand in his and tenderly pulled her around to stand in front of him, changing places by wrapping his arms around her waist protectively.

"You must have missed me this morning." He smiled against the side of her head and pressed his lips to her hair. "I missed you, too."

"I did miss you. Not that I haven't enjoyed our company, but it's always better when you're here with me."

"I'm here now. Just had to wrap up some loose ends this morning. How's your mom holding up?"

"Subtle change of subject, Brax. She alternates between a complete nervous breakdown and saying she's fine."

"And how are you holding up?"

"I alternate between a complete nervous breakdown and saying I'm fine."

He turned her in his arms to face him. "If it's too soon for everyone to be here, just say the word. They'll understand."

"No, it actually helps to have them here. Mom and I have been able to share stories about Dad with them. Talking about him helps because it makes me feel like he's still here with me. Like you said."

He lowered his head and softly kissed her lips. "If it's any consolation, you're completely safe now."

"You got him?"

"He'll never be seen or heard from again. I promise."

She threw her arms around his neck and murmured against his skin, her words in a breathy staccato. "Thank you. So much. I'm so relieved."

Rebel looked up to find Tucker watching them, his head cocked to the side and his eyebrow arched in silent questioning. "Fine. Tucker helped. A little."

Heather chuckled and turned to locate him. "Thank you for helping, Tucker. I really appreciate it."

"My pleasure." He winked and chuckled.

"Was he the secret contact you met in the park?" Rebel asked Silas.

"Yeah. Tucker had been following Bill since he faked his death and skipped out of Miami. We knew he'd eventually meet back up with Rashad," Silas confirmed. "We couldn't risk taking them out too soon, but unfortunately, our sources didn't have all the information about their plans."

"You warned us about that from the beginning, Silas. We don't blame either of you for what they did." Rebel knew the guilt of that night stayed with Silas, and he tried to reassure him no one on the team held him responsible.

Roman dropped his eyes to the floor, and he didn't seem to hold his shoulders as strong and proud as he normally did.

Heather noticed Roman's remorseful expression. "We don't blame you either, Roman. You tried to warn me, I remember that very vividly."

"That's right. Everyone in this room went above and beyond to help and support us during that time. We couldn't ask for a better family." Rebel made it a point to look each person in the eye, conveying the seriousness of his message.

"Speaking of family, I think Steve has an announcement he'd like to make now." Heather released Rebel and moved to stand next to Steve.

The aggressive chemotherapy treatments had taken a toll on his body, leaving his muscles weak and his energy level at a negative number based on a scale of one to ten. Ever the nurse, Heather reached down to steady and assist him when he began to stand up and address the crowd.

"Yes, I do, my favorite nurse in the world." Steve winked. "I've been a fighter all my life. I've worked hard, built a successful company, and took no prisoners. On the outside, everything in my life appeared to be the epitome of success. Houses, cars, money, nice things—on the surface, I had it all.

"It wasn't until many years later when I realized everything I'd worked for and spent my hard-earned money on was worthless without my family by my side. As hard as this is to say, finding out I had advanced cancer was a blessing in disguise because it brought my kids back to me. With them, I gained another son, another daughter, and now a granddaughter. If I could just get Silas married off, I'd have one more daughter. Hint, hint."

The room erupted in laughter, and all eyes swung to Silas.

"Yeah, don't hold your breath on that, old man." Silas laughed good-naturedly with his father.

"By extension, my new daughter brought Liz into the fold, who brought her son, my doctor, in. The cancer brought me here to Houston for treatment, where I met my favorite nurse in the world, only to find out her husband is one of my son's best friends. While I hate cancer and what it's done to my body, I wouldn't trade one thing I've lost during the last several months of treatment for all the wonderful things I've gained.

"I love you all. I want to thank you for standing by me, checking on me, taking care of me, and making sure I got the best care possible. I would've been dead long ago if it weren't for all of you. I would've missed my daughter's wedding, getting to hold my granddaughter, and so many important events in my family's lives."

Sara sat behind Steve, sniffling and attempting to control her emotions. He turned to take her hand and jerk his head to the side, indicating for her to join him. The room was silent as Sara stood next to her husband, hand in hand, waiting for Steve to continue. The air hung thick with apprehension as they tried to gauge what he would say next.

"We received some unexpected news recently we haven't had a chance to share with you because of everything that's occurred. We wanted to tell everyone at the same time because of how much you all mean to us. Dr. Stanton put me through the full gamut of blood work and body scans, and he said the experimental treatment has been a success. There's no sign of any cancer cells or tumors anywhere in my body."

Tears of happiness and relief flowed freely among the shouts and cheers of excitement.

"It's been a long, hard road. Many times, we weren't convinced he could withstand another round of treatment. But he refused to give up. He kept saying his kids needed him, so he had to try anything they threw at him." Sara spoke through her tears, sharing a tiny portion of the months of hell she'd witnessed firsthand. "With all the sadness that wicked man caused, we thought everyone could use some good news."

"That is truly wonderful news, and I'm so grateful you shared it with us today. Seeing something good emerge after all the evil of the last few days lifts my spirits and renews my faith," Kay replied. "I'm sure some will think I've made a rash decision, and maybe I have, but everything Steve said only reinforces to me it's the right one."

"What decision, Mom?"

"I'm moving to the Miami area to be close to my family. With Emmett gone, there's nothing holding me here now. Honestly, we'd talked about moving there in a couple of years when he retired. He wanted to see the merger through first to make sure everyone's jobs were preserved. My timetable has just changed. As soon as I can get odds and ends wrapped up here, I'll join you in sunny Florida."

"Mom, I'm so glad. I've been sick just thinking about leaving you." Heather hobbled in her boot over to Kay and wrapped her arms around her.

"Bryan and Jackie, no pressure or anything." Shadow playfully teased Rebel's parents. "It's not like everyone here is going back to Miami soon or anything."

"We may just surprise you one day. You never know," Bryan replied with a gleam of challenge in his eye.

"Joe and Emily, all eyes are on you now," Silas added. "Don't think you're immune from the peer pressure of this group."

"We are definitely going back to Miami," Emily confirmed. "I never wanted to leave in the first place."

"Since we're all sharing good news, Colton and I have some news to share." Chaise looked lovingly at her husband before turning back to her expanded family. "We're pregnant!"

After a boisterous round of congratulations for Chaise and intentionally harsh backslaps for Bull, the mood in the group was decidedly upbeat and hopeful for the future. Everyone gathered on the back porch where the men argued over grilling burgers and hot dogs and the women chatted about the excitement their futures held.

Throughout the day, Heather and Rebel passed unspoken messages to each other. Messages that conveyed how thankful one was to have the other. Messages of the deep-rooted need for the other they shared. Messages that said they knew tomorrow wasn't promised, so love would be given freely as if every day were their last day.

The wicked intentions of one man only served to strengthen their bonds of steel.

EPILOGUE

Two Years Later

"Yes!" Bull used his most commanding voice.

"No." Chaise replied with her hand on her hip and a definitive dare in her gaze.

"Chaise, it's time."

"Colton, no it's not." She mimicked his take-charge stance and assertive tone.

"Baby." He quickly changed his tactic and his tone, showing his charming side that was reserved only for Chaise. "Cason needs a little sister."

"Cason is barely a year and a half old. He doesn't need a little sister yet."

"But Rebel and Heather are already talking about having another baby. We can't let them beat us."

"Colton, this is not a race."

"Brianna is due any day now," he continued his argument. With a bogus pout, Bull tried to make her feel sorry for him.

"That look doesn't work on me."

"I know what works on you." Bull scooped her up in his arms, threw her over his shoulder, and marched toward their bedroom. "You love it when I'm a caveman."

"You know I love it," she replied seductively. "And I gladly invite you to try all you want, but it won't work since I'm still on the pill."

"Dammit, woman." He playfully popped the rounded globe of her ass cheek. "Where are they? I'm flushing them."

Chaise's laughter echoed off the walls as he carried her down the hall toward the bedroom. "What if I told you I've actually already quit taking them?"

Bull stopped in his tracks and lowered her to her feet. His eyes narrowed in suspicion as he leveled her with his penetrating stare. "Are you fucking with me right now?"

"No, honey, I'm not. You've been after me for months to have another baby. I quit taking them about two months ago, so we should be good to seriously try now."

"First man to the finish wins." Bull replied confidently.

"Don't even think about finishing before I do." Chaise arched one brow in mock threat.

"You will 'finish' many times before I do. I *guaran-damn-tee* you that."

~

"Babe, can you put Kinsley down for her nap? I need to change Elias before I put him down."

"You mean they're both going to take a nap at the same time, so I can spend some alone time with my wife? Come with me, my beautiful baby girl. It's nap time for my Kinsley." He lifted his daughter, held her against his chest, and her head automatically lowered to rest on his broad shoulder. "I get Mommy all to myself for the next hour."

"Don't jinx us, Brax. I don't think they've taken a nap at the same time more than once or twice in the last eighteen months since they were born."

"I'm already getting a semi just thinking about it. Do you think we'll have twins again?"

Heather's jaw dropped open and she stared incredulously at Rebel. "Why would you even wish that on me again? Do you have any idea how hard it is to carry two of your babies at the same time?"

"I'll help."

After she quit laughing, she wiped the tears from her eyes and shook her head at him. "And how, exactly, do you propose to help with that?"

"Oh, you meant carrying them while you're pregnant." Each word was pronounced exaggeratedly, as if he had just caught onto her meaning.

"Yeah, don't play dumb with me. What's this about? You've been obsessed with having another set of twins. As quickly as possible."

"I've just been thinking about it a lot lately. You know Brianna is due any day, so they'll have two kids. Bull and Chaise are talking about getting pregnant again, so they'll have two kids before long."

"And?" Heather's eyebrows disappeared under her bangs, she held her hands out, palms up, and narrowed her eyes.

"And," he hesitated. "I just think it's time we have another baby so we don't fall behind."

"Wait. Hold up a second. You want to have another baby, or two, right away, so our friends don't beat us in the 'how many kids do you have' category?"

He shrugged one shoulder but avoided direct eye contact. "I like having more kids than they have. Makes me feel proud. Plus, I love seeing you pregnant, my baby growing inside you, knowing we made that little person you're carrying. It turns me on."

"I guess we'd better get them down soon, then. While they're both sleepy. My husband just made my ovaries explode inside my body. I'll be surprised if we don't have triplets now."

"Don't tease me, woman." He followed her into the twins' bedroom and placed Kinsley in her crib while Heather put Elias in his.

"I wouldn't dare tease a big, bad, Delta Force operative. You're liable to handcuff me to bed and torture me in all kinds of devious ways."

"Definitely." He advanced on her, a predatory gleam in his eye and a determined gait in his swagger. "I'll show you all the ways I play dirty."

~

"You know, princess. I almost feel sorry for Bull and Rebel." Noah casually broached the subject as he massaged lotion on his wife's very pregnant belly.

"Why?" Brianna ask, her face scrunched in confusion.

"It's purely conjecture, really. A vicious rumor about me. But apparently, somehow I instigated a bet with them. Just a little wager between friends, as they say. My understanding is Shadow and Silas declined to participate."

"A bet, huh? And what was the alleged bet, exactly?" Brianna cut her eyes at Noah, titled her head to the side, and silently challenged him to confess.

"Somehow they got the idea that whoever has the highest number of kids by the end of next year wins bragging rights for life."

Brianna threw her head back in laughter, picturing the three men arguing over who was the most virile. "Bull and Rebel both fell for that?"

"Hook. Line. And sinker. They're just too easy."

"Yeah, 'too easy' describes Bull and Rebel," Brianna replied sardonically. "Let me guess. Not one of them has any idea we're having twins in a couple of weeks, do they?"

"Nope. Not a clue." Noah smiled widely and leaned over to kiss Brianna's swollen belly. "You two little miracles will give me bragging rights for life."

Brianna ran her fingers through his hair, lovingly stroking his scalp and watching him talk animatedly with their unborn children. Noah looked up and locked eyes with her, love radiating from every ounce of him.

"Actually, I have to take that back. Brianna, you gave me bragging rights for life the day you agreed to be mine. Now with our girls Amelia and soon-to-be Emery, and our soon-to-be son, Gray, my life is more than complete. It's absolutely perfect."

~

More Steele Security is coming soon in Wicked Shadows

BOOK 5: WICKED SHADOWS

Devon "Shadow" Kane chose a life of anonymity the moment he entered the clandestine world of the CIA. His training made him a killer, a skill he had no qualms using.

The younger sister of his childhood friend was far from the girl next door. She was also the one he couldn't have. The bright flash bulbs in her celebrity world were at odds with the stealth and invisibility required in his.

Then she disappeared—without a trace.

The stakes were high, but Shadow would risk his all for her. The only sure bets were the threat of blowing his cover and the likelihood he wouldn't reach her in time.

PROLOGUE

Twenty-One Years Prior

Elle Moore crouched low to the ground, darting from her hiding spot behind a shrub to a new position behind a tree. Her best friend and partner-in-crime, Beth Condra, followed her, staying close on her heels until she joined Elle behind the huge oak tree. Elle covered her lips with her index finger, indicating for her cohort to remain silent before she pointed toward the driveway they were casing.

"He's standing beside Jeff's car," Elle whispered and dropped to her knees on the ground. "Peek around the tree, but don't let them see you."

Beth slowly knelt, keeping her eyes locked on Elle's. "What if they see me? What should I do?"

"Just do it real slow." Elle emphasized the words with an emphatic pump of her arms, her fingers spread wide and her palms down.

"Okay." Beth put one hand on the ground to steady herself and peered around the tree, her movements painstakingly measured. "I see him. He's with Jeff. And he's not wearing a shirt!"

"What? Let me see!"

Elle jerked Beth back and quickly assumed her partner's vantage point. She was mesmerized by the black-haired, muscular young man with her brother. "Oh my gosh," she gasped. "Is he supposed to do that out here? He's almost naked. What if someone calls the cops on him?"

His athletic shorts sat low on his waist, revealing all of his upper body, from his broad shoulders to his narrow, muscular waist. Elle blatantly stared, completely enraptured by his presence, and wished there were a tree closer to the driveway so she could get a closer look at him, her hero.

"I don't know why we're even doing this. I mean, he's *old*, Elle. He's, like, in high school or something," Beth complained, suddenly bored with their mission. "Why don't you just go out with Scott? He likes you a lot. He keeps asking you to be his girlfriend."

Elle shook her head from side to side but kept her eyes trained on her singular focus. "Scott's all right, I guess. But no one else will ever compare to Devon Kane. I'm gonna marry him one day, Beth. You just wait. Besides, the house down the street is for sale. Maybe we can live there."

"Yeah, that's a good idea. Then you'll still be close to home," Beth agreed, with all of her youthful wisdom. "It's too hot for this, Elle. Let's go swimming already. You promised we'd get in your pool today."

"In a minute." Elle automatically dismissed her friend's demand. "They're washing Jeff's car. They don't know we're here."

Unable to tear her eyes away, embarrassment and panic grew wild when Devon turned his gaze and met hers. His dazzling smile made her blush just before he raised his hand beside his face and gave her a small, knowing wave of his fingers. Her jaw dropped, her eyes flew open wide, and her muscles froze in place.

She was so busted.

Jeff was leaned over, washing the side of his Mustang GT when Devon's movement caught his eye. Jeff followed Devon's line of sight, and anger hit him as soon as he spotted the girls hiding behind the tree.

"Elle Marie Moore, get over here right now!" Jeff yelled across the front yard and threw his soapy mitt in the bucket.

"He used your whole name," Beth whispered, her tone rife with fear. "That's not good."

Elle considered her options. She could pretend she didn't hear him and run like the wind to the backyard, or accept the consequences and get it all over with at once by doing what he said. Resigned to the fact that there was no other choice but to live in the same house with her brother for the next few years, Elle decided to go with the latter rather than the former. Her eyes downcast, her bottom lip quivered as she maintained a death grip on her best friend's hand. The pair of seven-year-old, towheaded girls marched across the grass toward Jeff and Devon. Each step brought more dread than the last and made Elle's feet feel like they were weighted down with cement blocks.

She chanced a glance at Jeff but quickly dropped her eyes again when she saw his arms folded over his chest and an irritated expression boring straight through her. She'd been caught spying on them in the past, but that had been many spy missions before this one. She thought she'd improved her technique since then, but apparently, she was too sloppy. Future excursions would require more stealth, more craftiness, and much better hiding places.

"Elle, what have I told you about spying on us?" Jeff demanded.

"Not to," she mumbled.

"Why do you keep doing it? It's weird. You're creeping me out."

"Because she's in lov—" Beth almost told on Elle, but Elle jerked her arm down hard and cut her eyes at her friend.

"Shut up, Beth," she hissed. Glancing up at her brother, she continued. Her voice quivered almost as much as her legs shook. "We're playing a game. It's not a big deal, Jeff."

"Would it be a big deal if I tell Mom to ground you from the pool all summer?" Jeff taunted.

Tears filled her eyes and spilled over her lower lids then slid down her cheeks before they dropped onto the concrete below. "No, Jeff," she pleaded. "I didn't do anything to you."

Two large hands slid under her arms and hoisted her up in the air. Before she knew what was happening, she was held by protective, muscular arms against a warm, bare chest. "Leave her alone, man." Devon's tone held a strict warning. "She's just a little kid having fun playing outside. Quit being so damn mean to her all the time."

Elle looked up at Devon, devotion shining in her big, gorgeous, hazel eyes. He wiped the lingering tears from her cheeks and talked to her with the kindest timbre in his voice. "Hey, it's okay, Elle. Don't cry, sweetheart. You're my girl, aren't you?"

Unable to speak, she nodded her head enthusiastically.

"Then you should know I'll take care of you. I'll kick Jeff's ass if he's mean to you again. No more crying. Okay?"

That elicited a small smile from her, and shyness took over, forcing her to avert her eyes. "Okay."

"Whatever game y'all are playing isn't bothering us. Go have fun, darlin'."

"Okay, we will."

Devon put her down, and Elle stood rooted to her spot for a few seconds before she tilted her head back to look up at him again. Even at sixteen years old, Devon was taller and thicker than any of Jeff's other friends, but he never once made her feel like she was a nuisance to him. A small smile played on his lips while he waited for her to say what was on her mind.

"You're my hero, Devon."

"And you'll always be my girl, Elle. You remember that when you get to be my age and all those boys are hitting on you." Devon winked at her, causing the butterflies in her stomach to flutter and turn somersaults in her belly.

"Let's go swim already," Beth complained.

With her heart full and a smile permanently affixed to her face, Elle wordlessly grabbed Beth's hand. The two rushed to the backyard to join Elle's mom in the pool.

The scorching Georgia sun didn't faze Elle at all that day as she and Beth jumped into the lukewarm pool water. Devon's words kept ringing in her ears. *"You're my girl, aren't you?"*

"What the hell was that about?" Jeff's tone was accusatory when he turned to Devon.

"She wasn't doing anything but watching us, man. You're way too mean to her. We did a lot worse when we were her age. In case you haven't noticed, your little sister is already pretty for her age. She's going to be a knockout when she gets older. And she's smart as a whip.

"If you don't quit being such a dick to her, she won't come to you later when she needs your help. And believe me, she'll have guys all over her when she hits our age. She'll need you, and you'd better be there for her, or I'll kick your ass then, too. You should be glad you have a little sister who even wants to be around you."

"I fucking hate it when you're right," Jeff huffed.

"Then I guess you're always hating on me, huh?" Devon laughed, lightening the mood.

"Hey, you weren't right about that algebra test. I almost had to go to summer school over that."

"No, my answers were right. You weren't wearing your glasses and wrote down the wrong thing."

The two best friends finished washing their cars before they joined the rest of Jeff's family in the pool. Jeff's parents, Danny and Tanya, best friends and long-time neighbors of Devon's parents, were like a second mom and dad to Devon. Mark, Jeff's younger brother and the middle child, worshiped the older boys almost as much as Elle did.

Watching the interactions between the close-knit family was bittersweet for Devon. The shadows of memories from his childhood were always on the fringe of his happiness, waiting to bring him down.

~

"You're doing *what?*" Tracey asked. Her hands dropped to her side, and she leaned toward her son.

"I'm joining the CIA. They offered me the perfect job, so I can't very well turn it down."

"You didn't say it was just a CIA job. You said you were joining the black ops team. That means you'll be a spy, doen't it?"

"Among other things. Yes."

"Why are you doing this, Devon? You just got out of the Army. How many tours did you do in the Middle East? I lost count! Now you'll be permanently undercover, and I'll have no way of knowing if you're dead or alive. I'm your mother—I need more of a reason than it's 'the perfect job.' You have to help me out here."

He pulled a chair out and sat, joining his father Phil at the table. His fingers traced invisible patterns on the table while he avoided their heavy stares. His voice was uncharacteristically low when he spoke. "When Ava disappeared, I was supposed to be watching her. But I got distracted—I don't even know for how long. When I looked up, she was gone. The whole time we searched for her, I wanted to tell you it was all my fault but I couldn't bring myself to say it. I figured when we found her, you'd be too happy to punish me for not watching her. But we never found her. And I've never forgiven myself. This is my way of helping other people, even if they never know I've helped them."

Phil cleared his throat nervously, fighting the emotions welling up in his throat and constricting his ability to breathe. Tears flowed across Tracey's cheeks as she rushed to her son's side. She stroked his hair before holding his face in her hands, forcing him to look at her when she spoke.

"Devon, you were only nine years old. You were not responsible for watching your little sister. You were not responsible for Ava's abduction, and you couldn't have stopped it even if you tried. A grown man took her, and he could've taken you too. There isn't a day that goes by your father and I don't thank God to have you. You don't have to do this to make amends for Ava. We love you. Ava worshiped you. We've never blamed you for what happened, and we never will."

"I need to do this, Mom. It's important to me. I'll be okay—I'm a big boy, and I can take care of myself now." He gave her a small, reassuring smile before standing and pulling her into his arms. "I love you both. Don't worry."

"Devon, I'm your mother. It's my job to worry about you."

"If I find the man who took Ava, we'll never have to worry about him taking another child again."

Tracey sank into his arms a little farther, half in hope and half in fear he'd do just that.

CHAPTER ONE

Current Day

"Miss Sinclair, they're ready for you." One of the many runners announced through the closed door, letting her know the production crew had finished lighting the set for the next scene.

"I'll be right there," Elle called back.

So many other actresses would kill to be in her position. Her long, perfectly coiffed hair fell straight against her shoulders, the highlights and lowlights accentuating her facial features. Professionally applied makeup hid any minor skin imperfections that would've been magnified a hundred times on the big screen. She stared at her reflection in the mirror, barely remembering who she'd been before the madness of her life as a celebrity began. The one goal she'd worked so hard to attain had become the very thing she wanted to run away from most.

A second knock on the door meant the crew grew more impatient, ready to finish the scene so they could go home, only to start it all again early the next morning. Like a robot, Elle rose from her seat and plastered a smile on her face as she rejoined the cast and crew. She hid her irritation when she realized the set had been opened to a select group of entertainment news reporters to help create early buzz for the movie.

Even on lower-budget films she'd starred in, she normally insisted on a closed set to keep the paparazzi out—and anyone else hoping to capture the perfect shot to twist and misconstrue into sensationalized lies for headlines. Such was the life of a movie star, even one classified as an on-the-cusp A-lister like Elle. She'd already experienced the backlash of the vicious rumors that ran rampant through the entertainment circuit. The general public apparently believed every word printed in big, bold letters, even without one shred of credible evidence.

Sex sells, but so do lies, she thought as she took her place beside her costar.

In front of the cameras, Jax Hart was charming and charismatic. His commanding presence on-screen filled the theater seats around the world and produced record-breaking opening weekends with each new release. Cast opposite him in any role was the absolute dream of every single actress, a sure bet to thrust her into the stratosphere of fame and fortune.

Off-screen, Jax Hart was actually Jason Hartman, and he was a far cry from the dashing and daring hero he pretended to be. Elle's agent, Ray Burke, often reminded her how hard he worked to land her the leading role, rather than a brief cameo appearance so many other models-turned-actresses would find themselves cast in. But she'd been in the entertainment business long enough to know exactly what Ray *wasn't* saying.

He was getting something out of the deal.

A trade-off had been made to benefit him. Otherwise, Ray would've pushed one of his established A-list clients instead. Judging by Jax's daily diva-worthy demands, she couldn't help but think somehow, she'd drawn the short straw in Ray's under-the-table deal. Regardless, if all the stars aligned, and the directors and editors worked their magic on this movie, she'd be able to pick and choose her future roles *and* possibly have a say regarding who the studio cast as her leading man.

With everyone in place, Elle switched gears in her mind and fully immersed herself into character. They'd reached another sex scene in the romantic drama storyline, and thankfully, it would be the last shot of the night. While Elle wanted nothing more than to get it over with and get away from her costar, she had to be convincing when she portrayed her character's desperate love for Jax's alter ego. As with every other scene, the only way she could even remotely do *that* was to lose herself in the memories of another man.

When Jax cupped her cheek with his hand, it wasn't his palm that radiated the heat through her body. Jax's lips brushed against hers, but her lips remembered the feel of another's instead. Every touch, every sound, and every scent pushed her further into the dream world she'd created and used as an escape from her unpleasant reality. Even though she was fully clothed, the flesh-colored suit gave the illusion of nudity while it added to the ambiance of the scene. In her mind, there were no barriers between her and the man of her dreams, their bodies completely intertwined in an erotic dance.

"Cut!" Vince, the director, yelled. "Holy shit, that was so fucking hot. If I didn't know better, I'd swear you two have been practicing that scene quite a few times in private."

Elle was abruptly pulled from her fantasy when Jax rolled off, leaving her feeling exposed and self-conscious, despite the fact that the bodysuit covered her completely. The smirk on Jax's face after Vince's comment said it all. He thought her performance was because she wanted *him*. Nothing could be further from the truth, but Elle couldn't tell him that and risk the repercussions.

"I guess it was okay," Jax replied with a dismissive shrug. "I'll know better when we review the film."

"You won't be reviewing the film, Jax. That's my job. Elle, you keep that up, and you'll have to prepare an acceptance speech before you know it." Vince clapped his hands and rubbed them together vigorously. "Hopefully, so will I."

Elle responded with her best smile, putting her acting skills to the test again. "Thanks, Vince. That would be a dream come true for us both, wouldn't it?"

Vince's response didn't register in Elle's mind, because Jax jumped into the conversation concerning awards and statues, showing no humility in his quest for validation of being loved for his abilities and not just his face. Annoyed, Elle walked toward her dressing room to change, lost in the make-believe world with the man she missed more every day. She silently mused over how he'd invaded all of her senses yet again, when he wasn't anywhere near her.

It'd be another long night of tossing and turning, dreaming of him and what they couldn't have. No amount of cold water could douse the fire he'd lit in her long ago.

"It's been a long day," Beth grumbled, echoing Elle's thoughts when Elle stepped into the trailer. "I'm beyond ready to crawl into bed and zone out in front of the TV until I pass out from exhaustion."

"That sounds perfect. We're out of here as soon as I throw my clothes on."

Elle grabbed her shorts and T-shirt off the clothes rack and quickly changed while Beth gathered their belongings. When they walked out, Elle heard Vince's and Jax's voices carrying across the lot. "Let's go the other way. I don't want them to see us and start another conversation. I've had all I can stand of Jax for one day."

"That guy is a serious jerk. He propositioned me again while I was doing his makeup today. I've only told him 'no' about a hundred times now." Beth shuddered at the thought.

"Yes, he's a complete ass. This movie can't wrap soon enough. But I'm so glad we're on the same set. After I accept my award, my first diva-demand will be to have you as my personal makeup artist for every movie."

"Hey, getting assigned as your personal makeup artist for life is my dream job. Don't tease me."

The forty-five-minute drive to their shared apartment in Westwood seemed to fly by, and they were home in no time. Beth would no doubt assume Elle's long day of filming wore her out, but the truth was she felt like she was revved up on a triple-shot of espresso. Her thoughts stayed on her dream man, reliving every moment of every encounter, remembering every word spoken, and wishing circumstances were different.

True to her word, Beth retreated to her bedroom and was soon sound asleep in her bed. The TV volume was high enough to drown out any other noise, and the light from the screen cast a soft blue hue over her room, changing with an occasional flicker. Elle paced in the living room, close to wearing a path in the rug with her back-and-forth marching. She gripped her phone, sorely tempted to dial the number she'd memorized by heart years before.

She couldn't bring herself to do it, though it tore her to shreds inside to deny herself the pure pleasure. She desperately wanted to hear his voice, but she knew once she did, it wouldn't be enough. Frustrated, she walked into her bathroom, started the shower, and washed away any remnant of Jax's scent from her. No amount of water could remove the other man from her thoughts, her fantasies.

When she dragged her soapy washcloth between her legs, her sex clenched from the slightest friction. The intensity of the sensation nearly brought her to her knees. Need for a release mixed with her desire for him, and it rippled through her, heightening all of her nerve endings. She removed the handheld shower head from its cradle to rinse the soap from her body and then let it linger at the apex of her thighs. She closed her eyes, dropped her head back, and pictured him there in the shower with her.

Frustration transformed into exasperation when the jet stream of water did nothing to bring relief. Elle quickly dried off then climbed into bed. As soon as she closed her eyes, the image of him was there again, mocking and teasing her from afar. Her hand slid down, finding the silky wetness between her legs. Since he refused to leave her memories, she stopped resisting and allowed them to run rampant through her mind. With his name on her lips, she climaxed while she envisioned her initial rendezvous with him eight years earlier.

Though, it still felt like just yesterday.

Lying in bed alone after a long day on the set, eight years after their first night together, she could feel his touch on her skin. She smelled the masculine scent of his cologne. Wood, amber, and earthy spices mixed with the heady aroma that made up his signature scent. She rolled over in bed, pulled the extra pillow close to her in a lonely hug, and let the tears fall wherever they landed. She missed him so much. At twenty-eight, she was fatigued and burned-out from modeling since age twelve, and she found she wished for a simpler life. With him.

What would her life be like if she'd stayed with him all those years ago? That question had played on a constant loop in her mind since the day she told him she had to leave. When he asked her not to go. When she'd decided her career was more important.

As she slipped into a restless slumber, words from her youth returned and taunted her with what she couldn't have.

No one else will ever compare to Devon Kane.

~

The sun hadn't even made a hint of an appearance when the alarm went off. With her eyes still closed, she smacked the clock to stop the irritating noise that dared to pull her from one of the best dreams she'd had in months. The scene in her mind was more realistic than any movie set she'd been on. Cool wind blew on her face, sending her long locks flying in every direction, as she strode hand in hand with Devon through the grassy clearing on the mountaintop. The weight of the world was lifted from her shoulders, and she was without a care in the world for the first time since she entered the modeling contest. Her demure smile was genuine and conveyed the contentment she felt inside—her life with Devon was simple. Easy. Stress-free.

"Elle, time to get up," Beth said from the doorway. "We have an early morning scene to shoot, so we have to get you into hair and makeup before Jax gets there. He primps longer than any woman I've ever seen."

With the grace and elegance of a zombie, Elle slid out of bed and walked straight to the shower. The spray of hot water helped her to peel her eyes open and face the long day ahead of her. She was thankful for one advantage of being on a movie set—her hair, makeup, and clothes would be done for her, sparing her the time and energy it would take otherwise. After she towel-dried her hair and threw on comfortable clothes, she and Beth left together for the studio.

The lot was eerily quiet that early in the morning, when it was still dark and most of the cast and crew on the other sets hadn't yet arrived. Security patrolled the area in golf carts, their serious expressions daring anyone out of place to step foot inside the gates. Still, when Elle and Beth stepped out of the car, a troubled chill surged up Elle's spine, and she looked around the darkened lot nervously.

"Everything all right, Miss Sinclair?" a deep voice asked from behind her.

She quickly turned and immediately recognized the familiar face of one of the foot patrol security guards. "Yes. Just spooked myself, I guess."

"I'll escort you ladies to the makeup trailer to make sure you get there safely."

Elle smiled and nodded, relieved they weren't alone, and turned with Beth to cover the short distance to shelter.

"Will Mr. Hart be joining you this morning?" the guard asked.

Elle stifled a laugh, knowing all too well why he asked about Jax's presence. The reputation of diva-like demands from some stars preceded them. With Jax, however, his outrageous demands made him the ire of most lower-level cast and crew members who'd had the misfortune of working with him. One of Jax's main rules was no crew member was allowed by contract to make direct eye contact with him—including security.

"Mr. Hart will be here early this morning, but I'm not sure what time. We arrived earlier than usual," Elle explained.

Elle had vowed early in her movie career she'd never be known as one of those actors—the ones like Jax who distanced themselves from everyone who supported their work. Keeping her down-to-earth personality had benefited her more than once. She'd found out firsthand that the people who were paid to cater to her needs were much more willing to make her time on the set easier just because she was kind to them.

When they'd stepped inside the trailer, Elle turned to the guard and gave him her sincerest smile. "Thank you for walking with us, Roy."

"Yes, thank you so much. Same time tomorrow morning?" Beth flirted.

Roy's smile spread across his face. "My pleasure, ladies. Have a good day."

Elle closed and locked the door, the uneasy feeling still lingering in her chest. Beth watched her movements closely as she prepared her makeup supplies. "What's wrong, Elle?"

"I just have a bad feeling, Beth. Nothing's happened, but it just feels like we're being watched."

"It's probably all the rumors that have been flying around the studio lots the last few weeks," Beth replied offhandedly.

"What rumors?"

"You know," she insisted. "About the actress who was reported missing from one of the other stages."

"I have no idea what you're talking about, Beth."

"Have a seat. We need to get started," Beth replied. She continued talking while applying Elle's on-screen makeup. "It's been almost two weeks ago now, but one of the actresses on another movie set was rumored to be missing. She didn't show up for work after they'd already filmed several scenes with her, so production is on hold until she shows up or they find a replacement."

"What do they think happened to her?"

"Some say she's in rehab somewhere and the studio execs are keeping it secret for her. But when a couple of the makeup artists said that wasn't true and something bad happened to her, they got in a lot of trouble. They may not be able to work on the lot again."

"That's really scary, Beth."

"Why? Maybe the stress got to her, and she's in the hospital somewhere. You know how delicate all these actresses are."

"I beg your pardon," Elle replied jokingly, her Southern accent making a rare appearance in her tone.

Beth laughed at Elle's reply. "The first time you can't take a joke from me, I'll drag you out of this town and whip your ass."

"You've threatened me with that for years. Maybe I should try it and see if you'll really do it. I'd love to take a long vacation somewhere far away from here."

"You know, there's a way you can do that. Pick up the phone, have your assistant make the arrangements, then text your agent and tell him you're leaving after you're already gone."

Elle inhaled deeply and released her breath on a long, wistful sigh. "I wish I could."

"Why can't you?"

"Oh, no reason, other than the little obstacle called a contract obligation that says I have to finish filming this movie."

"Minor details. You could always check in to a spa, otherwise known as a mental hospital, and take a nice long break."

"At this point, I'd even take that. But that reminds me what I was going to say before you sidetracked me. A while back, before this movie started filming, I heard about another actress dropping off the face of the earth during production. Why isn't any of this on the news?"

"Probably because she isn't well-known enough, Elle. I hate to say it, but it's true. Unless you're the female equivalent of Jax Hart, you're replaceable in this town. As soon as they find someone who fits the wardrobe they already have, the latest gone girl will be forgotten."

Throughout the day, Beth's words stayed with Elle, weighing heavily on her shoulders while she did her best to pretend she was someone else. The best part about the day was none of her scenes included Jax. Even though every scene required multiple retakes from different angles, the time seemed more productive without his pretentious presence on the stage.

When she and two of her costars left the sound stage building during a set break, raised voices immediately caught their attention. The trio of women stopped and gawked at the awkward scene unfolding in front of them. The normally bustling area between the stages was subdued, with the crew members using any excuse to avoid leaving the area and missing the conclusion.

"If you ever, and I mean *ever in your entire miserable life,* touch me again, your junk will be stuffed and mounted as a trophy over my fireplace. I don't give a shit what kind of badass you play on the screen, you're not man enough to handle me."

Katrina Fox stood in Jax's personal space, as close to his face as she could get without actually touching him, and her shouts carried across the lot, echoing off the many buildings and returning to the onlookers like an instant replay.

"Calm your tits, babe," Jax replied, his tone patronizing and his expression one of disdain. "If you're not into men, you should still give me a try. I guarantee you'll be back for more."

Katrina's hands curled into fists as her anger reached a tipping point. "Don't you dare try to downplay what you did or pass it off as my fault. I am happily married, and I've put up with your bullshit long enough. If I bring my husband on the set, he will kick your chickenshit ass. Keep your fucking hands off me, Jax. Or, so help me God, you will regret it."

Unwilling to accept her refusal of his overt advances, Jax's temper flared, revealing his true self. "No, Katrina, *you'll* regret it if you don't shut your fucking mouth and take it. You're nobody. You really think the execs will side with you over *me*? I'm their golden cash cow, baby. I get what I want, when I want, and from whomever I want. Your only job is to say *'Yes, sir, may I have another'* when I come for you. Keep causing a scene like this, and you'll be gone with a snap of my fingers. All those fat, old men you had to fuck to get here will mean nothing."

Katrina's arm swung back as she prepared to power through his face with her fist. Elle caught Katrina's elbow just in time and stopped her from following through with it. Katrina's head whirled around, fire shooting from her eyes, and a deep shade of red covered her face.

"Don't, Katrina. The trouble this will cause you isn't worth it. Take care of it through the appropriate channels," Elle urged her.

"You know as well as I do the studio talking heads will just look the other way for him," Katrina countered. Jax's smug expression made Elle want to finish what Katrina had started.

"Not if you handle it the *right* way."

Understanding lit in Katrina's eyes, and she nodded at Elle. "You're right. Thank you, Elle."

Jax's arrogant air instantly deflated when Katrina's fiery gaze swung back to him. Katrina stormed back through the door to her assigned sound stage, and Jax glared at Elle.

"You shouldn't have done that."

"No, Jax. *You* shouldn't have done that."

CHAPTER TWO

The next morning on the set, Elle's bottom jaw dropped to her chest when she reviewed the updated call sheet outlining the scenes that would be filmed. The last-minute notice aside, the number of set changes required ensured everyone would be on set until the wee hours of the morning.

"Can they do this?" Beth whispered as she gawked at her call sheet. "With our union contracts, can they legally get away with this?"

"Maybe not legally," Elle whispered back. "But they have a long arm, Beth. Don't get blacklisted."

Throughout the tedious hours of filming, Elle had to endure scene after scene with Jax, not only pretending she didn't despise him, but that she was in love with him. On more than one occasion, she mused about that golden statue and how it would be hers if she could only convey to the world her true feelings for her costar. Since everything was filmed as the set was needed, rather than in order of the script, her numerous scenes had thankfully been short ones. Her longest scene was scheduled at the end of the day, and she knew it would be her hardest scene to date.

"Get Elle and Jax set up for the next scene," Vince instructed. "We need to get as many finished today as possible. We're already behind schedule, and we can't get another extension on the time we have this stage."

While the crew scurried about, quickly correcting last-minute set details, the second assistant director left to fetch the main stars. Their workday had already been longer than the updated call sheets indicated, causing every crew member to inwardly grumble about the extra hours. While several whispered threats of calling their union representative the next morning, none dared to show their displeasure with the working conditions. Getting called back to work on another movie in the near future was more important than going home at the scheduled time.

"Elle, sweetheart, you're being such a trooper today," Vince praised her as she walked to her mark.

"My job isn't as physically demanding as our crew's jobs. As long as they're working, the least I can do is keep going, too."

Several nearby crew members looked up and gave her small, appreciative smiles as she sat in the side-stage makeup chair. When their smiles faded, Elle knew exactly who had entered the sound stage from the door behind her without even turning around. Beth approached her to freshen her makeup before the cameras started rolling again.

"How are you holding up?" Beth murmured while she worked.

"Okay, other than wanting to shave Jax's head and tattoo a pile of shit on it so everyone knows what a shithead he is."

Beth barked out a laugh and quickly covered it with a mock coughing fit.

"If you're sick, you need to leave. We can't have Elle catching a cold right now," Vince snapped.

"I'm not sick, sir," Beth replied without elaborating, knowing Vince wouldn't want to hear it from her anyway. Lowering her voice, she glared at Elle. "You can take the girl out of the South, but you can't take the South out of the girl."

"You would know as well as I do," Elle whispered back with a smirk.

Beth stepped back and admired her work. "There. You're perfect. Go break a leg."

"That's for theater work," Elle disputed.

"Then go break Jax's leg."

"Now you're talking," Elle replied with a chuckle.

"What'd the jackass do this time?"

"He barged into my trailer, without knocking, while I was changing clothes. I know he does that shit on purpose. Anyway, he offered his services to make me the best-paid female actress, if I'd service him on my knees right then and there. My hands were shaking from being so mad.

"Beth, I didn't even think about what would happen before I picked up the vase of flowers from the table and threw it at his head. He ducked, and it hit the wall behind him. Shattered glass flew everywhere. He spewed some vague threats at me and stormed off, back to his trailer.

"Of course, the noise was loud, and a few of the crew members came running. It was so sweet how concerned they were for me. The cleaning team rushed in and cleaned up the mess before anyone else realized what had happened. I'm surprised he didn't go running to Vince about me."

"It's too late in the process to replace you now. Production will wrap in a couple of days if we keep going at the filming pace we have today. Besides, the scuttlebutt around the crew is Vince is covering up something major, something that could be a career-ender. Most bets are it has to do with Jax harassing actresses and other women on the set, that he's crossed the line with the wrong woman."

"If that were true, Jax wouldn't have propositioned me. Vince would've made sure he had Jax under control, especially if it's something serious enough to affect their careers. It has to be something else."

"Hide that worried look on your face, Elle. Here come Vince and Jax. Time to put your acting skills to the test," Beth whispered while pretending to style a strand of Elle's hair.

"Elle, we're shooting the last scene you and Jax have together next. It's the breakup scene, so I need to see some real tears, real emotions, real heartache. Take a few moments to be alone and do whatever it takes to get into your character's frame of mind. We need you in top form so we can get this in as few takes as possible," Vince explained.

"You got it." Elle gave the reply he expected to hear, but inwardly, all she could think about was how thrilled she'd be to break up with Jax at the end of filming. Then she'd just have to make it through the months of press junkets with him, with all the fake articles about how their love was what made the scenes so authentic rather than their acting expertise. "I'm going to wardrobe to change into my costume now. Then we can wrap up this scene as soon as I'm all sad and depressed."

"I should hit wardrobe, too," Jax replied.

Elle narrowed her eyes at him and gritted her teeth. She opened her mouth to reply, but Vince beat her to it.

"You can wait on changing clothes. You have other things to do first. Besides, with all the set changes the grips are working on for the next scene, the wardrobe room is the only quiet place left for Elle to get into character. You stay away from that room as long as she's in it, or you'll deal with me, Jax Hart."

After she changed, Elle made herself comfortable on the small sofa in the back of the room, closed her eyes, and transported herself to another place and time. She drew on the memories she kept locked inside her, the ones she both wanted to forget and wanted to relive every day. Emotions welled up inside her chest when she released the first scene and allowed every second, every feeling, and every sensation to flood her mind. Once she started reminiscing, she couldn't stop the onslaught of sorrow that followed.

When she reached the point of no return, she rose from the couch and walked directly to the stage. For Elle, the emotional scenes were the rare times she wouldn't speak to anyone who wasn't written into the script. To remain in character and give the best performance she could muster, she immersed herself in the role and became the character. The character's pain and hers became a singular state of mind, and she poured her broken heart and soul into her performance.

When the final take was finished, and she'd recited her lines a dozen times with more heartrending emotion each time, Vince yelled "Cut." Elle blinked repeatedly, seemingly waking from a trance, and her gaze swung around the room. The familiar sound of sniffles floated on the air as others rubbed their eyes while discreetly whisking away the moisture gathered in them.

"You're done for the day, Elle," Vince said softly. "You can go ahead and change."

Elle nodded and briskly walked back to the wardrobe room. Getting into character was fairly easy, but leaving it behind was another matter in itself. She was unable to speak to anyone with her pent-up feelings still entirely too raw and barely under control. She was thankful that scene was the last shot of the day. She'd need the rest of the night to put the beast back in its cage so she'd be ready to work again the following day.

On the way back to their apartment, she stared silently out the window while Beth drove. Her thoughts took her thousands of miles away, a year into the past, and reminded her of how carefree she'd once felt.

"You've had a pretty rough day. Are you all right?" Beth asked, her voice soft but full of concern.

"I miss him, Beth. I can't keep living like this. It's been a year. Either I have to contact him, or I have to let him go." Saying those words out loud marked the first time she'd admitted to her best friend what had been weighing heavily on her heart.

"Have you tried calling and talking to him about it, Elle? I really think you should before you make any decisions. You've held on to him for a long time."

"I've thought about calling him more times than I can count, Beth. But I come to the same conclusion every time. If I meant as much to him as he does to me, I'd already know it. I wouldn't have to ask or wonder. So, I'm sure as hell not calling him to hear him confirm it."

Beth stretched her arm out and squeezed Elle's hand, offering what little support and solace she could. Elle's gaze stayed trained on the window, not seeing anything in the blur rushing by outside. The tears she shed on the set were real, but they were for her character's situation. The tears sliding down her cheeks in the darkness of the car were all for herself. For what she wanted more than anything. For what she'd never have.

Beth's ringing cell phone pulled her attention away from Elle. After a quick glance at the screen, Beth's eyebrows drew downward and an ominous feeling settled in her chest. "It's Analise, one of the makeup artists on the lot," she told Elle before accepting the call through the car's Bluetooth.

"Hey, Analise, you're on speaker."

"Beth?" came the tearful reply.

"What's wrong?" Beth asked, gripping the steering wheel.

"Katrina is missing. They think they can explain this away and make me shut up, but I know better than the lies they're spreading about her."

"Analise, I have no idea what you're talking about. What do you mean she's missing? What lies? Who's trying to shut you up?" Beth asked.

"She didn't make it home last night, and she didn't show up for work today. The studio executive assigned to our movie released a statement to our crew. It was more like a gag order, really. His statement said Katrina was going through a rough patch with her husband and had to leave town so she can pull herself together. The movie has been put on hold until she regains her composure because it would cost too much to redo all her scenes. He also said if we told anyone about this, we'd never work on a movie lot again," Analise explained.

Beth and Elle exchanged concerned glances.

"From a financial standpoint, that would make sense, Analise. From what I've heard, Katrina was in more scenes than not. If the movie's almost wrapped, that would be a lot of wasted money." Beth tried to calm Analise's fears with rational reasons why a production hiatus would make sense.

"That's true, Beth," Analise agreed. "Except, Kat wasn't having marital problems. They're crazy in love with each other. They're even actively trying to get pregnant. I talked to her husband Jay late last night and several times today. We've been looking for Kat everywhere. Now I can't reach Jay."

"Analise," Beth faltered. "I don't even know what to say. I didn't know you were so close to her."

"We've been close for many years. I don't advertise it because it just invites more trouble than it's worth. But Kat is one of my best friends, and our husbands even hang out together a lot. Beth, I know we're being fed lies. I know something bad has happened to her and now maybe to Jay. She would've called me by now. I'm scared, Beth, for her, for Jay, and now for my husband and myself."

"Are you working tomorrow, Analise?" Beth asked.

"No, the first assistant director told the entire crew to stay home for the time being. The executive and the director have a meeting with the investors to explain what's happening. I'm going out to look for Kat and Jay everywhere I can think to look."

"Don't do that," Beth warned. "I don't know what's going on with Kat and Jay, but I can tell you're honestly terrified. If you believe something bad happened to them, you have to stay as far away from it as possible. Go to your mother's house and stay in Oregon until they call you back to work or you hear from Katrina."

"But, Kat—"

"There's nothing more you can do now, Analise. Protect yourself and your family." Beth disconnected the call after Analise promised to leave the state and remain at her mother's indefinitely.

"Katrina was fighting with Jax when I left the stage last night. She said he'd put his hands on her, and she threatened to have her husband kick his ass," Elle said quietly.

"You saw it yourself? You didn't tell me about this."

"I saw them fighting. Katrina was about to punch him, and I stopped her because I knew he'd have her blackballed, or at least make her life hell for as long as possible. I told her to handle him the right way instead, so he couldn't fight back. What if my advice backfired on her somehow and they fired her?"

"What's the right way?"

"Release proof to the press if the studio execs won't put a stop to his harassment, then start legal proceedings against all of them. The bad publicity from the scores of women who would come forward would be too much for even their public relations team to bury."

"Just promise me you'll be careful. I don't know what's going on or where Katrina and Jay are. But you're a witness, and I don't want them coming after you. Just finish your scenes and get away from the lot. It has bad juju all around it," Beth replied, uneasiness filling her tone.

"No argument here. My scenes will be wrapped up in a couple of days, and I'll be free of Jax Hart until the promotional tour begins."

The rest of the drive back to their shared apartment was made in silence. Concern for their friend on top of an overly long and draining day left them both too exhausted to carry on a conversation. An hour later, thanks to interstate construction slowing traffic, they arrived at their apartment and retreated to their separate bedrooms. After Elle finished washing before going to bed, the events of the day caught up with her, took over her mind, and kept her awake past the point of fatigue.

She rolled over and grabbed her cell phone from the nightstand. She stared at the list of her favorite contacts for a few seconds before selecting her brother, Jeff. She let it ring a couple of times before realizing how late it was on the East Coast. He answered just before she ended the call.

"Elle? What's wrong? Are you okay?" Jeff answered, his voice thick with both sleep and concern.

"I'm okay, Jeff. I'm sorry—I forgot how late it was there, or I guess, how early. Go back to sleep."

"I don't think so, little sis. You don't call me for no reason, especially not this late even on Pacific Time. So go ahead and tell your big brother what's bothering you."

"Something strange is happening on the lot, Jeff. This will sound crazy, and I know it's big and there are multiple movies filming at once, and—"

"Spit it out already. You can explain it away after you tell me."

"Over the past few months, more than a couple of women have disappeared from the lot. The last one has me rattled, though. I just talked to Kat yesterday. Kat's best friend, Analise, called Beth tonight on the way home. She said the studio execs are lying about Kat's whereabouts. Analise was terrified something bad has happened to her friend. And..." She paused, afraid to speak the words. "I've had the eerie feeling someone was watching me a few times after I left the sound stage."

"Elle, if there's even the slightest chance something is off, you need to have a bodyguard with you at all times. Don't take any chances."

"I'm sure I'm overreacting."

"And don't dismiss your gut feelings. I'd rather you have a huge entourage of security guards and be safe than put it off and be sorry later."

"Okay, Jeff, you're right. I'll have Ray contact a couple of bodyguards first thing in the morning."

"I'm coming out there. I don't trust your agent to do what he's supposed to do. Do whatever you have to do to get me full access to the studio lot. You're not leaving my sight." Jeff was suddenly wide awake, his unease over the situation at maximum capacity.

"Jeff, you can't just leave your job to come babysit me because I have the heebie-jeebies. I'm not even sure I can get a full-access pass for you. I'll make sure Ray does his job, and there are always security guards on the lot," Elle argued.

"Elle, there may be guards, but that place is huge. There's no way they can be everywhere at once."

"I'm sure it's nothing but my overactive imagination."

"Your imagination has never been overactive like this before, so stop trying to get rid of me. Do I need to call Mark and have him come down from Paso Robles? He can leave right now and be there in a few hours to keep an eye on you until I get there."

"No, don't bother him, or Mom and Dad. I shouldn't have called you with this. With all the sound stages, there are hundreds of crew members on the lot at any given time. I'll get a personal bodyguard, and it'll be fine. I'm sorry I worried you. Go back to sleep, and I'll call you at a decent hour tomorrow."

"Okay," Jeff replied reluctantly. "If I don't hear from you early in the morning, I'm calling Mark, and I'm booking my flight to LAX."

Elle laughed softly, glad she had two brothers who would do anything for her. "Fine. I'll call you twice tomorrow." Lowering her voice, she added, "Thank you. Good night, Jeff."

"Good night, Elle."

CHAPTER THREE

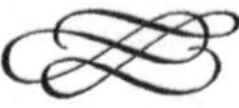

"It's your favorite sister, calling to report in as ordered by her older and demanding brother," Elle announced when Jeff answered his phone.

"Smartass little sister," he laughed. "Have you called Ray Burke, the worst agent in Hollywood yet?"

"I call him that every day," she joked.

"Very funny. You know what I mean. My mouse is hovered over the 'purchase' button for my plane ticket so I can kick your ass before I protect it myself."

"I've talked to Ray, and two bodyguards will be waiting outside my apartment first thing tomorrow morning."

"Why do you still live in an apartment, Elle? You've made more than enough money to buy an outrageously big house in Bel Air or Malibu with a security system to rival Tony Stark's."

"I have commitment issues. This way, I only have to agree to a year-long lease, and I can pay my way out of it if I need to break it. Plus, the threat of finding a new roommate is the only way I can guilt Beth into never leaving me."

"Have you told Mom, Dad, or Mark about this yet?" Jeff asked, suddenly serious again.

"No, there's no need to alarm them. I don't even know for sure anything's wrong. I could be overreacting to nothing at all."

"So, you only wanted to alarm me because I'm the one who's clear across the country from you? The one who'd get to you last if anything did happen?"

"Exactly!" She burst out laughing. "No, Jeff, because you're the level-headed one. You were supposed to tell me I was imagining things and I needed to get over myself. You broke the rules when you agreed with me."

"I could tell you were scared, and you don't get scared for no reason. Elle, I did some research this morning on what you told me about that missing girl. Do me a favor, and don't walk anywhere without an armed escort, even around the lot. Those bodyguards need to be there with you today. Since you haven't called Mark to get him to come down and stay with you, I'll call and talk to Ray myself if I have to. But those guards need to be there today."

"What did you find out, Jeff?" Elle asked slowly, clearly not actually wanting the answer.

"Let's just say the entire story has already been all neatly tied up with a pretty pink bow on top. Pictures are posted that any idiot with a smidgeon of technical savvy can tell have been doctored. Quotes from unnamed sources that draw sympathy for her circumstances without giving any details or verifiable information are plastered everywhere. The director wishes her well and has promised to be patient while she deals with what life has handed her."

"What's the story?"

"The articles claim Katrina and her costar Oliver fell in love on the set and took off to Cabo for an extended lovers' vacation. Both spouses were left at home, reeling from Katrina and Oliver's deceitful actions. The articles say both soon-to-be-former spouses left town, headed for undisclosed locations, so they can grieve without the prying eye of the media watching them."

"It's all a cover-up, from the highest level down," Elle replied in disbelief.

"No doubt about it."

"Okay, I'll call Ray back and insist he have two armed bodyguards waiting for me on the lot today."

"I'd rather you not go to the sound stage at all until they're with you," Jeff urged.

"Jeff, I don't have enough clout yet not to show up for work and have the director be okay with that. Today will be a long day. There's no break in the schedule until early afternoon, so I'll be inside the sound stage at least until then. I'll be fine."

Jeff released a heavy sigh, conveying his annoyance without words. "You are so hardheaded, you know that?"

"I love you, too. Thanks for looking out for me."

They disconnected with Elle promising to call Jeff immediately if her agent gave her any trouble over when her protection would be onsite. She repeated the conversation to Beth before calling Ray.

"Someone is lying, Elle. Katrina wouldn't have done that. Jeff needs to have someone check the pictures and verify the dates. I'd bet my entire year's salary none of them is recent," Beth objected.

"I agree, Beth. I'm calling Ray right now. Whatever is going on will not happen to us."

She scrolled through her contacts and hit the number for her agent. She held her breath, dread filling her with each ring that passed without an answer.

"Elle, my darling, it's not often I'm graced with two phone calls from you in one morning. What can I do for you?"

"Ray, I need those two armed bodyguards waiting for me at the sound stage by the time I leave today. Tomorrow is too late."

"Did something happen? Do I need to call the police right now?"

"No, nothing has happened yet, but I don't want to wait and leave anything to chance. Text me back with their names and pictures so I know who they are when I see them."

"Of course, of course. Consider it done, my love. Hey, aren't you due on the set in about twenty minutes?"

"Yes, I'm pulling into the lot right now. Don't worry, I have the best hair and makeup artists in the world to make sure I'm camera-ready on time."

"You're a natural beauty. You don't need makeup like everyone else does," Ray schmoozed. "Now, I'm off to ensure you feel safe and sound at all times. You'll hear back from me soon."

The busy schedule and moving to the various sets kept her busy throughout the day and well into the night. After the director yelled the final "Cut," she was exhausted and could no longer hide it.

"Vince, I need a break. I've been going nonstop since I got here this morning."

"I know, Elle. We're behind, and the studio can't extend our time with the sound stage. We'll call it a wrap for the night and start back tomorrow morning," Vince replied.

"Miss Sinclair? I have this message for you." A short, young girl smiled shyly as she passed the handwritten note to Elle.

"Thank you." Elle smiled warmly, despite her irritation with her situation. The young girl's smile brightened. She was clearly content with just being acknowledged by one of the main stars. Watching the girl walk away with an added spring in her step reminded Elle why she'd always been cognizant of how she treated the crew. Her positive thoughts changed immediately when she read the message. "You son of a bitch!"

"What's wrong, sailor?" Beth asked with a smirk.

"Listen to this. *'Elle, darling, your bodyguards will be on the set first thing in the morning, as you requested. –Ray'* They were supposed to be here *tonight* to escort us home. I need to find a better agent."

"Go change and let's go home. Your clothes are in your trailer. We'll deal with firing Ray and finding a competent agent in the morning. I'll meet you at the car and be your bodyguard for the night."

"I feel safer already," Elle replied with a sardonic chuckle. "I'll be right there."

When she stepped out of the sound stage door, she was surprised to see how busy the lot was so late. Crew members darted from one place to the other, various teams hustling to finish their work for the night. Once inside her trailer, she checked her phone for messages, chatted with her mother via text, then changed into her regular clothes. When she opened the door of her trailer and stepped out, the unnatural silence that met her frightened her.

Her skin prickled with cold chills in the warm Southern California air. The feeling of being watched hadn't left her for several days, but the shudders flowing over her in waves were stronger than they'd ever been. Someone was out there, watching and waiting. She knew it beyond a shadow of a doubt.

She rushed toward the car lot where they'd parked, wielding her apartment key like a weapon, ready to stab someone in the eye if necessary. Her thumb slid up the side of the key, holding it firmly in her grasp. The car was mere steps away—the safety and security of the interior were her homing beacon, and her feet instinctively carried her to it. A fleeting thought of having words with Vince about keeping security on the lot until everyone had cleared out crossed her mind as she reached the car. She extended her arm and grasped the handle, relief flooding her because she'd made it safely.

"Miss Sinclair."

Startled, she jumped and whirled around at the sound of a man behind her. Before her brain could register what her eyes witnessed, everything around her went completely black.

~

Strange noises roused Elle from her deep slumber. She fought against her own muscles to force her eyes to open. Sleep felt so good to her overexhausted mind and body, and she hadn't had a decent night's sleep in so long. But if Beth already had company over, then she'd apparently slept later than she realized. She rolled over in the bed and fought the grogginess that had overtaken her, covering her like a heavy blanket. After sitting up, she rubbed her eyes and realized when she felt the thick, stiff mascara still caked on her eyelashes she didn't wash her makeup off the night before.

That was her first red flag. As a model and actress, she never went to bed without completing her nighttime beauty regimen, no matter how late she'd returned home. The second red flag immediately followed the first when she realized how hard she'd slept. Running on fumes and a few hours of sleep every night had become her normal. She peeled her eyelids open, and a full-blown panic attack ensued. Her eyes traveled around the room, taking in the décor and furnishings. Reality and facts clashed with denial and self-preservation.

She wasn't in her bed.

She wasn't in her room.

She wasn't in her apartment.

She had no idea where she was.

The plush bedroom was as large as the entire apartment she shared with Beth. The furniture was all one-of-a-kind pieces from exclusive, appointment-only boutiques in Beverly Hills. The paintings adorning the walls were multimillion-dollar originals, not available for purchase to the average citizen. Vases of fresh flowers filled the room with their sweet fragrance. Floor-to-ceiling windows made up an entire wall, with what was sure to be a spectacular view when it wasn't still pitch-black outside.

She slid out of bed and panic nearly incapacitated her when she realized she wore a strange gown rather than her own clothes, but she had no memory of how she got in it. Determined to figure out where she was and why she was there, she began opening drawers to search for any clues. Every drawer only served to increase her anxiety, yielding nothing except more plain cotton nightgowns like the one she wore, mingled with various feminine toiletry items.

She rushed through the room, checking the expansive closets and the bathroom but finding nothing of use. Nothing that revealed any information and nothing that gave a single hint of where she was being held. Her chest heaved with heavy breaths, and her mind raced as she tried to recall what last happened to her and how she got there.

She moved to the door and quietly turned the knob, opening it slowly to peek into the hallway. When she found it was empty, she tiptoed out of the bedroom and ran barefoot toward the front of the house. The long hall was just one indication of how large the house was. The number of doors that lined the hallway was the other. Her anxiety ratcheted up another notch as she tried to formulate an escape plan in her jumbled thoughts. From whom she had to escape and why they'd taken her to start with were beyond her capacity to analyze at the time. All she could think about was finding the door that led outside, then when she was far enough away, she'd focus on who and why.

The end of the hall opened into an expansive family room, taking away the relative cover the smaller space had offered. A quick perusal around the room revealed much of what she already knew—she was held in a multimillion-dollar house. That fact frightened her more than if she'd awakened in a derelict house. With more resources came more security, more privacy, and less chance of anyone hearing her cries for help.

The large, wooden door to freedom came into view and propelled her body forward. Her feet smacked against the marble floor of the foyer, and her heart hammered against the inside of her chest. It was so close now—all she had to do was reach out and grab the door handle, then she'd be outside, one step closer to freedom.

She flung the door open, letting it slam against the wall when she released it. Across the spacious front porch, down the steps, into the thick, manicured grass of the sprawling front lawn, and toward the brick wall that encased the estate, she ran as hard as she could. The adrenaline coursing through her veins blocked the burning in her thighs and the pain from the lack of oxygen in her lungs.

Her sole focus was how she'd scale the brick wall that stood between her and the open road. A few more feet to go. A few more feet and she'd find help, learn what had happened to her, and stop long enough to cry her eyes out. But first things first—the wall.

Her legs carried her so fast, her body bent in half from the forward momentum when a strong, muscled arm grasped her around the waist. All the air was knocked out of her from the sudden stop, leaving her gasping for breath and nearly incapable of fighting back. The muscular arm easily lifted her off the ground and turned to face the house, carrying her away from freedom with every step.

From the outside, it was a gorgeous mansion she ordinarily would've admired. Palm trees lined the circular cobblestone driveway. Tall, white columns framed the archways along the entire front of the house and the matching detached garage. Ornate statues were evenly spaced along the drive. The stark white elegant marble figures were accentuated by the deep green privacy hedge.

The heavy thud of boots and clink of metal pulled her eye from the house and onto an approaching man. Dressed all in black and wearing a leather vest, he smirked as he strode toward her. His lewd smile made her skin crawl, and her breath hitched in her chest.

"Look who we have here, running around the yard like she owns the place," he said as his fingers slid down her cheek. "You woke up sooner than I thought you would. So, where were you going?"

Fear seized her from the inside out, stealing her ability to speak or think rationally. She shook her head from side to side, though she didn't know what it was she tried to convey. She only wanted to get away from both men. Seized by fear, all she could think was how she wanted to wake up from the nightmare that had become her life,

"You were trying to run from us. Don't lie to me now," he snarled. "You were trying to get out of here and call the police on us."

He waited for her to reply, but her vocal cords were paralyzed with fright.

"I'll tell you a secret, sweetheart. You would've been better off calling them from inside the house instead of trying to get over that high fence. But, we won't make the mistake of underestimating you again."

He raised his other hand to her face and gave a small spray bottle two swift pumps, sending the droplets directly into her nose and mouth. Within seconds, she was knocked out, her muscles as limp as a rag doll, and theirs to do with as they pleased.

CHAPTER FOUR

"Would you look at her? I wish I had her hair. And her eyes. And her face. And her body," Brianna mused as she watched TV. "She's perfect in every way."

"All of the tabloids are reporting she's dating Jax Hart. I bet that'll make for some interesting love scenes in their upcoming movie. The book they based it on is a scorcher." Chaise fanned herself.

"Was the book based on our sex life?" Bull questioned.

"Uh, no."

"Then it wasn't hot enough." He smirked with confidence.

"Do you believe the stories about them in those magazines are real?" Brianna probed, ignoring Bull.

"No," Shadow interjected. "They're not."

"You sound pretty sure. Has the CIA sanctioned stalking movie stars or something?" Brianna teased.

"Anything I do is sanctioned." His smile lit up his deep blue eyes and his handsome face.

"Because of tenure and all that jazz, huh?"

"Something like that." Shadow winked at Brianna before his gaze floated back to the TV and the beautiful woman's face filling the screen.

"Apparently, they want to make up their own happily-ever-after ending for the hottest silver screen costars," Chaise replied to Brianna, ignoring Shadow's interruption into their conversation.

"They can make up any ending they want," Shadow grumbled. "Her happily ever after won't be with that jackass."

Chaise and Bull casually laughed at Shadow's offhanded comment but otherwise continued the conversation about the movie still in production.

Brianna, however, wasn't as easily fooled by Shadow's aloofness. She locked her gaze on him, sensing she was finally in a position to use his tactics against him. Her inherent curiosity and journalistic instincts kicked into overdrive when he became unable to hide his discomfort with being under her scrutinizing gaze.

The muscles in the corners of her eyes squeezed together, narrowing in suspicion as she tilted her head to the side. He shifted positions in his seat and stared a little too hard at the TV, not allowing his eyes to move from the single spot. For a man who noticed everything about his surroundings, his choice to ignore the way she saw straight through him spoke volumes of what he'd never willingly verbalize.

"Shadow," Brianna gently chastised the giant of a man she loved like a brother, convinced he'd spook and run away from her otherwise. "You have to look at me at some point."

"Sunny," he replied with her nickname. "You are my little sister, and I love you. You know that, right?"

"I do. Without a doubt." She leaned over and put her hand on his arm. "And you know I love you. You're my brother, by love if not by blood."

"You realize some things are better left unsaid, right? Some questions don't need to be asked and answered."

"You literally saved my life, Shadow. If there's anything I can do to help you, I'll do it in a heartbeat. But if you don't want to talk, I'll respect that, too."

He nodded, deep in thought, and then lifted his eyes to hers. "Fine. Let's take a walk outside."

"I'd love to." She squeezed his arm in silent reassurance. "Noah, my love. Keep an eye on Amelia, Emery, and Gray, please. We'll be back in a little while."

"You're trusting me alone with all three of the kids at once?" Noah's grin lit up his face and made Brianna groan.

"I know that look. Don't force me to hide all the chocolate before I leave, Noah Steele," she warned in her stern, motherly voice.

"Yes, ma'am." He saluted her but couldn't hide his mischievous smile. "Whatever you say, princess." Noah turned his gaze to Shadow and issued his own directive. "Take care of my wife on your walk, Shadow."

"With my life, Reap."

"We're not even leaving the grounds, Noah," Brianna chuckled.

"You've been known to get into trouble a time or two without even leaving the house," Noah deadpanned.

"Fair enough. Ready to go, Shadow?"

"I know I'm going to regret this," Shadow mumbled under his breath. "Let's get it over with."

"You sound like you're about to be tortured." Bull didn't bother to hide his amusement at Shadow's discomfort. "Should I get the buckets of water ready?"

"I'd take waterboarding over talking about my *feelings* any day." Shadow shook his head and opened the door for Brianna to walk through first. Once she'd cleared the threshold, Shadow turned to Bull and whisper-shouted, "Come find me in five minutes. Save me!"

The door latched closed with the sound of roaring laughter on one side and complete silence on his side when he met Brianna's narrowed stare. His chest expanded with his deep breath, and he slid his sunglasses on his face. "Looks like I'm all yours now, Sunny."

"Uh-huh." She turned and began walking across the manicured lawn of the estate she shared with Noah, forcing Shadow to step quickly to keep up with her.

When they reached the terrace close to the pool, Brianna pulled out a chair and took a seat. Shadow followed suit, his sunglasses shading his eyes from the bright Florida sun, but his long face expressed his inner turmoil. He inhaled a deep breath and waited for the questions to begin.

"You know Elle Sinclair."

It wasn't a question. It was a direct statement, and she expected confirmation.

"I know Elle *Moore*," he corrected. "Sinclair is a stage name. But yes, I know her. I've known her most of her life, actually."

"Ah, finally. A look into the elusive Shadow's life." Brianna teased him to make it seem less formal and put him more at ease.

"Yeah, yeah, okay. I know her very well. We first started seeing each other about eight years ago, but it's been very…" He paused to search for the right word. "…sporadic."

"What do you mean by that? Why do I feel like there's more to the story?"

"I mean, for the first several years, we saw each other as much as we could. Between our jobs getting in the way. Sometimes, it was weeks apart. Sometimes, it was months apart."

The outer corner of her eyebrow lifted, arching in a silent question. Shadow shrugged one shoulder and continued.

"I'd show up out of the blue and surprise her. We'd spend a couple of weeks or more together, have the best time of my life, and then I'd leave again for the next job. I wouldn't see her again until the next time I had a break in the case or between assignments."

She studied his face, analyzed his words, and considered what he *wasn't* saying. "You're in love with her. Aren't you?"

"I can neither confirm nor deny your assumption."

"You just confirmed it. Why not just give it an honest try, stay together and see what you can have?"

"We already have too many strikes against us." He shook his head and dropped his shielded gaze to the ground.

"She's a good bit younger than you, isn't she?"

The humorless scoff before he replied confirmed her suspicion. "Yeah, that's actually the first strike against us."

"You're what? Thirty-five, close to thirty-six?"

Shadow nodded, and his full lips disappeared into a thin line.

"I think I read she's around twenty-eight now. That's honestly not a big deal, Shadow."

"Not now, no. But considering Elle's older brother was one of my best friends when we were growing up, the age gap doesn't help."

"I see." Brianna nodded slowly, realization settling in her mind. "You knew her as a little kid."

"When she was around seven, she developed a major crush on me. She'd follow Jeff and me around, spying on us from behind trees. It didn't matter what we were doing. She just wanted to be close to us. At the time, she was just my buddy's kid sister. You know? I never even considered..." His voice trailed off, leaving his thoughts unspoken, but there was no need to say it.

"You never considered anything would be kindled between you two, many years later, now that you're both adults," Brianna surmised.

With a heavy sigh, Shadow relented and decided to lay it all out for her, knowing she'd tell him the truth, regardless if he wanted to hear it or not. "Strike one, she's my buddy's little sister. That's just an unspoken rule every guy knows not to break."

"Wrong." Brianna shook her head vehemently and stopped his confession with her firm tone.

"What?" Shadow recoiled, jerking his head back as he openly gaped at her. "What do you mean 'wrong'?"

"Chaise is Noah's little sister, and she's happily married to one of his best friends. Do you think Noah would want anything less for her? Bull is his brother by choice, but now, also by marriage. Noah wouldn't change that for anything, no matter how much he enjoys giving Bull a hard time about it."

"Hmm," Shadow reflected. "You may have a point there."

"Of course I do. Please continue."

"I'm kind of afraid to now. Strike two, we've already covered. Elle's so much younger than I am. Believe me when I say I see the beautiful woman she's grown into. But I can't help but think, sometimes, that it's just wrong because of that little girl I remember."

His suspicion of Brianna's reaction was unmasked as he waited for the tongue-lashing he knew would come. His argument was weak, even he knew that. But his self-induced illusion had adequately sustained him for the past eight years. Somehow, he knew, deep down, Brianna would obliterate his delusion and smack him in the face with a dose of reality.

She tried to hide her mirth but failed magnificently. Her beautiful smile didn't last long, though, before it turned into a full belly laugh. Tears pooled in her eyes as she pointed at him, attempted to speak, but couldn't form the words over her outbursts of laughter. He crossed his arms over his chest, leaned back in the chair, forcefully blew out his breath, and refused to look at her.

"Okay." She finally managed to speak and wiped the tears from her eyes. "Let me catch my breath."

The thin line that formed his lips disappeared completely, and he attempted to project boredom with the entire conversation. It took all of Brianna's restraint not to start laughing again.

"Shadow, this is *me* you're talking to here. You know better than to say something stupid like that to me. She's not that little girl anymore, and you're not that young teenager anymore. Eight years' difference in age is nothing after you're both legal adults. The only reason you even mentioned knowing her as a child is because you're still hung up on her being the 'little' sister of your friend. She's his *younger* sister, but she's not *little* anymore. And you, my friend, are reaching, but you're only fooling yourself.

"Now, let's hear strike three."

"Strike three is a little harder to get around. Even you won't be able to argue with it," Shadow replied with confidence.

"Try me."

"She started modeling when she was twelve and moved to California with her parents after Jeff and I had already left home for college. When I first saw her in commercials, ads, and magazines, I was so proud of her. Kind of like a big brother would be. The older she got, the prettier she became. Then almost overnight, she was fucking drop-dead gorgeous. Even then, I only admired her from afar.

"While I was with the CIA, I was on assignment here in Miami, and she was sent here by the modeling agency. She called me when she landed, and our first three-week escapade began. When she first called me, I thought it was nothing more than a rekindled friendship. Getting to know each other again after so many years apart, mostly catching up on her life since I couldn't very well share the majority of mine.

"But the attraction was there from the beginning, and it was intense. Somehow, in those three weeks, I fell hard for her. The last night she was here, I knew I should just walk away and let it be her summer fling, but I couldn't. We'd spent every night together up until then, and I wanted that last night with her. I drove her to the airport early the next morning for her flight, and she shocked the hell out of me. She asked me to move to LA with her."

"What did you say?"

He removed his sunglasses and rubbed his eyes, stalling for as long as possible. He lifted his gaze, and Brianna was surprised at the sadness she recognized in them. "I asked her to stay here with me. Of course, she couldn't. But what shocked me even more than when she asked me to go with her was I honestly meant it when I asked her to stay here with me."

"But she couldn't. Her work was in LA, and she had to go back to it."

"Right, she had to go back to the bright lights and camera flashes that lit up everything around her. My job, my whole world, is in the darkness. In the shadows. Covert operations and instantly recognizable supermodels aren't exactly good bedfellows."

"Did you ever tell her you were with the CIA?"

"No. I couldn't tell her because I was still classified as an active covert agent."

Shadow turned to fully face Brianna before he continued. His expression became smug when he knew he had her dead to rights. She couldn't argue with his logic about their jobs. The odds of being a model who was also a household name were minuscule. The ability to conduct undercover governmental operations with invisibility was vital to national security and his very life. No way could she call him out on that.

"Strike three is our chosen professions. Neither of us can give up what we've worked so hard to attain, what we've invested so many years in perfecting."

"Bullshit."

"Huh?"

"I. Call. Bullshit." She emphasized each word and leaned toward him as she spoke. "That may have been true at first, but you've been out of the CIA for a while now. You've been with Steele Security for the last few years, not in some hostile, third-world country on a clandestine operation. If you hadn't been so stubborn this whole time, you could've rekindled this relationship long ago."

"Rekindled? Who says we've burned out?"

"Fine. You've had years to legitimize it, then. You've had plenty of opportunities to come out of the darkness and the shadows and walk with Elle in the light. But you haven't. Because you're scared."

"You think I'm scared?"

"I know you are." She smirked.

"Of what? I can't wait to hear this."

"You're a career bachelor, Shadow. You come and go as you please. Even in her life—you said you just show up out of the blue with no warning when it's convenient for you. She drops everything for you every time you appear, doesn't she? Gives up her plans without hesitation. Devotes every waking moment to you."

"Yeah." He drew out the one-syllable word, hesitant to hear the rest of Brianna's scolding.

"Hmm."

He didn't like that sound. Nothing good ever came from that sound. "What?"

"Just wondering. In the last eight years of this so-called relationship, what exactly have you given up for Elle?"

Her words hit him like a sledgehammer to his stomach, stealing his breath and rendering him speechless. He was unable to argue with her logic, because she'd been correct in everything she'd said to that point. He'd only fooled himself into believing his pathetic excuses. There were some events from the past year he couldn't bring himself to tell Brianna, though. Truths he had difficulties dealing with in his own mind, much less verbalizing. The most frightening unanswered questions popped into his mind without Brianna even addressing them first.

How long ago did Elle figure me out?

Are the rumors about her and Jax truths instead?

Has she given up on me and moved on to him?

"Yeah, that's what I thought. Shadow, only you can decide what you really want. You've been alone for a long time, and maybe you like it that way. But if she's the one you love, and you can't stand to think of her with someone else, you need to do something about this situation soon. That news about her and Jax could be complete hyperbole. But is that a chance you think you should take?"

"Thanks for the talk, Sunny. As usual, you've given me a lot to think about."

~

Shadow strode into his twelfth-floor condo and walked straight out onto the balcony overlooking the ocean. His thoughts had stayed on Elle since he left Noah's house, but his conversation with Brianna struck a sensitive chord he didn't even know he had. With his forearms resting on the railing, he stared off into the night, second-guessing his every decision and revisiting his every mistake.

His mind soon drifted back to their first night together eight years earlier.

He could still feel her quivering under his touch. She tried so hard to hide her apprehension, but he could be blind and deaf and still feel it rolling off her like the waves crashing on the shore. The rapid rise and fall of her chest, the pink tinge of her cheeks, and the dilation of her pupils were all telltale signs. Signs he was trained to identify.

But he couldn't deny her desire for him.

The ringing of his personal cell phone pulled him from his ruminations, giving him a welcome reprieve.

Until he saw the caller's name.

CHAPTER FIVE

"Devon, I need your help."

Jeff's frantic tone made the hair on the back of Shadow's neck stand at attention and salute. There was only one reason why Jeff would react with such strong emotion.

"Tell me."

"Elle is missing. She called me a couple of nights ago. It was late and she was scared. She said she thought someone was watching her. I should've listened to my gut and flew out there the minute we hung up. She convinced me she was just being paranoid. If anything has happened to her, I'll never forgive myself."

Jeff's agitated state had him spewing information at Shadow in half thoughts and out of sequence events. Shadow couldn't make sense of Jeff's ramblings, though he understood why he reacted so forcefully. The mere mention that Elle was missing was enough to push Shadow over the edge. But his friend called for a reason—for his expertise in high-pressure situations. He'd need all his wits about him, and all the details he could uncover, to get through it himself.

"Calm down and start over. This time, start from the beginning and walk me through everything. Every word she said. Don't leave anything out, no matter how small you think it is."

Shadow listened intently as Jeff took a deep breath, released it slowly, then recounted the entire conversation. He told Shadow about Elle calling late Pacific Time when she'd returned home from the lot, about the missing girls and fake press stories, and how she felt so uncomfortable she was at the point where she wanted armed bodyguards with her at all times.

"I'm kicking my own ass right now for staying here instead of flying out there to be with her. She said she'd call Mom, Dad, and Mark to alert them. Mark could've stayed with her until I got there." The guilt infused in Jeff's tone was palpable, thinking he'd let his little sister down when she needed him the most. "She never calls me that late, Devon. That should've been the first clue to slap me upside the head and make me see something was seriously wrong."

Shadow listened to his friend, soaked in every word and every detail, then tried to soothe him as best he could.

"Hey. Quit beating yourself up. That's my job. How long do you usually go without calling to check on her? Despite the number of times I've told you to stay close to her so you can protect her every second of every day."

"You're not helping. And I talk to my sister every few days. Our schedules aren't always conducive to multiple conversations per day. But this is different—she called me and she was scared. Now I can't reach her or Beth. Mark is on his way down there now, but he runs the winery for our parents. He doesn't have a clue where to start looking for her.

"I need your help, Devon. Elle needs you. I feel it—something bad has happened to her."

"I'm on the next flight to LAX. I'll find her no matter what it takes. You said you can't reach Beth either. Do you know if they were together on the set?"

"Yes, Elle said Beth is her makeup artist. They've been riding back and forth to work together, especially since they both work such long hours. It just makes sense since they live together. It's not a good sign that they're both missing, is it?"

"Jeff, I know you're on the verge of doing something really stupid. I can hear the panic in your voice. The more you obsess over what you should've, could've, would've done, the more likely you are to make a rash decision. Swear to me you'll give me time to do some digging around before you go off half-cocked and make things worse." Shadow's request more closely resembled an order.

"You have my word. I know you work for a security firm, but I didn't know who else to call. I'm sorry for dragging you into this."

"Don't be. I wouldn't have it any other way. I'll call you when I get to LA. But if you hear anything else before then, don't wait to contact me."

Shadow and Jeff hung up with the promise to keep each other updated on any new developments. Shadow retrieved a phone from a hidden safe in the wall. He stared at it longer than necessary, hating the fact that he was forced to use it at all. But she was worth it. He would do whatever it took to ensure she was safe and sound, even if that meant he'd be indebted to the CIA again.

With the phone powered on, he hit the send button and made the call. After two rings, the call connected and Shadow squeezed his eyes shut while he waited for the coded answer.

"Luigi's Pizza Delivery. What type of crust would you like?"

"Deep dish, extra garlic, extra cheese."

"Shadow," came the surprised response. "It's been a long time, my man. Must be something important for you to call in. What can I do for you?"

"Hey, Steadman. Good to hear your voice again. You know I need your help."

"Whatever you need. Lay it on me."

"What have you heard about actresses disappearing lately?"

"You sure you want to go there, Shadow? You're cleared to be read in, but once I do, there's no turning back," Steadman warned.

With his thumb and index finger firmly pinching the bridge of his nose, Shadow considered his options.

"If Elle Sinclair is involved, then read me in."

"Just remember you asked for it after you hear all the classified details. Don't show up in my apartment in the middle of the night and kill me," Steadman replied with a chuckle.

"You don't live in an apartment. Are you testing me, or did you really think you could hide from me?"

With a nervous clearing of his throat, Steadman gave Shadow the case details. Every point relayed made Shadow's heart move up into his throat a little bit more. By the time Steadman finished reading him in on the classified file, Shadow knew his involvement in the case was Elle's only chance.

"Create my new identity and backstory. Make it as bad as you can, then transfer the files to me. This won't be easy, but I need inside as of yesterday," Shadow commanded.

"There is another undercover agent who has embedded himself with the group. Maybe he can help you get inducted on a fast track. He may not agree to it, though. He's spent two years undercover, working his way up the chain, gathering intel. It could look too suspicious for him to bring you in now."

"Who is he?"

"Nick Tucker. DEA."

"I know him. Get a hold of his handler and get word to him that I'm coming in. You'll have to show me as an ex-con, recently paroled, and coming back home to California from a federal penitentiary. Don't leave anything out, Steadman, or you'll get us both killed."

"Have I ever gotten you killed before?" Steadman asked, taken aback at Shadow's lack of confidence in his abilities.

"Maybe you should transfer me to another analyst to handle my background cover."

"Come on, Shadow. You know I'm joking. It'll be flawless. Trust me."

"I'm CIA, Steadman, I don't trust anyone. But you can trust me when I say it better be the best backstory and fake identification you've ever created, or it'll be the last one you ever create."

"It'll be so good, even other analysts and operatives won't know it's fake. Guaranteed."

"Always a pleasure working with you, Steadman."

While he waited for his new identity and criminal record to be created, he called Jeff, knowing he couldn't share any information, but he had to warn Jeff and the rest of the family off the case. They couldn't actively search for her while Shadow was undercover, especially against the forces he'd be facing.

"Devon, have you already heard the news?" Jeff asked as soon as he answered the phone.

"What news?"

"Mark said a local news channel reported Elle and Jax eloped and took off on a secret honeymoon. They sent messages through their agents saying they're sorry for any concern they created for their well-being, but they're just so happy and so in love, they couldn't wait one more day.

"Devon, that is the biggest pile of horseshit I've ever heard. Elle can't stand Jax Hart. She sure as shit wouldn't run off and marry him. I'm looking for a privately chartered flight to get me out to California immediately."

"Jeff. Stop." Shadow's stern tone and terse words stopped Jeff's concerned tirade.

"What? Your turn to tell me," Jeff replied.

"You have to follow my instructions to the letter. You can't allow your feelings to overrule anything I'm about to tell you, regardless of how dire the situation seems. This is life or death, Jeff."

"I've always been amazed by your ability to find out things no one else could. That only became greater once you left the Army. So, I won't question you, Devon. I called you for a reason. Tell me what to do."

"You, Mark, Danny, and Tanya need to go to LA. Stay at her apartment and keep the media pressure up. Get in front of every camera you can and claim that story is a lie. Ask why the sheriff's department isn't taking you seriously. Whatever you have to do to keep her picture front and center in the news.

"Look for her in every trendy place a movie star would want to be seen. But Jeff, do not mention me. Do not look for me. Do not attempt to contact me in any way. You have to trust me on this. There's no other way. If you have any doubts, I need to know now."

"No doubts at all."

"You won't hear from me for long stretches of time. You, your parents, your brother—none of you can go getting all antsy on me. Let me do my job."

"I got it, Devon. I'll make sure Mom, Dad, and Mark get the message, too."

"You say that now. But when you're worried about her and don't hear from me, your mind will play tricks on you. You can't fall into that trap. When you start feeling despondent, remember this conversation."

"Thanks, Devon. I appreciate it more than you know. I trust you—no matter how bad the circumstances appear."

"If I send word instructing you to leave town, do not waste time. Leave immediately. No packing, no questions, just get to your parents' house and wait for me."

"Got it. Even though you're scaring the shit out of me. I know you won't tell me anything more."

"No, I won't. But for your own safety. Have a good flight. I'll be in touch as soon as I can."

The next call he needed to make was to Noah. A commercial flight wouldn't get him to LA fast enough from Miami. From what Steadman told him, time was definitely of the essence. Even telling Jeff what he'd told him was taking a huge risk, but keeping Elle's face and family in the news would hopefully buy more time. He only hoped his plan didn't backfire on him.

"Steele," Noah answered.

"Reaper, I need a favor—and I need it right now."

"Of course. Whatever you need. Name it."

"I need the private jet for a ride to LA."

"No problem. You need the team to go with you for backup or anything?"

"Not this time. I have to go this one alone."

"Understood. If anything changes, you know we're more than willing to jump into the fire with you," Noah replied, recognizing the code phrase they'd already established to identify Shadow's CIA missions.

"I know, Noah. If I don't make it back from this one, I want you and the guys to know how much I've relied on and valued your friendship."

"You know we feel the same way, Shadow. But I have to tell you, I'm more than a little worried about you, talking like this. You've never been hesitant to walk into a mission before."

"This one is different, Reap. This is a high-stakes poker round, and the dealer holds all the best cards. I'm going in on a long-shot gamble that I can pull it off successfully. But I can't and won't take you, Bull, and Rebel down with me if and when this mission goes wrong."

"We'll be in LA as soon as the plane returns and can take us out there. At least we'll be close if you need to pull us in."

"Actually, it would be helpful to have you there to cover a few people for me. They'll be making waves and could unknowingly draw the wrong attention to themselves. I'd feel better knowing you're there to watch their backs."

"Done. Fill me in on what they're doing."

Shadow packed while he recounted his conversations with Jeff and what he'd instructed Elle's family to do. After the time they'd spent together and all the missions they'd completed, Noah understood perfectly what Shadow hoped to achieve. With Noah's experience on highly classified operations, Shadow had no doubt he'd already deduced what the mission entailed, at least partially.

But the devil was in the details.

CHAPTER SIX

Eight Years Earlier

"I'm so glad you're here with me." Elle wrapped her arm around Beth's shoulders and squeezed as they walked along the shore, the water lapping at their feet.

Elle's parents, Danny and Tanya, moved her and Mark from their small town in Georgia to sunny Southern California a few years after Jeff and Devon went off to college. A modeling agency signed Elle at twelve years old after her mother submitted headshots in a competition Elle had read about in a fashion magazine. As thrilled as she'd been with the possibility of having her dream career, she knew what she'd miss most about Georgia were Devon and Beth. But her parents had concluded the once-in-a-lifetime chance was too good of an opportunity for their natural beauty to pass up.

Elle's thick, long blond hair was naturally wavy, and it perfectly framed her big hazel eyes, high cheekbones, and symmetrical facial features. Her teen years had ticked by with Elle gaining more and more popularity. Requests for magazine covers, cameo spots on established television sitcoms, and contracts to be the face of major name-brand designers poured in from her agent. By the time she'd turned twenty, her name was instantly recognized across the entertainment industry.

"What do you want now?" Beth asked, arching her eyebrow with a sideways glance at Elle. "I've been here with you for two years."

"I just found out I have to go to Miami for three weeks," Elle began explaining.

"Yes, I can see how that would be a hardship on you. Such a difficult and terrible life you live. Three weeks in Miami Beach. Photoshoots, bikinis, sun, sand, and salt water. Yes, I feel your pain."

"You're about to feel pain, all right," Elle laughed. "You're such a smartass. Before you so rudely interrupted me, I was going to ask if you can go with me. Now, I'm just not sure I want such negativity to taint my trip."

"Believe me, if I could get away to South Beach for three weeks, I would definitely taint your trip. I would taint the shit out of it. But the agency just contacted me about a small production that begins next week. You are looking at the newest member of the hair and makeup specialist team!"

"Congratulations, Beth! I'm so happy for you. Not that I ever had a doubt. I just know how hard it is to get in."

"Well, doing your hair and makeup and using those pictures in my portfolio didn't hurt my chances. With you being a hotshot supermodel and all."

"Supermodel. That's so funny, like I wear a mask and cape, parading around the city to fight crime. Maybe they'll create a comic book character based on me," Elle joked.

"I'm so glad fame never went to your head," Beth replied, her tone rife with sincerity. "You've never adopted the diva mentality no matter how much success you've achieved."

"You've never let me. You always remind me where I came from, and that you'd kick my ass all the way back to that small town in Georgia if my head got too big," Elle laughed.

"So, you could say I'm your brain trust. Your driving power behind the scenes."

"Let's not get carried away, Beth."

"Seriously, I wish I could go with you. What's the trip for and why will you be there so long?"

"I've just been selected as the new face of Kylie Rae Romano. Her new clothing line will be revealed soon, and they want me there for it. So over the next three weeks, they'll fit me, shoot me, and use me to help promote it. All while they use *her* status to promote *me*."

"Sounds like a lot of work." Beth scrunched up her nose in disagreement. "All work and no play."

"Beth..." Elle hesitated, capturing Beth's undivided attention. "Devon is in Miami. Jeff mentioned to Mom he'd talked to Devon the other day. I'm going to call him while I'm there."

"Elle, you've always had a crush on him. You know I'm all for having a good time, and hell if you don't need to let your hair down and have fun for once. You've worked since you got that first contract when you were twelve. But I know you. A fling with Devon wouldn't just be a fling to you."

"You're getting a few miles too far ahead of yourself, aren't you? How does seeing him again after all these years mean I'll have a fling with him?"

Beth stopped walking and turned to face her friend. Concern masked her face and burned in her eyes. "You didn't have the typical high school experience,

Elle. You were homeschooled while you shuffled from one photoshoot to another. From LA to New York and everywhere else in between. Your parents sheltered you, as they should have in this industry. You're twenty, riding high on your modeling career, but you've never really dated and had that whole experience of heartbreak, letdowns, and the occasional orgasm that makes up for it all."

Elle's cheeks flared red. After years of being on one set or another, with everyone looking at her with a critical eye, very few things embarrassed her at that point in her life. Her sex life, or lack of one, was one of those things that mortified her more than anything.

"I just haven't seen him in a long time, and this is the first chance I've had. He's been in the Army or something—and stationed all over the world. How can I not see him when we're finally in the same city?" Elle argued her point.

Beth smiled sadly, knowing she couldn't dissuade Elle from her course. "Just be careful. You're my best friend, Elle. I know you—I just don't want to see you hurt. So, when do you leave?"

"Saturday—three days away. Kylie Rae is a huge name in fashion. This will open so many doors for me—even small parts in more television shows and movies."

Elle's excitement was contagious, and soon, dreams of the movie parts were in both their eyes. "That would be so amazing, Elle. To see you on the silver screen and announce to the world, 'That's my best friend!' I wish I could be in Miami with you when this new era of your career kicks off. You can bet your ass I'll be on the set with you when you do your first major show—TV or movie."

The pair continued their trek along the shore, watching the waves and enjoying the warmth of the sunny day. They chatted about the upcoming possibilities and how life could drastically change in the very near future. But Elle's thoughts kept returning to her imminent trip to Miami—and the potential of seeing Devon again.

Perhaps it was the schoolgirl crush she'd had on him since the day she'd met him driving her need to contact him. Maybe Beth was right in her assessment, especially since Elle didn't have anyone else to compare to him. She still believed the impression she'd formed as a child.

No one compared to Devon Kane.

By the time the wheels touched down in Miami, her excitement couldn't be contained. As much as she couldn't wait to start a new venture in modeling, her thoughts were tied to Devon. The first second she had alone, she planned to call him. She'd managed to wrangle his cell number from Jeff, despite his protests and questions.

"Okay, ladies. You have today to rest and hydrate before we start shooting the swimsuit shots tomorrow morning. Call me if you need anything. Otherwise, I'll see you bright and early." Leslie, the photographer, and his crew left the dozen models assigned to the shoot to find their own way to the hotel.

Elle grabbed her suitcase off the conveyor belt and hit send on her phone before she changed her mind or lost her nerve. After two rings, the sexiest masculine voice answered.

"Kane."

"Hi, Devon. This is Elle Sin— Elle Moore. How have you been?"

"Is this *the* Elle Sinclair, model extraordinaire, calling me?" Devon teased, though his tone revealed he was thrilled to hear her voice. "I must've died and gone to heaven."

"Knock it off," she laughed. "I'm in Miami for the next few weeks. I just landed, actually. Jeff mentioned you're in town too. It's been a long time, but I'd hoped we could have dinner one night and catch up."

"I'd love to. I can't wait to see you. Do you have to work today?"

"No, there's nothing planned for today at all."

"I'm coming to pick you up right now, then. You need to get out and have some fun while you're here. Where are you staying?"

She gave him the name of her hotel, with the caveat to give her enough time to get out of the airport first. With his signature laugh, he agreed to wait a couple of hours before meeting her in the lobby. With the time set, she kept reminding herself to stop thinking of it as a date. They were simply two old friends who had a chance to become reacquainted as adults.

Of course, that didn't stop her from rushing to her room, showering, and dressing as if she had a date. It didn't stop the butterflies that danced in her stomach or her heart from racing with excitement. It didn't calm her jittery nerves from wondering what he looked like after all these years apart, or if she'd even recognize him when she went down to the lobby.

When she stepped out of the elevator, she saw heads turn and heard whispers as people recognized her. But his eyes were the only ones she felt. His stare was the only one she couldn't tear her eyes away from. His face was the only one that registered out of all the people milling about. Any concern of not knowing him faded into nothing when his dark blue eyes connected with hers.

The years apart had done nothing to diminish her feelings for Devon. Seeing him again after all the years made her heart turn flips in her chest. He'd always been an athletic, muscular young man, but the fully-grown man in front of her was even more impressive. Cut, defined muscles bulged under his shirt. From his wide, thick shoulders down to his tapered waist, the man was a specimen to behold. His jeans sat low on his hips. The snug-fitting denim gave a tantalizing hint at the muscular legs underneath.

"Elle, you're even more beautiful in person than on all those magazine covers," Devon said when he pulled her into his arms.

She slid her arms around his neck and returned his embrace. "You don't look so bad yourself, Devon. It's so good to see you again."

He kissed her cheek and flashed his dazzling smile. "I'll be the envy of every man in the world today. I get you all to myself. Are you ready for a day away from all the bright lights of the camera flashes?"

"You have no idea. In fact, you can even get us completely lost for a while, and you won't hear a single complaint from me."

"No chance of getting lost, but you'll feel like you're in another world. Let's blow this joint."

Devon extended his arm, and Elle wrapped her hand around it. The young, handsome boy she remembered had grown into a head-turning, gorgeous man with rippling muscles everywhere. He could give any male model a run for his money. The strength he naturally projected made her feel protected and safe. Even at her model height, he still stood taller than her. Their conversation flowed with a natural ease while they waited for the valet to bring his car around.

When a shiny red convertible Corvette stopped in front of them, Elle cut her eyes to him. "This is how you're whisking me away to anonymity? In a convertible Corvette that screams 'Look at me'?"

"Yep," he confirmed. "They can't snap pictures of you if you're flying by them in a blur."

Devon opened the passenger door and helped her into the car before his confident swagger carried him to the driver's side. On the interstate heading south with the top down, she felt carefree for the first time in what seemed like forever.

"Where are you taking me?"

"To a small but nice place in the Keys a friend owns. He rarely uses the house, and it's set on a private beach. It's a good place to go and not be seen or recognized by anyone. There are small, family-owned restaurants nearby."

"Sounds great. I should've brought my bathing suit, though, if we're going to the beach."

"Clothing is completely optional, so you don't even need one."

Her gasp followed by her chin hitting her chest made him laugh out loud. He couldn't keep up the façade even if he tried. Not with her.

"Have you lost your mind since the last time I saw you?"

"That's entirely possible, darlin'. But I'm only kidding about this. Partially anyway. If you twisted my arm really hard, I'd relent and let you skinny dip. Otherwise, we'll just walk around the small shops and find a tiny shred of cloth you can pretend is a bikini."

"I can already tell this outing will be memorable. Did you bring your loin-cloth or will you be going commando in the water?"

"One thing about me, darlin'. I'm always commando."

Heat filled her face, and she was infinitely appreciative of her sunglasses and the already hot South Florida temperature. The combination gave her the illusion of not being affected by him. She chose to ignore the deep rumble of his chuckle.

The small, unassuming beachfront home was surrounded by palm trees, giving the yard much-needed shade from the punishing rays of the sun. Devon strolled to the front door and unlocked it, pushing the door open for Elle to enter first.

"This is home for the day. It's not much, but it'll do for my plans."

"What are your plans?" Elle asked as she walked through the small beach cottage, trying to hide her nerves behind a quick perusal of the house. "What's on the agenda first?"

"First, I'll feed you. Then we'll grab a bathing suit, and we'll take my boat out for a spin. You still like to swim, don't you?"

"Are you kidding? I love it!"

"Let's go, then. You can leave your purse here. Everything is within walking distance from here. Today is all my treat."

"No. I called you, Devon," she protested. "You're not treating me when I proposed it."

"The hell I'm not. My momma raised me to be a Southern gentleman. You should already know that." With his hands firmly planted on her shoulders, he steered her toward the door, slipped her purse from her shoulder, and dropped it on the couch. "Now, let's go."

"You're such a stubborn man." She shook her head and rolled her eyes.

"You have no idea. I'll get my way no matter what I have to do." The smile in his voice only amplified his charm.

A quick stroll through the quaint streets led them to a small restaurant. If Devon hadn't pointed it out, Elle would've completely missed it. Though she was used to the attention from swarms of other people, it felt different coming from him. Opening doors, pulling out chairs, choosing the day's events, and taking care of her without being paid to do it made every gesture feel spontaneous and genuine. That was the exact opposite of how everyone else except Beth reacted to her celebrity status—being cordial because of what they could gain from her in return.

He ordered their lunches and turned his full attention to her. "You've grown up on me, Elle. I remember the little seven-year-old girl who followed me around all the time. Sneaking around cars, hiding behind trees, or using the corner of the house as cover to spy."

She smiled, remembering her favorite game of spying on Devon and Jeff. "I didn't know you were aware of all that at the time. I really thought I was being sly and that you didn't know you had a shadow."

An odd look flashed over his face, but it was gone as quickly as it had appeared. Unsure of what caused his discomfort, Elle kept talking, reminiscing over her childhood. "There was another time I'll never forget," she began, and she searched his eyes for a clue of his thoughts. "I never told you, I guess because I was so young and enamored of you. But you were always my hero. You made me feel welcome when Jeff tried to make me leave you two alone. You were always kind to me when he was my pain-in-the-ass older brother. Then you saved my life and put yours in jeopardy at the same time. I've never forgotten that, Devon. I never will."

"I was just in the right place at the right time. That doesn't make me a hero."

"You ran out in front of that speeding car and grabbed me, Devon. You almost got hit while saving me. That does make you a hero. I wouldn't be here right now if it weren't for you. I never thanked you. I was so shaken up at first, then an embarrassed nine-year-old afterward. So, thank you. You're still my hero."

"Enough about me. We're here to talk about you. What are you doing in Miami?"

"I just signed on as the model for Kylie Rae Romano's newest fashion line. Over the next three weeks, I have multiple photoshoots in different locations around Miami. I'm here with eleven other models for the swimsuit shoot, too."

"Such an exciting life. You're always in front of the camera. Your face has been on the cover of every major magazine. There's hardly anyone in the free world who doesn't know your name. That's so impressive, Elle. Your whole life is in the spotlight."

"It's surreal. Some days, it's more than I ever thought it could be. Other days, it's more than I can take. I guess it all equals out in the end, though."

"You'll get movie deals before you know it. With your innate beauty, they won't be able to resist you."

"I'm actually starting acting classes soon, so I'll be ready to break in to that market next."

Devon nodded, understanding her life was on a fast track to more stardom, more notoriety, and more spotlights. "Well, while I have you all to myself, let's go grab that bathing suit and take the boat out. There's a great reef we can snorkel about three miles offshore. You need a day away from your adoring fans every now and then, don't you?"

"That sounds like heaven on earth. You have no idea how ready I am for this."

CHAPTER SEVEN

They strode together in comfortable companionship to an island-themed boutique a few stores down from the restaurant. The locals were sheltered in their island lives, content to live in their own paradise and not invite the pressures of the mainland in. Elle's presence wasn't noticed any more than Devon's was. With a new bathing suit in hand, they walked to the marina and boarded his boat.

While he maneuvered out of the marina and the no-wake zone, Elle retreated below deck to the small cabin to change into her new bikini. She grabbed the bottle of sunblock on her way back to the deck and stopped in her tracks when she cleared the doorway. A shirtless Devon stood at the helm, navigating the boat away from the island. Behind his mirrored shades was the man she'd idolized for years from a distance. But he was suddenly very close.

She slid her sunglasses over her eyes and walked toward him. "Sunscreen?" She managed to utter the single-word question.

One corner of his lips twitched, but he kept his tone neutral. "Sure."

She stepped behind him and shook a dollop of lotion onto her hand then began rubbing it on his broad shoulders. Mesmerized by the ripples and ridges of his muscles, her movements slowed as her fingers memorized every inch of him. With deliberate concentration, she committed every sensation to memory so she could relive the moment repeatedly. She squeezed more from the bottle and continued exploring his arms and coated his lower back, taking her time since she'd run out of excuses to keep putting her hands on him. With reluctance and disappointment filling her, she took a step back and began coating herself.

"You missed a spot," he said casually.

She looked up at him, but his back still faced her. "Where?"

"You didn't get my chest or my ears. Do you want me to fry out here on the water in the harsh Florida sun?"

She grinned to herself, thrilled he'd challenged her the way he did. If it had been left up to her, she wouldn't have had the courage to do it on her own. But with him all but daring her to continue, she was more than happy to oblige.

Firm strokes of her fingers glided across the smooth skin of his chest. Though his eyes were hidden, she felt them moving over her face as if he'd physically touched her. His muscled body was firm and strong under her touch. At first, she hadn't noticed how rigid he'd become. The more she massaged the lotion into his skin, the faster his chest rose and fell with his breaths. His lips parted, and his eyebrows disappeared completely behind the rim of his sunglasses. Even with her inexperience, she loved knowing her touch affected him as much as his presence affected her, and even more so when he couldn't hide it as well as he thought.

Intentionally adding long, smooth strokes, she increased the pressure, massaging the thick striations of his muscles more than rubbing the lotion. Relishing in his masculine quality. Allowing her fingers to roam over the hard ridges of his defined stomach muscles. From the corner of her eye, she noticed his hand gripped the boat's steering wheel tighter, his knuckles turned white, and he became as stiff as a board.

Rising up on her toes, she brushed her breasts across his chest when she reached for his ears. She gingerly stroked over the lobes and the upper rim, drawing in the powerful scent of his cologne with every inhale.

"Have I missed anywhere else?" she asked breathily.

He silently raised one eyebrow, the arch appearing over the top of his sunglasses. One side of his mouth lifted in a slow smile, then the other side followed, revealing his white teeth against his tanned skin. "That's a dangerous question to ask me, Elle. I already have to keep reminding myself you're Jeff's little sister. That little towheaded girl still lives behind your eyes."

Being doused with a cold bucket of ice water would've felt better than the way his words dashed her hopes that something more than friendship could develop between them. His words, though they weren't meant to hurt her, left a sting in her chest that momentarily clogged her throat. The emotions welled up inside with the realization he didn't look at her at all the way she saw him.

Beth's warning reverberated in her mind, confirming she'd gotten her hopes raised for something that would never be reality. She'd misread cues and put too much emphasis on her own feelings, projecting them onto him and seeing what she wanted to see. But his reminder that she was simply his friend's sister brought her feet back to the ground and her head out of the clouds.

She snapped the lid of the sunscreen bottle closed with more force than necessary before stepping out of his personal space. "I haven't been known as

'Jeff's little sister' since you two graduated high school. Where are the masks, snorkels, and fins? I'll get them ready while you steer the boat."

"They're in the storage compartment under the bench seat in the back of the boat." He kept one hand on the wheel as he turned to watch her walk away. His head was leaned to the side, his eyebrows drawn together, and his gaze fixed.

Knowing he scrutinized her every move, she pushed her disappointment aside while preparing the snorkeling gear. After he'd planned an excursion to give her a reprieve from prying eyes, the last thing she wanted was to seem ungrateful. Feeling hurt was her own fault, she reasoned, for setting such unrealistic expectations. At least she had the answer she needed and could stop holding out for the one she couldn't have.

Lost in her thoughts as she knelt in front of the storage area, she was startled when she felt strong hands grip her arms from behind and lift her to stand. She was whirled around with no effort, instantly facing him. His sunglasses were pushed up on his head, and she saw the questions swimming in the depths of his blue eyes. Without changing his gaze, he removed her sunglasses and stared deep into her eyes.

"What's wrong, Elle?" He held her face in his hands, keeping their connection intact, refusing to let her look away from him.

Her lips parted to speak, but a reply wouldn't come. How could she explain how foolish she'd been? If she spilled her true feelings to him, the rest of their day together would be awkward. Uncomfortable. Ruined.

"Nothing's wrong." Her voice was intentionally more upbeat. She forced happiness into her eyes. Whatever it took to avoid being mortified by the truth.

He narrowed his eyes, crinkling them at the corners, and lowered his brows in a demanding gesture. "For the record, I know you're lying to me. You didn't even feel the boat come to a stop or hear me walk up behind you. What was on your mind just now?"

"Just the things I need to do." She was intentionally vague while stating the truth at the same time.

"Giving me a version of the truth isn't a loophole I'll let you get away with for long. Just remember that."

"Are we already at the reef?"

Her abrupt change of subject didn't go unnoticed, but he decided against challenging it for the time being.

"Yeah, we're here. Do you know how to snorkel?"

"Of course. Last one in the water buys dinner tonight." She grabbed her gear, climbed over the bench seat, and jumped off the boat's platform into the shallow water around the sandbar. "You're too late. Looks like you lose, Devon," she taunted.

"If 'losing' means I get more time with you tonight, I'll take 'losing' any day." With a flying leap, he jumped into the water next to her.

She squealed with laughter when the wall of water splashed her. It turned to playful laughter when his hand wrapped around her ankle, and she knew he was about to pull her underneath the water with him. Without a second to spare, she drew in a deep breath, and her head disappeared under the water. He wrapped his strong arms around her waist and resurfaced with her attached to him.

Water dripped off their faces, and the slight waves lapped around them while he kept a tight hold on her. "Now that you're at my mercy—" he smirked "—don't lie to me again. I can tell—I can *always* tell. You became upset with me when I said you're Jeff's little sister. Why?"

Resigned to being caught dead to rights, she decided to come clean with him. It was time to spill the secret she'd harbored for as long as she could remember. "I wanted you to see me as more than some little girl from your hometown. More than your friend's little sister. But apparently, our roles are set. I was just disappointed. That's all. It's fine—don't worry about it.

He nodded slowly, studying her face and her eyes. "You think the way I look at you is simply as my friend's little sister? I don't think you heard exactly what I said. I have to *remind* myself of it constantly, because that's not at all what I see when I look at you now.

"You're gorgeous, without a doubt. You're strong and fearless and smart and determined. You are kind, genuine, loving, and funny. I couldn't have made a more perfect woman if I'd made you myself. You're fucking sexy as hell, every inch of you, every part of you, inside and out. Before you get it in your head that I don't want you, think again."

He watched with rapt attention as a droplet of water rolled down her cheek and onto her lips. In a rare lapse of self-control, he couldn't resist licking the water from her lips. With a light swipe of his tongue across the part in her lips, he sampled her unique flavor and was immediately addicted. One taste only made him want more. He took every bit of what she willingly offered. With his head tilted to the side, he slanted his mouth over hers and drove his tongue inside.

His tongue slid against hers, and she gripped his hair tightly. Every silky-smooth pass of her tongue on his pushed him closer to the edge of losing all restraint. Low moans emanated from her chest when she wrapped her legs around his waist, crushing her thinly covered chest to his bare one. His hips surged upward involuntarily, brushing against her clit through her barely there bikini bottoms.

He gripped the hair on the back of her head and pulled lightly, separating them and ending their sensual hold. His voice deepened, and his intent gaze pierced her soul. "Don't ever think I don't want you. It takes all my willpower to think of anything other than the things I want to do to you. With you. Things I want to watch you do."

"Maybe you should reserve your willpower for more important things."

"You'll be the death of me yet." With a surrendering groan, he crushed his lips to hers for one more taste. "Now swim over to the sandbar and get your gear on so we can snorkel while we're out here. Before I change my mind and choose more interesting activities." He lowered his head and licked up her neck, sending chill bumps across her skin.

He reluctantly released her as they made their way to the shallow water. Once they were both ready, he led the way to the reef. They explored the underwater sanctuary like two overgrown kids who'd found sunken treasure. Minutes turned to hours, and by the time they climbed back aboard Devon's boat, Elle's energy had been depleted.

With the gear stowed, she plopped down on the bench seat and lay back, her arm bent across her face to shield her eyes. "I just remembered something. I was supposed to rest and hydrate today so I'd be ready for the lights and cameras tomorrow. Guess I completely messed that one up, huh?"

"Yeah, you really did. Maybe they'll fire you, then I'll have you all to myself for even longer." He stood over her holding a cold bottle of water, letting the small pieces of ice and water droplets fall on her bare skin.

When the ice hit her stomach, she jerked up with a start and came face-to-face with the bottled water. "I heard you need to hydrate."

"So thoughtful of you."

"It's good of you to notice. I do try."

When they returned to land, it was late afternoon, and Devon found he wasn't ready to let Elle leave. "You're tired, aren't you, darlin'? It's been a long day. Flying across the country late last night, shopping, snorkeling, trying to have your way with me. You've been very busy."

"Trying to have my *what?*" she laughed, playfully punching him in the arm.

"Why don't you go take a hot shower, curl up in the bed for a nap, and I'll wake you when it's time to eat? We're only about an hour from your hotel, so I can still have you home before your curfew."

She eyed him suspiciously for a few seconds, then relented. She didn't want their time together to end, and she decided taking him up on his offer was the best all-around solution. "I can't turn that offer down. Don't let me sleep too long, or I'll be up all night tonight."

"That's not much of an incentive for me to wake you up soon."

"You are going to be the death of me," she quipped, throwing his earlier words back at him.

That odd expression quickly passed over his face then disappeared again. She watched him closer this time, waiting to see if he revealed anything else. His eyes softened, but his face gave nothing else away. She raised up on her toes and placed a light kiss on his full lips. He returned it and cupped her face with his hands. He continued holding her face when she broke off the kiss. "What was that for?"

"You said you can tell when I'm lying. Well, I can tell when you're hiding something. For whatever reason, you don't want to tell me what it is. But I want you to know, I'm here when you're ready to talk about it."

She left him alone to mull over her offer while she showered, changed back into her clothes, and crawled into the bed. Once her head hit the pillow, she was fast asleep with dreams of Devon replaying the day's events. His words. Their kiss. The feel of her body crushed to his. How protected she felt in his arms. Every superb sensation brilliantly repeated in her mind's eye, where she felt loved, desired, and sheltered.

The scent of food cooking pulled her from the best sleep she'd had in weeks—and the best dream she'd ever had, period. She rolled off the side of the bed and walked into the kitchen. Finding Devon shirtless, in his form-fitting jeans, and barefoot would've been enough to ignite any woman's libido. When she realized he was cooking dinner, her heart melted. When he turned and saw her standing in the doorway, he smiled and pitched the hand towel over his bare shoulder. Her gaze traveled down his chest, over his stomach, taking in the happy trail and sexy V, and landed on his unbuttoned jeans.

Her mouth opened, and she sucked in a surprised breath. Her tongue darted out, reflexively wetting her lips as she continued to stare. When she met his knowing gaze, she didn't have enough wits about her to be embarrassed. She was too busy enjoying the view.

"See something you like?" He pushed off the counter and stalked toward her with slow and deliberate steps. "Elle, if you keep staring like you'd rather have *me* for dinner than this food, I'll make sure you're fed all night long."

Caged between his arms with her back against the wall, she watched as he fought his desire for her. The war between what he wanted to do and what he should do played out in his blue depths, and she wanted it to be the last time the thought of hesitation ever crossed his mind. She reached up and gently touched his lips, lightly gliding her fingertip over them. Over his chin. Down his neck, over his Adam's apple, to the hollow dip at the base of his throat. She lifted her eyes to meet his when her fingers continued their journey. She splayed her hand flat against his chest and raised her other hand to match.

The uncertainty in his expression changed to a raging inferno before her. He leaned in closer. His lips barely hovered over hers, grazing with the lightest touch when he spoke.

"Don't think I don't know what you're doing. Fuck if it isn't working, though. You seem damned and determined to have this your way. Be careful what you wish for, Elle. In this case, you may get more than you can handle."

Shocked by his words and the way he saw through her, she stood rooted to the floor and drank in his closeness, his masculinity, his commanding presence. The words she wanted to say wouldn't come. Not that she'd blurt them out even if she could speak, though she doubted her feelings were a secret from him. He seemed to be a mind reader, and she was apparently an open book.

"For tonight, I'll keep my gentlemanly reputation intact and save you from yourself. If you look at me like that tomorrow night, I won't be responsible for my actions."

"Tomorrow night?" Her voice was low and unsure, a complete contradiction to the confident persona she projected in her pictures.

"You're here for three weeks, right?"

"Right."

"Then you're mine every spare minute for the next three weeks. I may have to disappear for work now and then, but I won't leave you for very long. So, before you test my resolve again, let's eat and then I'll take you back to your hotel."

"You're not staying with me tonight?"

He narrowed his eyes at her, gauging the motive behind her question. Satisfied it was legitimate, he placed a warm kiss on her cheek before replying. "I'd love to stay with you tonight, but I have work to do. It'll be late before I finish, and I know you start work early tomorrow. If there were any way I could get out of it, I would. Believe me."

"Stop. I just showed up and called you out of the blue. I don't expect you to drop your whole life for me." She cut her eyes playfully to the side. "I only expect you to drop all your other girlfriends for me. That's all."

His brilliant smile lit up his gorgeous face, amusement sparkling in his eyes. "Done. I don't have any girlfriends, so that's not a problem."

He retreated to the stove to serve their dinner, his demeanor unchanged from his usual cheerful self. Though, she couldn't help but notice he didn't make the same request of her.

CHAPTER EIGHT

"You look like you've been up all night. What did you do? I said to rest and hydrate." Leslie glared at Elle from around his camera.

"I tried to rest last night, Leslie. The room above mine apparently pulled an all-nighter. They'd stop the music and noise long enough for the manager to threaten to kick them out, then they started up again." She struck a pose and moved slowly through the constantly clicking of the shutter.

"You should've called me. I'll take care of it right now, though." He put the camera down and snapped his fingers. On cue, his assistant appeared at his side. "Meechelle, Miss Sinclair needs a new room, with silence and tranquility on all sides. Not around loud revelers."

A few minutes later, Meechelle reappeared, apprehension covering her face. "Leslie, the hotel is sold out. There are no rooms to move her into."

"Must I handle everything?" he sighed. "As soon as the shoot is over, you'll have a new room, Elle."

She didn't have the heart to tell him she had no intentions of sleeping that night either. Devon promised he'd stay with her all night. She had twenty days with him, and she planned to make the most of every opportunity she was given. "Maybe the partiers will check out today," she offered.

"Meechelle, take her to the spa for a couple of hours while I shoot the others. Come back to me when she looks rested and photogenic again."

Two hours later, Elle emerged from the spa, refreshed and renewed. Leslie and Elle focused on the various moods he needed for the project, directing her into poses and sexy pouts to complete his overall vision.

She felt the change in the air and heard the low murmurs of whispers around the outdoor set. Without visual verification, she knew what had everyone buzzing—or rather, *who* had everyone's attention. Devon stepped into her direct line of sight, and their eyes met in an instant.

"That! Yes! That look!" Leslie yelped and moved in for a closeup shot.

Devon watched Elle, ignoring the obvious stares and questioning eyes all around him. In truth, he'd been watching her since she walked out of the spa. His training made him stealthy. Deadly. Invisible, when he wanted to be. He'd been invisible long enough at that point—he wanted her to see him. He wanted to see her reaction, to gauge her response, to read her body language when she was surprised by his presence.

What he got wasn't at all what he expected.

The look she gave him was more lethal than any he'd encountered. It was deadly to his way of life. The way it struck his core was detrimental to the plans he'd made. The fact that he liked it more than he should warned him to run while he still could.

But he knew it was already too late for that plan to work in his favor. Three weeks. He could handle three short weeks of being exclusive with a beautiful cover model.

Even if she was the younger sister of his friend.

Even if she'd celebrate her twenty-first birthday during their time together, further accentuating the age difference between them.

Even if it meant he had to give up the cover of shadows temporarily and live in her limelight.

"The spa must've been exactly what you needed. I've never seen you look more beautiful, my dear." Leslie stepped to the side, the camera all but glued to his face, while another man held Elle's singular focus. "Oh, honey, I love the fierce look, too. You're giving me so much to work with today, it'll be hard to choose just one."

The smirk covering Devon's face confirmed he'd heard Leslie, and he knew exactly what prompted the change in her expression. It was bad enough when the buxom sable-haired beauty in the string bikini approached him, but when the overtly flirtatious intruder put her hand on his arm, Elle became irrationally jealous and possessive.

Relief flooded her senses instantly when his response included a gesture toward Elle. The bikini-girl looked over her shoulder, immediately recognized Elle, and scurried away from Devon. Pride over witnessing the small victory swept over her, and Devon's smirk transformed into a beaming smile.

Smooth, Moore. Real smooth, she thought.

"And that's a wrap for you, my love. Rest. Hydrate. Come back to me even more gorgeous tomorrow." Leslie kissed the air on either side of her face and dismissed her when he called the next model into range of his viewfinder.

"I didn't expect to see you here today." Elle approached Devon, delighting in the sensation of his eyes heavy on her barely clad skin.

"Where the fuck was that bathing suit when we were on the boat yesterday? It's probably a good thing you weren't wearing it. You'd still be held in a secure, remote location where no one except me could find you."

"Promises, promises."

He wrapped his arm around her bare waist and pulled her to him. "I've warned you about that." He leaned down and captured her mouth with his, not caring that dozens of cell phone cameras captured their every move. "Let's go. I have more plans for you today. Do you get to keep the bikini?"

With a chuckle, she shook her head. "Not this time. Are we going back to the boat?"

"That's not what I had planned, but I'm game if that's what you want to do."

"Honestly, I don't care if we go play Skee-Ball for six straight hours. Just take me with you."

"Who told you my plans?"

"I'll never tell. Let me change, and I'll be ready to get out of here."

"Shorts. T-shirt. Bikini. Then dress for dinner and dancing tonight."

She stopped walking, waiting for him to give the punch line of his joke, but none came. "You're serious?"

"Of course. You're mine today. Remember? Move that fine ass. You're wasting daylight." He playfully smacked her on the ass, making her jump and squeal with laughter at the same time.

"Come on up. I'll have to pack a bag with all my makeup, hair stuff, shoes, clothes, jewelry—"

"Fine. Start with a bikini, T-shirt, and shorts. We'll come back here for the rest later. I'm still coming up to your room with you right now, though."

Devon roamed around her room, making himself at home and checking every nook and cranny of the space while she changed clothes. When she emerged from the bathroom, she found him standing on a chair, checking the smoke detector.

"Everything okay?"

"Absolutely. Just can't be too careful." He stepped down from the chair and raked his eyes up and down her. "You could wear a black plastic garbage bag and make it look sexy as hell."

"Such a sweet talker." She patted him on the cheek with her palm, accepting any excuse to touch him.

"We need to go now. Or we won't leave this room at all for a very long time. Then we'll miss our reservations."

"By all means, lead the way. I'm curious to see what you have planned for me today."

"A day you'll never forget." He laced their fingers together, picked up her bag, and pulled her into his side after they were through the hotel doorway.

~

"It'll be extremely hard for you to top today. That was so amazing! If we do that every day for the next three weeks, it'd never get old."

"Hmph." Devon had sulked since they left the research center.

"Are you still pouting?"

"Yes. Yes, I am." He crossed his arms over his chest.

"You're not even going to hold my hand now?" She managed not to laugh, but hiding her smile was impossible.

"Nope."

"He was just so amazing, Devon. I couldn't help but fall in love with him."

He cut his eyes sideways at her, his mouth gaped open in shock, and his eyes narrowed in disbelief. "You're still defending your actions? Unbelievable."

"But I'll probably never see him again," she argued.

The elevator doors opened, and they stepped in together. Devon punched the button for the seventeenth floor and waited for the doors to slide shut. As soon as they were alone, he pinned her to the wall with his body and kept his eyes trained on hers. "For the record, you're not allowed to have any other boyfriends. Ever. Not when I'm not around. And especially not when I'm there to witness it."

"But I've always loved dolphins…and you're the one who took me to see him."

"He got more kisses than I did. That's not acceptable by any stretch of the imagination. He knew it, too. Did you see how he smirked at me?"

"I saw the smile all dolphins appear to have on their faces. But I don't think that was a malicious smirk toward you."

"It's an alpha-male thing. You wouldn't understand," Devon countered.

"Ah, I see. Well, I'll make it up to you. Just tell me, in alpha-male code, how to do that."

"I'd much rather show you." He covered her mouth with his and gently licked across the part in her lips. "After dinner. You're making us late again, distracting me, and wreaking havoc on my plans. Go shower and get ready, woman. I'll be back in an hour to pick you up. You'd better be ready, or you'll be in even more trouble."

"Yes, sir." She saluted him in a joking fashion and slid out of his embrace. "Whatever you say."

Elle rushed to dress for a night of dinner, dancing, and more with the man she'd never been able to get out of her mind. Giddy with excitement, she hurried through her hotel room, threw on a dress and heels, and perfected her hair and makeup. She was putting the last earring in when the knock on her door came. One hour, on the dot. After peeking through the peephole, she flung the door open and grabbed her clutch from the table.

"I'm ready. On time, even."

Devon quirked one eyebrow upward. "Damn. I was looking forward to your punishment for making me wait."

Their date night would forever be etched in her memory. Beth was correct when she said Elle's professional life didn't leave her much time for a personal life. After their dinner over candlelight, Devon took her to a loud, packed club to dance. Approaching the bouncer, she was seized by fear at the thought of being turned away for being underage. Devon shook hands with the enormous man guarding the roped entrance, leaned in to his ear to whisper something, and stepped back to give the bouncer room to unhook the velvet barrier.

"Come on in, Shadow. It's been a long time, brother."

"Thanks, man. Good to see you."

"Your private room on the third floor is ready when you are. Enjoy."

Devon tipped his head at the bouncer, put his hand on the small of Elle's back, and led her through the crowded nightclub with ease. Whether it was his size or his dark expression, she wasn't sure, but the sea of people seemed to part willingly to move out of his path. The curved staircase leading to the private rooms gave the hopping club an air of glamour and class. They made their way to the third floor, and he led her to their exclusive corner room.

"Shadow?" she asked when he'd closed the door behind them.

"It was my nickname when I was in the service. The bouncer is an old Army buddy of mine."

A rapid knock on the door was immediately followed by several waitresses entering with trays of drinks and hors d'oeuvres. They placed them on the private bar and left as quickly as they appeared.

"You've thought of everything. I was worried they wouldn't let me in and I'd be mortified after being turned away in front of the crowd outside," Elle confessed.

"I'd never let anyone do that to you." He brushed a strand of hair away from her face, his fingers grazing across her skin and heating her from the inside out.

She stepped into him, held his face in her hands, then raised up on her tiptoes to initiate a kiss. When their lips connected, his reaction was tentative at first, but she was undeterred. Swiping the part of his lips with her tongue, she moved in when his mouth opened to her.

At first, she thought she was in control of their encounter. But he quickly proved her wrong. His fingers weaved through her hair, gripping at the roots, and he angled her head where he wanted it. The urgency and demanding nature of his tongue's caress overwhelmed her senses with a feeling of sheer perfection. When he broke the kiss, she was afraid he would pull away from her altogether, tell her he thought it was a bad idea, and then disappear from her life.

"Let's have a drink," he suggested then moved to the trays. He returned with two glasses—a beer mug for him and a glass of Moscato d'Asti for her. "We need a poignant toast."

They held up their glasses, and she waited for him to continue.

"To old friends reuniting, creating new memories, and never regretting a single moment."

"To us," she added.

"Ready to go dance?" he asked after they'd finished their drinks.

"Absolutely. You don't have two left feet, do you?"

"You just want to insult me again, don't you? After repeatedly kissing Sammy right in front of me."

"Sammy. The dolphin," she clarified.

"Come on." He chuckled under his breath as he took her hand. "Let's go dance so I can pretend to accidentally grope you on purpose while we're on the dance floor."

"Mr. Kane, if you keep talking like that, you will absolutely sweep me off my feet. You are such a romantic."

On the dance floor, in the middle of the throngs of bodies writhing to the music, Devon and Elle moved to their own beat. He held her close to him, bumping and grinding, rubbing and caressing, blocking out every other person in the room. A few hours later, the alcohol had been consumed, the food was eaten, and neither could deny where their course would take them next.

"I heard Leslie say you're supposed to rest and hydrate tonight. I seemed to have single-handedly screwed that up for you. Maybe we should head back to the hotel now."

"Absolutely," she agreed. But sleep was the last thing she wanted.

The ride back to the hotel was quiet, each lost in their own thoughts of how the night would end. Or wouldn't end. When he turned into the hotel drive, the lines separating the valet parking from self-parking loomed before them.

"Valet." Her single-word instruction was enough to convince him.

They exited the car, and he escorted her into the lobby. With the bank of elevators in sight, she sensed his second thoughts were getting the better of him. She took his hand in hers and faked confidence she in no way felt.

"Come upstairs with me, Devon. Stay with me tonight."

Without waiting for a reply, she pulled him toward the bank of elevators and pushed the call button. His hesitation had lasted a split second before they stepped onto the elevator. But once he relented after the doors closed, he gave her hope and reinforced her confidence. He wanted her as much as she wanted him, and there was no way in hell she'd let him back out on her after they stepped out of the elevator.

Holding his hand, she opened the door to her room and mentally noted how he hadn't even attempted to release hers. With the door closed and locked behind them, she turned to face him, meeting his heated stare.

"You're sure about this?" he asked, though she knew he still unsure.

"I've never been more positive of anything else in my life, Devon."

With a slight shake of his head, he stepped into her and took complete control of her body. "Then I should warn you first. This is my domain, and when we're in the bedroom, I'm in complete command."

Her lips parted with her sudden inhale, her cheeks flushed, and her eyes grew wider at his declaration. Waves of shock and excitement rolled through her. "Okay." Her reply came out as a raspy whisper.

His blue eyes darkened to nearly black when he leaned in closer to her, a glint of realization sparkling before he masked it. "Have you ever done this before?"

She shook her head. "No."

Devon hid his shock.

He remained her hero. After all the years apart, he couldn't help but look out for her best interests. "I warned your brother to keep the guys away from you. I never thought I'd be one of those guys I warned him about. I'm not sure how he'd feel about this."

"I guess this is where I should confess something to you." She watched his expression for any subtle changes. "I always knew you'd be—" she air-quoted his words "—'one of those guys.'" Elle searched his face and witnessed his expression soften before she spoke next. "And I don't care what my brother thinks about it. This is my life."

"Elle." Her name on his lips signaled his surrender and issued a warning.

"Devon."

A sudden passionate embrace had her in his arms, and their bodies melded together in perfect harmony. Their clothes disappeared, strewn in various places around the hotel room. She barely registered the sound of the condom package ripping open before he deftly rolled it onto his impressive length. He lifted her in his arms and carried her to the bed, then placed her in the center before he covered her body with his own.

His deep, searing kisses branded her with a brush of his tongue, leaving his invisible mark and claiming her as his and only his. He rolled her onto her side and slid his finger along her slit, stroking the sensitive skin and dragging the moisture from her sex around her clit in a deliciously teasing movement. Her gasps filled the air as his murmurs filled her ears when his fingers filled her body. Her pleasure coated his hand when her body could no longer contain the intense sensations building from within.

His powerfully strong muscles expanded and contracted when he rolled back on top of her. His hips pushed forward, delightfully teasing her limits. She arched her back as he slid his manhood across her drenched opening. He hovered above her, waiting for her consent while he maintained eye contact. She nodded. Her gaze never left his; her certainty never faltered. Slowly, his long, thick cock slid into her, and he became acutely aware that he was her first. The twinge of pain she undoubtedly felt would soon get replaced with waves of pleasure. He'd make sure of that. Sweat-covered skin slid across sweat-covered skin, heating each other almost to the point of spontaneous combustion.

Their eyes remained locked as he surged into her, over and over, and a deeper connection passed between them. The knowledge they'd never be as they once were, along with the realization they both wanted more settled between them. He gripped her legs and drove into her until she screamed his name in ultimate bliss, and her body shook from the intensity.

When he asked if she'd ever done that before, he had referred to being submissive to another man in the bedroom. She'd answered truthfully, and that excited him more than he'd allow himself to show. But the moment he realized she'd never been with another man in any way, he knew he was in over his head. The way her body wrapped around his cock, tight and wet, snug and soft, feeling as if she was custom made to fit him.

She'd fallen asleep after their first time, but he couldn't sleep even if his life had depended on it. She lay beside him with the sheet pushed down to her waist and the moonlight streaming across her breasts. He watched her sleep for the first hour, holding on to his last shred of willpower to avoid waking her and taking her again. The cool breeze from the air conditioner drifted over her, causing her nipples to pebble.

That was the exact moment his resolve broke.

He leaned over and covered one of her firm peaks with his mouth, instantly warming her cold skin. One taste of her wasn't enough, and his careful ministrations turned to voracious feasting. He slid his hand down her stomach as her fingers weaved through his hair. His fingers crawled over her slit slowly at first, testing the tenderness of her sensitive tissues before delving deeply inside her.

She slid her other hand down and covered his. His immediate thought was she was stopping him because she was too sore. But she surprised him when she spread her legs and pushed his fingers inside her wetness. Her hips bucked involuntarily, and she moaned with pleasure.

"Mmm, that's my girl," he murmured in her ear. "You like that, don't you?" He thrust two fingers into her while rubbing her clit with the callused pad of his thumb.

Her fingers gripped his hair as she rode his hand, the waves of ecstasy rippling through her body. He slid down and settled between her legs. His mouth teased her clit with more pleasure than she'd ever known. When his warm tongue laved her from bottom to top, the pleasure dragged her over the edge, past the point of no return, and her body shook from the intensity of it.

After lapping up every last bit of her essence, he crawled up her body until his cock was poised at her still wet entrance. "Are you ready for me, Elle?"

"I'm more than ready for you, Devon," she purred. "I must have died and gone to heaven. I've never felt anything like this before."

His hips surged forward, driving into the hilt with one forceful lunge. In one hand, he held Elle's hands above her head. The other hand reached behind her knee and pulled her thigh toward her chest, changing his angle and deepening his penetration. Her screams of pleasure echoed off the walls, and his name rang in the air. It was a sound he wasn't likely ever to forget.

Over their three weeks together, every spare minute she had away from modeling was spent with him. They took long strolls on the beach, they talked, they shared, they laughed, they played, and they inevitably grew closer. Their three weeks together felt like both the longest and shortest period of her life.

Her last night in Miami, he'd suggested they meet for dinner at the restaurant in her hotel's lobby, knowing she had an early-morning flight out the following day. She dreaded the moment when their dinner was over, and he stood to leave the restaurant. Something stopped him, though, and their eyes locked in a heated but silent debate.

He stayed with her the rest of the night, making love to her twice more while he demonstrated a few of his other masterful bedroom skills before she had to leave for California. He insisted on driving her to the airport early that next morning for her flight, though the other models planned to ride together. Part of her wanted to deny his request, knowing it would be hard enough to say goodbye. But, a bigger part of her heart needed to know how he'd react to her departure.

Would it affect him in the way she knew it would her?

He parked in the unloading zone and left the car running. Without saying a word, she reached for the door handle, but he grabbed her other hand in his and stilled her movements. "Elle, don't leave here thinking this was just a long one-night stand. It's not, by a long shot."

"Then, what is it?"

"It's more complicated than that."

"Come to LA with me." She blurted out the words before she realized what she was asking, what she hoped, what she begged of him.

"Stay in Miami with me." His eyes were sincere, his voice held no humor.

She tried hard to fight back the tears before she replied, "I can't."

He nodded, and disappointment flashed in his eyes. "I understand."

With heavy hearts, they exited the car. He grabbed her bags from the trunk and checked them with the curbside valet. A tender kiss was their only goodbye before she watched him drive away from inside the terminal.

CHAPTER NINE

Five Years Earlier

"Elle, you know how much I love you, right?"

"I know you love me when you want something. What is it this time? My shoes? My brand-new gray ostrich leather Hermes purse that I haven't even used yet? Spill it."

Beth's devilish grin made Elle stop dead in her tracks. "Dear God. What have you done? I'll be forced to kill you any minute now, won't I?"

Beth dismissed the threat with a shrug of her shoulder and the broadening of her smile. "I may have let it slip to Bruce and Josh that you're single. Josh may have expressed considerable interest in changing your relationship status. Bruce may have suggested we go out on a double date this weekend so you can give Josh a chance. Josh and Bruce may have already made plans for the four of us."

"No." The firm tone of Elle's rebuttal contradicted her normal demeanor, catching Beth off guard even after years of being at her best friend's side. "Beth, you know better than to set me up on a date with anyone. I'm not interested, and I won't go out just for the sake of going and then have our pictures splashed across the front page of every rag magazine. You know how vicious they can be. I can't believe you'd do that to me."

Elle's hands shook, her voice quavered, and her heart raced. She was angry with Beth and her boyfriend of the month, Bruce, for being so presumptuous and cavalier with her career. But she didn't want to face the deeper underlying reasons fanning the flames of her anger. At that moment, she found it was easier—safer—to place the brunt of it squarely on Beth's shoulders.

"I'm sorry, Elle. You know I'd never hurt you. It hurts me to see you pining your life away for a man who obviously doesn't feel the same about you. It's been three years since you started this insane relationship with him in Miami. It's not even a relationship." Beth search for the right word, and her agitation grew with each passing second. "It's an *arrangement* to benefit him! He just happens to show up out of the blue, and you drop everything to spend a few weeks with him. Then he leaves again, and you don't hear from him for several months.

"Think about it, Elle. Who's here to pick up the pieces of your shattered heart when he kills every hope and dream you have? Me. I'm the one who loves you and shows you every single day. How could you even think for a second I'd do anything to hurt you?"

The verbal slap from Beth's words didn't sting nearly as much as knowing she was right did. A vision of all the times Beth had stayed up all night, whispered comforting words, and kept her arm wrapped around Elle until they'd both fallen asleep from sheer exhaustion flashed through Elle's mind. Beth had been her best friend for more years than not, had been with her through the best and worst moments of her life, and had only ever shown loyalty.

"Beth, I—"

"You know what? Save it. Bruce and I have a date tonight, but I think I'll just go to his place instead of him coming here. Don't wait up for me."

With that, Beth stormed out of the apartment and slammed the door behind her. Elle sank down onto the couch, bent at the waist, and rested her face in her hands. As usual, Beth called it like she saw it—no holds barred, no sugarcoating, and no excuses. Almost every other time Beth had interjected, her frankness had been Elle's saving grace. The exception to the rule was when the discussion involved anything remotely related to Devon.

"Beth, I'm sorry. You're absolutely right," she confessed to the empty apartment. "Everything in my life fades to background noise when Devon shows up. It's not even a conscious choice that I make. Every time there's a knock at the door, my heart races and thumps like a bass drum because I hope he's there. I look for him everywhere I go, hoping he'll appear out of thin air.

"And you know what else? I wouldn't even question it if he did. I'd just be *so fucking happy* that he was beside me, the reason why wouldn't matter. I guess that creates another question, doesn't it? I'm so in love with him. I'm so happy to get a few weeks with him now and then, I don't ever question why that's all I get. Why do I settle for less than I want or deserve?"

Even though she couldn't say the words to Beth, she believed getting the thoughts out of her head and into the open was a step in the right direction. She looked up, dried her tears with her fingers, and released an exasperated breath. A rap on the door caused her to jump, then her eyes dropped to the side table where Beth's keys laid. She'd stomped out of the apartment in such a huff, she didn't grab her keys first.

"I'm glad you forgot your keys," Elle called out through the closed door.

She swung the door open wide and held the forgotten keys out in the palm of her hand.

"You haven't given me any keys," Devon replied with a sexy smirk. His eyes traveled up and down her body, drinking in every inch, branding her without a single touch. "But whatever you're offering, I certainly won't refuse."

She squeezed her fist around the keys. The sharp metal tips bit into her skin, but all she felt was complete exhilaration that he was there. The initial ardent expression in his gaze, the sexy timbre of his voice, and the confident air he projected create the ultimate lady-killer package. But the way he looked at her when his eyes softened said he never wanted to leave her. When his arms snaked around her waist and held her tightly against him, he revealed he'd missed her every bit as much as she'd missed him. The way he buried his face in her hair and deeply inhaled her scent exposed his vulnerable side, the one that wanted to hide away with her and never be found.

This is why I can never refuse him, she reflected. *This is what keeps me coming back for more. Every. Single. Time.*

Still holding her in their intimate embrace, he gently pushed her backward until they'd walked into the apartment and locked the door behind them. Time passed while they clung to one another, but neither was prepared—or capable—of letting go. He returned with a different demeanor each time. Just as she never knew when to expect him to show up, she also had no idea what kind of mood he'd be in.

When he returned sullen and quiet, she automatically knew his only solace was found in her touch. For the first few days, while he worked through whatever weighed on his mind, she'd learned not to move out of his reach. Though she had no idea what drove his need, she knew he needed the closeness their physical contact provided.

On the rare occasions when he was agitated and easily annoyed upon his reappearance, he took his dominance in the bedroom to a stratospheric level. His commands were direct and without mirth. He expected and accepted nothing less than full submission from her. She complied with his instructions the moment they were spoken, offered more than he requested, and bit her tongue. Once he'd worked through what bothered him, he became more like himself again, albeit a more subdued version.

As she stood there in his embrace, she tried to assess his frame of mind. His sexy, playful remark when she opened the door more resembled his usual demeanor. But the way he held her signaled something was different. Something had happened that affected him deeply.

"What are you thinking about, Devon? What's bothering you?" Her tone urged him to talk to her, to share a part of his life she knew nothing about.

His arms tightened around her in response.

"You have to let me in. I *want* to be part of your life."

"Darlin', believe me when I say, you're the *best* part of my life." Though his voice was partially muffled, the sincerity of his words flowed through her, filling her with hope. He lifted her with ease, held her tightly against his chest, and she wrapped her legs around his waist. He sat on the couch and adjusted her position without releasing his hold. He raised his head, met her questioning eyes, and felt compelled to share what he could.

"You know I spent time in the Army, in Special Forces. There's a lot of bad shit going on with a buddy from my old unit. He's more than a friend—he's part of my family. He's the brother I never had. His whole world has just been turned upside down. I have no doubt he can take care of himself. But he doesn't know the people he's mixed up with like he thinks he does—or what they can do to him."

"But you know they're corrupt. Why haven't you told him?"

"Because I can't—not yet anyway."

"I don't understand, Devon. If he's your brother, how can you not warn him about these people? Are you part of them—or in business with them?"

"It's a little more complicated than that, darlin'."

The suspicion in her eyes and the difference in how she looked at him were the very reasons he'd avoided discussing anything to do with the cases he worked. In their three years together, she'd accepted his ambiguous reasons for not calling regularly and the months he wasn't accessible at all. When he explained the classified nature of the missions he carried out in the Army, he implied his current work had the same conditions. But that was the extent of how much he divulged about his job and the activities it required of him.

After hearing he was aware of and involved with shady people, Elle naturally had more questions about his job, about his friends, and even about him. Questions he couldn't answer. Answers he couldn't give. Secrets he couldn't share. His undercover missions lasted months on end at times. But when the assignment concluded, he'd always made his way back to her. There were times his investigations brought him to LA, and though it went against his better judgment, those nights were spent in her bed.

He'd agonized over those decisions. Had he been careful enough not to be seen? Had he inadvertently made her a target? Too many times to count, he'd considered what he'd do if anyone hurt her, especially if he was the reason why. There was no hole deep enough, no island remote enough, and no place too far away for that man to escape the wrath of Shadow's blade. Any shred of information she had about his operations put her in more danger than she could imagine. He'd already crossed a line by sharing what little he'd said.

The hero light she'd always cast over him had begun to dim. The doubts about him started taking root in her mind. She had no idea of the dark, dangerous, and deadly exploits he'd carried out. She was utterly unaware of the horrible acts he was capable of doing—and frequently performed in the line of duty. While he had no qualms about doing whatever the job called for, there were facts about him he never wanted *her* to know.

Yet, he witnessed the skepticism and wariness mix with her feelings for him. He felt her body stiffen ever so slightly when the anger rolled through her, though she tried to hide it. Her eyes narrowed faintly as she pondered her next question—how to ask, and if she genuinely wanted the answer.

"Do you still talk to Jeff?"

"Occasionally."

"Have you told him about us?"

"No, I haven't."

The corners of her eyes squeezed together perceptibly. "Why not?"

"Because I don't feel the need to announce and advertise my private life to anyone."

"Wow." She pushed off his lap to stand in front of him. She ran her fingers through her hair in frustration as she began to pace. "I don't know which statement to be offended by first. That I'm lumped into the 'anyone' category. That you shut me out of your public and private life. Or that there are underhanded people who don't deserve your allegiance, but they seem to know more about you than I do. Beth was right."

And there's the resentment, he thought.

"What was Beth right about?"

"She and I had an argument right before you showed up. About you."

I know. I heard the entire conversation, then disappeared before she walked out. He kept his face impassive, concealing his true thoughts and feelings. "What about me?"

"What are we doing, Devon? What is really happening between us? Are we simply friends with benefits, or do you genuinely have feelings for me?"

Unshed tears glistened in her eyes as she fought with all her might to keep the fears at bay. He watched her chin quiver, her chest rise and fall with the deep breaths she took to calm herself, and the way she squared her shoulders to prepare for his response. She was the most beautiful woman he'd ever seen, inside and out. She deserved so much better than him, so much more than he could give her. But he'd be damned if he could do the gallant thing and walk away to let her move on without him.

"After three years together, you're asking this now? You're asking me if I have feelings for you? Of course I do, Elle. Strong feelings. But my job isn't a conventional nine-to-five, home-for-dinner type of work. There have been so many times I've wanted to tell you everything, but it's because of my feelings for you that I don't share the details of it—for your benefit."

"It doesn't feel like I'm important to you."

"You are not just *anyone* to me, Elle. The only other people who get a glimpse of the real me are the men from my unit. We worked in life-and-death situations twenty-four-seven, so we knew everything there was to know about each other. We were all well-trained for our roles and never let each other down. But even they don't get the side of me I give you.

"Don't think I haven't recognized all the ways you help me when I show up here. You were trying to determine what state my mind was in as soon as I walked in here. The weeks and months I'm away, I miss you every bit as much as you miss me, if not more. I tried to explain to you early on in this relationship how I'd be in and out of town, unreachable at times, but I'd always be back for you."

"You're right. You did tell me that, but I didn't realize it would always be this way."

"What are you saying, Elle? Just spit it out. Lay it on the line so there's no confusion."

"I'm saying I want more than this. I want more than you showing up occasionally, then leaving for extended periods again. I love you, Devon. I've loved you for so long. But if you're telling me we'll never have a full life together, that I'll never know more about you than I do right now...I'm saying I don't know if I can do this anymore."

He stood and walked to her, his once-hidden emotions instantly palpable in his eyes. "Elle, I don't want to lose you. If you're giving me an ultimatum of choosing between you and my job, at this moment, there's no way I can choose. Not tonight anyway. There's too much at stake to walk away now—from you or the job. It's a no-win situation for me. If you love me, give me more time to see this through."

"Give me a time frame. How much more time do you mean? Days? Weeks? Months? Years?"

"At the rate it's going now, it'll only take a couple more weeks to wrap it up once I go back. Of course, anything can happen between now and then."

"Go back where?"

He smiled, knowing she was testing him. "Miami."

"When are you going back?"

"In a couple of days."

"You flew all the way across the country to stay here for a couple of days?"

"I'd fly here from anywhere in the world if it means I'll have a couple of days with you."

Tears spilled over her bottom lashes, and Devon gently wiped them away with the pad of his thumb while he waited for her decision. "Well, that sweet-talking just earned you two weeks. You'd better finish whatever it is you're doing and get back here to me two weeks from the day you leave me. *Two. Weeks. Devon.*"

"Yes, ma'am."

They spent the following forty-eight hours in Elle's bed, only leaving her bedroom to restock their supply of food and drinks. Devon alternated between being dominant and possessive, gentle and affectionate, employing his full arsenal of moves and maneuvers to help remind her how much she missed him when he was away.

He waited until she'd passed out from exhaustion the first night, then raised up on one elbow to watch her sleep. Thoroughly relaxed, she wore a peaceful and contented expression—he'd even dare to say she was truly happy. She'd confessed her true feelings to him when she said those magic words. Naturally, he already knew she was in love with him and had been since their first encounter. No doubt she'd waited for him to confess his undying love first, then decided she couldn't wait any longer when she issued her ultimatum.

"Here's something you don't know about me," he said, his whisper barely audible. "I love you, Elle. You captured my heart that first day in Miami. The first time we made love, I knew I never wanted it back. But you can't know any of this. If the day ever comes that I let you go, believing I don't love you is the only way to make sure you'll stay far away from me."

Neither of them slept the second night. Devon had an early flight out of LA to get back to Miami and finish the job. The hours of driving into her core, slow and deep, didn't quench his desire. It only caused him to crave her more. The taste of her skin, the aroma of her arousal, the sound of her moans and screams were the equivalent of throwing gasoline on a raging fire. Hour after hour, their sweat-slick bodies remained joined as one, drawing out their pleasure and delaying their separation as long as possible.

Just before daylight broke, Devon begrudgingly left her bed to head to the airport, with the promise of returning two weeks later. He settled into the private jet and waited for the pilot and crew to finish their preflight check. The taste of her wet, salty goodbye kiss lingered in his memory. He wasn't likely to forget the feeling of releasing her from his arms either. Every time he had to leave her was harder than the last. That realization drove him to make a decision right then and there.

Once this case was over, he'd resign from the CIA and only work for Steele Security. With the way Noah's company had grown since its inception and continued to thrive, a bicoastal security firm was most definitely in the cards. Ideas formed one after the other, visions of how his life would change created excitement for the future. He spent the flight working up a full plan of attack for their new life together once his current assignment ended.

Wheels down in Miami, his undercover cell immediately began ringing.

"Shadow, our business associates are lined up and ready to move forward with our joint venture. I hope you've kept your promise to me."

"Of course, Richard. Have I ever let you down before?"

"Our meeting with the board of directors is in one week. I need you to be there with me. They want to meet you in person," Richard demanded.

"Let me know where and what time. I'll be there," Shadow replied.

"One of my men will contact you the day of the meeting with the exact location. It's been a pleasure doing business with you."

Richard Hollingsworth had been in the Army with Shadow and his brothers. He was missing for three years, presumed dead, after an illegal arms deal went south on him. He'd recently been released by his captors in the Middle East and was back in the States, in the market for a dirty CIA operative who could reestablish his supply chain without questions. Part of Shadow's covert operation was to be the middle man and take down all the players financing Richard's treasonous acts at once.

"My plans are already falling into place," Shadow said to himself as he jogged down the plane's steps to the tarmac.

After switching to his secure cell, he called Steadman. "Hi, Uncle Steadman. Just wanted to let you know the order for the birthday cake is being placed. They'll call me back later to give me a time to pick it up."

"I hope you ordered the chocolate cake. You know it's my favorite," Steadman replied with a chuckle.

"Is there any other kind? I'll call back later when I have more information. Get the family ready for our big dinner celebration next week. This cake has several layers."

Over the following week, Shadow gave his all to his assignment. He ensured every T was crossed and every I was dotted. The stars seemed to align when the cache of weapons arrived on time, cementing his cover and ensuring the deal would go through as planned. Once the money was exchanged and they took possession of the illegal arms, every federal agency identified by initials would swarm the spot and take them all in.

Then his undercover life would come to an eventful end.

He knew something was wrong when his secure cell began ringing. Those calls were normally one-way only. For Steadman to call him meant there was a major new development in the intelligence community.

"Uncle Steadman, I'm surprised to hear from you. Did you change your mind on the flavor of cake?"

"Shadow," Steadman replied with all seriousness. "He has Reaper's girlfriend, Brianna. He's going to kill her." He rattled off the address of the abandoned warehouse where Richard held Brianna captive.

Shadow glanced at his watch as he sprinted to his car, calculating how long it would take him to reach her. He loved Brianna like a sister and was almost as close to her as he was to Noah. Her only hope of survival was if he intervened, and he knew her death would be more than Noah could endure. His tires slid to a halt behind the warehouse, and he chambered a round in his gun as he ran toward the back door, praying he wasn't too late to stop a cold-blooded murder.

When the plane landed at LAX, Devon walked unhurriedly toward the baggage claim area. He'd lost the spring in his step and the gleam in his eye.

He was in LA to get them both back, along with the love of his life.

After dropping his suitcase off at his hotel room, he drove to her apartment and parked on the street outside. He already knew she wasn't home, but he'd wait until she showed up. If it meant getting down on his knees and begging, then so be it. One way or another, she had to talk to him and hear him out. He was ready to tell her everything.

When a couple of hours had passed and she still hadn't shown up, he turned on the radio to help pass the time. The local station's disc jockey was reporting a celebrity sighting at a trendy new restaurant.

"I just heard the one and only Miss Elle Sinclair is about to roll up in a long, black limousine. I can't even tell you how jealous I am of the guy she's with tonight. She is even hotter in person than she is in the pictures, if you can imagine that. And believe me, I can imagine a lot with her."

The car's engine roared to life, and his foot stomped on the gas pedal, pulling out of his space with peeling tires. The car deftly weaved through traffic, and he ignored blaring horns and angry shouts as he passed the other cars. Luckily, he found an empty parking spot a block away from the restaurant, not caring he'd illegally parked in someone's reserved spot. When he was as close as the throngs of people and photographers would allow him to get, he spotted her exiting the limo.

The man she was with extended his tuxedo-clad arm toward her, and she wrapped her dainty one around it with a beaming smile on her beautiful face. Dressed to kill in a short black dress that clung to her curves and showed off all her best assets, she stopped several times for pictures as the paparazzi yelled one question after another at her.

"Elle, who's your date?"

"Is he an actor?"

"Is he a model?"

"Where did you two meet?"

"Is this a serious relationship?"

"Are you off the market now? Are you exclusive?"

Lightbulbs flashed. People elbowed each other out of the way, vying for the perfect spot to snap the best picture. Young girls screamed Elle's name, yelling they loved her and wanted to be her.

It was the first time he'd seen in person how crazy her fans were over her. He knew she was famous, had hordes of fans, and was sought after for modeling gigs and movie parts. Living in the limelight was a foreign concept that he thought he was ready for and had a handle on. But that was before he watched that scene unfold. He realized even if he left the CIA, he couldn't be recognizable to that degree and still be effective as a security team member.

Their lives were just too different. Regardless of how much they tried to make it work, it was still as if they were attempting to fit a square peg in a round hole. It would never be as good as it should be. And he couldn't hold her back from happiness anymore. She'd moved on, though he'd never had the chance to explain that he was two weeks late because he'd saved Brianna from being shot, but her condition had been touch and go for a while. He couldn't leave Brianna, Noah, or his assignment until all the loose ends were tied up. He'd called repeatedly and left messages, but Elle wouldn't accept them.

Seeing how happy she was with her new date seemed to explain why he couldn't reach her. It was time to let her go, so she could have her career and the type of relationship she wanted. With a heavy heart, he drove back to his hotel, considering what his next move would be. Leaving the life of a spy was a definite. He'd had enough of that world to last a lifetime.

"To what do I owe the pleasure?" Steadman asked as a way of a greeting. "You're not on a sanctioned assignment."

"I'm calling in my 10-42."

"That's not funny, Shadow."

"No, it's not. This is my official end tour of duty notice. I'm not accepting missions as of now."

"Shadow," a stern voice replaced Steadman's. "What the hell is this?"

"This is my official resignation. I don't know where the confusion is. I quit."

"Your leave is approved. No one quits the CIA. We'll be in touch when we need you. Keep the phone. Don't make us have to find you."

The line went dead, and he chuckled a humorless laugh. "Well, that went better than I expected."

After finding there were no flights available until the following afternoon, he lay on his back on the bed, staring at the ceiling. The pictures in magazines and on television of Elle with other men over the prior three years had been bad enough, even though he knew she was his. But seeing her earlier was different. It wasn't a movie promotion or a platonic date to a premiere. She'd moved on without him, and as much as he wanted to wait at her apartment for her, he knew himself too well.

His personal cell woke him from a restless sleep. At first, he thought he'd let it roll to voice mail, but a glance at the name on the screen made him scramble to answer it instead.

"Hello."

"Devon? I swore I wouldn't do this when you didn't show up, but I can't move on without having this talk with you. Tell me it's over. Tell me you don't want me. Tell me I don't mean anything to you," Elle demanded through slightly slurred words.

His mind yelled at him to tell her what she wanted so she'd finally be happy without him. But his heart was selfish and couldn't lie to her. Wouldn't lie to her. "I can't tell you any of those things, Elle."

Her watery reply drove a searing hot knife through his heart. "You don't want me, but you don't want anyone else to have me either. Is that it?"

"No, that's not it at all. In fact, if you're finished with your date for the night, why don't you come on over to my hotel room and I'll show you how much I don't want you."

"How did you know about my date?"

"Because I'm fucking here and watched you walk into the restaurant on the arm of another man." His teeth were clenched together as he spoke, and the muscles in his jaw jumped in anger. "And I have called you, repeatedly, but you haven't answered any of them."

"Why were you late?"

"Because my friend's fiancée was in the hospital, fighting for her life, and I couldn't just leave them. Wrapping up the job took a little longer than I thought it would, but then I told you that was a possibility when I was here last time."

"My phone was mysteriously misplaced when I woke up on day fifteen. My assistant ordered a new phone, with a new number, and none of my existing contacts would download to my new phone for some odd reason. I tore Beth's room apart tonight until I found my old phone. Where are you?"

"Already on my way to you."

CHAPTER TEN

Three Years Earlier

One button at a time, he moved down the front of her blouse. His eyes stayed locked on hers, establishing his dominance and enjoying every second of it. Her arms hung loosely at her sides as he'd instructed, submissive regardless of how badly she wanted to speed things along. They'd been apart for too long and she was dying to touch him, but he loved how making her wait only increased her eagerness for him.

"I can almost hear your thoughts, Elle," Devon chided gently. "Are you trying to will me to go faster with your mind?"

"I would never, Devon. That would rob you of your favorite part—building the anticipation of what you're planning to do to me."

One eyebrow lifted in amusement, along with one side of his lips. She'd repeated his words from another time together back to him almost verbatim. "To be honest, that's not my favorite part. But it does rank fairly high on the list."

"You do have more self-control than anyone I've ever met. You'll have to share some of that with me one day."

"What I want to share with you has nothing to do with my self-control. You can have all you want."

He pushed her shirt off her shoulders and let it fall to the floor. Her bra quickly followed, leaving her standing completely bare to him. Exactly the way he wanted her. He bent his head and sucked her nipple into his mouth. The warmth of his tongue laved it, tasting and teasing with each pass. Her peak hardened and his teeth grazed over it, eliciting a moan of pleasure from deep inside her chest.

"Touch me," he instructed, and she readily complied. Her fingers wrapped around his girth and stroked back and forth along his length. "That's my girl. You don't know how many times I've had to do this myself, while thinking of you."

Her knees suddenly buckled when his fingers found her wet center. When he plunged them inside her without warning, the intensity of the welcome intrusion stole her breath. As he pumped his fingers deep inside her, his mouth continued to work magic on her breasts, giving ample and equal attention to both. One of her hands kept stroking him while the other gripped his shoulder tightly as his ministrations brought her closer to the edge of her climax.

"Oh my God, Devon!"

Before her body had recovered, he was on his knees in front of her, pushing her legs farther apart. "That was one. You'll give me several more tonight."

Before she could reply, his mouth covered her core. His warm tongue circled her clit, deliberately avoiding making direct contract with the most sensitive spot on her body. He leisurely trailed his finger along her slit with just enough pressure to let her know he was there. Waiting for him to take his attentions to the next level was sweet torture, but she knew he'd make her wait longer if she asked for it.

Patience, my girl. Have I ever left you anything but completely satisfied? He'd asked that the first few times she'd tried to rush him, before she learned her lesson and let him have his way with her in the bedroom. Or the living room. Or outside, depending on where they were when they'd reunited.

She watched with rapt attention as he pulled her leg over his shoulder. He smirked up at her, his smile smug and knowing, and she couldn't contain her smile.

"You're trying to rush me again. For the record, I'm not making you wait because of how badly I want to taste you. But you'll have to be punished for that later."

"I didn't say a word," she replied through a giggle. "I've been a good girl."

"It's the thought that counts," he countered, his smug smile still in place.

She knew better than to argue any further, so she let him believe he'd won that round. While he enjoyed being the dominant one, the aggressor, he certainly didn't mind when she took charge to please him. She'd easily learned how to distract him, and in doing so, she'd enjoyed even more pleasure at his hand...and mouth...and enormous cock. While her mind momentarily wandered to their other escapades, he effectively brought her back to the present with a swift move.

Simultaneously, he sucked hard on her clit and thrust two fingers deep into her channel. Her inner muscles clamped around his fingers while her essence soaked his hand. His tongue licked and lapped her, and he pulled her closer to him until she straddled his face. She grasped his hair, tugging with abandon as each wave rolled through her. Her hips moved of their own accord, riding out the force of her orgasm, and she threw her head back when she screamed in pleasure.

"Mmm," he hummed against her. "That's number two."

One strong arm circled her, lifted her, and carried her to the bedroom. He lay on his back, his erection standing tall and proud, and he waggled his eyebrows at her. "Ready to go for a wild and wet ride?"

While taking in the perfect male form stretched out on her bed, she licked her lips instinctively. "I'm more than ready."

"Do that again."

She met his gaze with confusion. "Do what again, love?"

"Lick your lips like you're dying to take every inch of my cock down your throat."

"Now that you mention it," she purred seductively and crawled up his body. Poised over his thick cock, she repeated licking her lips in an exaggerated manner and watched his eyes darken with desire. With his recent torture of her in mind, she took her time exploring him. She ran her tongue lightly around the rim of his head, reveling in the way all his muscles tightened with her slightest touch.

When his eyes were squeezed shut, she opened her mouth widely and took him in fully, the tip hitting the back of her throat. Each time he drew in a harsh breath, the air barely passing over his gritted teeth, she increased her pressure and tempo. His hips bucked, rising to meet her movements, and his hands gripped her hair. "Fuck, darlin'. This kills me to say, but you have to stop."

"Oh? And why would I do that?"

"Because as much as I love the feel of your soft, warm mouth wrapped around me, it's been too damn long since I've been inside that sweet little pussy of yours. I plan on wearing it out tonight. And tomorrow night. Hell, every night I'm here with you. So, what are you waiting for? Climb on board."

With her sly smile in place, she straddled his lap and hovered over him. Her hand wrapped around his cock firmly and guided him to her waiting entrance. The slight burn of her body stretching to accept his size only increased her yearning for him. She slid down his length and stilled for a second when he was fully seated inside her. Her hips began rocking back and forth, then side to side. His fingers gripped her hips just before he began thrusting upward. She leaned back slightly, throwing her head back and focusing on the pleasure, when his thumb found her clit.

The mixture of erotic stimulation caused stars to ignite into fireworks behind her closed eyes. As she pushed down, he plunged upward. The erotic connection in the middle hit the spot every time, with each pulse building into an overpowering culmination before they reached the summit and tumbled over together. Elle fell forward, lying on his chest, as they fought to catch their breath and slow their speeding hearts.

"That was amazing," she said groggily, her energy spent. "I don't have the strength to move now, so I'm sleeping right here all night."

"Sounds like a wonderful idea to me. When I wake up in the middle of the night, you'll be in the perfect position to start all over again."

"Devon, I could sleep cocooned inside a mummy sleeping bag, and you'd say I was in the perfect position."

"Well, you are very fuckable no matter what position you're in. I'll give you that one."

Wrapped in his arms, warmed by the natural heat of his body, she fell into a deep sleep with her cheek resting on his chest. Hours later, she was pulled from a beautiful dream by a noise that seemed far away at first. When she gained her bearings, she realized the noises were coming from Devon.

He was talking in his sleep. Unintelligible words at first. Nothing she could make out to understand what he dreamed about. Then the next words, spoken with a more forceful tone, caught her full attention.

"Ava? Ava, no! Don't leave me. Stay with me, Ava. Stay with me."

~

"Are you ready, superstar?" Devon asked playfully. "Have you penciled me in for the weekend on your appointment calendar?"

"No, I most certainly have not penciled you in," Elle replied, mock offense rife in her tone. "That's my assistant's job. Those menial tasks are beneath me."

"My knee is the only thing that'll be beneath you. When I turn you over it and spank that ass for being so sassy with me."

"You love it when I'm sassy, and you know it."

"I can't deny it. I do love that sassy mouth of yours."

A flash of disappointment passed over her eyes for a split second before she tamped it down. "Okay, I'm packed and ready to go. I can't believe you're actually taking a whole weekend off from your six different cell phones."

"It's kind of hard not to take the weekend off when we're going to your parents and they live in the middle of nowhere. One of the last places on Earth that doesn't have cell reception." He shook his head in disgust and picked up their suitcases. "Move that fine ass. We have a three-hour drive ahead of us. Six if I have to pull over on the side of the road and have my wicked way with you."

"We are not stopping on the side of the road to have sex before we go spend the weekend with my parents and brothers." She put her hands on her hips and dared him to argue with her stern expression.

"Spoilsport," he muttered on his way out the door.

In the car on their way north to the vineyard country, they chatted mindlessly about anything and everything. When she could no longer take not knowing, she prepared herself to ask him about Ava. They'd never verbally agreed to an exclusive relationship, but that had always been Elle's expectation. From Devon's reaction to her going on a meaningless date with another man, she believed he'd felt the same.

"What's on your mind? Let's have it." Devon cut his eyes over to her.

"How do you always know?"

"It's my job to know, darlin'. What's bothering you?"

"Something you said in your sleep last night," she admitted.

He turned his head toward her, waiting to see the laughter in her eyes. But she was dead serious. "I talked in my sleep? What did I say?"

"You asked Ava not to leave you," she replied quietly. "Who is Ava?"

"Not who you think she is, darlin'. I know it bothers you, but I need you to trust me. I want to tell you about her, but not right now—not in the car. She's not an old flame by any stretch of the imagination, if that helps calm your mind."

From the way his naturally bronzed skin paled at the mention of Ava's name, Elle believed he spoke the truth. The innate happiness that was usually clear in his eyes had dimmed, leaving a sadness she'd never seen in them before that moment. Whoever Ava was, and whatever made her leave him, left a profound impact on him. Elle was confident he'd tell her everything when the time was right. As far as she was concerned, he'd always been true to his word.

"Okay, Devon. You can tell me later, when you're ready. I'll be here."

He gripped her hand in his, pulled it to his mouth, and pressed his lips to the back of it tenderly. "You have no idea how much that means to me, Elle. Knowing you're here for me. Some days, it's all I have."

"When are you going to tell me what your work involves? What you do. Where you go. Why you only show up for a few weeks or days at a time, then leave again. Even after all this time, there's still so much I don't know about you. But you know everything there is to know about me."

"It's not fair, I know, and I'm truly sorry it has to be this way. My occupation is dangerous, to say the least, and has always demanded unquestionable loyalty. My path hasn't been as well-lit as yours. When you step outside, hundreds of bright lights from cameras flash from every direction to capture a glimpse of you. My world has been in the shadows, where I'm invisible."

"That's why you refuse to be photographed with me? Because of your job?"

A mixture of pain and relief permeated her tone, instinctively prompting him to jerk his gaze to hers. "I'm such a fucking idiot. Darlin', I never realized I'd hurt you over that. My...activities...mandate I stay out of the public eye. I've gone to great lengths to keep my fugly mug out of the papers. If I could, I'd be in every picture with you. The world would know without a doubt you're mine."

"Does your world know you're mine?" She dared to ask, taking a gamble with her heart in a new way.

"To protect you, my world doesn't know you're associated with me in any way. But I think what you're really asking me is if the other ladies of the world know I'm yours. The answer is no, they don't know anything about you. Or me, for that matter." He paused and looked at her again. "But *I* know who has my heart, Elle. That's all that matters."

Devon turned onto a long, winding driveway lined with sycamore trees and followed it through the rolling hills covered with rows upon rows of grapevines. Danny and Tanya Moore had bought the one-hundred-thirty-acre property soon after they'd migrated west and transformed it into a family business. Their son Mark had successfully managed and built the winery operations, establishing a lucrative vintner's private reserve with a long waiting list.

"Look who beat us here," Elle remarked, inclining her head toward the car parked outside the garage.

Devon's disbelief over what sat directly before his eyes prevented his keen eyes from identifying it first.

"What are my parents doing here?"

Elle laughed out loud, leaned forward in her seat, and fixed her eyes on his shocked expression. "I can't believe I actually pulled it off. You've always known when I've tried to hide anything from you. Not this time, though. My acting skills are definitely improving."

"You're an incredibly bad distraction, because there's no way I'm losing my touch. I'll just have to watch you closer and use different tactics in the future. Now, seriously, what are they doing here?"

"They're vacationing at my parents' house for a couple of weeks. They don't get to see each other as often as they'd like. Or you, from what they've told me." Elle pierced him with her perceptive stare.

"Sometimes I have to choose between going to visit them in Georgia or you in California. The odds of me picking *anyone* over you are slim to none, darlin'."

"You're going to blame me when we get inside, aren't you?"

"Abso-fucking-lutely." He grinned, and the mischief sparkled in his eyes.

Ready to face both families and get the questions out of the way, they exited the car and walked to the front door hand in hand. Elle glanced over her shoulder at Devon when she crossed the threshold into the sprawling home. "Are you ready for this?"

"As ready as I'll ever be."

A concurrence of laughter and voices engaged in multiple conversations at once echoed off the walls, emanating from the kitchen. Elle was greeted by a moment of silence when the families realized she'd arrived. Then the entire group jumped to their feet and rushed to Elle and Devon upon seeing them together. Hugs, handshakes, and squeals of delight filled the home—along with love.

"Devon, what are you doing here?" Tracey, his mom, asked as she wrapped her arms around him.

"Do you want me to leave?" he asked playfully and started moving toward the door.

"No!" She laughed and shook her head. "You know what I meant. How did you even know we were here?"

"He didn't have a clue until we were already here and I told him," Elle bragged. "I was finally able to keep a secret from him after all these years we've been seeing each other."

Devon shut his eyes tight and winced, waiting for the onslaught of questions to begin.

"Years?" Tracey's whirled back to Devon. "You've been seeing each other for *years,* and I'm just now hearing about it?"

Without even looking at Elle, he felt the heartache radiating off her from his mother's innocent declaration. Elle turned on her heel and started to walk away, but he caught her before she could get away. One muscled arm circled around her waist and pulled her back to his front, holding her firmly against his chest. His other arm wrapped around her, securing his hold. With his chin resting lightly on her shoulder, he kissed her sweetly on the cheek.

"That's right, Mom. Elle and I have been together since just before her twenty-first birthday. She came to Miami while I was working there, and we've been together ever since."

"You never tell me anything, Devon," Tracey accused, her finger pointed at him and her other hand on her hip. "I hope you don't keep everything a secret from Elle like you do from me."

"Tracey, stop harassing our son. We haven't seen him in months, and now it'll be months before he comes home again." Phil, Devon's father, affectionately pulled his wife into his arms. "How long are you staying?"

"However long Elle says we're staying." He squeezed her gently, attempting to elicit a response.

"Unfortunately, with the tight production schedule, we can only stay a few days. I'll have to get back to review the script changes, meet with the other cast members, and get my costumes fitted."

"You're here now, so let's make the most of it. We were just about to have dinner, so you got here just in time." Tanya led the group back to the table and grabbed extra place settings for Elle and Devon while the others began filling their plates.

"That was a subtle change of plans," Devon murmured under his breath.

"Yeah, well, that was a blatant slap in the face that Tracey didn't know about me after four years," she retorted.

Tracey and Tanya carried on a separate conversation that quickly silenced all the other sidebars. With all eyes and ears on them, they continued talking, unaware they held the room's engrossed attention.

"Mom and I had to have 'the talk' the other day. I think that was the hardest conversation I've ever had in my life," Tracey said.

"What do you mean 'the talk'?" Devon asked.

She met Devon's inquisitive gaze with a heavy heart. "She's declining quickly, son. We had to talk about her end-of-life wishes before it's too late. I needed to know exactly what she wants so we can respect her needs. She already has the burial plot beside Dad, but she didn't have an advance directive for medical procedures. We completed one together and sent it to all her doctors. Afterward, we hugged and cried for a solid fifteen minutes."

"I want to be cremated when I die," Devon announced definitively and impassively. Tracey and Elle both gaped at him over his announcement. "What?"

"You're too young. Don't even joke about that." Tracey shuddered, the mere thought too much to bear.

"I'm serious. Any of us could go at any time. If you needed to know Grandma's wishes, you need to know mine, too. I want to be cremated—it's important to me. I've left specific instructions that will be delivered to you, but I also want you to hear it from me."

The conversation continued, taking natural twists and turns, until they had covered a broad spectrum of topics. While Elle joined in, listening to their parents share amusing and embarrassing stories from both her and Devon's childhoods and laughing along with them, she mentally pieced together the brief glimpses she'd gained into his secret life. The sum of each individual part added up to one disturbing conclusion.

His work is dangerous.

He lives in the shadows.

He avoids photographs.

He hides me from his world to protect me.

He has "in case of death" instructions.

Who is Devon Kane? Do I even know him?

CHAPTER ELEVEN

One Year Earlier

"Elle Sinclair, best known for her supermodel days, had her big break on the big screen with minor, but memorable, secondary characters. Confidential sources have told us that's all about to change. One of Hollywood's most influential leading men, Matt Lane himself, has specifically requested Elle be his leading lady in the highly anticipated romantic comedy.

"Filming is scheduled to begin late next month, but the beautiful pair has been spotted together several times already. Is it too early to hope this pairing is more than just great casting? We may be looking at Hollywood royalty in the making. We'll keep our eyes on this couple and bring you more updates as they become available."

Watching television normally bored Shadow to tears, but seeing Elle cozied up to Hollywood's "good guy" on the nightly entertainment news certainly caught his attention. With his eyes glued to the screen, his hands curled into fists, and his nostrils flaring from agitation, he watched Matt put his arm around Elle's waist and pull her into his side. When she curled into Matt willingly, Shadow's blood began to boil. But when Matt placed a lingering kiss on Elle's cheek, Shadow finally moved.

"Hey, Reap. Just wanted to let you know I'll be away for a couple of weeks. I'll call you when I get back."

"No problem. Everything okay?"

"Yeah. Just a few things I need to take care of."

After he finished talking to Noah, he called Steadman.

"Shadow, my man. What do you have for me today?"

"I'll be off the grid for a couple of weeks. Don't send anything my way because I won't be checking in at all."

After a few clicks on his laptop, his ticket to LAX was booked. Then he started planning the ultimate destination—and that place didn't include *Matt Lane*. With his surprise plans securely in place, he threw his clothes into a suitcase and hurried to the airport. Every element of his actions went against the grain of his personality.

He didn't make rash decisions. He always carefully planned every move he made.

He only appeared to be spontaneous. Every move and countermove were considered ahead of time.

Logic ruled his mind, heart, and actions. He wasn't a slave to his emotions. Rational thinking, sound decision-making skills, and careful analysis of every possible outcome had kept him alive in some of the worst places in the world.

All the years of extensive training and having the rules of working undercover drilled into his subconscious evaporated where Elle was concerned. No risk was too great, no stakes were too high, no matter what the cost to himself would be. She was worth it. She was more than worth it—she was the only light he could see at the end of his tunnel.

It appeared the only thing he couldn't do for her was the very thing she'd asked of him. He couldn't stay away from her and give her the time apart like she'd requested. He'd stayed away for as long as he could stand, and seeing her happy with another man was the tipping point. There was no doubt he'd pay the price of her wrath when he showed up out of the blue, demanding she see him. Even more so when he sprang the tickets to Jade Mountain in St. Lucia. For two. For two weeks of total seclusion.

His life of secrecy and disappearing with no word for weeks on end had taken an adverse toll on their relationship. Questions gave way to suspicions. The silence between them became deafening. He couldn't say the words she needed to hear, and she couldn't accept the way their lives had to be.

"Devon." She'd begun tentatively, and he read the signs of what was to come next. "There's still so much I don't know about you. Where you go. What you do. I feel like an outsider in your life, when I want nothing more than to know everything about you."

"I know you do, Elle. I don't know what to say to make you feel better about us."

She wrung her hands, and tears shimmered in her eyes. "This isn't working for me, Devon. As much as I want it to, as much as I love you, this isn't the life I want. We need some time apart to reevaluate our relationship and what we want out of it."

Devon nodded slowly. Not agreeing with her, but giving himself an extra moment to rein in his feelings before he spoke. "Time apart to reevaluate our relationship," he repeated. "How much time will that take? How much more time do you need apart from me than you already have?"

"I don't want you to come back until I call you. I don't know how long it'll take, but I can't constantly watch for you to show up and live my life at the same time. The longest we've been apart is four months—"

"That only happened once, and it couldn't be helped. I explained that to you."

"You did—you said it couldn't be helped. That's the only explanation you gave. Knowing how I felt at the end of those four months, I'm guessing I should know one way or another after six months apart."

"You want me to stay away for six months while you decide if you want me to come back at all?" The timbre of his voice lowered while the volume raised. He ran his fingers through his hair and clasped his hands behind his neck before releasing a forced exhale.

The tears spilled over her lower lids and slid down her cheeks. One quickly followed the previous, soaking her cheeks and leaving her eyes red and swollen. "Yes. But I understand if you'd rather end it now."

She's testing me, he thought. *Will I wait for her like she's waited for me so many times? Yes, Elle, I will wait for you however long it takes to prove my love for you.*

"Six months it is, then. I'll stay away until you call. When I hear from you, I'll run back to your side."

Unable to walk away without one more taste, he pressed his lips to hers, skimmed his tongue along the part in her mouth, and plunged inside when she gave him the slightest opportunity. Salty tears mixed with the heady flavor that belonged solely to Elle.

With a step backward serving as the foreboding symbol of their relationship, he left her apartment and her life, giving her the time and space she needed. He gave her what she asked of him to prove his love was real. He was willing to do for her what she'd always done for him—wait, and welcome her back with open arms when she was ready.

But seeing her with Matt Lane made him realize that proving he loved her hadn't been her plan at all. He'd misread her intentions completely. The time of separation was her chance to move on without him, to forget what they'd had, and to leave all the memories of their time together in the past. Moving on would be easier with someone new to occupy her time and her mind.

And her bed.

Then, Matt Lane would be a dead man.

Hours later, the plane landed at LAX, and he made a mad dash to Elle's apartment. His heavy fist beat on the door, demanding entrance.

"Let me in, or I'll break the door down and come in anyway. I know you're in there."

The deadbolt turned, unlocking the door, and she slowly opened it. "What are you doing here, Devon? I haven't called you."

"That's exactly why I'm here. You've tried to forget me, but it won't work. You love me, Elle. You've loved me too long to stop, and I won't let you just walk away from me without putting up one hell of a fight for you. I tried to give you space and time to come to this conclusion on your own. But you're too stubborn and headstrong. So if I have to camp out here in the hallway outside your door until you come to your senses, so be it."

She sighed deeply. "Come on in."

"Good call," he replied and stepped into the room. "Now, go pack. We're going away for two weeks. You won't need many clothes."

"Have you lost your mind? I'm not going away with you. I haven't seen or talked to you in months."

"That was your idea, not mine. You wanted that, I didn't."

"I needed it for my own sanity."

"Are you happy without me?" He crossed his arms over his chest and dared her to lie.

"No. I'm not any happier at all. I'm miserable, and I'm driving Beth crazy."

"Beth needs a break from you for two uninterrupted weeks. Come away with me."

"Bikinis, sand, and surf?" She knew him too well. His idea of uninterrupted paradise would be somewhere warm, with tropical breezes, the bare minimum of clothes, and no cell or internet access.

"You know it, darlin'."

Elle questioned her sanity while packing her suitcase. He just showed up after more than four months apart, and she was right back in the same position as if they'd never been apart. She couldn't resist him—didn't even want to. There was a certain romantic element to the way he insisted they couldn't remain apart. She wanted to believe him. More than anything she'd ever wanted in her life, she wanted to believe what he'd said. Her heart was convinced, but her mind still had serious doubts their lives would ever progress past the rut they'd been stuck in for ages.

"You won't regret it," he said from behind her.

She turned to face him. His hip was leaned against the doorframe, his eyes drinking her in from top to bottom, obviously delighted to see her again. His self-control was at all all-time high. From his heated gaze and darkened eyes, she knew he wanted nothing more than to entangle his body with hers so thoroughly they'd never be separate again. But he was still giving her time and space—in his own way.

"Reading my mind again?" She kept her voice low and quiet. Uncertainty clouded her mind and her judgment.

His thoughtful expression gave her an unusual insight into his thoughts and feelings. "Something like that. I know you, Elle, and while you think you don't know me, nothing could be further from the truth. You know I always find my way back to you. Even if you question everything else, you know there's nothing I wouldn't do for you."

"Where are we going?" She knew his words were meant to help heal—but they only seemed to cut deeper. She turned back to packing her clothes, anything to avoid his scrutiny.

Before she even felt his presence or his hands on her arms, he'd whirled her around to face him. He held her firmly in his grasp, as if he thought she'd try to escape from him. So many times, he'd almost told her what kept him away. That was one of those times when he wanted to blurt it all out. The covert missions. The classified details. The undercover assignments. He wanted to tell her everything. Would she even believe him? Some of the details of his life and what he'd encountered were beyond belief in the normal realm of civilian existence.

When he'd turned in his resignation to Steadman through the end of watch code, he had hope they'd allow him simply to walk away. No more clandestine missions, infiltrating areas angels feared to tread. No more eluding questions from family and friends. He'd be home for every holiday and special occasion.

He'd had high hopes for a normal life.

The CIA had other plans for him. A highly trained, seasoned assassin who'd had access to every secret the country had, along with those of several other countries, was not someone they were prepared to just let go. When he'd first joined, many members had given him the same dire warning. "You can never really quit the CIA." He soon realized what they meant: "You can quit when you die." Since he wasn't ready for that extreme measure, he answered when they called.

The two weeks away with Elle had been taken without negotiation. He'd learned the best way to avoid having his plans interrupted was not to share them until the very last second. By the time they were in the air, he would be completely unreachable, and all his attention would be hers. Until then, he knew he had to give her more reason to go away with him before she changed her mind. She was on the cusp of walking away from him forever.

"We're going to spend two weeks away from everyone and everything else in the world. We're going to discover and rediscover everything about each other all over again. We're going to remember why we're together, why we first got together, why we've stayed together, and why we'll always be together. After the next two weeks, if you still want me to leave, I'll stay away and you'll never see me again. I guarantee it."

"Remembering how much I love you and why I do isn't the problem, Devon. But you have two weeks." *You have two weeks to convince me you love me.*

"We have two weeks." He bent his knees to put them both at eye level. "I can't wait to steal you away."

"You picked the perfect time. Filming starts soon on the movie with Matt Lane. When that starts, I won't be able to get away for several months."

His eyebrows twitched ever so slightly, but she caught the movement nonetheless. That small gesture gave his thoughts away completely.

"That's why you're here. You believed all the rumors about Matt and me being a couple. Unbelievable." She twisted out of his grip and stepped away. "This is about you claiming what you think belongs to you, isn't it?"

"No. It's really very simple. I don't want to lose you. This isn't what I want at all—I don't want us to be apart. And I sure as hell don't want you to be with another man. But if you're with me, I want it to be because that's what you want, too."

She exhaled sharply, releasing her exasperation as she gripped the suitcase. Her thoughts vacillated between telling him to leave and giving him the two weeks, for no other reason than she'd never have to wonder "what if." She dropped her chin to her chest and shook her head. "Okay, Devon. Two weeks it is. When do we leave?"

"Tomorrow morning."

"Not wasting any time, are you?"

"Not one minute."

The following morning came both too soon and not fast enough. Devon kept his arm draped over Elle all night, his front to her back. Though, he didn't sleep much, with his desire for her trying to take control of his willpower. But the last idea he wanted to reinforce in her mind was the assumption he only wanted to claim his property. Much more was at stake than his ego or pride. Their two weeks in a private island retreat would provide ample time to show her how he felt about her.

Before the sun rose, Devon was up and showered, ready to depart on their early-morning flight. Elle soon joined him in the living room, the tension between them still thick with uncertainty for the future.

"You still haven't told me exactly where we're going." Elle broke the heavy silence between them by focusing on the positive aspect of the situation.

"It's a secret. I can't tell you until we get there." He winked at her and smiled broadly, clearly pleased with himself.

Elle fought to tamp down the mistrust and stabbing pain in her heart from having one more secret between them. Even one she should appreciate—like a two-week exotic vacation.

"There are people who need to know where I am and when I'll return, Devon. There are contract clauses I'm required to honor, last-minute engagements that may come up, and someone will need to provide a statement for my absence. Even if I wanted to escape from everyone and everything, I wouldn't shirk my responsibilities and just disappear off the face of the earth. Other people depend on me to uphold my commitments."

The more she talked, the angrier she became that she even had to explain those simple facts to him. Facts that anyone else who had spent time in her life would already know about her. Yet the very man she'd devoted years to loving didn't give a second thought to the career she'd worked hard to build.

"We're going to St. Lucia. We're staying at Jade Mountain. Do you need to leave the number to the hotel with anyone? Beth, or your parents?" He gave her a card he retrieved from his shirt pocket. It contained all the information anyone would need to know about their location. Flight numbers, times, phone numbers, and the dates they'd be away.

"You knew I'd ask for this."

"Of course. You don't think I'd need to leave the same information with others, too?"

"I'm sorry. I obviously wasn't thinking straight. This is all happening so fast, and I still don't know what to make of it."

"We'll slow down to island time when we get there. Can we call a truce for now? When we land and you see it for yourself, you can decide if you want to be trapped in a tropical paradise with me for two weeks."

"Truce."

Island time sounded perfect to Elle. She slowed her racing thoughts long enough to study Devon intentionally for the first time in many months. She memorized every feature and expression that crossed his face. She began to realize his outward actions didn't always reflect what his eyes revealed to her. An odd thought popped into her mind from nowhere.

He is actually a very skilled actor. The only people he can't fool are those who know him best.

She suspected those people were few and far between, and she questioned if even she fell into that category.

I suppose I'll know for sure two weeks from today.

She rose and left a note for Beth on the kitchen counter, instructing her to share Elle's whereabouts with her assistant and her agent. Devon waited at the door until she'd finished, then carried their bags down to the waiting taxi.

Once they were in the air, she expressed her delight over flying first class. "You keep spoiling me like this, I'll start to expect it all the time."

"This is nothing compared to what awaits you, darlin'. You'll never want to leave once you see it."

"You know, it just occurred to me you flew across the country to my apartment, only to fly east again to the island. That's a lot of time in the air."

"You're worth every second of it. I've already told you there's nothing I wouldn't do for you. All you have to do is say the word."

"That's it? Just say the word, and it's mine?"

"Absolutely."

"What is the secret word that unlocks this magical treasure trove?"

"It's no secret, Elle. You own my heart. Whatever you need from me is yours, whenever you need it."

There, in his eyes, was the truth that matched his words. He'd never actually said the words "I love you," but she couldn't deny she'd always loved him. And she always would. Time and distance hadn't diminished her feelings in the least. She leaned over and placed a long kiss on his lips, savoring the moment of truth and the time they had to spend together.

CHAPTER TWELVE

The resort was more magnificent than she could've imagined in her most luxurious dreams. The sweeping mountainside suites featured a wall completely open to the elements and provided a stunning view of the twin volcanic peaks and the Caribbean Sea. At the edge of the open-air suite sanctuary was a private infinity pool, providing the guests an incredible sense of floating out into nature.

When Elle entered their expansive suite, she was instantly awestruck. One room flowed directly into another, so the panoramic view was never obscured. Entering that room felt as if she were entering an entirely new world. The sparkling water, the lush green trees, and the steep peaks of the mountains transported her to a place where stress and worries couldn't exist.

"Devon, this is...beyond words. There's no way I'll want to leave after being here for two weeks. I don't want to leave after being here for two seconds. Can we get lost in the jungle and stay here forever?"

"The *rain forest* is amazing. Forget the real world exists. Erase any memory of responsibilities waiting for us back home. Spend every day right here on this amazing island, exploring every inch of it and each other. Making love at all hours of the day and night. Having you all to myself and never sharing you with anyone else."

"The same goes for you," she retorted. "No more disappearing on me. By my side every day and night."

"You'd get tired of me real fast."

She looked over her shoulder, meeting his gaze. "Never."

They reached for each other at the same time. Arms encircled, lips clashed, and tongues demanded entrance. Hands moved with fluid precision, shedding clothes with no regard to where they landed. The urgency to have, hold, and feel each other commanded them, demanding their submission.

His arms slid down her back, and his hands cupped her ass and lifted her off the floor. She wrapped her legs around his waist and held on to him, their mouths fused together in an erotic union while he moved to the wall. With her back pushed against it and her legs tight around him, he freed one hand and reached down between her legs. His fingers, long and deft, found her wet center and gently pushed inside. The whimper that escaped her throat urged him on until her soft moans became cries of ardent passion.

"I love the fucking sexy sounds you make when you come. They're music to my ears, and this song will be on repeat all night."

He moved to the bed and set her down on the edge. On his knees in front of her, he buried his face between her legs. His warm, wet tongue licked up her slit before pushing inside to taste her fully. On cue, her eyes closed and her head dropped back. He wrapped his arms around her legs, his fingers gripped her thighs, and he pushed them up and farther apart. Her arms folded, and she gently fell backward until she lay flat on the bed.

His tongue circled and tantalized her clit while one hand traced her entrance, teasing her pussy until she'd coated his fingers with her desire. When he forcefully sucked her clit into his mouth, he thrust his fingers deep inside her waiting channel. She gripped his hair tightly, instinctively drawing him closer to her. He increased the tempo and pressure of his dual assault until her screams filled the air. When he'd lapped up every bit of her ecstasy, he raised his eyes and met hers.

A slow, sexy smile spread across his handsome face. His eyes were so dark blue, they looked almost black. Knowing he'd only begun and had so many more plans for ravaging her body made the butterflies in her stomach turn somersaults.

"Fuck, that is the best sound in the world. I need to record that and listen to it while we have phone sex."

"As long as no one else hears it."

"My thoughts exactly. I'd kill a man for less than that."

His words should've given her pause, but when he lowered his head and began again, all logical thought and reasoning left her faculties. The feel of his mouth on her, so intimate yet so intense, rendered her speechless and incoherent. The orgasm built in increasing levels until it ripped through her with an unstoppable ferocity. The swirling and thrusting of his tongue mixed with the filling and stretching sensation of his fingers was too much to handle. The addictive part was that every time with Devon was equally as thrilling and pleasing. Every time, her body was left spent and satisfied. Every time was better than the last.

"Mmm, you taste so good." His lips brushed against her pussy as he spoke. His deep voice reverberated against her thighs, sending chills up her spine.

"You've set my body on fire. I don't think I can bear for you to touch me right now." Her words came out in a breathy staccato. "That was intense."

"I'm just getting warmed up. That was my appetizer."

"Now it's time for mine," she replied. She tugged on his hand lightly, and he let her pull him onto the bed beside her. She moved down his muscular chest and rippled stomach, leaving a wet, open mouthed swath of kisses until she reached his cock. It was standing at attention, hard and proud, when she wrapped her fingers around it. She slid her hand up and down the shaft while circling the head with her tongue, simultaneously teasing and pleasing.

Without warning, she took him deep into her mouth. The tip of his cock hit the back of her throat repeatedly while she worked him into a frenzy. Her head bobbed up and down, matching the speed of her hand. His fingers threaded through her hair, holding on while her soft, wet mouth worked wonders on his control.

"Elle, if you keep doing that, I'm going to come."

His warning was an aphrodisiac to her. Being the one who made him give up his control and give in to her ministrations made her feel emboldened, empowered. His release came soon after she increased her fervor, intent to see it through to the end. When she'd taken the very last drop, she swallowed it down and looked up at him through her lashes.

"You know, the noises you make when I make you come are pretty damn sexy too."

He smirked in reply, his smug smile sexy as sin on his handsome face. Then he reached under her arms and pulled her back up beside him. In one swift move, he rolled over on top of her and thrust his thick cock inside her to the hilt. She cried out in pleasure. The sweet burn of his cock stretching her only added to the intense pleasure. He pushed forward and arched back over and over again. His mouth covered the beaded tip of her nipple, laving her skin with his wet tongue. Each thrust became harder. Every sensation became stronger.

"You are mine, Elle," he stated definitively. "No matter how hard you try, you'll never be free of me."

"I don't want to be. I've never wanted that."

He stopped abruptly and stood beside the bed. Then he positioned her in front of him, bent over with her chest on the mattress. "I want you in every way imaginable." He ran his finger down the ridge of her spine, along the crack of her ass, and brushed against the puckered rosebud of her virgin ass. "This, one day soon, will be mine. There's no part of you I'd share with another man, Elle. Your every first will be with me."

"Yes." A one-word reply was all she could manage. Yes—to everything he wanted, anything he wanted.

He held his cock in his hand and rubbed it up and down her center, coating the head with the wetness pooled between her legs. He suddenly pushed inside her, his fingers gripped her hips, and he drove relentlessly until neither of them could wait another second. When she screamed his name, her body locked down around him and forced his tumble over the edge in concert with hers.

After they'd cleaned up, they slipped into their private infinity pool. The healing touch of the cool water soothed her delicate skin. Wrapped in each other's embrace, they shared no less intimacy while talking about their hopes and dreams for the future than while in the throes of passion just moments before. Elle felt as if she'd met a new side of Devon. For the first time in several years, she thought they might actually have a shot at a happily-ever-after story of their own.

"Are you ready to go explore the island?" he asked.

"Yes, I can't wait to see everything this place has to offer."

They changed into shorts and sandals before leaving the suite, and the tension and doubts that hung between them only hours before had disappeared. Hand in hand, they strode through the hillside terraces of the resort, excited about the plentiful activities their vacation destination would provide.

The luxurious spa and raving reviews over the couple's massage caught Elle's attention immediately. Devon insisted on booking the zip line tour of the rain forest for them both. Just off the beach at the bottom of the multilevel terraces and winding staircase was a shallow coral reef where they could relive their first date. They wound down the sweeping steps until they reached the beach below.

"We can't miss the tour of the volcanoes while we're here." Elle bounced on her toes in excitement while taking in the grandeur around her.

"If we have time in between our indoor activities," Devon teased. "We may not have time to put clothes on again after today."

"Then we'll go naked and really cause a stir around here." The spark of defiance in her eyes made Devon narrow his in return.

"If you think I'd let another man see you naked, you've got another thing coming."

"You know it turns me on when you go all Neanderthal man on me. Just no pissing on my leg to mark your territory. I have to draw the line there."

His steps were casual, but his gaze held a playful warning. His advance toward Elle was slow but calculated, forcing her to back up in an automatic, self-preservation response. "Elle, you're the only person who's gotten away with mocking me more than once. The bodies of the other unfortunate people will never be found. Don't make me have to take you and hide you away, too."

"That depends. Where would you hide me? Is it as beautiful a place as this island? If so, I'll be sure to mock you again so we can stay. You'd have to stay with me to make sure I don't escape, of course." She smiled from ear to ear while she attempted to see how far she could push his ultra-controlled demeanor before he revealed more of his true self to her.

"It's not punishment if you like it and want it. I'm afraid you're not leaving me much choice."

Her watchful eyes never left him, waiting for him to made a sudden move on her, but she didn't see him move until she was already in his grasp. His speed was unbelievable, putting him on top of her before her brain even comprehended he'd made a move. She was in his arms and tossed over his shoulder in the blink of an eye.

He charged toward the water and dove in, turning on his back and positioning her on top of him at the last moment. Submerged in the aqua blue waters of the Caribbean, he pushed up and they surfaced with sputtering and hysterical laughter.

"You were getting a little hotheaded. I thought you could use some cooling off," he explained.

"Is that so?" She laughed as she wrapped her arms around his neck and her legs around his waist. He supported her in the water with his strong, muscular arms. "Always looking out for my well-being, aren't you?"

"Always have. Always will."

The following day, he woke her early for their zip line tour of the rain forest. High in the canopy of the lush green trees, she stood on a platform with nothing but a harness and a line stretched through the trees to keep her from plunging to her death on the forest floor.

"I think I'm going to be sick." She peered over the edge of the platform and quickly retreated when she saw the dizzying height.

He wrapped his arms around her from behind to make her feel more secure. "When the fear is too much and you feel like it's overtaking you, close your eyes. Feel me with you. Remember how this feels in my arms and let it calm you. I'm your shadow, Elle. I'm always with you."

"Next," the tour guide called out.

Elle opened her eyes and stepped out of Devon's embrace, her courage renewed. The guide connected her harness to the line and gave her a reminder demonstration of what to do.

"Now, just sit down in your harness, and simply let go. Soar through the trees and have the time of your life. There's nothing to fear."

She did as he said, keeping Devon's encouragement close to her heart. In an instant, she was zipping through the canopy. Amazing sights and beauty she'd never seen before quickly made her forget about her fears. The tree height became her friend, introducing her to new and wonderful experiences she never would've risked on her own. Her squeals of delight rang through the trees, quickly followed by Devon's laughter.

"I'm so glad you made me do this!" She jumped into his arms as soon as he landed on the next stop. "This is so much fun. Makes me wish I had a video camera on my helmet so I could watch it over and over again."

When they'd finished flying through the trees, Devon pulled her into his arms and kissed her on the tip of her nose. "I'm proud of you. Even though you were scared out of your mind, you handled it like a pro."

"I did what you told me to do. When I felt your arms around me, I felt safe and protected. You didn't seem to have any problem jumping off that platform at all."

He shrugged. "That wasn't high. I had to jump out of planes in the Army, so being able to see the ground while attached to a line was a walk in the park."

"You never talk about what you did in the service. I never knew you had to skydive."

He grinned at her reference. "I went to Jump School to become a *paratrooper*. But that was a long time ago. Nothing to talk about now." He quickly dismissed the subject, regretting bringing it up, while also wishing he could tell her everything about his life so she'd better understand his position.

"What's on the agenda for tonight?"

"I thought we'd spend some time enjoying the privacy of our suite before our dinner reservations. Then maybe a romantic walk on the beach, find a quiet spot, enjoy more privacy, and start all over again tomorrow."

"Enjoy the privacy, huh?"

"Yep, and by that, I mean we'll explore every inch of each other's body. I can't wait to strip you down and taste you all over again."

"Maybe we should skip the dinner reservations completely and just eat in tonight."

"Don't think the thought hasn't crossed my mind a dozen or so times. But, with only having two weeks and so much I want to experience with you, it's best we go out. Besides, I want to show you off without the paparazzi around us."

"Fair enough. But only because I'd hate to deprive you of showing me off tonight." She tried to keep a straight face while teasing him, but she was unable to hold the expression when he stared at her suspiciously. "Especially considering you won't even be seen with me any other time."

"That's it. I'm spanking that ass tonight." His sly grin covered his face, the mirth of his words gleaming in his expression. "Keep talking to me like that. I'll come up with more punishment that's exciting to dole out."

"Promises, promises." She stepped out of his arms but held on to his hand. "Let's head back to the privacy of our room and begin that thorough exploration you mentioned."

Hours later, they emerged from the suite for dinner.

"I love how you have that just-thoroughly-fucked glow. I love even more that I'm the only one who knows what it looks like. It makes me want to take you back to the room and start all over again."

"You can after you feed me."

"Oh, I'll feed you all right."

"I need actual food for energy to keep up with you." She walked faster toward the restaurant before he changed her mind. Again. "We're already almost late. If they give our table away…" Her words trailed off, but the warning had been appropriately issued.

His responding chuckle left no doubt of how scared he was in the face of her threat. The deep timbre of his laugh rumbled through his chest, reverberating through her body and leaving tingling chills from the sexy undertones of it. She was forced to acknowledge part of her attraction to him was his dangerous and mysterious air. It only added to his appeal and her inability to resist him.

The open-air restaurant overlooked the mountains and ocean, giving them an incredible view of the moon shimmering off the surface of the calm water. The exclusive resort attracted the type of traveler who preferred privacy and offered it to others. Elle's presence didn't cause the slightest stir, giving them at least the illusion of anonymity during their meal.

"Today has been perfect," Elle gushed. "I've loved every minute of it. We should've done this long ago."

"I agree, so we'll have to make it a standing date. A yearly escape to a remote location."

"Absolutely."

"Great. Then you agree to let me kidnap you and take you away whenever I want."

"Well, I won't object, but my director may if I'm filming at the time you decide to kidnap me."

"Technically," he quipped, "I can find ways around that inconvenience."

"You have so many talents, I can't say I doubt that at all."

"To us." He raised his wineglass. "And to our lifelong commitment of standing dates in hidden locations."

"To never having to worry that a date with you will be boring or awkward." Elle raised her goblet and giggled during the clinking of glasses.

After dinner, they took a stroll along the shore, the gentle waves lapping at their feet. The ocean breeze kept them cool in the tropical heat, though Elle could've sworn she saw sparks arc from the heated glances Devon shot her.

"We're all alone out here," he whispered. "I can do anything I want to you, and no one would be the wiser. It's so very tempting."

"That goes both ways, actually."

His dark blue eyes flashed with a mixture of desire, admiration, and amusement. "Just when I think I have you figured out." He pulled her into his side, his big arm wrapped securely around her, and they walked back to their room with their bodies stuck together.

Their remaining time on the island was spent in much the same manner. By day, their exciting excursions took her to places she never would've dared or dreamed of going without Devon. Perilous journeys to volcanic peaks. Dizzying heights of rock climbing expeditions. Day-long hikes deep inside the rain forest. Underwater excursions to a beautiful coral reef.

Nights were spent in their open-air suite with room service delivering their meals more times than not. The in-suite infinity pool provided all the privacy they needed while allowing them to enjoy the moonlit views. Wrapped in a sensual embrace, they made love nightly, with one waking the other for a second round at some point before the morning sun lit up their room. The closer they were to the end of their two-week escape, the more desperate they both became for one more touch, one more embrace, one more kiss.

CHAPTER THIRTEEN

The morning before they were scheduled to leave, Devon snuck out of the room while Elle showered. He had a special surprise planned for her and didn't want to risk her hearing him on the phone arranging it.

"Hello, sir. How can I help you?" The suites had butlers assigned to cater to the guests' every need. Though they hadn't needed his services before, Devon knew he didn't have long before Elle would notice his absence, so he provided the basics and left the man to finalize the details.

"I need to arrange a spa package for my companion—after we return from a helicopter sight-seeing tour." Devon gave the butler his specific instructions, speaking low and looking over his shoulder frequently to make sure she hadn't overheard him.

"I'll be glad to arrange every aspect of it." With a few keystrokes, Devon and Elle were booked on the morning helicopter tour, and her complete spa package would begin immediately afterward.

"Thank you," Devon replied and turned to walk away after the butler handed him the itinerary.

"Sir?" the butler called to him. "This was left for you late last night. We don't allow unscheduled visitors in the suite area after the resort doors are locked. The gentleman was adamant you were to receive this first thing this morning."

He handed Devon a large manila envelope, and Devon's heart sank. No one knew precisely where he was or exactly when he'd return, so there was only one explanation for the unscheduled visitor. The fact that someone had tried to access the room he shared with Elle enraged him. Had that man been successful, his body would've been shark food, never to be found again—

company man or not. The agent in him suddenly cringed at the room he'd chosen for their escape.

On paper, the idea was perfect. Secluded. Romantic. Private. Tropical.

In practice, he'd given whoever had followed him to the island a full-frontal view of every move they'd made. The unobstructed view looking out on the island was equally as open looking in with high-powered binoculars or a scope. His lapse in judgment and following of security protocol could've cost both his and Elle's lives.

He thanked the butler absently before rushing back to the room to check on Elle. His paranoia was engaged with a renewed ferocity. He'd been so busy living the carefree life, his guard had been down completely. He hadn't even sensed eyes on him or footsteps following him. With all his time and attention devoted to Elle, he'd unknowingly put them both at risk. He berated himself over his own stupidity as he stomped back to their door.

Elle stepped out of the bathroom just as Devon entered the suite. "Where have you been?"

He was relieved to see her wearing the short robe, though the belt was loosely tied and the fabric gaped open at her chest. "Just making sure our last day here is off the charts unforgettable."

"Care to share what awaits me today?"

"Nope. I don't want to share at all. I want every second to be a surprise. But do me one favor—get dressed in the bathroom. I overheard one of the butlers say they've caught people with binoculars trying to get a peep show before."

Elle laughed incredulously. "We've been parading around here naked and having sex on every surface in every position imaginable for the last thirteen nights. One more won't hurt now."

"You're probably right," he conceded. He decided there was no need to alarm her unnecessarily. If anyone from the company had seen them, he'd find out. If it had been someone with the press, the pictures would've already been all over the web.

He stole into the bathroom, locked the door for privacy, and silently opened the manila envelope. With the contents in his hands, he squeezed his eyes shut and shook his head. The death stipulation for leaving the CIA had suddenly become more appealing.

After memorizing the details, he put the documents under hot water and watched as they completely disintegrated. Though he couldn't deny that handy little trick was better than eating them to erase all traces, the fact that he was activated on his vacation didn't escape him. It was a clear message sent from high up the chain.

We can find you wherever you are.

The helicopter tour of the island was better than Elle ever expected. Though she'd seen many of the sights up close and personal, the morning tour bundled all the memories they'd made into a neat package and tied them together with a pretty bow on top. Thirteen days of perfection and bonding with the man of her dreams, the man she loved and had always loved. It had been the best time of her life, hands down.

"You've been quiet today. Are you ready to get rid of me? Run out of things to talk about with me?" She teased Devon, knowing he dreaded the end of their escapade as much as she did. She had simply decided to reserve her quiet suffering for the flight home the next morning.

"You know better than that. I wish I could keep you with me always."

"Don't go back," she pleaded. She'd decided long before never to ask him to choose between his job and her. Truth be told, she'd been laser-focused on her own career, and she took advantage of the mostly out-of-town-boyfriend to avoid splitting her own time and attention. But her career was no longer the most important aspect of her life. She wanted more—with Devon. "Stay with me. Quit your job, whatever it is that takes you away from me."

His eyes searched hers, but his expression was unreadable.

"Or take me with you, and I'll quit my job. Either way you want it—I don't care which. It's just too hard to let you go again now."

"I feel the same way, Elle. But I can't let you quit what you've worked so hard to attain. I also can't quit my job, even though I can't explain why. And I certainly can't take you with me. You are far too valuable to me to do that."

Her crestfallen face tore at his heart, though he hid his deep disappointment behind his passive façade. "Don't worry, darlin'. One day, we'll be together without all these obstacles between us. I'm working on it."

She snuggled into his side and swallowed the tears that threatened to fall. Crying wouldn't help and would rob them of the time they had left together. That also reminded her. "Hey, you said you had another surprise for me after the helicopter tour. I can't imagine anything could top this. So, what's next after we land?"

"It's two-fold, actually. First, you're going to the spa for a lot of pampering and girly stuff. After that is a surprise I refuse to spoil, so you'll just have to wait and see."

"You're not going to the spa with me? For a couple's massage?"

"No, I'm not letting some guy put his hands all over me—or you. I booked the only lady masseuse who was open for you, and I'll just wait patiently until you're finished."

"You could've booked the guy for me, you know."

"Hell, no, I couldn't have either."

Elle snorted with laughter at his refusal. "You know the studio brings in massage therapists for us, and sometimes they're male. It's okay. Just because he's a man doesn't mean it's wrong or bad."

"It is wrong for another man to have his hands on you, and it will be bad when my hands are on him."

"What about when I have to film a nude scene or a sex scene with another actor? How wrong or bad will that be?"

"Deadly. It'll be deadly wrong all the way around."

"You'd better hurry with that plan for us to be together all the time, then. That scenario will arise if I stay in movies long enough. Not that you have anything to worry about because there's nothing romantic about the scene itself. But the camera and editing magic can definitely fool you."

His responding growl conveyed his displeasure with her answer.

"And we're back at the heliport. I hope you've both enjoyed your flight," the pilot said into their headphones.

Elle and Devon cut their eyes to each other at the same time. They'd become so comfortable with their privacy that they'd forgotten the pilot could hear their entire conversation. She chuckled lightly and dropped her head in her hands, shielding her face in embarrassment.

"Yes, we loved it. Sorry you had to suffer through our whole conversation. I'm afraid you've spoiled us here with a sheltered vacation, and we've enjoyed the seclusion a little too much."

"Not to worry, miss. This radio has a convenient button that mutes your conversation for the pilot. When I have it muted, I just watch to see if you're speaking to me or not. Usually, the passengers talk amongst themselves and relive their stay. It's all part of the appeal of this resort."

When they exited the helicopter, Devon walked Elle to the spa and left her at the front desk. "Enjoy your Princess Elle package."

"Thank you. I'm sure I will." She rose up on her toes and kissed him before he got away.

Once outside the spa, he walked to the railing of the terrace and waited. Within minutes, he felt the weight of eyes on him and sensed the presence of someone too close to be a coincidence.

"Just a suggestion, but if you value your eyes and limbs where they are, I suggest you get out here now." Shadow spoke to the air, letting his voice carry to his watcher.

"I've heard your skills were incredible. But the stories could never match the real-life action."

"Rogers. You son of a bitch. If I find out you've been lurking outside my room and getting your rocks off watching my girl and me, I'll force-feed those rocks to you before I snap your fucking neck."

"I'm not that stupid. Besides, I just got here late last night. They wouldn't let me anywhere near your room. The target just arrived yesterday, and this is the only chance we've had to take him out of play. He's preparing to move a shipment of children. We're sanctioned to neutralize him. The syringe is taped under the bench beside you.

"Older man, completely white hair, naturally bronze skin. He has lunch reservations on the veranda in fifteen minutes. Table for one. He likes to eat alone. His table will be in a secluded spot. Handle this, and go enjoy the rest of your vacation. You picked a hell of a spot."

"Why don't you handle it and save us both the trouble?"

"He's above my pay grade. Should something go wrong, we'll need your unique skill set to handle it."

"It's past time for you to upgrade, then. Stop depending on me when you're afraid to get your hands dirty. Or when you're simply afraid."

"I'm not supposed to tell you, but the analysts think he could be connected to Ava's abduction. They didn't give me concrete intel, but for them to even mention it tells me they're at least one thousand percent certain."

"Oh, he's definitely a fucking dead man then."

Shadow reached under the bench seat beside him and retrieved the syringe. He knew it well—he'd helped perfect the current design. Small and easy to conceal in the palm of his hand, a simple push of a button released the needle and the contents in quick succession. He could be in and out of the area before the effects of the medication took hold.

The emergency team that would pick up the victim during his medical crisis were prearranged personnel from the company. Their only task was to help him along to the light and complete the mission. The medical examiner, also on the payroll, would rule his death as natural causes, the mixture of his blood pressure medication in combination with the elevated levels of potassium chloride in his blood would appear to be no more than he ingested too much table salt and didn't get enough exercise. In short—he ate and drank too much while not caring for his overall health.

It was easy to make the report say what was necessary to carry out orders when it was all orchestrated well in advance. Even the autopsy report with an official cause of death had already been completed, leaving only a few standard fill-in-the-blanks, and his death wouldn't be questioned by anyone who could do anything about it.

With the device in hand, Shadow strode casually to the area where his target sat alone, reading a paper and occasionally looking out at the spectacular view. Just beyond the unfortunate target was another terrace overlooking the trees and ocean below. With his sights set on the vacant terrace, Shadow wound his way through the tables and chairs, passing the man as he returned his glass to the table.

Shadow waited a few seconds on the terrace behind his target before he continued moving down more stairs to other areas of the sprawling resort. Each step took him farther from the man who'd grabbed his chest in pain. His request for a table away from everyone else would aid in his demise. The resort staff was busy serving larger parties at busier clusters of tables, oblivious to his emergent situation and his inability to cry out for help.

In his peripheral vision, Shadow saw the man's body go limp, and he knew the mission was complete. He kept moving down the side of the mountain, away from the commotion that would no doubt ensue within minutes. He planned to be as far away as possible when that happened.

~

"My appointment didn't show up," the lovely massage therapist grumbled.

"Was it for right now?" Elle asked, an idea already quickly forming.

"Yes. He was adamant about booking this time then didn't even show up. Now I can't find him on the guest roster at all." Her brows furrowed in confusion. "That's so odd."

"Is there any chance I can grab his spot for my boyfriend? He won't let a man touch him, but we could do a couple's massage with two female therapists." Elle's excitement over the possibility was contagious.

"I'd be glad to do that for you. I'm Layla, by the way. Go grab your boyfriend, and I'll get the room set up for two."

Elle rushed out of the spa, thinking she'd find Devon just outside the door since he'd left her only minutes before. Another man stood at the rail instead. When he turned and met her gaze, Elle's blood ran cold. He didn't appear to belong in such an exclusive, high-end resort.

His hair was long and unkempt, even pulled back in the messy ponytail he wore. Faded black tattoos covered his arms, chest, and neck. Not the colorful, sexy tattoos that every man-candy with six-pack abs seemed to sport. These were decidedly prison tattoos—an ex-convict who'd been inked with a makeshift method while incarcerated. The letters across his fingers were distinguishable, even from where she stood.

EVILONES

As if she were propelled by some invisible force, her feet moved on their own to carry her away from him. His horrifying smile slowly crept across his haggard face, revealing missing and rotten teeth, but deeper than that, his evil nature. She moved quicker, her eyes scanning the area for Devon and the safety his presence inherently provided. She spotted him walking with his casual swagger across one of the private terraces where a guest sat alone, reading the paper and sipping on his drink.

Devon passed behind him just as the man put his glass down. She opened her mouth to yell his name when she saw something that couldn't have been. Even in the far reaches of her mind, she wouldn't accept what her eyes insisted she'd seen.

Devon's arm swung loosely at his side when he passed the guest, then made a quick stabbing motion before Devon had moved past the man. Elle's feet halted at the action, her mouth hung open, and her heart raced at breakneck speed. Consciously willing her feet to move again, she dismissed it and assumed she'd misjudged the entire scene.

Then the man slumped in his chair, and Devon rapidly descended the stairs, disappearing from her sight. By the time she reached him, she knew he was dead and wouldn't be revived by the time medical crews arrived. She wanted to help him, but she'd never learned CPR. The frothy spittle just inside his still open lips convinced her to alert the waiter so others who were more qualified could help him instead.

She ran back up the stairs, yelling for help as she ascended. She was met by two waiters, their faces panic-stricken as she described the man's condition.

"Call an ambulance. I think he may already be dead." Tears welled up in her eyes, and panic rose in her chest. "Do you know how to perform CPR?" she asked one of the men on their way back down the stairs.

"No," he replied while staring blankly at the dead man. He finally snapped out of his trance and began instructing the other waiter. "I'll go call the first responder team. You get an ambulance." They hurried away from the scene, calling for others to help, and left Elle alone with the dead man again.

Was I seeing things?

She didn't want an answer—but she needed one. She had to satisfy her overactive imagination. She had *not* just seen Devon jab something into the back of the man's neck moments before he slouched in his seat. Devon did *not* palm some sort of device before sliding his hand down into his pocket. The *only* logical explanation was that she had hallucinated all of it.

With painfully slow steps, she moved toward the dead man's back with her eyes glued to his neck and her breaths frozen in her chest. She didn't know what she'd find there, and she didn't know what she'd do with whatever she did find.

How can I report Devon?

How can I not report Devon?

Will I be implicated and investigated, too?

Will I go to prison for being his accomplice?

How can I believe he had any part to play in this stranger's death?

She knew him—the best side of him he didn't show anyone else. She felt she'd betrayed him for allowing her thoughts to stray as far as they had. He'd done nothing but love and care for her for the last several years.

Still.

One more step, and any doubt would be erased—one way or another.

She moved directly behind him, and her eyes searched the skin on the back of his neck. The way his head dropped to the side created folds of skin that obscured part of her view. A half step closer and her upper body slightly bent over to get a better look, she steeled her nerves and looked again.

"Excuse me, miss," a frantic man bellowed from beside her.

"Elle, what are you doing?" The familiar voice spoke in her other ear at the same time, causing her to jump backward. Devon lifted her up and away from the dead man as the medical crews began to move him.

There, in the folds of his skin, appeared to be something out of place. Something that didn't belong. Something so small, it would've been missed had she not specifically looked for it. A pinprick that could've just as easily been a bug bite. *In fact, it's more likely to be a bug bite than what caused his death,* she thought.

Who returns to the scene of a murder?

Cold chills ran over her body in the tropical heat of the afternoon at her next thought.

The murderer does, that's who.

Devon carried her up the stairs, giving the medical team room to work on the hotel guest. He pulled her into his arms, and she willingly buried her face in his chest.

"What are you doing out here alone? You were supposed to be getting pampered for our date tonight."

"I was looking for you," she stuttered, her teeth chattering.

"Darlin', even at this resort, you have to be careful. You're a celebrity. People know your face—and this is a small island. Word travels fast when famous people arrive." He pulled her closer, tightening his arms around her. "If anything happened to you, I'd never forgive myself for not being there to protect you."

Guilt further consumed her. How could she think so lowly of someone who obviously cared so much for her? What did that say about her character? These thoughts and feelings flew through her mind, mixing with flashes of what she thought she'd seen. Then he'd adjust his embrace and remind her how much she loved him all over again.

"Let's get you out of here. You don't need to see this," he murmured against her temple and placed a reassuring kiss there.

When they reached the top of the terrace, the sinister-looking ex-convict was still standing in the same spot. His cold stare drifted between Devon and Elle with no attempt to hide his interest in them. He kept his eyes trained on Devon for a second longer than normal, then cut his eyes to Elle again. That same unnerving smile covered his face, enhancing the evil and ugliness inside him.

For the first time in a very long time, Elle felt genuinely frightened and didn't know which way to turn. Her rock was beside her, and he was also the one she questioned. The scary-looking man didn't belong there, but he seemed to recognize them both. The dead man had rattled her beyond belief—but the events leading up to it caused her to question everything about Devon and herself.

And their relationship.

CHAPTER FOURTEEN

"You're treating me like I'm a fragile doll you're convinced will shatter any second now." The curt undertone in Elle's voice left no room for doubt regarding her frustration.

"For a while there, I thought you might." Devon watched her cautiously, unconvinced she was as "fine" as she professed.

"Who was that man standing outside the spa? Did you know him?" Her eyes held a challenge he hadn't seen before. She was asking more than her words conveyed, though she didn't want to admit it, even to herself.

"What man? Why would you think I know anyone here?"

"Don't think I haven't noticed how you answer with a question and keep everything as vague as possible." She moved from the dresser to the bed, packing her clothes for the flight home.

Devon could only watch with his heart in his throat. She'd only sampled a small taste of his life—and he'd even tried to keep her out of that, as easy as it had been. She wasn't cut out for the life of a spy, or a spy's wife. She was too well-known. She'd be used against him. She was truly his weakness—his Achilles' heel.

A simple mission had all but ruined his last night on the island with her. His last night ever. The events of the day revealed what he'd known all along. But like Elle, he didn't want to face or accept the truth he already knew. He had to let her go, once and for all. For both of their sakes, he had to sever their ties and allow her to live her life in the light of the stars, while he remained in the shadows where he belonged.

She folded a shirt and placed it in her suitcase. When she moved to the closet to get the next one, he stood and moved into her path, stopping her with his sheer size.

"Elle, it's our last night together," he began. His words struck a chord in her, forcing her eyes to fly up and meet his. "Our last night of vacation on this gorgeous island, with the incredible suite and warm infinity pool. I don't want to spend it fighting or being distant. Today was upsetting for you, I know. But do you think we can enjoy what little time we have left?"

Her expression softened, and she smiled lovingly up at him. "I would love that, Devon. I'd love to pretend this afternoon never happened and move back into our bubble of happiness where nothing bad can touch us. Care to pretend with me?"

"I'd love nothing more than to pretend all night with you." He leaned down and captured her mouth with his.

She expected his usual dominant side to emerge and start giving her orders. Not that she'd ever minded his take-charge attitude or his ability to make her feel like a rag doll by the time she'd snuggled beside him to sleep. But his gentleness surprised her. He took his time undressing her and laid her on the bed. He quickly shed his clothes and joined her.

His fingers glided over her skin as if they had a singular purpose of memorizing every inch of her body. Heated eyes followed their path, but his self-control kept his urges in check. Soft lips placed numerous kisses all over her, worshiping her body with palpable reverence and devotion. The intensity of his emotions streamed out of him without a single word to convey his thoughts. Every articulation he couldn't voice was clearly pronounced in the way he made love to her soul by simply caressing her body.

His nose skimmed along her stomach, and he inhaled deeply, drawing in her scent. The first splinter in her heart appeared.

His tongue blazed a trail over the sensitive skin between her breasts, greedily ingesting her flavor like a man starved. The splinter in her heart became a fissure.

He nibbled on the delicate skin along the side of her neck and watched with rapt attention as the cold chills flared out across her skin. One side of his mouth lifted slightly in amusement, but the smile never reached his eyes.

The fissure became a fracture.

Positioned between her legs, he straightened his arms to hover over her. He pushed forward, his cock brushing against her pussy before he nudged his way inside. Her eyes closed automatically when she moaned, relishing the sensation of him rocking into her. He stopped abruptly and waited for her to look at him again. With her eyes opened and locked on his, he began surging into her again with full, controlled movements. With bent arms, he framed her face and continued, never moving his eyes from hers. When he reached around to wrap his arms under her knees, his gaze never strayed—and he didn't allow hers to move from him. His message and intentions were clear.

Their connection was more than physical. In any other circumstance, long periods of direct eye contact would've been uncomfortable. But not that night

—not with him. The feelings they conveyed to each other with only a slight shift of expressions communicated much more than words could.

When she thought he couldn't extract one more scream from her, he proved her wrong. When her skin became slick with sweat and her breaths became labored from exertions, he seemed to gain his second wind. When she didn't think her body could take his sensual form of torture one more second, he slowed his efforts to let her recover but didn't break their union.

When his body forced his release, a moment of grave sadness flashed across his face, deepening his already dark blue eyes further. She searched his face wordlessly, questioning him without verbalizing the fears inside. Everything about their encounter was different than every other time. Part of her tried to rationalize it was symbolic of the two weeks coming to an end and knowing they'd be apart for weeks on end again. But a dire warning registered, and she knew that wasn't the reason behind their profound lovemaking experience.

He dipped his head and brushed his lips across hers—lightly at first, then more firmly until a rift in his self-control revealed an instant of desperation in his caress.

Her heart shattered in her chest.

After rolling onto his side, he pulled her flush against him and clung to her as if she were his only lifeline in the sea raging out of control in a storm. Even after his exhaustive actions during their carnal union, tension streamed from him with full blunt force. She eventually drifted off into a fitful sleep in his arms.

One advantage a predawn flight held was no one actually wanted to speak to anyone else unless it was absolutely necessary. Elle was thankful for that, and for Devon packing the rest of their clothes while she showered, trying to wake up after their late-night endeavors. When she emerged from the bathroom, the butler had already taken their luggage down to the waiting taxi.

Devon closed his hand around hers, threw her carry-on bag over his other shoulder, and led her out of the room. The door clicked shut behind them, automatically locking them out of the room without giving them a chance for one final glance back.

When their plane reached cruising altitude, she yawned repeatedly while attempting to fight back the sleep that tried relentlessly to overtake her. He reached over to press the button to recline her seat then covered her with both her and his blankets.

"Rest," he commanded softly.

Her lips parted, ready to protest sleeping through more of their time together than absolutely necessary, but he stopped her.

"I enjoy watching you sleep. You're tired. Take a nap. I'll still be right here when you wake."

"Not sure I can sleep now, knowing you'll be watching me." A hint of melancholy bled through her attempt at levity.

Devon responded by covering her hand with his warm one. In the dimly lit first-class cabin, Elle ached to confess to every thought, feeling, and desire in her mind and heart. She wanted to tell him all her fears about their future, about her career, about him. She needed him to acknowledge and accept they were a vital part of each other's lives. More than anything else, she longed for him to explain what she'd witnessed the day before.

He squeezed her hand and inclined his head ever so slightly, urging her to close her eyes. She clasped her other hand on top of his as she rolled to her side and faced him. With the words on the tip of her tongue, the fatigue and weariness won when her heavy eyes closed and she slipped off to sleep.

When she opened her eyes, the flight attendant was passing out meals to the other passengers. Her tray and drink sat in front of her, already prepared for her to eat.

"Did you fix this for me?"

"Yes. We didn't make it to the special date I had planned last night, so this is my pathetic replacement."

"Thank you for doing that. Did you get any sleep?"

"No. But I watched you sleep, and that always relaxes me." He picked up her fork and handed it to her.

"Very subtle clue that you want me to eat, Devon." Her teasing sounded good to his ears. She sounded more like his Elle—the one who still thought he hung the moon and stars.

She chatted about the plot of the upcoming production in between bites of her in-flight meal. Devon pretended he listened to her every word, but mostly, he found himself staring at her to memorize small details no one else would notice. Like the small flecks of green and gray in her hazel eyes. How she couldn't enjoy her food unless she had at least two napkins. The way she loved tomatoes, but not on her sandwiches. She always ate them separately. But mostly he pictured his life without her in it and what that would mean for both of them.

He tried to remember what filled his time before he jetted off to LA every chance he had to see her. What did he do to occupy his days? How would he cope with all of that after having Elle in his life and his heart for so long?

For her sake, he had to let her go. He'd selfishly held on to her for far too long—and she'd allowed it to happen because she loved him. But it was time to show her how much he loved her—by doing the right thing, even if it was also the hardest pill to swallow.

"That was actually pretty good for airline food," Elle remarked, pulling him from his internal thoughts. "You've been quiet, listened to me blabber on nonstop, and stared at me while I ate. What's on your mind?"

The words were right there—waiting to be said.

"Just thinking about how busy you'll be with production and promotion. You'll have me pushed out of the picture in no time."

If he made it seem like it was her idea, his absence would be easier for her to accept. He wanted to give her that much peace about it.

"You really think I'd choose any role over you?"

"You'd have to, Elle. You're bound by contract. If you ever want to work on another movie, you can't worry about me."

Her eyes lit with fiery anger, though she contained her voice. "I know exactly what you're doing, Devon Kane, and it won't fucking work on me."

Her change in demeanor was unexpected. He immediately realized his reverse psychology tactic would fail miserably on her, and he needed to contain the situation.

"Elle—"

"Don't Elle me. I offered to quit and go with you wherever you go. That's how much you mean to me and how little acting means compared to you. Yes, I love it, but I've achieved it. I don't need more and more of it to feed my self-worth. I need you, more than anything or anyone.

"I've allowed this long-distance romance because it was convenient and what we both needed at the time. But that's not how I want the rest of my life to be, and I don't believe you do either."

He couldn't argue—and she was on a roll and wouldn't let him get a word in anyway.

"Whatever happened that made you so closed off has to be dealt with in some way. Talk to me about it, talk to a therapist, decide to let it all go and move on—whatever works for you. But I didn't get this far by being a shrinking violet who's afraid to speak up for what I want. And I'm no one's doormat. You've had time to come to this conclusion on your own, but you haven't. Not fully committed anyway. So I'm calling your bluff. What was it you and Jeff used to say? Oh, yeah—shit or get off the pot."

Fuck, you have no idea how much I love you, he thought.

The flight attendant returned to pick up their items before the captain announced they were arriving at LAX. Though she was disappointed they hadn't finished their conversation, she had every intention of resuming it as soon as they were locked away in her bedroom. And she wouldn't let Devon out until he'd given his word and a solid commitment for their future.

Before she'd fallen asleep on the plane, her mind and heart were heavy with turmoil and pain. All those awful thoughts about Devon had taken a serious toll on her ability to be rational. The sight of the dead man, Devon's proximity to him, the evil man who kept smiling at her—it all crashed down on her at once, compounded by the end of the best two weeks she'd ever had.

When she'd opened her eyes after her nap, Devon was the first person she saw. His proximity was the protective and calming presence she needed. There was never a time when he didn't hold a special place in her heart, in one way or another. And there wasn't a day she wanted to pass without him in it. The clarity she had was refreshing; the vision she had of their future was bright.

She knew who she wanted, needed, and loved. It was time for Devon to admit the same.

The cab ride back to her apartment was a stark contrast from the laid-back atmosphere of the island. Despite how long she'd lived in LA, she was amazed at how easily she adapted to St. Lucia and the privacy it afforded. The packed LA interstates, with all the angry drivers and crowded lanes, assaulted the island tranquility she brought home with her.

Devon carried her bags up to the apartment, walking behind her as she fished her keys from her purse. She breezed in, quickly reacclimating to the four walls with city-street-view accommodations she called home.

"Beth, we're back. Are you here?" Elle moved through the small living space, looking for but not finding her best friend. "Looks like we have the place to ourselves."

Devon gave her a small smile and set her suitcases down beside where he stood. It was then she realized he didn't have his own bags in his hands. She began shaking her head from side to side, fighting back the lump in her throat and the tears in her eyes.

Unsuccessfully.

In a couple of steps, he stood directly in front of her and began his prepared speech. He kept reminding himself his decision was best for her. He'd put her in enough danger. He'd risked her safety too many times. He'd wasted enough of her time.

His big hand cupped her cheek, and she leaned into it. The tears spilled over her bottom lids and covered her face. She didn't bother to wipe them away—they wouldn't stop anytime soon.

"Elle, I should've told you this a long time ago, but I couldn't. I've selfishly tried to hold on to you, and to keep you holding on to me. You deserve better—you deserve to have everything you've ever wanted."

His other hand covered her other cheek and held her gaze directly on his face. He leaned in and kissed her sweetly, longingly, hauntingly. When he pulled back, he finally muttered the words that would release her. She'd finally know the truth.

"I love you, Elle. More than my life. More than anyone or anything. I'll love you and only you, all my life. You're my girl—forever."

Her heart disintegrated.

He released his hold on her and backed away. With his hand on the doorknob, he pulled it shut as he backed into the corridor. The symbolic wall separated them. The door had literally been shut. She no longer questioned his feelings for her or how much he loved her. But he had to walk away. He had to give her her life back, no matter how much it killed him to live without her, without the anticipation of seeing her again, without the thrill of making love to her again.

He slid into the back seat of the waiting taxi and rode back to LAX. To the gate with the Miami-bound flight. To the only life he'd ever really known.

To a quiet condo.

With an ocean view that reminded him of Elle.

To a cold, empty bed that only taunted him with a chance to sleep but not exactly delivering on that promise.

And to a life of loneliness and emptiness in the wicked shadows of what once might have been.

~

The door closed between them with Elle frozen where she stood. Though she'd known and felt a major shift in his demeanor, she ignored her instincts, all the red flags her heart tried to warn her about. Unable to move, she waited where he left her standing, hoping he'd return on his own.

She had no idea how much time had passed when the door finally began to swing open. Hope sprang up in her chest, ratcheting her heart rate up as excitement and anticipation grew. She waited to see his handsome face, read his thoughts behind his dark blue eyes, and lose herself when his muscular arms wrapped her in the safety of his embrace.

"Elle? What's wrong? What happened?" The questions rushed from Beth the moment she saw the despondent expression on her friend's face. The tears flowed freely down Elle's cheeks, leaving tracks in her makeup.

Afraid to tear her eyes from Elle in her current condition, Beth made a quick glance around the apartment and spotted the suitcases still sitting beside Elle. Then she knew whatever had caused the current dilemma, it revolved around Devon.

Beth's heart hurt for her friend, knowing only time would lessen the pain, while never fully eliminating it. She locked the door, took Elle by the hand, and led her to the bathtub. She ran a hot bath and tossed in a lavender bath bomb.

"Undress and get in, love. I'll make us both some chamomile tea, and you can fill me in on what happened. Or, you can just lay your head in my lap and cry while I pet your hair. Whatever you need."

Elle nodded mindlessly, the blank expression she wore showed her thoughts were a million miles away. But she did as Beth instructed and sank further into the steaming water. Relief was nowhere to be found, however, because everything around her was tied to a memory of him.

When the water cooled, she wrapped a thick robe around her and joined Beth in the living room.

"Want me to reheat your tea?"

Elle shook her head and stretched out on the couch. With her head in Beth's lap, she let her hot tears flow. Beth stroked her hair and tried to comfort her as best she could, but the end of a dream left a hole in Elle's heart that couldn't be filled with promises of a better day to come.

Her only consoling thought before she fell asleep on Beth was how she'd lived through other heartbreaking and difficult situations. She'd come through this one stronger and wiser.

But first, she would hurt.

CHAPTER FIFTEEN

Current Day

On the private jet to LAX, Shadow planned his every move and how he'd infiltrate a well-known and dangerous motorcycle club past the probie level. Hell, even a probie was a step up from where he'd normally have to prove his worth. But he didn't have enough time to go through the standard process.

Elle and Beth didn't have enough time.

Over the past year, he'd kept his distance from her and let her live her life. He'd watched with a mixture of extreme pride and sorrowful regret how her career skyrocketed when she put all her energies into it. She was frequently sought out for leading roles, and the most popular strutting peacocks vied for her attention.

"Fuckers," he mumbled to himself. "Why couldn't it be those dickheads disappearing instead of Elle?"

The prior twelve months were the hardest Shadow could remember enduring since he was a kid. His trips to LA had not lessened. He still visited Elle, checked on her well-being, watched her work—though she never knew he was there. He wanted her to forget him and have the life he couldn't give her.

Only he couldn't let her go, and he didn't want a life that didn't include her.

"Maybe this is my ticket away from the CIA operations. If they knew how fucking crazy messed up I am, they wouldn't send me out anymore."

He glanced around the cabin of the luxurious Steele Security jet, thankful the flight attendant was out of earshot. While he wouldn't mind the company directors thinking he was crazy, he didn't want to share his instability with anyone else.

"That wouldn't work anyway," he realized. "They'd just send me to even worse places."

For the time being, his focus had to be solely on Elle and Beth if he was to have any chance of saving them. From the intelligence Steadman had shared, there was little hope of rescuing one of them, much less both. If two were missing, there were bound to be more.

Fortifying his mind and steeling his resolve, he cracked open the dossier on the outlaw motorcycle club he'd soon pledge to as a new member.

The Devil's Dominion Motorcycle Club.

He leaned back in his seat and began memorizing all the details and planning his offensive. Every word solidified his belief the chance of success was low and the risk of death was high. The Devil's Dominion was not known to suffer fools—or traitors.

Based out of LA, the motorcycle gang had spread to multiple states through smaller gangs brought into the fold—either by their request or via a hostile takeover and violent orientation. With the additions to their ranks, their total member count was estimated to be close to two thousand men.

An enterprise that size would have considerable resources at their beck and call. It would also need a mixture of criminal activities to fund it. With more than 150 chapters, their reach was far and wide. He had no doubt the case would require all his skill to pull off. On paper, they were a formidable opponent. Reality would be much worse.

Little information was known about their initiation process. Those who had endured it were either still part of the club and didn't talk about it, or had been killed trying to leave the gang. His inside man, Nick Tucker, gave a detailed report two years prior, but he stressed the leaders of the group created new scenarios frequently. Each new round of probies endured more humiliating and sinister acts than the last. The harsh induction helped ensure they maintained their cruel nature as full-fledged members.

The highest concentration of members was in the LA chapter. With nearly 300 members, it was by far the most dangerous and least predictable. Fortunately, it was also the chapter Nick had infiltrated and worked his way up the chain during his two years undercover. As the current club treasurer, he was trusted implicitly and had proven his commitment.

According to Nick's handler, the two years with the gang had taken a significant toll on him. Shadow could only imagine what Nick had been forced to do to show his allegiance and gain their trust. For any criminal organization to accept an outsider, they would require the probationary member to commit a heinous crime—to prove his mettle and to have leverage to hold over his head.

The leader of all the chapters was an ex-convict by the name of Bobby Blalock, but his club nickname was Headbanger. He required every member to be a convicted felon, adding to the notoriety of the club overall. Every new member was assigned a nickname when they joined unless they already had one from an associated gang—but the club officers were the most notorious.

Using his secure phone, Shadow contacted Nick's handler, Jack Collins, to get the information directly from those closest to the action. "Jack, I'm on my way to LA. Tell me everything is ready for me."

"Steadman and I have been working on your background. It's airtight. They'll hire a private investigator to check you out. They've become very careful about any new members."

"Recently?"

"Fairly. In the last several months. Headbanger, the club president, has been extremely paranoid lately. His vice president, Nutcrusher, personally oversees every new pledge, comparing their formal application to whatever the PI digs up."

"Headbanger and Nutcrusher. I'm sure there's a joke in there somewhere."

Jack chuckled darkly. "Not one they'd find funny. Nick joined at the most opportune time, before they became so suspicious of everyone. We built his arrest record and background around what he'd already told them."

"What is Nick's club name?"

"Renegade. He's the club treasurer, so they trust him with all the money. He and their sergeant at arms, Bonebreaker, convinced Headbanger to allow officers to nominate new members at the probie stage, so you'll skip the pledge stage. They still won't trust you until you've proven yourself, though."

"I've been reading up on their initiation process. It's fairly grueling but nothing I haven't been through before."

"Don't expect it'll be anything you've read about. They pride themselves on new and improved torture tactics. They have been known to order probies to kill someone for them, too."

Jack and Shadow discussed how he'd get in touch with Nick once he was ready to ride with the club. The only part of the agreement Shadow was leery over was waiting two to three weeks to allow changes to his features to occur naturally. His normally kempt hair needed to be longer and shaggy. His beard must be full and scraggly. Tattoos would be strategically placed to show his prison allegiance and felon status.

His motorcycle and leathers would be waiting for him at his run-down, sparsely furnished apartment, complete with dust and road grime to portray his recent ride across the country after his prison release. His photographic memory and training taught him how to blend in with any type of element and gave him a decided advantage, but earning the trust of a group of very suspicious criminals wouldn't be easy. He used the rest of the flight to pore over every detail of their known hangouts.

By the time he landed at a private airstrip in LA County, he'd moved past concerned and straight to murderous rage. Jack waited outside the fence in a beat-up truck. He looked the part of a retired lifetime club member in case he was ever spotted near Nick Tucker. In Shadow's case, Jack would lend credence to his cover story if anyone saw them pull up to the apartment together.

"Good flight?" Jack asked when Shadow had settled in the passenger seat.

"As good as can be under the circumstances. Have you talked to Nick directly?"

Jack chuckled. "Not since we last talked a couple of hours ago. We go weeks without speaking. But I got a message to him, and he'll meet us tonight at your place. Your cover story will be enough to explain how the three of us know each other if anyone questions it. Or, I should say, *when* someone questions it. Bonebreaker will suspect you immediately. He spent twelve years in prison because of a snitch who turned out to be an undercover agent. He suspected Nick, too, so don't take it personally."

"As long as he doesn't take it personally when I serve his cock and balls to him chilled before I finish killing him."

Jack arched one brow as he looked over his shoulder at Shadow. "Angry much?"

"Jack, I'm more than angry after reading that file. What they're most likely doing with Elle makes my blood boil. I'm already a deadly man, but I could wipe out every single one of them and not lose a wink of sleep at night."

"Your director at the CIA warned me about turning you loose on this club."

"Yeah? What was his warning?"

"He said I may not have anyone left to arrest if they pissed you off. Apparently, you have a reputation in the company for taking care of business, no matter how messy the situation may be."

"You've been warned correctly. Think of all the money we'll save the taxpayers in the long run." His tone held no mirth or indication Jack shouldn't take his words at full face value.

"Just remember there's always more to the story. Someone else behind the scenes, calling the plays, directing the activities, reading the field. We need to take that person down, too. So we need them alive to flush out who's financing the big ventures."

"The money isn't coming from their drug operations? I read they're in league with the Mexican cartels and pulling in major dollars from street-level dealers all the way up the chain to the manufacturers."

"They are, no doubt. But their new business is much more expensive—at least, initially. The number of people we think they're paying off leads to a staggering amount of money. We'll get into that more with Nick when he drops by later."

Jack pulled alongside the curb in front of an old, dilapidated building that probably should've been condemned decades before. The sparsely remaining paint was peeling, the overhangs were rotten, and the gutters had long ago fallen away.

"Charming place. You didn't have anything a little less pretentious? I'm not sure I can afford a room here," Shadow deadpanned.

"Sorry. Everywhere else was full," Jack retorted. "Come on in, and I'll show you around."

He unlocked the door and stepped inside. With his arm extended, he smiled at Shadow. "Here's your apartment. Try not to get lost."

Shadow stepped through the doorway and did a full 360-degree turn. "The janitor's closet at my old high school was bigger than this apartment. It's a good thing I'm not claustrophobic."

The only privacy in the small room was behind the bathroom door that would undoubtedly fall off the hinges at any time. It was barely hanging on as it was, but the slightest breeze or softest tremor would surely separate it from the hinges completely.

"No chance of getting lost in here. Bright side," Jack laughed and closed the door. "We've already stocked your fridge and cupboard. Here are your keys—one to the door, one to the garage, and one to the bike. That's the best thing about this place. The small garage next door is yours too. Your bike is parked over there."

"Let's go check out the garage, then." Shadow left the apartment with a quickness in his step that made Jack chuckle under his breath when he fell into step behind him. Shadow rounded the corner of the building and stopped in his tracks. "I'm sleeping in the garage, Jack."

The garage was formerly a service station, abandoned at least a decade before. The gas pump had been removed, weeds grew in the huge cracks in the concrete, and some of the upper windows had been busted out. The single roll-up door was all metal, shielding the inside from prying eyes.

Shadow unlocked the door to the small office area and turned to Jack. "It smells better in here than over there. Does this bathroom work?"

"Yeah. We actually just had it redone last year. You could open this place up and take in small jobs. Get your name and face known in the area to help draw them in to you."

"Good idea. I think I may just do that, with a back-office business of my own to make extra money. Make myself indispensable to the club before they even know what hit them."

"You are dangerous. Maybe you should quit the CIA and come to the DEA."

"No one ever quits the CIA, Jack. Haven't you heard?"

"I've heard stories. Never knew if they were true or not. So you can only quit when you die?"

"Only if you give a two-week notice first."

"Got it. Well, we'll do our best to avoid the notice and the death stipulation while you're here. Don't want you tarnishing my good record."

Jack and Shadow busied themselves with moving the small bed from the apartment over to the office behind the front counter, then the refrigerator and all the food. After they'd straightened up the tools left behind by the last tenant, Shadow inspected his new abode.

"I can't believe you were going to put me over in that little shithole instead of this nice, roomy garage."

"Honestly, I'm surprised no one before you thought of doing this. I'm going to take this as a good sign for things to come. Maybe you're just what we need to wrap this case up. Two years undercover is changing Nick. This group is merciless and ice-cold."

"Jack, I'll do what I can to help close the case against them and shut down their operations for good. But my primary objective is to find Elle and Beth before it's too late."

The low, mean rumble of a motorcycle engine grew louder until it stopped just outside the garage. Jack and Shadow exchanged glances and moved to the office area where they could see outside. A tall, muscular man swung his leg over the Harley and slid his skullcap off his head.

"Well, if it isn't Renegade himself." Shadow walked toward him, no expression on his face to give away his thoughts. He felt eyes on him, searing his skin and heightening his senses.

"Shadow," Nick replied, keeping his voice level and glancing up and down the street. "You all moved in?"

"Yeah. What little I have anyway."

"Well," Nick paused. "There goes the fucking neighborhood."

With raucous laughter and manly hugs, the two men greeted each other like long-lost friends. Appearances weren't a far cry from reality. They'd worked a couple of cases together—one before Nick joined the DEA and one afterward. They hadn't seen each other in quite a while, but they'd initially established a close working relationship while protecting Dominic Powers that carried forward to that very day.

"What's up with this hairstyle and manscaped beard? You turn into a pussy in prison or what?"

"You're still so fucking funny. I've been in admin-seg for the last year. One of my punishments was to cut my hair and beard."

"Administrative segregation. Why'd they put you in time-out for so long?"

"For killing another convict after he called me a pussy."

Nick threw his head back and roared with laughter. "Fair enough, brother. I brought you a housewarming gift. Maybe that'll keep you from killing me."

"Depends on what you brought."

Nick opened his saddlebag and withdrew two six-packs of beer. "Guessing it's been a while since you've had one of these if you've been on lockdown for the past year."

"You're forgiven. Come on in and pop a top with us. Jack is here too."

With the door closed, the three men sat in the office and talked. To anyone outside, they were laughing and becoming reacquainted after a prolonged absence. Cans of beer were tossed, fingers were pointed as smiles turned to laughter, and hands moved wildly through the air in animated displays.

Every move and gesture were carefully orchestrated to maintain the façade they'd created. While they shared pertinent, detailed information in private, their secret spectator would be none the wiser. Looks could be very deceiving, and assumptions were downright deadly. Their ruse was perfected over time and with intense training. It was as ingrained in them as riding a bike.

"Who's watching us?" Shadow asked.

"Not sure. It's not Bonebreaker. I just left him with his ole lady. Not saying he didn't send someone to watch Jack or me, though." Nick took a swig of his beer.

"Are you any closer to cracking the case and finding out who's funding the change in their MO?" Jack asked.

"Not who's funding it, but I did find an interesting puzzle piece today. Large sums of money are being transferred from the club's accounts, routed through several dummy corporations, and finally deposited into an offshore account. Someone is already checking the dummy corporations' names and officers for me."

"What if no one is funding their newest venture? It could be the exact opposite," Shadow contemplated. "Maybe we've been too focused on it being one way to see other possibilities."

"Let's go over what we know, then. Lay it all out on the table." Jack stood and walked into the service bay area. "Come in here so we can quit playing those damn charades."

Nick and Shadow rose, laughing over Jack's description of their actions, and followed him into the garage.

"Jack tell you this place is kept clean by a perpetual de-bugger device?" Nick asked.

"No, but it's good to hear y'all are using that technology now. I'm having some of my own installed as we speak. I'll let them know to work around it."

"So, what do we know? Start from the beginning."

"Devil's Dominion has been involved in the usual illegal trades—drugs, prostitution, and weapons. Their main drug supplier is the Mexican cartel. They make regular runs to the border and meet their contacts. Then they come back, disperse their product to the satellite clubs for distribution, and collect the money from them weekly."

"The same guys travel to the border and back? No one left behind at the meeting?" Shadow clarified.

"No one left behind. Same set of guys because the cartel members know them. They rotate schedules randomly to avoid overeager DEA agents. But nothing other than drugs and money is exchanged."

"Same with weapons?"

"Yeah. Certain guys are tagged to gain weapons. They use their own ole lady, or some of the better-looking sheep they keep around the clubhouse, to lure guys from the local military bases. Once they get the supply chain established, all transactions are kept way under the radar. There's way too much press coverage on this to be tied to the weapons deals."

"That leaves the prostitution ring," Jack surmised.

Shadow crushed the beer can between his palms until it was as flat as a pancake.

"Calm down. Let's talk it through before you go all rogue on us," Jack said.

"Jack's right. The prostitution ring is fairly straightforward. They use the same sheep they keep around the club—or new girls they pick up hitchhiking. But as far as I know, they always bring them back to the clubhouse for the members to pass around."

"As far as you know. So there could be a deviation from the norm going on." Shadow stood and began pacing. "I'm reading you both in on a highly classified piece of intel we have."

"Highly classified piece of intel means it was obtained illegally." Nick raised his eyebrows at Shadow. "Blurring lines?"

"I have no lines where Elle is concerned. If I had to storm the gates of hell itself to bring her back, that's exactly what I'd do. If I have to kill every single member of the Devil's Dominion with my bare hands to get her out of their clutches, it won't bother me one bit.

"So, one of our analysts was combing through all the data and chatter from the time surrounding the disappearances and found something interesting. Katrina Fox was the first actress I'd heard about going off the grid, but she actually wasn't the first. A girl by the name of Carrie Snow was the first one.

"A similar story was given—she quit the film industry and settled down somewhere in suburbia. There were rumors of drug and alcohol addiction that plagued her. While our analyst was checking for anything related to Elle, Carrie's name came up. He marked it to research it later and called me on the flight today. Seems Carrie's name is hot on the chatter wheel these days."

"So your analyst hacked into the NSA's program and has been monitoring cell phone conversations for you across Southern California?" Nick was barely holding on to his sense of right and wrong after being a full-fledged officer in an outlaw motorcycle club for two years. He needed his friends outside the club to be his moral compass when his own was askew.

"You're completely missing the point. That's three missing actresses and a makeup artist who happened to be with Elle when she disappeared. The first one was weeks before Katrina—but her name is still active in the chatter. The goods haven't been delivered yet. Not with the intel he gave me.

"Where would they hide the girls they're not using yet? We've checked the known properties, and nothing jumps out as an obvious hideaway."

"Nowhere. The club has nowhere to hide girls like that. You're talking high-profile, instantly recognizable, the-whole-world-looking-for-them actresses. Our sheep are taken out in broad daylight and paraded in front of men on the street. They're openly offered to potential Johns on the sidewalks downtown.

"Most of these boys don't have a pot to piss in on their own. Your apartment over there would be a palace to more than half of our local chapter members. Did your analyst come across any other names that would be helpful in our search?"

"No, but he's still doing his analysis. He picked up on her name and searched every hit on that match first. It'll take him a little while longer to sort through the rest."

"And that doesn't bother you? Eavesdropping illegally?"

"Not a bit. It's not for my monetary gain. It's to save the lives of four young women and to prevent more from being taken. We know it was Devil's Dominion members who took Elle and Beth. That was confirmed by the patches on their vests. He followed them with local cameras as far as he could. The truck disappeared in an alley and never came back out."

"And you've already had the buildings scanned by satellites." Nick wasn't even asking at that point.

"Of course. One of the buildings is a parking garage. Too many large vehicles went in and out to identify one to home in on. Plus, they could've separated Elle and Beth and taken them on different routes. An incursion at one location could mean death to the others. I can't take that risk—I need absolutes in this case."

"Then I guess your friend needs to perform more illegal searches and find a connection to the money." Nick didn't try to hide his sarcasm or his disapproval.

"It's not illegal when they're suspected of domestic terrorism and treason." Shadow shot his words back at Nick, not hiding his disgust with the turn in the conversation.

"Domestic terrorism? By kidnapping a starlet and depriving America of their ninety-minute worship time?"

"You don't honestly believe their end game is to kidnap three beautiful, well-known stars and use them for a local prostitution ring, do you? They're going to trade them—desirable human slaves in exchange for weapons from a Middle Eastern country known for using biological weapons on their own people, Chinese syndicates who sell them into slavery in exchange for large amounts of laundered money, or anything else in between.

"Think like a DEA agent, Nick. Not like a low-level thug who only does what 'big boss Headbanger' tells him to do. Your biker gang is attempting to break in to the big leagues for a reason. Whether they want to use the weapons themselves or sell them to others for a shitload of money doesn't matter."

CHAPTER SIXTEEN

Elle's parents, Danny and Tanya, and her brothers, Jeff and Mark, arrived at her apartment and frantically searched for any sign of her return. A small clue that confirmed she was fine, just avoiding the world. But none of her close personal belongings were there—purse, cell phone, or wallet. Beth's parents were scheduled to arrive later that evening, and Jeff had shared Devon's strict instructions with them.

"Mr. and Mrs. Moore?" The deep, authoritative voice boomed from the doorway. "I'm Noah 'Reaper' Steele. I believe you're expecting my team and me."

"Yes, though I've only heard Devon call you Reaper. He told us all about you. Please come in." Tanya urged him into the apartment, her eyes growing wider with each man who followed him.

"This is the rest of my team. Colton 'Bull' Lanier and Braxton 'Rebel' Reed. We'll be watching your backs at all times. I wanted to make sure you met us first. You won't see us unless we want you to know we're there, but when that happens, it'll be for a specific reason."

"Do you think we're in danger?" Danny glanced around the room at his family, his concern for their safety etched in his features. They were all anxious to start hounding anyone and everyone over his daughter's whereabouts, but he had to consider the safety of the rest of his family as well.

"There's nothing to indicate that," Rebel replied. "But there's also no reason to take chances."

"Right. Our information shows you own a lucrative winery. If this is a ransom case, the more leverage they have, the harder it'll be for us to gain traction. We'd rather be more cautious than necessary." Bull explained the situation in his usual straightforward manner.

"So let's get started. We'll take shifts and follow you when you leave. No one goes anywhere alone for any reason—even if that's their only demand. This is not up for discussion." Noah had the family sit and memorize the coverage schedule and how to contact them in case of an emergency. "First stop will be the studio office. You need to demand to speak with the executive in charge of production on Elle's movie. He'll refuse. Leave, and go back with a reporter and camera. Then don't take no for an answer."

"I can do that," Tanya replied. "If I need to pitch a tent and sleep in their office, I can do that too."

"Let's hope it doesn't come to that." The admiration on Bull's face contradicted his words.

Early the next morning, the Moore family arrived at the executive offices, their sights set on forcing the hand of the one responsible for releasing lies about Elle's disappearance. The secretary looked up, confused and concerned, when she heard the commotion behind the double doors that separated the executive suite. Tanya burst through the opening, threats and promises of relieving the security guard of everything that made him a man if he touched her again.

"Barry Jacobson," she yelled down the long hallway of executive offices. "We demand to speak with you this instant."

With Danny, Jeff, and Mark running interference with the guards, Tanya walked briskly down the corridor, calling his name loudly. "If I'm forced to leave without speaking to you, it will be much worse when I return."

A door swung open, and a graying man in his midfifties stepped out. "What can I do for you, Ms.—?" His voice trailed off as he searched her face for recognition. She knew the moment he realized who she was. "You must be Elle Sinclair's mother because she is the spitting image of you."

"That's right. Elle Moore is my daughter, and I want to know where she is right now."

He tried to hide his shock, but the way the color drained from his face couldn't be denied. "You haven't heard from her yet?"

"Would I be here if I had?"

"I'm sure she and Jax are still enjoying their honeymoon on some remote island. No need to worry."

"She's not with Jax on some remote island or anywhere else. We both know that is a lie, and I'll make sure the entire world knows it, too. You'll answer for why no police report has been filed, no questions asked, no searches performed. What are you hiding?"

"Ma'am, you need to leave the premises immediately before we call the police and have you arrested for trespassing." The security guard had finally gotten around the Moore men and approached Tanya.

"Tell you what," she replied calmly when she rounded on him. "You go ahead and call the police and have them wait right here for me. Because when I come back, the whole world will see it."

"Mrs. Moore—wait. Let's talk about this. Elle and Jax are perfectly fine."

"You have one hour to produce her," she replied to Barry. To the guard, she continued, "And you have one hour to get the LAPD here to protect you. We'll be back."

Once outside the building, Tanya's phone began ringing. With shaky hands, she dug it out of her purse.

"Very nice work," Reaper chuckled darkly. "You need a job with my team?"

She released a much-needed laugh before replying. "I'm not sure I could handle that on a daily basis. I was sure the guard would toss me over his shoulder and carry me out."

"You riled Barry up enough that he's making stupid mistakes. His first call was to Jax. We're working on getting an exact location for him now, then one of my team members will pay him a visit."

"You don't believe Elle is with Jax either, do you?" Tanya asked the question, but she didn't exactly want an answer. The trepidation he'd confirm her worst fears overwhelmed her coping skills.

"No, Tanya, I don't believe it at all. But that gives us concrete proof to put more pressure on them both. Even if they don't know where she is, they know more than they're saying. Don't give up hope—we're just getting started. You know Devon won't rest until she's home again."

With Reaper's direction, they left the studio offices and drove straight to the entertainment news station. Within minutes, they'd arranged an exclusive first interview and had a pushy reporter with a crew of cameramen at their disposal. Upon returning to the executive offices, they found the police and the lot guards waiting for them.

"This is perfect," the reporter hungry for the juicy scoop exclaimed. She grabbed the microphone and ordered the cameramen to take their places to get multiple angles.

"Hello, officers. Mary Ellen Gallie with Hollywood Biz News. Can you tell me why you've locked down the offices of Timeless and Classic Entertainment Studios?"

"We had a previous issue with trespassing. The offices are closed to any visitors for the rest of the day." The guard glanced nervously between her and the cameras.

"Is that because executive Barry Jacobson is hiding the truth from the world? Is that why he won't speak with the parents and brothers of Elle Sinclair?" Mary Ellen thrust the microphone into his face and waited for an answer.

"She didn't have an appointment," he stammered.

"Let me get this straight so that I—and all of our viewers watching this live broadcast—understand. This family maintains Elle Sinclair is actually missing, but they can't speak with Barry Jacobson...because they didn't have an appointment?"

The guard opened his mouth to reply, but he was abruptly interrupted when Barry stepped outside.

"Thank you, officers, for your assistance, but I believe we can take it from here." Barry took a few steps toward the camera and turned on the charm. "Mary Ellen, so good to see you again."

"Barry, I've spoken with Elle Sinclair's family, and they've provided some very damning information that directly contradicts your assertion Elle and Jax ran away together. Your reply?"

"Mary Ellen, I completely understand their concern and need for concrete proof that their beloved daughter is safe and sound. Here at Timeless and Classic Entertainment, we are one big family. When one hurts, we all hurt.

"As soon as I realized their level of concern, and that they haven't heard from Elle yet, I tracked Jax down myself. Mrs. Moore had already left when I spoke with him, but he assured me he'll have Elle contact them as soon as possible. She was indisposed when we spoke, but he promised the call would be made soon."

"Did Jax give you any indication of where they are?"

"No, and I didn't ask. I've tried to respect their privacy, but I couldn't let this loving family continue to suffer." Barry's smile was warm and sincere, but something else burned in his eyes when he met Tanya's gaze.

Conceit. Victory.

Fury. Resentment.

"You are lying, Barry Jacobson. We both know it. Shall we wait together in your office for this make-believe call? So we can all hear my daughter's voice at once? Or better yet, see her beautiful face? Surely, if you reached Jax once today, you can do it again for all of us." Tanya challenged him, meeting his fiery gaze with one of her own.

"I'm afraid I have other commitments I can't break, but I look forward to hearing all about their trip."

With that, Barry turned and walked back into the building, his guards maintaining their position between the Moores and the entrance. Mary Ellen turned to the camera and spoke to her live audience.

"Danny and Tanya Moore, parents of Elle Sinclair, will be with me in the studio for an exclusive interview on the sudden disappearance of one of Hollywood's favorite sweethearts. Tune in tonight to hear why they're adamant foul play cannot be ruled out. If Elle calls to check in, you'll be the first to know."

On the way back to the studio for the interview, Tanya's phone rang, and her heart nearly jumped out of her chest. She'd love to be wrong about Elle. She prayed she was wrong—but she knew her daughter better than anyone. Jax Hart held no position in Elle's heart. She'd reserved that spot for Devon Kane years ago. Even over the past year when Tanya encouraged her to date and get over him, Elle's reply was always the same.

No one else will ever compare to Devon Kane.

Elle's elation at being cast opposite Jax turned to ire after the first day on the set with him. Her frequent conversations with Tanya revealed growing tensions between them. Tanya talked her off the proverbial ledge many times when Elle threatened to quit the film. In the end, her strong work ethic and loyalty to her fans won, and she endured "just one more day with Jax Hart."

Tanya's heart sank when she saw the number on the caller ID. It wasn't Elle calling to confirm Barry's story.

"Nice move with the live feed. We're helping Barry along with the promise to hear from Elle. He has people in the sound booth now creating a recorded message from her. The clips will be spliced together to make her say what they want her to say. Let him hang himself with it. We'll send you the unedited version to air on Mary Ellen's show immediately after his."

"How do you know all this, Reaper?"

"We're all Special Forces—it's our job to know. My men are the best at what they do. Barry won't be able to take all the pressure we'll put on him. Just remember—no mention of Devon. We can't call attention to him. If you even hint she has another love interest, they'll demand you produce him. And they'll want to know why he hasn't stepped forward before now. For both Elle's and Devon's safety, don't forget that."

Tanya silently questioned if Reaper could read her mind, since that was the exact thought she had before he called. "You're right. I don't know what Devon is doing, but he stressed to Jeff it's a matter of life or death to leave him out of the conversation. That's not an exaggeration, is it?"

"No, Tanya. It's actually an understatement. You don't want to know what could happen to them if anything is accidentally leaked."

They disconnected, and Tanya relayed the conversation to Danny and her sons. With a new understanding of what was at stake and how far the studio was willing to go to hide their involvement, the family of four silently reflected on the dangerous situation they were in. And how much worse that danger was for Elle and Devon.

"Mary Ellen Gallie will love this scoop," Mark chortled when he envisioned her reaction. "You know this could backfire on us. Every major news outlet in the world will run the edited versus unedited versions day and night. The internet will break from people on social media. What if exposing their lies just makes them mad?"

"Son, I've considered that too, and I've decided I'd rather lose her knowing I did everything I could to fight for her than lose her because I just rolled over and let them run over me," Danny replied solemnly. "Your mother and I talked about this very scenario all night. Beth's family agreed. We'd all rather do anything than nothing at all."

They remained silent for the remainder of the ride, each fortifying the resolve needed to see the plan through. Trusting that Devon and his friends knew what they were doing and wouldn't advise them wrong. Brokenhearted over the fate of one of their own and livid they couldn't do more, the feeling of helplessness that saturated the interior of their car was stifling.

~

Elle woke with a start but couldn't force her eyes to remain open. Throwing the covers back, she swung her legs off the side of the bed, her vision blurry, but the panic of being late to the set controlled her movements. If the sun was already peeking over the horizon, she was already late for work. Apparently so was Beth since she hadn't pounced on Elle yet.

"Beth!"

The memories came rushing back to her. The strange house. The terrifying man who stopped her escape. The elegant mansion that was her prison. The spray that rendered her unconscious—twice—with merely a misting.

And Beth, her best friend, was nowhere to be seen when Elle left the sound stage late that night she was abducted. Terror filled her chest at the thought they didn't take Beth also but did something far worse to her. Elle had to force her body to comply with her will to move. Finding Beth was her first order of business. They would escape together—two heads were better than one.

She padded barefoot across the ornate wood floor toward the door. While holding a deep breath, she slowly turned the knob and was both relieved and surprised to find it wasn't locked from the other side. The soft squeak of the hinge made her freeze in place and actively listen for her captors.

Without opening the door wider, she slid through the narrow opening into the hallway. She decided to check each room behind the closed doors in the long corridor. If they put her in one, maybe Beth still slept in another. The first few rooms were empty, but set up nearly identical to the one she'd snuck out of. The view waiting behind door number four reduced her to tears.

Tied to the four-poster bed was her best friend and confidante, still deep in slumber and blissfully unaware of their current situation. Elle rushed to her side and began tugging at the ropes to free her. Beth's head lolled to the other side, as if she were simultaneously trying to sleep and wake.

"Beth," Ellie whisper-shouted at her. "Beth, it's me. Wake up. We have to find a way out of here."

Beth's mumbled reply was incoherent, leaving no doubt she'd been drugged. The struggle between leaving without her and bringing help back, or staying with her until the effects wore off enough for Beth to stand was unbearable. Elle kept working at untying the knots while she weighed the pros and cons of each, hoping Beth would become coherent in the meantime.

When she'd finished with the last figure eight knot, Beth's arm fell limply against the bed. "What have they done to you?" Elle whispered through her tears and pushed the hair out of Beth's face.

"We just helped her sleep. She's quite combative and feisty when she's awake."

Elle jumped and whirled around to find a distinguished older man in a butler's uniform standing in the doorway.

"I assure you, no one has harmed or assaulted her in any way. The ropes were used for her ultimate protection. She has already slapped two of our staff members. Should she assault the wrong man, I cannot guarantee her safety."

"Where are we? Why have you taken us? Just let us both go, and nothing else has to happen. I'm sure my disappearance is all over the news. People everywhere will be looking for me. She's my makeup artist on the set and my best friend from childhood. They'll know something is wrong. You'll never get away with this."

Elle rambled on, not taking a breath between sentences as she tried to convince her captor of the folly of his plan.

He smiled at her, the kind of sneer that confirmed she was wasting her breath by trying to convince him to let her go. She knew then she wasn't the first person they'd abducted, and she likely wouldn't be the last.

"I've been sent to bring you to the media room. There's a documentary of sorts my employer would like for you to watch. If you come quietly and willingly, there will be no need for your own restraints."

"What about Beth?"

"She will be here when the documentary has concluded, likely beginning to awaken by then. You may rejoin her at that time if you wish."

Such a cordial captor, Elle thought as she followed him to the high-tech-equipped media room. The chairs were arranged in theater seating, plush recliners providing clear views of the wall-sized flat-screen TV. The surround sound system added to the theater experience, topping off the opulence and wealth of the state-of-the-art room.

The butler placed a glass of water on the table beside her and moved to the back of the room while her eyes remained glued to the enormous screen. The vibrant colors lit up the screen as Mary Ellen Gallie greeted her viewers.

"Hello, and thank you for joining us tonight. We have a full show, so I'm going to jump straight in without delay. As many of you saw earlier this morning, Elle Sinclair's family has arrived in LA, adamant she and Jax Hart have *not* eloped. They insist something terrible has happened to Elle.

"The family confronted Timeless and Classic Entertainment executive Barry Jacobson, and Hollywood Biz News was there to capture part of it live for you. During that confrontation, Mr. Jacobson claims he spoke to Jax Hart today and that Jax will make sure Elle contacts her family as soon as possible. According to the studio executive, Elle was 'indisposed' at the time he spoke to Jax.

"I'm excited to tell you we have a recorded message from Elle to share with you and with her family. It was emailed to the studio just minutes ago with a note saying the internet service is spotty at their secluded resort, but the local news channel was kind enough to record her message in return for autographs for the staff.

"It's now my pleasure to show you this message from Miss Elle Sinclair. Or should I say, Mrs. Elle Hart? Let's watch."

Elle stared at the screen in sheer disbelief. Before her eyes, an image of herself appeared on the screen, extolling the romance between her and Jax, how they were perfect for each other, and she'd never been happier than she was at that moment.

Words she'd never uttered.

A message she'd never sent.

Lies that sealed her fate.

Complex deceptions that took talent to achieve.

She'd cried too many tears over her circumstances. At that moment, she was absolutely numb. From the moment she saw herself deliver a falsified message to the world, her emotions automatically shut down in a self-preservation and coping mechanism.

"Most people would accept that prerecorded message as the gospel and move on with their lives, allowing Jax and Elle to live and love in peace. However, Elle's parents have maintained from the start that this is all a ruse and a far more sinister agenda is afoot.

"Ladies and gentlemen, our video department received a second file of Elle Sinclair, with an email urging our station to compare the two videos and see for ourselves that the first one is an edited farce. So we did. Industry film editors have reviewed them and formed an expert opinion. Before we hear from them, have a look for yourselves."

The screen cut to a series of press junket interviews with Elle, where a long line of journalists entered the room one at a time and were given fifteen minutes to ask their questions. Her answers, all conveying the excitement and enthusiasm she displayed while speaking of Jax, her fake new love, were projected toward working with him on the movie. Each time one journalist was escorted out of the room, another one was brought in to ask additional questions.

"After reviewing these two videos, all our industry experts agree the first video is a spliced and fake recreation, using clips of the second video. The unanimous decision is there is no possible way the purported message from Elle is valid. This evidence has been sent to local law enforcement to urge them to open a missing person's case for Elle Sinclair, Beth Condra, and Jax Hart. Hollywood Biz News suggests the detectives start with Barry Jacobson as the primary person of interest."

The screen went black before Mary Ellen finished speaking, but Elle caught just a glimpse of her parents and brothers when the camera panned in their direction. Knowing they were close and pushing for the truth gave her an instant swelling of hope. Whatever plan her captors had for her would surely fail.

"Your family is very tenacious. We expected your video message would be enough to satisfy them for a few weeks, giving us time to complete our business deals before they started looking for you. Make no mistake, Miss Sinclair, this wrinkle temporarily changes our plans but does not cancel them in any way. You will not be returned to your family or to the life you used to have."

Elle stared at the woman, dumbfounded, and shook her head. Her eyes floated between the badge she wore on her belt and her angry eyes. Her words and her attire were direct opposites.

"Oh, I'm so sorry. I know who you are, but I haven't introduced myself. I'm Detective Joanna Gough, and I've just been assigned to your missing person's case. Since they're so closely related, I also volunteered to take Beth Condra's and Jax Hart's cases. Unfortunately, my stellar record for solving cases will take a major hit, but I'll just have to find a way to live with it."

"Why? Why would you do this?" Elle wailed.

"Don't be stupid," Detective Gough replied. "So naïve and stupid. Take her back."

The butler wrapped his hand around her bicep and pulled her to her feet. Once they were out of earshot of the detective, Elle turned to him.

"I don't understand what's happening. What are you going to do with us?"

"Do you want to go to your room or to your friend's room?" His reply was cordial, but his avoidance of her direct question was blatant.

"Take me to Beth."

He opened the door to find Beth pacing back and forth across the bedroom, shouting obscenities and her own terroristic threats. When Beth saw Elle in the doorway, she rushed to her and pulled her into a death-grip hug.

"I thought I dreamed you earlier. You really were here, weren't you?"

The butler pushed them into the room and closed the door again. Elle waited until his footsteps could no longer be heard before she told Beth what had happened. When she finished repeating every word for the third time, Beth paled and quickly sat.

"What? What are you thinking?" Elle had to push her friend to speak her mind for the first time in their friendship.

"They abducted us. Drugged us to bring us to this secret mansion prison. Put us in separate rooms. Concocted this elaborate video of how happy you are with Jax. The detective assigned to our case is in on this scheme. But now they're letting us talk and stay together? Something about that last part doesn't sit well with me. It's the complete opposite of everything else they've done."

Dread settled in Elle's gut.

CHAPTER SEVENTEEN

"Do you know where they're keeping Katrina?" Elle asked.

"No. You think she's here too?" Beth rose from the bed and walked to the window. "It would make sense. Honestly, I haven't been able to think past finding you and getting out of here."

"They don't lock the bedroom doors. Maybe we should go look around. I don't even know how long we've been here, but when I first woke up, I got as far as the front yard. There's a tall brick fence around the property as far as I could see."

Elle told Beth the rest of the details she remembered from that night. Together, they agreed to explore as much of the house as they could before anyone stopped them. Since no one knew where they were, they couldn't wait and chance being rescued. They'd have to be their own heroes in this real-life thriller.

Elle opened the door and stepped into the hall. Something about the dead space gave her a sick feeling each time, as if a monster hid behind one of the doors, waiting to devour her. *That's probably not far off the mark, actually,* she thought as she approached the next closed door. Much like she'd done when she searched for Beth, she inspected the room for any sign of inhabitants and moved to the next one. Beth checked the doors on the opposite side, also holding her breath until a flood of relief washed over her when she realized the coast was clear.

"Katrina?" Beth's voice carried down the hall to Elle.

Elle's gaze snapped to Beth's, waiting to learn the fate of their mutual friend.

Beth stepped inside the room, and Elle heard muffled cries. Without a second thought, she ran to the room and found the two women in a tight embrace. Katrina looked up at Elle and stretched out one of her arms to her. Elle immediately joined in, wrapping her arms around them both and clinging to them in the comfort of shared misery. When Katrina could release them, Elle and Beth stepped back to visually inspect her for wounds.

"I'm okay. No one has hurt me. It's so odd, though. Not that I want them to do anything to me, but I almost feel like we're part of some rich, eccentric guy's collection. A life-size doll collection." Katrina walked to the window and pointed outside. "Look. Do you recognize where we are? I don't see any landmarks I know from around LA."

They joined her at the window and took a minute to memorize the landscape. Knowing the layout of the grounds and what awaited on the other side of the brick wall would be helpful in an escape attempt.

"Wait a minute—that looks so familiar." Elle pointed at a rocky outcrop in the distance.

"Rocks on the Pacific shore look familiar?" Beth asked. "They all look the same to me."

"No, it's the unique shape they make. Mark and I used to laugh about how it's shaped like a breast. I think we're close to my family's vineyard."

"Where no one is looking for us," Beth replied gloomily.

Elle and Beth gave Katrina a condensed version of what they knew, ending with Detective Gough's involvement with their imprisonment while being assigned to find them. Katrina listened carefully, doing her best to keep up with the details while keeping her panic under control.

"Wait—did you just say she's assigned to Jax's disappearance case, too?" Katrina asked.

"Yeah. What are you thinking?" Elle asked.

"It just seems like Jax is a common denominator in this whole sordid mess. Do you think he could be behind it?"

"Even he couldn't afford this place," Elle replied. "But that doesn't mean he's not involved somehow. I just don't know how or why. The movie production will be put on hiatus with me gone—it's too late to replace me, and the sound stage has already been booked for the next movie anyway."

"So it's a coincidence I rejected him just before I was taken?"

"I don't believe in coincidences." Elle turned the facts over in her mind, examining them from various angles. But like a jigsaw puzzle with the picture missing, she couldn't make the pieces fit together and make any sense. Her only hope was she knew her family wouldn't give up until they got to the bottom of her recorded message fiasco.

"Ladies, come with me, please." The butler stood in the doorway eying them, no doubt eavesdropping on their conversation.

"Where are you taking us?" Beth asked defiantly.

"My employer wishes to have a word with you. It's best not to keep him waiting."

The three ladies followed him down the hall, across the foyer, and down the stairs at the back of the kitchen. The narrow staircase opened into a large basement. Bile rose in Elle's throat, and her neck muscles worked to swallow it down. The floor, walls, and ceiling were covered in thick black sheets of plastic. In Elle's mind, there was only one reason why that would be found in a multimillion-dollar mansion.

"Ladies, have a seat, please," the voice behind them instructed. They gasped and turned to see who'd joined them. A handsome older man, distinguished by the strands of gray at his temples and salt-and-pepper smattering throughout, gestured to the four folding chairs. His face was vaguely familiar, though Elle couldn't place where she'd seen him before.

"Carrie? Carrie Snow?" With a slack jaw and wide eyes, Katrina stared at the woman beside him.

He gently pushed Carrie forward as she nodded at Katrina, confirming her identity.

"Have you been here the entire time?" Katrina whispered and walked with her to the brown metal chairs.

"Yes. Is anyone even looking for me anymore?" Tears welled up in Carrie's eyes, and her voice broke on her last word. Katrina didn't have the heart—or the time—to tell her no one suspected foul play in her case. Widespread rumors of her repeat drug and alcohol addiction just weeks before she went missing provided more than enough of a cover story to explain her absence.

The older man began speaking, drawing their attention to him and the empty chair beside him. "Ladies, I've brought you down here to ensure we understand each other. As long as you obey my rules, you are free to roam to any unlocked area of the house. I know you didn't reach your current star status because you played by the rules, so I'm sure at least one of you will try me. In fact, I understand one of you has already tried to escape, so I'll give you a demonstration of what happens when someone pushes me past my limit."

The man dressed in black leather, the one who sprayed Elle's face the night she attempted her escape, stepped into the room. He had another man with him—gagged, bound, and blindfolded. He directed the man's steps to the empty chair, forcefully shoved him down onto the chair, and removed his blindfold.

Still unable to speak, the man's frightened gaze darted around the room, searching for someone to help him. He made direct contact with each woman, using his eyes to plead for help. The black plastic shrouding the room only added to his frantic behavior, and he attempted to stand. The rough man in black halted his movement with a firm hand on his shoulder, pushing him back down.

"This man has been a member of my private parties for many years. I've trusted him enough to allow him into my home. He'd been welcome, until I learned he's been running his mouth to others, boasting about his status with me, and revealing private details he swore to secrecy.

"To show you how seriously I value my personal affairs, you will watch what happens to those I consider to be a traitor. Spider." He nodded to the man in black. "You're up."

The older man stepped out of the way, but he stayed close to the women to ensure they didn't look away. The gagged traitor grunted loudly, obviously trying to beg for his life or explain some misunderstanding. The man's cries had no effect on Spider as he leveled the gun against the traitor's temple.

"Do not look away," the older man reminded sternly.

"Any last words?" Spider asked mockingly. "Oh, that's right. You can't speak. Guess not, then."

The man yelled, his gaze locked on to Elle's, begging for her to intervene on his behalf. Before she could murmur a word, a loud noise rang through the room. In slow motion, she watched matter spray from the opposite side of the man's head while a single stream of blood ran down the entrance side. Spider returned his gun to its holster, an amused sneer covering his face while he watched the man slump to one side, lifeless.

Gasps followed by muffled cries filled the room, each woman afraid to make too much noise and call undue attention to herself. Elle couldn't cry and she couldn't breathe. Her lungs seized in her chest, refusing to cooperate and do their job.

"This is what happens to those who disappoint me. Spider has no problem killing them—in fact, I think he prefers it. If you try to escape in any way, you will be stopped. But one of your silver screen sisters will die in your place while you watch."

That visual prompted Elle's body to inhale sharply, reminding her lungs of their intended function a little too well. Her rapid breaths on top of her racing heart pushed her closer to hyperventilation. The older man walked over to her and placed his hands on her shoulders.

"Calm down, Elle. Take deep breaths and clear your head. As long as you cooperate, everything will be fine. You'll have nothing to worry about at all."

The butler returned to escort the ladies upstairs, locking the basement door behind him. That was one door Elle didn't mind being forbidden from entering again.

"You may return to your rooms or any other unlocked room. The kitchen is always open and well-stocked with anything you may need. You have nothing and no one to fear if you adhere to the instructions. My employer has strict rules about that, and none of his associates will cross the line."

Elle ushered the others into her room, away from anyone else who may be watching or listening. She stood on the threshold, watching for their captors, and spoke quickly in hushed tones. Her voice quivered and her hands shook, but she knew they only had two alternatives. Have a nervous breakdown and let them win, or pretend they didn't just witness a man get shot in the head in front of them so they could focus on an escape plan.

"Listen. There's no way they'll let us go unharmed. Whatever their plans are for us are obviously bad, or we wouldn't be here at all." Her voice broke, and she pressed the back of her hand against her lips. "When he said we had nothing to fear—that was just to placate us. But I do believe if one of us runs, they'll kill one of the others. So we have to go together. No one gets left behind."

"When? How?" Katrina's eagerness surged through her posture, readying herself to run at that moment. Carrie's apprehension was equally as obvious when she shrank back and wrapped her arms around her midsection. Beth jumped to her feet, prepared to fight the devil and rescue herself.

"As soon as we can safely do it together. We can't wait too long, though. It's time we start checking out the house thoroughly and find anything of use."

~

Shadow spent the first week in his service-station apartment setting up his legal and illegal businesses, letting his beard grow out, and brooding in his anger and hatred toward the ones who took Elle. Through his contacts, he set up a collection of small arms to sell in backroom deals. The sooner his name became established, the sooner Nick could get him inside.

With the service bay door open, he sat on a mechanic's chair, working on a customer's bike Jack had thrown his way. It was a simple job he could do blindfolded—a meaningless task to busy his hands and legitimize his business. He sensed the presence of another person before he lifted his eyes. He'd memorized the faces and names of every major player in the Devil's Dominion motorcycle club. There was no denying who approached him.

Spider Skull—the club secretary. The one who kept the membership list, the bylaws, the club rules, and the appointment book for every club officer. The one who knew the comings and goings of everyone—where they were, who they met with, and why. He had every piece of information and correspondence on the club members—the epitome of a field asset.

But he wasn't the sergeant at arms.

So why is he here?

"I heard this old place was in business again." Spider walked into the garage and looked around, like he belonged there as much as Shadow did.

"Word travels fast, then, since it's only been a week."

"I have friends who keep me updated on things of interest around here."

"A small-engine repair and bike detail shop, with one customer, is interesting to you?" Shadow stood and turned, following his visitor around the room.

"Don't like anyone behind you?"

"No. Prison will do that to a man if life doesn't do it first."

"Where were you?"

"Federal pen. Atlanta."

"Federal charges, huh? What were you convicted of?"

"Drugs and weapons. Fucking undercover DEA agent." He tossed his wrench into the toolbox, the loud clanking emphasizing his disgust.

"Something similar happened to a friend of mine. He wasn't dumb enough to get caught with drugs, though."

"You want to tell me your name first?" Shadow asked, narrowing his eyes.

"First? Before what?"

"Before I kick your ass and have to notify your next of kin."

He burst out laughing. "Name's Spider. Jack's a friend of a friend, and he suggested I drop by here."

"Jack's a good man. Strange I didn't hear your bike pull up. Did you pedal?"

Spider smiled. His sneer sickened Shadow, but he hid his contempt. "Maybe. Or maybe I cut the engine and coasted in to test your reflexes. Took you a minute to realize I was on top of you."

It was Shadow's turn to flash his smug grin. "The hell you say. You cut the engine a block and a half back, just when you passed the fire hydrant. If the car in front of you had turned, you would've lost your element of surprise completely."

"I'm impressed. And I'm not impressed easily. You're Shadow, right?"

"That's right. Something I can do for you, Spider? Or did you just drop by for tea?"

"After Jack told me about you, I did some checking up on you. Seems you already have a lucrative business starting, and not only with your one customer." Spider inclined his head toward the work Shadow had done on the bike. "Some of the items you've acquired could be good for my club. But it would be bad for you if they find out about your extracurricular activities. It could be seen as an act of war against us."

"Interesting perspective, since I'm not part of any club. You don't see any colors on my back. I'm just doing some minor work on motorcycles for avid riders, restoring classics for rich collectors. What business are you referring to?"

Spider nodded slowly, mentally sizing Shadow up. With a couple of steps, he sauntered up to Shadow, reached into his vest pocket, and pulled out a business card. "Come by here tomorrow night at eight. I want you to meet the officers of the club, maybe become a pledge if they like you."

"You trying to move in on my turf, Spider?" Nick asked from the doorway.

"Renegade. What are you doing here?"

"Shadow is a friend of mine. I've already arranged a meeting with the prez and VP," Nick replied.

"Strange it's not on my radar since I keep the calendars for both of them."

Nick held up his cell phone and shook it from side to side. "Just hung up with Headbanger. You should get a call any minute now."

Just as Nick finished speaking, Spider's phone began ringing. When he walked off to take the call, Nick and Shadow exchanged knowing glances.

Word on the street spread fast when the information was given to the right people.

Spider rejoined them, his suspicious gaze cutting back and forth between Nick and Shadow. "Good thing we all agree how Shadow could be an asset to the club. Of course, that just makes Bonebreaker even more suspicious than he normally is."

"Should make for an interesting meeting, then," Shadow retorted.

The clubhouse was a two-story cinder block building with no windows, painted completely black, sitting on the corner of the block. The long string of buildings attached also belonged to the club and were used for storefront businesses. The long corridor that attached to the clubhouse at the back provided a quick getaway when rival clubs took cheap shots, or when the federal agents arrived for a raid.

Nick and Shadow arrived early, before the rest of the officers returned. Nick showed him around, being careful with his words since the paranoia had escalated and he never knew when extra eyes and ears were around. Headbanger made the food and drink run while he was already out on official club business. Nights when the entire club was required to attend church, their club meeting, the probies and pledges carried all the food and beer in. But they weren't allowed in the officers' area unless specifically called, so Nick and Shadow watched for Headbanger to arrive so they could assist.

The thundering rumble of several motorcycles approaching at once drew Shadow to the door. Angry voices and loud threats streamed through the closed metal door. Shadow opened it and stood face-to-face with Headbanger. Nutcracker and Bonebreaker stood immediately behind him. All six eyes bore into the outsider, anger rolling off them in waves at finding him in the officers' area.

Shadow opened the door wider and stepped out of the way to give them room to pass. The first two stepped by him, and Nick stepped forward to take some of the cases of beer from Headbanger's hands. Bonebreaker stopped directly in front of Shadow and glared at him menacingly. Instant suspicion lit his expression.

"Who the fuck are you? The doorman?"

"That's me. The Devil's Doorman." He knew on one hand he was expected to be respectful to the officers and to every other lifelong member. His place among them was the lowest of the ranks, and they enjoyed reminding newbies of their place. On the other hand, it would take minimal effort for him to snap Bonebreaker's neck and be done with him, so taking insults from him asked too much of Shadow's patience.

A stare down between the two brutes ensued, with neither man showing an ounce of weakness. Headbanger began laughing loudly, his booming voice filling the room and drawing their attention. "Looks like you have a new nickname, Shadow. You're the Doorman now. Renegade told me all about you. Then you hit Spider's radar, and he had our PI check you out immediately. Seems you've made quite an impression on our little club."

"All the more reason to suspect him," Bonebreaker grumbled.

"I told you to cut that shit out. I've known him for years. You're doubting and disrespecting me when you question him. Why don't you try questioning my loyalty to my face and see what happens?" Nick changed into his role of Renegade flawlessly, issuing his dare as a threat rather than a question. His glare taunted Bonebreaker to try him. His muscles tensed, and his hands curled into fists.

"Fine. You're responsible for him, then." Bonebreaker stomped away, conceding to Renegade. Shadow noted to ask Nick about it later. There was obviously bad blood somewhere in their history.

Nutcrusher, the VP, called for several of the sheep they kept at the clubhouse. "Get this food and beer ready for us," he barked at the women when they entered the room. "We're hungry and thirsty, so don't take all damn day."

Shadow's blood boiled over at how the girls were treated. They took women who'd already had a hard life and used them in any and every way. Some of them admittedly volunteered for the position, feeling like they were part of a larger family and protected by the nature of the club. The members could abuse them, but no one else could.

The thought of the same men having their hands on Elle made Shadow the most lethal man in the world. He couldn't find her soon enough. Every minute that passed added another vision of horrible acts Elle had to endure.

When the women finished with the food, they delivered heaping plates and chilled beer to the table. Headbanger told everyone to take their seats and gave Shadow the rare opportunity to join them.

"You're here because you obviously built quite a network before you were sent off. You trusted the wrong person. Bone did the same once. Now he trusts no one."

"It only takes one mistake for the house of cards to fall." Shadow's cryptic reply had a purpose. Showing his distrust of others gave him and Bone something in common. "What is it you're looking to acquire?"

"We have a list of things." Bone sat back in his chair and continued. "Are you not good enough to get more than one piece?"

"I'm good enough to get whatever I set my sights on."

"All right, boys. Enough." Headbanger's brows furrowed when he slammed his fist on the table. "We'll meet your contact and decide if he's good enough ourselves."

"Then there's no reason for us to continue this conversation. My contact is just that—mine. He deals with me. If you don't want to work through me, find your own supply chain." Shadow crumpled his napkin and threw it on his plate of half-eaten food. "Thanks for lunch. You can send me a bill for it. You know where to find me."

He stood, pushing his chair back with the force of his movement, and turned to leave.

"You're right, Renegade. He is a stubborn one." Headbanger chuckled, his laughter reaching his eyes and mixing with the malice. The combination only revealed the madness he hid underneath his calm exterior. "Sit down, Doorman. We're extending an honorary lifelong member position to you. We've never done this before, but you bring an advantage we need at the moment. You'll still have to go through our initiation process."

"I can take whatever you dish out." *If it means I'll get Elle back.*

Headbanger motioned to the chair. "Sit down. Let's discuss the specifics before we arrange your initiation tonight. You may not be able to speak for a while after we're done with you."

Spider burst through the door, breathing heavily from running. He was late to an officers' meeting, and that didn't go without punishment in their paramilitary rank and order. "Sorry about that, Headbanger. Had to take care of an issue at the country club, and it took longer than I thought."

"Everyone okay up there?"

"Yeah. Except I had to move one to the old clubhouse. Bitch was a troublemaker, so she had to be reminded who's in charge. Now she knows not to fuck with me."

"Did you leave a mark on her face?" Headbanger put his palms on the table, ready to push up and lunge at Spider.

"No, boss. Didn't have to do that. She slept the whole trip down."

"You'd better have a good excuse for taking a risk like that this late in the game. The pressure hasn't let up at all. Everyone is still talking about it. You said you had that under control, too."

"I'm working on a new plan to draw attention away."

"Your schemes and excuses will get you in a lot of trouble one day, Spider."

Under the table, Shadow's knuckles turned white from curling his fists so tight. His facial expression remained passive, indifferent. Too much interest in anything other than why they'd brought him in would get both Elle and him killed. Spider's comments had sealed his fate, though. He'd be the first to die. Painfully. The moment Elle was safe. Shadow had already made that decision.

CHAPTER EIGHTEEN

"Everyone knows what to do, right?" Elle whispered, her lips barely moving, as if she were a ventriloquist.

"Yes," came three hushed replies, their voices shaky.

Every day for a week, each one had a specific area of the house to roam, to check for information, to find a way out. Something—anything—that wasn't locked down and could be used to fight back. The kitchen was open to them, but every knife was in a locked drawer. The drinking glasses were plastic—and not very effective for self-defense.

All exterior doors were locked and guarded by the hired thugs. The inside rooms were monitored by a recording system. Elle had seen the monitors once when the butler opened the door. She'd gone back to her bedroom and searched high and low for a camera in there, but she didn't find one. She wanted inside that room to see where the camera blind spots were or where there were no guards. The need to have access to the one room with a view to the whole house kept her awake at night.

She'd seen him go into the room earlier and decided she and the other ladies had officially outstayed their welcome. It was time for the four of them to get out together. True to his word, their captor had ensured their stay was comfortable and none of them had been harmed. As much as she hated to admit it, that was the very thing that worried her the most. The ladies were being kept in pristine condition for a very specific reason—and she knew that reason would be worse than death.

Elle had tried to explain her fear in depth to the others. While Katrina and Beth were visibly upset and afraid, they appeared to grasp the urgency of their escape better than Carrie. After witnessing what their captor was capable of doing, Carrie was even more afraid of escaping than remaining in his custody. Keeping him placated. Elle was concerned what continued captivity would do to Carrie. She'd already been there the longest—alone for many weeks.

Though Elle was taking a big gamble with their lives, Carrie's mental status was the exact reason why Elle chose her for their elaborate scheme. It gave Carrie a specific task, something to focus on that would help her friends as much as it would help herself. To remind her she had a say in what others could do to her, and she had a right to a happy life.

"Carrie, remember what we agreed to do. Just like we practiced. Okay?" Elle grasped Carrie's arm and squeezed it gently. The terrified glint in Carrie's gaze cleared enough to seal their sisterly bond.

"Okay," she agreed, nodding her head. "I can do this."

"That's right—because you're a damn good actress. This will work."

Using every trick and tactic she'd learning in acting classes, Elle drew in a deep breath, stood tall, and showed Carrie her most confident stance. "We are all getting out of here together—and as soon as possible."

"Let's do this. We're in this together, and we're getting out of this together. Places, everyone. This may be our only chance to pull this off," Carrie replied.

Beth waited in her bedroom, and Elle walked past the door to the monitors to wait in the kitchen. She'd sat on the barstool every day staring out the window to establish a pattern no one would question when they were ready to make their move. When they heard the lock on the door turn, Carrie and Katrina rose from their seats and hurried across the room, banking on the fact that he had his back turned to the monitors.

Elle rose from her place in the kitchen and prepared to rush to the door before it closed behind him. Timing was everything. One second too late could mean certain death for one or all of them. On Carrie's cue, Elle sprinted down the short hall between the kitchen and the monitoring room.

"Help! Oh, my God, someone help us! She's dying!" Carrie shrieked. Her voice held genuine fear, though not for Katrina's fake condition. "Help us!"

The butler flew out of the room, leaving the door standing open in his haste. "What the hell happened? What did you do?"

"I only handed her some crackers. She ate one and said she felt funny. So I was taking her back to her room. She just collapsed."

"Why do I smell peanut butter?"

"I had some with my crackers. What does that matter? Help her!"

"I'm trying to," he growled. "She has a severe peanut allergy. If you just ate it and didn't wash your hands, you've now put her into anaphylactic shock."

Elle quickly checked each monitor, identifying where all the cameras and guards were located. She kept one monitor on the scene outside the door, her gaze returning to it every few seconds to ensure the situation was still under control. With a few clicks on the computer, she found a way to scroll through all the views quickly. Her heart raced and tears of joy sprang to her eyes when she found their way out.

Just as quickly, her heart stopped and she felt as if she'd been punched in the gut when a familiar face filled the screen.

The scary, evil man in St. Lucia who smiled at her and made her skin crawl.

The one she was certain Devon knew.

The one who didn't belong there.

The one watching them when the man died right in front of her, when she thought she'd seen Devon stab the back of the dead man's neck.

There was no way his presence at her palatial prison was a coincidence.

"Does this mean Devon is involved?" She shook her head from side to side, disbelieving how far her thoughts had strayed from the possible and probable. "But, still..."

"She's coming to—look!" Carrie yelled loud enough for Elle to hear her through the door had she not seen the cue on the screen. "Katrina, are you okay?"

"What? What happened?" Her eyes fluttered open and darted between the two people hovering over her.

"You fainted—passed out cold. I thought you were dying." Carrie wiped tears from her cheeks and sniffled. "You scared me to death. Don't ever do that to me again."

"My blood sugar must've dropped too low. It does that sometimes and I get the shakes, but I've only passed out once before. I didn't recognize the signs this time."

They helped Katrina sit up, the butler watching her closely for signs of any other problems. Katrina glanced over his shoulder and saw Elle watching them. Relief washed over her with the knowledge they'd given her enough time to get out of the room without being seen.

"Katrina, what can I do? What can I get you?" Elle asked, joining the commotion.

"Some orange juice would be great. Thank you, Elle."

"Are you sure you're okay? Do you need the doctor?" the butler asked, genuine concern filling his tone.

We're under his watch, and apparently, he'll be held responsible if anything happens, Elle thought as she poured the juice. *Interesting.*

"I'm sure," Katrina replied, taking the plastic cup from Elle. She sipped the juice, giving an Oscar-worthy performance and holding his full attention with the most mundane scene ever written. "I feel better already. Maybe I'll just relax on the couch in here for a few minutes."

He helped her onto the couch and went out of his way to make her comfortable. Pillows, a blanket, and more juice as a precaution. "I'll be back to check on you in a few minutes. I thought for sure you'd been exposed to peanuts."

"No, nothing like that. I wouldn't be breathing if I had. No need to worry about me now."

"We'll stay with her for a while." Carrie sat beside her, still playing the guilt-ridden, despondent friend.

"Was it worth it?" Katrina whispered when he'd left them alone.

"Definitely," Elle replied. "We have a plan."

Elle and Carrie helped Katrina up to take her back to her room. Elle glanced over at the room she'd just left and saw the door had been shut. The narrow window of opportunity she'd been given wasn't lost on her, nor was the slim chance of success they'd have to escape. But she'd take that chance and make it count for all it was worth. If she died trying, at least her death would be for a noble reason. Rolling over and being a good little doormat was never her style anyway.

Beth joined them in Katrina's room, anxious to hear what Elle had found. "Great performances, ladies. That's why you make the big bucks and I do your makeup. Let's hear it, Elle. How do we get out of here?"

"We have to go through the basement."

"No." Carrie's stern tone mixed with her clenched fists, and she shook her head in vehement rejection.

"I don't want to go back down there either, but it's our best option. There are no active cameras in that room—only in the stairwell down and outside the outer door. They must specifically activate the cameras down there. And with us up here, there's no reason to. Plus, I may have taken them offline completely while I was in there.

"That door leads to a separate driveway on the back of the house. There's a smaller gate at the back of the brick fence. We can climb it and get out. We'll have to run like hell once we get out the door. I say we do it at night when we won't be seen as easily."

"Yes. Let's go tonight. We're pushing our luck more and more the longer we stay here," Katrina agreed.

"I'm in. Tonight, it is. I'm ready to get home," Beth added.

All eyes turned to Carrie and waited for her assent. "Okay, I can do this."

When the house was silent late that night, they each left their rooms at different times in case anyone was watching the monitors. They made their way to the kitchen and listened for anyone else stirring. When Elle was satisfied they hadn't been seen, she led the group down the back stairs to the basement door.

"How do we get past the door without making noise and alerting the entire house what we're doing?" Beth asked.

Elle pulled a key from her pocket. "I stole this from their control room." She slid the key into the lock and said a silent prayer. The tumblers disengaged, and the knob turned in her hand. Like a shot in the dark, the foursome sprinted across the basement, now void of all the eerie black plastic that covered it before.

The door leading outside was easily unlocked from the inside; the owner obviously didn't consider his captives would make it that far. Elle threw the door open, and they dashed across the lush, green grass behind the house. Their adrenaline was at an all-time high—the gate to freedom was in view, glowing like a beacon in the pale moonlight, illuminating their path.

Freedom was almost within their reach when the yard was lit up by floodlights that seemed to come from everywhere. Angry male voices shouted orders and four-wheelers skidded to a halt between them and the gate. Men jumped off and rushed at them, much like a linebacker targets a quarterback to stop the play. The four women scattered, running in different directions to draw attention and give the others a chance to escape. If only one got free, the rest would be saved.

Screams filled the night, echoing on the breeze as they were corralled and caught one by one. All four were brought together by a host of clean-cut guards in uniforms mixed with scary men dressed all in black, wearing leather vests, and sporting long beards and shaggy hair. The thugs' presence was a direct contradiction to their palatial prison, exactly how the man in St. Lucia appeared to be out of his element at the überposh resort.

As they were forced to their knees with their hands behind their backs, their reactions were as varied as the women themselves. Carrie bowed her head and cried, knowing one of them had to die for their actions. Katrina was terrified of the dozens of men leering at her. Beth's gaze kept returning to the gate as she calculated the odds of actually making it to it and over it without getting caught.

Elle spoke first when the owner arrived in the middle of the scene. "It was my idea. The only reason they're out here is because I coerced them. Put all the punishment on me. Just don't hurt them."

The distinguished-looking man regarded her, contemplating her words for a moment. The tension around the ladies was thick and heady, feeding his controlling nature. "Take the other three back inside and leave your gun with me."

"No!" Beth screamed as one man lifted her to her feet. She fought against him, struggling in vain against his strength. "No, Elle! Leave her alone!"

They were forcefully taken back to the house while Elle remained kneeling on the ground alone. Just as they stepped into the basement, a gunshot rang out in the night, followed by the screaming wails of the three who still lived.

"Move—or I'll make you move," the man behind Beth threatened.

With tears streaming down her face and sobs racking her body, she forced her feet to move, following the others back up the staircase and down the hall to her room. The door was slammed and locked behind her. Resigned to her fate, she fell onto the bed and cried herself into a restless, fitful sleep.

Elle remained motionless in a heap on the ground outside while the two men stood over her. "Spider, she has to go first thing in the morning. The rest can stay here for now, but we need to arrange to transfer them soon."

"You got it." Spider picked up Elle and slung her over his shoulder. "Guesthouse for tonight?"

"That's fine. Just make sure she's gone by the time I leave for work."

"Don't worry. I got you covered, Uncle B."

Spider walked off toward the guesthouse, his brother-in-colors, Axle, falling into step at his side. "She's hot, isn't she? We could fuck every hole she has twice tonight, and she wouldn't know it. I gave her an extra spray of our sleeping juice for good measure."

"No way, man," Axle replied. "You know I wouldn't normally give a shit what you do to some sheep, but this one brings a special price. Your dick isn't going to rob me of my retirement fund."

"Just as well, I guess. I do prefer them to be conscious when they suck my dick. Can't get enough of those girls who can suck better than a Hoover." Spider laughed and opened the door to the guesthouse. He dropped her on the bed and shook his head. "Shit. I don't want to sleep in the fucking guesthouse to babysit her all night."

"Head on back to the main house. I'll stay. This place is nicer than my shitty apartment."

After Spider left, Axle moved into the living room, leaving the bedroom door open so he could see her, and dropped down on the couch. He raked his hands over his face before removing his phone from his pocket. "Hey. Yeah. I got eyes on her now. It's just a matter of time."

Deception seems to be the name of the game with these guys, Elle thought. *I can play that game, too*

After she'd been caught and they'd taken the others inside, Spider sprayed the sleeping serum in her face. When she slumped on the ground, her captor fired his gun into the air as a scare tactic to keep the others in line. She'd prepared herself by holding her breath to avoid inhaling the spray when she saw Spider moving toward her. With one eye barely open, she saw the older man lift his arm above his head and knew what would come next. She kept perfectly still, not giving away her advantage or her subterfuge.

She waited for Axle to fall asleep in front of the television, hoping the noise would mask her movements. When his breaths became even and he didn't move for an extended time, she silently rolled off the bed and tiptoed to the door. With her hand on the knob, she began to turn it.

"If you open that door, every alarm in this place will go off. You'll be sorry this time, trust me. You've already tried twice. Third time will be lights-out for you."

She gasped and jumped at the same time, turning to look at him. He remained on the couch in the same position he was in when she'd thought he was asleep.

"Best just to go on back to bed and wait until tomorrow. You'll be moved from here. They won't let you escape. Even if you get away this time, they won't let you live. They can't take the chance you'll talk."

"So I'm just supposed to take it? To let them do what they want with me?" Fire lit in her eyes, and her lips formed a thin line. Rage built up inside her, pushing her to the limit.

"You don't have much choice. You're in this now, so you'll just have to ride it out till the end. Whatever that may be."

"Why are you here? I remember seeing you in St. Lucia. Were you following me then? Helping them to kidnap me?"

"Nope."

She waited for him to continue, to elaborate on his single-word answer, but he didn't. "That's helpful. Thanks for the detailed explanation."

He chuckled and sat up, his gaze finally meeting hers. "Go to bed. You're safe in here with me. I won't let Spider back in until morning when we move you. Might want to remember that handy trick you used earlier when you see us coming for you, though."

"Why are you helping me?"

"Because I'm selfish."

She rolled her eyes, huffed, and spun on her heel, heading back to the bedroom. She stopped in the doorway, the question she wanted to ask searing her mind. It was there, on the tip of her tongue, and she desperately wanted to know. Almost as much as she didn't want to know at all.

"Don't ask, Elle. Just try to get some sleep. You'll need it for tomorrow."

Dread filled her heart, then her feisty anger took control. She wasn't giving up without a fight. She refused to bow down to them. Though she didn't trust Axle, he had spared her more than once in a short time. Crawling back on the bed felt a lot like defeat, making it difficult for her to rest and sleep as he prompted.

She heard the door open and recognized Spider's voice before he saw she was already awake. She waited for the two men to enter her room, sensing they were close, before opening her eyes. They were closing in on her, leaning down toward her in a surprise attack.

"Hey!" she yelled in mock surprise.

Spider sprayed three short bursts of liquid into her face, and her body went limp. "Works every time," he boasted. "I love this shit. Used it on this one slut the other night, and she didn't remember anything."

"Man, you know if Headbanger gets wind of you flaunting that, he'll cut your balls off and mount them on his handlebars as a warning to the rest of us." Axle released a harsh huff toward Spider and snaked his arms under Elle's back. "Grab her feet. I've got her head."

They carried her out to the waiting van and put her in the back. Spider climbed on his motorcycle and pitched the keys to the van to Axle. "Drive her to the old clubhouse. I'll meet you there to help get her inside. Headbanger will have my head on a platter because I'll be late for our officers' meeting by the time we're done."

Axle slid behind the wheel and followed Spider off the property. "Just stay down and pretend to be asleep. He'll be gone soon enough. The club takes the officers' meetings seriously. He's already on thin ice with the prez, so he won't risk being too late."

"You can just let me go, you know?" She had to try—he was looking out for her well-being for a reason.

"Ah, you know I can't do that. And if you know what's good for you, don't act like I'm your friend. None of us are good guys, sweetheart. You wouldn't want to be our friend."

"You're not as good of an actor as you like to think you are, Axle."

She barely heard his laugh over the roar of the road. "I guess I'd better go back to acting classes, then. Evidently, I won't win one of those little gold statues anytime soon. Or maybe I will. Maybe I've completely played you to get you to cooperate."

"Maybe," she conceded. "You wouldn't be the first. Hopefully, you won't be the last either."

At the former clubhouse, a wide metal door opened for the van to pull completely inside, fully hidden from the outside. Once the door was shut, the blackness covered everything. "Pretend you're still asleep. He's coming now," Axle whispered.

The back door of the van swung open, and Spider grabbed her ankles, dragging her roughly toward the edge. "Grab her head. I've got to get going. I'm so fucking late."

Axle grabbed Elle under the arms and helped carry her inside. The musty, mildewed smell of the interior was a stark difference to the opulent mansion she'd been expelled from the night before. Dust and dirt covered everything, infiltrating her nose and threatening to make her sneeze. She held her breath until Spider dumped her on an old, filthy mattress thrown on the floor in the corner of the room.

"Want me to send someone by with food and beer?" Spider asked on his way out.

"Nah. I'll call one of the probies and put him to work. Get to your meeting before you get kicked out of the officers' club."

When she heard the rumble of Spider's motorcycle and the loud metal clank of the roll-up door, she bolted up from the mattress and searched her new cell. The lights barely cast dim rays around the windowless room. The interior doors were thick steel, designed for maximum security. The rooms with working lightbulbs were near mirror images of the first room.

"You must be hungry. Come in here and choose what you want. I'll order takeout," Axle called from the other room.

"Is this what I needed my rest for?" She held out her arms and gestured to the dilapidated furnishings.

He cut his gaze to her, and his lips lifted on one side in amusement. But something closer to remorse shone in his dark eyes. "No, sweetheart. Not hardly."

~

The midday sun in Southern California was hot. In the remote, arid hangout of the Devil's Dominion initiation grounds, the heat was nearly unbearable. But the members of the club didn't mind, because the Doorman's induction into the group was cause for celebration. And for beating up the new guy.

"Gather 'round," Headbanger yelled over the roar of the crowd. A hush immediately fell over the group as they did as he commanded. "Some of you have met our newest member. He had a nickname before he came to us, but we've changed it. He's now known as the Doorman. Tonight is his official induction into the club. Some of you will be pissed to know he's entering the ranks higher than any of you pussies did because he's of better use to me than you are. What do you think of that?"

A loud rumble of discord and outright threats floated over the crowd of angry bikers. "What the hell? What the fuck's so special about him?"

"He has contacts we need to complete our next weapons shipment. AR-16s, fully auto, locked and loaded. We're keeping a few dozen for ourselves and selling the rest. Military-grade aerosol canisters, gas masks, and whatever else we need. He's our man." Headbanger smiled broader the more the men grumbled and groaned.

He loved riling them up before an initiation. The extra surge of testosterone and adrenaline produced much more creative consequences for the new recruit. It also kept the men sharp, ready to dole out pain for pleasure. As long as no one killed or permanently incapacitated the new member, nothing else was off-limits.

"All right, boys. Make the Doorman feel at home." Headbanger stepped back, his snide sneer in place.

A group of twenty handpicked men closed in on Shadow, taunting him with insults as they shuffled around him. He braced himself, knowing the first hit would be a sucker punch meant to disorient before the brood jumped on him at once.

The biker tried to be nonchalant, but Shadow saw the punch coming and turned his head away from it slightly, softening the blow. The others immediately jumped at the chance, fists flying, flesh smacking against flesh. He ducked and shielded his head with his thick arms as much as he could. Several banded together and pushed him to the ground, where they commenced kicking and punching him repeatedly.

He heard Headbanger's laughter roar over the angry mob surrounding him.

From between his arms, he saw the crowd part to allow another man a wide berth to pass. He could barely make out the outline of what the guy carried in his hand, but the glowing red end left no room for mistaking it. They were getting ready to hold him down and brand him.

Elle's face flashed in his mind. Amid the kicks to the back and legs, the punches to his jaws and ribs, he focused on her safety as a reminder of why he allowed the beating to occur in the first place. His revenge would be swift and terrible as soon as she was out of harm's way. It was the feel of her embrace and smell of her smooth skin that prevented him from screaming out in pain when the skin on his back sizzled from the searing hot branding iron.

"Enough." One word from Headbanger halted all action. "Get up, Doorman. Greet your brothers."

Shadow stood and faced the man holding the branding iron. His mocking laugh was met by the cold, fierce stare of a man who tortured people for a living to gain intel from them. For that dickhead, Shadow decided he'd do it for free.

With his lightning reflexes, Shadow snatched the brand from the biker's hand and had him flat on his back before anyone knew what had happened. With his heavy boot across the guy's neck holding him in place, Shadow twirled the hot iron in his fingers, watching the fear fill his victim's eyes. The angry mob stood stock-still, shocked at the sudden turn of events and unsure of how they should react.

"We're brothers now, right?" Shadow asked, taunting his mocker. "We need matching tattoos, then."

On a downward twirl, Shadow pushed the brand into his chest. The biker screamed in pain, his arms flailing as he tried to hit Shadow's leg, the brand—anything he could reach that would stop the pain. Shadow lifted the brand and inspected the angry, burnt skin in the middle of the biker's chest.

"That's better." Shadow released him and spat on the ground, barely missing his shocked face. He threw the branding iron, making several of his new brothers jump out of the way. He turned his sights on the men who had so brutally inducted him, ready to return the favor tenfold. The first one within reach was the unlucky poster boy for the others. Shadow held him with one hand and repeatedly punched him with the other.

When the rest of the initiators attempted to stop him, he released his victim and let his fists fly. When they thought they had him contained, he outwitted and outmaneuvered them, while hurling insults about their inability to overpower him, even with twenty men to one. Every word and every blow only added to his determination. At the end of the case, he would be surprised if a single Devil was still standing.

"Stop." Headbanger moved into the crowd and surveyed Shadow from top to bottom. Then he turned to do the same to the men he'd picked to induct Shadow. "You're beat to shit—your face, arms, everywhere. But you give as good as you get. These boys look like they've been through a meat grinder."

"And I was only getting warmed up."

Headbanger laughed at his response, but Shadow wasn't joking.

"You're part of the Devil's Dominion now. But you have to complete a couple of tasks to get your rocker panels and patch. You ready?"

"Absolutely."

He pulled a picture from his vest pocket and handed it to Shadow. Nick moved around the crowd so he was in a direct line of sight behind Headbanger, reading Shadow's expression. "Find her. Take her. Don't get caught or be seen by anyone."

"Take her where? Who is she?"

"To the country club. Spider can fill you in. And who she is doesn't matter. Complete this, and you get the bottom rocker and the club patch."

"And the top rocker?"

"You are ambitious." Headbanger smiled, knowing Shadow wasn't the type to do anything half-assed. "Someone has been a thorn in my side. You can take care of that for me, right?"

"Of course." Shadow shrugged, as if a request to kill someone was an everyday occurrence. "Who?"

"The girl first. Then the top rocker. One step at a time."

Shadow shifted his eyes slightly over Headbanger's shoulder and connected with Nick's. An imperceptible nod was all it took to confirm his suspicions.

"Spider, take the Doorman to the old clubhouse with you. Explain our process to him. Take Axle and Renegade with you, too."

"Axle is already there, babysitting our company."

"Even better. You head on over to the old clubhouse and keep him company, then. Renegade and Doorman can handle this one on their own. Can't you, boys?"

"Piece of cake," Shadow replied.

"Renegade, come talk to me before you leave," Headbanger called over his shoulder when he walked away.

CHAPTER NINETEEN

Silas Steele, Noah's brother, pulled up to the gate and pressed the call button, holding it an extra few seconds longer than necessary.

"Can I help you?" the female voice asked.

"Yeah. You can open the gate and let me in. I need to talk to Jason Hartman immediately—it's urgent."

"What is your name? Do you have an appointment for today?" she asked, hesitant to let him in or send him away.

"My name is Silas Steele, and I'm a federal agent. Tell Jason he can either willingly talk to me now, or I can come back with the SWAT team and a warrant for his arrest. Either way, this gate will open for me." Silas removed his badge and held it in front of the camera. The automatic gate began to swing open, giving him access to drive in. "Good call."

When Silas reached the secluded house in the woods, Jason Hartman, also known as Jax Hart, stepped out of the house with his private security detail surrounding him. Even though he stood between three men who could double as club bouncers, Jax wore a leery expression. His gaze roamed over the cab of Silas's truck, trying to see through the blacked-out windows.

With a glance, Silas knew Jax Hart wasn't involved in the kidnapping scheme, but he definitely knew something about it. He took his time exiting the truck, letting Jax make all the wrong assumptions before Silas even asked the first question.

"Are you alone?" Jax asked as Silas rounded the front of his truck.

"Yes, I'm alone."

The three security guards chuckled to themselves, confident they'd have the upper hand on him. Silas smirked to himself, stifling a laugh at their expense. *It's not about size, guys. It's about who's meaner.*

"What do you want?" one of the bodyguards asked.

"I have questions for Jason." Silas intentionally used his given name and inclined his head toward Jax. "He can refuse to answer them, but then he'd be refusing to cooperate in a federal investigation and he'd be under arrest. Is that what you want? I can haul his ass in right now, then."

Silas produced a set of handcuffs, held them in position to slap them on Jax's wrists, and advanced on him.

"Whoa, whoa, whoa!" Jax shouted, backing up. "I didn't say I wouldn't cooperate. What's this about?"

"We need to speak inside," Silas stated, looking past the security detail and directly at Jax. "I believe you know what it's about."

Fear and acceptance flashed across his face. He was hiding in a remote location and the press had been fed lies about his true whereabouts, but he had to face the truth sometime. With a gloomy nod, he commanded his security team to stand down. "Come on in. Let's get it over with as soon as possible."

Silas followed him into the sprawling log cabin. The family room covered half of the entry level. The entire back wall was made of folding glass patio doors to give an unobstructed view of the mountains and lake surrounding the property. Jax motioned for Silas to have a seat.

"Nice house. Knowing your Hollywood persona, I wouldn't have pegged you as the outdoorsy type. But then, you were probably banking on the true facts of your background remaining hidden when you chose to hide here."

Even Hollywood's leading man couldn't hide his shock after that statement. "Guess what the conspiracy theorists say is true. We have no secrets from Big Brother."

"It's actually worse than they think. Do you want to be called Jason or Jax?"

"Jason is fine. No more pretending, at least while we're here."

"Fair enough. Jason, tell me why you're hiding in Idaho at your aunt and uncle's vacation home."

"Getting right to the point, huh? Okay." He released a harsh breath. "I'm here because I'm scared for my life. Literally. And I get that makes me a complete shit because Elle and Beth are missing, so they're even more afraid than I am."

He shook his head and dropped his face into his hands, shame and guilt consuming him. "The night they disappeared, they left the sound stage before me. When I walked out, I rounded the corner and expected my driver to be waiting for me. But he wasn't. Two rough-looking men dressed in black, with leather motorcycle vests, were putting Elle in the back of a van—the kind of long cargo van they use for deliveries and stuff. No windows on the side panels."

"Did you get a good look at the insignia on their vests?"

"Yeah, I saw it plain as day. It said Devil's Dominion."

"When you saw them put Elle in the van, was she conscious at the time?"

"No. She was completely limp. Honestly, I didn't even know if she was alive at first. It was only after everything was over when I realized I'd seen her chest rising and falling when they put her down. After they closed the doors, they turned, and that's when they saw me standing there. One of them used his finger and thumb to make the sign like a gun and 'shot' me. Then he laughed, like he thought it was so damn funny, and climbed in the van. They drove off, didn't even stop at the guard station to the lot, and left me standing there."

Silas watched Jason's face as he relived the scene from that night, giving him time to remember any other details he'd tried to forget. Jason was visibly shaken by the entire incident and believed they'd kill him, and he was correct. They would, without a second thought. They had no use for him—they were after the women. When Jason appeared to have checked out of the conversation, Silas drew him back in.

"What did you do next?"

"I tucked my tail between my legs and ran back inside the sound stage. When I found Vince Rossi, the director, I told him to call the police. Then I explained everything, just like I told you. He told me to go home and he'd take care of it."

"Did he take care of it?"

"At the time, I honestly thought he did. He grabbed his cell and began barking orders, yelling he needed the police right away. When he realized I was still there, he called my driver and basically pushed me into the car. On the way home, my agent called and said they were putting the publicity tour on hold, but they'd finish editing the movie so we'd be ready to go when it was time. I told him I didn't care about that—what about Elle and Beth? He said the police were there, and the studio was handling it. They didn't want me involved in the case because it would hurt more than it would help."

"Hurt what?"

"My career—because I didn't rush to stop them, like the hero I play in my movies. Elle's career—because our onscreen relationship wouldn't be believable after people realized I allowed her to be taken. The movie itself—since it would get bad reviews and no one would go see it. Everything from our reputations to being cast in future movies would be destroyed. That's how he sold it to me anyway, and I went along with it."

"When the van left the lot, you said it didn't stop at the guard station. Does your driver always stop to check out with the guard?"

"Yes. Always. They're supposed to check everyone in and out of the lot."

"Did your driver stop that night?" Silas asked.

Jason's brows drew down and he stared straight ahead, his eyes slightly downcast while he tried to remember. "You know, I was so shaken up by the time I got in the car, I didn't even think about it. I just wanted to get home, as far away from there as I could get. But, no, we didn't check out." His eyes jerked up to meet Silas's. "What does that mean? They're all in on it?"

"I can't comment on an open investigation," Silas replied. "Which way did the van turn when they left the lot?"

"Right. Why are you not taking any notes?"

"I don't need notes to remember. Were you aware that Vince Rossi left LA this morning for an undetermined length of time?"

Jason blanched and sat back against the couch. "No, I didn't know. Why did he leave?"

"The official statement said there was a medical emergency, and he was returning home to be with his family." Silas studied Jason, watching for clues to confirm he honestly didn't know about the director's abrupt departure from the studio.

"*Returned home?* Where—all the way to Orange? That's where his family lives."

"Yes, I'm aware. I found it interesting too." Silas stood and walked to the large bank of patio doors. "Jason, there's something I want you to do. They're planning to do something terrible to the ladies they've kidnapped. We must force their hand so we can stop this before it's too late."

"What do you want me to do?"

"Call Mary Ellen Gallie and tell her you're not with Elle. You don't have to give any details of that night, simply confirm you left LA for an extended vacation off the grid before the promotional tour started. Then you were hit with all this nonsense about you and Elle running away to get married. So you wanted to set the record straight, because if she's in danger, law enforcement needs to do something about it.

"The video they sent of her talking about how happy you two are has already been proven a fake. The people need to hear it from you now, so your fans will demand action on your behalf, and hers."

"Of course. I'll do whatever you need me to do."

Silas checked his watch and nodded to the phone. "Her show is about to come on now. Perfect time to set the public straight on the facts." Jason grabbed his phone, scrolled through his contacts, and dialed the line dedicated to celebrities. Silas listened while Jason donned his Jax personality. Without giving details of that night, he answered questions from the host and call-in viewers. By the end of the hour-long show, word had spread across the waves. Calls and emails flooded law enforcement offices across the state. From the governor to the mayor to the chief of police, concerned fans demanded immediate action and questioned the effectiveness of assigning only Detective Gough to such a complex case.

"Stay here with around-the-clock security until this is over. When Elle is home safely, you'll know you can return to LA." Silas stepped out the front door and turned back to Jason. "You should know, Jason, there's no shame in what you did. If you'd tried to stop them, they *would've* killed you and still left with Elle and Beth. These are not the kind of men the average person tangles with, and you have no reason to be ashamed. What you did today will do more to help save them than you know. Thanks for your help."

"Thank you, Agent Steele. I can't tell you how much I appreciate you saying that."

Once Silas was back in the truck, he called his brother. "Jax Hart handled that very well. Turned on the charm and rallied his troops. That should help with the message Elle's and Beth's parents are pushing daily."

"His message was perfect. Did he say anything that could help?"

"Nothing we don't already know." Silas repeated the conversation for Reaper, who also wasn't surprised to hear the director appeared to be involved.

"Sounds like we need to pay a visit to his sick family member in Orange. We know who to look at, but we haven't figured out why they're doing this yet. Have you heard anything from your analyst with the agency?"

"Coded messages sent to a buyer in Hong Kong were intercepted. Nick Tucker has been trying to identify the name on an offshore account. My analyst is helping unravel that a little faster. We should have the details soon. Nick is a little more by-the-book than I am," Silas chuckled.

"Most everyone is more by-the-book than you are, Silas. Other than Shadow. Must be part of the training manual for all spies to break the rules as much as possible," Reaper retorted. "Speaking of, have you heard anything about our boy? Even through unofficial channels?"

"Not yet. I've got his analyst, Steadman, and my analyst, Chris, watching him on satellite as much as possible. He put himself and Nick at more risk by going in as quickly as he did. I'm concerned it'll backfire, and they won't be able to handle the backlash from it."

"Agreed. Are you on your way here now?"

"I'm heading to the airport now and will be in LA County soon."

~

"What did Headbanger want to talk to you about?" Shadow asked as Nick climbed into the van, sparing no time.

Nick rubbed the back of his neck, trying to ease the tension and stress accumulating in his muscles. "Your initiation—he was impressed with how you handled yourself, so he wants to replace Spider with you as an officer."

"How's Spider going to take that news?" Shadow chuckled.

"He won't. That's the other news he sprang on me. The way you'll earn your top rocker is to kill Spider, the thorn in his side."

"What's the problem? I can take him out easily."

"Seriously? What is wrong with you spooks? You can't just kill everyone." Nick openly gaped at Shadow, incredulous at his blasé attitude toward taking another man's life.

"I most certainly can. I'm a trained soldier. I protect our country every day, from all kinds of threats. Sometimes I *have* to be the bigger threat to get the job done. Spider is a dangerous man who takes lives indiscriminately—innocent people, defenseless women—and he does it for pleasure. The more he gets away with it, the worse he'll be. Taking him out of the game is a public service."

"I'm genuinely concerned you're missing the entire point of this conversation," Nick deadpanned. "You do remember I've been undercover for two fucking years, right? I'd like to actually arrest someone for all my trouble."

Shadow glanced over his shoulder at Nick, understanding his angst. "Undercover life is hard. I know. Truly, I get it. You want to see someone pay for all the time you've given up of your own life. You want the satisfaction of putting them behind bars for a very long time, knowing it was your dedication to your job and country, and that time has been repaid.

"I hate to be the bearer of bad news, but you'll be sorely disappointed with the due process. The lawyers, the trials, the delays, the deals. Years of your life already spent collecting irrefutable proof, only to have your every past mistake paraded through court to discredit you. The slap on the wrist they get for being 'brainwashed and coerced' into being part of this gang. You'll wish you'd killed him yourself when it's all over."

"It's a good thing we only have to kidnap another Hollywood starlet in the meantime," Nick replied dully.

"Do we have a plan for this abduction? Shall we surprise her, or give her a heads-up before we grab her off the sidewalk and pitch her in the back of our Chester Molester van?"

"Does the CIA require regular brain CT scans? Check for changes or anomalies? Seriously, Shadow."

He threw his head back and released a deep belly laugh. "Man, it feels good to laugh again. It's been a long time. I'm joking about the kidnapping. While you were chatting with Headbanger, I made some calls on my secure cell to make the arrangements. She's being briefed and convinced to cooperate as we speak."

"Who's prepping her?"

"Bull and Rebel—they're demonstrating how the GPS injected in her arm works regardless of where she is, assuring her that the two big, scary guys sweeping her off her feet are both undercover agents who will take care of her, and we'll return her home, safe and sound, as soon as possible. Reaper went to pick up Silas at the airport."

"We can't possibly guarantee she's safe while we're not around. We have no idea what they're doing to them," Nick protested.

The temperature in the van dropped instantly when Shadow turned his gaze to Nick. Or maybe it was from the chills running up Nick's spine when he recognized the dark, lethal expression on Shadow's face.

"Shadow, I'm sorry, man. I didn't even think... Besides, I don't think they'd hurt them. They're planning something else for them, I can feel it. They want more money. Manufacturing meth, selling for the cartels, and running guns isn't making them enough for some reason."

Before Shadow could reply, his secure cell began vibrating in his pocket. "Talk to me, Bull."

"Lori Hensley is ready for her chauffeured ride," Bull replied. "She's been tagged and is ready for an extra special surprise visit."

"She does understand what's really happening, right? You didn't trick her into thinking she's going on a blind date or anything?"

Bull chuckled. "I'm giving you the one-finger salute right now, in case you're wondering. I know how to do my damn job. Just come kidnap the girl. We're waiting on the lot, just outside the sound stage door. Let me know when you pull up. I'll step back inside."

"Copy that. See you soon, princess."

"Bite me."

Shadow and Nick turned into the lot and were waved on by the guard. Checking the side mirror, Shadow noted the guard immediately left his station and pointed it out to Nick. He circled slowly around the buildings until he found the perfect spot to avoid detection. If they'd been followed, he didn't want to take any chances that would blow their cover.

Lori walked across the drive toward the area where her driver should have been waiting and stopped, looking around for her ride. Shadow and Nick jumped out of the van and walked up stealthily behind her. Nick tapped on her shoulder, raised his hand up to her face, and squeezed the spray twice in quick sequence. She slumped in Shadow's arms, and he placed her in the back of the van.

"I hated to knock her out, but we can't take the chance of anyone else realizing she's not asleep. We can't make the slightest move out of character now."

"It's not a big deal, man. I would've done the same in your place."

Nick's cell began ringing, and he exchanged a leery glance with Shadow. "Renegade."

"Change of plans. When you get the girl, take her to the old clubhouse instead of the country club."

"We just got her, in fact. They must have wrapped up early today. Her driver hadn't even arrived to pick her up yet."

"Good work, Renegade. I'm glad to hear that. We're moving up the schedule, so it only makes sense to take her to the old clubhouse rather than risk moving her again."

Nick relayed the message to Shadow then directed him to the old building. Bonebreaker waited in the garage with the large metal door rolled up so they could pull straight into the covered area. While Bone closed the door, Shadow and Nick circled to the back of the van to pick up Lori. Shadow snaked his arms underneath her and pulled her to his chest. He hauled her body weight over his shoulder with ease and carried her inside.

"Where does this one go?" he asked, looking around the dingy room.

"Throw her in there," Bone replied, pointing to the closed door.

Shadow swung the door open with one hand, flipped the light on, and turned his head when Bone issued a warning. "Be careful of the other one in there. She's mouthy and gets on my fucking nerves."

Shadow turned back to the bedroom, stepped inside, and deposited Lori on the grungy bed. His skin tingled, and the air sparked with electricity.

She's here.

When he turned, Elle stood rooted to her spot behind the door. Shock and anguish crushed her spirit. Devastation rocked her foundation, driving her down to her knees.

"No," she breathed, defeat overtaking her. "*No.*"

CHAPTER TWENTY

"You've been there every day for the last three days, and she hasn't even made eye contact with you. You're going to draw attention to us that we don't need." Nick ran his fingers through his hair and stomped across the floor of his ratty apartment.

"I know how to operate an undercover investigation, Nick."

"But you're not running one, are you? You're only here to get your girlfriend. Fuck my case. Fuck the last two years of my life. Fuck my career. As long as you get what you want."

"I can't leave her there any longer and risk something happening to her."

"You're not thinking clearly. You will get her killed by pulling her out now. You'll get both of us killed. Who will be there to protect her, then? You're too close. You need to get out."

"What you're really asking is if you need to push me out," Shadow countered. "The hell you will. I'm not leaving *without* Elle."

"And you're not leaving *with* her yet. I need more information—like exactly who is behind this and why."

"You know who—Barry Jacobson and Vince Rossi. Who else do you need?"

"The DEA requires this little thing called evidence. We can't prosecute someone and stop them unless we have everything on them—and more. If you bothered to check the rules, you'd know that.

"Look, I let you come in on this case as a favor. Not so you'd blow it all to hell. You've seen her. You know she's okay. She's fed well, she's taken care of, no one has hurt her. They're moving the other girls there with her soon. We're tracing the money, unraveling the tangled web of fake companies to get to the offshore account. We know something's going down—likely this week. Just be patient so I don't have to shoot you myself."

"I'm going over there to relieve Bone. He said you have an officers' meeting this morning." Shadow slid his fingers into his leather gloves and picked up his keys. "I'm sure I'll see you after the meeting."

"Expect a phone call from Headbanger as soon as the meeting is over. Spider has been fucking up more over the last couple of days. He's on his way out. Oh, and Shadow?"

"Yeah?"

"Don't do anything stupid while I'm gone."

Shadow grinned, the mischief playing in his eyes once again. "Cross my heart."

Nick glared at Shadow's back as he walked out. As if he didn't have enough to manage with all the fast-paced, confusing pieces of the case, his old friend added more stress to an already unbearable situation. He was doing all his thinking with the head between his legs instead of the one between his shoulders. But Nick had to get his own head in the game at play that day instead of worrying about Shadow doing something crazy.

Shadow strode into the old clubhouse and found Bone in the large common room. The bedroom doors that lined the long wall were all closed, leaving Shadow to question which one Elle used to hide from him that visit.

"Fuck, I'm glad you're here. I'll never complain about our new clubhouse again. This building is a fucking dump. The last rat that ran by was as big as a fucking gopher. Damn thing may carry me off in my sleep." Bone paced back and forth, speaking fast, and his eyes darted aimlessly around the room.

Great—he's as high as a fucking kite, Shadow thought.

"Yeah, well, I'm here to cover for you while you're at the officers' meeting. Whenever you're ready to take off is fine."

"I'm ready now. Have fun, man. They're both in that room." Bone motioned to the room farthest from the kitchen area, at the end of the long room. "We have an unspoken agreement to stay away from each other. The mouthy one pisses me off, and I don't want the prez taking my head off over her."

Shadow stood in the same spot, staring at the closed door, when he heard Bone's Harley fire up. The familiar thump, thump, thump of the engine rattled the metal door in the garage when he rode away. The metal grinding against metal sound of the door closing drew his attention. He moved quickly through the room toward the kitchen until he reached the door leading out to the garage to see who had joined him.

And why.

The door swung open, and Axle stepped into the room. He had a knack for seeing everything while remaining in the background. Extra-cautious and suspicious of everyone, Axle had every classic sign of a man who'd served hard time in a maximum-security prison—and didn't want to go back.

"Wasn't expecting to see you here." Shadow tried to keep the disappointment out of this tone. He wanted time alone with Elle more than anything.

Axle narrowed his eyes and tilted his head slightly. "I'll just bet you didn't. What are you up to, Doorman?"

"Nothing. Just entertaining our guests in Bone's absence."

"Uh-huh," Axle replied. "You can go if you want. I got it."

"I just got here. Maybe I'll hang out for a while."

"Suit yourself." Axle shrugged and opened the drawer to go through the delivery menus. "Hungry?"

Shadow chuckled. "Always."

"I'll ask the ladies what they want." Axle walked to the last bedroom door and knocked lightly. The door barely cracked open at first, then opened wide when they realized who stood on the other side.

Lori and Elle walked out into the main room, their postures at ease and small smiles lighting their faces. They weren't afraid of Axle in the least, despite his rough appearance and outlaw gang ties. Shadow's heart leapt up into his throat watching Elle, knowing he couldn't tell her the truth but dying to pull her into his arms.

After he'd dropped Lori off and Elle had seen him in the act, he knew the crushed expression she wore was because she believed his act. Why wouldn't she? He looked and dressed the part. Elle had been abducted by the very men he openly called brothers. Then she watched him put an unconscious Lori on the bed.

After Elle's momentary breakdown, she found her strength and her anger flared. When she stood, she beat her fists against Shadow's chest and let her rage flow. "How could you help them do this to me? To her? Did she think you loved her too?" Though her heart was broken, her defiance was strong. She wanted to cause him as much physical pain as he'd caused her emotionally.

As much as Shadow wanted to tell her the truth, he already knew what Nick had scolded him over that morning. She couldn't know the truth and risk giving them away. Lori didn't know which men had nabbed her—she couldn't have identified either man if she'd had to. If he'd told Elle, she would've reacted differently toward him and raised everyone's suspicions.

So he turned his back on her and left, leaving her to think the worst about him. Without telling her he'd walked away from his life to save hers. Without her knowing about the beating he'd taken—and given—to join the club. He'd kept the branding mark hidden while it healed. The scar would require plastic surgery to correct. The faded black-ink prison tattoos he'd had strategically placed were a special ink developed by the CIA. The removal would be painful, but if it meant she was safe, he'd gladly endure it. And more.

Three days later, she still refused to make eye contact or acknowledge his presence. But she seemed to enjoy Axle's company. A small part of him was thankful she'd found someone who could comfort her in the middle of the worst time of her life. But a bigger part of him was angry with himself for not being the man she needed. The war playing out between his head and his heart was unrelenting.

She walked with Lori into the kitchen, keeping her distance from him. Lori cast furtive glances in his direction, apprehension and fear rolling off her in waves. His size was intimidating. His intense glare exposed his deadly inclinations. People naturally moved out of his way when they saw him coming. Her reaction to him was typical, even if it stung strangely.

He opened his mouth to speak to Elle, but his phone rang and stopped him just in time. "Yeah," he snapped. He listened wordlessly to the instructions from the other end for a moment. "Understood."

He turned to Axle and pocketed his phone. "Never mind my order. I have to go. I'll see you later."

~

Spider sauntered through the hall of the mansion they called the country club. He'd already rendered Beth unconscious and moved her to the van. He whistled as he made his way to Katrina's room to collect her. Then to Carrie's room. With the three women sleeping in the back of the van, Spider started his trek to move them to the old clubhouse, reuniting them with Elle.

When he strolled in with Beth thrown over his shoulder, Elle visibly withdrew away from him, toward Axle, until she realized who he carried. She watched silently as he brought them in, one by one.

"What's happening? Why are you bringing them here? What are you doing with us?" she demanded sharply.

"Nothing at all, sweetheart," Spider replied with a smirk. He stepped outside and called Headbanger. "It's done, boss. All the girls are here. You can make the call for the sale now."

"That's good news. I'll get the ball rolling. Head back over here to the clubhouse so we can make our final arrangements with your uncle." Headbanger disconnected and turned to Bone. "Go get his uncle."

"You got it."

Once Bone left, Headbanger turned on the television to catch the promised news update on the search for Elle Sinclair and her makeup artist, Beth Condra. He'd been following the updates religiously, waiting for any clue the authorities were closing in on them. He'd agreed to include Detective Gough in their scheme as a precaution, someone who had the inside track to cover their asses while putting her own on the line.

He turned up the volume when the ticker at the bottom of the screen showed the district attorney's name.

"Thank you, Mayor Porter. As the district attorney, I'm here to assure you the chief of police and I are working together to ensure the missing entertainment industry professionals are found and returned, safe and sound. I can't go into details about the steps we're taking, but know that we've heard your concerns loud and clear. We're taking this situation very seriously and have had agreements from all the major studios to increase their security presence. We encourage everyone involved with the industry, regardless of job title, to be diligent about their surroundings and to move around the lots in groups, never alone."

The governor, mayor, DA, and chief of police all stood shoulder-to-shoulder on the stage, showing their solidarity. To the side of the stage stood Detective Gough, her shoulders held back in her staunch military stance, her back rod straight, and her face expressionless.

"One of the city's best detectives has been assigned to the case. She has the highest percentage of cases successfully solved and is one of our most decorated officers. We will update you as we can without jeopardizing the case."

The DA closed the press conference by saying she wouldn't accept any questions, and they filed off the stage and into the justice building behind them. Headbanger watched Detective Gough's body language when she walked away. He didn't trust anyone for a reason—most everyone had disappointed or double-crossed him at some point. The club was his family, a proven brotherhood of men who had his back and proved water was thicker than blood.

He put all of his trust in his brothers, making any act of betrayal acutely devastating to him. Like a wild animal when it's wounded, he became more dangerous when he was hurt. After he discovered he'd been fooled, his trust had been thrown back in his face, he was wounded. A wounded wild animal. That kind of betrayal couldn't be forgiven and forgotten. It was premeditated, well planned-out, and overtly deliberate. They wanted to make him look like a fool, to play him—but they'd be the ones played when he was finished with them.

He moved to the back room and began setting up his interrogation tools. One way or another, he'd get the answers he needed. And when he was finished, his ferocity would never be doubted again.

"Hey, Prez," Spider said when he entered the club.

Headbanger glanced up at him. "Everything go okay?"

"Smooth as glass."

"Good. Take a load off." Headbanger gestured to the open chair. "Just watching a little TV, waiting for Bone to get back."

"Want a beer?"

"Sure. I'll take one."

When Bone arrived, he forced their guest into the clubhouse and locked the door behind them. "Look who I found," Bone announced when they entered the club's media room.

Spider looked up and saw his uncle, who was beaten and battered and wore a terrified expression, compliments of the gun held to his back. "What the fuck? Uncle Barry? What's going on?" Spider stood and met Bone's hard stare with one of his own. "What the fuck have you done to my uncle?"

"He did what I told him to do," Headbanger replied from behind him. "We need to talk."

They led Spider and Barry into the interrogation room. All color drained from Spider's face as realization of what was to come set in. Bone shoved them both into the waiting chairs and strapped them down.

"I have a few questions you're going to answer. Some I already know the answers to, some I don't. So I dare you to lie to me." Headbanger reared his fist back and smashed it into Spider's face amid his protests to wait, to explain what was wrong. But he didn't stop. Spider's pleas didn't register through his rage.

"Stop!" Barry bellowed. His tone, a mixture of terror and alarm, caught Headbanger's attention.

"Did you think I forgot about you?"

"You haven't even asked anything yet. You haven't told us what's wrong."

"You're absolutely right," he replied, leaning down to stare directly into Barry's eyes. "Where the fuck is my money?"

"What money? What are you talking about?"

He grabbed Spider's mangled face and turned it toward Barry. "Tell him, Spider. Tell your uncle why he's about to die with you."

"Boss, wait. It's not what you think."

"Let's go over the facts. Renegade is the treasurer and you're the secretary. At first, I did question Renegade's loyalty, so I had an outside contact comb through everything from my companies all the way to my offshore account. You did a good job of covering your tracks and making me suspect someone else. But you also did a good job of keeping club records.

"Money started disappearing from my account immediately before Renegade became the treasurer, so it couldn't have been him. The timing was close, but no dice. You've mastered signing my signature. The outside auditor noticed the change in it over time to more closely match my real signature.

"So you set up a new account in my name and transferred money from my actual account a little at a time. When the amounts started adding up, you covered up my account balance by showing me the fake account instead. Renegade wouldn't have had any reason to suspect a second account, thanks to your club records."

One of Spider's eyes had already swollen shut, but his one good eye was open wide and filled with fear. "No, boss. I was just trying to protect you and your money. It's still in your name. It's yours. This is how money is laundered, small amounts transferred to different accounts over time."

"You know what, Spider? I could almost believe that—if you hadn't booked a one-way flight to the Bahamas leaving one week from today. You almost made it, didn't you? You almost pulled off a great heist. But not quite. I trust no one implicitly, I double-check everything. Surely you know that about me if you know nothing else."

"No, boss. You've got it all wrong."

"You know I hate a liar. The more I have to spend time proving I know this beyond a shadow of a doubt, the worse it'll be for you."

He motioned to Bone, and they pushed Spider over onto his side. Bone grabbed Spider's wallet from his back pocket and stepped back, his disgusted glare firmly set on his victim. Bone dug through the wallet, removing Spider's license along with the fake identification he'd had made.

Spider's whole body sagged in defeat as his prez read the name on the fake license. "Bobby Blalock. Is that your name, Spider?"

He shook his head from side to side.

"Whose name is it?"

"Yours."

"Spider, what have you done?" Barry asked, surprise and dread equally infused in his whisper.

"I'm sorry, boss. I was just trying to protect you."

"It's a good thing I don't need your protection, isn't it?" He nodded to Bone, who stepped out of the room and got Shadow.

When Shadow walked in and realized who sat beside Spider, his skin pricked, knowing the case was unraveling quickly.

"Doorman, take Spider out and get rid of him. I have other plans for Uncle Barry." Headbanger mocked Barry, emphasizing his name with a blatant sneer.

Bone slid a pair of zip-tie handcuffs over Spider's wrists and tied a gag around his mouth. Shadow drew Spider to his feet and shoved him through the door with Spider's grunts begging for his uncle's safety.

"Now, Barry, how much do you think the studio will pay for your safe return? Bet they'd pay a pretty penny if we return all their talent at once, wouldn't they?"

Shadow couldn't delay his departure any longer without drawing attention to himself. Once outside, he put Spider in the club's truck and slid behind the wheel. Spider glanced over at Shadow and grunted when he tried to speak. Shadow shook his head and sighed loudly. He should be in that room, preventing them from killing the studio executive, but he was with Spider instead.

"Barry Jacobson is your uncle?" Shadow verified.

Spider nodded, grief covering his features.

"You screwed over your uncle, didn't you?"

Spider nodded.

"And it never occurred to you they'd suspect he was in on it after you disappeared? Or that they'd take it out on him because he's your uncle?"

Spider shook his head, understanding of what he'd done beginning to sink in.

Shadow dialed Nick to give him the news. After he'd explained what had happened and what he was doing, Nick advised him to take Spider to Jack's place.

"He's been tracing the fake companies and offshore account. He'd just uncovered the discrepancies in the accounts today. What Headbanger doesn't know yet is there's a third account. The full balance of both accounts under Bobby Blalock's name is scheduled to transfer to the third account one week from today."

"Whose name is that one in?"

"Barry Jacobson."

Shadow looked over at Spider. "You don't say."

"Yeah. Great family, huh? I'm heading to the clubhouse now to try to keep them from killing Barry. If they find out Barry has double-crossed them all, there'll be a long line of people who want to kill him."

Shadow parked at Jack's apartment and marched Spider inside, where two DEA agents waited to take him into custody. With fake blood and a staged scene, Shadow took pictures of Spider's "dead" body as proof for Headbanger.

"You're undercover DEA?" Spider finally asked, still dumbfounded with the turn of events.

"No, I'm not DEA at all. But I did just save your life," Shadow replied. "So, you're going to tell me everything."

Over the next hour, Shadow questioned Spider and listened to his rendition of the kidnapping scheme.

"It was my uncle's idea. He's a big-time executive, but he'd spent too much of the money that was earmarked to go to movie production on himself. He couldn't finalize the movie without being found out, so he wanted us to take the girls until he fixed his money problems. Once he got more funding, we were supposed to let them go, and he'd pay us for grabbing them.

"But it took a lot longer than he thought it would, and another movie was wrapping up before he had the money to finish. Then another. It just kept adding up on him, so Boss decided to sell the girls. The cartels gave us the spray to knock them out, and they got it from a guy in Hong Kong. They arranged a deal for us, with the cartel getting a cut, of course. The girls are supposed to be moved through Mexico to the port in the next few days. That's why I moved them from Barry's house."

"Selling them to whom?"

"The cartel's contact in Hong Kong."

Shadow cut his gaze to the DEA agents. One spoke up. "We'll cast a wide net across the border—land and sea. They won't leave the States."

Shadow nodded and stood to leave. Spider had lost all his bravado when he searched Shadow's face. "Are you going to save my uncle's life too?"

"I'll try," he replied after a few seconds. "No promises. I have no idea what those two are doing to him since we left." He turned to leave when Spider stopped him again.

"Bone suspects you, ya know? He told Boss this morning. He thinks there's something up with you and that actress. He swears he heard the two of you talking the night you brought the new girl in. But when he moved to the door to listen, she'd quit talking. Since then, she's avoided you. He wants to off both of you."

"Thanks for the heads-up." He nodded to Spider and left, calling Nick as soon as he got into the truck. "Tell me you saved Jacobson."

"Oh, he's alive, Guess you haven't seen the news over the last hour."

"No. What now?"

"Now we're into extortion via ransom demands. Headbanger sent a video showing Jacobson tied up and beaten, and he demanded the studio pay for the release of their executive and actresses. The money is supposed to be wired to his offshore account."

"The same one that's about to be drained dry?"

Nick chuckled at the irony. "The same. Karma can be such a bitch."

"What's his exchange plan?"

"When the money transfer is confirmed, he'll leave them all at one location and send the address when he's long gone."

"Because those schemes always work exactly as planned."

"Don't underestimate him. He's likely to have another plan in mind but not tell any of us. We need eyes on him at all times."

Shadow told Nick the last words Spider said to him. "Don't let them hurt my girl, Nick. I swear to you, I will mow every one of those bastards down if she's harmed."

"I hear you, man."

CHAPTER TWENTY-ONE

Brianna, Chaise, Heather, and Liz entered the enormous suite that had become the temporary headquarters of Steele Security. The Moore and Condra families had been moved to the same floor for their own safety, traveling to interviews under the watchful eye of Reaper, Bull, or Rebel.

"We're here. You can all take a break now. We've got this," Liz exclaimed upon her entrance.

"Case is closed, boys. Liz is here. We can all go home," Rebel teased as he rose to greet Heather. He enjoyed seeing Liz's feathers ruffled.

"You think you're better at this than me? As far as I can tell, you only started solving cases after I showed up to help you."

Bull snorted, then coughed exaggeratedly to hide his gaffe. "We were just saying we couldn't wait until you got here. We've missed you, Liz."

Liz beamed with pride as every other eye in the room bore through Bull's skin with a burning intensity.

"Yes, that's exactly what we were just saying," Reaper added, his tone rife with sarcasm and humor.

"Never fear, my boys. Mama Liz is here to protect you."

"When did you become Mama Liz?" Heather asked as she wrapped her arms around Rebel, happy to be in her husband's arms again.

"Since I started my own day care with just Steele Security kids. Have any of you figured out what causes repeat pregnancies yet?" Liz moved through the expansive adjoining suites, checking every bedroom before claiming hers. "I'm glad you reserved several suites on this floor. We'll need one just for my headquarters."

Reaper had learned not to argue with Liz more than absolutely necessary. Over the years with her as their nanny and friend, she'd trapped him by his own words one time too many. He rushed to Brianna and scooped her up in his arms. "Hey, baby. I'm so glad you're here."

"Me, too. Your parents and my parents argued over who would babysit while I'm here with you." She laughed then kissed him. "I gave them each a week, so you need to wrap up this case and take me away for some adult time."

"Oh, lord. Another Steele baby coming right up," Liz groaned.

Reaper and Brianna chuckled while they continued their kiss hello.

Chaise melted into Bull's arms, and their lips fused together. "Hello, gorgeous," he said against her lips. "'Bout time you showed up."

"Got here as soon as I could. Your parents and my parents are taking turns with the kids, too. I agree with Bri—we all need an adults-only vacation once this is over," Chaise replied.

"What can we do to help?" Brianna asked.

"Elle's and Beth's parents have had a hard time with this. We've tried to calm them as much as possible without giving them much information on Shadow."

"Where is my man?" Liz asked, reappearing in the living room decked out in black leather pants, a long-sleeve black Henley shirt, and a black leather vest. The matching black leather hat and fingerless gloves completed her biker look. "I'm his ride-or-die chick. Gotta support my man no matter which road he chooses."

"Uh, Liz," Rebel began, wiping the smile off his face with his big hand. "Your man is deep undercover. In an outlaw motorcycle gang. We can't just insert you undercover with him. It'll get him killed. Besides, I'm not sure your slip-on Skechers are approved by the Devil's Dominion."

"What's wrong with them? They're comfortable and easy to get on and off my feet when they swell."

"Maybe we should let her loose on the gang. She'd probably take them down single-handedly," Bull quipped.

"Damn straight. Let me at 'em." Liz stood in front of the entry mirror and adjusted her hat. "Did anyone bring me a gun?"

"No!" came the unified reply from all three men.

Liz turned slowly and glared at each man. "Wait a minute. Where's Silas?"

Reaper buried his face in Brianna's neck, his body shaking so hard with laughter he couldn't speak to respond to her question.

"Silas is working a different angle of the case, Liz. He's protecting Jax Hart and working through his CIA contact to help Shadow. I'm sure we'll see him soon."

"Not when he finds out Liz is here," Reaper whispered to Brianna. She immediately shushed him.

Liz narrowed her eyes at Brianna and Reaper. "Noah Steele. Silas taught me how to be a spy. I know everything he knows. Call him right now—in front of me and on speaker—and tell him to get over here. Jax Hart can stay here with the others and be just fine. Silas needs backup, though."

"You'll have to lose your biker chick outfit. He's not in the gang. In fact, if they find out he's here, they'll kill him. He infiltrated the gang years ago and was 'sent to prison' to get out of it. But he's sure his cover was blown in the process," Rebel countered.

"Like I said, I'm Shadow's ride-or-die girl, so the leather stays. If anyone sees me with Silas, I can vouch for him as a real biker chick." Liz lowered her gaze to Reaper's phone pointedly and raised her eyebrows.

With a resigned sigh, he picked up his phone and pressed the button for Silas. When the call connected, he smiled and hit the speaker button. "Hey, big brother, you're on speaker. There's someone here who wants to see you."

A few seconds of pregnant silence filled the line before Silas replied. "Oh, yeah? Who's that?"

"You know damn well who it is, Silas Steele," Liz called. "You lied to me. You said you couldn't bring me with you as a matter of national security."

"It is a matter of national security, Liz. The nation is not secure when you're on the loose as a rogue quadruple agent. You missed the whole point of a double agent."

"There's no reason why I should be limited to just double. I can play many sides against each other. Just because I'm more talented and flexible than you are is no reason to let envy keep me from helping you."

Another punctuated silence stalled the conversation.

"Silas?"

"Yes, Liz?"

"Come on over to the hotel and bring this Jax person. He can stay here while we wrap up this case and bring Shadow home."

Silas dropped his head backward and stared at the ceiling, ceding to Liz's demand before disconnecting. "Fine. We'll be there later tonight."

Silas turned to Jax and smiled a devious smile. "I know I just moved you here from your Idaho mountain hideout, but Liz actually does have a valid point for once. I'm moving you to another location tonight. It's secure and under armed protection. Elle's and Beth's families are also staying there."

"Okay. But why the creepy smile?"

"You're going to help me with Liz."

"Who's Liz?"

"You'll see." Silas laughed out loud. "You'll see."

When darkness began to fall over LA, Silas had Jax put on his disguise so they could leave the building without him being recognized. They reached the hotel and stepped off the elevators to find Liz waiting impatiently with her foot tapping.

"It's about time." She crossed her arms over her chest and huffed loudly. "Do you know how much time we've already wasted?"

"Patience, Liz. Let's get Jason set up in his room."

She looked at Jason suspiciously. "I thought your name was Jax."

"Jax is his spy name. To everyone else, he's Jason." Silas made his statement so matter-of-factly, so nonchalantly, knowing Liz's interest in Jason would double.

"Hold up. You're a spy?"

"Of course. He's in disguise right now. What's really interesting is he used to be a special-effects makeup artist here in LA. He has mad skills with a makeup brush and a little putty." Silas pulled out the big guns early, hoping his distraction was enough to entice Liz.

"Well. We'll just see about his mad skills, won't we?" Liz challenged.

Hook, line, and sinker, Silas thought as he smiled to himself.

"Let's practice on Silas before he and I go out to help Shadow tonight," Liz continued, effectively bursting his happy bubble.

"What? Who's Shadow?" Jason asked, looking at Silas for help.

"Never mind. You don't need to know anything about him. Now, my outfit is already perfect to join a motorcycle club, but I need more of a kick to my makeup. A good disguise to protect my real identity," Liz decided.

Jason started with the leather cap on her head and worked his way down to her white slip-on Skechers. He jerked his head up and opened his mouth to object when Silas stopped him.

"That's a great idea, Liz. Why don't the two of you work on your makeup while I go check in with Noah."

"All right, Silas. But you know what happens if you sneak off without me," Liz warned.

He rolled his eyes, knowing full well what Liz would do. He'd made that mistake once before on a far less important grocery store run on a group trip. When he awoke that night, Liz stood over him with her bright pink nail polish in hand. Not only had she painted his nails, but also his lips. To date, he still hadn't figured out how she'd pulled that off, and she refused to divulge her own trade secrets.

But removing her as his self-proclaimed spy partner was worth the painted lips and nails he'd endure later. For the time being, his focus had to be on getting Shadow and the others out of the Devil's clutches. Events had been escalating in severity, ramping up the danger Shadow and Nick faced if their covers were blown and increasing the probability someone would be killed before the sting was finished.

"Noah," he called out when they entered the suite.

"Back here," Reaper answered.

Liz escorted Jason to another room so they could begin work on her disguise. Silas breathed a sigh of relief when he joined the other men in their temporary command center.

"I just got here, and she's already threatening me."

The others laughed at his misfortune. "We're just glad she's taken a liking to you, Silas," Reaper replied.

"Noah, you're my brother. You're supposed to have my back."

"Brother, you know I'd take a bullet for you. But when it comes to Liz, we've all agreed it's every man for himself," Reaper replied.

"Bastards," Silas mumbled under his breath.

"What have you found out, Silas?" Rebel asked.

Silas filled them in on his entire conversation with Jason and what he'd seen. Noah, in turn, brought Silas up to speed on the events of the day. "Jack, Nick's handler, called and gave us the rundown of Shadow's interrogation of Spider. He was singing like a songbird, hoping Shadow could save his uncle after he'd double-crossed his club and his family. He has no idea his uncle planned to double-cross him in the end, though."

Silas listened intently, following the explanation of the first account feeding the second, until both were to be transferred to the third account held by the studio executive Barry Jacobson. It was a good scheme, he had to give Barry that. Mismanage funds, run out of production money, have the girls kidnapped by his nephew's gang until he could secure more investors or recover money from somewhere else, all while the studio covered for him because losing their insurance policy would shut them down forever.

Barry never considered Shadow's commitment to Elle, though.

Shadow returned to the old clubhouse, per Nick's request. Since he hadn't been invited to take Spider's place as an officer, his presence around the officers' area would be suspicious. Nick tried to keep Shadow's interactions with Headbanger and Bone to a minimum. The wrong word uttered regarding Elle would result in all-out war, something Nick wasn't prepared to initiate just yet. They'd had another disagreement over the phone.

"You have all the info you need on the bank accounts. You said that's what you were waiting for—to find out who was behind this. Now we know the funds came from the club's drug and weapons money funneling into the offshore account through shell corporations, and Jacobson is behind the abductions on the lot. There's no reason to continue this charade. We need to get them out of that clubhouse before Headbanger kills them all out of spite." Shadow had argued his points until he was blue in the face, but Nick wouldn't back down.

"I have orders from my superiors. Since Headbanger is openly taunting the police and the feds, they want to tack on extra charges and make sure he never sees the outside of the prison walls again. This isn't over until we have the all-clear and our teams are in place to ensure everyone's safety," Nick shot back.

"While you follow orders and your superiors look to add one more charge to a list already a mile long, those civilians' lives are in mortal danger. That should be your first priority—not an extra star for the agency. Is there something else you're not telling me?"

"No. It'll be over soon. Don't jump the gun."

"You'd better hope Headbanger and Bone don't jump the gun." Shadow hung up on Nick, angry and frustrated his friend wouldn't listen to reason.

Shadow killed the engine outside the old clubhouse and sat on his bike, fighting the urge to storm into the old clubhouse and ride off into the sunset with Elle on the back. With an impatient growl, he climbed off and sauntered up the steps to the door. He stepped inside and came face-to-face with Elle.

At least she's looking at me, Shadow thought.

"Didn't expect to see you," Axle said, throwing Shadow's words back at him.

Shadow grinned knowingly. "I like to keep you guessing."

Elle huffed and walked out of the room, carrying her meal with her and leaving the others at the table. Shadow glanced over at them, hoping Beth wouldn't give him away. The expression on her face matched the hatred in her eyes. She wanted to relieve him of his head. When her lips parted and she prepared to speak, he moved quickly out of the kitchen and in the direction Elle had gone.

He heard a chair scrape against the floor, followed by Axle's command. "Sit down and eat." The distant sound of the chair sliding across the floor confirmed she'd obeyed.

With one person in mind, his feet carried him straight to her. She sat with her back to him when he approached. The closer he got, the more he realized she wasn't simply sitting on the couch to eat. Her shoulders shook softly at first, but the shaking grew more intense with his every step. Her quiet sobs and muffled wails reached his chest before his ears, causing a tightening he could only describe as a vise around him. Her face was mashed into a pillow, giving her the only private place she had to completely melt down.

He wasn't sure which was worse—seeing her like that and not being able to comfort her, allowing her to believe he'd helped put her in that predicament, or walking away to give her the privacy she needed and deserved.

His hand hovered over her head, waiting to stroke her hair.

His arms ached to lift her from the couch and cradle her against his chest until her tears dried.

His lips craved to claim hers, to kiss away the pain she felt until she remembered the love they shared.

His ego strained against his loyalty, wanting to defy Nick and burn the case down around them when he freed the girls and kidnapped Elle for himself.

Instead, he backed away from her. And decided that was definitely the worst-case scenario.

"How could you? I loved you. I thought you loved me." She whispered each sentiment to herself between gasps for air.

I was so wrong, he thought. *I've never been so wrong. Letting her think I'm behind any of this is definitely the worst.*

CHAPTER TWENTY-TWO

"Are you and your boys a bunch of ignorant, inbred assholes?" Detective Gough barged into the officers' area of the Devil's Dominion clubhouse. "I mean, I've busted some dumbass criminals before, but you and your boys take the fucking cake."

Headbanger leaned back in his chair and leveled his death-glare at her. "Either you were dropped on your head repeatedly as a child, or you've lost your bitch mind."

"Is that right?" She pinned him with her own pissed-off stare. "Well, I haven't lost my bitch mind enough to let a fucking undercover federal agent join my outlaw motorcycle club and not even fucking know it."

Headbanger's face turned beet red. "What the fuck did you just say?"

"You heard me. Shit rolls downhill, you know? After all your fuck-ups with a simple snatch and grab of a couple of actresses, I really shouldn't be surprised. But you've effectively fucked us both. Your boys grabbed Elle Sinclair and her makeup artist in front of Jax Hart. Jax went to the media with it. Do you have any clue how much pressure gets put on us to quickly solve anything to do with our stars?

"The governor called the mayor. The mayor called the DA. The DA called the chief of police. The chief chewed my ass up one side and down the other. Somewhere in the chain of command, they demanded to let the FBI take over, but the DEA confirmed there's already an undercover agent in your club. So they have jurisdiction to protect their asset.

"How the fuck can you not tell one of your men is a federal agent? That's why you and your boys are stupid, inbred assholes. That undercover agent has already made me, I can guarantee that. He just hasn't been debriefed to rat me out yet."

"Get the fuck out of here. You ever come at me with one ounce of disrespect again, I'll put a bullet between your fucking eyes and feed your goddamn body to the sharks." He stood and rounded his desk, charging toward her like an out-of-control bull. When she didn't move fast enough, he grabbed her with one hand, opened the door with the other hand, and shoved her outside. Before she could speak, he slammed the door shut in her face.

"Bone," he bellowed. "Get in here."

Within seconds, his sergeant at arms stood in his office awaiting orders. "Yes, sir?"

"Take Nutcrusher, and you two put a bullet in Gough's, Doorman's, and Renegade's skulls. Then rip the patches and rockers off their vests and bring them back to me, soaked in their blood."

Shock crossed Bone's face before he nodded. "Renegade? He betrayed us?"

"That fucking detective just said we have an undercover agent in our club. Doorman is the first man I suspected. The way he got up and fought back after his initiation should've tipped me off, but I ignored it. If he's an agent, Renegade must be too. Either way, he endorsed a fed, and he has to go."

"I fucking knew it. Renegade was behind my brother getting busted at that bar, I'm sure of it. I'll gladly take care of them both."

Bone went into the armory and took four Glock 9mm pistols and extra clips, two for him and two for Nutcrusher. One bullet to each of their skulls wouldn't be enough. He walked through the clubhouse, calling for his friend, when a door opened suddenly and a half-dressed Nutcrusher rushed out.

"What? Where's the fucking fire?" He buttoned his pants and pulled up the zipper. The girl he was with sat up on the bed, wide-eyed while she watched him.

"We have orders." Bone handed him two of the handguns, effectively conveying the rest of the message.

"Who?" Nutcrusher asked, tucking the guns into the back of his pants.

"Renegade and the fucking Doorman. But first, Gough."

"What? Why?"

"They're undercover feds, and that bitch detective rubbed the prez the wrong way."

The two men left in the truck, heading toward the detective's apartment. Bone couldn't help but hear what Headbanger threatened Gough with—and he knew his boss didn't make idle threats. She'd die exactly as he'd described, and when she saw them approaching, she'd know exactly why.

Nutcrusher knocked on her door while Bone flattened his back against the wall and waited. The peephole darkened as she peeked through it, but Nutcrusher left his expression neutral. He sensed her hesitancy and considered kicking the door in just before the deadbolt turned.

"What do you want?" Her bravado was fake, but he had to give her credit for trying.

Bone swung around, his gun drawn, and ordered her out of the apartment. Her eyes cut to the side, and Nutcrusher knew she planned to run. He grabbed her arm and jerked her toward him. She lost her balance and fell against his chest. With a gun pressed into her spine, they walked her to the truck and forced her into the cab between them.

"What's going on? Where are you taking me?"

"Detective Gough, we thought you were smart," Bone taunted.

"You fucked up royally, sweetheart," Nutcrusher added, knowing she hated that endearment. "Not only did you threaten the prez, you disrespected him and failed to identify a fed in our midst before he'd gained too much intel on us. You're supposed to be our police protection. You suck at your job."

The false bravado she had just moments before was nowhere to be found. Realization dawned, and she understood how dire her situation was. "Guys, come on. We can fix this. I'll help you find him, and we'll take him out of play. I have a lot riding on him being out of the picture too."

"Not anymore, sweetheart. You're out completely. No sense in worrying about your job anymore. Remember how Headbanger said you'd die? One custom-made death package coming up." Bone loved his club and was loyal to his boss. If he'd learned one valuable lesson in life, that lesson was loyalty was most important.

They drove to an abandoned mall and marched her inside, with Detective Gough pleading for her life the entire way. With every word, they mocked her, repeating her pleas in abnormally high-pitched voices. Nutcrusher pushed her down on her knees while Bone chambered a round. He lowered the top of the barrel to her forehead, lining it up directly between her eyes, and smiled when he pulled the trigger, despite her flowing tears and frantic requests.

"Well, that was easy." Bone smirked and spread out the plastic tarp. "Grab her feet and put her on this. We'll drive up toward the country club and dump her into the ocean."

They rolled her up and carried her back to the truck, throwing her in the back with no regard. Nutcrusher slid across the driver's seat, fired up the truck, and drove north out of the city until they reached an isolated area along the coast. From the top of the cliff overlooking the rocky shore, they unwrapped her from the tarp and tossed her lifeless body over the side. The waves crashed against the rocks, and the foamy plumes leapt into the air from the force and claimed her as part of the sea.

"Goodbye, sweetheart." Nutcracker watched the ebb and flow of the waves pull her out into the deeper water until she was no longer visible. "The current and the fishes have her now," he heckled.

"Let's go kill those undercover pigs now," Bone replied.

"You really think it's them? She didn't say two agents. She said she'd help us find *him*. What if we kill two brothers, and they're not undercover agents?"

"It's them, all right. My gut has told me it was Renegade from the start. The Doorman made his way into the group all too easy with his weapons and endorsement from Renegade."

"Spider wanted him too."

"And where is Spider now?"

"Same place these two will be. I say we make them talk first. Find out what they know and who they've told. May be useful info to have in the near future. We may be able to avoid a federal raid—or at least laugh at them while they look in the wrong place."

"Good idea. Maybe we'll cut their fingers off one knuckle at a time—whether they talk or not. My castration shears have been feeling unappreciated lately."

By the time Bone and Nutcrusher reached the old clubhouse, night had settled in and darkness permeated the dimly lit rooms. The tension between Shadow and Nick had subsided, but neither had been overly talkative. Shadow watched the two bikers stroll through the house, nonchalantly checking each bedroom and demanding they all come out to the main room. The feeling something major was going down grew with each step they took.

Their demeanor was off. The more they tried to act natural, the more obvious it was they were anything but natural.

The longer they delayed their intentions, the more they showed their hand.

They thought they were smooth and stealthy, when they were transparent as glass and nervous.

Shadow caught Nick's attention and slid his left index finger along the right side of his nose. An innocuous move to signal his friend to get ready—they would have to fight their way out of the clubhouse at any minute. Shadow's gaze traveled over their outlines and quickly spotted the two guns each man carried. They came more prepared than they normally were.

"What's going on?" Nick asked and leaned against the doorframe. His stance hid his right arm, which was bent behind his back so he could reach his gun in a split second.

"Headbanger sent us. Seems there's a new development and a change in plans for the girls," Bone replied. "The deal is off, so we can do what we want with them before we put a bullet in their brains."

"Prez didn't tell us about any change of plans." Nick's fingers firmly gripped the butt of his gun.

"I'm telling you now. He doesn't have to tell you when I can do it for him." Bone walked toward Katrina. "Maybe I'll start with this one." He ran his callused fingers along her cheek, his sneer conveying the images conjured by his imagination.

"You're not doing anything to any of these girls unless I hear it directly from the prez. He didn't give me the okay, so I sure as fuck don't take your word for anything. These girls have a specific purpose, and I won't be the one to fuck that up for him."

"No, you won't be the one to fuck anything up. I'll be the one who fucks you up if you talk to me like that again. Call him yourself. While you wait to talk to him, this one will be sucking me off. Come back later," Nutcrusher replied and wrapped his fingers around Elle's wrist.

Shadow flinched, an uncharacteristic reaction for him after what years of training and work had drilled into him, but the man in him responded before the spy did when another man touched her or even thought about enjoying any part of her body. Though she still believed the worst about him, he'd protect her with his life. He had to make her believe he was part of the scheme so she wouldn't give them a reason to suspect or kill her. But there was no way in hell he'd allow Nutcrusher to do anything to her.

"Get your hand off her." Shadow stepped forward—threatening him openly. "Unless you want to lose that hand for good."

Nutcrusher looked over at Shadow, a small smile playing on his lips. "You know, Bone always said you were sweet on this one. You wanna watch? See how good she is before you give her a try?"

"You only get one warning. I'm counting down. When I get to zero, I'll snap that hand off and shove it up your ass. Three, two, one." Shadow stomped across the floor, his face dark with malicious intent.

Nutcrusher released her wrist, turned to face Shadow, and took a couple of steps backward. When Shadow had moved in front of Elle, effectively blocking her from Nutcrusher's view with his sheer size, he stopped abruptly. "Just in time. Maybe you're not as stupid as your nickname suggests. To be clear, the countdown doesn't start over if you touch her again."

The room became eerily quiet with the only sounds coming from the ladies' rapid breathing. Tension filled every square inch as time ticked by slowly. Shadow stood motionless, daring Nutcrusher to say or do the wrong thing one more time. Shadow arched one eyebrow, lifting it slowly as he wordlessly questioned the other man's intelligence.

"Fine. She's all yours," Nutcrusher ceded. "It is strange, though, how protective you are over a girl you don't even know."

"I'm protective over this entire play we're making. You screw it up, you screw me over. Any man who screws me over ends up without a fucking head."

"You two can't take a joke for shit," Bone chimed in. His easy laugh was meant to lighten the mood in the room. But the nervous edge to it contradicted his intent.

"We can take a joke just fine. None of this was fucking funny, though." Nick adjusted his stance but kept his gun arm hidden.

Nutcrusher moved away from Shadow and Elle, back toward Bone. Shadow sensed they were refortifying their positions, moving back into attack mode by aligning their combined force. Bone pulled his hands from his front pockets, giving Shadow a quick glimpse of something in his hand. He began walking toward Nick, palming something suspicious.

Nick's keen eyes homed in on Bone's movements. His fingers gripped his gun, and he mentally prepared for a shootout. The problem was his conscience got in the way. He made a note of where every woman stood and the likelihood she'd be hit in the cross fire. Bone and Nutcrusher wouldn't care about collateral damage. Nick's gaze drifted to Shadow, and he caught the tail end of a secret signal.

Shadow slid two fingers across his throat.

Their cover was blown.

Though Nick saw it coming, he remained in place and let Bone think he had the upper hand in his surprise attack. Bone lifted his hand to Nick's face and pumped the sprayer several times in quick succession. Nick threw his hand up, forcefully knocking Bone backward while wiping his face with his other arm. Bone, shocked Nick wasn't unconscious on the floor, was temporarily confused and didn't see Nick's right hook until it was too late. His head jerked violently to the side, his feet stumbled under his shaky legs, and he went down to the ground. Nick drew his gun and held it on Bone.

Shadow corralled the ladies and rushed them into the kitchen area, toward the door to the garage, and out of the line of fire. He turned in the doorway, ready to fight to the death. With his gun in his hand, he faced Bone and Nutcrusher, resisting the urge to shoot them both in the head, take Elle home, and be done with the entire farce.

"What the fuck was that, Bone?" Nick roared, testing whether their covers were truly blown.

Bone pushed up to stand and glared at Nick, his face hard and angry. "We all know what you are, pig. You and your friend here. At least one of you is undercover. I don't really care which one of you is the rotten pig and which one isn't—or if you both are. Our orders are to kill you both, and that's exactly what we're going to do."

"You two think you can take us?" Shadow asked, the first genuine smile in weeks covering his face. "By all means, let's see what you've got."

"Everyone just calm the fuck down. Why would you accuse me of being undercover? I've ridden beside you for the last two years, had your back countless times, and you've repeatedly insulted me. What the fuck have I ever done to you?"

"You're the one who put my little brother away. You are an undercover cop, and you had him arrested at that bar almost two years ago. We never had one problem until you joined." Bone's face turned beet red, anger and hatred welling up inside him.

"It wasn't him," Axle said, entering the room behind Bone. "It was me."

"You?" Bone whirled around, his jaw slack and his eyes wide. "You've been with us for years."

"And I have so much shit on you, I could put you away tomorrow and you'd never see the light of day again."

Bone roared with thunderous rage. He moved with lightning speed and drew his gun on Axle. In an instant, Axle's gun was out, and he fired at Bone first. Bone dropped to the floor, narrowly missing the bullet that passed by his head. Nutcrusher pulled his gun and began shooting, the adrenaline flowing out of control, making his hands shake and the bullets fly indiscriminately.

"Get out of here, wait in the garage," Shadow yelled to the ladies.

Once they were out of harm's way, Shadow moved beside Nick, behind cover. "We can't let them shoot Axle, man. We have to take them out."

Nick nodded. Uncertainty clouded his eyes, but his sense of right and wrong won. If that meant revealing his true identity, he could live with that easier than knowing he'd let a fellow agent die in his place.

What seemed to take hours had literally only been seconds. The events escalated so quickly, Shadow lost count of the number of shots that had been exchanged. He raised up from behind the overturned table and aimed his gun at Axle. When Nutcrusher saw Shadow's movement, a broad smile of victory covered his face. Shadow knew Axle had taken all suspicion off Nick and him.

When Nutcrusher turned his gaze back in Axle's direction, Shadow adjusted his arm and his cross hairs. Directly on Nutcrusher's temple. He centered and squeezed the trigger, incapacitating him instantly.

"You want Bone, or want me to take him?" Shadow whispered to Nick while Axle and Bone continued to exchange fire. Screams of terror emanated from the garage, echoing off the high ceiling with every shot.

"I'll take him. I've hated that guy for two fucking years."

Nick eased around the table and crouched behind a chair, lining his sights up with Bone's head. While Axle had him occupied, Nick pulled the trigger. Just as the bullet left the barrel, Bone dropped his extra clip and bent to grab it. The shot whizzed by, obviously coming from a different direction. Bone jerked his head up, his eyes met Nick's, and the disgusted expression on his face confirmed he knew Axle wasn't the only undercover officer. Nick's choice was gone—he couldn't let Bone live and expose them to the other 300 chapter members.

Axle sprinted to a new position and squeezed off another shot. The bullet hit Bone's shoulder. He spun around and fell to the floor with a howl of pain. Axle moved closer and fired another shot just as Bone rolled behind the door. Silence filled the clubhouse one heartbeat too long.

"Bone! You can't hide from me for long. Come out here and face me like a man, you pussy!" Axle yelled.

"Move to that side and check. I'll take the other. Let's get this motherfucker." Shadow took a covering position beside the door, and Nick joined him on the opposite side. With precision and determination, Shadow slowly pushed the door open to give Nick a better view inside. Not seeing Bone in his field of view, Nick moved farther into the room, his gun drawn and his senses heightened.

"He's gone!" Nick yelled. "He's fucking gone. There's a hidden hallway behind this fucking room!"

Shadow bolted toward the garage, where he'd left Elle waiting. Where he thought she'd be safest. Where she was now a sitting duck for an evil man who would kill her simply out of spite. He jerked the door open and flew into the open room, seeing the ladies huddled together in terror. All he could see was Elle—he had to get to her and protect her from Bone's wrath. An arm extended toward Elle. A finger slid across the trigger. A second passed while Bone focused his aim.

A shot rang out, the noise amplified by the echoes, quickly followed by a second shot. The first one tore through Shadow's upper side, and the second bullet hit his upper chest. Shadow stumbled as he turned, using his body as a shield for Elle. He raised his gun, seeing Bone was injured worse than he originally thought, and fired six shots into his body—the final shot hitting his head.

The white-hot pain seared his torso, making it hard to breathe. The room began to spin, and his vision began to fade as he turned to Elle. Every move he made took tremendous effort and used up what little strength he had left.

"Elle," he choked out then coughed. He looked down and saw blood on his hand.

Her eyes were wide, filled with fear, and her face was wet with rivers of tears. She wanted to run to him, to comfort him, but she was frozen in place by the growing bloodstains on his shirt. The two enormous spots were quickly becoming one. Her gaze traveled up his body to meet his eyes, and she snapped out of her haze instantly. The sparkle in his eyes that made him unique, that enhanced his entire personality, was fading.

He collapsed to the floor as Nick emerged from the hidden hallway, and Axle appeared in the doorway from the kitchen. "Call an ambulance!" Nick yelled and ran toward Shadow.

Elle lurched from where she'd knelt on the floor and sprinted to his side. "Devon," she cried repeatedly while stroking his face and hair. "Talk to me, Devon. Stay with me."

Sirens rang out from many blocks away, but Elle only heard her own wails when Nick yelled into his phone.

"Tell them to hurry! He has no pulse—I've lost him! He's dead! Man down, we have a man down!" Nick dropped his phone and began doing chest compressions, yelling at his friend to hold on with each push. "Don't you dare die on me now."

Axle opened the roll-up door and flagged down the ambulance. The paramedics rushed to his side and took over CPR from Nick. Elle watched in shock and anguish while they attempted to revive him. Chest compressions continued once they had him loaded into the back of the ambulance.

"I've got no pulse, no respirations. Pupils are nonreactive to light. Patient is nonresponsive to pain stimulation. We're running emergency with lights and sirens. Have the trauma team on standby for our arrival," the paramedic relayed through his radio. The back doors of the ambulance were closed, and they sped away.

CHAPTER TWENTY-THREE

Elle and Beth rushed into the emergency room, frantically searching for Devon. The agents who'd swarmed the old clubhouse told her she couldn't leave. The cops who showed up after the federal agents forbade her from leaving before they'd completed their paperwork. Axle had been her saving grace in that moment. When everyone else told her to wait, he told her to go—before it was too late.

"Where is Devon Kane?" she shrieked at the triage nurse.

"We don't have anyone here by that name," the nurse stammered. "When was he brought in?"

"About thirty minutes ago, by ambulance. Gunshot wound."

"Okay, I know which patient you're talking about now. Are you family?"

"She's his wife," Beth interjected. "She'd like to see her husband."

The nurse looked at her computer screen and back up at Elle. "He's in surgery. They took him straight to the operating room when they got here—didn't stop in the emergency room at all. Go up to the fifth-floor surgical waiting room. The surgeon will come out and talk to you when they're finished."

Elle and Beth made their way to the waiting room, expecting to be the only ones there, but they found a room full of sad, anxious faces instead. They found two seats and sat quietly, holding hands and waiting for an update from the doctor. Elle's eyes stayed glued to the door, willing the surgeon to magically appear, though she could feel eyes on her. She waited for the moment cell phones emerged to snap pictures of her to sell to the paparazzi or for someone to tip off the media where she was.

But she didn't care. She needed answers. She needed to understand what had happened. She needed an explanation that made sense of the chaotic state her emotions lived in.

How can he be part of this?

All the time we spent together, was it all a lie?

No, it couldn't have been. But then, why did he do this?

Is he in trouble? Was he forced to help them?

Doesn't he care about me at all anymore?

Has this been his life all along? Is this why he never let me be part of his life? Why he said it was too dangerous?

Some of the federal agents who'd rushed in after Devon was shot walked into the waiting room. At first, she thought they'd tracked her down, but they moved past her and sat against the wall. Their expressionless faces gave nothing away of their intentions, but Elle assumed they wanted to question Devon almost as much as she did.

"Beth, we have to call our families and Devon's. I've been so crazy, I didn't even think about them until right this second."

"That makes two of us. When I saw him get shot, and all that blood, I think my brain just shut down. I'll go call them right now. You can wait here."

Elle was lost in her thoughts when she heard familiar voices from the hallway. She looked up to see her parents and brothers enter. She rushed into her parents' open arms, feeling safe for the first time in weeks. With hugs and kisses and tears all around, they had a family reunion in the hospital waiting room. She couldn't answer their questions about anything regarding her time held captive by the gang. There were too many aspects of it she needed to understand first.

Her father wrapped his arm around her shoulders and led her back to the chairs. Beth stepped in front of her and knelt. "Elle, my parents are taking me to the station to answer their questions, then we're going to the apartment. I'll grab some clothes for you. Do you need anything else?"

"No. Thank you, though." She touched Beth's face, thankful to have such a loyal friend.

Beth squeezed her hand and smiled through her tears. "You and I will need therapy after this. You know that, right?"

"Without a doubt."

Beth kissed her cheek before leaving, then lingered in the doorway when second thoughts clouded her mind. She gave Elle a questioning look, but Elle waved her on. It had been quite an ordeal, and Elle understood her need for normalcy, or a semblance of it.

Elle watched Beth disappear around the corner, then kept her vigil over the door while waiting on any news about Devon. Time seemed to stand still and fly by at the same time. She was desperate to know. When a tall doctor's frame darkened the doorway, she decided she was definitely not ready to hear.

"Kane family?" he called into the room.

Elle and her family stood to greet the doctor, and she was startled when eight others quickly stood and gathered around her. She glanced at the men and women around her, not recognizing the first face. She met the doctor's surprised gaze when he asked, "You're all here for Devon Kane?"

"Yes," came the simultaneous reply.

"Okay, looks like we have the room to ourselves. Please have a seat." He waited until everyone sat before he began. "I'm sorry to tell you all Devon died during the surgery. We did everything we could to stabilize him, but the damage from the two bullets was just too much. We couldn't repair it fast enough to stop the internal bleeding. I'm very sorry."

"No! God, please, no!" Elle began screaming. The emotional toll of the past few weeks suddenly took a back seat to the pain rippling through her entire body. "Don't tell me that. Tell me you got him back. He can't be gone. It can't end this way."

Elle's father pulled her close to him, and she sobbed into his chest.

"I'm really very sorry. We did everything we could," the doctor consoled.

"Thank you, Doctor. We're sure you did. It's just a hard pill to swallow," her father replied.

Cries filled the room as the news sank in. He was gone, and they'd never get him back. After everything they'd been through, losing him had never been a thought. It wasn't ever an option. Facing one of their worst fears collectively but separately was their only bond. Everyone in that room loved Devon and felt the loss in their own way. That feeling of profound bereavement covered Elle like a heavy blanket, threatening to crush her and steal the air from her lungs. The pain was becoming unbearable and only increased with each tick of the clock.

"Can we see him?" someone in the room asked.

"I'm sorry. The federal officers have already taken custody of his body as part of their investigation. They're collecting evidence and taking pictures of the gunshot wounds. When they finish, I'm sure we can arrange for you to see him."

"Take me home," Elle whispered to her father. "Please get me out of here. I can't take it anymore." The walls began closing in on her, and she felt as if she were in a shrinking box. If she didn't leave immediately, the whole world would witness her complete and total breakdown. She needed the privacy of her bedroom to process her feelings and work through them one at a time. For as long as it took.

Sympathetic faces watched her stand and walk toward the door, but she couldn't stop to address anyone. All her energy and focus were spent on simply putting one foot in front of the other. One step at a time away from the nightmare. One step at a time in a desperate attempt to flee from the pain and heartbreak. One step at time toward a life that would never be the same again.

~

The day of the funeral was harder than the day he died. Elle thought the pain couldn't get any worse, until the morning she opened her eyes and realized that was the last day she would ever see him. Every night before she fell asleep, she prayed she'd wake up and all the events would fade away, like a bad dream long forgotten. But her prayer hadn't been answered, and on that day, she had to say goodbye forever.

Goodbye to the only man she'd ever loved.

Goodbye to all the hopes and dreams of their future.

Goodbye to all the lingering questions and doubts that nagged her.

Goodbye to her heart—he'd had it in one way or another since she was a little kid. It was his as much as it was hers, only she didn't want it anymore.

Tracey, Devon's mother, had visited Elle at her apartment since Elle refused to leave home. Their conversation replayed through her mind, further driving her aversion to the memorial service.

"Elle, sweetheart, how are you doing?" Tracey sat on the edge of the bed and studied Elle's appearance and demeanor.

"I should be asking you that, Tracey. This has to be your worst nightmare come true." Elle covered Tracey's hand with hers, their bond of mourning sealed.

"It's our *worst nightmare, love. We'll get through it together." Tracey smoothed her hair down. "Devon really loved you, ya know?"*

"I thought he did," she replied sadly. "He never said he did, until the day he left me."

Tracey drew back and furrowed her brow. "Of course he did, Elle. He never brought dates around us. Only you. He never went on vacation with anyone else. Every break he had on his job was spent right here with you. Every decision he made was with you in mind—what you needed, what you wanted, what was best for you. He showed you he loved you with everything he did."

"And helping my kidnappers? Was that out of love too?"

"There's actually no greater love than what he did," Tracey replied with tears streaming down her cheeks. "Which brings me to the other reason why I'm here. This is so hard to say, but I have to. Devon's wish was to be cremated."

"I remember him saying that."

"So, we'll have an open casket viewing for one hour only. That's the longest we can do it...since he won't be embalmed. They'll take him away for cremation after that, but we'll still have the chapel. Do you want to stand up and say a few words?"

"Tracey, I'm sorry to let you down, but I can't speak at his funeral. I can barely make it from here to the shower without becoming hysterical. I'm not even sure how I'll make it through the service at all."

"It's okay." Tracey hushed her when the oncoming panic attack became obvious. "You don't have to. I can't do it either, but I didn't want to take that opportunity away from you. Our pastor is coming to preside over it."

Elle forced herself out of bed and into the shower. She moved through the motions of getting dressed—hair, makeup, dress, shoes. But every task only brought her closer to what she didn't want to do.

"Elle, it's time to go, honey," Beth said from her doorway.

Elle's eyes focused, and she realized she'd been staring at herself in the full-length mirror without even really seeing anything. "Okay."

"Your mom came by last night. You were asleep. She left this and wanted you to take it before we leave." Beth held her hand out and offered the small blue pill.

"What is it?"

"It's for anxiety, to help you get through the day."

She stared at the medication while making up her mind. Did she want to feel everything? Or did she want to simply move through the motions and get it all over with? She snatched the pill from Beth's hand and swallowed it quickly. *I've felt enough*, she thought. *I can't handle more feelings.*

By the time they reached the funeral home, the effects had set in and rendered Elle next to numb. Devon's casket sat at the other end of the room, amid all the flowers. A large US flag was draped over him, the corner of it attached to the inside of the casket lid so it flowed over him in memorium. His picture while on active duty in the Army was displayed on an easel at his feet. She walked on unsteady heels toward him, *for the last time* on repeat in her mind. The closer she got, the slower she walked, until she could no longer deny the truth.

Devon Kane lay in wake in the casket in front of her.

Her knees buckled, and she crumpled to the floor before anyone could grab her. She felt strong arms snake under hers and lift her off the floor then place her in the pew. She looked up and recognized the face of one of the men from the hospital waiting room.

"Thank you," she mumbled.

"You're welcome, my dear," he replied and went back to his seat.

The pastor was talking to Devon's parents when he moved behind the pulpit. Her stomach dropped, knowing his memorial service was actually about to begin. It was all real. Every last horrible detail of it. Everything seemed to happen in slow motion, as if she watched from outside her own body.

"Shadow!" An older woman bellowing drew her out of her misery for a moment. "Get up out of that casket right now!"

"Liz, this is not the time," one of the women hissed at her. Elle continued watching the scene play out, feeling detached from reality.

"It's the perfect time. I'm not falling for his trickery. We all know he's not really dead. This is just to throw everyone off his trail. Shadow, this is your last warning!"

One of the women jumped up and rushed to Liz, trying to stop her. But Liz was obviously a spry little old lady because she evaded capture and rushed the casket. While attempting to climb on top of it, she yelled, "I'm coming to collect my kiss, Shadow. And I'm going to use the tongue. You'd better jump up out of there unless you want *le tongue* in *le French kiss*."

Two of the big, burly men jumped up and ran to her, picking her up off the casket just before she reached his face. She struggled against them, craning her neck in an attempt to reach him.

"For the love of God and all things holy, get off Shadow's casket, Liz!"

"Wait a minute," Liz replied solemnly. "Then Shadow's really gone?"

"Yes, Liz. Shadow is really gone." He pulled her into his arms and consoled her while they made their way back to the pew. Elle knew exactly how Liz felt, even though she didn't know Liz at all.

"I'm so sorry, everyone. Shadow and I always teased and played jokes on each other. I meant no disrespect," Liz announced.

"We know, Liz. Devon told us all about you." Tracey smiled through her tears. "It's okay."

Several men entered the room and took Devon away, wheeling the casket out of the room and away from them. The pastor cleared his throat, choking back emotion, and began the eulogy.

"We're here to celebrate the life of a man who lived his life shrouded in darkness so others may enjoy the freedom of living in the light. His selfless sacrifices didn't lessen the impact he had on others' lives, as we can see from simply looking around the room. His many friends and family are here to pay last respects to a man who rushed into situations everyone else ran away from.

"His wish was to be cremated, but I don't know if most of you were aware of the stipulations he made. He asked that his ashes not be put into an urn. There will be no remains or plaque to visit. He wanted his ashes to be made into a white gold ring that bears his fingerprint. The inscription will read, 'You're my girl—forever,' and it's for someone very special to him."

Elle's gaze snapped up to the pastor's in shock. Tears ran down her cheeks though she paid no attention to them. The pastor smiled sadly at her before he continued. "Miss Elle Moore, his mother told me just this morning the ring will be delivered to you in about four weeks. He loved you very much and wanted you to be happy above all else."

The rest of the eulogy was lost to Elle. Once the tears started, they wouldn't stop. Once the tidal wave of feelings hit her, she drowned in them—every single one. The onslaught was terrible, but the memories they evoked also brought the many happy times, and that comforted her. By the end of the service, she was completely spent.

The four weeks following the funeral were hell on earth for Elle. The first week, everyone stayed to help tie up loose ends. And all of them hovered over her as if she would shatter into a million pieces at any time, putting more pressure on her to be "okay" all the time.

But she wasn't okay and never would be again. That was a given. The brief reprieve from sympathetic eyes came from the demands of the government agencies identified with an initial that demanded to speak with her regarding her ordeal. She'd delayed it as long as she could. Reliving the moment Devon was shot brought it all rushing back to her mercilessly, but she maintained her composure long enough to give them the info they needed. She only hoped it was enough to put those sons of bitches away forever.

Week two brought a different kind of suffering because everyone returned to their regularly scheduled lives, leaving Elle feeling as if she were drifting aimlessly through life. There was no one around to watch her every move except Beth, who was busy looking for a new job. Elle envied her friend in a way. A new job would bring a new start, a clean slate to put all the ghosts of their abduction ordeal behind her. While Elle felt a little bit stronger every day, her heart wasn't in returning to the fake life of a Hollywood starlet.

With the newfound free time she had, her thoughts kept returning to that moment when Devon was shot. She began to remember details that didn't stand out to her at first. Fear had gripped her so tightly while she was in the middle of the chaos, she didn't realize she'd blocked the memory of Bone leveling his gun at her. The panicked expression on Devon's face when he'd entered the garage. The way he'd sprinted across the floor and stopped when he was directly in front of her.

"Did he do that to save me?" she asked herself, pacing back and forth across the room.

"Elle?" Beth asked softly. Elle looked up at her concerned eyes. "Why don't you come with me to therapy? I wasn't kidding when I said we needed it."

"I know. But I'm not ready. I'm just remembering the sequence of events and trying to make sense of everything."

"Okay. Did you hear about the studio?"

"No, I haven't heard anything about anything. What's going on?"

"The studio is closing the lot and filing for bankruptcy." Elle's brows drew downward, her eyes narrowed, and her lips parted. Beth understood Elle's confusion was because she'd cut herself off from the outside world. "Okay, from the beginning. The person behind our abduction was actually a studio executive. He mismanaged investor funds and tried to hide it by delaying movie releases. Anyway, once the gang took him hostage because he double-crossed them, the investors figured out what happened and they withdrew all funding, so the studio has no capital to operate with. They're closing the doors for good."

"What about the movie we just finished? It's scrapped too?"

"Maybe not. Another studio is asking about buying it. There's also talk about a group of investors producing it independently," Beth replied.

"I like option number two better."

Week three post-funeral, Elle started watching the news and began entering the world of the living again. The television was safer than going out in public—not because she was afraid but because she'd become indifferent to everything. For the sake of her own career, should she ever go back to it, she had to maintain appearances. At that moment, she recognized she simply didn't care about anything.

Then the images of the Devil's Dominion club officers flashed across the screen, and she turned the volume up to catch every word the news anchor said.

"These high-ranking members of the Devil's Dominion motorcycle club, one of the infamous one-percenter gangs, have been arrested and denied bail because of their flight risk. Their charges include human trafficking, kidnapping, murder, extortion, and drug trafficking. Federal agencies say they expect to file more charges soon, including organized crime and money laundering.

"Two weeks ago, Detective Joanna Gough's body washed ashore. The gang has been linked to her murder. You'll remember she was the detective in charge of the kidnapping investigation involving Elle Sinclair, Beth Condra, Katrina Fox, Carrie Snow, and Lori Hensley. Director Vince Rossi and agent Ray Burke have also been indicted on conspiracy charges."

Fueled by rage over what they'd stolen from her, Elle flew up from her seat and moved into action. Just the sight of their faces was enough to turn her stomach, but more than that, she was ashamed of what she'd allowed them to reduce her to.

"No more," she decided. "No more living my life behind closed doors. Devon would've wanted more for me. I want more for me."

CHAPTER TWENTY-FOUR

"I'm so glad you started coming to therapy with me. In group, there are so many people who've decided to speak out because you had to courage to do it. You've changed already from just a week ago. I was honestly getting worried about you." Beth threw her arm around Elle as they strolled on the beach, enjoying the warmth of the sun and the sand beneath their toes.

"Me, too. It's been very helpful. And I'm glad my big mouth helps others when I give them a chance to speak."

"Yeah, you have to take a breath every now and then," Beth teased. "Man, it feels good to laugh and joke again."

They had lunch at an outdoor oceanside café, carefully avoiding certain topics so they wouldn't step back into melancholy, but still enjoying each other's company. "I think it's time we stop tiptoeing around each other and get back to saying what's on our minds like we used to. The more we act normal, the faster we'll feel normal," Elle said between bites.

"Agreed. So, I'm glad you're showering again. That made a nice change to the smell coming from your room."

"Bitch," Elle laughed and threw a piece of her bread at Beth.

With the tension finally broken, she found a new spring in her step and could breathe easier. One step at a time, she was beginning to feel better. She was actually beginning to feel anything again.

Later that evening, Elle and Beth were watching a movie together in Beth's bedroom when the doorbell rang. "I'll get it," Beth announced. "Elle, it's a package for you. Come sign for it," she called from the door.

Elle froze in place, suddenly remembering the date. Four weeks to the day since his funeral. The ring with his fingerprint made partly from his ashes. The last piece of Devon Kane waited for her.

She padded across the apartment toward the front door and grabbed the knob while she steeled her nerves. Anything remotely related to Devon was still a trigger for her, but she was learning to embrace the memories of their good times. She swung the door open with her best face forward, even though it put her acting skills to the ultimate test.

"Elle Moore, this is the only confirmed fingerprint of Devon Kane. Every other print has been expunged from every file accessible anywhere as a safety precaution to national security. I want you to wear it, as part of your bridal set, as a constant reminder of my promise that I'll never leave you again."

She couldn't move. She couldn't breathe. She couldn't speak.

Devon Kane was kneeling down on one knee outside her apartment door. There was only one explanation for that—she'd had a complete break with reality.

"Elle, will you marry me?" Devon extended the ring to her.

To test her sanity, she reached out, took it from him, and slid it onto her finger. It fit perfectly. She admired the unique lines and grooves his fingerprint created.

"Elle?" He stood slowly and slid his hand across her cheek until his fingers threaded through her hair. "Darlin', talk to me. You're scaring me."

She leaned into the warmth of his hand and closed her eyes, lost in her fantasy. Then her eyes flew open when she realized she could feel this daydream. She reached up and touched his face, several days of stubble covering his jaws.

"Devon? Are you real?" she whispered, scared she'd interrupt the best dream she'd ever had if she spoke too loud.

"I'm real, darlin'. It's me, Elle. I know I have a lot to explain, but believe me when I say you'll understand everything when I'm done. I love you, Elle. And I want to spend my life with you as my wife."

Her hands flew to her mouth, covering it after a loud gasp. Her eyes grew big and locked wide open, staring at him and shaking her head from side to side.

"You died. I saw you get shot twice. The ambulance. The surgeon said… The funeral. I went to your funeral!"

"Just listen, okay?" He spoke softly, calmly and approached her cautiously. "I know it was all hell on you. It was on me, too. I've been in the hospital recovering. At my funeral, I was in a medically induced coma, with a special medication to slow my breathing. I knew nothing that happened. That's why my casket was only open for an hour, so they tell me. They had to get me back to the hospital.

"From the beginning, here it is. After I left the Army, I joined the CIA's clandestine black ops team. I've spent most of my life undercover and pretending to be someone else. That's why I was part of the motorcycle gang. I went in undercover to save you. I would never do anything to hurt you or put you in any kind of jeopardy. Letting you think I was actually part of all that killed me, but I couldn't risk telling you the truth and letting it get out. We'd both have been killed. The best I could do was stay close to you and protect you, so that's what I did."

He explained how Nick, Axle, and Jack were all working together as part of a joint task force to bring the club down. With Nick undercover DEA, Axle undercover CIA and working through Silas, and Jack being Nick's handler, they had her and the other ladies well covered.

"You brought another actress in." Her statement was disguised as a question, hoping he had a valid answer.

"The actress you saw me bring in the old clubhouse that night was one of their targets, but she participated willingly. She was prepped by trained agents and knew we were coming to get her, but she didn't know which of the gang members were undercover agents. She never saw our faces so she couldn't give us away."

"She never told me."

"She was strongly warned not to say anything. Her life depended on it too. She had a tracking device inserted into her arm just in case." He stepped toward her, tentative in his approach, afraid she would bolt away from him forever. "The past eight years, the only reason I've left your side was because I was on a case. In between working assignments, I was with you. If I was in town on assignment, I checked on you and watched you from a distance, like an obsessed fan. But only because I've hated every second I've been away from you.

"You once asked me who Ava is. She's my little sister, but she was taken from us when she was only five. Kidnapped by a monster. My parents had just bought me a new bicycle for my birthday, and at nine years old, I was preoccupied with tricking out my ride. I took my eyes off her for too long. They must have driven by and snatched her out of the front yard.

"Remember the man who died while we were in St. Lucia? He was a party to her disappearance, and he was there to coordinate the movement of more abducted children. Since I was completely off the grid while we were away, Axle showed up to deliver my orders in person. It was a sanctioned hit, but I gladly killed the man who took my sister away from us. I've blamed myself for what happened all my life, and I've dedicated my every move to protecting innocents as best as I could.

"So many times, I've wanted to lay all my cards out on the table for you to know all about me. I've said repeatedly the only way to leave the CIA is to die. Shadow was my nickname, the only name most people have ever known me as. Shadow died on his last operation and is finally released from the CIA. Devon now stands in front of you, asking for, I believe, the third time—will you marry me?"

"I'm sorry," she replied and watched his face fall. "I'm still trying to catch up to you actually being alive and deciding if I should be mad at how much anguish you've put me through. When I opened the door and saw you there, I actually thought, if I was hallucinating because I'd had a mental breakdown, I didn't want to be put back together. So now I know I'm not crazy, you are real, and you've been a spy and an undercover agent the entire time we've been together. It's…a lot to take in.

"Plus, as I recall, you left me a year ago and haven't been back."

"I've been back many times," he replied quietly. "But I can understand how you're hurt over the secrets and the month since my funeral. To be fair, I've been in the hospital all that time, but you didn't know that. It is a lot to accept and forgive. So I'll go and give you the time to think about everything that's happened. Mull it over. Decide what you want."

He turned to leave, and she noticed his grimace when he moved, the slow pace of his steps, and his hand on the wall for support. The pallor of his skin struck her hard, as did the noticeable weight loss.

"I never said I didn't know what I want, Devon."

He stopped in his tracks, but he didn't turn to face her. "And that is?"

"You. All I've ever wanted is you. All I'll ever want is you. Had you asked me to leave the glamour and glitz of modeling and movies to join the undercover world in the shadows, I wouldn't have thought twice about it as I packed my bags. My first choice has always been you."

She slipped under his arm on his injured side and wrapped her arm around him, gripping the other side tightly. He looked down at her, his eyes overflowing with love. "Let me help you into my apartment. You need to lie down before you fall down."

"You're just trying to get me into your bed."

"Damn straight." She smirked.

His thumb and index finger found the ring on her finger and tilted it slightly from side to side. "Does this mean yes?"

"It means yes. With all of my heart, body, mind, and soul—yes."

She walked him toward her bedroom, and her steps faltered only when she saw Jeff standing in Beth's bedroom doorway with his hand firmly over Beth's mouth.

"It's the only way I could keep her from blabbing." Jeff shrugged and winked, clearly enjoying his role in the game. "I'll be on my way now." He nodded to Devon, his eyes conveying the sincere gratitude he felt inside.

Elle smiled at her brother and continued assisting Devon to her room, then watched with tears brimming in her eyes as he struggled to crawl into the bed. Tears for so many reasons—elation, sadness, concern, and relief. Euphoria topped the list of feelings overwhelming her senses, though. Completely grateful for everything she'd gone through because it only made her that much more thankful to have him back in her life.

"When did you get out of the hospital?"

"About thirty minutes before I rang your doorbell."

She slid into the bed beside him, his back to her front, and gently draped her arm over his side. "Does that hurt?"

"No." He wrapped his hand around hers and pulled her closer to him. "You feel like heaven."

"I have so many questions to ask you."

"Ask away."

"I don't even know where to start," she laughed.

"We have the rest of our lives, darlin'."

She raised up on one elbow and put her chin on his shoulder. "So, black ops. Does that mean you know how to torture people for information?"

He slowly turned his head until he could see her. "That's the first thing you want to know? Out of everything you could possibly ask?"

"It was the first question that popped up in my mind," she giggled.

"Fuck, I've missed you so much."

"Can I see your scars?"

One corner of his mouth lifted slightly, then he grabbed the hem of his shirt and began pulling it up. She sat up on the bed behind him and helped. She expected to see raised lines of red, angry skin from the bullet holes and surgeries, but the wounds barely had a pink tinge. The outer edges already matched his normal skin tone. She ran her fingers over the barely visible scars.

"I can't believe the wounds are completely healing without leaving a scar," she marveled.

"The agency called in the best doctors. I was lucky to be in LA and have immediate access to the best plastic surgeons in the world."

She continued her examination of his wounds, letting her hands roam freely over his back and side. When she reached his lower back, she stopped and examined the raised white skin. There were two larger letters on top—DD—and three smaller letters curved underneath it—KSD. "What is this?"

"Nothing you need to worry about, darlin'."

"Devon, no more secrets. Please."

He raked his hand down his face and exhaled slowly. "It's not a secret, Elle. You can see what it says. *Devil's Dominion. Kill, Steal, and Destroy*. The same wording as on their patches. They branded me as part of the initiation."

Elle dropped her chin to her chest, closed her eyes, and quieted the frantic thoughts running through her mind. The ordeal was over, and the memories couldn't hurt her. She inhaled deeply, a peaceful calm enveloping her as specific memories returned to her and reality dawned.

I prayed he'd return to me, and he's here.

"You're my girl—forever."

"I love you and only you, all my life."

He was undercover to save me.

He risked his life multiple times for me.

"That's not all they did to you, is it?"

"During initiation? No. But I'm okay, Elle. You don't need to worry about me. I'm a big boy. I can take care of myself."

She crawled over him, careful of his healing wounds, and lay facing him. "You can, there's no doubt about that. But you don't have to do it alone, in the darkness of the wicked shadows anymore. You've protected me so I can walk freely in the light. Now it's time for us to walk together."

"Every day, Elle, for the rest of your life. Just try to get rid of me. I'm your shadow now."

He slid his hand to the back of her neck and pulled her face to his. When their lips touched, the intense yearning consumed them, burning with a new intensity. The year apart hadn't extinguished the flames of their desire. The gentle peck quickly became a passionate embrace. Hands desperate to touch. Skin demanding to be caressed. Bodies hungry for more of anything and everything they could get.

Gentle hands slid her shirt off, revealing the smooth, creamy skin beneath. Deft fingers unhooked her bra before he rolled her to her back. His lips trailed down her jaw, to her neck, over the hollow space at her collarbone, continuing until he reached her bare breast. The warmth of his mouth covered the hardened tip of her nipple, sending electricity zinging along every nerve ending in her body. The sensation shot directly between her legs, igniting the craving for what only he could give her.

Devon took his time, ignoring her no-so-subtle cues to rush him. He'd thought about this moment so often, planning every move he'd make in his mind. He ravished her body in his designed sequence with no conscious effort. Every second was committed to memory. Every sound she made. The scent of her skin. The weight of her breast in his hand. The aroma of her arousal that grew with his ministrations. The sharp intake of breath when he slid lower down her body. The way her fingers gripped his hair when his tongue laved her abdomen. Her enthusiasm and eagerness to remove the rest of their clothes.

He shifted lower, anchoring his body between her legs, spreading them to make enough room to carry out his mission. He changed positions gingerly, ignoring the lingering pains and focusing on the incredible pleasure that awaited him. He lowered his head, lightly brushed his face against her sex, and inhaled her unique bouquet before covering her clit with his lips. He looped his tongue around it, his forcefulness increasing with each circle.

Her hips bucked under his grip as the intensity grew. He flicked her sensitive nub with his tongue, her moans spurring him to take what belonged to him. At that moment, her ultimate pleasure was what he wanted most. To hear his name fall from her lips in the culmination of her gratification. He licked up her slit, lapping up the proof of her desire, until he reached her swollen core. His teeth grazed across her clit when he pulled it into his mouth, sucking harder on it before teasing her entrance with his finger, gliding up and down until her essence coated his fingertip.

Hungry for more, he slid his finger inside her wet channel, easy at first then with more vigor when her body naturally adapted to accept the carnal invasion. She lifted her hips higher, giving him full access and wordlessly asking for more. Her fingers dug into his shoulders, her nails biting into his skin while her inner muscles contracted around his finger. His lips, his tongue, his teeth, his hands—they all claimed her, wanted to own her, needed to possess her.

When his name rang out through the room, carried on the sweetest music he'd ever heard, he made a decision he'd never thought possible. He surrendered, willingly. Deliberately. Purposely. He acknowledged his feelings ran deeper than the usual declaration of love. Only she awakened the part of him that wanted a normal life. Only she matched him in every way, complemented his flaws with her perfection, and propelled him to forsake everything he'd worked toward in exchange for a new life goal.

"Devon." Her voice was breathy, still reeling from her carnal high. "Let me help you out of your clothes. You've spent enough energy. It's time for you to lie on your back and enjoy the view for a while."

His cock twitched from the visual her offer inspired. After he stood, she scooted to the edge of the bed and began removing his jeans. She unconsciously licked her lips when her eyes landed on the bulge in his boxer briefs. She looked up at him from under her lashes, emboldened by how desire had darkened his eyes to almost black, and smiled seductively.

"I thought you were always commando."

"Now that I'm out of the hospital and never leaving your side, you'll be lucky to get me in pants again, much less briefs. You can keep these as a souvenir—the last pair I'll ever wear."

She kept her gaze locked on his while she slid them down his legs. His cock sprang free and stood at attention against his abdomen. Her soft hand flowed up his shaft, gripping tightly as she teased and tormented him in the most delicious manner. Her fingers clutched the hem of his shirt and carefully pulled it over his head. With his clothes shed and his body bared, she motioned for him to take his place on the bed.

Propped up on pillows, he watched with hooded eyes as she placed open-mouthed kisses across his chest. Her tongue darted out, leaving a wet trail of affection on his skin. Across his ripped abdominal muscles, she licked and tasted every ridge and dip. Her fingers glided over his body until they touched the tip of his cock. The bead of moisture drew her attention downward, and she hungrily took him into her mouth, as far as she could until he hit the back of her throat. She relaxed the muscles, taking him deeper, and he groaned in ecstasy.

While working her mouth and hand in tandem up and down him, she focused on giving him as much pleasure as he'd given her. When she went down, she held the tip at the back of her throat and intentionally mimicked swallowing, forcing her neck muscles to contract around his head like a soft, velvety clamp. His hands gripped her hair, and he called her name with a throaty grunt. Sensing he was close to the edge, she pumped and sucked until the overload of pleasure left him no choice but to abandon his control and succumb to his release.

He tugged on her arm and guided her to lie next to him, securely tucked into his side, wrapped in his arms, and enveloped by his love. The roller coaster of emotions she'd lived on came to a crashing halt after she relaxed, melting into him. The tears she was sure had dried came back with a renewed vengeance. She couldn't hold them back. The hot, salty tracks covered her face and soaked his chest. He lifted his hand to her face, cradled her wet cheek in his palm, and gently raised her head to look at him.

"Talk to me, darlin'. Don't try to hold it all in."

She smiled through her tears, a bright, happy smile that lit up her whole face. "For the first time in a long time, I am so happy." She emphasized each word, amazement prevalent in her voice. "You're here with me—alive, on the mend, but otherwise healthy—and you proposed to me."

"And you said yes. That means you've agreed to be my sex slave for the rest of your life. This is a binding legal agreement with no exit clause. You belong to me and only me for all time."

"Like any of that is a surprise to me," she joked, her giggles filling the air with joy and love. "But the best part is you belong to me for all time."

"Yes, I do, darlin'. Always have—always will. I'd walk into hell and slay the devil for you."

"I believe you. You already have."

Despite her protests that he hadn't healed enough, he rolled her over onto her back and covered her body with his. His hard cock rested between her legs at the entrance to her wet core. She was ready for him with a single touch. Her body craved his, but she'd been too concerned with his injuries to encourage him. Who was she to deny him when he was so insistent, though? Her body hummed with need, waiting for him to finish what he'd started.

His arms framed her face, and his expression conveyed his profound love. He sank into her one inch at a time until he was fully seated inside, giving her body a moment to accept and adapt to his size. Her muscles quivered around him, gripping him tightly and urging him to keep moving. With slow, deliberate strokes, he surged into her repeatedly until his sweat mixed with hers during an erotic dance built for two. All their emotions poured out of them as promises of a forever love fell from their lips. The crescendo of their encounter built to an unbelievable high that ended in their mutual climax.

"You are my world, Elle. The last year has shown me I'm dead without you. You are the breath that sustains me. You bring me to life, make me feel, and give me hope for a normal life. I wouldn't even be here now it if weren't for you. Thoughts of seeing you, talking to you, and loving you are what pulled me through the darkest days in the hospital. I couldn't die with you thinking I'd done anything but protected you with my last breath."

"I should've known. Maybe a part of me did. None of it made sense to me.

I couldn't reconcile the Devon I knew with the Doorman I met. But I have no doubts now—you've always been my Devon."

The next morning over breakfast, Elle cast furtive glances toward him. A few times, she started to ask another question but stopped herself before she started. Devon finally set his fork down and rested his elbows on the table.

"If you don't ask me whatever it is you want to know, I'm going to hold you down and use my torture techniques to make you talk." The mischievous gleam in his eyes was back, the signature twinkle a little brighter.

"Who knew you weren't really dead?"

He knew that question would come, and he braced himself for her reaction. "Besides the agency, only my parents and the guys at Steele Security."

"They knew, but no one could tell me for a whole month? I could've been at the hospital with you. I could've helped you, and knowing you were alive would sure as hell have helped me. Do you have any idea how miserable and depressed I've been?" The more she thought about it, the angrier she became. "That was really shitty, Devon."

"Can I explain?"

"That would be best."

"Easy there, tiger. My condition was touch and go there at first. If I didn't pull through, there was no reason to put you through that again. My parents were my beneficiaries and had medical power of attorney, so they had to be there to make decisions for my care. The guys have a high enough security clearance to be read in on the plan. While evidence was gathered and charges brought against the gang, my condition had to be kept secret for my safety. When I was coherent enough to make my own decisions, I planned my return to the living and my marriage proposal. Though, I did see it all going very differently in my mind."

"Oh, yeah? How?"

"You know…you falling at my feet, grasping my leg, thanking God for my safe return." He smiled and winked, instantly defusing her anger over his deception.

"If you ever fake your death again without telling me first, I'll kill you."

"Fair enough. You'll be the first to know next time."

She threw her wadded-up napkin at him while laughing. She couldn't be mad if she tried—she was simply too happy and blessed to let anything from the past impact her bright future.

"Oh, and, darlin'? Can you clear your schedule next week?"

"What do you have in mind?"

"There are four other women in Miami I have to go face and take my lashes. I want you to go with me and meet everyone. They're dying to meet you."

"I'd love to meet them, and my schedule happens to be wide open for the foreseeable future."

"Good. I have plans for you every single day. Forever."

CHAPTER TWENTY-FIVE

"You're moving around so much better than you were last week." Elle watched Devon get out of the bed and walk to the bathroom. The light pink scars had faded to his natural skin color even more. Her eyes drifted to the brand seared into his skin. *Funny how the memory of what happened doesn't bother me as much as it did last week,* she thought. *My scars are fading too.*

"I can feel your eyes on my ass." He smirked at her over his shoulder. "Don't be shy. You can look all you want."

"Yeah, I know I can. As fine as it is, that's not actually where my eyes landed this time."

"You're staring at my brand again. Does it bother you that much? Do you want me to have it removed?" He turned to face her, sincerely interested in her reply. Then he shook his head and chuckled when her eyes dropped to his package. "Hey. My eyes are up here."

"It's your fault for going commando and pantless." She met his amused gaze and continued. "The brand doesn't bother me. And no, I don't want you to have it removed because that would mean more surgery and pain for you. A month ago, it may have freaked me out, but I can't honestly say. It already feels like a lifetime ago. I'm just thankful everything worked out the way it did in the end."

"Okay. If you're sure."

"I'm positive."

"Now get your fine ass out of bed so we don't miss our flight to Miami. I'm taking you home to meet the family of Steele."

Packed and ready to leave, they climbed into the taxi and Devon gave the address. Elle looked at him, her eyebrows raised in question. "Private airport. I have a little surprise for you."

When they reached the small airport, Elle stepped out of the car, and the private Steele Security jet on the tarmac immediately caught her attention. She helped Devon get their bags since he was still under strict orders not to lift anything heavy, and she'd packed her entire wardrobe for the trip.

"I've never been on a private jet before. This is exciting."

"You really need to use your star status more effectively. There's no reason why you shouldn't have already had a private flight. Unless it means you fly privately with some other guy. In which case, you fly coach."

"No one else will ever compare to Devon Kane," she replied automatically.

"What?" He stopped walking and waited for an explanation. "You said that so offhandedly, like you've said it a thousand times."

"I have—at least that many times. Whenever anyone encouraged me to move on, date someone else, tried to convince me there are other fish in the sea, that was my standard response. You have no reason to worry or be jealous of anyone. No other man has ever compared to you—and no other man ever will."

"Just when I think there's no way I could love you more, you prove me wrong again." He bent his head and kissed her sweetly. "I love you."

"I love you too." She beamed.

Devon took his seat while Elle examined every square inch of the private Steele Security jet. "Oh, my God—there's a bedroom back here!"

Devon laughed at her excitement, thrilled he was experiencing it with her. Unable to sit still, he joined her at the back of the plane. "There is a bedroom. And it has a bed." He leaned against the door and watched her, his libido kicking into overdrive.

"I know that look. You can stop devouring me with your eyes right now, mister. The flight attendant will know exactly what we're doing back here. No, Devon." She tried to sound stern, serious. But even she wasn't that good of an actress.

"Elle, you worry way too much about what others think. What's the worst that would happen if she heard us? She'd tell the rag magazines, they'd run an article saying you're part of the mile-high club, and every man in the world would know it was with me. I don't see the downside. But the upside is we get to have sex and join the mile-high club." He closed the door behind him and advanced on her like a tiger stalking its prey.

Four hours later, they emerged from the bedroom in time to prepare for landing. Devon couldn't hide his amusement over Elle's red face every time the flight attendant approached them. "She knows what we were doing back there," Elle hissed at him. "I'm so embarrassed."

The ride from the airport to Noah's secluded mansion passed quickly. Before she knew it, they'd turned into the driveway and the driver pressed the call button on the state-of-the-art security system. The gate slid open, giving them access to the grounds with no questions asked. Elle watched intently as the estate came into view.

"Devon, what's going on? What are they doing?" She pointed to the odd scene on the ornate front lawn. In the middle of the expertly manicured and professionally landscaped setting stood four women, four men...and five large doghouses.

"Is it too late to pretend our flight was delayed?" Devon deadpanned.

"Yes, considering they can see us, and they're already motioning for us to come to them."

He sighed, resigned to accept his punishment like a man, and opened the door. "Here we go. Oh, before we get out, I'm sorry now for whatever Liz does or says."

"Liz?"

"Shadow, get out of that car right this second." Liz stood a few feet away with her hands on her hips, her lips in a tight, firm line, and her eyes on fire with anger.

"That's Liz," he replied to Elle. "Liz, sweetheart, how are you?"

"Don't try to sweet-talk me. It didn't work for these four, and it won't work for you either."

Elle watched as men emerged from the house and took their luggage inside the stately mansion. A quick glance in Devon's direction told her to relax, as their actions must be commonplace. He laced his fingers with hers and walked toward the waiting hosts. The closer they got, the more confused Elle became.

She recognized the men from Devon's funeral, though she didn't know their names. Except Liz. But then, everyone in the chapel knew her name that day.

"Elle, this is Noah 'Reaper' Steele and his wife, Brianna."

"Hello, nice to meet you," she said to Brianna first and shook her hand.

"Elle, we wanted to approach you in the hospital waiting room, but it just didn't seem like the right time. You'd been through so much already, and we didn't want to appear to be insensitive fans. I'm so glad to meet you now."

"Thank you. I wasn't in the best frame of mind, so keeping your distance was probably best," Elle chuckled.

Her gaze drifted up to Noah's, and she reacted before she could stop herself. Her eyes grew wide and her lips parted—but no words would come out. "Umm," she stammered. "It's nice to meet you."

Noah offered his hand, and Elle hesitated briefly before accepting it. From the corner of her eye, she saw Devon cover the smile that split his face in two. "Very nice to meet you, Elle."

"You're the one who picked me up off the floor and set me in the pew," she said while staring a little too long at his lips. "Thank you so much for doing that. I would've stayed on the floor had you not."

"It was the least I could do for you."

Devon snickered beside her and tried to hide it with a fake cough.

"Something to say, Shadow?" Reaper asked, lifting one eyebrow in challenge.

"Nope. Not a thing. Elle, this is Colton 'Bull' Lanier and his wife, Chaise. Noah and Chaise are brother and sister."

Elle found herself in the same predicament when she greeted Bull and Chaise. And Devon didn't help when he unsuccessfully tried to hide his laughter. After Bull cordially addressed Elle, he threatened Devon with, "I'm kicking your ass as soon as you're healed. Fucker."

Devon wore a huge, shit-eating grin when he steered Elle away from Bull and to the next couple. "This is Braxton 'Rebel' Reed and his wife, Heather."

"Elle, it's great to meet you. My condolences to you on what will happen to Shadow the second he's healed enough to take his beating."

She had no idea what they meant, but she couldn't take her eyes off Rebel's lips or his fingernails.

"Don't pay any attention to Rebel, Elle. The heat down here fries his brain sometimes," Devon explained. "This is Silas Steele, Noah and Chaise's older brother."

"Elle, I'm so glad everything turned out well for you after your ordeal. You should probably purchase big-and-tall-sized diapers for Shadow as soon as possible. He'll need them for a while after we get through with him."

"You too, Silas? That hurts," Devon lied through his smiling teeth.

"And, my love, this is Liz."

"I knew you were faking it at the funeral. Hello, sweet girl. How are you? You didn't fool me for one minute, Shadow. I'm so sorry you have to witness this, Elle, but it's best for us all. What you did is just unforgivable and inexcusable, Shadow. Did you have a nice flight, dear? Now that you're here, it's time for you to face the music."

Elle attempted to keep up with Liz's conversation. She was terrifying and angry when she addressed Devon, then loving and grandmotherly when she spoke to Elle. Liz had carried on two entire conversations, in two distinctly different tones, without taking a single breath.

Liz picked up a small black makeup bag and retrieved two vials of fingernail polish. Her keen eyes snapped up to Devon's and held an inherent threat. The other men smiled broadly.

Reaper's pink leopard-print-colored lips spread across his face. Bull's lips were white with pink, blue, and green dots covering them. Rebel's lips had been painted with a bright, sparkling blue polish. Silas's appeared to be black stripes on a bright orange background, until he closed his lips. Then the word "TRAITOR" could be read clearly. Their fingernails matched the colors used on their lips. And apparently, Devon was her next target.

"What's the story behind the nail polish?" Elle finally asked.

"It goes with the doghouses. Each man out here has one. We even painted names on their specific homes. They lied to us, let us believe Shadow was dead instead of letting us in on the ruse. They didn't trust us enough, so they had to be punished," Liz explained. "Did you know?"

"No, I knew even less than you did. And I was mad at him for about a second, but then I remembered how hard I'd prayed to wake up from that nightmare and have him back with me. Being left out of the loop when his life was in danger didn't seem like a big deal then. Though, I did threaten him if he ever pulls that on me again."

"Oh." Liz dropped the polish back into the bag, her voice flat and her eyes downcast. "I didn't think of it that way. Maybe I should've talked to you before I painted these guys. You're right. His life is more important, and we were all so thrilled to learn he was okay."

Four large and angry men began shouting and pointing at once.

"Do you know how long we've been wearing this shit?"

"I actually slept all night in the fucking doghouse!"

"No way does he get out of his punishment! I'll hold him down and paint him myself!"

"I took my punishment like a man! Now he will too!"

Liz kept talking to Elle as if a brawl weren't about to break out in front of them. "If you're not upset, then I'm not either. Besides, I knew it was all fake. Tracey told me before the funeral."

All the yelling stopped cold.

"You knew?" Silas asked.

"Of course. Took you long enough to get me off the casket. I thought I'd actually get that kiss I've been hankering for."

Silas glared at her, the ability to connect letters into those things they made had escaped him.

"What? What's the problem?" Liz prompted him.

"We all took our punishment…but you knew."

"Did you hide it from us?"

"Yes, but—"

"No buts. You knew. You hid it. You got punished. Now, imagine what I would've done if I hadn't known the truth. Chew on that for a while."

Devon leaned down and kissed Liz's cheek, then winked. "Thanks for always having my back."

"My pleasure, my boy. Now it's time for us to get to know this pretty little lady." Liz took Elle's hand in hers and led her to the house, leaving everyone else standing on the front lawn, by their assigned doghouses, in shock. Devon watched them walk together, then realized he'd been left alone with the angry mob. He sprang into action, holding his side while he took long strides to reach Elle's side and Liz's protection.

Later that evening, after the men had scrubbed all of the skin off their lips and removed the polish from their nails, they sat on the back deck. Steaks, chicken, and seafood cooked on the grill. The team was all together, laughing and sharing stories again as if nothing had happened. Elle felt welcomed with open arms and became instant best friends with the ladies.

Devon leaned over and placed a chaste kiss on her cheek while she talked with Brianna. She turned and looked at him thoughtfully. "What was that for?"

"Because I love you. Because I'm so glad you never gave up on me all the years I was such an idiot. Because I can't imagine ever being happy again if I lost you. Because I finally understand why these guys can't function without their better halves and why they'd move hell and earth to reach their loves, and God help anyone who gets in their way. Because if I had to choose between having decades to live alone undercover, or only one night, but it was with you, I'd choose you every time."

Elle kissed his lips, lingering and savoring the moment. "We'll never have to be apart again, my love. There's never been a remote possibility of you losing me. No matter what happened, I've always loved you. And I'll always love you, no matter what happens."

"I'm so happy for you two," Brianna gushed. "Have you decided on a wedding date yet?"

"No, we haven't even talked about it yet. Devon has been healing and getting stronger. I haven't decided what I'm going to do now that the studio closed and my movie hasn't released yet. I don't even know if it will release now. Nothing in my life is definite except this man beside me."

"We're getting married as soon as possible, and I'm keeping her chained to the bed the entire first year," Shadow added.

The group laughed, but they didn't doubt he'd actually try to do what he'd threatened. Silas leaned forward and steepled his fingers. "Actually, I wanted to talk to you both about that."

"About chaining my woman to the bed? Do you have a death wish?" Shadow fired back.

"No and no," Silas replied sardonically. "I mean talk about what you're going to do next. Steele Security is here. The studio lots are in LA. Are you moving to California? Is Elle moving to Miami? Have you thought about what you're going to do next, Shadow?"

"Not really. I'm waiting for inspiration to hit me. Or for Elle to demand I move in with her. Or for Elle to demand to move in with me. Or for Elle to demand we move to Kansas and commute to work."

"That's what I thought. So I have an early wedding present for you." Silas pulled a business card out of his wallet. "The offshore account the gang used to launder money, courtesy of the CIA for your years of valuable service to your country. You were grievously injured in the line of duty during a joint CIA-DEA-ATF-FBI investigation, so you've been awarded hazard pay, too."

Silas handed the card to Elle. "Since Shadow died during the investigation, the funds go to his beneficiary. As of today, that's you. Don't spend it all in one place."

Elle narrowed her eyes at Silas, unsure if he was joking, before inspecting the card. "Holy shit! The motorcycle club made that much money?"

"Yes, and more, but they made it for you when they kidnapped you and killed my friend. Payback is a bitch."

"Thank you, Silas. I don't even know what else to say. This is incredible." Elle showed the card to Devon and turned to him, bouncing in her seat with excitement. "Babe, I have an idea. This is perfect."

"Let's hear it. I'm all ears."

"What if we split this with the other ladies, and we all executive produce the movie on our own? Buying it from the bankruptcy court will cost a lot less than trying to buy it from the studio. The royalties we'll make on it will pay out for years."

"That's a great plan," Silas interjected. "Except, each of the ladies has their own account. Not as hefty as yours, but enough."

"Perfect. What do you think, Devon?"

"I'm with you, sugar momma." He leaned over and kissed her.

"Do you need more executive producers?" Reaper asked and turned to Brianna with a smile.

"You have something in mind, Reap?" Shadow asked.

"Yeah. We've all discussed what would happen when we decided we're coming out of the firefight and into suburban life. I see an excellent opportunity for us to get out of the security field and into the movie industry. If we buy in now, we'll start on the ground floor with a major A-lister movie for a fraction of the cost."

"You want to close Steele Security?" Bull asked.

"If all of you are in on this, yes. This can be our new business, and we won't have to worry about making it home to our wives and kids in one piece," Reaper replied.

"We're in," Rebel replied, hugging Heather to him. "Come on, Bull—you know it's time to hang up your camouflage hat and ghillie suit."

Bull turned to Chaise, silently asking her opinion. "Let's do it, babe. A brand-new adventure for the crew."

"All right, then. We're in too," Bull replied. "Let's own this bitch and take Hollywood by storm."

"Silas?" Reaper asked.

"I'll be a silent partner. You can't put my name on anything, but I'll buy in."

"Look what you did, darlin'," Shadow teased Elle. "You just got me fired."

EPILOGUE

Fall at the winery was the perfect time of year for an outdoor wedding. The sycamore trees lining the driveway from the main road to the house were in full spectacular color. The bright yellows, oranges, and reds in the surrounding oak and aspen grove mixed with the changing grapevines and provided the perfect backdrop against the still lush green grass.

Devon stood with the pastor under the canopy, waiting for Elle to make her grand entrance. While he waited, he soaked in the features around him so he wouldn't forget a single detail. The garden area was beautifully decorated with a variety of fall-colored planters and flowers. The October air was crisp and invigorating, the slight breeze gentle enough to be comfortable in the setting sun.

The path Elle would take to him was adorned with thick grass, manicured hedges, and white marble statues. The walking bridge over the reflection pool was what sealed the deal for Elle, but the reception area was a close second. Pergolas over linen-covered tables with hanging paper lanterns and candles in glass jars on the tables completed the ambiance. Knee-high hurricane candles were staggered along the pathway and around the pool. The guest chairs were draped in matching linens, completing her dream wedding theme.

Beth, Brianna, Chaise, and Heather emerged first, escorted by Jeff, Reaper, Bull, and Rebel. When the music changed to the wedding march, Shadow craned his neck to see Elle. She'd insisted on keeping her wedding gown a secret from him and had spent the night at her parents' house, away from him, the night before. One night away from her was more than enough. Over the past year while they'd worked the movie junkets and planned their wedding, he hadn't spent more than a few hours apart from her. The sudden change was not welcomed or appreciated.

Then she stepped into view, escorted by her father, and he forgot every other detail. All he could see was the most beautiful woman in the world walking to him. To stand by his side. For better or for worse. Through sickness and health. Till death claimed them both, for real this time.

She wore a floor-length gown, the train extending behind her only slightly. The top was sheer, with lace appliques strategically placed to give the illusion of much less fabric. The waist tapered in to show off her figure and elegance. Her hair was curled and piled high on her head in a perfectly messy heap. Small flowers and baby's breath were secured inside the ringlets, giving her a graceful and carefree effect.

When she reached the last row of guest chairs, she smiled at him, and pride swelled in his chest. The moment he'd always said would never happen couldn't happen soon enough. He was marrying the love of his life. He was giving her his name. She moved closer to him, her eyes sparkling with unshed tears of happiness.

Her father passed her hand to Devon, and she gripped his tightly. Her lifeline, her rock, her love—her everything. The demons of the past no longer plagued her because the life she'd built with Devon drove out all the wicked shadows. They lived every moment in the light, grateful for one more day together, thankful for every night in each other's arms.

The pastor went through the usual verbiage found in a wedding, but they'd written their own vows to each other.

"Elle, I promise you will never regret agreeing to be my wife. My sole purpose in life is simultaneously to make you happy, give you more love than you've ever known, and fill our home with light and laughter. I promise to be the best husband, friend, confidant, and partner I can be. Your needs will come first, always. All I ask in return is that you're my girl—forever."

He slid the wedding band onto her finger and raised it to his lips.

"Devon, since the day I met you, you've owned my heart in one way or another. As a little kid, you were my hero. When I was a young adult, you were my love. Our love and relationship progressed, and you became so much more. My champion, my cheerleader, my savior, my best friend, my partner, my very heart. I promise I will be all these things and more for you. I promise to love you until my dying breath, and then take that love to the afterlife with me, where I'll wait for you to join me again. I promise to be there when you wake in the morning and when you go to sleep at night, giving you whatever you need or want. I promise to love you and only you unconditionally for all time."

She slid the wedding band onto his finger.

With a long, lingering kiss, they sealed their union in front of their family and friends. The bond had always been there—tried, tested, and true.

After the reception dinner, Mark turned on the lights around the dance floor and had the DJ fire up the sound system. Devon and Elle took the floor alone for their first dance as husband and wife. She melted into his arms, still eager for his embrace after having him at her beck and call for more than a solid year. She accepted and embraced she'd never grow tired of him. She'd never not want him with her.

The night she spent alone was proof of that. She awoke several times and picked up her phone, nearly calling him to her each time. She was amazed she'd been strong enough to resist.

"I missed you last night," she admitted.

"Darlin', I missed you too. I almost drove up here to climb in your window. I don't know how I ever slept without you."

"Same. I got no sleep last night."

"You won't get any sleep tonight either."

"I don't want to sleep tonight. I want you."

"You have me—all night, every night, forever."

"It's a good thing we're already packed for our honeymoon then, isn't it?"

"Yes, ma'am. I'm so looking forward to our two weeks in St. Lucia. Back to our spot. Our room. Our happy place."

"I've found my happy place. It's wherever you are."

"That's all I want. Because I'll be wherever you are. You're my girl —forever."

And they lived...*happily ever after.*

~

Want more of Nick Tucker? FINE LINE, the first book in a new stand-alone series, is available now! You can read more about Silas in BLURRED LINE! HARD LINE will be released soon!

CROSSING LINES: FINE LINE, BLURRED LINE, & HARD LINE

WICKED WEEKEND

BONUS CONTENT

This short story appeared in the
USA Today bestselling
F*cking Awkward anthology.

WICKED WEEKEND

Featuring Colton "Bull" Lanier & Chaise Lanier
Characters from Wicked Ties, book two in the Steele Security Series

"Finally," Colton grumbled. "That was the longest fucking case we've ever worked. I can't wait to take you away and have you all to myself for the next five days."

"I'm so ready, Colton," Chaise agreed. "We barely had a honeymoon because of that case. You're leaving your phone behind. There's no way I'm sharing you with Steele Security for our long weekend away."

"Deal. No fucking way I'm leaving your side for one second. I have so many things planned for that sexy body of yours."

"Oh, yeah? Like what?"

"Let's just say I've definitely upped the game in my bag of tricks." He shot her a sly smile and a mischievous wink. "Trust me, babe."

Chaise zipped her suitcase closed and flashed Colton her sexy smile. "I'm ready."

"Keep talking like that, and I'll be ready right now," Colton warned as he picked up her suitcase. "Get that fine ass of yours in the car and let's hit the road."

Colton keyed the address into the GPS, and they set out for their destination–a private bed-and-breakfast on a secluded part of a barrier island in the Gulf of Mexico. As a key member of the security firm, Colton was often needed to oversee critical assignments. With the last one completed and behind him, he decided a getaway with his wife of only a few months was the best reward for a job well done.

"I can't believe we're finally doing this," Chaise remarked. "I thought this day would never come. You realize you've been on a case since the day I met you?"

"Yeah, I sure have." He raised her hand to his lips and kissed the back of it. "But for the next five days, I'll only be on you."

"You know I do love that mouth of yours, Colton."

"My mouth will be on you, too. All over you, baby."

"Just hurry up and get there. You're killing me," Chaise demanded.

Colt chuckled and turned up the radio. "Anything you say, my love."

After a couple of hours of driving and fantasizing about everything he planned to do to his wife, he needed a distraction before his urges forced him to pull over on the side of the road. Glancing over at Chaise, all he saw were her toned, tanned legs. The smooth skin begging him to glide his tongue across every inch of them before reaching her soft, delicious center. He quickly averted his eyes, moving his focus back to the road.

"How'd you find this place anyway?" He sounded calm and casual, but the blood surged through his veins and had started to collect between his legs. The uncomfortable swelling that pushed against the inside of his zipper was hard to ignore.

"I didn't find it. I thought you did."

"No, Liz gave me the paper and said you printed it."

Liz was an adopted member of the Steele Security family. In her late sixties, her eccentric ways and lack of a brain-mouth filter kept everyone on their toes. Somehow, she always seemed to get away with whatever crazy new stunt she pulled, regardless of how embarrassed it made the team.

"Oh, shit."

"Yeah, oh, shit. What have we done?"

"It's too late now. We're almost there, and our reservation is nonrefundable. I'm sure Liz wouldn't send us somewhere awful. Right?"

"Not if she knows what's good for her. She'll have to see us again in a few days."

"We're about to find out. Take the next left," Chaise pointed.

Across the bridge, at the end of a road devoid of anything resembling civilization, Colt pulled into the driveway and put his truck in park. His eyes roamed over the grounds, took in the buildings on the lot, and gripped the steering wheel with both hands. "I've never seen a bed-and-breakfast like this before."

"You're right," Chaise agreed. "It doesn't look like a regular B&B. Let's just go in and check it out. If it's too bad, we'll just go stay somewhere else."

They climbed out of the truck and approached the front door of the main house. As they reached the door, they were met by a woman who was the exact image of Liz, only slightly older. Colt and Chaise stopped in their tracks and flashed each other a tentative glance.

"You must be Bull and Chaise," the lady addressed them with a knowing nod. "Liz told me all about you, young man. Your name is Colton, but your code name is Bull. I like code names. They're all dangerous and sexy.

"You're even sexier than she described. Look at those broad shoulders. Women love that, you know. Bulging muscles, strong back. You don't skip leg day at the gym, do you?"

"Uh, no, ma'am, I don't," Colt stuttered. "Do you know Liz Stanton?"

"I'm Bea Lee, her older sister." She extended her hand and shook their hands. "My husband, Earl, is around here somewhere."

"Do you own this bed-and-breakfast?" Chaise asked.

"Bed-and-breakfast?" She chuckled sarcastically. "I guess you could call it that. I rent out a couple of rooms in this big house from time to time. Like right now, I have two couples staying here for the week on their vacation."

A young, black Labrador retriever suddenly came bounding out the door behind Bea, nearly knocking her down on its way out. Chaise jumped out of the way in the nick of time, but Colt wasn't as lucky. The lab's big nose plowed into Colt's family jewels as she rushed through the space between his legs. Colt's knees buckled, his hands instinctively flew to cover his wounded package, and he bent at the waist with a groan of pain.

"Harper, bad dog!" Bea yelled. "Bad dog!"

Harper apparently didn't care what her owner thought of her behavior as she continued bouncing around the yard, chasing the flying insects, and marking her territory on the tires of Colt's truck.

"Damn dog," Bea huffed. "Thinks she's a boy. I've never seen a girl dog hike her leg and piss on everything like that one does. Craziest thing I've ever seen. You two come on in, and I'll grab the key to the private cottage. That's the one Liz said you'd want."

"Harper Lee?" Chaise laughed. "You must be a big fan."

"Always have been," Bea confirmed. "Always will be."

Chaise and Colt followed Bea inside, still not convinced they should stay, but they knew they couldn't very well leave now. The inside of the large beach house was decorated in a nautical theme throughout. Each room flowed into the next, giving the feel of a welcoming, lived-in home. Seeing the home so clean and well-kept, Chaise began to feel less apprehensive about spending their time away there.

"You have a lovely home, Bea," she complimented. "Colton and I live more inland, but after seeing this, I may have to work on him to move to a beachfront home."

"We love it here. Let me show you the back deck." Bea led the way to the back French patio doors and swung them open to give a full view.

"It's breathtaking," Chaise replied. "I'd live right here, in this space, all the time. You have a perfect view of the beach and the ocean."

"We like it." Bea shrugged one shoulder nonchalantly, trying to downplay the importance of the location. "We can go this way to your room. I'll unlock this door in the mornings so you can come in for breakfast and coffee."

The smaller building on the property was a petite version of the main house, just slightly larger than a mother-in-law's apartment. The living room and kitchen were one large, open space. The short hallway led to the master bedroom, bath, and a laundry room. A small formal dining area was situated off the kitchen and had a large sliding glass door leading to the patio area.

"I'm so glad we have the same perfect view you have," Chaise said to Bea. "Look, Colton, we have a hot tub on the patio."

"It's still early enough in the season to use it without burning up, too," Bea replied. "You'll have plenty of privacy out here. You're far enough from the main house to feel like you're alone but close enough to let me know if you need anything."

"Thank you. This looks perfect. I'll just grab our bags from the truck, and we'll be out of your hair." Colt turned and started back toward the front door.

"Here are the keys. You kids have fun." Bea winked mischievously, and Chaise knew without a doubt she had the same eccentric streak Liz had. When Bea reached the door, she stopped before going through it. "Oh, and since we're the only ones out here, we let Harper run free as much as possible. She's still a pup and has too much energy to sit still. I hope you don't mind."

"Not at all. We love dogs," Chaise assured her.

"Glad to hear it. Tell Bull he can pull his truck into the carport to get it out of the sun. That door leads straight into the laundry room, and those keys are for it, too. Enjoy your stay."

When Colton came in with the bags, Chaise relayed the message and started unpacking while he moved the truck to the shaded carport. "Ready for a dip in the ocean? I can't wait to see you in that skimpy bikini. On this deserted beach. Where no one else can see you."

Chaise laughed and shook her head. "I'm definitely ready for a dip in the ocean. Get those clothes off, and put your swimming shorts on."

"I love when you get demanding. Tell me to undress again."

She peeled her shirt off, slowly pulling it over her head. "Colton. Get naked. Now."

"Fuck, that's hot. I expect you to say that again later tonight."

She shimmied her shorts and panties down her legs and let them fall into a heap at her feet. She stepped out of them slowly and kept her eyes locked on him. "Colton, you're not naked yet. If you want this," she replied teasingly and squeezed her breasts together with her upper arms, "you have to get naked *right now*."

"Fuck swimming. We're staying in."

"No, we're not!" She pulled her bikini bottoms on before grabbing her top. "Tie me."

His fingers trailed down her skin, lighting her on fire as they went, but she refused to give in to his kind of torture tactics. She held her breath as he pulled the strings together and intentionally took his time tying them. "I promise my surges will make you feel better than the waves will."

"You don't play fair," she complained.

"Never claimed to." His lips touched the skin on the back of her neck, and she naturally leaned backward into his embrace. His hands snaked around her, lightly brushing against her skin along her ribcage until they met in the middle, while he licked and nipped at the sensitive skin beneath her ear.

"No, Colton!" She jumped out of his arms and took a couple of steps away. "Once we start, we'll never leave this room again. We're getting in the water. Come on."

"Okay," he agreed. A little too easily. "We'll get in the water." Within a few seconds, he'd shed his clothes and pulled his swimming trunks on. With a playful grin, he took her hand in his. "Let's go get wet, Chaise."

They walked across the hot sand and straight into the warm waters of the Gulf. When they reached chest-deep water, Colt pulled Chaise into his arms. One hand slid down her leg until he lifted it. She immediately lifted the other one and locked them around his waist, her arms around his neck, and their mouths fused together. Feeling his length growing between them, she tilted her hips to rub her core against it.

Within seconds, he'd freed his cock from his shorts and slid his fingers to her bikini bottoms. He slid the small patch of fabric to the side and pushed his fingers deep inside her. He moved his hand rapidly in and out. She tilted her head back, the inner walls of her pussy tightened around his fingers, and he knew she was close.

"Ow! Shit! Fuck! Goddammit!" Colton yelled and began squirming.

"What's wrong?"

"Something fucking stung me right on my dick. We're getting the fuck out of the water now." Colt adjusted his shorts and started moving through the water toward the shore.

Chaise looked down into the water and tried to withhold her laugh. "Look, honey, there are all kinds of little blobs around us. I think it's parts of jellyfish."

"No fucking wonder it stings. That's it for ocean sex."

"Take me to the room, and I'll make it all better."

"Later. When the stinging stops. Let's go shower and grab something to eat."

Hiding her smile, Chaise placed her head on his shoulder and let him carry her back to the shore. She noticed he kept adjusting himself as they walked back to their private cottage. "Are you okay, babe?"

"Yeah. But I still feel jellyfish tentacles on me."

"You don't have tentacles on your testicles. You're fine."

"You won't say that when my dick falls off in the shower. Right in my damn hand."

~

After an uneventful shower, Chaise and Colton ventured out to the more populated areas for a late lunch and shopping before returning to their secluded getaway. Settled in and relaxed, they snuggled together on a large, round lounger covered by a canopy, just off of their patio. "Maybe we can try again now," Colton murmured against her neck.

"Right here?" Chaise's eyes grew wide and darted back and forth between his.

"There's no one around, babe. It's just you and me."

He moved to cover her body with his, to claim her mouth, and to finish what they'd started in the ocean. His erection pushed against the denim of his shorts, and he pressed it into her heated core with each lunge forward. The friction of their clothes between them only drove the anticipation higher. Her legs parted wider, his hands roamed along her body before unfastening her shorts, and he was more than ready to dive deep inside her.

"Howdy, neighbor." A man's voice with a deep Southern drawl interrupted their impromptu make-out session. "It's a beautiful day, ain't it? We thought we'd go ahead and get the fire pit ready for tonight. Roast some weenies and marshmallows, sing a few songs. Y'all game?"

Colton raised his head and gazed deeply into Chaise's eyes. "Son of a bitch," he whispered, trying to keep his anger under control.

With his cock still at full-staff, he couldn't roll off Chaise without revealing his current state. With the man speaking directly to them, he couldn't very well stay on top of her and carry on a conversation either. He felt Chaise push him to the side, so he reluctantly rolled off her. He was relieved when she followed him and rolled onto her side, hooking her leg over him to help hide his state of arousal.

"Maybe later. We'll have to see. We honestly came here to spend some time alone because our lives have been so hectic," Colton replied.

"Man, I hear ya. I own my own business, and it keeps me running."

Not wanting to keep the conversation going any longer than necessary, Colt replied as vaguely as he could. "So you understand."

"I definitely understand. My lawn-mowing business is crazy busy. Especially down here where it never gets cold enough for grass to stop growing. Lawns need maintenance care. Landscaping needs new mulch. Always something to do. Oh, I'm Tim, by the way." He stepped more into their space to extend his hand to Colt.

Withholding a groan, Colt sat up and shook the man's hand. "Colt. Chaise." *Tim is obviously an idiot*, Colt decided.

"Well, I'll let you two get back to it then. See y'all later."

"Inside, woman. Right now. It's time to barricade the doors, draw all the shades, and have you all to myself. No damn jellyfish stings. No intruding, rude-ass strangers. Just you, me, the bed, and several other places over the course of the night."

"You know I love it when you get bossy like that."

"Come on, I'll show you bossy."

After locking every door, closing all the blinds, and setting the mood music to drown out any outside sounds, Colt led Chaise to the bedroom. "Finally. No interruptions. If anyone knocks on the door, we'll just ignore them. If they won't go away, I'll shoot them. Let the damn house burn down around us, I don't care. This is *our* time."

"You're overdressed for our date."

"So are you. But I can fix that right now."

Colton grabbed his bag of special tricks while Chaise undressed and positioned herself on the bed.

"Uh, babe? I'm not sure how sturdy this bed is." She scrunched her face up in concern as she tested the vintage bed. The wrought-iron headboard was beautiful, but the entire structure felt a little too shaky when she moved.

He grabbed the iron post of the footboard and shook the bed. "It's fine. It's just old and feels different than our bed."

After quickly shedding his clothes, he climbed on the bed with her and began removing items from his arsenal. With each item, Chaise's eyes grew wider and so did her smile. "You have been prepping for this."

"Damn straight. Hope our friendly neighbors don't need much sleep tonight." He waggled his eyebrows and picked up the Duotone balls first. "I want to try these on you."

"What are they?"

"They're like Ben Wa balls, but these have smaller balls inside that roll around when you move. They're supposed to increase sensations and stimulation. This string just makes it easier to remove them. Let's see if they work while I work on you."

"Death by orgasm. Sounds like heaven."

Using the lubricant he'd bought with the toy, Colt gently pushed the pleasure balls into her pussy. With a devilish smirk, he settled between her legs and covered her clit with his mouth. The sensation made her back involuntarily arch in pleasure, and she cried out to him.

"Baby, you feel so good," she moaned. When he pushed his finger inside her, her fingers gripped his short, blond hair and held on tightly. His second finger, in addition to the feel of his mouth on her and the Duotone balls inside her, was all it took to push her over the edge. "Oh fuck, Colton!"

"I'm going to fuck you with these balls inside your sweet pussy," Colt stated resolutely. "If it hurts at all, tell me and I'll stop immediately."

"Okay," she nodded, her excitement obvious.

Unsure of how she would like the feel of both his cock and the balls inside her, Colt pushed into her slowly at first. Her body adjusted to accept his size, and she soon began moving in time with him. Knowing she wasn't in pain gave him the push he needed, and his thrusts became more forceful. The more his cock glided across the balls and the more her inner muscles clenched him, the more he had to hold back to make it last longer.

The room grew hotter and hotter, their bodies became slick with sweat, and Chaise drew nearer and nearer to an earth-shattering climax. She gripped his back with her fingers, her nails digging in as he brought her body closer and closer to ecstasy. With his restraint tested to the limits, he surged into her with reckless abandon, and she screamed loudly in pleasure as her orgasm tore through her.

A split second later, her grip slipped off of his back slick with sweat, and her fisted hand flew toward her face, connecting directly with her eye. In the midst of screaming his name in desire, she shouted curses in pain. "Oh my God, Colton! Oh, God! Fuck, that hurt! Shit! Oooooowww!"

"Are you okay, babe?" He unsuccessfully tried to hide his chuckle.

"Yeah. Damn, that hurt." She laughed at herself. "Rough sex souvenir."

"Lucky for you, we're not finished. Turn over and get on your knees for me."

Eagerly doing as he asked, she turned over and waited on all fours. He pushed inside her, gripping her hips with his fingers, and slammed into her repeatedly. Working up to his own release, his head dropped back and he tuned out everything else except the exquisite feel of her pussy clenched around his cock.

The unexpected cold, wet intrusion in the crack of his ass made him immediately jump to his feet without conscious thought. There behind him, on the bed, stood Harper, the gender-confused black Lab overgrown puppy. Her mouth was parted, her tongue hanging out, and she genuinely seemed to be smiling at him. "What the fuck? How'd you get in here?"

"What?" Chaise turned her head and locked eyes with the dog. "What? How? I don't understand."

Colt jumped down, grabbed Harper's collar, and led her to the carport door. "The damn doggie door wasn't locked. She just came in on her own."

He rejoined Chaise on the bed. "Now, where were we?" His fingers glided up her legs to her pussy, where the string from the balls hung. Giving it a light tug, he tried to remove them. But they wouldn't budge.

"Relax, babe."

"I am relaxed."

He pulled again. But they wouldn't move. "Lie down on your stomach for me."

She glanced over her shoulder at him, giving him a dubious look, but lay flat on her stomach just the same. With another pull, he felt them shift slightly, but he still couldn't remove them without pulling harder and possibly hurting his wife.

"Colt. What the hell is going on?"

"They won't come out."

"What? What do you mean they won't come out?"

"I mean, they won't come out. They're stuck."

She buried her face in the pillow and shouted obscenities into it. "You have to get them out, Colt. I refuse to go to the emergency room with Ben Wa balls in my hoo-ha and become the poster child of the hospital for a safe-sex campaign."

"They're not Ben Wa. They're Duotone."

"I don't care. I do not care. Do you hear me? Get them out."

"I'll try more lube. Hang on a second." He searched for the lubricant he'd used to insert them, but he couldn't find the tube. "Shit. Just give me a minute. I'll open the other bottle. I can't find the one I used a few minutes ago."

After rattling around in his bag, he pulled out another tube and squirted a generous amount on his fingertips. Gently inserting his fingers inside her, he coated her insides with the slick substance, making sure to cover the balls as well. He gently tugged on the string but with no luck. Giving it a harder tug proved even less helpful, as the string broke in his hand.

"Oh, shit," he murmured, more to himself than to her.

"Oh, shit! Oh, shit!" she screamed.

"What? What's wrong?"

"I'm on fire! Holy shit, what did you do?" Chaise jumped out of bed and ran to the bathroom, her hands cupping her sex as she ran, yelling curse words every step of the way. "What the hell kind of lube is that?"

Colt's jaw fell slack, and he picked up the bottle. "*Wickedly ultra-warming lube with ultra-wicked sensations*" was the tag line he'd failed to read before he so generously applied it. "Just everyday, normal lube, babe. You must have sensitive skin."

"The hell you say," she yelled from the bathroom, over the rush of water flowing into the tub. After several minutes of soaking in the tub, she rejoined him in the bedroom and pitched the Duotone balls at him. "Seems like the string was longer when you first showed them to me."

"It may have snapped in two when I pulled on it too hard."

"Uh-huh. Let's see that bottle of lube now."

"I lost it."

"Both bottles?"

"Yep," he lied. "Ready to finish now?"

Her stare bored holes into him at first, but she finally relented, remembering the reason why they arranged the getaway in the first place. "Okay, but no more toys. No more lube made by the habanero farmers. No more public, indecent-exposure sexcapades. Just you, me, and the bed. At this point, I'm even afraid of trying shower sex."

"You can be on top and in control. I'll just lie here and please you."

"Deal."

After a repeat of the foreplay, without the added toys, Chaise straddled Colt and eased herself onto his cock until he was fully inside her. She began rocking her hips, moving them up and down, and relishing in the sensations as he thrust his hips upward to meet hers. With the recent events forgotten, they once again moved rapidly in tandem and became lost in their passion-fueled frenzy. Colt grabbed the wrought-iron headboard in an attempt to stop it from banging against the wall as Chaise continued to ride him, milking every last drop from him.

"Babe." Colt hated to interrupt her bliss, especially with the beautiful expression of complete satisfaction on her face and her head thrown back in fervor. But he had to tell her.

As if on cue, the corner of the bed frame broke the moment he started to warn her about the headboard banging against the wall. With both of his hands holding the headboard up, he could only watch as Chaise toppled over with the momentum of the mattresses suddenly falling to the side. He released the headboard, but he was too late to stop her as she fell headfirst into the nightstand. After hitting her forehead on the corner of the table, she landed on the hard floor in a complete daze.

Her stunned expression, coupled with her naked body lying on the floor, nursing a quickly growing bump on her forehead, pushed Colt into action. He jumped out of the broken bed and scooped her up in his arms. "Baby, are you okay?"

"Yeah. That hurt like hell, though." She began to laugh hysterically when her gaze landed on the bed. "I'm kind of proud of that, in a strange way."

Colton began to laugh along with her and kissed the throbbing knot on her forehead. "I'm kind of proud of my wife, too. I can't wait to tell the guys this story. Well, part of it anyway."

She smacked his chest playfully. "Leave out the part where I hit my head."

"Oh no, I'm sharing that part. I'll just add that it didn't stop you in the least bit."

After he checked her head to make sure she was really okay, they took a quick shower and Colt fixed the bed. "No big deal. The screw just came loose from the frame."

"Colton, I know we have this place for the next several days, but I think I'd really like to go home tomorrow."

"I'm so fucking glad you said that. I don't know if we'll survive another night here. Don't worry, we'll still have four days alone at home. No one has to know we're back."

"That sounds like the perfect getaway to me. No more adventures for a while!"

"The only adventure I want is to plan our revenge against Liz for sending us here in the first place," Colton deadpanned. "I think she's about to win an all-expense paid vacation to a place of our choice, with activities hand-picked just for her, and every moment captured on video for our amusement."

~

Want more of Nick Tucker? FINE LINE, the first book in a new stand-alone series, is available now! Keep reading for free sneak peek! Two more stories will be available soon!

CROSSING LINES: FINE LINE, BLURRED LINE, & HARD LINE

FINE LINE

FINE LINE.

A CROSSING LINES NOVEL.

Cover photo by Wander Aguiar.

Cover model is Jonny James.

Cover design by Sommer Stein, Perfect Pear Creative Covers

PROLOGUE

A Terrible Idea
Nick

"For the record, this is a terrible idea."

My director, Calvin Montgomery, locks his angry eyes on me while speaking to the handler who will be assigned to me—if Calvin approves the operation, that is.

"Sir, Special Agent Nick Tucker has repeatedly proved what a valuable asset he is in the field. He's one of our best. He has outscored most of his peers in both field and psychological profile tests—even those who have previous undercover experience. We can't deny the man has the skills we need on this assignment. He deserves this chance."

"Yes, I can read the reports as well as you can, Jack. But Nick doesn't have any true undercover experience—not even on short-term cases, and the others do. Maybe they didn't score as well on the psych tests because they're already accustomed to living among the criminal element and acting as one of them. Did that ever occur to you? We both know how hard this life is even for a few months, but the case you're asking me to put Nick on is potentially a multiyear mission."

Calvin turns his penetrating gaze to me, constantly assessing my every reaction, looking for a weakness and a reason to deny my involvement. I've been in hectic firefights before and kept my cool, though. My time in the military, working for Steele Security, and providing private security for billionaire Dominic Powers before joining the DEA prepared me for most every perilous situation they can throw at me. Drawing on my inner strength, I keep my expression passive, my breathing regular, and my instinct to remind him he's driven a desk for too many years to remember what working in the field is actually like under wraps.

"You'll be cut off from everyone you know, Nick. You'll essentially divorce your entire life—for years. Your friends, your family, wife, girlfriend, boyfriend. *Everyone.* You hear me? And that's the easy part of the job. Even contact with Jack will be sparse, especially due to the group you'll infiltrate, so you'll be making decisions on the fly. Any outside affiliation will be scrutinized—and these guys won't ask questions first. They'll shoot you in the head and replace you with the next guy in line. I'm not convinced you truly understand what you'll have to do to be one of them."

"I can assure you, I do understand."

"Is that right? This UC op has been issued special permission to break the very laws you've sworn to uphold. Your psych profile shows a strong sense of duty and a penchant for following the rules to the letter. So, you'd be fine if they order you to force some young kid to sell drugs on the street corner and bring you every penny of the money he made? Then rough him up if he doesn't bring you enough?"

The visual that pops into my brain before I can stop it makes my heart rate increase instantly, the artery in my neck jerking and giving away my reaction.

"Or maybe it's not a him. Maybe it's a her. You'd willingly force a young woman into prostitution, selling her to any Joe Blow off the street, who'll do whatever the fuck he wants to do to her? You can make them believe you don't care about her at all, just how much money she brings in for getting her John's rocks off? What if that means her customer gets to beat the shit out of her just because he has mommy issues? I mean, as long as he doesn't kill her and she can perform for her next trick, what the fuck does it matter, right?"

My stomach churns with disgust, and the room around me turns red with my rage. But I tamp down those feelings inside my chest until they form a mangled ball full of drive and determination to see this through to the end.

"I'll do whatever the fuck I have to do to stop these bastards. The longer we sit here repeatedly arguing the same points and imagining hypothetical situations, the more time they have to commit those very crimes. Sir."

"I'm sure I don't have to remind you we're after the major charges to shut them down for good. Small-time hoods are a dime a dozen. We want the source—their suppliers. Local reports say this group is using a prescription drug that hasn't even cleared the FDA yet. It's highly effective and lethal in the wrong hands. That's in addition to the influx of opioids and other controlled substances from their Mexican drug cartel affiliation. We can't blow the entire operation because you feel the need to feed your savior complex over every sob story you hear. Most of those women asked for it anyway—they probably even enjoy it."

"I'm well aware of what we're after and how to do my job." Inside, I'm seething; outside, I display a calm demeanor.

He's testing me, that much I know. His last comment was to gauge my knee-jerk reaction because that's exactly how this gang thinks. If Calvin approves my request for undercover work, the group I'll join will say and do a lot worse to me than my director has ever even thought about. If I can't handle my boss yanking my chain inside the comfort of his office in our secure, air-conditioned building, I have no business being an undercover agent where anything and everything can go wrong.

Will go wrong.

Something always does.

To stay alive, I have to think fast on my feet, improvise, and give an award-winning performance.

No time like the present to start earning a few of those golden statuettes.

"Sir, I can handle anything they throw at me. I've been in intense situations in my career, starting in the Army, through private details, and in my time with the DEA. I'm ready to take my career to the next level, and I need undercover experience to do that. This wasn't Jack's idea—I requested to be assigned to this case."

The muscles around Calvin's eyes contract, crinkling the skin until only small slits remain. He draws a slow circle around his mouth with his thumb and forefinger before resting his chin on his hand. With my gaze locked on to his, I wait for him to make his decision. The first one to blink will be Calvin, because I am all in.

"All right, Special Agent Tucker, you've convinced me to give you a chance. On one condition."

"What condition is that?"

"If at any time you suspect your cover is blown, or your gut warns you that something is off and they've turned on you, get out of there. To hell with the case and the charges. Call Jack, get to the safe house, do whatever it takes to extract yourself from the situation."

"I appreciate your concern, sir, but it won't come to that. I'll see this through till the end."

"All right. We'll get your name, background, and criminal history established. Congratulations, Nick. You have the distinct honor of pledging to one of the most notorious motorcycle gangs in the world. The Devil's Dominion rules their LA territory with an iron fist. I only hope they don't turn that fist on you."

"Thank you, sir. I won't let you down."

~

Six Months Later

"Are you sure you're ready to approach them, Nick? No need to rush things." Jack paces in his kitchen while I sit at the table and finish my coffee.

Jack Collins fits the bill for a retired biker. He is a handler, but he's curated his entire life around the motorcycle club lifestyle to avoid arousing any suspicions. He hasn't pledged to any outfit, but he is known by enough bikers that no one questions his presence, and no one crosses him. He has the don't-fuck-with-me air down pat.

His long black and gray hair is pulled back in a low ponytail. His sun-weathered skin bears the ravages of years on the open road—the deep-set wrinkles, the sunspots, the year-round dark tan. His brown eyes are keen, assessing a man and his intentions with a quick glance. The skin on his hands matches his face, but his grip is as strong as a man half his age. The long span of his career gives him advantages others could only hope to attain one day.

"It's time, Jack. You're my handler, you know I'm ready, and you know that shit is escalating out there. My hair has grown out, along with my beard. All my ink is finished—nothing overly distinguishable but still believable. My criminal background is airtight, and my stints in San Quentin and Pelican Bay legitimize my badass felon status."

"You can't use words like *legitimize* around these guys, Nick." Jack scrubs his hand down his face.

"I can talk real dumb too, Jack. Like I ain't got no schooling or nothing."

"Make fun of this all you want, Nick. But I'm telling you, these guys have a grittiness about them, a certain way they talk, a language all their own. It's a combination of the motorcycle gang lingo and prison slang."

"Trust me, I got this. I've mastered how they speak, the motorcycle gang terms, and the prison slang. I've memorized my background and rehearsed how I became a badass ex-convict, looking to join the baddest MC club around. One point that is pure genius on your part is showing I was part of a Tijuana-based gang before I was sent to prison. Thanks for that."

"Anything I can do to keep you from having to murder someone as part of your initiation. Because that's what they usually require—and could still order you to do it. But we'll cross that bridge when we have to. If you can patch in, you won't have to do the lowly probie bullshit. That'll at least give you a leg up in earning their trust and working your way up the chain faster than most.

"If you have to improvise and add anything to your history, don't forget to tell me immediately. We can build your experience around whatever you need, but it could take a little time to get it on paper. And don't say gang. You know how one-percenters feel about that word."

"Striking the word gang from my vocabulary now. And I'll try to keep the improvisation to a minimum, but I'm sure it'll come up. My documented history is solid, but that doesn't account for the things I never got caught doing. If you happen to have any former gang members in your back pocket, that would be useful too."

"I'll see what I can do. You never know, this old dog may still have a few tricks you don't know about."

One thing about Jack Collins, he always has another trick up his sleeve no one else knows about. How he stayed one step ahead of the agents under his charge when he went weeks without hearing from them is a mystery in our world. He takes his job home with him every night, and the safety of his agents is his first priority. I know I am in good hands.

"Thanks for the coffee. I'm heading back to my dinky little apartment to get into character. They're having a party at their clubhouse tomorrow night, so I'll use that opportunity to make my presence known."

"Good luck, kid. Don't die."

"That's the nicest thing you've ever said to me, Jack." I smile over my shoulder as I leave his bachelor pad and climb onto my bike.

My new life waits for me, in the gritty, dirty underbelly of the criminal world. Getting the approval for this level of undercover work is a boost to my ego and a rush to my senses. The heightened danger, constantly surveilling my surroundings, and testing my ability to decipher friend from foe within a matter of seconds will take my career to the next level.

I feel as if I've found my purpose in life. Finally.

~

Major Mistakes
Savannah

The woman staring at me looks familiar, but I don't know her. Not anymore anyway. Her red hair is longer than when she was younger. Her deep green eyes hold so many secrets, ones she'll never tell. She's also much thinner than she used to be—a telltale sign of stress and depression settling in over the long haul. The sad fact is, I used to know her very well. But now she's only the outer shell of the vibrant, bubbly personality I remember from just a couple of years ago. The light in her eyes is dim now, barely perceptible even when I'm searching for it.

"When did this happen, exactly? How did I become *this* woman?" I stare into the hollow green eyes reflected in the mirror, talking to myself. Again.

A loud bang on my apartment door abruptly ends my one-sided conversation. My heart drops, and a groan escapes from my throat. Dread covers me like a lead blanket. There's only one person that can be...the one person I really don't want to see, much less spend the evening around. But I don't have a choice. I'm trapped, like a frightened, timid animal in a cage.

After removing the door chain and unlocking the multiple bolts I had installed, the door swings open before I can even grab the knob.

"Why the fuck do you have the door locked like that? Who are you hiding in here?" Butch pushes past me, moving from one room to the next through my apartment as he searches for the invisible man.

"There's no one here except me. Just like last time. And the time before that. You know I always keep all the door locks in place when I'm here alone."

It's a phobia I have—an intense fear that drives me to check the locks several times before going to bed every night. He knows this about me, because he's complained about it every time he's stayed at my apartment. Thankfully, that hasn't happened in a very long time.

He stomps toward me in his heavy leather boots, the ones he wears every day because they best protect his feet and ankles while he's riding his motorcycle. It's strange how what I initially thought was intriguing, dangerous, and sexy about him when we met are the very traits that make me want to run away and start a new life somewhere else today.

I just haven't figured out how to get away from him yet.

"Pack all your shit. We're leaving."

"What?" I whirl around on my heel and stare at him, completely dumbfounded.

"We're moving. Prez is sending me and a couple of other guys to DC to induct a smaller club into ours. We have to try them out, see if they're worthy enough to wear the Devil's Dominion colors. This is my chance to show him I'm officer material and get on the voting ballot to move up in the club. I've been waiting years for this day."

The only thought in my mind is that my opportunity to get away from him is finally here. The day I've been waiting to come for far too long. There's no way I can move from LA to DC—they're at completely opposite ends of the country. Literally from one coast to the other. My entire life is here in LA, including my job and the few friends I had before I started seeing Butch.

Maybe my friends will take me back when I get rid of him.

"That's great news for you, Butch. I'm glad the president finally sees your potential in the club, and I hope they make you an officer soon. But I can't just up and move across country with you. My job is here—my entire career I've worked years to establish. I also have a lease on this apartment I can't just break."

I'm listing every logical reason I can think of, no matter how lame it will inevitably sound to him. He doesn't care about excuses—he only cares about results. More specifically, he only cares about the results he wants to see.

"Wouldn't that just fucking thrill you? Wouldn't you just love for me to go across the fucking country for the next six months and leave you here alone so you can fuck every swinging dick that crosses your path? Of course you're going with me, you stupid bitch. Who the fuck do you think is gonna drive the truck behind us and haul our shit across the country? All our stuff won't fit on our fucking bikes, you moron. Now, pack your shit like I said."

With his final command, he shoves me and slams my head into the wall, catching the edge of the doorframe with the full blunt force of the impact. Even with my eyes closed, I can feel the room spinning. Nausea settles into my gut and the bile churns, threatening to work its way up my throat. The pain in my skull makes me whimper. His only reply is a disgusted huff.

"Now, rent the fucking moving truck, pack your shit, and let's go to DC before I'm too old to ride my damn bike anymore."

After I hear the door open, he hurls one last threat at me. "If you even think of trying to get out of this, I'll kill every single person you love. All your fucking friends from the hospital. Your mom. Your sister. Try me, bitch. I dare you."

He stomps out, the chains on his boots and belt clinking with every step, growing fainter until I hear the engine of his bike roar to life. Funny, or not funny, how it reminds me so much of his own terrible roar. After he rides away, I open my eyes and gingerly move off the wall where he left me.

The door to my apartment is standing wide open.

He knows my paralyzing fear of leaving the door unlocked. Irrational or not, it's still there.

I want to rush to lock every bolt, but the first step in that direction reminds me of my head injury. The disorientation, nausea, and I are not new friends. With slow movements, I lift my hand to feel the goose egg forming behind my ear. I'm not even surprised to find blood on my fingers when I lower my arm again.

My walk to the door is slow as I calculate each step and how much farther I have to go. My chest is heaving from the building anxiety. When the door is finally locked—every bolt is secured and every chain is in place, my pounding heart slows enough so I can breathe normally again.

After I put a cold compress on the back of my head, I slide onto the couch and carefully lie back on the throw pillows. I waste a few minutes daydreaming about never leaving my apartment again, never unlocking the door again, while waiting for the throbbing in my head to subside. As often as I dream about this, I should've already found the master plan for leaving Butch in my dust.

Since nothing else I've tried so far has worked, I pick up my laptop and rent the moving van as the asshole commanded. A one-way trip to Washington, DC coming up, sans the excitement a cross-country trip should elicit. The only way I can describe how I feel about what I just did is I'm positive I've just signed my own death certificate.

In fact, the longer I'm around Butch, the more I realize that outcome is inevitable—it's only a matter of time. The odds there will come a day when it's him or me increase with our every encounter. I let my eyes drift up to the ceiling, staring at nothing in particular while thinking about my situation. My job as an emergency room nurse is stressful and adrenaline-filled, but it pales in comparison to a single interaction with Butch. In an ironic twist, I would be required by law to report potential domestic abuse if one of my patients presented with the same signs I bear.

He wasn't always like this. When I first met him, the tall, muscular, brooding man was much sexier. His brown hair was longer than other men I'd dated before, but it gave him an edgier appearance. Eyes so brown they're almost black sparkled with playfulness and teasing. But it was all a charade—he was pretending to be someone he wasn't. And he was so good at it for so long—long enough to ensure I fell for him. Long enough to ensure I was caught in his trap. When I look at him now, all I see is the ugliness inside. Any desire that once burned for him has long been doused.

Thankfully, those nights with him have dwindled to an occasional visit—and only when he needs me to do something for him. He disappeared for a couple of weeks one time, and I thought he'd found someone else to prey upon. Selfishly, I hoped he had—but then I immediately felt bad for wishing him on anyone else. Unfortunately, one day, he simply walked back into my apartment as if he'd been here all along. No explanation. No questions.

His visits have been sporadic since that day. Usually when he's drunk and looking for somewhere to crash after a night out with his friends. He passes out in my bed, and I sleep on the couch, unable to stand being in the same room with him any longer than absolutely necessary. His insane jealousy makes no sense to me whatsoever. We are not a couple and haven't been for a very long time, yet he calls me every name in the book when he accuses me of seeing other men.

Not that I'm the least bit interested in even trying to date. I still can't get rid of the last mistake I made.

Now he shows up and demands I move across the country with him. I'm having a hard time wrapping my head around this one. It's not like either of us wants to be with the other. That much is clear. But I believe he'll make good on his threat to kill everyone I love. In fact, I have no doubt he will.

One problem at a time, though. Before we even reach the East Coast, I have to survive the actual 3,000-mile trip with him and his buddies. That should be fun—waiting for them to pass out on the bed from the abundance of drugs and alcohol so I can grab the extra linens and sleep on the nasty floor. But I prefer the floor over touching any of them. Maybe I'll sleep in the truck...with the doors locked...under the guise of protecting our belongings.

A few hours later when I walk into the hospital for the night shift, my heart is heavy, and all my feelings show on my face. My coworker takes one look at me, and her face falls.

"What has Butch done now?" Stella puts her hands on her hips and draws in a deep breath. She already knows she won't like the answer.

After explaining the series of events and the commandment Butch issued, I watch her face for the disappointment I know will come. On one hand, I completely understand it, and I was even the same way...before I became the abused and battered victim. Life is now divided into two sections: BB and AB. Before Butch and After Butch.

Before Butch, I said no man would ever lay a hand on me and live to tell about it.

No man would ever abuse me in any way—physically, mentally, or verbally. I would leave him in a heartbeat.

No man would replace my job, my dreams, or my friends—the sacred relationships I'd always held so dear.

After Butch, I withdrew from my friends.

My dreams took a back seat.

Self-esteem was what others had, but not me.

I miss the Before Butch version of myself. But now I feel as if I'm in too deep and can't claw my way out. One thing I've realized after looking back over the past eighteen months is none of this happened suddenly. He chipped away at the very core of me little by little, bit by bit, day by day. Until the very spark that made me *me* disappeared. And I allowed him to do it.

It's my fault.

If I'd been stronger, smarter, faster...maybe I would've seen the warning signs for what they really were.

Huge signs that flashed "Bridge Out Ahead."

But his apologies were so sincere at first. So heartfelt. He was remorseful and promised those bad things would never happen again.

He'd drunk too much. He always liked to fight when he drank. Such a man's man.

He was under too much stress. Work was a constant sore spot. His coworkers or his boss never liked him. They always made up a reason to get rid of him.

Of course, that was before I found out the truth about him. Before I understood what being in a one-percenter motorcycle club really meant. When I made the mistake of calling his club a gang during a heated argument, I saw stars after he backhanded me for disrespecting his brothers.

That was the day the apologies stopped and the real threats began. Old ladies didn't leave bona fide club members. Ever. It wasn't the woman's decision whether to stay or go. She just did what she was told and lived with what she got. He warned me to be glad I wasn't a sheep—one of the women they pass around to each other indiscriminately, using at will for any hedonistic pleasure they wanted to indulge in at the moment.

Ignoring the pleas and concern in Stella's eyes, I continue updating her on my plans. "I'm turning in my two-week notice tonight. That date was the earliest I could get a moving truck big enough for my stuff plus theirs anyway. I'm so glad it has a towing hitch for my car too."

I leave Stella, disappointed expression and all, to start my rounds and focus on the emergency cases. I wish I could stop time so my shift would never end. But working in busy emergency rooms always makes the time go by faster than the slower pace, comparatively, on the medical-surgical floors. Before I know it, the sun rises and a new day dawns, and I have to face the unpleasantness of packing all my belongings.

Two weeks will pass in the blink of an eye.

~

The Initiation
Nick

"You ready for tonight?" Jack's serious expression gives away his thoughts. Unusual for him after the years of handling undercover officers.

"I'm as ready as I'll ever be." I slide my arm into my cut and complete the persona of Renegade.

Turns out, the idea to convince them I was part of a Tijuana-based club was a stroke of genius on Jack's part. The Devils' ties to the Mexican cartel are already in place, but with my joining them, the full backing of the cartel is implied, giving them more muscle than they already have. An ATF agent has been working a few members of that gang over the last several years, so interagency cooperation kicked in, and my alibi was instantly airtight. With my background in prison and ties to the Mexican cartel-sanctioned motorcycle club firmly in place, I approached the Devils with an offer they couldn't refuse.

The Devils' already long reach just increased with no effort on their part. At least as far as their reputation with rival clubs is concerned. Keeping those other clubs at arm's length while the Devils conduct business is vital to maintaining their dominance in the territory. When the club president realized the possibilities I could bring, the dollar signs in his eyes were so bright, they rivaled the neon signs of the Vegas strip.

Headbanger, also known as Bobby Blalock, is the club president. He has a rap sheet longer than my leg, along with countless other crimes he's never been charged with committing. Or ordering. His officers and many other members are all too eager to carry out plans on his behalf. They're brothers in colors, but they're also all vying for the attention of one man. The one who can make or break them in the club.

Tonight is initiation for a few new prospects who are on their way to becoming full patch members. The ceremony to patch in is a big deal to these guys—it seals their identity and their place in the family.

I've been riding with the Devils for the past two weeks. Hanging out with them in the clubhouse provides a completely unique perspective on the inner workings of a notorious outlaw gang. Some of the guys have done hard time, and it's a miracle most aren't still in prison. I've had to bite my tongue way too many times already—something my director knew about me before he approved the assignment.

My moral compass always points due north. Always.

Their skewed sense of right and wrong doesn't mesh well with me. In fact, we're like oil and water at the very core. The only peace I have is when we're on the open road, the wind whipping around me, and the road rushing by under my wheels. The sense of freedom on a motorcycle is the sole only thing I have in common with these guys. It's the only time we're even remotely on the same page.

The long ride to the initiation grounds in the hot, arid desert of Southern California gives me time to get myself back into character. Jack stressed over and over how I have to be part of the group to avoid suspicion. Because of the high stakes, I've been given special clearance to break the laws I've sworn to uphold. But there are oaths I've taken, and I have no intention of reneging on them.

There are lines I refuse to cross.

There are rules I refuse to break—even for the greater good and the thrill of closing the case.

But I have to act like there are no lines I won't cross. To be convincing, I have to put Nick Tucker away and be Renegade to the bone. In my mind, I have to think of Renegade as a completely different person. It's the only way I can pull this off.

He's an ex-con, fresh out of a maximum-security prison, and that has to be my persona. As a convicted felon on parole, I can't legally cross the border to ride with my old club because the pigs will nab Renegade immediately. I can't exactly drive my motorcycle through the underground tunnels to cross the border. Of course, as Renegade, I have the contacts, so I could find an illegal way, like a fake passport or hidden in a caravan. But I'd take that risk only for a golden opportunity, a sure thing.

Renegade has talked a good game in his two weeks with the Devils. Tonight, Prez will present me with the final piece of my colors—the top rocker panel for my cut—because I scored the largest shipment of meth and negotiated the best deal for the club he's ever seen. Compliments of my DEA and ATF friends.

When I finally roll up to their private hideaway in the desert, my Renegade character is in full swing. After grabbing a couple of beers from the cooler, I stroll over to where the officers are hanging out with a few of the lifers—the men who have been part of the club for so long, they aren't required to attend all church meetings and outings anymore, but they're every bit a part of the club as any other member. They can come and go as they please, though most stay more than they leave. This is the only life they know.

"Good of you to bring me a beer, Renegade." Axle reaches for one of the longneck bottles I'm carrying, so I hand it over without a fuss. He's one of the most respected lifers in the group. His experience combined with his naturally level head makes for a powerful ally in a group of trigger-happy thugs. Despite Axle's advanced age and lack of officer status, no man in this group wants to tangle with him.

"You know I always got your back, Ax."

"Back atcha, kid." He takes a long pull from the bottle but keeps his eyes locked on mine. "Heard about that big score you got for us. I'm impressed—and I don't impress easily. Good job."

"Appreciate it, man. Just glad I could help out."

"Well, well, look who's coming our way. The new prospects are here, and they brought their offerings to the Devils with them." Nutcrusher, the club vice president, stands and rubs his hands together, eager to get down to business.

When I glance over my shoulder at the approaching prospects, my stomach drops to my knees and my empty hand curls into a tight fist.

Their "offerings" are new sheep, women being shoved into the midst of the already rowdy scene. The three prospects are each forcing a woman to walk in front of them. The women alternate from stumbling ahead a few steps to digging their heels in to try to stop, only to be shoved from behind and start the process all over again. Their eyes are wide and full of fear. Their faces are tear-stained and their hair is disheveled—and not from the ride here since they arrived in the club van.

I'm positive these three women have already been used as offerings before the new patches ever brought them to meet the brothers. Before I consciously realize I'm moving, my feet develop a mind of their own and take a step forward. Then I feel a hand on my shoulder, holding me back.

"What you see tonight will test your mettle, boy. You've never been around anything like this, I can already tell. But I guarantee, if you blow your cover now, you'll never see anything at all, ever again."

Shocked by his words, I whip my head around and meet Axle's knowing gaze.

"Use it, kid. Use everything you have to see and do as a member to take them down. As shitty as it sounds, you can't save these women and do what you came here to do at the same time. Keep your eyes on the end goal, son, and make them pay for their crimes when it's all said and done."

"What are you talking about, Axle?" He knows. We both know he knows. But I'll be damned if I'll blow my own cover.

"I'm CIA, Nick Tucker from the DEA family. I've been on this case for a long time, waiting for my foreign target to make his move so I can take him down. I told you, I got your back."

"The CIA can't operate on US soil, Ax. Everyone knows that."

His grin resembles one connected to an inside joke. Everyone else is clueless, and one person holds all the aces in his hand. "Sure we don't. I'm on loan to whichever agency wants to take the credit for the bust when it goes down. If you're still here when it happens, maybe that'll be the DEA."

Before I can reply, the shrill shriek of a woman's scream combined with ripping fabric fills the air, making my guts churn with disgust. Any man who would lay a hand on a woman in anger or abuse is no man at all. He's a pussy who knows he couldn't stand toe-to-toe with a real man.

The crowd that gathers around the three women—to watch, to encourage, or to participate—are the worst of the underworld. Preying on the defenseless and taking advantage of those who are hanging on by a thread as it is.

"Come with me, Renegade. This is as good as this scene gets. It's all downhill from here, and I don't think you can stop yourself from intervening yet." Axle guides me away from the ruckus.

I can still hear their pleas to stop. Their screams that echo through the desert air. Their cries for someone to please help them...to make it stop.

But I do nothing.

What kind of man does that make me?

"When they finish with the girls, they'll take them back to the clubhouse, and the club doctor will patch them up. They'll use them as sheep, or they'll cycle them into the prostitution ring and run them on the streets. They're not easy on them, but they don't permanently damage them either. Headbanger has a strict rule on that part since it affects his cash flow."

"Axle, your explanation doesn't help me one fucking bit. Do you even hear yourself? Of course they're permanently damaged now. Maybe not in the way you meant, but they still are." He nods in understanding, and he knows he can't say much more to justify what we've witnessed. "Where did they get those girls? Did they kidnap them?"

"No. They pick up hitchhikers or strays. Bring them into the family. Give them food, a place to sleep, and the protection of a notorious motorcycle club. But they expect the girls to earn their keep one way or another. This may be the first time you've ever seen this, but it won't be the last. It won't even be the worst thing you've seen by the time your undercover operation ends."

The silence between us only seems to amplify the mixture of screams and catcalls behind us.

"Talk to me, Axle. Tell me about life in the CIA. Were you in the service? Anything, man. Talk about the fucking weather. I don't care."

"This gets easier, kid. You'll learn to compartmentalize shit like this. Picture those assholes in prison orange, enduring the same fate they're subjecting those girls to right now at the hands of a big, angry brute in their cell, where they have nowhere else to run. Then make that your end goal and sole mission in life. Find what gets you through the rough spots one day at a time. Your assignment will be over before you know it. Then you can put all this bullshit behind you."

I don't see that happening.

CHAPTER ONE

Savannah—Two Years Later

"We're moving you out of that apartment today. I've been waiting for this day forever. No more excuses about waiting until your lease is up." Karen slings her backpack over her shoulder and jingles her car keys in her hand. "Let's go do this."

"What if he's still there?"

"That's why my husband and his friends are meeting us. We need their muscles to carry your furniture, and the fact that they're all cops doesn't hurt either." Karen smiles broadly, knowing Butch wouldn't dare start something with them around. "You know, you're welcome to stay with Spencer and me anytime you want. For example, if you wake up in the middle of the night scared and don't want to be alone anymore. Or if you just want to have a slumber party full of alcohol and junk food. Just show up at my house and make yourself at home."

"That sounds like so much fun. I don't know how to thank you for this, Karen." The shame of my situation is almost unbearable. All the time I've wasted, being afraid of Butch and what he'd do if I said or did the wrong thing when he was around. Not living my life to the fullest, enjoying every minute of every day. Not doing all the things I've wanted to do when I wanted to do them. Not spending time with my family so I could keep them as far away from that bastard as possible.

Being controlled and dominated by a cruel man.

"You can thank me by staying away from him for good. By calling the police if he comes anywhere near you again. By asking for help if he finds a way to back you into a corner again. I will get you out—one way or another. You are not alone in this, and you are not to blame." Karen grabs my arms to emphasize her words, and I consciously avoid wincing in pain from the pressure on my bruised skin. She doesn't know the bruises are there; I've hid them well.

Guess old habits do die hard.

"You have my word. Once I'm rid of him, it will be once and for all. There will be no going back or letting him in again for any reason. I've honestly wanted this for a long time, but I never could make it work. I think this time will definitely be different. For the first time in a long time, I have hope for a better life."

"It's all yours, babe. All yours for the taking. Once we get you moved, we'll work on finding you a real man. I'm sure Spencer has at least one single, handsome friend we can set you up with."

"Oh, no. No, no, no. I'm not interested in anything remotely resembling a man in my life. I'll just borrow your husband and his friends for heavy-lifting duties and scaring away bad guys. That's as close to having another man as I want to get."

"Woman-to-woman…friend-to-friend…I have to be brutally honest with you, Savannah."

"Go ahead. I know you. You'll explode if you don't get it out."

"It's not you I'm worried about as much as it's your poor, neglected, prune-shriveled va-jay-jay. I mean, it's seriously been three years since you took it out for a sit and spin? No squats in the cucumber patch? No gland-to-gland combat? We're both mandatory reporters, and you are definitely way past neglecting the old bearded clam. I think I need to turn you in to the nearest hot policeman."

Before meeting Karen, I'd almost forgotten how good it felt to simply laugh with a friend. To say whatever crazy thought came to my mind without fear of ridicule or reprisal. To have someone on my side, in my corner, standing by me no matter where the chips may fall. Stella was the last person I was semi-close to, but my friendship with Stella was nothing like the one I now have with Karen. We tease each other relentlessly, and I always tell her she elbowed her way into my heart, never taking no for an answer.

And saved my life in the process.

Now she's adding fun, love, and laughter too. Maybe the old me will emerge like a butterfly coming out of a cocoon.

We arrive at my apartment complex and find Spencer is already here waiting for us with his own small army. He pulls Karen into his arms, a warm, sweet smile on his face as he looks at her and kisses her hello. He's not at all shy or embarrassed by public displays of affection—or showing how completely and utterly in love he is.

Watching the two of them embrace, I'd swear the depth of their love for each other is their source of strength.

Butch insisted love was a weakness. A way other people could use you without explanation or a chance for retribution. He didn't believe anything that exposed your vulnerabilities could possibly make you stronger.

Butch was wrong.

I see it so clearly now, watching my friends. They give me something to aspire to reach in relationship goals—one day, possibly. The way I feel right now, I'd never trust a man enough to feel safe with him. To give him all of me and believe he'd do the same. Perhaps I'll find that man at some point in my life, but I plan to focus on myself first.

My goals.

My hopes.

My dreams.

I've put them on the back burner for a man who wasn't worth even a second of my time. Today is the first day of the new me.

"Hi, Savannah. Good to see you." Spencer turns his attention to me, keeping his arm wrapped around Karen's waist.

"Thank you for doing this, Spence. I don't know how to repay your kindness—and all your friends. I wish you'd let me pay you for your trouble." My gaze drifts to each of his friends standing by the moving truck—and I immediately regret it. Though they try to mask their thoughts, I see the judging stares and disgusted glances.

I can't exactly hide the black eye I'm sporting, though it has mostly faded to light green bruising.

They're asking why I've stayed so long.

They're questioning what I've done to deserve this.

They want to know why I'm so weak and spineless to let someone treat me this way.

I've experienced these reactions so many times from other people. Until they've walked a mile in my shoes, they'll never understand what it takes to be able to get out of a situation like this. Now that I've lived it, I can honestly say I didn't have a fucking clue what I was talking about when I used to pass those same judgments on other women.

"You're not paying us one single penny. We're happy to help." Spencer releases Karen and steps toward me. "Can I have your keys? Jake and I are going up to your apartment to make sure it's safe. Stay here with Terry, Jarod, and Trent until you hear from us. Then you and Karen can pack your things and we'll get you away from this asshole." Jake steps up next to Spencer and inclines his head at me as Spencer speaks.

"Sure. This one is the door key, this one is to the top bolt, and this one is the bottom bolt." I hand the keys over, feeling guilty for allowing complete strangers to stick their necks out for me. They're off duty, doing this as a favor to Spencer.

"I sure hope he's up there. And I hope he puts up a fight. At the very least, a little resistance. All I need is one good reason to take him down." Jake cracks his knuckles and sneers his lip. "I'm more than willing to pay him back on your behalf, Savannah."

Could I have been wrong? Could their expressions I took for judgment against me have been disgust with Butch instead? Have I read others wrong too?

"I appreciate the offer, Jake. But I don't want you to get in trouble because of me."

"You're looking at it all wrong, sweetheart. All he has to do is touch me wrong one time and he's assaulted a police officer. That's a serious offense, one he'd be hauled away in handcuffs over." Jake smiles, hopeful for the chance to arrest Butch and avenge me in one fell swoop.

One can hope he's in my apartment. Right?

~

Both fortunately and unfortunately, Butch wasn't in my apartment, and he never showed up while we were there, packing and moving all my belongings out, cleaning up afterward, and leaving the complex without a trace we'd ever been there. While I would've enjoyed seeing him hauled away in handcuffs by a few of DC's finest detectives, I'll take the stealthy approach we pulled off over a confrontation with him any day.

My new home is actually in a newer apartment, but the rent is affordable, and the neighborhood is on the trendier side. This area is nice and safe. I spotted a small coffee shop down the street. Cozy and quaint, it looks like the perfect place to work on my secret project. Something I've decided to do just for myself as much as for others.

"This place looks great!" Karen walks in like she lives here—after unlocking all my locks and bolts with the extra key I gave her—and I wouldn't have it any other way. "You must've been up all night, unpacking and decorating your new place."

"I couldn't sleep. I was too excited to close my eyes."

She drops her purse on the couch, places her hand on her hip, and quirks one eyebrow up at me. "For the record, I'm letting you get away with that abbreviated answer because there is some truth to it. Don't think for one second you'll get away with that shit in the future, though."

"Fine. I was also checking the door and window locks every five minutes and thirty-six seconds. And my ears were oddly in tune with every loud engine that drove past, regardless of the hour."

"I knew I should've spent the night with you last night, even though you insisted you'd be fine. It's really too bad Butch didn't show up yesterday. I would've enjoyed seeing the guys take care of him. But that also means he has no idea where you are now. There are over six million people in the DC metro area. You could live in Virginia or Maryland now for all he knows."

"But he knows where I work. He could follow me home from the hospital." With that thought, I can't help but glance nervously around my small condo, even knowing he isn't inside it. It's a reflex, as if mentioning his name will actually conjure the man out of thin air. "And it's not like you can just move in with me, so enough of the guilt trip for not spending the night."

"Let's devise a plan in case he does show up at the hospital or spots you on the road on the way home." Karen gives me her undivided attention. "Watch your surroundings at all times. We'll alert human resources and arrange for a security guard to escort you to your car every morning. If you think anyone is following you, don't go home. Drive straight to the police station and call me on the way. I'll get Spencer and the guys on the case immediately. Stay in public sight, and never yell for help. Always yell 'Fire.' That draws more people faster than screaming for help does."

"You are definitely married to a cop."

"I need to ask Spencer about self-defense classes. I'll go with you. We can do it on our days off." The wheels in Karen's head are spinning, making plans and mental to-do lists. All to ensure my safety and security.

My best friend is the best person.

"Have a seat. I'll get us a couple of sodas from the fridge, and we'll just bask in the newness of my new little home." True to her nature, she refuses the seat and checks out my decorating skills instead.

"You have great taste, Savannah. I don't know why you chose the noble but overworked profession of nursing over interior design. You could star in your own remodeling TV show by now." Karen pops the top on the Coke can and sips as she strolls to the master bedroom. "I love how you arranged this. You need to come over to my house and help me figure out how to rearrange and redecorate."

"You want to change your bedroom?"

"Oh no, not just the bedroom. My house. I want you to redo my whole house."

"That's more than just a weekend project, Karen."

"Yeah, I know. I'm good with however long it takes. Gives me time to parade Spencer's friends around and see which one you mesh with best."

"Sit. Stop with the matchmaking. Talk to me about more important topics."

We settle on the couch, facing the floor-to-ceiling windows that let in all the natural light I could ever want, and stare at the landscape of Meridian Hill Park only a block away. A light dusting of snow covers the bare trees, shrubs, and grassy areas. The temperatures haven't dropped enough for the snow to stick to the pavement yet, and the cold wind hasn't stopped anyone from enjoying the park.

"You know I only want you to be happy and loved, right? The way Spence loves me and puts me first in everything he does. I want that happy home life for you too." Karen's unusually serious tone makes my breath catch. I swing my eyes up to read her expression. Should've known I'd only find kindness and compassion there.

"I do know that, Karen. Sometimes when I watch you and Spence together, I'm overwhelmed by how much I wish I had what you two have. It's not envy—it's a goal I've set for myself. But whether the man for me is one of Spencer's friends or not doesn't make a difference right now.

"I've lost myself over the last three years. Butch was a different man when I first met him, though I should've recognized the warning signs and red flags for what they really were. The blinders I wore were my fault, and I accept the blame for that. But when the switch flipped and the abuse started, it wasn't just physical injuries. The mental damage he caused nearly destroyed me. Before I even consider looking at another man, I have to be okay with looking at myself in the mirror again.

"There's a fine line between love and hate. I need to find my way back across that line."

"You know I don't judge you for staying with him as long as you did. The threats, the violence, and being in the constant state of fight-or-flight takes a terrible toll on your overall well-being. But I am so thankful you're away from him now, and I'm so proud of you for finding the courage and strength to do it. Just to be clear, though. I will have you committed on a seventy-two-hour psychiatric hold if you let him back in now. You have all the support you need from me, Spence, and a host of DC's finest."

"That seventy-two-hour hold kind of sounds appealing. A little vacation. I could use a long weekend away. Can you arrange for that evaluation to be done in the Bahamas?"

"Your sarcastic humor is what first told me we'd be best friends. You know you're not going off to a Caribbean island for a mental-health check and leaving me here to work your shifts. We go mental together, or we don't go at all."

"Good to know your priorities are in order."

"Did you expect anything less of me?" A sly smile spreads across her face.

"No. In fact, I would've been very disappointed in you if you had replied any other way."

"You know me too well. There's no mystery left in our relationship…no hidden gems for you to uncover."

"I haven't met all of your personalities yet. I'm sure you have plenty of mysteries left for me to figure out."

~

Days bled into weeks with no sign or word from Butch. Over that time, I began to find purpose in my work again. Meaning in my life. A new direction to take and a way to use what I've been through for good. The exciting prospects of new projects, secret plans, and shifts at the hospital consumed my time. I fell into bed every day completely exhausted and thoroughly content for the first time in years.

"Have a good day. I'm off for the next four days, and I am not coming in for anyone or anything." I've already briefed the incoming day nurse on the status of each patient and completed all my charting from the night shift. All that's left is to clock out and stroll through the doors.

The snow flurries swirl in the wind outside and the skies are a gloomy shade of gray, but nothing can dampen my mood today. My neighborhood has a quaint little coffee shop at the end of the block. The scents and the scenery are calling my name. My laptop, a table with a view, and a piping hot cup of coffee are all I need to work on my life-defining purpose—a new business venture to help other women in my predicament. I'm writing a book for women in abusive relationships, and I need time and inspiration to add another chapter to the hardest story I've ever told.

My own.

No time like the present.

FINISH READING FINE LINE!

BLURRED LINE & HARD LINE ALSO ARE AVAILABLE NOW!

BOOKS BY A.D. JUSTICE

Steele Security Series

Wicked Games (Book 1)

Wicked Ties (Book 2)

Wicked Nights (Book 3)

Wicked Intentions (Book 4)

Wicked Shadows (Book 5)

Crossing Lines Series

Fine Line

Blurred Line

Hard Line

The Vault Series

Warning Part One

Warning Part Two

Warning Part Three

The Crazy Series

Crazy Maybe (Book 1)

Crazy Baby (Book 2)

Crazy Love (Book 3, Free Short Story)

Dominic Powers Series

Her Dom (Book 1)

Her Dom's Lesson (Book 2)

Stand—alone Novels

Saving Grace

Completely Captivated

Intent

Mistletoe Not Required

Immortal Envy

Just One Summer

ABOUT THE AUTHOR

A.D. Justice is the USA Today bestselling author of the Steele Security Series (Wicked Games, Wicked Ties, Wicked Nights, Wicked Intentions, Wicked Shadows), the Crazy Series (Crazy Maybe, Crazy Baby), the Dominic Powers series (Her Dom, Her Dom's Lesson), the Immortal Obsessions series (Immortal Envy) and a few stand—alone romance novels, such as Saving Grace, Completely Captivated, Just One Summer, Envy, and Intent.

When she's not writing, she's spending time with her own alpha male character in their North Georgia mountain home. She is also an avid reader of romance novels, a master at procrastination, a chocolate sommelier, a twister of words, and speaks fluent sarcasm. An avid animal lover, A.D. Justice has two horses, three cats, and two very spoiled dogs.

While the primary focus of her books has been romantic suspense, she has expanded into different sub—genres of romance. Stay tuned to read what she has in store for you!

Connect with her online!

Newsletter
Facebook Reader Group
Website

facebook.com/adjusticeauthor
instagram.com/authoradjustice
bookbub.com/authors/a-d-justice
amazon.com/author/adjustice
pinterest.com/adjusticeauthor

www.ingramcontent.com/pod-product-compliance
Lightning Source LLC
Chambersburg PA
CBHW020533310726
48979CB00014B/2322/J

* 9 7 8 1 7 3 3 9 0 7 0 4 0 *